AUTHOR
MCAULEY, P.

CLASS  AFSF

TITLE
Child of the river

D0774104

By the same author

FOUR HUNDRED BILLION STARS

SECRET HARMONIES

THE KING OF THE HILL

ETERNAL LIGHT

RED DUST

PASQUALE'S ANGEL

FAIRYLAND

THE INVISIBLE COUNTRY

ANCIENT OF DAYS
The Second Book of Confluence

IN DREAMS
(edited with Kim Newman)

PAUL J. McAULEY

CHILD OF THE RIVER

THE FIRST BOOK OF CONFLUENCE

CASSELL PLC

VISTA

07852715

ub

First published in Great Britain 1997
by Victor Gollancz

This Vista edition published 1998
Vista is an imprint of the Cassell Group
Wellington House, 125 Strand, London WC2R OBB

A catalogue record for this book is
available from the British Library.

ISBN O 575 60168 X

Typeset by SetSystems Ltd, Saffron Walden, Essex
Printed in Great Britain by
Caledonian International Manufacturing Ltd, Glasgow

98 99   10 9 8 7 6 5 4 3 2 1

For Caroline,
shelter from the storm

Praise the Lord! for He hath spoken
Worlds His mighty voice obeyed
Laws, which never shall be broken
For their guidance He hath made.

Kempthorn

1 ~ The White Boat

The Constable of Aeolis was a shrewd, pragmatic man who did not believe in miracles. In his opinion, everything must have an explanation, and simple explanations were best of all. 'The sharpest knife cuts cleanest,' he often told his sons. 'The more a man talks, the more likely it is he's lying.'

But to the end of his days, he could not explain the affair of the white boat.

It happened one midsummer night, when the huge black sky above the Great River was punctuated only by a scattering of dim halo stars and the dull red swirl, no bigger than a man's hand, of the Eye of the Preservers. The heaped lights of the little city of Aeolis and the lights of the carracks riding at anchor outside the harbour entrance were brighter by far than anything in the sky.

The summer heat was oppressive to the people of Aeolis. For most of the day they slept in the relative cool of their seeps and wallows, rising to begin work when the Rim Mountains clawed the setting sun, and retiring again when the sun rose, renewed, above the devouring peaks. In summer, stores and taverns and workshops stayed open from dusk until dawn, fishing boats set out at midnight to trawl the black river for noctilucent polyps and pale shrimp, and the streets of Aeolis were crowded and bustling beneath the flare of cressets and the orange glow of sodium vapour lamps. At night, in summer, the lights of Aeolis shone like a beacon in the midst of the dark shore.

That particular night, the Constable and his two eldest sons were rowing back to Aeolis in their skiff with two vagrant river traders who had been arrested while trying to run bales of cigarettes to the unchanged hill tribes of the wild shore downstream of Aeolis. Part of the traders' contraband cargo, soft bales sealed in plastic wrap and oiled cloth, was stacked in the forward well of the skiff; the traders lay in the stern, tied up like shoats for the slaughter. The skiff's powerful motor had been shot out in the brief skirmish, and the Constable's sons, already as big as their father, sat side by side on the centre thwart, rowing steadily against the current. The Constable was perched on a button cushion in the skiff's high stern, steering for the lights of Aeolis.

The Constable was drinking steadily from a cruse of wine. He was a large man with loose grey skin and gross features, like a figure hastily moulded from clay and abandoned before it was completed. A pair of tusks protruded like daggers from his meaty upper lip. One tusk had been broken when he had fought and killed his father, and the Constable had had it capped with silver; silver chinked against the neck of the cruse each time he took a swig of wine.

The Constable was not in a good temper. He would make a fair profit from his half of the captured cargo (the other half would go to the Aedile, if he could spare an hour or so from his excavations to pronounce sentence on the traders), but the arrest had not gone smoothly. The river traders had hired a pentad of ruffians as an escort, and they had put up a desperate fight before the Constable and his sons had managed to despatch them. The Constable's shoulders had taken a bad cut, cleaving through blubber to the muscle beneath, and his back had been scorched by reflection of the pistol bolt which had damaged the skiff's motor. Fortunately, the weapon, which had probably predated the foundation of Aeolis, had misfired on the second shot and killed the man using it, but the Constable knew that he could not rely on good luck for ever. He was getting old, ponderous and muddled when once he had been quick and strong. He knew that sooner or later one of his sons would challenge him, and he was worried that this night's botched episode was a harbinger of his decline. Like all strong men, he feared his own weakness more than death, for strength was how he measured the worth of his life.

Now and then he turned and looked back at the pyre of the smugglers' boat. It had burnt to the waterline, a flickering dash of light riding its own reflection far out across the river's broad black plain. The Constable's sons had run it aground on a mudbank, so that it would not drift amongst the banyan islands which at this time of year spun in slow circles in the shallow sargasso of the Great River's nearside shoals, tethered only by fine nets of feeder roots.

Of the two river traders, one lay as still as a sated cayman, resigned to his fate, but his mate, a tall, skinny old man naked but for a breechclout and an unravelling turban, was trying to convince the Constable to let him go. Yoked hand to foot, so that his back was bent like a bow, he stared up at the Constable from the well, his insincere frightened smile like a rictus, his eyes so wide that white showed clear around their slitted irises. At first he had tried to gain the Constable's attention with flattery, now he was turning to threats.

'I have many friends, captain, who would be unhappy to see me in your jail,' he said. 'There are no walls strong enough to withstand the force of their friendship, for I am a generous man. I am known for my generosity across the breadth of the river.'

The Constable rapped the top of the trader's turban with the butt of his whip, and for the fourth or fifth time advised him to be quiet. It was clear from the arrowhead tattoos on the man's fingers that he belonged to one of the street gangs which roved the ancient wharves of Ys. Any friends he might have were a hundred leagues upriver, and by dusk tomorrow he and his companion would be dead.

The skinny trader babbled, 'Last year, captain, I took it

upon myself to sponsor the wedding of the son of one of my dear friends, who had been struck down in the prime of life. Bad fortune had left his widow with little more than a rented room and nine children to feed. The son was besotted; his bride's family impatient. This poor lady had no one to turn to but myself, and I, captain, remembering the good company of my friend, his wisdom and his friendly laughter, took it upon myself to organize everything. Four hundred people ate and drank at the celebration, and I count them all as my friends. Quails' tongues in aspic we had, captain, and mounds of oysters and fish roe, and baby goats tender as the butter they were seethed in.'

Perhaps there was a grain of truth in the story. Perhaps the man had been one of the guests at such a wedding, but he could not have sponsored it. No one desperate enough to try to smuggle cigarettes to the hill tribes would have been able to lavish that kind of money on an act of charity.

The Constable flicked his whip across the legs of the prisoners. He said, 'You are a dead man, and dead men have no friends. Compose yourself. Our city might be a small place, but it has a shrine, and it was one of the last places along all the river's shore where avatars talked with men, before the heretics silenced them. Pilgrims still come here, for even if the avatars are no longer able to speak, surely they are still listening. We'll let you speak to them after you've been sentenced. I suggest you take the time to think of what account you can give of your life.'

One of the Constable's son's laughed, and the Constable gave their broad backs a touch of his whip. 'Row,' he told them, 'and keep quiet.'

'Quails' tongues,' the talkative trader said. 'Anything you want, captain. You have only to name it and it will be yours. I can make you rich. I can offer you my own home, captain. Like a palace it is, right in the heart of Ys. Far from this stinking hole—'

The boat rocked when the Constable jumped into the

well. His sons cursed wearily, and shipped their oars. The Constable knocked off the wretched trader's turban, pulled up the man's head by the greasy knot of hair that sprouted from his crown and, before he could scream, thrust two fingers into his mouth and grasped his writhing tongue. The trader gagged and tried to bite the Constable's fingers, but his teeth scarcely bruised their leathery skin. The Constable drew his knife, sliced the trader's tongue in half and tossed the scrap of flesh over the side of the skiff. The trader gargled blood and thrashed like a landed fish.

At the same moment, one of the Constable's sons cried out. 'Boat ahead! Leastways, there's running lights.'

This was Urthank, a dull-witted brute grown as heavy and muscular as his father. The Constable knew that it would not be long before Urthank roared his challenge, and knew too that the boy would lose. Urthank was too stupid to wait for the right moment; it was not in his nature to suppress an impulse. No, Urthank would not defeat him. It would be one of the others. But Urthank's challenge would be the beginning of the end.

The Constable searched the darkness. For a moment he thought he glimpsed a fugitive glimmer, but only for a moment. It could have been a mote floating in his eye, or a dim star glinting at the edge of the world's level horizon.

'You were dreaming,' he said. 'Set to rowing, or the sun will be up before we get back.'

'I saw it,' Urthank insisted.

The other son, Unthank, laughed.

'There!' Urthank said. 'There it is again! Dead ahead, just like I said.'

This time the Constable saw the flicker of light. His first thought was that perhaps the trader had not been boasting after all. He said quietly, 'Go forward. Feathered oars.'

As the skiff glided against the current, the Constable fumbled a clamshell case from the pouch hung on the belt of his white linen kilt. The trader whose tongue had been cut out was making wet, choking sounds. The Constable kicked him into silence before opening the case and lifting out the spectacles that rested on the waterstained silk lining. The spectacles were the most valuable heirloom of the Constable's family; they had passed from defeated father to victorious son for more than a hundred generations. They were shaped like bladeless scissors, and the Constable unfolded them and carefully pinched them over his bulbous nose.

At once, the hull of the flat skiff and the bales of contraband cigarettes stacked in the forward well seemed to gain a luminous sheen; the bent backs of the Constable's sons and the supine bodies of the two prisoners glowed with furnace light. The Constable scanned the river, ignoring flaws in the old glass of the lenses which warped or smudged the amplified light, and saw, half a league from the skiff, a knot of tiny, intensely brilliant specks dancing above the river's surface.

'Machines,' the Constable breathed. He stepped between the prisoners and pointed out the place to his sons.

The skiff glided forward under the Constable's guidance. As it drew closer, the Constable saw that there were hundreds of machines, a busy cloud swirling around an invisible pivot. He was used to seeing one or two flitting through the sky above Aeolis on their inscrutable business, but he had never before seen so many in one place.

Something knocked against the side of the skiff, and Urthank cursed and feathered his oar. It was a waterlogged coffin. Every day, thousands were launched from Ys. For a moment, a woman's face gazed up at the Constable through a glaze of water, glowing greenly amidst a halo of rotting flowers. Then the coffin turned end for end and was borne away.

The skiff had turned in the current, too. Now it was broadside to the cloud of machines, and for the first time the Constable saw what they attended.

A boat. A white boat riding high on the river's slow current.

The Constable took off his spectacles, and discovered that the boat was glimmering with a spectral luminescence. The water around it glowed too, as if it floated in the centre of one of the shoals of luminous plankton that sometimes rose to the surface of the river on a calm summer night. The glow spread around the skiff; each stroke of the oars broke its pearly light into whirling interlocking spokes, as if the ghost of a machine lived just beneath the river's skin.

The tongue-cut trader groaned and coughed; his partner raised himself up on his elbows to watch as the white boat turned on the river's current, light as a leaf, a dancer barely touching the water.

The boat had a sharp, raised prow, and incurved sides that sealed it shut and swept back in a fan, like the tail of a dove. It was barely larger than an ordinary coffin. It made another turn, seemed to stretch like a cat, and then it was alongside the skiff, pressed right against it without even a bump.

Suddenly, the Constable and his sons were inside the cloud of machines. It was as if they had fallen headfirst into a nebula, for there were hundreds of them, each burning with ferocious white light, none bigger than a rhinoceros beetle. Urthank tried to swat one that hung in front of his snout, and cursed when it stung him with a flare of red light and a crisp sizzle.

'Steady,' the Constable said, and someone else said hoarsely, 'Flee.'

Astonished, the Constable turned from his inspection of the glimmering boat.

'Flee,' the second trader said again. 'Flee, you fools!'

Both of the Constable's sons had shipped their oars and were looking at their father. They were waiting for his lead. The Constable put away his spectacles and shoved the butt end of his whip in his belt. He could not show that he was afraid. He reached through the whirling lights of the machines and touched the white boat.

Its hull was as light and close woven as feathers, and at the Constable's touch, the incurved sides peeled back with a sticky, crackling sound. As a boy, the Constable had been given to wandering the wild shore downriver of Aeolis, and he had once come across a blood orchid growing in the cloven root of a kapok tree. The orchid had made precisely the same noise when, sensing his body heat, it had spread its fleshy lobes wide to reveal the lubricious curves of its creamy pistil. He had fled in terror before the blood orchid's perfume could overwhelm him, and the ghost of that fear stayed his hand now.

The hull vibrated under his fingertips with a quick, eager pulse. Light poured out from the boat's interior, rich and golden and filled with floating motes. A body made a shadow inside this light, and the Constable thought at once that the boat was no more than a coffin set adrift on the river's current. The coffin of some lord or lady no doubt, but in function no different from the shoddy cardboard coffins of the poor or the enamelled wooden coffins of the artisans and traders.

And then the baby started to cry.

The Constable squinted through the light, saw something move within it, and reached out. For a moment he was at the incandescent heart of the machines' intricate dance, and then they were gone, dispersing in flat trajectories into the darkness. The baby, a boy, pale and fat and hairless, squirmed in the Constable's hands.

The golden light was dying back inside the white boat. In moments, only traces remained, iridescent veins and dabs that fitfully illuminated the corpse on which the baby had been lying.

It was the corpse of a woman, naked, flat-breasted and starveling thin, and as hairless as the baby. She had been shot, once through the chest and once in the head, but there was no blood. One hand was three fingered, like the grabs of the cranes of Aeolis's docks; the other was monstrously swollen and bifurcate, like a lobster's claw. Her skin had a silvery-grey cast; her huge eyes, divided into a honeycomb of cells, were like the compound lenses of certain insects, and the colour of blood rubies. Within each facet lived a flickering glint of golden light, and although the Constable knew that these were merely reflections of the white boat's fading light, he had the strange feeling that things, malevolently watchful things, lived behind the dead woman's strange eyes.

'Heresy,' the second trader said. Somehow, he had got up on his knees and was staring wide-eyed at the white boat.

The Constable kicked the trader in the stomach; the man coughed and flopped back into the bilge water alongside his partner. The trader glared up at the Constable and said again, 'Heresy. When they allowed the ship of the Ancients of Days to pass beyond Ys and sail downriver, our benevolent bureaucracies let heresy loose into the world.'

'Let me kill him now,' Urthank said.

'He's already a dead man,' the Constable said.

'Not while he talks treason,' Urthank said stubbornly. He was staring straight at his father.

'Fools,' the trader said. 'You have all seen the argosies and carracks sailing downriver to war with their cannons and siege engines. But there are more terrible weapons let loose in the world.'

'Let me kill him,' Urthank said.

The baby had caught at the Constable's thumb, although he could not close his fingers around it. He grimaced, as if trying to smile, but blew a saliva bubble instead.

The Constable gently disengaged the baby's grip and set him on the button cushion at the stern. He moved carefully, as if through air packed with invisible boxes, aware of Urthank's burning gaze at his back. He turned and said, 'Let the man speak. He might know something.'

The trader said, 'The bureaucrats are trying to wake the

Hierarchs from their reveries. Some say by science, some by witchery. The bureaucrats are so frightened of heresy consuming our world that they try anything to prevent it.'

Unthank spat. 'The Hierarchs are all ten thousand years dead. Everyone knows that. They were killed when the Insurrectionists threw down the temples and destroyed most of the avatars.'

'The Hierarchs tried to follow the Preservers,' the trader said. 'They rose higher than any other bloodline, but not so high that they cannot be called back.'

The Constable kicked the man and said roughly, 'Enough theology. Is this one of their servants?'

'Ys is large, and contains a multitude of wonders, but I've never seen anything like this. Most likely it is a foul creature manufactured by the forbidden arts. Those trying to forge such weapons have become more corrupt than the heretics. Destroy it! Return the baby and sink the boat!'

'Why should I believe you?'

'I'm a bad man. I admit it. I'd sell any one of my daughters if I could be sure of a good profit. But I studied for a clerkship when I was a boy, and I was taught well. I remember my lessons, and I know that the existence of this thing is against the word of the Preservers.'

Urthank said slowly, 'We should put the baby back. It isn't our business.'

'All on the river within a day's voyage is my business,' the Constable said.

'You don't know everything,' Urthank said. 'You just think you do.'

The Constable knew then that this was the moment poor Urthank had chosen. So did Unthank, who subtly shifted on the thwart so that he was no longer shoulder to shoulder with his brother. The Constable met Urthank's stare and said, 'Keep your place, boy.'

There was a moment when it seemed that Urthank would

not attack. Then he inflated his chest and let out the air with a roar and, roaring, threw himself at his father.

The whip caught around Urthank's neck with a sharp crack that echoed out across the black water. Urthank fell to his knees and grabbed hold of the whip as its loop tightened under the slack flesh of his chin. The Constable gripped the whip's stock with both hands and jerked it sideways as if he held a line which a huge fish had suddenly struck. The skiff tipped wildly and Urthank tumbled headfirst into the glowing water. But the boy did not let go of the whip. He was stupid, but he was also stubborn. The Constable staggered, dropped the whip – it hissed over the side like a snake – and fell overboard too.

The Constable kicked off his loose, knee-high boots as he plunged down through the cold water, kicked out again for the surface. Something grabbed the hem of his kilt, and then Urthank was trying to swarm up his body. Light exploded in the Constable's eye as his son's hard elbow hit his face. They thrashed through glowing water and burst into the air, separated by no more than an arm's length.

The Constable spat a mouthful of water and gasped, 'You're too quick to anger, my son. That was always your weakness.'

He saw the shadow of Urthank's arm sweep through the milky glow, and countered the thrust with his own knife. The blades clashed and slid along each other, locking at their hilts. Urthank growled and pressed down. He was very strong. The Constable felt a terrific pain as his knife was twisted from his grasp and Urthank's blade buried its point in his forearm. He kicked backwards in the water as Urthank slashed at his face; spray flew in a wide fan.

'Old,' Urthank said. 'Old and slow.'

The Constable steadied himself with little circling kicks. He could feel his hot blood pulsing into the water; Urthank had caught a vein. There was a heaviness in his bones; the wound on his shoulder throbbed. He knew that Urthank was right, but he also knew that he was not prepared to die.

He said, 'Come to me, son, and find out who is strongest.'

Urthank grinned, freeing his tusks from his lips. He kicked forward, driving through the water with his knife held out straight, trying for a killing blow. But the water slowed him as the Constable had known it would, and the Constable kicked sideways, always just out of reach, while Urthank stabbed wildly, sobbing curses and uselessly spending his strength. Father and son circled each other. In the periphery of his vision, the Constable was aware that the white boat had separated from the skiff, but he could spare no thought for it as he avoided Urthank's next onslaught.

At last Urthank stopped, paddling to keep in one place and gasping heavily.

'Strength isn't everything,' the Constable observed. 'Come to me, son. I'll grant you a quick release and no shame.'

'Surrender, old man, and I'll give you an honourable burial on land. Or I'll kill you here and let the little fishes strip your bones.'

'O Urthank, how disappointed I am! You're no son of mine after all!'

Urthank lunged with a sudden, desperate fury, and the Constable punched precisely, hitting the boy's elbow where the nerve travelled over the bone. Urthank's fingers opened in reflex and his knife fluttered away through the water. He dove for it without thinking, and the Constable bore down on him with all his weight, enduring increasingly feeble blows to his chest and belly and legs. It took a long time, but at last he let go and Urthank's body floated free, face down in the glowing water.

'You were the strongest of my sons,' the Constable said, when he had his breath back. 'You were faithful after your fashion, but you never had a good thought in your head. If you had killed me and taken my wives, someone else would have killed you in a year.'

Unthank paddled the skiff over and helped his father clamber into the well. The white boat was a dozen oarlengths off, glimmering against the dark. The skinny trader whose tongue the Constable had cut out lay face-down in the bilge water, drowned in his own blood. His partner was gone. Unthank shrugged, and said that the man had slipped over the side.

'You should have brought him back. He was bound hand and foot. A big boy like you should have had no trouble.'

Unthank returned the Constable's gaze and said simply, 'I was watching your victory, father.'

'No, you're not ready yet, are you? You're waiting for the right moment. You're a subtle one, Unthank. Not like your brother.'

'He won't have got far. The prisoner, I mean.'

'Did you kill him?'

'Probably drowned by now. Like you said, he was bound hand and foot.'

'Help me with your brother.'

Together, father and son hauled Urthank's body into the skiff. The milky glow was fading out of the water. After the Constable had settled Urthank's body, he turned and saw that the white boat had vanished. The skiff was alone on the wide dark river, beneath the black sky and the smudged red whorl of the Eye of the Preservers. Under the arm of the tiller, on the leather pad of the button cushion, the baby grabbed at black air with pale starfish hands, chuckling at unguessable thoughts.

2 ~ The Anchorite

One evening early in spring, with the wheel of the Galaxy tilted waist-deep at the level horizon of the Great River, Yama eased open the shutters of the window of his room and stepped out on to the broad ledge. Any soldier looking up from the courtyard would have seen, by the Galaxy's blue-white light, a sturdy boy of some seventeen years on the ledge beneath the overhang of the red tile roof, and recognized the long-boned build, pale sharp face and cap of black hair of the Aedile's foundling son. But Yama knew that Sergeant Rhodean had taken most of the garrison of the peel-house on patrol through the winding paths of the City of the Dead, searching for the heretics who last night had tried to firebomb a ship at anchor in the floating harbour. Further, three men were standing guard over the labourers at the Aedile's excavations, leaving only the pack of watchdogs and a pentad of callow youths under the command of old one-legged Rotwang, who by now would have finished his nightly bottle of brandy and be snoring in his chair by the kitchen fire. With the garrison so reduced there was little chance that any of the soldiers would leave the warm fug of the guardroom to patrol the gardens, and Yama knew that he could persuade the watchdogs to allow him to pass unreported.

It was an opportunity for adventure too good to be missed. Yama was going to hunt frogs with the chandler's daughter,

Derev, and Ananda, the sizar of the priest of Aeolis's temple. They had agreed on it that afternoon, using mirror talk.

The original walls of the Aedile's peel-house were built of smooth blocks of keelrock fitted together so cunningly that they presented a surface like polished ice, but at some point in the house's history an extra floor had been added, with a wide gutter ledge and gargoyles projecting into the air at intervals to spout water clear of the walls. Yama walked along the ledge as easily as if on a pavement, turned a corner, hooked his rope around the eroded ruff of a basilisk frozen in an agonized howl, and abseiled five storeys to the ground. He would have to leave the rope in place, but it was a small risk.

No one was about. He darted across the wide, mossy lawn, jumped the ha-ha and quickly and silently threaded familiar paths through the dense stands of rhododendrons which had colonized the tumbled ruins of the ramparts of the peel-house's outer defensive wall. Yama had played endless games of soldiers and heretics with the kitchen boys here, and knew every path, every outcrop of ruined wall, all the holes in the ground which had once been guardrooms or stores and the buried passages between them. He stopped beneath a mature cork-oak, looked around, then lifted up a mossy stone to reveal a deep hole lined with stones and sealed with polymer spray. He pulled out a net bag and a long slender trident from this hiding place, then replaced the stone and hung the bag on his belt and laid the trident across his shoulders.

At the edge of the stands of rhododendrons, the ground dropped away steeply in an overgrown demilune breastwork to a barrens of tussock grass and scrub. Beyond was the patchwork of newly flooded paeonin fields on either side of the winding course of the Breas, and then low ranges of hills crowded with monuments and tombs, cairns and cists: league upon league of the City of the Dead stretching to the foothills of the Rim Mountains, its inhabitants outnumbered the living citizens of Aeolis by a thousand to one. The tombs glimmered in the cold light of the Galaxy, as if the hills had been dusted with salt, and little lights flickered here and there, where memorial tablets had been triggered by passing animals.

Yama took out a slim silver whistle twice the length of his forefinger and blew on it. It seemed to make no more than a breathy squeak. Yama blew three more times, then stuck his trident in the deep, soft leaf-mould and squatted on his heels and listened to the peeping chorus of frogs that stitched the night. The frogs had emerged from their mucus cocoons a few weeks ago. They had been frantically feeding ever since, and now they were searching for mates, every male endeavouring to outdo his rivals with passionate froggy arias. Dopey with unrequited lust, they would be easy prey.

Behind Yama, the peel-house reared above the rhododendrons, lifting its freight of turrets against the Galaxy's blue-white wheel. A warm yellow light glowed near the top of the tall watchtower, where the Aedile, who had rarely slept since the news of Telmon's death last summer, would be working on his endless measurements and calculations.

Presently, Yama heard what he had been waiting for, the steady padding tread and faint sibilant breath of a watchdog. He called softly, and the strong, ugly creature trotted out of the bushes and laid its heavy head in his lap. Yama crooned to it, stroking its cropped ears and scratching the ridged line where flesh met the metal of its skullplate, lulling the machine part of the watchdog and, through its link, the rest of the pack. When he was satisfied that it understood it was not to raise the alarm either now or when he returned, Yama stood and wiped the dog's drool from his hands, plucked up his trident, and bounded away down the steep slope of the breastwork towards the barren ruins and the flooded fields beyond.

Ananda and Derev were waiting at the edge of the ruins. Tall, graceful Derev jumped down from her perch halfway up a broken wall cloaked in morning glory, and half-floated, half-ran across overgrown flagstones to embrace Yama. Ananda kept his seat on a fallen stele, eating ghostberries he had picked along the way and pretending to ignore the embracing lovers. He was a plump boy with dark skin and a bare, tubercled scalp, wearing the orange robe of his office.

'I brought the lantern,' Ananda said at last, and held it up. It was a little brass signal lantern, with a slide and a lens to focus the light of its wick. The plan was to use it to mesmerise their prey.

Derev and Yama broke from their embrace and Ananda added, 'I saw your soldiers march out along the old road this noon, brother Yama. Everyone in the town says they're after the heretics who tried to set fire to the floating harbour.'

'If there are heretics within a day's march, Sergeant Rhodean will find them,' Yama said.

'Perhaps they're still hiding here,' Derev said. Her neck seemed to elongate as she turned her head this way and that to peer into the darkness around the ruins. Her feathery hair was brushed back from her shaven forehead and hung to the small of her back. She wore a belted shift that left her long, slim legs bare. A trident was slung over her left shoulder. She hugged Yama and said, 'Suppose we found them! Wouldn't that be exciting?'

Yama said, 'If they are stupid enough to remain near the place they have just attacked, then they would be easy to capture. We would need only to threaten them with our frog-stickers to force their surrender.'

'My father says they make their women lie with animals to create monstrous warriors.'

Ananda spat seeds and said, 'Her father promised to pay a good copper penny for every ten frogs we catch.'

'Derev's father has a price for everything,' Yama said, smiling.

Derev smiled too – Yama felt it against his cheek. She said, 'My father also said I should be back before the Galaxy sets. He only allowed me to come here because I told him that one of the Aedile's soldiers would be guarding us.'

Derev's father was very tall and very thin and habitually dressed in black, and walked with his head hunched into his shoulders and his white hands clasped behind him. From the back he looked like one of the night storks that picked over the city's rubbish pits. He was invariably accompanied by his burly bodyservant; he was scared of footpads and the casual violence of sailors, and of kidnapping. The latter was a real threat, as his family was the only one of its bloodline in Aeolis. He was disliked within the tight-knit trading community because he bought favours rather than earned them, and Yama knew that Derev was allowed to see him only because Derev's father believed it brought him closer to the Aedile.

Ananda said, 'The soldier would be guarding something more important than your life, although, like life, once taken it cannot be given back. But perhaps you no longer have it, which is why the soldier is not here.'

Yama whispered to Derev, 'You should not believe everything your father says,' and told Ananda, 'You dwell too much on things of the flesh. It does no good to brood on that which you cannot have. Give me some berries.'

Ananda held out a handful. 'You only had to ask,' he said mildly.

Yama burst a ghostberry between his tongue and palate: the rough skin shockingly tart, the pulpy seed-rich flesh meltingly sweet. He grinned and said, 'It is spring. We could stay out all night, then go fishing at dawn.'

Derev said, 'My father—'

'Your father would pay more for fresh fish than for frogs.'

'He buys all the fish he can sell from the fisherfolk, and the amount he can buy is limited by the price of salt.'

Ananda said, 'It's traditional to hunt frogs in spring, which is why we're here. Derev's father wouldn't thank you for making her into a fisherman.'

'If I don't get back before midnight he'll lock me up,' Derev said. 'I will never see you again.'

Yama smiled. 'You know that is not true. Otherwise your father would never have let you out in the first place.'

'There should be a soldier here,' Derev said. 'We're none of us armed.'

'The heretics are leagues away. And I will protect you, Derev.'

Derev brandished her trident, as fierce and lovely as a naiad. 'We're equally matched, I think.'

'I cannot stay out all night either,' Ananda said. 'Father Quine rises an hour before sunrise, and before then I must sweep the naos and light the candles in the votary.'

'No one will come,' Yama said. 'No one ever does any more, except on high days.'

'That's not the point. The avatars may have been silenced, but the Preservers are still there.'

'They will be there whether you light the candles or not. Stay with me, Ananda. Forget your duties for once.'

Ananda shrugged. 'I happen to believe in my duties.'

Yama said, 'You are scared of the beating you will get from Father Quine.'

'Well, that's true, too. For a holy man, he has a fearsome temper and a strong arm. You're lucky, Yama. The Aedile is a kindly, scholarly man.'

'If he is angry with me, he has Sergeant Rhodean beat me. And if he learns that I have left the peel-house at night, that is just what will happen. That is why I did not bring a soldier with me.'

'My father says that physical punishment is barbaric,' Derev said.

'It is not so bad,' Yama said. 'And at least you know when it is over.'

'The Aedile sent for Father Quine yesterday,' Ananda said. He crammed the last of the ghostberries into his mouth and got to his feet. Berry juice stained his lips; they looked black in the Galaxy's blue-white light.

Yama said unhappily, 'My father is wondering what to do with me. He has been talking about finding a clerkship for me in a safe corner of the department. I think that is why Dr Dismas went to Ys. But I do not want to be a clerk – I would rather be a priest. At least I would get to see something of the world.'

'You're too old,' Ananda said equitably. 'My parents consecrated me a hundred days after my birth. And besides being too old, you are also too full of sin. You spy on your poor father, and steal.'

'And sneak out after dark,' Derev said.

'So has Ananda.'

'But not to fornicate,' Ananda said. 'Derev's father knows that I'm here, so I'm as much a chaperon as any soldier, although more easily bribed.'

Derev said, 'Oh, Ananda, we really are here to hunt for frogs.'

Ananda added, 'And I will confess my sin tomorrow, before the shrine.'

'As if the Preservers care about your small sins,' Yama said.

'You're too proud to be a priest,' Ananda said. 'Above all, you're too proud. Come and pray with me. Unburden yourself.'

Yama said, 'Well, I would rather be a priest than a clerk, but most of all I would rather be a soldier. I will run away and enlist. I will train as an officer, and lead a company of myrmidons or command a corvette into battle against the heretics.'

Ananda said, 'That's why your father wants you to be a clerk.'

Derev said, 'Listen.'

The two boys turned to look at where she pointed. Far out across the flooded fields, a point of intense turquoise light was moving through the dark air towards the Great River.

'A machine,' Yama said.

'So it is,' Derev said, 'but that isn't what I meant. I heard someone crying out.'

'Frogs fornicating,' Ananda said.

Yama guessed that the machine was half a league off. It seemed to slide at an angle to everything else, twinkling as if stitching a path between the world and its own reality.

He said, 'We should make a wish.'

Ananda smiled, 'I'll pretend you didn't say that, brother Yama. Such superstitions are unworthy of someone as educated as you.'

Derev said, 'Besides, you should never make a wish in case it is answered, like the story of the old man and the fox maiden. I know I heard something. It may be heretics. Or bandits. Quiet! Listen!'

Ananda said, 'I hear nothing, Derev. Perhaps your heart is beating so quickly it cries out for relief. I know I'm a poor priest, Yama, but one thing I know is true. The Preservers see all; there is no need to invoke them by calling upon their servants.'

Yama shrugged. There was no point debating such niceties with Ananda, who had been trained in theology since birth, but why shouldn't machines at least hear the wishes of those they passed by? Wishing was only an informal kind of praying, after all, and surely prayers were heard, and sometimes even answered. For if praying did not bring reward, then people would long ago have abandoned the habit of prayer, as farmers abandon land which no longer yields a crop. The priests taught that the Preservers heard and saw all, yet chose not to act because they did not wish to invalidate the free will of their creations; but machines were as much a part of the world which the Preservers had created as the Shaped bloodlines, although of a higher order. Even if the Preservers had withdrawn their blessing from the world after the affront of the Age of Insurrection, as the divarica-tionists believed, it was still possible that machines, their epigones, might recognize the justice of answering a particular wish, and intercede. After all, those avatars of the Preservers which had survived the Age of Insurrection had spoken with men as recently as forty years ago, before the heretics had finally silenced them.

In any event, better the chance taken than that lost and later regretted. Yama closed his eyes and offered up the quick wish, hostage to the future, that he be made a soldier and not a clerk.

Ananda said, 'You might as well wish upon a star.'

Derev said, 'Quiet! I heard it again!'

And Yama heard it too, faint but unmistakable above the frogs' incessant chorus. A man's angry wordless yell, and then the sound of jeering voices and coarse laughter.

Yama led the others through the overgrown ruins. Ananda padded right behind him with his robe tucked into his girdle – the better to run away if there was trouble, he said, although Yama knew that he would not run. Derev would not run away either; she held her trident like a javelin.

One of the old roads ran alongside the fields. Its ceramic surface had been stripped and smelted for the metals it had contained thousands of years ago, but the long straight track preserved its geodesic ideal. At the crux between the old road and a footpath that led across the embankment between two of the flooded fields, by a simple shrine set on a wooden post, the Constable's twin sons, Lud and Lob, had ambushed an anchorite.

The man stood with his back to the shrine, brandishing his staff. Its metal-shod point flicked back and forth like a watchful eye. Lud and Lob yelled and threw stones and clods of dirt at the anchorite but stayed out of the staff's striking range. The twins were swaggering bullies who believed that they ruled the children of the town. Most especially, they picked on those few children of bloodlines not their own. Yama had been chased by them a decad ago, when he had been returning to the peel-house after visiting Derev, but he had easily lost them in the ruins outside the town.

'We'll find you later, little fish,' they had shouted cheerfully. They had been drinking, and one of them had slapped his head with the empty bladder and cut a clumsy little dance. 'We always finish our business,' he had shouted. 'Little fish, little fish, come out now. Be like a man.'

Yama had chosen to stay hidden. Lud and Lob had scrawled their sign on a crumbling wall and pissed at its base, but after beating about the bushes in a desultory fashion they had grown bored and wandered off.

Now, crouching with Derev and Ananda in a thicket of chayote vine, Yama wondered what he should do. The anchorite was a tall man with a wild black mane and wilder beard. He was barefoot, and dressed in a crudely stitched robe of metallic-looking cloth. He dodged most of the stones thrown at him, but one had struck him on the head; blood ran down his forehead and he mechanically wiped it from his eyes with his wrist. Sooner or later, he would falter, and Lud and Lob would pounce.

Derev whispered, 'We should fetch the militia.'

'I don't think it's necessary,' Ananda said.

At that moment, a stone struck the anchorite's elbow and the point of his staff dipped. Roaring with glee, Lob and Lud ran in from either side and knocked him to the ground. The anchorite surged up, throwing one of the twins aside, but the other clung to his back and the second knocked the anchorite down again.

Yama said, 'Ananda, come out when I call your name. Derev, you set up a diversion.' And before he could think better of it he stepped out onto the road and shouted the twins' names.

Lob turned. He held the staff in both hands, as if about

to break it. Lud sat on the anchorite's back, grinning as he absorbed the man's blows to his flanks.

Yama said, 'What is this, Lob? Are you and your brother footpads now?'

'Just a bit of fun, little fish,' Lob said. He whirled the staff above his head. It whistled in the dark air.

'We saw him first,' Lud added.

'I think you should leave him alone.'

'Maybe we'll have you instead, little fish.'

'We'll have him all right,' Lud said. 'That's why we're here.' He cuffed the anchorite. 'This culler got in the way of what we set out to do, remember? Grab him, brother, and then we can finish this bit of fun.'

'You will have to deal with me, and with Ananda, too,' Yama said. He did not look around, but by the shift in Lob's gaze he knew that Ananda had stepped out onto the road behind him.

'The priest's runt, eh?' Lob laughed, and farted tremendously.

'Gaw,' his brother said, giggling so hard his triple chins quivered. He waved a hand in front of his face. 'What a stink.'

'Bless me your holiness,' Lob said, leering at Ananda, and farted again.

'Even odds,' Yama said, disgusted.

'Stay there, little fish,' Lob said. 'We'll deal with you when we've finished here.'

'You wetbrain,' Lud said, 'we deal with him first. Remember?'

Yama flung his flimsy trident then, but it bounced uselessly off Lob's hide. Lob yawned, showing his stout, sharp tusks, and swept the staff at Yama's head. Yama ducked, then jumped back from the reverse stroke. The staff's metal tip cut the air a finger's width from his belly. Lob came on, stepping heavily and deliberately and sweeping the staff back and forth, but Yama easily dodged his clumsily aimed blows.

'Fight fair,' Lob said, stopping at last. He was panting heavily. 'Stand and fight fair.'

Ananda was behind Lob now, and jabbed at his legs with his trident. Enraged, Lob turned and swung the staff at Ananda, and Yama stepped forward and kicked him in the kneecap, and then in the wrist. Lob howled and lost his balance, and Yama grabbed the staff when it clattered to the ground. He reversed it and jabbed Lob hard in the gut.

Lob fell to his knees in stages. 'Fight fair,' he gasped, winded. His little eyes blinked and blinked in his corpulent face.

'Fight fair,' Lud echoed, and got off the anchorite and pulled a knife from his belt. It was as black as obsidian, with a narrow, crooked blade. He had stolen it from a drunken sailor, and claimed that it was from the first days of the Age of Enlightenment, nearly as old as the world. 'Fight fair,' Lud said again, and held the knife beside his face and grinned.

Lob threw himself forward then, and wrapped his arms around Yama's thighs. Yama hammered at Lob's back with the staff, but he was too close to get a good swing at his opponent and he tumbled over backwards, his legs pinned beneath Lob's weight.

For a moment, all seemed lost. Then Ananda stepped forward and swung his doubled fist; the stone he held struck the side of Lob's skull with the sound of an axe sinking into wet wood. Lob roared with pain and sprang to his feet, and Lud roared too, and brandished his knife. Behind him, a tree burst into flame.

'It was all I could think of,' Derev said. She flapped her arms about her slim body. She was shaking with excitement. Ananda ran a little way down the road and shouted after the fleeing twins, a high ululant wordless cry.

Yama said, 'It was well done, but we should not mock them.'

'We make a fine crew,' Ananda said, and shouted again.

The burning tree shed sparks upwards into the night, brighter than the Galaxy. Its trunk was a shadow inside a roaring pillar of hot blue flame. Heat and light beat out across the road. It was a young sweetgum tree. Derev had soaked its trunk with kerosene from the lantern's reservoir, and had ignited it with the lantern's flint when Lob had fallen on Yama.

'Even Lob and Lud won't forget this,' Derev said gleefully.

'That is what I mean,' Yama said.

'They'll be too ashamed to try anything. Frightened by a tree. It's too funny, Yama. They'll leave us alone from now on.'

Ananda helped the anchorite sit up. The man dabbed at the blood crusted under his nose, cautiously bent and unbent his knees, then scrambled to his feet. Yama held out the staff, and the man took it and briefly bowed his head in thanks.

Yama bowed back, and the man grinned. Something had seared the left side of his face; a web of silvery scar tissue pulled down his eye and lifted the corner of his mouth. He was so dirty that the grain of his skin looked like embossed leather. The metallic cloth of his robe was filthy, too, but here and there patches and creases reflected the light of the burning tree. His hair was tangled in ropes around his face, and bits of twig were caught in his forked beard. He smelt powerfully of sweat and urine. He fixed Yama with an intense gaze, then made shapes with the fingers of his right hand against the palm of his left.

Ananda said, 'He wants you to know that he has been searching for you.'

'You can understand him?'

'We used hand speech like this in the seminary, to talk to each other during breakfast and supper when we were supposed to be listening to one of the brothers read from the Puranas. Some anchorites were once priests, and perhaps this is such a one.'

The man shook his head violently, and made more shapes with his fingers.

Ananda said uncertainly, 'He says that he is glad that he remembered all this. I think he must mean that he will always remember this.'

'Well,' Derev said, 'so he should. We saved his life.'

The anchorite dug inside his robe and pulled out a ceramic disc. It was attached to a thong looped around his neck, and he lifted the thong over his head and thrust the disc towards Yama, then made more shapes.

'You are the one who is to come,' Ananda translated.

The anchorite shook his head and signed furiously, slamming his fingers against his palm.

'You will come here again. Yama, do you know what he means?'

And Derev said, 'Listen!'

Far off, whistles sounded, calling and answering in the darkness.

The anchorite thrust the ceramic disc into Yama's hand. He stared into Yama's eyes and then he was gone, running out along the footpath between the flooded fields, a shadow dwindling against cold blue light reflected from the water, gone.

The whistles sounded again. 'The militia,' Ananda said, and turned and ran off down the old road.

Derev and Yama chased after him, but he soon outpaced them, and Yama had to stop to catch his breath before they reached the city wall.

Derev said, 'Ananda won't stop running until he's thrown himself into his bed. And even then he'll run in his dreams until morning.'

Yama was bent over, clasping his knees. He had a cramp in his side. He said, 'We will have to watch out for each other. Lob and Lud will not forgive this easily. How can you run so fast and so far without getting out of breath?'

Derev's pale face glimmered in the Galaxy's light. She gave him a sly look. 'Flying is harder work than running.'

'If you can fly, I would love to see it. But you are teasing me again.'

'This is the wrong place for flying. One day, perhaps, I'll show you the right place, but it's a long way from here.'

'Do you mean the edge of the world? I used to dream that my people lived on the floating islands. I saw one—'

Derev suddenly grabbed Yama and pulled him into the long grass beside the track. He fell on top of her, laughing, but she put her hand over his mouth. 'Listen!' she said.

Yama raised his head, but heard only the ordinary noises of the night. He was aware of the heat of Derev's slim body pressing against his. He said, 'I think the militia have given up their search.'

'No. They're coming this way.'

Yama rolled over and parted the long dry grass so that he could watch the track. Presently a pentad of men went past in single file. None of them were of the bloodline of the citizens of Aeolis. They were armed with rifles and arbalests.

'Sailors,' Yama said, when he was sure that they were gone.

Derev pressed the length of her body against his. 'How do you know?'

'They were strangers, and all strangers come to Aeolis by the river, either as sailors or passengers. But there have been no passenger ships since the war began.'

'They are gone now, whoever they are.'

'Perhaps they were looking for the anchorite.'

'He was crazy, that holy man, but we did the right thing. Or you did. I could not have stepped out and challenged those two.'

'I did it knowing you were at my back.'

'I'd be nowhere else.' Derev added thoughtfully, 'He looked like you.'

Yama laughed.

'In the proportion of his limbs, and the shape of his head. And his eyes were halved by folds of skin, just like yours.'

Derev kissed Yama's eyes. He kissed her back. They kissed for a long time, and then Derev broke away.

'You aren't alone in the world, Yama, no matter what you believe. It shouldn't surprise you to find one of your own bloodline.'

But Yama had been looking for too long to believe it would be that easy. 'I think he was crazy. I wonder why he gave me this.'

Yama pulled the ceramic disc from the pocket of his tunic. It seemed no different from the discs the Aedile's workmen turned up by the hundred during their excavations: slick, white, slightly too large to fit comfortably in his palm. He held it up so that it faintly reflected the light of the Galaxy, and saw a distant light in the crooked tower that stood without the old, half-ruined city wall.

Dr Dismas had returned from Ys.

3 ~ Dr Dismas

Dr Dismas's bent-backed, black-clad figure came up the dry, stony hillside with a bustling, crabbed gait. The sun was at the height of its daily leap into the sky, and, like an aspect, he cast no shadow.

The Aedile, standing at the top of the slope by the spoil-heap of his latest excavation site, watched with swelling expectation as the apothecary drew near. The Aedile was tall and stooped and greying, with a diplomat's air of courteous reticence which many mistook for absent-mindedness. He was dressed after the fashion of the citizens of Aeolis, in a loose-fitting white tunic and a linen kilt. His knees were swollen and stiff from the hours he had spent kneeling on a leather pad brushing away dirt, hairfine layer after hairfine layer, from a ceramic disc, freeing it from the cerements of a hundred thousand years of burial. The excavation was not going well and the Aedile had grown bored with it before it was halfway done. Despite the insistence of his geomancer, he was convinced that nothing of interest would be found. The crew of trained diggers, convicts reprieved from army service, had caught their master's mood and worked at a desultory pace amongst the neatly dug trenches and pits, dragging their chains through dry white dust as they carried baskets of soil and limestone chippings to the conical spoil heap. A drill rig taking a core through the reef of land coral which had overgrown the hilltop raised a plume of white dust that feathered off into the blue sky.

So far, the excavation had uncovered only a few potsherds, the corroded traces of what might have been the footings of a watchtower, and the inevitable hoard of ceramic discs. Although the Aedile had no idea what the discs had actually been used for (most scholars of Confluence's early history believed that they were some form of currency, but the Aedile thought that this was too obvious an explanation), he assiduously catalogued every one, and spent hours measuring the faint grooves and pits with which they were decorated. The Aedile believed in measurement. In small things were the gauge of the larger world which contained them, and of worlds without end. He believed that all measurements and constants might be arithmetically derived from a single number, the cypher of the Preservers which could unlock the secrets of the world they had made, and much else.

But here was Dr Dismas, with news that would determine the fate of the Aedile's foundling son. The pinnace on which the apothecary had returned from Ys had anchored beyond the mouth of the bay two days before (and was anchored there still), and Dr Dismas had been rowed ashore last night, but the Aedile had chosen to spend the day at his excavation site rather than wait at the peel-house for Dr Dismas's call. Better that he heard the news, whatever it was, before Yama.

It was the Aedile's hope that Dr Dismas had discovered the truth about the bloodline of his adopted son, but he did not trust the man, and was troubled by speculations about the ways in which Dr Dismas might misuse his findings. It was Dr Dismas, after all, who had proposed that he take the opportunity offered by his summons to Ys to undertake research into the matter of Yama's lineage. That this trip had been forced upon Dr Dismas by his department, and had been entirely funded from the Aedile's purse, would not reduce by one iota the obligation which Dr Dismas would surely expect the Aedile to express.

Dr Dismas disappeared behind the tipped white cube of one of the empty tombs which were scattered beneath the brow of the hill like beads flung from a broken necklace – tombs of the dissolute time after the Age of Insurrection and the last to be built in the City of the Dead, simple boxes set at the edge of the low, rolling hills, crowded with monuments, tombs and statues of the ancient necropolis. Presently, Dr Dismas reappeared almost at the Aedile's feet and laboured up the last hundred paces of the steep, rough path. He was breathing hard. His sharp-featured face, propped amongst the high wings of his black coat's collar and shaded by a black, broad-brimmed hat, was sprinkled with sweat in which, like islands in the slowly shrinking river, the plaques of his addiction stood isolated.

'A warm day,' the Aedile said, by way of greeting.

Dr Dismas took out a lace handkerchief from his sleeve and fastidiously dabbed sweat from his face. 'It *is* hot. Perhaps Confluence tires of circling the sun and is falling into it, like a girl tumbling into the arms of her lover. Perhaps we'll be consumed by the fire of their passion.'

Usually, Dr Dismas's rhetorical asides amused the Aedile, but this wordplay only intensified his sense of foreboding. He said mildly, 'I trust that your business was successful, doctor.'

Dr Dismas dismissed it with a flick of his handkerchief, like a conjuror.

'It was nothing. Routine puffed up with pomp. My department is fond of pomp, for it is, after all, a very old department. I am returned, my Aedile, to serve, if I may, with renewed vigour.'

'I had never thought to withdraw that duty from you, my dear doctor.'

'You are too kind. And more generous than the miserable termagants who nest amongst the dusty ledgers of my department, and do nothing but magnify rumour into fact.'

Dr Dismas had turned to gaze, like a conqueror, across the dry slope of the hill and its scattering of abandoned tombs, the patchwork of flooded fields along the Breas and the tumbled ruins and cluster of roofs of Aeolis at its mouth, the long finger of the new quay pointing across banks of green mud towards the Great River, which stretched away, shining like polished silver, to a misty union of water and air. Now he stuck a cigarette in his holder (carved, he liked to say, from the finger-bone of a multiple murderer; he cultivated a sense of the macabre), lit it and drew deeply, holding his breath for a count of ten before blowing a riffle of smoke through his nostrils with a satisfied sigh.

Dr Dismas was the apothecary of Aeolis, hired a year ago by the same council which regulated the militia. He had been summoned to Ys to account for several lapses since he had taken up his position. He was said to have substituted glass powder for the expensive suspensions of tiny machines which cured river blindness – and certainly there had been more cases of river blindness the previous summer, although the Aedile attributed this to the greater numbers of biting flies which bred in the algae which choked the mud banks of the former harbour. More seriously, Dr Dismas was said to have peddled his treatments amongst the fisherfolk and the hill tribes, making extravagant claims that he could cure cankers, blood cough and mental illness, and halt or even reverse aging. There were rumours, too, that he had made or grown chimeras of children and beasts, and that he had kidnapped a child from one of the hill tribes and used its blood and perfusions of its organs to treat one of the members of the Council for Night and Shrines.

The Aedile had dismissed all of these allegations as fantasies, but then a boy had died after blood-letting, and the parents, mid-caste chandlers, had lodged a formal protest. The Aedile had had to sign it. A field investigator of the Department of Apothecaries and Chirurgeons had arrived a hundred days ago, but quickly left in some confusion. It seemed that Dr Dismas had threatened to kill him when he had tried to force an interview. And then the formal summons had arrived, which the Aedile had had to read out to

Dr Dismas in front of the Council of Night and Shrines. The doctor had been commanded to return to Ys for formal admonishment, both for his drug habit and (as the document delicately put it) for certain professional lapses. The Aedile had been informed that Dr Dismas had been placed on probation, although from the doctor's manner he might have won a considerable victory rather than a reprieve.

The apothecary drew deeply on his cigarette and said, 'The river voyage was a trial in itself. It made me so febrile that I had to lay in bed on the pinnace for a day after it anchored before I was strong enough to be taken ashore. I am still not quite recovered.'

'Quite, quite,' the Aedile said. 'I am sure you came here as soon as you could.'

But he did not believe it for a moment. The apothecary was up to something, no doubt about it.

'You have been working with those convicts of yours again. Don't deny it. I see the dirt under your nails. You are too old to be kneeling under the burning sun.'

'I wore my hat, and coated my skin with the unguent you prescribed.' The sticky stuff smelled strongly of menthol, and raised the fine hairs of the Aedile's pelt into stiff peaks, but it seemed uncharitable to complain.

'You should also wear glasses with tinted lenses. Cumulative ultraviolet will damage your corneas, and at your age that can be serious. I believe I see some inflammation there. Your excavations will proceed apace without your help. Day by day, you climb down into the past. I fear you will leave us all behind. Is the boy well? I trust you have taken better care of him than of yourself.'

'I do not think I will learn anything here. There are the footings of a tower, but the structure itself must have been dismantled long ago. A tall tower, too; the foundations are very deep, although quite rusted away. I believe that it might have been made of metal, although that would have been fabulously costly even in the Age of Enlightenment. The geomancer may have been misled by the remains into thinking that a larger structure was once built here. It has happened before. Or perhaps there is something buried deeper. We will see.'

The geomancer had been from one of the hill tribes, a man half the Aedile's age, but made wizened and toothless by his harsh nomadic life, one eye milky with a cataract which Dr Dismas had later removed. This had been in winter, with hoarfrost mantling the ground each morning, but the geomancer had gone about barefoot, and naked under his red wool cloak. He had fasted three days on the hilltop before scrying out the site with a thread weighted with a sliver of lodestone.

Dr Dismas said, 'In Ys, there are buildings which are said to have once been entirely clad in metal.'

'Quite, quite. If it can be found anywhere on Confluence, then it can be found in Ys.'

'So they say, but who would know where to begin to look?'

'If there is any one person, then that would be you, my dear Dr Dismas.'

'I would like to think I have done my best for you.'

'And for the boy. More importantly, the boy.'

Dr Dismas gave the Aedile a quick, piercing look. 'Of course. That goes without saying.'

'It is for the boy,' the Aedile said again. 'His future is constantly in my thoughts.'

With the thumb and forefinger of his left hand, which were as stiffly crooked as the claw of a crayfish, Dr Dismas plucked the stub of his cigarette from the bone holder and crushed its coal. His left hand was almost entirely affected by the drug; although the discrete plaques allowed limited flexure, they had robbed the fingers of all feeling.

The Aedile waited while Dr Dismas went through the ritual of lighting another cigarette. There was something of Dr Dismas's manner that reminded the Aedile of a sly, sleek nocturnal animal, secretive in its habits but always ready to pounce on some scrap or titbit. He was a gossip, and like all gossips knew how to pace his revelations, how to string out a story and tease his audience – but the Aedile knew that like all gossips, Dr Dismas could not hold a secret long. So he waited patiently while Dr Dismas fitted another cigarette in the holder, and lit and drew on it. The Aedile was by nature a patient man, and his training in diplomacy had inured him to waiting on the whims of others.

Dr Dismas blew streams of smoke through his nostrils and said at last, 'It wasn't easy, you know.'

'Oh, quite so. I did not think it would be. The libraries are much debased these days. Since the librarians fell silent, there is a general feeling that there is no longer the need to maintain anything but the most recent records, and so everything older than a thousand years is considerably compromised.'

The Aedile realized that he had said too much. He was nervous, there on the threshold of revelation.

Dr Dismas nodded vigorously. 'And there is the present state of confusion brought about by the current political situation. It is most regrettable.'

'Quite, quite. Well, but we are at war.'

'I meant the confusion in the Palace of the Memory of the People itself, something for which your department, my dear Aedile, must take a considerable part of the blame. All of these difficulties suggest that we are trying to forget the past, as the Committee for Public Safety teaches we should.'

The Aedile was stung by this remark, as Dr Dismas had no doubt intended. The Aedile had been exiled to this tiny backwater city after the triumph of the Committee for Public Safety because he had spoken against the destruction of the records of past ages. It was to his everlasting shame that he had only spoken out, and not fought, as had many of his faction. And now his wife was dead. And his son. Only the

Aedile was left, still in exile because of a political squabble mostly long forgotten.

The Aedile said with considerable asperity, 'The past is not so easily lost, my dear doctor. Each night, we have only to look up at the sky to be reminded of that. In winter, we see the Galaxy, sculpted by unimaginable forces in ages past; in summer, we see the Eye of the Preservers. And here in Aeolis, the past is more important than the present. After all, how much greater are the tombs than the mudbrick houses down by the bay? Even stripped of their ornaments, the tombs are greater, and will endure in ages to come. All that lived in Ys during the Golden Age once came to rest here, and much remains to be discovered.'

Dr Dismas ignored this. He said, 'Despite these difficulties, the library of my department is still well-ordered. Several of the archive units are still completely functional under manual control, and they are amongst the oldest on Confluence. If records of the boy's bloodline could be found anywhere, it is there. But although I searched long and hard, of the boy's bloodline, well, I could find no trace.'

The Aedile thought that he had misheard. 'What is that? None at all?'

'I wish it were otherwise. Truly I do.'

'This is – I mean to say, it is unexpected. Quite unexpected.'

'I was surprised myself. As I say, the records of my department are perhaps the most complete on Confluence. Certainly, I believe that they are the only fully usable set, ever since your own department purged the archivists of the Palace of the Memory of the People.'

The Aedile failed to understand what Dr Dismas had told him. He said weakly, 'There was no correspondence . . .'

'None at all. All Shaped bloodlines possess the universal sequence of genes inserted by the Preservers at the time of the remaking of our ancestors. No matter who we are, no matter the code in which our cellular inheritance is written, the meaning of those satellite sequences are the same. But although tests of the boy's self-awareness and rationality show that he is not an indigen, like them he lacks that which marks the Shaped as the chosen children of the Preservers. And more than that, the boy's genome is quite different from anything on Confluence.'

'But apart from the mark of the Preservers we are all different from each other, doctor. We are all remade in the image of the Preservers in our various ways.'

'Indeed. But every bloodline shares a genetic inheritance with certain of the beasts and plants and microbes of Confluence. Even the various races of simple indigens, which were not marked by the Preservers and which cannot evolve towards transcendence, have genetic relatives amongst the flora and fauna. The ancestors of the ten thousand bloodlines of Confluence were not brought here all alone; the Preservers also brought something of the home worlds of each of them. It seems that young Yamamanama is more truly a foundling than we first believed, for there is nothing on record, no bloodline, no plant, no beast, nor even any microbe, which has anything in common with him.'

Only Dr Dismas called the boy by his full name. It had been given to him by the wives of the old Constable, Thaw. In their language, the language of the harems, it meant *Child of the River*. The Council for Night and Shrines had met in secret after the baby had been found on the river by Constable Thaw, and it had been decided that he should be killed by exposure, for he might be a creature of the heretics, or some other kind of demon. But the baby had survived for ten days amongst the tombs on the hillside above Aeolis, and the women who had finally rescued him, defying their husbands, had said that bees had brought him pollen and water, proving that he was under the protection of the Preservers. Even so, no family in Aeolis would take in the baby, and so he had come to live in the peel-house, son to the Aedile and brother to poor Telmon.

The Aedile thought of this as he tried to fathom the implications of Dr Dismas's discovery. Insects chirred all around in the dry grasses, insects and grass perhaps from the same long-lost world as the beasts which the Preservers had shaped into the ancestors of his own bloodline. There was a comfort, a continuity, in knowing that you were a part of the intricate tapestry of the wide world. Imagine then what it would be like to grow up alone in a world with no knowledge of your bloodline, and no hope of finding one! For the first time that day, the Aedile remembered his wife, dead more than twenty years now. A hot day then, too, and yet how cold her hands had been. His eyes pricked with the beginnings of tears, but he controlled himself. It would not do to show emotion in front of Dr Dismas, who preyed on weakness like a wolf which follows a herd of antelope.

'All alone,' the Aedile said. 'Is that possible?'

'If he were a plant or an animal, then perhaps.' Dr Dismas pinched out the coal of his second cigarette, dropped the stub and ground it under the heel of his boot. Dr Dismas's black calf-length boots were new, the Aedile noted, hand-tooled leather soft as butter.

'We could imagine him to be a stowaway,' Dr Dismas said. 'A few ships still ply their old courses between Confluence and the mine worlds, and one could imagine something stowing away on one of them. Perhaps the boy is an animal, able to mimic the attributes of intelligence, in the way that certain insects mimic a leaf or a twig. But then we must ask, what is the difference between the reality and the mimic?'

The Aedile was repulsed by this notion. He could not bear to think that his own dear adopted son was an animal imitating a human being. He said, 'Anyone trying to pluck such a leaf would know.'

'Exactly. Even a perfect mimic differs from what it is imitating in that it *is* an imitation, with the ability to dissemble, to appear to be something it is not, to become something else. I know of no creature which is so perfect a

47

mimic that it becomes the thing it is imitating. While there are insects which resemble leaves, they cannot make their food from sunlight. They cling to the plant, but they are not part of it.'

'Quite, quite. But if the boy is not part of our world, then where is he from? The old mine worlds are uninhabited.'

'Wherever he is from, I believe him to be dangerous. Remember how he was found. "In the arms of a dead woman, in a frail craft on the flood of the river." Those, I believe, were your exact words.'

The Aedile remembered old Constable Thaw's story. The man had shamefully confessed the whole story after his wives had delivered the foundling to the peel-house. Constable Thaw had been a coarse and cunning man, but he had taken his duties seriously.

The Aedile said, 'But my dear doctor, you cannot believe that Yama killed the woman – he was just a baby.'

'Someone got rid of him,' Dr Dismas said. 'Someone who could not bear to kill him. Or was not able to kill him.'

'I have always thought that the woman was his mother. She was fleeing from something, no doubt from scandal or from her family's condemnation, and she gave birth to him there on the river, and died. It is the simplest explanation, and surely the most likely.'

'We do not know all the facts of the case,' Dr Dismas said. 'However, I did examine the records left by my predecessor. She performed several neurological tests on Yamaman-ama soon after he was brought to your house, and continued to perform them for several years afterwards. Counting backwards, and allowing for a good margin of error, I formed the opinion that Yamamanama had been born at least fifty days before he was found on the river. We are all marked by our intelligence. Unlike the beasts of the field, we must all of us continue our development outside the womb, because the womb does not supply sufficient sensory input to stimulate growth of neural pathways. I have no reason to doubt that this is not a universal law for all intelligent races. All the tests indicated that it was no newborn baby that Constable Thaw rescued.'

'Well, no matter where he came from, or why, it seems that we are all he has, doctor.'

Dr Dismas looked around. Although the nearest workers were fifty paces away, chipping in a desultory way at the edge of the neat square of the excavated pit, he stepped closer to the Aedile and said confidingly, 'You overlook one possibility. Since the Preservers abandoned Confluence, one new race has appeared, albeit briefly.'

The Aedile smiled. 'You scoff at my theory, doctor, but at least it fits with what is known, whereas you make a wild leap into thin air. The ship of the Ancients of Days passed downriver twenty years before Yama was found floating in his cradle, and no members of its crew remained on Confluence.'

'Their heresies live on. We are at war with their ideas. The Ancients of Days were the ancestors of the Preservers, and we cannot guess at their powers.' Dr Dismas looked sideways at the Aedile. 'I believe,' he said, 'that there have been certain portents, certain signs . . . The rumours are vague. Perhaps you know more. Perhaps it would help if you told me about them.'

'I trust you have spoken to no one else,' the Aedile said. 'Talk like this, wild though it is, could put Yama in great danger.'

'I understand why you have not discussed Yamamanama's troublesome origin before, even to your own department. But the signs are there, for those who know how to look. The number of machines that flit at the borders of Aeolis, for instance. You cannot hide these things for ever.'

The machines around the white boat. The woman in the shrine. Yama's silly trick with the watchdogs. The bees which had fed the abandoned baby had probably been machines, too.

The Aedile said carefully, 'We should not talk of such things here. It requires discretion.'

He would never tell Dr Dismas everything. The man presumed too much, and he was not to be trusted.

'I am, and shall continue to be, the soul of discretion.'

Never before had Dr Dismas's dark, sharp-featured face seemed so much like a mask. It was why the man took the drug, the Aedile realized. The drug was a shield from the gaze and the hurts of the world.

The Aedile said sternly, 'I mean it, Dismas. You will say nothing of what you found, and keep your speculations to yourself. I want to see what you found. Perhaps there is something you missed.'

'I will bring the papers tonight, but you will see that I am right in every particular. Now, if I may have permission to leave,' Dr Dismas said, 'I would like to recover from my journey. Think carefully about what I told you. We stand at the threshold of a great mystery.'

When Dr Dismas had gone, the Aedile called for his secretary. While the man was preparing his pens and ink and setting a disc of red wax to soften on a sunwarmed stone, the Aedile composed in his head the letter he needed to write. The letter would undermine Dr Dismas's already blemished reputation and devalue any claims the apothecary might make on Yama, but it would not condemn him outright. It would suggest a suspicion that Dr Dismas, because of his drug habit, might be involved with the heretics who had recently tried to set fire to the floating docks, but it must be the merest of hints hedged round with equivocation, for the Aedile was certain that if Dr Dismas was ever arrested, he would promptly confess all he knew. The Aedile realized then that they were linked by a cat's cradle of secrets that was weighted with the soul of the foundling boy, the stranger, the sacrifice, the gift, the child of the river.

4 ~ Yamamanama

Yama remembered nothing of the circumstances of his birth, or of how he had arrived at Aeolis in a skiff steered by a man with a corpse at his feet and the blood of his own son fresh on his hands. Yama knew only that Aeolis was home, and knew it as intimately as only a child can, especially a child who has been adopted by the city's Aedile and so wears innocently and unknowingly an intangible badge of privilege.

In its glory, before the Age of Insurrection, Aeolis, named for the winter wind that sang through the passes of the hills above the broad valley of the river Breas, had been the disembarkation point for the City of the Dead. Ys had extended far downriver in those days, and then as now it was the law that no one could be buried within its boundaries. Instead, mourners accompanied their dead to Aeolis, where funeral pyres for the lesser castes burned day and night, temples rang with prayers and songs for the preserved bodies of the rich and altars shone with constellations of butter lamps that shimmered amongst heaps of flowers and strings of prayer flags. The ashes of the poor were cast on the waters of the Great River; the preserved bodies of the ruling and mercantile classes, and of scholars and dynasts, were interred in tombs whose ruined, empty shells still riddled the dry hills beyond the town. The Breas, which then had been navigable almost to its source in the foothills of the Rim Mountains, had been crowded with barges bringing slabs of land coral, porphyry, granite, marble and all kinds of precious stones for the construction of the tombs.

An age later, after half the world had been turned to desert during the rebellion of the feral machines, and the Preservers had withdrawn their blessing from Confluence, and Ys had retreated, contracting about its irreducible heart, funeral barges no longer ferried the dead to Aeolis; instead, bodies were launched from the docks and piers of Ys onto the full flood of the Great River, given up to caymans and fish, lammer-geyers and carrion crows. As these creatures consumed the dead, so Aeolis consumed its own past. Tombs were looted of treasures; decorative panels and frescoes were removed from the walls; preserved bodies were stripped of their clothes and jewellery; the hammered bronze facings of doors and tomb furniture were melted down – the old pits of the wind-powered smelters were still visible along the escarpment above the little city.

After most of the tombs had been stripped, Aeolis became no more than a way station, a place where ships put in to replenish their supplies of fresh food on their voyages downriver from Ys. This was the city that Yama knew. There was the new quay which ran across the mudflats and stands of zebra grass of the old, silted harbour to the retreating edge of the Great River, where the fisherfolk of the floating islands gathered in their little coracles to sell strings of oysters and mussels, spongy parcels of red river moss, bundles of riverweed stipes, and shrimp and crabs and fresh fish. There were always people swimming off the new quay or splashing about in coracles and small boats, and men working at the fish traps and the shoals at the mouth of the shallow Breas where razorshell mussels were cultivated, and divers hunting for urchins and abalone amongst the holdfasts of stands of giant kelp whose long blades formed vast brown slicks on the surface of the river. There was the long road at the top of the ruined steps of the old waterfront, where tribesmen from the dry hills of the wild shore downriver of Aeolis squatted at blanket stalls to sell fruit and fresh meat, and dried mushrooms and manna lichen, and bits of lapis lazuli and marble pried from the wrecked facings of ancient tombs. There were ten taverns and two whorehouses; the chandlers' godowns and the farmers' cooperative; straggling streets of mudbrick houses which leaned towards each other over narrow canals; the one surviving temple, its walls white as salt, the gilt of its dome recently renewed by public subscription. And then the ruins of the ancient mortuaries, more extensive than the town, and fields of yams and raffia and yellow peas, and flooded paddies where rice and paeonin were grown. One of the last of Aeolis's mayors had established the paeonin industry in an attempt to revitalize the little city, but when the heretics had silenced the shrines at the beginning of the war there had been a sudden shrinkage in the priesthood and a decline in trade of the pigment which dyed their robes. These days, the mill, built at the downriver point of the bay so that its effluent would not contaminate the silty bay, worked only one day in ten.

Most of the population of Aeolis were of the same bloodline. They called themselves the Amnan, which meant simply *the human beings*; their enemies called them the Mud People. They had bulky but well-muscled bodies and baggy grey or brown skin. Clumsy on land, they were strong swimmers and adept aquatic predators, and had hunted giant otters and manatees almost to extinction along that part of the Great River. They had preyed upon the indigenous fisherfolk, too, before the Aedile had arrived and put a stop to it. More women were born than men, and sons fought their fathers for control of the harem; if they won, they killed their younger brothers or drove them out. The people of Aeolis still talked about the fight between old Constable Thaw and his son. It had lasted five days, and had ranged up and down the waterfront and through the net of canals between the houses until Thaw, his legs paralysed, had been drowned in the shallow stream of the Breas.

It was a barbaric custom, the Aedile said, a sign that the Amnan were reverting to their bestial nature. The Aedile went into the city as little as possible – rarely more than once every hundred days, and then only to the temple to attend the high day service with Yama and Telmon sitting to the right and left side of their father in scratchy robes, on hard, ornately carved chairs, facing the audience throughout the three or four hours of obeisances and offerings, prayer and praise-songs. Yama loved the sturdy square temple, with its clean high spaces, the black disc of its shrine in its ornate gilded frame, and walls glowing with mosaics picturing scenes of the end times, in which the Preservers (shown as clouds of light) ushered the re-created dead into perfect worlds of parklands and immaculate gardens. He loved the pomp and circumstance of the ceremonies, too, although he thought that it was unnecessary. The Preservers, who watched all, did not need ritual praise; to walk and work and play in the world they had made was praise enough. He was happier worshipping at the shrines which stood near the edge of the world on the far side of the Great River, visited every year during the winter festival when the triple spiral of the Home Galaxy first rose in its full glory above the Great River and most of the people of Aeolis migrated to the farside shore in a swarm of boats to set up camps and bonfires and greet the onset of winter with fireworks, and dance and pray and drink and feast for a whole decad.

The Aedile had taken Yama into his household, but he was a remote, scholarly man, busy with his official duties or preoccupied with his excavations and the endless measurements and calculations by which he tried to divide everything into everything else in an attempt to discover the prime which harmonized the world, and perhaps the Universe. It left him with little in the way of small talk. Like many unworldly, learned men, the Aedile treated children as miniature adults, failing to recognize that they were elemental, unfired vessels whose stuff was malleable and fey.

As a consequence of the Aedile's benign neglect, Yama and Telmon spent much of their childhood being passed from one to another of the household servants, or running free amongst the tombs of the City of the Dead. In summer, the Aedile often left the peel-house for a month at a time, taking most of his household to one or another of his excavation sites in the dry hills and valleys beyond Aeolis. When they were not helping with the slow, painstaking work, Yama and Telmon went hunting and exploring amongst desert suburbs of the City of the Dead, Telmon searching for unusual insects for his collection, Yama interrogating aspects – he had a knack for awakening them, and for tormenting and teasing them into revealing details of the lives of the people on whom they were based, and for whom they were both guardians and advocates.

Telmon was the natural leader of the two, five years older, tall and solemn and patient and endlessly inquisitive, with a fine black pelt shot through with chestnut highlights. He was a natural horseman and an excellent shot with bow, arbalest and rifle, and often went off by himself for days at a time, hunting in the high ranges of hills where the Breas ran white and fast through the locks and ponds of the old canal system. He loved Yama like a true brother, and Yama loved him in turn, and was as devastated as the Aedile by news of his death.

Formal education resumed in winter. For four days each decad Yama and Telmon were taught fencing, wrestling and horsemanship by Sergeant Rhodean; for the rest, their education was entrusted to the librarian, Zakiel. Zakiel was a slave, the only one in the peel-house; he had once been an archivist, but had committed an unspeakable heresy. Zakiel did not seem to mind being a slave. Before he had been branded, he had worked in the vast stacks of the library of the Palace of the Memory of the People, and now he was librarian of the peel-house. He ate his simple meals amongst dusty tiers of books and scrolls, and slept in a cot in a dark corner under a cliff of quarto-sized ledgers whose thin metal covers, spotted with corrosion, had not been disturbed for centuries. All knowledge could be found in books, Zakiel declared, and if he had a passion (apart from his mysterious heresy, which he had never renounced) it was this. He was perhaps the happiest man in the Aedile's household, for he needed nothing but his work.

'Since the Preservers fully understand the Universe, and hold it whole in their minds, then it follows that all texts, which flow from minds forged by the Preservers, are reflections of their immanence,' Zakiel told Yama and Telmon more than once. 'It is not the world itself we should measure, but the reflections of the world, filtered through the creations of the Preservers and set down in these books. Of course, boys, you must never tell the Aedile I said this. He is happy in his pursuit of the ineffable, and I would not trouble him with these trivial matters.'

Yama and Telmon were supposed to be taught the Summalae Logicales, the Puranas and the Protocols of the Department, but mostly they listened to Zakiel read passages from selected works of natural philosophy before engaging in long, formal discussions. Yama first learned to read upside-down by watching Zakiel's long, ink-stained forefinger tracking glyphs from right to left while listening to the librarian recite in a sing-song voice, and later had to learn to read all over again, this time the right away up, to be able to recite in his turn. Yama and Telmon had most of the major verses of the Puranas by heart, and were guided by Zakiel to read extensively in chrestomathies and incunabulae, but while Telmon dutifully followed the programme Zakiel set out, Yama preferred to idle time away dreaming over bestiaries, prosopographies and maps – most especially maps.

Yama stole many books from the library. Taking them was a way of possessing the ideas and wonders they contained, as if he might, piece by piece, seize the whole world. Zakiel retrieved most of the books from various hiding places in the house or the ruins in its grounds, using a craft more subtle than the tracking skills of either Telmon or Sergeant Rhodean, but one thing Yama managed to retain was a map of the inhabited half of the world. The map's scroll was the width of his hand and almost twice the length of his body, wound on a resin spindle decorated with tiny figures of a thousand bloodlines frozen in representative poses. The map was printed on a material finer than silk and stronger than steel. At one edge were the purple and brown and white ridges of the Rim Mountains; at the other was the blue ribbon of the Great River, with a narrow unmarked margin at its far shore. Yama knew that there were many shrines and monuments to pillar saints on the farside shore – he visited some of them each year, when the whole city crossed the Great River to celebrate with fireworks and feasting the rise of the Galaxy at the beginning of winter – and he wondered why the map did not show them. For there was so much detail crammed into the map elsewhere. Between the Great River and the Rim Mountains was the long strip of inhabited land, marked with green plains and lesser mountain ranges and chains of lakes and ochre deserts. Most cities were scattered along the Great River's nearside shore, a thousand or more which lit up with their names when Yama touched them. The greatest of them all stood below the head of the Great River: Ys, a vast blot spread beyond the braided delta where the river gathered its strength from the glaciers and icefields which buried all but the peaks of the Terminal Mountains. When the map had been made, Ys had been at the height of its glory and its intricate grids of streets and parks and temples stretched from the shore of the Great River to the foothills and canyons at the edge of the Rim Mountains. A disc of plain glass, attached to the spindle of the map by a reel of wire, revealed details of these streets. By squeezing the edges of the disc the magnification could be adjusted to show individual buildings, and Yama spent long hours gazing at the crowded rooftops, imagining himself smaller than a speck of dust and able to wander the ancient streets of a more innocent age.

More and more, as he came into manhood, Yama was growing restless. He dreamed of searching for his bloodline. Perhaps they were a high-born and fabulously wealthy clan, or a crew of fierce adventurers who had sailed their ships downstream to the midpoint of the world and the end of the Great River, and fallen from the edge and gone adventuring amongst the floating islands; or perhaps they belonged to a coven of wizards with magic powers, and those same powers lay slumbering within him, waiting to be awakened. Yama elaborated enormously complicated stories around his imagined bloodline, some of which Telmon listened to patiently in the watches of the night, when they were camped amongst the tombs of the City of the Dead.

'Never lose your imagination, Yama,' Telmon told him. 'Whatever you are, wherever you come from, that is your most important gift. But you must observe the world, too, learn how to read and remember its every detail, celebrate its hills and forests and deserts and mountains, the Great River and the thousands of rivers that run into it, the thousand cities and the ten thousand bloodlines. I know how much you love that old map, but you must live in the world as it is to really know it. Do that, and think how rich and wild and strange your stories will become. They will make you famous, I know it.'

This was at the end of the last winter Telmon had spent at home, a few days before he took his muster to war. He and Yama were on the high moors three days' ride inland, chasing the rumour of a dragon. Low clouds raced towards the Great River ahead of a cold wind, and a freezing rain, gritty with flecks of ice, blew in their faces as they walked at point with a straggling line of beaters on either side. The moors stretched away under the racing clouds, hummocky and drenched, grown over with dense stands of waist-high bracken and purple islands of springy heather, slashed with fast-running peaty streams and dotted with stands of wind-blasted juniper and cypress and bright green domes of bog moss. Yama and Telmon were walking because horses were driven mad by the mere scent of a dragon. They wore canvas trousers and long oilcloth slickers over down-lined jackets, and carried heavy carbon-fibre bows which stuck up behind their heads, and quivers of long arrows with sharply tapered ceramic heads. They were soaked and windblasted and utterly exhilarated.

'I will go with you,' Yama said. 'I will go to war, and fight by your side and write an epic about our adventures that will ring down the ages!'

Telmon laughed. 'I doubt that I will see any fighting at all!'

'Your muster will do the town honour, Tel, I know it.'

'At least they can drill well enough, but I hope that is all they will need to do.'

After the Aedile had received the order to supply a muster of a hundred troops to contribute to the war effort, Telmon had chosen the men himself, mostly younger sons who had little chance of establishing a harem. With the help of Sergeant Rhodean, Telmon had drilled them for sixty days; in three more, the ship would arrive to take them downriver to the war.

Telmon said, 'I want to bring them back safely, Yama. I will lead them into the fighting if I am ordered, but they are set down for working on the supply lines, and I will be content with that. For every man or woman fighting the heretics face to face, there are ten who bring up supplies, and build defences, or tend the wounded or bury the dead. That is why the muster has been raised in every village and town and city. The war needs support troops as desperately as it needs fighting men.'

'I will go as an irregular. We can fight together, Tel.'

'You will look after our father, first of all. And then there is Derev.'

'She would not mind. And it is not as if—'

Telmon understood. He said, 'There are plenty of metic marriages, if it does become that serious.'

'I think it might be, Tel. But I will not get married before you return, and I will not get married before I have had my chance to fight in the war.'

'I'm sure you will get your chance, if that is what you want. But be sure that you really want it.'

'Do you think the heretics really fight with magic?'

'They probably have technology given to them by the Ancients of Days. It might seem like magic, but that is only because we do not understand it. But we have right on our side, Yama. We are fighting with the will of the Preservers in our hearts. It is better than any magic.'

Telmon sprang onto a hummock of sedge and looked left and right to check the progress of the beaters, but it was Yama, staring straight ahead with the rain driving into his face, who saw a little spark of light suddenly blossom far out across the sweep of the moors. He cried out and pointed, and Telmon blew and blew on his silver whistle, and raised both arms above his head to signal that the beaters at the far end of each line should begin to walk towards each other and close the circle. Other whistles sounded as the signal was passed down the lines, and Yama and Telmon broke into a run against the wind and rain, leaping a stream and running on towards the scrap of light, which flickered and grew brighter in the midst of the darkening plain.

It was a juniper set on fire. It was burning so fiercely that it had scorched the grass all around it, snapping and crackling as fire consumed its needle-laden branches and tossed yellow flame and fragrant smoke into the wind and rain. Telmon and Yama gazed at it with wonder, then hugged and pounded each other on the back.

'It is here!' Telmon shouted. 'I know it is here!'

They cast around, and almost at once Telmon found the long scar in a stand of heather. It was thirty paces wide and more than five hundred long, burnt down to the earth and layered with wet black ashes.

It was a lek, Telmon said. 'The male makes it to attract females. The size and regularity of it shows that he is strong and fit.'

'This one must have been very big,' Yama said. The excitement he had felt while running towards the burning tree was gone; he felt a queer kind of relief now. He would not have to face the dragon. Not yet. He paced out the length of the lek while Telmon squatted with the blazing tree at his back and poked through the char.

'Four hundred and twenty-eight,' Yama said, when he came back. 'How big would the dragon be, Tel?'

'Pretty big. I think he was successful, too. Look at the claw marks here. There are two kinds.'

They quartered the area around the lek, moving quickly because the light was going. The tree had mostly burned out when the beaters arrived and helped widen the search. But the dragon was gone.

Three days later, Telmon and the muster from Aeolis boarded a carrack that had anchored at the floating harbour on its way from Ys to the war at the midpoint of the world. Yama did not go to see Telmon off, but stood on the bluff above the Great River and raised his fighting kite into the wind as the little flotilla of skiffs, each with a decad of men, rowed out to the great ship. Yama had painted the kite with a red dragon, its tail curled around its long body and fire pouring from its crocodile jaws, and he flew it high into the snapping wind and then lit the fuses and cut the string. The kite sailed out high above the Great River, and the chain of firecrackers exploded in flame and smoke until the last and biggest of all set fire to the kite's wide diamond, and it fell from the sky.

After the news of the death of Telmon, Yama began to feel an unfocused restlessness. He spent long hours studying the map or sweeping the horizons with the telescope in the tower which housed the heliograph, most often pointing it upriver, where there was always the sense of the teeming vast city, like a thunderstorm, looming beyond the vanishing point.

Ys! When the air was exceptionally clear, Yama could glimpse the slender gleaming towers rooted at the heart of the city. The towers were so tall that they rose beyond the limit of visibility, higher than the bare peaks of the Rimwall Mountains, punching through the atmosphere whose haze hid Ys itself. Ys was three days' journey by river and four times that by road, but even so the ancient city dominated the landscape, and Yama's dreams.

After Telmon's death, Yama began to plan his escape with meticulous care, although at first he did not think of it as escape at all, but merely an extension of the expeditions he had made, first with Telmon, and latterly with Ananda and Derev, in the City of the Dead. Sergeant Rhodean was fond of saying that most unsuccessful campaigns failed not because of the action of the enemy but because of lack of crucial supplies or unforeseeable circumstances, and so Yama made caches of stolen supplies in several hiding-places amongst the ruins in the garden of the peel-house. But he didn't seriously think of carrying out his plans until the night after the encounter with Lud and Lob, when Dr Dismas had an audience with the Aedile.

Dr Dismas arrived at the end of the evening meal. The Aedile and Yama customarily ate together in the Great Hall, sitting at one end of the long, polished table under the high, barrel-vaulted ceiling and its freight of hanging banners, most so ancient that all traces of the devices they had once borne had faded, leaving only a kind of insubstantial, tattered gauze. They were the sigils of the Aedile's ancestors. He had saved them from the great bonfires of the vanities when, after coming to power, the present administration of the Department of Indigenous Affairs had sought to eradicate the past.

Ghosts. Ghosts above, and a ghost unremarked in the empty chair at the Aedile's right hand.

Servants came and went with silent precision, bringing lentil soup, then slivers of mango dusted with ginger, and then a roast marmot dismembered on a bed of watercress. The Aedile said little except to ask after Yama's day.

Yama had spent the morning watching the pinnace which had anchored downriver of the bay three days ago, and now he remarked that he would like to take a boat out to have a closer look at it.

The Aedile said, 'I wonder why it does not anchor at the new quay. It is small enough to enter the mouth of the bay, yet does not. No, I do not think it would be good for you to go out to it, Yama. As well as good, brave men, all sorts of ruffians are recruited to fight the heretics.'

For a moment, they both thought of Telmon.

Ghosts, invisibly packing the air.

The Aedile changed the subject. 'When I first arrived here, ships of all sizes could anchor in the bay, and when the river level began to fall I had the new quay built. But now the bigger ships must use the floating harbour, and soon that will have to be moved further out to accommodate the largest of the argosies. From its present rate of shrinkage I have calculated that in less than five hundred years the river will be completely dry. Aeolis will be a port stranded in a desert plain.'

'There is the Breas.'

'Quite, quite, but where does the water of the Breas come from, except from the snows of the Rim Mountains, which in turn fall from air pregnant with water evaporated from the Great River? I have sometimes thought that it would be good for the town to have the old locks rebuilt. There is still good marble to be quarried in the hills.'

Yama mentioned that Dr Dismas was returned from Ys, but the Aedile only said, 'Quite, quite. I have even talked with him.'

'I suppose he has arranged some filthy little clerkship for me.'

'This is not the time to discuss your future,' the Aedile said, and retreated, as was increasingly his habit, into a book. He made occasional notes in the margins of its pages with one hand while he ate with the other at a slow, deliberate pace that was maddening to Yama. He wanted to go down to the armoury and question Sergeant Rhodean, who had returned from his patrol just before darkness.

The servants had cleared away the great silver salver bearing the marmot's carcass and were bringing in a dish of iced sherbet when the major domo paced down the long hall and announced the arrival of Dr Dismas.

'Bring him directly.' The Aedile shut his book, took off his spectacles, and told Yama, 'Run along, my boy. I know you want to quiz Sergeant Rhodean.'

Yama had used the telescope to spy on the Aedile and Dr Dismas that afternoon, when they had met and talked on the dusty hillside at the edge of the City of the Dead. He was convinced that Dr Dismas had been to Ys to arrange an apprenticeship in some dusty corner of the Aedile's department.

And so, although he set off towards the armoury, Yama quickly doubled back and crept into the gallery just beneath the Great Hall's high ceiling, where, on feast days, musicians hidden from view serenaded the Aedile's guests. Yama thrust his head between the stays of two dusty banners and found that he was looking straight down at the Aedile and Dr Dismas.

The two men were drinking port wine so dark that it was almost black, and Dr Dismas had lit one of his cigarettes. Yama could smell its clove-scented smoke. Dr Dismas sat stiffly in a carved chair, his white hands moving over the polished surface of the table like independently questing animals. Papers were scattered in front of him, and patterns of blue dots and dashes glowed in the air. Yama would have dearly loved to have had a spyglass just then, to find out what was written on the papers, and what the patterns meant.

Yama had expected to hear Dr Dismas and the Aedile discuss his apprenticeship, but instead the Aedile was making a speech about trust. 'When I took Yama into my household, I also took upon myself the responsibility of a parent. I have brought him up as best I could, and I have tried to make a decision about his future with his best interests in my heart. You ask me to overthrow that in an instant, to gamble my duty to the boy against some vague promise.'

'It is more than that,' Dr Dismas said. 'The boy's bloodline—'

Yama's heart beat more quickly, but the Aedile angrily interrupted Dr Dismas. 'That is of no consequence. I know what you told me. It only convinces me that I must see to the boy's future.'

'I understand. But, with respect, you may not be able to protect him from those who might be interested to learn of him, who might believe that they have a use for him. I speak of higher affairs than those of the Department of Indigenous Affairs. I speak of great forces, forces which your few decads of soldiers could not withstand for an instant. You should not put yourself between those powers and that which they may desire.'

The Aedile stood so suddenly that he knocked over his glass of port. High above, Yama thought that for a moment his guardian might strike Dr Dismas, but then the Aedile turned his back on the table and closed his fist under his chin. He said, 'Who did you tell, doctor?'

'As yet, only you.'

Yama knew that Dr Dismas was lying, because the answer sprang so readily to his lips. He wondered if the Aedile knew, too.

'I notice that the pinnace which brought you back from

Ys is still anchored off the point of the bay. I wonder why that might be.'

'I suppose I could ask its commander. He is an acquaintance of mine.'

The Aedile turned around. 'I see,' he said coldly. 'Then you threaten—'

'My dear Aedile, I do not come to your house to threaten you. I have better manners than that, I would hope. I make no threats, only predictions. You have heard my thoughts about the boy's bloodline. There is only one explanation. I believe any other man, with the same evidence, would come to the same conclusion as I, but it does not matter if I am right. One need only raise the possibility to understand what danger the boy might be in. We are at war, and you have been concealing him from your own department. You would not wish to have your loyalty put to the question. Not again.'

'Be careful, doctor. I could have you arrested. You are said to be a necromancer, and it is well known that you indulge in drugs.'

Dr Dismas said calmly, 'The first is only a rumour, and while the second may be true, you have recently demonstrated your faith in me, and your letter is lodged with my department. As, I might add, is a copy of my findings. You could arrest me, but you could not keep me imprisoned for long without appearing foolish or corrupt. But why do we argue? We both have the same interest. We both wish no harm to come to the boy. We merely disagree on how to protect him.'

The Aedile sat down and ran his fingers through the grey pelt which covered his face. He said, 'How much money do you want?'

Dr Dismas laughed. It was like the creaking of old wood giving beneath a weight. 'In one pan of the scales is the golden ingot of the boy; in the other the feather of your worth. I will not even pretend to be insulted.' He stood and plucked his cigarette from the holder and extinguished it in the pool of port spilled from the Aedile's glass, then reached into the glowing patterns. There was a click: the patterns vanished. Dr Dismas tossed the projector cube into the air and made it vanish into one of the pockets of his long black coat. He said, 'If you do not make arrangements, then I must. And believe me, you'll get the poorer part of the bargain if you do.'

When Dr Dismas had gone, the Aedile raked up the papers and clutched them to his chest. His shoulders shook. High above, Yama thought that his guardian might be crying, but surely he was mistaken, for never before, even at the news of Telmon's death, had the Aedile shown any sign of grief.

5 ~ The Siege

Yama lay awake long into the night, his mind racing with speculations about what Dr Dismas might have discovered. Something about his bloodline, he was sure of that at least, and he slowly convinced himself it was something with which Dr Dismas could blackmail the Aedile. Perhaps his real parents were heretics or murderers or pirates ... but who then would have a use for him, and what powers would take an interest? He was well aware that like all orphans he had filled the void of his parents' absence with extreme caricatures. They could be war heroes or colourful villains or dynasts wealthy beyond measure; what they could not be was ordinary, for that would mean that he too was ordinary, abandoned not because of some desperate adventure or deep scandal, but because of the usual small tragedies of the human condition. In his heart he knew these dreams for what they were, but although he had put them away, as he had put aside his childish toys, Dr Dismas's return had awakened them, and all the stories he had elaborated as a child tumbled through his mind in a vivid pageant that ravelled away into confused dreams filled with unspecific longing.

As the sun crept above the ragged blue line of the Rim Mountains, Yama was woken by a commotion below his window. He threw open the shutters and saw that three pentads of the garrison, in black resin armour ridged like the carapaces of sexton beetles and kilts of red leather strips, and with burnished metal caps on their heads, were climbing onto their horses. Squat, shaven-headed Sergeant Rhodean leaned on the pommel of his gelding's saddle as he watched his men settle themselves and their restless mounts. Puffs of vapour rose from the horses' nostrils; harness jingled and hooves clattered on concrete as they stepped about. Other soldiers were stacking ladders, grappling irons, siege rockets and coils of rope on the loadbed of the grimy black steam waggon. Two house servants manoeuvred the Aedile's palanquin, which floated a handspan above the ground, into the centre of the courtyard and then the Aedile himself appeared, clad in his robe of office, black sable trimmed with a collar of white feathers that ruffled in the cold dawn breeze.

The servants helped the Aedile over the flare of the palanquin's skirt and settled him in the backless chair beneath its red and gold canopy. Sergeant Rhodean raised a hand above his head and the procession, two files of mounted soldiers on either side of the palanquin, moved out of the courtyard. Black smoke and sparks shot up from the steam waggon's tall chimney; white vapour jetted from leaking piston sleeves. As the waggon ground forward, its iron-rimmed wheels striking sparks from concrete, Yama threw on his clothes; before it had passed through the arch of the gate in the old wall he was in the armoury, quizzing the stable hands.

'Off to make an arrest,' one of them said. It was the foreman, Torin. A tall man, his shaven bullet-head couched in the hump of muscle at his back, his skin a rich dark brown mapped with paler blotches. He had followed the Aedile into exile from Ys and, after Sergeant Rhodean, was the most senior of his servants. 'Don't be thinking we'll saddle up your horse, young master,' he told Yama. 'We've strict instructions that you're to stay here.'

'I suppose you are not allowed to tell me who they are going to arrest. Well, it does not matter. I know it is Dr Dismas.'

'The master was up all night,' Torin said, 'talking with the soldiers. Roused the cook hours ago to make him early breakfast. There might be a bit of a battle.'

'Who told you that?'

Torin gave Yama an insolent smile. His teeth were needles of white bone. 'Why it's plain to see. There's that ship still waiting offshore. It might try a rescue.'

The party of sailors. What had they been looking for? Yama said, 'Surely it is on our side.'

'There's some that reckon it's for Dr Dismas,' Torin said. 'That's how he came back to town, after all. There'll be blood shed before the end of it. Cook has his boys making bandages, and if you're looking for something to do you should join them.'

Yama ran again, this time to the kitchens. He snatched a sugar roll from a batch fresh from the baking oven, then climbed the back stairs two steps at a time, taking big bites from the warm roll. He waited behind a pillar while the old man who had charge of the Aedile's bedchamber locked the door and pottered off, crumpled towels over one arm, then used his knife to pick the lock, a modern mechanical thing as big as his head. It was easy to snap back the lock's wards one by one and to silence the machines which set up a chorus of protest at his entrance, although it took a whole minute to convince an alembic that his presence would not upset its delicate settings.

Quickly, Yama searched for the papers Dr Dismas had brought, but they were not amongst the litter on the Aedile's desk, nor were they in the sandalwood travelling chest, with its deck of sliding drawers. Perhaps the papers were in the room in the watchtower – but that had an old lock, and Yama had never managed to persuade it to let him pass.

He closed the chest and sat back on his heels. This part of the house was quiet. Narrow beams of early sunlight slanted through the tall, narrow windows, illuminating a patch of the richly patterned carpet, a book splayed upside-down on the little table beside the Aedile's reading chair. Zakiel would be waiting for him in the library, but there were more important things afoot. Yama went back out through the kitchen, cut across the herb garden and, after calming one of the watchdogs, ran down the steep slope of the breastwork and struck off through the ruins towards the city.

Dr Dismas's tower stood just outside the city wall. It was tall and slender, and had once been used to manufacture shot. Molten blackstone had been poured through a screen at the top of the tower, and the droplets, rounding into perfect spheres as they fell, had plummeted into an annealing bath of water at the base. The builders of the tower had sought to advertise its function by adding slit windows and a parapet with a crenellated balustrade in imitation of the watchtower of a castellan, and after the foundry had been razed, the tower had indeed been briefly used as a lookout post. But then the new city wall had been built with the tower outside it, and the tower had fallen into disuse, its stones slowly pried apart by the tendrils of its ivy cloak, the platform where molten stone had been made poured to make shot for the guns of soldiers and hunters becoming the haunt of owls and bats.

Dr Dismas had moved into the tower shortly after taking up his apothecary's post. Once it had been cleaned out and joiners had fitted new stairs and three circular floors within it and raised a tall slender spire above the crenellated balustrade, Dr Dismas had closed its door to the public, preferring to rent a room overlooking the waterfront as his office. There were rumours that he performed all kinds of black arts in the tower, from necromancy to the surgical creation of chimeras and other monsters. It was said that he owned a homunculus he himself had fathered by despoiling a young girl taken from the fisherfolk. The homunculus was kept in a tank of saline water, and could prophesy the future. Everyone in

Aeolis would swear to the truth of this, although no one, of course, had actually seen it.

The soldiers had already begun the siege by the time Yama reached the tower, and a crowd had gathered at a respectful distance to watch the fun. Sergeant Rhodean stood at the door at the foot of the tower, his helmet tucked under one arm as he bawled out the warrant. The Aedile sat straight-backed under the canopy of the palanquin, which was grounded amongst the soldiers and a unit of the town's militia, out of range of shot or quarrel. The militiamen were a motley crew in mismatched bits of armour, armed mostly with home-made blunderbusses and rifles but drawn up in two neat ranks as if determined to put on a good show. The soldiers' horses tossed their heads, made nervous by the crowd and the steady hiss of the steam waggon's boiler.

Yama clambered to the top of a stretch of ruined wall near the back of the crowd. It was almost entirely composed of men; wives were not allowed to leave the harems. They stood shoulder to shoulder, grey- and brown-skinned, corpulent and four square on short, muscular legs, barechested in breechclouts or kilts. They stank of sweat and fish and stale riverwater, and nudged each other and jostled for a better view. There was a jocular sense of occasion, as if this were some piece of theatre staged by a travelling mountebank. It was about time the magician got what he deserved, they told each other, and agreed that the Aedile would have a hard time of it winkling him from his nest.

Hawkers were selling sherbet and sweetmeats, fried cakes of riverweed and watermelon slices. A knot of whores of a dozen different bloodlines, clad in abbreviated, brightly col-oured nylon chitons, their faces painted dead white under fantastical conical wigs, watched from a little rise at the back of the crowd, passing a slim telescope to and fro. Their panderer, no doubt hoping for brisk business when the show was over, moved amongst the crowd, cracking jokes and handing out clove-flavoured cigarettes. Yama looked for the whore he had lain with the night before Telmon had left for the war, but could not see her, and blushingly looked away when the panderer caught his eye and winked at him.

Sergeant Rhodean bawled out the warrant again, and when there was no reply set his helmet on his scarred, shaven head and limped back to where the Aedile and the other soldiers waited. He leaned on the skirt of the Aedile's palanquin and there was a brief conference.

'Burn him out!' someone in the crowd shouted, and there was a general murmur of agreement.

The steam waggon jetted black smoke and lumbered forward; soldiers dismounted and walked along the edge of the crowd, selecting volunteers from its ranks. Sergeant Rhodean spoke to the bravos and handed out coins; under his supervision, they lifted the ram from the loadbed of the steam waggon and, flanked by soldiers, carried it towards the tower. The soldiers held their round shields above their heads, but nothing stirred in the tower until the bravos applied the ram to its door.

The ram was the trunk of a young pine bound with a spiral of steel, slung in a cradle of leather straps with handholds for eight men and crowned with a steel cap shaped like a caprice, with sturdy, coiled horns. The crowd shouted encouragement as the bravos swung it in steadily increasing arcs. 'One!' they shouted. 'Two!'

At the first stroke of the ram, the door rang like a drum and a cloud of bats burst from the upper window of the tower. The bats stooped low, swirling above the heads of the crowd with a dry rustle of wings, and the men laughed and jumped up, trying to catch them. One of the whores ran down the road screaming, her hands beating at two bats which had tangled in her conical wig. Some in the crowd cheered coarsely. The whore stumbled and fell flat on her face and a militiaman ran forward and slashed at the bats with his knife. One struggled free and took to the air; the man stamped on the other until it was a bloody smear on the dirt. As if blown by a wind, the rest of the bats rose high and scattered into the blue sky.

The ram struck again and again. The bravos had found their rhythm now. The crowd cheered the steady beat. Someone at Yama's shoulder remarked, 'They should burn him out.'

It was Ananda. As usual, he wore his orange robe, with his left breast bare. He carried a small leather satchel containing incense and chrism oil. He told Yama that his master was here to exorcise the tower and, in case things got out of hand, to shrive the dead. He was indecently pleased about Dr Dismas's impending arrest. Dr Dismas was infamous for his belief that chance, not the Preservers, controlled the lives of men. He did not attend any high day services, although he was a frequent visitor to the temple, playing chess with Father Quine and spending hours debating the nature of the Preservers and the world. The priest viewed Dr Dismas as a brilliant mind that might yet be saved; Ananda knew the doctor was too clever and too proud for that.

'He plays games with people,' Ananda told Yama. 'He enjoys making people believe that he's a warlock, although of course he has no such powers. No one has, unless they flow from the Preservers. It's time he was punished. He's been revelling in his notoriety too long.'

'He knows something about me,' Yama said. 'He found it out in Ys. I think that he is trying to blackmail my father with it.'

Yama described what had happened the night before, and Ananda said kindly, 'I shouldn't think that Dismas has found out anything at all, but of course he couldn't return and tell the Aedile that. He was bluffing, and now his bluff has been called. You'll see. The Aedile will put him to question.'

'He should have killed Dr Dismas on the spot,' Yama said. 'Instead, he stayed his hand, and now he has this farce.'

'Your father is a cautious and judicious man.'

'Too cautious. A good general makes a plan and strikes

before the enemy has a chance to find a place to make a stand.'

Ananda said, 'He could not strike Dr Dismas dead on the spot, or even arrest him. It would not be seemly. He had to consult the Council for Night and Shrines – Dr Dismas is their man, after all. This way, justice is seen to be done, and all are satisfied. That's why he chose volunteers from the crowd to break down the door. Everyone is involved in this.'

'Perhaps,' Yama said, but he was not convinced. That this whole affair was somehow hinged about his origin was both exciting and shameful. He wanted it over with, and yet a part of him, the wild part that dreamed of pirates and adventurers, exulted in the display of force, and he was more certain than ever that he could never settle into a quiet tenure in some obscure office within the Department of Indigenous Affairs.

The ram struck, and struck again, but the door showed no sign of giving way.

'It is reinforced with iron,' Ananda said, 'and it is not hinged, but slides into a recess. In any case we've a long wait even after they break down the door.'

Yama remarked that Ananda seemed to be an expert on the prosecution of sieges.

'I saw one before,' Ananda said. 'It was in the little town outside the walls of the monastery where I was taught, in the high mountains upriver of Ys. A gang of brigands had sealed themselves in a house. The town had only its militia, and Ys was two days' march away – long before soldiers could arrive, the brigands would have escaped under cover of darkness. The militia decided to capture the brigands themselves, but several were killed trying to break into the place, and at last they burned the house to the ground, and the brigands with it. That's what they should do here; otherwise the soldiers will have to break into every floor of the tower to catch Dismas. He could kill many of them before that – and suppose he has something like the palanquin? He could fly away.'

'Then my father could chase him.' Yama laughed at the vision this conjured up: Dr Dismas fleeing the tower like a black beetle on the wing and the Aedile swooping behind in his richly decorated palanquin like a hungry bird.

The crowd cheered. Yama and Ananda pushed to the front, using their elbows and knees, and saw that the door had split from top to bottom.

Sergeant Rhodean raised a hand and there was an expectant hush. 'One more time, lads,' the sergeant shouted, 'and put some back into it!'

The ram swung and the door shattered and fell away. The crowd surged forward, carrying Ananda and Yama with it, and soldiers pushed them back. One recognized Yama. 'You should not be here, young master,' he said. 'Go back now. Be sensible.'

Yama dodged away before the soldier could grab him and, followed by Ananda, retreated to his original vantage point on the broken bit of wall, where he could see over the heads of the crowd and the line of embattled soldiers. The team of bravos swung the ram with short brisk strokes, knocking away the wreckage of the door; then they stood aside as a pentad of soldiers (the leader of the militia trailing behind) came forward with rifles and arbalests at the ready.

Led by Sergeant Rhodean, this party disappeared into the dark doorway. There was an expectant hush. Yama looked to the Aedile, who sat upright under the canopy of his palanquin, his face set in a grim expression. The white feathers which trimmed the high collar of his sable robe fluttered in the morning breeze.

There was a muffled thump. Thick orange smoke suddenly poured from one of the narrow windows of the tower, round billows swiftly unpacking into the air. The crowd murmured, uncertain if this was part of the attack or a desperate defensive move. More thumps: now smoke poured from

76

every window, and from the smashed doorway. The soldiers stumbled out under a wing of orange smoke. Sergeant Rhodean brought up the rear, hauling the leader of the militia with him.

Flames mingled with the smoke that poured from the windows, which was slowly changing from orange to deep red. Some of the crowd were kneeling, their fists curled against their foreheads to make the sign of the Eye.

Ananda said to Yama, 'This is demon work.'

'I thought you did not believe in magic.'

'No, but I believe in demons. After all, demons tried to overthrow the order of the Preservers an age ago. Perhaps Dismas is one, disguised as a man.'

'Demons are machines, not supernatural creatures,' Yama said, but Ananda had turned to look at the burning tower, and did not seem to have heard him.

The flames licked higher; there was a ring of flames around the false spire that crowned the top of the tower. Red smoke hazed the air. Fat flakes of white ash fell through it. There was a stink of sulphur and something sickly sweet. Then there was another muffled thump and a tongue of flame shot out of the doorway. The tower's spire blew to flinders. Burning strips of plastic foil rained down on the heads of the crowd and men yelled and ran in every direction.

Yama and Ananda were separated by the sudden panic as the front ranks of the crowd tried to flee through the press of those behind and dozens of men clambered over the broken wall. A horse reared up, striking with its hooves at a man who had grabbed hold of its bridle. The steam waggon was alight from one end to the other. The driver jumped from its burning cab, rolled over and over to smother his smouldering clothes, and staggered to his feet just as the charges on its loadbed exploded and blew him to red ruin.

Siege rockets flew in crisscross trajectories, trailing burning lengths of rope. A cask of napalm burst in a ball of oily flame, sending a mushroom of smoke boiling into the air.

Flecks of fire spattered in a wide circle. Men dived towards whatever cover they could find. Yama dropped to the ground, his arms crossed over his head, as burning debris pattered around.

There was a moment of intense quiet. As Yama climbed to his feet, his ears ringing, a heavy hand fell on his shoulder and spun him around.

'We've unfinished business, small fry,' Lob said. Behind his brother, Lud grinned around his tusks.

6 ~ The House of Ghost Lanterns

Lud took Yama's knife and stuck it in his belt beside his own crooked blade. 'Don't go shouting for help,' he said, 'or we'll tear out your tongue.'

People were making a hasty retreat towards the gate in the city wall. Lob and Lud gripped Yama's arms and carried him along with them. The tower was burning furiously, a roaring chimney belching thick red fumes that, with the smoke of the burning waggon and countless lesser fires, veiled the sun. Several horses had thrown their riders and were galloping about wildly. Sergeant Rhodean strode amidst the flames and smoke, organizing countermeasures; already, soldiers and militiamen were beating at small grass fires with wet blankets.

The fleeing crowd split around Ananda and the priest. They were kneeling over a man and anointing his bloody head with oil while reciting the last rites. Yama turned to try and catch Ananda's eye, but Lud snarled and cuffed his head and forced him on.

The fumes of the burning tower hung over the crowded flat roofs of the little city. Along the old waterfront, peddlers were bundling wares into their blankets. Chandlers, tavern owners and their employees were locking shutters over windows and standing guard at doors, armed with rifles and axes. Men were already looting the building where Dr Dismas had his office. They dragged furniture onto the second floor veranda and threw it into the street; books rained down like broken-backed birds; jars of simples smashed on the concrete, strewing arcs of coloured powder. A man was methodically smashing all the windows with a heavy iron hammer.

Lob and Lud bundled Yama through the riot and turned down a sidestreet that was little more than a paved walkway above the green water of a wide, stagnant canal. The single-storey houses which stood shoulder to shoulder along the canal had been built with stone looted from older, grander buildings, and their tall, narrow windows were framed by collages of worn carvings and broken tablets incised with texts in long-forgotten scripts. Chutes led down into the scummy water; this part of the city was where the bachelor field labourers lived, and they could not afford private bathing places.

For a moment, Yama thought that the two brothers had dragged him to this shabby, unremarked sidestreet so that they could punish him for interfering with their fun with the anchorite. He braced himself, but was merely pushed forward. With Lud leading and Lob crowding behind, he was hustled through the street doorway of a tavern, under a cluster of ancient ghost lanterns that squealed and rustled in the foetid breeze.

A square plunge pool lit by green underwater lanterns took up half the echoing space. Worn stone steps led down into the slop of glowing water. An immensely fat man floated on his back in the middle of the pool; his shadow loomed across the galleries that ran around three sides of the room. As Lob and Lud hustled Yama past the pool, the man snorted and stirred, expelling a mist of oily vapour from his nostrils and opening one eye. Lob threw a coin. The fat man caught it in the mobile, blubbery lips of his horseshoe-shaped mouth. His lower lip inverted and the coin vanished into his maw. He snorted again and his eye closed.

Lud jabbed Yama with the point of his knife and marched him around a rack of barrels and along a narrow passage which opened into a tiny courtyard. The space, roofed with glass speckled and stained by green algae and black mould, contained a kind of cage of woven wire that fitted inside the whitewashed walls with only a handsbreadth to spare on either side. Inside the cage, beneath its wire ceiling, Dr Dismas was hunched at a rickety table, reading a book and smoking a clove-scented cigarette stuck in his bone cigarette holder.

'Here he is,' Lud said. 'We have him, doctor!'

'Bring him inside,' the apothecary said, and closed his book with an impatient snap.

Yama's fear had turned to paralysing astonishment. Lob roughly pinioned his arms behind his back while Lud unlocked a door in the cage; then Yama was thrust through and the door was closed and locked behind him.

'No,' Dr Dismas said, 'I am far from dead, although I have paid a heavy price for this venture. Close your mouth, boy. You look like one of the frogs you are so fond of hunting late at night.'

Outside the cage, Lud and Lob nudged each other. 'Go on,' one muttered, and the other, 'You do it!' At last, Lud said to Dr Dismas, 'You'll pay us. We done what you asked.'

'You failed the first time,' Dr Dismas said, 'and I haven't forgotten. There's work still to be done, and if I pay you now you'll turn any money I give you into drink. Go now. We'll start on the second part of this an hour after sunset.'

After more nudging, Lob said, 'We thought maybe we get paid for the one thing, and then we do the other.'

'I told you that I would pay you to bring the boy here. And I will. And there will be more money when you help me take him to the man who has commissioned me. But there will be no money at all unless everything is done as I asked.'

'Maybe we only do the one thing,' Lob said, 'and not the other.'

'I would suggest it is dangerous to leave something unfinished,' Dr Dismas said.

'I don't know if this is right,' Lud said. 'We did what you asked—'

Dr Dismas said sharply, 'When did I ask you to begin the second part of your work?'

'Sunset,' Lob said in a sullen mumble.

'An hour after. Remember that. You will suffer as much as I if the work is done badly. You failed the first time. Don't fail again.'

Lud said sulkily, 'We got him for you, didn't we?'

Lob added, 'We would have got him the other night, if this old culler with a stick hadn't got in the way.'

Yama stared at the brothers through the mesh of the cage. They would not meet his eyes. He said, 'You should allow me to go. I will say you rescued me from the mob. I do not know what Dr Dismas promised, but my father will pay double to have me safe.'

Lud and Lob grinned, nudging each other in the ribs.

'Ain't he a corker,' Lud said. 'Like a proper little gentleman.'

Lob belched, and his brother sniggered.

Yama turned to Dr Dismas. 'The same applies to you, doctor.'

'My dear boy, I don't think the Aedile can afford my price,' Dr Dismas said. 'I was happy in my home, with my research and my books.' He put a hand on his narrow chest and sighed. He had six fingers, with long nails filed to points. 'All gone now, thanks to you. You owe me a great deal, Yamamanama, and I intend to have my price in full. I don't need the Aedile's charity.'

Yama felt a queer mixture of excitement and fear. He was convinced that Dr Dismas had found his bloodline, if not his family. 'Then you really have found where I came from! You have found my family — that is, my real family—'

'O, far better than that,' Dr Dismas said, 'but this is not the time to talk about it.'

82

Yama said, 'I would know it now, whatever it is. I deserve to know it.'

Dr Dismas said with sudden anger, 'I'm no house servant, boy,' and his hand flashed out and pinched a nerve in Yama's elbow. Yama's head was filled with pain as pure as light. He fell to his knees on the mesh floor of the cage, and Dr Dismas came around the table and caught Yama's chin between long, stiff, cold fingers.

'You are mine now,' he said, 'and don't forget it.' He turned to the twins. 'Why are you two still here? You have your orders.'

'We'll be back tonight,' Lud said. 'See you pay us then.'

'Of course, of course.' Once the twins had gone, Dr Dismas said to Yama in a confiding tone, 'Frankly, I would rather work alone, but I could hardly move amongst the crowd while everyone thought I was in the tower.' He got his hands under Yama's arms and hauled him up. 'Please, do sit. We are civilized men. There, that's better.'

Yama, perched on the edge of the flimsy metal chair, simply breathed for a while until the pain had retreated to a warm throb in the muscles of his shoulder. At last he said, 'You knew the Aedile was going to arrest you.'

Dr Dismas resumed his seat on the other side of the little table. As he screwed a cigarette into his bone holder, he said, 'Your father is a man who takes his responsibilities seriously. Very properly, he confided his intentions to the Council for Night and Shrines. One of them owed me a favour.'

'If there is any problem between you and my father, I am sure it can be worked out, but not while you hold me captive. Once the fire in the tower burns out, they will look for a body. When they do not find one, they will look for you. And this is a small city.'

Dr Dismas blew a riffle of smoke towards the mesh ceiling of the cage. 'How well Zakiel has taught you logic. It would be a persuasive argument, except that they will find a body.'

'Then you planned to burn your tower all along, and you

should not blame me. I expect you removed your books before you left.'

Dr Dismas did not deny this. He said, 'How did you like the display, by the way?'

'Some are convinced that you are a magician.'

'There are no such creatures. Those who claim to be magicians delude themselves as much as their clients. My little pyrotechnic display was simply a few judiciously mixed salts ignited by electric detonators when the circuit was closed by some oaf stepping on a plate I'd hidden under a rug. No more than a jape which any apprentice apothecary worthy of the trade could produce, although perhaps not on such a grand scale.' Dr Dismas pointed a long forefinger at Yama, who stifled the impulse to flinch. 'All this for you. You do owe me, Yamamanama. The Child of the River, yes, but which river, I wonder. Not our own Great River, I'm certain.'

'You know about my family.' Yama could not keep the eagerness from his voice. It was rising and bubbling inside him – he wanted to laugh, to sing, to dance. 'You know about my bloodline.'

Dr Dismas reached into a pocket of his long coat and drew out a handful of plastic straws. He rattled them together in his long pale hands and cast them on the table. He was making a decision by appealing to their random pattern; Yama had heard of this habit from Ananda, who had reported it in scandalized tones.

Yama said, 'Are you deciding whether to tell me or not, doctor?'

'You're a brave boy to ask after forbidden knowledge, so you deserve some sort of answer.' Dr Dismas tapped ash from his cigarette. 'Oxen and camels, nilgai, ratites and horses – all of them work under the lash, watched by boys no older than you, or even younger, who are armed with no more than fresh-cut withes to restrain their charges. How is this? Because the part in those animals which yearns for freedom has been broken and replaced by habit. No more than a twitch of a stick is required to reinforce that habit; even if those beasts were freed of their harness and their burden, they would be too broken to realize that they could escape their masters. Most men are no different from beasts of burden, their spirits broken by fear of the phantoms of religion invoked by priests and bureaucrats. I work hard to avoid habits. To be unpredictable – that is how you cheat those who would be the masters of men.'

'I thought you did not believe in the Preservers, doctor.'

'I don't question their existence. Certainly they once existed. This world is evidence; the Eye of the Preservers and all the ordered Galaxy is evidence. But I do question the great lie with which the priests hypnotize the population, that the Preservers watch over us all, and that we must satisfy them so that we can win redemption and live for ever after death. As if creatures who juggled stars in their courses would care about whether or not a man beats his wife, or the little torments one child visits upon another! It is a sop to keep men in their places, to ensure that so-called civilization can run on its own momentum. I spit on it.'

And here Dr Dismas did spit, as delicately as a cat, but nevertheless startling Yama.

The apothecary fitted his cigarette holder back between his large, flat-topped teeth. When he smiled around the holder, the plaques over his cheekbones stood out in relief, their sharp edges pressing through brown skin with the coarse, soft grain of wood-pulp.

Dr Dismas said, 'The Preservers created us, but they are gone. They are dead, and by their own hand. They created the Eye, and fell through its event horizon with all their worlds. And why? Because they despaired. They remade the Galaxy, and could have remade the Universe, but their nerve failed. They were cowardly fools, and anyone who believes that they watch us still, yet do not interfere in the terrible suffering of the world, is a worse fool.'

Yama had no answer to this. There was no answer. Ananda was right. The apothecary was a monster who refused to serve anyone or anything except his own swollen pride.

Dr Dismas said, 'The Preservers are gone, but machines still watch us, and regulate the world according to out-of-date precepts. Of course, the machines can't watch everything at once, so they build up patterns and predict the behaviour of men, and watch only for deviation from the norm. It works most of the time for most of the people, but there are a few men like me who defy their predictions by basing important decisions on chance. The machines cannot track our random paths from moment to moment, and so we become invisible. Of course, a cage such as the one in which we sit also helps hide us from them. It screens out the probing of the machines. I wear a hat for the same reason – it is lined with silver foil.'

Yama laughed, because Dr Dismas confessed this ridiculous habit with complete solemnity. 'So you are afraid of machines.'

'Not at all. But I am deeply interested in them. I have a small collection of parts of dead machines excavated from ruins in the deserts beyond the midpoint of the world – one is almost intact, a treasure beyond price.' Dr Dismas suddenly clutched his head and shook it violently for a moment, then winked at Yama. 'But that's not to be spoken of. Not here! They might hear, even in this cage. One reason I came here is because machine activity is higher than anywhere else on Confluence – yes, even Ys. And so, my dear Yamamanama, I found you.'

Yama pointed at the straws scattered on the table. They were hexagonal in cross-section, with red and green glyphs of some unknown language incised along their faces. He said, 'You refuse to acknowledge the authority of the Preservers over men, yet you follow the guidance of these bits of plastic.'

Dr Dismas looked crafty. 'Ah, but I choose which question to ask them.'

Yama had only one question in his mind. 'You found something about my bloodline in Ys, and told my father what you had learned. If you will not tell me everything, will you at least tell me what you told him? Did you perhaps find my family there?'

'You will have to look further than Ys to find your family, my boy, and you may be given the opportunity to do so. The Aedile is a good enough man in his way, I suppose, but that is to say he is no more than a petty official barely capable of ruling a moribund little region of no interest to anyone. Into his hands has fallen a prize which could determine the fate of all the peoples of Confluence – even the world itself – and he does nothing about it. A man like that deserves to be punished, Yamamanama. And as for you, you are very dangerous. For you do not know what you are.'

'I would like very much to know.' Yama had not understood half of what Dr Dismas had said. With a sinking heart, he was beginning to believe that the man was mad.

'Innocence is no excuse,' Dr Dismas said, but he appeared to be speaking to himself. He moved the plastic straws about the tabletop with a long, bony forefinger, as if seeking to rearrange his fate. He lit another cigarette and stared at Yama until Yama grew uncomfortable and looked away.

Dr Dismas laughed, and with sudden energy took out a little leather case and opened it out on the table. Inside, held by elastic loops, were a glass syringe, an alcohol lamp, a bent silver spoon, its bowl blackened and tarnished, a small pestle and mortar, and several glass bottles with rubber stoppers. From one bottle Dr Dismas shook out a single dried beetle into the mortar; from another he added a few drops of a clear liquid that filled the room with the smell of apricots. Dr Dismas ground the beetle into a paste with finicky care and scraped the paste into the bowl of the spoon.

'Cantharides,' he said, as if that explained everything. 'You are young, and will not understand, but sometimes the world becomes too much to bear for someone of my sensibilities.'

'My father said this got you into trouble with your department. He said—'

'That I had sworn to stop using it? Oh yes, of course I said that. If I had not said that, they would not have let me return to Aeolis.'

Dr Dismas lit the wick of the alcohol lamp with a flint and steel and held the spoon over the blue flame until the brown paste liquified and began to bubble. The smell of apricots intensified, sharpened by a metallic tang. Dr Dismas drew the liquid into the hypodermic and tapped the barrel with a long thumbnail to loosen the bubbles which clung to the glass. 'Don't think to escape,' he said. 'I have no key.'

He spread his left hand on the tabletop and probed the web of skin between thumb and forefinger until he hit a vein. He teased back the syringe's plunger until a wisp of red swirled in the thin brown solution, then pressed the plunger home.

He drew in a sharp breath and stretched in his chair like a bow. The hypodermic dropped to the table. For a moment, his heels drummed an irregular tattoo on the mesh floor, and then he relaxed, and looked at Yama with half-closed eyes. His pupils, smeary crosses on yellow balls, contracted and expanded independently. He giggled. 'If I had you long enough . . . ah, what I'd teach you . . .'

'Doctor?'

But Dr Dismas would say no more. His gaze wandered around the cage and at last fixed on the spattered glass which roofed the courtyard. Yama tested the cage's wire mesh, but although he could deform its close-woven hexagons, they were all of a piece, and the door was so close-fitting Yama could not get his fingers into the gap between it and its wire frame. The sun crept into view above the little courtyard's glass ceiling, filling it with golden light, and began its slow reversal.

At last, Yama dared to touch the apothecary's outstretched hand. It was clammy, and irregular plaques shifted under the loose skin. Dr Dismas did not stir. His head was tipped back, his face bathed by the sunlight.

Yama found only one pocket inside the apothecary's long black coat, and it was empty. Dr Dismas stirred as Yama withdrew his hand, and gripped his wrist and drew him down with unexpected strength. 'Don't doubt,' he murmured. His breath smelt of apricots and iron. 'Sit and wait, boy.'

Yama sat and waited. Presently the immensely fat man he had seen floating in the tavern's communal pool shuffled down the passage. He was naked except for blue rubber sandals on his broad feet, and he carried a tray covered with a white cloth.

'Stand back,' he told Yama. 'No, further back. Behind the doctor.'

'Let me go. I promise you will be rewarded.'

'I've already been paid, young master,' the fat man said. He unlocked the door, set the tray down, and relocked the door. 'Eat, young master. The doctor, he won't want anything. I never seen him eat. He has his drug.'

'Let me go!' Yama banged at the cage's locked door and yelled threats at the fat man's retreating back before giving up and looking under the cloth that covered the tray.

A dish of watery soup with a cluster of whitened fish eyes sunk in the middle and rings of raw onion floating on top; a slab of black bread, as dense as a brick and almost as hard; a glass of small beer the colour of stale urine.

The soup was flavoured with chili oil, making it almost palatable, but the bread was so salty that Yama gagged on the first bite and could eat no more. He drank the sour beer and somehow fell asleep on the rickety chair.

He was woken by Dr Dismas. He had a splitting headache and a foul taste in his mouth. The courtyard and the cage was lit by a hissing alcohol lantern which dangled from the cage's wire ceiling; the air beyond the glass that roofed the courtyard was black.

'Rise up, young man,' Dr Dismas said. He was filled with barely contained energy and hopped from foot to foot and banged his stiff fingers together. His shadow, thrown across the whitewashed walls of the courtyard, aped his movements.

'You drugged me,' Yama said stupidly.

'A little something in the beer, to take away your cares.' Dr Dismas banged on the mesh of the cage and shouted, 'Ho! Ho! Landlord!' and turned back to Yama and said, 'You have been sleeping longer than you know. The little sleep just past is my gift to make you wake into your true self. You don't understand me, but it doesn't matter. Stand up! Stand up! Look lively! Awake, awake awake! You venture forth to meet your destiny! Ho! Landlord!'

7 ~ The Warlord

In the darkness outside the door of the tavern, Dr Dismas clapped a wide-brimmed hat on his head and exchanged a few words with the landlord, who handed something to the apothecary, knuckled his forehead, and shut the heavy street door. The cluster of ghost lanterns above the door creaked in the breeze, glimmering with a wan pallor that illuminated nothing but themselves. The rest of the street was dark, except for blades of light shining between a few of the closed shutters of the houses on the other side of the wide canal. Dr Dismas switched on a penlight and waved its narrow beam at Yama, who blinked stupidly at the light; his wits were still dulled by sleep and the residue of the drugged beer.

'If you are going to be sick,' Dr Dismas said, 'lean over and don't spatter your clothes or your boots. You must be presentable.'

'What will you do with me, doctor?'

'Breathe, my dear boy. Slowly and deeply. Is it not a fine night? There is a curfew, I'm told. No one will be about to wonder at us. Look at this. Do you know what it is?'

Dr Dismas showed Yama what the landlord had given him. It was an energy pistol, silver and streamlined, with a blunt muzzle and a swollen chamber, and a grip of memory plastic that could mould itself to fit the hands of most of the bloodlines of the world. A dot of red light glowed at the side of the chamber, indicating that it was fully charged.

'You could burn for that alone,' Yama said.

'Then you know what it can do.' Dr Dismas pushed the muzzle into Yama's left armpit. 'I have it at its weakest setting, but a single shot will roast your heart. We will walk to the new quay like two old friends.'

Yama did as he was told. He was still too dazed to try to run. Besides, Sergeant Rhodean had taught him that in the event of being kidnapped he should not attempt to escape unless his life was in danger. He thought that the soldiers of the garrison must be searching for him; after all, he had been missing all day. They might turn a corner and find him at any moment.

The dose of cantharides had made Dr Dismas talkative. He did not seem to think that he was in any danger. As they walked, he told Yama that originally the tavern had been a workshop where ghost lanterns had been manufactured in the glory days of Aeolis.

'The lanterns that advertise the tavern are a crude representation of the ideal of the past, being made of nothing more than lacquered paper. Real ghost lanterns were little round boats made of plastic, with a deep weighted keel to keep them upright and a globe of blown nylon infused with luminescent chemicals instead of a sail. Ghost lanterns were floated on the Great River after each funeral to confuse any restless spirits of the dead and make sure that they would not haunt their living relatives. There is, as you will soon see, an analogy to be made with your fate, my dear boy.'

Yama said, 'You traffic with fools, doctor. The owner of the tavern will be burnt for his part in my kidnap – it is the punishment my father reserves for the common people. Lud and Lob too, though their stupidity almost absolves them.'

Dr Dismas laughed. His sickly sweet breath touched Yama's cheek. He said, 'And will I be burnt, too?'

'It is in my father's power. More likely you will be turned over to the mercies of your department. No one will profit from this.'

'That's where you are wrong. First, I do not take you for

92

ransom, but to save you from the pedestrian fate to which your father would consign you. Second, do you see anyone coming to your rescue?'

The long waterfront, lit by the orange glow of sodium vapour lamps, was deserted. The taverns, the chandlers' godowns and the two whorehouses were shuttered and dark. Curfew notices fluttered from doors; slogans in the crude ideograms used by the Amnan had been smeared on walls. Rubbish and driftwood had been piled against the steel doors of the big godown owned by Derev's father and set alight, but the fire had done no more than discolour the metal. Several lesser merchants' offices had been looted, and the building where Dr Dismas had kept his office had been burnt to the ground. Smouldering timbers sent up a sharp stench that made Yama's eyes water.

Dr Dismas marched Yama quite openly along the new quay, which ran out towards the mouth of the bay between meadows of zebra grass and shoals of mud dissected by shallow stagnant channels. The wide bay faced downriver. Framed on one side by the bluff on which the Aedile's house stood, and by the chimneys of the paeonin mill on the other, the triple-armed pinwheel of the Galaxy stood beyond the edge of the world. It was so big that when Yama looked at one edge he could not see the other. The Arm of the Warrior rose high above the arch of the Arm of the Hunter; the Arm of the Archer curved in the opposite direction, below the edge of the world, and would not be seen again until next winter. The structure known as the Blue Diadem, that Yama knew from his readings of the Puranas was a cloud of fifty thousand blue-white stars each forty times the mass of the sun of Confluence, was a brilliant pinprick of light beyond the frayed point of the outflung Arm of the Hunter, like a drop of water flicked from a finger. Smaller star clusters made long chains of concentrated light through the milky haze of the galactic arms. There were lines and threads and globes and clouds of stars, all fading into a general misty radiance notched by dark lanes which barred the arms at regular intervals. The core, bisected by the horizon, was knitted from thin shells of stars in tidy orbits concentrically packed around the great globular clusters of the heart stars, like layers of glittering tissue wrapped around a heap of jewels. Confronted with this ancient grandeur, Yama felt that his fate was as insignificant as that of any of the mosquitoes which danced before his face.

Dr Dismas cupped his free hand to his mouth and called out, his voice shockingly loud in the quiet darkness. 'Time to go!'

There was a distant splash in the shallows beyond the end of the quay's long stone finger. Then a familiar voice said, 'Row with me, you bugger. You're making us go in circles.'

A skiff glided out of the darkness. Lud and Lob shipped their oars as it thumped against the bottom of a broad stone stair. Lob jumped out and held the boat steady as Yama and Dr Dismas climbed in.

'Quick as you like, your honour,' Lud said.

'Haste makes waste,' Dr Dismas said. Slowly and fussily he settled himself on the centre thwart, facing Yama with the energy pistol resting casually in his lap. He told the twins, 'I hope that this time you did exactly as I asked.'

'Sweet as you like,' Lob said. 'They didn't know we were there until the stuff went up.' The skiff barely rocked when he vaulted back into it; he was surprisingly nimble for someone of his bulk. He and his brother settled themselves in the high seat at the stern and they pushed off from the rough stones of the quay.

Yama watched the string of orange lights along the water-front swiftly recede into the general darkness of the shore. The cold breeze off the river was clearing his head, and for the first time since he had woken from his drugged sleep he was beginning to feel fear.

He said, 'Where are you taking me, doctor?'

Dr Dismas's eyes gleamed with red fire beneath the brim

of his hat; his eyes were backed with a reflective membrane, like those of certain nocturnal animals. He said, 'You return to the place of your birth. Yamamanama. Does that frighten you?'

'Little fish,' Lud said mockingly. 'Little fish, little fish.'

'Fish out of water,' Lob added.

They were both breathing heavily as they rowed swiftly towards the open water of the Great River.

'Keep quiet if you want to earn your money,' Dr Dismas said, and told Yama, 'You must forgive them. Good help is so hard to find in backwater places. At times I was tempted to use my master's men instead.'

Lud said, 'We could tip you overboard, doctor. Ever think of that?'

Dr Dismas said, 'This pistol can kill you and your brother just as easily as Yamamanama.'

'If you shoot at us, you'll set fire to the boat, and drown as neat as if we'd thrown you in.'

'I might do it anyway. Like the scorpion who convinced the frog to carry him across the river, but stung his mount before they were halfway across, death is in my nature.'

Lob said, 'He don't mean anything by it, your honour.'

'I just don't like bad-mouthing of our city,' Lud said sullenly.

Dr Dismas laughed. 'I speak only the truth. Both of you agree with me, for why else would you want to leave? It is an understandable impulse, and it raises you above the rest of your kind.'

Lud said, 'Our father is young, that's all it is. We're strong, but he's stronger. He'd kill either of us or both of us, however we tried it, and we can't wait for him to get weak. It would take years and years.'

Dr Dismas said, 'And Yamamanama wants to leave, too. Do not deny it, my boy. Soon you will have your wish. There! Look upriver! You see how much we do for you!'

The skiff heeled as it rounded the point of the shallow,

silted bay and entered the choppier waters of the river proper. As it turned into the current, Yama saw with a shock that one of the ships anchored at the floating harbour half a league upstream was ablaze from bow to stern.

The burning ship squatted over its livid reflection, tossing harvests of sparks into the night, as if to rival the serene light of the Galaxy. It was a broad-beamed carrack, one of the fleet of transports which carried troops or bulk supplies to the armies fighting the heretics at the midpoint of the world. Four small boats were rowing away from it, sharply etched shadows crawling over water that shone like molten copper. Even as Yama watched, gape-mouthed, a series of muffled explosions in the ship's hold blew expanding globes of white flame high above the burning mastheads. The ship, broken-backed, settled in the water.

Lud and Lob cheered, and the skiff rocked alarmingly as they stood to get a better view.

'Sit down, you fools,' Dr Dismas said.

Lud whooped, and shouted, 'We did it, your honour! Sweet as you like!'

Dr Dismas said to Yama, 'I devised a method so simple that even these two could carry it out successfully.'

Yama said, 'You tried to burn a ship a few days ago, did you not?'

'Two barrels of palm oil and liquid soap. One at the bow, one at the stern,' Dr Dismas said, ignoring the question, 'armed with clockwork fuses. It makes a fine diversion, don't you think? Your father's soldiers are busy rescuing sailors and saving the rest of the floating harbour while we go about our business.'

'There is a pinnace anchored further out,' Yama said. 'It will investigate.'

'I think not,' Dr Dismas said. 'Its commander is most anxious to make your acquaintance, Yamamanama. He is a cunning warlord, and knows all about the fire. He under-stands that it is a necessary sacrifice. The heretics will be blamed for the burning of the ship, as will your disappearance. Your father will receive a ransom note tomorrow, but even if he answers it there will, alas, be no reply. You will disappear without trace. Such things happen, in this terrible war.'

'My father will search for me. He will not stop searching.'

'Perhaps you won't want to be found, Yamamanama. You want to run away, and here you are, set on a great adventure.'

Yama knew now who the sailors had been searching for. He said, 'You tried to kidnap me two days ago. Those burning rafts were your work, so my father's soldiers would chase after imaginary heretics. But these two failed to get hold of me, and you had to try again.'

'And here we are,' Dr Dismas said. 'Now please be quiet. We have a rendezvous to keep.'

The skiff drifted on a slow current parallel to the dark shore. The burning ship receded into the night. It had grounded on the river bottom, and only the forecastle and the masts were still burning. The fisherfolk were abroad, and the lanterns they used to attract fish to their lines made scattered constellations across the breast of the Great River, red sparks punctuating the reflected sheen of the Galaxy's light.

Dr Dismas stared intently into the glimmering dark, swearing at Lud and Lob whenever they dipped their oars in the water. 'We got to keep to the current, your honour,' Lud said apologetically, 'or we'll lose track of where we're supposed to be.'

'Quiet! What was that?'

Yama heard a rustle of wings and a faint splash.

'Just a bat,' Lud said. 'They fish out here at night.'

'We catch 'em with glue lines strung across the water,' Lob explained. 'Make good eating, bats do, but not in spring. After winter they're mainly skin and bone. They need to fatten up—'

'Do shut up!' Dr Dismas said in exasperation. 'One more

word and I'll fry you both where you sit. You have so much fat on your bodies that you'll go up like candles.'

The current bent away from the shore and the skiff drifted with it, scraping past young banyans that raised small crowns of leaves a handspan above the water. Yama glimpsed the pale violet spark of a machine spinning through the night. It seemed to be moving in short stuttering jerks, as if searching for something. At any other time he would have wondered at it, but now its remote light and unguessable motives only intensified his feeling of despair. The world had suddenly turned strange and treacherous, its wonders traps for the unwary.

At last Dr Dismas said, 'There! Row, you fools!'

Yama saw a red lamp flickering to starboard. Lud and Lob bent to their oars and the skiff flew across the water towards it. Dr Dismas lit an alcohol lantern with flint and steel and held it up by his face. The light, cast through a mask of blue plastic, made his pinched face, misshappen by the plaques beneath its skin, look like that of a corpse.

The red lantern was hung from the stern of a lateen-rigged pinnace which swung at anchor beside a solitary banyan. It was the ship which had returned Dr Dismas to Aeolis. Two sailors had climbed into the branches of the tree, and they watched over the long barrels of their rifles as the skiff came alongside. Lob stood and threw a line up to the stern of the pinnace. A sailor caught the end and made the skiff fast, and someone vaulted the pinnace's rail, landing so suddenly and lightly in the well of the skiff that Yama half rose in alarm.

The man clamped a hand on Yama's shoulder. 'Easy there, lad,' he said, 'or you'll have us in the river.' He was only a few years older than Yama, bare-chested, squat and muscular, with an officer's sash tied at the waist of his tight, white trousers. His broad, pugnacious face, framed by a cloud of loose, red-gold hair, was seamed with scars, like a clay mask someone had broken and badly mended, but his look was frank and appraising, and enlivened by good-humoured intelligence.

The officer steadied the skiff as Dr Dismas unhandily clambered up the short rope ladder dropped down the side of the pinnace, but when it was his turn Yama shook off the officer's hand and sprang up and grabbed the stern rail. His breath was driven from him when his belly and legs slammed against the clinkered planks of the pinnace's hull, and pain shot through his arms and shoulders as they took his weight, but he pulled himself up, got a leg over the rail and rolled over, coming up in a crouch on the deck of the stern platform at the bare feet of an astonished sailor.

The officer laughed and sprang from a standing jump to the rail and then, lightly and easily, to the deck. He said, 'He has spirit, doctor.'

Yama stood up. He had banged his right knee, and it throbbed warmly. Two sailors leaned on the steering bar and a tall man in black stood beside them. The pinnace's single mast was rooted at the edge of the stern platform; below it, three decads of rowers, naked except for breechclouts, sat in two staggered rows. The sharp prow was upswept, with a white stylized hawk's eye painted on the side. A small, swivel-mounted cannon was set in the prow's beak; its gunner had turned to watch Yama come aboard, one arm resting on the cannon's fretted barrel.

Yama looked at the black-clad man and said, 'Where is the warlord who would buy me?'

Dr Dismas said querulously, 'I dislike doing business with guns pointed at me.'

The officer gestured, and the two sailors perched in the banyan branches above the pinnace put up their rifles. 'Just a precaution, Dismas, in case you had brought along uninvited guests. If I had wanted you shot, Dercetas and Diomedes would have picked you off while you were still rowing around the point of the bay. But have no fear of that, my friend, for I need you as much as you need me.'

Yama said again, loudly, 'Where is he, this warlord?'

The barechested officer laughed. 'Why here I am,' he said, and stuck out his hand.

Yama took it. The officer's grip was firm, that of a strong man who is confident of his strength. His fingers were tipped with claws that slid a little from their sheaths and pricked the palm of Yama's hand.

'Well met, Yamamanama,' the officer said. His large eyes were golden, with tawny irises; the only beautiful feature of his broken face. The lid of the left eye was pulled down by a deep, crooked scar that ran from brow to chin.

'This war breeds heroes as ordure breeds flies,' Dr Dismas remarked, 'but Enobarbus is a singular champion. He set sail last summer as a mere lieutenant. He led a picket boat smaller than his present command into the harbour of the enemy and sank four ships and damaged a dozen others before his own boat was sunk under him.'

'It was a lucky venture,' Enobarbus said. 'We had a long swim of it, I can tell you, and a longer walk afterwards.'

Dr Dismas said, 'If Enobarbus has one flaw, it is his humility. After his boat was sunk, he led fifteen men – his entire crew – through twenty leagues of enemy lines, and did not lose one. He was rewarded with command of a division, and he is going downriver to take it up. With your help, Yamamanama, he will soon command much more.'

Enobarbus grinned. 'As for humility, I always have you, Dismas. If I have any failing, you are swift to point it out. How fortunate, Yamamanama, that we both know him.'

'More fortunate for you, I think,' Yama said.

'Every hero must be reminded of his humanity, from time to time,' Dr Dismas said.

'Fortunate for both of us,' Enobarbus told Yama. 'We'll make history, you and I. That is, of course, if you are what Dismas claims. He has been very careful not to bring the proof with him, so that I must keep him alive. He is a most cunning fellow.'

'I've lied many times in my life,' Dr Dismas said, 'but this time I tell the truth. For the truth is so astonishing that any lie would pale before it, like a candle in the sun. I think we should leave. My diversion was splendid while it lasted, but already it is almost burned out, and while the Aedile of that silly little city may be a weak man, he is no fool. His soldiers searched the hills after my men set fire to the first ship, and they will search the water this time.'

'You should have trusted my men, Dismas,' Enobarbus said. 'We could have taken the boy two nights ago.'

'And the game would have been up at once if anyone had seen you. We should move on at once, or the Aedile will wonder why you do not come to the aid of the burning ship.'

'No,' Enobarbus said, 'we'll tarry here a while. I have brought my own physician, and he'll take a look at your lad.'

Enobarbus called the man in black forward. He was of the same bloodline as Enobarbus, but considerably older. Although he moved with the same lithe tread, he had a comfortable swag of a belly and his mane, loose about his face, was streaked with grey. His name was Agnitus.

'Take off your shirt, boy,' the physician said. 'Let's see what you're made of.'

'It's better you do it yourself,' Dr Dismas advised. 'They can tie you down and do it anyway, and it will be more humiliating, I promise you. Be strong, Yamamanama. Be true to your inheritance. All will be well. Soon you will thank me.'

'I do not think so,' Yama said, but pulled his shirt over his head. Now he knew that he was not going to be killed, he felt a shivery excitement. This was the adventure he had dreamed of, but unlike his dreams it was not under his control.

The physician, Agnitus, sat Yama on a stool and took his right arm and turned the joints of his fingers and wrist and elbow, ran cold hard fingers down his ribs and prodded at his backbone. He shone a light in Yama's right eye and gazed closely at it, then fitted a kind of skeletal helmet over Yama's scalp and turned various screws until their blunt ends gripped his skull, and recorded the measurements in a little oilskin-covered notebook.

Dr Dismas said impatiently, 'You'll see that he has a very distinctive bone structure, but the real proof is in his genotype. I hardly think you can conduct that kind of test here.'

Agnitus said to Enobarbus, 'He's right, my lord. I must take a sample of the boy's blood and a scraping of the skin from the inside of his cheek. But I can tell you now that his bloodline is not one I recognize, and I've seen plenty in my time. And he's not a surgical construct, unless our apothecary is more cunning than I am.'

'I would not presume,' Dr Dismas said.

'A proof by elimination is less satisfactory than one by demonstration,' Enobarbus said. 'But unless we storm the library of the Department of Apothecaries and Chirurgeons, we must be content with what we have.'

'It is true,' Dr Dismas said. 'Haven't I sworn it so? And does he not fulfil the prophesy made to you?'

Enobarbus nodded. 'Yamamanama, you've always believed yourself special. Do you have a clear view of your destiny?'

Yama pulled his shirt over his head. He liked Enobarbus's bold candour, but mistrusted him because he was clearly an ally of Dr Dismas. He realized that everyone was looking at him, and he said defiantly, 'I would say that you are a proud and ambitious man, Enobarbus, a leader of men who would seek a prize greater than mere promotion. You believe that I can help you, although I do not know how – unless it is to do with the circumstances of my birth. Dr Dismas knows about that, I think, but he likes to tease.'

Enobarbus laughed. 'Well said! He reads us both as easily as reading a book, Dismas. We must be careful.'

'The Aedile would have made him a clerk,' Dr Dismas said with disgust.

'The Aedile belongs to a part of our department that is not noted for its imagination,' Enobarbus said. 'It is why men like him are entrusted with the administration of unimportant towns. They can be relied upon precisely because they have no imagination. We should not condemn him for what, in his office, is a virtue.

'Yamamanama, listen to me. With my help, the world itself lies within your grasp. Do you understand? You have always considered yourself to be of special birth, I know. Well, Dismas has discovered that you are unique, and he has convinced me that you are a part of my destiny.'

And then this powerful young man did an extraordinary thing. He knelt before Yama and bowed his head until his forehead touched the deck. He looked up through the tangle of his mane and said, 'I will serve you well, Yamamanama. I swear with my life. Together we will save Confluence.'

'Please get up,' Yama said. He was frightened by this gesture, for it marked a solemn moment whose significance he did not fully understand. 'I do not know why I have been brought here, or why you are saying these things, but I did not ask for any of it, and I do not want it.'

'Stand fast,' Dr Dismas hissed, and grasped Yama's upper arm in a cruel pinch.

Enobarbus stood. 'Let him alone, Dismas. My lord . . . Yamamanama . . . we are about to embark upon a hard and perilous journey. I have worked towards it all my life. When I was a cub, I was blessed by a vision. It was in the temple of my bloodline, in Ys. I was praying for my brother, who had died in battle a hundred days before. The news had just reached me. I was praying that I could avenge him, and that I could play my part in saving Confluence from the heretics. I was very young, as you might imagine, and very foolish, but my prayers were answered. The shrine lit and a woman arrayed in white appeared, and told me of my destiny. I accepted, and I have been trying my best to carry it out ever since.

'Yamamanama, to know one's fate is a privilege granted only to a few men, and it is a heavy responsibility. Most men live their lives as they can. I must live my life in pursuit of an ideal. It has stripped me of my humanity as faith strips an eremite of worldly possessions, and honed my life to a single point. Nothing else matters to me. How often have I wished that the obligation be lifted, but it has not, and I have come to accept it. And here we are, as was predicted long ago.'

Enobarbus suddenly smiled. It transformed his wrecked face as a firework, bursting across the dark sky, transforms the night. He clapped his hands. 'I have spoken enough for now. I will speak more, Yamamanama, I promise, but it must wait until we are safe. Pay your men, Dismas. We are at last embarked on our journey.'

Dr Dismas pulled out his pistol. 'It would be well if your boat put some distance between their miserable skiff. I'm not sure of the range of this thing.'

Enobarbus nodded. 'It's probably for the best,' he said. 'They might guess, and they'll certainly talk.'

'You overestimate them,' Dr Dismas said. 'They deserve to die because they endangered my plans by their stupidity. Besides, I cannot stand boorishness, and I have been exiled amongst these uncivilized creatures for an entire year. This will be a catharsis.'

'I'll hear no more. Kill them cleanly, and do not seek to justify yourself.'

Enobarbus turned to give his orders, and at that moment one of the sailors perched in the branches of the banyan to which the pinnace was moored cried out.

'Sail! Sail ahead!'

'Thirty degrees off the starboard bow,' his mate added. 'Half a league and bearing down hard.'

Enobarbus gave his orders without missing a beat. 'Cut the mooring ropes fore and aft. Dercetas and Diomedes, to your posts at once! Ready the rowers, push off on my word! I want thirty beats a minute from you lads, and no slacking or we're dead men.'

In the midst of the sudden rush of activity, as oars were raised and sailors hacked at mooring lines, Yama saw his opportunity. Dr Dismas made a grab for him, but was too slow. Yama vaulted the rail and landed hard in the well of the skiff.

'Row!' Yama yelled to Lob and Lud. 'Row for your lives!'

'Catch hold of him!' Dr Dismas shouted from above. 'Catch him and make sure you don't let go!'

Lud started forward. 'It's for your own good, little fish,' he said.

Yama dodged Lud's clumsy swipe and retreated to the stern of the little skiff. 'He wants to kill you!'

'Get him, you fools,' Dr Dismas said.

Yama grabbed hold of the sides of the skiff and rocked it from side to side, but Lud stood foursquare. He grinned. 'That won't help, little fish. Keep still, and maybe I won't have to hurt you.'

'Hurt him anyway,' Lob said.

Yama picked up the alcohol lantern and dashed it into the well of the skiff. Instantly, translucent blue flames licked up. Lud reared backwards, and the skiff pitched violently. Unbearable heat beat at Yama's face; he took a deep breath and dived into the river.

He swam as far as he could before he came up and drew a gulp of air that burned all the way down the inverted trees of his lungs. He pulled at the fastenings of his heavy boots and kicked them off.

The skiff was drifting away from the side of the pinnace. Flames flickered brightly in its well. Lud and Lob were trying to beat out the fire with their shirts. Sailors threw ropes down the side of the pinnace and shouted to them to give it up and come aboard. A tremendous glow was growing brighter and brighter beyond the pinnace, turning everything into a shadow of its own self. The cannon in the prow of the pinnace spoke: a crisp rattling burst, and then another.

Yama swam as hard as he could, and when he finally turned to float on his back, breathing hard, the whole scene was spread before him. The pinnace was sliding away from the banyan tree, leaving the burning skiff behind. A great glowing ship was bearing down towards the pinnace. She was a narrow-hulled frigate, her three masts crowded with square sails, and every part of her shone with cold fire. The pinnace's cannon spoke again, and there was a crackling of rifle fire. And then Dr Dismas fired his pistol, and for an instant a narrow lance of red fire split the night.

8 ~ The Fisherman

Dr Dismas's shot must have missed the glowing frigate, for it bore down on the pinnace relentlessly. The bristling oars of the pinnace set a steady, rapid beat as it left the burning skiff behind and began to turn towards its pursuer. Yama saw that Enobarbus was planning to come around to the near side of the frigate to pass beneath its cannons and rake its sides with her own guns, but before he could complete his manoeuvre the frigate swung about like a leaf blown by the wind. In a moment, its bow loomed above the stricken pinnace. The pinnace's cannon hammered defiantly, and Yama heard someone cry out.

But at the instant the frigate struck the pinnace, it dissolved into a spreading mist of white light. Yama backstroked in the cold water watching as the pinnace was engulfed by a globe of white fog that boiled up higher than the outflung arm of the Galaxy. A point of violet light shot up from this spreading bank of luminous fog, rising into the night sky until it had vanished from sight.

Yama did not stop to wonder at this miracle, for he knew that Enobarbus would start searching for him as soon as the pinnace had escaped the fog. He turned in the water and began to swim. Although he aimed for the dark, distant shore, he quickly found himself in a swift current that took him amongst a scattered shoal of banyans. They were rooted in a gravel bank that at times Yama could graze with his toes;

if he had been as tall as the Aedile he could have stood with his head clear of the swiftly running water.

At first, the banyans were no more than handfuls of broad, glossy leaves that stood stiffly above the water, but the current carried Yama deeper into a maze of wide channels between stands of bigger trees. Here, they rose in dense thickets above prop roots flexed in low arches. The prop roots were fringed by tangled mats of feeder roots alive with schools of tiny fish that flashed red or green dots of luminescence as they darted away from Yama.

With the last of his strength, Yama swam towards one of the largest of the banyans as he was swept past it. The cold water had stolen all feeling from his limbs and the muscles of his shoulders and arms were tender with exhaustion. He threw himself into floating nets of feeder roots and, scraping past strings of clams and bearded mussels, dragged himself onto a smooth horizontal trunk, and lay gasping like a fish that had just learned the trick of breathing air.

Yama was too cold and wet and scared to sleep, and something in the tangled thickets of the tree had set up a thin, irregular piping, like the fretting of a sick baby. He sat with his back against an arched root and watched the uppermost arm of the Galaxy set beyond the bank of faintly luminescent fog that had spread for leagues across the black river. Somewhere in the fog was Enobarbus's pinnace, lost, blinded. By what strange allies, or stranger coincidence? The top of the wide fog bank seethed like boiling milk; Yama watched the black sky above it for the return of the machine's violet spark. Answered prayers, he thought, and shivered.

He dozed and woke, and dozed again, and jerked awake from a vivid dream of standing on the flying bridge of the ghostly frigate as it bore down on the pinnace. The frigate was crewed neither by men nor even by ghosts or revenants, but by a crowd of restless lights that responded to his unspoken commands with quick unquestioning intelligence.

Zakiel had taught him that although dreams were usually stitched from fragments of daily experience, sometimes they were more, portents of the future or riddles whose answers were keys to the conduct of the dreamer's life. Yama did not know if this dream was of the first or second kind, let alone what it might mean, but when he woke it left him with a clinging horror, as if his every action might somehow be magnified, with terrible consequences.

The Galaxy had set, and dawn touched the flood of the river with flat grey light. The bank of fog was gone; there was no sign of the pinnace. Yama dozed again, and woke with sunlight dancing on his face, filtered through the restless leaves of the banyan. He found himself on a wide limb that gently sloped up from the water and ran straight as an old road into the dense leafy tangles of the banyan's heart, crossed by arching roots and lesser branches that dropped prop roots straight down into the water. The banyan's glossy leaves hung everywhere like the endlessly deep folds of a ragged green cloak, and the bark of its limbs, smoothly wrinkled as skin, was colonized by lichens that hung like curtains of grey lace, the green barrels of bromeliads, and the scarlet and gold and pure white blossoms of epiphytic orchids.

Yama ached in every muscle. He drew off his wet shirt and trousers and hung them on a branch, then set to the exercises Sergeant Rhodean had taught him until at last his joints and muscles loosened. He drank handfuls of cold water, startling shoals of fairy shrimp that scattered from his shadow, and splashed water on his face until his skin tingled with racing blood.

Yama had come ashore on the side of the banyan that faced towards the far side of the river. He slung his damp clothes over his shoulder and, naked, set off through the thickets of the tree, at first following the broad limb and then, when it joined another and bent upwards into the high, sunspeckled canopy, scrambling through a tangle of lesser branches. There was always still, black water somewhere beneath the random lattice of branches and prop roots. Tiny hummingbirds, clad in electric blues and emerald greens, as if enamelled by the most skilful of artists, darted from flower to flower. When Yama blundered through curtains of leaves, clouds of blackflies rose up and got in his eyes and mouth. At last, he glimpsed blue sky through a fall of green vines. He parted the soft, jointed stems and stepped through them onto a sloping spit of mossy ground, where a round coracle of the kind used by the fisherfolk was drawn up on the miniature shore.

The blackened, upturned shell of a snapping turtle held the ashes of a small fire, still warm when Yama sifted them through his fingers. Yama drew on his damp shirt and trousers and called out, but no one answered his call. He cast around and quickly found a winding path leading away from the spit. And a moment later found the fisherman, tangled in a crude net of black threads just beyond the second bend.

The threads were the kind that Amnan used to catch bats and birds, resin fibres as strong as steel covered with thousands of tiny blisters that exuded a strong glue at a touch. The threads had partly collapsed when the fisherman had blundered into them, and he hung like a corpse in an unravelling shroud, one arm caught above his head, the other bound tightly to his side.

He did not seem surprised to see Yama. He said, in a quiet, hoarse voice, 'Kill me quick. Have mercy.'

'I was hoping for rescue,' Yama said.

The fisherman stared at him. He wore only a breechclout, and his pale skin was blotched with islands of pale green. Black hair hung in greasy tangles around his broad, chinless froggy face. His wide mouth hung open, showing rows of tiny triangular teeth. He had watery, protuberant eyes, and a transparent membrane flicked over their balls three times before he said, 'You are not one of the Mud People.'

'I come from Aeolis. My father is the Aedile.'

'The Mud People think they know the river. It's true they can swim a bit, but they're greedy, and pollute her waters.'

'One of them seems to have caught you.'

'You're a merchant's son, perhaps. We have dealings with them, for flints and steel. No, don't come close, or you'll be caught too. There is only one way to free me, and I don't think you carry it.'

'I know how the threads work,' Yama said, 'and I am sorry that I do not have what is needed to set you free. I do not even have a knife.'

'Even steel will not cut them. Leave me. I'm a dead man, fit only to fill the bellies of the Mud People. What are you doing?'

Yama had discovered that the surface of the path was a spongy thatch of wiry roots, fallen leaves and the tangled filaments of epiphytic lichens. He lay on his belly and pushed his arm all the way through the thick thatch until his fingers touched water. He looked at the fisherman and said, 'I have seen your people use baited traps to catch fish. Do you have one on your coracle? And I will need some twine or rope, too.'

While Yama worked, the fisherman, whose name was Caphis, told him that he had blundered into the sticky web just after dawn, while searching for the eggs of a species of coot which nested in the hearts of banyan thickets. 'The eggs are good to eat,' Caphis said, 'but not worth dying for.'

Caphis had put into the banyan shoal last night. He had seen a great battle, he explained, and had thought it prudent to take shelter. 'So I am doubly a fool.'

While the fisherman talked, Yama cut away a section of lichenous thatch and lashed the trap upright to a prop root. He had to use the blade of the fisherman's short spear to cut the twine, and several times sliced his palm. He sucked at the shallow cuts before starting to replace the thatch. It was in the sharp bend of the path; anyone hurrying down it would have to step there to make the turn.

He said, 'Did you see much of the battle?'

'A big ship caught fire. And then the small boat which has been lying offshore of the Mud People's city for three days must have found an enemy, because it started firing into the dark.'

'But there was another ship – it was huge and glowing, and melted into fog . . .'

The fisherman considered this, and said at last, 'I turned for shelter once the firing started, as anyone with any sense would. You saw a third ship? Well, perhaps you were closer than I, and I expect that you saw more than you wanted to.'

'Well, that is true enough.' Yama stood, leaning on the stout shaft of the spear.

'The river carries all away, if you let it. That's our view. What's done one day is gone the next, and there's a new start. He might not come today, or even tomorrow. You will not wait that long. You will take the coracle and leave me to the fate I deserve.'

'My father outlawed this.'

'They are a devious people, the Mud People.' Sunlight splashed through the broad leaves of the banyan, shining on the fisherman's face. Caphis squinted and added, 'If you could fetch water, it would be a blessing.'

Yama found a resin mug in the coracle. He was dipping it into the water at the edge of the mossy spit when he saw a little boat making its way towards the island. It was a skiff, rowed by a single man. By the time Yama had climbed into a crotch of the banyan, hidden amongst rustling leaves high above the spit, the skiff was edging through the slick of feeder roots that ringed the banyan.

Yama recognized the man. Grog, or Greg. One of the bachelor labourers who tended the mussel beds at the mouth of the Breas. He was heavy and slow, and wore only a filthy kilt. The grey skin of his shoulders and back was dappled with a purple rash, the precursor of the skin canker which affected those Amnan who worked too long in sunlight.

Yama watched, his mouth dry and his heart beating quickly, as the man tied up his boat and examined the coracle and the cold ashes in the turtle shell. He urinated at the edge of the water for what seemed a very long time, then set off along the path.

A moment later, while Yama was climbing down from his hiding place, made clumsy because he dared not let go of the fisherman's short spear, someone, the man or the fisherman, cried out. It startled two white herons which had been perching amongst the topmost branches of the banyan; the birds rose up into the air and flapped away as Yama crept down the path, clutching the spear with both hands.

There was a tremendous shaking in the leaves at the bend of the path. The man was floundering hip-deep amongst the broken thatch which Yama had used to conceal the trap. The big trap was wide-mouthed and two spans long, tapering to a blunt point. It was woven from pliable young prop roots, and bamboo spikes had been fastened on the inside, pointing downwards, so that when a fish entered to get at the bait it could not back out. These spikes had dug into the flesh of the man's leg when he had tried to pull free, and he was bleeding hard and grunting with pain as he pushed down with his hands like a man trying to work off a particularly tight boot. He did not see Yama until the point of the spear pricked the fat folds of speckled skin at the back of his neck.

After Yama had used the spray which dissolved the threads' glue, Caphis wanted to kill the man who would have killed and eaten him, but Yama kept hold of the spear, and at last Caphis satisfied himself by tying the man's thumbs together behind his back and leaving him there, with his leg still in the trap.

The man started to shout as soon as they were out of sight. 'I gave you the stuff, didn't I? I didn't mean no harm. Let me go, master! Let me go and I'll say nothing! I swear it!'

He was still shouting when Caphis and Yama put out from the banyan.

The fisherman's scrawny shanks were so long that his knees jutted above the crown of his head as he squatted in the coracle. He paddled with slow, deliberate strokes. The threads of the trap had left a hundred red weals across the mottled yellow skin of his chest. He said that once he had warmed up his blood he would take Yama across to the shore.

'That is, if you don't mind helping me with my night lines.'

'You could take me to Aeolis. It is not far.'

Caphis nodded. 'That's true enough, but it would take me all day to haul against the current. Some of us go there to trade, and that's where I got that fine spear-point last year. But we never leave our boats when we go there, because it is a wicked town.'

Yama said, 'It is where I live. You have nothing to fear. Even if the man gets free, he would be burnt for trying to murder you.'

'Perhaps. But then his family would make a vendetta against my family. That is how it is.' Caphis studied Yama, and said at last, 'You'll help me with my lines, and I'll take you to the shore. You can walk more quickly to your home than I can row. But you'll need some breakfast before you can work, I reckon.'

They landed at the edge of a solitary grandfather banyan half a league downstream. Caphis built a fire of dried moss in the upturned turtle shell and boiled up tea in the resin mug, using friable strips of the bark of a twiggy bush that grew, he said, high up in the tangled tops of the banyans. When the tea started to boil he threw in some flat seeds that made it froth, and handed Yama the mug.

The tea was bitter, but after the first sip Yama felt it warm his blood, and he quickly drained the mug. He sat by the fire, chewing on a strip of dried fish, while Caphis moved about the hummocky moss of the little clearing where they had landed. With his long legs and short barrel of a body, and his slow, deliberate, flatfooted steps, the fisherman looked something like a heron. The toes of his feet were webbed, and the hooked claws on his big toes and spurs on his heels helped him climb the banyan's smooth, interlaced branches. He collected seeds and lichens and a particular kind of moss, and dug fat beetle grubs from rotten wood and ate them at once, spitting out the heads.

All anyone could want could be found in the banyans, Caphis told Yama. The fisherfolk pounded the leaves to make a fibrous pulp from which they wove their clothes. Their traps and the ribs of their coracles were made from young prop roots, and the hulls were woven from strips of bark varnished with a distillation of the tree's sap. The kernels of banyan fruit, which set all through the year, could be ground into flour. Poison used to stun fish was extracted from the skin of a particular kind of frog that lived in the tiny ponds cupped within the living vases of bromeliads. A hundred kinds of fish swarmed around the feeder roots, and a thousand kinds of plants grew on the branches; all had their uses, and their own tutelary spirits which had to be individually appeased.

'There's hardly anything we lack, except metals and tobacco, which is why we trade with you land folk. Otherwise we're as free as the fish, and always have been. We've never risen above our animal selves since the Preservers gave us the banyans as our province, and that is the excuse the Mud People use when they hunt us. But we're an old folk, and we've seen much, and we have long memories. Everything comes to the river, we say, and generally that's true.'

Caphis had a tattoo on the ball of his left shoulder, a snake done in black and red that curled around so that it could swallow its own tail. He touched the skin beneath this tattoo with the claw of his thumb and said, 'Even the river comes to its own self.'

'What do you mean?'

'Why, where do you think the river goes, when it falls over the edge of the world? It swallows its own self and returns to its beginning, and so renews itself. That's how the Preservers made the world, and we, who were here from the first, remember how it was. Lately, things are changing. Year by year the river grows less. Perhaps the river no longer bites its own tail, but if that is so I cannot say where it goes instead.'

'Do you – your people, do they remember the Preservers?'

Caphis's eyes filmed over. His voice took on a sing-song lilt. 'Before the Preservers, the Universe was a plain of ice. The Preservers brought light that melted the ice and woke the seeds of the banyans which were trapped there. The first men were made of wood, carved from a banyan tree so huge that it was a world in itself, standing in the universe of water and light. But the men of wood showed their backs to the Preservers, and did not respect animals or even themselves, and destroyed so much of the world-tree that the Preservers raised a great flood. It rained for forty days and forty nights, and the waters rose through the roots of the banyan and rose through the branches until only the youngest leaves showed above the flood, and at last even these were submerged. All of the creatures of the world-tree perished in the flood except for a frog and a heron. The frog clung to the last leaf which showed above the flood and called to its own kind, but the lonely heron heard its call and stooped down and ate it.

'Well, the Preservers saw this, and the frog grew within the heron's stomach until it split open its captor, and stepped out, neither frog nor heron but a new creature which had taken something from both its parents. It was the first of our kind, and just as it was neither frog nor heron, neither was it man or woman. At once the flood receded. The new creature lay down on a smooth mudbank and fell asleep. And while it slept, the Preservers dismembered it, and from its ribs fifty others were made, and these were men and women of the first tribe of my people. The Preservers breathed on them and clouded their minds, so that unlike the men of wood they would not challenge or be disrespectful to their creators. But that was long ago, and in another place. You, if you don't mind me saying so, look as if your bloodline climbed down from the trees.'

'I was born on the river, like you.'

Caphis clacked his wide flat lower jaw – it was the way the fisherfolk laughed. 'Sometime I'd like to hear that story. But now we should set to. The day does not grow younger, and there is work to do. It is likely that the Mud Man will escape. We should have killed him. He would bite off his own leg, if he thought that would help him escape. The Mud People are treacherous and full of tricks – that is how they are able to catch us, we who are more clever than they, as long as our blood is warmed. That is why they generally hunt us at night. I was caught because my blood had the night chill, you see. It made me slow and stupid, but now I am warm, and I know what I must do.'

Caphis pissed on the fire to extinguish it, packed away the cup and the turtle shell beneath the narrow bench which circled the rim of the coracle, and declared himself ready.

'You will bring me luck, for it was by luck that you saved yourself from the phantom and then found me.'

With Yama seated on one side and Caphis wielding a leaf-shaped paddle on the other, the coracle was surprisingly stable, although it was so small that Yama's knees pressed against Caphis's bony shins. As the craft swung out into the current, Caphis paddled with one hand and filled a long-stemmed clay pipe with ordinary tobacco with the other, striking a flint against a bit of rough steel for a spark.

It was a bright clear afternoon, with a gentle wind that barely ruffled the surface of the river. There was no sign of the pinnace; no ships at all, only the little coracles of the fisherfolk scattered across the broad river between shore and misty horizon. As Caphis said, the river bore all away. For a while, Yama could believe that none of his adventures had happened, that his life could return to its normal routines.

Caphis squinted at the sun, wet a finger and held it up to the wind, then drove his craft swiftly between the scattered tops of young banyans (Yama thought of the lone frog in Caphis's story, clinging to the single leaf above the universal flood, bravely calling but finding only death, and in death, transfiguration).

As the sun fell towards the distant peaks of the Rim Mountains, Yama and Caphis worked trotlines strung between bending poles anchored in the bottom of the gravel bank. Caphis gave Yama a sticky, odourless ointment to rub on his shoulders and arms to protect his skin from sunburn. Yama soon fell into an unthinking rhythm, hauling up lines, rebaiting hooks with bloodworms and dropping them back. Most of the hooks were empty, but gradually a pile of small silver fish accumulated in the well of the coracle, frantically jinking in the shallow puddle there or lying still, their gill flaps pulsing like blood red flowers as they drowned in air.

Caphis asked forgiveness for each fish he caught. The fisherfolk believed that the world was packed with spirits which controlled everything from the weather to the flowering of the least of the epiphytic plants of the banyan shoals. Their days were spent in endless negotiations with these spirits to ensure that the world continued its seamless untroubled spinning out.

At last Caphis declared himself satisfied with the day's catch. He gutted a pentad of fingerlings, stripped the fillets of pale muscle from their backbones, and gave half to Yama, together with a handful of fleshy leaves.

The fillets of fish were juicy; chewed, the leaves tasted of sweet limes and quenched Yama's thirst. Following Caphis's example, he spat the leaf pulp overboard, and tiny fish promptly swarmed around this prize as it sank through the clear dark water.

Caphis picked up his paddle and the coracle skimmed

across the water towards a bend of the stony shore, where cliffs carved and socketed with empty tombs rose from a broad pale beach.

'There's an old road that leads along the shore to Aeolis,' Caphis told Yama. 'It will take you the rest of this day, and a little of the next, I reckon.'

'If you would take me directly to Aeolis, I can promise you a fine reward. It is little enough in return for your life.'

'We do not go there unless we must, and never after nightfall. You saved my life, and so it is always in your care. Would you risk it so quickly, by taking me into the jaws of the Mud People? I do not think you would be so cruel. I have my family to consider. They'll be watching for me this night, and I don't want to worry them further.'

Caphis grounded his frail craft in the shallows a little way from the shore. He had never set foot on land, he said, and he wasn't about to start now. He looked at Yama and said, 'Don't walk after dark, young master. Find shelter before the sun goes down and stick to it until first light. Then you'll be all right. There are ghouls out there, and they like a bit of live meat on occasion.'

Yama knew about the ghouls. He and Telmon had once hidden from a ghoul on one of their expeditions into the foothills of the City of the Dead. He remembered the way the man-shaped creature's pale skin had glimmered in the twilight like wet muscle, and how frightened he had been as it stooped this way and that, and the stench it had left. He said, 'I will be careful.'

Caphis said, 'Take this. No use against ghouls, but I hear tell there are plenty of coneys on the shore. Some of us hunt them, but not me.'

It was a small knife carved from a flake of obsidian. Its hilt was wrapped with twine, and its exfoliated edge was as sharp as a razor.

'I reckon you can look after your own self, young master, but maybe a time will come when you need help. Then my family will remember that you helped me. Do you recall what I said about the river?'

'Everything comes around again.'

Caphis nodded, and touched the tattoo of the self-engulfing snake on his shoulder. 'You had a good teacher. You know how to pay attention.'

Yama slid from the tipping coracle and stood knee-deep in ooze and brown water. 'I will not forget,' he said.

'Choose carefully where you camp this night,' Caphis said. 'Ghouls are bad, but ghosts are worse. We see their lights sometimes, shining softly in the ruins.'

Then he pushed away from the shallows and the coracle waltzed into the current as he dug the water with his leaf-shaped paddle. By the time Yama had waded to shore, the coracle was already far off, a black speck on the shining plane of the river, making a long, curved path towards a raft of banyan islands far from shore.

9 ~ The Knife

The beach was made of deep, soft drifts of white shell fragments; it was not until Yama began to climb the worn stone stair that zigzagged up the face of the carved cliff that he remembered how difficult it was to walk on firm ground, where each step sent a little shock up the ladder of the spine. At the first turn of the stair, a spring welled inside a trough cut from the native stone. Yama knelt on the mossy ground by the trough and drank clear sweet water until his belly sloshed, knowing that there would be little chance of finding any potable water in the City of the Dead. Only when he stood did he notice that someone else had drunk there recently – no, to judge by the overlapping footprints in the soft red moss, it had been two people.

Lud and Lob. They had also escaped Dr Dismas. Yama had tucked the obsidian knife into his belt under the flap of his shirt, snug against the small of his back. He touched the handle for reassurance before he continued his ascent.

An ancient road ran close to the edge of the cliff, its flat pavement, splashed with the yellow and grey blotches of lichens, so wide that twenty men could have ridden abreast along it. Beyond, the alkaline, shaley land shimmered in the level light of the late afternoon sun. Tombs stood everywhere, casting long shadows towards the river. This was the Silent Quarter, which Yama had rarely visited – he and Telmon preferred the ancient tombs of the foothills beyond the Breas, where aspects could be wakened and the flora and fauna was richer. Compared to the sumptuously decorated mausoleums of the older parts of the City of the Dead, the tombs here were poor things, mostly no more than low boxes with domed roofs, although here and there memorial steles and columns rose amongst them, and a few larger tombs stood on artificial stepped mounds, guarded by statues that watched the river with stony eyes. One of these was as big as the peel-house, half hidden by a small wood of yews grown wild and twisted. In all the desiccated landscape nothing stirred except for a lammergeyer high in the deep blue sky, riding a thermal on outspread wings.

When Yama was satisfied that he was not about to be ambushed, he set off down the road towards the distant smudge that must surely be Aeolis, halfway towards the vanishing point where the Rim Mountains and the misty horizon of the farside seemed to converge.

Little grew in the stone gardens of this part of the City of the Dead. The white, sliding rocks weathered to a bitter dust in which only a few plants could root, mostly yuccas and creosote bushes and clumps of prickly pear. Wild roses crept around the smashed doorways of some of the tombs, their blood-red blooms scenting the warm air. The tombs had all been looted long ago, and of their inhabitants scarcely a bone remained. If the cunningly preserved bodies had not been carted away to fuel the smelters of old Aeolis, then wild animals had long ago dismembered and consumed them once they had been disinterred from their caskets. Ancient debris was strewn everywhere, from fragments of smashed funeral urns and shards of broken furniture fossilized on the dry shale, to slates which displayed pictures of the dead, impressed into their surfaces by some forgotten art. Some of these were still active, and as Yama went past scenes from ancient Ys briefly came to life or the faces of men and women turned to watch him, their lips moving soundlessly or shaping into a smile or a coquettish kiss. Unlike the aspects of older tombs, these were mere recordings without

ne
and
of the
out the
ront of the
nished from
at were covered
rown water.
rning.'
fall, little fish.'
Lob stood on top of a
de of the road. Both wore
e over his bare shoulder; the
dened and blistered by a bad

ng,' Lud advised. 'It's too hot for
water, and you know you can't get

Dismas tried to have you killed. There is
en us.'
know about that,' Lud said. 'I reckon we've a
e.'
we us,' Lob said.
not see it.'
explained patiently, 'Dr Dismas would have paid us
our trouble, and instead we had to swim for our lives
hen you pulled that trick. I got burnt, too.'

'And he lost his knife,' Lob added. 'He loved that knife,
you miserable culler, and you made him lose it.'

Lud said, 'And then there was the boat you put on fire.
You owe for that, I reckon.'

intelligence; the slates played the same meaningless loop over
and over, whether for the human eye or the uncomprehend-
ing gaze of any lizard that flicked over the glazed surfaces in
which the pictures were embedded.

Yama was familiar with these animations; the Aedile had
an extensive collection of them. They had to be exposed to
sunlight before they would work, and Yama had always
wondered why, for they were normally found inside the
tombs. But although he knew what these mirages were, their
unpredictable flicker was still disturbing. He kept looking
behind him, fearful that Lud and Lob were stalking him
through the quiet solitude of the ruins.

The oppressive feeling of being watched grew as the sun
fell towards the ragged blue line of the Rim Mountains and
the shadows of the tombs lengthened and mingled across the
bone-white ground. To be walking through the City of the
Dead in the bright sunshine was one thing, but as the light
faded Yama increasingly glanced over his shoulder as he
walked, and sometimes turned and walked backwards a few
paces, or stopped and slowly scanned the low hills with their
freight of empty tombs. He had often camped in the City of
the Dead with the Aedile and his retinue of servants and
archaeological workers, or with Telmon and two or three
soldiers, but never before alone.

The distant peaks of the Rim Mountains bit into the
reddened disc of the sun. The lights of Aeolis shimmered in
the distance like a heap of tiny diamonds. It was still at least
half a day's walk to the city, and would be longer in darkness.
Yama left the road and began to search the tombs for one
that would give shelter for the night.

It was like a game. Yama knew that the tombs he rejected
now would be better than the one he would choose of
necessity when the last of the sun's light fled the sky. But he
did not want to choose straight away because he still felt that
he was being watched and fancied, as he wandered the
network of narrow paths between the tombs, that he heard a

padding footfall behind him that stopped when he stopp[ed]
and resumed a moment after he began to move forw[ard]
again. At last, halfway up a long, gentle slope, he turned
called out Lud and Lob's names, feeling both fearf[ul]
defiant as the echoes of his voice died away amon[g]
tombs spread below him. There was no answer, but [as he]
moved on he heard a faint squealing and splashing
the crest of the slope.

Yama drew the obsidian knife and crept forw[ard]
thief. Beyond the crest, the ground fell away in
drop, as if something had bitten away half the
foot of the drop, a seep of brackish water gleam[ed]
in the sun's last light, and a family of hyraces
in the muddy shallows.

Yama stood and yelled and plunged down
The hyraces bolted in every direction and
squealing in blind panic into the middle of
It saw Yama charging towards it and st[opped so]
that it tumbled head over heels. Befor[e it could]
direction, he threw himself on its sli[ppery back,]
wrestled it onto its back and slit its thro[at.]

Yama built a fire of twisted strands
from the centres of prickly pear clu[sters and a]
friction bow made from two twigs
hyrax's carcass. He cleaned and skinned and [gutted the]
hyrax, roasted its meat in the hot ashes, and ate until h[is]
stomach hurt, cracking bones for hot marrow and licking the
fatty juices from his fingers. The sky had darkened to reveal
a scattering of dim halo stars, and the Galaxy was rising,
salting the City of the Dead with a blue-white glow and
casting a confusion of shadows.

The tomb Yama chose as a place to sleep was not far from
the seep, and as he rested against its granite façade, which
still held the day's heat, he heard something splash in the
pool – an animal come to drink. Yama laid the remains of

The cliffs there were sheer and high; if the peel-house had
stood in the seething water at their bases, its tallest turret
would not have reached to their tops. Yama got down on his
belly and hung over the edge and looked right and left, but
could not see any sign of a path or of stairs, although there
were many tombs cut into the cliff faces – there was o[ne]
directly below him. Birds nested in the openings,
thousands floated on the wind that blew up the face
cliff, like flakes of restlessly sifting snow. Yama spa[red]
pebble and watched it bounce from the ledge in
tomb directly below and dwindle away; it [was lost to]
sight before it hit the tumbled slabs of rock t[hat]
and uncovered by the heave of the river's b[ed]

Behind him, someone said, 'A hot mo[rsel']
And someone else: 'Watch you don'[t]
Yama jumped to his feet. Lud an[d Lob,]
bank of white shale on the far si[de]
only kilts. Lob had a coil of ro[pe]
skin of Lud's chest was red[dened by]
burn.

'Don't think of runn[ing,']
you to get far withou[t]
away.'

Yama said, 'Dr[...]
no enmity betw[een...]
'I wouldn't [...]
score to set[tle...]
'You o[...]
'I do[...]
had been looki[ng...]
narrow paths that meande[red...]
rials and up and down the gentle slop[es...]
all alike, and not one ran for more than a h[undred...]
before meeting with another, or splitting into two, but [Yama]
kept the sun at his back, and by midmorning had reached
the wide straight road again.

'That was not yours.'

Lud scratched at the patch of reddened skin on his chest and said, 'It's the principle of the thing.'

'In any case, I can only pay you when I get home,' Yama said.

'"In any case",' Lud echoed in a mocking voice. 'That's not how we see it. How do we know we can trust you?'

'Of course you can.'

Lud said, 'You haven't even asked how much we want, and then you might just think to tell your father. I don't think he'd pay us then, would he, brother?'

'It's doubtful.'

'Very doubtful, I'd say.'

Yama knew that there was only one chance to escape. He said, 'Then you do not trust me?'

Lud saw Yama's change in posture. He started down the slope, raising a cloud of white dust, and yelled, 'Don't—'

Yama did. He turned and took two steps backwards, and then, before he could have second thoughts, ran forward and jumped over the edge of the cliff.

He fell in a rush of air, and as he fell threw back his head and brought up his knees (Sergeant Rhodean was saying, 'Just let it happen to you. If you learn to trust your body it's all a matter of timing.'). Sky and river revolved around each other, and then he landed on his feet, knees bent to take the shock, on the ledge before the entrance to the tomb.

The ledge was no wider than a bed, and slippery with bird excrement. Yama fell flat on his back at once, filled with a wild fear that he would tumble over the edge – there had been a balustrade once, but it had long ago fallen away. He caught a tuft of wiry grass and held on, although the sharp blades of grass reopened the wounds made by Caphis's spearhead.

As he carefully climbed back to his feet, a stone clipped the ledge and tumbled away towards the heaving water far below. Yama looked up. Lob and Lud capered at the top of the cliff, silhouetted against the blue sky. They shouted down at him, but their words were snatched away by the wind. One of them threw another stone, which smashed to flinders scarcely a span from Yama's feet.

Yama ran forward, darting between the winged figures, their faces blurred by time, which supported the lintel of the gaping entrance to the tomb. Inside, stone blocks fallen from the high ceiling littered the mosaic floor. An empty casket stood on a dais beneath a canopy of stone carved to look like cloth rippling in the wind. Disturbed by Yama's footfalls, bats fell from one of the holes in the ceiling and dashed around and around above his head, chittering in alarm.

The tomb was shaped like a wedge of pie, and behind the dais it narrowed to a passageway. It had once been sealed by a slab of stone, but that had been smashed long ago by robbers who had discovered the path used by the builders of the tomb. Yama grinned. He had guessed that the tombs in the cliffs would have been breached and stripped just like those above. It was his way of escape. He stepped over the sill and, keeping one hand on the cold dry stone of the wall, felt his way through near darkness.

He had not gone far when the passage struck another running at right angles. He tossed an imaginary coin and chose the left-hand way. A hundred heartbeats later, in pitch darkness, he went sprawling over a slump of rubble. He got up cautiously and climbed the spill of stones until his head bumped the ceiling of the passage. It was blocked.

Then Yama heard voices behind him, and knew that Lud and Lob had followed him. He should have expected it. They would lose their lives if he was able to escape and tell the Aedile about the part they had played in Dr Dismas's scheme.

As Yama slid down the rubble, his hand fell on something cold and hard. It was a metal knife, its curved blade as long as his forearm. It was cold to the touch and gave off a faint glow; motes of light seemed to float in the wake of its blade when Yama slashed at the darkness. Emboldened, he felt his way back to the tomb.

The dim light hurt his eyes; it spilled around one of the twins, who stood in the tomb's narrow entrance.

'Little fish, little fish. What are you scared of?'

Yama held up the long knife. 'Not you, Lud.'

'Let me get him,' Lob said, peering over his brother's shoulder.

'Don't block the light, stupid.' Lud pushed Lob out of the way and grinned at Yama. 'There isn't a way out, is there? Or you wouldn't have come back. We can wait. We caught fish this morning, and we have water. I don't think you do, or you would have set out for the city straight away.'

Yama said, 'I killed a hyrax last night. I ate well enough then.'

Lud started forward. 'But I bet you couldn't drink the water in the pool, eh? We couldn't, and we can drink just about anything.'

Yama was aware of a faint breath of air at his back. He said, 'How did you get down here?'

'Rope,' Lob said. 'From the boat. I saved it. People say we're stupid, but we're not.'

'Then I can climb back up,' Yama said, and advanced on Lud, making passes with the knife as he came around the raised casket. The knife made a soft hum, and its rusty hilt pricked his palm. He felt a coldness flowing into his wrist and along his arm as the blade brightened with blue light.

Lud retreated. 'You wouldn't,' he said.

Lob pushed at his brother, trying to get past him. He was excited. 'Break his legs,' he shrieked. 'Break his legs! See how he swims then!'

'A knife! He's got a knife!'

Yama swung the knife again. Lud crowded backwards into Lob and they both fell over.

Yama yelled, words that hurt his throat and tongue. He did not know what he yelled and he stumbled, because suddenly his legs seemed too long and bony and his arms hung wrong. Where was his mount and where was the rest of the squad? Why was he standing in the middle of what looked like a ruined tomb? Had he fallen into the keelways? All he could remember was a tremendous crushing pain, and then he had suddenly woken here, with two fat ruffians threatening him. He struck at the nearest and the man scrambled out of the way with jittery haste; the knife hit the wall and spat a shower of sparks. It was screaming now. He jumped onto the casket – yes, a tomb – but his body betrayed him and he lost his balance; before he could recover, the second ruffian caught his ankles and he fell heavily, striking the stone floor with hip and elbow and shoulder. The impact numbed his fingers, and the knife fell from his grasp, clattering on the floor and gouging a smoking rut in the stone.

Lud ran forward and kicked the knife out of the way. Yama scrambled to his feet. He did not remember falling. His right arm was cold and numb, and hung from his shoulder like a piece of meat; he had to pull the obsidian knife from his belt with his left hand as Lud ran at him. They slammed against the wall and Lud gasped and clutched at his chest. Blood welled over his hand and he looked at it dully. 'What?' he said. He stepped away from Yama with a bewildered look and said again, 'What?'

'You killed him!' Lob said.

Yama shook his head. He could not get his breath. The ancient knife lay on the filthy floor exactly between him and Lob, sputtering and sending up a thick smoke that stank of burning metal.

Lud tried to pull the obsidian knife from his chest, but it snapped, leaving a fingerswidth of the blade protruding. He blundered around the tomb, blood all over his hands now, blood running down his chest and soaking into the waistband of his kilt. He didn't seem to understand what had happened to him. He kept saying over and over again,

'What? What?' and pushed past his brother and fell to his knees at the entrance to the tomb. Light spilled over his shoulders. He seemed to be searching the blue sky for something he could not find.

Lob stared at Yama, his grey tongue working between his tusks. At last he said, 'You killed him, you culler. You didn't have to kill him.'

Yama took a deep breath. His hands were shaking. 'You were going to kill me.'

'All we wanted was a bit of money. Just enough to get away. Not much to ask, and now you've gone and killed my brother.'

Lob stepped towards Yama and his foot struck the knife. He picked it up – and screamed. White smoke rose from his hand and then he was not holding the knife but a creature fastened to his arm by clawed hands and feet. Lob staggered backwards and slammed his arm against the wall, but the creature only snarled and tightened its grip. It was the size of a small child, and seemed to be made of sticks. A kind of mane of dry, white hair stood around its starveling face. A horrid stink of burning flesh filled the tomb. Lob beat at the creature with his free hand and it vanished in a sudden flash of blue light.

The ancient knife fell to the floor, ringing on the stone. Yama snatched it up and fled down the passage, barely remembering to turn right into the faint breeze. He banged from wall to wall as he ran, and then the walls fell away and he was tumbling through a rush of black air.

10 ~ The Curators of the City of the Dead

The room was in some high, windy place. It was small and square, with whitewashed stone walls and a ceiling of tongue-and-groove planking painted with a hunting scene. The day after he first woke, Yama managed to raise himself from the thin mattress on the stone slab and stagger to the deep-set slit window. He glimpsed a series of stony ridges stepping away beneath a blank blue sky, and then pain overcame his will and he fainted.

'He is ill and he does not know it,' the old man said. He had half-turned his head to speak to someone else as he leaned over Yama. The tip of his wispy white beard hung a finger's width from Yama's chin. The deeply wrinkled skin of his face was mottled with brown spots, and there was only a fringe of white hair around his bald pate. Glasses with lenses like small mirrors hid his eyes. Deep, old scars cut the left side of his face, drawing up the side of his mouth in a sardonic rictus. He said, 'He does not know how much the knife took from him.'

'He's young,' an old woman's voice said. She added, 'He'll learn by himself, won't he? We can't—'

The old man curled and uncurled the end of his wispy beard around his fingers. At last, he said, 'I cannot remember.'

Yama asked them who they were, and where this cool white room was, but they did not hear him. Perhaps he had not spoken at all. He could not move even a single fingertip, although this did not scare him. He was too tired to be scared. The two old people went away and Yama was left to stare at the painted hunting scene on the ceiling. His thoughts would not fit together. Men in plastic armour over brightly coloured jerkins and hose were chasing a white stag through a forest of leafless tree trunks. The turf between the trees was starred with flowers. It seemed to be night in the painting, for in every direction the slim trunks of the trees faded into darkness. The white stag glimmered amongst them like a fugitive star. The paint had flaked away from the wood in places, and a patch above the window was faded. In the foreground, a young man in a leather jacket was pulling a brace of hunting dogs away from a pool. Yama thought that he knew the names of the dogs, and who their owner was. But he was dead.

Some time later, the old man came back and lifted Yama up so that he could sip thin vegetable soup from an earthenware bowl. Later, he was cold, so cold that he shivered under the thin grey blanket, and then so hot that he would have cast aside the blanket if he had possessed the strength.

Fever, the old man told him. He had a bad fever. Something was wrong with his blood. 'You have been in the tombs,' the old man said, 'and there are many kinds of old sicknesses there.'

Yama sweated into the mattress, thinking that if only he could get up he would quench his thirst with the clear water of the forest pool. Telmon would help him.

But Telmon was dead.

In the middle of the day, sunlight crept a few paces into the little room before shyly retreating. At night, wind hunted at the corners of the deep-set window, making the candle gutter inside its glass sleeve. When Yama's fever broke it was night. He lay still, listening to the wuthering of the wind. He felt very tired but entirely clearheaded, and spent hours piecing together what had happened.

Dr Dismas's tower, burning like a firework. The strange

133

cage, and the burning ship. The leonine young war hero, Enobarbus, his face as ruined as the old man's. The ghost ship, and his escape – more fire. The whole adventure seemed to be punctuated by fire. He remembered the kindness of the fisherman, Caphis, and the adventure amongst the dry tombs of the Silent Quarter, which had ended in Lud's death. He had run from something terrible, and as for what had happened after that, he remembered nothing at all.

'You were carried here,' the old woman told him, when she brought him breakfast. 'It was from a place on the shore somewhere downstream of Aeolis, I'd judge. A fair distance, as the fox said to the hen, when he gave her a head start.'

Her skin was fine-grained, almost translucent, and her white, feathery hair reached to the small of her back. She was of the same bloodline as Derev, but far older than either of Derev's parents.

Yama said, 'How did you know?'

The old man smiled at the woman's shoulder. As always, he wore his mirrored lenses. 'Your trousers and your shirt were freshly stained with river silt. It is quite distinctive. But I believe that you had been wandering in the City of the Dead, too.'

Yama asked why he thought that.

'The knife, dear,' the woman said.

The old man pulled on his scanty white beard and said, 'Many people carry old weapons, for they are often far more potent than those made today.'

Yama nodded, remembering Dr Dismas's energy pistol.

'However, the knife you carried has a patina of corrosion that suggests it had lain undisturbed in some dark, dry place for many years. Perhaps you have carried it around without scrupling to clean it, but I think that you are more responsible than that. I think that you found it only recently, and did not have time to clean it. You landed at the shore and began to walk through the City of the Dead, and at some point found the knife in an old tomb.'

'It's from the Age of Insurrection, if I'm a judge,' the woman said. 'It's a cruel thing.'

'And she has forgotten a good deal more than I ever knew,' the old man said fondly. 'You will have to learn its ways, or it could kill you.'

'Hush!' the old woman said sharply. 'Nothing should be changed!'

'Perhaps nothing can be changed,' the old man said.

'Then I would be a machine,' the old woman said, 'and I don't like that thought.'

'At least you would not need to worry. But I will be careful. Pay no attention to me, youngster. My mind wanders these days, as my wife will surely remind you at every opportunity.'

They had been married a long time. They both wore the same kind of long, layered shifts over woollen trousers, and shared the same set of gestures, as if love were a kind of imitation game in which the best of both participants was mingled. They called themselves Osric and Beatrice, but Yama suspected that these were not their real names. They both had an air of sly caution which suggested that they were withholding much, although Yama felt that Osric wanted to tell him more than he was allowed to know. Beatrice was strict with her husband, but she favoured Yama with fond glances, and while he had been stricken with fever she had spent hours bathing his forehead with wet cloths infused with oil of spikenard, and had fed him infusions of honey and herbs, crooning to him as if he were her child. While Osric was bent by age, his tall, slender wife carried herself like a young dancer.

Later, husband and wife sat side by side on the ledge beneath the narrow window of the little room, watching Yama eat a bowl of boiled maize. It was his first solid food since he had woken. They said that they were members of the Department of the Curators of the City of the Dead, an office of the civil service which had been disbanded centuries ago.

'But my ancestors stayed on, dear,' Beatrice explained. 'They believed that the dead deserved better than abandonment, and fought against dissolution. There was quite a little war. Of course, we're much diminished now. Most would say that we had vanished long ago, if they had heard of us at all, but we still hold some of the more important parts of the city.'

'You might say that I am an honorary member of the department, by marriage,' Osric said. 'Here, I cleaned the knife for you.'

Osric laid the long, curved knife at the foot of the bed. Yama looked at it and discovered that although it had saved his life he feared it; it was as if Osric had set a live snake at his feet. He said, 'I found it in a tomb in the cliffs by the river.'

'Then it came from somewhere else,' Osric said, and laid a bony finger beside his nose. The tip of the finger was missing. He said, 'I used a little white vinegar to take the bloom of age from the metal, and every decad or so you should rub it down with a cloth touched to mineral oil. But it will not need sharpening, and it will repair itself, within limits. It had been imprinted with a copy of the personality of its previous owner, but I have purged that ghost. You should practise with it as often as you can, and handle it at least once a day, and so it will come to know you.'

'Osric—'

'He needs to know,' Osric told his wife. 'It will not hurt. Handle it often, Yama. The more you handle it, the better it will know you. And leave it in the sunlight, or between places of different temperature – placing the point in a fire is good. Otherwise it will take energy from you again. It had lain in the dark a long time – that was why you were hurt by it when you used it. I would guess it belonged to an officer of the cavalry, dead long ages past. They were issued to those fighting in the rain forests two thousand leagues downriver.'

Yama said stupidly, 'But the war started only forty years ago.'

'This was another war, dear,' Beatrice said. 'I found it by the river. In a tomb there. I put out my hand in the dark.'

Yama remembered how the knife had kindled its eldritch glow when he had held it up, wonderingly, before his face. But when Lob had picked it up, the horrible thing had happened. The knife was different things to different people.

Yama had been brought a long way from the river. This was the last retreat of the last of the curators of the City of the Dead, deep in the foothills of the Rim Mountains. He had not realized until then the true extent of the necropolis.

'The dead outnumber the living,' Osric said, 'and this has been the burial place for Ys since the construction of Confluence. Until this last, decadent age, at least.'

Yama gathered that there were not many curators left now, and that most of those were old. This was a place where the past was stronger than the present. The Department of the Curators of the City of the Dead had once been responsible for preparation and arrangement of the deceased, whom they called clients, and for the care and maintenance of the graves, tombs and memorials, the picture slates and aspects of the dead. It had been a solemn and complex task. For instance, Yama learned that there had been four methods of dealing with clients: by interment, including burial or entombment; by cremation, either by fire or by acids; by exposure, either in a byre raised above the ground or by dismemberment; and by water.

'Which I understand is the only method used these days,' Osric said. 'It has its place, but many die a long way from the Great River, and besides, many communities are too close together, so that the corpses of those upriver foul the water of those below them. Consider, Yama. Much of

Confluence is desert or mountain. Interment in the soil is rare, for there is little enough land for cultivation. For myriad upon myriad days, our ancestors built tombs for their dead, or burned them on pyres or dissolved them in tanks of acid, or exposed them to the brothers of the air. Building tombs takes much labour and is suitable only for the rich, for the badly constructed tombs of the poor are soon ransacked by wild animals. Firewood is in as short supply as arable land, for the same reasons, and dissolution in acid is usually considered aesthetically displeasing. How much more natural, in the circumstances, to expose the client to the brothers of the air. It is how I wish my body to be disposed, when my time comes. Beatrice has promised it to me. The world will end before I die, of course, but I think there will still be birds . . .'

'You forgot preservation,' Beatrice said sharply. 'He always does,' she told Yama. 'He disapproves.'

'Ah, but I did not forget. It is merely a variation on interment. Without a tomb, the preserved body is merely fodder for the animals, or a curiosity in a sideshow.'

'Some are turned into stone,' Beatrice said. 'It is mostly done by exposing the client to limy water.'

'And then there is mummification, and desiccation, either by vacuum or by chemical treatment, and treatment by tar, or by ice.' Osric ticked off the variations on his fingers. 'But you know full well that I mean the most common method, and the most decadent. Which is to say, those clients who were preserved while still alive, in the hope of physical resurrection in ages to come. Instead, robbers opened the tombs and took what there was of value, and threw away the bodies for wild animals to devour, or burned them as fuel, or ground them up for fertilizer. The brave cavalry officer who once wielded your knife in battle, young Yama, was in all probability burned in some furnace to melt the alloy stripped from his tomb. Perhaps one of the tomb robbers picked up the knife, and it attacked him. He dropped it

138

where you would find it an age later. We live in impoverished times. I remember that I played amongst the tombs as a child, teasing the aspects who still spoke for those beyond hope of resurrection. There is a lesson in folly. Only the Preservers outrun time. I did not know then that the aspects were bound to oblige my foolishness; the young are needlessly cruel because they know no better.'

Beatrice straightened her back, held up her hand, and recited a verse:

> Let fame, that all hunt after in their lives,
> Live registered upon our brazen tombs,
> And then grace us in the disgrace of death;
> When, spite of the cormorant devouring time,
> The endeavour of this present breath may buy
> That honour which shall bate his scythe's keen edge,
> And makes us heirs to all eternity.

Yama guessed that this was from the Puranas, but Beatrice said that it was far older. 'There are too few of us to remember everything left by the dead,' she said, 'but we do what we can, and we are a long-lived race.'

There was much more to the tasks of the curators than preparation of their clients, and in the next two days Yama learned something about care of tombs and the preservation of the artefacts with which clients had been interred, each according to the customs of their bloodline. Osric and Beatrice fed him vegetable broths, baked roots and succulent young okra, corn and green beans fried in airy batter. He was getting better, and was beginning to feel a restless curiosity. He had not broken any bones, but his ribs were badly bruised and muscles in his back and arms had been torn. There were numerous half-healed cuts on his limbs and torso, too, and the fever had left him very weak, as if most of his blood had been drained.

Beatrice cleaned out the worst of his wounds; she explained that the stone dust embedded in them would otherwise leave scars. As soon as he could, Yama started to exercise, using the drills taught him by Sergeant Rhodean. He practised with the knife, too, mastering his instinctive revulsion. He handled it each day, as Osric had suggested, and otherwise left it on the ledge beneath the narrow window, where it would catch the midday sun. To begin with, he had to rest for an hour or more between each set of exercises, but he ate large amounts of the curators' plain food and felt his strength return. At last, he was able to climb the winding stairs to the top of the hollow crag.

He had to stop and rest frequently, but finally stepped out of the door of a little hut into the open air under an achingly blue sky. The air was clean and cold, as heady as wine after the stuffy room in which he had lain for so long.

The hut was set at one end of the top of the crag, which was so flat that it might have been sheared off by someone wielding a gigantic blade. Possibly this was more or less what had been done, for during the construction of Confluence, long before the Preservers had abandoned the ten thousand bloodlines, energies had been deployed to move whole mountains and shape entire landscapes as easily as a gardener might set out a bed of flowers.

The flat top of the crag was no bigger than the Great Hall of the peel-house, and divided into tiny fields by low drystone walls. There were plots of squash and yams, corn and kale and cane fruits. Little paths wandered between these plots, and there was a complicated system of cisterns and gutters to provide a constant supply of water to the crops. At the far end, Beatrice and Osric were feeding doves which fluttered around a round-topped dovecote built of unmortared stone.

The crag stood at the edge of a winding ridge above a gorge so deep that its bottom was lost in shadow. Other flat-topped crags stood along the ridge, their smooth sides fretted with windows and balconies. There was a scattering of tombs on broad ledges cut into the white rock of the gorge's steep sides, huge buildings with blind, whitewashed walls under pitched roofs of red tile that stood amidst manicured lawns and groves of tall trees. Beyond the far side of the gorge, other ridges stepped up towards the sky, and beyond the furthest ridge the peaks of the Rim Mountains seemed to float free above indistinct blue and purple masses, shining in the light of the sun.

Yama threaded the winding paths to the little patch of grass where Beatrice and Osric were scattering grain. Doves rose up in a whir of white wings as he approached. Osric raised a hand in greeting and said, 'This is the valley of the kings of the first days. Some maintain that Preservers are buried here, but if that is true, the location is hidden from us.'

'It must be a lot of work, looking after these tombs.'

The mirror lenses of Osric's spectacles flashed light at Yama. 'They maintain themselves,' the old man said, 'and there are mechanisms which prevent people from approaching too closely. It was once our job to keep people away for their own good, but only those who know this place come here now.'

'Few know of it,' Beatrice added, 'and fewer come.'

She held out a long, skinny arm. A dove immediately perched on her hand, and she drew it to her breast and stroked its head with a bony forefinger until it began to coo.

Yama said, 'I was brought a long way.'

Osric nodded. His wispy beard blew sideways in the wind. 'The Department of the Curators of the City of the Dead once maintained a city that stretched from these mountains to the river, a day's hard ride distant. Whoever brought you here had a good reason.'

Beatrice suddenly flung out her hands. The dove rose into the wind and circled high above the patchwork of tiny fields. She watched it for a minute and then said, 'I think it's time we showed Yama why he was brought here.'

'I would like to know who brought me here, to begin with.'

'As long as you do not know who saved you,' Osric said, 'there is no obligation.'

Yama nodded, remembering that after he had saved Caphis from the trap, the fisherman had said that his life was for ever in Yama's care. He said, 'Perhaps I could at least know the circumstances.'

'Something had taken one of our goats,' Beatrice said. 'It was in a field far below. We went to look for her, and found you. It is better if you see for yourself why you have been brought here. Then you'll understand. Having climbed so high, you must descend. I think that you are strong enough.'

Descending the long spiral of stairs was easier than climbing up, but Yama felt that if not for him, Osric and Beatrice would have bounded away eagerly, although he was so much younger than they. The stairs ended at a balcony that girdled the crag halfway between its flat top and its base. A series of arched doorways opened off the balcony, and Osric immediately disappeared through one. Yama would have followed, but Beatrice took his arm and guided him to a stone bench by the low wall of the balcony. Sunlight drenched the ancient stone; Yama was grateful for its warmth.

'There were a hundred thousand of us, once,' Beatrice said, 'but we are greatly reduced. This is the oldest part of all that still lies within our care, and it will be the last to fall. It will fall eventually, of course. All of Confluence will fall.'

Yama said, 'You sound like those who say that the war at the midpoint of the world may be the war at the end of all things.'

Sergeant Rhodean had taught Yama and Telmon the major battles, scratching the lines of the armies and the routes of their long marches in the red clay floor of the gymnasium.

Beatrice said, 'When there is a war, everyone believes that it will end in a victory that will bring an end to all conflict, but in a series of events there is no way of determining which is to be the last.'

Yama said stoutly, 'The heretics will be defeated because they challenge the word of the Preservers. The Ancients of Days revived much old technology which their followers use against us, but they were lesser creatures than the Preservers because they were the distant ancestors of the Preservers. How can a lesser idea prevail against a greater one?'

'I forget that you are young,' Beatrice said, smiling. 'You still have hope. But Osric has hope too, and he is a wise man. Not that the world will not end, for that is certain, but that it will end well. The Great River fails day by day, and at last all that my people care for will fall away.'

'With respect, perhaps you and your husband live for the past, yet I live for the future.'

Beatrice smiled. 'Ah, but which future, I wonder? Osric suspects that there might be more than one. As for us, it is our duty to preserve the past to inform the future, and this place is where the past is strongest. There are wonders interred here which could end the war in an instant if wielded by one side, or destroy Confluence, if used by both against each other.

'The living bury the dead and move on, and forget. We remember. Above all, that is our duty. There are record keepers in Ys who claim to be able to trace the bloodlines of Confluence back to their first members. My family preserves the tombs of those ancestors, their bodies and their artefacts. The record keepers would claim that words are stronger than the phenomena they describe, and that only words endure while all else fails, but we know that even words change. Stories are mutable, and in any story each generation finds a different lesson, and with each telling a story changes slightly until it is no longer the thing it was. The king who prevails against the hero who would have brought redeeming light to the world becomes after many tellings of the story a hero saving the world from fire, and the light-bringer becomes a fiend. Only things remain what they are. They are themselves. Words are merely representations of things; but we have the things themselves. How much more powerful they are than their representations!'

Yama thought of the Aedile, who put so much trust in the objects that the soil preserved. He said, 'My father seeks to understand the past by the wreckage it leaves behind. Perhaps it is not the stories that change but the past itself, for all that lives of the past is the meaning we invest in what remains.'

Behind him, Osric said, 'You have been taught by a record keeper. That is just what one of those beetle-browed near-sighted bookworms would say, bless them all, each and every one. Well, there is more of the past than can be found in books. That is a lesson I had to learn over and over, young man. All that is ordinary and human passes away without record, and all that remains are stories of priests and philosophers, heroes and kings. Much is made of the altar stones and sacraria of temples, but nothing of the cloisters where lovers rendezvoused and friends gossiped, and the courtyards where children played. That is the false lesson of history. Still, we can peer into random scenes of the past and wonder at their import. That is what I have brought you.'

Osric carried something square and flat under his arm, covered with a white cloth. He removed the cloth with a flourish, revealing a thin rectangle of milky stone which he laid in a pool of sunlight on the tiled floor of the balcony.

Yama said, 'My father collects these picture slates, but this one appears blank.'

'He collected them for important research, perhaps,' Osric said, 'but I am sorry to hear of it. Their proper resting place is not in a collection, but in the tomb in which they were installed.'

'I have always wondered why they need to drink sunlight to work, when they were buried away in darkness.'

'The tombs drink sunlight, too,' Osric said, 'and distribute it amongst their components according to need. The pictures respond to the heat given off by a living body, and in the darkness of the tomb would waken in the presence of any watcher. Outside the tomb, without their usual power source, the pictures also require sunlight.'

'Be quiet, husband,' Beatrice said. 'It wakens. Watch it, Yama, and learn. This is all we can show you.'

Colours mingled and ran in the slate, seeming to swirl just beneath its surface. At first they were faint and amorphous, little more than pastel flows within the slate's milky depths, but gradually they brightened, running together in a sudden silvery flash.

For a moment, Yama thought that the slate had turned into a mirror, reflecting his own eager face. But when he leaned closer, the face within the slate turned as if to speak to someone beyond the frame of the picture, and he saw that it was the face of someone older than he was, a man with lines at the corners of his eyes and grooves at either side of his mouth. But the shape of the eyes and their round blue irises, and the shape of the face, the pale skin and the mop of wiry black hair: all these were so very like his own that he cried out in astonishment.

The man in the picture was talking now, and suddenly smiled at someone beyond the picture's frame, a frank, eager smile that turned Yama's heart. The man turned away and the view slid from his face to show the night sky. It was not the sky of Confluence, for it was full of stars, scattered like diamond chips carelessly thrown across black velvet. There was a frozen swirl of dull red light in the centre of the picture, and Yama saw that the stars around it seemed to be drawn into lines that curved in towards the red swirl. Stars streaked as the viewpoint of the picture moved, and for a moment it steadied on a flock of splinters of light hung against pure black and then it faded.

Osric wrapped the white cloth around the slate. Immediately, Yama wanted to strip the cloth away and see the picture blossom within the slate again, wanted to feast on the stranger's face, the stranger who was of his bloodline, wanted to understand the strange skies under which his long-dead ancestor had stood. His blood sang in his ears.

Beatrice handed him a square of lace-trimmed cloth. A handkerchief. Yama realized then that he was weeping.

Osric said, 'This is the place where the oldest tombs on Confluence can be found, but the picture is older than anything on Confluence, for it is older than Confluence itself. It shows the first stage in the construction of the Eye of the Preservers, and it shows the lands which the Preservers walked before they fell into the Eye and vanished into the deep past or the deep future, or perhaps into another universe entirely.'

'I would like to see the tomb. I want to see where you found this picture.'

Osric said, 'The Department of the Curators of the City of the Dead has kept the picture a long time, and if it once rested in a tomb, then it was so long ago that all records of that tomb are lost. Your bloodline walked Confluence at its beginning, and now it walks it again.'

Yama said, 'This is the second time that someone has hinted that I have a mysterious destiny, but no one will explain why or what it is.'

Beatrice told her husband, 'He'll discover it soon enough. We should not tell him more.'

Osric tugged at his beard. 'I do not know everything. What the hollow man said, for instance, or what lies beyond the end of the river. I have tried to remember it all over again, and I cannot!'

Beatrice took her husband's hands in her own and told Yama, 'He was hurt, and sometimes gets confused about what might happen and what has happened. Remember the slate. It's important.'

Yama said, 'I know less than you. Let me see the slate again. Perhaps there is something—'

Beatrice said, 'Perhaps it is your destiny to discover your past, dear. Only by knowing the past can you know yourself.'

Yama smiled, because that was precisely the motto which Zakiel used to justify his long lessons. It seemed to him that the curators of the dead and the librarians and archivists were so similar that they amplified slight differences into a deadly rivalry, just as brothers feuded over nothing at all simply to assert their individuality.

'You have seen all we can show you, Yama,' Osric said. 'We preserve the past as best we can, but we do not pretend to understand everything we preserve.'

Yama said formally, 'I thank you for showing me this wonder.' But he thought that it proved only that others like him had lived long ago – he was more concerned with discovering if they still lived now. Surely they must – he was proof of that – but where? What had Dr Dismas discovered in the archives of his department?

Beatrice stood with a graceful flowing motion. 'You cannot stay, Yama. You are a catalyst, and change is most dangerous here.'

Yama said, 'If you would show me the way, I would go home at once.'

He said it with little hope, for he was convinced that the two curators were holding him prisoner. But Beatrice smiled and said, 'I will do better than that. I will take you.'

Osric said, 'You are stronger than you were when you arrived here, but not, I think, as strong as you can be. Let my wife help you, Yama. And remember us. We have served as best we can, and I feel that we have served well. When you discover your purpose, remember us.'

Beatrice said, 'Don't burden the poor boy, husband. He is too young. It is too early.'

'He is old enough to know his mind, I think. Remember that we are your friends, Yama.'

Yama bowed from the waist, as the Aedile had taught him, and turned to follow Beatrice, leaving her husband sitting in a pool of sunlight, his ravaged face made inscrutable by the mirror lenses of his spectacles, the blue uncharted mountain ridges framed by the pillars behind him, and the picture slate, wrapped in white cloth, on his lap.

Beatrice led Yama down a long helical stair and through chambers where machines as big as houses stood half-buried in the stone floor. Beyond these were the wide, circular mouths of pits in which long narrow tubes, made of a metal as clear as glass, fell into white mists a league or more below. Vast slow lightnings sparked and rippled in the transparent tubes. Yama felt a slow vibration through the soles of his feet, a pulse deeper than sound.

He would have stayed to examine the machines, but Beatrice urged him past and led him down a long hall with black keelrock walls, lit by balls of white fire that spun beneath a high curved ceiling. Parts of the floor were transparent and Yama saw, dimly, huge machines crouched in chambers far below his feet.

'Don't gawp,' Beatrice said. 'You don't want to wake them before their time.'

Many narrow corridors led off the hall. Beatrice ushered Yama down one of them into a small room which, once its door slid shut, began at once to hum and shake. Yama felt for a moment as if he had stepped over a cliff, and clutched at the rail which ran around the curved walls of the room.

'We fall through the keelways,' Beatrice said. 'Most people live on the surface now, but in ancient times the surface was a place where they came to play and meet, while they had their dwelling and working places underground. This is one of the old roads. It will return you to Aeolis in less than an hour.'

'Are these roads everywhere?'

'Once. No more. We have maintained a few beneath the City of the Dead, but many more no longer function, and beyond the limits of our jurisdiction things are worse.

Everything fails at last. Even the Universe will fall into itself eventually.'

'The Puranas say that is why the Preservers fled into the Eye. But if the Universe will not end soon, then surely that is not why they fled. Zakiel could never explain that. He said it was not for me to question the Puranas.'

Beatrice laughed. It was like the tinkling of old, fragile bells. 'How like a librarian! But the Puranas contain many riddles, and there is no harm in admitting that not all the answers are obvious. Perhaps they are not even comprehensible to our small minds, but a librarian will never admit that any text in his charge is unfathomable. He must be the master of them all, and is shamed to admit any possible failure.'

'The slate showed the creation of the Eye. There is a sura in the Puranas, the forty-third sura, I think, which says that the Preservers made stars fall together, until their light grew too heavy to escape.'

'Perhaps. There is much we do not know about the past, Yama. Some have said that the Preservers set us here for their own amusement, as certain bloodlines keep caged birds for amusement, but I would not repeat that heresy. All who believed it are safely dead long ago, but it is still a dangerous thought.'

'Perhaps because it is true, or contains some measure of the truth.'

Beatrice regarded him with her bright eyes. She was a head taller than he was. 'Do not be bitter, Yama. You will find what you are looking for, although it might not be where you expect it. Ah, we are almost there.'

The room shuddered violently. Yama fell to his knees. The floor was padded with a kind of quilting, covered in an artificial material as slick and thin as satin.

Beatrice opened the door and Yama followed her into a very long room that had been carved from rock. Its high roof was held up by a forest of slender pillars and wan light fell from narrow slits in the roof. It had once been a stonemasons' workshop, and Beatrice led Yama around half-finished carvings and benches scattered with tools, all abandoned an age ago and muffled by thick dust. At the door, she took out a hood of soft, black cloth and said that she must blindfold him.

'We are a secret people, because we should not exist. Our department was disbanded long ago, and we survive only because we are good at hiding.'

'I understand. My father—'

'We are not frightened of discovery, Yama, but we have stayed hidden for so long that knowledge of where we are is valuable to certain people. I would not ask you to carry that burden. It would expose you to unnecessary danger. If you need to find us again, you will. I can safely promise that, I think. In return, will you promise that you won't mention us to the Aedile?'

'He will want to know where I have been.'

'You were ill. You recovered, and you returned. Perhaps you were nursed by one of the hill tribes. The Aedile will be so pleased to see you that he won't question you too closely. Will you promise?'

'As long as I do not have to lie to him. I think that I am done with lies.'

Beatrice was pleased by this. 'You were honest from the first, dear heart. Tell the Aedile as much of the truth as is good for him, and no more. Now, come with me.'

Blinded by the soft, heavy cloth of the hood, Yama took Beatrice's hot, fine-boned hand, and allowed himself to be led once more. They walked a long way. He trusted this strange old woman, and he was thinking about the man of his bloodline, dead ages past.

At last she told him to stand still. Something cold and heavy was placed in his right hand. After a moment of silence, Yama lifted the hood away and saw that he was in a dark passageway walled with broken stone blocks, with stout tree roots thrust between their courses. A patch of sunlight fell through a narrow doorway at the top of a stair whose stone treads had been worn away in the centre. He was holding the ancient metal knife he had found in the tomb by the river's shore – or which had found him. A skirl of blue sparks flared along the outer edge of its blade and sputtered out one by one.

Yama looked around for Beatrice and thought he saw a patch of white float around the corner of a passageway. But when he ran after it, he found a stone wall blocking his way. He turned back to the sunlight. This place was familiar, but he did not recognize it until he climbed the stair and stepped out into the ruins in the Aedile's garden, with the peel-house looming beyond masses of dark green rhododendrons.

11 ~ Prefect Corin

Lob and the landlord of *The House of Ghost Lanterns* were arrested before Yama had finished telling his story to the Aedile, and the next day were tried and sentenced to death for kidnap and sabotage. The Aedile also issued a warrant for the arrest of Dr Dismas, although he confided to Yama that he did not expect to see the apothecary again.

Although it took a long time to explain his adventures, Yama did not tell the whole story. He suppressed the part about Enobarbus, for he had come to believe that the young warlord had somehow been caught by Dr Dismas's spell. He kept his promise to Beatrice, too, and said that after he had escaped from the skiff and had been helped ashore by one of the fisherfolk, he had fallen ill after being attacked by Lob and Lud amongst the ransacked tombs of the Silent Quarter, and had not been able to return to the peel-house until he had recovered. It was not the whole truth, but the Aedile did not question him closely.

Yama was not allowed to attend the trial; nor was he allowed to leave the grounds of the peel-house, although he very much wanted to see Derev. The Aedile said that it was too dangerous. The families of Lob and the tavern landlord would be looking for revenge, and the city was still on edge after the riots which had followed the failed siege of Dr Dismas's tower. Yama tried to contact Derev using mirror talk, but although he signalled for most of the afternoon there was no answering spark of light from the apartments

Derev's father had built on top of his godown by the old waterfront of the city. Sick at heart, Yama went to plead with Sergeant Rhodean, but the Sergeant refused to provide an escort.

'And you're not to confuse the watchdogs and go sneaking out on your own, neither,' Sergeant Rhodean said. 'Oh yes, I know all about that trick, lad. But see here, you can't rely on tricks to keep yourself out of trouble. They're more likely to get you into it instead. I won't risk having any of my men hurt rescuing you from your own foolishness, and think how it would look if we took you down there in the middle of a decad of armed soldiers. You'd start another riot. My men have already spent too much time looking for you when you were lost in the City of the Dead, and they'll have their hands full in a couple of days. The department is sending a clerk to deal with the prisoners, but no extra troops. Pure foolishness on their part, and I'll get blamed if something goes wrong.'

Sergeant Rhodean was much exercised by this. As he talked, he paced in a tight circle on the red clay floor of the gymnasium. He was a small, burly man, almost as wide as he was tall, as he liked to say. As always, his grey tunic and blue trousers were neatly pressed, his black knee-boots were spit-polished, and the scalp of his heavy, ridged skull was close-shaven and burnished with oil. He favoured his right leg, and the thumb and forefinger of his right hand were missing. He had been the Aedile's bodyguard long before the entire household had been exiled from the Palace of the Memory of the People, and had celebrated his hundredth birthday two years ago. He lived quietly with his wife, who was always trying to overfeed Yama because, she said, he needed to put some muscle on his long bones. They had two married daughters, six sons away fighting the heretics, and two more who had been killed in the war; Sergeant Rhodean had mourned Telmon's death almost as bitterly as Yama and the Aedile.

Sergeant Rhodean suddenly stopped pacing and looked at Yama as if for the first time. He said, 'I see you're wearing that knife you found, lad. Let's take a look at it.'

Yama had taken to hanging the knife from his belt by a loop of leather, with its blade tied flat against his thigh by a red ribbon. He undid the ribbon, unhooked the loop and held out the knife, and Sergeant Rhodean put on thick-lensed spectacles, which vastly magnified his yellow eyes, and peered closely at it for a long time. At last, he blew reflectively through his drooping moustache and said, 'It's old, and sentient, or at least partly so. Maybe as smart as one of the watchdogs. A good idea to carry it around. It will bond to you. You said you were ill after using it?'

'It gave out a blue light. And when Lob picked it up, it turned into something horrible.'

'Well now, lad, it had to get its energy from somewhere for tricks like that, especially after all the time in the dark. So it took it from you.'

'I leave it in sunlight,' Yama said.

'Do you?' Sergeant Rhodean gave Yama a shrewd look. 'Then I can't tell you much more. What did you clean it with? White vinegar? As good as anything, I suppose. Well, let's see you make a few passes with it. It will stop you brooding over your true love.'

For the next hour, Sergeant Rhodean instructed Yama on how to make best use of the knife against a variety of imaginary opponents. Yama found himself beginning to enjoy the exercises, and was sorry when Sergeant Rhodean called a halt. He had spent many happy hours in the gymnasium, with its mingled smell of clay and old sweat and rubbing alcohol, its dim underwater light filtered through green-tinted windows high up in the whitewashed walls, the green rubber wrestling mats rolled up like the shed cocoons of giant caterpillars and the rack of parallel bars, the open cases of swords and knives, javelins and padded staves, the straw archery targets stacked behind the vaulting horse, the battered wooden torsos of the tilting dummies, the frames hung with pieces of plastic and resin and metal armour.

'We'll do some more work tomorrow, lad,' Sergeant Rhodean said at last. 'You need to work on your backhand. You aim too low, at the belly instead of the chest, and any opponent worth their salt would spot that in an instant. Of course, a knife like this is really intended for close work by a cavalryman surrounded by the enemy, and you might do better carrying a long sword or a revolver when walking about the city. It's possible that an old weapon like this might be proscribed. But now I have to drill the men. The clerk is coming tomorrow, and I suppose your father will want an honour guard for him.'

But the clerk sent from Ys to oversee the executions slipped unnoticed into the peel-house early the next morning, and the first time Yama saw him was when the Aedile summoned him to an audience that afternoon.

'The townspeople already believe that you have blood on your hands,' the Aedile said. 'I do not wish to see any more trouble. So I have come to a decision.'

Yama felt his heart turn over, although he already knew that this was no ordinary interview. He had been escorted to the Aedile's receiving chamber by one of the soldiers of the house guard. The soldier now stood in front of the tall double doors, resplendent in burnished helmet and corselet and scarlet hose, his pike at parade rest.

Yama perched on an uncomfortable curved backless seat before the central dais on which the Aedile's canopied chair stood. The Aedile did not sit down but paced about restlessly. He was dressed in a tunic embroidered with silver and gold, and his sable robe of office hung on a rack by his chair.

There was a fourth person in the room, standing in the shadows by the small private door which led, via a stairway, to the Aedile's private chambers. It was the clerk who had been sent from Ys to supervise the executions. Yama watched him out of the corner of his eye. He was a tall, slender man of the Aedile's bloodline, bareheaded in a plain homespun tunic and grey leggings. A close-clipped black pelt covered his head and face, with a broad white stripe, like a badger's marking, on the left side of his face.

Yama's breakfast had been brought to his room that morning, and this was the first chance he had to study the man. He had heard from the stable hands that the clerk had disembarked from an ordinary lugger, armed with only a stout ironshod staff and with no more than a rolled blanket on his back, but the Aedile had prostrated himself at the man's feet as if he were a Hierarch risen from the files.

'I don't think he expected someone so high up in the Committee for Public Safety,' the foreman, Torin, had said.

But the clerk did not look like an executioner, or anyone important. He could have been any one of the thousands of ordinary scribes who plied pens in cells deep in the Palace of the Memory of the People, as indistinguishable from each other as ants.

The Aedile stood before one of the four great tapestries that decorated the high, square room. It depicted the seeding of Confluence. Plants and animals rained out of a blaze of light towards a bare plain crossed by silvery loops of water. Birds soared through the air, and little groups of naked men and women of various bloodlines stood on wisps of cloud, hands modestly covering their genitals and breasts.

Yama had always loved this tapestry, but now that he had talked with the curators of the City of the Dead he knew that it was a lie. Since he had returned, everything in the peel-house seemed to have changed. The house was smaller; the gardens cramped and neglected; the people preoccupied with small matters, their backs bent to routine labour so that, like peasants planting a paddy field, they failed to see the great events of the world rushing above their heads.

At last, the Aedile turned and said, 'It was always my plan to apprentice you to my department, Yama, and I have not changed my mind. You are perhaps a little young to begin proper apprenticeship, but I have great hopes of you. Zakiel says that you are the best pupil he has known, and Sergeant Rhodean believes that in a few years you will be able to best him in archery and fencing, although he adds that your horse riding still requires attention.

'I know your determination and ambition, Yama. I think that you will be a great power in the department. You are not of my bloodline, but you are my son, now and always. I would wish that you could have stayed here until you were old enough to be inducted as a full apprentice, but it is clear to me that if you stay here you are in great danger.'

'I am not afraid of anyone in Aeolis.'

But Yama's protest was a formality. Already he was dizzy with the prospect of kicking the dust of this sleepily corrupt little city from his heels. In Ys, there were records which went back to the foundation of Confluence. Beatrice had said as much. She and Osric had shown him a slate which had displayed the likeness of an ancestor of his bloodline; in Ys, he might learn who that man had been. There might even be people of his bloodline! Anything was possible. After all, surely he had come from Ys in the first place, borne downstream on the river's current. For that reason alone he would gladly go to Ys, although more than ever he knew that he could not serve as a clerk. But he could not tell his father that, of course, and it burned in his chest like a coal.

The Aedile said, 'I am proud that you can say that you are unafraid with such conviction, and I think that you truly believe it. But you cannot spend your life looking over your shoulder, Yama, and that is what you would have to do if you stayed here. One day, sooner or later, Lob and Lud's brothers will seek to press their need for revenge. That they are the sons of the Constable of Aeolis makes this more likely, not less, for if any one of them killed you, it would not only satisfy their family's need for revenge, it would also be a triumph over their father.

'It is not the townspeople I fear, however. Dr Dismas has

fled, but he may try to revive his scheme, or he may sell his information to others. In Aeolis you are a wonder; in Ys, which is the fount of all the wonders of the world, less so. Here, I command only three decads of soldiers; there, you will be in the heart of the department.'

'When will I go?'

The Aedile clasped his hands and bowed his head. It was a peculiarly submissive gesture. 'You will leave with Prefect Corin, after he has concluded his business here.'

The man in the shadows caught Yama's gaze. 'In cases like this,' he said in a soft, lilting voice, 'it is not advisable to linger once duty has been done. I will leave tomorrow.'

No, the clerk, Prefect Corin, did not look like an executioner, but he had already visited Lob and the landlord of the tavern, who had been held in the peel-house's oubliette since their trial. They were to be burned that evening outside the town's walls, and their ashes would be scattered on the wind so that their families would have no part of them as a memorial and their souls would never have rest until the Preservers woke all the dead at the end of the Universe. Sergeant Rhodean had been drilling his men ever since the trial. If there was any trouble, he could not rely on the Constable and the city militia for aid. Every bit of armour had been polished, and every weapon cleaned or sharpened. Because the steam waggon had been destroyed in the siege of Dr Dismas's tower, an ordinary waggon had been sequestered to transport the condemned men from the peel-house to the place of execution. It had been painted white, and its axles greased and its wheels balanced, and the two white oxen which would draw it had been brushed until their coats shone. The entire peel-house had been filled with bustle over the affair, but as soon as he had arrived, Prefect Corin had become its still centre.

The Aedile said, 'It is abrupt, I know, but I will see you in Ys, as soon as I can be sure that there will be no more trouble here. In the meantime, I hope you will remember me with affection.'

'Father, you have done more for me than I ever can deserve.' It was a formal sentiment, and sounded trite, but Yama felt a sudden flood of affection for the Aedile then, and would have embraced him if Prefect Corin had not been watching.

The Aedile turned to study the tapestry again. Perhaps Prefect Corin made him uncomfortable, too. He said, 'Quite, quite. You are my son, Yama. No less than Telmon.'

Prefect Corin cleared his throat, a small sound in the large room, but father and son turned to stare at him as if he had shot a pistol at the painted ceiling.

'Your pardon,' he said, 'but it is time to shrive the prisoners.'

Two hours before sunset, Father Quine, the priest of the temple of Aeolis, came in his orange robes, walking barefoot and bareheaded up the winding road from the city to the peel-house. Ananda accompanied him, carrying a chrism of oil. The Aedile greeted them formally and escorted them to the oubliette, where they would hear the final confessions of the prisoners.

Again, Yama had no part in the ceremony. He sat in one corner of the big fireplace in the kitchen, but that had changed, too. He was no longer a part of the kitchen's bustle and banter. The scullions and the kitchen boys and the three cooks politely replied to his remarks, but their manner was subdued. He wanted to tell them that he was still Yama, the boy who had wrestled with most of the kitchen boys, who had received clouts from the cooks when he had tried to steal bits of food, who had cheeked the scullions to make them chase him. But he was no longer that boy.

After a while, oppressed by polite deference, Yama went out to watch the soldiers drilling in the slanting sunlight, and that was where Ananda found him.

Ananda's head was clean-shaven; there was a fresh cut above his right ear, painted with yellow iodine. His eyes were enlarged by clever use of blue paint and gold leaf. He gave off a smell of cloves and cinnamon. It was the scent of the oil with which the prisoners had been anointed.

Ananda knew how to judge Yama's mood. For a while, the two friends stood side by side in companionable silence and watched the soldiers make squares and lines in the dusty sunlight. Sergeant Rhodean barked orders which echoed off the high wall of the peel-house.

At last, Yama said, 'I have to go away tomorrow.'

'I know.'

'With that little badger of a clerk. He is to be my master. He will teach me how to copy records and write up administrative reports. I will be buried, Ananda. Buried in old paper and futile tasks. There is only one consolation.'

'You can look for your bloodline.'

Yama was astonished. 'How did you know?'

'Why, you've always talked about it.' Ananda looked at Yama shrewdly. 'But you've learnt something about it, haven't you? That's why it's on your mind.'

'A clerk, Ananda. I will not serve. I cannot. I have more important things to do.'

'Not only soldiers help fight the war. And don't change the subject.'

'That is what my father would say. I want to be a hero, Ananda. It is my destiny!'

'If it's your destiny, then it will happen.' Ananda pulled a pouch from inside his robe and spilled hulled pistachios into his meaty palm. 'Want some?'

Yama shook his head. He said, 'It has all changed so quickly.'

Ananda put his palm to his lips and said, around a mouthful of pistachios, 'Is there time to tell me all that happened? I'm never going to leave here, you know. My master will die, and I will take his place, and begin to teach the new sizar, who will be a boy just like me. And so on.'

'I am not allowed to go to the execution.'

'Of course not. It would be unseemly.'

'I want to prove that I am brave enough to see it.'

'What did happen, Yama? You couldn't have been lost for so long, and they couldn't have taken you far if you said you escaped on the night you were taken.'

'A lot of things happened after that. I do not understand all of them, but one thing I do understand. I found something . . . something important.'

Ananda laughed. 'You mustn't tease your friends, Yama. Share it with me. Perhaps I can help you understand everything.'

'Meet me tonight. After the executions. Bring Derev, too. I tried to send a message to her by mirror talk, but no one replied. I want her to hear my story. I want to . . .'

'I know. There will be a service. We have to exculpate Prefect Corin after he sets the torch to . . . well, to the prisoners. Then there's a formal meal, but I'm not invited to that, of course. It begins two hours after sunset, and I'll come then. And I'll find a way of bringing Derev.'

'Have you ever seen an execution, Ananda?'

Ananda poured more pistachios into his palm. He looked at them and said, 'No. No, I haven't. Oh, I know everything that will happen, of course, and I know what I have to do, but I'm not sure how I'll act.'

'You will not disgrace your master. I will see you two hours after sunset. And make sure to bring Derev.'

'As if I would forget.' Ananda tipped the pistachios into the dirt and brushed his hands together. 'The landlord of the tavern was an addict of the drug that Dismas used, did you know that? Dismas supplied him with it, and he'd do anything asked of him. It didn't lessen the sentence, of course, but it was how he pleaded.'

Yama remembered Dr Dismas grinding dried beetles and

clear, apricot-scented liquid into paste, the sudden relaxation of his face after he had injected himself.

'Cantharides,' he said. 'And Lob and Lud did it for money.'

'Well, Lob had his payment, at least,' Ananda said. 'He was drunk when he was arrested, and I hear he'd been buying the whole town drinks for several days before that. I think he knew that you'd be back.'

Yama remembered that Lob and Lud had not been paid by Dr Dismas. Where then had Lob got the money for his drinking spree? And who had rescued him from the old tomb, and taken him to the tower of Beatrice and Osric? With a cold pang, he realized who it must have been, and how she had known where to find him.

Ananda had turned to watch the soldiers wheel out on the parade square, one line becoming two that marched off side by side towards the main gate, with Sergeant Rhodean loudly counting the pace as he marched at their head. After a while, Ananda said, 'Did you ever think that Lob and Lud were a little bit like you? They wanted to escape this place, too.'

Yama wanted to watch Lob and the landlord of the tavern leave the peel-house for the place of execution, but even that was denied him. Zakiel found him at a window, staring down at the courtyard where soldiers were harnessing the stamping horses to the white waggon, and took him off to the library.

'We have only a little time, master, and there is so much to tell you.'

'Then why begin to try? Are you going to the executions, Zakiel?'

'It is not my place, master.'

'I suppose that my father told you to keep me occupied. I want to see it, Zakiel. They are trying to exclude me from it all. I suppose it is to spare my feelings. But imagining it is worse than knowing.'

'I have taught you something, then. I was beginning to wonder.'

Zakiel rarely smiled, but he smiled now. He was a tall, gaunt man, with a long, heavy-browed face and a shaven skull with a bony crest. His black skin shone in the yellow light of the flickering electric sconce, and the muscles of his heavy jaws moved under the skin on either side of the crest when he smiled. As a party piece, on high day feasts, he would crack walnuts between his strong square teeth. As always, he wore a grey tunic and grey leggings, and sandals soled with rubber that squeaked on the polished marquetry of the paths between the library stacks. He wore a slave collar around his neck, but it was made of a light alloy, not iron, and covered with a circlet of handmade lace.

Zakiel said, 'I could tell you what will happen, if you like. I was instructed in it, because it is believed that to tell the prisoner exactly what will happen to him will make it endurable. But it was the cruellest thing they did, far crueller than being put to question.'

Zakiel had been sentenced to death before he had come to work for the Aedile. Yama, who had forgotten that, was mortified. He said, 'I was not thinking. I am sorry. No, do not tell me.'

'You would rather see it. You believe your senses, but not words. Yet the long-dead men and women who wrote all these volumes which stand about us had the same appetites as us, the same fears, the same ambitions. All we know of the world passes through our sensory organs and is reduced to electric impulses in certain sensory nerve fibres. When you open one of these books and read of events that happened before you were born, some of those nerve fibres are stimulated in exactly the same way.'

'I want to see for myself. Reading about it is different.'

Zakiel cracked his knuckles. They were swollen, like all of his joints. His fingers looked like strings of nuts.

'Why, perhaps I have not taught you anything after all. Of course it is different. What books do is allow you to share the perceptions of those who write them. There are certain wizards who claim to be able to read minds, and mountebanks who claim to have discovered ancient machines that print out a person's thoughts, or project them in a sphere of glass or crystal metal, but the wizards and mountebanks lie. Only books allow us to share another's thoughts. By reading them, we see the world not through our senses, but through those of their authors. And if those authors are wiser than us, or more knowing, or more sensitive, then so are we while we read. I will say no more about this. I know you would read the world directly, and tomorrow you will no longer have to listen to old Zakiel. But I would give you something, if I may. A slave owns nothing, not even his own life, so this is in the nature of a loan, but I have the Aedile's permission.'

Zakiel led Yama deeper into the stacks, where books stood two-deep on shelves that bent under their weight. He pulled a ladder from a recess, set its hooked top on the lip of the highest shelf, and climbed up. He fussed there for a minute, blowing dust from one book after another, and finally climbed down with a volume no bigger than his hand.

'I knew I had it,' he said, 'although I have not touched it since I first catalogued the library. Even the Aedile does not know of this. It was left by one of his predecessors; that is the way this library has grown, and why there is so much of little value. Yet some hold that gems are engendered in mud, and this book is such a gem. It is yours.'

It was bound in a black, artificial stuff that, although scuffed at the corners, shone as if newly made when Zakiel wiped away the dust with the hem of his tunic. Yama riffled the pages of the book. They were stiff and slick, and seemed to contain a hidden depth. When he tilted the pages to the light, images came and went in the margins of the crisp double-columned print. He had expected some rare history of Ys, or a bestiary, like those he had loved to read when he was younger, but this was no more than a copy of the Puranas.

Yama said, 'If my father told you to give me this book, then how is it that he does not know he owns it?'

'I asked if I could give you a volume of the Puranas, and so I have. But this edition is very old, and differs in some details from that which I have taught you. It is an edition that has long been suppressed, and perhaps this is the only copy of that edition which now exists.'

'It is different?'

'In some parts. You must read it all to find out, and remember what I have taught you. So perhaps my teachings will continue, in some fashion. Or you could simply look at the pictures. Modern editions do not, of course, have pictures.'

Yama, who had been tilting the pages of the book to the light as he turned them, suddenly felt a shock of recognition. There in the margin of one of the last pages was the view he had glimpsed behind the face of his ancestor, of stars streaming inwards towards a dull glow.

He said, 'I will read it, Zakiel. I promise.'

For a moment Zakiel stared at Yama in silence, his black eyes inscrutable beneath the bony shelf of his brow. Then the librarian smiled and clapped dust from his big, bony hands. 'Very good, master. Very good. Now we will drink some tea, and talk on the history of the department of which, when you reach Ys, you will be the newest and youngest member.'

'With respect, Zakiel I am sure that the history of the department will be the first thing I will be taught when I arrive in Ys, and no doubt the clerk will have some words on it during our journey.'

'I do not think that Prefect Corin is a man who wastes words,' Zakiel said. 'And he does not see himself as a teacher.'

'My father would have you occupy my mind. I understand. Well then, I would like to hear something of the history of another department. One that was broken up a long time ago. Is that possible?'

12 ~ The Execution

After sunset, Yama climbed to the heliograph platform that circled the top of the tallest of the peel-house's towers. He uncapped the observation telescope and, turning it on the heavy steel gimbals which floated in sealed oil baths, lined up its declination and equatorial axes in a combination he knew as well as his own name.

Beyond the darkening vanishing point, the tops of the towers that rose up from the heart of Ys shone in the last light of the sun like a cluster of fiery needles floating high above the world, higher than the naked peaks of the Rim Mountains. Ys! In his room, Yama had spent a little time gazing at his old map before reluctantly rolling it up and putting it away. He had traced the roads that crossed the barrens of the coastal plains, the passes through the mountains that embraced the city. He vowed now that in a handful of days he would stand at the base of the towers as a free man.

When he put up the telescope and leaned at the rail, with warm air gusting around him, he saw prickles of light flickering in the middle distance. Messages. The air was full of messages, talking of war, of far-away battles and sieges at the midpoint of the world.

Yama walked to the other side of the tower and stared out across the wide shallow valley of the Breas towards Aeolis, and saw with a little shock that the execution pyre had already been kindled. The point of light flickered like a baleful star fallen to the ground outside the wall of the little city.

'They would have killed me,' he said, trying out the words, 'if there was money in it.'

Yama watched for a long time, until the distant fire began to dim and was outshone by the ordinary lights of the city. Lob and the landlord of *The House of Ghost Lanterns* were dead. The Aedile and the colourless man, the clerk, Prefect Corin, would be in grave procession towards the temple, led by Father Quine and flanked by Sergeant Rhodean's men in polished black armour.

His supper had been set out in his room, but he left it and went down to the kitchen and, armoured by his new authority, hacked a wedge from a wheel of cheese and took a melon, a bottle of yellow wine, and one of the heavy date loaves that had been baked that morning. He cut through the kitchen gardens, fooled the watchdogs for the last time, and walked along the high road before plunging down the steep slope of the bluff and following the paths along the tops of the dikes which divided the flooded paeonin fields.

The clear, shallow Breas made a rushing noise in the darkness as it ran swiftly over the flat rocks of its bed. At the waterlift, two oxen plodded side by side around their circle, harnessed to the trimmed trunk of a young pine. This spar turned the shaft that, groaning as if in protest at its eternal torment, lifted a chain of buckets from the river and tipped them in a never-ending cascade into the channels which fed the irrigation system of the paeonin fields. The oxen walked in their circle under a roof of palm fronds, their tails rhythmically slapping their dung-spattered flanks. Now and then they snatched a mouthful of the fodder scattered around the perimeter of their circular path, but mostly they walked with their heads down, from nowhere to nowhere.

No, Yama thought, I will not serve.

He sat on an upturned stone a little distance off the path and ate meltingly sweet slices of melon while he waited. The oxen plodded around and around, turning the groaning shaft. Frogs peeped in the paeonin fields. Beyond the city, at the mouth of the Breas, the misty light of the Arm of the Warrior was lifting above the farside horizon. It would rise a little later each night, a little further downriver. Soon it would not rise at all, and the Eye of the Preservers would appear above the upriver vanishing point, and it would be summer. But before then Yama would be in Ys.

Two people were coming along the path, shadows moving through the Galaxy's blue twilight. Yama waited until they had gone past before he whistled sharply.

'We thought you might not be here,' Ananda said as he walked up to where Yama sat.

'Well met,' Derev said, at Ananda's shoulder. The Galaxy put blue shadows in the unbound mass of her white hair and a spark in each of her large, dark eyes. 'O, well met, Yama!'

She rushed forward and hugged him. Her light-boned body, her long slim arms and legs, her heat, her scent. Yama was always surprised to discover that Derev was taller than himself. Despite the cold certainty he had nursed ever since Ananda's remark about Lob's drunken spree, his love rekindled in her embrace. It was an effort not to respond, and he hated himself because it seemed a worse betrayal than anything she might have done.

Derev drew back a little and said, 'What's wrong?'

Yama said, 'I am glad you came. There is something I want to ask you.'

Derev smiled and moved her arms in a graceful circle, making the wide sleeves of her white dress floatingly glimmer in the half-dark. 'Anything! As long, of course, as I can hear your story. All of it, not just the highlights.'

Ananda found the wedge of cheese and began to pare slices from it. 'I've been fasting,' he explained. 'Water for breakfast, water for lunch.'

'And pistachios,' Yama said.

'I never said I would make a good priest. I am supposed

to be cleaning out the narthex while Father Quine dines with the Aedile and Prefect Corin. This is a strange place to meet, Yama.'

'There was something Dr Dismas once said to me, about the habits we fall into. I wanted to be reminded of it.'

Derev said, 'But you are all right. You have recovered from your adventures.'

'I learned much from them.'

'And you will tell all,' Ananda said. He handed around slices of bread and cheese, and pried the cork out of the wine bottle with his little knife. 'I think,' he said, 'that you should start at the beginning.'

The story seemed far stranger and more exciting than the actual experience. To tell it concisely, Yama had to miss out the fear and tension he had felt during every moment of his adventures, the long hours of discomfort when he had tried to sleep in wet clothes on the trunk of the banyan, his growing hunger and thirst while wandering the hot shaly land of the Silent Quarter of the City of the Dead.

As he talked, he remembered a dream he had had while sleeping on the catafalque inside the old tomb in the Silent Quarter. He had dreamed that he had been swimming in the Great River, and that a current had suddenly caught him and swept him towards the edge of the world, where the river fell away in thunder and spray. He had tried to swim against the current, but his arms had been trapped at his sides and he had been helplessly swept through swift white water towards the tremendous noise of the river's fall. The oppressive helplessness of the dream had stayed with him all that morning, right up to the moment when Lud and Lob had caught up with him, but he had forgotten about it until now. And now it seemed important, as if dream and reality were, during the telling of his tale, coterminous. He told his two friends about the dream as if it were one more part of his adventures, and then described how Lob and Lud had surprised him, and how he had killed Lud by accident.

'I had found an old knife, and Lob got hold of it, ready to kill me because I had killed his brother. But the knife hurt him. It seemed to turn into something like a ghoul, or a giant spider. I ran, I am ashamed to say. I left him with his dead brother.'

'He would have killed you,' Derev said. 'Of course you should have run.'

Yama said, 'I should have killed him. The knife would have done it for me if I had not taken it, I think. It helped me, like the ghost ship.'

'Lob escaped,' Ananda said. 'He wanted his father to condemn you for the murder of his brother, the fool, but then you came back. Lob had already convicted himself, and Unprac confessed to his part as soon as he was arrested.'

Unprac was the name of the landlord of *The House of Ghost Lanterns*. Yama had not known it until the trial.

'So I killed Lob anyway. I should have killed him then, in the tomb. It would have been a cleaner death. It was a poor bargain he got in the end.'

'That's what they said about the farmer,' Derev said, 'after the girl fox had lain with him and took his baby in payment.'

Suddenly, with a feeling like falling, Yama saw Derev's face as a stranger might. All planes, with large dark eyes and a small mouth and a bump of a nose, framed by a fall of white hair that moved in the slightest breeze as if possessed with an independent life. They had pursued each other all last summer, awakened to the possibilities of each other's bodies. They had lain in the long dry grasses between the tombs and tasted each other's mouths, each other's skin. He had felt the swell of her small breasts, traced the bowl of her pelvis, the elegant length of her arms, her legs. They had not made love; they had sworn that they would not make love together until they were married. Now, he was glad that they had not.

He said, 'Do you keep doves, Derev?'

'You know that my father does. For sacrifice. Some

171

palmers still come here to pray at the temple's shrine. Mostly they don't want doves, though, but flowers or fruit.'

'There were no palmers this year,' Ananda said.

'When the war is over, they'll come again,' Derev said. 'My father clips the wings of the doves. It would be a bad omen if they escaped in the middle of the sacrifice.'

Ananda said, 'You mean that it would be bad for his trade.'

Derev laughed. 'Then the desires of the Preservers are equal to those of my father, and I am glad.'

'There is one more mystery,' Yama said, and explained that he had been knocked unconscious by a fall and had woken elsewhere, in a little room of a hollowed crag far from the Great River's shore, watched by an old man and an old woman who claimed to be curators of the City of the Dead.

'They showed me a marvel. It was a picture slate from a tomb, and it showed someone of my bloodline. It was as if they had been waiting for me, and I have been thinking about what they showed me ever since I was returned here.'

Derev had the bottle of wine. She took a long swallow from it and said, 'But that's good! That's wonderful! In less than a decad you have found two people of your bloodline.'

Yama said, 'The man in the picture was alive before the building of Confluence. I imagine he is long dead. What is interesting is that the curators already knew about me, for they had the picture slate ready, and they also had prepared a route from their hiding place to the very grounds of the peel-house. That was how I returned. One of them, the woman, was of your bloodline, Derev.'

'Well, so are many. We are traders and merchants. We are to be found throughout the length and breadth of Confluence.'

Derev looked coolly at Yama when she said this, and his heart meltingly turned. It was hard to continue, but he had to. He said, 'I did not think much of it for that very reason, and I did not even make very much of the fact that, like you, they had a fund of cautionary sayings and stories concerning magical foxes. But they kept doves. I wonder, if I looked amongst your father's doves, if I would find some that were not clipped. I think you use them to keep in touch with your people.'

Ananda said, 'What is this, Yama? You make a trial here.'

Derev said, 'It's all right, Ananda. Yama, my father said that you might have guessed. That was why he did not allow me to go to the peel-house, or to talk with you using the mirror. But I came here anyway. I wanted to see you. Tell me what you know, and I'll tell you what we know. How did you guess that I helped you?'

'I think that the old woman, Beatrice, had a son, and that he is your father. When Lob returned to Aeolis, you gave him money and got him drunk to learn his story. I know that he had not been paid by Dr Dismas, so he had to get the money from somewhere. You found me, and took me to your grandparents. They made up a story about looking for a lost goat and finding me instead, but they ate only vegetables. As do you and your parents, Derev.'

'They make cheese from goats' milk,' Derev said. 'And they *did* lose one last year, to a leopard. But you more or less have the truth. I'm not sure what scared me more, getting Lob drunk, or climbing down the cliff using the rope he had left behind and picking my way through the dark tomb to find you.'

'Did your family come here because of me? Am I so important, or am I merely foolish to believe it? Why are you interested in me?'

'Because you are of a bloodline which vanished from the world long ago. My family have stayed true to the old department as no others of my bloodline have. We revere the dead, and keep the memory of their lives as best we can, but we do not remember your bloodline, except in legends from the beginning of the world. Beatrice isn't my grandmother, although she and her husband came to live at the tower after my great-grandparents died. My grandparents wanted a normal life, you see. They established a business downriver and my father inherited it, but Beatrice and her husband persuaded him to move here because of you.' She paused. She said, 'I know you are destined for great things, but it doesn't change what I feel for you.'

Yama remembered Beatrice's verse and recited, '*Let fame, that all hunt after in their lives, Live registered upon our brazen tombs.*'

Derev said, 'Yes, it's a favourite verse of Beatrice's. She has always said that it was far older than Confluence. But we keep the memory of all the dead alive, even if no one else will.'

Yama said, 'Am I then of the dead?'

Derev walked about, pumping her elbows in and out as was her habit when agitated. Her white dress glimmered in the light of the outflung arm of the Galaxy. 'You were very ill when I found you. You had been lying there all night. I took you to Beatrice and Osric by the keel road and they saved your life, using old machines. I didn't know what else to do. I thought you might die if I took you to Aeolis, or if I went to fetch the soldiers who were looking for you. Well, it is time you knew that my family have been watching over you. After all, Dr Dismas found out about you and put you in peril. So might others, and you should be ready.'

Ananda said, 'What are you saying, Derev? That you're some kind of spy? On which side?'

Yama laughed. 'Derev is no spy. She is anxious that I should receive my inheritance, such as it is.'

'My father and mother know, too. It isn't just me. At first, I didn't even know why we came here.'

Ananda had drunk most of the wine. He tipped the bottle to get the last swallow, wiped his mouth on his sleeve, and said gravely, 'So you don't want to sell rubbish to sailors and Mud Men, Derev? There's no harm in that. It's good that you want to keep to the old ways of your people.'

'The Department of the Curators of the City of the Dead was disbanded long ago,' Yama said, looking at Derev.

'It was defeated,' Derev said, 'but it endures. There are not many of us now. We mostly live in the mountains, or in Ys.'

'Why are you interested in me?'

'You've seen the picture,' Derev said. She had turned her back to Yama and Ananda, and was looking out across the swampy fields towards the ridge at the far side of the Breas's valley. 'I don't know why you're important. My father thinks that it is to do with the ship of the Ancients of Days. Beatrice and Osric know more, I think, but won't tell even me all they know. They have many secrets.'

Ananda said, 'The ship of the Ancients of Days passed downriver long before Yama was born.'

Derev ignored his interruption. 'The Ancients of Days left to explore the neighbouring galaxy long before the Preservers achieved godhead. They left more than five million years ago, while the stars of the Galaxy were still being moved into their present patterns. It was long before the Puranas were written, or the Eye of the Preservers was made, or Confluence was built.'

'So they claimed,' Ananda said. 'But there is no word of them in the Puranas.'

'They returned to find all that they knew had passed into the Eye of the Preservers, and that they were the last of their kind. They landed at Ys, travelled downriver and sailed away from Confluence for the galaxy they had forsaken so long ago, but they left their ideas behind.'

'They turned innocent unfallen bloodlines against the word of the Preservers,' Ananda said. 'They woke old technologies and created armies of monsters to spread their heresies.'

'And twenty years later you were born, Yama.'

'So were many others,' Ananda said. 'All three of us here were born after the war began. Derev makes a fantasy.'

'Beatrice and Osric think that Yama's bloodline is the one which built Confluence,' Derev told Ananda. 'Perhaps the Preservers raised his bloodline up for just that task and then dispersed it, or perhaps as a reward it passed over with the Preservers when they fell into the Eye and vanished from the Universe. In any event, it disappeared from Confluence long ago. And yet Yama is here now, at a time of great danger.'

Ananda said, 'The Preservers needed no help in creating Confluence. They spoke a word, and it was so.'

'It was a very long word,' Derev said. She lifted her arms above her head, and raised herself up on the points of her toes, as graceful as a dancer. She was remembering something she had learned long ago. She said, 'It was longer than the words in the nuclei of our cells which define what we are. If all the different instructions for all the different bloodlines of Confluence were put together it would not be one hundredth of the length of the word which defined the initial conditions necessary for the creation of Confluence. That word was a set of instructions or rules. Yama's bloodline was part of those instructions.'

Ananda said, 'This is heresy, Derev. I'm a bad priest, but I know the sound of heresy. The Preservers needed no help in making Confluence.'

'Let her explain,' Yama said.

Ananda stood. 'It's lies,' he said flatly. 'Her people deceive themselves that they know more of Confluence and the Preservers than is written in the Puranas. They spin elaborate sophistries, and delude themselves with dreams of hidden power, and they have snared you, Yama. Come with me. Don't listen any more. You leave for Ys tomorrow. Don't be fooled into thinking that you are more than you are.'

Derev said, 'We don't pretend to understand what we remember. It is simply our duty. It was the duty of our bloodline since the foundation of Confluence, and my family are among the last to keep that duty. After the defeat of the department, my bloodline were scattered the length and breadth of the Great River. They became traders and merchants. My grandparents and my father wanted to be like them, but my father was called back.'

Yama said, 'Sit down, Ananda. Please. Help me understand.'

Ananda said, 'I don't think you're fully recovered, Yama. You've been ill. That part I believe. You have always wanted to see yourself as the centre of the world, for you have no centre to your own life. Derev is treating you cruelly, and I'll hear no more. You've even forgotten about the execution. Let me tell you that Unprac died badly, screaming to the Preservers for aid with one breath, and cursing them and all who watched with the next. Lob was stoic. For all his faults, he died a man.'

'That is cruel. Ananda.' Yama said.

'It's the truth. Farewell, friend Yama. If you must dream of glory, dream of being an ordinary soldier and of giving your life for the Preservers. All else is vanity.'

Yama did not try to stop Ananda. He knew how stubborn his friend could be. He watched as Ananda walked away beside the noisy river, a shadow against the blue-white arch of the Galaxy. Yama hoped that the young priest would at least turn and wave farewell.

But he did not.

Derev said, 'You must believe me, Yama. At first I became your friend because it was my duty. But that quickly changed. I would not be here if it had not.'

Yama smiled. He could not stay angry at her; if she had deceived him, it was because she had believed that she was helping him.

They fell into each other's arms and breathlessly kissed and rekissed. He felt her heat pressing through their clothes, the quick patter of her heart like a bird beating at the cage of her ribs. Her hair fell around his face like a trembling veil: he might drown in its dry scent.

After a while, he said, 'If you took me to Beatrice and

Osric, and they nursed me back to health, then what of the ghost ship? Do they claim that, too?'

Derev's eyes shone a handspan from his. She said, 'I'd never heard of it before you told me your story. But there are many strange things on the river, Yama. It is always changing.'

'Yet always the same,' Yama said, remembering Caphis's tattoo, the snake swallowing its own tail. He added, 'You thought that the anchorite we saved from Lud and Lob was one of my bloodline.'

'Perhaps he was the first generation, born just after the ship of the Ancients of Days arrived.'

'There may be hundreds of my bloodline by now, Derev. Thousands!'

'That's what I think. I told Beatrice and Osric about the anchorite, but they didn't seem to be very interested. Perhaps I was mistaken about him being of your bloodline, but I do not think I was. He gave you a coin. You should take it with you.'

'So he did. I had forgotten it.'

13 ~ The Palmers

Yama discovered the knife at the bottom of his satchel on the first evening of his journey to Ys in the company of Prefect Corin. Yama had given the knife to Sergeant Rhodean that morning because Prefect Corin had said that it was not the kind of thing an apprentice should own. The Prefect had been quite specific about what Yama could and could not carry; before they had set off he had looked through Yama's satchel and had removed the knife and the carefully folded map of Ys and the horn-handled pocket-knife which had once belonged to Telmon. Yama had been able to take little with him but a change of clothes and the money given to him by the Aedile. He had the copy of the Puranas and the anchorite's coin, which he wore around his neck, inside his shirt, but because they had been given to him so recently they did not yet seem like proper possessions.

Sergeant Rhodean must have slipped the knife back into the satchel when Yama had been making his farewells. It was sheathed in brown and white goatskin and tucked beneath Yama's spare shirt and trousers. Yama was pleased to see it, even though it still made him uneasy. He knew that all heroes carried weapons with special attributes, and he was determined to be a hero. He was still very young.

Prefect Corin asked him what he had found. Reluctantly, Yama slipped the knife from its sheath and held it up in the firelight. A blue sheen slowly extended from its hilt to the

179

point of its curved blade. It emitted a faint high-pitched buzz, and a sharp smell like discharged electricity.

'I am certain that Sergeant Rhodean meant well,' Prefect Corin said, 'but you will not need that. If we are attacked, it will do nothing but put you in danger. In any case, it is very unlikely that we will be attacked.'

Prefect Corin sat crosslegged on the other side of the small campfire, neat and trim in his homespun tunic and grey leggings. He was smoking a long-stemmed clay pipe which he held clenched between his small even teeth. His ironshod staff was stuck in the ground behind him. They had walked all day at a steady pace, and this was the most he had said to Yama at any one time.

Yama said, 'That is why I gave it away, dominie, but it has come back.'

'It is not regulation.'

'Well, but I am not yet an apprentice,' Yama said. He added, 'Perhaps I could make a gift of it to the Department.'

'That is possible,' Prefect Corin allowed. 'Tributes are not unknown. Weapons like that are generally loyal to their owner, but loyalty can be broken with suitable treatment. Well, we cannot leave it here. You may carry it, but do not think to try to use it.'

But after Prefect Corin had fallen asleep, Yama took out the knife and practised the passes and thrusts that Sergeant Rhodean had taught him, and later slept sweetly and deeply, with the point of the knife thrust into the warm ashes of the campfire.

The next day, as before, Yama dutifully walked three paces behind Prefect Corin along raised paths between the flooded fields that made an intricate green and brown quilt along the margin of the river. It was the planting season, and the fields were being ploughed by teams of water buffalo commanded by small, naked boys who controlled their charges with no more than shouts and vigorous application of long bamboo switches.

A cool wind blew from the Great River, ruffling the brown waters which flooded the fields, stirring the bright green flags of the bamboos and the clumps of elephant grass that grew at the places where the corners of four fields met. Yama and Prefect Corin rose just before dawn and prayed and walked until it was too hot, and sheltered in the shade of a tree until early evening, when, after a brief prayer, they walked again until the Galaxy began to rise above the river.

Ordinarily, Yama would have enjoyed this adventure, but Prefect Corin was an impassive, taciturn companion. He did not comment on anything they saw, but was like a machine moving implacably through the sunlit world, noticing only what was necessary. He responded with no more than a grunt when Yama pointed to a fleet of argosies far out across the glittering waters of the Great River; he ignored the ruins they passed, even a long sandstone cliff-face which had been carved with pillars and friezes and statues of men and beasts around gaping doors; he ignored the little villages which could be glimpsed amongst stands of palms, flowering magnolias and pines on the ridge of the old river bank in the blue distance, or which stood on islands of higher ground amongst the mosaic of flooded fields; he ignored the fishermen who worked the margin of the Great River beyond the weedy gravel banks and mud flats revealed by the river's retreat, fishermen who stood thigh-deep in the shallows and cast circular nets across the water, or who sat in tiny bark boats further out, using black cormorants tethered by one leg to catch fish. (Yama thought of the verse which the old curator, Beatrice, had recited to him. Had its author seen the ancestors of these fishermen? He understood then a little of what Zakiel had tried to teach him, that books were not obdurate thickets of glyphs but transparent windows, looking out through another's eyes on to a familiar world, or on to a world which lived only when the book was read, and vanished when it was set down.)

The mud walls of the straw-thatched huts of the villages often incorporated slates stolen from tombs, so that pictures from the past (as often as not sideways or upside down) flashed with vibrant colours amongst the poverty of the peasants' lives. Chickens and black pigs ran amongst the huts, chased by naked toddlers. Women pounded grain or gutted fish or mended fishing nets, watched by impassive men sitting in the doorways of their huts or beneath shade trees, smoking clay pipes or sipping green tea from chipped glasses.

In one village there was a stone pen with a small dragon coiled on the white sand inside it. The dragon was black, with a double row of diamond-shaped plates along its ridged back, and it slept with its long, scaley snout on its forelegs, like a dog. Flies clustered around its long-lashed eyes; it stank of sulphur and marsh gas. Yama remembered the abortive hunt at the end of last winter, before poor Telmon went away, and would have liked to see more of this wonder, but Prefect Corin strode past without sparing it a single glance.

Sometimes the villagers came out to watch Yama and Prefect Corin go by, and little boys ran up to try and sell them wedges of watermelon or polished quartz pebbles or charms woven of thorny twigs. Prefect Corin ignored the animated crowds of little boys; he did not even trouble to use his staff to clear a way but simply pushed through them as through a thicket. Yama was left behind to apologize and ask for indulgence, saying over and over that they had no money. It was almost true. Yama had the two gold rials which the Aedile had given him, but one of those would buy an entire village, and he had no smaller coins. And Prefect Corin had nothing but his staff and his hat, his leggings and his homespun tunic, his sandals and his blanket, and a few small tools packed inside the leather purse that hung from his belt.

'Be careful of him,' the Aedile had whispered, when he had embraced Yama in farewell. 'Do all he asks of you, but no more than that. Reveal no more than is necessary. He will seize on any weakness, any difference, and use it against you. It is their way.'

The Prefect was a spare, ascetic man. He drank tea made from fragments of dusty bark and ate only dried fruit and the yeasty buds of manna lichen picked from rocks, although he let Yama cook the rabbits and lizards he caught in wire snares set each evening. As he walked, Yama ate ghostberries picked from thickets which grew amongst ruined tombs, but the ghostberries were almost over now and difficult to find under the new leaves of the bushes, and Prefect Corin would not allow Yama to move more than a few paces from the edge of the path. There were traps amongst the tombs, he said, and ghouls and worse things at night. Yama did not argue with him, but apart from the necessities of toilet he was never out of Prefect Corin's sight. There were a hundred moments when he wanted to make a run for it. But not yet. Not yet. He was learning patience, at least.

The stretches of uncultivated country between the villages grew wider. There were fewer flooded fields and more ruined tombs, overgrown with creepers and moss amidst rustling stands of bamboo or clumps of date or oil palms, or copses of dark green swamp cypress. Then they passed the last village and the road widened into a long, straight pavement. It was like the ancient road that ran between the river and the edge of the Silent Quarter downriver of Aeolis, Yama thought, and then he realized that it was the same road.

It was the third day of the journey. They camped that night in a hollow with tall pines leaning above. Wind moved through the doffing branches of the pines. The Great River stretched away towards the Galaxy, which even at this late hour showed only the upper part of the Arm of the Warrior above the horizon, with the Blue Diadem gleaming cold and sharp at the upflung terminus of the lanes of misty starlight.

Halo stars were like dimming coals scattered sparsely across the cold hearth of the sky; the smudged specks of distant galaxies could be seen here and there.

Yama lay near the little fire on a soft, deep layer of brown pine needles and thought of the Ancients of Days and wondered what it might be like to plunge through the emptiness between galaxies for longer than Confluence had been in existence. And the Ancients of Days had not possessed one hundredth of the power of their distant children, the Preservers.

Yama asked Prefect Corin if he had ever seen the Ancients of Days after they had arrived at Ys. For a long time, the man did not answer, and Yama began to believe that he had not been heard, or that Prefect Corin had simply ignored the question. But at last the Prefect knocked out his pipe on the heel of his boot and said, 'I saw two of them once. I was a boy, a little older than you, and newly apprenticed. They were both tall, and as alike as brothers, with black hair and faces as white as new paper. We say that some bloodlines have white skin – your own is very pale – but we mean that it has no pigmentation in it, except that it is suffused by the blood in the tissues beneath. But this was a true white, as if their faces had been powdered with chalk. They wore long white shirts that left their arms and legs bare, and little machines hung from their belts. I was in the Day Market with the oldest of the apprentices, carrying the spices he had bought. The two Ancients of Days walked through the aisles at the head of a great crowd and passed by as close to me as you are now.

'They should have been killed, all of them. Unfortunately, it was not a decision the Department could make, although even then, in Ys, it was possible to see that their ideas were dangerous. Confluence survives only because it does not change. The Preservers unite us because it is to them that each department swears its loyalty, and so no department shows particular favour to any of the bloodlines of Confluence. The Ancients of Days have infected their allies with the heresy that each bloodline, indeed every individual, might have an intrinsic worth. They promote the individual above society, change above duty. You should reflect on why this is wrong, Yama.'

'Is it true that there are wars in Ys now? That different departments fight each other, even in the Palace of the Memory of the People?'

Prefect Corin gave him a sharp look across the little fire and said, 'You have been listening to the wrong kind of gossip.'

Yama was thinking of the curators of the City of the Dead, whose resistance had dwindled to a stubborn refusal to yield to the flow of history. Perhaps Derev would be the last of them. He said, trying to draw out the Prefect, 'But surely there are disputes about whether one department or another should carry out a particular duty. I have heard that outmoded departments sometimes resist amalgamation or disbandment, and I have also heard that these disputes are increasing, and that the Department of Indigenous Affairs is training most of its apprentices to be soldiers.'

'You have a lot to learn,' Prefect Corin said. He tamped tobacco into the bowl of his pipe and lit it before adding, 'Apprentices do not choose the way in which they serve the Department, and you are too young to be an apprentice in any case. You have had an odd childhood, with what amounts to three fathers and no mother. You have far too much pride and not enough education, and most of that in odd bits of history and philosophy and cosmology, and far too much in the arts of soldiering. Even before you can be accepted as an apprentice, you will have to catch up in all the areas your education has neglected.'

Yama said, 'I think I might make a good soldier.'

Prefect Corin drew on his pipe and looked at Yama with narrowed eyes. They were small and close together, and gleamed palely in his black-furred face. The white stripe ran past the outer corner of his left eye. Eventually he said, 'I came down here to execute two men because their crimes involved the Aedile's private life. That is the way it is done in the Department. It demonstrates that the Department supports the action of its man, and it ensures that none of the local staff have to do the job. That way, there is no one for the locals to take revenge on, with the exception of the Aedile himself, and no one will do that as long as he commands his garrison, because he has the authority of the Preservers. I agreed to bring you to Ys because it is my duty. It does not mean I owe you anything, especially answers to your questions. Now get some sleep.'

Later, long after the Prefect had rolled himself in his blanket and gone to sleep, Yama cautiously stood and backed away from the fire, which had burnt down to white ash around a dimming core of glowing coals. The road stretched away between hummocks of dry friable stone and clumps of pines. Its paved surface gleamed faintly in the light of the Galaxy. Yama settled his pack on his shoulders and set off. He wanted to go to Ys, but he was determined not to become an apprentice clerk, and after the final dismissal of his worth he thought that he could not bear Prefect Corin's company a day longer.

He had not gone very far down the road when he heard a dry rattle in the darkness ahead. Yama put his hand on the hilt of his knife, but did not draw it from its sheath in case its light betrayed him. He advanced cautiously, his eyes wide, his whole skin tingling, his blood rustling in his ears. Then a stone smashed onto the paved road behind him! He whirled around, and another stone exploded at his feet. A fragment cut his shin, and he felt blood trickle into his boot.

He gripped the knife tightly and said, 'Who is it? Show yourself.'

Silence, and then Prefect Corin stepped up behind Yama and gripped the wrist of his right hand and said in his ear, 'You have a lot to learn, boy.'

186

'A clever trick,' Yama said. He felt oddly calm, as if he had expected this all along.

After a moment Prefect Corin released him and said, 'It is lucky for you I played it, and no one else.' Yama had never seen Prefect Corin smile, but in the blue light of the Galaxy he saw the man's lips compress in what might have been the beginning of a smile. 'I promised to look after you, and so I will. Meanwhile, no more games. All right?'

'All right,' Yama said.

'Good. You need to sleep. We still have a long way to go.'

Early the next day, Yama and Prefect Corin passed a group of palmers. They soon left the group behind, but the palmers caught up with them that night and camped a little way off. They numbered more than two decads, men and women in dust-stained orange robes, their heads cleanly shaven and painted with interlocked curves which represented the Eye of the Preservers. They were a slightly built people, with pinched faces under swollen, bicephalic foreheads, and leathery skin mottled with brown and black patches. Like Prefect Corin, they carried only staffs, bedrolls, and little purses hung from their belts. They sang in clear high voices around their campfire, welding close harmonies that carried a long way across the dry stones and the empty tombs of the hillside.

Yama and Prefect Corin had made camp under a group of fig trees beside the road. A little spring rose amongst the trees, a gush of clear water that fell from the gaping mouth of a stone carved with the likeness of a fierce, bearded face into a shallow pool curbed with flat rocks. The road had turned away from the Great River, climbing a switchback of low, gentle hills dotted with creosote scrub and clumps of saw-toothed palmettos as it rose towards the pass.

The priest who was in charge of the palmers came over to talk with Prefect Corin. His group was from a city a thousand leagues downriver. They had been travelling for half a year, first by a merchant ship and then by foot after the ship had been laid up for repairs after having been attacked by water bandits. The palmers were archivists on their way to the Palace of the Memory of the People, to tell into the records the stories of all those who had died in their city in the last ten years, and to ask for guidance from the prognosticators.

The priest was a large smooth-skinned man by the name of Belarius. He had a ready smile and a habit of mopping sweat from his bare scalp and the fat folds of skin at the back of his neck with a square of cloth. His smooth, chrome-yellow skin shone like butter. He offered Prefect Corin a cigarette and was not offended when his offer was refused, and without prompting started to talk about the risks of travelling by foot. He had heard that there were roving bands of deserters abroad in the land, in addition to the usual bandits.

'Near the battlelines, perhaps,' Prefect Corin said. 'Not this far upriver.' He drew on his pipe and stared judiciously at the fat priest. 'Are you armed?'

Belarius smiled – his smile was as wide as a frog's, and Yama thought that he could probably hold a whole watermelon slice in his mouth. The priest said, 'We are palmers, not soldiers.'

'But you have knives to prepare your food, machetes to cut firewood, that kind of thing?'

'Oh yes.'

'A large group like yours need not worry. It is people travelling alone, or by two or by three, who are vulnerable.'

Belarius mopped at his scalp. His smile grew wider. He said eagerly, 'And you have seen nothing?'

'But for the chattering of this boy, it has been a quiet journey.'

Yama smarted at Prefect Corin's remark, but said nothing. Belarius smoked his cigarette – it smelt overpoweringly of cloves – and gave a rambling account of exactly how the ship on which he had hoped to take his charges all the way to Ys had been ambushed one night by water bandits in a decad of small skiffs. The bandits had been beaten off when the ship's captain had ordered pitch spread on the water and set on fire.

'Our ship put every man to the oars and rowed free of the flames,' Belarius said, 'but the bandits were consumed.'

Prefect Corin listened, but made no comment.

Belarius said, 'The bandits fired chainshot. It damaged the mast and rigging and struck the hull at the waterline. We were taking on water in several places, and so we limped to the nearest port. My charges did not want to wait out the repairs, so we walked on. The ship will meet us at Ys, when we have finished our business there. A ghoul has been following us the past week, but that is the only trouble we have had. Such are the times, when the road is safer than the Great River.'

After Belarius had filled his waterskin from the spring and taken his leave, Yama said, 'You do not like him.'

Prefect Corin considered this, then said in a measured tone, 'I do not like veiled insults about the competence of the Department. If the Great River is no longer safe, it is because of the war, and those who travel on it should take suitable precautions and travel in convoy. Not only that, but our well-upholstered priest did not hire any bodyguards as escort on the road, which would have been prudent, and it would have been more prudent to have waited until the ship was repaired than to have gone forward on foot. I rather think that he has told us only half of the story. Either he does not have the money to hire men or to pay for repairs to the ship, or he is willing to risk the lives of his charges to make extra profit. And he put aboard with a bravado captain, which says little for his judgement. If the ship was able to outdistance the fire it set on the water, then it could have outdistanced the bandits. Often flight is better than fight.'

'If less honourable.'

'There is no honour in needless fighting. The captain could have destroyed his ship as well as the bandits with his trick.'

'Will we stay with these people?'

'Their singing will wake every bandit in a hundred leagues,' Prefect Corin said. 'And if there are any bandits, then they will be attracted to the larger group rather than to the lesser.'

14 ~ The Bandits

The next day, Yama and Prefect Corin drew ahead of the group of palmers, but never so far ahead that the dust cloud the palmers raised was lost from sight. That night, the palmers caught up with them and camped nearby, and Belarius came over and talked to Prefect Corin about the day's journey for the length of time it took him to smoke two of his clove-flavoured cigarettes. The palmers' songs sounded clear and strong in the quiet evening.

When Prefect Corin woke Yama from a deep sleep it was past midnight, and the fire was no more than warm ashes. They had camped by a square tomb covered in the scrambling thorny canes of roses, on top of a bluff that overlooked the Great River. He was leaning on his staff. Behind him, the white roses glimmered like ghosts of their own selves. Their strong scent filled the air.

'Something bad nearby,' Prefect Corin said in a quiet voice. Galaxy light put a spark in each of his close-set eyes. 'Take up your knife and come with me.'

Yama whispered, 'What is it?'

'Perhaps nothing. We will see.'

They crossed the road and circled the palmers' camp, which had been pitched in a grove of eucalyptus. Low cliffs loomed above. The openings of tombs carved into the rock were like staggered rows of hollow eyes: a hiding place for an army. Yama heard nothing but the rustle of eucalyptus leaves, and, far off, the screech of a hunting owl. In the camp, one of the palmers groaned in his sleep. Then the wind shifted, and Yama caught a faint, foul odour above the medicinal tang of the eucalyptus.

Prefect Corin pointed towards the camp with his staff and moved forward, dry leaves crackling beneath his feet. Yama saw something scuttle away through the trees, man-sized yet running on all fours with a lurching sideways movement. He drew his knife and gave chase, but Prefect Corin overtook him and sprang onto an outcrop of rock beyond the trees with his staff raised above his head. He held the pose for a moment, then jumped down.

'Gone,' he said. 'Well, the priest is right about one thing. They have a ghoul following them.'

Yama sheathed his knife. His hand was trembling. He was out of breath and his blood sang in his head. He remembered the time he and Telmon had hunted antelope, armed only with stone axes like the men of the hill tribes. He said, 'I saw it.'

'I will tell them to bury their rubbish and to make sure that they hang their food in branches.'

'Ghouls can climb,' Yama said. He added, 'I am sorry. I should not have chased after it.'

'It was bravely done. Perhaps we scared it off.'

Yama and Prefect Corin reached the pass the next day. It was only a little wider than the road, cutting through a high scarp of rough-edged blocks of grey granite which rose abruptly from the gentle slope they had been climbing all morning. A cairn of flat stones stood at the edge of the road near the beginning of the pass, built around a slab engraved with a list of names. Prefect Corin said that it was the memorial of a battle in the Age of Insurrection, when those few men whose names were engraved on the slab had held the pass against overwhelming odds. Every man defending the pass had died, but the army they had fought had been held up long enough for reinforcements from Ys to arrive and drive them back.

Across the road from the shrine was a house-sized platform of red rock split down the middle by a single, straight-edged crack. Prefect Corin sat in the shade of the rock's overhang and said that they would wait for the palmers to catch up before they tried the pass.

'Safety in numbers,' Yama said, to provoke a reaction.

'Quite the reverse, but you do not seem to understand that.' Prefect Corin watched as Yama restlessly poked about, and eventually said, 'There are supposed to be footprints on top of this rock, one either side of the crack. It is said that an aesthetic stood there an age past, and ascended directly to the Eye of the Preservers. The force of his ascent cracked the rock, and left his footprints melted into it.'

'Is it true?'

'Certainly a great deal of energy would be required to accelerate someone so that they could fall beyond the influence of Confluence's gravity fields, more than enough to melt rock. But if the energy was applied all at once a normal body would be flash-heated into a cloud of steam by friction with the air. I do not blame you for not knowing that, Yama. Your education is not what it should be.'

Yama did not see any point replying to this provocation, and continued to wander about in the dry heat, searching for nothing in particular. The alternative was to sit by Prefect Corin. Small lizards flicked over the hot stones; a scarlet and gold hummingbird hung in the air on a blur of wings for a few moments before darting away. At last, Yama found a way up a jumble of boulders to the flat top of the outcrop. The fracture was straight and narrow, and its depths glittered with shards of what looked like melted glass. The fabled prints were just as Prefect Corin had described them, no more than a pair of foot-sized oval hollows, one on either side of the crack.

Yama lay down on warm, gritty rock and looked up at the

empty blue sky. His thoughts moved lazily. He started to read his copy of the Puranas, but did not find anything that was different from his rote learning and put the book away. It was too bright and hot to read, and he had already looked long and hard at the pictures; apart from the one which showed the creation of the Eye of the Preservers, they were little different from the scenes of the lost past captured in the slates of tombs – and unlike the pictures in the slates, the pictures in the book did not move.

Yama idly wondered why the ghoul was following the palmers, and wondered why the Preservers had created ghouls in the first place. For if the Preservers had created the world and everything in it, as was written in the Puranas, and had raised up the ten thousand bloodlines from animals of ten thousand worlds, then what were the ghouls, which stood between animals and the humblest of the indigenous races?

According to the argument from design, which Zakiel had taught Yama and Telmon, ghouls existed because they aided the processes of decay, but there were many other scavenger species, and ghouls had a particular appetite for the flesh of men, and would take small children and babies if they could. Others said that ghouls were only imperfectly raised up, their natures partaking of the worst of men and of beasts, or that their bloodline had not advanced like those of other kinds of men, or remained unchanged, like the various indigenous races, but had run backwards until they retained nothing of the gifts of the Preservers but the capacity for evil. Both arguments suggested that the world which the Preservers had created was imperfect, although neither denied the possibility of perfectibility. Some claimed that the Preservers had chosen not to create a perfect world because such a world would be unchanging, and only an imperfect world allowed the possibility of evil and, therefore, of redemption. By their nature, Preservers could do only good, but while they could not create evil, the presence of evil was an inevitable consequence in their creation, just as light casts shadows when material objects are interposed. Others argued that since the light of the Preservers had been everywhere at the construction of the world, where then could any shadows lie? By this argument, evil was the consequence of the rebellion of men and machines against the Preservers, and only by rediscovering the land of lost content which had existed before that rebellion could evil be banished and men win redemption.

Still others argued that evil had its use in a great plan that could not be understood by any but the Preservers themselves. That such a plan might exist, with past, present and future absolutely determined, was one reason why no one should rely on miracles. As Ananda would say, no use praying for intercession if all was determined from the outset. If the Preservers wanted something to be so, then they would have created it already, without waiting to hear prayers asking for intercession, without needing to watch over every soul. Everything was predestined in the single long word which the Preservers had spoken to bring the world into existence.

Yama's mind rebelled against this notion, as a man buried before his death might fight against a winding sheet. If everything was part of a predetermined plan, then why should anyone in it do anything at all, least of all worship the Preservers? Except that too was a part of the plan, and everyone in the world was a wind-up puppet ratcheting from birth to death in a series of preprogrammed gestures.

It was undeniable that the Preservers had set the world in motion, but Yama did not believe that they had abandoned it in disgust or despair, or because, seeing all, they knew every detail of its destiny. No, Yama preferred to think that the Preservers had left the world to grow as it would, as a fond parent must watch a child grow into independence. In this way, the bloodlines which the Preservers had raised up from animals might rise further to become their equals, and that could not occur if the Preservers interfered with destiny, for just as a man cannot make another man, so gods cannot make other gods. For this reason, it was necessary that individuals must be able to choose between good and evil – they must be able to choose, like Dr Dismas, not to serve goodness, but their own appetites. Without the possibility of evil, no bloodline could define its own goodness. The existence of evil allowed bloodlines to fail and fall, or to transcend their animal natures by their own efforts.

Yama wondered if ghouls had chosen to fall, revelling in their bestial nature as Dr Dismas revelled in his rebellion against the society of men. Animals did not choose their natures, of course. A jaguar did not delight in the pain it caused its prey; it merely needed to eat. Cats played with mice, but only because their mothers had taught them to hunt by such play. Only men had free will and could choose to wallow in their base desires or by force of will overcome them. Were men little different from ghouls, then, except they struggled against their dark side, while ghouls swam in it with the innocent unthinking ease of fish in water? By praying to the Preservers, perhaps men were in reality doing no more than praying to their own as yet unrealized higher natures, as an explorer might contemplate the untravelled peaks he must climb to reach his goal.

If the Preservers had left the world to its own devices and there were no miracles, except the existence of free will, what then, of the ghost ship? Yama had not prayed for it, or at least had not known that he had done so, and yet it had come precisely when he had needed a diversion to make good his escape. Was something watching over him? If so, to what purpose? Or perhaps it was no more than a coincidence: some old machinery had been accidentally awakened, and Yama had seized the moment to escape. It was possible that there was another world where the ghost ship had not appeared, or had appeared too early or too late, and Yama had gone with Dr Dismas and the warlord, Enobarbus. He would be travelling downriver on the pinnace even now, a willing or unwilling participant in their plans, perhaps to death, perhaps to a destiny more glorious than the apprenticeship which now lay ahead of him.

Yama's speculations widened and at some point he was no longer in control of them but was carried on their flow, like a twig on the Great River's flood. He slept, and woke to find Prefect Corin standing over him, a black shadow against the dazzling blue of the sky.

'Trouble,' the man said, and pointed down the long gentle slope of the road. A tiny smudge of smoke hung in the middle distance, trembling in the heat haze, and at that moment Yama realized that all along Prefect Corin had been protecting the palmers.

They found the dead first. The bodies had been dragged off the road and stacked and set on fire. Little was left but greasy ash and charred bones, although, bizarrely, a pair of unburnt feet still shod in sandals protruded from the bottom of the gruesome pyre. Prefect Corin poked amongst the hot ashes with his staff and counted fourteen skulls, leaving nine unaccounted for. He cast about in one direction, bending low as he searched the muddle of prints on the ground, and Yama, although not asked, went in the other. It was he, following a trail of blood speckles, who found Belarius hiding inside a tomb. The priest was cradling a dead woman, and his robe was drenched in her blood.

'They shot at us from hiding places amongst the tombs,' Belarius said. 'I think they shot Vril by accident because they did not shoot any of the other women. When all the men had been killed or badly wounded, they came for the women. Small fierce men with bright red skin and long arms and legs, some on foot, some on horse, three or four decads of them. Like spiders. They had sharp teeth, and claws like thorns. I remember they couldn't close their hands around their weapons.'

'I know the bloodline,' Prefect Corin said. 'They are a long way from home.'

'Two came and looked at me, and jeered and went away again,' Belarius said.

'They would not kill a priest,' Prefect Corin said. 'It is bad luck.'

'I tried to stop them despoiling the bodies,' Belarius said. 'They threatened me with their knives or spat on me or laughed, but they didn't stop their work. They stripped the bodies and dismembered them, cut what they wanted from the heads. Some of the men were still alive. When they were finished, they set the bodies on fire. I wanted to shrive the dead, but they pushed me away.'

'And the women?'

Belarius started to cry. He said, 'I meant no harm to anyone. No harm. No harm to anyone.'

'They took the women with them,' Prefect Corin said. 'To despoil or to sell. Stop blubbering, man! Which way did they go?'

'Towards the mountains. You must believe that I meant no harm. If you had stayed with us instead of getting ahead – no, forgive me. That is unworthy.'

'We would have been killed, too,' Prefect Corin said. 'These bandits strike quickly, and without fear. They will attack larger groups better armed than themselves if they think that the surprise and fury of their assault will overcome their opponents. As it is, we may yet save some of your people. Go and shrive your dead, man. After that you must decide whether you want to come with us or stay here.'

When Belarius was out of earshot, Prefect Corin said to Yama, 'Listen carefully, boy. You can come with me, but only if you swear that you will do exactly as I say.'

'Of course,' Yama said at once. He would have promised anything for the chance.

It was not difficult to track the bandits and the captured women across the dry, sandy land. The trail ran parallel to the granite scarp across a series of flat, barren salt pans. Each was higher than the next, like a series of giant steps. Prefect Corin set a relentless pace, but the priest, Belarius, kept up surprisingly well; he was one of those fat men who are also strong, and the shock of the ambush was wearing off. Yama supposed that this was a chance for Belarius to regain face. Already, the priest was beginning to speak of the attack as if it was an accident or natural disaster from which he would rescue the survivors.

'As if he did not invite the lightning,' Prefect Corin said to Yama, when they stopped to rest in the shade of a tomb. 'At the best of times, bringing a party of palmers on the land route to Ys without proper escort is like herding sheep through a country of wolves. And these were archivists, too. Not proper archivists – those are from the Department, and are trained in the art of memory. These use machines to record the lives of the dying. If you had looked closely at the skulls, you would have seen that they had been broken open. Some bandits eat the brains of their victims, but these wanted the machines in their heads.'

Yama laughed in disbelief. 'I have never heard of such a thing!'

Prefect Corin passed a hand over his black-furred face, like a grooming cat. 'It is an abomination, promulgated by a department so corrupt and debased that it seeks to survive by coarse imitation of the tasks properly carried out by its superiors. Proper archivists learn how to manage their memories by training; these people would be archivists in a few days, by swallowing the seeds of machines which migrate to a certain area of the brain and grow a kind of library. It is not without risks. In one in fifty of those who swallow the seeds, the machines grow unchecked and destroy their host's brains.'

'But surely only the unchanged need archivists? Once changed, everyone is remembered by the Preservers.'

'Many no longer believe it, and because the Department

will not supply archivists to the cities of the changed, these mountebanks make fortunes by pandering to the gullible. Like real archivists, they listen to the life stories of the dying and promise to transmit them to the shrines of the Palace of the Memory of the People.'

Yama said, 'No wonder the priest is upset. He believes that many more died than we saw.'

'They are all remembered by the Preservers in any event,' Prefect Corin said. 'Saints or sinners, all men marked by the Preservers are remembered, while true archivists remember the stories of as many of the unchanged blood-lines as they can. The priest is upset because his reputation will be blemished, and he will lose trade. Hush. Here he comes.'

Belarius had ripped away the blood-soaked part of his orange robe, leaving only a kind of kilt about his waist. The smooth yellow skin of his shoulders and his fat man's breasts had darkened in the sun to the colour of blood oranges, and he scratched at his sunburnt skin as he told Yama and Prefect Corin that he had found fresh horse droppings.

'They are not more than an hour ahead of us. If we hurry, we can catch them before they reach the foothills.'

Prefect Corin said, 'They make the women walk. It slows them down.'

'Then their cruelty will be their undoing.' Belarius curled his right hand into a fist and ground it into the palm of his left. 'We will catch them and we will crush them.'

Prefect Corin said calmly, 'They are cruel but not stupid. They could tie the women to their horses if they wanted to outpace us, yet they do not. They taunt us, I think. They want sport. We must proceed carefully. We will wait until night, and follow them to their camp.'

'They will leave us behind in the darkness!'

'I know this bloodline. They do not travel by night, for their blood slows as the air cools. Meanwhile we will rest.

You will pray for us, Belarius. It will set our minds to the struggle ahead.'

They waited until the sun had fallen behind the Rim Mountains and the Galaxy had begun to rise above the farside horizon before they set off. The tracks left by the bandits ran straight across the flat white land into a tangle of shallow draws which sloped up towards a range of low hills. Yama tried his best to imitate Prefect Corin's ambling gait, and remembered to go flatfooted on loose stones, as Telmon had taught him. Belarius was less nimble, and every now and then would stumble and send stones clattering away down-slope. There were tombs scattered at irregular intervals along the sides of the draws, unornamented and squarely built, with tall narrow doors which had been smashed open an age ago. A few had picture slates, and these wakened when the three men went by, so that they had to walk along the tops of the ridges between the draws to avoid being betrayed by the light of the past. Belarius fretted that they would lose the trail, but then Yama saw a flickering dab of light brighten ahead.

It was a dry tree set on fire in the bottom of a deep draw. It burned with a white intensity and a harsh crackling, sending up volumes of acrid white smoke. Its tracery of branches made a web of black shadows within the brightness of its burning. The three men looked down on it, and Prefect Corin said, 'Well, they know that we are following them. Yama, look after Belarius. I will not be long.'

He was gone before Yama could reply, a swift shadow flowing down the slope, circling the burning tree and disappearing into the darkness beyond. Belarius sat down heavily and whispered, 'You two should not die on my account.'

'Let us not talk of death,' Yama said. He had his knife in his hand – he had drawn it upon seeing the burning tree. It showed not a spark, and he sheathed it and said, 'A little while ago, I was taken aboard a pinnace by force, but a white ship appeared, glowing with cold fire. The pinnace attacked the white ship and I was able to escape. Yet the white ship was not real; even as it bore down on the pinnace it began to dissolve. Was this a miracle? And was it for my benefit? What do you think?'

'We shouldn't question the plan of the Preservers. Only they can say what is miraculous.'

It was a rote reply. Belarius was more intent on the darkness beyond the burning tree than on Yama's tale. He was smoking one of his clove-scented cigarettes, cupping it hungrily to his wide mouth. The light of the burning tree beat on him unmercifully; shadows in his deep eye sockets made a skull of his face.

Prefect Corin came back an hour later. The tree had burnt down to a stump of glowing cinders. He appeared out of the darkness and knelt between Belarius and Yama. 'The way is clear,' he said.

Yama said, 'Did you see them?'

Prefect Corin considered this. Yama thought he looked smug, the son-of-a-bitch. At last he said, 'I saw our friend of last night.'

'The ghoul?'

'It is following us. It will feed well tonight, one way or the other. Listen carefully. This ridge rises and leads around to a place above a canyon. There are large tombs at the bottom of the canyon, and that is where the bandits are camped. They have stripped the women and tied them to stakes, but I do not think they have used them.' Prefect Corin looked directly at Belarius. 'These people come into heat like dogs or deer, and it is not their season. They display the women to make us angry, and we will not be angry. They have built a big fire, but away from it the night air will make them sluggish. Yama, you and Belarius will create a diversion, and I will go in and cut the women free and bring them out.'

Belarius said, 'It is not much of a plan.'

'Well, we could leave the women,' Prefect Corin said, with

such seriousness that it was plain he would do just that if Belarius refused to help.

'They'll sleep,' the priest said. 'We wait until they sleep, and then we take the women.'

Prefect Corin said, 'No. They never sleep, but simply become less active at night. They will be waiting for us. That is why we must make them come out, preferably away from their fire. I will kill them then. I have a pistol.'

It was like a flat, water-smoothed pebble. It caught the Galaxy's cold blue light and shone in Prefect Corin's palm. Yama was amazed. The Department of Indigenous Affairs was surely greater than he had imagined, if one of them could carry a weapon not only forbidden to most but so valuable, because the secret of its manufacture was lost an age past, that it could ransom a city like Aeolis. Dr Dismas's energy pistol, which merely increased the power of light by making its waves march in step, had been a clumsy imitation of the weapon Prefect Corin held.

Belarius said, 'Those things are evil.'

'It has saved my life before now. It has three shots, and then it must lie in sunlight all day before it will fire again. That is why you must get them into the open, so I have a clear field of fire.'

Yama said, 'How will we make the diversion?'

'I am sure you will think of something when you get there,' Prefect Corin said.

His lips were pressed together as if he was suppressing a smile, and now Yama knew what this was all about.

Prefect Corin said, 'Follow the ridge, and be careful not to show yourself against the sky.'

'What about guards?'

'There are no guards,' Prefect Corin said. 'Not any more.'

And then he was gone.

The canyon was sinuous and narrow, a deeply folded crevice winding back the hills. The ridge rose above it to a tabletop bluff dissected by dry ravines. Lying on his belly, looking over the edge of the drop into the canyon, Yama could see the fire the bandits had lit on the canyon floor far below. Its red glow beat on the white faces of the tombs that were set into the walls of the canyon, and the brushwood corral where a decad of horses milled, and the line of naked women tied to stakes.

Yama said, 'It is like a test.'

Belarius, squatting on his heels a little way from the edge, stared at him.

'I have to show initiative,' Yama said. 'If I do not, Prefect Corin will not try to rescue the women.'

He did not add that it was also a punishment. Because he carried the knife; because he wanted to be a soldier; because he had tried to run away. He knew that he could not allow himself to fail, but he did not know how he could succeed.

'Pride,' Belarius said sulkily. He seemed to have reached a point where nothing much mattered to him. 'He makes himself into a petty god, deciding whether my poor clients live or die.'

'That is up to us, I think. He is a cold man, but he wants to help you.'

Belarius pointed into the darkness behind him. 'There's a dead man over there. I can smell him.'

It was one of the bandits. He was lying on his belly in the middle of a circle of creosote bushes. His neck had been broken and he seemed to be staring over his shoulder at his doom.

Belarius mumbled a brief prayer, then took the dead man's short, stout recurved bow and quiver of unfledged arrows. He seemed to cheer up a little, and Yama asked him if he knew how to use a bow.

'I'm not a man of violence.'

'Do you want to help rescue your clients?'

'Most of them are dead,' Belarius said gravely. 'I will shrive this poor wight now.'

Yama left the priest with the dead man and quartered the ground along the edge of the canyon. Although he was tired, he felt a peculiar clarity, a keen alertness sustained by a mixture of anger and adrenalin. This might be a test, but the women's lives depended on it. That was more important than pleasing Prefect Corin, or proving to himself that he could live up to his dreams.

A round boulder stood at the edge of the drop. It was half Yama's height and bedded in the dirt, but it gave a little when he put his back to it. He tried to get Belarius to help him, but the priest was kneeling as if in prayer and either did not understand or did not want to understand, and he would not stand up even when Yama pulled at his arm. Yama groaned in frustration and went back to the boulder and began to attack the sandy soil around its base with his eating knife. He had not been digging for long when he struck something metallic. The little knife quivered in his hands and when he drew it out he found that the point of the blade had been neatly cut away. He had found a machine.

Yama knelt and whispered to the thing, asking it to come to him. He did it more from reflex than hope, and was amazed when the soil shifted between his knees and the machine slid into the air with a sudden slipping motion, like a squeezed watermelon seed. It bobbed in the air before Yama's face, a shining, silvery oval that would have fitted into his palm, had he dared touch it. It was both metallic and fluid, like a big drop of hydrargyrum. Flecks of light flickered here and there on its surface. It emitted a strong smell of ozone, and a faint crepitating sound.

Yama said, slowly and carefully, shaping the words in his mind as well as his mouth as he did when instructing the peel-house's watchdogs, 'I need to make this part of the edge of the canyon fall. Help me.'

The machine dropped to the ground and a little geyser of dust and small stones spat up as it dug down out of sight. Yama sat on his heels, hardly daring to breathe, but although he waited a long time, nothing else seemed to happen. He had started to dig around the base of the boulder again when Belarius found him.

The priest had uprooted a couple of small creosote bushes. He said, 'We will set these alight and throw them down onto those wicked men.'

'Help me with this boulder.'

Belarius shook his head and sat by the edge and began to tie the bushes together with a strip of cloth torn from remnants of his robe.

'If you set fire to those bushes, you will make yourself a target,' Yama said.

'I expect that you have a flint in your satchel.'

'Yes, but—'

In the canyon below, horses cried to each other. Yama looked over the edge and saw that the horses were running from one corner of the corral to the other. They moved in the firelight like water running before a strong, choppy wind, bunched together and flicking their tails and tossing their heads. At first, Yama thought that they had been disturbed by Prefect Corin, but then he saw something white clinging upside-down to the neck of a black mare in the middle of the panicky herd. The ghoul had found the bandits. Men were running towards the horses with a scampering crabwise gait, casting long crooked shadows because the fire was at their backs, and Yama threw his weight against the boulder, knowing he would not have a better chance.

The ground moved under Yama's feet and he lost his footing and fell backwards, banging the back of his head against the boulder. The blow dazed him, and he was unable to stop Belarius pawing through his satchel and taking the flint. The ground moved again and the boulder stirred and sank a handspan into the soil. Yama realized what was happening and scrambled out of the way just as the edge of the canyon collapsed.

The boulder dropped straight down. A cloud of dust and

dirt shot up and there was a crash when the boulder struck the side of the canyon, and then a moment of silence. The ground was still shaking. Yama tried to get to his feet, but it was like trying to stand up in a boat caught in cross-currents. Belarius was kneeling over the bundle of creosote bushes, striking the flint against its stone. Dust puffed up behind him, defining a long crooked line, and a kind of lip opened in the ground. Little lights swarmed in the churning soil. Yama saw them when he snatched up his satchel and jumped the widening gash. He landed on hands and knees and the ground moved again and he fell down. Belarius was standing on the other side of the gash, his feet planted wide apart as he swung two burning bushes around his head. Then the edge of the canyon gave way and fell with a sliding roar into the canyon. A moment later a vast cloud of dust boiled up amidst a noise like a thunderclap, and lightning lit the length of the canyon at spaced intervals. Once, twice, three times.

15 ~ The Magistrate

At first the houses were no more than empty tombs that people had moved into, making improvised villages strung out along low cliff terraces by the old edge of the Great River. The people who lived there went about naked. They were thin and very tall, with small heads and long, glossy black hair, and skin the colour of rust. The chests of the men were welted with spiral patterns of scars; the women stiffened their hair with red clay. They hunted lizards and snakes and coneys, collected the juicy young pads of prickly pear and dug for tuberous roots in the dry tableland above the cliffs, picked samphire and watercress in the marshes by the margin of the river and waded out into the river's shallows and cast circular nets to catch fish, which they smoked on racks above fires built of creosote bush and pine chips. They were cheerful and hospitable, and gave food and shelter freely to Yama and Prefect Corin.

Then there were proper houses amongst the tombs, four-square and painted yellow or blue or pink, with little gardens planted out on their flat roofs. The houses stepped up the cliffs like piles of boxes, with steep narrow streets between. Shanty villages had been built on stilts over the mudbanks and silty channels left by the river's retreat, and beyond these, sometimes less than half a league from the road, sometimes two or three leagues distant, was the river, and docks made of floating pontoons, and a constant traffic of little cockle-shell sailboats and barges and sleek fore-and-aft rigged cutters and three-masted xebecs hugging the shore. Along the old river road, street merchants sold fresh fish and oysters and mussels from tanks, and freshly steamed lobsters and spiny crabs, samphire and lotus roots and water chestnuts, bamboo and little red bananas and several kinds of kelp, milk from tethered goats, spices, pickled walnuts, fresh fruit and grass juice, ice, jewellery made of polished shells, black seed pearls, caged birds, bolts of brightly patterned cloth, sandals made from the worn rubber tread of steam waggon tyres, cheap plastic toys, tape recordings of popular ballads or prayers, and a thousand other things. The stalls and booths of the merchants formed a kind of ribbon market strung along the dusty margin of land at the shoulder of the old road, noisy with the cries of hawkers and music from tape recorders and itinerant musicians, and the buzz of commerce as people bargained and gossiped. When a warship went past, a league beyond the crowded tarpaper roofs of the shanty villages and the cranes of the floating docks, everyone stopped to watch it. As if in salute, it raised the red and gold blades of its triple-banked oars and fired a charge of white smoke from a cannon, and everyone watching cheered.

That was when Yama realized that he could see, for the first time, the farside shore of the Great River, and that the dark line at the horizon, like a storm cloud, were houses and docks. The river here was deep and swift, stained brown along the shore and dark blue further out. He had reached Ys and had not known it: the city had crept up on him like an army in the night, the inhabited tombs like scouts, these painted houses and tumbledown shanty villages like the first ranks of footsoldiers. It was as if, after the fiasco of the attempted rescue of the palmers, he had suddenly woken from a long sleep.

Prefect Corin had said little about the landslide which had killed the bandits, the kidnapped women and their priest, Belarius. 'You did what you could,' he had told Yama. 'If we had not tried, the women would be dead anyway.'

Yama had not told Prefect Corin about the machine. Let him think what he liked. But Yama had not been able to stop himself reliving what had happened as he had trudged behind the Prefect on the long road to Ys. Sometimes he felt a tremendous guilt, for it had been his foolish pride which had prompted him to use the machine, which had led to the deaths of the bandits and the kidnapped women. And sometimes he felt a tremendous anger towards Prefect Corin, for having laid such a responsibility upon him. He had little doubt that the Prefect could have walked into the bandits' camp, killed them all, and freed the women. Instead he had used the situation to test Yama, and Yama had failed, and felt guilt for having failed, and then anger for having been put to an impossible test.

Humiliation or anger. At last, Yama settled for the latter. As he walked behind Prefect Corin, he often imagined drawing his knife and hacking the man's head from his shoulders with a single blow, or picking a stone from the side of the road and using it as a hammer. He dreamed of running fast and far and, until the warship passed, had been lost in his dreams.

Yama and Prefect Corin ate at a roadside stall. Without being asked, the owner of the stall brought them steamed mussels, water lettuce crisply fried in sesame oil with strands of ginger, and tea made from kakava bark; there was a red plastic bowl in the centre of the table into which fragments of bark could be spat. Prefect Corin did not pay for the food – the stall's owner, a tall man with loose, pale skin and rubbery webs between his fingers, simply smiled and bowed when they left.

'He is glad to help someone from the Department,' Prefect Corin explained, when Yama asked.

'Why is that?'

Prefect Corin waved a hand in front of his face, as if at a fly. Yama asked again.

'Because we are at war,' the Prefect said. 'Because the

Department fights that war. You saw how they cheered the warship. Must you ask so many questions?'

Yama said, 'How am I to learn, if I do not ask?'

Prefect Corin stopped and leaned on his tall staff and stared at Yama. People stepped around them. It was crowded here, with two- and three-storey houses packed closely together on either side of the road. A string of camels padded past, their loose lips curled in supercilious expressions, little silver bells jingling on their leather harness.

'The first thing to learn is when to ask questions and when to keep silent,' Prefect Corin said, and then he turned and strode off through the crowd.

Without thinking, Yama hurried after him. It was as if this stern, taciturn man had made him into a kind of pet, anxiously trotting at his master's heels. He remembered what Dr Dismas had said about the oxen, trudging endlessly around the water lift because they knew no better, and his resentment rose again, refreshed.

For long stretches, now, the river disappeared behind houses or godowns. Hills rose above the flat roofs of the houses on the landward side of the road, and after a while Yama realized that they were not hills but buildings. In the hazy distance, the towers he had so often glimpsed using the telescope on the peel-house's heliograph platform shone like silver threads linking earth and sky.

For all the long days of travelling, the towers seemed as far away as ever.

There were more and more people on the road, and strings of camels and oxen, and horse-drawn or steam waggons bedecked with pious slogans, and sleds gliding at waist height, their loadbeds decorated with intricately carved wooden rails painted red and gold. There were machines here, too. At first, Yama mistook them for insects or hummingbirds as they zipped this way and that above the crowds. No one in Aeolis owned machines, not even the Aedile (the watchdogs were surgically altered animals, and did not count), and if a machine strayed into the little city's streets everyone would get as far away from it as possible. Here, no one took any notice of the many machines that darted or spun through the air on mysterious errands. Indeed, one man was walking towards Yama and Prefect Corin with a decad of tiny machines circling above his head.

The man stopped in front of the Prefect. The Prefect was tall, but this man was taller still – he was the tallest man Yama had ever seen. He wore a scarlet cloak with the hood cast over his head, and a black tunic and black trousers tucked into thigh-high boots of soft black leather. A quirt like those used by ox drivers was tucked into the belt of his trousers; the ends of the quirt's hundred strands were braided with diamond-shaped metal tags. The man squared up to Prefect Corin and said, 'You're a long way from where you should be.'

Prefect Corin leaned on his staff and looked up at the man. Yama stood behind the Prefect. People were beginning to form a loose circle with the red-cloaked man and Prefect Corin in its centre.

The man in the red cloak said, 'If you have business here, I haven't heard of it.'

A machine landed on Prefect Corin's neck, just beneath the angle of his jaw. Prefect Corin ignored it. He said, 'There is no reason why you should.'

'There's every reason.' The man noticed the people watching and slashed the air with his quirt. The tiny, bright machines above his head widened their orbits and one dropped down to hover before the man's lips.

'Move on,' the man said. His voice, amplified by the machine, echoed off the faces of the buildings on either side of the street, but most of the people only stepped back a few paces. The machine rose and the man told Prefect Corin in his ordinary voice, 'You're causing a disturbance.'

Prefect Corin said, 'There was no disturbance until you stopped me. I would ask why.'

'This is the road, not the river.'

Prefect Corin spat in the dust at his feet. 'I had noticed.'

'You are carrying a pistol.'

'By the authority of my Department.'

'We'll see about that. What's your business? Are you spying on us?'

'If you are doing your duty, you have nothing to fear. But do not worry, brother, I am no spy. I am returning from a downriver city where I had a task to perform. It is done, and now I return.'

'Yet you travel by road.'

'I thought I would show this boy something of the countryside. He has led a very sheltered life.'

A machine darted forward and spun in front of Yama's face. There was a flash of red light in the backs of Yama's eyes and he blinked, and the machine flew up to rejoin the spinning dance above the man's head. The man said, 'This is your catamite? The war is going badly if you can't find better. This one has a corpse's skin. And he is carrying a proscribed weapon.'

'Again, by the authority of my Department,' Prefect Corin said.

'I don't know the bloodline, but I'd guess he's too young for an apprenticeship. You had better show your papers to the officer of the day.'

The man snapped his fingers and the machines dropped and settled into a tight orbit around the Prefect's head, circling him like angry silver wasps. The man turned then, slashing the air with his quirt so that those nearest him fell back, pressing against those behind. 'Make way!' the man shouted as he hacked a path through the crowd with his quirt. 'Make way! Make way!'

Yama said to Prefect Corin, as they followed the man, 'Is this the time to ask a question?'

'He is a magistrate. A member of the autonomous civil authority of Ys. There is some bad blood between his department and mine. He will make a point about who is in charge here, and then we will be on our way.'

'How did he know about the pistol and my knife?'

'His machines told him.'

Yama studied the shuttling weave of the little machines around Prefect Corin's head. One still clung to the Prefect's neck, a segmented silver bead with four pairs of wire-like legs and mica wings folded along its back. Yama could feel the simple thoughts of the machines, and wondered if he might be able to make them forget what they had been ordered to do, but he did not trust himself to say the right thing to them, and besides, he was not about to reveal his ability by helping the Prefect.

The road opened onto a square lined with flame trees just coming into leaf. On the far side, a high wall rose above the roofs of the buildings and the tops of the trees. It was built of closely fitted blocks of black, polished granite, with gun platforms and watch-towers along its top. Soldiers lounged by a tall gate in the wall, watching the traffic that jostled through the shadow of the gate's arch. The magistrate led Prefect Corin and Yama across the square and the soldiers snapped to attention as they went through the gate. They climbed a steep stair that wound widdershins inside the wall to a wide walkway at the top. A little way along, the wall turned at a right-angle and ran beside the old bank of the river, and a faceted blister of glass, glittering in the sunlight, clung there.

It was warm and full of light inside the glass blister. Magistrates in red cloaks stood at windows hung in the air, watching aerial views of the road, of ships moored at the docks or passing up and down the river, of red tile rooftops, of a man walking along a crowded street. Machines zipped to and fro in the bright air, or spun in little clouds. At the centre of all this activity, a bareheaded officer sat with his boots up on a clear plastic table, and after the magistrate had talked with him the officer called Prefect Corin over.

'Just a formality,' the officer said languidly, and held out his hand. The eight-legged machine dropped from the Prefect's neck and the officer's fingers briefly closed around it. When they opened again the machine sprang into the air and began to circle the magistrate's head.

The officer yawned and said, 'Your pass, Prefect Corin, if you please.' He ran a fingernail over the imprinted seal of the resin tablet Prefect Corin gave him, and said, 'You didn't take return passage by river, as you were ordered.'

'Not ordered. I could have taken the river passage if I chose to, but it was left to my discretion. The boy is to be apprenticed as a clerk. I thought that I would show him something of the country. He has led a sheltered life.'

The officer said, 'It's a long, hard walk.' He was looking at Yama now. Yama met his gaze and the officer winked. He said, 'There's nothing here about this boy, or his weapon. Quite a hanger for a mere apprentice.'

'An heirloom. He is the son of the Aedile of Aeolis.' Prefect Corin's tone implied that there was nothing more to be said about the matter.

The officer set the tablet on the desk and said to the magistrate, 'Nym, fetch a chair for Prefect Corin.'

Prefect Corin said, 'There is no need for delay.'

The officer yawned again. His tongue and teeth were stained red with the narcotic leaf he had wadded between gum and cheek. His tongue was black, long and sharply pointed. 'It'll take a little while to confirm things with your department. Would you like some refreshment?'

The tall, red-cloaked magistrate set a stool beside Prefect Corin. The officer indicated it, and after a moment Prefect Corin sat down. He said, 'I do not need anything from you.'

The officer took out a packet of cigarettes and put one in his mouth and lit it with a match he struck on the surface of the desk. He did all this at a leisurely pace; his gaze did not leave the Prefect's face. He exhaled smoke and said to the magistrate, 'Some fruit. And iced sherbet.' He told Prefect

Corin, 'While we're waiting, you can tell me about your long walk from—' he glanced at the tablet '—Aeolis. A party of palmers has gone missing somewhere around there, I believe. Perhaps you know something. Meanwhile, Nym will talk with the boy, and we'll see if the stories are the same. What could be simpler?'

Prefect Corin said, 'The boy must stay with me. He is in my charge.'

'Oh, I think he will be safe with Nym, don't you?'

'I have my instructions,' Prefect Corin said.

The officer stubbed out his half-smoked cigarette. 'You cleave to them with admirable fidelity. We'll take care of the boy. You'll tell your story to me. He'll tell his to Nym. Then we'll see if the stories are the same. What could be simpler?'

Prefect Corin said, 'You do not know—'

The officer raised an eyebrow.

'He is in my charge,' Prefect Corin said. 'We will go now, I think.'

He started to rise, and for an instant was crowned with a jagged circle of sparks. There was a sudden sharp smell of burnt hair and he fell heavily onto the stool. The little machines calmly circled his head, as if nothing had happened.

'Take the boy away, Nym,' the officer said. 'Find out where he's been and where he's going.'

Prefect Corin turned and gave Yama a dark stare. His shoulders were hunched and his hands were pressed between his knees. A thin line of white char circled his sleek black head, above his eyes and the tops of his tightly folded ears. 'Do what you are told,' he said. 'No more than that.'

The magistrate, Nym, took Yama's arm and steered him around the windows in the air. The machines quit their orbits around Prefect Corin's head and followed the magistrate in a compact cloud. In the hot sunlight outside the dome, Nym looked through Yama's satchel and took out the sheathed knife.

'That was a gift from my father,' Yama said. He half-hoped that the knife would do something to the magistrate, but it remained inert. Yama added, 'My father is the Aedile of Aeolis, and he told me to take good care of it.'

'I'm not going to steal it, boy.' The magistrate pulled the blade half-way out of its sheath. 'Nicely balanced. Loyal, too.' He dropped it into Yama's satchel. 'It tried to bite me, but I know something about machines. You use it to cut firewood, I suppose. Sit down. There. Wait for me. Don't move. Try to leave, and the machines will knock you down, like they did with your master. Try to use your weapon and they'll boil you down to a grease spot. I'll come back and we'll have a little talk, you and me.'

Yama looked up at the magistrate. He tried not to blink when the machines settled in a close orbit around his head. 'When you fetch refreshments for my master, remember that I would like sherbet, too.'

'Oh yes, we'll have a nice talk, you and me. Your master doesn't have a pass for you, and I'll bet you don't have a permit for your knife, either. Think about that.'

Yama waited until Nym had gone down the stairway, then told the machines to leave him alone. They wanted to know where they should go, so he asked them if they could cross the river, and when they said that they could he told them to go directly across the river and to wait there.

The machines gathered into a line and flew straight out over the edge of the wall, disappearing into the blue sky above the crowded roofs of the stilt shanties and the masts of the ships anchored at the floating docks. Yama went down the stairs and walked boldly past the soldiers. None of them spared him more than a glance, and he walked out of the shadow of the gate into the busy street beyond the wall.

16 ~ The Cateran

At first the landlord of the inn did not want to rent a room to Yama. The inn was full, he said, on account of the Water Market. But when Yama showed him the two gold rials, the man chuckled and said that he might be able to make a special arrangement. Perhaps twice the usual tariff, to take account of the inconvenience, and if Yama would like to eat while waiting for the room to be made up . . .? The landlord was a fat young man with smooth brown skin and short, spiky white hair, and a brisk, direct manner. He took one of the coins and said that he'd bring change in the morning, seeing as the money changers were closed up for the day.

Yama sat in a corner of the taproom, and presently a pot boy brought him a plate of shrimp boiled in their shells and stir-fried okra and peppers, with chili and peanut sauce and flat discs of unleavened bread and a beaker of thin rice beer. Yama ate hungrily. He had walked until the sun had fallen below the roofs of the city, and although he had passed numerous stalls and street vendors he had not been able to buy any food or drink – he had not realized that there were men whose business was to change coins like his into smaller denominations. The landlord would change the coin tomorrow, and Yama would begin to search for his bloodline. But now he was content to sit with a full stomach, his head pleasantly lightened by the beer, and watch the inn's customers.

They seemed to fall into two distinct groups. There were

ordinary working men of several bloodlines, dressed in home-spun and clogs, who stood at the counter drinking quietly, and there was a party of men and a single red-haired woman eating at a long table under the stained glass window which displayed the inn's sign of two crossed axes. They made a lot of noise, playing elaborate toasting games and calling from one end of the table to the other. Yama thought that they must be soldiers, caterans or some other kind of irregulars, for they all wore bits of armour, mostly metal or resin chestplates painted with various devices, and wrist guards and greaves. Many were scarred, or had missing fingers. One big, barechested man had a silver patch over one eye; another had only one arm, although he ate as quickly and as dextrously as his companions. The red-haired woman seemed to be one of them, rather than a concubine they had picked up; she wore a sleeveless leather tunic and a short leather skirt that left her legs mostly bare.

The landlord seemed to know the caterans, and when he was not busy he sat with them, laughing at their jokes and pouring wine or beer for those nearest him. He whispered something in the one-eyed man's ear and they both laughed, and when the landlord went off to serve one of the other customers, the one-eyed man grinned across the room at Yama.

Presently, the pot boy told Yama that his room was ready and led him around the counter and through a small hot kitchen into a courtyard lit by electric floodlights hung from a central pole. There were whitewashed stables on two sides and a wide square gate shaded by an avocado tree in which green parrots squawked and rustled. The room was in the eaves above one of the stable blocks. It was long and low and dark, with a single window at its end looking out over the street and a tumble of roofs falling towards the Great River. The pot boy lit a fish-oil lantern and uncovered a pitcher of hot water, turned down the blanket and fussed with the bolster on the bed, and then hesitated, clearly reluctant to leave.

'I do not have any small coins,' Yama said, 'but tomorrow I will give you something for your trouble.'

The boy went to the door and looked outside, then closed it and turned to Yama. 'I don't know you, master,' he said, 'but I think I should tell you this, or it'll be on my conscience. You shouldn't stay here tonight.'

'I paid for the room with honest money left on account,' Yama said.

The boy nodded. He wore a clean, much-darned shirt and a pair of breeches. He was half Yama's height and slightly built, with black hair slicked back from a sharp, narrow face. His eyes were large, with golden irises that gleamed in the candlelight. He said, 'I saw the coin you left on trust. I won't ask where you got it, but I reckon it could buy this whole place. My master is not a bad man, but he's not a good man either, if you take my meaning, and there's plenty better that would be tempted by something like that.'

'I will be careful,' Yama said. The truth was that he was tired, and a little dizzy from the beer.

'If there's trouble, you can climb out the window onto the roof,' the boy said. 'On the far side there's a vine that's grown up to the top of the wall. It's an easy climb down. I've done it many times.'

After the boy left, Yama bolted the door and leaned at the open window and gazed out at the vista of roofs and river under the darkening sky, listening to the evening sounds of the city. There was a continual distant roar, the blended noise of millions of people going about their business, and closer at hand the sounds of the neighbourhood: a hawker's cry; a pop ballad playing on a tape recorder; someone hammering metal with quick sure strokes; a woman calling to her children. Yama felt an immense peacefulness and an intense awareness that he was there, alone in that particular place and time with his whole life spread before him, a sheaf of wonderful possibilities.

He took off his shirt and washed his face and arms, then pulled off his boots and washed his feet. The bed had a lumpy mattress stuffed with straw, but the sheets were freshly laundered and the wool blanket was clean. This was probably the pot boy's room, he thought, which was why the boy wanted him to leave.

He intended to rest for a few minutes before getting up to close the shutters, but when he woke it was much later. The cold light of the Galaxy lay on the floor; something made a scratching sound in the rafters above the bed. A mouse or a gecko, Yama thought sleepily, but then he felt a feathery touch in his mind and knew that a machine had flown into the room through the window he had carelessly left open.

Yama wondered sleepily if the machine had woken him, but then there was a metallic clatter outside the door. He sat up, groping for the lantern. Someone pushed at the door and Yama, still stupid with sleep, called out.

The door flew open with a tremendous crash, sending the broken bolt flying across the room. A man stood silhouetted in the broken frame. Yama rolled onto the floor, reaching for his satchel, and something hit the bed. Wood splintered and straw flew into the air. Yama rolled again, dragging his satchel with him. He cut his hand getting his knife out but hardly noticed. The curved blade shone with a fierce blue light and spat fat blue sparks from its point.

The man turned from the bed, a shadow in the blue half-light. He had broken the frame and slashed the mattress to ribbons with the long, broad blade of his sword. Yama threw the pitcher of water at him and he ducked and said, 'Give it up, boy, and maybe you'll live.'

Yama hesitated, and the man struck at him with a sudden fury. Yama ducked and heard the air part above his head, and slashed at the man's legs with the knife, so that he had to step back. The knife howled and Yama felt a sudden coldness in the muscles of his arm.

'You fight like a woman,' the man said. Knife-light flashed on something on his intent face.

Then he drove forward again, and Yama stopped thinking. Reflexes, inculcated in the long hours in the gymnasium under Sergeant Rhodean's stern instruction, took over. Yama's knife was better suited to close fighting than the man's long blade, but the man had the advantage of reach and weight. Yama managed to parry a series of savage, hacking strokes – fountains of sparks spurted at each blow – but the force of the blows numbed his wrist, and then the man's longer blade slid past the guard of Yama's knife and nicked his forearm. The wound was not painful, but it bled copiously and weakened Yama's grip on his knife.

Yama knocked the chair over and, in the moment it took the man to kick it out of the way, managed to get out of the corner into which he had been forced. But the man was still between Yama and the door. In a moment he pressed his attack again, and Yama was driven back against the wall. The knife's blue light blazed and something white and bone-thin stood between Yama and the man, but the man laughed and said, 'I know that trick,' and kicked out, catching Yama's elbow with the toe of his boot. The blow numbed Yama's arm and he dropped the knife. The phantom vanished with a sharp snap.

The man raised his sword for the killing blow. For a moment, it was as if he and Yama stood in a tableau pose. Then the man grunted and let out a long sighing breath that stank of onions and wine fumes, and fell to his knees. He dropped his sword and pawed at his ear, then fell on his face at Yama's feet.

Yama's right arm was numb from elbow to wrist; his left hand was shaking so much that it took him a whole minute to find the lantern and light it with his flint and steel. By its yellow glow he tore strips from the bedsheet and bound the shallow but bloody wound on his forearm and the smaller, self-inflicted gash on his palm. He sat still then, but heard only horses stepping about in the stables below. If anyone had heard the door crash open or the subsequent struggle, which was unlikely given that the other guests would be sleeping on the far side of the courtyard, they were not coming to investigate.

The dead man was the one-eyed cateran who had looked at Yama across the taproom of the inn. Apart from a trickle of dark, venous blood from his right ear he did not appear to be hurt. For a moment, Yama did not understand what had happened. Then the dead man's lips parted and a machine slid out of his mouth and dropped to the floor.

The machine's teardrop shape was covered in blood, and it vibrated with a brisk buzz until it shone silver and clean. Yama held out his left hand and the machine slid up the air and landed lightly on his palm.

'I do not remember asking you for help,' Yama told it, 'but I am grateful.'

The machine had been looking for him; there were many of its kind combing this part of Ys. Yama told it that it should look elsewhere, and that it should broadcast that idea to its fellows, then stepped to the window and held up his hand. The machine rose, circled his head once, and flew straight out into the night.

Yama pulled on his shirt and fastened his boots and set to the distasteful task of searching the dead cateran. The man had no money on him and carried only a dirk with a thin blade and a bone hilt, and a loop of wire with wooden pegs for handles. He supposed that the man would have been paid after he had done his job. The pot boy had been right after all. The landlord wanted both coins.

Yama sheathed his knife and tied the sheath to his belt, then picked up his satchel. He found it suddenly hard to turn his back on the dead man, who seemed to be watching him across the room, so he climbed out of the window sideways.

A stout beam jutted above the window frame; it might once have been a support for a hoist used to lift supplies from the street. Yama grasped the beam with both hands and swung himself once, twice, and on the third swing got his leg over the beam and pulled himself up so that he sat astride it. The wound on his forearm had parted a little, and he retied the bandage. Then it was easy enough to stand on the beam's broad top and pull himself on to the ridge of the roof.

17 ~ The Water Market

The vine was just where the pot boy had said it would be. It was very large and very old – perhaps it had been planted when the inn had been built – and Yama climbed down its stout leafy branches as easily as down a ladder. He knew that he should run, but he also knew that Telmon would not have run. It was a matter of honour to get the coin back, and there in the darkness of the narrow alley at the back of the inn Yama remembered the landlord's duplicitous smile and felt a slow flush of anger.

He was groping his way towards the orange lamplight at the end of the alley when he heard footsteps behind him. For a moment he feared that the cateran's body had been found, and that his friends were searching for his killer. But no cry had been raised, and surely the city was not so wicked that murder would go unremarked. He forced himself not to look back, but walked around the corner and drew his knife and waited in the shadows by the inn's gate, under the wide canopy of the avocado tree.

When the pot boy came out of the alley, Yama pushed him against the wall and held the knife at his throat. 'I don't mean any harm!' the boy squealed. Above them, a parrot echoed his frightened cry, modulating it into a screeching cackle.

Yama took away the knife. The thought came to him that if the one-eyed cateran had crept into the room to cut his throat or use the strangling wire, instead of bursting in with his sword swinging wildly, he, and not the cateran, would now be dead.

'He came for you,' the pot boy said. 'I saw him.'

'He is dead.' Yama sheathed his knife. 'I should have listened to you. As it is, I have killed a man, and your master still has my coin.'

The pot boy fussily straightened his ragged jerkin. He had regained his dignity. He looked up at Yama boldly and said, 'You could call the magistrates.'

'I do not want to get you into trouble, but perhaps you could show me where your master sleeps. If I get back the coin, half of it is yours.'

The boy said, 'Pandaras, at your service, master. For a tenth of it, I'll skewer his heart for you. He beats me, and cheats his customers, and cheats his provisioners and wine merchants, too. You are a brave man, master, but a poor judge of inns. You're on the run, aren't you? That's why you won't call on the magistrates.'

'It is not the magistrates I fear most,' Yama said, thinking of Prefect Corin.

Pandaras nodded. 'Families can be worse than any lock-up, as I know too well.'

'As a matter of fact, I have come here to search for my family.'

'I thought you were from the wrong side of the walls – no one born in the city would openly carry a knife as old and as valuable as yours. I'll bet that dead man in your room was more interested in the knife than your coins. I may not be much more than a street urchin, but I know my way around. If hunting down your family is what you want, why then I can help you in a hundred different ways. I'll be glad to be quit of this place. It never was much of a job anyway, and I'm getting too old for it.'

Yama thought that this pitch was little more than a gentler form of robbery, but said that for the moment he would be glad of the boy's help.

'My master sleeps as soundly as a sated seal,' Pandaras said. 'He won't wake until you put your blade to his throat.'

Pandaras let Yama into the inn through the kitchen door and led him upstairs. He put a finger to his black lips before delicately unlatching a door. Yama's knife emitted a faint blue glow and he held it up like a candle as he stepped into the stuffy room.

The landlord snored under a disarrayed sheet on a huge canopied bed that took up most of the space; there was no other furniture. Yama shook him awake, and the man pushed Yama's hand away and sat up. The sheet slipped down his smooth naked chest to the mound of his belly. When Yama aimed the point of the knife at his face, the man smiled and said, 'Go ahead and kill me. If you don't, I'll probably set the magistrates on you.'

'Then you will have to explain that one of your guests was attacked in his room. There is a dead man up there, by the way.'

The landlord gave Yama a sly look. The knife's blue glow was liquidly reflected in his round, black eyes and glimmered in his spiky white hair. He said, 'Of course there is, or you wouldn't be here. Cyg wasn't working for me, and you can't prove different.'

'Then how did you know his name?'

The landlord's shrug was like a mountain moving. 'Everyone knows Cyg.'

'Then everyone will probably know about the bargain he made with you. Give me my coin and I will leave at once.'

'And if I don't, what will you do? If you kill me you won't find it. Why don't we sit down over a glass of brandy and talk about this sensibly? I could make use of a sharp young cock like you. There are ways to make that coin multiply, and I know most of them.'

'I have heard that you cheat your customers,' Yama said. 'Those who cheat are always afraid that they will be cheated in turn, so I would guess that the only place you could have hidden my coin is somewhere in this room. Probably under your pillow.'

The landlord lunged forward then, and something struck at Yama's knife. The room filled with white light and the landlord screamed.

Afterwards, the landlord huddled against the headboard of his bed and wouldn't look at Yama or the knife. His hand was bleeding badly, for although he had wrapped his sheet around it before grabbing at the knife, the blade had cut him badly. But he took no notice of his wound, or Yama's questions. He was staring at something which had vanished as quickly as it had appeared, and would only say, over and over, 'It had no eyes. Hair like cobwebs, and no eyes.'

Yama searched beneath the bolster and the mattress, and then, remembering the place where he had hidden his map in his own room in the peel-house, rapped the floor with the hilt of his knife until he found the loose board under which the landlord had hidden the gold rial. He had to show the landlord his knife and threaten the return of the apparition to make the man roll onto his belly, so that he could gag him and tie his thumbs together with strips torn from the bedsheet.

'I am only taking back what is mine,' Yama said. 'I do not think you have earned any payment for hospitality. The fool you sent to rob me is dead. Be grateful you are not.'

Pandaras was waiting outside the gate. 'We'll get some breakfast by the fishing docks,' he said. 'The boats go out before first light and the stalls open early.'

Yama showed Pandaras the gold rial. His hand shook. Although he had felt quite calm while looking for the coin, he was now filled with an excess of nervous energy. He laughed and said, 'I have no coin small enough to pay for breakfast.'

Pandaras reached inside his ragged shirt and lifted out two

worn iron pennies hung on a string looped around his neck. He winked. 'I'll pay, master, and then you can pay me.'

'As long as you stop calling me master. You are hardly younger than I am.'

'Oh, in many ways I'm much older,' Pandaras said. 'Forgive me, but you're obviously of noble birth. Such folk live longer than most; relatively speaking, you're hardly weaned from the wet nurse's teat.' He squinted up at Yama as they passed through the orange glow of a sodium vapour lamp. 'Your bloodline isn't one I know, but there are many strange folk downriver of Ys, and many more in her streets. Everything may be found here, it's said, but even if you lived a thousand years and spent all your time searching you'd never find it all. Even if you came to the end of your searching so much would have changed that it would be time to start all over again.'

Yama smiled at the boy's babble. 'It is the truth about my bloodline I have come to discover,' he said, 'and fortunately I think I know where to find it.'

As they descended towards the waterfront, down narrow streets that were sometimes so steep that they were little more than flights of shallow steps, with every house leaning on the shoulder of its neighbour, Yama told Pandaras something of the circumstances of his birth, of what he thought Dr Dismas had discovered, and of his journey to Ys. 'I know the Department of Apothecaries and Chirurgeons,' Pandaras said. 'It's no grand place, but stuck as an afterthought on the lower levels of the Palace of the Memory of the People.'

'Then I must go there after all,' Yama said. 'I thought I had escaped it.'

'The place you want is on the roof,' Pandaras said. 'You won't have to go inside, if that's what's worrying you.'

The sky was beginning to brighten when Yama and Pandaras reached the wide road by the old waterfront. A brace of camels padded past, loaded with bundles of cloth and led by a sleepy boy, and a few merchants were rolling up the shutters of their stalls or lighting cooking fires. On the long piers which ran out to the river's edge between shacks raised on a forest of stilts above the wide mud flats, fishermen were coiling ropes and taking down nets from drying poles and folding them in elaborate pleats.

For the first time, Yama noticed the extent of the riverside shanty town. The shacks crowded all the way to the edge of the floating docks, half a league distant, and ran along the river edge for as far as the eye could see. They were built mostly of plastic sheeting dulled by smoke and weather towards a universal grey, and roofed with tarpaper or sagging canvas. Channels brimming with thick brown water ran between mudbanks under the tangle of stilts and props. Tethered chickens pecked amongst threadbare grass on drier pieces of ground. Already, people were astir, washing clothes or washing themselves, tending tiny cooking fires, exchanging gossip. Naked children of a decad or more different bloodlines chased each other along swaybacked rope walkways.

Pandaras explained that the shanty towns were the home of refugees from the war. 'Argosies go downriver loaded with soldiers, and return with these unfortunates. They are brought here before they can be turned by the heretics.'

'Why do they live in such squalor?'

'They know no better, master. They are unchanged savages.'

'They must have been hunters once, or fishermen or farmers. Is there no room for them in the city? I think that it is much smaller than it once was.'

'Some of them may go to the empty quarters, I suppose, but most would be killed by bandits, and besides, the empty quarters are no good for agriculture. Wherever you dig there are stones, and stones beneath the stones. The Department of Indigenous Affairs likes to keep them in one place, where they can be watched. They get dole food, and a place to live.'

'I suppose many become beggars.'

Pandaras shook his head vigorously. 'No, no. They would be killed by the professional beggars if they tried. They are nothing, master. They are not even human beings. See how they live!'

In the shadows beneath the nearest of the shacks, beside a green, stagnant pool, two naked men were pulling pale guts from the belly of a small cayman. A boy was pissing into the water on the other side of the pool, and a woman was dipping water into a plastic bowl. On a platform above, a woman with a naked baby on her arm was crumbling grey lumps of edible plastic into a blackened wok hung over a tiny fire. Beside her, a child of indeterminate age and sex was listlessly sorting through wilted cabbage leaves.

Yama said, 'It seems to me that they are an army drawn up at the edge of the city.'

'They are nothing, master. We are the strength of the city, as you will see.'

Pandaras chose a stall by one of the wide causeways that ran out to the pontoon docks, and hungrily devoured a shrimp omelette and finished Yama's leavings while Yama warmed his hands around his bowl of tea. In the growing light Yama could see, three or four leagues downriver, the wall where he and Prefect Corin had been taken yesterday, a black line rising above red tile roofs like the back of a sleeping dragon. He wondered if the magistrates' screens could be turned in this direction. No, they had set machines to look for him, but he had dealt with them. For now he was safe.

Pandaras called out for more tea, and told Yama that there was an hour at least before the money changers opened.

Yama said, 'I will make good my debt to you, do not worry. Where will you go?'

'Perhaps with you, master,' Pandaras said, grinning. 'I'll help you find your family. You do not know where you were born, and wish to find it, while I know my birthplace all too well, and want to escape it.'

The boy had small, sharp teeth all exactly the same size. Yama noticed that his black, pointed fingernails were more like claws, and that his hands, with leathery pads on their palms and hooked thumbs stuck stiffly halfway up the wrists, resembled an animal's paws. He had seen many of Pandaras's bloodline yesterday, portering and leading draft animals and carrying out a hundred other kinds of menial jobs. The strength of the city.

Yama asked about the caterans who had been eating in the taproom of the inn, but Pandaras shrugged. 'I don't know them. They arrived only an hour before you, and they'll leave this morning for the Water Market by the Black Temple, looking for people who want to employ them. I thought that you might be one of them, until you showed my master the coin.'

'Perhaps I am one, but do not yet know it,' Yama said, thinking of his vow. He knew that he was still too young to join the army in the usual way, but his age would be no bar to becoming an irregular. Prefect Corin might think him young, but he had already killed a man in close combat, and had had more adventures in the past two decads than most people could expect in a lifetime. He said, 'Before we go anywhere else, take me to the Water Market, Pandaras. I want to see how it is done.'

'If you join up then I'll go with you, and be your squire. You've enough money to buy a good rifle, or better still, a pistol, and you'll need armour, too. I'll polish it bright between battles, and keep your devices clean—'

Yama laughed. 'Hush! You build a whole fantasy on a single whim. I only want to find out about the caterans; I do not yet want to become one. After I know more about where I come from, then, yes, I intend to enlist and help win the war. My brother was killed fighting the heretics. I have made a vow to fight in his place.'

Pandaras drained his cup of tea and spat fragments of bark onto the ground. 'We'll do the first before the Castellan of the Twelve Devotions sounds its noon gun,' he said, 'and the second before the Galaxy rises. With my help, anything is possible. But you must forgive my prattle. My people love to talk and to tell stories, and invent tall tales most of all. No doubt you see us as labourers little better than beasts of burden. And that is indeed how we earn our bread and beer, but although we may be poor in the things of the world, we are rich in the things of imagination. Our stories and songs are told and sung by every bloodline, and a few of us even gain brief fame as jongleurs to the great houses and the rich merchants, or as singers and musicians and storytellers of cassette recordings.'

Yama said, 'It would seem that with all their talents, your people deserve a better station than they have.'

'Ah, but we do not live long enough to profit from them. No more than twenty years is the usual; twenty-five is almost unheard of. You're surprised, but that's how it is. It is our curse and our gift. The swiftest stream polishes the pebbles smoothest, as my grandfather had it, and so with us. We live brief but intense lives, for from the pace of our living comes our songs and stories.'

Yama said, 'Then may I ask how old you are?'

Pandaras showed his sharp teeth. 'You think me your age, I'd guess, but I've no more than four years, and in another I'll marry. That is, if I don't go off adventuring with you.'

'If you could finish my search in a day, I would be the happiest man on Confluence, but I think it will take longer than that.'

'A white boat and a shining woman, and a picture of one of your ancestors made before the building of Confluence. What could be more distinctive? I'll make a song of it soon enough. Besides, you said that you know to begin your search in the records of the Department of Apothecaries and Chirurgeons.'

'If Dr Dismas did not lie. He lied about much else.'

The sky above the crowded rooftops was blue now, and

traffic was thickening along the road. Fishing boats were moving out past the ends of the piers of the floating docks, their russet and tan sails bellying in the wind and white birds flying in their wake as they breasted the swell of the morning tide. As he walked beside Pandaras, Yama thought of the hundred leagues of docks, of the thousands of boats of the vast fishing fleets which put out every day to feed the myriad mouths of the city, and began to understand the true extent of Ys.

How could he ever expect to find out about his birth, or of the history of any one man, in such a mutable throng? And yet, he thought, Dr Dismas had found out something in the records of his department, and he did not doubt that he could find it too, and perhaps more. Freshly escaped from his adventure with the cateran and from the fusty fate the Aedile and Prefect Corin had wished upon him, Yama felt his heart rise. It did not occur to him that he might fail in his self-appointed quest. He was, as Pandaras had pointed out, still very young, and had yet to fail in anything important.

The first money changer refused Yama's rials after a mere glance. The second, whose office was in a tiny basement with a packed dirt floor and flaking pink plaster walls, spent a long time looking at the coins under a magnifying screen, then scraped a fleck from one coin and tried to dissolve it in a minim of aqua regia. The money changer was a small, scrawny old man almost lost in the folds of his black silk robe. He clucked to himself when the fleck of gold refused to dissolve even when he heated the watchglass, then motioned to his impassive bodyguard, who fetched out tea bowls and a battered aluminium pot, and resumed his position at the foot of the steps up to the street.

Pandaras haggled for an hour with the money changer, over several pots of tea and a plate of tiny honeycakes so piercingly sweet that they made Yama's teeth ache. Yama felt cramped and anxious in the dank little basement, with the tramp of feet going to and fro overhead and the bodyguard blocking most of the sunlight that spilled down the stair, and was relieved when at last Pandaras announced that the deal was done.

'We'll starve in a month, but this old man has a stone for a heart,' he said, staring boldly at the money changer.

'You are quite welcome to take your custom elsewhere,' the money changer said, thrusting his sharp face from the fold of black silk over his head and giving Pandaras a fierce, hawkish look. 'I'd say your coins were stolen, and any price I give you would be fair enough. As it is, I risk ruining my reputation on your behalf.'

'You'll not need to work again for a year,' Pandaras retorted. Despite the money changer's impatience, he insisted on counting the slew of silver and iron coins twice over. The iron pennies were pierced – for stringing around the neck, Pandaras said. He demonstrated the trick with his share before shaking hands with the money changer, who suddenly smiled and wished them every blessing of the Preservers.

The street was bright and hot after the money changer's basement. The road was busier than ever, and the traffic crowding its wide asphalt pavement moved at walking pace. The air was filled with the noise of hooves and wheels, the shouts and curses of drivers, the cries of hawkers and merchants, the silver notes of whistles and the brassy clangour of bells. Small boys darted amongst the legs of beasts and men, collecting the dung of horses, oxen and camels, which they would shape into patties and dry on walls for fuel for cooking fires. There were beggars and thieves, skyclad mendicants and palmers, jugglers and contortionists, mountebanks and magicians, and a thousand other wonders, so many that as he walked along amongst the throng Yama soon stopped noticing any but the most outrageous, for else he would have gone mad with wonder.

A black dome had been raised up amongst the masts of the ships and the flat roofs of the godowns at the edge of the river, and Yama pointed to it. 'That was not there when we first came here this morning,' he said.

'A voidship,' Pandaras said casually, and expressed surprise when Yama insisted that they go and look at it. He said, 'It's just a lighter for a voidship really. The ship to which it belongs is too big to make riverfall and hangs beyond the edge of Confluence. It has been there a full year now, unloading its ores. The lighter will have put in at the docks for fresh food. It's nothing special.'

In any case, they could not get close to the lighter; the dock was closed off and guarded by a squad of soldiers armed with fusiliers more suited to demolishing a citadel than keeping away sightseers. Yama looked up at the lighter's smooth black flank, which curved up to a blunt silver cap that shone with white fire in the sunlight, and wondered at what other suns it had seen. He could have stood there all day, filled with an undefined longing, but Pandaras took his arm and steered him away.

'It's dangerous to linger,' the boy said. 'The star-sailors steal children, it's said, because they cannot engender their own. If you see one, you'll understand. Most do not even look like men.'

As they walked on, Yama asked if Pandaras knew of the ship of the Ancients of Days.

Pandaras touched his fist to his throat. 'My grandfather said that he saw two of them walking through the streets of our quarter late one night, but everyone in Ys alive at that time claims as much.' He touched his fist to his throat and added, 'My grandfather said that they glowed the way the river water sometimes glows on summer nights, and that they stepped into the air and walked away above the rooftops. He made a song about it, but when he submitted it to the legates he was arrested for heresy, and he died under the question.'

The sun had climbed halfway to zenith by the time Yama and Pandaras reached the Black Temple and the Water

Market. The Black Temple had once been extensive, built on its own island around a protrusion or plug of keelrock in a wide deep bay, but it had been devastated in the wars of the Age of Insurrection and had not been rebuilt, and now the falling level of the Great River had left it stranded in a shallow muddy lagoon fringed with palm trees. The outline of the temple's inner walls and a row of half-melted pillars stood amongst outcrops of keelrock and groves of flame trees; the three black circles of the temple's shrines glittered amongst grassy swales where the narthex had once stood. Nothing could destroy the shrines, not even the energies deployed in the battle which had won back Ys from the Insurrectionists, for they were only partly of the world of material existence. Services were still held at the Black Temple every New Year, Pandaras said, and Yama noticed the heaps of fresh flowers and offerings of fruits before the shrines. Although most of the avatars had disappeared in the Age of Insurrection, and the last had been silenced by the heretics, people still came to petition them.

At the mouth of the bay which surrounded the temple's small island, beyond wrinkled mudflats where flocks of white ibis stalked on delicate legs, on rafts and pontoons and barges, the Water Market was in full swing. The standards of a hundred condottieri flew from poles, and there were a dozen exhibition duels under way, each at the centre of a ring of spectators. There were stalls selling every kind of weapon, armourers sweating naked by their forges as they repaired or reforged pieces, provisioners extolling the virtue of their preserved fare. A merchant blew up a water bottle and jumped up and down on it to demonstrate its durability. Newly indentured convicts sat in sullen groups on benches behind the auction block, most sporting fresh mutilations. Galleys, pinnaces and picket boats stood offshore, their masts hung with bright flags that flapped in the strong, hot breeze.

Yama eagerly drank in the bustle and the noise, the exotic costumes of the caterans and the mundane dove-grey uniforms of regular soldiers mingled together, the ringing sound of the weapons of the duellists, and the smell of hot metal and plastic from the forges of the armourers. He wanted to see everything the city had to offer, to search its great temples and the meanest of its alleys and courts for any sign of his bloodline.

As he followed Pandaras along a rickety gangway between two rafts, someone stepped out of the crowd and hailed him. His heart turned over. It was the red-haired woman who last night had sat eating with the man he had killed. When she saw that he had heard her, she shouted again and raised her naked sword above her head.

18 ~ The Thing in the Bottle

'They are yours by right of arms,' Tamora, the red-haired cateran, said. 'The sword is too long for you, but I know an armourer who can shorten and rebalance it so sweetly you'd swear afterwards that's how it was first forged. The corselet and the greaves can be cut down to suit, and you can sell the trimmings. That way it pays for itself. Old armour is expensive because it's the best. Especially plastic armour, because no one knows how to make the stuff any more. You might think my breastplate is new, but that's only because I polished it this morning. It's a thousand years old if it's a day, but even if it's better than most of the clag they make these days, it's still only steel. But, see, these greaves are real old. I could have taken them, but that wouldn't be right. Everyone says we're vagabonds and thieves, but even if we don't belong to any department, we have our traditions. So these are your responsibility now. You won them by right of arms. You can do what you want with them. Throw them in the river if you want, but it would be a fucking shame if you did.'

'She wants you to give them back to her as a reward for giving them to you,' Pandaras said.

'I talk to the master,' Tamora said, 'not his fool.'

Pandaras struck an attitude. 'I am his squire.'

'I was the fool,' Yama said to Tamora, 'and because I was a fool your friend died. That is why I cannot take his things.'

Tamora shrugged. 'Cyg was no friend of mine, and as far as I'm concerned he was the fool, getting himself killed by a scrap of a thing like you. Why, you're so newly hatched you probably still have eggshell stuck to your back.'

Pandaras said, 'If this is to be your career, then you must arm yourself properly, master. As your squire, I strongly suggest it.'

'Squire, is it?' Tamora cracked open another oyster with her strong, ridged fingernails, slurped up the flesh and wiped her mouth with the back of her hand. The cateran's bright red hair, which Yama suspected was dyed, was cut short over her skull, with a long fringe in the back that fell to her shoulders. She wore her steel breastplate over a skirt made of leather strips and a mesh shirt which left her muscular arms bare. There was a tattoo of a bird sitting on a nest of flames on the tawny skin of her upper arm, the flames in red ink, the bird, its wings outstretched as if drying them in the fire which was consuming it, in blue.

They were sitting in the shade of an umbrella at a table by a food stall on the waterfront, near the causeway that led from the shore to the island of the Black Temple. It was sunstruck noon. The owner of the stall was sitting under the awning by the ice-chest, listening with half-closed eyes to a long antiphonal prayer burbling from the cassette recorder under his chair.

Tamora squinted against the silver light that burned off the wet mudflats. She had a small, triangular, feral face, with green eyes and a wide mouth that stretched to the hinges of her jaw. Her eyebrows were a single brick-red rope; now the rope dented in the middle and she said, 'Caterans don't have squires. That's for regular officers, and their squires are appointed from the common ranks. This boy has leeched onto you, Yama. I'll get rid of him if you want.'

Yama said, 'It is just a joke between the two of us.'

'I *am* his squire,' Pandaras insisted. 'My master is of noble birth. He deserves a train of servants, but I'm so good he needs no other.'

Yama laughed.

Tamora squinted at Pandaras. 'You people are all the same to me, like fucking rats running around underfoot, but I could swear you're the pot boy of the crutty inn where I stayed the night.' She told Yama, 'If I was more suspicious, I might suspect a plot.'

'If there was a plot, it was between your friend and the landlord of the inn.'

'Grah. I suspected as much. If I survive my present job, and there's no reason why I shouldn't, then I'll have words with that rogue. More than words, in fact.'

Tamora's usual expression was a sullen, suspicious pout, but when she smiled her face came to life, as if a mask had suddenly dropped, or the sun had come out from behind a cloud. She smiled now, as if at the thought of her revenge. Her upper incisors were long and stout and sharply pointed.

Yama said, 'He did not profit from his treachery.'

Pandaras kicked him under the table and frowned.

Tamora said, 'I'm not after your fucking money, or else I would have taken it already. I have just now taken on a new job, so be quick in making up your mind on how you'll dispose of what is due to you by right of arms. As I said before, you can throw it in the river or leave it for the scavengers if you want, but it's good gear.'

Yama picked up the sword. Its broad blade was iron and had seen a lot of use. Its nicked edge was razor sharp. The hilt was wound with bronze wire; the pommel an unornamented plastic ball, chipped and dented. He held the blade up before his face, then essayed a few passes. The cut on his forearm stickily parted under the crude bandage he had tied and he put the sword down. No one sitting at the tables around the stall had looked at the display, although he had hoped that they would.

He said, 'I have a knife that serves me well enough, and

the sword is made for a strong unsubtle man more used to hewing wood than fighting properly. Find a woodsman and give it to him, although I suspect he would rather keep his axe. But I will take the armour. As you say, old armour is the best.'

'Well, at least you know something about weapons,' Tamora said grudgingly. 'Are you here looking for hire? If so, I'll give some advice for free. Come back tomorrow, early. That's when the best jobs are available. Condottieri like a soldier who can rise early.'

'I had thought to watch a duel or two,' Yama said.

'Grah. Exhibition matches between oiled corn-fed oafs who wouldn't last a minute in real battle. Do you think we fight with swords against the fucking heretics? The matches draw people who would otherwise not come, that's all. They get drunk with recruiting sergeants and the next day find themselves indentured in the army, with a hangover and the taste of the oath like a copper penny in their mouth.'

'I am not here to join the army. Perhaps I will become a cateran eventually, but not yet.'

'He's looking for his people,' Pandaras said.

It was Yama's turn to kick under the table. It was green-painted tin, with a bamboo and paper umbrella. He said, 'I am looking for certain records in one of the departmental libraries.'

Tamora swallowed the last oyster and belched. 'Then sign up with the department. Better still, join the fucking archivists. After ten years' apprenticeship you might just be sent to the Palace of the Memory of the People; more likely you'll be sent to listen to the stories of unchanged toads squatting in some mudhole. But that's a better chance than trying to bribe your way into their confidence. They're a frugal lot, and besides, if any one of them was caught betraying his duty he'd be executed on the spot. The same penalty applies to any who try to bribe them. Those records are all that remains of the dead, kept until they're resurrected at the end of time. It's serious shit to even look at them the wrong way.'

'The Puranas say that the Preservers need no records, for at the end of time an infinite amount of energy becomes available. In the last instant as the Universe falls into itself all is possible, and everyone who ever lived or ever could have lived will live again for ever, in that eternal now. Besides, the records I am looking for are not in the Palace of the Memory of the People, but in the archives of the Department of Apothecaries and Chirurgeons.'

'That's more or less the same place. On the roof rather than inside, that's all.'

'Just as I told you, master,' Pandaras said. 'You don't need her to show you what I already know!'

Tamora ignored him. 'Their records are maintained by archivists, too. Unless you're a sawbones or a sawbones' runner, you can forget about it. It's the same in all the departments. The truth is expensive and difficult to keep pure, and so getting at it without proper authority is dangerous.' Tamora smiled. 'But that doesn't mean that there aren't ways of getting at it.'

Pandaras said, 'She is baiting a hook. Be careful.'

Yama said to Tamora, 'Tell me this. You have fought against the heretics – that is what the tattoo on your arm implies, anyway. In all your travels, have you ever seen any other men and women like me?'

'I fought in two campaigns, and in the last I was so badly wounded that I took a year recovering. When I'm fit I'll go again. It's better pay than bodyguard or pickup work, and more honourable, although honour has little to do with it when you're there. No, I haven't seen anyone like you, but it doesn't signify. There are ten thousand bloodlines on Confluence, not counting all those hill tribes of indigens, who are little more than animals.'

'Then you see how hard I must search,' Yama said.

Tamora smiled. It seemed to split her face in half. 'How much will you pay?'

'Master—'

'All I have. I changed two gold rials for smaller coins this morning. It is yours, if you help me.'

Pandaras whistled and looked up at the blue sky.

'Grah. Against death, that is not so much.'

Yama said, 'Do they guard the records with men, or with machines?'

'Why, mostly machines of course. As I said, the records of any department are important. Even the poorest departments guard their archives carefully – often their archives are all they have left.'

'Well, it might be easier than you suppose.'

Tamora stared at Yama. He met her luminous green gaze and for a long moment the rest of the world melted away. Her pupils were vertical slits edged with closely crowded dots of golden pigment that faded to copper at the periphery. Yama imagined drowning in that green-gold gaze, as a luckless fisherman might drown in the Great River's flood. It was the heart-stopping gaze that a predator turns upon its prey.

Tamora's voice said from far away, 'Before I help you, if I do help you, you must prove yourself.'

Yama said faintly, 'How?'

'Don't trust her,' Pandaras said. 'If she really wanted the job, she'd have asked for all your money. There are plenty like her. If we threw a stone in any direction, we'd hit at least two.'

Tamora said, 'In a way, you owe it to me.'

Yama was still looking into Tamora's gaze. He said, 'Cyg was going to partner you, I think. Now I know why you came here. You were not looking for me, but for a replacement. Well, what would you have me do?'

Tamora pointed over his shoulder. He turned, and saw the black, silver-capped dome of the voidship lighter rising beyond the flame trees of the island of the Black Temple. The cateran said, 'We have to bring back a star-sailor who jumped ship.'

They sold the sword to an armourer for rather more than Yama expected, and left the corselet and the greaves with the same man to be cut down. Tamora insisted that Yama get his wounds treated by one of the leeches who had set up their stalls near the duelling arena, and Yama sat and watched two men fence with chainsaws ('Showboat juggling,' Tamora sneered) while the cut on his forearm was stitched, painted with blue gel and neatly bandaged. The shallow cut on Yama's palm should be left to heal on its own, the leech said, but Tamora made him bandage it anyway, saying that the bandage would help Yama grip his knife. She bought Pandaras a knife with a long thin round blade and a fingerguard chased with a chrysanthemum flower; it was called a kidney puncher.

'Suitable for sneaking up on someone in the dark,' Tamora said. 'If you stand on tiptoe, rat-boy, you should be able to reach someone's vitals with this.'

Pandaras flexed the knife's blade between two clumsy, clawed fingers, licked it with his long, pink tongue, then tucked it in his belt. Yama told him, 'You do not have to follow me. I killed the man who would have helped her, and it is only proper that I should take his place. But there is no need for you to come.'

'Well put,' Tamora said.

Pandaras showed his small sharp teeth. 'Who else would watch your back, master? Besides, I have never been aboard a voidship.'

One of the guards escorted them across the wharf to the voidship lighter. Cables and flexible plastic hoses lay everywhere, like a tangle of basking snakes. Labourers, nearly naked in the hot sunlight, were winching a cavernous pipe towards an opening which had dilated in the lighter's black hull. An ordinary canvas and bamboo gangway angled up to a smaller entrance.

Yama felt a distinct pressure sweep over his skin as, following Tamora up the gangway, he ducked beneath the port's rim. Inside, a passageway sloped away to the left, curving as it rose so that its end could not be seen. Yama supposed that it spiralled around the inside of the hull of the lighter like the track a maggot leaves in a fruit. It was circular in cross-section, and lit by a soft directionless red light that seemed to hang in the air like smoke. Although the lighter's black hull radiated the day's heat, inside it was as chilly as the mountain garden of the curators of the City of the Dead.

A guard waited inside. He was a short, thickset man with a bland face and a broad, humped back. His head was shaven, and ugly red scars criss-crossed his scalp. He wore a many-pocketed waistcoat and loose-fitting trousers, and did not appear to be armed. He told them to keep to the middle of the passageway, not to touch anything, and not to talk to any voices which might challenge them.

'I've been here before,' Tamora said. She seemed subdued in the red light and the chill air of the passageway.

'I remember you,' the guard said, 'and I remember a man with only one eye, but I do not remember your companions.'

'My original partner ran into something unexpected. But I'm here, as I said I would be, and I vouch for these two. Lead on. This place is like a tomb.'

'It is older than any tomb,' the guard said.

They climbed around two turns of the passageway. Groups of coloured lights were set at random in the black stuff which sheathed the walls and ceiling and floor. The floor gave softly beneath Yama's boots, and there was a faint vibration in the red-lit air, so low-pitched that he felt it more in his bones than in his ears.

The guard stopped and pressed his palm against the wall, and the black stuff puckered and pulled back with a grating noise. Ordinary light flooded through the orifice, which opened onto a room no more than twenty paces across and ringed round with a narrow window that looked out across the roofs of the city in one direction and the glittering expanse of the Great River in the other. Irregular clusters of coloured lights depended from the ceiling like stalactites in a cave, and a thick-walled glass bottle hung from the ceiling in the middle of the clusters of lights, containing some kind of red and white blossom in turgid liquid

Yama whispered to Tamora, 'Where is the captain?'

He had read several of the old romances in the library of the peel-house, and expected a tall man in a crisp, archaic uniform, with sharp, bright eyes focused on the vast distances between stars, and skin tanned black with the fierce light of alien suns.

Pandaras snickered, but fell silent when the guard looked at him.

The guard said, 'There is no captain except when the crew meld, but the pilot of this vessel will talk with you.'

Tamora said, 'The same one I talked with two days ago?'

'Does it matter?' the guard said. He pulled a golden circlet from one of his pockets and set it on his scarred scalp. At once, his body stiffened. His eyes blinked, each to a different rhythm, and his mouth opened and closed.

Tamora stepped up to him and said, 'Do you know who I am?'

The guard's mouth hung open. Spittle looped between his lips. His tongue writhed behind his teeth like a wounded snake and his breath came out as a hiss that slowly shaped itself into a word.

'Yessss.'

Pandaras nudged Yama and indicated the bottled blossom with a crooked thumb. 'There's the star-sailor,' he said. 'It's talking through the guard.'

Yama looked more closely at the thing inside the bottle. What he had thought were fleshy petals of some exotic flower were the lobes of a mantle that bunched around a core woven of pink and grey filaments. Feathery gills rich with red blood waved slowly to and fro in the thick liquid in which they were suspended. It was a little like a squid, but instead of tentacles it had white, many-branching fibres that disappeared into the base of its bottle.

Pandaras whispered, 'Nothing but a nervous system. That's why it needs puppets.'

The guard jerked his head around and stared at Yama and Pandaras. His eyes were no longer blinking at different rates, but the pupil of the left eye was much bigger than that of the right. Speaking with great effort, as if forcing the words around pebbles lodged in his throat, he said, 'You told me you would bring only one other.'

Tamora said, 'The taller one, yes. But he has brought his . . . servant.'

Pandaras stepped forward and bowed low from the waist. 'I am Yama's squire. He is a perfect master of fighting. Only this night past he killed a man, an experienced fighter better armed than he, who thought to rob him while he slept.'

The star-sailor said through its puppet, 'I have not seen the bloodline for a long time, but you have chosen well. He has abilities you will find useful.'

Yama stared at the thing in the bottle, shocked to the core.

Tamora said, 'Is that so?'

'I scanned all of you when you stepped aboard. This one—' the guard slammed his chest with his open hand '—will see to the contract, following local custom. It will be best to return with the whole body, but if it is badly damaged then you must bring a sample of tissue. A piece the size of your smallest finger will be sufficient. You remember what I told you.'

Yama said, 'Wait. You know my bloodline?'

Tamora ignored him. She closed her eyes and recited, ' "It will be lying close to the spine. The host must be mutilated to obliterate all trace of occupation. Burn it if possible."' She opened her eyes. 'Suppose we're caught? What do we tell the magistrates?'

'If you are caught by your quarry, you will not live to tell the magistrates anything.'

'He'll know you sent us.'

'And we will send others, if you fail. I trust you will not.'

'You know my bloodline,' Yama said. 'How do you know my bloodline?'

Pandaras said, 'We aren't the first to try this, are we?'

'There was one attempt before,' Tamora said. 'It failed. That is why we're being so well paid.'

The guard said, 'If you succeed.'

'Grah. You say I have a miracle worker with me. Of course we'll succeed.'

The guard was groping for the circlet on his head. Yama said quickly, 'No! I want you to tell me how you know my bloodline!'

The guard's head jerked around. 'We thought you all dead,' he said, and pulled the circlet from his scalp. He fell to his knees and retched up a mouthful of yellow bile which was absorbed by the black floor, then got to his feet and wiped his mouth on the sleeve of his tunic. He said in his own voice, 'Was it agreed?'

Tamora said, 'You'll make the contract, and we put our thumbs to it.'

'Outside,' the guard said.

Yama said, 'He knew who I was! I must talk with him!'

The guard got between Yama and the bottled star-sailor. He said, 'Perhaps when you return.'

'We should get started straight away,' Tamora said. 'It's a long haul to the estate.'

The door ground open. Yama looked at the star-sailor in its bottle, and said, 'I will return, and with many questions.'

19 ~ Iachimo

When the giant guard went past the other side of the gate for the third time, Tamora said, 'Every four hundred heartbeats. You could boil an egg by him.'

She lay beside Yama and Pandaras under a clump of thorny bushes in the shadows beyond the fierce white glare of a battery of electric arc lamps that crackled at the top of the wall. The gate was a square lattice of steel bars set in a high wall of fused rock, polished as smoothly as black glass. The wall stretched away into the darkness on either side, separated from the dry scrub by a wide swathe of barren sandy soil.

Yama said, 'I still think we should go over the wall somewhere else. The rest of the perimeter cannot be as heavily guarded as the gate.'

'The gate is heavily guarded because it's the weakest part of the wall,' Tamora said. 'That's why we're going in through it. The guard is a man. Doesn't look it, but he is. He decides who to let in and who to keep out. Elsewhere, the guards will be machines or dogs. They'll kill without thinking and do it so quick you won't know it until you find yourself in the hands of the Preservers. Listen. After the guard goes past again, I'll climb the wall, kill him, and open the gates to let you in.'

'If he raises the alarm—'

'He won't have time for that,' Tamora said, and showed her teeth.

'Those won't do any good against armour,' Pandaras said. 'They'll snap off your head if you don't swallow your tongue. Be quiet. This is warrior work.'

They were all tired and on edge. It had been a long journey from the waterfront. Although they had travelled most of the distance in a public calash, they had had to walk the final three leagues. The merchant's estate was at the top of one of a straggling range of hills that, linked by steep scrub-covered ridges, rose like worn teeth at the edge of the city's wide basin. An age ago, the hills had been part of the city. As Yama, Tamora and Pandaras had climbed through dry, fragrant pine woods, they had stumbled upon an ancient paved street and the remains of the buildings which had once lined it. They had rested there until just after sunset. Yama and Pandaras had eaten the raisin cakes they had bought hours before, while Tamora had prowled impatiently amongst the ruins, wolfing strips of dried meat and snicking off the fluffy seeding heads of fireweed with her rapier.

The merchant who owned the estate was a star-sailor who had jumped ship the last time it had lain off the edge of Confluence, over forty years ago. He had amassed his wealth by surreptitious deployment of technologies whose use was forbidden outside the voidships. For that alone, quite apart from the crime of desertion, he had been sentenced to death by his crewmates, but they had no jurisdiction outside their ship and, because of the same laws which the merchant had violated, could not use their powers to capture him.

Tamora was the second cateran hired to carry out the sentence. The first had not returned, and was presumed to have been killed by the merchant's guards. Yama thought that this put them at a disadvantage, since the merchant would be expecting another attack, but Tamora said it made no difference.

'He has been expecting this ever since his old ship returned. That's why he has retreated to this estate, which has better defences than the compound he maintains in the city. We're lucky there aren't patrols outside the walls.'

In fact, Yama had already asked several machines to ignore them as they had toiled up the hill through the pine woods, but he did not point this out. There was an advantage in being able to do something no one suspected was possible. He already owed his life to this ability, and it was to his benefit to have Tamora believe that he had killed the cateran by force of arms rather than by lucky sleight of hand.

Now, crouched between Tamora and Pandaras in the dry brush, Yama could faintly sense other machines beyond the high black wall, but they were too far away to count, let alone influence. He was dry-mouthed, and his hands had a persistent uncontrollable tremor. All his adventures with Telmon had been childhood games without risk, inadequate preparation for the real thing. His suggestion to try another part of the wall was made as much from the need to delay the inevitable as to present an alternative strategy.

Pandaras said, 'I have an idea. Master, lend me your satchel, and that book you were reading.'

Tamora said fiercely, 'Do as I say. No more, no less.'

'I can have the guard open the gates for me,' Pandaras said. 'Or would you rather break your teeth on steel bars?'

'If you insist that we have to go through the gate,' Yama told Tamora, as he emptied out his satchel, 'at least we should listen to his idea.'

'Grah. Insist? I *tell* you what to do, and you do it. This is not a democracy. Wait!'

But Pandaras stood up and, with Yama's satchel slung around his neck, stepped out into the middle of the asphalt road which ran through the gateway. Tamora hissed in frustration as the boy walked into the glare of the arc lights, and Yama told her, 'He is cleverer than you think.'

'He'll be dead in a moment, clever or not.'

Pandaras banged on the gate. A bell trilled in the distance

and dogs barked closer at hand. Yama said, 'Did you know there were dogs?'

'Grah. Dogs are nothing. It is easy to kill dogs.'

Yama was not so sure. Any one of the watchdogs of the peel-house could bring down an ox by clamping its powerful jaws on the windpipe of its victim and strangling it – and to judge by the volume and ferocity of the barking there were at least a dozen dogs beyond the gate.

The guard appeared on the other side of the gate. In his augmented armour, painted scarlet as if dipped in fresh blood, he was more than twice Pandaras's height. His eyes were red embers that glowed in the shadow beneath the bill of his flared helmet. Energy pistols mounted on his shoulders trained their muzzles on Pandaras and the guard's amplified bass voice boomed and echoed in the gateway.

Pandaras stood his ground. He held up the satchel and opened it and showed it to the guard, then took out the book and flipped through its pages in an exaggerated pantomime. The guard reached through the gate's steel lattice, his arm extending more than a man's arm should reach, but Pandaras danced backwards and put the book back in the satchel and folded his arms and shook his head from side to side.

The guard conferred with himself in a booming mutter of subsonics; then the red dots of his eyes brightened and a bar of intense red light swept up and down Pandaras. The red light winked out and with a clang the gate sprang open a fraction. Pandaras slipped through the gap. The gate slammed shut behind him and he followed the monstrously tall guard into the shadows beyond.

'He's brave, your fool,' Tamora remarked, 'but he's even more of a fool than I thought possible.'

'Let us wait and see,' Yama said, although he did not really believe that the pot boy could do anything against the armoured giant. He was as astonished as Tamora when, a few minutes later, the dogs began to bark again, the gate clanged open, and Pandaras appeared in the gap and beckoned to them.

The giant guard sprawled on his belly in the roadway a little way beyond the gate. His helmet was turned to one side, and one of his arms was twisted behind him, as if he was trying to reach something on his back. Yama knew that the guard was dead, but he could feel a glimmer of machine intelligence in the man's skull, as if something still lived there, gazing with furious impotence through its host's dead eyes.

Pandaras returned Yama's satchel with a flourish, and Yama stuffed his belongings into it. Tamora kicked the guard's scarlet cuirass, then turned on Pandaras.

'Tell me how you did it later,' she said. 'Now we must silence the dogs. You're lucky they weren't set on you.'

Pandaras calmly stared up at her. 'A harmless messenger like me?'

'Don't be so fucking cute.'

'Let me deal with the dogs,' Yama said.

'Be quick,' Pandaras said. 'Before I killed him, the guard sent for someone to escort me to the house.'

The dogs were baying loudly, and other dogs answered them from distant parts of the grounds. Yama found the kennel to the left of the gate, cut into the base of the wall. Several dogs thrust their snouts through the kennel's barred door with such ferocity that their skull caps and the machines embedded in their shoulders struck sparks from the iron bars. They howled and whined and snapped in a ferocious tumult, and it took Yama several minutes to calm them down to a point where he could ask them to speak with their fellows and assure them that nothing was wrong.

'Go to sleep,' he told the dogs, once they had passed on the message, and then he ran back to the road.

Tamora and Pandaras had rolled the guard under the partial cover of a stand of moonflower bushes beside the road. Tamora had stripped the guard's heavy pistols from their shoulder mountings. She handed one to Yama and showed him how to press two contact plates together to make it fire.

'I should have one of those,' Pandaras said. 'Right of arms, and all that.'

Tamora showed her teeth. 'You killed a man in full powered armour twice your height and armed with both of these pistols. I'd say you are dangerous enough with that kidney puncher I chose for you. Follow me, if you can!'

She threw herself into the bushes, and Yama and Pandaras ran after her, thrashing through drooping branches laden with white, waxy blossoms. Tamora and Pandaras quickly outpaced Yama, but Pandaras could not sustain his initial burst of speed and Yama soon caught up with him. The boy was leaning against the trunk of a cork oak, watching the dark stretch of grass beyond while he tried to get his breath back.

'She has the blood rage,' Pandaras said, when he could speak again. 'No sense in chasing after her.'

Yama saw a string of lights burning far off through a screen of trees on the far side of the wide lawn. He began to walk in that direction, with Pandaras trotting at his side.

Yama said, 'Will you tell me how you killed the guard? I might need the trick myself.'

'How did you calm the watchdogs?'

'Do you always answer a question with a question?'

'We say that what you know makes you what you are. So you should never be free with what you know, or strangers will take pieces of you until nothing is left.'

'Nothing is free in this city, it seems.'

'Only the Preservers know everything, master. Everyone else must pay or trade for information. How did you calm the dogs?'

'We have similar dogs at home. I know how to talk to them.'

'Perhaps you'll teach me that trick when we have time.'

'I am not sure if that is possible, Pandaras, but I suppose that I can try. How did you get through the gate and kill the guard?'

'I showed him your book. I saw you reading in it when we rested in the ruins. It's very old, and therefore very valuable. My former master—' Pandaras spat on the clipped grass '—and that stupid cateran you killed would have taken the gold rials and left the book, but my mother's family deals in books, and I know a little about them. Enough to know that it is worth more than the money. I talked with someone through the guard, and they let me in. The rich often collect books. There is power in them.'

'Because of the knowledge they contain.'

'You're catching on. As for killing the guard, it was no trick. I'll tell you how I did it now, master, and you must tell me something later. The guard seemed a giant, but he was an ordinary man inside that armour. Without power, he could not move a step; with it, he could sling a horse over his shoulders and still run as fast as a deer. I jumped onto his back, where he couldn't reach me, and pulled the cable that connected the power supply to the muscles in his armour. Then I stuck my knife in the gap where the cable went in, and pierced his spinal cord. A trick one of my stepbrothers taught me. The family of my mother's third husband work in a foundry that refurbishes armour. I helped out there when I was a kit. You get to know the weak points that way – they're where mending is most needed. Do we have to go so fast?'

'Where is the house, Pandaras?'

'This man is rich, but he is not one of the old trading families, who have estates upriver of the city. So he has a compound by the docks where he does his business, and this estate in the hills on the edge of the city. That is why the wall is so high and strong, and why there are many guards. They all fear bands of robbers out here, and arm their men as if to fight off a cohort.'

Yama nodded. 'The country beyond is very wild. It used to be part of the city, I think.'

'No one lives there. No one important, anyhow. The robbers come from the city.'

'The law is weaker here, then?'

'Stronger, master, if you fall foul of it. The rich make their own laws. For ordinary people, it's the magistrates who decide right and wrong. Isn't that how it was where you come from?'

Yama thought of the Aedile, and of the militia. He said, 'More or less. Then the house will be fortified. Sheer force of arms might not be the best way to try and enter it.'

'Fortified and hidden. That's the fashion these days. We could wander around for a day and not find it. Those lights are probably where the servants live, or a compound for other guards.' Pandaras stopped to untangle the unravelling edge of his sleeve from the thorny canes of a bush. 'If you ask me, this crutty greenery is all part of the defences.'

Yama said, 'There is a path through there. Perhaps that will lead to the house.'

'If it was that simple, we'd all be rich, and have big houses of our own, neh? It probably leads to a pit full of caymans or snakes.'

'Well, someone is coming along it, anyway. Here.'

Yama gave the pistol to Pandaras. It was so heavy that the boy needed both hands to hold it. 'Wait,' he said, 'you can't—'

But Yama ran towards the lights and the sound of hooves, carried by a rush of exhilaration. It was better to act than to hide, he thought, and in that moment understood why Tamora had charged off so recklessly. As he ran, he took the book from his satchel; when lights swooped towards him through the dark air, he stopped and held it up. A triplet of machines spun to a halt above his head and bathed him in a flood of white light. Yama squinted through their radiance at the three riders who had pulled up at the edge of the road.

Two guards in plastic armour reined in their prancing mounts and levelled light lances at him. The third was a mild old man on a grey palfrey. He wore a plain black tunic and his long white hair was brushed back from the narrow blade of his face. His skin was yellow and very smooth, stretched tautly over high cheekbones and a tall, ridged brow.

Yama held the book higher. The white-haired man said, 'Why aren't you waiting at the gate?'

'The guard was attacked, and I got scared and ran. Thieves have been after what I carry ever since I have come to this city. Only last night I had to kill a man who wanted to steal from me.'

The white-haired man jogged his palfrey so that it stepped sideways towards Yama, and he leaned down to peer at the book. He said, 'I can certainly see why someone would want to steal this.'

'I have been told that it is very valuable.'

'Indeed.' The white-haired man stared at Yama for a full minute. The two guards watched him, although their lances were still pointed at Yama, who stood quite still in the light of the three machines. At last, the man said, 'Where are you from, boy?'

'Downriver.'

Did he know? And if he knew, how many others?

'You've been amongst the tombs, have you not?'

'You are very wise, dominie.'

It was possible that the Aedile knew. Perhaps that was why he had wanted to bury Yama in a drab clerkship, away from the eyes of the world. And if the Aedile had known, then Prefect Corin had known too.

One of the guards said, 'Take the book and let us deal with him. He won't be missed.'

'I allowed him in,' the white-haired man said. 'Although he should have waited by the gate, I will continue to be responsible for him. Boy, where did you get that book? From one of the old tombs downriver? Did you find anything else there?'

Before Yama could answer, the second guard said, 'He has the pallid look of a tomb-robber.'

The white-haired man held up a hand. His fingers were very long, with nails filed to points and painted black. 'It isn't just the book. I'm interested in the boy too.'

The first guard said, 'He carries a power knife in his satchel.'

'More loot, I expect,' the white-haired man said. 'You won't use it here, will you, boy?'

'I have not come to kill you,' Yama said.

The second guard said, 'He's a little old for you, Iachimo.'

'Be silent,' the white-haired man, Iachimo, said pleasantly, 'or I'll slice out your tongue and eat it in front of you.' He told Yama, 'They obey me because they know I never make an idle threat. I wish it were otherwise, but you cannot buy loyalty. You must win it by fear or by love. I find fear to be more effective.'

The second guard said, 'We should check the gate.'

Iachimo said, 'The dogs have not raised any real alarm, and neither has the guard.'

The first guard said, 'But here's this boy wandering the grounds. There might be others.'

'Oh, very well,' Iachimo said, 'but be quick.' He swung down from his palfrey and told Yama, 'You'll come with me, boy.'

As they crossed the road and plunged into a stand of pine trees beyond, Iachimo said, 'Is the book from the City of the Dead? Answer truthfully. I can smell out a lie, and I have little patience for evasion.'

Yama did not doubt it, but he thought to himself that Iachimo was the kind of man who believed too strongly in his cleverness, and so held all others in contempt and did not pay as much attention to them as he should. He said, 'It was not from the City of the Dead, dominie, but a place close by.'

'Hmm. As I remember, the house occupied by the Aedile of Aeolis has an extensive library.' Iachimo turned and looked at Yama and smiled. 'I see I have hit the truth. Well, I doubt that the Aedile will miss it. The library is a depository of all kinds of rubbish, but as the fisherfolk of that region have it, rubies are sometimes engendered in mud by the light of the Eye of the Preservers. Nonsense, of course, but despite that it has a grain of truth. In this case, the fisherfolk are familiar with pearls, which are produced by certain shellfish when they are irritated by a speck of grit, and secrete layers of slime to enclose the irritation. This slime hardens, and becomes the black or red pearls so eagerly sought by gentlemen and ladies of high breeding, who do not know of the base origin of their beloved jewels. Your book is a pearl, without doubt. I knew it as soon as I saw it, although I do not think it was you who held it up at the gate.'

'It was my friend. But he got scared and ran off.'

'The guards will catch him. Or the dogs, if he is unlucky.'

'He's only a pot boy from one of the inns by the waterfront. I struck up a friendship with him.'

'From which he hoped to profit, I expect,' Iachimo said, and then stopped and turned to look back at the way they had come.

A moment later, a thread of white light lanced through the darkness, illuminating a distant line of trees. Yama felt the ground tremble beneath his feet; a noise like thunder rolled through the grounds.

Iachimo grasped Yama's shoulders and pushed him forward. 'One of the weapons mounted by the gatekeeper, unless I am mistaken. And I am never mistaken. Your friend has been found, I believe. Do not think of running, boy, or you'll suffer the same fate.'

Yama did not resist. Both Tamora and Pandaras were armed with the pistols taken from the gatekeeper, and

Iachimo did not yet know that the gatekeeper was dead. Besides, he was being taken to the very place the others were looking for.

Yama and Iachimo descended into a narrow defile between steep rock walls studded with ferns and orchids. Another white flash lit the crack of sky above. Pebbles rattled down the walls in the aftershock. Iachimo tightened his grip on Yama's shoulder and pushed him on. 'This matter is consuming more time than I like,' he said.

'Are you in charge of the guards? They do not seem to be doing a very good job.'

'I am in charge of the entire household. And do not think I turned out for you, boy. It was the book. But I admit you are a curiosity. There could be some advantage here.'

Yama said boldly, 'What do you know about my bloodline? You recognized it, and that was why I was not killed.'

'You know less than I, I think. I wonder if you even know your parents.'

'Only that my mother is dead.'

A silver lady in a white boat. The old Constable, Thaw, had said that he had plucked Yama from her dead breast, but as a young boy Yama had dreamed that she had only been profoundly asleep, and was searching for him in the wilderness of tombs around Aeolis. Sometimes he had searched for her there – as he was searching still.

Iachimo said, 'Oh, she's dead all right. Dead ages past. You're probably first generation, revived from a stored template.'

The narrow defile opened out into a courtyard dimly lit by a scattering of floating lanterns, tiny as fireflies, that drifted in the black air. Its tiled floor was crowded with grey, life-sized statues of men and animals in a variety of contorted poses. Iachimo pushed Yama forward. Horribly, the statues stirred and trembled, sending up ripples of grey dust and a dry scent of electricity. Some opened their eyes, but the orbs they rolled towards Yama were like dry, white marbles.

Iachimo said in Yama's ear, 'There's worse that can happen to you than being returned to storage. Do we understand each other?'

Yama thought of his knife. It occurred to him that there were situations in which it might be more merciful to use it against himself rather than his enemies. He said, 'You are taking me to your master.'

'He wants only to see the book. You will be a surprise gift. We'll see what shakes out, and afterwards we'll talk.'

Iachimo smiled at Yama, but it was merely a movement of certain muscles in his narrow, high-browed face. He was lost in his own thoughts, Yama saw, a man so clever that he schemed as naturally as other men breathed.

Yama said, 'How do you know about my bloodline?'

'My master's bloodline is long-lived, and he is one of the oldest. He has taught me much about the history of the world. I know that he will be interested in you. Of course, he may want you killed, but I will try to prevent it. And so you owe me your life twice over. Think of that, when you talk with him. We can do things for each other, you and I.'

Yama remembered that the pilot of the voidship lighter had said that it knew his bloodline, and understood that he was a prize which Iachimo would offer to his master in the hope of advancement or reward. He said, 'It seems to me that this is a very one-sided bargain. What will I gain?'

'Your life, to begin with. My master may want to kill you at once, or use you and then kill you, but I can help you, and you can help me. Damn these things!'

Iachimo was standing beside the statue of a naked boy – or perhaps it had once been a living boy, encased or transformed in some way – and the statue had managed to grasp the hem of his tunic. Iachimo tugged impatiently, then broke off the statue's fingers, one by one. They made a dry snapping sound, and fell to dust when they struck the floor.

Iachimo brushed his hands together briskly and said, 'My master has revived certain technologies long thought forgotten. It is the basis of his fortune and his power. You understand why you will be of considerable interest to him.'

Yama realized that this was a question, but he did not know how to begin to answer it. Instead, he said, 'It is a very old edition of the Puranas.'

'Oh, the book. Like you, it is not an original, but it is not far removed. You have read it?'

'Yes.'

'Don't tell my master that. Tell him you stole it, nothing more. Lie if you must; otherwise he may well have you killed on the spot, and that is something that will be difficult for me to prevent. He controls the guards here. Let us go. He is waiting.'

On the far side of the courtyard was an arched doorway and a broad flight of marble steps that led down towards a pool of warm white light. Iachimo's long, pointed nails dug into Yama's shoulder, pricking his skin through his shirt.

'Stand straight,' Iachimo said. 'Use your backbone as it was intended. Remember that you were made in the image of the Preservers, and forget that your ancestors were animals that went about on all fours. Good. Now walk forward, and do not stare at anything. Most especially, do not stare at my master. He is more sensitive than he might appear. He has not always been as he is now.'

20 ~ The Hollow Man

Even before Yama reached the bottom of the stairs, he knew that there was a large number of machines ahead of him, but the size of the room was still surprising. Golden pillars twisted into fantastic shapes marched away across an emerald green lawn, lending perspective to a space perhaps a thousand paces long and three hundred wide. The lawn was studded with islands of couches upholstered in brilliant silks, and fountains and dwarf fruit trees and statues – these last merely of red sandstone or marble, not petrified flesh. Displays of exotic flowers perfumed the air. Constellations of brilliant white lights floated in the air beneath a high glass ceiling. Above the glass was not air but water – schools of golden and black carp lazily swam through illuminated currents, and pads of water lilies hung above them like the silhouettes of clouds.

Thousands of tiny machines crawled amongst the closely trimmed blades of grass or spun through the bright air like silver beetles or dragonflies with mica wings, their thoughts a single rising harmonic in Yama's head. Men in scarlet and white uniforms and silver helmets stood in alcoves carved into the marble walls. They were unnaturally still and, like the fallen guard at the gate, emitted faint glimmers of machine intelligence, as if machines inhabited their skulls.

As Yama walked across the lawn, with Iachimo following close behind, he heard music in the distance: the chiming runs of a tambura like silver laughter over the solemn pulse of a tabla. A light sculpture twisted in the air like a writhing column of brightly coloured scarves seen through a heat haze.

The two musicians sat in a nest of embroidered silk cushions to one side of a huge couch on which lay the fattest man Yama had ever seen. He was naked except for a loincloth, and as hairless as a seal. A gold circlet crowned his shaven head. The thick folds of his belly spilled his flanks and draped his swollen thighs. His black skin shone with oils and unguents; the light of the sculpture slid over it in greasy rainbows. He was propped on his side amongst cushions and bolsters, and pawed in a distracted fashion at a naked woman who was feeding him pastries from a pile stacked high on a silver salver. Without doubt, this was the master of the house, the merchant, the rogue star-sailor.

Yama halted a few paces from him and bowed from the waist, but the merchant did not acknowledge him. Yama stood and sweated, with Iachimo beside him, while the musicians played through the variations of their raga and the merchant ate a dozen pastries one after the other and stroked the gleaming pillows of the woman's large breasts with swollen, ring-encrusted fingers. Like her master, the woman was quite without hair. The petals of her labia were pierced with rings; from one of these rings a fine gold chain ran to a bracelet on the merchant's wrist.

When the concluding chimes of the tambura had died away, the merchant closed his eyes and sighed deeply, then waved at the musicians in dismissal. 'Drink,' he said in a high, wheezing voice. The woman jumped up and poured red wine into a bowl which she held to the merchant's lips. He slobbered at the wine horribly and it spilled over his chin and chest onto the grassy floor. Yama saw now that the cushions of the couch were stained with old spillages and littered with crumbs and half-eaten crusts; underlying the rich scents of spikenard and jasmine and the sweet smoke of candles which floated in a bowl of water was a stale reek of old sweat and spoiled food.

The merchant belched and glanced at Yama. His cheeks were so puffed with fat that they pushed his mouth into a squashed rosebud, and his eyes peered above their ramparts like sentries, darting here and there as if expecting a sudden attack from any quarter. He said petulantly, 'What's this, Iachimo? A little old for your tastes, isn't he?'

Iachimo inclined his head. 'Very amusing, master, but you know that I would never trouble you with my bed companions. Perhaps you might look more closely. I believe that you will find he is a rare type, one not seen on Confluence for many an age.'

The merchant waved a doughy paw in front of his face, as if trying to swat a fly. 'You are always playing games, Iachimo. It will be your downfall. Tell me and have done with it.'

'I believe that he is one of the Builders,' Iachimo said.

The merchant laughed – a series of grunts that convulsed his vast, gleaming body as a storm tosses the surface of the river. At last he said, 'Your inventive mind never ceases to amaze me, Iachimo. I'll grant he has the somatype, but this is some river-rat a mountebank has surgically altered, no doubt inspired by some old carving or slate. You've been had.'

'He came here of his own accord. He brought a book of great antiquity. I have it here.'

The merchant took the copy of the Puranas from Iachimo and pawed through it, grunting to himself, before casually tossing it aside. It landed face down and splayed open amongst the cushions on which the merchant sprawled. Yama made a move to retrieve it, but Iachimo caught his arm.

'I've seen better,' the merchant said. 'If this fake says he brought you an original of the Puranas, then that too will be a fake. I'm no longer interested. Take this creature away, Iachimo, and its book. Dispose of it in the usual way, and dispose of its companion, too, once you've caught it. Or do I have to take charge of the guards and do that myself?'

'It won't be necessary, master. The other boy is certainly no more than a river-rat. He won't be missed. But this one is something rarer.' Iachimo prodded Yama in the small of the back with a fingernail as sharply pointed as a stiletto and whispered, 'Show him what you can do.'

'I do not understand what you want of me.'

'Oh, you understand,' Iachimo hissed. 'I know what you can do with machines. You got past the gatekeeper, so you know something of your inheritance.'

The merchant said, 'I'm in an indulgent mood, Iachimo. Here's your test. I'm going to order my soldiers to kill you, boy. Do you understand? Stop them, and we'll talk some more. Otherwise I'm rid of a fraud.'

Four of the guards started forward from their niches. Yama stepped back involuntarily as the guards, their faces expressionless beneath the bills of their silver helmets, raised their gleaming falchions and marched stiffly across the lawn towards him, two on the right, two on the left.

Iachimo said in a wheedling tone, 'Master, surely this isn't necessary.'

'Let me have my fun,' the merchant said. 'What is he to you, eh?'

Yama put his hand inside his satchel and found the hilt of his knife, but the guards were almost upon him and he knew that he could not fight four at once. He felt a tingling expansion and shouted at the top of his voice. 'Stop! Stop now!'

The guards froze in midstep, then, moving as one, knelt and laid down their falchions, and bent until their silver helmets touched the grass.

The merchant reared up and squealed, 'What is this? Do you betray me, Iachimo?'

'Quite the reverse, master. I'll kill him in a moment, if

you give the word. But you see that he is no mountebank's fake.'

The merchant glared at Yama. There was a high whine, like a bee trapped in a bottle, and a machine dropped through the air and hovered in front of Yama's face. Red light flashed in the backs of his eyes. He asked the machine to go away, but the red light flashed again, filling his vision. He could see nothing but the red light and held himself still, although panic trembled in his breast like a trapped dove. He could feel every corner of the machine's small bright mind, but by a sudden inversion, as if a flower had suddenly dwindled down to the seed from which it had sprung, it was closed to him.

Somewhere beyond the red light, the merchant said, 'Recently born. No revenant. Where is he from, Iachimo?'

'Downriver,' Iachimo said, close by Yama's ear. 'Not far downriver, though. There's a small town called Aeolis amongst the old tombs. The book at least comes from there.'

The merchant said, 'The City of the Dead. There are older tombs elsewhere on Confluence, but I suppose you aren't to know that. Boy, stop trying to control my machines. I have told them to ignore you, and fortunately for you, you don't know the extent of your abilities. Fortunate for you, too, Iachimo. You risked a great deal bringing him here. I'll not forget that.'

Iachimo said, 'I am yours to punish or reward, master. As always. But be assured that this boy does not understand what he is. Otherwise I would not have been able to capture him.'

'He's done enough damage. I have reviewed the security systems, something you haven't troubled to do. He blinded the watchdogs and the machines patrolling the grounds, which is why he and his friend could wander the grounds with impunity. I have restored them. He has killed the gatekeeper too, and his friend is armed. Wait – there are two of them, both armed, and loose in the grounds. The security

268

system was told to ignore them, but I'm tracking them now. You have let things get out of hand, Iachimo.'

'I had no reason to believe the security system was not operating correctly, master, but it proves my point. Here is a rare treasure.'

Yama turned his head back and forth, but could see nothing but red mist. There was a splinter of pain in each of his eyes. He said, 'Am I blinded?' and his voice was smaller and weaker than he would have liked.

'I suppose it isn't necessary,' the merchant said, and the red mist was gone.

Yama knuckled his stinging eyes, blinking hard in the sudden bright light. Two of the guards stood at attention behind the merchant's couch, their red and white uniforms gleaming, their falchions held before their faces as if at parade.

The merchant said, 'Don't mind my toys. They won't harm you as long as you're sensible.' His voice was silkily unctuous now. 'Drink, eat. I have nothing but the best. The best vintages, the finest meats, the tenderest vegetables.'

'Some wine, perhaps. Thank you.'

The naked woman poured wine as rich and red as fresh blood into a gold beaker and handed it to Yama, then poured another bowl for the merchant, who slobbered it down before Yama could do more than sip his. He expected some rare vintage, and was disappointed to discover that it was no better than the ordinary wine of the peel-house's cellars.

The merchant smacked his lips and said, 'Do you know what I am? And do stop trying to take control of my servants. You will give me a headache.'

Yama had been trying to persuade one of the machines which illuminated the room to fly down and settle above his head, but despite his sense of expansion, as if his thoughts had become larger than his skull, he might as well have tried to order an ossifrage to quit its icy perch in the high foothills of the Rim Mountains. He stared at the gold circlet on the merchant's fleshy, hairless pate, and said, 'You are really one of those things which crew the voidships. I suppose that you stole the body.'

'As a matter of fact I had it grown. Do you like it?'

Yama took another sip of wine. He felt calmer now. He said, 'I am amazed by it.'

'You have been raised to be polite. That's good. It will make things easier, eh, Iachimo?'

'I'm sure he could stand a little more polishing, master.'

'I've yet to find a body that can withstand my appetites,' the merchant told Yama, 'but that's of little consequence, because there are always more bodies. This is my – what is it, Iachimo? The tenth?'

'The ninth, master.'

'Well, there will soon be need for a tenth, and there will be more, an endless chain. How old are you, boy? No more than twenty, I'd guess. This body is half that age.'

The merchant pawed at the breasts of the woman. She was feeding him sugared almonds, popping them into his mouth each time it opened. He chewed the almonds mechanically, and a long string of pulp and saliva drooled unheeded down his chin.

He said, 'I've been male and female in my time, too. Mostly male, given the current state of civilization, but now that I've made my fortune and have no need to leave my estate, perhaps I'll be female next time. Are there others like you?'

'That is what I want to discover,' Yama said. 'You know of my bloodline. You know more than me, it seems. You called me a builder. A builder of what?'

But he already knew. He had read in the Puranas, and he remembered the man in the picture slate which Osric and Beatrice had shown him.

Iachimo said, '"And the Preservers raised up a man and set on his brow their mark, and raised up a woman of the same kind, and set on her brow the same mark. From the

270

white clay of the middle region did they shape this race, and quickened them with their marks. And those of this race were the servants of the Preservers. And in their myriads this race shaped the world after the ideas of the Preservers." There's more, but you get the general idea. Those are your people, boy. So long dead that almost no one remembers—'

Suddenly, the room brightened: white light flashed beyond the lake which hung above the long room. Rafts of waterlily pads swung wildly on clashing waves and there was a deep, heavy muffled sound, as if a massive door had slammed in the keel of the world.

The merchant said, 'No hope there, boy. You put some of my guards to sleep, but they're all under my control again, and almost have your two friends. Iachimo, you did not say that one of them was a cateran.'

'There was another boy, master. I knew of no other.'

The merchant closed his eyes. For a moment, Yama felt that a thousand intelligences lived in his head. Then the feeling was gone and the merchant said, 'She has killed several guards, but one caught a glimpse of her. She's of the Fierce People, and she's armed with one of the gatekeeper's pistols.'

'There are still many guards, master, and many machines. Besides, the lake will absorb any blast from the pistol.'

The merchant pulled the woman close to him. 'He's an assassin's tool, you idiot! Why else would a cateran come here? You know I have been expecting this ever since my old ship returned through the manifold.'

'There was the man who broke into the godown,' Iachimo said, 'but we dealt with him easily enough.'

'It was just the beginning. They won't rest—'

There was another flash of white light. A portion of water above the glass ceiling seethed into a spreading cloud of white bubbles, and the glass rang like a cracked bell.

The merchant closed his eyes briefly, then relaxed and drew the naked woman closer. 'Well, it doesn't matter now.

There's a weapon in his satchel, Iachimo. Take it out and give it to me.'

The white-haired man lifted out the sheathed knife and said, 'It is only a knife, master.'

'I know what it is. Bring it here.'

Iachimo offered the sheathed knife, hilt first. Yama implored it to manifest the horrible shape which had frightened Lob and the landlord of *The Crossed Axes*, but he was at the centre of a vast muffling silence. The merchant squinted at the knife's goatskin sheath, and then the woman drew it and plunged it into Iachimo's belly.

Iachimo grunted and fell to his knees. The knife flashed blue fire and the woman screamed and dropped it and clutched her smoking hand. The knife embedded itself point first in the grass, sizzling faintly and emitting a drizzle of fat blue motes. Iachimo was holding his belly with both hands. There was blood all over his fingers and the front of his black tunic.

The merchant looked at the woman and she fell silent in mid-scream. He said to Yama, 'So die all those who think to betray me. Now, boy, you'll answer all my questions truthfully, or you'll join your two friends. Yes, they have been captured. Not dead, not yet. We'll talk, you and I, and decide their fate.'

Iachimo, kneeling over the knife and a pool of his own blood, said something about a circle, and then the guards seized him and jerked him upright and cut his throat and lifted him away from the merchant, all in one quick motion. They dropped the body onto the neatly trimmed grass beneath the light sculpture and returned to their position behind the merchant's couch.

'You're trouble, boy,' the merchant said. The woman tremblingly placed the mouthpiece of a clay pipe between his rosebud lips and lit the scrap of resin in its bowl. He drew a long breath and said, dribbling smoke with the words, 'Your people were the first. The rest came later, but you were the first. I had never thought to see your kind again, but this is an age of wonders. Listen to me, boy, or I'll have you killed too. You see how easy it is.'

Yama was holding the wine goblet so tightly that he had reopened the wound in his palm. He threw it away and said as boldly as he could, 'Will you spare my friends?'

'They came to kill me, didn't they? Sent by my crewmates, who are jealous of me.'

Yama could not deny it. He stared in stubborn silence at the merchant, who calmly drew on his pipe and contemplated the wreathes of smoke he breathed out. At last, the merchant said, 'The woman is a cateran, and their loyalty is easily bought. I might have a use for her. The boy is no different from a million other river-rats in Ys. I could kill him and it would be as if he had never been born. I see that you want him to live. You are very sentimental. Well then. You must prove your worth to me, and perhaps the boy will live. Do you know exactly what you are?'

Yama said, 'You say that I am of the bloodline of the Builders, and I have seen an ancient picture showing one of my kind before the world was made. But I also have been told that I might be a child of the Ancients of Days.'

'Hmm. It's possible they had something to do with it. In their brief time here they meddled in much that didn't concern them. They didn't achieve anything of consequence, of course. For all that they might have appeared as gods to the degenerate population of Confluence, they predated the Preservers by several million years. Their kind were the ancestors of the Preservers, but with about as much relation to them as the brainless plankton grazers which were the ancestors of my own bloodline have to me. It is only because the Ancients of Days were timeshifted while travelling to our neighbouring galaxy and back at close to the speed of light that they appeared so late, like an actor delayed by circumstance who incontinently rushes on stage to deliver his lines and finds that he has interrupted the closing soliloquy instead of beginning the second act. We are in the end times, young Builder. This whole grand glorious foolish experiment has all but run its course. The silly little war downriver begun by the Ancients of Days is only a footnote.'

The merchant seemed exhausted by this speech, and drank more wine before he continued. 'Do you know, I haven't thought about this for a long time. Iachimo was a very clever man, but not a brave one. He was doomed to a servant's role, and resented it. I thought at first you were some scheme of his, and I haven't fully dismissed the thought from my mind. I do not believe that it was through simple carelessness that he allowed the cateran to roam free, or that you were allowed to carry a knife into my presence.'

'I have never seen him before tonight. I am not the servant of any man.'

The merchant said, 'Don't be a fool. Like most here, your bloodline was created as servants to the immediate will of the Preservers.'

'We all serve the Preservers as we can,' Yama said.

'You've been in the hands of a priest,' the merchant said. His gaze was shrewd. 'You parrot his pious phrases, but do you really believe them?'

Yama could not answer. His faith was never something he had questioned, but now he saw that by disobeying the wishes of his father he had rebelled against his place in the social hierarchy, and had not that hierarchy proceeded from the Preservers? So the priests taught, but now Yama was unsure. For the priests also taught that the Preservers wanted their creations to advance from a low to a high condition, and how could that happen if society was fixed, eternal and unchanging?

The merchant belched. 'You are just a curiosity, boy. A revenant. An afterthought or an accident – it's all the same. But you might be useful, even so. You and I might do great things together. You asked why I am here. It is because I have remembered what all others of my kind have long forgotten. They are lost in ascetic contemplation of the mathematics of the manifolds and the secrets of the beginning and end of the cosmos, but I have remembered the pleasures of the real world, of appetite and sex and all the rest of the messy wonderful business of life. They would say that mathematics is the reality underlying everything; I say that it is an abstraction of the real world, a ghost.' He belched again. 'There is my riposte to algebra.'

Yama made a wild intuitive leap. He said, 'You met the Ancients of Days, didn't you?'

'My ship hailed theirs, as it fell through the void towards the Eye of the Preservers. They had seen the Eye's construction by ancient light while hundreds of thousands of years out, and were amazed to discover that organic intelligent life still existed. We merged our mindscapes and talked long there, and I followed them out into the world. And here I am. It is remarkably easy to make a fortune in these benighted times, but I'm finding that merely satisfying sensual appetites is not enough. If you're truly a Builder, and I am not quite convinced that you are, then perhaps you can help me. I have plans.'

'I believe that I am no man's servant. I cannot serve you as Iachimo did.'

The merchant laughed. 'I would hope not. You will have to unlearn your arrogance to begin with; then I will see what I can make of you. I can teach you many things, boy. I can realize your potential. There are many like Iachimo in the world, intelligent and learned and quite without the daring to act on their convictions. There is no end to natural followers like him. You are something more. I must think hard about it, and so will you. But you will serve, or you will die, and so will your friends.'

The twisting scarves of colour in the light sculpture ran together into a steely grey and widened into a kind of window, showing Tamora and Pandaras kneeling inside tiny cages suspended in dark air.

For a moment, Yama's breath caught in his throat. He said, 'Let them go, and I will serve you as I can.'

The merchant shifted his immense oiled bulk. 'I think not. I'll give you a taste of their fate while I decide how I can make use of you. When you can make that promise from your heart, then we can talk again.'

The two guards turned towards Yama, who stared in sudden panic into their blank, blind faces. His panic inflated into something immense, a great wild bird he had loosed, its wings beating at the edges of his sight. In desperation, quite without hope, his mind threw out an immense imploring scream for help.

The merchant pawed at his head and far down the room something struck the glass ceiling with a tremendous bang. For a moment, all was still. Then a line of spray sheeted down, and the glass around it gave with a loud splintering crash. The spray became a widening waterfall that poured down and rebounded from the floor and sent a tawny wave flooding down the length of the room, knocking over pillars and statues and sweeping tables and couches before it.

The merchant's couch lurched into the air. The woman gave a guttural cry of alarm, and clung to her master's flesh as a shipwrecked sailor clings to a bit of flotsam. Yama dashed forward through surging water (for a moment, Iachimo's corpse clutched at his ankles; then it was swept away), made a desperate leap and caught hold of one end of the rising couch. His weight rocked it on its long axis, so violently that for one moment he hung straight down, the next tipped forward and fell across the merchant's legs.

The merchant roared and his woman clawed at Yama with sudden fury, her long nails opening his forehead so that blood poured into his eyes. The couch turned in a dizzy circle above the guards as they struggled to stay upright in the seething flood. The merchant caught at Yama's hands, but his grasp was feeble, and Yama, half-blinded, grabbed the golden circlet around the man's fleshy scalp and pulled with all his strength.

For a moment, he feared that the circlet would not give way. Then it snapped in half and unravelled like a ribbon. All the lights went out. The couch tipped and Yama and the merchant and the woman fell into the wash of the flood. Yama went under and got a mouthful of muddy water and came up spitting and gasping.

The guards had fallen; so had all the machines.

Yama asked a question, and after a moment points of intense white light flared down the length of the room, burning through the swirling brown flood. Yama wiped blood from his eyes. The current swirled around his waist. He was clutching a tangle of golden filaments tipped with stringy fragments of flesh.

At the far end of the huge room, something floated a handspan above the water, turning slowly end for end. It was as big as Yama's head, and black, and decorated all over with spikes of varying lengths and thickness, some like rose thorns, others long and finely tapered and questing this way and that with blind intelligence. The thing radiated a black icy menace, a negation not only of life, but of the reality of the world. For a moment, Yama was transfixed; then the machine rose straight up, smashing through the ceiling. Yama felt it rise higher and higher, and for a moment felt all the machines in Ys turn towards it – but it was gone.

The merchant sprawled across the fallen couch like a beached grampus. A ragged wound crowned his head, streaming blood; he snorted a jelly of blood and mucus through his nose. The woman lay beneath him, entirely submerged. Her head was twisted back, and her eyes looked up through the swirling water. Up and down the length of the room, the guards were dead, too.

Yama held the frayed remnants of the circlet before the merchant's eyes, and said, 'Iachimo told me about this with his last breath, but I had already guessed its secret. I saw something like it on the lighter.'

'The Preservers have gone away,' the merchant whispered.

The floodwaters were receding, running away into deeper levels of the sunken house. Yama knelt by the couch and said, 'Why am I here?'

The merchant drew a breath. Blood ran from his nostrils and his mouth. He said wetly, 'Serve no one.'

'If the Preservers are gone, why was I brought back?'

The merchant tried to say something, but only blew a bubble of blood. Yama left him there and went to find Tamora and Pandaras.

21 ~ The Fierce People

Tamora came back to the campfire at a loping run. She was grinning broadly and there was blood around her mouth. She threw a brace of coneys at Yama's feet and said proudly, 'This is how we live, when we can. We are the Fierce People, the Memsh Tek!'

Pandaras said, 'Not all of us can live on meat alone.'

'Your kind have to exist on leaves and the filth swept into street gutters,' Tamora said, 'and that is why they are so weak. Meat and blood are what warriors need, so be glad that I give you fine fresh guts. They will make you strong.'

She slit the bellies of the coneys with her sharp thumbnail, crammed the steaming, rich red livers into her mouth and gulped them down. Then she pulled the furry skins from the gutted bodies, as someone might strip gloves from their hands, and set about dismembering them with teeth and nails.

She had attacked the merchant's carcass with the same butcher's skill, using a falchion taken from one of the dead guards to fillet it from neck to buttocks and expose the thing which had burrowed into the fatty flesh like a hagfish. It was not much like the bottled creature Yama had seen on the lighter. Its mantle was shrunken, and white fibres had knitted around its host's spinal column like cords of fungus in rotten wood.

Tamora kept most of the coney meat for herself and ate it raw, but she allowed Yama and Pandaras to cook the haunches over the embers of the fire. The unsalted meat was half-burned and half-raw, but Yama and Pandaras hungrily stripped it from the bones.

'Burnt meat is bad for the digestion,' Tamora said, grinning at them across the embers of the fire. She wore only her leather skirt. Her two pairs of breasts were little more than enlarged nipples, like tarnished coins set on her narrow ribcage. In addition to the bird burning in a nest of fire on her upper arm, inverted triangles were tattooed in black ink on her shoulders. There was a bandage around her waist; she had been seared by backflash from a guard's pistol shot. She took a swallow of brandy and passed the bottle to Yama. He had bought the brandy in a bottleshop and used a little to preserve the filaments Tamora had flensed from the merchant's body and placed in a beautiful miniature flask, cut from a single crystal of rose quartz, which Yama had found in the wreckage left by the flood when he had been searching for his copy of the Puranas.

Yama drank and passed the bottle to Pandaras, who was cracking coney bones between his sharp teeth.

'Drink,' Tamora said. 'We fought a great battle today.'

Pandaras spat a bit of gristle into the fire. He had already made it clear how unhappy he was to be in the Fierce People's tract of wild country, and he sat with his kidney puncher laid across his lap and his mobile ears pricked. He said, 'I'd rather keep my wits about me.'

Tamora laughed. 'No one would mistake you for a coney. You're about the right size, but you can't run fast enough to make the hunt interesting.'

Pandaras took the smallest possible sip from the brandy bottle and passed it back to Yama. He told Tamora, 'You certainly ran when the soldiers came.'

'Grah. I was trying to catch up with you to make sure you went the right way.'

'Enough stuff to set a man up for life,' Pandaras said, 'and we had to leave it for the city militia to loot.'

'I'm a cateran, not a robber. We have done what we contracted to do. Be happy.' Tamora grinned. Her pink tongue lolled amongst her big, sharp teeth. 'Eat burnt bones. Drink. Sleep. We are safe here, and tomorrow we are paid.'

Yama realized that she was drunk. The bottle of brandy had been the smallest he could buy, but it was still big enough, as Pandaras put it, to drown a baby. They had needed only a few minims to fill the crystal flask, and Tamora had drunk about half of what was left.

'Safe?' Pandaras retorted. 'In the middle of any number of packs of bloodthirsty howlers like you? I won't sleep at all tonight.'

'I will sing a great song of our triumph, and you will listen. Pass that bottle, Yama. It is not your child.'

Yama took a burning swallow of brandy, handed the bottle over, and walked out of the firelight to the crest of the ridge. The sandy hills where the Fierce People maintained their hunting grounds looked out across the wide basin of the city towards the Great River. The misty light of the Arm of the Warrior was rising above the farside horizon. It was past midnight. The city was mostly dark, but many campfires flickered amongst the scrub and clumps of crown ferns, pines and eucalyptus of the Fierce People's hunting grounds, and from every quarter came the sound of distant voices raised in song.

Yama sat on the dry grass and listened to the night music of the Fierce People. The feral machine still haunted him, like a ringing in the ears or the afterimage of a searingly bright light. And beyond this psychic echo he could feel the ebb and flow of the myriad machines in the city, like the flexing of a great net. They had also been disturbed by the feral machine, and the ripples of alarm caused by the disturbance were still spreading, leaping from cluster to cluster of machines along the docks, running out towards the vast bulk of the Palace of the Memory of the People, clashing at the bases of the high towers and racing up their lengths out of the atmosphere.

Yama still did not know how he had called down the feral machine, and although it had saved him he feared that he might call it again by accident, and feared too that he had exposed himself to discovery by the network of machines which served the magistrates, or by Prefect Corin, who must surely still be searching for him. The descent of the feral machine was the most terrifying and the most shameful of his adventures. He had been paralysed with fear when confronted with it, and even now he felt that it had marked him in some obscure way, for some small part of him yearned for it, and what it could tell him. It could be watching him still; it could return at any time, and he did not know what he would do if it did.

The merchant – Yama still found it difficult to think of him as the parasitic bundle of nerve fibres burrowed deep within that tremendously fat body – had said that he was a Builder, a member of the first bloodline of Ys. The pilot of the voidship had said something similar, and the slate that Beatrice and Osric had shown him had suggested the same thing. His people had walked Confluence in its first days, sculpting the world under the direct instruction of the Preservers, and had died out or ascended ages past, so long ago that most had forgotten them. And yet he was here, and he still did not know why; nor did he know the full extent of his powers.

The merchant had hinted that he knew what Yama was capable of, but he might have been lying to serve his own ends, and besides, he was dead. Perhaps the other star-sailors knew – Iachimo had said that they were very long-lived – or perhaps, as Yama had hoped even before he had set out from Aeolis, there were records somewhere in Ys that would explain everything, or at least lead him to others of his kind. He still did not know how he had been brought into the world, or why he had been found floating on the river on the breast of a dead woman who might have been his mother or nurse or something else entirely, but surely he had been born to serve the Preservers in some fashion. After the Preservers had fallen into the event horizon of the Eye, they could still watch the world they had made, for nothing fell faster than light, but they could no longer act upon it. But perhaps their reach was long – perhaps they had ordained his birth, here in what the merchant had called the end times, long before they had withdrawn from the Universe. Perhaps, as Derev believed, many of Yama's kind now walked the world, as they had at its beginning. But for what purpose? All through his childhood he had prayed for a revelation, a sign, a hint, and had received nothing. Perhaps he should expect nothing else. Perhaps the shape of his life was the sign he sought, if only he could understand it

But he could not believe he was the servant of the feral machines. That was the worst thought of all.

Yama sat on a hummock of dry grass, with the noise of crickets everywhere in the darkness around him, and leafed through his copy of the Puranas. The book had dried out well, although one corner of its front cover was faintly but indelibly stained with the merchant's blood. The pages held a faint light, and the glyphs stood out like shadows against this soft effulgence. Yama found the sura which Iachimo had quoted, and read it from beginning to end.

The world first showed itself as a golden embryo of sound. As soon as the thoughts of the Preservers turned to the creation of the world, the long vowel which described the form of the world vibrated in the pure realm of thought, and re-echoed on itself. From the knots in the play of vibrations, the crude matter of the world curdled. In the beginning, it was no more than a sphere of air and water with a little mud at the centre.

And the Preservers raised up a man and set on his brow their mark, and raised up a woman of the same kind, and

set on her brow the same mark. From the white clay of the
middle region did they shape this race, and quickened them
with their marks. And those of this race were the servants
of the Preservers. And in their myriads this race shaped the
world after the ideas of the Preservers.

Yama read on, although the next sura was merely an exhaustive description of the dimensions and composition of the world, and he knew that there was no other mention of the Builders, nor of their fate. This was towards the end of the Puranas. The world and everything in it was an afterthought at the end of the history of the Galaxy, created in the last moment before the Preservers fell into the Eye and were known no more in the Universe. Nothing had been written about the ten thousand bloodlines of Confluence in the Puranas; if there had been, then there would have never been a beginning to the endless disputations amongst priests and philosophers about the reason for the world's creation.

Tamora said, 'Reading, is it? There's nothing in books you can't learn better in the world, nothing but fantastic rubbish about monsters and the like. You'll rot your mind and your eyes, reading too much in books.'

'Well, I met a real monster today.'

'And he's dead, the fucker, and we have a piece of him in brandy as proof. So much for him.'

Yama had not told Tamora and Pandaras about the feral machine. Tamora had boasted that one of her pistol shots had weakened the ceiling and so caused the flood which had saved them, and Yama had not corrected her error. He felt a rekindling of shame at this deception, and said weakly, 'I suppose the merchant was a kind of monster. He tried to flee from his true self, and let a little hungry part of himself rule his life. He was all appetite and nothing else. I think he would have eaten the whole world, if he could.'

'You want to be a soldier. Here's some advice. Don't think

about what you have to do and don't think about it when it's done.'

'And can you forget it so easily?'

'Of course not. But I try. We were captured, your rat-boy and me, and thrown into cages, but you had it worse, I think. The merchant was trying to bend you towards his will. The words of his kind are like thorns, and some of them are still in your flesh. But they'll wither, and you'll forget them.'

Yama smiled and said, 'Perhaps it would be no bad thing, to be the ruler of the world.'

Tamora sat down close beside him. She was a shadow in the darkness. She said, 'You would destroy the civil service and rule instead? How would that change the world for the better?'

Yama could feel her heat. She gave off a strong scent compounded of fresh blood and sweat and a sharp musk. He said, 'Of course not. But the merchant told me something about my bloodline. I may be alone in the world. I may be a mistake thrown up at the end of things. Or I may be something else. Something *intended*.'

'The fat fuck was lying. How better to get you to follow him than by saying that you are the only one of your kind, and he knows all about you?'

'I am not sure that he was lying, Tamora. At least, I think he was telling part of the truth.'

'I haven't forgotten what you want, and I was a long time hunting coneys because I really went to ask around. Listen. I have a way of getting at what you want. There is a job for a couple of caterans. Some little pissant department needs someone to organize a defence of its territory inside the Palace of the Memory of the People. There are many disputes between departments, and the powerful grow strong at the expense of the weak. That's the way of the world, but I don't mind defending the weak if I get paid for it.'

'Then perhaps maybe they are stronger than you after all.'

'Grah. Listen. When a litter is born here, the babies are exposed on a hillside for a day. Any that are weak die, or are taken by birds or foxes. We're the Fierce People, see? We keep our bloodline strong. The wogs and wetbacks and snakes and the rest of the garbage down there in the city, they're what we prey on. They need us, not the other way around.' Tamora spat sideways. Yes, she had drunk a lot of brandy. She said, 'There's prey, and there's hunters. You have to decide which you are. You don't know, now is the time you find out. Are you for it?'

'It seems like a good plan.'

'Somewhere or other you've picked up the habit of not speaking plain. You mean yes, then say it.'

'Yes. Yes, I will do it. If it means getting into the Palace of the Memory of the People.'

'Then you got to pay me, because I found it for you, and I'll do the work.'

'I know something about fighting.'

Tamora spat again. 'Listen, this is a dangerous job. This little department is certain to be attacked and they don't have a security office or they wouldn't be hiring someone from outside. They're bound to lose, see, but if it's done right then only their thralls will get killed. We can probably escape, or at worse lose our bond when we're ransomed, but I won't deny there's a chance we'll get killed, too. You still want it?'

'It is a way in.'

'Exactly. This department used to deal in prognostication, but it is much debased. There are only a couple of seers left, but it is highly placed in the Palace of the Memory of the People, and other more powerful departments want to displace it. It needs us to train its thralls so they can put up some kind of defence, but there will be time for you to search for whatever it is you're looking for. We will agree payment now. You'll pay any expenses out of your share of the fees for killing the merchant and for this new job, and I keep my half of both fees, and half again of anything that's left of yours.'

'Is that a fair price?'

'Grah. You're supposed to bargain, you idiot! It is twice what the risk is worth.'

'I will pay it anyway. If I find out what I want to know, I will have no need of money.'

'If you want to join the army as an officer, you'll need plenty, more than you're carrying around now. You'll have to buy the rest of your own armour, and mounts, and weaponry. And if you're looking for information, there will be bribes to be paid. I'll take a quarter of your fees, bargaining against myself like a fool, and share expenses with you. You'll need the rest, believe me.'

'You are a good person, Tamora, although I would like you better if you were more tolerant. No one bloodline should raise itself above any other.'

'I'll do well enough out of this, believe me. One other thing. We won't tell the rat-boy about this. We do this without him.'

'Are you scared of him because he killed the gatekeeper?'

'If I was scared of any of his kind, I would never dare spit in the gutter again, for fear of hitting one in the eye. Let him come if he must, but I won't pretend I like it, and any money he wants comes from you, not me.'

'He is like me, Tamora. He wants to be other than his fate.'

'Then he's certainly as big a fool as you.' Tamora handed Yama the brandy bottle. It was almost empty. 'Drink. Then you will listen to me sing our victory song. The rat-boy is scared to sit with my brothers and sisters, but I know you won't be.'

Although Yama tried not to show it, he was intimidated by the proud, fierce people who sat around the campfire: an even decad of Tamora's kin, heavily muscled men and women marked on their shoulders by identical tattoos of inverted triangles. Most intimidating of all was a straight-backed matriarch with a white mane and a lacework of fine scars across her naked torso, who watched Yama with red-backed eyes from the other side of the fire while Tamora sang.

Tamora's victory song was a discordant open-throated ululation that rose and twisted like a sharp silver wire into the black air above the flames of the campfire. When it was done, she took a long swig from a wine skin while the men and women murmured and nodded and showed their fangs in quick snarling smiles, although one complained loudly that the song had been less about Tamora and more about this whey-skinned stranger.

'That is because it was his adventure,' Tamora said.

'Then let him sing for himself,' the man grumbled.

The matriarch asked Tamora about Yama, saying that she had not seen his kind before.

'He's from downriver, grandmother.'

'That would explain it. I'm told that there are many strange peoples downriver, although I myself have never troubled to go and see, and now I am too old to have to bother. Talk with me, boy. Tell me how your people came into the world.'

'That is a mystery, even to myself. I have read something in the Puranas about my people, and I have seen a picture of one in an old slate, but that is all I know.'

'Then your people are very strange indeed,' the matriarch said. 'Every bloodline has its story and its mysteries and its three names. The Preservers chose to raise up each bloodline in their image for a particular reason, and the stories explain why. You won't find your real story in that book you carry. That's about older mysteries, and not about this world at all.' She cuffed one of the women and snatched a wine skin from her. 'They keep this from me,' she told Yama, 'because they're frightened I'll disgrace myself if I get drunk.'

'Nothing could make you drunk, grandmother,' one of the men said. 'That's why we ration your drinking, or you'd poison yourself trying.'

The matriarch spat into the fire. 'A mouthful of this rotgut will poison me. Can no one afford proper booze? In the old days we would have used this to fuel our lamps.'

Yama still had the brandy bottle, with a couple of fingers of clear, apricot-scented liquor at its bottom. 'Here, grandmother,' he said, and handed it to the matriarch.

The old woman drained the bottle and licked her lips in appreciation. 'Do you know how we came into the world, boy? I'll tell you.'

Several of the people around the fire groaned, and the matriarch said sharply, 'It'll do you good to hear it again. You young people don't know the stories as well as you should. Listen, then.

'After the world was made, some of the Preservers set animals down on its surface, and kindled intelligence in them. There are a people descended from coyotes, for instance, whose ancestors were taught by the Preservers to bury their dead. This odd habit brought about a change in the coyotes, for they learned to sit up so they could sit beside the graves and mourn their dead properly. But sitting on cold stone wore away their bushy tails, and after many generations they began standing upright because the stone was uncomfortable to their naked arses. When that happened, their forepaws lengthened into human hands, and their sharp muzzles shortened bit by bit until they became human faces. That's one story, and there are as many stories as there are bloodlines descended from the different kinds of animals which were taught to become human. But our own people had a different origin.

'Two of the Preservers fell into an argument about the right way to make human people. The Preservers do not have sexes as we understand them, nor do they marry, but it is easier to follow the story if we think of them as wife and husband. One, Enki, was the Preserver who had charge of the world's water, and so his work was hard, for in those early times all there was of the world was the Great River, running from nowhere to nowhere. He complained of his hard work to his wife, Ninmah, who was the Preserver of earth, and she suggested that they create a race of marionettes or puppets who would do the work for them. And this they did, using the small amount of white silt that was suspended in the Great River. I see that you know this part of the story.'

'Someone told me a little of it today. It is to be found in the Puranas.'

'What I tell you is truer, for it has been told from mouth to ear for ten thousand generations, and so its words still live, and have not become dead things squashed flat on plastic or pulped wood. Well then, after this race was produced from the mud of the river, there was a great celebration because the Preservers no longer needed to work on their creation. Much beer was consumed, and Ninmah became especially light-headed. She called to Enki, saying, "How good or bad is a human body? I could reshape it in any way I please, but could you find tasks for it?" Enki responded to this challenge, and so Ninmah made a barren woman, and a eunuch, and several other cripples.

'But Enki found tasks for them all. The barren woman he made into a concubine; the eunuch he made into a civil servant, and so on. Then in the same playful spirit he challenged Ninmah. He would do the shaping of different races, and she the placing. She agreed, and Enki first made a man whose making was already remote from him, and so the first old man appeared before Ninmah. She offered the old man bread, but he was too feeble to reach for it, and when she thrust the bread into his mouth, he could not chew it for he had no teeth, and so Ninmah could find no use for this unfortunate. Then Enki made many other cripples and monsters, and Ninmah could find no use for them, either.

'The pair fell into a drunken sleep, and when they wakened all was in uproar, for the cripples Enki had made were spreading through the world. Enki and Ninmah were summoned before the other Preservers to explain themselves, and to escape punishment Enki and Ninmah together made a final race, who would hunt the lame and the old, and so make the races of the world stronger by consuming their weak members.

'And so we came into the world, and it is said that we have a quick and cruel temper, because Enki and Ninmah suffered dreadfully from the effects of drinking too much beer when they made us, and that was passed to us as a potmaker leaves her thumbprint in the clay.'

'I have heard only the beginning of this story,' Yama said, 'and I am glad that now I have heard the end of it.'

'Now you must tell a story,' one of the men said loudly. It was the one who had complained before. He was smaller than the others, but still a head taller than Yama. He wore black leather trousers and a black leather jacket studded with copper nails.

'Be quiet, Gorgo,' the matriarch said. 'This young man is our guest.'

Gorgo looked across the fire at Yama, and Yama met his truculent, challenging gaze. Neither was willing to look away, but then a branch snapped in the fire and sent burning fragments flying into Gorgo's lap. He cursed and brushed at the sparks while the others laughed.

Gorgo glowered and said, 'We have heard his boasts echoed in Tamora's song. I simply wonder if he has the heart to speak for himself. He owes that courtesy, I think.'

'You're a great one for knowing what's owed,' someone said.

Gorgo turned on the man. 'I only press for payment when it's needed, as you well know. How much poorer you would be if I didn't find you work! You are all in my debt.'

The matriarch said, 'That is not to be spoken of. Are we

not the Fierce People, whose honour is as renowned as our strength and our temper?'

Gorgo said, 'Some people need reminding about honour.'

One of the women said, 'We fight. You get the rewards.'

'Then don't ask me for work,' Gorgo said petulantly. 'Find your own. I force no one, as is well known, but so many ask for my help that I scarcely have time to sleep or catch my food. But here is our guest. Let's not forget him. We hear great things of him from Tamora. Hush, and let him speak for himself.'

Yama thought that Gorgo could speak sweetly when he chose, but the honey of his words disguised his envy and suspicion. Clearly, Gorgo thought that Yama's was one of the trash or vermin bloodlines.

Yama said, 'I will tell a story, although I am afraid that it might bore you. It is about how my life was saved by one of the indigens.'

Gorgo grumbled that this didn't sound like a true story at all. 'Tell something of your people instead,' he said. 'Please do not tell me that such a fine hero as yourself, if we are to believe the words of our sister here, is so ashamed of his own people that he has to make up stories of sub-human creatures which do not carry the blessing of the Preservers.'

Yama smiled. This at least was easy to counter. 'I wish I knew such stories, but I was raised as an orphan.'

'Perhaps your people were ashamed of you,' Gorgo said, but he was the only one to laugh at his sally.

'Tell your story,' Tamora said, 'and don't let Gorgo interrupt you. He is jealous, because he hasn't any stories of his own.'

When Yama began, he realized that he had drunk more than he intended, but he could not back out now. He described how he had been kidnapped and taken to the pinnace, and how he had escaped (making no mention of the ghostly ship) and cast himself upon a banyan island far from shore.

'I found one of the indigenous fisher-folk stuck fast in a trap left by one of the people of the city which my father administers. The people of the city once hunted the fisher-folk, but my father put a stop to it. The unfortunate fisherman had become entangled in a trap made of strong, sticky threads of the kind used to snare bats which skim the surface of the water for fish. I could not free him without becoming caught fast myself, so I set a trap of my own and waited. When the hunter came to collect his prey, as a spider sidles down to claim a fly caught in its web, it was the hunter who became the prey. I took the spray which dissolves the trap's glue, and the fisherman and I made our escape and left the foolish hunter to the torments of those small, voracious hunters who outnumber their prey, mosquitoes and black-flies. In turn, the fisherman fed me and took me back to the shore of the Great River. And so we saved each other.'

'A tall tale,' Gorgo said, meeting Yama's gaze again.

'It is true I missed out much, but if I told everything then we would be up all night. I will say one more thing. If not for the fisherman's kindness, I would not be here, so I have learnt never to rush to judge any man, no matter how worthless he might appear.'

Gorgo said, 'He asks us to admire his reflection in his tales. Let me tell you that what I see is a fool. Any sensible man would have devoured the fisherman and taken his coracle and escaped with a full belly.'

'I simply told you what happened,' Yama said, meeting the man's yellow gaze. 'Anything you see in my words is what you have placed there. If you had tried to steal the hunter's prey, you would have been stuck there too, and been butchered and devoured along with the fisherman.'

Gorgo jumped up. 'I think I know something about hunting, and I do know that you are not as clever as you imagine yourself to be. You side with prey, and so you're no hunter at all.'

Yama stood too, for he would not look up from a lesser

to a higher position when he replied to Gorgo's insult. Perhaps he would not have done it if he had been less drunk, but he felt the sting of wounded pride. Besides, he did not think that Gorgo was a threat. He was a man who used words as others use weapons. He was taller and heavier than Yama, and armed with a strong jaw and sharp teeth, but Sergeant Rhodean had taught Yama several ways by which such differences could be turned to an advantage.

'I described what happened, no more and no less,' Yama said. 'I hope I do not need to prove the truth of my words.'

Tamora grabbed Yama's hand and said, 'Don't mind Gorgo. He has always wanted to fuck me, and I've always refused. He's quick to anger, and jealous.'

Gorgo laughed. 'I think you have me wrong, sister. It is not your delusion I object to, but his. Remember what you owe me before you insult me again.'

'You will both sit down,' the matriarch said. 'Yama is our guest, Gorgo. You dishonour all of us. Sit down. Drink. We all lose our temper, and the less we make of it the better.'

'You all owe me,' Gorgo said, 'one way or another.' He glared at the circle of people, then spat into the fire and turned and stalked away into the night.

There was an awkward pause. Yama sat down and apologized, saying that he had drunk too much and lost his judgment.

'We've all slapped Gorgo around one time or another,' one of the women said. 'He grows angry if his advances are ignored.'

'He is more angry than fierce,' someone said, and the rest laughed.

'He's a fucking disgrace,' Tamora said. 'A sneak and a coward. He never hunts, but feeds off the quarry of us all. He shot a man with an arbalest instead of fighting fair—'

'Enough,' the matriarch said. 'We do not speak of others to their backs.'

'I'd speak to his face,' Tamora said, 'if he'd ever look me in the eye.'

'If we say no more about this,' Yama said, 'I promise to say no more about myself.'

There were more drinking games, and more songs, and at last Yama begged to be released, for although Tamora's people seemed to need little sleep, he was exhausted by his adventures. He found his way back to his own campfire by the faint light of the Arm of the Warrior, falling several times but feeling no hurt. Pandaras was curled up near the warm ashes, his kidney puncher gripped in both hands. Yama lay down a little way off, on the ridge which overlooked the dark city. He did not remember wrapping himself in his blanket, or falling asleep, but he woke when Tamora pulled the blanket away from him. Her naked body glimmered in the near dark. He did not resist when she started to undo the laces of his shirt, or when she covered his mouth with hers.

22 ~ The Country of the Mind

The next morning, Pandaras watched with unconcealed amusement as Tamora swabbed the scratches on Yama's flanks and the sore places on his shoulders and neck where she had nipped him. Pandaras sleeked back his hair with wrists wet by his own saliva, slapped dust from his ragged jerkin, and announced that he was ready to go.

'We can buy breakfast on the way to the docks. With all the money we have earned, there's no reason to live like unchanged rustics.'

'You slept soundly last night,' Yama said.

'I was not sleeping at all. When I had not fainted away with fright I was listening to every sound in the night, imagining that some hungry meat-eater was creeping up on me. My people have lived in the city for ever. We were not made for the countryside.'

Yama held up his shirt. It was stained with silt from the flood which had fallen through the ceiling of the merchant's house, and flecked with chaff where he and Tamora had used it as a pillow. He said, 'I should wash out my clothes. This will make no impression on our new employers.'

Pandaras looked up. 'Are we away then? We'll collect our reward, and go to our new employer in the Palace of the Memory of the People, and find your family, all before the mountains eat the sun. We could already be there, master, if you had not slept so late.'

'Not so quickly,' Yama said, smiling at Pandaras's eagerness.

'I'll be an old man before long, and no use to you at all. At least let me wash your clothes. It will take but a minute, and I am, after all, your squire.'

Tamora scratched at reddened skin at the edge of the bandage around her waist. 'Grah. Some squire you'd make,' she said, 'with straws in your hair and dirt on your snout. Come with me, Yama. There's a washing place further up.'

Pandaras flourished his kidney puncher and struck an attitude and smiled at Yama, seeking his approval. He had an appetite for drama, as if all the world were a stage, and he was the central player. He said, 'I will guard your satchel, master, but do not leave me alone for long. I can fight off two or three of these ravenous savages, but not an entire tribe.'

A series of pools in natural limestone basins stepped away down the slope of the hill, with water rising from hot springs near the crest and falling from one pool to the next. Each pool was slightly cooler than the one above. Yama sat with Tamora in the shallow end of the hottest pool he could bear and scrubbed his shirt and trousers with white sand. He spread them out to dry on a flat rock already warm from the sun, and then allowed Tamora to wash his back. Little fish striped with silver and black darted around his legs in the clear hot water, nipping at the dirt between his toes. Other people were using pools higher up, calling cheerfully to each other under the blue sky.

Tamora explained that the water came from the Rim Mountains. 'Everyone in the city who can afford it uses mountain water; only beggars and refugees drink from the river.'

'Then they must be the holiest people in Ys, for the water of the Great River is sacred.'

'Grah, holiness does not cleanse the river of all the shit put into it. Most bathe in it only once a year, on the high

297

day celebrated by their bloodline. Otherwise those who can avoid it, which is why water is brought into the city. One of the underground rivers which transports the mountain water passes close by. It's why we have our hunting grounds here. There are waterholes where animals come to drink and where the hunting is good, and at this place we have hidden machines to heat the water.'

'It is a wonderful place,' Yama said. 'Look, a hawk!'

Tamora lifted the thong around Yama's neck and fingered the coin which hung from it. 'What's this? A keepsake?'

'Someone gave it to me. Before I left Aeolis.'

'You find them everywhere, if you bother to dig for a few minutes. We used to play with them when we were children. This is less worn than most, though. Who gave it to you? A sweetheart, perhaps?'

Derev. This was the second time Yama had betrayed her trust. Although he did not know if he would ever see Derev again, and although he had been drunk, he felt suddenly ashamed that he had allowed Tamora to take him.

Tamora's breath feathered his cheek. It had a minty tang from the leaf she had plucked from a bush and folded inside her mouth between her teeth and her cheek. She fingered the line of Yama's jaw and said, 'There's hair coming in here.'

'There is a glass blade in my satchel. I should have brought it to shave. Or perhaps I will grow a beard.'

'It was your first time, wasn't it? Don't be ashamed. Everyone must have a first time.'

'No. I mean, no, it was not the first time.'

Telmon's high, excited voice as he threw open the door of the brothel's warm, scented, lamp-lit parlour. The women turning to them like exotic orchids unfolding. Yama had gone with Telmon because he had been asked, because he had been curious, because Telmon had been about to leave for the war. Afterwards, he had suspected that Derev had known all about it, and if she had not condoned it, then perhaps at least she had understood. That was why Yama had been so fervent with his promises on the night before he left Aeolis, and yet how easily he had broken them. He felt a sudden desolation. How could he even think of being a hero?

Tamora said, 'It was your first time with one of the Fierce People. That should burn away the memory of all others.' She nipped his shoulder. 'You have a soft skin, and it tastes of salt.'

'I sweat everywhere, except the palms of my hands and the soles of my feet.'

'Really? How strange. But I like the taste. That's why I bit you last night.'

'I heal quickly.'

Tamora said, 'Yama, listen to me. It won't happen again. Not while we're working together. No, stay still. I can't clean your back if you turn around. We celebrated together last night, and that was good. But I won't let it interfere with my work. If you don't like that, and think yourself used, then find another cateran. There are plenty here, and plenty more at the Water Market. You have enough money to hire the best.'

'I was at least as drunk as you were.'

'Drunker, I'd say. I hope you didn't fuck me just because you were drunk.'

Yama blushed. 'I meant that I lost any inhibitions I might otherwise have had. Tamora—'

'Don't start on any sweet talk. And don't tell me about any sweetheart you might have left at home, either, or about how sorry you are. That's there. This is here. We're battle companions. We fucked. End of that part of the story.'

'Are all your people so direct?'

'We speak as we find. Not to do so is a weakness. I like you, and I enjoyed last night. We're lucky, because some bloodlines are only on heat once a year – imagine how miserable they must be – and besides, there's no danger of us making babies together. That's what happens when my people fuck, unless the woman is already pregnant. I'm not ready for that, not yet. In a few years I'll find some men to run with and we'll raise a family, but not yet. A lot of us choose the metic way for that reason.'

Yama was interested. He said, 'Can you not use prophylactics?'

Tamora laughed. 'You haven't seen the cock of one of our men! There are spines to hold it in place. Put a rubber on that? Grah! There's a herb some women boil into a tea and drink to stop their courses, but it doesn't work most of the time.'

'Women of your people are stronger than men.'

'It's generally true of all bloodlines, even when it doesn't seem so. We're more honest about it, perhaps. Now you clean my back, and I'll go use the shittery, and then we'll find the rat-boy. If we're lucky, he's run back to where he belongs.'

As they went back down the hill, along the path that wandered between stands of sage and tall sawgrasses, Yama saw someone dressed in black watching them from the shade at the edge of a grove of live oaks. He thought it might have been Gorgo, but whoever it was stepped back into the shadows and was gone before Yama could point him out to Tamora.

The city was still disturbed by Yama's drawing down of the feral machine. Magistrates and their attendant clouds of machines were patrolling the streets, and although Yama asked the machines to ignore him and his companions, he was fearful that he would miss one until it was too late, or that Prefect Corin would lunge out of the crowds towards him. He kept turning this way and that until Tamora told him to stop it, or they'd be arrested for sure. Little groups of soldiers lounged at every major intersection. They were the city militia, armed with fusils and carbines, and dressed in loose red trousers and plastic cuirasses as slick and cloudily transparent as ice. They watched the crowds with hard, insolent eyes, but they did not challenge anyone. They did not dare, Pandaras said, and Yama asked how that could be, if they had the authority of the Preservers.

'There are many more of us than there are of them,' Pandaras said, and made the sign Yama had noticed before, touching his fist to his throat.

The boy did not seem scared of the soldiers, but instead openly displayed a smouldering contempt, and Yama noticed that many of the other people made the same sign when they went by a group of soldiers. Some even spat or shouted a curse, safe in the anonymity of the crowd.

Pandaras said, 'With the war downriver, there are even fewer soldiers in the city, and they must keep the peace by terror. That's why they're hated. See that cock there?'

Yama looked up. An officer in gold-tinted body armour stood on a metal disc that floated in the air above the dusty crowns of the ginkgoes which lined one side of the broad, brawling avenue.

'He could level a city block with one shot, if he had a mind to,' Pandaras said. 'But he wouldn't unless he had no other choice, because there'd be riots and even more of the city would be burned. If someone stole a pistol and tried to use it against soldiers or magistrates, then he might do it.'

'It seems an excessive punishment.'

Tamora said, 'Energy weapons are prohibited, worse luck. *I'd* like one right now. Clear a way through these herds of grazers in a blink.'

'One of my uncles on my mother's side of the family was caught up in a tax protest a few years back,' Pandaras said. 'It was in a part of the city a few leagues upriver. A merchant bought up a block and levelled it to make a park, and the legates decided that every tradesman living round about should pay more tax. The park made the area more attractive, neh? The legates said that more people would come because of the open space, and spend more in the shops round about. So the tradesmen got together and declared a tax strike in protest. The legates called up the magistrates, and they came and blockaded the area. Set their machines spinning in the air to make a picket line, so no one could get in or out. It lasted a hundred days, and at the end they said people inside the picket line were eating each other. The food ran out, and there was no way to get more in. A few tried to dig tunnels, but the magistrates sent in machines and killed them.'

Yama said, 'Why did they not give up the strike?'

'They did, after twenty days. They would have held out longer, but there were children, and there were people who didn't live there at all but happened to be passing through when the blockade went up. So they presented a petition of surrender, but the magistrates kept the siege going as punishment. That kind of thing is supposed to make the rest of us too frightened to spit unless we get permission.'

Tamora said, 'There's no other way. There are too many people living in the city, and most are fools or grazers. An argument between neighbours can turn into a feud between bloodlines, with thousands killed. Instead, the magistrates or the militia kill two or three, or even a hundred if necessary, and the matter is settled before it spreads. There are a dozen bloodlines they could get rid of and no one would notice.'

'We're the strength of Ys,' Pandaras said defiantly, and for once Tamora didn't answer back.

They reached the docks late in the afternoon. The same stocky, shaven-headed guard met them in the shadow of the lighter. He looked at the brandy-filled flask and the strings of nerve tissue that floated inside and said that he had already heard that the merchant was dead.

Tamora said, 'Then we'll just take our money and go.'

Yama said to the guard, 'You said you would need to test what we brought.'

The guard said, 'The whole city knows that he was killed

last night. To be frank, we would have preferred less attention drawn to it, but we are happy that the task was done. Do not worry. We will pay you.'

'Then let's do it now,' Tamora said, 'and we'll be on our way.'

Yama said quickly, 'But we have made an agreement. I would have it seen through to the letter. Your master wanted to test what we brought, and I would have it done no other way, to prove that we are honest.'

The guard stared hard at Yama, then said, 'I would not insult you by failing to carry out everything we agreed. Come with me.'

As they followed the guard up the gangway, Tamora caught Yama's arm and whispered fiercely, 'This is a foolish risk. We do the job, we take the money, we go. Who cares what they think of us? Complications are dangerous, especially with the star-sailors, and we have an appointment at the Water Market.'

'I have my reasons,' Yama said stubbornly. 'You and Pandaras can wait on the dock, or go on to the Water Market, just as you please.'

He had thought it over as they had walked through the streets of the city to the wharf where the voidship lighter was moored. The star-sailor who piloted the lighter had said that it knew something of Yama's bloodline, and even if it was only one tenth of what the merchant had claimed to know, it was still worth learning. Yama was prepared to pay for the knowledge, and he thought that he knew a sure way of getting at it if the star-sailor refused to tell him anything.

Inside the ship, in the round room at the top of the spiral corridor, the guard uncapped the crystal flask and poured its contents onto the black floor, which quickly absorbed the brandy and the strings of nervous tissue. He set the gold circlet on his scarred, shaven scalp and jerked to attention. His mouth worked, and he said in a voice not his own, 'This one will pay you. What else do you want of me?'

Yama addressed the fleshy blossom which floated inside its bottle. 'I talked with your crewmate before he died. He said that he knew something of my bloodline.'

The star-sailor said through its human mouthpiece, 'No doubt he said many things to save his life.'

'This was when he had me prisoner, and my friends, too.'

'Then perhaps he was boasting. You must understand that he was mad. He had corrupted himself with the desires of the flesh.'

'I remember you said that I had abilities that might be useful.'

'I was mistaken. They have proved ... inconvenient. You have no control over what you can do.'

Tamora said, 'We should leave this. Yama, I'll help you find out what you want to know, but in the Palace of the Memory of the People, not here. We made a deal.'

Yama said stubbornly, 'I have not forgotten. The few questions I want to ask will not end my quest, but they may aid it.' He turned back to the thing in the bottle. 'I will waive my part of the fee for the murder of your crewmate if you will help me understand what he told me.'

Tamora said, 'Don't listen to him, dominie! He hasn't the right to make that bargain!'

The guard's mouth opened and closed. His chin was slick with saliva. He said, 'He was driven mad by the desires of the flesh. I, however, am not mad. I have nothing to say to you unless you can prove that you know what you are. Return then, and we can talk.'

'If I knew that, I would have nothing to ask you.'

Tamora grabbed Yama's arm. 'You're risking everything, you fool. Come on!'

Yama tried to free himself, but Tamora's grip was unyielding and her sharp nails dug into his flesh until blood ran. He stepped in close, thinking to throw her from his hip, but she knew that trick and butted him on the bridge of his nose with her forehead. A blinding spike of pain shot through his head and tears sprang to his eyes. Tamora twisted his arm up behind his back and started to drag him across the room to the dilated doorway, but Pandaras wrapped himself around her legs and fastened his sharp teeth on her thigh. Tamora howled and Yama pulled free and flung himself at the guard, ripping the gold circlet from the man's head and jamming it on his own.

White light.

White noise.

Something was in his head. It fled even as he noticed it and he turned in a direction he had not seen before and flew after it. It was a woman, a naked, graceful woman with pale skin and long black hair that fanned out behind her as she soared through clashing currents of light. Even as she fled, she kept looking back over her bare shoulder. Her eyes blazed with a desperate light.

Yama followed with mounting exhilaration. He seemed to be connected to her through a kind of cord that was growing shorter and stronger, and he twisted and turned after his quarry without thought as they plunged together through interlaced strands of light.

Others were pacing them on either side, and beyond these unseen presences Yama could feel a vast congregation, mostly in clusters as distant and faint as the halo stars. They were the crews of the voidships, meeting together in this country of the mind, in which they swam as easily as fish in the river. Whenever Yama turned his attention to one or another of these clusters, he felt an airy expansion and a fleeting glimpse of the combined light of other minds, as if through a window whose shutters are flung back to greet the rising sun. In every case the minds he touched with his mind recoiled; the shutters slammed; the light faded.

In his desperate chase after the woman through the country of the mind, Yama left behind a growing wake of confused and scandalized inhabitants. They called on something, a guardian or watchdog, and it rose towards Yama like a pressure wave, angling through unseen dimensions like a pike gliding effortlessly through water towards a duckling paddling on the surface. Yama doubled and redoubled his effort to catch the woman, and was almost on her when white light blinded him and white noise roared in his ears and a black floor flew up and struck him with all the weight of the world.

23 ~ The Temple of the Black Well

When Yama woke, the first thing he saw was Pandaras sitting cross-legged by the foot of the bed, sewing up a rip in his second-best shirt. Yama was naked under the scratchy starched sheet, and clammy with old sweat. His head ached, and some time ago a small animal seemed to have crept into the dry cavern of his mouth and died there. Perhaps it was a cousin of the bright green gecko which clung upside down in a patch of sunlight on the far wall, its scarlet throat pulsing. This was a small room, with ochre plaster walls painted with twining patterns of blue vines, and dusty rafters under a slanted ceiling. Afternoon light fell through the two tall windows, and with it the noise and dust and smells of a busy street.

Pandaras helped him up, fussing with the bolster, and brought him a beaker of water. 'It has salt and sugar in it, master. Drink. It will make you stronger.'

Yama obeyed the boy. It seemed that he had been asleep for a night and most of the day that followed. Pandaras and Tamora had brought him here from the docks.

'She has gone out to talk with the man we should have met yesterday. And we didn't get paid by the star-sailor, so she's angry with you.'

'I remember that you tried to help me.' Yama discovered that at some time he had bitten his tongue and the insides of his cheeks. He said, 'You killed the guard with that kidney puncher she gave you.'

'That was before, master. At the gate of the merchant's estate. After that there was the voidship lighter, when you snatched the circlet from the guard and put it on your head.'

'The merchant was wearing the circlet. It was how he controlled his household. But I broke it when I took it away from him.'

'This was in the voidship lighter. Please try and remember, master! You put the circlet on your head and straightaway you collapsed with foam on your lips and your eyes rolled right back. One of my half-sisters has the falling sickness, and that's what it looked like.'

'A woman. I saw a woman. But she fled from me.'

Pandaras pressed on with his story. 'I snatched the circlet from your head, but you didn't wake. More guards came, and they marched us off the lighter. The first guard, the one you took the circlet from, he and Tamora had an argument about the fee. I thought she might kill him, but he and his fellows drew their pistols, and there was no argument after that. We took some of your money to pay for the room, and for the palanquin that carried you here. I hope we did right.'

'Tamora must be angry with you, too.'

'She doesn't take any account of me, which is just as well. I bit her pretty badly when she tried to stop you taking the circlet, but she bandaged up her legs and said nothing of it. Wouldn't admit I could hurt her, neh? And now I'm not frightened of her because I know I can hurt her, and I'll do it again if I have to. I didn't want to fight with her, master, but she shouldn't have tried to stop you. She didn't have the right.'

Yama closed his eyes. Clusters of lights hanging from the ceiling of the round room at the top of the voidship lighter. The thing in the bottle, with rose-red gills and a lily-white mantle folded around a thick braid of naked nerve tissue. 'I remember,' he said. 'I tried to find out about my bloodline. The country of the mind—'

Pandaras nodded eagerly. 'You took the circlet from the guard and put it on your own head.'

'Perhaps it would have been better if Tamora had stopped me. She was worried that I would no longer have any need of her.'

Pandaras took the empty beaker from Yama and said, 'Well, and do you need her, master? You stood face to face with that thing and talked to it direct. Did it tell you what you wanted to know?'

It seemed like a dream, fading even as Yama tried to remember its details. The woman fleeing, the faint stars of other minds. Yama said, 'I saw something wonderful, but I did not learn anything about myself, except that the people who crew the voidships are scared of me.'

'You scared me too, master. I thought you had gone into the place where they live and left your body behind. I'll have some food sent up. You haven't eaten in two days.'

'You have been good to me, Pandaras.'

'Why, it's a fine novelty to order people about in a place like this. A while ago it was me running at any cock's shout, and I haven't forgotten what it was like.'

'It was not that long ago. A few days.'

'Longer for me than for you. Rest, master. I'll be back soon.'

But Pandaras was gone a long time. The room was hot and close, and Yama wrapped the sheet around himself and sat at one of the windows, where there was a little breeze. He felt weak, but rested and alert. The bandage was gone from the wound on his forearm and the flesh had knitted about the puckers made by the black crosses of the stitches; the self-inflicted wound on his palm was no more than a faint silvery line. All the bruises and small cuts from his recent adventures were healed, too, and someone, presumably Pandaras, had shaved him while he had been sleeping.

The inn stood on a broad avenue divided down the centre by a line of palm trees. The crowds which jostled along the dusty white thoroughfare contained more people than Yama had ever seen in his life, thousands of people of a hundred different bloodlines. There were hawkers and skyclad mendicants, parties of palmers, priests, officials hurrying along in groups of two or three, scribes, musicians, tumblers, whores and mountebanks. An acrobat walked above the heads of the crowd on a wire strung from one side of the avenue to the other. Vendors fried plantains and yams on heated iron plates, or roasted nuts in huge copper basins set over oil burners. Ragged boys ran amongst the people, selling flavoured ice, twists of licorice, boiled sweets, roast nuts, cigarettes, plastic trinkets representing one or another of the long-lost aspects of the Preservers, and medals stamped with the likenesses of official heroes of the war against the heretics. Beggars exhibited a hundred different kinds of mutilation and deformity. Messengers on nimble genets or black plumaged ratites rode at full tilt through the crowds. A few important personages walked under silk canopies held up by dragomen, or were carried on litters or palanquins. A party of solemn giants walked waist high amidst the throng as if wading in a stream. Directly across the avenue, people gathered at a stone altar, burning incense cones bought from a priest, muttering prayers and wafting the smoke towards themselves. A procession of ordinands in red robes, their freshly shaven heads gleaming with oil, wound in a long straggling line behind men banging tambours.

In the distance, the sound of braying, discordant trumpets rang above the noise of the crowded avenue, and presently the procession heralded by the trumpeters hove into view. It was a huge cart pulled by a team of a hundred sweating, half-naked men, with priests swinging fuming censers on either side. It was painted scarlet and gold and bedecked with garlands of flowers, and amidst the heaps of flowers stood a screen, its black oval framed by ornate golden scrollwork. The cart stopped almost directly opposite Yama's window, and people gathered on the rooftops and threw down bucketfuls of water on the men who pulled it, and dropped more garlands of flowers onto the cart and around the men and the attendant priests in a soft, multicoloured snowstorm. Yama leaned out further to get a better view, and at that moment heard a noise in the room behind him and turned, thinking it was Pandaras.

A patch of ochre plaster on the wall opposite the window was cracked in a spiderweb pattern, and in the centre of the web stood an arbalest bolt.

The bolt was as long as Yama's forearm, with a shaft of dense, hard wood and red fight feathers. From the downward pointing angle at which the bolt had embedded itself in the plaster, it must have been fired from one of the flat roofs on the other side of the avenue, for all of them were higher than the window. Yama crouched down and scanned the rooftops, but there were hundreds of people crowded along their edges, scattering flowers and pitching silvery twists of water at the cart. He tried to find a machine which might have been watching, but it seemed that there were no magistrates here.

Still crouching, Yama closed and bolted the heavy slatted shutters of both windows, then pulled the arbalest bolt from the wall.

A few minutes later, Pandaras returned ahead of a pot boy who set a tray covered in a white cloth on the low, round table which, apart from the bed and the chair in which Yama sat, were the only pieces of furniture in the room. Pandaras dismissed the pot boy and whipped away the tray's cover like a conjuror, revealing a platter of fruit and cold meat, and a sweating earthenware pitcher of white wine. He poured wine into two cups, and handed one to Yama. 'I'm sorry it took so long, master. There's a festival. We had to pay double rates just to get the room.'

The wine was cold, and as thickly sweet as syrup. Yama said, 'I saw the procession go by.'

'There's always some procession here. It's in the nature of

311

the place. Eat, master. You must break your fast before you go anywhere.'

Yama took the slice of green melon Pandaras held out. 'Where are we?'

Pandaras bit into his own melon slice. 'Why, it's the quarter that runs between the river and the Palace of the Memory of the People.'

'I think we should go and find Tamora. Where are my clothes?'

'Your trousers are under the mattress, to keep them pressed. I am mending one of your shirts; the other is in your pack. Master, you should eat, and then rest.'

'I do not think so,' Yama said, and showed Pandaras the arbalest bolt.

The landlady called to Yama and Pandaras as they pushed through the hot, crowded taproom of the inn. She was a plump, broad-beamed, brown-skinned woman, her long black hair shiny with grease and braided into a thick rope. She was sweating heavily into her purple and gold sarong, and she waved a fretted palm leaf to and fro as she explained that a message had been left for them.

'I have it here,' she said, rummaging through the drawer of her desk. 'Please be patient, sirs. It is a very busy day today. Is this it? No. Wait, here it is.'

Yama took the scrap of stiff paper. It had been folded four times and tucked into itself, and sealed with a splash of wax. Yama turned it over and over, and asked Pandaras, 'Can Tamora read and write?'

'She put her thumb to the contract, master, so I'd guess she has as much reading as I have, which is to say none.'

The landlady said helpfully, 'There are scribes on every corner. The seal is one of theirs.'

'Do you know which one?'

'There are very many. I suppose I could have one of my boys . . .' The landlady patted her brow with a square of yellow cloth that reeked of peppermint oil. Her eyes were made up with blue paint and gold leaf and her eyebrows had been twisted and stiffened with wax to form long tapering points, giving the effect of a butterfly perched on her face. She added, 'That is, when we are less busy. It is a festival day, you see.'

Yama said, 'I saw the cart go by.'

'The cart? Oh, the shrine. No, no, that is nothing to do with the festival. It passes up and down the street every day, except on its feast day, of course, when it is presented at the Great River. But that is a hundred days off, and just a local affair. People have come here from all over Ys for the festival, and from downriver, too. A very busy time, although of course there are not so many people as there once were. Fewer travel, you see, because of the war. That is why I was able to find you a room at short notice.'

'She moved two palmers into the stables, and charges us twice what they paid,' Pandaras remarked.

'And now they are paying less than they would have,' the landlady said, 'so it all evens out. I hope that the message is not bad news, sirs. The room is yours as long as you want it.' Despite her claim to be busy, it seemed that she had plenty of time to stick her nose in other people's business.

Yama held up the folded paper and said, 'Who brought this?'

'I didn't see. One of my boys gave it to me. I could find him, I suppose, although it's all a muddle today—'

'Because of the festival.' Yama snapped the wax seal and unfolded the paper.

The message was brief, and written in neatly aligned glyphs with firm and decisive downstrokes and fine feathering on the upstrokes. Most likely it had been set down by a scribe, unless Tamora had spent as long as Yama learning the finer nuances of penmanship.

I have gone on. The man you want is at the Temple of the Black Well.

Pandaras said, 'What does it say?'

Yama read the message to Pandaras, and the landlady said, 'That's not too far from here. Go down the passage at the left side of the inn and strike towards the Palace. I could get you a link boy if you'd like to wait . . .'

But Yama and Pandaras were already pushing their way through the crowded room towards the open door and the sunlit avenue beyond.

The narrow streets that tangled behind the inn were cooler and less crowded than the avenue. They were paved with ancient, uneven brick courses, and naked children played in the streams of dirty water that ran down the central gutters. The houses were flat-roofed and none were more than two storeys high, with small shuttered windows and walls covered in thick yellow or orange plaster, walls that were crumbling and much-patched. Many had workshops on the ground floor, open to the street, and Yama and Pandaras passed a hundred tableaus of industry, most to do with the manufacture of the religious mementoes which were displayed in shops which stood at every corner of every street, although none of the shops seemed to be open.

It was a secretive, suspicious place, Yama thought, noting that people stopped what they were doing and openly stared as he and Pandaras went past. But he liked the serendipitous geography, so that a narrow street might suddenly open onto a beautiful square with a white fountain splashing in its centre, and liked the small neighbourhood shrines set into the walls of the houses, with browning wreaths of flowers and pyramids of ash before a flyspotted circle of black glass that poorly mimicked the dark transparency of true shrines.

The domes and pinnacles and towers of temples and shrines reared up amongst the crowded flat roofs of the ordinary houses like ships foundering in the scruffy pack ice of the frozen wilderness at the head of the Great River hundreds of leagues upstream. And beyond all these houses and temples and shrines, the black mountain of the Palace of the Memory of the People climbed terrace by terrace towards its distant peak, with the setting sun making the sky red behind it.

Pandaras explained that this part of the city was given over to the business of worship of the Preservers and of the governance of Ys. Civil service departments displaced from the interior of the Palace of the Memory of the People occupied lesser buildings on its outskirts, and a thousand cults flourished openly or skulked in secret underground chambers.

'At night it can be a dangerous place for strangers,' Pandaras said.

'I have my knife. And you have yours.'

'You should have worn your armour. We collected it from the Water Market, cut down neatly and polished up as good as new.'

Yama had found it when he had taken his shirt from the satchel. He said, 'It would attract attention. Someone might take a fancy to it. Already I feel as if I am a procession, the way people turn to stare.'

'They might want our blood. Or want to scoop out our brains and put them in tanks, all alive-o like the star-sailors.'

Yama laughed at these fantasies.

Pandaras said darkly, 'This is a place of good and evil, master. It is the New Quarter, built on a bloody battle-ground. You are a singular person. Don't forget it. You would be a great prize for a blood sacrifice.'

'New? It seems to me very old.'

'That's because nothing here has been rebuilt since the Age of Insurrection. The rest of the city is far older, but people are always knocking down old buildings and putting up new ones. The Hierarchs built the Palace of the Memory of the People where the last battle between machines was fought, and the bones and casings of all the dead were tipped into great pits and the ground around about was flattened and these houses were built.'

'I know there was a battle fought near Ys, but I thought it was much further upriver.' Yama remembered now that the Temple of the Black Well had something to do with that last battle, although he could not quite remember what it was.

Pandaras said, 'They built the houses over the battle-ground, and nothing's changed since, except for the building of shrines and temples.'

'I had thought the houses were built around them.'

'Houses have to be knocked down each time a new temple is built. It's a dangerous business. There are old poisons in the ground, and old weapons too, and sometimes the weapons discharge when they are uncovered. There's a department which does nothing but search by divination for old weapons, and make them safe when they're found. And some parts of the quarter are haunted, too. It's why the people are so strange hereabouts, neh? The ghosts get inside their heads, and infect them with ideas from ages past.'

Yama said, 'I have never seen a ghost.' The aspects which haunted the City of the Dead did not count, for they were merely semi-intelligent projections. And while the Amnan claimed that the blue lights sometimes seen floating amongst the ruins below the peel-house were wights, the eidolons of the restless dead, Zakiel said that they were no more than wisps of burning marsh gas.

Pandaras said, 'These are machine ghosts mostly, but some were human, once, and they say that those are the worst. That's why they make so many icons hereabouts, master. If you were to look inside one of these houses, you'd find layer upon layer of them on the walls.'

'To keep out the ghosts.'

'They don't usually work. That's what I heard, anyway.'

'Look there. Is that our temple?'

It reared up a few streets ahead, a giant cube built of huge, roughly hewn stone blocks stained black with soot, and topped by an onion dome lapped in scuffed gilt tiles.

Pandaras squinted at it, then said, 'No, ours has a rounder roof, with a hole in the top of it.'

'Of course! Where the machine fell!'

The Temple of the Black Well had been built long after the feral machine's fiery fall, but its dome had been left symbolically uncompleted, with the aperture at its apex directly above the deep hole made when the machine had struck the surface of the world and melted a passage in the rock all the way down to the keel. Yama had been told the story by the aspect of a leather merchant who had had his tannery near the site of the temple's construction. Mysyme, that had been the merchant's name. He had had two wives and six beautiful daughters, and had done much charitable work amongst the orphaned river rats of the docks. Mysyme was dead an age past, and Yama had lost interest in the limited responses of his aspect years ago, but now he remembered them all over again. Mysyme's father had seen the fall of the machine, and had told his son that when it hit, a plume of melted rock had been thrown higher than the atmosphere, while the smoke of secondary fires had darkened the sky above Ys for a decad.

'It's a little to the left,' Pandaras said, 'and maybe ten minutes' walk. That place with the gold roof is a tomb of a warrior-saint. It's solid all the way through except for a secret chamber.'

'You are a walking education, Pandaras.'

'I have an uncle who used to live here, and one time I stayed with him. He was on my mother's side, and this was when my father ran off and my mother went looking for him. She was a year at it, and never found him. And a year is a long time for my people. So she came back and married another man, and when that didn't work out she married my stepfather. I don't get on with him, and that's why I took the job of pot boy, because it came with a room. And then you came along, and here we are.' Pandaras grinned. 'For a long time after I left this part of the city, I thought maybe I was haunted. I'd wake up and think I'd been hearing voices, voices that had been telling me things in my sleep. But I haven't heard them since I met up with you, master. Maybe your bloodline is a cure for ghosts.'

'All my bloodline are ghosts, from the little I have learned,' Yama said.

The Temple of the Black Well stood at the centre of a wide, quiet plaza of mossy cobbles. It had been built in the shape of a cross, with a long atrium and short apses; its dome, covered in gold leaf that shone with the last light of the sun, capped the point where the apses intersected the atrium. The temple was clad in lustrous black stone, although here and there parts of the cladding had fallen away to reveal the greyish limestone beneath. Yama and Pandaras walked all the way around the temple and saw no one, and then climbed the long flight of shallow steps and went through the tall narthex.

It was dark inside, but a thick slanted column of reddish light fell through the open apex of the dome at the far end of a long atrium flanked by colonnades. Yama walked towards the light. There was no sign of Tamora or her mysterious contact; the whole temple seemed deserted. The pillars of the colonnades were intricately carved and the ruined mosaics of the floor sketched the outlines of heroic figures. The temple had been splendid once, Yama thought, but now it had the air of a place that was no longer cared for. He thought it an odd choice for a rendezvous – far better for an ambush.

Pandaras clearly felt the same thing, for his sleek head continually turned this way and that as they went down the atrium. The reddish light, alive with swirling motes of dust, fell on a waist-high wall of undressed stone which ringed a wide hole that plunged down into darkness. It was the well, the shaft the fallen machine had melted. The wide coping on top of the wall was covered in the ashy remnants of incense cones, and here and there were offerings of fruit and flowers. A few joss sticks jammed into cracks in the wall sent up curls of sweet-smelling smoke, but the flowers were shrivelled and brown, and the little piles of fruit were spotted with decay.

'Not many come here,' Pandaras said. 'The ghost of the machine is powerful, and quick to anger.'

Yama gripped the edge of the coping and looked into the depths of the well. A faint draught of cold, stale air blew up around him from the lightless depths. The walls of the shaft were long glassy flows of once-melted rock, veined with impurities, dwindling away to a vanishing point small as the end of his thumb. It was impossible to tell how deep the well really was, and in a spirit of enquiry Yama dropped a softening pomegranate into the black air.

'That isn't a good idea,' Pandaras said uneasily.

'I do not think a piece of fruit would wake this particular machine. It fell a long way as I recall – at least, it was two days in falling, and appeared in the sky as a star clothed in burning hair. When it struck the ground, the blow knocked down thousands of houses and caused a wave in the river that washed away much of the city on the farside shore. And then the sky turned black with smoke from all the fires.'

'There might be other things down there,' Pandaras said. 'Bats, for instance. I have a particular loathing of bats.'

Yama said, 'I should have thrown a coin. I might have heard it hit.'

But a small part of his mind insisted that the fruit was still falling through black air towards the bottom, two leagues or more to the keel. He and Pandaras walked around the well, but apart from the smoking joss sticks there was no sign that Tamora or anyone else had been there recently, and the hushed air was beginning to feel oppressive, as if it held a note endlessly drawn out just beyond the range of hearing.

Pandaras said, 'We should go on, master. She isn't here.' He added hopefully, 'Perhaps she has run off and left us.'

'She made a contract with me. I should think that is a serious thing for someone who lives from one job to the next. We will wait a little longer.' He took out the paper and read it again. '"The man you want . . ." I wonder what she meant.'

'It'll be dark soon.'

Yama smiled, and said, 'I believe that you are scared of this place.'

'You might not believe in ghosts, master, but there are many who do – most of the people in the city, I reckon.'

'I might have more cause to believe in ghosts, because I was brought up in the middle of the City of the Dead, but I do not. Just because a lot of people believe in ghosts does not make them real. I might believe that the Preservers have incarnated themselves in river turtles, and I might persuade a million people to believe it, too, but that does not make it true.'

'You shouldn't make jokes like that,' Pandaras said. 'Especially not here.'

'Surely the Preservers will forgive a small joke.'

'There's many who would take offence on their account,' Pandaras said stubbornly. He had a deep streak of superstition, despite his worldly-wise air. Yama had seen the care with which he washed himself in a ritual pattern after eating and upon waking, the way he crossed his fingers when walking past a shrine – a superstition he shared with the citizens of Aeolis, who believed that it disguised the fact that you had come to a shrine without an offering – and his devotion at prayer. Like the Amnan, who could not or would not read the Puranas and so only knew them secondhand through the preaching of priests and iconoclasts, Pandaras and the countless millions of ordinary folk of Ys believed that the Preservers had undergone a transubstantiation, disappearing not into the Eye but dispersing themselves into every particle of the world which they had made, so that they were everywhere at once, immortal, invisible and, despite their limitless power, quick to judge and requiring constant placation. It was not surprising, then, that Pandaras believed in ghosts and other revenants.

Pandaras said, 'Ghosts are more like ideas than you might think. The more people believe in them, the more powerful they become. Listen! What was that?'

'I heard nothing,' Yama said, but even as he said it there was a faint brief rumble, as if the temple, with all its massy stones, had briefly stirred and then settled again. It seemed to come from the well, and Yama leaned over and peered into its depths. The wind which blew out of the darkness seemed to be blowing a little more strongly, and it held a faint tang, like heated metal.

'Come away,' Pandaras pleaded uneasily. He was shifting his weight from foot to foot, as if ready to run.

'We will look in the apses. If anything was going to happen, Pandaras, it would have happened by now.'

'If it does happen, it'll be all the worse for waiting.'

'You go left and I will go right, and if we find nothing I promise we will go straight out of this place.'

'I'll come with you, master, if you don't mind. I've no liking for being left alone in this hecatomb.'

The archway which led into the apse to the right of the well was curtained by falls of fine black plastic mesh. Beyond was a high square space lit by shafts of dim light striking through knotholes that pierced the thick walls just beneath the vaulted roof. There was a shrine set in the centre of the space, a glossy black circle like a giant's coin or eyeglass stood on its side.

Statues three times the height of a man stood in recesses all around the four walls, although they were not statues of men, and nor were they carved from stone, but were made of the same slick, translucent stuff as ancient armour. Yama could dimly see shapes and catenaries inside their chests and limbs.

Pandaras went up to a statue and knocked his knuckles

against its shin: it rang with a dull note. 'There's a story that these things fought against the Insurrectionists.'

'More likely they were made in the likeness of great generals,' Yama said, looking up at their grim visages.

'Don't worry,' a woman's voice said. 'They've been asleep so long they've forgotten how to wake.'

24 ~ The Woman in White

Yama turned, and streamers of blazing white light suddenly raced through the shrine's black disc. He raised an arm to shade his eyes, but the white light had already faded into a swirling play of soft colours.

Pandaras's clenched paw fluttered under his open mouth. He said, 'Master, this is some horrid trick.'

Cautiously, Yama stepped through polychromatic light and touched the shrine's slick, cold surface. He was possessed by the mad idea that he could slip into it as easily as slipping into the cool water of the river.

Like a reflection, a hand rose through swirling colours to meet his own. For a moment he thought that he felt its touch, like a glove slipping around his skin, and he recoiled in shock.

Laughter, like the chiming of small silver bells. Streaks and swirls and dabs of a hundred colours collapsed into themselves, and a woman was framed in the disc of the shrine. Pandaras shouted and ran, flinging himself in a furious panic through the black mesh curtains which divided the apse from the main part of the temple.

Yama knelt before the shrine, fearful and amazed. 'Lady . . . what do you want from me?'

'Oh do get up. I can't talk to the top of your head.'

Yama obeyed. He supposed that the woman was one of the avatars of the Preservers, who, as was written in the Puranas, stood between the quotidian world and the glory of their masters, facing both ways at once. She was tall and slender, with a commanding, imperious gaze, and wore a white one-piece garment which clung to her limbs and body. Her skin was the colour of newly forged bronze, and her long black hair was caught in a kind of net at her right shoulder. A green garden receded behind her: smooth lawns and a maze of high, trimmed hedges. A stone fountain sent a muscular jet of water high into the sunlit air.

'Who are you, domina? Do you live in this shrine?'

'I don't know where I live, these days. I'm scattered, I suppose you could say. But this is one of the places where I can look out at the world. It's like a window. You live in a house made of rooms. Where I live is mostly windows, looking out to different places. You drew me to this window and I looked out and found you.'

'Drew you? Domina, I did not mean to.'

'You wear the key around your neck. You have discovered that, at least.'

Yama lifted out the coin which hung on the thong around his neck, the coin which the anchorite had given him the spring night when Dr Dismas had returned to Ys, and everything had changed. Yama had gone out to hunt frogs, and caught something far stranger. The coin was warm, but perhaps only because it had lain next to his skin.

The woman in the shrine said, 'It works by light, and briefly talked with this transceiver. I heard it, and came here. Don't be afraid. Do you like where I live?'

Yama said, with reflexive politeness, 'I have never seen a garden like yours.'

'Of course you haven't. It is from some long-vanished world, perhaps even from Earth. Do you wish me to change it? I could live anywhere, you know. Or at least anywhere on file that hasn't been corrupted. The servers are very old, and there's much that has been corrupted. Atoms migrate; cosmic rays and neutrinos corrupt the lattices ... Anyway, I like gardens. It stirs something in my memory. My original ruled many worlds once, and surely some of those possessed gardens. It's possible she owned a garden just like this, once upon a time. But I've forgotten such a lot, and I was never really whole in the first place. There are peacocks. Do you know peacocks? No, I suppose not. Perhaps there are autochthonous creatures like peacocks somewhere on Confluence, but I don't have the files to hand. If we talk long enough perhaps one will come past. They are birds. The cocks have huge fan-shaped tails, with eyes in them.'

Yama was suddenly overwhelmed by the image of an electric blue long-necked bird with concentric arcs of fiery eyes peering over its tiny head. He turned away, the heels of his palms pressed into his eye sockets, but the vision still beat inside his head.

'Wait,' the woman said. Was there a note of uncertainty in her voice? 'I didn't mean ... The gain is difficult to control ...'

The sheaves of burning eyes vanished; there was only ordinary bloodwarm darkness behind his eyelids. Cautiously, Yama turned back to the shrine.

'It isn't real,' the woman said. She stepped up to the inner surface of the shrine and pressed her hands against it and peered between them as if trying to see through the window of a lighted room into a dark landscape. Her palms were dyed red. Paeonin. She said, 'That it isn't real is the important thing to remember. But isn't everything an illusion? We're all waves, and even the waves are really half-glimpsed strings folded deeply into themselves.'

She seemed to be talking to herself, but then she smiled at Yama. Or no, her eyes were not quite focused on him, but at a point a little to one side of the top of his head.

Yama said, prompted by a flicker of suspicion, 'Excuse me, domina, but are you really an avatar? I have never seen one before.'

'I'm no fragment of a god, Yamamanama. The clade of my original ruled a million planetary systems, once upon a time, but she never claimed to be a god. None of the transcendents ever claimed that, only their enemies.'

Fear and amazement collapsed into relief. Yama laughed and said, 'An aspect. You are an aspect. Or a ghost.'

'A ghost in the machine. Yes, that's one way of looking at it. Why not? Even when my original walked the surface of this strange habitat she was a copy of a memory, and I suppose that would make me a kind of a ghost of a ghost. But you're a ghost, too. You shouldn't be here, not at this time. You're either too young, or too old, a hundred thousand years either way . . . Do you know why you are here?'

'I wish with all my heart to find out,' Yama said, 'but I do not believe in ghosts.'

'We have spoken before.' The woman tilted her head with a curiously coquettish gesture, and smiled. 'You don't remember, do you?' she said. 'Well, you were very young, and that foolish man with you hid your face in a fold of his robes. I think he must have done something to the shrine, afterwards, because that window has been closed to me ever since, like so many others. There is much old damage in the system from the war between the machines. I could only glimpse you now and then as you grew up. How I wish I could have spoken to you! How I wish I could have helped you! I am so happy to meet you again, but you should not be here, in this strange and terrible city. You should be on your way downriver, to the war.'

'What do you know about me? Please, domina, will you tell me what you know?'

'There are gates. Manifolds held open by the negative gravity of strange matter. They run in every direction, even into the past, all the way back to when they were created. I think that is where you come from. That, or the voidships. Perhaps your parents were passengers or stowaways on a voidship, time-shifted by the velocity of some long voyage. We did not learn where the voidships went. There was not enough time to learn a tenth of what we wanted to know. In

326

any case, you come from the deep past of this strange world, Yamamanama, but although I have searched the records, I do not know who sent you, or why. Does it matter? You are here, and there is much to be done.'

Yama could not believe her. For if he had been sent here from the deep past when his people, the Builders, had been constructing the world according to the desires of the Pre-servers, then he could never find his family or any others like him. He would be quite alone, and that was unthinkable.

He said, 'I was found on the river. I was a baby, lying on the breast of a dead woman in a white boat.' He suddenly felt that his heart might burst with longing. 'Please tell me! Tell me why I am here!'

The woman in the shrine lifted her hands, wrists cocked in an elegant shrug. She said, 'I'm a stranger here. My original walked out into your world and died there, but not before she started to change it. And before she died part of her came here, and here I am still. I sometimes wonder if you're part of what she did after she left me here. Would that make you my son, if it were true?'

Yama said, 'I am looking for answers, not more riddles.'

'Let me give an example. You see the statues? You think them monuments to dead heroes, but the truth is simpler than any story.'

'Then they are not statues?'

'Not at all. They are soldiers. They were garrisoned here after the main part of the temple was built, to guard against what the foolish little priests of the temple call the Thing Below. I suppose that when the apses were remodelled many years later it was easier to incorporate the soldiers into the architecture than to move them. Most of their kind have been smelted down, and small pieces of armour have been cast from their remains, so in a sense they still defend the populace. But the soldiers around us are the reality, and the human soldiers who wear reforged scraps of the integuments of their brothers are but the shadows of that reality, as I am a shadow of the one for whom I speak. Unlike the soldiers, she is quite vanished from this world, and only I remain.'

Yama looked up at the nearest of the figures. It stared above his head at one of its fellows on the opposite side of the square apse, but Yama fancied that he saw its eyes flicker towards him for an instant. They were red, and held a faint glow that he knew had not been there before.

He said, 'Am I then a shadow too? I am searching for others like me. Can I find them?'

'I would be amazed and delighted if you did, but they are all long dead. I think that you will be sufficient, Yamamanama. Already you have discovered that you can control the machines which maintain this habitat. There is much more I can teach you.'

'My bloodline was made by the Preservers to build the world, and then they went away. That much I have learnt, at least. I will discover more in the Palace of the Memory of the People.'

'They were taken back,' the woman said. 'You might say that if I am a shadow of what I was, then your kind were a shadow of what you call the Preservers and what I suppose I could call my children, although they are as remote from me as I am from the plains apes which walked out of Afrique and set fire to the Galaxy.'

Someone had recently said something similar to Yama. Who? Trying to remember, he said automatically, 'All are shadows of the Preservers.'

'Not quite all. There are many different kinds of men on this strange world – I suppose I must call it a world – and each has been reworked until it retains only a shadow of its animal ancestors. Most, but not all, have been salted with a fragment of inheritable material derived from the Preservers. The dominant races of this habitat are from many different places and many different times, but they all are marked by this attribute, and all believe that they can evolve to a higher state. Indeed, many seem to have evolved out of existence, but it is not clear if they have transcended or merely become extinct. But the primitive races, which resemble men but are little better than animals, are not marked, and have never advanced from their original state. There is much I still do not understand about this world, but that much I do know.'

'If you can help me understand where I came from, perhaps I can help you.'

The woman smiled. 'You try to bargain with me. But I have already told you where you came from, Yamamanama, and I have already helped you. I have sung many songs of praise in your honour. I have told many of your coming. I have raised up a champion to fight for you. You should be with him now, sailing downriver to the war.'

Yama remembered the young warlord's story. He said, 'With Enobarbus?'

'The soldier too. But I meant Dr Dismas. He found me long ago, long before I spoke with Enobarbus. You should be with them now. With their help, and especially with mine, you could save the world.'

Yama laughed. 'Lady, I will do what I can against the heretics, but I do not think I can do more than any other man.'

'*Against* the heretics? Don't be silly. I have not been able to speak to you, but I have watched you. I heard your prayers, after your brother's death. I know how desperately you wish to become a hero and avenge him. Ah, but I can make you more than that.'

After the news of Telmon's death, Yama had prayed all night before the shrine in the temple. The Aedile had sent two soldiers to watch over him, but they had fallen asleep, and in the quiet hour before dawn Yama had asked for a sign that he would lead a great victory in Telmon's name. He had thought then that he wanted to redeem his brother's death, but he understood now that his prayers had been prompted by mere selfishness. He had wanted a shape to his own life, to know its beginning and to be given a destiny.

He realized that perhaps his prayer had been answered after all, but not in the way he had hoped.

'You must take up your inheritance,' the woman said. 'I can help you. Together we can complete the changes my original began. I think you have already begun to explore what you can do. There is much more, if you will let me teach you.'

'If you had listened to me, domina, you would know that I pledged to save the world, not change it.'

Did her gaze darken? For a moment, it seemed to Yama that her strange beauty was merely a mask or film covering something horrible.

She said, 'If you want to save the world, it must be changed. Change is fundamental to life. The world will be changed whichever side wins the war, but only one side can ensure that stasis is not enforced again. Stasis preserves dead things, but it suffocates life. A faction of the servants of this world realized that long ago. But they failed, and those which survived were thrown into exile. Now they are our servants, and together we will succeed where they alone did not.'

Yama remembered the cold black presence of the feral machine he had inadvertently called down at the merchant's house, and it took all his will not to run from the woman, as Pandaras had run at first sight. He knew now which side this avatar was on, and where Enobarbus and Dr Dismas would have taken him if he had not escaped. Dr Dismas had lied about everything. He was a spy for the heretics, and Enobarbus was not a champion against them, but a warlord secretly fighting on their side. He had not escaped when his ship had been sunk, but had been captured by the heretics and made into one of them. Or perhaps he had been granted safe passage because he already was one of them – for had he not spoken of a vision which had spoken to him from the shrine of the temple of his people? Yama knew now who had spoken to the young soldier, and knew what course he had been set upon. Not against the heretics, but for them. What a fool he had been to believe otherwise!

He said, 'The world cannot be saved by contesting the will of those who made it. I will fight the heretics, not serve them.'

Silver bells, ringing in the air all around. 'You are still so young, Yamamanama! You still cling to the beliefs of your childhood! But you will change your mind. Dr Dismas has promised that he has already sown the seeds of change. Look on this, Yamamanama. All this can be ours!'

The shrine flashed edge to edge with white light. Yama closed his eyes, but the white light was inside his head, too. Something long and narrow floated in it, like a needle in milk. It was his map. No, it was the world.

Half was green and blue and white, with the Great River running along one side and the ranges of the Rim Mountains on the other, and the icecap of the Endpoint shining in the sunlight; half was tawny desert, splotched and gouged with angry black and red scars and craters, the river dry, the icecap gone.

It floated before Yama, serene and lovely, for a long moment. And then it was gone, and the woman smiled at him from the window of the shrine, with the green lawn and the high hedges of the garden receding behind her.

'Together we will do great things,' she said. 'We will remake the world, and everyone in it, as a start.'

Yama said steadfastly, 'You are an aspect of one of the Ancients of Days. You raised up the heretics against the will of the Preservers. You are my enemy.'

'I am no enemy of yours, Yamamanama. How could an enemy speak from a shrine?'

'The heretics silenced the last avatars of the Preservers. Why shouldn't something else take their place? Why do you tempt me with foolish visions? No one can rule the world.'

The woman smiled. 'No one does, and there is its problem. Any advanced organism must have a dominating principle, or else its different parts will war against each other, and it will be paralysed by inaction. As with organisms, so with worlds. You have so many doubts. I understand. Hush! Not another word! Someone comes. We'll talk again. If not here, then at one of the other transceivers that are still functioning. There are many on the farside shore.'

'If I talk with you again, it will be because I have found some way of destroying you.'

She smiled. 'I think you will change your mind about that.'

'Never!'

'Oh, but I think that you will. Already it has begun. Until then.'

And then she was gone, and with her the light. Once more, Yama could see through the darkly transparent disc of the shrine. On the far side of the apse, the curtain of black mesh stirred as someone pushed it aside.

25 ~ The Assassin

It was not Pandaras, nor even Tamora, but a barechested giant of a man in black leather trews. His skin was the colour of rust and his face was masked with an oval of soft black moleskin. He carried a naked falchion, and there was a percussion pistol tucked into his waistband. His muscular arms were bound tightly with leather thongs; plastic vambraces, mottled with extreme age, were laced around his forearms.

As soon as he saw Yama, the man quickly advanced around the shrine. Yama stepped backwards and drew his long knife. It ran with blue fire, as if dipped in flaming brandy.

The man smiled. His mouth was red and wet inside the slit in his black mask. The pointed teeth of a small fierce animal made a radiating pattern around the mask's mouth slit and little bones made a zig-zag pattern around the eyeholes, exaggerating their size. The man's rust-coloured skin shone as if oiled, and a spiral pattern of welts was raised on the skin of his chest. Yama thought of the friendly people who had colonized the abandoned tombs at the edge of Ys. This was one of their sons, corrupted by the city. Or perhaps he had left his people because he was already corrupted.

'Who sent you?' Yama said. He was aware that one of the statues was only a few paces from his back. Remembering what Sergeant Rhodean had taught him, he carefully watched as the man moved towards him, looking for weaknesses he might exploit if it came to a fight.

'Put up that silly pricking blade, and I'll tell you,' the man said. His voice was deep and slow, and set up echoes in the vaulted roof of the apse. 'I was asked to kill you slowly, but I promise to make it quick if you don't struggle.'

'It was Gorgo. He hired you at the Water Market.'

The man's eyes widened slightly under the mask and Yama knew that he had guessed right, or had struck close to the truth.

He said, 'Or you are a friend of Gorgo, or someone who owes him a favour. In any case, it is not an honourable act.'

The man said, 'Honour has nothing to it.'

Yama's fingers sweated on the hilt of the knife and the skin and muscles of his forearm tingled as if held close to a fire, although the knife blade gave off no heat. Pandaras had not known to leave the knife in sunlight while I was ill, he thought. Now it takes the energy it needs from me, and I must strike soon.

He said, 'Did Gorgo tell you who I killed? He cannot have forgotten, because it was only two nights ago. It was a rich and powerful merchant, with many guards. I was his prisoner, and my knife was taken from me, but he is dead and I stand here before you. Go now, and I will spare you.'

He was calling out to any machine for help, but there were none close by. He could only feel their distant, directionless swarm, as a man hears the many voices of a city as an unmodulated roar.

The assassin said, 'You think to keep me talking, that I may spare you or help will come. Those are foolish hopes. Put up your knife and it'll be a quick dispatch. You have my word.'

'And perhaps you talk because you do not have the stomach for it.'

The assassin laughed, a rumble like rocks moving over each other in his belly. 'It's the other way around. I was paid to kill you as slowly as possible, and to withhold the name of my client until the last possible moment. You won't put away your silly little blade? You choose a slow death, then.'

Yama saw that the assassin favoured his right arm; if he ran to the left, the man must turn before striking. In that instant Yama might have a chance at a successful blow. Although the shrine was dark and fading sunlight had climbed halfway up the walls, laying a bronze sheen on the cloudily opaque torsoes of the gigantic soldiers, everything in the square apse shone with an intense particularity. Yama had never felt more alive than now, at the moment before his certain death.

He yelled and ran, striking at the man's masked face. His opponent whirled with amazing speed and parried automatically with such force that Yama was barely able to fend off the blow. The knife screamed and spat a stream of sparks, and notched the assassin's sword.

The assassin did not press his advantage, but stared distractedly at something above Yama's head. Yama struck again, lunging with the point of his knife; Sergeant Rhodean had taught him that the advantage of a shorter blade is the precision with which it can be directed. The assassin parried with the same casual, brutal force as before and stepped back, pulling the percussion pistol from his waistband.

Suddenly, dust boiled around them in a dry, choking cloud. Chips of stone rained down like hail, ringing on the stone flags of the floor. In the midst of this, Yama lunged again. It was a slight, glancing blow that barely grazed the assassin's chest, but the knife flashed and there was a terrific flash of blue light that knocked the man down. Yama's arm was instantly numbed from wrist to shoulder. As he shifted the knife to his left hand, the assassin got to his feet and raised the percussion pistol.

The man's mouth was working inside the mask's slit, and his eyes were wide. He fired and fired again at something behind Yama. The pistol failed on the third shot and the assassin threw it hard over Yama's head and ran, just as

Pandaras had run when the woman had appeared in the shrine.

Yama chased after the assassin, his blood singing in his head, but the man plunged through the curtain of black mesh and Yama stopped short, fearing an ambush on the other side. He turned and looked up at the soldier which had stepped from its niche, and asked it to go back to sleep until it was needed again. The soldier, its eyes glowing bright red in its impassive face, struck its chestplate with a mailed fist, and the apse rang like a bell with the sound.

26 ~ The Thing Below

A long way down the shadow-filled atrium, in the glow of a palm-oil lantern which had been lowered on a chain from the lofty ceiling, two men bent over something. Yama ran forward with his knife raised, but they were only priests tending to Pandaras. The boy lay sprawled on the mosaic floor, alive but unconscious. Yama knelt and touched his face. His eyes opened, but he seemed unable to speak. There was a bloody gash on his temple; it seemed to be his only wound.

Yama sheathed his knife and looked up at the two priests. They wore homespun robes and had broad, wide-browed faces and tangled manes of white hair: the same bloodline as Enobarbus. Although Yama had guessed that this was the place where the young warlord had received his vision, he still felt a small shock of recognition.

He asked the priests if they had seen who had wounded his friend, and they looked at each other before one volunteered that a man had just now run past, but they had already discovered this poor boy. Yama smiled to think of the spectacle the masked assassin must have made, running through the temple with a sword in his hand and blood running down his bare chest. Gorgo must be nearby – if he had sent the assassin, surely he would want to witness what he had paid for – and he would have seen the rout of his hireling.

The priests looked at each other again and the one who

had spoken before said, 'I am Antros, and this is my brother, Balcus. We are keepers of the temple. There is a place to wash your friend's wound, and to tend to your own wounds, too. Follow me.'

Yama's right arm had recovered most of its strength, although it now tingled as if it had been stung by a horde of ants. He gathered up Pandaras and followed the old priest. The boy's skin was hot and his heartbeat was light and rapid, but Yama had no way of knowing whether or not this was normal.

Beyond the colonnade on the left-hand side of the atrium was a little grotto carved into the thick stone of the temple's outer wall. Water trickled into a shallow stone trough from a plastic spout set in the centre of a swirl of red mosaic. Yama helped Pandaras kneel, and bathed the shallow wound on his temple. Blood which had matted the boy's sleek hair fluttered into the clear cold water, but the bleeding had already stopped and the edges of the wound were clean.

'You will have a headache,' Yama told Pandaras, 'but nothing worse. I think he struck you with the edge of his vambrace, or with his pistol, rather than with his falchion. You should have stayed with me, Pandaras.'

Pandaras was still unable to speak, but he clumsily caught Yama's hand and squeezed it.

The old priest, Antros, insisted on cleaning the shallow cuts on Yama's back. As he worked, he said, 'We heard two pistol shots. You are lucky that he missed you, although I would guess that he did not miss you by much, and you were hurt by stone splinters knocked from the wall.'

'Fortunately, he was not aiming at me,' Yama said.

Antros said, 'This was a fine place once. The pillars were painted azure and gold, and beeswax candles as tall as a man scented the air with their perfume. Our temple was filled with mendicants and palmers from every town and city along the length of the river. That was long before my time, of course, but I do remember when an avatar of the Preservers still appeared in the shrine.'

'Was this avatar a woman, dressed in white?'

'It was neither man nor woman, and neither young nor old.' The old priest smiled in recollection. 'How I miss its wild laughter – it was filled with fierce joy, and yet it was a gentle creature. But it is gone. They have all gone. Men still come to pray at the shrine, of course, but although the Preservers hear every prayer, men have fallen so far from grace that there are no longer answers to their questions. Few come here now, and even fewer to bare themselves humbly before their creators. Most who come do so to ask the one below to curse their enemies, but there are not even very many of them.'

'I suppose that most people fear this place.'

'Just so, although we do have problems with cultists from time to time, for they are attracted by the same thing which the ordinary folk fear. My brother and I come here each evening to light the lamps, but otherwise the temple is not much used, even by our own bloodline. Of course, we have our high day when the atrium is decorated with palm fronds and wreaths of ivy and there is a solemn procession to aspurge every corner and to propitiate the Thing Below. But otherwise, as I have said, most people keep away. You are a stranger here. A palmer, perhaps. I am sorry that you and your friend were attacked. No doubt a foot-pad followed you, and saw his chance.'

Yama asked Antros if the Thing Below was the machine which had fallen in the final battle at the end of the Age of Insurrection.

'Indeed. You must not suppose it was destroyed. Rather, it was entombed alive in rock made molten by its fall. It stirs, sometimes. In fact, it has been very restless recently. Listen! Do you hear it?'

Yama nodded. He had supposed that the high singing in

his head was his own blood rushing through his veins with the excitement of his brief skirmish.

'It is the second time in as many days,' Antros said. 'Most of our bloodline are soldiers, and part of our duty is to guard the well and the thing entombed at its bottom. But many have gone downriver to fight in the war, and many of those have been killed there.'

'I met one,' Yama said. He did not need to ask when the machine had begun to be restless, and felt a chill in his blood. He had called for help in the merchant's house, and the feral machine which had answered his call was not the only one to have heard him. What else? What else might he have inadvertently awakened?

Out in the atrium, someone suddenly started to shout, raising overlapping echoes. The old priest looked alarmed, but Yama said, 'Do not be afraid, dominie. I know that voice.'

Tamora had returned to the inn, she said, and had had to threaten the painted witch who ran it to find out where Yama and Pandaras had gone. 'Then I realized what the game was, and came straightaway.'

'It was Gorgo,' Yama said, as he tied the laces of his torn, blood-stained shirt. 'I appear to have a knack of making enemies.'

'I hope you gouged out his eyes before you killed him,' Tamora said.

'I have not seen him. But someone shot an arbalest bolt at me earlier, and I remember that you said Gorgo had killed someone with an arbalest. He missed, and then he sent another man to kill me. Fortunately, I had some help, and was able to scare off the assassin.'

'I will have his eyes,' Tamora said with venomous passion, 'if I ever see him again! His balls and his eyes! He is a disgrace to the Fierce People!'

'He must be very jealous, to want to kill me because of you.'

Tamora laughed, and said, 'O Yama, at last you show some human weakness, even if it is only conceit about your cockmanship. The truth is, I owe Gorgo money. He's not one for fighting, but for making deals. He finds work for others, and takes a cut of the fees for his trouble. And he loans money, too. I borrowed from him to buy new armour and this sword after I was wounded in the war last year. I lost my kit then, you see. I was working on commission to pay off the debt and the interest. I got enough to live on, and he took the rest.'

'Then the job I did with you—'

'Yes, yes,' Tamora said impatiently. 'On Gorgo's commission. He didn't really expect me to succeed, but he was still angry when I told him that we'd killed the merchant and hadn't been able to collect the fee.'

'And that is why you agreed to help me.'

'Not exactly. Yama, we don't have time for this.'

'I need to know, Tamora.'

Yama understood now why Tamora had embarked on such a risky enterprise, but he still did not understand why Gorgo wanted him dead.

Tamora hung her head for a moment, then said with a mixture of vulnerability and defiance, 'I suppose it's only fair. The star-sailor job would have paid well, but we lost the fee because you went crazy and grabbed that circlet. And I still owe Gorgo, and I was going off to work for you, as he saw it. I said he should wait and I'd pay back everything, but he's greedy. He wants the liver and the lights as well as the meat and bones.'

Yama nodded. 'He decided to kill me and steal the money I have.'

'He said that he would rob you, not kill you. He said it was only fair, because you'd lost him the fee for killing the merchant. I didn't know he'd try and kill you. I swear it.'

'I believe you,' Yama said. 'And I know that Gorgo found someone else to help you with the job in the Palace of the Memory of the People. He wanted me out of the way.'

'A man with red skin and welts on his chest. I told Gorgo that I was going to work with you, Yama, and no other, but Gorgo said the man would be waiting for me at the Palace gate. I went there, but I couldn't find the man and I went back to the inn and found that you had come here.'

'Well, the man you were waiting for was here. It was he who tried to kill me.'

'I was going to tell you everything,' Tamora said. 'I decided something, while I was waiting. Hear me out. I made an agreement with you, and I will stick with it. Fuck Gorgo. When the job is finished I'll find him and kill him.'

'Then you will work for me, and not Gorgo?'

'Isn't that what I said?' Tamora said impatiently. 'But there isn't time to stand and talk a moment longer, not now! You've been lying around in bed, and then fooling about in this mausoleum, and meanwhile I have been busy. We have already missed one appointment, and we must not miss the second, or the contract will be voided. Can you ride?'

'A little.'

'That had better mean you can ride like the wind.' Tamora seemed to notice Pandaras for the first time. 'What happened to the rat-boy?'

'A blow to the head. Luckily, the assassin Gorgo hired had some scruples.'

'Maybe it'll have knocked some of his airs out and let some sense in. I suppose you still want to bring him? Well, I'll carry him for you. Why are you staring at me? Do you call off our contract after all this?'

'I have already woken things best left sleeping. If I go on, what else might I do?'

Tamora said briskly, 'Would you emasculate yourself, then? If you don't know who you are and where you came from, then you can't know what you can become. Come with me, or not. I'm taking the job anyway, because I'll get paid for it with you or without you. And when I've finished there, I'll kill Gorgo.'

She slung Pandaras over her shoulder and walked away with a quick, lithe step, as if the boy weighed nothing at all. After a moment, Yama followed.

It was dusk. Warm lights glowed in windows of the houses around the mossy plaza. Two horses were tethered to a pole topped by a smoky, guttering cresset. Tamora and Yama lifted Pandaras on to the withers of her mount, and then she vaulted easily into the saddle behind him. She leaned down and told Yama, 'I had to pay the painted witch a fortune for the hire of these. Don't stand and gape. Already it may be too late.'

The horses were harnessed cavalry fashion, with light saddles and high stirrups. Yama had just grasped the horn of his mount's saddle and fitted his left foot in the stirrup, ready to swing himself up, when the ground shook. The horse jinked and as Yama tried to check it, he saw a beam of light shoot up through the aperture of the domed roof of the Black Temple.

The light was as red as burning sulphur, with flecks of violet and vermilion whirling in it like sparks flying up a chimney. It burned high into the sky, so bright that it washed the temple and the square in bloody light.

Yama realized at once what was happening, and knew that he must confront what he had wakened. He was horribly afraid of it, but if he did not face it then he would always be afraid.

He threw the reins of his mount to Tamora and ran up the steps into the temple. As he entered the long atrium, the floor groaned and heaved, like an animal tormented by biting flies. Yama fell headlong, picked himself up, and ran on towards the column of red light that burned up from the well and filled the temple with its fierce glare.

The temple was restless. The stone of its walls squealed

and howled; dust and small fragments rained down from the ceiling. Several of the pillars on either side had cracked from top to bottom; one had collapsed across the floor, its heavy stone discs spilled like a stack of giant's coins. The intricate mosaics of the floor were fractured, heaved apart in uneven ripples. A long ragged crack ran back from the well, and the two old priests stood either side of it, silhouetted in the furnace light. Balcus had drawn his sword and held it above his head in pitiful defiance; Antros knelt with the heels of his hands pressed to his eyes, chanting over and over an incantation or prayer.

The language was a private dialect of the priests' bloodline, but its rhythm struck deep in Yama. He fell to his knees beside the old priest and began to chant too.

It was not a prayer, but a set of instructions to the guards of the temple.

He was repeating it for a third time when the black mesh curtain which divided the right-hand apse from the atrium was struck aside. Two, four, five of the giant soldiers marched out. The red light gleamed like fresh blood on their transparent carapaces.

The two old priests immediately threw themselves full-length on the floor, but Yama watched with rapt fascination. The five soldiers were the only survivors of the long sleep of the temple's guards. One dragged a stiff leg, and another was blind and moved haltingly under the instructions of the others, but none of them had forgotten their duty. They took up position, forming a five-pointed star around the well, threw open their chest-plates and drew out bulbous silver tubes as long as Yama was tall. Yama supposed that the soldiers would discharge their weapons into the well, but instead they aimed at the coping and floor around it and fired as one.

One of the weapons exploded, blowing the upper part of its owner to flinders; from the others, violet threads as intensely bright as the sun raked stone until it ran like water into the well. Heat and light beat at Yama's skin; the atrium filled with the acrid stench of burning stone. The floor heaved again, a rolling ripple that snapped mosaics and paving slabs like a whip and threw Yama and the priests backwards.

And the Thing Below rose up from the white-hot annulus around its pit.

It was brother to the feral machine that Yama had inadvertently drawn down at the merchant's house, although it was very much larger. It barely cleared the sides of the well – black, spherical, and bristling with mobile spines. It had grown misshapen during its long confinement, like a spoiled orange that flattens under its own weight.

The giant soldiers played violet fire across the machine, but it took no notice of them. It hung in the midst of its column of red light and looked directly into Yama's head. *You have called me. I am here. Now come with me, and serve.*

Pain struck through Yama's skull like an iron wedge. His sight was filled with red and black lightnings. Blind, burning inside and out, he gave the soldiers a final order.

They moved as one, and then Yama could see again. The four soldiers were clinging to the machine as men cling to a bit of flotsam from a wreck. They were shearing away the machine's spines with the blades of their hands.

The spines were what enabled the machine to bend the gravity field of the world to its will. It spun and jerked, like a hyrax attacked by dire wolves, but it was too late. It fell like a stone into the well, and the temple shuddered again. There was a long roaring sound, and the column of red light flickered and then went out.

27 ~ The Palace of the Memory of the People

Yama and the two priests helped each other through the smoky wreckage of the temple. A great cheer went up when they emerged into the twilight, scorched, blinking, coughing on fumes and covered in soot. The people who lived in the houses around and about the temple had run out of their homes convinced that the last day of the world was at hand, and now they knew that they were saved. Men of the priests' bloodline ran up and helped them away; Tamora urged her horse up the shallow steps, leading Yama's mount by its reins.

Yama fought through the crowd. 'It is gone!' he shouted to her. 'I woke the soldiers and I defeated it!'

'We may be too late!' Tamora shouted back. 'If you're done here, follow me!'

By the time Yama had climbed into the saddle of his horse, she was already galloping away across the square. He whooped and gave chase. His horse was a lean, sure-footed gelding, and needed little guidance as he raced Tamora through the narrow streets. The rush of warm evening air stung his scorched skin but cleared his head. His long hair, uncut since he had left Aeolis, streamed out behind him.

A bell began to toll, and Tamora looked back and yelled, 'The gate! Ten minutes before it closes!'

She lashed the flanks of her mount with her reins, and it laid back its ears and raised its tail and doubled its speed. Yama shouted encouraging words in the ear of his own horse, and it took heart and gave chase. A minute later, they shot out of the end of the narrow street and began to plough through crowds that clogged a wide avenue beneath globes of blue fire floating high in the air.

They were petitioners, penitents and palmers trying to gain entrance to the Palace of the Memory of the People, their numbers swelled by those panicked by earth tremors and strange lights. Tamora laid about her with bunched reins, and people pressed back into each other as she forced a way through, with Yama close behind. The tolling of the bell shivered the air, drowning the screams and shouts of the crowd.

When Tamora and Yama reached the end of the avenue, they found a picket line of machines spinning in the air, burning with fierce radiance like a cord of tiny suns. Overhead, more machines flitted through the dusk like fireflies. They filled Yama's head with their drowsy hum, as if he had plunged head-first into a hive of bees. Robed and hooded magistrates stood behind the glare of the picket line. Beyond them the avenue opened out into a square so huge it could easily have contained the little city of Aeolis. At the far side of the square a high smooth cliff of keelrock curved away to the left and right, punctuated by a gateway that was guarded by a decad of soldiers in silvery armour who stood on floating discs high in the blue-lit air.

The black mountain of the Palace of the Memory of the People loomed above all of this, studded with lights and blotting out the sky. Its peaks vanished into a wreath of clouds. Yama stared up at it. He had come so far in a handful of days, from the little citadel of the peel-house of the Aedile of Aeolis to this, the greatest citadel of all, which the preterites claimed was older than the world itself. He had learned that his bloodline was older than the world, and that he could bend to his will the machines which maintained the world. He had learned that the heretics considered him a great prize, and had resolved to fight against them with all his might – and he had confronted and defeated one of their dark angels.

He had left behind his childhood. Ahead lay the long struggle by which he would define himself. Perhaps it would end in death; certainly, countless men had already died in the war, and many more would die before the heretics were defeated. But at this moment, although he was exhausted and bruised, his clothes scorched and tattered, he felt more alive than ever before. Somewhere in the great citadel that reared above him, in the stacks of its ten thousand libraries, in the labyrinths of the hundreds of temples and shrines and departments, must be the secret of his origin. He did not doubt it. The woman in the shrine had said that he had come from the deep past, but she was his enemy, and surely she had been lying. He would prove her wrong. He would find the secrets that Dr Dismas had uncovered and discover where his bloodline still lived, and learn from them how to use his powers against the heretics.

Tamora caught the bridle of Yama's horse and shouted that they would do better to return tomorrow. 'The gates are about to close!'

'No! We must go now! It is my destiny!'

Pandaras raised his head and said weakly, 'My master wills it.'

Tamora grinned, showing the rack of her sharp white teeth, and held up something that flashed with red light. The picket line of incandescent machines spun apart before her. People started towards the gap and magistrates moved forward, lashing out with their quirts, driving those at the front into those pressing forward from behind. In the midst of the mêlée, a fat woman reclining on a pallet born by four oiled, nearly naked men suddenly clutched at the swell of her bosom. Under her plump hands, a vivid red stain spread over her white dress. She slumped sideways and the pallet tipped and foundered, sending a wave of confusion spreading out through the close-packed people.

Yama did not understand what had happened until a man right by his horse's flank flew forward and folded over and fell under the feet of his neighbours. Yama glimpsed the red fletching of the bolt in the dead man's back, and then the crowd closed over him.

Tamora had drawn her sword and was brandishing it about her as she forced a way through the crowd. Yama kicked at hands which tried to grasp the bridle of his plunging mount, and fought through the tumult to her side.

'Gorgo!' he shouted at Tamora. 'Gorgo! He is here!'

But Tamora did not hear him. She was leaning against Pandaras and shouting at the magistrates who barred her way. Yama reached for her shoulder and something went past his ear with a wicked crack, and when he jerked around to see where it had come from another bolt smashed the head of a man who had been trying to catch hold of the bridle of his horse.

Yama lashed out in panic and anger then. Red and black lightning filled his head. And suddenly he saw the square from a thousand points of view that all converged on a figure on a flat roof above the crowded avenue. Gorgo screamed and raised the arbalest in front of his face as hundreds of tiny machines smashed into him, riddling his torso and arms and legs. He must have died in an instant, but his body did not fall. Instead, it rose into the air, the sole of one boot brushing the parapet as it drifted out above the packed heads of the crowd.

Yama came to himself and saw that Tamora had forced her way through the line of magistrates. He galloped after her. On the far side of the vast square, the great iron gates of the Palace of the Memory of the People were closing. The bell fell silent, and there was a shocking moment of silence. Then people felt drops of blood falling on them and looked up and saw Gorgo's riddled body sustained high above, head bowed and arms flung wide, the arbalest dangling by its strap against his ruined chest.

A woman screamed and the crowd began to yell again, ten thousand voices shouting against each other. The discs which bore the soldiers swooped towards the crowd as Yama and Tamora raced their horses across the square and plunged through the gates into the darkness beyond.

Prime Suspect
The sensational thriller behind the hit TV series *Prime Suspect*. DCI Jane Tennison fights for the right to lead a murder enquiry, but the boys will do anything to stop her.

A Face in the Crowd
The coroner's report identifies a body as young, black, female and impossibly anonymous. DCI Jane Tennison is up against a brutal killer in a city where racial tensions are running high.

Silent Victims
DCI Tennison is now head of the Vice Squad. On her first day in the new job, a high-profile case, one that might threaten to destroy everything she has worked for.

Above Suspicion
The first instalment in the bestselling Anna Travis series. Anna tackles her first murder case, one that might bring down a much-loved actor.

The Red Dahlia
Anna Travis and James Langton return, and must work together to capture one of the most terrifying killers they have ever encountered.

Clean Cut
For DI Anna Travis, this time it's personal, as DCI James Langton is almost fatally injured by a suspect and Anna must keep them both alive.

Deadly Intent
DI Anna Travis is pulled onto a case that has already claimed the life of an ex-police officer. As the body count rises, the police wonder if this is the work of a killer from the past.

Silent Scream
Young British film star Amanda Delany had the world at her feet, until she's found murdered. As DI Anna Travis strives for promotion, this might be the case that breaks her career.

Blind Fury

The body of an unidentifiable young woman is discovered. And then DI Anna Travis receives a letter from an imprisoned murderer: he knows the killer.

Blood Line

Under the watchful eye of DCS James Langton, Anna Travis is given her first case. But is it a full-blown murder investigation or purely a missing person case?

Backlash

The police arrest a murder suspect, but then the man tells them this is his third victim. Cold cases will come back to haunt DCS James Langton and DCI Anna Travis.

Wrongful Death

A suicide case suddenly starts to look like a murder, as DCI Anna Travis is torn between her London team and a new opportunity with the FBI in America.

Cold Shoulder

The first novel in the thrilling Lorraine Page series. Lieutenant Page was thrown out of the homicide squad, but as they search for a serial killer, she is the witness they need.

Cold Blood

A movie star's daughter vanishes in New Orleans. Lorraine Page tackles her first case as a private eye, which threatens to drag her back to the world she fought to escape.

Cold Heart

A movie mogul is found dead in Beverly Hills and his wife is charged with murder. Private investigator Lorraine Page is the only one who believes she is innocent.

The Legacy

From the poverty of the Welsh pit valleys to the glories of the prize ring, from the dangers of prohibition America to the terror of Britain at war, this is the story of a remarkable family and its fortunes, and the curse that forged their name . . .

The Talisman
Sequel to *The Legacy*. For each new generation, the talisman is the key to a fortune. It should have been buried with Freedom Stubbs, but his spirit is restless in his grave.

Entwined
No matter how cruelly twins are separated, their lives will always be entwined. In the newly liberated streets of modern Berlin, two extraordinary women are drawn together.

Sleeping Cruelty
Sir William Benedict has always desired acceptance from society's elite. But after a political scandal erupts around him, he turns to his sisters to help him get revenge.

Royal Flush
A wealthy race horse owner has set high hopes on a magnificent colt, Royal Flush. Afraid he will lose everything, he pursues a diamond worth dying for.

Twisted
Marcus and Lena Fulford are the envy of their friends. But when their daughter Amy goes missing, the perfect facade starts to slip.

Tennison
From the creator of the award-winning ITV series *Prime Suspect*, starring Helen Mirren, comes the fascinating back story of the iconic DCI Jane Tennison.

Hidden Killers
Newly promoted Jane Tennison is conflicted as she becomes inextricably involved in a multiple rape case, and must put her life at risk in her search for answers.

Good Friday
When rookie detective constable Jane Tennison survives a deadly explosion, the race is on to unmask the terrorists. Before the Metropolitan Police's Good Friday dinner, Jane must convince her senior officers that her instincts are right before there's another bloodbath.

Murder Mile

Jane Tennison, now a Detective Sergeant, has been posted to Peckham CID, one of London's toughest areas. As the rubbish on the streets begins to pile up, so does the murder count: two bodies in as many days. With press headlines claiming police incompetence, Jane is under immense pressure to catch the killer – before they strike again . . .

The Dirty Dozen

Jane Tennison has worked hard to become the first female detective ever post to the infamous Flying Squad. But the Dirty Dozen is a notorious boys' club. Determined to prove she's as good as the men, Jane discovers from a reliable witness that a gang is going to carry out a massive robbery.

Widows

A security van heist goes disastrously wrong and three women are left widowed. When Dolly Rawlins discovers her gang boss husband's plans for the failed hijack, an idea starts to form. Could she and the other wives finish the job their husbands started?

Widows' Revenge

Against all the odds, Dolly Rawlins and her gangland widows managed the impossible: a heist their husbands had failed to pull off. But then Dolly discovers that Harry Rawlins isn't dead. He knows where the four women are and he wants them to pay.

Lynda La Plante

SHE'S OUT

**SIMON &
SCHUSTER**

London · New York · Sydney · Toronto · New Delhi

A CBS COMPANY

First published in Great Britain by Pan Books, 1995
First published by Simon & Schuster UK Ltd, 2012
This edition published by Simon & Schuster UK Ltd, 2019
A CBS COMPANY

1 3 5 7 9 10 8 6 4 2

Simon & Schuster UK Ltd
1st Floor
222 Gray's Inn Road
London WC1X 8HB

Simon & Schuster Australia, Sydney
Simon & Schuster India, New Delhi

www.simonandschuster.co.uk
www.simonandschuster.com.au
www.simonandschuster.co.in

A CIP catalogue record for this book
is available from the British Library

Paperback ISBN: 978-1-4711-7901-3
Trade paperback ISBN: 978-1-4711-8714-8
eBook ISBN: 978-1-4711-0029-1

Typeset in Bembo by M Rules
Printed and bound by CPI Group (UK) Ltd, Croydon, CR0 4YY

MIX
Paper from
responsible sources
FSC® C020471

SHE'S OUT

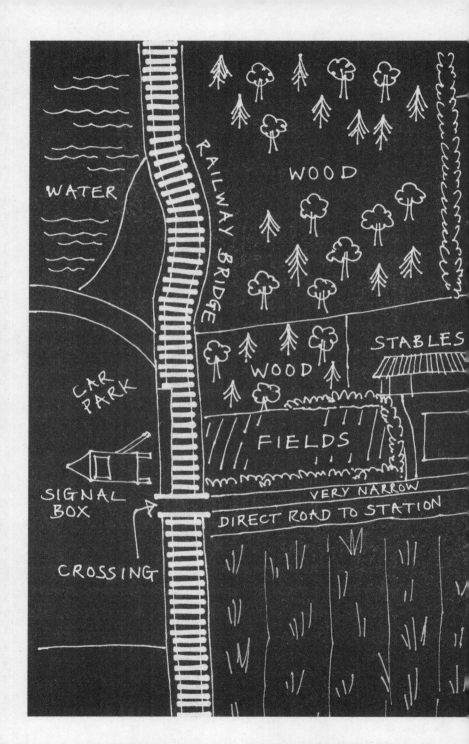

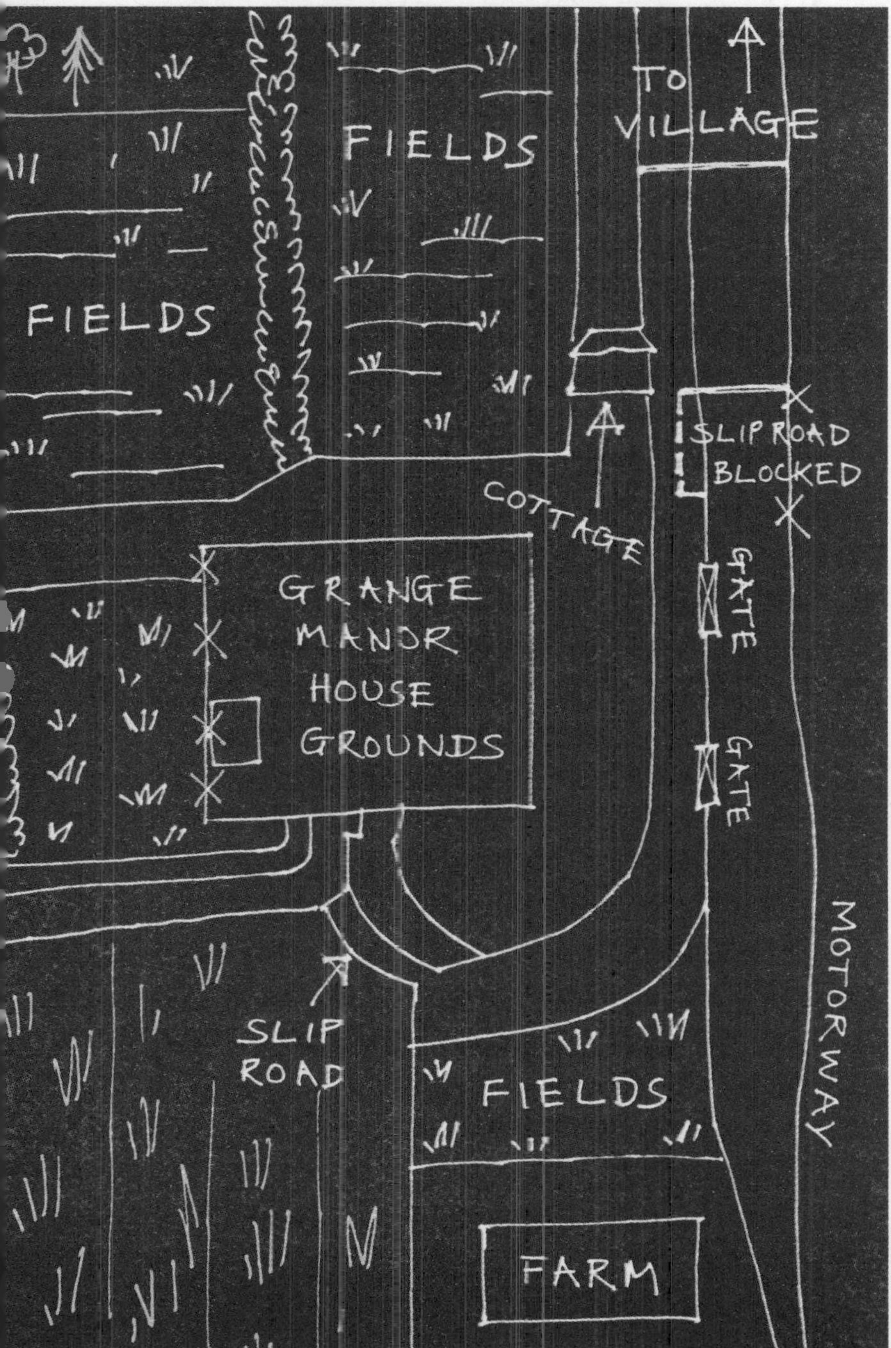
FIELDS
TO VILLAGE
FIELDS
SLIP ROAD BLOCKED
COTTAGE
GATE
GRANGE MANOR HOUSE GROUNDS
GATE
MOTORWAY
SLIP ROAD
FIELDS
FARM

Chapter 1

The date was ringed with a fine red biro circle: 15 March 1994. It was the only mark on the cheap calendar pinned to the wall in her cell. There were no photographs, no memorabilia, not even a picture cut out of a magazine. She had always been in a cell by herself. The prison authorities had discussed the possibility of her sharing with another inmate but it had been decided it was preferable to leave Dorothy Rawlins as she had requested – alone.

Rawlins had been a model prisoner from the day she had arrived. She seemed to settle into a solitary existence immediately. At first she spoke little and was always polite to both prisoners and prison officers. She rarely smiled, she never wrote letters, but read for hours on end alone in her cell, and ate alone. After six months she began to work in the prison library; a year later she became a trusty. Gradually the women began to refer to Rawlins during recreational periods, asking her opinion on their marriages, their relationships. They trusted her opinions and her advice but she made no one a close friend. She wrote their letters, she taught some of the inmates to read and write, she was always patient, always calm and, above all, she would always listen. If you had a problem, Dolly Rawlins would sort it out for you. Over the following years she became a dominant and highly respected figure within the prison hierarchy.

The women would often whisper about her to the new inmates, embroidering her past, which made her even more of a queen-like figurehead. Dorothy Rawlins was in Holloway for murder. She had shot her husband, the infamous Harry Rawlins, at point-blank range. The murder took on a macabre undertone as throughout the years the often repeated story was embellished, but no one ever discussed the murder to her face. It was as if she had an invisible barrier around her own emotions. Kindly towards anyone who needed comfort, she seemed never to need anything herself.

So the rumours continued: stories passed from one inmate to another that Rawlins had also been a part of a big diamond raid. Although she had never been charged and no evidence had ever been brought forward at her trial to implicate her, the idea that she had instigated the raid, and got away with it, accentuated her mystique. More important was the rumour that she had also got away with the diamonds. The diamonds, some said, were valued at one million, then two million. The robbery had been a terrifying, brutal raid and a young, beautiful girl called Shirley Miller had been shot and killed. It was never discovered that Shirley Miller had been one of the women who took part in the infamous robbery at the Strand underpass.

Four years into her sentence, Rawlins began to write letters to request a better baby wing at Holloway. She began to work with the young mothers and children. The result was that she became even more of a 'Mama' figure. There was nothing she would not do for these young women, and it was on Rawlins's shoulders that they sobbed their hearts out when their babies were taken from them. Rawlins seemed to have an intuitive understanding, talking for hour upon hour with these distressed girls. She also had the same quiet patience with the drug offenders.

Five years into her sentence, Dolly Rawlins proved an invaluable inmate. She kept a photo album of the prisoners who had left, their letters to her, and especially the photographs of their children. But only the calendar was pinned to the chipboard on the wall of her cell. Nothing ever took precedence over the years of waiting.

She would always receive letters when the girls left Holloway. It was as if they needed her strength on the outside, but usually the letters came only for a couple of weeks then stopped. She was never hurt by the sudden silence, the lack of continued contact, because there were always the new inmates who needed her. She was a heroine, and the whispers about her criminal past only grew. Sometimes she would smile as if enjoying the notoriety, encouraging the stories with little hints that maybe, just maybe, she knew more about the diamond raid than she would ever admit. She was also aware by now that the mystery surrounding her past enhanced her position within the prison pecking order, allowing her to remain top dog without fighting or arguments.

After seven years, Rawlins was the 'Big Mama' – and it was always Dolly who broke up the fights, Dolly who was called on to settle arguments, Dolly who received the small gifts, the extra cigarettes. The prison officers referred to her as a model prisoner, and she was consequently given a lot of freedom by the authorities. She organized and instigated further education, drug rehabilitation sessions and, with a year to go before she was released, Holloway opened an entire new mother-and-baby wing, with a bright, toy-filled nursery. This was where she spent most of her time, helping the staff care for the children. For Dolly, who had no visitors, no one on the outside to care for or about her, the babies became her main focus – and began to shape a future dream for when she would finally be free.

Dolly Rawlins did have those diamonds waiting and, if they had been worth two million when she was sentenced, she calculated they now had to be worth double. Alone in her cell she would dream about just what she was going to do with all that money. Fencing them would bring the value down to around two million. She would have to give a cut to Audrey, Shirley Miller's mother, and a cut to Jimmy Donaldson, the man holding them for her. She would then have enough to open some kind of home, buy a small terraced house for herself, maybe in Islington or an area close to the prison, so she could come and visit the girls she knew would still need her. She contemplated opening the home specifically for the children of pregnant prisoners, who, she knew, would have their babies taken away. Then they would at least know their babies were in good care, as many of the girls were single parents and their babies might otherwise be put up for adoption.

This daydreaming occupied Dolly for hours on end. She kept her idea to herself, afraid that if she mentioned it to anyone they would know for sure she had considerable finances. She did have several thousand pounds in a bank account set up for her by her lawyer and she calculated that with that, a government grant and the money from the gems the home could be up and running within a year of her release. She even thought about offering a sanctuary for some of the drug addicts who needed a secure place to stay when they were released. And, a number of the women inside were battered wives: perhaps she could allocate a couple of rooms for them. The daydreaming relieved the tension. It was like a comforter, a warm secret that enveloped her and helped her sleep. But the dream would soon be a reality as the months disappeared into weeks, and then days. As the ringed date was drawing closer and closer, she could hardly contain herself: at last she would have a reason to live. Being so close to newborn babies had opened up the terrible, secret pain of her own childlessness. But soon she would have a houseful of children who needed her. Then she could truly call herself 'Mama'.

They all knew she would soon be leaving. They whispered in corners as they made cards and small gifts. Even the prison officers were sad that they would lose such a valuable inmate, not that any of them had ever had much interaction with her on a personal level. She rarely made conversation with them unless it was strictly necessary, and some of them resented the fact that she seemed to have more power over the inmates than they did. A few years back, Rawlins had struck a prison officer, slapped her face, and warned her to stay away from a certain prisoner. She had been given extra days and been locked up in her cell. The result had been that Rawlins was fêted when she was eventually unlocked and the officer, a thickset, dark-haired woman called Barbara Hunter, never spoke to or looked at Rawlins again. The animosity between Hunter and Rawlins remained throughout the years. Hunter had tried on numerous occasions to needle Dolly, as if to prove to the Governor that the model prisoner 45688 was in reality an evil manipulator. But Dolly never rose to the bait, just looked at her with ice-cold eyes, and it was that blank-eyed stare that, Hunter suspected, concealed a deep hatred, not just of herself, but of all the prison officers.

Finally the day came, 15 March, and Dolly carefully packed her few possessions from her cell. She had already given away all her personal effects: a radio, some tapes, skin cream, books and packets of cigarettes. She had lost a considerable amount of weight, and the suit she had worn the day she arrived hung on her like a rag as she waited for the call to the probation room for the usual chat with the Governor before she would finally be free. The years she had spent banged up had made her face sallow and drawn; her grey hair was cut short in an unflattering style.

As she sat, hands folded on her lap, until they called her to go into the first meeting, she appeared as calm as always but her heart was beating rapidly. She would soon be out. Soon be free. It would soon be over.

*

The old Victorian Grange Manor House was in a sorry state of disrepair, although at a distance it still looked impressive. The grounds, orchards and stables were all in need of serious attention. The grass was overgrown and weeds sprouted up through the gravel driveway. A swimming pool with a torn tarpaulin was filled with stagnant water, and even the old sign 'Grange Health Farm' was broken and peeling like the paint on all the woodwork of the house. The once handsome stained-glass double-fronted door had boards covering the broken panes, many of the windows had cracks and some of the tiles from the roof lay shattered on the ground below. The double chimney-breasts were tilting dangerously. The house seemed fit only for demolition, while the vast acreage that had belonged to the manor had been sold off years before to local farmers, and the dense, dark wood that fringed the lawns had begun to creep nearer with brambles and twisted shrubs.

A motorway had been built close to the edge of the lane leading to the manor, cutting off the house from the main road. Now the only access was down a small slip road that had been left, like the house, to rot, with deep potholes that made any journey hazardous. The rusted, wrought-iron gates were hanging off their hinges, and the chain threaded through them with the big padlock hung limply as if no one would want to enter anyway.

The Range Rover bumped and banged along the lane as it made its slow journey towards the house, the hedges either side hiding the fields and grazing cows.

Ester Freeman swore as the Range Rover hit a deep rut; it was even worse than the last time she'd been there. She was a handsome woman in her late forties. Five feet six and slender, she was a smart dresser, who always wore designer labels, and there was an elegance to her that belied the inner toughness that even her well-modulated voice sometimes couldn't disguise. Now, with her dark hair scraped back from her face and her teeth clenched, she looked anything but ladylike. She continued to swear as the Range Rover splashed through yet another water-filled pothole on its lurching course down the lane.

Sitting beside Ester, Julia Lawson looked equally unhappy. She was much younger than Ester and taller, almost six feet, with a strong, rangy body made to seem even more mannish by her jeans and leather jacket. She wore beat-up cowboy boots and a worn denim shirt, and there was an habitual arrogance to her expression that sometimes made her seem attractive, at other times plain. She had a deep, melodic, cultured voice, and was swearing fruitily as they bounced along. 'Jesus Christ, Ester, slow down. You're chucking everything over the back of the car!'

Ester paid no attention as she heaved on the handbrake, jumped out and crossed to the wrought-iron gates. She didn't bother with a key to open the padlock – she just wrenched it loose and pushed back the old gates.

As they drove up the Manor House driveway, Julia laughed. 'My God, I think it needs a demolition crew.'

'Oh, shut up,' Ester snapped as they veered round a pothole.

'You know, I don't think they'll find it.'

'They'll find it, I gave them each a map. Don't be so negative. She's out today, Julia. Come on, move it!'

Julia followed Ester slowly out of the car and looked around, shaking her head. She stepped back as a front doorstep crumbled beneath her boot. 'You know, it looks unsafe.'

'It's been standing for over a hundred years so it's not likely to fall down now. Get the bags out.'

Julia looked back to the piles of suitcases and bulging black bin liners in the back of the Range Rover and ignored her request, following Ester into the manor.

The hallway was dark and forbidding: the William Morris wallpaper hung in damp speckled flaps from the carved cornices and there were stacks of old newspapers and broken bottles everywhere. The old wooden reception desk was dusty, the key-rack behind it devoid of keys.

Their feet echoed in the marble hall as Ester opened one door after another, the smell of must and mildew hanging in the air.

'You'll never get it ready in time, Ester.'

Ester marched into the drawing room, shouting over her shoulder, 'Oh yes I will, if everybody helps out.'

Julia picked up the dust-covered telephone with a look of surprise. 'Well I never. The phone's connected.'

Ester stood looking around the drawing room: old-fashioned sofas and wing-backed chairs, threadbare carpet and china cabinets. The massive open stone fireplace was still filled with cinders. 'I had it connected,' she snapped as she began to draw back the draped velvet curtains, turning her face away as years of dust spiralled down. Even when Ester had occupied the place, no one had ever been that interested in dusting.

The Grange Health Farm had been defunct when Ester bought the manor with all its contents, but she had no plans to refurbish the old house as it was a perfect cover for her real profession. All Ester had done was spread a few floral displays around the main rooms and bring in fourteen girls, a chef, a domestic and two muscle-bound blokes in case of trouble. The Grange Health Farm reopened, catering to clients who wanted a massage and a sauna, but if they wanted a little bit more physical contact, Ester provided that too ... at a price.

'We should have started weeks ago,' Julia said as she lolled in the doorway, looking around with undisguised distaste.

'Well, I didn't, so we're gonna have to work like the

clappers.' Ester looked up to the chandelier, trying the light switch. Two of the eighteen bulbs flickered on.

'Bravo, the electricity's on as well,' laughed Julia.

Ester glared around the room. 'We'll clean this room, the dining room and a few bedrooms. Then that's it, we won't need to do any more.'

'Really?' Julia smiled.

Ester pushed past her, wiping her dusty hands on a handkerchief, and Julia followed her back into the hall, watching as she banged open shutters.

The dining room was in the same condition but with empty bottles and glasses scattered on the table and smashed on the floor. Ester was flicking on lights, dragging back curtains with manic energy. But she seemed to deflate when she saw the wrecked kitchen, broken crockery and more smashed bottles. 'Shit! I'd forgotten how bad it was.'

'I hadn't. I told you this was a crazy idea from the start.'

Ester crossed to the back door. She unlocked it, pushing it open to get the stench of old wine and rotten food out of the kitchen.

'Must have been some party,' Julia mused.

'It was,' Ester said, as she looked at the big black rubbish bags bursting at the seams.

'Surprised the rats haven't been in here.'

'They have,' Ester said as she spotted the droppings.

She hadn't realized just how bad the place was. When

she and Julia had visited a few weeks earlier, there had been no electricity and they had arrived at dusk. Ester sighed: it had been some party all right. There used to be one every night but she had not been able to see the last one through to the end. She had been arrested along with her girls. She reckoned most of the damage had been done by the few who were left behind or who had come back when they knew she had been sentenced to grab whatever they could. A lot of the rooms looked as if they had been stripped of anything of value.

She had not bothered to come to see the damage before; she knew the bank held the deeds as collateral for her debts. She had dismissed the place from her mind until she got the news that Dolly Rawlins was going to be released. Then she had begun thinking – and thinking fast: just how could she use the old Grange Manor House to her benefit? But only if she could get it ready in time.

Julia strolled to the back door and looked out into the stable yard. The old doors were hanging off their hinges and even more rubbish and rubble had piled up.

Ester began banging open one bedroom door after another. Every room stank of mildew, and most of the beds hadn't been touched since the occupants had rolled out of them. In a few rooms clothes and dirty underwear lay discarded on the floor.

Julia started to walk up the old wide staircase, when Ester appeared at the top. 'Go and get the cases.'

'You're not serious, are you, Ester? This is madness.'

'No, it isn't. I've already laid out cash for a bloody Roller and a chauffeur. There are caterers, florists ... so we'll just have to get stuck in while we wait for the others to give us a hand.'

Julia sat on the stairs and began to roll a cigarette. 'So, you gonna tell me who you've invited to this celebration?'

Ester looked down at her. Sometimes she wanted to slap her – she could be so laid-back.

'You don't know them all. There's Connie Stevens, Kathleen O'Reilly, and I've asked that little black girl, Angela, to act as a maid.'

Julia laughed. 'She's gonna be wearing a pinny and a little hat, is she?'

Ester pursed her lips. 'Don't start with the sarcasm. We need them, and they all knew Dolly.'

Julia looked up at her. 'They all inside with her like us?'

'Not Angela, but the others. And I don't want you to start yelling – but Gloria Radford's coming.'

Julia stood up. 'You joking?'

'No, I'm not.'

'Well, count me out. I can't stand that demented cow. I spent two years in a cell with her and I'm not going to spend any more time with her if I can help it. What the hell did you rope her into it for?'

'Because we might need her, and she knows Dolly.'

Julia turned and began to march down the stairs in a fury. 'She reads aloud from the newspapers, she drove me crazy, I nearly killed her. I'm out of here.'

'Fine, you go. I don't give a shit, but it's a long walk to the station.'

Julia looked up. 'Gloria Radford on board and this is a fiasco before we even start. She's cheap, she's coarse, she's got the mental age of a ten-year-old.'

'What makes you so special, Doctor? We needed as many of us as I could get, Julia, especially ones that were as desperate as us. Now, are you staying or are you going?'

Julia lit her roll-up and shrugged. 'I'm leaving.'

Ester moved down the stairs. 'Fine, you fuck off, then, and don't think you'll get a cut of anything I get. You walk out now, and I'll never see you again. I mean it, we're through.'

Julia hesitated, looked back at Ester standing at the top of the stairs. Her face, her dark eyes, now blazing with anger, made her heart jump. Despite everything she'd said, she knew she'd be staying. She couldn't stand the thought of never seeing or touching Ester again.

She dropped her roll-up and ground it into the floor with her boot. 'I'll get the cases but just don't ask me to be nice to that midget.'

Ester smiled, and headed back to the bedroom. 'The only person you've got to be nice to is Dolly Rawlins.'

Julia got to the front door. 'What if she doesn't come, Ester? *Ester*?'

Ester reappeared, leaning on the banister rail. 'Oh, she'll come, Julia, I know it. She'll be here. She's got nobody else.'

Julia gave a small nod and walked out to the car. She began to collect all the cases and bin liners, then paused a moment as she looked over the grounds. There was a sweet peacefulness to the place. She was suddenly reminded of her childhood, of the garden at her old family home. She had been given her own pony and suddenly she remembered cantering across the fields. She had been happy then ... it seemed a lifetime ago.

The bedroom Ester chose for Dolly was spacious, with a double bed and white dressing table. Even though the carpet was stained, the curtains didn't look too bad, and with a good polish and hoover, a few bowls of flowers, it would be good enough. After all, she had spent the last eight years in a cell. This would be like a palace in comparison.

Julia appeared at the door. 'You know, we could call the local job centre if they've got one here, get a bunch of kids to start helping us. What do you think?'

Ester was dragging off the dirty bedlinen. 'Go and call them. We'll have to pay them, though. How are you off for cash?'

'I've got a few quid.'

Ester suddenly gave a beaming smile. 'We'll be rich soon, Julia. We'll never have to scrabble around for another cent.'

'You hope.'

'Why are you always so negative? I know she's got those diamonds, I know it . . .'

'Maybe she has, maybe she hasn't. And maybe, just maybe, she won't want us to have a cut of them.'

Ester gathered the dirty sheets in her arms. 'There'll be no maybes. I've worked over more people than you've had hot dinners, and I'll work her over. I promise you, we'll get to those diamonds, two million quid's worth, Julia. Just thinking about it gives me an orgasm.'

Julia laughed. 'I'll go call a job centre. This our bedroom, is it?'

'No, this one's for Dolly.'

Ester patted the bed, then sat down and smiled, thinking of how rich she was going to be.

Mike Withey looked over the newspaper cuttings. They were yellow with age, some torn from constantly being unfolded, and one had a picture of Shirley Miller, Mike's sister. It was a photograph from some job she had done as a model, posed and airbrushed. The same photograph was in a big silver frame on the sideboard, this time in colour. Blonde hair, wide blue eyes that always appeared to follow you around the room, as if she was trying to tell you something. She had been twenty-one years old when she had been shot, and even now Mike was still unable to believe that his little blue-eyed sweetheart sister had been involved in a robbery. He had been stationed in Germany when he received the hysterical call from his mother, Audrey. It had been hard to make out what she was saying, as she alternated between sobs and rantings, but there was one name he would never forget, one sentence. 'It was Dolly Rawlins, it was her, it was all her fault.'

The following year Mike married Susan, the daughter of a sergeant major. His mother was not invited to the wedding. Their first son was born before he left Germany and his second child was on the way when he was given a posting to Northern Ireland. By this stage he was a sergeant, but he didn't tell Audrey about his promotion. Susan was worried about him being stationed in Ireland and since she was heavily pregnant with a toddler to look after and all her friends were in Germany, she persuaded Mike to quit the Army. He was reluctant at first, having signed up at seventeen: it was the only life he knew. It had been his salvation, it had educated him and, most importantly, given him a direction and discipline lacking in his own home.

Mike's second son was born on the day he found out that he had been accepted by the Metropolitan Police, and with an excellent recommendation from his CO, it was felt that Mike Withey was a recruit worth keeping an eye on. He proved them right: he was intelligent, hard-working, intuitive and well liked. Mike became a 'high-flyer', never missing an opportunity to further his career prospects. No sooner was a new course pinned up on the board than he would be the first to apply. It was the many courses, the weekends away at special training colleges that made Susan, now coping with two toddlers, suggest that Mike should contact his mother again, not just for company but because she hoped Audrey could give her a hand or even babysit. Mike's refusal resulted in a big argument. Susie felt his boys had a right to know their grandmother as her own parents were still in Germany.

Mike took a few more weeks to mull it over. He supposed he could have been honest with Susan about his younger brother Gregg, who had been in trouble with the law, but he didn't want her knowing that his sister was Shirley Ann Miller, killed in an abortive robbery. It had been easy for him to conceal it because they all had different fathers, different surnames, though he was unsure if his mother had actually ever been married.

Audrey was working on the fruit and veg stall when Mike turned up as a customer, asking for a pound of Granny Smiths. She was just as he remembered her, all wrapped up, fur-lined boots, headscarf, woollen mittens with their fingers cut off.

'Well, hello, stranger. You want three or four? If it's four it'll be over the pound.' She took each apple, dropping it into the open brown-paper bag, trying not to cry, not to show Mike how desperately pleased she was to see him. She wanted to shout out to the other stallholders, 'This is my son. I told yer he'd come back, didn't I?' but she had always been a tough one, and never showed her feelings. It had taken years of practice — but get kicked hard enough and in the end it comes naturally. She didn't even touch his hand, just twisted the paper bag at the corners. 'There you go, love. Fancy a cuppa, do you?'

He had not expected to feel so much, to hurt inside so much as he followed her into the same council flat in which he had been brought up. No recriminations, no questions, talking nineteen to the dozen about people she thought he might remember: who had died on the market stalls, who had got married, who had been banged up. She never stopped talking as she chucked off her coat, kicked off the boots and busied herself making tea.

She still chattered on, shouting to him from the kitchen, as he saw all his postcards, the photo of his wedding, his boys, laid out on top of the mantelshelf, pinned into the sides of the fake gilt mirror. There had been a few changes: new furniture, curtains, wallpaper and some awful pictures from one of the stalls.

'Gregg's doin' a stint on one of the oil rigs,' Audrey

shouted. 'He's trying to go on the straight an' narrow, there's a postcard from him on the mantel.'

Mike picked up the card of two kittens in a basket and turned it over. His brother's childish scrawl said he was having a great time and earning a fortune, saving up for a motorbike. The postmark was dated more than eight months ago. He replaced the card and stared at himself in the mirror. It was then that he saw her. The thick silver frame, placed in the centre of the sideboard, a small posy of flowers in a tiny vase in front of it. She was even more beautiful than he remembered. It was one of the pictures taken when she was trying to be a model, very glamorous. Shirley's smile went straight to his heart.

'It's her birthday tomorrow,' said Audrey, 'and you've not seen her grave.'

'I'm on duty tomorrow, Mum.'

She held on to his hand. 'We can go now.'

Audrey hung on to his arm. It was dusk, the graveyard empty. Shirley was buried alongside her husband Terry Miller. The white stone was plain and simple, but the ornate flowers in a green vase were still fresh. 'Tomorrow she'll have a bouquet. They do it up for me on the flower stall, never charge me neither.' Her voice was soft as she stared at the headstone. 'She came to me straight after it had happened.'

'I'm sorry, what did you say?'

She remained focused on her daughter's name. 'That bitch – that bitch Dolly Rawlins came to see me and I've never forgiven myself for letting her take me in her arms.'

'We should go, Mum.'

She turned on him, hands clenched at her sides. 'She was behind that robbery, she organized the whole thing. They never got the diamonds . . .'

Mike stepped forward, not wanting to hear any more, but there was no stopping her. 'No, you listen. That bitch held me in her arms and I let her, let her use me just like she used my Shirley. She had them, she had the bloody things.'

'What?'

'The diamonds! She had them – got me to – she got me to give 'em to a fence, said she would see I was looked after, see I'd never want for anythin'.'

Mike's heart began to thud. He was unable to comprehend what he was hearing, as Audrey's voice became twisted with bitterness. 'I *did it*, I bloody did it. She got me so I couldn't say nothin', couldn't do anything, and then . . . she fuckin' shot her husband.'

Mike took her to a pub, gave her a brandy, and watched as she chain-smoked one cigarette after another. 'No mention of the diamonds at her trial – they never had any evidence that put her in the frame. She got done for manslaughter.'

Mike was sweating. 'You ever tell anybody what you did?'

'What do you think?' she snapped back at him. 'She got me involved, didn't she? I could have been done for fencin' them, helpin' her. No, I never told anybody.'

'Did you get paid?'

She stubbed out her cigarette. 'No. Payday is when the bitch comes out. Bitch thinks she's gonna walk out to a fortune.'

Mike gripped Audrey's hand. 'Listen to me! *Look at me!* You know what I am. You know what it means for you to tell me all this?'

Audrey lit another cigarette. 'What you gonna do, Mike, arrest your own mother?'

He ran his fingers through his hair; he could feel the sweat trickling down from his armpits. 'You got to promise me you will never, *never* tell a soul about those diamonds. You got to swear on my kids' lives. You don't touch them – don't even think about them.'

'She'll be out one day. Then what?'

Mike licked his lips.

'She as good as killed Shirley,' Audrey continued. 'I had to identify her, watch them pull the sheet down from her face.'

'*Stop it!* Look, I promise you I'll take care of you. You won't need any more dough – but I'm asking you, Mum, don't screw it up for me, please.'

23

She stared at him, then leaned forward and touched his blond hair – the same texture, same colour as Shirley's. 'I'll make a deal with you, love. If you make that bitch pay for what she done to my baby, you get her locked up—'

'Mum, she *is* away, she's in the nick right now.'

Audrey prodded his hand with her finger. 'But when she comes out she'll be rich and free. I don't care about the money, all I want is . . .'

Audrey never said the word 'revenge' but it hung in the air between them. So Mike made a promise. It felt empty to him but he had no option. He promised that, when Dolly Rawlins came out of Holloway, he would get her back for her part in the diamond robbery.

Five years later, the promise came back to haunt him, because his mother had never forgotten it. She called him and asked him to come round. As if unconcerned, Audrey was tut-tutting over some character's downfall on the TV, then offhandedly suggested he look in the left-hand drawer of the side table. Every single newspaper article about the diamond robbery was there, along with calendars with dates marked one year, two years, three years in thick red-tipped pen. He flicked through the news-clippings and his eye was drawn to a photograph, taken at some West End nightclub. He had never seen Dolly Rawlins, wouldn't know her if he was to come face to face with her in the street, but he instantly knew which one she was: she had to be the blonde, hard-faced woman sitting at the centre of the large round table. She had a champagne glass in her hand, a half-smile on her face, but there was something about her eyes: unsmiling, hard, cold eyes ... The handsome man seated next to her had almost an angry expression, as if annoyed by the intrusion of the photographer. Mike recognized his brother-in-law, dead before Shirley. Terry Miller had always looked like he never had a care in the world: his wide smile was relaxed, one arm resting along the cushioned booth seat as if protecting his pretty, innocent, child-like wife. Shirley Miller.

The TV was turned off and Audrey turned to Mike. She was crying, clutching a sodden tissue in her hand. She pointed to the photo of Dorothy Rawlins. 'You never seen her, have you, love?'

Beneath her picture was a smaller one with the heading: 'Gangland Boss Murdered by His Wife'. Harry Rawlins had been a handsome, elegant, if cruel-faced, man, and his picture made him look like a movie star. Dolly's hard gaze made them seem an unlikely couple but they had been married twenty years nonetheless. Harry Rawlins was one of the most notorious gangsters in London, a man who had never been caught, never spent a day behind bars, and yet had been questioned by the police so many times he was a familiar face to most of the Met officers. He had lived a charmed life until his wife shot him. The newspaper article stated that Dorothy Rawlins had shot and killed her husband when she had discovered that he had a mistress and a child. There was no mention that he had planned a robbery in which Shirley Miller's husband had been burnt to death. They had nicknamed Dolly the 'Black Widow' because throughout her trial she had always been dressed in black.

Audrey prodded Dolly's face in the paper. 'Nine years. Nine years. Well, she'll be out any day now,' she said, wiping her eyes.

Audrey had never told Mike that she had been pregnant when Dolly had come to see her and had lost the baby. She blamed that on Dolly Rawlins as well. Dolly had not sat down but stood in the small hallway, her head slightly bowed, her voice a low whisper. 'I'm sorry about Shirley. I am deeply sorry for Shirley.'

Audrey had been unable to reply, she was in such a state.

'Nothing will make up to you for her loss, I know that.'

Still Audrey couldn't speak. Then Dolly had lifted her head, her pale washed-out eyes brimming with tears. 'You'll get a cut of the diamonds, that I promise you. Just hand them over to Jimmy Donaldson. Jimmy'll keep them safe. When this is all over, I'll see you're taken care of, Audrey.'

But that hadn't been the end of it. Everything had changed when Audrey read in the paper that a small-time fence called Jimmy Donaldson had been arrested for dealing in stolen property. Audrey had then done something she would never have believed herself capable of. She had done it all by herself and, having done it, she had been terrified. But the weeks passed and gradually she grew more and more confident that what she had done was right.

But now she was scared, really scared, and she didn't know if she should tell Mike or not, because Dolly Rawlins was coming out and she would come out looking for her, Audrey was sure of that.

Mike was feeling uneasy. It was back again, that constant undercurrent of guilt whenever he was with his mother. He had made that promise, but how could he keep it? He held on to his temper. 'Mum, there is nothing I can do—'

'You're a ruddy police officer, aren't you? Re-arrest her. She did that robbery, Mike – I know it, you know it. She as good as killed our Shirley, never mind her bloody husband.'

The tears started again. He was due at his station in half an hour; he wished he'd never called in. 'Look, Mum, the problem will be if it implicates you – and it could.'

Audrey clung to him. 'I've got an offer. Friend's got

a villa in Spain. I can stay as long as I like. That way I can keep out of it.'

'Look, I'll see what I can do, okay?'

Audrey kissed him. 'Just let her sleep in peace, let my little girl sleep in peace.'

Mike turned on the ignition of the car but the last thing he felt like doing was going into the station. He checked his watch again and then drove to Thornton Avenue in Chiswick. He worried that he was making a mistake, this was a stupid move, but he needed to get his head straightened out. He parked the car and walked up the scruffy path. He was about to ring the front doorbell when he heard someone calling his name.

Angela was running up the road, waving, with a big wide smile. 'Mike, Mike . . .'

Mike turned as she threw herself into his arms.

'I knew you'd come and see me again, I just knew it.'

He walked hand in hand with her to his car, already wanting to kick himself for coming to her place.

'I've missed you,' she said, hanging on to his arm.

Mike released his hand. 'Look, I shouldn't have come, Angela. It was just . . . I'm sorry.'

'Oh, please stay, please. Me mum's down at the centre, there's no one in the house, and, please, I got something to tell you, please . . .'

Mike locked the car and followed Angela into her

mother's ground-floor flat. It was dark and scruffy and kids' pushchairs and toys littered every inch of the floor. Angela guided him towards the small back bedroom, and all the time he kept on saying to himself that he was dumb, he was stupid to start this up again. Angela began to undress as soon as she shut the door but he shook his head. 'No, I can't stay. Angela, I'm on duty in an hour. I just . . .'

She slumped onto the bed. 'I been waitin' for you to call for weeks. You know the way I feel about you. Why did you come here, then?'

He shook his head. He was feeling even worse. 'I dunno, I was over at my mum's place and she starts doing my head in over my sister, and I just . . .' She wrapped her arms around him, kissing his face 'No, don't, Angela, I shouldn't have come.'

She broke away. 'Well, get out, I don't care, I'm goin' away anyway.'

'Where you goin'?'

'Friend's place, just a few days, bit of work.'

Mike looked at her, shaking his head. 'What kind of work?'

Angela plucked at her short skirt.

'You're not going back on the game, are you?'

'*No, I am not,*' she shrieked.

Mike sat on the bed and rested his head against the wall. He closed his eyes.

'I was never on the game and you know it. You of all people should know it. I just worked as her maid, Mike.'

'This Ester Freeman, is it?' he asked.

Angela crawled onto the bed to sit next to him. Mike had been on the Vice Squad when Ester Freeman had been busted for running a brothel. Angela was one of the girls who had been arrested along with twelve other women but they had all, including Ester, insisted that little Angela was not on the game, just serving drinks. Mike and Angela, who was then only fifteen, had begun an affair, a stupid, on-off scene that he constantly tried to break. He never saw her more than once a month, sometimes twice, over the years, but he was very fond of her. He even gave her money sometimes but he had no intention of ever leaving his wife. If it hadn't been for him, Angela might have been sent to an approved school, but that was just an excuse. The sex was good and he simply refused to admit that that was what he used her for.

'Ester called yesterday. Wants me to go to her old manor house.'

'Oh yeah? She back running another brothel?'

'No way. She's holding some kind of party, for a woman called . . .'

Angela frowned as she tried to remember, and then grinned. 'Oh, I dunno, but she was in Holloway wiv her, shot her old man, you know. She was famous. He was a big-time villain. Anyway, she's comin' out of the nick and Ester is arranging a group of old friends to sort of welcome her, you know, give a party, and she wants me to act as a waitress.'

Mike fingered the knot in his tie. His mouth was dry. It couldn't be, could it? 'Dolly Rawlins? Is that who it is?'

'Yeah, she was in Holloway with Ester.'

Mike started undoing the buttons of her shirt. 'Who else is going?'

'I dunno, but it'll be some kind of scam, you can bet on it. I got to wear a black dress an' apron. Ester never did nothin' for nobody without there being something in it for her. She's a hard cow but I need the cash. Said she'll pay me fifty quid.'

Mike eased off Angela's shirt, reaching round to the clasp of her lacy bra. 'She say anything else about Dolly Rawlins?'

Two young prisoners peeked into Dolly Rawlins's cell, looking at the small neatly packed brown suitcase, a coat placed alongside it. Apart from these two items the cell was empty.

Footsteps echoed on the stone-flagged floor. The two girls scuttled back down the corridor as Rawlins, with a prison officer, walked towards her cell. But whatever they were expecting to see, they were disappointed. The infamous Dolly Rawlins seemed pale and worn out. The officer stood outside the cell waiting for Dolly to get her case and coat.

The corridors were strangely silent. Nearly all of the women were waiting, hiding, whispering.

The tannoy repeated a message that Rawlins, prisoner 45688, was to go to landing B. They all knew that was the check-out landing. She was almost out.

The coat was too large now she had lost so much weight, but it was good quality and she had always liked the best. She did up each button slowly and then reached for her case. None of the girls had spoken to her or said goodbye, but she refused to show that she was hurt. She looked to the officer and gave a brief nod. She was ready.

As Dolly headed towards landing B, the singing began, low at first, then rising to a bellow as every woman joined in.

'Goodbye, Dolly!'

They bellowed and stamped their feet, they called out her name and clapped their hands. 'Goodbye, Dolly, you must leave us . . .' They screeched out their thank yous for the cigarettes, for her radio, her cassettes, for every item she had passed around. Some of the girls were sobbing, openly showing how much they would miss 'Big Mama'. One old prisoner shouted at the top of her voice, 'Don't turn back, Dolly, don't look back, keep on walking out, gel . . .'

She could feel the tears welling up, her mouth trembling, but she held on, waving like the Queen as they walked onto the landings. They continued to sing, their voices echoing as she was ushered along the corridor towards the Governor's office. It wouldn't be long now.

Mike thumbed through the files and then sat, drumming his fingers on the mug shot of Dorothy Rawlins. He had read enough about Dolly Rawlins and her husband to know that if the diamonds existed she would go after them. He thought about Angela on her way to Ester Freeman. He wondered about a lot of things, trying to think if there was any possibility of doing something for his sister, for his mother – if he could get Dolly Rawlins back inside.

Mike was just starting to go through Harry Rawlins's files when he received a phone call – nothing to do with Dolly Rawlins, nothing to do with his mother or his sister. It was from Brixton Prison: a boy called Francis Lloyd wanted to give some information.

A lot of police officers had their private snitches in the prisons. Lloyd was a youngster Mike had arrested during a burglary eighteen months ago. He had been sentenced to two years because of a previous conviction. He was a likeable kid, and Mike had even got to know his mum and dad, so he returned the call – and for the second time in one day he heard the name Dolly Rawlins. Francis had some information but he didn't want to talk about it over the phone.

Governor Ellis rose to her feet from behind the desk as Dolly Rawlins was ushered into her bright, friendly office. She offered tea, a usual ritual when a long-serving prisoner was leaving. Mrs Ellis was a good governor, well liked by the inmates for her fairness and, in many instances, even for her kindness and understanding. Rawlins, however, seemed never to have needed her kindness and, as she passed Dolly her tea in a floral china cup, Mrs Ellis couldn't help but detect an open antagonism.

She eased the conversation round, discussing openings and contacts should Dolly feel in need of assistance outside, making sure she was fully aware that she would, because of the nature of her crime, be on parole for the rest of her life. When she asked if Dolly had any plans for the future she received only a quiet, 'Yes, I have plans, thank you.'

'Well, rest assured there is a network of people who will give you every assistance to readjust to being outside. Eight years – it should have been nine but, as you know, you're being released early for good behaviour – is a long time, and you will find many changes.'

'I'm sure I will,' Dolly replied, returning the half-empty cup to the tray.

Barbara Hunter remained with her back to the door, staring at Rawlins, whose calm composure annoyed the hell out of her. She listened as Mrs Ellis passed over leaflets and phone numbers should Rawlins require them. She kept her eyes on Rawlins's face, wanting to see some kind of reaction, but Dolly remained impassive.

'You have been of invaluable help with many of the young offenders and especially with the mother-and-baby wing. I really appreciate all your hard work and I wish you every success in the future.'

Dolly leaned forward and asked, bluntly, if she could leave.

'Why, of course you can, Dorothy.' Mrs Ellis smiled.

'Anything I say now, it can't change that, can it?' Dolly seemed tense.

'No, Dorothy, you are free to go.'

'Good. Well, there is something I would like to say. That woman ...' Dolly turned an icy stare on Barbara Hunter, who straightened quickly. 'You know what she is. I've got no quarrel with anyone's sexual preferences so don't get me wrong, Mrs Ellis, but that woman should not be allowed near the young girls comin' in. She shouldn't be allowed to get her dirty hands on any single kid in this place, but she does, and you all know it. She messes with the most vulnerable, especially when they've just had their babies taken from them. You got any decency inside you, Mrs Ellis, you should get rid of her.'

Mrs Ellis stood up, flushing, as Dolly sprang to her feet, adding, 'I know where she lives.'

Mrs Ellis snapped, 'Are you making threats, Mrs Rawlins?'

'No, just stating a fact. I'll be sending her a postcard. Can I go now?'

Mrs Ellis pursed her lips and gave a nod as Hunter opened the office door. Dolly walked out, past Hunter, and never looked back. Two more officers were waiting outside for her as the door closed.

Mrs Ellis sat down and drew the file of prisoner 45688, Dorothy Rawlins, towards her. She opened it and stared at the police file photographs, then slapped the file closed. 'I think we'll be seeing Dorothy Rawlins again before too long.'

Hunter agreed. 'I've never trusted her. She's devious, and a liar.'

Mrs Ellis stared at Hunter. 'Is she?' she said softly.

'Jimmy Donaldson was in the canteen two nights ago and I was next to him, I couldn't help but hear.' Francis Lloyd looked right and left, lowering his voice. 'He said that he was holding diamonds for Rawlins, that you lot copped him for peanuts compared to what he'd got stashed at his place. Diamonds . . .'

Mike leaned back in the chair. 'You sure about this, Francis?'

'Yes, on my life. Diamonds, he was braggin' about them, honest. Said he'd held on to them for eight years – diamond robbery, I swear that's what he said.'

Mike leaned forward and pushed two packs of Silk Cut cigarettes forward. They'd been opened and there was a ten quid note tucked in each of them.

'Thanks, thanks a lot.'

On his way back to the station, Mike went over everything he had picked up and started to piece it together. By the time he'd parked his car in the underground car park at the station he was feeling more positive, and even thinking that maybe, just maybe, he would be able to get Dolly Rawlins put back inside. He couldn't wait to see his mother's face when he told her, but he had to go by the book and first run it by his guv'nor.

Detective Chief Inspector Ronald Craigh was a sharp officer, a high-flyer with a good team around him. His other sidekick was Detective Inspector John Palmer, steady, cool-headed and a personal friend. The pair of them often joked about Mike being over-eager but that was not a stroke against him – far from it. Craigh listened attentively as Mike discussed the information he had received that day.

'I have a good reliable informant who told me Rawlins is going to a big manor house. There's a bunch of ex-cons waiting for her. I then get a tip-off from my informant in Brixton nick.'

Craigh leaned forwards. 'Hang about, son, this informant ... are they in my file?'

'Yes, it's Francis Lloyd – he's in Brixton.' Mike made no mention of Angela. She was not on the guv'nor's informant list. He presented the old files on the diamond robbery, explaining how Dorothy Rawlins would be out any minute and would, he estimated, go for the diamonds.

'Well, that'll be tough, won't it?' Craigh smiled. 'If Jimmy Donaldson is holdin' them for her and he's banged up, how's she gonna get to them?'

Mike paced up and down. 'What if we were to bring him out, talk it over with him, see what he has to say? I mean, we might be able to have a word with his probation officer or the Governor at Brixton, see if we couldn't get him shipped to a cushy open prison.'

'No way,' Craigh said.

Palmer held up his hand. 'We might be able to swing something that'll make him play ball with us.'

Craigh shook his head again. 'Come on, you know we got no pull to move any friggin' prisoner anywhere – and if we get him out, then what?'

'We get the diamonds,' Mike said, grinning like a Cheshire cat. 'One, there's still a whopper of a reward out for them, two, we clean up that robbery – nobody was pulled in for it. What if it was Rawlins all along? We'll find out if she contacts Donaldson. It'll be proof she knows about the diamonds.'

Craigh was still iffy about it. 'According to the old files, it was suspected that Harry Rawlins was behind it—'

'She shot him,' Mike interrupted.

'I know she did. What I'm saying is there was never any evidence to connect her to that blag.'

'There will be if she goes for those diamonds.'

Craigh sucked on his teeth and then picked up all the old files. 'Okay, I'll run it by the Super, see what he's got to say about it.'

Mike followed him to the door. 'She's out today, guv.'

Craigh opened his office door. 'I know that, son, just don't start jumping over hurdles until we know what the fuck we're gonna do.'

Mike looked glumly at Palmer as Craigh slammed the door. 'It's just that she's out, and she might call Donaldson, find out he's in the nick and . . .'

'Maybe she knows already,' Palmer said, doodling on a notepad.

'Just sit tight. If the Super gives the go-ahead, we'll see what they decide. In the meantime . . .'

Mike sighed. He had a load of reports to complete so he took himself off to the incident room. As he reached his desk, his phone rang. It was Craigh. They were going to talk to Donaldson, if he wanted to come along. Mike grinned; it was going down faster than he'd thought.

Ester ordered the six boys from the job centre to collect every bottle and piece of broken glass before they started to hoover and dust. A florist's van had arrived with two massive floral displays that were propped up in the hall. Julia was using a stiff brush to sweep the front steps when she saw the taxi at the open manor gates. 'Someone's coming now,' she called out.

The taxi drove slowly down the drive, skirted the deep hole in the gravel and stopped by the front steps. Kathleen O'Reilly peered from the back seat. She had boxes and cases and numerous plastic bags. 'Hi. You moving in or on the move, Kathleen?' asked Julia.

Kathleen opened the car door. 'They're all me worldly possessions. I had to do a bit of a moonlight but Ester said I could doss down here for a few days. Will you give the driver a fiver? I'm flat broke.'

Kathleen: overweight, wearing a dreadful assortment of ill-matched clothes – a cotton skirt with two hand-knitted sweaters on top of a bright yellow blouse. She had red hair spilling over a wide moon face and her false teeth, yellow with tobacco stains, needed bleaching. But she had a marvellous, generous feel to her, an open Irish nature. Julia delved into her pocket to pay off the driver as Kathleen hauled out her belongings. 'They said this was closed down,' she bellowed as she staggered into the hallway. Kathleen dumped her bags in the hall and looked around. 'Holy Mother of God, what a dump! Is that chandelier safe, Julia?'

Julia dropped one of Kathleen's cases. 'Ask Ester – she's running the show.'

At that moment Ester came down the stairs. 'You made it here, then?'

'Well, of course I did.' Kathleen embraced her. 'I was glad you called, darlin'. I was in shit up to me armpits, I can tell you, with not a roof over my head. So . . . is she here, then?'

Julia turned, listening.

'Not yet, and I hope she won't be for a few hours. We've got to get the place ready.'

Kathleen plodded to the stairs. 'Well, let me unpack me gear, darlin', and I'll give you a hand.'

Ester instructed Kathleen to use one of the second-landing bedrooms and went into the kitchen, squeezing past the boys as they scrubbed the floor. Julia picked up the broom again, trying to remember what Kathleen had been in prison for, but her attention was diverted by yet another car making its slow progress down the driveway.

Connie Stevens sat next to the railway-station attendant, a nice man who, seeing Connie outside the small local station waiting for a taxi, had offered her a lift. Men did that kind of thing for Connie: she had such a helpless Marilyn Monroe quality to her, they went weak at the knees. She even had a soft breathy voice, hair dyed blonde to match her heroine's, and recent plastic surgery that gave a dimple to her chin, tightened her jaw and removed the lines from her baby eyes. She worked hard to retain her curvaceous figure as she was already in her mid-thirties – not that she ever admitted it to anyone: she had been twenty-five for the past ten years.

Julia watched as the man, red-faced, struggled to remove an enormous case on wheels from the boot of his car.

'Thank you, I really appreciate this so much,' Connie cooed. The station attendant returned to his car, and, embarrassed by Julia's obvious amusement, drove out as fast as he could, crashing into the pothole as he went.

Ester leaned out of an upstairs window. 'Hi, Connie, come on in. Kathleen's already arrived.'

Connie dragged her case towards the steps. Julia tossed away the broom and took her case by the handle. 'Here, lemme help, Princess.'

Connie gave a breathy 'aaw' as she looked at the hall. 'It's changed so much since I was last here.'

Ester jumped down the stairs and embraced Connie warmly, then held her at arm's length to admire her new face. 'You look good – *really* good. Just drag your case upstairs and get into some old gear. We've got to clear the place up and make it ready for Dolly.'

'How many more are coming?' asked Kathleen. 'I mean, are we gonna cut it between us all?'

'I don't know. Like I said, Ester's in charge, ask her. She hasn't told me what she plans on doing.'

Kathleen moved closer. 'They're worth millions, the diamonds, everyone used to talk about them. Are you certain she'll be coming?'

Julia picked up the broom and started sweeping the steps again. 'Ester seems to think so, that's why she's got us all here.'

Kathleen started hoovering with venom. She certainly hoped this wasn't all a waste of time. She was in deep trouble: her three kids had been taken into care and she needed money, a lot of it, and fast. Dolly Rawlins's diamonds would be her only way out of the mess she had got herself into.

Way down the lane, Gloria Radford threw up her hands in fury. She'd been down one dead end after another, up onto the motorway three times, and still not found the Manor House. She got out of her dilapidated Mini Traveller and headed towards a man on a tractor in the middle of a field. 'Oi, mate, can you direct me to the Grange Manor House?'

The old farmhand turned in surprise as Gloria, small, plump and wearing spike-heeled shoes and skin-tight black pants, waved from the field gates. Her make-up was plastered on thick: lip gloss-smudged teeth, mascara-clogged lashes with bright blue eye-shadow on the lids – she was like someone from the late Sixties stuck in a time-warp. Gloria Radford waved the hand-drawn map Ester had sent her. The old boy wheeled his tractor towards her.

'Down there.' He pointed.

'I been down there and I been back up there and I keep gettin' back on the bleedin' motorway.'

'Ay, yes, they cut off the access road. Just keep on this slip road and you'll get to it. The manor's off to the right.'

Gloria stepped over the clods of earth and headed back to her Mini. The farmhand remained watching as she reversed straight into a pothole and let rip with a stream of expletives.

Ester was now checking the cutlery. Some of it was quite good but it all needed cleaning, as did every plate and cup and saucer. Kathleen was on duty in the dining room, dusting the chairs, when the crate of wine was delivered. She was ready for a drink and about to open a bottle when they all heard the tooting of a car horn and the sound of Gloria Radford arriving, towed in by a tractor.

They all stood crowded on the doorstep, watching the spectacle. Julia turned to Ester. 'Subtle as ever. I suppose you wanted the entire village to know we were here.'

'Me bleedin' back end's fucked!' yelled Gloria, as she heaved out a case.

Julia winced as Gloria negotiated some complicated financial arrangement with the old man on his tractor to tow the car to the nearest garage. She was so loud and brassy that she was almost comical: her fake-fur leopard coat slung round her shoulders, her too-tight, puce, wrap-around shirt. 'Er, Ester, you got a few quid I can bung 'im?'

Julia saw Ester purse her lips and join Gloria at the tractor.

Ester paid ten quid to the tractor driver and directed him to the nearest garage that would be able to repair the Mini.

Gloria banged into the hallway. 'Cor blimey, this is the old doss-house, is it? Hey, Kathleen, how are you doin', kid?' Kathleen said she was doing fine, then Gloria pointed at Connie. 'I know you, don't I?'

Connie shook her head. 'I don't think so, I'm Connie.'

'You one of Ester's tarts, then, are you?'

Connie's jaw dropped. 'No, I am not.'

Gloria seemed unaware of how furious Connie was. She turned to Julia. 'I didn't know you was on this caper, Doc.'

'Likewise,' said Julia sarcastically.

'You sure you got Dolly comin'? I mean, I come a hell of a long way to get here, you know.' Julia had to turn away because she wanted to laugh out loud.

Ester clenched her fists: Gloria had only been there two minutes and she was getting under her skin already. 'She'll be here, Gloria. Just get some old gear on and start helping us, we've got a lot to do.'

'Right, you tell me what you want done, sweet face. I'm ready, I'm willin' and nobody ever said Gloria Radford wasn't able.'

Ester looked at her watch. She thought she should have received a call from Dolly by now but she said nothing, just hoped to God she had played her cards right. She had laid out a lot of cash already and if wily old Dolly Rawlins copped out, she was in trouble. All the women she had chosen were desperate for cash, but Ester more than any of them.

Dolly was out. She became a free woman two hours ago. The fear crept up unexpectedly. Suddenly she felt alone. She stood on the pavement as her heart began to race and her mouth went bone dry. She was out – and there was no one to meet her, no one to wrap their arms around her, no place to go. She saw the white Rolls Corniche; it was hard to miss, parked outside the prison gates. She stepped back, afraid for a moment, when a uniformed chauffeur got out and looked over.

'Excuse me, are you Mrs Rawlins, Mrs Dolly Rawlins?'

Dolly frowned, gave a small nod, and he smiled warmly, walking towards her. 'Your car, Mrs Rawlins.'

'I never ordered it.'

He touched her elbow gently. 'Well, my docket says you did, Mrs Rawlins, so, where would you like to go?'

Nonplussed, she allowed herself to be ushered towards the Rolls. He opened the door with a flourish. 'Anywhere you want. It's hired for the entire day, Mrs Rawlins.'

'Who by?' she asked suspiciously.

'You, and it's paid for, so why not? Get in, Mrs Rawlins.' Dolly looked at the prison, then back to the car. On the back seat was a small bouquet of roses, a bottle of champagne, and an invitation. 'I don't understand, who did this?'

The chauffeur eased her in and shut the door. Dolly opened the invitation.

Dear Dolly,
    Some of your friends have arranged a 'SHE'S
OUT' party. Take a drive around London and then
call us. Here's to your successful future, and hoping
you will join us for a slap-up dinner and a knees-up,

Ester

Dolly read and reread the invitation. She knew Ester Freeman but she'd not been that friendly with her.

'Where would you like to go, Mrs Rawlins?'

She leaned back, still nonplussed. 'Oh, just drive around, will you? So I can see the sights.'

'Right you are.'

She saw the portable phone positioned by his seat. She leaned forward and picked up the phone.

'Call any place you want, Mrs Rawlins.'

She turned the phone over in her hand, never having seen one before, and then she smiled softly. 'My husband would have loved one of these,' she whispered.

Chapter 2

James 'Jimmy' Donaldson was a small, sandy-haired man. With his trim physique and thick hair with a deep widow's peak at the temple, he looked younger than his fifty-five years. He was exceedingly nervous, having been brought from a woodwork class to be confronted by DCI Craigh and DS Mike Withey. The prison officers left the three men alone, which seemed to unnerve Donaldson even more, and his eyes darted nervously from one man to the other.

Craigh asked quietly if he knew a woman called Dorothy Rawlins. Donaldson shook his head, then shifted his buttocks on the chair to sit on his hands, as if afraid they would give him away because they were shaking.

'You sure about that, Jimmy?'

He nodded, blinking rapidly, as Craigh, still speaking softly, asked him about the diamonds.

'I d–d–don't know anything about them,' he stuttered.

'She's out today, Jimmy. Dolly Rawlins is out.'

Donaldson went white.

Craigh spoke soothingly. 'No need to worry, Jimmy. If you help us, then maybe we can make things easier for you, maybe even get the authorities to move you to a nice, cushy open prison.'

Two hours later, Donaldson was taken from Brixton Prison to their local nick. It was done fast and Craigh made sure that it was put out that Donaldson required a small operation, so that when and if they sent him back he wouldn't be subjected to threats for grassing. All he had admitted so far was that he might know about the diamonds but he refused to say anything more unless he was taken out of the jail.

On the journey he brightened up at the prospect of being moved, even going home to visit his wife. Craigh had laughed. 'Don't get too excited, Jimmy, because we'll need to know more – a lot more. You're doing time for fencing hot gear right now and we've not got much sway with the prison authorities. All we do is catch 'em, the rest is not down to us unless you have some very good information.'

It was almost six thirty by the time Donaldson was taken into the station, and he was given some dinner before they really began to pressure him. He admitted that he knew Dolly Rawlins but he had known her husband better, and had held the stones for her as a favour. When asked if Rawlins instigated the diamond raid, he swore he didn't know and he was certain that Mrs Rawlins couldn't have done it because she was a woman. He knew she had killed her husband but word was he'd been fooling around with a young bit of fluff who'd had a kid by him. At the time of the shooting, there were many rumours around as to what had happened, but the truth had always been shrouded in mystery – and fear, because Harry Rawlins was a formidable and exceptionally dangerous man, nicknamed the 'Octopus' because he seemed to have so many arms in so many different businesses. A lot of men known to have crossed him had disappeared.

Harry Rawlins had masterminded a raid on an armoured truck. The plan had been to ram it inside the Strand underpass but the raid had gone disastrously wrong. The explosives used by his team had blown their own truck to smithereens; four men inside had died, their charred bodies unrecognizable. Dolly Rawlins had been given a watch, a gold Rolex, from the blackened wrist of one of the dead men. She had buried his remains, the funeral an ornate affair, with wreaths from every main criminal in England. In many instances they were sent not out of sympathy, but relief.

Dolly had been in deep shock. The husband she had worshipped for twenty years was gone, her loss made worse by the pressure from villains trying to take over her husband's manor. Her grief had turned to anger when they approached her at his graveside, and then to icy fury. When she found Harry's detailed plans for the abortive robbery, Dolly drew together the widows of the men who had died alongside Harry in the truck. She manipulated and cajoled them into repeating the raid that had taken their men. Always a strong-minded woman, Dolly grew more confident and arrogant each day. Her belief that they could handle it quelled their fears, and her constant encouragement and furious determination ensured that they not only succeeded in pulling off one of the most daring armed robberies ever, but she also made sure they got away with it. She had been doing it for Harry, using his carefully crafted plans. Never for one moment had she believed or even contemplated his betrayal.

Harry Rawlins was alive. He had been the only one to escape from the nightmare raid that killed his men. Rawlins had arranged that when the raid was over he would never return to his wife, and would leave Dolly for his twenty-five-year-old mistress. To his amazement, Harry Rawlins had found himself watching as Dolly went ahead with the raid, and then laughed because he knew that if she succeeded he would take the money. Her audacity amused him. Safe in his girlfriend's apartment, he had watched and waited, had played with his baby boy, the child Dolly had been desperate to give him.

But Harry Rawlins had underestimated his wife.

Dolly succeeded in the raid and she also found out the terrible truth. She never confronted him – it would have been too dangerous, not for herself but for the other women concerned. Instead she planned their escape from England, leaving him penniless and desperate.

For a while the widows had lived high but the bulk of the money became a monster they could not control. Dolly had chosen to hide out in Rio, not only for safety, but because she knew Harry had a bank account there with over fifty thousand in it, and as she had his death certificate she knew she would be able to claim it. Their sojourn in Rio did not last long, though, as Dolly discovered Harry had arrived there and when he found out she had cleaned out his bank account, he would come after her. She was able to move the money from the security raid from a convent where she had worked to beneath the stage of the local church hall. She also discovered that Harry, desperate to track her down, was organizing a jewellery raid. As she recalled the women back to London, her plan was to tip off the police about the diamond heist, but tragically, not everything had gone according to plan. One of them, Linda Pirelli, was killed in a car accident, a second, the young beautiful Shirley Miller, who had unwittingly become involved as a catwalk model wearing some of the diamonds, was shot during the robbery.

Dolly got away with a large portion of the diamonds, but the police net was drawing in.

Yet again she reacted as her husband would have. She knew Jimmy Donaldson could be trusted; small-time he might be but he had done a lot of work for Harry in the past and had never been charged so she used that as a lever to ensure that he would keep the diamonds safe. She could have got away with it but something was more important than the diamonds: her guilt about little Shirley. She went to Audrey, Shirley's mother, because she felt she owed her a debt. Audrey would also be unlikely to go to the police, because Dolly had used Audrey in the first raid when they had escaped from England. Dolly was hoping the promise of a cut of the diamonds would atone for Shirley's death. All Dolly had asked Audrey to do was wait, and in time she would get her share. Audrey wept but had delivered the diamonds to Jimmy that same night, as Dolly had instructed, agreeing that they would have no further contact until Dolly gave the word. Neither Jimmy nor Audrey knew that while they were organizing a hiding place for the diamonds, Dolly had arranged a meeting with her husband and was waiting for him with a .22 handgun. Harry had been sure as soon as she saw him that he would be able to talk her round, make her believe that he'd had to lie low because he would have been arrested. He had allowed her to go through the charade of a funeral because if he hadn't, the filth would have known he was still alive. So he had waited, confident he could manipulate her. Never had he properly considered the pain he had caused her, the terrible grief he had put her through – the wife who had stood by him for twenty years.

Harry had smiled when Dolly approached and had taken a few steps towards her. He had still been smiling when she fired at point-blank range into his heart.

Dolly Rawlins was arrested and charged with manslaughter, resulting in a nine-year sentence to be served at Holloway Prison. She had never stopped loving him and the pain never did go away, but the years eased it. In prison she embraced the hurt inside her, like the child she was never able to conceive.

Even after Harry's death, Jimmy Donaldson's fear of Harry Rawlins remained. All he had admitted to was having received a package from Dolly Rawlins. Even after his subsequent arrest for fencing, he had remained silent about the diamonds. In reality, he had been too scared to fence them or mention them to anyone else. But now he began to talk.

'She's a tough bitch, you know, hard as nails. Everyone knew how much her old man depended on her – gave him more alibis than you've had hot dinners, mate.'

Donaldson became quite cocky as he told them how

Dolly had promised he'd get a nice reward for keeping her property safe.

'So where are they, Jimmy?' asked Craigh.

Donaldson pursed his lips. 'Well, that would be telling. I mean, you gonna let me see my wife?'

Craigh became tougher, prodding him with his finger. 'We make the deals, Jimmy, not you. You're lucky we're not gonna slap more years on for not coming out with this at your trial.'

'Fuckin' hell, you bastards, you just been stringing me along. Well, no more, no way, I retract everythin' I said, I dunno anythin'.'

The truth was that Craigh was in no position to offer a deal until he had spoken to the prison authorities and to Donaldson's parole officer to see if they could get him moved. Mike was eager for them to make any promise and he was the one who asked Donaldson if Dolly Rawlins had contacted him since she had been in Holloway.

'No, never – she's not stupid. But a few times I sort of felt a finger on the back of the neck, so to speak.'

Donaldson never divulged that Dolly Rawlins had quite a hold over him because of all the other times he had fenced stolen gear for her husband, knowing he could be put away for a lot longer than five years. Now he felt a bit of relief because they seemed to want to put her away again and it would mean he was free of her.

Mike Withey was also relieved. At no point had Donaldson mentioned the part his own mother, Audrey, had played.

'How is she going to collect the diamonds?'

'Well, she'll call me. She was never arrested or charged for that gig, was she? I mean, nobody knows she's got them, do they?' Still not knowing the location of the diamonds, Craigh and Palmer talked it over with the Super and decided to take Donaldson to his home and give it a few days to see if Rawlins made contact.

Once Donaldson knew he was going home to see his wife – even if a police officer would be with him at all times – he told them where the stones were hidden. His wife still ran his junk and antique shop and the main wall had a four-brick hideaway; if they removed the bricks, they would find the gems.

Craigh and Palmer high-fived each other, thinking of the big reward for the return of the stones. Mike was more pleased about the fact that, if Donaldson handed the diamonds over to Dolly, they could send her straight back to prison. Rest in peace, Shirley Miller.

Dolly stood outside her old house in Totteridge. She stared at the new curtains, the fresh paint. For the twenty years of her marriage this was where she had lived. She had always been house-proud, and had done her best to make it into a place Harry would be proud of. Harry entertained regularly and she had always set a nice table with good, home-cooked food. She had thought she was happy, had believed he was too. As she stood there now, thinking of his betrayal, she clenched her hands, trying not to break down, refusing to after all these years. He had forced her into a grief-driven fury – she had even buried him when all the time he had been alive. Alive and cheating on her. It was so bizarre, so insane what she had done, what she had become. And even when he had faced her, knowing that she knew everything, he had still been so sure of her love that he had opened his arms and said, 'I love you, Doll.'

She had pulled the trigger then, almost nine years ago. She had served the sentence for his murder and now she was free. She walked back to the waiting chauffeur and he opened the car door. Dolly had sold the house and all its contents for a lot of money through her lawyers, and now wanted to go to the bank to collect enough to buy herself a small flat.

'That was my home,' she said softly.

He helped her inside the car.

'Now it's someone else's.' She sounded so sad, but she suddenly gave him a sweet smile.

'Can I use this portable phone, then?'

Ester grabbed the phone after two rings, knowing it had to be Dolly. She'd got a new number when the phone had been reconnected and only Dolly knew it. She listened for a moment, then put the phone down. Dolly was on her way. Ester sighed with relief and then hurried into the dining room.

The table was almost ready but Gloria and Kathleen were having a go at each other. 'She's drinking, Ester,' said Gloria. 'I keep telling her not to get pissed.'

Ester snatched up one of the bottles, recorked it and banged it onto the table as Kathleen shouted that all she was doing was getting them ready for the decanters. 'She's on her way, and as soon as those lads are finished we'd all better have a talk, get sorted. She's not stupid so we got to make this look good. Where's Connie?'

'I'm here. I've been repairing my nails. I've chipped two already – they're not supposed to be in too much water, you know.'

Gloria raised her eyes to heaven as Connie showed off her false-tipped nails. Ester told her to start bringing up extra chairs from the basement. She had to show her the way and as they walked down the hall, Connie pulled her to one side. 'What were they in prison for?'

Ester told her that Gloria had been in for a long stretch for fencing stolen guns and Kathleen was in for forgery and kiting.

'And what about Julia? What was she in for?'

Gloria appeared. 'The Doc was in for sellin' prescriptions. She was a junkie.'

Connie flushed with embarrassment.

'I heard you, Ester. I wasn't done for the guns, that was a total frame-up. I was stitched up,' Gloria said.

Ester sighed, already sick and tired of Gloria. She ushered Connie to the cellar door, which led down to the sauna, the steam room and the old laundry. There was also a gymnasium, and there were showers and changing cubicles, all from the days when the manor had been a health farm.

Connie went down to inspect the chairs as most of the ones in the dining room were broken. Confronted by banks of mirrors, she couldn't resist looking at herself and pouting, then jumped when Julia asked what she was doing in her droll voice. Connie squinted in the semi-darkness, looking over the stack of chairs. 'I love to work out, I do it whenever I can – it's like a fix.' She put her hand to her mouth. 'Oh, I'm sorry, I didn't mean that the way it came out...'

'I know what you meant,' Julia said. 'You worked for Ester, right? What were you, then?'

'I'm a model. I don't do any of that kind of thing now, not any more.'

Julia smiled. 'Well, I don't use drugs, and you're not selling that lovely body, so we both seem to have improved our lives, don't we?'

Julia turned and left and Connie sighed. She hated it when anyone assumed she had been a prostitute. But that was what she had been, like it or not. Then when Lennie, who she had trusted, who she believed had loved her, had tried to make her go back on the game it had really hurt because she had dreamed of one day being a model, a proper one, one that kept her clothes on. She had written to agents and now, with all the work done on her face, she reckoned she might even get a TV commercial. She had big plans for herself: she would have a big-time photographer do a good contact sheet, send out a portfolio. She was sure she had a chance. Lennie had laughed and told her she was too old, told her that was the reason he had paid for her surgery, so she could make some money on her back, but she had refused.

Connie sat down on one of the dusty chairs and started to cry. He never touched her face, at least he didn't ruin that, but her body was still covered in bruises. She had said she would do whatever he wanted, if he just left her alone. The following morning Ester had called, not to ask her to go on the game as she had first thought, but to give her a chance of making a lot of money. Connie had immediately thrown a few things into a case and done a runner. She knew Lennie would be going crazy, knew he would be out looking for her: he'd want his money back for the surgery at the very least, but Ester had said that she'd have more money than she would know what to do with. She hoped Ester was right. Connie had never really met Dolly Rawlins.

'What the hell are you doin' down here?' Gloria suddenly yelled.

Connie picked up the chair and brushed past her.

'You see any big trays around here? Ester said we need one,' Gloria added.

Connie hadn't, so Gloria began to sort through the odd bits and pieces of furniture in the gym. She sighed when she caught her dirt-streaked reflection. Then she inspected the black roots of her hair. She needed a tint badly; she had to have it done before she went to see Eddie.

Eddie Radford was serving eighteen years for arms dealing and armed robbery. He was going to be away for so long that sometimes Gloria wondered if it was worth going back and forth to the prisons. He'd spent most of their marriage in one or another. To be honest, they were two bad pennies, as she had been in and out for this and that since she was a teenager. But Eddie was trouble – she'd known it when she first met him. He was even worse than her first husband. Now he'd got a stash of weapons hidden at their old house with two of his bastard friends trying to get them. She had no money but Eddie kept telling her he'd arrange a deal, that she just had to sit tight and wait until he'd made the contact. Gloria was behind with the rent, and the council had told her to leave. It seemed like everyone was always telling her what to do and it always ended up a mess. She was scared of sitting on such a big stash of guns, scared of his so-called contacts and she was sick to death of always being on the move, always looking over her shoulder in case one of Eddie's friends tracked her down.

When Ester had called, it had been like a breath of fresh air. The thought of getting away from that pressure, away from Eddie's bloody heavies, was intoxicating. And with the promise of big money tied in with it, who could refuse?

Ester checked the table. It was looking good. As it grew darker it got harder to see the dilapidation, and she had bought boxes of candles and incense sticks, plus room sprays, so gradually the stench of mildew was disappearing. Gloria said it smelt like someone had farted in a pine forest.

The food had been delivered on big oval throwaway platters, and all they had to do was heat it up. The Aga was on, the boiler was working and fires were lit in the dining room and drawing room. Julia had cut logs and carried them in, and slowly the firelight and the candlelight had given warmth to the old house. The kids from the job centre had gone and only the women remained. Ester shouted for them all to meet up and have a confab as Dolly would be arriving in a couple of hours.

The doorbell rang and Ester swore, looking at her watch. It couldn't be her yet . . . Then she remembered Angela.

'You took your bloody time getting here. I said this afternoon. It's almost six,' she snapped.

Angela dumped her overnight bag. 'I had to bleedin' walk all the way from the station, it took hours. And I missed the train so I had to wait . . .' She looked at the bank of candles. 'Eh, this looks great, I thought it was wrecked.'

'It was, it is, we've done a good bandage job.'

Angela hadn't seen the old house for years, not since it was busted, so she was impressed by the big floral displays in the hall, the banisters gleaming from the hours Kathleen had spent polishing.

Gloria walked out from the dining room and glared at Angela. 'Who's this? What're you doing?'

Ester said that Angela was a friend who had come to serve the dinner.

'Oh yeah? We cut this any more ways and there's not gonna be much to go round, you know.'

Ester pushed Gloria against the wall. 'She doesn't know anything, she doesn't know Dolly and she's not in for a cut. She gets fifty quid to wait on us at dinner. Now will you get the others in the dining room so we can have a talk?'

Angela went into the kitchen. Ester pointed to what food needed heating, what was to be served cold and showed her the low oven of the Aga for the plates to be heated. Angela looked around, nodding, then trailed after Ester to the dining room.

'There's a room ready for you. Dump your bag. Did you bring a black dress and an apron?'

'Yes, ma'am,' said Angela with a little curtsy.

'Okay, all of you read these.' Ester handed round old newspaper clippings she had Xeroxed about the diamond raid: there were photographs of Dolly Rawlins after the shooting of her husband and several of Shirley Miller.

'Holy shit, you read this?' said Gloria. '"Diamonds worth more than five million were last night stolen in a daring raid."'

Julia grabbed the clippings. 'Gloria, we can read it for ourselves, okay?'

Gloria picked up another. 'Fuckin' hell, listen to this, "Harry Rawlins was last night shot at point-blank range by his wife. His body was discovered in a lake in—"'

Julia snatched it from her. 'Shut up, just shut up.'

Kathleen looked at Ester. 'This was some raid. Did she set it up? Dolly?'

'She was never shopped for it if she did.'

Gloria frowned. 'This was no doodle at Woolworth's. Look at the gear they got away with, and guns. See this?' She held up a cutting. '"Shirley Miller, aged twenty-one, was shot and killed during a terrifying armed raid that took place at a fashion show last night. The models were wearing *over ten million pounds' worth of diamonds* . . ."'

Julia glanced at Ester in exasperation. She had had to

put up with Gloria reading aloud when they had shared the same prison cell and she was about to make her shut up when Ester stopped them all short.

'If they were worth ten million nearly nine years ago, you can double the value now. Even if Dolly didn't get the motherlode.'

Kathleen whistled in awe. Gloria's face was puckered in concentration. 'I mean, I know there were rumours, Ester, but, like, she might have started them. How can you be sure she's really got these diamonds?'

'Because nobody ever found them after the raid.'

'That don't mean she got 'em,' said Gloria.

Julia sighed. 'Let's take it that she does have them.'

'Okay, she's got them, and now she's out and she's coming here tonight.'

'Right. She's coming here, to be with friends, and that's what we are going to be for her, dear old friends,' said Ester.

Gloria shook her head. 'You must be joking. She don't know the meaning of the word.'

'Gloria, will you keep it shut for ten minutes and *fucking listen to me*?' Ester ran her hands through her hair. 'I know she has no one, had no visitors. She's going to be very lonely, even frightened, so we make her welcome, we make her have a great night . . .'

Gloria nodded. 'Then what? When do we get our hands on the stones?'

'None of you, not one of you, mentions diamonds. We just want her to feel like we're her friends, that she can trust us. She might need a good fence – Kathleen knows plenty. She might have trouble getting the stones – Gloria's got contacts. She will need us, you understand? Above all, we make her trust us. When she tells us about the diamonds, we go for them, we take them if we feel like it, and we share them between us.'

'The five of us?' asked Gloria.

'Yes, Gloria, the five of us, or six—'

'Who's the sixth, then? Not that little black chick you got in for the nosh?'

'No, Gloria, Angela is not the sixth, but I reckon Dolly might want a cut of her own gear.'

'Well, if I was her I'd just say piss off. I mean, why give us a cut?'

Ester sighed, beginning to think the whole thing was turning into a fiasco, when Connie suddenly giggled. 'Five million! Oh, *yes!*'

They all started to laugh so Ester decided it was time to break it up and told them to start getting changed: Dolly was on her way and would be there within the hour. Like kids they trooped out.

Julia began to rub Ester's neck, feeling the tension. 'I hope to God this works, Julia, and works fast, because I don't think I could stand more than a few hours cooped up with that bloody Gloria Radford.'

Julia cupped Ester's face in her hands and kissed her lips. 'Don't say I didn't warn you. If anyone can pull it off, you can. I just hope there really are diamonds. It could all be a fantasy – you know that, don't you, darling?'

Ester gripped her wrists. 'No. There's diamonds, believe me, I know it. And I know that bitch has got them somewhere . . . and we'll get them away from her and then . . .'

Julia stepped back. 'Then?' she said softly.

'I'm free, Julia. I'll be free. No bastard trying to slit my throat. I'll even airmail their wretched tape back to them. With all those millions I won't need to grovel or beg from anyone. I don't reckon in all honesty I've ever in my life been free but this time I will be.'

'I hope for your sake you get them, then. I love you, Ester.'

Ester was already walking out of the room. She didn't hear or if she did she pretended not to. Alone, Julia looked round the once magnificent room. Maybe Dolly would be taken in if she didn't look too carefully, if she didn't see the cracks, if she believed that Ester was her friend, all of them were her friends. Julia sighed. In some ways she felt sorry for Dolly Rawlins because she was walking into a snake pit and Julia was ashamed to be a part of it.

The candles threw shadows on the wall and she raised her hand to make a silhouette of a bird flying, flapping its wings. Dolly Rawlins's first day of freedom in eight years. Julia watched the shadow bird flutter and then broke the shadow as she moved her hands away from the candle. Ester had planned this evening carefully, each one of them chosen because they were desperate, herself included. She was desperate not to lose Ester, desperate to safeguard the lies she had told her ailing elderly mother, lies she had spun round her arrest and prison sentence. Julia's mother didn't know her daughter the doctor was an ex-drug addict, that she had been struck off and for the last four years had been in prison. She had arranged an elaborate charade via friends who passed Julia's letters written in Holloway to look as if they were sent from abroad. Julia's mother had never suspected her daughter was leading a double life, just as she had no notion that her daughter could or would be deeply in love with another woman. It was beyond her comprehension, and Julia was determined her mother would never know. Keeping up the pretence had taken money, and still took every penny she could lay hands on, as she paid all her mother's bills. Julia needed those diamonds just like the rest of them. The only difference was, she was ashamed of the awful con they were all about to begin on Dolly Rawlins.

Chapter 3

Jimmy Donaldson's wife had been informed that her husband was returning home on a 'special leave' from prison. She was asked not to mention the visit to anyone and to remain in the house until he was brought home. When he did arrive, in the company of two plainclothes officers, they had only one or two moments alone before he was taken into their sitting room. One officer placed a tape recorder and bugging device on their telephone in the hope that Dolly Rawlins would make contact. The small antique shop was already being searched. DCI Craigh arranged for a rota of officers to remain in the house and keep an eye on Jimmy. Mike Withey was to take the following morning shift. Mike couldn't wait to see his mother and tell her what was happening.

*

At the same time Dolly Rawlins was about to arrive at Grange Manor House. The women had all changed into cocktail dresses. Ester had laid out one of her own dresses for Dolly to change into and, as she saw the headlamps of the Corniche turning into the driveway, she gave hurried orders for the women to remain in the dining room and stay silent. Next she briefed Angela that when the doorbell rang she was to open the front door and welcome Dolly into the house. Ester would then make her appearance.

Dolly stepped out of the car. She looked around, feeling unsure, even more so than when she'd been driving down the dark, potholed lane leading to the house. Now that she was here, it was difficult to see what state it was in. The chauffeur guided her towards the front steps. She stopped.

'Are you staying?'

'If you would like me to, Mrs Rawlins. It's entirely up to you.' He rang the bell. Some of the stained glass was broken but Dolly wasn't paying much attention; she was feeling edgy.

Angela opened the door, wearing a neat black dress and white apron.

'Good evening, Mrs Rawlins. Welcome to the Grange.'

Dolly hesitated and then saw Ester, elegant as ever, standing with her arms wide. 'Dolly. Come on in.'

She walked into the hall.

'What's going on?'

'It's a welcome-out party for you. All your old mates, Dolly, from Holloway.'

She watched as Angela closed the door, taking Dolly's small case from the chauffeur, and then Ester embraced her warmly, kissing her on both cheeks.

'Come on, let me show you around. You'll want a bath, won't you?'

Dolly looked at the banks of flickering candles, still nonplussed as Ester guided her up the stairs. She stopped. 'Why are you doing this?'

Ester continued up the stairs. 'We all know what it feels like, coming out to nothing and no one, Dolly. We wanted to make sure you got a special party, to sort of start you off in the right direction.'

Dolly followed Ester up the stairs, impressed by the state of the house, then the clean room with the black lace dress laid out on the bed. There were stockings and clean underwear, even a couple of pairs of high-heeled shoes.

'You did all this for me?' Dolly said, still nonplussed.

'It's not a new dress but it is a Valentino. Would you like me to run a bath for you? Wash your hair?'

Angela slipped in with Dolly's suitcase and placed it by the bed. She was out again before Dolly could say a word. 'Who's that?'

'Oh, she's just a kid that used to work for me.'

'A tart, is she?'

'No, she's just here to serve us so we don't have to do anything but enjoy ourselves.'

Dolly wandered around the room. 'Who else is here?'

Ester went into the ensuite, turned on the taps, felt the hot water — it wasn't what you'd call *hot* hot — and poured in bath salts.

'Kathleen O'Reilly, you remember her?' Ester told her the other names.

Dolly sat on the bed. 'Well, I wouldn't call any of them friends, Ester. They all here, are they?'

'Yes, well, I tried to get as many women as I thought you knew so it'd be a bit of a knees-up.'

'I'm not sure what to say.'

Ester smiled. 'Just have a nice bath. I'll go and tell them you'll be down soon, okay?'

Dolly slowly took off her coat, and then smiled. 'Yeah, why not? I could do with a drink.'

They all looked towards the double doors as Ester came into the dining room. 'She's getting ready, won't be long.'

'I hope not, I'm starving,' Gloria muttered.

Julia lolled in her chair. 'She knows who's down here?'

'Yes, she does,' Ester said, looking round the room. 'Please don't drink any more, Kathleen. We've got to work her over and if you get pissed you'll open that yapping mouth. That goes for you too, Gloria.'

She glanced over the table and then went to the kitchen. Angela had her feet up and was reading a magazine. 'We'll have the first course, then I'll ring for you.'

'Yeah, you told me that before.'

'When she's ready to come down, I want you to bring her in. Go up to her room when I tell you. I don't want her wandering around.'

'You told me that as well.'

Ester walked out. Angela waited a moment, then followed. As soon as she saw her heading up the stairs she crept to the phone, eased it off the hook, and dialled. She waited, eyes on the dark, candlelit hallway.

Susan was dishing up dinner and Mike answered the phone. He spoke softly and then replaced the receiver. He was smiling like he'd just been given good news.

'Who was that?'

'Mum. I said I'd go over later after dinner.'

'Oh, I'd liked to have come with you. Why didn't you tell me? I could ask the girl next door to babysit.'

'I'm only going for a few minutes.'

Mike sat down as Susan passed him a plate of stew. She had long blonde hair, like Mike's sister Shirley, and was almost as pretty. Their two boys had already been put to bed and she'd half-hoped they could have an evening together.

'Is your mum still planning to go to Spain?'

Mike nodded, his mouth full. 'Yeah, that's why I said I'd drop in, see if she needed me to do anything.'

'Funny time to go, isn't it, winter?'

Mike shrugged, forking in another mouthful. 'Got some friend there with a villa, be good for her, she needs to get away.'

'Don't we all. It's been ages since we had a holiday – be nice to get away.'

'We will,' he said, eyes on the clock, wondering if they'd found the diamonds yet.

Susan watched him: he'd been very distracted of late, moody and snapping at the kids. 'Everything all right at work, is it?'

'Yep.' He pushed the plate aside, only half finished, and wiped his mouth with a napkin. 'I'll shove off. Sooner I go, sooner I'll be home.'

He leaned over and kissed her forehead.

'There's nobody else, is there, Mike?'

'What?'

'It's just I hardly have time to talk to you, you're always out, and most weekends you've been on duty. If there is somebody else ...'

He sat down again. 'There isn't anyone else, Sue, okay? It's been a bit heavy lately, I've got a lot on and ...'

'Yes?'

'Well, it's to do with Shirley. The woman Mum blames for her being killed, Dolly Rawlins, got released today, so Mum's been a bit hysterical, you know the way she always harps on about it.'

'Well, you can't blame her. If one of our boys was killed I'd feel the same.'

'I won't be long, I promise, okay?'

Once he'd gone, Susan tried to finish her supper but she wasn't hungry any more. She was sure Mike was seeing someone else – she'd even searched his suit pockets, looking for evidence. She hadn't found anything but that didn't prove anything because he was a detective so he wouldn't be stupid enough to leave anything incriminating, would he? She told herself to stop it: it was just as he said, overwork, he was tired and she was reading more into his moods than she should. She pushed her plate away, muttering to herself. What about *her* moods? Nobody ever seemed concerned about her or the way she felt.

Ester cocked her head to one side, sprayed lacquer over Dolly's hair and stepped back. 'That's much nicer, softer round your face with a bit of a wave. So, we all set to go down?' Dolly stood up and admired herself in the wardrobe mirror. 'This is a lovely frock.'

Ester opened the bedroom door. 'It was a lovely price, too, a few years back, Dolly. Come on, they're all starving down there.'

They walked down the stairs together, Angela waiting at the bottom.

'No men invited, then?' Dolly asked.

Ester laughed. 'Well, we could always get the chauffeur back.'

'Couldn't you get the Chippendales? They're all the rage in the nick – girls have got their posters on the walls. Good-looking lads, they do dances just for women.'

'I know who they are, Dolly, but they're a bit passé now. That's always the problem in the nick. Years behind what's going on.'

Angela opened the dining-room doors wider and Ester stepped back to allow Dolly to walk in ahead of her.

The women all rose to their feet and began to sing. 'Good luck, God bless you ...'

The banks of candles, their dresses and the beautifully laid table made Dolly gasp: it seemed almost magical. The room with its ornately carved ceiling, the huge stone hearth with a blazing log fire, the women all raising their glasses in a toast.

'To Dolly Rawlins. She's out!'

Dolly slowly moved from one woman to the next. Like a princess, she touched their shoulders or kissed their cheeks.

Ester drew out the carved chair at the head of the table. 'Sit down, Dolly. This is your night, one we won't let you forget.'

Dolly sat down, seeming near to tears. She accepted a glass of champagne and lifted it. 'God bless us all.'

In the soft firelight with the flickering candles, they looked almost surreal: six women enjoying a celebration dinner. No one caught the strange glint behind the star guest's eyes because she was smiling, seemingly enjoying every precious moment. In reality she was waiting, knowing they wanted something, and she had a pretty good idea what it was. But she could wait. She was used to waiting.

The officers found it difficult to search the dark, poky little antique shop. There was a lot of junk and clutter to be moved aside and Donaldson had said the diamonds were hidden in a wall recess, but by ten o'clock they still had not been found. The men decided to call it quits for the night and to start again early the following morning.

Audrey was in her dressing gown when she opened the door to Mike. He beamed as he hugged her. 'Have I got news for you.'

She shut the door, a look of anticipation on her face.

'She's out, Mum, and I know exactly where she is, and ...'

Audrey sat on the settee as Mike gave her all the details about what had gone down that day, ending by clapping his hands together and laughing. 'Right now we got blokes searching for the diamonds, right? When they find them, we'll have Jimmy Donaldson wired up. If she calls, and she will, she'll go straight for them. We'll be ready and waiting. She's going to go right back inside, Mum, just what you wanted.'

Audrey had gone pale. 'You should have warned me, told me what you were doing.'

'How could I? It all happened today. It was such a bloody coincidence I couldn't believe it. First Angela—'

'You're not still messing around with that little tart, are you?'

'For Chrissakes, Mum, she's very useful. Because of her, right now I know where Dolly Rawlins is. Then I got a tip-off about Jimmy Donaldson. It was beautiful, just beautiful, I got my guv'nor jumping around. You know there was a reward for those stones and—'

'You got to stop this, Mike,' Audrey said sharply.

'Why? It's what you've been bleatin' on about for the past eight years, isn't it? Well, I'm going to have Dolly Rawlins put back inside for that robbery. She's going to be copped for those diamonds.'

'No, she isn't, love.'

'What are you talking about?'

'The diamonds.'

'Yeah, we got blokes stripping Donaldson's place for them.'

'They won't find them.'

'Why not?'

'Because they're not there.'

'How do you know?'

'Because I took them.'

Mike's jaw dropped. He couldn't take it in.

Audrey started to cry. 'When I read about Jimmy being arrested, I . . . You see, she always said I'd get a cut. I couldn't risk him telling the police where they were.'

'Jesus Christ, I don't believe this.'

'So I went round to his shop. I've known his wife for years and, well, she asked if I wanted a coffee, then she went round to a café to bring it back and I knew where he'd stashed them, so I took them.'

'You've got them?'

'No, I had them.'

'So what the fuck have you done with them?'

'Sold them.'

Mike stood up. He was shaking. 'You sold them?'

Audrey took out a tissue and blew her nose. 'Yes. God help me, I didn't know what to do with them once I'd got them here and I was scared. I mean, they just sat there and I got more and more scared having something worth that much in the flat.'

Mike slumped into a chair, his head in his hands. 'Holy shit, you've really landed me in it. Who's got them now?'

Audrey twisted the tissue. 'Well, I couldn't really shop around, could I? I knew this dealer, Frank Richmond. He's dodgy but I took them to him and he said he'd get what he could for them. But you know, they weren't easy because they were still hot. Well, that's what he said.'

'He paid you for them?'

'He gave me four hundred and fifty grand.'

Mike leaned back, his eyes closed.

'They were worth millions, I knew that, but I wasn't gonna start pushing for more money, was I? I was desperate – I knew she'd be out, knew she'd go to Jimmy and then come here.'

Mike jumped to his feet. 'You've been bullshitting me, haven't you? All that crap about Shirley. You've lied to me.'

'*No, I haven't!*'

'Yes, you bloody have. This wasn't for Shirley. It was for you, *you*, and now you've got me caught up in it.'

Audrey sobbed as he paced up and down the room.

'Where's the money?' Mike demanded.

'Well, some of it's in my bank, some's in a building society but the bulk of it's in Spain.'

'*Spain?*' Mike wanted to shake or slap her, he didn't know which. 'Is that why you're going there?'

She sniffed. 'Yes. Wally Simmonds bought a villa for me.'

Mike gaped. 'A villa?'

She nodded. 'It was ever such a good buy and we did a cash deal. I'm leaving for good. I was gonna tell you when I'd sorted myself out.'

Mike swallowed. It was getting worse by the second. He could feel the floor shifting under his feet.

'What am I going to do, Mike?'

'I don't know.'

'Do you want a cup of tea?'

He turned on her in a fury. '*No, I bloody don't.* Just shut up and let me think this one out.'

She sat snuffling as he sat with his head in his hands. Eventually he asked flatly, 'Do you know anyone who could make us up some dud stones that'd look like the real things?'

Audrey licked her lips, trying to think.

Mike continued, 'I could stash them at Donaldson's. It could still work but we'd only have a few hours, a day maybe, to get the stuff ready. Do you know anyone?'

'I'm sorry I've done this to you, love. Will you get into trouble?'

He stared at his mother. 'I could lose my fucking job – that good enough for you? Now, do you know anyone?'

Audrey took a worn address book from her handbag. 'There's Tommy Malin – he's probably the best – and if we said we'd pay cash for it he might do us a favour.'

'Us now, is it?'

'Well, I'll just do whatever you tell me to.' Her brain was a jumbled mess of questions. Why, why had she been so stupid? Why had she done it? Was it because she just wanted to get back at Dolly? Was that it? But there was another element: greed. Audrey wanted money. She had always wanted it but it had always been out of her reach. When she read about Jimmy's arrest, all the waiting seemed to have been for nothing and it was her fury at being cheated that pushed her into getting the diamonds. She had not foreseen how deeply she would bring her son into it all. Somehow she had thought he'd just arrest the bitch and put her away, out of reach.

'I'm so scared of her, Mike. I know she'll come after me. She won't understand what it was like having them stones in the flat, why I just had to …'

Mike sighed as she started crying again. 'Mum, you're up to your neck in it, whatever excuses you make. Gimme the address book. I'll call this fence bloke but I can only do so much. Then I gotta walk away from it – and from you if necessary.'

They had all had a considerable amount to drink: champagne, white and red wine. The booze had eased the tension and now they were all talking freely. Kathleen, well away, was telling an elaborate story about how she found her ex-husband in bed with a lodger and how she'd locked him in a coal hole. Connie was sketching the details of her plastic surgery operations on a paper napkin. Gloria was having a heated argument with Julia about body fat. Their voices were like music to Dolly. She didn't listen to whatever anyone was saying:

it was the freedom, the roaring laughs, and the relaxed atmosphere. Ester did not drink as much as the others but watched Dolly throughout, noting how often her glass was refilled, waiting for the right moment to start a conversation about Dolly's future arrangements.

Angela carried in a tray and said that coffee and brandy would now be served in the drawing room.

Ester saw Dolly stumble slightly as she pushed back her chair. She was obviously enjoying herself and even took hold of Gloria's hand as they wove their way into the drawing room, where there were more candles and another big blazing fire, the perfumed incense disguising the damp smell, the gentle light hiding the darkened patches on the wallpaper.

Julia whispered to Ester to keep her eye on Kathleen as she started thumping out a song on the piano, having a ball, almost forgetting why she was there. Julia handed out the drinks as Gloria picked up the box of After Eight mints. 'Here you go, Dolly, love. Have a mint and tell us what you're gonna be up to now you're out?'

Ester edged closer, wanting Gloria to shut up. Not subtle at the best of times, Gloria now plunged right in. 'So you got yourself a nice nest egg, have you, Dolly?'

Dolly laughed as she sipped her brandy. 'I might have.'

'I bet that old man left you a few quid, didn't he?' Gloria continued, and then grimaced as Ester stood firmly on her foot.

'He left me comfortable.' Dolly shrugged, moving towards the mantelpiece.

Then she turned to face them all as Kathleen staggered away from the piano stool to slump into a big winged chair.

'So, why don't you all come clean? What you all after?' Dolly said it calmly but there was an edge to her voice.

Ester sounded convincingly bemused. 'After? What's that supposed to mean?'

'Well, this is all very nice but none of us were what you would call friends. So I just wondered what you wanted.'

Ester stood up, a furious look on her face. 'Oh, thanks a lot, Dolly. We all worked our butts off today to get this place ready for you. You think we did it for what? What you got that any of us would want? We did it, I arranged it, because in the nick you belted that cow Barbara Hunter. I admired that, we all admired that, but if you think we've all come here for some ulterior motive, then screw you. We only wanted you to come out to friends, to have one night to find your feet.' She marched angrily towards the door as if about to make an exit.

'I'm sorry,' Dolly said quietly.

'So you bloody should be. I know it's hard to trust people inside but we're not inside. We're all out. All we wanted was to give you a bit of a party.'

'I said I'm sorry. Come on, sit down.'

Ester gave a tiny wink to Julia as she grudgingly sat

on the arm of the easy chair, close to Gloria so she could keep a watchful eye on her.

Dolly turned towards the fire. 'Truth is, I do have a few quid put by.'

A low murmur from them all, and sly glances flashed between them.

'Well, that's good to know,' said Connie. 'I hope you have a secure and successful future.'

They all raised their glasses and toasted Dolly yet again.

'So how much you got, then?' asked Gloria, getting an immediate dig in the ribs from Ester.

'It's not a fortune but . . . I'm all right, comfortable.'

They waited with bated breath as Dolly drained her glass and placed it on the tray. 'I'm going to tell you something.'

They all leaned forward, listening attentively, hoping she was now about to say 'diamonds'.

'For eight years, I've been sort of planning it, in my head. It's my dream, my future.'

A row of expectant faces waited.

'I want to put back something into society. It might sound crazy, but I really want to do something useful with the rest of my life.'

No one spoke. They felt a trifle uneasy, though – she was coming on like something from *The Sound of Music*.

Dolly took a deep breath. 'I want to buy a house and

I want to open it up as a home, a foster home for kids, battered wives, a home run by me, for all those less fortunate than me.'

None of them could speak. They looked at Dolly as if she had two heads. She had taken the carpet from beneath every one of them.

Tommy Malin agreed that he could make up a bag of fake stones, using some real settings and some fake ones. He could do it for two grand cash and have it ready by the following afternoon. Mike tried to push him to have them done by the following morning but he refused, saying if they wanted the stuff to look good, really good, they'd have to wait. He'd have to shop around for some good cut-glass fakes, maybe throw in a couple of zircons, and that took time. Mike agreed and said Audrey would collect them as soon as he called to say they were ready.

By the time Mike got home it was after twelve and he was exhausted. Susan heard the front door shut and turned over to her side of the bed, not wanting to speak to him or confront him. She was sure now he had another woman and it was breaking her heart.

Mike cleaned his teeth. His eyes were red-rimmed, his face chalk-white; he was in it up to his neck now, just like Audrey. He had to find some way of stashing the fakes in Jimmy Donaldson's place. He splashed cold water over his face, half hoping that Dolly Rawlins would never make contact about the bloody diamonds.

Susan heard him undressing and then he got into bed beside her, turning his back to her. Neither said a word, Susan because she was sure he was cheating on her, Mike hearing his own heart thudding as he went over the mess he had got himself caught up in. Whatever excuses he tried to make for Audrey, the fact was that she had dragged him back into the world he had tried so hard all his life to escape. Shirley had been well caught up in it, together with her husband, and she had ended up getting shot. In the end, though, it all came back to Dolly Rawlins. If he could get her put away, it would get them all out of trouble. And even if he had to frame her, she still deserved everything she got.

Ester had a mink coat slung round her shoulders and Dolly wore Gloria's fluffy wrap as they walked towards the stables. 'I mean, look at this place, Dolly. You could have ten, twelve kids here, get a horse even. And there's a swimming pool, needs a bit of work, the whole house does, but it's crying out for kids. It'd be perfect.'

Dolly looked back at the vast house. 'I dunno, Ester. I was sort of thinking about a small terraced job, near Holloway.'

'No. This is much better. Country air, grounds, and it'd be cheaper than any terraced house. I'll even throw in all the linen, crockery and furniture. I put it on the market for two hundred and fifty grand, but you can have the lot for two hundred. I've got the surveyors' reports. But if it's out of your league . . .'

It wasn't out of her league – in fact it was smack in it: she'd got two hundred and fifty grand to be exact but after shelling out here and there it'd be around the two hundred mark.

They walked on round the stables to the front of the house, Ester pointing over towards the swimming pool. 'There's an orchard, vegetable patch. You could grow your own veg, be self-sufficient. It's a dream place for kids, Dolly.'

Dolly sighed. 'I dunno, Ester, it's an awfully big house.'

'All the better. And we can all give you a hand, stay on and work it up for you, get the place shipshape. Hell, none of us have got anythin' better going for us. We'd be your helpers, it's a brilliant idea.'

The women watched from the slit in the curtains. Kathleen turned away. 'Home for battered wives! She's out of her mind. I've been one most of me life and I'm not about to start livin' with a bunch of them. She's got a screw loose.'

Gloria kicked at the dying embers of the fire. 'Well, I'm pissed off. I think this was all Ester was after from the start. She wanted us to break our backs cleaning the fuckin' place up so she can flog it to Dolly. That's what she got us here for – she's used the lot of us to sell this bleedin' place.'

Julia poured another brandy and swirled it in her glass. 'No, she hasn't, she's just being clever.'

'You can say that again. We all done it up and she's the only one that's gonna make any dough out of it,' Gloria retorted.

Connie joined in. 'I didn't even know she was selling this place, she never told me.'

Julia shook her head. 'You really are dumb, all of you, aren't you? Dolly has got to have a lot of money. Well, this place will swallow that right away so where's she going to get the money to get this place up and running as a kids' home?' She drained her glass. 'She'll have to go for those diamonds. Ester knows it. Can't you see what she's doing? She's creaming her, you stupid cows.'

They looked at each other and then Kathleen yawned. 'Well, in that case I'm staying on.'

The rest of them quickly agreed it was the best thing to do.

Ester showed Dolly all the estate agents', valuers' and solicitors' letters, and all the old surveys of the Manor House. 'Two hundred's a bargain, Dolly.'

Dolly frowned. 'That wipes me out, Ester.'

Ester felt her belly tighten: she'd guessed right. It

tickled her that she could always suss out people's cash-flow. It came with dealing for the girls, pushing the punters to the limit. She gave a wide smile. 'But you'll get big grants for the kids.'

Dolly looked over the documents again. 'I dunno, Ester. What if the others won't stay on? I can't run this place on my own.'

'Listen, none of them have got a place to go. They'll stay on, believe you me. And then we got Julia, she's a doctor, just what you need.'

Dolly was still unsure.

'Look, don't do anything right away,' Ester said breezily. 'Think about it, take your time. If you're not interested, fine, I'll sell it to someone else. No skin off my back ...'

Dolly suddenly took out her chequebook. 'You're on. Here, I'll give you a cheque right now.'

Ester put a hand on her arm. 'Now don't do anything you're going to be sorry for. Maybe you should sleep on it. I don't want you thinking I bamboozled you into this. It's your choice. The only thing that might be a problem is the other offer that I got, but it can wait at least until tomorrow.'

Dolly wrote out the cheque there and then, still heady from the wine. She insisted Ester take it and she did, pocketing it quickly.

'Where's the phone?' Dolly asked.

'In the hall.'

Ester slipped out of the kitchen, leaving Dolly looking over the papers. The women had all gone up to bed, the fires were dead, the candles burnt out. She went upstairs to her own bedroom where Julia was waiting, lying on the bed with her hands behind her head. Ester showed her the cheque. 'I'll put this in the bank first thing tomorrow before the old cow changes her mind. Not that she will, because we're going to work that woman over, every one of us. We'll make her believe we love the idea, want the home to be up and running. We all egg her on and keep it going until she ...'

'Goes for the diamonds.'

Ester smiled. 'Right, and then ...' She made a plucking motion with her fingers.

Julia stared at the cheque for two hundred thousand pounds. 'You could do okay on this, you know.'

Ester sighed. 'I got debts that'd eat up more than two hundred grand. We need those diamonds – two, three million quid's worth, Julia, and we're going to have them.'

'I love you when you're like this,' Julia whispered.

'Like what?'

'Cruel. Come to bed.'

Ester gave a soft sexy laugh as she sidled towards Julia and then froze halfway and turned to listen at the door.

*

Dolly stood in the marbled hall, the phone in her hand. 'Jimmy, is that you?'

Jimmy Donaldson was in his pyjamas, his hand shaking, as DI Palmer gestured for him to keep talking.

'Yes, this is Jimmy Donaldson. Who's this? You know what time it is?'

'Oh, I'm sorry to ring so late. It's Dolly, Dolly Rawlins.'

Palmer leaned forward, hardly able to contain himself. It was going down even faster than any one of them had thought. Mike Withey had been right. Dolly Rawlins was going for the diamonds. Again he gestured for Donaldson to keep talking.

'I need to see you,' Dolly said softly. 'Tomorrow. I'm out, Jimmy. Have you got my things for me?'

'Yes, yes, I've got them.'

'Well, what say we meet up tomorrow, about noon?'

Jimmy looked to Palmer. They still didn't have the stones but he reckoned they would by the following day. He wrote on a notepad. Jimmy nodded. 'Can you make it later – like late afternoon?'

'They are safe, aren't they, Jimmy?'

'Yes, of course.'

'Fine, I'll call you tomorrow, then.'

Dolly hung up.

Donaldson looked at Palmer. 'She's gonna call me tomorrow. She hung up before I could say anythin' different.'

Frowning, Palmer drummed his fingers on the telephone table. 'We better find those diamonds, then, Jimmy. You sure they're where you said they are?'

'If they're not, then some bastard's nicked them.'

Palmer jerked his head for Donaldson to return to his bed. He checked the time and replayed the message. Dolly Rawlins had carefully not said the word 'diamonds' but she certainly hadn't wasted much time. She'd only been released that afternoon. She was out all right.

Chapter 4

D olly woke with a start, unable for a moment to
orientate herself, and it scared her. Her heart thudded, she started to pant, then realized it was the sound
of birds, rooks cawing from the woods, a sound she had
not heard for a long, long time.

She got up and drew the curtains, then looked out
of the window. 'Holy shit.' In the harsh light of day,
for the first time she saw the derelict gardens, the dank,
dark poolside. 'Oh my God, what have you got yourself
into, gel?'

She listened at her door, could hear no sound of movement so she went out onto the landing. In the cold light
of morning, she moved silently round the old manor,
peeking into each unoccupied room, from the attic to
the ground floor, her heart sinking at every turn as she
realized what she had let herself in for. The rundown

state of the house was obvious, from the peeling wall-paper to the cracked ceilings and crumbling woodwork. The banister rail was fine, thick mahogany, but many of the pegs were missing and the carpets worn and dangerous on the old wide stairs. The smell of mould, damp and mildew made her nostrils flare but she kept on moving from room to room until she finally entered the old kitchen, easing back the bolts from the back door to walk outside into the stable yard.

She inspected the pool, the woods, the neglected orchard, and the wild, overgrown mess of brambles and throttling weeds that was the vegetable garden. She returned to the kitchen, her shoes covered in mud, her legs scratched from the brambles, and the hem of her coat sodden. No one was up so she put on the kettle, working out how to use the big lidded Aga, fetching a mug and making a cup of tea, her mind working overtime.

The house was a dog, she knew that, but she couldn't help liking it all the same. Perhaps it was fate; it was meant to be. Dolly sat with her hands cupping the chipped mug. From what she could see, the place could certainly accommodate at least ten, fifteen kids with ease, and she hadn't even been down to the basement. She went over the survey reports, all a few years out of date. She started to calculate on the back of an envelope just how much money it would take to get a place this size back into order. All her cash would go with the one cheque to Ester so it would mean she was dependent on the sale of the diamonds. Although she knew she hadn't got all of the stolen gems, she calculated that what she had would be valued at two or three million. The need to fence them quickly would bring the price down, but if she was able to work with Jimmy Donaldson she reckoned she would probably clear one to two million cash. The house would need a hell of a lot of money spent on it but she could use ex-prisoners to help her, perhaps even the women from last night.

Dolly spent over an hour making notes and working out costs and then went down to the basement. There was a sauna, a steam room, an old gym and a large laundry room. None of the machines appeared to be in working order and the stench of damp was even worse down there. She looked over the old boilers and knew they'd all have to be replaced. Maybe it really was all too much ...

By the time she returned to the kitchen, Gloria was up and Ester and Julia were washing dishes in the big stone sink. Angela was clearing the debris in the dining room and came in carrying a tray filled with dirty glasses. 'Good morning, you're up bright and early, Mrs Rawlins.'

Dolly gave a brittle smile. 'Yes. Is everyone else up yet?'

'No, not yet. Do you want breakfast?'

'Yes.'

'Eggs and bacon coming up.'

Dolly opened the front door to look down the big wide drive.

'Good morning, Dolly.' Connie beamed, wrapping a silk kimono round herself.

Dolly turned round as Kathleen appeared. 'My God, I've got a bastard of a headache. How about you, Dolly?'

Watching the women coming and going made Dolly feel a bit better. 'Get some coffee down you,' she said to Kathleen, and then walked behind the old reception desk to look for a telephone directory.

Ester appeared at the kitchen door. 'Good morning, Dolly. You looking for something?'

'Directories.'

Ester wandered to the desk. 'Be out of date, get the operator. Who are you calling?'

Dolly sighed. 'Well, I should have a word with the local social services, just to see about the possibilities of opening this place up as a home.'

'You don't waste much time, do you?'

'Nor do you, Ester. You did a good job hustling me into buying this place.'

'What? Look, it was up to you, love. I mean, I'm not forcing you into anything you don't want to do.'

Dolly raised an eyebrow. 'Fine, just don't bank the cheque until I'm sure.'

*

Ester moved into action, instructing the women to get the breakfast on the table and to look as if they loved the place. By the time Dolly joined them, the kitchen was filled with the smell of sizzling bacon and eggs, hot toast and coffee, all laid out ready and waiting. Their smiling faces greeted Dolly warmly as she sat down.

'I been all round the grounds. Place is in a terrible state.'

'Get a few locals to clear the gardens. It used to be beautiful, in the summer especially.' Ester continued to sell the manor, hinting time and again what a wonderful place it would be for children.

Angela gave Dolly the number for the social services but it was almost nine thirty when Dolly put in a call and arranged for a meeting at the town hall. She was still unsure and not giving much away. She had only the few things she had brought with her so she would need to do some shopping, but it would be a good opportunity to see what the local village was like.

As soon as Dolly was out of earshot, they started whispering about the diamonds. Ester hissed at them to keep their mouths shut.

'Yeah, well, that's why we're all here, Ester, and so far she's not said a dickie about them. All that's gone down is you're two hundred grand up. What if they don't exist?' Gloria muttered irritably.

'Oh, they exist,' snapped Ester. She crossed the kitchen

and looked out into the hallway, drawing the door shut. 'Make her think we're all behind the project, right? Offer to stay and help out, start clearing the place up. She's gonna need hard cash to get this place up and rolling so we watch her like a hawk and—'

Dolly called from the stairs, asking if the boiler was working as she wanted to have a bath before she left. Ester opened the door and shouted that the water was on and hot. She waited until she could hear the thud of the old pipes before she went to give the women more instructions. She then paid off Angela and said that when they went into the village she could catch the next train home.

'I got to go and see Eddie,' Gloria said tetchily.

'Fine, you go,' said Ester.

'I need my gear.' Connie pouted.

Ester sighed. 'Look, you all do what you have to but, whatever you do, keep your mouths shut about being here and especially about the diamonds. Is that clear?'

By eleven they were all waiting for Dolly, Ester out in the yard in her Range Rover. Julia was looking into the stables. 'You know, this place must have been something,' she said.

'It was. What the hell is she doing in there?'

Ester paced up and down, impatient to go into Aylesbury to bank the cheque.

Julia came close. 'You going to be okay?'

Ester nodded. 'Yeah. Nobody knows I'm here and besides, I got to bank the cheque and get her the deeds of the house.'

Julia cocked her head to one side. 'Well, you take care.'

Gloria teetered out with Connie behind her. 'I'm off to see Eddie. I'm givin' Connie a lift in. Can you take us to the garage to see if me car's ready?'

Connie put her bag into the back of the Range Rover. 'I won't even see Lennie. He always leaves by twelve so I'll just get my stuff and come straight back.'

Kathleen wandered out. 'Where you all going?'

Ester sighed. 'Into Aylesbury. Where's Dolly?'

'She's on the phone, the social services again, asking what they want her to bring in.'

'Are you stopping, then?' Ester demanded.

'Yeah, I got nowhere else to go, have I?' muttered Kathleen.

Angela joined them, followed by Dolly, so they all squashed into the Range Rover and drove off, leaving Kathleen alone.

Gloria's car wasn't ready so Connie and Angela were dropped off at the local railway station. Ester took Dolly on to the Aylesbury town hall. 'I'll wait here for you.' She smiled.

Dolly nodded but seemed ill at ease. 'I'll just see what

they say. I shouldn't be too long, then I'll need to do a bit of shopping, tights and stuff like that.'

As soon as Dolly walked into the town hall, Ester drove straight to the bank. She kept a good lookout for anyone following her and hurried inside.

Dolly waited in the anteroom and eventually a pleasant-faced woman called Deirdre Bull asked if she would come into her office. Dolly was offered a seat and coffee as Deirdre sat down behind her cluttered desk. The walls were lined with posters for foster carers and adoption societies.

'Now, it's Mrs Rawlins, isn't it?'

'Yes, Dorothy Rawlins. I've come to ask you about opening a foster home. I've done a bit of research with a probation officer but I thought I'd just run a few things by you.'

Deirdre nodded and began opening drawers. 'First there are some forms you'll need to look over and fill in. Have you ever been a foster carer before?'

'No, I haven't, but I'm buying a big house and I could accommodate up to ten or twelve kids easily.'

Deirdre was so relaxed and friendly that Dolly began to ease up, as Deirdre patiently passed her one form after another to look over.

'Are you married?'

'I'm a widow.'

'Do you have children?'

'No, but I have worked with a lot of babies recently, and I have some letters from . . .'

Ester finally handed the cheque to the cashier. Impatient, her eyes on the clock, she'd had to stand in a queue for ten minutes. The cashier took his time, working methodically, which Ester found infuriating. He looked first at the cheque, then at Ester's paying-in slip.

'There's nothing wrong, is there?' Ester asked sharply, leaning closer into the counter. 'I'm in rather a hurry and I have someone waiting.'

The cashier peered at Ester. 'It's Miss Freeman, isn't it? Could you wait one moment?'

'Why? All I want are the documents I've listed. Can't you just get them for me? I'm in a hurry.'

'The manager will need to speak to you, Miss Freeman,' the cashier said pleasantly.

'But there's nothing wrong with the cheque, is there?'

'No, not that I can see, but he will need to talk to you. Your account has been frozen.'

'I know that,' Ester retorted. It was impossible to forget what her financial situation was. She was in debt up to her eyeballs, tax inspectors breathing down her neck, and the only asset she had was the manor – and that was frozen, like her accounts.

She tried a different approach. 'I just want the deeds

to Grange Manor House.' She gave a soft smile. 'I have a cash buyer, so part of the overdraft could be paid off. If the bank tried to sell the house, they'd not get as good a price. And I'm sure I'll be able to cover any further outstanding debts within a few weeks.'

She was sure she sounded entirely convincing. The cashier looked up and gave her a tight nod: he was going to release the deeds of the house. He excused himself and left Ester waiting. She checked her watch again, willing him to move his arse.

Deirdre looked through Dolly's forms, and showed not a flicker when she read that she had only just been released from prison.

'The house is well situated, with gardens and a swimming pool. It will need a lot of work and I don't know how I apply for grants and allowances – or if I am acceptable as a foster carer,' Dolly said.

Deirdre nodded. 'Well, you'll have to go before a board of committee members – I can't say whether or not you'll be acceptable, Mrs Rawlins. All this takes considerable time and your property will have to be reviewed and assessed by the committee.'

'But you don't think it's out of the question?'

'I can't say. If you like, I can ask my superior, Mrs Tilly, to come and talk to you.'

Dolly leaned closer. 'I would be grateful if you would.

I don't want to go ahead with buying the house if I don't stand a chance with my application – if my background goes against me, you understand?'

Deirdre smiled warmly. 'Mrs Rawlins, there are so many children in need. Obviously your background will be taken into consideration but, that said, there are so many ways we can approach the board. If you can give me ten minutes I'll go up and have a word with Mrs Tilly, see if she can tell you the best way.'

'I'll wait,' Dolly said, becoming more confident by the second. As soon as the door closed behind Deirdre, Dolly inched round the desk and drew the telephone closer. She looked to the door a moment before she dialled.

Jimmy Donaldson was sitting with a mug of tea. It was almost twelve and there had not been any further contact from Dolly Rawlins. DI Palmer was sitting reading the morning paper. In the hall another officer sat on duty. Mrs Donaldson was confused about what was going on, especially as she had had little time alone with her husband. Even when they slept, an officer sat outside their bedroom. Jimmy was nervous and twitchy, but said with a bit of luck he'd be home for good sooner than they had anticipated. The police told her to speak to no one, to remain at home and continue with her housework as if they weren't there, which was easier said than done. Right now she was preparing lunch in the kitchen, trying to pretend the house wasn't full of cops.

The phone rang and she turned from the sink. The door to the sitting room was closed, the officer in the hallway giving her a pleasant smile. With a sigh, she went back to making lunch.

In the sitting room, Palmer gave a brisk nod for Donaldson to pick up the phone as he slipped on his headphones to listen to the call.

'Jimmy? It's Dolly.'

Jimmy looked nervously at Palmer, who gestured for him to continue the call.

'Hello, Dolly. How are you?'

'I'm fine. I'd like to collect.'

Palmer nodded and Donaldson hesitated. 'Okay. When do you want to come over?'

'I won't come to your place, you bring them to me. You know Thorpe Park?'

'What?'

'It's a big amusement park. About four o'clock this afternoon. I'll see you there.'

She hung up before Donaldson could reply. He sat looking at the receiver in his hand. Palmer swore, told him to hang up and then put a trace on the call.

'Have they found them yet?' Donaldson asked.

Palmer said nothing as he waited for the results of the trace. DCI Craigh came in as Palmer was jotting something down. He passed the note to Craigh. 'She made contact from Aylesbury town hall, social services. She's asked for a meet. You want to hear the call?'

Craigh nodded. 'What the hell is she doing at the town hall? She's moving fast, isn't she? We've still not found the stones. They're ripping his entire shop apart because it was so long ago he can't remember which wall he hid the stones behind.'

'Shit.'

'Yeah, well, we'll just have to stall her, or Jimmy will.'

Palmer looked back to the closed door. 'You think he's spinnin' yarns? If we've not found the ruddy diamonds maybe they're not there.'

Craigh sighed. This wasn't working out the way he'd hoped. Now they'd have to drag Donaldson out to Thorpe Park, and they'd be screwed if they didn't find the stones by four o'clock.

'Look, see if you can get his wife shipped out – to a relative or something. I don't like her being around. Meanwhile I'll go and see what I can work up for the four o'clock meet. Why Thorpe Park?'

Palmer shrugged. 'I dunno. She said it, then hung up.'

Tommy Malin had worked until late the previous night and went straight back to it in the morning. He reset the stones one by one, using a lot of settings from a previous little job he'd done, only then they had contained some beautiful emeralds and diamonds. He had never been asked to make up a whole bag of glass before but he wasn't going to turn his nose up at an easy two grand cash. Audrey called to ask if they were ready and he said they'd be finished later on in the afternoon. He had some business to attend to at lunchtime.

'They're not ready yet,' Audrey said to her son as he paced up and down the living room. 'Has she called? Do you know if she's talked to Jimmy yet?'

'No, I'm going over there now. I'll come back later and pick them up. And for Chrissakes don't tell anyone about this.'

'Who'd I tell? I've got the cash ready,' Audrey said nervously.

Mike stared at her, his anger at what she had got him involved with still close to the surface. 'Just get the stones, Mum, and as soon as you've got them, call me on my bleeper.'

Mike walked out of the flat and hurried to his patrol car as his bleeper went off. When he managed to call in, he was instructed to meet DCI Craigh at the station and not, as he had previously been told, at Donaldson's house.

Mrs Tilly looked over Dolly's forms. She then stacked them in a neat pile. 'Well, I think you stand a good chance but you'll have to be interviewed by the board and have your details assessed. It will take time for us to give you a positive answer and you'll obviously require grants, which is another area where you'll need to be instructed. There are so many different sections and application forms.'

Dolly was feeling good, her dream already turning into reality. Mrs Tilly frowned as she reread the top form.

'Grange Manor House? It had a bad reputation, you know.'

Dolly looked confused. 'I'm sorry? I don't understand. It was a health farm, wasn't it?'

'It used to belong to an Ester Freeman. Oh, I'm going back maybe five or six years. It's been closed — I thought it had been demolished, to tell you the truth, not just because the motorway was built across the main access, but because it was such a scandal—'

'I'm sorry, I don't know what you mean,' Dolly interrupted.

'Grange Manor House was run as a brothel. The police arrested, oh, fourteen women, I think. It was run by Ester Freeman. I think she went to prison.' Suddenly Mrs Tilly flushed. 'Did you buy it from Miss Freeman?'

'No, I did not,' Dolly lied, her hands clenched tightly. 'Thank you for all your help.' She managed to keep a smile on her face but she was so angry she could have screamed. This was all she needed. Trying to open a foster home as an ex-prisoner was one hurdle to get over, but now she knew that the place had been run as a brothel any association with Ester would obviously go against her.

Dolly stormed out of the town hall. Ester was not waiting as she had promised. Dolly forced herself to remain calm. She'd have to get out of this, and fast. She'd do a bit of shopping, get the next train to London, collect the diamonds and do just as she had planned: buy a small terraced house near Holloway and screw that bitch Ester Freeman.

Ester faced the bank manager, a dapper little man with a faint blond moustache. He shuffled Ester's thick file of documents. The cheque from Mrs Rawlins, he assured Ester, was cleared or would be soon, as he had already contacted Mrs Rawlins's bank, but this still left Ester three hundred thousand pounds in debt. She would be declared bankrupt unless she had means to cover the outstanding balance.

'But I've just paid in a cheque for two hundred thousand.'

The manager nodded patiently. 'Yes, I know, Miss Freeman, but the bank are holding the house as collateral for the outstanding monies. I cannot release the property deeds.'

'Fine. Then I'll withdraw the cheque. The money is for the sale of the manor and you know that it won't get that price on the open market. You sell it and the bank'll lose out. This way, at least I've paid off some of it and I give you my word you'll get the rest within a few weeks.'

He sighed. What she was saying made sense. 'So, Miss Freeman, is this cheque from Mrs Rawlins for the sale of the property?'

'Yes. That's why I've got to have the deeds returned to me. If you refuse, there will be no sale. You then have to put it on the market and—'

He interrupted, drawing back his chair, 'Fine. I will, however, have to wait for the cheque to be cleared, Miss Freeman. That still leaves your balance over three hundred thousand pounds in the red, and unless this situation is rectified we have no alternative but to begin proceedings against you.'

She leaned on his desk. 'Give me just one more month – you'll get the money. I am waiting to be paid a considerable amount more than enough to cover my overdraft.'

Ester would have liked to scream at him, 'Try three million quid's worth of diamonds, you fuckin' little prat,' but instead she smiled sweetly as he flipped through her bank statements.

'Well, we'll give it three weeks, Miss Freeman, but then—'

'You'll get me the deeds? Yes?'

He nodded. 'Yes. I'm prepared to trust you, Miss Freeman.'

'You won't regret it,' she said softly, having no intention whatsoever of paying in another penny. She was going to skip the country and fast, just as soon as she laid her hands on Dolly Rawlins's diamonds.

Mike met up with DCI Craigh in the station corridor. 'She only called from the Aylesbury social services and you won't believe where she's asked Donaldson to meet her.'

'Oh, they find the diamonds?' Mike asked casually, knowing it was an impossibility.

Craigh shook his head. 'I'm gonna need extra men, sort this out at the bloody theme park, and we'll get Donaldson wired up. He'll just have to stall her or get her to implicate herself. I'm beginning to wish we'd never started this whole thing.'

Craigh had no idea just how much Mike wished he had never mentioned Dolly Rawlins's name, let alone the diamonds.

Gloria eased her way round the visitor tables, crowded with the wives and mothers, girlfriends, kids. It never ceased to amaze her how many women were always there every visiting day. Never as many men – they were all banged up like her old man.

Eddie Radford was staring at his folded hands, a glum expression on his Elvis Presley lookalike features. Eight years younger than Gloria, he'd never even bought an Elvis record but she had. She'd been a great fan and the first time she'd set eyes on Eddie she'd seen the similarity, with his slicked-back hair. If he'd had sideburns he'd have been the spitting image.

'You're bleedin' late,' he muttered.

'I had to get a train, missed the tube, waited fifteen minutes.'

'Oh shuddup. Every time you come I got to listen to a bleedin' travelogue of how you got here. You get me some fags?'

'Yes.'

'Books? Any cash?'

'Yeah, in me left sleeve, can you feel it?'

Eddie leaned over and kissed her as he slipped his hand up her sleeve and palmed the money. 'How much?'

'Sixty quid, and that's cleaned me out. I got to pick up me giro.'

'Where've you been? I called the house three times.' Eddie opened the cigarettes and lit one, looking around the room at the men and their visitors. The racket was deafening.

'The council have given me my marching orders for non-payment of rent.'

'Oh, great! What you let them do that for?'

'Could be because I've not got any cash and that Mrs Rheece downstairs is a bloody moron. She let them in, found that bloke kipping down and so they said I was sublettin'.'

'What bloke?'

'You know, him with the squint, friend of your brother's. I asked him to leave an' all but he wouldn't. Pain in the arse, he is.'

'So where've you been stayin'?'

'I'm near Aylesbury, with some friends. You don't know them, Eddie. I wish you wouldn't grill me every time I come, it gets on my nerves.'

'Who you staying with then?'

She sighed. 'Ester Freeman, you don't know her. She did time with me. Julia Lawson, she was also in Holloway, Kathleen O'Reilly, a stupid cow called Connie and—'

'Ester Freeman? They all tarts then, are they?'

'No, they're not. Dolly Rawlins, she's there.'

'Oh yeah, Dolly Rawlins, yeah, I remember Harry. So what you all there for?'

'For God's sake, I needed a place to doss down, all right? So we're all sort of helping Dolly out until—'

'Until what?'

Gloria flushed. 'I always get a headache in here. They should keep the kids to another section.'

Eddie reached out and gripped her wrist. 'I said, *what are you doing there?*'

She wrenched her wrist free and rubbed it. 'Word is,

she's got some diamonds stashed and we're, well, we're waiting for her to get them.'

'And then what?'

She smiled. 'Well, we want a cut and if she doesn't like it, we're gonna take it. But you keep your mouth shut about it.'

'Who would I tell?' he said bitterly.

She touched his hand. 'You'll have some nice things, I'll get you anything you want, Eddie.'

He pulled his hand away. 'Who's looking after my guns?'

Gloria looked round nervously, then leaned close to whisper, 'They're still out in the coal hut. I ain't touched them.'

Eddie closed his eyes. 'Brilliant! You're not even at the fuckin' house, that idiot bloke is hanging around and I got thirty grand's worth of gear stashed out back. You fuckin' out of your mind, Gloria?'

'I don't want anythin' to do with them. I get picked up again and that's me for ten years, Eddie. It's too dangerous.'

'You listen to me, slag, you move them out of that place. I'll get you a decent contact, you'll flog them when I say so, understand me? You move them, you do that, Gloria. Get the gear, stash it where you're staying with all the tarts, then I'll get my friends to contact you. Gimme the number there.'

'I can't, the phone's not connected, Eddie, on my mother's life.'

He swore and then the bell rang for the first section of visitors to move out. He gripped her hand tightly. 'Just get them. Then next time you come I'll arrange for you to meet someone. You do it, Gloria, they're all I got left in the world, them and you, so I'm depending on you, understand me?'

He drew her towards him and they kissed. She always felt like crying when he did that but this afternoon she was too much on edge, having gone and told him about Dolly Rawlins. For a second she hoped he'd forgotten but he suddenly smiled. 'And if that cow don't want to part with her diamonds, you got the gear to make her, haven't you? Use them, sweetheart. You get me some dough and we'll go abroad, have a nice holiday when I get out.'

The officers were pointing for him to go back to the corridor outside and be returned to his cell.

'I love you, Eddie,' she said softly.

'I should hope so, Gloria. Ta-ra, see you next week.'

He smiled wryly as he walked after the prison officer. He'd got eighteen years and there he was talking about when they would go on a bloody holiday together. She'd be in a Zimmer frame by the time he got out.

Dolly paid off the taxi and carried her purchases inside the manor. Ester's Range Rover was nowhere to be seen. She went straight to her bedroom and sorted out what

she would wear for the afternoon, then started to pack
her few things. She would leave without a goodbye and
then get the cheque stopped. She swore at herself: she
should have done that as soon as she came home. Dolly
headed down the stairs as Ester breezed in, waving a big
brown envelope.

'Hi! They said you'd left when I went to the town hall
so I did a grocery shop. Here you go, Dolly, the lease all
signed, and now the place is really all yours.'

'Oh, is it? Well, you can take it and stuff it. I don't
want this place, I don't want anything to do with you
and I'm gonna stop that cheque.'

'What?'

Dolly glared at Ester. 'You really did me in, didn't
you? Never thought to mention this place was a brothel.'

Ester tossed the envelope down. 'You knew
what I was.'

'I didn't know you ran a whorehouse from here,
though, did I?'

'All you had to do was ask.'

'They all know about this place, they told me at the
social services.'

'So what?'

'This place has got such a bad reputation. What
with that and my record, you think they'll give us the
go-ahead?'

Dolly was about to walk back up the stairs when Ester

yelled, 'They'll be more likely to give you the go-ahead on a place like this that's crying out for kids than any terraced place in fucking Islington or Holloway – and they cost, Dolly. You've been away a long time, any house in that area's gonna cost you at least a hundred and fifty grand. Here you got beds, furniture, linen, all thrown in, but if you don't want it, then that's up to you . . .'

Julia walked out and leaned on the kitchen door. 'She's right, you know, Dolly. This is a fabulous place for kids.'

Dolly hesitated. Julia's soft voice seemed to calm her. 'The orchard and the gardens, the pool doesn't need much doing to it, then you can even get a horse for the stables . . .'

Ester winked at Julia. 'She's right, Dolly. I mean, each kid would bring in about two hundred a week. I'm right, aren't I, Julia?'

'Yep, and then you'd get grants to rebuild and convert . . .'

Dolly sat down on the stairs, more confused than ever. Ester glanced at her watch. All she needed was a few more hours for the cheque to go into the system then Dolly couldn't stop it.

Dolly frowned. 'I got to go to London, let me think about it.'

'You want a lift, do you? To the station?'

Dolly nodded, then got up and went to her room.

'By tomorrow the cheque will have gone through,' Ester said quietly to Julia. 'Where do you think she's going?'

'I don't know, do I?'

Ester pulled her into the kitchen. 'What if she's going for the diamonds?' She thought for a moment. 'You make some excuse, say you got to go to London as well, see where she goes and who she talks to.'

'Oh, for Chrissakes, Ester, that's ridiculous. You mean follow her around?'

'What the hell do you think I mean?'

By the time Dolly came back downstairs, Julia was already sitting in the Range Rover.

'Julia's got to go and see her mother so she'll catch the train with you,' Ester explained as Dolly followed her out.

'She's still being kept in the lap of luxury by her beloved daughter. She has no idea Julia was even picked up and put in the slammer, never mind that she was a junkie. Julia's been paying for her for years, she's in a wheelchair or somethin', so that's housekeepers and cleaners and . . . you name it. That's why Julia's broke.'

As soon as Dolly got into the car, she started asking Julia about her mother. 'She's very old, Dolly. I don't want her to know what a mess I've made of my life. It would devastate her.'

'Where does she think you are, then?' Dolly asked.

'Well, when I was in Holloway I got friends to send

postcards from Malta. She thought I was working over there with the Red Cross.'

'And now?' Dolly asked.

'Well, since my release, I told her I've been looking for a new practice. She doesn't know I was struck off – she doesn't know anything about my life, really.'

Dolly nodded and looked at her watch: she was going to be late for the meeting with Jimmy Donaldson. She didn't know how she was going to get all the way to the theme park on time. Well, if he left, he left. She'd just have to rearrange the meeting.

Connie had asked the cab driver to wait while she hurried into the mansion block. Lennie always left just before lunch, did the rounds of his girls, then checked his club for the previous night's takings. He would then come home, change and have something to eat. Connie usually cooked him a light meal before running his bath. He would change and leave the flat between eight and eight thirty in the evening, rarely returning until the early morning.

For Lennie his girls, his club, his Porsche and his well-furnished flat came before any love or relationship. Connie knew that now. She had been with him for three years, cooking, cleaning, keeping his flat spotless. Occasionally she went to the club and they dined out frequently, but then he had started knocking her around and a few times told her to be 'very nice' to friends of his. When that became a regular weekly session, she knew that it was all over between them, she was no longer his 'special'. He was getting ready for a change, as if she was part of the fixtures and fittings.

He had beaten her up so badly one night, breaking her nose, that he had arranged for her to have plastic surgery. She had her eyes done, her nose remodelled, a cheek implant and a breast implant. At first she had felt wonderful. He had visited her in the clinic and been kind to her when she came home in the bandages. She had believed he'd changed, that perhaps he really did care for her, but when the bandages came off and she admired herself in front of him as he lay in bed, he had said, lighting a ciga-rette, 'Well, now, girl, you can make up the money, seven grand you owe. I reckon you've a few more years in you now so you're going to share with Carol and Leslie.'

Connie couldn't believe it. They were two of his girls and he was moving her out and in with them, as if there had been nothing between them. 'But, Lennie, I want to try going straight. You know, get a proper agent and do some modelling.'

He had laughed. 'No way. You can earn more for me on your back than doing any bleedin' cereal advert . . .'

She hadn't said anything, hadn't argued back, afraid he'd maybe whack her again. She had simply waited for him to leave at his usual time, then Ester had called her and said she would be free to come to the manor. She had packed fast and run off. Now Connie was back, she let herself in and went straight to the kitchen. She began unplugging all the movable stuff she could lay her hands on. She then went into the bedroom and cleared out her side of the wardrobe. At least she was alone; he hadn't moved anyone else in yet.

Lennie's portable phone was on the stand, recharging. She was so busy filling the suitcase that she didn't notice it. Lennie never went anywhere without his portable. At that moment he was swearing as he realized he'd forgotten to put it in his pocket, right now doing a U-turn and heading back to the flat to pick it up.

The cab driver watched the metallic-blue Porsche park, and saw the dapper West Indian straighten his draped suit as he headed towards the mansion block. He went back to reading the *Sun*, after a quick look at the meter. The girl had said she'd be ten minutes but she'd already been gone that. He swore, wondering for a moment if she'd just done a Marquess of Blandford on him and wouldn't be coming out, but then he saw she had left a bag on the back seat.

Connie had filled two cases when she heard the front door slam and instantly backed away in terror. He kicked open the bedroom door and looked at her.

'Hello, Lennie,' she said in a trembling voice. 'I was just packing me gear.'

'I can see that. You missed anything? Like the light fittings?'

'I've not taken anything that wasn't mine, Lennie.'

'I gave you the cash for everything you're standing up in, sweetheart. Now what the fuck do you think you're doing and where've you been?'

'Near Aylesbury ... with some friends.' He came closer. 'Don't hurt me, please don't.'

He laughed. 'Aylesbury? You kiddin'? Who you staying there with?'

'Dolly Rawlins, you don't know her, but listen, Lennie, I might be on to a good thing. She's got diamonds, a lot of diamonds and—' Connie panicked, trying anything to stop him coming closer, pressing herself against the wardrobe, bracing herself for what she knew was coming. She raised her hands in a feeble gesture. 'Please don't hit me in the face, Lennie.'

The cab driver saw the West Indian guy walk out quickly and roar off in his Porsche. Then Connie came out, walking unsteadily as she carried a suitcase. She was wearing dark glasses and a headscarf. He took the case from her. 'You all right, love?'

'Take me to Marylebone Station, please,' she said, getting into the back seat.

'Right, the station ...' He looked at her in the mirror. She had a blood-soaked handkerchief pressed to her face. 'You sure you're okay, love?'

'Yes, yes, I'm fine, thank you.' She could feel the swelling coming up under her eyes. Her nose was bleeding, but she didn't think he'd broken it, though her neck was covered in dark red bruises. She thought he was going to kill her, and he had only stopped when she had pretended to be unconscious.

'Kathleen? *Kathleen*?' Ester shouted. Kathleen was on her bed. She'd had a few drinks earlier and was now sleeping it off. Ester barged into the room. 'Didn't you hear me calling you?'

'What do you want?'

Ester shut the door. 'I think she might be going for the diamonds today. Who do you know that we could trust to fence them?'

Kathleen lifted her head a little. 'Well, it depends, doesn't it? I mean, they're still hot but I've got a few people I'd trust.'

Ester was pacing up and down. 'If they were valued at God knows how many million when they were nicked almost nine years ago, what do you reckon they're worth now?'

'Could be double, it all depends on the quality. Soon as I see them I'll be able to tell you the best man. When do you reckon that's going to be, Ester?'

'I think she's maybe doing something about them this afternoon.'

Kathleen sat up, rubbing her head. 'Well, shouldn't someone be with her?'

'Julia's on her, I hope.'

'Have you told Dolly you know about them?'

Ester shook her head. 'No. Let's just take it one step at a time.'

'Fine by me, but she's such a wily old cow she might pick them up and that's the last we see of her.'

'No, she'll be back. All her gear's still in her room.'

'Ah, she might be back, but will she be bringin' back the diamonds?'

'I bloody hope so. And in the meantime, you just stop nicking the booze,' she added, walking out.

Kathleen slowly got off the bed. She splashed her face with cold water then patted it dry. The photographs of her three daughters were on the dressing table, positioned so she could see them from her bed. They were the last thing she saw at night and the first in the morning: the nine-year-old twins, Kate and Mary, and five-year-old Sheena. They were in care, a convent home, but how long they would remain together Kathleen couldn't be sure. All she knew was that when she got the cut of the diamonds they were going home, all of them, going back to Dublin. She'd be safe, the cops wouldn't find her there. 'You get the diamonds, Dolly, love,' she whispered to herself. 'Pray God you get them before the cops find me.'

Kathleen, like every one of them, was in trouble. But Kathleen's problem was not some bloke out to make her a punchbag: a warrant was out for her arrest on two charges of cheque-card fraud. She had simply not turned up for the hearing and Ester's invitation to come to the manor not only gave her hope for a lot of cash, but also a safe place to hide.

Dolly finally found a taxi for the last stage of the journey to Thorpe Park, and Julia was right on her heels, grabbing the next cab in the rank.

At the theme park Julia concentrated on keeping Dolly in sight, keeping her distance until she saw Dolly heading towards the funfair section.

What Julia didn't know was that she wasn't the only one watching Dolly. Far from it. Unmarked patrol cars and plainclothes officers were positioned at each exit, while a moody Jimmy Donaldson sat in another one. They had arrived at three fifteen and he'd been in the car for over an hour and a half. They were all almost giving up when they got the contact. 'Suspect has entered gate C, over.'

Donaldson was wired up, instructed to move slowly, and told not to approach any of the officers. He would be monitored at all times. He was still fuming that they had not found the diamonds because it meant that some other bugger had, and he spent his time trying to think who could have shifted them. Only Audrey and Dolly had known where they were – and maybe his wife. Could she have moved them? He wished he'd never agreed to the whole thing. It would only be worth it if they got him transferred to a nice, cushy open prison. He'd be safe there. It was, after all, nearly nine bloody years ago, and there'd been renovations in his back yard, so some bastard could have come across the diamonds, he supposed. Dolly Rawlins was a hard-nosed cow but, without her old man, just how much of a threat could she be? It was Harry who had had enough on him to put him behind bars for years. And now he was dead. On the other hand, Dolly was the one who had shot him, so she might decide to have a pop at him, too. Jimmy Donaldson was not a happy man, and getting more and more pissed off by the minute.

DCI Craigh beckoned him out of the car, pressing his earpiece into his ear, listening. 'Okay, Jimmy. She moved to the hoopla stand or something, so you start walking in by gate B, the one closest to us. Just act nice and casual, and don't keep looking round. Off you go.'

Donaldson shook his head. 'She's not gonna like it, me not having them with me.'

Craigh sighed. None of them liked it, but they couldn't do anything about it. 'Just do the business. Tell her to meet you back at your place, it was unsafe to bring them here – tell her anything.'

'This is entrapment, you know,' Donaldson whined.

'You fuckin' do the business, Jimmy, or you'll be trapped all right, and for longer than you got in the first place.'

He moved off with a scowl. When he got to the hoopla stand he couldn't see Dolly so he went over to the shooting arcade and handed over two quid for three shots. 'Let her find me,' he said to himself as he took aim. 'Let her bloody find me.'

Dolly walked casually around, enjoying the stands, marvelling at the amazing rides. It was all beyond anything they had when she was a kid, and it all cost a hell of a lot more, too. She fingered the hoops, fifty pence a throw. In her day it had been threepence but she paid over her money and took aim with the wooden hoop.

'Rawlins is at the hoopla stand. She's throwing hoops now.' Palmer wandered past, not even looking at Dolly as she threw her third hoop and was presented with a goldfish in a plastic bag. As she reached for the fish, she caught sight of Julia, hovering at another stand. She did a double-take.

Julia sighed. No matter how hard she tried to stay in the background she was so tall she stuck out like a sore thumb. As Dolly walked towards her, she smiled weakly.

'Hello, Julia. You just won yourself a prize,' said Dolly, handing over the bag. 'Here, take it back to the manor.'

As Julia took the goldfish bag, Dolly looked up at her. 'So why you following me?'

'Ester told me to.'

'Oh, I see, and what she tells you to do, you do, right?'

'Yeah. Well, now you've caught me at it, I'll push off.'

'You do that, love. I'm only here for a bit of fun.'

Julia couldn't help but smile but Dolly remained poker-faced, watching the tall woman as she threaded her way out of the area. Dolly was piecing it all together: they were definitely after her diamonds. Well, they were going to be in for a shock. As soon as she had them, she would be on her way and they could all rot in hell as far as she was concerned. Apart from Angela: she liked that little kid.

Dolly wondered if she'd missed Jimmy Donaldson — maybe he'd got tired of waiting.

'She's looking around now, handed a fish to a woman who's walked out. Should be coming through exit E. Check her out.'

Julia made her way to the courtesy bus stop, thinking she would go and see her mother. It had been a long time.

Dolly finally spotted Donaldson and walked off in the opposite direction towards a Ferris wheel.

'I think she saw him but she's walked off, straight past him. Now at the Ferris wheel. She's talking to the boy on the ticket box.'

Dolly smiled at the spotty young kid and slipped him a tenner. 'I'll be back for a ride in a bit and you'll get another tenner if you make sure I get a nice view from the top of the wheel. Say about five minutes' worth of view, all right, love?'

He grinned. It was not unusual to get requests like that, and for twenty quid, why not? He watched as she strolled back into the crowd.

Donaldson had another three shots. On his last he got a bull's-eye and the stall owner begrudgingly handed over a stuffed white rabbit. He turned to see Dolly standing directly in front of him.

'Okay, they're together. He's just won a white rabbit so we can't miss them. He's walking off with her to the other stands.'

'You're looking well, Dolly. Long time no see.'

'I am well, Jimmy, very well. How's your wife?'

'Oh, she's her usual. Gone to see her sister in Brighton.'

'That's nice for her. Would you like a ride?'

He looked at the Ferris wheel. 'No. Can't stand those things.'

'Oh, come on, it'll be fun. Might as well enjoy ourselves now we're here. I saw an article saying Princess Diana brings the princes here. Did you know that?'

He nodded. 'That's the big theme rides over the other side. This is just the fairground. It's not part of the main park.'

'I fancied that water ride, down a chute. I saw it in the paper. Never mind, we'll make do with this.'

Dolly winked at the spotty boy and slipped him another tenner. He unbuckled the seat bar and helped her sit down.

'Dolly, I've not got a head for heights.'

'Oh, get in, Jimmy. I want to see the view.'

Donaldson was ushered into the seat and locked into his safety harness; below, the static interference was breaking up on the radios. Jimmy's and Dolly's voices were coming and going with a crackle and a buzz.

'They're on the Ferris wheel,' an officer said into his radio.

'We can see that,' DCI Craigh muttered back. They could hear them too, just about, but so far not one word about the diamonds. Mike was in the car, listening on the radio, clocking the time, wondering if his mother had picked up the fakes yet, getting more and more agitated. He hadn't even seen Dolly Rawlins yet, and he didn't know how he'd deal with it if he did.

'They're on the ride,' crackled his radio.

Mike pushed his earpiece further into his ear, wincing as the static caused by the steel girders on the Ferris wheel deafened him.

Donaldson clung to the safety bar as the wheel turned slowly. 'There's nobody else getting on,' he panted.

'Oh, there will be,' she said, smiling.

'Why are they doing it so slowly?' he gasped as they inched higher.

'They got to allow for the punters to get on. So, have you got them for me?'

She said it so casually, he felt even sicker. 'Er, not with me, it's too dangerous.'

She stared ahead, and the wheel turned higher until they were almost at the top.

'You've not got them at all, is that right?'

'Yes – no – I've got them but not on me. You crazy? I couldn't carry them around . . . Oh, oh, holy shit, is this bleedin' thing safe?'

They remained poised at the top of the wheel and Dolly leaned forward, looking around at the views. 'Isn't it lovely, Jimmy?'

'No, I'm gonna be sick.'

She faced him, her eyes hard. 'You will be sick, Jimmy, if you're trying it on. Are you trying it on with me, Jimmy?'

'No, no, I swear. Listen, is there an alarm? I'm feeling sick, really I am. I hate swings, I hate heights, I'm dying, Dolly.'

She pushed at the seat with her feet. It swung backwards and forwards. 'Where are they?'

'*At home! I got them at home!*' He was shaking in terror, his knuckles white from gripping the safety bar.

She looked down, waving to the boy, and the wheel

began to move down. 'I'll come for them tomorrow, then. I'll call you.'

'All right, all right, anythin' you say . . .'

She nodded, and then leaned closer. 'Life is too short to mess around. You won't mess with me, will you, Jimmy? I've been waiting eight years.'

'Yeah, well, I got to get a good fence. I mean, you're talking millions so you'll need the very best.'

'No, love, you don't need to get anything but what belongs to me. I'll do the rest and then you'll get your cut.'

DCI Craigh was ripping his hair out. They still hadn't mentioned the word 'diamonds'. 'Jesus Christ, say it, woman, *say* it.'

Dolly left a white-faced Jimmy Donaldson leaning against the fence, throwing up, as she went out of the exit, carrying the white rabbit. They could follow her all day, but she hadn't said the word 'diamonds', and neither had the stupid bastard Jimmy Donaldson.

Julia arrived at the station and put in a call to Ester, who instantly went into a screaming fit. Julia yelled back, saying she should have followed Dolly herself. 'I'm going to see my mother, okay?' Then she slammed down the phone, picked up the bag with the goldfish and walked onto the platform to wait for the train. She wished she'd never agreed to the Dolly Rawlins business. She wished she'd never met Ester, she wished she hadn't fucked herself up so badly, she wished she could start her life over again. She was such an idiot, such a stupid bitch to have got herself into such a mess.

It was after eight by the time Gloria arrived at her old place, which looked even more rundown in the dark. Mrs Rheece was coming out of the front door. Gloria ran up the path. 'Mrs Rheece, it's me, Gloria Radford. I just come to pick up my stuff. Is that okay?'

'You can do what you like, no business of mine. I don't give a shit what anyone does. The council have been round askin' after you and that bloke was here last night again, the one with the squint. I said to him you wasn't here and he was fuckin' abusive.'

'Oh, I'm sorry. You tell him to sod off the next time.'

'There won't be a next time, Mrs Radford, 'cos I'll call the law on him.'

The old woman went off with her shopping trolley down the road, still muttering to herself about the council, as Gloria slipped round the back of the house to the old coal hut. It had been used as a bike shed, and rubbish bins were stacked up inside and out. She shone a torch round and began to move aside all the junk, swearing as she ripped her tights in the process. She squeezed her way into the back of the hut and then eased away some old wooden boards. Scared of being disturbed, she switched off the torch and fumbled around in the inky darkness.

Soon she felt the big canvas bag and began to heave with all her might. It was very heavy, but she finally managed to drag it out. She went back for two more bags before she shut the coal-hut door. She dragged each bag out to the Mini Traveller and hauled it inside, terrified that someone would see her. Then she went up into her old flat, washed her hands and face, and collected a suitcase full of clothes.

She drove slowly, frightened of every passing police car. She knew that if she was stopped and the car was searched, she'd be arrested. Eddie's stash, Eddie's retirement money, was all in the back of the Mini: thirty thousand pounds' worth of weapons.

She got on to the motorway towards Aylesbury, her hands gripping the wheel tightly, her whole body tense. 'Please, God, nobody stop me, please, God, don't break down, please, God, let me get to the manor.'

Ester heard the front door slam and looked over the banisters. Connie, still wearing her dark glasses and headscarf, was dragging in her case.

'Where the hell have you been all day?'

'I need a fiver for the taxi, Ester.'

Ester thudded down the stairs. 'I'm not a bloody charity, you know. I paid for everyone's taxi yesterday.' Ester stopped in her tracks as she saw Connie's face. 'What the hell happened to you?'

*

Audrey was in a right state. She had twice paged Mike on his mobile and he'd not returned her call. She now had the fake diamonds from Tommy and just having them in the flat made her freak. She kept on opening the pouch and looking at them. She'd never seen the original diamonds properly, but Jimmy had seen right away they were in gold or platinum settings, some from around 1920. She closed the pouch up again, and stood over the telephone. 'Ring, come on, ring me. I've got them, I've got them.'

Mike didn't call until after ten, saying he was just coming off duty and he'd come round to collect them. As he put the phone down, Angela paged him. He arranged to meet her outside Edgware Road tube station, then called his wife to tell her he would be late home. He had just finished the call when DCI Craigh wandered over to his desk.

'We've got Donaldson back at his place. He says that maybe we should take him over to his shop, maybe they've not been looking in the right place. I said to him, "You drew the map, Jimmy, we're looking just where you told us to look." Jimmy got very evasive and described in detail how he'd removed the bricks from one of the walls, scraped out the cement and stuffed the jewellery bag inside. He replaced the bricks and cemented them in.'

Mike could feel the sweat trickle under his armpits. 'You want me to go over there and have a look?'

Craigh rubbed his nose. 'Yeah, okay, I'm taking myself off home. We've been over all the tapes from the fairground. Useless. They could have been talking about anything. He's a smart-arsed prick, you know, Donaldson.'

Mike nodded. 'Yeah, well, we know what she meant though, don't we?'

'Yeah, we know, but it wouldn't stand up in court. Still, we'll see what we get tomorrow – she's calling him again then.'

Mike put his coat on. It was another hour, sitting in traffic, before he picked up Angela She told him as far as she knew the women were all still together at the manor; Dolly had bought it from Ester, paid her by cheque. She hadn't heard any mention of diamonds but they were all edgy, especially Ester.

Mike paid her a tenner. She wanted him to take her out for a burger, but he said he didn't have the time. 'When will I see you again, then?' she asked him.

Mike cleared his throat. 'Soon as I get some free time. It's getting a bit heavy with Susan right now – she's asking a lot of questions about where I am. We just have to cool it for a bit.'

She started to sniffle and he hugged her. 'Come on, now, don't start. I've got to be on duty in half an hour.'

'You just used me.'

He turned away from her. 'I'm sorry if it feels that

way but you knew I was married right from the start, Angela, I got kids.'

She sniffed again and opened the car door. 'All the same, you used me, Mike. I give you all that information and you can't spare ten minutes for me. How do you think that makes me feel?'

'Look, let me get this Rawlins business sorted, then I promise I'll call you, okay?'

He reached over and squeezed her hand and she watched as he drove off. She felt cheated but also slightly guilty. Mrs Rawlins had seemed quite nice, not like the others. She hunched her shoulders and went back into the tube station, heading for her mother's place.

Audrey showed Mike the fake diamonds. 'Two grand, I paid. Tommy's a real professional. What do you think?'

Mike was tired out. He stuffed the bag into his pocket without looking inside it. 'Okay. Now you should get packed and out of here as soon as you can. I'll stash these tonight.'

'Did she meet up with Jimmy, then, today?'

'Yeah, but they played games.'

'She's clever, Mike. Don't trust her.'

He looked at his mother. 'You mean like I trusted you?'

'How can you say that? You know why I did it! You *know* why!'

He pursed his lips. 'You did it for the money, so don't

give me the sob story about Shirley because it won't wash
any more. I'm doing this tonight and then that's it, you
hear me? I want you out of here, out of my life.'

'You don't mean that, do you?'

'Yes, I do.'

'But the villa! You and the kids can come for holidays.'

'No, Mum, I don't want to know about the fucking
villa. You got it, you stay in it. Now pack your bags.'

Audrey burst into tears and started talking about how
she had every right to do what she did, how Dolly had
killed Shirley. Mike couldn't take any more.

'Don't give me that crap. I'm only doing this for
Shirley and I never want to see you again.'

He ran down the stone steps, his mother's screeching
voice in his ear, and he hated her. At that moment, he
even hated his sister. But there was one person he hated
even more. If he was caught replacing the stones at
Jimmy Donaldson's antique shop he'd be arrested and it
would all be Dolly Rawlins's fault!

Crashing the gears, he sped off down the road, the
pouch of fake diamonds feeling like a red-hot coal in
his jacket pocket.

Chapter 5

Julia kissed her mother's soft powdery cheek and then stepped back, holding up the goldfish. 'I got you a present.'

Mrs Lawson smiled, gently stroking Bates the cat, who eyed the bag hungrily. 'Well, I'll have my work cut out watching Bates to make sure he doesn't eat it.'

'We used to have a fish bowl somewhere, didn't we? I remember it.' Julia searched in the kitchen and eventually found it, filled it with water and tipped in the fish. Then she carried it into the drawing room. Her mother was still stroking Bates, sitting in her wheelchair, a cashmere shawl wrapped round her knees. The room was oppressively hot, the gas fire turned on full.

'So, how are you?' Julia said as she sat down, peeling off her sweater.

'Oh, Mrs Dowey takes good care of me and her husband still looks after the garden.'

Julia could think of nothing to say so she got up and looked over a stack of bills placed in a wooden tea-caddy on the sideboard. 'Are these for me?'

'Yes, dear. I was going to send them to your accountant as I always do, but as you're here ...'

They were the usual telephone, gas and electricity bills, Mrs Dowey's and her husband's wages, and bills for repairs and maintenance to the house. Julia even paid for the groceries.

'You know, dear, if this is too much for you ...'

Julia turned the wheelchair round to face her. 'If it was I'd say so. Besides, who else have I got to look after?'

'I always hope you'll meet someone nice, marry and settle down. It would be nice to have a grandchild before I die.'

Julia smiled, touching her mother's wrinkled hand. 'I am trying, Mother, but you know my job – it's always taken precedence over my personal life.'

'You look very well, dear.' Mrs Lawson smiled, changing the subject. 'Will you be staying tonight?'

'No, sadly I can't. I've got surgery this evening.'

'Ah, yes, of course. Perhaps a cup of tea?'

Julia nodded and stood up. She was so tall that the low ceiling felt as if it was pressing on her head. 'I'll put the kettle on.'

'That would be nice, dear, thank you.'

Julia stood at the window, wanting to cry. Everything was exactly as she remembered it. Nothing had changed for years. Only her mother had got older and more frail, her voice light and quavery. It always seemed so strange that her mother never noticed how different she was. Couldn't she tell?

'I'll make the tea.' Julia left the room and Mrs Lawson turned to stare at the solitary goldfish swimming round and round in the empty glass bowl.

'We should get some green things for the fish, shouldn't we, Bates? He seems very lonely.'

Mrs Lawson continued to stare as if hypnotized while the fish went round and round. 'Poor little soul,' she whispered.

Angela let herself in, hating the smell that always hung in the air − babies' vomit and urine. 'I'm back, Mum,' she yelled, dropping her bag.

Mrs Dunn was making a half-hearted attempt to iron, feed the two kids and cook all at once. Everything about her looked tired − her face, her hair, her clothes and, worst of all, her eyes. They seemed devoid of any expression.

'Where've you been?' It came out as a single sigh, the iron thudding over the drip-dry shirt that always creased.

'Working.'

Mrs Dunn thumped the iron back on its stand. She pulled more semi-damp clothes from the wooden rail, tossed them into an already laden basket, switched off a steaming kettle and took an empty Mars Bar paper out of her youngest son's mouth, all in one slow, tired swing.

'Here's a tenner for you.'

'Put it in the tin on the sideboard. Eric's going crazy – you don't pay any rent or anything towards the food, we don't know where you are, when you're coming in, you treat this place like it was a hotel. There's been call after call for you.'

'Who from?'

'I don't know, that girl Sherry? John at the ice rink? I'm not your social secretary. Where've you been?'

Angela sat down, kicking her heels against the table leg. 'Ester Freeman gimme a job for a night – *just* waitressin'.'

Mrs Dunn moved slowly back to the ironing. 'I've told you not to mix with her, she's no good, she'll have you on the game next. Eric said he wouldn't be surprised if you're not on it anyway.'

'Eric would know, wouldn't he? He's a pest, a dirty-minded, two-faced shit. This is your house and he has no right to ask me to pay rent in it.'

'He does if he's paying the bills, love, and he is. And don't speak about him like that.'

'He's not my dad.'

'No, he isn't, thank Christ, or we'd have no roof over our heads. Eric's taken you on.'

Angela snorted, looking around the dank kitchen. 'Yeah, I'm sure. This is a dump, it always was, and it's got worse over the years. You should complain to the council – you got every right, you know. There's empty flats either side, they're moving everyone else round here. You'd be up for a new place, five kids, no husband.'

Mrs Dunn banged down the iron. 'Now, don't start. Just because you've got nothing in your life you got to have a go at me! Well, just stop it or you're out on your ear.'

Angela sighed. She hated being home – hated everything about it – even more since Eric had taken over as 'man of the house'. He was half her mother's age and constantly made moves on Angela, but her mother refused to believe it, fearful that if Eric was confronted he would walk out on her.

'So, where have you been?'

'I just told you. You don't listen to what I say. I went to Aylesbury.'

'Oh, yes, Ester Freeman.' Mrs Dunn suddenly sagged into a chair. 'Don't go back to working for her, Angela, she's no good. I just don't know what to do about you, I really don't.'

Angela got up and slipped her arms around her mother. 'Mum, I've got a boyfriend, I was sort of working for him in a way. He's asked me to go and live with him. He's got a nice house and—'

'Oh, just stop it, Angela, you make up stories all the time. What man is this now? That copper?'

Mrs Dunn put her head in her hands. 'I don't know what to do with you. You won't go back to school, you got no qualifications. How you gonna get a job with no qualifications? You tell me that.'

Angela stuck out her lower lip. Since she'd been picked up after the bust at Ester's, she'd had a string of part-time jobs. Nothing kept her interested for more than a few weeks and the pay was bad in all of them. She'd been a waitress, a barmaid, a clerk, a trainee at two hair salons, part-time sales girl in numerous boutiques and she'd even helped out a few market-stall owners at Camden Lock. But in reality she was just drifting around and she knew it. She didn't know how to stop it and she'd hoped Mike would help her – but he just fucked her, like everyone else.

'I dunno what to do, Mum. Nothin' seems to work out for me.'

Mrs Dunn kissed her daughter. She was such a pretty girl: her thick hair hung in a marvellous Afro spiral cascade and she was a pale tawny colour with big, wide, amber eyes. 'I want you to go and talk to your old teachers, see what they say, maybe get on some government training course. You can't just live your life wanderin' from one part-time job to another, you got to have a purpose.'

'You mean like you?' Angela said sarcastically, and saw the pain flash across her mother's face.

'No, what I don't want is for you to have a life like mine, I wouldn't want it for my worst enemy.'

Angela started to cry. She just felt so screwed up, with nothing in the future. She knew Mike didn't want to see her any more – he hadn't for a while now. 'I'll go and see them tomorrow, okay?'

Mrs Dunn smiled and suddenly all the tiredness evaporated. 'Just stay away from Ester, that woman's a bad influence.'

Angela nodded and went upstairs. She packed her bag, stuffing anything that came to hand into it. She'd had enough; there was nothing to do but leave. She heard Eric come in and start shouting and yelling at her mother in the kitchen, so she never even said goodbye.

She had no place to go, so she called Mike at home but his wife answered and she put the phone down. She had no place to go but back to the Grange. She just needed somewhere to stay until she sorted herself out. Maybe when she told Mike he would help her, find a job for her. Then she'd come back to London.

By the time Dolly returned it was after eleven and she was still carrying the white rabbit. Ester had seen Dolly's arrival from the bedroom window and was waiting in the hall.

'Did you have a nice day?'

'Didn't Julia tell you? Here, she got the fish, you get the rabbit.' Dolly threw the fluffy toy at her and walked slowly up the stairs as Connie wandered out of the kitchen.

'I got some stew on.'

Dolly looked at her. She had cotton wool stuffed up her swollen nose, both eyes were black and she was crying. 'What the hell happened to you?'

Connie snivelled and went back into the kitchen just as Kathleen was coming down the stairs. 'Boyfriend, if you can call him that, whacked her one.'

Kathleen passed Dolly, raising an eyebrow at Ester. 'Nice bunny. Where'd you get it?'

Dolly washed her face and hands. She heard the doorbell ring and went downstairs, thinking it must be Julia. Ester came hurrying out from the kitchen. 'I'll get it. You go on in and sit down and have your dinner, Dolly.' She pulled open the front door to see Angela huddled on the doorstep.

'What do you want?' Ester snapped.

'Oh, please, Ester I've had to leave me mum's house and I had no other place to go.'

'Well, you can't stay here.'

Dolly walked further down into the hall. 'What's this?'

'It's Angela. I said we don't want her here.'

147

'Well, she can't go back at this hour. Let her in, we've got enough room.'

Ester stepped aside. 'Thank you very much, Mrs Rawlins,' Angela said, giving Ester a superior look.

'There's some stew on so put your bag in a room and come into the kitchen,' Dolly said, smiling. She headed into the kitchen.

Julia was already sitting at the table, helping a still tearful Connie serve up the stew, when Gloria banged in from the back yard. She went straight to wash her hands. 'I brought me gear from the house.'

Dolly cleared her throat. 'Right. Things have changed since last night. I'm not taking on this house. I'm sorry, but I've had time to think and I reckon it'll be too expensive to do up, so I'm going back to my original plan and opening up a smaller place back in town.' She placed her knife and fork together.

'You should have told me this morning, Dolly,' Ester said.

'I'm telling you now. I want my money back, Ester.'

'Well, if you'd told me this morning that might have been possible but you're too late now. I put it in the bank.'

'You can take it out again, can't you?'

'No. I'm bankrupt. I've still got about three hundred grand to pay off, and they won't cash a cheque for a tenner right now.' Ester looked dutifully crestfallen and her voice took on an apologetic tone. 'I'm really sorry, Dolly. Like I said, you should have told me this morning.'

Dolly's face tightened. 'If you'd told me you were bankrupt I'd never have walked out without getting my money.'

'But you did and now there's nothing I can do about it. The house is yours, Dolly, lock, stock and barrel.'

Dolly pursed her lips. 'You really stitched me up, didn't you, Ester? I really walked into this one, didn't I?'

'With your eyes open, Dolly, I never pushed you. I told you to think about it, if you recall. Now there's nothing I can do. But we're all here, we can all lend a hand, get this place up and rolling.'

Dolly clenched her hands. 'You any idea how much this will cost to get fixed up?'

'No, but we can start getting estimates in tomorrow. Local builders are cheaper than up in London.'

'And how do I pay them?' Dolly said quietly.

Ester flicked a look at Julia. 'Well, they give you grants, don't they? Unless you've got more dough stashed away.'

Dolly got up and fetched a glass. 'Any wine left from last night?'

Ester sent Angela to get a bottle from the dining room. All the women were looking at Ester, then back to Dolly as if at a tennis match.

Dolly went into the drawing room, where Angela

was at the desk, reading a stack of newspaper cuttings. When she saw Dolly, she tried to stuff them back into the drawer. 'I couldn't find any wine, Mrs Rawlins.'

'It wouldn't be in a drawer, would it, love?' She pushed past Angela and opened the drawer as Angela backed away from her. She flicked through the cuttings: headlines about the murder of her husband, headlines about the shooting of Shirley Miller – and the diamond raid, then folded them and picked up her handbag.

'What you staring at me like that for?' she demanded.

Angela stuttered, 'I'm not, I just – just didn't know about all that.'

'What? That I'd been in prison? You knew, they all know. Now go and get the bottle. Try the dining room, dear.'

Angela scuttled out, and Dolly, taking a deep breath, walked back into the kitchen. The room fell silent.

Angela uncorked the wine as Dolly sat waiting, her hands clenched over her handbag. As soon as the wine was poured, Ester lifted her glass. 'Well, here's to the Grange Foster Home.' Dolly took only a small mouthful before she put her glass down.

'Isn't it about time you all cut the pretence and came clean?'

'About what, Dolly? Ester asked innocently.

'Why you're all here,' Dolly replied calmly.

Again they looked at Ester to take the lead. She smiled

sweetly. 'You know why. We were all at a bit of a loose end and thought it would be nice, you know, to have a little welcome-out party, that's all. As it turned out, you bought the place.'

'No other reason?' said Dolly.

'I don't know what you mean, Dolly,' Gloria said.

'Don't you?' Dolly threw the newspaper cuttings onto the table. 'Not too clever leaving them lying around, was it? That's why you're all here. That's what you're all after, isn't it?'

'The diamonds?' Connie asked, and received a kick under the table from Ester.

'Yes. The bloody diamonds.' Dolly rarely swore.

Mike drew up outside Jimmy Donaldson's rundown antique shop. The lights were on and a patrol car was parked outside. He patted his pocket, felt the pouch, and walked into the shop.

Arc-lights were turned on and three uniformed officers were searching the place. It was a tough job as furniture, junk and bric-a-brac were crowded into every inch of the shop space. An officer looked up at Mike as he entered. 'There's another floor even more stuffed than down here, plus a back yard crammed full, and an outside lav.'

'You not found them, then?' Mike asked.

'No. According to Donaldson, they were hidden behind a wall. Well, we've nearly had the place come down on us, we've pulled out so many bricks, but we've come to the conclusion he's playing silly buggers.'

Mike eased his way round a Victorian washstand. 'Well, carry on. I was just passing so I'll give you a hand for an hour or so.'

The officer nodded. 'You want a cup of tea? We're about to brew up out back.'

'Yeah, milk, one sugar.'

Left alone, Mike looked round the shop. He could see the wall where they had been removing bricks and he inched towards it. He had to be fast as the men were within yards of him. He pulled back two bricks and stuffed in the pouch, then shoved the bricks back into place. When the officer returned with two mugs of tea, Mike was standing by the opposite wall. He was inspecting the brickwork. 'Go over every inch of all the walls again. Donaldson is still insisting it's behind the brickwork.'

Mike stayed for another half-hour, helping move furniture around but keeping well away from where he had stashed the pouch, concentrating on the opposite wall. As he left, he suggested they stay at it.

He got home after twelve. His wife was already in bed and when he got in beside her, she didn't move.

'You awake?'

'Yes.'

'Sorry I'm so late. It's this bloke we brought out of the nick, taking up a lot of extra time.'

'Phone call for you.'

'Oh yeah, who?'

'I don't know. She put the phone down.'

Susan turned to face him. He sighed. 'If whoever it was put the phone down, how do you know it was a she?'

'I can tell. And that's what I'm asking you to do, Mike. Tell me if there's somebody else, just tell me.'

'There isn't, Sue, honestly, there's no one. This is starting to get on my nerves, you know.'

She turned over again, and lay awake for about ten minutes, crying silently, until she couldn't stand it any longer and turned back to him, but he was fast asleep. She'd been through his pockets earlier and this time she'd found a crumpled half-page torn from an old diary. There was a phone number and a name. Angela. She'd called the number, asked to speak to Angela, but a woman had said she no longer lived there, had no idea where she was, and slammed down the receiver. Susan realized she should have said that the girl on the phone had said her name was Angela. She punched the pillow. Nothing in the world was worse than lying next to someone who was sleeping soundly, when you couldn't. She lay on her back and stared at the ceiling with tears in her eyes.

The bottle was empty. The women sat listening to Dolly as she twisted the wine glass round by the stem. 'There were the four of us, all widows, Linda Pirelli, Bella, Shirley Miller and me. They're all dead.'

Angela stared. She knew the name Shirley Miller, knew it very well, because Mike was always talking about her: his sister.

'Anyway, when it was over, I knew it would be just a matter of time before they picked me up so I left the stones with a friend of mine, someone I knew I could trust.'

'You left them with someone for eight years?' Ester asked uneasily.

'Yes, but, like I said, I knew he wouldn't try anything because I had so much on him. Well, my husband did.'

'Harry,' Gloria said eagerly.

'You've read about him, have you?' Dolly looked at the old newspaper cuttings, the photocopies. One had his face on the front page: 'Harry Rawlins Murdered', screamed the headline. 'I know what I did was wrong,' Dolly said softly. 'I killed him. And I paid the price. And probably I'm the only person who still mourns him. I always will. In some ways I tried to be him, before I knew what he'd done to me, before I knew he had a cheap little tart of a girlfriend, before I knew she'd had his kid. I tried to be him, keeping him alive inside me, but the laugh was on me because he really was alive.'

No one spoke, watching and listening intently as Dolly bared her soul.

'I'm serious about putting something back into society. He just took, for years and years, and I want to make up for it. I really do want to open a foster home ... I want to have a purpose for the rest of my life.'

Ester nodded. 'Yeah, well, we all agree it's a great idea, and I know you may regret buying this place now, but when you've done it up, Dolly, think how many kids you can give a place to.'

Dolly sighed. 'Yeah, it's just the finances, isn't it? And that's what I'm going to use the diamonds for. Now, if any of you have any thoughts about getting a cut, then let me tell you, you've not got a hope in hell. They are mine, all mine, and I'll need every penny.'

'But we know that. All we're doing is offering to help you run this place,' Ester said warmly. The other women muttered in agreement.

Julia leaned forward. 'Will you need any help in getting the diamonds back from this guy? Any help fencing them? Surely we can help you there.'

'For what? A cut?' Dolly asked.

'Hell, no, just to show you how we all feel,' Ester said, beaming. She could almost feel the money in her hands, she was so close.

Dolly leaned back. 'Well, maybe I will need some help. I've been away a long time, and I'm not sure who to fence them to.'

Kathleen received a nudge beneath the table. 'Eh, Dolly, leave that to me, I know the best. You get them and we'll soon have them sorted out, and cash in your hand. How much you reckon they're worth?'

Dolly paused before she answered. 'Maybe three and a half million . . . I doubt if I'll see more than one, maybe one and a quarter back.'

There was a lot of murmuring and quiet sneaky looks as they each suddenly felt rich. Then Dolly stood up. 'I'm collecting them tomorrow so we'll soon see what the value is. Now I'm off to bed, maybe just have a walk around. Goodnight.'

They all chorused goodnight, as Dolly fetched her coat, refusing everyone's offer to join her.

As soon as the door closed behind her, Ester put out her hand. 'Put it there. What did I tell you?'

A few slapped Ester's hand, but Julia rocked in her chair. 'She doesn't seem eager to give us a cut, Ester. Maybe you're starting to celebrate a bit too early.'

Ester gazed at her. 'She brings them here and we don't get a cut, we don't wait for her to fence them, we simply take them! Agreed?'

They all nodded. They seemed to have forgotten Angela, who had not said a word throughout. Ester reached out to prod her. 'You just got lucky, darlin', but open your mouth to her about this and you'll be sorry, very sorry.'

Angela hunched her shoulders. 'I won't say anything to anyone.' But her mind was buzzing. Mike would definitely talk to her if she told him about the diamonds.

Ester pulled back her bedroom curtains an inch, the room in darkness. 'She's still out there, Julia, looking at the house, as if she's checking us out.'

'Try just checking out what you lumbered her with,' Julia drawled from the bed.

Ester jumped on the bed, crawling towards Julia on her hands and knees.

'Can I ask you something?' Julia said as Ester nuzzled her neck. 'Would you kill her for them?'

Ester lay back against the pillows. 'No. Let me ask *you* something. If she caught us taking them, do you think Dolly would kill us?'

Julia thought for a moment and then said, very quietly, 'I'm sure of it.'

Dolly paced round the garden. The night was chilly and she was cold, but she didn't want to go inside. It was talking about him; it brought it all back. She walked slowly towards the swimming pool: the dank, dark water made her remember even more clearly. The way he smiled at her, waiting there by the lake. She would never forget the look of utter surprise on his face when she brought out the gun and fired: a half-mocking smile, then that moment of fear. And then he was dead, his body falling backwards into the water.

She rubbed her arms, turning back to the house. She was going to make her dream come true, on a bigger scale than she had ever hoped for – with or without that bunch of slags.

Chapter 6

Dolly was up at six. She went through the *Yellow Pages* and earmarked the local building companies. She couldn't wait to get started. At nine, she had Angela sitting at the reception desk, calling all the companies and asking for them to come and give estimates. She gave the women orders to list what they felt needed to be done in different parts of the house, and they all went about the delegated duties with a zest and energy that sparkled like the diamonds they all expected to get a slice of.

By ten o'clock, the drive was filled with an odd assortment of trucks as builders arrived and started looking over the house, all vying with each other to win the business. Mrs Rawlins wanted an immediate verbal estimate, and she wanted the work to start immediately, that afternoon if possible.

Dolly felt more alive than she had for years. She drove

into the village in Gloria's Mini and bought provisions, wellington boots, sweaters and jeans. If the women weren't genuine, she'd soon find out. She then went into the town hall to speak to Mrs Tilly again, feeling more confident than the last time, asking if there was any possibility of being interviewed by the board before she gave the go-ahead for structural work to begin on the house.

Mrs Tilly liked Dolly, her forthrightness, her eagerness and, above all, her genuineness. When she went to see the chairman of the board, she would ask if there was any possibility of moving Mrs Rawlins's application forward.

Back at the house, Dolly handed out the wellington boots, sweaters and jeans and asked for the groceries to be unloaded. She had ordered a giant deep freeze, plus a new fridge. The women looked on as trucks delivered wheelbarrows, spades, brooms and cleaning equipment. It was still only twelve o'clock when the builders began to ask to speak to Dolly about their estimates, and she sat in the dining room listening to each man. She eventually chose John Maynard, Builder and Carpenter. He was a one-man business that hired in workmen. His yard was only a mile from the manor and his estimates were lower than any of the others. The reason she hired 'Big John' was not only because his estimates were low; she reckoned that as he was a one-man show she could make a cash deal and cut down on the VAT payments.

Working from the top of the house down to the cellars, he pointed out what structural work was required.
Firstly the roof needed to be replaced and the chimneys
were also dangerous. Every window sash had to be
renewed, and all the plumbing in every bathroom, as
well as the boilers; and ceilings had to be re-plastered.
In other words, the manor needed to be stripped back
to the bare boards and rebuilt. He said it would cost
between sixty and seventy thousand pounds, and that
excluded fixtures and fittings; with those it would come
to at least a hundred and fifty thousand. And that was
without taking into consideration the gardens, stables,
swimming pool and orchard. But even with the extra
work that would mean, his charges were still way under
any of the larger firms'.

'How long will it all take?' Dolly asked.

'Six months at least.'

Dolly frowned: she would have to have that meeting at
the town hall to find out what grants she would be entitled
to because it was now obvious that Ester's big deal about
all the furnishing being part of the sale meant nothing.
Everything needed to be replaced – cutlery, linen, beds,
mattresses, carpets. She knew she was looking at around
half a million to get the manor back into shape – and that
was for only the bare necessities because she would still
have to install fire alarms and child safety equipment. Even
so, she couldn't help feeling excited. She felt confident she

could finance the place and still come out with money in the bank for emergencies, perhaps schooling and further education for the kids, home helps, nannies.

Big John agreed to cut out the VAT for cash payment and departed a happy man to begin hiring workmen, plumbers, carpenters and brickies.

The women began to 'look busy', with a lot of comings and goings, without actually over-exerting themselves. They were more intent on keeping an eye on Dolly, but monitoring her phone calls was difficult as Angela was constantly on the phone making calls for her.

Ester passed Angela twice. 'You're not still on the phone, are you, Angela? Maybe Dolly wants to call somebody.'

'I'm calling people for her. She's given me a list.'

Angela was telephoning the social services, trying to find out what the building requirements and stipulations were, but she kept on being switched from one department to another.

Out in the stables, the women were half-heartedly clearing away years of rubbish, old wine crates and bottles.

Ester marched out. 'That bloody Angela is *still* on the phone. It's crazy, she's been on it all morning.'

'I thought Dolly was gonna call about the diamonds,' bellowed Gloria.

'Can you say that any louder, Gloria? Maybe the station attendant didn't pick it up!'

Kathleen hurled a crate down from the loft. 'Well, get her off the bloody phone.' She climbed down the ladder as Ester started pacing up and down. 'If she's paying cash to that builder, she's either got to have more than she let on or she's going for them later today.'

Kathleen began to load the wheelbarrow and yelled that somebody else should also look as if they were working apart from her. Ester climbed up the ladder and began to kick down crates as Gloria dragged out an old table with three legs.

'Gloria, come up here. *Gloria!*'

'*What do you want?*' she yelled back, and then looked up at Ester as she peered down from the loft.

'You come up here, Gloria!' Gloria sighed and went up the ladder. As her nose appeared at the top, Ester pointed to some old straw covering several large canvas bags. 'Are these yours?'

Gloria shrugged. 'Maybe. What's your problem?'

Ester knelt down and dragged forward one of the open bags. 'They're full of guns, Gloria.'

'So bleedin' what? What's that got to do with you?'

'A lot. There's gonna be builders coming back this afternoon, and they'll be swarming all over the place. If they find them, they'll think the bloody IRA have taken up residence. Move them.'

'Where to, for Chrissakes?'

'Somewhere out of sight, not left up here for anyone to find.'

'I'll move 'em but I'll need you to help. They weigh a ton.'

Dolly was reading the leaflets from the social services when she heard a yell from below. She crossed to the window to see Gloria staggering towards the house with Ester, carrying what looked like a body bag.

They stumbled through the kitchen, all the guns wrapped in an old piece of carpet. As they went into the hall, they found Angela on the phone.

'Well, I have to see you, it's important.'

'Get off the phone,' Ester snapped.

Angela whipped round. 'I'm still calling for Dolly,' she lied, and began to redial.

The two women continued on towards the cellar door and down into the sauna. Dolly watched from the landing, wondering what they were taking down there. She moved slowly down the stairs as Angela hurriedly dialled again. 'Keep getting put into different departments, Mrs Rawlins.'

Dolly pressed her finger over the button and then lifted it up. She asked Angela to dial a number for her and ask for Jimmy. Angela did as she was told. Dolly leaned forward, listening. 'Ask him if he's got them,' she whispered, as Angela held her hand over the phone.

'Got what?'

Dolly gave her one of her strange, sweet smiles. 'I'll maybe tell you about it later but just do as I say, love.'

Angela hesitated and then spoke into the phone. 'Have you got them?' she stammered.

Donaldson looked at Palmer. They still hadn't found the stones but Palmer nodded for him to say that he had them, and to stall for time. 'Yes, I've got them, but not here.'

Dolly wrote on a notepad and passed it to Angela. She read it and then said into the phone, 'I'll collect them at two o'clock tomorrow afternoon.'

Dolly pressed on the button to cut off the call, and told Angela to carry on chasing the social services, as Ester and Gloria came up from the cellars. 'Still clearing the junk from the stable, Dolly,' Ester told her.

'Good, keep at it. We'll have some skips delivered soon so a lot of it can be chucked into them. I'm going to London tomorrow afternoon.'

They went out smiling, and reported to the women outside that it looked like Dolly was going to pick up the diamonds the following afternoon. They all started clearing the rubbish with renewed vigour.

Dolly waited until Angela had started telephoning again before she slipped down into the basement to see what Gloria and Ester had been carrying. She went into the old sauna locker room. Some of the cupboards were dented and hanging open but a row of three was locked, dusty fingerprints showing they had been opened and used recently. Dolly looked around and found an old screwdriver left on a bench. She prised open a locker and found herself looking at a thick canvas bag. She swore, and then sighed, leaning against the old locker. 'Stupid, stupid, stupid . . .'

At seven the workmen erecting scaffolding finally left. The women sat watching TV, all of them knackered, apart from Dolly who remained at the kitchen table making notes, and all went up to bed early. Julia was fast asleep when Ester suddenly sat bolt upright, nudging her. 'Somebody's downstairs, can you hear?'

Julia listened, and then crept to the doorway. She couldn't hear anything. Ester looked out of the window and whispered, 'She's out there again – look, up by the woods.'

Dolly was standing, staring at the manor, looking from one window to the next. She wore wellington boots and a raincoat she had found in a closet, a man's raincoat, stained and torn.

'What's she doing out there?'

'Who cares? Come back to bed,' Julia yawned.

'I don't trust her one bit,' Ester said, reluctantly returning to bed. A couple of hours later she woke again as she
heard someone on the stairs. She listened and then heard
Dolly's bedroom door opening and closing.

'I don't trust her,' she murmured, falling back into a
troubled sleep.

The workmen arrived at six the next morning. They
were still putting up the scaffolding, but they had also
begun to clear out old carpets and broken furniture, lay
down planks for wheelbarrow access into the hallway,
and put bags of cement by the open front door. Dolly
was up and having breakfast when Big John tapped on
the door. 'Scaffolding should be up by this afternoon and
we'll start clearing out anything you don't want, and get
ready for the roof. Er, I've hired eight men, so . . .'

'You'll get the first payment end of the week, if that's
okay, just a couple of days.'

'Oh, fine. It's just I'm laying out cash for all the tiles
and the men'll want wages come Friday.'

'I know, John, but I have to go to London to get the
cash. You'll have it, don't worry.'

'Okay, Mrs Rawlins.'

'Thank you, John.' She sat a moment, tapping her
teeth with a pencil, as one by one the women drifted
down for breakfast.

'Will you all start clearing the vegetable patch? I got

bags and bags of seeds we can start planting,' Dolly said, as they started frying bacon and eggs.

Julia walked in, face flushed. 'You know, those old stables are in quite good nick – be nice to get a horse. I used to have one when I was a kid. They're not that expensive to keep, you'd be surprised.'

Dolly paid no attention, concentrating on her notes.

'Did you hear what I said, Dolly?' Julia said as she threw off her jacket.

'Last thing we need right now, love, is a horse. Let's get the garden in order first. We can start that while the house is being done over, no need to fork out for gardeners.'

The women looked at one another, having no desire to 'shift' anything but the eggs and bacon.

'I'm going up to London this afternoon. I'll take Angela with me.' Dolly left the kitchen and went to the yard.

Ester closed the door behind her. 'Told you, she's going for them this afternoon. Get Angela in here, go on.'

Gloria caught Angela dialling. She crooked her finger. 'Who you callin'?'

'My mum, let her know where I am.'

'Well, do it later. Come in here, we want to talk to you.'

It was a beautiful clear day and Dolly was walking up to the woods. She stopped as she heard the sound of a train, and looked over to see the level-crossing gates open and close. A square-faced boy was sitting on a stool, obviously a trainspotter. He was making copious notes in a black schoolbook, checking his watch, face set in concentration. Dolly strolled down onto the narrow lane by the crossing.

'Good morning,' she said cheerfully.

The boy looked up: his face was even squarer close up and his thick black hair stuck up in spikes. 'Good morning. My name is Raymond Dewey,' he said loudly. 'I'm here every day, checking on the trains. I'm the time-keeper. That was the nine o'clock express, on time, always on time.'

'Really? You have an important job then, don't you? Raymond, was it?'

'That is correct, Raymond Dewey of fourteen, Cottage Lane. Who are you?'

'Well, Raymond, I'm Dolly. Dolly Rawlins.'

'Hello, Dolly, very nice to meet you.'

She smiled at his over-serious face. Bright button eyes glinted back as he licked his pencil tip and returned to his work.

'Well,' Dolly said, 'I won't disturb you. Bye-bye.'

He stuck out his stubby-fingered hand and she shook it. His grasp was strong, almost pulling her off her feet. Close to, he looked much older than at first sight but she thought no more of him as she wandered back up to the woods.

*

At the town hall, Mrs Tilly replaced the receiver and checked her watch. She thought it was probably best to discuss what she'd just heard with Mrs Rawlins personally, so she left her office.

The women were grouped around the vegetable patch. Connie was peering at seed packets as Julia dug the soil, turning it over. Two wheelbarrows were filled with weeds and rubbish.

'Should these be goin' in now?' Gloria asked, as she opened another packet.

Julia began to stick in rods. 'Bit late, but if the weather keeps fine it'll be okay.'

Gloria sprayed out the contents of the packet.

'*Not there!* Over here, what do you think I'm putting the rods in for?' Julia shouted.

'Well, I didn't know. What you got in your packet, Connie?'

Connie pulled at the top to open it and the seeds all fell out.

'Pick them up,' said Julia, bad-tempered.

'What, all of them?' asked Connie. 'There's hundreds!'

Gloria laughed and kicked at the seeds. 'Who gives a bugger?'

They saw a Mini Metro pull up by the front path. 'Who's that?' Julia asked.

'I dunno, she's driving this way now.'

Mrs Tilly wound down the window. 'I'm looking for Mrs Rawlins.'

'Try the back door,' said Gloria. 'Round the back, past the stables. She was in the kitchen.'

Mrs Tilly smiled her thanks and pulled away.

Connie, on her hands and knees, was picking up one seed at a time. 'Ugh, the dirt's gettin' under my nails.'

'Take them off, then,' said Gloria as she kicked more soil over a mound of seeds.

'No chance – do you know what they cost?'

Gloria peered down at her. 'With a bit of luck, you'll soon be able to buy all the nails you want. Come on, let's go and see what the Metro lady wanted.'

Mrs Tilly tooted the horn and stepped out of the car as Dolly hurried out from the kitchen.

'Mrs Tilly, good morning.'

'Good morning, Mrs Rawlins. I can't stop but I wanted to tell you personally. We had a cancellation for this afternoon so the board are reviewing your case and, if you're available, they can see you this afternoon at four thirty. I'm sorry it's such short notice but as they're all gathered, it seemed a shame not to jump the queue, so to speak.'

Dolly beamed. 'Is there any advice you can give me, anything I should take with me?'

Mrs Tilly smiled. 'My advice to everyone applying for

foster caring is always tell the truth because everything is always checked and double-checked.'

'Thank you very much, Mrs Tilly. Are you sure you won't come in for a cup of tea?'

'No, I shouldn't have really left the office unattended.'

'I'll see you later then.'

Angela had been listening. She came to the kitchen door. 'Mrs Rawlins, about this afternoon—'

Dolly turned and frowned at Angela to shut her up, then turned back to Mrs Tilly. 'Four thirty, then, Mrs Tilly. Should I wear a suit, do you think?'

'You'll be asked a lot of questions, some very personal, so wear whatever you feel most confident and relaxed in. Goodbye.'

Dolly felt like skipping – everything was coming together so fast. She waited until Mrs Tilly's car had disappeared before she clapped her hands. 'Did you hear, Angela? I've got a meeting with the social services board this afternoon!'

Angela wrinkled her nose. 'But what about that Jimmy bloke? You said you'd see him this afternoon. I phoned him yesterday, remember? You can't go to London for two and be back by four thirty. It's after eleven now.'

Dolly's face fell. How could she have forgotten? It was the excitement. She'd not felt like this since she was a kid. She hugged her arms tightly around herself. 'Get the others in. Tell them we need to talk.'

Dolly hurried up to her room to sort out what she would wear for the afternoon's meeting.

Sitting on the dressing-table stool, Dolly started brushing her hair, talking to herself, trying to sort out exactly what she should do. She didn't like leaving Jimmy Donaldson holding the stones for too long. He could get itchy fingers and she'd kind of given him an ultimatum. She didn't like going back on that as it made her look weak, as if she didn't mean business. Harry had something on Donaldson but without him, Donaldson might just try it on.

They were sitting at the table in the big kitchen, obviously waiting. As soon as she walked in, she could feel the tension. 'Okay, this is how we work it. One of you will have to collect the stones for me. I can't risk losing this opportunity with the board members. They're doing me a big favour as it is. So . . .'

'What do you want us to do?' Ester asked.

Dolly sat down. 'Jimmy's waiting for me to come at two o'clock. One of you'll have to go and do it for me.'

There was a unanimous 'I'll do it' but Dolly shook her head.

'What, don't you trust us?' Julia asked.

'No, if you want my honest opinion, but if I say I'll give you each a cut, then whoever picks them up better not do a runner or she ll do every one of you in. So that's a bit of an incentive to come back, isn't it?' Dolly's mind was racing. She'd never said how much of a cut but they could fight that out later, when she'd fenced the diamonds.

She looked them all over: Ester was Julia's partner, so it wouldn't do to put them together; Kathleen she wouldn't trust with a loaf of bread, or Gloria for that matter.

'Okay, Ester, you go.'

Ester couldn't hide her smile.

'You sure, Dolly? I mean, what do you think, Ester?' Julia said, and Ester could have smacked her.

'I'll do it. Don't be stupid,' she said quickly.

Julia shrugged her shoulders. She knew that Ester had people after her. 'Okay, if you say so.'

'Take Angela with you, the pair of you do it. Ester collects, you drive, Angela.'

Angela seemed too scared to speak, looking from one to the other.

'Why Angela?' Ester demanded.

Dolly gave an icy smile. 'I trust her.'

'And you don't trust me?'

'No, but I don't think you'd leave Julia in the lurch – leave us all in the lurch – would you?'

They glared at Ester, warning her that she'd better not try anything.

'So get yourselves together, take the Range Rover and get moving.'

*

Julia walked in as Ester was changing, and shut the door.
'You're coming back, aren't you?'

Ester snapped, 'Of course I am. She's not as dumb
as you think. She knows I've got people after me. I'm
not likely to fence the gear all by myself in one afternoon, am I?'

Julia sat on the bed. 'I dunno. Just seems odd she'd
choose you, not me.'

'Why would she choose you?'

'Because she knows I'd come back if you were here,
whereas I don't know if you would – that answer your
question?'

Ester leaned over Julia. 'She's tied me to Miss Goody-
Two-Shoes, so she'll be watching me like a hawk. I'll be
back, Julia, don't you worry about that.'

'Then what?'

Ester clenched her fists. 'Well, you said it the other
night. You reckoned Dolly would kill for those diamonds. Maybe, just maybe, I would too.'

'What about the others?'

'Fuck 'em. Now, how do I look?'

'Great, but then I'm biased.' Julia smiled: Ester
always turned her on when she was hard like this.
Dangerous.

Dolly spoke softly, and Angela had to listen closely to
hear every word. 'You watch her all the time. You see

her collect, then you put your foot down and come straight back here. This is the address, twenty-one, Ladbroke Grove Estate. You all right?'

'I wish you'd ask one of the others.'

'No, love, you're the only one who hasn't been inside. You've still got some honesty about you, some integrity none of the others has left. They'd have 'em and be away, I know it.'

Angela was in turmoil but couldn't see any way out of it. She was still shaking as Ester walked in, dangling the car keys. 'Okay, we're all set, sweet-face, let's go and collect.'

Gloria looked at the clock. 'Well, you got plenty of time.'

'Maybe we'll stop off for lunch.'

'Just as long as you don't stop off anywhere after you've picked them up.'

Ester laughed, unaware that Dolly had already searched her room and pocketed her passport.

Ester gave Julia a little wink as they climbed into the Range Rover. 'Right, might as well get on with it then.'

Julia banged on the side of the door. 'Take care, Ester, see you later.'

Gloria, leaning on a rake, watched the Range Rover drive away. 'Well, if she doesn't show, I'll shove this up her arse.'

*

Dolly dialled and waited. She recognized Tommy's laboured breathing immediately. 'Hello, Tommy, it's Dolly, Harry Rawlins's widow.'

'Good God, you're out then, are you, gel?'

'Yeah, I'm out, but I need a favour.'

'You know old Tommy, lovey, if he can do you one, he will.'

'Just so long as you get paid for it, right?' Dolly chuckled.

'On the nail. So what can I do you for?'

Dolly lowered her voice. 'I've got a few things I want to run by Jimmy Donaldson, then maybe bring to you.'

'Jimmy Donaldson?' Tommy wheezed.

'Yeah, you know him?'

'Course I do. Runs a gig over in Hackney, or he did. You know he's been away for a few years – still is as far as I know.'

'Away? Where?'

'Banged up. Got pinched for floggin' some stolen Georgian silver. Didn't you know?'

'You sayin' he's still in the nick? You sure?'

'Yeah, a few days back someone was asking after him and ... hello? Hello?'

Dolly felt cold, her hand still gripping the receiver. If Donaldson was nicked, how come he was answering his phone? She sat down and ran her hands through her hair, trying to remember everything he had said at the fairground. The more she thought about it, the more she began to think that maybe she was being set up.

The women turned as they heard Dolly calling for Ester. 'She's gone. Dolly?'

Dolly ran towards them. 'They've gone already? But why...?'

'Well, they couldn't wait.' Gloria started to laugh, but seeing Dolly's expression quickly became serious. 'What is it?'

'I'm being set up. Jimmy Donaldson's supposed to be in the nick.'

Julia looked distraught.

Gloria hurled aside her rake. 'Get me car – we can catch them up. Come *on!*'

Julia ran after her, Dolly following close behind. Kathleen looked at Connie, who was still half-heartedly digging a drainage trench. 'What did you make of that?'

'I don't know. What do you think?'

Kathleen gazed down at the trench. She rammed in her spade. 'Keep digging. This looks like a grave, and maybe we'll be putting somebody in it . . .'

Chapter 7

The Mini backfired again and this time Dolly hit the dashboard. 'Next turning there's a hire firm. Pull in and get a car with something under the bonnet.'

'Who's paying for it?' Gloria grumbled.

'I will! Just do it!' Julia shouted. Gloria turned left towards Rodway Motors.

'They should have waited!' Dolly seethed, as Gloria pulled onto the forecourt and went to reception. 'If they'd just waited I'd have told them not to go.'

'Well, they didn't,' said Julia, looking at her watch, 'but we can still be there in plenty of time.'

Dolly was clenching and unclenching her hands. 'If I miss this board meeting, I'll – I'll—'

Julia glanced at Dolly curiously. She didn't seem to care about the diamonds, only that she had been set up. 'What about the diamonds, Dolly?' she said.

'If Jimmy has done me over, he'll regret it. I'll take everything he's got, then I'll have him taken out. I might even do it myself.'

Julia blinked, and then heard the *toot-toot* of a horn as Gloria drove up in a red Volvo. 'Right,' said Dolly, getting out of the Mini, 'move over, I'm driving.'

At twelve fifteen, one of the officers at long last returned to the wall they had first checked, but it wasn't until almost one o'clock that they found the pouch of diamonds. It was driven at top speed to Donaldson's house on the Ladbroke estate and handed over to DI Palmer, who snatched it unceremoniously.

'I've not logged it yet, guv,' the officer told him.

'I'll do it, thanks.'

DCI Craigh was standing in the hall. 'They got them,' Palmer gasped.

Craigh grinned. 'Talk about cutting it fine. Let's have a look at them.'

'They've not put it on record yet.'

'I'll do it when I go in,' Craigh said as he eased open the velvet pouch. 'Holy shit, look at the size of some of those stones,' he said in awe, then pulled the drawstring tight. 'Look, we don't let these out of our sight – that's your job and yours only, you watch these babies, okay?'

Craigh walked into the living room and held up the

bag to Jimmy Donaldson. 'Saved by the bell, Sunny Jim, we got them.'

Donaldson looked over with baleful eyes. 'Just so long as you put her away. She plugged her old man and I don't want her going after me.'

Craigh smirked. 'That's the whole point of the exercise, Jimmy. We want her back inside for nicking these.'

Mike stared blankly from his position by the window. He'd just about given up on them finding the stones in time but knew he couldn't risk going back to Donaldson's shop or it would look suspicious. All that had to happen now was for Rawlins to arrive and get nicked, and him and his bloody mother would be in the clear.

'What time is it?' he asked. Everyone looked at their watches, including Donaldson.

'We've almost an hour to go until she collects.'

Ester liked driving fast, and they were in London with time to spare. They were parked close to Ladbroke Grove tube station, eating burgers. At least, Ester was; Angela couldn't stomach anything. She was a bag of nerves, wondering if she would have to face Mike.

'I don't drive.'

Ester turned to her with her mouth full. 'What did you say?'

'I said I don't drive. Well, I do, but not very well. I

never passed my driving test and now, with my nerves I – I just don't think I'll be able to drive.'

Ester tossed the half-eaten hamburger out of the window. 'Well, it's a fucking brilliant time to tell me.'

'I'm sorry.'

Ester sighed. 'Okay, we switch. You collect, I'll drive.'

Angela chewed at her nails. 'I don't think we should do this, Ester. I'm scared. What if we get arrested?'

'For Chrissakes, stop bleatin'. It's one thirty – we can start to head up the road soon.'

'It's one thirty,' squawked Gloria.

'You tell me the time just once more . . .' snarled Julia, and then looked at the road ahead. 'Oh shit, look at the traffic! It's jammed solid.'

Dolly slowed down, and glanced at the clock on the dashboard. 'We can still make it. We get onto the flyover, it's only about fifteen minutes from there.'

'We're nowhere near the bloody flyover!' yelled Gloria, and Julia reached over and whacked her one. Dolly pulled out and drove alongside the rows of orange cones and roadworks signs. 'Fuckin' hell, you'll get us arrested next,' Gloria screeched. But they made it to the front of the traffic jam, and nudged into the line of cars while an irate driver gave them a V sign and a flow of verbals. Gloria wound down her window. 'We got a pregnant woman here on the way to the hospital, you prick, so *fuck off*.'

The man stared open-mouthed as Dolly pressed on, horn blaring as she bullied her way through the traffic and accelerated towards the Edgware Road.

Ester checked her watch. It was ten minutes to two. She put the car into gear. 'Let's go for it. We wait any longer and you'll have chewed down to your knuckles.'

They drove down Ladbroke Grove, passing the police station on the right. 'Police station,' Angela whispered.

'Thank you, I might not have noticed it,' Ester said, but she drove carefully all the same, not wanting any aggro.

Driving fast from the opposite direction, turning off the Harrow Road, came Dolly.

'It's off to the right,' said Julia. 'If they keep to two o'clock, we'll just catch them.'

Craigh looked at the clock. It was nine minutes to two. Donaldson was sweating now. 'When she rings the door-bell,' Craigh told him, 'you answer it, bring her in here, the bag is open, and all she's got to do is . . .'

Mike turned from the window. He pressed his radio earpiece closer. 'Nothing yet, road's still clear.'

The two officers outside waited, scanning the road in front of them and checking their wing and rear-view mirrors. But the road was empty.

Then it happened. The Range Rover was coming

towards them just as the red Volvo raced in from the opposite direction. They saw the Range Rover stop and Angela get out and then all hell broke loose as the Volvo mounted the pavement, Gloria hanging out of the window. *'Get back, get out of here!'*

The door opened and Angela was hauled bodily into the Volvo, while Julia leapt out, ran towards the Range Rover and jumped aboard. The two cars then roared away. The two officers got out of the patrol car, staring down the road in disbelief as DCI Craigh hurtled out of the house.

'What the fuck is going on?'

'We dunno. Woman ran from one car, driven off in another.'

Craigh clenched his fists in frustration. 'Was it her? *Was it Dolly Rawlins?'*

Mike was at the window. 'What the hell is going on? It was her – it was Dolly Rawlins, for Chrissakes. Why aren't they going after the goddamned car?'

Palmer turned on Mike. 'What the fuck for? Speeding? We dunno if it was her or not.'

Mike ran out of the house. It was a total cock-up and it was at this moment Jimmy Donaldson saw his chance. He saw the stones, he saw Palmer with his back to him, and he was alone. He picked up the heavy glass ashtray, whacked Palmer over the back of the head, picked up the bag of diamonds and then he was out, closing the door behind him.

He let himself out the back, leapt over a fence and took off down the narrow alley running between the houses.

Craigh leaned into the patrol car. He couldn't believe what had happened. They had three digits of the number plate, but the two officers were confused as to what they'd seen.

'We saw a Range Rover, right? Cruised up behind us, I mean, it wasn't a blonde at the wheel, right? It was a brunette. We saw it stop, young kid gets out, sort of walks a few paces, next minute this other fucking car screams up.'

Craigh rubbed his head. 'You see the driver at all?'

The officer pulled at his collar. 'Yeah, it looked like a friggin' car full of women, but one was blonde.'

The second officer peered at the sweating Craigh. 'No, there were two blondes. There was one hanging out the window doin' all the screamin'.'

Craigh breathed in, then told them to see if there was any police car in the vicinity.

'What you want, guv?'

Craigh turned on him in a fury. 'Not this fuckin' mess, for starters. Just see if we can get a full reg on the car.'

'Which one? One with the blondes or the Range Rover?'

The Range Rover was already at the Shepherd's Bush flyover, Julia panting with fear as Ester put her foot down. 'Not too fast, keep in the near lane.'

'What the fuck happened?' Ester bellowed.

Julia was white-faced with fear, hearing sirens now. 'Dolly sussed she was being set up, that's all I know.'

'You're out of your mind!' Gloria screamed, as Dolly drove all the way round the Shepherd's Bush roundabout and started to head back the way they had come. 'You're driving us right back to Ladbroke Grove – you should have gone up on the motorway.'

Dolly said nothing. She turned left onto Ladbroke Grove again and then onto a side street.

'*What* are you *doing*?'

'If they're trying to find us, they won't be looking for us right on his bloody doorstep, will they? I'm going back onto the Harrow Road and then to the station. There's a train at three and I'm gonna be on it.'

Palmer was sitting dabbing his neck with a handkerchief. DCI Craigh was out in one of the cars searching for Donaldson while Mike sat on the stairs, shaking his head in disbelief. Things were now bordering on farce and they knew they were all in deep trouble.

Jimmy Donaldson had no idea he'd risked everything for a bag of glass as he dodged down the alleyways, hugging the pouch bag to his chest. He reached the end of Ladbroke Grove and took a quick look round to see if he was still in the clear. He jogged down Portobello Road, weaving in and out of the stallholders, catching his breath in antique shops. He was making his way towards a cut-through that led onto Harrow Road, where he knew he'd be able to nick a motor easy. They were sometimes being worked on by blokes he knew so he reckoned if he made it there he'd be away.

Dolly pushed Gloria into the back seat of the Volvo as she knew they'd be looking for a middle-aged blonde. Then she dragged Angela out of the car and shoved her into the driving seat. 'Get in and drive.'

Angela had never driven an automatic in her life. Dolly made herself small in the back seat with Gloria. 'Just put the gear into "Drive", Angela, and take it nice and easy. Go up to the end and take a right onto the Harrow Road.'

Dolly sat back, feeling things were going to be all right – until Angela took a left instead of a right, then she almost punched the back of Angela's head.

Donaldson was panting now, feeling like he was going to throw up, having run himself into the ground as he picked his way in and out of the parked cabs and trucks. He saw the car, the door open with the keys inside, and a surge of adrenalin gave him new strength.

As he made for the car, Angela careered down the

alley, terrified that she couldn't control the Volvo, shouting to Dolly that she had never driven an automatic and hadn't even passed her test on an ordinary car.

'Stay fucking calm!' Gloria shouted back. 'Where the hell are we? It's a dead end, Dolly.'

Dolly knew exactly where they were and told Angela to keep going straight ahead. Either side of the road were garages, some with their doors open, mechanics working on vehicles, and no one was paying them any attention. By now they were moving more slowly. As they neared the end of the narrow road and Dolly told Angela to put her foot down, Jimmy Donaldson suddenly appeared from behind a truck. He was looking back over his shoulder, and ran out straight into the Volvo.

The car hit him side on, tossing him up into the air. He rolled across the bonnet and slithered to the ground with a sickening thump. Angela slammed on the brakes, throwing Gloria and Dolly forward in their seats. 'What the bloody hell was that?' Angela wailed.

'You've gone an' hit a bloke, for Chrissakes!' bellowed Gloria. She then screamed as Donaldson, pushing himself to his knees, pressed his face to the window, while clawing at the door.

'Back up,' shouted Dolly. Angela shoved the car into reverse with a shaking hand and, as the car lurched backwards, Donaldson's body disappeared.

'He's under the fucking car,' shrieked Gloria. She

leaned over and rammed the car into 'Drive'. Angela started sobbing hysterically as the car lurched forward. They all felt the hideous bump and heard the crunching sound beneath the wheels.

Hearing the women screaming, two mechanics from a nearby garage looked over. Donaldson lay unmoving in the gutter, his chest crushed.

Dolly leapt out of the car and almost fainted when she recognized Jimmy Donaldson. As she felt his pulse, she saw the black velvet pouch still clutched in his hand. Without missing a beat she snatched it, stuffed it into her pocket, and got back in the car. Neither Gloria nor Angela saw her do it. Both were in a state of shock.

'Get out of here and fast. *Move it, Angela!*' Dolly shouted.

The Volvo's tyres screeched as it hurtled round the corner and disappeared.

By the time DCI Craigh arrived at the scene, Donaldson's body was being lifted onto a stretcher. He quickly ascertained that the bag of diamonds was nowhere to be seen. All he had were useless witnesses who couldn't tell him the make of the car or give a description of the driver. What he did know was that Jimmy Donaldson was dead and no one had seen Dolly Rawlins anywhere near his home. If she had been in the car that killed Jimmy, they had no evidence. They had, as he put it to DI Palmer, fuck all.

*

Dolly made it to the train just in time. She had to run along the platform and opened one of the doors as the train was moving off. She scrambled on, ignoring the shouts of the guards, and hauled Angela after her. They slumped into two vacant seats, heaving for breath. Dolly felt the pouch in her pocket pressing into her stomach. She leaned back, closing her eyes.

'We made it.'

Angela was still panting, scared to death. 'That – that man I ran over.'

Dolly opened her eyes. 'Not your fault – you couldn't stop. Anyway, we've got other things to worry about; this is where we both get arrested for not having tickets.'

She smiled, trying to lighten the mood, but Angela couldn't stop thinking about the collision. She kept seeing that big grey object as it hit the windscreen, kept feeling that hideous bump as she ran over him, not once but twice. She started to cry.

'Pull yourself together, Angela, we don't want anyone to . . . remember us. So I'll sit up front, away from you, all right, love?'

Dolly made her way up the train, slipped into the toilet and held the bag of diamonds tightly to her chest. Whatever else had happened, she'd got them and she'd still make the meeting.

*

Gloria took a scenic route back to the rental garage, after stopping at a car wash to check for any signs of damage or blood on the bumpers – but the car didn't even have a dent. The windscreen wasn't cracked either. The Volvo was a solid piece of machinery, she thought, but her feelings of relief were soon punctured by the realization that they hadn't got the diamonds. By the time she collected her Mini and drove back to the manor, she was feeling thoroughly depressed. She knew she should have stuck with what she knew, and not allowed herself to be swayed by Ester Freeman and her big ideas – especially not with her luck.

At the town hall, Dolly told Angela to see which room the meeting was in while she went into the ladies' and carefully stashed the bag of diamonds on top of one of the old toilet cisterns. If some bastard had set her up, they were bound to come sniffing around at the manor.

She turned as Angela slipped in and whispered, 'They said they're running a bit behind and for you to go into the waiting room outside the boardroom.'

Dolly examined her face in the mirror. Not too bad, she thought. It was only when she tried to put on some lipstick that she realized she was shaking.

Angela was biting her nails as she sat next to Dolly in the waiting room. Ten minutes ticked by, during which two women came in and walked out again, Dolly making a point each time of politely saying, 'Good afternoon.'

Angela suddenly started to cry again.

'I think he was dead, Dolly. I'm sure I killed him.'

Dolly squeezed her hand tightly. 'Yes, I think you did, love,' she said, just as the boardroom doors opened and Mrs Tilly walked out.

'I'm so sorry to have kept you waiting, Mrs Rawlins. Please do come in.'

As the door closed behind them, Angela sniffed and pressed her hand to her mouth. She'd killed that poor man, she'd killed him and she couldn't face it. She pressed her hands to her mouth, then got up and hurried out.

Mike's wife picked up the phone. She could hear someone sobbing on the other end of the line. 'Look, whoever this is, don't keep calling here, do you hear me? Leave us alone.'

'No, please,' Angela begged, 'I've got to talk to Mike – it's urgent.' There was something in her terrified voice that stopped Susan from putting down the receiver. 'Do you have a number he can contact you on? What's your name?'

'It's Angela, it's—' Susan couldn't make out any more because of the sobbing, and then the phone went dead. She called the office but they said Mike was out. Then she called her mother-in-law.

'Is Mike there, Mum?'

'No, love, I'm waiting for him to call. Did he tell you? I'm going to Spain.'

Susan asked Audrey to get Mike to phone her straight away if he called.

'Are you all right, Susan?' Audrey asked, hearing the tension in her voice.

'No, Mum, I'm not. If I ask you something, will you be honest? I mean it, Audrey, I don't want you to lie to me.'

'I won't, love.' Audrey had never heard Susan so agitated.

'I think Mike is seeing someone else. I'm getting hysterical phone calls and then sometimes they just put the receiver down on me.'

'Oh, Mike wouldn't, love. It'll be somethin' to do with his work; he wouldn't carry on.'

Susan clutched the receiver tighter. 'You ever heard him mention a girl called Angela?'

Audrey sighed. The fact was, he'd called an Angela a couple of times from her flat. When she'd asked about her, he'd said she was just a kid he was trying to help out. Maybe he'd been doing a bit more than helping her out. 'Look, I'll talk to him, don't you worry about it. But I think you've got it wrong – I've got to go now, love, but don't you worry.'

Audrey could hear Susan crying and then the phone

went dead. She replaced the receiver, feeling guilty, but the truth was, she had more important things on her mind. She looked at the clock: it was almost five. She crossed her fingers. Dolly Rawlins should have been arrested by now. She went back to packing her clothes, half an ear listening for the phone, while the face of her dead daughter Shirley looked on with that sweet, vague smile from the picture frame.

The women were huddled in the kitchen as Gloria told her side of it, then Ester hers. Julia said nothing. Kathleen looked glum and Connie wanted to cry. 'So, there's no diamonds?' she said.

Ester gave a slow, burning stare. 'That's fucking bright of you to fathom out, Connie. What the hell do you think we've been talking about, a box of Smarties?'

Mr Arthur Crow, the chairman of the board, looked over Dolly Rawlins's forms and listened intently to her answers. She seemed nervous but that was only to be expected. She described the manor and her intentions, how many staff she felt would be required, how many children she could easily accommodate. That section was impressive: she was concise and to the point, saying the grounds were ample, there were stables and a swimming pool, but truthfully that the house was in a poor state of repair.

They now turned to her criminal record and she quickly made it clear that, as she had been convicted of murder, she would be on parole for the rest of her life. She said quietly that she had never been involved in any criminal activity before the shooting of her husband and that it had been at a time when she was emotionally unstable, having been told he was dead, then discovering he was alive and living with another woman who had borne his child. She spoke candidly about the therapy sessions she had been given at Holloway but said she had required no therapy for the past five and a half years.

'I found great solace in working with the young female offenders, especially in the maternity section of the prison. I developed an interest in the group-therapy sessions for the inmates and became a trusty, working with probation officers and therapists, but not as a patient.'

Deirdre gave Dolly small encouraging nods and Mrs Tilly was a constant source of encouragement. The men, however, were offhand and cool, showing much more restraint.

Dolly was asked further questions about whether she would be prepared to work with a foster carer and resident-home advisory officers, and she agreed to be available and prepared to do anything the board suggested that would enable her to open the manor as a home.

'Mrs Rawlins, how are you at this present moment financing the running of the Grange?'

Dolly explained that she had a considerable private income that had enabled her to purchase the manor.

'Do you know the previous owner?' It was slipped in fast.

'No, I do not. I believe her name was Ester Freeman and the place had a very bad reputation. Perhaps that is why I think, and my lawyers agree, I paid a fair price for such a substantial property.'

Eventually, after over an hour and a half of questions and answers with Dolly maintaining her composure, she was asked if she would allow a visit within the next few days to assess the property. She said they were free to come at any time – in fact, the sooner the better. Mr Crow ended the meeting by saying that everything she had said would be assessed and obviously her past checked into in some detail. They thanked her for her honesty and wished her every success.

She walked out confidently, and was further gratified by Mrs Tilly's light touch on her arm as she left. 'Thank you so much for coming in to see us at such short notice, and sorry again for keeping you waiting.'

Dolly returned to the manor by taxi. At the level crossing they were held up for almost ten minutes. The cab driver shook his head and turned to the back seat. 'Sorry about this, it's the mail train. Holds us up for

sometimes ten, twelve minutes. One night it was fifteen.'
The gates opened, and they drove on down the narrow
country lane back to the manor.

Dolly breezed in, all smiles, saying how well the meeting
had gone, trailed by a downcast Angela. She shut the
back door and tossed her handbag onto the table. 'I don't
know about anyone else but I'm starving. Who's on the
dinner tonight?'

Ester stared at her in disbelief. 'Is that all you've got to
say? I'm glad everything went well for *you*!'

The police cars moved silently up the driveway, two
officers from Thames Valley in front, followed by DCI
Craigh, accompanied by DS Mike Withey with one uniformed driver. Craigh was first out. He walked up the
manor steps, sidestepping the sacks of cement, and waited
as more local police moved around to the back yard to enter
from there. Then he radioed in that he was about to enter.

He gave one soft knock and murmured it was the
police and that they had a warrant to search the premises.
He then stepped back as the two Thames Valley officers
banged on the door. They didn't need much force as it
was only on the latch, and they burst into the hallway,
Craigh holding up the warrant.

'We have a warrant to search the premises. This is
the police.'

Kathleen ran up the stairs onto the first landing and legged it out onto a low roof at the back. The other women ran in all directions, only Dolly remaining unflustered as she picked up the kettle to put it on the stove. Angela curled into a ball, making herself as small as she could, terrified that they had come to arrest her for the hit-and-run.

Dolly put a firm hand on her shoulder. 'Angela, keep your mouth shut. Just give them your name, nothing more. Understand me?'

Gloria pulled at Ester's arm. 'What the fuck do we do?'

Ester shrugged her away. 'Nothing. There's nothing here.'

Gloria was white-faced. 'Yes, there is,' she hissed. 'We put the bloody guns in the cellar.'

Ester froze, but could do nothing as they were sur-rounded by police and herded into the drawing room.

Craigh looked at Dolly as she calmly opened a tea caddy. 'I am Detective Chief Inspector Craigh.'

Dolly smiled. 'Dorothy Rawlins.' She held out her hand for him to shake.

'Do you mind if I talk to you first? Do you want to see the warrant?'

'Of course. I'd also like to know what this is about.'

Craigh passed her the warrant and watched her study it. He looked into the hallway towards Mike. 'I'll take

Mrs Rawlins's statement first, then the others'. Get their names, addresses, you know the drill.'

He looked back at Dolly. 'My men will begin searching the entire house and outbuildings.'

She nodded, seemingly still carefully reading the warrant. He waited patiently.

The women wandered around the drawing room; Gloria was now crying along with Angela. Julia nudged Ester. 'What the hell are they getting so upset about?'

Ester's face was tight with anger. 'There's an arsenal of weapons down in the sauna. Gloria's husband's guns, three bags full of them.'

Julia looked at Gloria, stunned. 'Are you serious?' But before Ester could say anything more Mike Withey walked in.

'I'll need all your names, dates of birth, present and past addresses.'

Behind Mike, the women could see the officers moving up the stairs, while others headed down to the cellar. No one spoke. All they could do now was wait for the police to find the weapons.

Chapter 8

Craigh sat with his notebook open as Dolly drank a cup of tea. She hadn't offered him one. She had admitted that she knew James 'Jimmy' Donaldson, and seemed shocked when told he was dead.

'Dead? But he can't be. I only spoke to him yesterday. I met up with him a few days ago.' She sat down with a heavy sigh.

'Would you mind telling me why you met Mr Donaldson?'

'He was keeping something for me. I've been in prison, you see, and, oh, this is a shock . . .'

Craigh tapped his pen on the table. 'What was he holding for you, Mrs Rawlins?'

'Well, they were nothing to look at, really. You wouldn't even think they were valuable, but they are, they're worth a lot of money.'

He leaned close. 'What exactly, Mrs Rawlins?'

'They used to be in my front garden at Totteridge. Gnomes – two Victorian garden gnomes. Not the bright plastic things but proper old carved stone ones. Jimmy was holding them for me until I got out. I called to see if he still had them and we arranged for me to collect them today, as a matter of fact.'

Craigh wrote down every word, gritting his teeth. 'Did you in fact collect them from Mr Donaldson?'

'I couldn't get away because I had a very important meeting at the town hall.'

'What time?'

Dolly said she'd been at the town hall from three fifteen until after five – shortly before they had arrived, in fact: she had been there for an assessment interview.

'Can anyone verify that, Mrs Rawlins?'

'Oh yes.'

Craigh dug the pen in deeply as he wrote one name after the other. He had a terrible sinking feeling in the pit of his stomach that he had been well and truly stitched up.

The officers searched every room, lifted the floorboards, opened cupboards and cases. They went into the attic, they were out in the stables. Kathleen remained stuck on the roof, half hidden by the gables, not moving a muscle. For eight hours, fifteen men searched the grounds, the swimming pool and the cellars.

Finally Kathleen crawled back into the room she'd escaped from and fell asleep under the bed. The police were now concentrating on the sauna and steam room. The women waited, expecting any moment for the shout to go up but it never came. They smelt bacon being cooked and, to their amazement, Dolly walked in with a tray of bacon butties. Gloria was about to blurt out to Dolly how much trouble they were in, but Dolly shoved a sandwich into her hand. 'Eat it and say nothing.'

Gloria stuffed a big bite of the sandwich into her mouth and sat down.

Craigh was picking through the sauna when Mike joined him. 'They're searching the grounds now, but so far nothing.'

Craigh felt knackered and, even worse, foolish. 'She's got about eight or nine people giving her alibis. She was at the ruddy social services.'

Mike was as tired out as Craigh and couldn't work out if this was good news or bad.

'This all stinks, you know that, don't you?' Craigh started pacing up and down. 'The Super's gonna have a seizure about the whole cock-up – Donaldson was in our custody.'

'I'm sorry,' Mike muttered.

'You're sorry. Jesus Christ, *sorry*? Have you any idea what kind of a mess we're in? Donaldson dead, no sign of the diamonds ...' Craigh hesitated and then licked his lips. 'Look, until we've sorted this, keep schtum about those stones. I never put it in the record sheets so maybe we can—'

'Fine by me.'

Mike nodded, his brain ticking away. He concentrated on looking as glum as Craigh obviously felt, while he thanked God nothing had been found. He was off the hook.

Dolly watched the London mob, as she referred to Craigh and Withey, leaving, then let the curtain fall back into place. 'Right,' she yawned. 'I'm off to bed.'

'How the hell can you sleep?' Ester said.

Dolly shrugged. 'I've got a lot of thinking to do.'

Gloria was pulling at a piece of sodden tissue. 'Did you move them, Dolly? Did you?'

She gave her a hard look. 'What the hell do you think, you stupid idiot? Of course I bloody moved them – and a good thing too or we'd all have been arrested. I've been waiting for you to mention them.'

'I got nothing to do with them,' said Ester.

'But you bloody knew they was in the house.'

Ester turned away. It was always the same: instead of being grateful to Dolly, she just said nothing, whereas Gloria would have kissed her feet. But none of them was prepared for Dolly's next admission, dropping the line in quietly, with a little smile. 'I also got the diamonds but I'm not talking about it yet. Like I said, I need to sleep, get my head straight.'

'You got them?' Ester said in wonder.

'Yes, Ester, I got them but they're not here. What is here smells, because someone tipped off the police. Somebody here's grassing on me – *one of you*. One of you hates me enough to get me put back inside and I'm going to find out which one of you it is.'

She walked out, slamming the door. No one spoke, not quite believing what they had heard her say, hardly daring to believe they still had a chance of a cut of the diamonds. Then Gloria said, 'Grassin'? What she friggin' talkin' about? None of us'd do it, I mean, we want them diamonds as much as she does. She's nuts if she thinks it's one of us!'

Angela started to cry again and ran out of the room before anyone could tell her off, bumping into Kathleen, who was creeping down the stairs as the last of the Thames Valley police drove away. They all looked as she walked into the drawing room.

'Where the hell have you been?' asked Ester.

Dolly couldn't sleep. She stared at a stain on the wall, wondering. Who would hate her enough to want to put her back inside? Because that's what it came down to. If she'd been picked up with the diamonds, virtually holding Donaldson's hand, the cops would have had her. Even if they couldn't pin the old robbery on her, they'd have had her for fencing the stolen diamonds. Either way, with her out on parole, she'd have been back in a cell straight away and with no hope of bail. Was it just that dirty little conman, Jimmy? If it was, then he'd got his just deserts, but something inside her said there had to be more to it than that. Harry had taught her, 'Always remember, sweetheart, it takes two to tango. One leads, the other follows.' So who was Jimmy's dance partner? If it was one of the women she would find out and God help them.

The next morning Dolly left the house and drove straight to the town hall. She hurried into the ladies' and found the pouch bag exactly where she had left it. She kissed it with relief. She then got down, straightened her skirt and slipped out, bumping into a surprised Mrs Tilly in the corridor.

'Mrs Rawlins?'

'I was just passing. I know there's no possibility of you having any answers for me yet but I just wanted to ask you how I did. Was I all right?'

'Yes, you were. I thought you handled yourself very well but it'll be some time before we have any definite news. I'll let you know as soon as I hear anything.'

'Thank you. I really appreciate all your help.'

As Dolly hurried out, Mrs Tilly went in to speak to Mr Crow.

'You know, Mrs Rawlins is so keen, I think we should push forward an on-site visit. I worry she may spend too much money without approval and I don't want her to waste her savings.'

He looked up from his diary. 'Well, we'll have to get some appraisals from her probation officer and the prison authorities. And we're nowhere near ready even to discuss the project yet.'

'Well, I would just like us to inspect the Manor House. She was so enthusiastic.'

He smiled, flattening down his few strands of hair. 'I'll see what I can do. If we're visiting anyone near the location we can possibly have a look over the place as well. I was also impressed by her. I very much doubt if she will ever be allowed access to very young children – not enough experience – but she might be good with the older children, the problem ones particularly. Leave it with me.'

Mrs Tilly smiled and left the office. She doubted if Mr Crow would show Dolly Rawlins any favours. He was a stickler for rules and regulations, after all. But if he was going to make an exception for anyone, she thought it might be Dolly.

Dolly stopped at a phone booth and called Tommy Malin. She asked if he was still in business – unlike

Jimmy Donaldson. They had a few laughs, and she said she would be around later in the afternoon as she had something that might interest him. She then returned to the manor. As she came in she saw Angela on the telephone. 'Who you calling, love?'

Angela spun round. 'Oh – my mum. I've not told her where I am.'

'Well don't, and don't make private calls – that goes for all of you. Fewer people who know what's going on here the better.'

'Okay.'

'I'm going to London. You want to come with me?' Angela nodded. 'Good, in about an hour, then.'

The others, who had overheard the conversation from the kitchen, whispered and nudged each other, sure that Dolly was off to fence the stones. Ester gave them all a quiet talking-to: they were to show a lot more willing, they were to get out to that vegetable patch and look like they were working and loving every minute of it. They got to their feet, went out and began to trudge around with wheelbarrows, spades and rakes. When Dolly and Angela left in the local taxi, they appeared to be too intent on their labour even to notice them go.

As the cab passed them, Dolly laughed. 'Amazing what a bit of incentive can do, isn't it?'

'I don't understand,' Angela said.

'Well, they all know I'm going to fence the diamonds

this morning and they all want a slice so "Let's show Dolly how hard we're working!"'

Angela very nearly smiled. 'Oh, yes, I see what you mean.'

Mike had waited after Angela put down the receiver. He was hoping she would call back right away but after half an hour he gave up. It had unnerved him to be told that Dolly Rawlins had the diamonds but there was nothing he could do about it. If he told Craigh, he could just feel himself sinking deeper into the hole he'd dug for himself.

Susan walked in with a bag of groceries. 'Hi, I didn't wake you when I went out, did I?'

'No, I'm up. I've had something to eat. I was just going to go, actually.'

'Oh, were you? You stayed out all night. Surely they can't expect you to work today?'

He sighed. 'Yes, they can.'

'There was another call from your girlfriend yester-day – I tried to contact you, she seemed upset.'

'What?'

'She was crying, in a terrible state.' She stared at him, waiting. 'She said her name was Angela.'

'I heard you,' he snapped.

'What's going on with her, then?'

He took a deep breath. 'She's a tart, sweetheart, a

young kid I helped out a while back when I was on Vice. Now sometimes she acts as an informant. There is nothing going on between us, it's business, all right? *Is that all right with you?'*

'I don't like tarts having your home phone number or ringing me up screaming and yelling. *Is that all right with you?'* Susan went into the kitchen. He dithered, knowing he should talk to her, try and straighten things out, but instead he grabbed his car keys and left without a word.

Sitting in the back of a taxi heading for Tommy Malin's address, Dolly took Angela's hand. 'Don't you worry about that hit-and-run. Gloria said there wasn't a mark on the car and if they'd got anything on you – on any of us – we'd have been pulled in last night.' Angela clutched Dolly's hand tightly, desperate to believe her. 'Will you want to stay on and help me?' Angela nodded. 'I'll be able to pay you a decent wage and you could even have cookery classes. Would you like that?'

Angela sniffed. 'Yes. I would.'

She wanted to tell Dolly about Mike, about everything. She liked her so much, felt protected by her – but how *could* she tell her? And now, with that poor man she'd run over, it was all so complicated. She wanted to talk to Mike, needed to ask his advice.

The cab headed towards Elephant and Castle and then turned off down a small one-way road, stopping outside a paint yard. Dolly got out, saying, 'You wait here, love, I shouldn't be too long.'

Angela watched as Dolly knocked on the door and disappeared inside the yard.

A young kid in filthy overalls pointed Dolly towards the office and then re-joined his colleagues stripping down some pine furniture.

'Dolly Rawlins,' wheezed Tommy Malin, leaning against the doorframe.

'Hello, Tommy.' They shook hands and he gestured for her to go in ahead of him. He waved at the workmen and closed the door.

'I'll put the kettle on.'

'That'd be nice,' she said, taking in the cheap desk, rows of bulging and dented filing cabinets and the massive cast-iron safe. Dolly eased herself onto a newspaper-filled chair. She looked over the equally cluttered desk: the scales, the rows of diamond cutters and pinchers, and rolls of velvet cloth, the only indication that perhaps Mr Malin's paint and pine-stripping factory was also used for other purposes. Tommy Malin would deal in literally anything he could turn round fast. He was famous for his high percentage and his 'no risk' attitude. He would deal in hot stuff but always insisted on a long chilling period. That was why he was so wealthy and had so far avoided arrest. He was very, very careful.

*

The women had done a half-day's work. Rods had been fixed up, more seeds sown, and the rubbish was now tipped into a skip left for them by the builder. Big John was getting a bit edgy; it was almost payday, he'd used up all his savings to buy the materials, and still Mrs Rawlins hadn't given him the down payment. He'd seen all the women working out in the garden but Mrs Rawlins wasn't among them. He'd even looked for her inside the house, but she wasn't there, either.

Connie was testing the sauna temperature when he asked if he could have a word. She turned and gave him a wonderful smile that made him flush.

'I'm sorry to bother you but is Mrs Rawlins around?'

'No, I'm sorry, she's gone into London. Can I help at all?'

He could feel his cheeks burning. 'Well, it was just we had an arrangement and Mrs Rawlins is a bit behind with the first instalment, you see, and I have to pay the men, pay for the materials and—'

'Oh, she's gone to get some money this afternoon.' Connie gave another beaming smile. 'You couldn't have a look at the sauna for me, could you? I think I've got it working but I'm not sure.'

She brushed against him as they went into the small Swedish sauna hut. John checked the temperature dials and the coals. 'Do you like it hot?' he asked seriously.

'Oh yes, as hot as you can give it to me.' He flushed

again but she seemed to be concentrating on the temperature gauge. 'Do you work out?'

He stepped back – he couldn't deal with her closeness. She was the most glamorous woman he had ever been this close to in his entire life. 'Yes, there's a good local gym, very well equipped.'

'Ah, I thought you did, I can always tell. You've got marvellous shoulders.'

Now the heat of the sauna was making him sweat but he didn't want to go. He found himself automatically flexing everything, even tightening his bum cheeks.

John breathed in gratefully as she opened the sauna door. He was getting dizzy.

'Thanks for your help, John.'

When Connie joined the others, they were sweating and filthy. 'Sauna's working, it's really hot. Do any of you want to work out first?'

She received a barrage of abuse in reply – as if after all the digging and wheeling stuff in barrows they needed to work out! All they wanted was a cold drink and a long afternoon in the sauna.

Tommy's wheezing breath and halitosis were overpowering. The drawn blinds, the bolted door and the hissing gas fire made Dolly feel light-headed. She took off her coat. Tommy's thick stubby fingers began to unfurl the cord round the pouch bag. He pulled it open and laid it out flat.

'Is this some kind of joke?'

'No. Why?'

'I just made these up for somebody.'

'What?'

He turned his lamp out and pushed his eye-glass onto his forehead. 'You didn't pay a bundle for these, did you, sweetheart?'

'What are you talking about?'

'I made them up. They're glass, good settings ... I mean, I did spend quite a few hours—'

'*You made these?*'

Tommy stared at Dolly, whose face was now chalk white.

'Who for, Tommy?'

He wouldn't usually have said – clients are clients, and he was always a man to keep his mouth shut – but he had a feeling she wasn't going to leave his office until he told her.

'I nearly went back inside for this crap, Tommy, so you tell me who ordered you to make them up.'

Mike knew something was up the moment the message came over the tannoy for him to go into DCI Craigh's office. Craigh looked up at him as he knocked sheepishly and entered. He pointed to the chair in front of his desk and told Mike to sit down. Mike could see a stack of files on his desk, including one with Dolly Rawlins's name printed across it. 'Right, let's go from the top and don't bullshit me.'

'I don't follow.'

'I think you do. I am in it right up to my fucking ears over this Donaldson business. I've got the Super, the prison authorities, Donaldson's wife, his parole officer, all breathing fire all over me so let's start at the beginning, shall we? How did you know that Rawlins had bought the Manor House?'

'My informant.'

'Oh yeah? Which one?'

Mike explained about Angela, how he'd busted her along with Ester Freeman.

'You booked her, did you?'

'No, she was never charged. She wasn't on the game, she was just serving drinks at the house for the tarts and their punters.'

'So she told you all about Rawlins, and her buying the manor?'

'Yes.'

'So what about the diamonds? Same source? You said it was a kid in Brixton with Donaldson. That's the only name I've got down as an informant.'

'Yes, that's true. When he told me, I contacted Angela and that's how I knew all the women were staying there.'

Craigh pushed his chair back and walked around the

office, hands stuffed in his pockets. 'Anything else? I mean, is there anything else you've not told me?' Mike licked his lips nervously as Craigh leaned down so his face was almost touching Mike's. 'What about that diamond robbery, Mike? You want to tell me about that? Better still, tell me about Shirley Miller.' Mike closed his eyes. Craigh prodded him and he flinched. 'This was personal, wasn't it?' Mike nodded. 'Your sister was killed on that diamond raid.'

'Yes.'

'Not on your original application form, Mike. There is no mention that you even had a fucking sister.'

Mike gave a half-smile. 'I didn't reckon it'd look good on my CV, guv.'

'Don't you fucking joke with me, this isn't funny. Let's go from the top again. Your sister worked with Dolly Rawlins and—'

Mike interrupted. 'She used her, she manipulated her, she was only twenty-one, a beauty queen and . . .'

Craigh returned to his desk. Mike was close to breaking down, his voice faltering. 'I didn't have all that much to do with Shirley. I was in the Army, stationed in Germany, when she was killed. Then when I joined the Met it was, like, all in the past, but my mum, er ...' He was floundering, trying not to implicate Audrey. The sweat was pouring off him. 'I saw her grave, right? And I felt guilty that I'd never come home, never even sent flowers, and ... my mum was always on and on about Dolly Rawlins. I'm sorry, I am really sorry ...'

Mike sniffed, trying to hold on to his emotions because he wasn't acting any more. The more he tried to explain about Shirley, the more her face kept flashing into his mind and in the end he bowed his head. 'I loved her a lot. She was a lovely kid.' Craigh remained silent, staring at him. 'I know Rawlins instigated that robbery, I know it.'

'Mike, son, Rawlins was sent down for murder, she killed her husband. It was never proved that she had anything to do with that diamond heist.'

'But she had.'

'You don't have any proof.' Craigh pursed his lips. 'Listen to what I'm saying, Mike. Dolly Rawlins was *never* charged with anything to do with that heist. There was never a shred of evidence to link her to it. But your sister was no angel, her husband was a known villain, so don't give me all this whiter-than-white Mother Teresa stuff. All I know is you instigated a full-scale operation from personal motives, drawing me, DI Palmer, the whole team in on a crazy caper that has landed us in shit, making us all look like prize fucking idiots.'

'I know she was going for those diamonds,' Mike insisted.

'*No, you don't.* You don't know anything. It's all been supposition because *you* had a personal grudge against Rawlins.'

'She got away with murder.'

'No she didn't. She served her sentence, and as far as being implicated in the Donaldson business is concerned, she has an alibi, and a very strong one, saying she wasn't anywhere near Ladbroke Grove yesterday.'

Mike frowned. 'We had any joy tracing the car?'

'What car? How many red Rovers or Volvos are there in London?'

Mike remained silent as Craigh jangled the change in his pockets.

'We've got Traffic running around like blue-arsed flies – they always love a challenge. But we got nothing from the road where Donaldson got hit, we've not got one decent eyewitness. In fact we've got bugger all. But we do have a nasty, dirty mess that I've got to clear up.'

'I'm sorry.'

'I hope to Christ you are. And from now on you stay clear of this Rawlins bitch or I'll have you back to wearing a big hat in seconds flat, understand me?'

'Yes, sir.'

'Now piss off and I'll see if I can iron all this out.'

Craigh watched Mike walk out with his head bent. Picking up Rawlins's file, he stared at her harsh expression in the mug shots and began to flick through her record sheet. He put in a call to the Aylesbury social services to double-check one more time that Rawlins was, as she had stated, being interviewed by the board members.

*

Angela knew something was very wrong when Dolly walked stiffly back to the taxi. She opened the door and got in. 'Go back to the manor – get the train home.'

'Aren't you coming with me?'

'No. Just get on your way. I've got someone to see.'

'Well, don't you need a lift?'

'No, I want to be on my own for a while.'

Dolly passed over a ten-pound note and walked off down the road as Angela directed the cab driver to take her to Marylebone Station.

Mike let himself in and called out to Susan, but the house was silent. He checked the time, assuming she was collecting the kids. He sat down in the hall, knowing he'd had a narrow escape. The phone rang and he jumped.

Angela was at the station in a phone booth. She was relieved when Mike answered but shocked when he yelled at her never to call his home again.

'Well, I needed to speak to you. I'm in London, I came here with Dolly. She got the diamonds, Mike, she had them with her.'

Mike stood up, trying to keep his voice calm. 'You sure? Where is she now?'

Angela told him where she had been, and then Mike said he had to go, he couldn't talk any more. His head felt as if it was blowing apart. If Dolly Rawlins had the diamonds then she had to have run over Jimmy Donaldson, and she had to know by now the diamonds were fakes. It seemed that any way he moved he just sank in deeper and deeper into the mud. There was one thing in his favour: she wouldn't go to the law. But he knew one place she would go and his panic went into overdrive. He hoped to Christ his mother was out of the country. He grabbed the phone and dialled her number.

Angela sat on the station platform. She had tried to call Mike again but the number was engaged. She kept trying but it was constantly busy. She was near to tears, sure he'd taken it off the hook. There was something else she had to tell him: she'd missed two periods.

Audrey picked up the phone and Mike started yelling before she'd even said hello. 'She knows about Tommy. She's been to see him about the diamonds this afternoon.'

'Who?'

'Who the hell do you think? Dolly Rawlins. She got the diamonds then went to Tommy Malin.'

Audrey's legs were like jelly. 'I've got me ticket, but I don't leave until tomorrow.'

Mike rubbed his chin. 'You'd better go tonight.'

'You think she'll come here?'

He closed his eyes. 'Look, the best thing you can do is go away, just clear out.'

Audrey burst into tears and he yelled at her to pull herself together. He said he'd see if he could come round later, and hung up.

She sat for a moment, still cradling the phone before shakily going back to her packing. Half an hour later the doorbell rang shrilly and Audrey dropped her case as she ran to the door. She thought it would be Mike but when she swung the door open she froze.

'Hello, Audrey. It's Dolly – Dolly Rawlins.'

Audrey forced a smile. 'Good heavens! So you're out then, are you?'

'Yes. You going to ask me in?'

Audrey swallowed and held the door wider.

Dolly walked past her, straight into the sitting room. The first thing she saw was the big eight-by-ten colour photograph of Shirley. She reached out, touched it, and laid it face down on the sideboard. Then she spotted the passport and plane ticket. 'Going away?'

Audrey could hardly breathe. She gestured to the half-packed suitcases in her bedroom. 'Just to Brighton, to see a friend for the weekend.'

'Taking a lot of gear for just a weekend, aren't you?' Audrey flushed as Dolly held up her passport. 'Won't be needing this then, will you?'

Audrey's eyes almost popped out of her head as Dolly slipped it into her pocket. 'Why did you do that?'

Dolly sat down on the settee, unbuttoning her coat. 'Because, Audrey, we've got to talk. Sit down.'

Audrey moved to a hard-backed chair and perched on the edge of the seat.

'How long have you been out?'

Dolly gave an icy smile. 'I bet you know the exact minute. Come on, Audrey, how much did you get for the diamonds?'

She knew it was pointless to deny she'd taken them. 'It's not the way it looks.'

'I'm all ears.'

Audrey gulped. 'Well, when I read that Jimmy Donaldson had been arrested—'

Dolly interrupted, 'You went round and collected. But you never thought to contact me, did you?'

'Well, it was too risky, wasn't it?'

'How much did you get?'

'Not a lot.' Audrey cleared her throat.

'How much?'

'Four hundred and fifty thousand.'

Dolly leaned back and gave a short humourless laugh. 'Don't mess me around. *How much?*'

Audrey began to blubber, swearing on her life that was all she got, and said Dolly could even check it out with Frank Richmond.

'Frank Richmond? You fenced them through him, that cheap bastard? Why didn't you fence them with Tommy?'

'I didn't think – I was scared – I mean, they were here in the flat.'

Dolly leaned back and closed her eyes. 'Eight years I waited, Audrey, eight years . . .'

'Shirley's been dead eight years,' Audrey said. Then she got even more scared as Dolly went rigid, her eyes shut tight, hands clenched. 'I've only got a few thousand cash I can give you. I put the bulk of it in Spain.'

'Spain?'

'I bought a villa and . . . it was all done in such a hurry because I was terrified I'd be nicked.'

'I was, Audrey. I did almost nine years for killing Harry and right now I'd do ten for you. You get me my share and I want it by tomorrow.'

'But I haven't got it.'

'*Then get it!* And when you have, call me. This is my number.' Dolly opened her bag and scrawled her phone number. She stood up to pass it to her, leaning in close, her face almost touching Audrey's. 'Until I get it, I'll hold your passport. You call me by tomorrow or, like I said, I'll shop you, go down for you and don't think for a second I don't mean it.'

Mike listened in stunned silence as Audrey told him about Dolly's visit. 'I got to get money, Mike, or she'll shop me.'

Mike could feel that mud turning into cement round his ankles now. 'Does she know about me?'

'She thinks it was just me. Mike, I got until tomorrow to get the money.'

'What the fuck do you want me to do?'

'I'll need the money I put in the kids' building society savings accounts.'

'*What*? Are you telling me some of that cash is in *my kids' accounts*?' Audrey started sobbing. He couldn't make any sense of what she was saying. 'Mum, get in a cab and come round. Now.'

Mr Crow looked out of the window as he drove up the Manor House driveway. Mrs Tilly sat in the back seat with Mr Simms, another member of the board.

'There's a lot of land. A wonderful place for kids,' he observed.

They drove slowly up to the front door, where workmen's tools were lying around.

'Looks like work has already started,' mused Mr Crow, looking up at the scaffolding.

They got out and looked over the grounds again before walking to the front door. Mrs Tilly had wanted to warn Dolly of their arrival, but they had been to visit another foster family and only just decided to make an on-site visit to the manor.

As the door was open they all entered the house. Mrs

Tilly called out for Dolly and, receiving no reply, peered into the lounge. 'It's huge. I had no idea it was such a big property,' she said.

'Hello? Anyone at home?' Mr Crow called as he looked into the kitchen. The others followed him and stood in the doorway, impressed by the size of the old-fashioned kitchen. They were about to leave the leaflets and documents they had brought on the hall table when they heard the screams and laughter from the cellar.

Kathleen tried the first shower but nothing came out except a low rumbling from the pipes. She banged the pipes with a shoe as Gloria came out of the sauna. 'Showers aren't working,' Kathleen said, grinning when she saw the hosepipe. 'How about bein' hosed down, shall we try that?'

Gloria pulled a face. 'Forget it. I'm gonna have a bath in me own room.' She hitched a towel round her and wandered out, heading up the cellar stairs. Mr Crow and his party were just coming out of the dining room when she appeared. She took one look, shrieked and dived back down to the cellar.

'Was that Mrs Rawlins?' Mr Crow asked.

Mrs Tilly shook her head on her way to the cellar door. She called again for Dolly but could hear only more shrieks from below.

Connie, stark naked, had her hands up as Kathleen

turned the hosepipe on her full blast. Gloria yelled for her to switch it off but Kathleen pointed the hose at her just as the three visitors appeared in the doorway, spraying them with water as the women screamed and yelled like schoolgirls. There was a lot of fumbling for towels as Gloria shot out past them.

Mrs Tilly was red-faced with embarrassment as she opened the sauna door. She gasped and slammed it shut.

'I think we should leave.' She hurried out, appalled at what she had just seen: Ester and Julia, both naked, locked in each other's arms.

Ester grabbed her towel and ran out after them as they disappeared up the cellar stairs. 'Just a minute! *Wait!* Wait a minute.'

But they couldn't get out fast enough.

Ester called down the stairs to Julia, 'I think they were from the social services. Better not mention this to Dolly.'

It was getting dark when Angela appeared. When they saw her alone the women downed tools and asked her where Dolly was.

'I don't know, she sent me home.'

'Shit!' Ester marched over. 'Where did she go? She's coming back, isn't she?' she demanded, her heart sinking. Would Dolly just up, take the cash and leave them all here? She went into Dolly's room. All her belongings were there, including the deeds of the house, so she felt a little easier.

By the time Dolly did come back, a few hours later, the women were all having supper. When she walked in, they all started talking at once about how much work they had been doing, how they loved the house, but slowly their conversation petered out as Dolly chucked the pouch onto the table.

'Take a look. They're worthless, glass, all of them.'

They fingered the glittering stones, before looking at Dolly in confusion.

'There's no money, so you all get a cut of nothing.'

Kathleen picked up one of the biggest stones, holding it in her pudgy hand, then pressed it against her cheek. It felt cold but quickly warmed up. She hurled it against the side of the Aga where it shattered into tiny fragments. 'Fucking glass, all right.'

Each one of them would have liked to smash something, anything, as their initial confusion turned to anger, their dreams shattered just like the fake diamond. Gradually their anger subsided and a dark depression hung in the air. Dolly slowly sat down and picked up a piece of bread, picking bits off it as she looked from one crestfallen face to another. 'So, will you be staying on, Ester?'

'Well, I've got to admit it, Dolly, I've never been one for kids so I guess I'm out of here.'

'What about you, Julia?'

Julia shrugged her shoulders, then looked at Ester. 'I guess I'll leave with Ester. That's not to say I don't love this place because I do but—'

Dolly interrupted, looking at Connie. 'What about you?'

Connie flushed. 'Well, to be honest, I know I've got this problem with Lennie and I need a place to lie low for a while, but as a long-term thing I want to start off my career proper, you know, get an agent and . . .' She trailed off, head bent, not able to meet Dolly's eyes.

Kathleen coughed. 'I'll stay put with you, love. I need a place, I got nowhere else.'

Angela reached out and touched Dolly's hand. 'I'll stay too. I'm sure we can . . .'

Dolly held Angela's hand tightly, as Gloria pushed back her chair. 'I'll be here for a few weeks.' Dolly looked up at her, surprised. 'You got Eddie's gear some place and we'll have to sort something out about that.'

'I see,' Dolly said quietly. 'Well, at least I know where I stand. So, those of you that are going, pack up and leave. It'll save on food bills. Goodnight.'

Dolly stared at her reflection in the dressing-table mirror. She calculated that with the money from Audrey she might still be able to pull off something. It might even be better that it had worked out this way – at least she knew who she could trust, now that she'd found out it was Audrey, poor Shirley Miller's mother, who'd grassed on her.

Chapter 9

Dolly had only just come down to breakfast when John asked to speak to her. He was obviously angry: the men wanted paying; he wanted paying. She had successfully put off the first instalment but now it was Friday and there was still no cash.

Guiltily, Dolly said she was having problems releasing the cash but assured him that he would have it by the following morning.

John didn't like the sound of it, but what could he do? His workers were less stoical about it, immediately downing tools and walking off the site, saying they would come back when he paid up.

The house, with the scaffolding and debris surrounding the grounds, looked in an even more dilapidated condition than before. Loose tiles had been thrown from the roof, the chimneys were still at a dangerous angle, windows were out in some rooms, sections of the front of the house had no plaster, leaving the rough old bricks exposed. It was a depressing sight, but Dolly didn't let it dampen her spirits: not only was some money coming her way, but she had impressed the social services.

Audrey, in a state of nerves matched only by her son's, gathered all the money she could lay her hands on. At least Dolly still had no knowledge of Mike's part and, thankfully for him, neither did the police. DCI Craigh had played down Mike's part to the Chief and the fact that the police had succeeded in tracing the stolen gems at Donaldson's antique shop had been swept under the carpet.

Traffic, however, had been pressured to trace the car that killed Donaldson and now, with the incentive to pull out all the stops, they really went to work. They had only a part registration and a vague description of the vehicle, but they checked on paint colour co-ordination with both Rover and Volvo companies, their computers triggering further developments as they began slowly to narrow down the make and year of the vehicle. All they required was time.

Julia knew that she would be in deep trouble if she returned to London. But Ester was set on leaving: 'You do what the hell you like.'

Julia had flounced out of the house and taken herself off to the local pub. She ordered a double Scotch on the rocks and leaned on the bar. Across the room, seated at one of the bay windows, was Norma Hastings, wearing jodhpurs and a hacking jacket. Norma looked at Julia curiously from behind her newspaper. Norma was an attractive woman, thick red hair, a pleasant round face and obviously fit: her cheeks had that ruddy glow. In comparison, Julia looked pale, her skinny frame mannish and her long, wiry brown hair like an unruly mop-head. Norma continued to watch her, pretending to read the paper, until she could not be bothered to hide her interest any longer and tossed the paper aside. She reckoned she was right about the gangly woman at the bar – it was rare that she wasn't. It was also clear she was unhappy, ordering one double Scotch after another, knocking them back in one gulp, then staring at the polished wood counter. As she dug into her pockets to count out the cash to pay the barman, Norma also couldn't help noticing her perfect, tight arse in her skin-tight trousers.

As Julia's boots were mud-spattered, Norma reckoned it would be a good opener to ask if she liked to ride – horses, of course, not herself; at least not yet. She wasn't often so blatant about it – in her job she couldn't be. If the Metropolitan Police knew that one of their mounted officers was gay ... she could only imagine the snide cracks. She'd had enough of them just being a woman, without them knowing she was a lesbian as well.

Norma decided to go for it and walked towards the bar, but her confidence slipped as Julia turned to her. She had not expected such dark, angry eyes. 'Hello, I'm Norma Hastings.' She put out her hand.

'Are you now. Good for you,' said Julia sarcastically.

Norma was undeterred. 'Can I buy you a drink?'

'Why not? Double Scotch.'

An hour later, Julia's cheeks were as flushed as Norma's, not from fresh air but from all the alcohol. She felt really very tipsy as the two climbed over a gate and into a field with a couple of grazing horses.

'She's called Helen of Troy and if you can stable her, I'll provide the feed. It's just that I've got Caper and he's a bit of a handful.' Norma pointed to a three-year-old stallion and then smiled at the quietly grazing Helen of Troy.

Julia pressed her cheek against Helen's nose. 'She's beautiful,' she whispered.

'Well, I even put an advert in the local papers but I've had no offers yet. I was going to let the local riding school have her – she's still got a lot of life in her. '

Julia was still plastered as she wove her way along the manor's drive. She wasn't alone. Dolly looked out from the drawing-room window. 'Oh my Gawd!' she exclaimed.

'What?' asked Kathleen, trying to remove a bursting hoover bag.

'Julia's only gone and got a horse.'

Gloria peered up into Helen's face. 'Cor blimey, it's enormous this, isn't it?'

Connie reached out to stroke the horse and then stepped back as Norma drove up in a clapped-out Land Rover. 'I've brought her tack and feed. Is that the stable?' she asked, hopping down.

The women looked at one another, not sure what was going on, as now Dolly and Kathleen came to the kitchen door.

'Hi, Dolly. This is Norma and this is Helen of Troy.' Julia grinned like a schoolgirl. 'She's been given to us, for free.'

'Oh, yeah ...' Dolly looked on as Angela squeezed out, running over to the horse.

Norma walked over and gave Dolly a bone-crushing handshake. 'She'll be marvellous with kids. She's thirteen years old, retired now, but if you're opening this as a children's home she'll be ideal. You can drop a bomb in front of her and she won't even flinch. She can walk through a band or a riot and she's as cool as a cucumber.'

Julia looked pleadingly at Dolly. 'She's a police horse, Dolly.'

Kathleen flinched as if the horse was about to arrest her.

'A minute, love,' Dolly said, and went back into the kitchen, followed by a flushed Julia.

'She's beautiful, isn't she? And free! We don't even have to pay for her feed.'

Dolly folded her arms. 'Really? And Norma's a police-woman, is she?'

Julia nodded, grinning inanely. She reeked of booze.

Dolly sighed. 'I don't like the filth, mounted or other-wise, poking their nose around.'

Julia looked crestfallen. 'Oh, well, I can take it back. I just thought . . .'

'You thought what? I don't ride, there's no kids here yet and you're leaving, so what the hell am I gonna do with a horse?'

Julia gripped the back of the chair. 'I want to stay on, Dolly. I'll groom her, feed her . . . You wouldn't have to do a single thing, and I'll make sure Norma keeps her distance.'

'You better. We got an arsenal of guns on the property and none of us are what you might call upright citizens.'

Julia was about to return to the yard when Dolly put her hand on her arm. 'Ester's gone.'

Julia was stunned. 'Gone?'

'About fifteen minutes ago. And if you don't mind me saying so, it's good riddance.'

*

Julia couldn't believe Ester had walked out without even saying goodbye. She had to check that all her belongings had gone from their bedroom before finally accepting it. She slipped downstairs for a bottle of vodka, and started drinking it straight from the bottle. Ester had left her without so much as a note. Julia rested back against the pillow that still smelt of her perfume and started to cry, those awful, silent tears she had learnt to cry in prison. Ester had chosen Julia, walked straight up to her. The other girls sitting with their dinner trays had moved away from the table, but Julia had said nothing, just continued to eat, her eyes down, afraid of what Ester wanted.

'You shooting up?' Ester had said.

Julia had swallowed, still unable to look at her.

'Bad stuff in here. You'd better go cold turkey. I'll take care of you.'

Julia reached for the bottle, wanting to pass out. She didn't want to hear that wonderful gravelly voice in her head, smell that thick sweet-scented perfume. Ester was the love of Julia's life and without her the fear returned, her confidence dwindled and her deep-seated guilt and shame threatened to overwhelm her.

'I'm at the station,' Audrey said.

'I'll be there, just wait in the car park.' Dolly put down the phone and went out to find Gloria. She was with Kathleen, hanging over the stable door. Dolly held up the keys to Gloria's Mini. 'I won't be long, just getting some groceries.'

Gloria rushed over. 'I need Eddie's guns, Dolly. I got to get some cash.'

Dolly opened the Mini and got inside. 'We'll talk about them later.'

'They're worth around thirty grand, Eddie said.'

Dolly wound down the window. 'And they could have got us arrested. When I come back we'll talk.'

'I'll cut you in, Dolly, that's only fair.' Dolly started the engine and backed the Mini down the drive, Gloria still following her. 'Say twenty per cent?'

Gloria watched the car disappear down the drive.

Audrey was standing in the centre of the car park clutching her handbag when Dolly pulled up. Audrey climbed into the Mini. The level-crossing gates were closed. 'What's up?' Audrey asked, staring at the railway crossing.

'Must be a train due.'

Raymond Dewey saw Dolly and waved. She lowered the window. 'Hello, Raymond, you on duty, are you?' He came over to the car and shook her hand, then introduced himself to Audrey. She pressed herself back in her seat as his square head poked through the window. 'How long will we have to wait?' Dolly asked.

'Oh, might be a few minutes. Not like the mail train,

and Connie were sitting at the kitchen table play-
ts and crosses when Dolly got back. 'Did you
nie asked.
e closed, wasted journey.'
up the paper. 'About Eddie's

'We'll go and get them when
a cup of tea, if that's all
n't got any milk.'

always a long delay every Thursday. This is the three twenty, local.' He returned to his stool to jot down more notes in his precious book as Audrey and Dolly sat in silence. They watched the train chugging past them before the gates slowly lifted.

'Bloody nutter,' said Audrey as they passed him, now waving them on like a traffic controller.

They went into the local pub and Audrey took a corner seat at the bay window as Dolly got the drinks. When Dolly put a large gin and tonic down in front of her she knocked it back in two gulps to try to calm her nerves. 'Right, I've got you all I could. Twenty grand.'

Dolly sipped her drink. 'I hope you're joking.'

'No, I'm not. I brought bank statements, everything, you can see for yourself that's all I could get. The rest, like I told you, went into the villa. I'll sell it, split the profits, but it'll take a while.' Audrey opened her bag and took out a thick envelope. She was about to pass it to Dolly when Norma walked over.

'Hello, Mrs Rawlins.'

Dolly gave a tight, brittle smile. 'Hello, Norma. I'd offer to buy you a drink but we're just leaving. Audrey, this is Norma. She's a mounted police officer.'

Audrey gaped in horror. 'Oh, nice to meet you.'

Dolly waved at Raymond as they passed him again and ʼove into the station car park. Audrey still clutched her bag tightly, sweating with nerves and wishing Dolly would say something to break the tension. But she drove in tight-lipped silence.

'I'll need my passport, Dolly, and me ticket for Spain.'

Dolly engaged the handbrake and leaned over to open the glove compartment. 'Here, take them. Just give me the money.' Audrey passed her the envelope. She shoved it into her pocket without counting it. 'I don't want to see you or hear from you again, Audrey. Just get out of my sight.'

Audrey fumbled with the door handle in her haste to get away. She ran into the station, still afraid Dolly might get out and attack her – she'd turned those chipped-ice eyes on her with such hatred. Dolly sat in the car and watched her go. Twenty thousand pounds! And she'd thought she would have millions. How was she going to make things work now?

Gloria and Connie were sitting at the kitchen table playing noughts and crosses when Dolly got back. 'Did you get milk?' Connie asked.

'No. Shops were closed, wasted journey.'

Gloria screwed up the paper. 'About Eddie's guns, Dolly.'

Dolly took off her coat. 'We'll go and get them when it's dark but right now I'd like a cup of tea, if that's all right with you – even if we haven't got any milk.'

*

Julia was lying face down on the bed. She didn't look up when Dolly tapped on the door and walked in. 'I need a hand, Julia. We're going to get the guns and—' Julia tried to sit up then flopped down again. Dolly saw the empty bottle on the floor. 'You'd better sleep it off, we'll manage without you.'

'We'll need spades and a wheelbarrow,' Dolly said to Gloria and then, as Connie, all dressed up, walked into the kitchen, added, 'You leaving too, are you?'

Connie shook her head. 'No, I'm going out with that builder bloke.'

Gloria nudged Dolly. 'I told her earlier to get the old leg over and he'd maybe work for nothin'.'

Dolly shook her head at Gloria, as if she was a naughty kid, and then asked Connie to come into the room she now used as an office. She handed over an envelope with ten thousand pounds cash inside. 'Give this to him, will you? Tell him he'll get the rest next week and if he could get the men back to work over the weekend, I'd be grateful.'

'Okay.' Connie slipped the envelope into her pocket.

Dolly hesitated, then patted Connie's arm. 'Be nice to him. Be a help to me, know what I mean?'

Connie bit her lip. 'Sure, pay my way, so to speak.'

Dolly nodded. 'Good. You have a nice evening, then.'

*

Connie met John outside the manor gates. He'd changed into a suit and Connie was touched by the effort he'd made. 'Sorry about the state of the van,' he said nervously as they drove off. 'Do you like Chinese?'

Connie hated Chinese. She flashed him a beaming smile. 'That would be lovely.'

'God, I'm hungry,' complained Gloria as she trundled the wheelbarrow through the woods.

Kathleen trudged along behind with two spades. 'Got to hand it to you, Dolly, if you hadn't stashed them, we'd be in a right old mess.'

Gloria scowled, all the time wondering just how much Dolly would squeeze her for Eddie's guns, but she couldn't help being impressed by the fact she'd hidden them so far from the house and done it all on her own. As if she was reading her mind, Dolly looked at her. 'I did it in three trips, Gloria, took half the night.'

Julia woke up, her dulled senses finally making out the sound of the telephone ringing and ringing. She stumbled out of her room and almost fell down the stairs.

She lurched towards it, snatching it up. 'Ester? Is that you?'

'Is Connie there?' said a man's voice.

Julia swung round and looked into the kitchen. 'Connie? *Connie?*'

'She ... she's not here,' Julia slurred.

'Okay. I'm coming to meet her but I seem to be in a dead-end road. How do I get to the Grange?'

Julia began to give him directions, assuming Connie had arranged for Lennie to collect her. She was too drunk to remember that Connie was terrified of him.

Lennie slipped the portable back into the glove compartment of his shining Porsche and started to reverse. He swore when the car sank into a pothole, the mud splashing the gleaming paintwork. Then he drove slowly down the lane.

Connie giggled as the waiter presented John with the bill and his eyes almost popped out of his head. But he paid up, digging into the envelope Connie had given him. She felt a bit bad about ordering champagne and pressed her leg against his under the table. He flushed as she kicked off her shoe and let her toes stroke his crotch. He had never before come across a woman like Connie and felt excited and terrified at the same time.

'Do you think she'll be able to pay the rest?' he asked, trying to appear nonchalant as Connie's toes stroked the fly of his trousers.

'Oh, so you asked me out to find out about Mrs Rawlins?'

'No, no! It's just that I'm a one-man firm and I could go broke over this. I've ordered a lot of equipment.'

'If Mrs Rawlins says she'll pay you, then she will,' Connie purred, leaning towards him over the table as her toes did all the walking below.

'I'd better get you home,' he gulped.

Gloria had taken over the digging as Kathleen heaved the first bag onto the wheelbarrow. 'You're stronger than you look, Dolly Rawlins. These weigh a ton.'

Angela pulled the brambles away from the third hiding place as Gloria stuck in the spade. They were on the brow of a small hill just outside the wooded perimeter of the manor's land, and could see clearly the signal box below.

'Who's at the gates?' Kathleen pointed.

Dolly looked up. She could see the flashing signal lights, the barred gates, and the stationary builder's van.

Gloria prodded her in the ribs. 'You think he's givin' her one or is it just light relief?'

Dolly grimaced. Sometimes Gloria's crudeness really irritated her but she couldn't help taking another look to see what was going on in the van.

John had Connie's top undone and was nuzzling her breasts as she kept one eye on the signal lights.

'Train's coming,' she whispered.

He moaned, and for a moment she thought he was coming too but then he sat back. 'I'm sorry.'

She buttoned her blouse and snuggled up to him. 'Are you married?'

'No, but I live with someone.'

'And where does she think you are tonight?'

'At the gym.'

She grinned. 'Can I work out with you one day? I love doing weights.'

The train thundered past and the gates slowly opened. 'Any time you like.' John put the van into gear and they headed down the narrow lane back towards the manor.

Lennie reversed into a field through an open gate. He'd already driven past the manor, taken a quick look and decided that the element of surprise would be more beneficial. He was just about to get out when the van passed him. He waited until it parked by the manor, then followed on foot, keeping close to the overhanging hedgerow.

They'd finally loaded the wheelbarrow and were pushing it back towards the manor. Dolly walked ahead, her arm slung around Angela's shoulder. 'You know you can go on special government courses, get further education, proper training in something. You're welcome to stay on here for as long as you like, you know that, but you should think about it. Do you like kids?'

'Oh yeah, and I'm used to them. I've got younger brothers still at school.'

Connie leaned in to John and gave him a long, lingering kiss. 'You'd better check your face before you go in. Lipstick!' She giggled as he wiped his mouth. 'I'll see you tomorrow?'

He watched her wiggle and sashay her way to the front door, then turn and do her Marilyn Monroe pout. He blew her a kiss, felt stupid and quickly put the van into reverse. He drove past Lennie, waiting in the shadows, without seeing him.

'Connie!'

She knew his voice immediately. 'Lennie?'

He stepped forward. 'Surprise, surprise!'

She began to shake with terror. 'You stay away from me, Lennie. Don't hurt me!'

He walked towards her, his arms out wide, smiling. 'I'm not going to hurt you, Connie. Why would I do that? I've just come to take you home.'

'I'm not coming with you, Lennie. You got to leave me alone.'

He came closer and now he wasn't playing games. 'You owe me, Connie, and you're gonna pay it off or work it off. Suit yourself.'

'I won't go anywhere with you.'

He lunged for her but she kicked out, screaming, catching him in the groin. He lost his footing, tripping over a plank left by the builders, while clutching his balls. 'Don't you dare fuck with me!' he snarled through gritted teeth.

She was running in no particular direction, anywhere to get away from him, sobbing with fear. He started after her, yelling with rage, as she ran on, weaving her way erratically towards the woods.

Dolly went rigid as the sound of screaming made them stop in their tracks.

Gloria let go of the handles of the wheelbarrow. 'It's Connie.' She ran towards the manor.

Dolly started to follow and then turned to Kathleen and Angela. 'You stay put, the pair of you, until I come back and get you.' She tore after Gloria through the woods, hearing another high-pitched scream.

Connie had run straight into Gloria and Gloria had to slap Connie's face. 'It's me, Connie, it's me, Gloria.'

Connie clung to her. 'He's here. Oh God, Gloria, he's here and he's gonna kill me. He was chasing me, he's going to kill—'

'Connie, listen to me.' Gloria smacked her hard again. 'Nobody is going to touch you, all right? We're all here.'

Dolly was breathless when she reached them. 'What's going on?'

'It's that bloke, her pimp. He's come after her.'

Dolly gripped Connie's arm. 'We won't let him lay a finger on you. Gloria, go and get the other two. I'll take Connie back to the house with me.'

A terrified Connie clung to Dolly as they made their way cautiously, then ran the last few yards past the stables and into the safety of the house. Dolly quickly latched the door behind them but Connie still didn't feel safe. 'What if he's here, in the house?'

Gloria, Kathleen and Angela wheeled the rest of the guns into the stable yard and then carried them inside. Connie was sitting with a large brandy, her eyes red-rimmed from crying, as Julia sat with her head in her hands, so hungover she could hardly speak.

Gloria held up a shotgun. 'Right, we got enough of these. If that prick shows his face, I'll blow it off.'

'We'll search the house,' Dolly said. 'Some of the windows are out so if he's here, we'd better find him. We'll have a good look round, then, Connie, you lock yourself in a room with Angela.'

Connie began to sob again and Dolly lost her patience. 'Shut up, for God's sake! And you, Julia, get some coffee down you and try and sober up.'

Connie wiped her face with the back of her hand. 'He said he's going to take me back.'

Dolly shook her by the shoulders. 'Nobody's going to make you do anything you don't want to do, okay? We'll sort it.'

Gloria went over the grounds with the shotgun at the ready. She checked the stables, the outhouses and the yard, and even went up to the woods, but an owl suddenly hooting gave her the willies, so she quickly scuttled back to the front door of the manor. It was ajar and she pushed it slowly. 'Anyone here?'

Dolly stood there with her hands on her hips. 'Yes. Me, you fool. Did you see anything out there?'

'Nope. Maybe he saw us and decided to piss off.'

'Let's hope you're right,' Dolly said, shutting the door.

Ester drove into the underground car park of the Club Cabar. She'd been to three other clubs and this was her last hope: it was Steve Rooney or back to the Grange. She locked up the Range Rover, checked her hair and make-up, pulled her black dress down a bit further to show off her shoulders and tits and changed her driving shoes for spiked heels. 'Right, gel, let's do the business.'

She walked in casually, full of confidence, towards the private lift to the club. The car park was used by a number of offices in the day but taken over by the club at night so they had their own small lift leading directly to their reception. As the grille slid back, a muscle-bound bouncer in an ill-fitting evening suit nodded at Ester.

She gave him a cursory wave. 'Is Steve in?'

'Yeah, he's wiv someone. But I'll tell 'im you're 'ere.'

'Thank you,' she said crisply, heading towards the main room of the club. Its small sunken dance floor was empty but you could hardly see your hand in front of your face for the blinking neon strips. At least the ornate, over-brassy bar was well lit and the row of red velvet-topped high stools had only one male occupant: a swarthy, fat little man, drinking from a long glass with a profusion of fruit and paper umbrellas sticking out of it. He was surrounded by a gaggle of sexy blondes with tight mini-skirts and tied blouse tops showing a lot of cleavage, tottering on heels even higher than Ester's. They were giggling and whispering to each other as the poor sucker with the paper umbrella almost up his nose slurped a drink that had probably set him back a tenner. The girls would make sure he was parted from a lot more than that before the night was out.

Ester perched on a stool as far away from the fat man as possible. The slant-eyed barman was doing an impressive performance with his Martini shaker to the deafening, thudding rock music that made it impossible for anyone to have a conversation.

'Hi, Eth-ter, how ya doin?' the barman lisped.

'I'm doing fine. Gimme a Southern Comfort, lemonade, slice of lemon and crushed ice, easy on the lemonade.' She lit a cigarette as she spoke, but he knew what she liked and was already searching through the array of bottles. He shimmied up and down the bar and then whisked out a paper napkin and a bowl of peanuts before placing her drink down with a smile.

'On the house.'

'Cheers.' She sipped, then winced. He'd overdone it with the lemonade. In the mirror she saw Steve Rooney talking to the bouncer, who gestured towards the bar. Ester turned and Rooney held up his hand to indicate five minutes.

A few more punters arrived and wandered around. Ester signalled for a refill, then grabbed a handful of peanuts. It was strange. She'd been out of the business a long time, and didn't know any of the girls now. She hated the whole scene, which was why she'd moved to the Grange, but for a while she had been coining it. Rooney tapped her shoulder and pointed at his office, interrupting her thoughts. She slid off the stool, drained her glass and followed, shooting a look at the little fat man. 'I'd get out while you're still on top, fella.'

Rooney perched on his fake antique desk. 'So, how's tricks, darlin'? I just hope you've not come to touch me for a few quid. As you can see, it's Friday night and we're not exactly filling the joint.'

'It'll pick up, it always used to.'

His polished Gucci loafer tapped the side of the desk. 'What do you want, Ester? I know you've schlepped round a few places tonight.'

'Warned off me, were you?'

He smiled. His eyes were pale blue behind tinted glasses. 'You're not still wheeling around in that Range Rover, are you?'

She flicked her lighter and lit a cigarette.

'You really are stupid, you know that, don't you? You tried it on with the wrong people, Ester. They got a lot of dough and they'll use it to find you.'

'No kidding. Doesn't scare me.'

'It should. That was a stupid move. They paid out a lot of cash for you, and what do you do?'

'I did three years and I kept my mouth shut. They ripped me off.'

'No, they didn't. How were they to know you had a string of offences as long as both arms? They paid your taxes and your lawyer, and you come out, try to nail them for more cash, then nick the kid's motor.'

She stubbed out the cigarette. 'They got enough of them. What's one little Range Rover?'

'It wasn't what it was, it was you doin' it. It was stupid.'

Ester shrugged. 'You seem to know a lot about my business.'

Rooney sighed, picking a bit of fluff off his Armani jacket. 'Because I supply them now, okay? I'm not gonna hide anything from you. It's not as if I nicked your clients. You were inside.'

'Yes, I was, and now I need a job, Rooney.'

'Well don't look in my direction. I'm not going to put

myself out for you, Ester. You never gave me a leg-up when I needed it.'

'But I sent a lot of clients your way, you cheap shit.'

His face tightened and Ester would have liked to smack him. Rooney had once been a barman she'd hired for special parties, back in the old days when she ran a house for two major club owners. They'd have the clients drinking and eating at their respectable joints and when they wanted a girl Ester supplied them. She kept ten good-looking tarts, and they were always busy. There were private parties for movie stars, MPs, titled perverts; in fact anyone the club owners gave membership to would at some time or another end up at the Notting Hill Gate house . . . until it was busted. Ester had served a few years back then, and when she came out of prison she had been determined that the next place would be her own. So she turned tricks solo for four years, working the main hotels until she had enough to put down on Grange Manor House. Rooney had learnt fast, and soon after her bust, which he was never questioned about, he had gone to work for the club owners.

It had been Rooney who had sent her the Arab clients for the manor, and he'd taken a cut. But, just like her bust at Notting Hill Gate, when it went down at the Grange, Rooney's name was never mentioned. Rooney had even suggested to her that, if she played her cards right, she might even earn extra by making a couple of videos of certain clients at the manor. He had sold a few for her, just light porn stuff, but when she told him about the tape she'd made of his Arab clients' kids, he had walked away. He told her that if she had any sense she would as well. A couple of movie stars caught with their pants down was one thing but not the so-called flowing-robed royalty: that was asking for trouble.

'You don't know how to say thank you, do you?' she said curtly.

Rooney leaned close. 'Sweetheart, I owe you fuck all. You done nothing for me. Whatever I done, I done all by meself.'

She laughed. 'You're still an illiterate shit.'

'Maybe I am, but I'm a fucking sight richer than you are and I don't look for trouble. That's why I'm in business and you're nowhere.'

She was about to remind him who gave him his first job, but there was a rap at the door and Brian, the bouncer, appeared.

'There's a party of six kids, they said to ask for you. None of them are members but they look as if they got a few readies.'

Ester stood up, smoothed down her dress and saw the car keys on the desk. She whipped them up fast and then picked up her handbag. 'Well, I'll be going.'

Rooney asked her to go out of the back entrance. 'I don't want any aggro, Ester. I'm sorry.'

She pushed past him and he looked at Brian. 'If she's in that fucking Range Rover, get it.'

Rooney closed his office door and headed into the club's reception.

Ester went out through the kitchens, down the fire escape and into the car park. She was searching in her bag for the Range Rover keys when she saw Brian stepping out of the lift, accompanied by another equally heavy-set bouncer. They walked nonchalantly towards the Range Rover and leaned against it. 'This isn't yours, is it, Ester? Give me the keys, darlin'.'

'Piss off.'

Brian made a grab for her but she quickly twisted the keys into her fist, jabbing hard at his face. She caught his right eye a beaut, and he backed away. Ester felt her hair being torn out by the roots by his friend and screamed, hurling the keys at him. But Brian was back, slapping her hard across the face. Ester fell onto the dirty garage floor and tried to crawl away, but they kicked her in the head, the ribs and the groin. She curled up in a tight ball to protect herself, but they kept on kicking until she half rolled beneath a car.

She stayed there, wedged under it, as they threw her belongings onto the ground before driving the Range Rover out of the car park. She moaned, gingerly feeling her ribs and her face before searching for her handbag. Finally she pulled her body upright. It was agony.

When she pressed the alarm on the keys she'd taken from Rooney they lit up a brand-new Saab convertible and, as sick as she felt, she couldn't help but smile. It was beautiful. She was just about to drag her belongings together when she heard the lift opening. Rooney slid back the gate. 'I'm sorry about that, Ester, but I've got to take the Range Rover back and if you've got any sense you'll take that tape back as well.'

She picked up her case. 'Thanks for the advice.'

Rooney peeled off two fifty-pound notes and tossed them towards her. 'Take a cab.'

She wouldn't let him see her grovel and pick up the notes, so she stood there until the lift had disappeared, then picked up the money, wincing in pain, and opened the boot of the Saab, tossing in her case.

'Fuck you, Rooney.' She got in and drove out fast, smiling.

Gloria had all the guns laid out on the kitchen table, and it was a formidable collection. She was in her element as she handled them expertly, showing them off as if they were fashion accessories. Kathleen hung back, eyes popping. She wouldn't go near them. But Julia was brave enough to reach out and touch the barrel of the Heckler and Koch machine gun. 'My God! You had these stashed in the house?'

Dolly wasn't happy having such heavy-duty weaponry

in the house, but at the same time knew she was looking at cold, hard cash. 'What are they worth, did you say?'

'Thirty grand at least,' Gloria said, beaming.

Dolly nodded. 'Well, the sooner they're out of here the better. You tell that husband of yours I want a cut, fifty per cent. If he doesn't like it . . .'

Gloria sniggered. 'He can't really do a lot about it. He's doing eighteen, Dolly.'

'I know that,' Dolly replied. 'I Just don't want him sending any goons round. So get a contact and get rid of them – fast.'

Gloria began to roll up the shotguns in their padded cloths. She obviously knew what she was doing and Julia couldn't help but be impressed. 'Do you know how to use them?'

'Course I do. I belong to one of the top gun clubs in the country. You got to know what you're sellin' or buyin'.' She picked up a .45 and held it out in front of her at arm's length as if she was about to take aim.

Dolly turned on her angrily. 'Just put them away, Gloria!'

'Right, right.' As Dolly walked out, Gloria grinned at Julia. 'You know, they say Hitler's mistress never died in the bunker with him. That one, dead ringer for Eva Braun.'

Julia smiled, and put the kettle on.

*

Angela was sitting holding Connie's hand. She was still scared, jumping at every creak in the house, and sprang up when Dolly walked in.

'I'm going to bed. Julia will stay downstairs just in case he comes back but I think he's gone.'

Connie stammered, 'He'll be back, Dolly. He'll never leave me alone.'

Dolly didn't want to hear it all over again. 'How did he know you were here?'

Connie paused. 'I might have mentioned it, I don't remember.'

'Well, then, you got nobody else to blame, have you? Goodnight, Angela, love.'

Angela shut the door and went back to sit with Connie. 'Why don't you tell the police about him?'

Connie sniffed. 'Don't be stupid.'

'Well, he can't just knock you around and get away with it.'

'He can't? Who're you kidding?' Connie wiped her nose with a sodden piece of tissue. 'All my life I've been on the end of a fist. First my dad, only he did a lot more than knock me around. My poor mum was so scared of him she used to lock herself in a cupboard. Even when she knew what he was doing to me, she didn't stop him. It meant that it wasn't *her* getting a beating and ... Every man I've been with has been the same. I dunno why but I always thought Lennie was different. I really thought he loved me.'

Angela slipped her arm around her.

'Can't hide out here for ever though, can I?' Connie continued. 'Because he'll come back. He thinks I'm his property.' Angela did sympathize with Connie's situation, but to be honest, she was getting bored with Connie going over and over the same ground. 'If I could get an agent, a decent one, I know I could make a living doing proper modelling, I know I could. I can't do anything else, that's for sure.'

'How old are you?' asked Angela innocently, and was taken aback when Connie turned on her.

'Mind your own fucking business.'

Ester kept her foot pressed to the floor. She hit a hundred and twenty, passing everything on the road, and then suddenly felt sick and quickly veered over onto the hard shoulder. She only just got out before she vomited, sitting with head bent, the driver's door open, as she waited for the dizziness to pass.

Julia saw the headlights and went to the window, wishing she had one of Gloria's guns. But then she heard the clip–clip of high heels coming towards the back door.

Angela woke and sat up. Connie was by the window. 'I just saw a car drive up.'

Angela listened. She heard a door open and close. The

next moment there was a light tap and Gloria appeared at the door with a loaded shotgun. 'Did you hear someone?' Angela nodded. 'Right, you lock the door and stay put. I'll see to him.'

Gloria crept down the landing and almost blasted Dolly. 'Cor, you give me a fright!' she exclaimed.

'What you think you're playing at? Put the gun away,' snapped Dolly.

'Somebody come in the house, we all heard it. Shush, listen.' They could hear a chair scraping and then Julia talking. They inched down the stairs together, Gloria in front with the shotgun.

Julia examined Ester's ribs. They were cracked, she reckoned, beneath the deep purple bruising.

'I just pranged the car – steering wheel hit me,' Ester said, gasping with pain.

Julia produced a large bandage and had just begun to wind it around Ester's midriff when the door burst open. Ester jumped out of her chair, flinching, as Dolly and Gloria marched in.

'Oh, it's you,' Gloria snarled.

'Yes. Sorry about this, Dolly. I had a bit of an accident in the car. Is it okay if I just stay for a night or two?'

Dolly folded her arms. 'An accident? Who you kidding?'

Ester turned her bruised face away, changing the

subject fast. 'Whose is the flash Porsche parked down the lane?'

Julia looked at Dolly, then back at Ester. 'Our lane?'

'I passed it on my way in.'

Gloria ran upstairs to ask Connie what car Lennie drove. She was back a moment later. 'It's his.'

Julia helped Ester to bed and then joined Gloria and Dolly to search the grounds. This time Dolly carried the shotgun, making Gloria hold up the flashlight. They toured the stables, the outhouses, and saw Ester's Saab.

'Where did she get this?'

Julia said Ester had told her she'd traded the Range Rover in.

'Did she?' Dolly said, already suspicious. They walked together round to the front of the manor, getting more and more anxious as they began to wonder if Lennie was hiding in the house. The beam of the flashlight moved slowly over the grounds, the overgrown bushes and hedgerows, and then swept across the swimming pool.

'Wait! Move it back, down the deep end of the pool.' Dolly was squinting in the darkness, trying to work out what she had seen. They walked slowly towards what looked like a bundle of rags but as they moved closer, it was obviously the body of a man.

Lennie was lying face down, his arms floating in the stagnant water in front of him, one leg caught round some old rope.

Dolly hesitated only for a moment. Already there were guns in the house. A body was all they needed. 'Get him out.'

Julia stared at her. 'Are you crazy?'

'No. We get him out and bury him as fast as we can. It's almost dawn.'

'Don't you think we should call the police?' Julia asked.

'No, I don't. What do you think the social services would make of it? Get Connie and Angela – we'll all have to help drag him out. We'll put him in the back of Gloria's car.'

'I don't think that's a good idea,' Julia said, and Dolly turned on her, her face like parchment in the dim light.

'Fine. You take care of it, then,' she said coldly, walking away.

Gloria went and fetched Connie, then waded into the filthy water with a hook, to pull the body closer. 'Is it him?'

Connie broke down, sobbing that she didn't do it, she never even touched him. Dolly re-joined them, standing slightly apart.

'Well, look at the gash on his head. He must have cracked it on the side of the pool. Nobody's accusing you of doin' anything. So stop howling.' Gloria waded in deeper, drawing the body closer to the steps.

It took three of them to drag him out of the pool. Julia had pulled a big sheet of polythene from the roof of the house and they heaved the body towards it. They turned out his pockets as Gloria drove the Mini round, then they rolled the body in the polythene and lifted it into the back of the car. 'Now what?' Gloria asked. Dolly checked the time: it was almost five o'clock and the builders would be starting at seven. It didn't give them enough time: and they couldn't dump it in broad daylight.

'Drive it back to the lean-to and we'll leave it there until tomorrow night.'

'What? In my car?'

'Yes, Gloria, unless you can think of somewhere better,' Dolly retorted.

By the time the others had returned to the house, Dolly had a pot of coffee on the stove and some toast made. They trooped in and started to wash their hands, all suddenly quiet.

Ester walked in. 'Everything okay?'

'What do you think? We got her bleedin' boyfriend stashed in the back of me car and a kitchen full of guns,' Gloria said angrily.

Connie broke down into heaving sobs again and this time Dolly turned on her. '*Shut up*, all of you. Now sit down and listen.' They sat like kids, seemingly grateful that she was taking charge. 'You, Connie, go out to his car. Here are his keys and wallet. Any money we take, but burn his cards. You then drive the car back to London, go to his flat, get the log book.' She proceeded to give Connie directions to a garage she knew in North London. She was to sell the car after cleaning it of all fingerprints, leave notes cancelling the milkman and newspapers, and make it look as if Lennie had gone away. Then clean any fingerprints from the flat and return to the manor.

Connie nodded dumbly, not really comprehending.

'Go on then, get started. Get rid of that car as soon as possible.' Dolly spooned sugar into her coffee. 'Right, Julia, and you, Kathleen, go through the local papers, find out when the next funerals are going to be, then check out the grave in the cemetery.'

'*What?*' Julia was about to laugh, but again she was thrown off balance by the coldness in Dolly's eyes.

'Best way to get rid of a body. Find a dug grave and dump him. Now, Ester, that car out back. Is it hot? How did you get it?'

'I bought it. Well, it's on the never-never in part exchange for the Range Rover. It's not nicked, if that's what you're thinking.'

'Okay. Gloria, you go and see Eddie. The sooner those guns are out of here the better.'

Angela had remained silent throughout. Dolly patted her shoulder. 'I'm sorry to get you involved in this, love, but I think it's the best thing for all of us and with you driving the car that took out Jimmy Donaldson, I just think the less we see of the filth the better.'

Suddenly hearing the name of the man she had run over made Angela's whole body tremble. 'I won't say anything,' she said.

Dolly frowned. 'Well, I hope not, and that goes for everyone here. Now I'm going to have a couple of hours' kip.'

She walked out. They were impressed by her – but a little afraid of her coldness.

Kathleen swallowed and nudged Gloria. 'Thank God she's not found out about that business down the sauna. I think she'd bloody kill us.'

Chapter 10

The Mini remained in the lean-to, pools of water slowly forming under its wheels. Julia and Kathleen checked the newspapers and then went to the cemetery. Connie was already driving to London to sell the Porsche and clean Lennie's flat. She parked it a good distance from his block, and set about finding the log book. Having so much to do calmed her.

Ester stayed in bed with some aspirin. Her ribs hurt and she felt dizzy if she so much as sat up. Dolly slept, the only one of them able to do so. Gloria caught the train to London and went to Brixton to visit Eddie.

Angela cleaned the kitchen; she was worrying herself into a panic about Jimmy Donaldson. As she cleared the dirty crockery, she saw the big bags of guns left by the kitchen cabinet.

*

Mike listened impatiently to his mother fretting because she'd missed her flight so she now had to rearrange her trip to Spain.

'You have to get out soon, Mum, I mean it.'

'I will, Mike, but I got to pack the whole place up, you know. At least it's over, love. She took the cash, said she didn't ever want to see me again.'

He hung up and the phone rang again immediately. Mike swore when he heard Angela's voice and was about to slam it down again when she whispered, 'Guns.' She was hysterical, and he had to calm her down before he could piece together what she was saying: Dolly Rawlins had bags full of weapons that belonged to Eddie Radford in the manor.

Ester walked slowly down the stairs and stopped when she saw Angela furtively hunched over the telephone in the hall.

'I'm positive, I got to see you.'

'Who you calling?' Ester asked.

Angela whipped round, dropping the phone back on the hook. 'Just my mum. I'll get you some breakfast.'

Ester continued her slow progress down the stairs; she felt terrible. She felt even worse when Norma drove into the yard, tooting the horn to herald her arrival. 'Get rid of her, Angela.'

Norma was hauling out some bags of feed for the

horse and smiled as Angela approached. 'I was just passing so I thought I'd drop this lot off.'

'Everybody's out,' Angela said lamely.

'Oh well, can you give me a hand then?'

Angela helped her take a sack out of her Land Rover and into the stables. She could see Gloria's Mini out of the corner of her eye.

'Say hello to Julia. Tell her I'll maybe drop by later, see if she wants a ride.'

Dolly felt the blood rush to her cheeks as she read the letter. Her application to open Grange Manor House as a children's home had been turned down. She walked stiffly into the drawing room as Ester appeared.

'Just a word of advice. That little Angela's making secret phone calls.'

Dolly nodded, not listening. Ester shrugged and went back to bed.

Angela came in a few moments later with a cup of tea. 'That Norma brought feed for the horse. She even looked right at the Mini – I was scared stiff.'

Dolly roused herself and sighed. 'I've been turned down.'

She showed the letter to Angela. 'But they don't even say why. Why don't you call them on Monday?'

Dolly considered. 'Yeah, I got a right to know why they rejected me.'

*

Connie drove Lennie's Porsche across the river and to the small garage Dolly had told her would buy it without asking too many questions. She was calmer now as two mechanics looked it over. She'd told them it was her boyfriend's and he had just got a job abroad. They continued checking the engine and left the cash negotiation to Ron Delaney, the garage owner, a young, flashy, overconfident man wearing a tracksuit and heavy gold chains. He didn't waste much time: if he had any suspicions about the car he didn't mention them but offered a cash deal price well below the 'book'. Connie accepted twelve thousand pounds in fifties and twenties, eager to get back to the manor.

Gloria waited to be searched before entering the visitors' section at Brixton. When her name was called, she hurried over to Eddie, who was already sitting at the table. He looked her up and down. 'You look different,' he said nonchalantly.

'Yeah, it's all the fresh air.'

'What you brought me?'

'Nothin'. I didn't have any time and I've not got any cash.'

'Every time you come you got a line of bullshit, Gloria. Last time you said—'

'I know what I said. It all went wrong, there's no pay-off.'

'No? What about the diamonds?'

'Fakes. So now I got to sell the gear, Eddie. I'm flat broke and I got to pay the rent. There's no need to flog the lot but if you got a contact then . . .'

'No way.'

Gloria leaned closer. 'Eddie, I got them at the manor. We've already had one bleedin' search – if they come back and . . .' Eddie peeled off a cigarette paper. Gloria bent closer. 'Eddie, she'll have to have a bit of a cut.'

'Who?'

'You know who. Dolly Rawlins. If it wasn't for her they could have arrested the lot of us. It's only fair.'

'Is it?'

'Oh, come on, Eddie, just gimme a name, I'll do the business. You know me, you can trust me.'

'Can I?'

Gloria pursed her lips. 'What's the matter with you?'

Eddie opened his baccy tin. 'That stash is mine, my insurance for when I get out. Now, if it was just you, maybe I'd be prepared to—'

'What you mean, if it was just me? Of course it is.'

'No, it isn't. Now you want to give her a cut, next she'll want more, so if she wants to make a deal you tell her to come and see me. Maybe I'll do a deal with her, maybe I won't.'

'She won't come in here, Eddie.'

He fingered his tobacco carefully, laying it out on the paper. Tell her she got no option.'

Dolly listened as Julia described the cemetery, where the recent burials were, and explained that graves already dug and waiting for funerals were at the far side. Connie returned with the money and handed it over to Dolly. She had seen no one at Lennie's flat and she had done exactly as Dolly had told her. She was rewarded with a frosty smile. Gloria arrived back later that afternoon and told Dolly what Eddie had said.

'He wants me to go and see him in the nick?' Dolly was livid. 'No way. I'll sort something. He won't be out, Gloria, for a very long time. In the meantime they're here, in the house, and I don't like it. The sooner we're rid of them the better.'

Tommy Malin wanted a 50 per cent cut. He agreed to arrange a buyer and they would make the exchange that night. Gloria was furious – Eddie would go out of his mind. Why pay some bloke 50 per cent? It was madness.

'We pay because I want cash and I want to get rid of them,' Dolly said.

'Then go and talk to Eddie.'

'No. I can trust Tommy.'

'You sayin' you can't trust Eddie?'

'Can you?'

Gloria was gobsmacked.

'He's in the nick. Who knows who he'll hook you up with. We do as I say. We sell the guns to Tommy Malin's contact.'

'We could bleedin' sell them to the Queen Mother for a fifty per cent cut,' stormed Gloria, but Dolly walked out. Conversation over.

Mike ran along the stone corridor and up the stairs to Audrey's flat. He banged hard on the door and she opened it with the chain still on. 'It's me – come on – let me in.'

She looked at him fearfully. 'What's happened?'

'I want you to put in a call for me. I just got a tip-off about something. Maybe we'll get her after all.'

'Who?'

'*Who the hell do you think?*'

'Dolly? What do you want me to do?'

'Call my guv'nor. I know he's at the station so we'll go to a pub and you put in a call.'

'Why me?'

'You won't say your name, for Chrissakes. I just want you to tip him off about something.'

'What?'

'Guns. Dolly Rawlins has got bags full of guns stashed at the manor.'

*

DCI Craigh replaced the phone. He was working over-time and was in a foul mood, but he had come in because Traffic reckoned they had now traced the vehicle used in the hit-and-run that killed James Donaldson. The car was registered to a hire garage called Rodway Motors, but what interested Craigh was that the garage was in the Aylesbury area – not far from Grange Manor House.

Craigh was about to leave his office when his desk phone rang. He reached out for it just as DI Palmer walked in.

'We might have got a trace on the vehicle,' Craigh said as he answered the phone.

Audrey had to cover one ear because of the racket in the pub. She turned to Mike, just able to see him sitting up at the bar, watching her. He gestured for her to hurry up and make the call, then checked his watch. When he looked at her again, she had already dialled. Audrey asked if she was speaking to Detective Chief Inspector Craigh. When he confirmed that she was, she said her carefully rehearsed speech. 'Dolly Rawlins is holding a stash of weapons owned by Eddie Radford. The guns are at Grange Manor House in Aylesbury, and worth at least thirty thousand pounds.' Then she replaced the receiver and went to join Mike at the bar.

'What did he say?' Mike asked.

'Well, nothin'. You told me to just say what I had to then put the phone down.'

Mike downed his pint. 'I'd better get back home in case he calls me there.'

'What do you want me to do?'

'Just leave, like you were planning to.'

Audrey sipped her gin and tonic. 'I got to wait, Mike. I've missed my flight again, so I'll have to go back to the travel agent. You know, you could come with me, all of you, Susan and the kids.'

Mike shook his head. 'No way. You don't seem to understand. I like my job, and I don't want to lose it.'

Mike had only just walked into his own home when the phone rang. It was DCI Craigh, and he wanted him back at the station.

'What's up?' Mike asked innocently.

'Just get in here fast as you can,' Craigh said.

'Okay, I'm on my way.' Mike hung up as Susan and the kids came into the hall.

'Are we going to the swimming pool, Dad?' his youngest boy said excitedly.

'No, I'm sorry. I just got a call – they want me in.'

'But it's Saturday,' Susan said, frowning.

'I know, but . . . I got to go.'

Susan didn't believe him. She stared at him, her face tight. 'Oh yes? Well, I hope they're paying you over-time – you seem to be on duty all hours lately. You sure you're not just going off with that girl?'

Mike sighed. 'Sue, don't keep on about that, all right? You want to call the station and check? Go ahead, but this is getting me down. You question every bloody move I make.'

She pushed the kids to the front door. 'Maybe you give me reason to.'

DCI Craigh told Mike about the car. 'We're going over there to check it out. And there's something else. I got a call, a woman – she may have been your contact but she asked for me. Guns. Come on, I'll tell you in the car.'

The builders finished early as it was the weekend. The coast was clear. Dolly ordered a disgruntled Gloria to start loading up the guns. They would use Ester's Saab to deliver them to Tommy Malin.

Ester was uneasy. She knew just how hot the car was. 'I can't let anyone drive it, Dolly. I'm the only one on the insurance.'

Dolly fixed her with a look. 'So you can drive. Gloria will go with you – unless you're planning on leaving?'

Ester said nothing and Dolly took her silence as confirmation that she agreed to help them out. 'Pack them up, go on, get started. Julia, Kathleen and I will do the graveyard shift.'

'What about Connie? She got us all into this mess

with her ruddy boyfriend, why can't she help bury him?'
Kathleen moaned.

'Because Connie will be doing something else.' Dolly
walked away before they could argue.

Connie was lying on her bed reading a magazine
when Dolly entered. She didn't bother to knock. 'That
builder bloke, the one that took you out?'

'What about him?'

'Well, you go out with him again, make him happy,
understand me? I owe him, but I don't want to fork out
all the cash we got, so you go see him, give him a few
more grand, and tell him the rest will be coming soon.'

Connie hesitated. 'What about all that cash from
Lennie's car?'

'I need to pay off electricity, phone connection and
keep a bit back for emergencies and groceries. Besides,
I think you should earn your keep after all we're doing
for you.' Dolly stared coldly at her.

'Okay,' Connie agreed. 'He said I could go to his gym
with him. I'll give him a call.'

'Good. Oh – this gym. Do they have lockers, ones
you can keep the key?'

'I dunno.'

'Check it out when you call him, ask about membership and if you can leave your gear there.'

'Why?'

'Don't ask questions, just do what I tell you to.'

Connie turned away. Dolly had a nasty way of lowering her voice when she was angry.

DCI Craigh drove into Rodway Motors' car-hire section and he and Mike went into the reception while DI Palmer walked over to the main garage. Craigh showed the receptionist his ID and waited as she thumbed through the log book. She then looked up. 'It was hired by a Mrs Gloria Radford.'

Craigh flicked a glance at Mike, then turned back to the receptionist. She pushed the log book towards him and he read that the Volvo had been hired for one day only, the same day James Donaldson was killed. Mrs Radford had listed her address as a flat in Clapham.

Craigh nodded to Mike. 'She was at the manor, wasn't she? The night we busted it?'

Gordon Rodway, the owner of the garage, walked in, followed by Palmer. The car had been returned, no damage recorded, and it had subsequently been hired out again. It had also been through a carwash three times, polished and hoovered.

'I want no one near it. I'll have my people check it over,' Craigh said, none too happy as they all followed Rodway back to the garage. The Volvo was still on the ramp where a mechanic had been checking the exhaust. 'What's the interest in this car, then? We recorded the mileage, if that's any help.'

Mike walked round to the front bumpers: no dents, no paintwork scratched, it looked immaculate. But the Forensic boys would be all over it with a fine-tooth comb; if this was the car that ran over James Donaldson, they would find the evidence.

Dolly looked at Connie in her skin-tight leotard. 'Well, do they have lockers?'

'Yes, and it's a hundred and fifty quid for membership.'

'Good. Join up, and when you get there tonight, put this in the locker and bring me the key.' Dolly handed her a bag, which weighed a ton.

'What's this?'

'Just some personal things of mine – call them a safe-guard. But not a word to any of the others. Just make John nice and happy. You don't have to screw him, I wouldn't ask you to do that, just string him along.'

Connie went out to the front pathway to wait for John to collect her. It was just growing dark but not dark enough yet to move the body.

Angela was cleaning the kitchen when Dolly came in. 'Julia's looking for you, she's out in the yard,' she said.

Dolly opened the back door. 'Julia?'

She came out of the stables and joined Dolly on the kitchen doorstep. 'Yeah. Look, I don't think it's a good idea for Kathleen to come along tonight. She's getting all twitchy, says she doesn't want to be a part of it.'

y sighed. She touched Julia's arm lightly; she
her, she was straightforward, you knew where you
ere with her. 'Right, you and me will sort the body,
Kathleen can stay here with Angela.'

'What about Connie?'

'She's doing something else. Are the guns all loaded
up?' Julia nodded. Dolly glanced at her watch. 'They
should get moving, Tommy said his contact will be there
about ten. Ester's all right to drive, isn't she?'

'I think so.'

'Is she staying on?' Dolly asked.

'I don't know.'

'If she isn't, does that mean you won't?'

Julia flushed. 'I guess so, but I don't think she's got
anywhere to go. She's got a big mouth but ... well,
maybe you should talk to her yourself.'

DCI Craigh got back into the car. Palmer was at the
wheel. 'Gloria Radford hasn't lived there for a few weeks.
Flat was taken over by the council but she returned to
collect something from out in the back shed. I had a look
round and it's mostly filled with junk. Maybe she took
the guns and stashed them at the manor.'

Mike leaned on the front seat. 'What are we waiting
for, then? If your tip-off was right and there are guns at
the manor, why don't we just bust the place?'

Craigh looked directly ahead. 'We already made

ourselves look like a bunch of arseholes, Mike. This ti.
we do it by the book. We cover ourselves and check out
the fucking information first – and apart from that I'd
like a day off. That all right with you, is it?'

Mike sat back, knowing not to push it. He stared out
of the window as they drove down the road. Palmer
looked back at Craigh. 'So far they've found nothing on
the vehicle, guv.'

Craigh lit a cigarette. 'Let's see if we can have a chat
to Eddie Radford on Monday. He might have some
information. That suit you, Mike?' he said sarcastically.

'Whatever you say, guv. Just, why wait until then?
They could shift her guns.'

Craigh checked his watch. 'Okay – we go see Eddie
Radford. Then we call it quits.'

Ester eased herself up and winced. The last thing she felt
like doing was driving back to London. She wondered
if she could get out of it when Dolly walked in, closing
the door behind her.

'How did you get the beating, Ester?' She sat on the
dressing-table stool and waited.

Ester was about to lie, but didn't have the energy.
'Okay, last time I got sent down I also got a raw deal.
When I was busted, a couple of my clients got scared –
you know, that I'd plead not guilty and they'd have to
prove it and name my clients. They got my little black

'Back here?'

Ester nodded. 'Yeah, but I won't be staying long, just enough time to get my face healed.'

Dolly stood up. 'Okay, at least you told me the truth. So, go do the business with Gloria and you can stay on here until you're recovered, then you do whatever you want . . .'

Ester smiled, instantly regretting it because of her cut lip. 'Thanks.'

Eddie Radford was really edgy. He knew word would be out he'd been lifted and . . . . was having a talk with the . . . . . . know within an . . . . k – and he . . . . he could

. . . they got some punk, after me, I mean, they're all crazy! So I kind of . . . . me with a fuck- . . . on my head, I mean, they won't leave me alone and the result . . . out here. They beat me up and I ran like hell!

279

. . . ate, I asked for five . . . around at . . . .

... as a whopper, and I got
o kiddin'. I was coining it,
Arab royal family. I was told
, my fine would be paid, my back
get a few quid on top. I was assured
down. Well, I was. I got five years. They
gal costs, a percentage of my taxes and then
pa... walk... away. Not one name was mentioned. So, I got
pissed off.'

Dolly fingered a perfume bottle, then looked
up. 'Go on.'

'I used to make private videos which clients would
take after the show. I never made copies but on the night
I got turned over, I stashed one and it was never found.
When I got out, I went to them straight, said I felt I was
owed some dough. They threw me out, told me that if I
showed my face again I'd be sorry. I then called them and
said they would now be very sorry, that I had a video and
I was gonna expose them.' Dolly tutted. Ester looked
her. 'It's not even that bad, just a few slags rolli...
with them, but you know how Arabs...
hundred grand.'

'And?'

'Next thing...

ɔlding something that belongs to you, is she?'

ɔnno.'

You're in for dealing in guns, armed robbery.'

'Yeah, that's right.'

'Eighteen years.'

'Great, you can count.'

'Can you, though? That's a long time, a very long time, Eddie. Be better spending time in an open prison – lot cushier than this dump,' Craigh said softly.

'Thinking of taking me out to Butlin's, are you?'

Mike changed his position, staring hard at Radford. Craigh flicked his cigarette packet over. 'We think your wife was driving the car that killed Jimmy Donaldson, Eddie.'

'Oh yeah? Well, she was never a blinder behind the wheel.'

'You know about it, do you?'

'Look, I dunno this Donaldson, I don't know what you got me up here for, I want to go back to my cell.'

'But she could be charged with murder, Eddie.'

'Tough luck. I want to go.'

'If she's picked up, who's gonna flog your guns, Eddie?' Eddie frowned. 'They're being held for you at Grange Manor House, aren't they?' Eddie chewed his lower lip. 'We know they're at the manor so if we arrest Gloria you're gonna lose your pension fund. All I need from you is confirmation that they're there and in return,

well, we can talk to people, recommend you get n.
We can't make promises but we can certainly talk to ι.
right people.'

Eddie shifted his weight on the chair and reached out for Craigh's cigarettes. 'I dunno anythin' about this Jimmy Donaldson bloke or whatever Gloria's done. I dunno anythin' about that.'

'But you know about the guns, don't you, Eddie?'

Eddie removed a cigarette, lit it, and let the smoke trail from his nostrils as he decided what he should say. He knew they were worth thirty grand, but what good was that if they were sold by that cow Dolly Rawlins? What good were they to him if he couldn't get his hands on them? What if they were gonna arrest Gloria?

'I want to be moved,' Eddie said quietly.

Craigh smiled. 'Open prison, swimming pool, tennis courts and, like you said, Eddie, some nicks are better than Butlin's . . .'

Eddie flicked ash from his cigarette and rested both elbows on the table. 'She's staying with her, with Dolly Rawlins.'

They were surprised at how quickly he'd given her up, but he didn't seem to give a damn about his wife or her possible arrest. All he seemed to care about was the money he was going to lose.

'They're worth thirty grand,' Eddie said, hardly audible.

Dolly sighed. She touched Julia's arm lightly; she liked her, she was straightforward, you knew where you were with her. 'Right, you and me will sort the body, Kathleen can stay here with Angela.'

'What about Connie?'

'She's doing something else. Are the guns all loaded up?' Julia nodded. Dolly glanced at her watch. 'They should get moving, Tommy said his contact will be there about ten. Ester's all right to drive, isn't she?'

'I think so.'

'Is she staying on?' Dolly asked.

'I don't know.'

'If she isn't, does that mean you won't?'

Julia flushed. 'I guess so, but I don't think she's got anywhere to go. She's got a big mouth but ... well, maybe you should talk to her yourself.'

DCI Craigh got back into the car. Palmer was at the wheel. 'Gloria Radford hasn't lived there for a few weeks. Flat was taken over by the council but she returned to collect something from out in the back shed. I had a look round and it's mostly filled with junk. Maybe she took the guns and stashed them at the manor.'

Mike leaned on the front seat. 'What are we waiting for, then? If your tip-off was right and there are guns at the manor, why don't we just bust the place?'

Craigh looked directly ahead. 'We already made

ourselves look like a bunch of arseholes, Mike. This time we do it by the book. We cover ourselves and check out the fucking information first – and apart from that I'd like a day off. That all right with you, is it?'

Mike sat back, knowing not to push it. He stared out of the window as they drove down the road. Palmer looked back at Craigh. 'So far they've found nothing on the vehicle, guv.'

Craigh lit a cigarette. 'Let's see if we can have a chat to Eddie Radford on Monday. He might have some information. That suit you, Mike?' he said sarcastically.

'Whatever you say, guv. Just, why wait until then? They could shift her guns.'

Craigh checked his watch. 'Okay – we go see Eddie Radford. Then we call it quits.'

Ester eased herself up and winced. The last thing she felt like doing was driving back to London. She wondered if she could get out of it when Dolly walked in, closing the door behind her.

'How did you get the beating, Ester?' She sat on the dressing-table stool and waited.

Ester was about to lie, but didn't have the energy. 'Okay, last time I got sent down I also got a raw deal. When I was busted, a couple of my clients got scared – you know, that I'd plead not guilty and they'd have to prove it and name my clients. They got my little black

book – well, it wasn't little, it was a whopper, and I got
K for kings, P for princes, no kiddin'. I was coining it,
specials laid on for this Arab royal family. I was told
that if I pleaded guilty, my fine would be paid, my back
taxes paid and I'd get a few quid on top. I was assured
I'd not be sent down. Well, I was. I got five years. They
paid my legal costs, a percentage of my taxes and then
walked away. Not one name was mentioned. So, I got
pissed off.'

Dolly fingered a perfume bottle, then looked
up. 'Go on.'

'I used to make private videos which clients would
take after the show. I never made copies but on the night
I got turned over, I stashed one and it was never found.
When I got out, I went to them straight, said I felt I was
owed some dough. They threw me out, told me that if I
showed my face again I'd be sorry. I then called them and
said they would now be very sorry, that I had a video and
I was gonna expose them.' Dolly tutted. Ester looked at
her. 'It's not even that bad, just a few slags rolling around
with them, but you know how Arabs are. I asked for five
hundred grand.'

'And?'

'Next thing they got some punk after me with a fucking price on my head. I mean, they're all crazy! So I kind
of hid out here. They won't leave me alone and the result
is what you can see. They beat me up and I ran like hell.'

'Back here?'

Ester nodded. 'Yeah, but I won't be staying long, just enough time to get my face healed.'

Dolly stood up. 'Okay, at least you told me the truth. So, go do the business with Gloria and you can stay on here until you're recovered, then you do whatever you want . . .'

Ester smiled, instantly regretting it because of her cut lip. 'Thanks.'

Eddie Radford was really edgy. He knew word would be out he'd been lifted and that he was having a talk with the filth. Every prisoner there would know within an hour or so – word travels fast in the nick – and he didn't like it, didn't like anyone even thinking he could be grassing.

'What's all this about?' he snapped.

DCI Craigh drew up a chair. Mike stood leaning against the wall as Craigh offered a cigarette.

'I don't want a fag. I want to know what this is about,' he repeated.

'You know someone called James Donaldson?'

'No.'

'Dolly Rawlins?'

'No.'

'Gloria Radford?'

Eddie looked at Craigh, shrugged. 'Yeah, she's my wife.'

'She holding something that belongs to you, is she?'

'I dunno.'

'You're in for dealing in guns, armed robbery.'

'Yeah, that's right.'

'Eighteen years.'

'Great, you can count.'

'Can you, though? That's a long time, a very long time, Eddie. Be better spending time in an open prison – lot cushier than this dump,' Craigh said softly.

'Thinking of taking me out to Butlin's, are you?'

Mike changed his position, staring hard at Radford. Craigh flicked his cigarette packet over. 'We think your wife was driving the car that killed Jimmy Donaldson, Eddie.'

'Oh yeah? Well, she was never a blinder behind the wheel.'

'You know about it, do you?'

'Look, I dunno this Donaldson, I don't know what you got me up here for, I want to go back to my cell.'

'But she could be charged with murder, Eddie.'

'Tough luck. I want to go.'

'If she's picked up, who's gonna flog your guns, Eddie?' Eddie frowned. 'They're being held for you at Grange Manor House, aren't they?' Eddie chewed his lower lip. 'We know they're at the manor so if we arrest Gloria you're gonna lose your pension fund. All I need from you is confirmation that they're there and in return, well, we can talk to people, recommend you get moved. We can't make promises but we can certainly talk to the right people.'

Eddie shifted his weight on the chair and reached out for Craigh's cigarettes. 'I dunno anythin' about this Jimmy Donaldson bloke or whatever Gloria's done. I dunno anythin' about that.'

'But you know about the guns, don't you, Eddie?'

Eddie removed a cigarette, lit it, and let the smoke trail from his nostrils as he decided what he should say. He knew they were worth thirty grand, but what good was that if they were sold by that cow Dolly Rawlins? What good were they to him if he couldn't get his hands on them? What if they were gonna arrest Gloria?

'I want to be moved,' Eddie said quietly.

Craigh smiled. 'Open prison, swimming pool, tennis courts and, like you said, Eddie, some nicks are better than Butlin's . . .'

Eddie flicked ash from his cigarette and rested both elbows on the table. 'She's staying with her, with Dolly Rawlins.'

They were surprised at how quickly he'd given her up, but he didn't seem to give a damn about his wife or her possible arrest. All he seemed to care about was the money he was going to lose.

'They're worth thirty grand,' Eddie said, hardly audible.

The same figure the anonymous caller had given to Craigh. He now reckoned the call was on the level, the tip-off legitimate. His weekend was well and truly blown. He knew they would have to act on the tip-off now.

Dolly and Julia drove to the cemetery. It was pitch dark and Julia drove without headlamps, guided by the white tombstones as they moved slowly down the dirt-track road towards the recently dug graves. Flowers and wreaths were still strewn across the ground. They parked as close as they could, then took out the spades and zigzagged their way through the tombstones towards the freshly dug grave. It was all ready for its occupant, the trench dug, boards placed across the gaping hole.

Julia carefully moved aside the wooden planks, and said, 'Let's get on with it.'

They began to dig, making the hole even deeper so they could bury Lennie's body and cover him up without anyone noticing the grave had been tampered with. The coffin would then be placed on top of him at the funeral. Goodbye, Lennie!

It was not too difficult because the earth was so fresh and they worked in silence. Only the swishing of the spades could be heard in the quiet of the cemetery.

While Dolly and Julia were at the cemetery, Ester and Gloria headed for London's West End to fence the guns. Gloria squinted at the *A to Z*. Ester had insisted they cut across London by various back streets and they were now somewhere in Elephant and Castle but neither had any idea exactly where.

'Wait a minute, go left, first left,' Gloria muttered.

Ester drove on and turned left, then swore. No entry. She sighed and snatched the book from Gloria. 'Let me see.'

'It's not my fault. Why you had to come your route I dunno. I mean, we been going round in circles for over an hour now.'

Ester squinted at the small squares on the map. 'We don't want to get stopped with what we've got in the boot, do we?'

'Gettin' lost with them's not a brilliant move neither,' Gloria retorted.

'Okay, I got it, we're not too far.' She began to do a U-turn, when, caught in the headlamps, they saw a police officer examining a locked gate. He turned and watched the car bump onto the pavement.

'Oh, bloody hell. Do you see what I see?' said Gloria.

Ester looked in the mirror. He was walking towards them. She turned off the lights, gunned the engine, careered up the road and screeched round the corner.

'Well, that was fucking subtle,' muttered Gloria.

*

Julia was waist deep and still digging.

Dolly peered down. 'Okay, just drop him in and cover him. It's deep enough, isn't it?'

Julia started to climb out. 'Yeah, the maggots'll have a field day.'

'Let's get him out of the car,' Dolly said as she chucked her spade aside. Julia stuck hers into the ground and followed. The body was wrapped in an old carpet and polythene sheeting. They dragged it towards them and, between them, eased it from the rear of the Mini. It was too heavy to carry easily and they resorted to dragging it across the uneven ground towards the grave.

'One shoe's missing,' Julia whispered.

'Shit! Go and see if it's in the car.'

Julia searched the car but found nothing. 'Maybe it's still in the pool,' she said, as she helped roll the body down into the grave. They began to shovel the earth back into the hole, both working flat out, as slowly, bit by bit, Lennie was covered up. Dolly stamped the earth down on top of him before clambering out, and Julia dragged the planks back to lay across the grave.

Gloria was furious. She found it hard to believe Ester could be so stupid but at least she now understood why they'd kept to the back streets.

'Hot? This bleedin' car's hot and you been driving it around London, almost ran over a bloody copper. I'm tellin' you, Ester, you need your head seeing to. If Dolly finds out ...'

'Oh, shut up. We're here now. Go on.'

Gloria got out of the car and knocked on a small door built into the big yard gates. It was opened by Tommy, who had a whispered conversation with her, and then the main gates eased back. Ester drove in, and Tommy and his contact began to unload the guns, carrying them into the warehouse.

Gloria had never met the buyer before, a small, softly spoken man wearing a camel coat, a good suit and pinkish-toned glasses. His expert began to check over each weapon as Gloria placed them on the desk. A large space had been cleared, the blinds had been drawn, and they quietly got on with the business in hand.

Ester was surprised by Gloria, who proved adept at handling the guns, making a convincing sales pitch with each piece. The weapons consisted of two 9mm Browning pistols, semi-automatic, four .38 Smith and Wessons, three .35 Magnum Colts, two .44s, two .455 Webley's specials, collector's items, with boxes of ammunition, two Westley Richards rifles, 26-inch barrels, bead foresight and stands, two Heckler and Koch machine guns and four Kalashnikovs.

While Gloria was doing her business, Ester was selling

Tommy the Saab for cash. She admitted it was a bit 'iffy' but not too hot. Tommy raised an eyebrow.

'Come on, man, you know it's a great deal. You can switch the plates on it and get it out of the country within twenty-four hours.'

'Okay. I've got an old van you can take in part exchange.'

Tommy glanced over at the gun dealers, then at Gloria who was searching one of the big bags. 'Ester, a minute,' she said, and Ester went to join her. 'Three shotguns missing. You know anything about that?'

Ester shook her head and whispered that Tommy was interested in buying the Saab.

'Good, I'm not driving around in it any more.' Gloria returned to the dealers.

'No shotguns, sorry, but I got a Desert Eagle that's the gun to have right now. You want to see it?'

The officers in the patrol car received the information that the Saab was stolen. The beat officer had succeeded in taking the Saab's registration number and had flagged down the patrol car, whose window he was now leaning against. 'I thought it might be. They drove off fast soon as they saw me, heading back towards Tower Bridge, but they could have turned off anywhere. Lot of old warehouses round that area.'

The patrol car moved off. As the officer watched it

disappear, he turned to continue his street patrol. An old, green-painted van passed him but he didn't give it a second glance. Inside, Gloria was counting the money, licking her fingers to flick through the notes. 'Ten grand! What a bleedin' rip-off. I couldn't believe the cheap bastard.'

'Well, we made up for it with the Saab.'

'Yeah, but that's not the point. I hate being skinned. They got a lot for their dough, you know. They were worth at least thirty grand. I mean, two of the rifles would cost you seven big ones alone.'

Ester headed over Tower Bridge. 'Well, I'll split the money from the car with you. Dolly needn't know.'

Gloria smirked. 'You mean about it being nicked?'

'Yeah, we just divide the cash between us.'

'No way. She gets the lot because she'll be on the blower to Tommy checking it out, you know her. And besides . . .'

'Besides what?'

Gloria stuffed the money up her skirt, wriggling it into her panties. 'Somebody kept those shotguns – and you never know . . .'

'Never know what?'

'Maybe she's got something in mind? I mean, she's pulled a couple of blinders, hasn't she? Way I see it, let's keep her happy, see what's going on in that old brain of hers.'

Ester laughed. 'Why not? In the meantime, you keep that cash warm.'

'Better to be safe than sorry,' Gloria said, as the wad of notes eased round her panties. 'They got bastards holding up motors in traffic jams to nick handbags now, you know. They push a gun into your face and nick your wallet. Shocking world nowadays.'

DCI Craigh, DI Palmer and Mike headed towards Grange Manor House, accompanied by twelve local officers from Thames Valley along with a search warrant, this time not for diamonds but weapons.

Julia and Dolly had carried the spare earth to the hedges and scattered it around. They were filthy dirty but the job had been done. They were just putting the spades back into the car when they heard the noise of engines. They froze, looking towards the lane as a police car drove past, followed by two more vehicles.

'What was that about?'

'I don't know and I don't care, just so long as they're not coming into the cemetery,' Dolly muttered.

Julia walked round to the driving seat. She got in and turned to Dolly.

'Connie really owes us a big favour.'

'Don't worry, she'll pay it back,' Dolly replied as they drove slowly out of the cemetery and onto the lane. 'Anyway, enough excitement for one evening. Let's go back to the house.'

Chapter 11

DCI Craigh gave the signal and all vehicle lights went out as the convoy moved slowly down the drive to the manor. The cars stopped and six men moved quickly to the rear of the house, while six more positioned themselves around the front. Craigh, accompanied by Palmer and Mike, walked up the front steps. He tapped lightly and called quietly that it was the police. Receiving no reply, he stepped back, and Palmer hit the lock on the front door with a sledgehammer. At the same time, the men at the rear of the house got a radio message to enter via the kitchen.

The sound of the forced entry echoed like thunder inside the manor. Down came the front door as the back door splintered.

Kathleen was putting coal into a scuttle when she heard the crash and the voices shouting: '*Police! Police!*'

She threw the scuttle aside, drew open the cellar window and climbed out.

Angela almost had heart failure. She was caught midway up the stairs and started screaming in terror.

Connie was the first to return. Big John had dropped her at the manor gates. She was picked up as she walked down the drive, two uniformed officers holding her between them as they pushed her towards the front door. By now every light was turned on, the place seemed to be swarming with police and she was as terrified as Angela. She thought they were arresting her because of Lennie, while Angela thought they had come for her because of James Donaldson. They were questioned, asked for their names, dates of birth, and shown the search warrant: neither said anything.

Kathleen was equally terrified and, once out of the cellar, made a run for it, heading towards the woods. Two officers gave chase. By the time she was brought back, gripped tightly by two police officers, she was sobbing hysterically.

Ester and Gloria drove in just as Kathleen was being escorted from the woods. Both women were asked to step out of their vehicle, place their hands on the top of the van and stand with their legs apart. Gloria was yelling her head off, demanding that a female officer search her, as Ester shouted that she wanted to know what the hell was going on. No one answered. They were shown the warrant as DCI Craigh walked out of the house. He instructed his men to run checks on all the women.

'What you talking about?' Gloria demanded.

Kathleen stood by the patrol car, head bowed, still crying.

'What you think we are? Bleedin' IRA? I'm from East Ham, she's from Liverpool, you got this all wrong.' Gloria was yelling while Ester nudged her to shut up. 'I want to go to the toilet,' Gloria shouted.

Ester warned her again to shut up but Gloria hissed back, 'Have you forgot I got the dough in me knickers?'

The police received information that Kathleen O'Reilly was wanted for absconding from a magistrates' court; there was an outstanding charge of fraud and kiting against her. She was ushered into the patrol car.

As Dolly and Julia drove up to the manor, they gaped at the scene: Ester and Gloria, spread-eagled over the van, Kathleen sobbing inside the patrol car, and everywhere uniformed officers carrying big-beamed torches.

'Shit, now what?' Dolly exclaimed.

'Will you get out of the car?' DCI Craigh gestured for more officers to assist in searching the new arrivals.

The women were herded into the house and taken into the drawing room where Connie sat with Angela while the room was searched by a uniformed officer. Dolly looked over the search warrant and then handed it back to Craigh. 'You mind if I make a pot of tea?'

He shook his head. If that woman had a stash of guns inside the house she was acting very cool about it, but he wasn't about to call the men off, far from it. They would comb every inch of the house and grounds.

The dawn came and with it better visibility. The search continued, both inside and out. The women sat drinking tea, eating sandwiches, but did not offer either to the police.

At half past eight on Sunday morning, Craigh gave up. He returned to London with Palmer and Mike. They had found nothing and all they had to show for eight hours' work was a missing felon, Kathleen O'Reilly.

Dolly examined the smashed doors and broken banister rails. She began making up a list of damages and she would make damned sure they paid through the nose for them. She was angry, not just because of the warrant and the search but because it was obvious they had a tip-off from someone. The question was, which one of them was it? She knew they had been very lucky: a few hours earlier and they would have been caught not only with the guns but with a dead body. The women were all on edge, waiting for the police to leave. They couldn't talk, too scared they might be overheard. By one o'clock the remaining police called it quits and left. As soon as the women saw them moving out, they all began to talk at once.

'Eh! Dolly, what about Kathleen?'

Dolly frowned. 'I don't know what to think.'

'I can't see her being a grass,' Gloria said as she hitched up her skirt.

'Somebody is, though,' Dolly said.

Gloria pulled the money from out of her panties. 'There you go. I had it stashed in me drawers – about the only thing I've had in them for a few years.'

Dolly arched an eyebrow. 'No need to be crude.'

They counted the money, discussed the sale of the car and then Dolly looked at her watch. 'Right, I'm going to have a sleep, then I'm going to church.'

They were astonished. She yawned, asking if the boiler was on as she needed a bath.

'Church?' Gloria asked.

'Yes, church. I want the locals to trust me – I've got to if I'm going to open up this place.' Dolly paused. 'Even though they turned me down, I'm not finished yet. I knew it wasn't going to be easy but —'

'Why don't you be realistic, Dolly?' Ester said. 'You don't stand a chance in hell. As if they would let kids come here.' She yawned.

'Why not?' Dolly persisted.

'Because you're an ex-con, darlin'. Now maybe you'd stand more of a chance if you applied for teenagers – better still, ex-cons, young ones coming out. They all need a home and—' Suddenly Ester laughed and clapped her hands. 'I tell you something, with my contacts, if you got a houseful of young girls we could open this place again. Coin it in! What a perfect cover.'

'Run this as a brothel?' Dolly asked, not believing what she was hearing.

'Why not? It ran before and, like I said, I have contacts. Put in the cash we got from the guns, from my car — we've at least got a kick-start.'

Julia turned on her. 'Use poor kids coming out of the nick? Is that what you'd do, Ester?'

'Why not? We've already got a couple of tarts here for starters.'

'Who you bleedin' callin' a tart?' Gloria snapped.

'Oh, come off it. You and Connie have been turning tricks and Angela's done a couple. All I'm saying is be realistic.'

Julia was furious. 'Well, before I'd get kids on the game, I'd pull a robbery. You make me sick, Ester.'

'Do I? Well, maybe we should think about pulling a robbery, then. What do you say, Dolly? You know this will never get opened as a foster home so what about it? You got any ideas?'

Dolly moved slowly to the door. 'The only thing I've got on my mind right now is trying to find out which one of you shopped me. Somebody here did — one of *you* did — and after I sort that out I'm going to bloody well open this place up, whatever anyone thinks. '

They waited until the door closed behind her, then started looking from one to another: was one of them a grass?

Gloria sighed. 'What about Kathleen, then? She was the only one of us the filth had anything on. Maybe she was scared and wanted to make a deal.'

'I told you, Kathleen's a lot of things but she's not a grass,' Julia said.

'That leaves one of us in here, doesn't it?' Gloria said, looking at Ester.

'It's not fucking me,' Ester snapped.

Julia opened the door. 'This is ridiculous. We're all knackered. Why don't we do what Dolly's doing and have some kip? We've been up all night.'

Dolly could hear toilets flushing, baths running. She was wide awake, couldn't sleep. Ester tapped lightly on the door and peeked in. 'Dolly, can I have a word?'

Dolly lay back on the pillow. 'Sure, sit down.'

'Look, I'm sorry if I spoke out of turn down there but I was just tired and right now I need a roof over my head.'

Dolly nodded. 'Sure. Anything else?'

'Maybe check out Angela. She's been making phone calls.' Ester backed out and closed the door.

Dolly sat up and thumped her pillow. Next to turn up was Connie. She wanted Dolly to know that she believed in the project and was sure it would work, she loved the old house. 'It wasn't me, Dolly, I wouldn't have told anyone about the guns, I mean, I wouldn't, not with Lennie here, now would I?'

Dolly smiled ruefully. 'No, love, but Lennie could have got us all in hot water.'

Connie was near to tears. 'I know, I know.'

A while after she left, Gloria tapped at the door. One by one they came, just to make sure Dolly knew it wasn't them.

The only one who did not appear was Angela.

She was lying wide awake in her bed, and jumped when Dolly walked in and closed the door behind her. 'I want to talk to you, Angela, and I want you to be honest with me. Who have you been calling?' Angela burst into tears and Dolly came and sat on the edge of her bed. 'Now don't cry, just tell me. We all know you're always making phone calls.'

'My mum and—'

Dolly listened as Angela blurted out how frightened she was about being arrested for running over Jimmy Donaldson. Between sobs and gasps she told Dolly about her boyfriend, who was married with kids, and now didn't want anything to do with her.

Dolly patted her hand. 'Well, maybe it's best that you're here.'

'I'm pregnant.'

She cradled Angela in her arms, comforting her,

asking if she wanted to keep the baby. When Angela sobbed that she didn't know, Dolly assured her that, as long as she was at the manor, she and the baby would have a home.

When Dolly came out Connie was passing Angela's room.

'She's pregnant,' Dolly said.

Connie looked at the closed door, then back at Dolly. 'So that's why she's been on the phone, is it?'

'Don't tell the others. She doesn't want anyone to know.'

Connie scooted down the stairs and into the kitchen. Gloria was sitting with Ester as Julia washed up.

'Okay, this is what we've decided, Connie,' Ester said.

Connie's eye was caught by a stack of bits and pieces of jewellery.

'We're all giving up what we can, you know, just to make it look like we're really behind this foster home crap. We don't think Dolly stands a chance in hell but . . .'

Connie pulled out a chair and sank into it. 'I got a few pieces I can give.'

'Good. It's just that she's got to trust us, Connie. We think she may be coming up with something. We don't know but Gloria said three shotguns are missing.'

'Yeah, I took them into the gym, they're in a locker there.'

Ester turned to Julia. 'See, what did I tell you? I knew she was planning something.'

Julia was putting away the dishes. 'So we all make out we love this place, is that right?'

Connie pouted. 'But I do.'

'So do I,' said Julia.

'Yeah, well, that's 'cos of that bleedin' horse. You're never off the friggin' thing.'

Julia glared at Gloria. 'Okay, so I love Helen of Troy, but I also like this place.'

Ester slapped the table. 'For Chrissakes, can we get done with *The Sound of Bleedin' Music*? All I am saying is she doesn't trust us.'

'Well, *I'm* not the fuckin' grass,' Gloria said angrily.

'I think it's Angela,' Ester said.

'No, she's not, she's pregnant,' Connie said, and they all turned on her. She shrugged her shoulders. 'She is, Dolly just told me, that's why she's been making all these calls.'

Gloria stood up. 'Well, she's a bloody little liar. She's not pregnant.'

'How do you know?' Ester demanded.

'Because she borrowed my Tampax yesterday.' Dolly walked in and Gloria whipped round. 'We think it's Angela. She's not pregnant, Dolly, she's a liar.'

Dolly clenched her hands in front of her. 'Is she? Well, one of you get her down here, then. Get her in here right now.'

Angela was hauled out of her bed by Gloria and

pushed down the stairs. She crept into the kitchen like a frightened rabbit.

'How many weeks gone are you?' demanded Dolly.

'Two months,' Angela said.

Gloria pushed her. 'No, you're not. Why did you borrow my Tampax if you was up the spout?'

'Because I had some blood, I did, I swear on my life.'

Connie went over to her and slipped her arms around her. 'Don't cry, we believe you.'

'I fucking don't,' yelled Gloria.

Dolly scratched her head, and then said to Julia, 'Take her upstairs and examine her.'

'Oh, for God's sake, Dolly, this is ridiculous,' Julia said.

'Is it? Well, I want to know, because if she isn't then she lied to me and she could have been lying from day one. Somebody is tipping off the police, so examine her. Go on, do it.'

Julia led Angela out of the room, then Ester tapped Dolly's shoulder. 'This is for you. It's from us, all of us. We want to help out in any way we can, Dolly. Some of it's gold and—'

Gloria pointed. 'That tie-pin belonged to Jack Dempsey and that Rolex Eddie gave me. It could be a fake, though,' she added.

Dolly picked up pieces of the jewellery, strangely moved even as she noted that they were still wearing their best items. But it was, as the old saying goes, the thought that counted.

About ten minutes later Julia returned. 'She was telling the truth. I think she's more like three months than two. You can often have a few spots, even a period, during the early months.'

Dolly felt awful but she had needed to know.

'So you think it's Kathleen?' Gloria asked.

'I don't know – I just don't know,' Dolly said, drumming her fingers on the table. 'I mean maybe, just maybe, it's no one. Have any of you had dealings with DCI Craigh before?'

No one could recall having been arrested by him on a previous occasion. Connie said that she quite liked him, he'd been very nice to her; it was the younger bloke she didn't like.

Angela was suddenly standing like a child in the doorway.

Dolly reached for her and took her hand. 'I'm sorry about that, love, but I needed to know.'

Angela backed away, pressing her body against the wall.

'We're just talking about the coppers,' Dolly said.

'Well, I don't like them, any of them,' Julia said.

'Me neither,' Gloria muttered.

'Funnily enough, I'm sure I've met that younger one, the blond-haired guy, the good-looking one,' Ester said.

Ester looked at Angela and everyone followed suit.

'I don't know him!' she wailed. But she was trembling.

Ester sprang forward. 'Yes, you do!'

Angela bolted, and Ester took off after her.

The rest of them followed, to see Angela running up the stairs, with Ester giving chase. Ester lunged forward and caught hold of Angela's foot. Angela fell forwards, then started bumping and slithering down the stairs as Ester climbed over her, hauling her by her hair.

'Ester! Don't! *Ester, she's pregnant!*' screamed Julia.

Angela fought off her attacker, pushing and screaming, and managed to escape up the stairs, but a furious Ester pursued her along the landing and caught up with her in a couple of strides.

'You little liar! You're a bloody liar, Angela!' Ester was terrifying as she punched and slapped like a whirlwind. 'Tell me the truth! Tell me the truth or I'll fucking kill you.'

Angela dived beneath Ester's arm and ran into her own room, but she didn't have time to lock the door before Ester kicked it open and slammed it behind her. Dolly was first in after them, then Julia. Dolly dragged Ester off Angela, who was hunched on the bed, trying to protect her face from Ester's blows. Ester was red-faced with fury.

'Ester! *Ester! Calm down!*' Dolly slapped her face.

'You just slapped the wrong face, sweetheart. Ask

that dirty piece of shit who her boyfriend is. He's that bloke that was here, isn't he? *Isn't he?*'

Angela clung to the pillow, as if it would shield her from any further onslaught.

'Is this true?' Dolly asked calmly.

Angela nodded through her tears. Crowding at the door, the other women stared at her angrily.

'You don't understand,' she wailed.

'Oh, I think I do,' Dolly spat, prepared to leave her to the women, just like a cell fight in the nick.

'He's Shirley Miller's brother,' Angela shrieked.

Dolly froze, her hands clenched at her sides. 'Get out and leave her with me. All of you, get out.'

'What you think she's doing up there?' Gloria asked. Dolly had been with Angela for about fifteen minutes.

'Suffocating her, I hope,' Ester muttered.

'So it was her all the time,' Connie sighed.

'Yeah, the two-faced little bitch,' Gloria snarled. 'She could have had the lot of us sent down. Ester was right. I just wish I'd got a few punches in.'

Gloria looked up. 'You don't think she'd bump her off, do you?'

Angela was still red-eyed from weeping but at least she was calmer now. She had explained how she had first met Mike after Ester was raided, how he had been kind to her as she was under-age. He had been helpful in getting her social workers and it was thanks to him that she was never reported. They had then become more than friendly after Ester was sent for trial, but recently Mike had refused to see her as his wife had found out. When Ester had called, Angela had contacted him and he'd asked her to report anything she found out about Dolly Rawlins.

'What did he tell you about Shirley?'

Angela snivelled. 'Only that you were responsible, and his mother . . .'

Dolly smiled inwardly. Audrey had such a big mouth but she'd kept her son's part in it very quiet.

'What are you going to do with me?' Angela asked.

Dolly opened the door and held up the key. 'You can stay here until tomorrow, then you pack up and leave. I never want to see you again. You betrayed me – the only one of them I trusted. Seems I was wrong. I'll never forgive you, love, so get packed.'

The door closed silently but to Angela the key turning in the lock was like thunder.

Dolly shuffled along a pew and bent to pray. Then, as the service began, she sat back and opened the hymn book. No one paid much attention to her. When the service was over, she shook hands with the vicar and made her way towards the gates. To her right was the big cemetery where only the night before she had buried Lennie. But she hardly gave it a second thought because up ahead she had seen Mrs Tilly opening her car door. She hurried towards her.

'Mrs Tilly!' Dolly called, and was taken aback by the cold, aloof stare she got in return. 'I got a letter,' Dolly said, a little out of breath.

Mrs Tilly was in two minds whether even to speak to Dolly but her own anger got the better of her. 'You lied to me, Mrs Rawlins. When I think how much work I did to persuade the board not only to see you but make an on-site visit.'

Dolly interrupted, 'I'm sorry. Are you saying you've been to the manor?'

'Oh yes, we came, Mrs Rawlins. Didn't Ester Freeman tell you?'

Gloria was looking out of the window as a stern-faced Dolly marched up the path. 'Well, the church has certainly done wonders for her! She looks ready for nine rounds with Mike Tyson.'

The door banged shut and promptly swung open again because of the damaged lock. The drawing-room door was thrown wide. Dolly hurled her handbag onto the sofa and threw off her coat.

'Something wrong?' Ester asked innocently.

'Oh yes, you can say that again. Now I know why

they turned me down. They only came here and found the lot of you bollock-naked in the sauna.'

'Oh, come on, we weren't all naked, Dolly,' said Julia.

'You, Julia, shut your mouth because you and that bitch over there were, and I quote, "in an obvious sexual embrace". I presume that was before you turned the hosepipe on the chairman of the board.'

They hadn't got any excuses, not that she gave them a chance to make any as she paced up and down. 'All of you knew you'd blown my chances and not one of you had the guts to tell me what you'd done. Eight years I planned this, eight years I waited and now you've ruined it. You've destroyed any hope I had of reversing the rejection. Well, the lot of you can pack up and piss off with Angela.'

She slammed the door so hard that the chandelier shook dangerously.

'Oh, bloody hell,' muttered Gloria. 'I knew it'd come out. How do we get round this one?'

Ester was up and heading for the door. She turned and winked. 'Leave it to me.'

Dolly banged the kettle onto the Aga as Ester walked in with her hands up as if at gunpoint. 'Just let me tell you something, okay? Don't shoot.'

Dolly was not amused. She threw tea-bags into the pot.

'Listen, Dolly. There may, just may, be a way round this.'

'Like what?'

'Just listen. That bloke who came with them, beaky-nosed, bald fella with a few hairs combed over the top of his head.'

'Mr Crow. He's chairman of the board.'

'Ah, crow by name, crow by nature. Well, Dolly, I recognized him and maybe one of the reasons why the board turned you down, or he did, was because—'

'You were all frolicking naked in the sauna?'

'No. He used to be a regular. I'm sure he wouldn't want that known, would he? You could pay him a private visit. Maybe *he* can do something for you.'

Dolly put her head in her hands. 'He was one of your clients?'

'Yeah. Work him over, Dolly. Make him sweat. It's got to be worth a shot.'

Mike was watching TV when the phone rang. He watched Susan jump up to answer it, making no effort to take it himself. He was sick and tired of being monitored.

Susan called from the hall. 'She wants to speak to you.'

He didn't know if she was referring to Angela or his mother. 'Who is it?'

'She said her name was Dolly Rawlins.'

Mike was half out of his seat when he fell back, his face drained of colour.

'Mike? She said it's important.'

*

Audrey was booked on the first flight to Spain on Monday morning, her third attempt to leave. She opened the door to Mike, all smiles, thinking he had called to say goodbye, but one look at his face made her step back, afraid.

'What's happened?'

He walked into the living room and threw himself down on the sofa.

'Dolly Rawlins just called my house.'

'Oh God.'

'She just wanted me to know that she knows about my involvement with the diamonds, with everything.'

'What's she going to do?'

'I don't know but I'm in deep shit because if she goes to my guv'nor, I'll be arrested. So will you.'

'She wouldn't do that. It'd implicate her.'

'I know. That's what I'm banking on.'

'What do we do?'

Mike sank lower into the sofa cushions. 'Well, maybe you should leave anyway.'

She went to him and put her arms around him. 'Come with me, love, you and the kids and Susan. We just up and run for it.'

He pushed her away. 'I can't do that.'

'Why not?'

'I can't do anything that'll throw any suspicion on me. Don't you understand? I'll just have to wait, see what she wants.'

Audrey broke down and sobbed. 'It's not fair, is it? Some people get away with murder. You know she killed that poor Jimmy Donaldson, just as she as good as killed our Shirley.'

Mike swung round and grabbed his mother's arm. 'I don't want to hear her name again. If it wasn't for Shirley I'd never have got into this mess. I mean it, Mum! And I don't want to see or hear from you either. You got me involved in this, Mum, and I got to get myself out of it, so leave, go away, get the hell out of my sight.'

He was almost at the car when he stopped and leaned against a brick wall. He started to cry – he couldn't stop the tears. He hadn't meant to say all that about Shirley. He sniffed, wiped his face with the back of his hand, then forced himself to get angry.

She was to blame, whatever way he looked at it, whatever guilt he felt. She'd married that cheap villain Terry Miller, she ... Shirley was dead and buried, he had to get his life sorted, he had to straighten things out. He was losing it, he was blowing everything that was important to him and if he didn't get hold of himself there was no one else to prop him up.

By the time he got into his car he was calmer and in control. He didn't look back to the lit-up window of his mother's flat. He really never wanted to see her again.

*

Audrey was all packed. She'd earmarked a few items for shipping out but now she was taking down the little personal items, the photographs from the gilt mirror above the mantel. She read her younger son Gregg's last postcard, looked at the stupid kittens, and sighed. Well, he'd just have to ask around to find out where she was. They would tell him down the market. She tossed the card into the bin. She didn't have the energy to worry about Gregg, or anyone but herself. Now she could even blame Dolly Rawlins for her son walking out on her. Everything was Dolly Rawlins's fault and Audrey felt the anger boiling up in her. But then she straightened herself out: she'd be in Spain this time tomorrow, with a villa and a few quid in the bank. At least she'd beaten that bitch over the money. At least she had something to show for poor Shirley. She turned towards the sideboard as if to confirm everything was all right but she'd already packed Shirley's photograph: there was nothing there, no sweet, smiling, beautiful Shirley. Audrey felt the tears, not of anger or fury or revenge: tears of guilt because she knew she had thought about and cared more for Shirley after she was dead than when she was alive.

Chapter 12

D olly was directed to sit on a row of chairs in the draughty town hall corridor. Mr Crow's secretary walked out of his office without even glancing in Dolly's direction. Dolly stood up, watched the squat-legged woman disappear, carrying a thick file, then quickly tapped on the door of Mr Crow's office and walked in. She was through with waiting.

Mr Crow looked up, frowning when he saw her close the door behind her. 'Mrs Rawlins, did my secretary tell you—'

'Yes, she said I could have a few moments. It won't take any longer.'

He pursed his lips and put his hands together, as if he was praying. 'I am a very busy man.'

'I'm busy too but, like I said, this won't take a moment. I've come about the letter.'

'Mrs Rawlins, the decision was unanimous. Obviously you can take private action if you wish, that is entirely up to you, but as far as I am concerned I do not at this stage feel you would be advised to proceed.'

'All I want is to make a home for kids without one.'

'I am aware of that, but it is my job to make sure any child placed into care will have not only the right supervision but also a suitable environment.'

'Is it my criminal record that went against me?'

'Obviously that was taken into consideration, and we are also aware that you have been questioned by a DCI Craigh regarding—' Again he was interrupted.

'You referring to the warrants? The house was searched, the police found nothing incriminating and—'

Mr Crow sucked in his breath. 'Mrs Rawlins, under the circumstances, and with reference to an on-site visit to your property, it was decided that—'

'You didn't really need one, though, did you?'

'I'm sorry?'

She leaned forward. 'A visit. You already know the Manor House well, don't you? According to Miss Freeman you were a regular visitor when it was a brothel. Isn't that right?'

Pink dots appeared on his cheeks. 'Just what are you inferring, Mrs Rawlins?'

'That perhaps you had an ulterior motive for rejecting

312

my application, that had nothing to do with me or my criminal background.'

'Be careful what you are insinuating, Mrs Rawlins. You are, I am sure, fully aware you remain on licence for the rest of your life and—'

'I'm just stating a fact,' she said quietly.

'Then please, Mrs Rawlins, be careful. I have told you this was a unanimous decision by all members of the board. We do not feel that you would be the right person to be given access to young children. We do not feel that the Manor House would be suitable accommodation. It is my only intention to make sure any foster carer recommended by the social services department is both mentally and physically—'

She stood up, this time leaning right over his desk. 'You know, my husband said he could never go straight because people like you, like the police, would never allow him to. Well, now I know about you.'

Mr Crow stood up, the pink blobs spreading, no longer with embarrassment but with anger. 'I'd like you to leave my office now.'

'Oh, I'm going, and I won't come back. I waited a long time to make a home for kids a reality but it was stupid, wasn't it? I never stood a chance. Don't worry, I won't let on that you're a two-faced bastard.'

She left, closing the door quietly behind her, and he could hear her footsteps on the marble corridor outside.

He was shaking with anger but he was now confident that he had made the right decision. He would add to her report that she had lied to the board. Contrary to Mrs Rawlins's denial, Ester Freeman was still resident at Grange Manor House.

Dolly drove back to the manor. She had to wait at the level crossing for ten minutes. This time she couldn't be bothered to talk to Raymond Dewey who sat, as usual, on his little trainspotter's stool, jotting down his times and numbers. He waved at her but she turned towards the lake and the small narrow bridge the railway crossed. She got out of the car and walked a few paces, still focusing on the bridge. Then she turned round, towards the station and the signal box. She sauntered over to Raymond and gave him a forced smile.

'Hello, Raymond, how are you today?'

'I'm very well. This is the twelve fifteen from Marylebone.'

'Is it? You know every train, do you? All the right times and the delays?'

'That's my job.'

'I bet there's one train you don't know the times of.'

'No, there isn't one. I know every train that passes through this station, how long they take to go over the bridge and—'

'So you write them all down, then?'

'Yes,' he said, proudly proffering his thick wedge of school exercise books. 'Each train has its own book.'

Dolly took one of the books with his thick scrawled writing across the front. 'Mail train.' She flipped over the pages. He had listed every delivery, time of arrival at and departure from the station, plus delays at the crossing.

'You're very thorough, Raymond,' Dolly said, as her eyes took in his dates and times. She then shut the book and passed it back to him as the lights changed and the train went by. As the gates opened, she returned to the Mini.

'Thank you very much, Raymond.' She smiled and waved as she drove past him. She felt strangely calm, almost as if it was fate. Had she been subconsciously thinking about it? It seemed so natural. It certainly wouldn't be easy but, then, she had always liked a challenge. This would be one – a terrifyingly dangerous one.

A few minutes later, Dolly parked the car and walked up into the woods. From there she had a direct view of the station, the bridge, the lake and the level crossing. She spent over half an hour carefully checking the lay of the land. She could tell with one look why the police had chosen this specific station to unload the money from the road onto the train. There were only two access roads, both very narrow, and room for only one vehicle at a time. Anyone attempting to hold up the security wagon as it delivered the money to the train would be cut off.

The station could easily be manned by four or five police officers and no one could hide out there. If they did, if they hit the train standing in the platform, they wouldn't have a hope in hell of transporting the money by road as there was no access for the getaway vehicles. The tracks were lined with hedgerows and wide-open fields, not a road in sight.

Dolly studied the bridge. Twenty-five feet high, the lake beneath, no access either side of the tracks, just a narrow walkway. Surely it would be impossible. How could you hold up the train on the bridge and get away with heavy mailbags on foot? It couldn't be done. She looked down at the lake, then back to the bridge. If you got a boat, you'd still have to reach the shore, and no vehicles could get down there. Again, there were no roads, just fields, hedges and streams.

Dolly was so immersed in her thoughts that when she heard twigs cracking she spun round in shock, her heart pounding. Julia appeared, riding Helen of Troy.

'Sorry if I made you jump. I did call out!'

Dolly covered her fright, smiling. 'I didn't hear you – I didn't even see you, come to think about it. You been here long?'

'No, I just rode up, cut across the fields.' Julia dismounted and tied up the horse. 'How did it go at the social services?' she asked.

'It didn't. It's finished.'

'I'm sorry.'

'So am I. Are they easy to ride?'

'Yeah. Why, you thinking of taking lessons?'

Dolly moved tentatively towards Helen, putting out her hand to stroke her nose.

'She won't bite you. Be confident, they know when you're nervous.' Julia moved to stand beside Dolly, putting an arm round her shoulders.

Dolly petted Helen's nose. 'That Norma ... she said this horse was police-trained?'

'Yep. She's very solid, nothing scares her. As Norma said, she's bomb-proof. Be good for kids to learn on.'

Dolly withdrew her hand, her face drawn. 'Yes, well, there won't be any kids to teach. I'll see you back at the house.'

She trudged off as Julia unhitched the reins and got back into the saddle. She rode away, unaware that Dolly had turned back to watch her as she cantered into the fields.

There *was* a way to get to that train. Julia was now galloping, disappearing from sight as she jumped the hedges.

DCI Craigh and DI Palmer looked over the forensic reports taken from the red Volvo. There was no indication that the car had been involved in any accident, no trace of blood, or body tissue. They didn't have enough to bring charges against Gloria Radford and, even if she had hired the car, they had no evidence that she had run over James Donaldson. In other words, they had fuck all.

'Now what?'

Craigh looked at Palmer and shrugged. 'Well, we're up for a hard rap around the knuckles from the Super, and that's just for starters, unless we can iron this out somehow.'

Palmer looked over their reports and noted the vast amount it had cost Thames Valley and the Met to mount the searches of the manor, together with the surveillance. And all they had to show for it was one arrest: Kathleen O'Reilly.

Craigh sucked his teeth. 'I'm going to interview O'Reilly again. So far she's not said a bloody word, but you never know.'

'Bring her in, shall I?'

Kathleen had been taken to Holloway. She would stand trial again for the previous charges of fraud and kiting but she insisted she was just staying at the manor and that Dolly Rawlins had no knowledge of her previous record or that she was on a wanted list. All she did was pay Rawlins rent.

Mike appeared and Craigh fixed him with a stare. 'I'm going to talk to O'Reilly again but the word from the guv is to stay well clear of Rawlins. We got to get ourselves out of this mess so you make sure your reports are tight as a nut.'

Mike hesitated. 'What about my sister?'

'Less said about her the better. We're in enough trouble as it is so just get on with the backlog of work on your desk.' Craigh glared at him. 'This isn't over yet, son. We could all be in trouble. We never found any diamonds so at least that's been sorted, understand?'

'Yes, sir.'

Mike sat down at his desk. His heart was thudding in his chest. Had he got away with it? Or was that call from Rawlins going to turn into a real threat? He felt sick to his stomach and when he reached for his files his hand was shaking. If Rawlins put him in the frame, he was finished.

Kathleen was as unforthcoming with Craigh as she had been the night she was arrested. She didn't know anything about any diamonds or guns; all she did was rent a room from Dolly Rawlins.

'What you think she is? Some kind of female Al Capone? Why don't you leave her alone? All she's doin' is tryin' to open a home for kids and you're just harassing her.'

Craigh thanked her for her observations and turned on his heel. Maybe she really didn't know anything about Rawlins and maybe, he began to wonder, they had been pressured into the searches and warrants by Mike Withey because he had personal motives. The more Craigh thought about it the more he made up his mind that if the Super tapped on his shoulder he'd point the finger at Mike. He wasn't going to take the fall.

Dolly sat with a mug of tea. She was deep in thought when Ester walked in. 'Angela's still in her room. Gloria took up a coffee at breakfast time, told her to get packed, but she's still in there.'

Dolly got up and poured the dregs of the tea into the sink. 'I don't care, just get rid of her. I got to go up to London, have a word with Kathleen.'

Connie walked in with three sheets of paper. 'Dolly, you wanted John to give estimates for the damage when the police raided the house.'

Dolly inspected the figures and smiled. 'These are good. Oh, Connie, can I have a word?' She turned to Ester. 'Can you leave us for a minute?'

Ester sloped off, and Dolly washed and dried the mug carefully, placing it back on its hook. 'There's a signal box at the station, young bloke on duty – I think there's two of them. Can you get to know them a bit? Find out what time they come on duty, when they're off and who does nights, that kind of thing.'

'Why?'

'Because I want you to.' Connie pulled a face and Dolly moved closer. 'This time, Connie, if needs be you fuck them, because I want that information. I want you to know that signal box layout better than the back of your hand, understand me?'

Connie stepped back. 'Yes . . . all right.'

'Good – but don't tell any of the others, just get on with it.'

Dolly went out of the back door and called Julia, who was leading Helen of Troy back into the stables. 'A minute, love.'

Ester caught Connie as she went up the stairs. 'What was that about?'

Connie looked back down the stairs. 'She said not to tell you.'

'So, what did she want?'

Connie repeated what Dolly had told her then carried on up the stairs. Ester was about to go into the kitchen when she overheard Dolly talking to Julia. 'You go and see Norma; try and find out about the security at the station.'

'Why?' Julia asked as she pulled off her boots.

'Don't ask questions, just do it. If she doesn't know, then fine, but test her out.'

Julia felt uneasy but Dolly didn't seem to be in the mood to take no for an answer, so she kept quiet.

Dolly walked into the hall. She saw the drawing-room door closing. 'Ester?'

Ester popped her head out, acting surprised. 'Oh! What do you want?'

'That kid, the trainspotter. He's got books, train times and—'

'We can get you a timetable, you know, Dolly.'

Dolly's mouth was set in a thin tight line. 'Yes, I know, but I want the times and details of one specific train. The mail train. Get his book off him but do it without him knowing.'

'That shouldn't be too hard – he's mental anyway.'

Dolly picked up the phone and began to dial. Ester hovered a moment before she went into the kitchen.

Julia was still there, drinking a cup of tea. 'She's planning something, isn't she?' she said.

Ester nodded. 'Yeah. I knew it. I always knew that if she had her back to the wall she'd come up with something.'

'Yeah, but what is it?'

Ester leaned close, one eye on the door. 'I think it's the security wagon that delivers the money to the mail train.'

Julia let out her breath. 'Jesus Christ.'

Ester kept her eye on the door, afraid Dolly would walk in. 'She held back three shotguns from Gloria's stash. She reckoned she was going to do something. Well, she was right.'

Julia rubbed her arms. 'Do we really want to be involved in it, though?'

Ester nudged her, grinning. 'What do you think? Let's

just play her along, see what happens. In the meantime, we got this place, we got bed and board, so why not?'

Dolly drove into George Fuller's car park. A clever, iron-faced man employed by many top-level crooks, he was the lawyer who had represented her at her trial. He was expensive but he was as tough as he looked and even when he smiled he seemed to be sneering.

'Hello, Dolly, good to see you. Sit down.'

She perched on a chair in his immaculate office and passed over the estimates from the builders. 'I'm being harassed. I want them off my back, George.'

He nodded, then lifted his briefcase onto the desk. 'Right. We can go there now and you can fill me in on the way. I'm in court at two so we've not much time.'

Dolly stood up. She liked the way George got straight to the point.

They drove to the police station in Fuller's immaculate green Jaguar and Dolly told him exactly what had occurred since she was released from Holloway. She also asked if he would take on Kathleen O'Reilly's case as a favour to her. He inclined his head a little, and then gave that icy smile. 'If she can meet the fees, then yes.'

'She can't but I will.'

Ester and Julia had already left to begin their assignments. Julia was calling at Norma's cottage and Ester went to talk to Raymond Dewey. Connie was already at the station, watching the man in the signal box. He had a pot belly and she had a feeling he would have bad BO. She shuddered. But then, crossing to the signal box, she saw the pleasant-faced young man who had given her a lift the day she arrived. She saw him walk up the steps as the pot-bellied man came out.

'You're late again, Jim.'

'Sorry, Mac, got held up.'

'Oh yeah? Who was it last night, then?'

Jim chuckled as he entered the signal box. Connie waited a moment and then ran out, colliding with the fat man. She was right. He was a walking deodorant advert. 'Oh, I'm sorry,' she gasped as she fell forward and then yelped. 'My ankle, oh . . .'

It didn't take long for Jim to come down the steps with a glass of water as Connie sat at the bottom. She sipped the water and then tried to stand but had to sit down again.

'I'm sorry, love, I just didn't see you. Do you need a doctor?' Pot-bellied Mac looked down at her with concern.

'I'm all right, just a bit dizzy.'

Jim helped her up and looked at his mate. 'You go off, Mac, I'll take care of her. Maybe she should just sit here for a while.'

Mac muttered that he just bet his mate would take care of her, and shuffled off towards his beat-up Ford Granada. 'See you tomorrow, Jim.'

...m wasn't listening. He was supporting Connie,
...m around her.

'Lucky sod,' mused Mac as he drove out. He wouldn't
have minded taking care of her – she was a cracker.

DCI Craigh stared at the estimates then at George Fuller
and at the impassive face of Dolly Rawlins. He didn't
really look at them properly – he was too edgy. Fuller
declared that on her release Rawlins had, in his opinion,
been harassed. If it was to be made public, not only the
waste of public money but also that a woman who had
served her sentence and been released with every good
intention of building a home for ex-prisoners had been
picked on, it would not look good for the force. Craigh
tried to interrupt but Fuller was in full flow and wouldn't
let him get a word in.

'We obviously know that a Mrs Kathleen O'Reilly
was arrested at Mrs Rawlins's establishment but she was
unaware of any of the outstanding charges levelled at
Mrs O'Reilly and all the women resident at the manor
are, as you must be aware, ex-prisoners. As Mrs Rawlins
was attempting to open a home to give these unfortunate
women a chance to straighten out their lives, then it is
only to be expected that residents would be, like herself,
ex-prisoners. To my mind this has been a flagrant misuse
of police resources. If it were to get into the papers, I'm
sure it would cause an outcry.'

Fuller hardly drew breath. His quiet, steely
firmly hammered home each point until finally h
dropped in his ace. 'Also, it is possible that one of the men
in your team, Detective Chief Inspector, has a private
vendetta against Mrs Rawlins. Not to mention the fact
that you have accused Mrs Rawlins of being associated
with a James Donaldson, who, I understand, recently
died while in your custody.'

Craigh felt the rug being pulled from under him but
he remained calm. His hands tightened into fists on the
desk as he gazed ahead at a small dot on the wallpaper.

'So if you would please give the estimates your due
care and attention, I would be most grateful if Mrs
Rawlins could receive payment for the damage to her
property as soon as possible.'

Fuller rose, and gestured to Dolly to accompany him
to the door.

'Thank you for your time, Detective Chief Inspector.'
Fuller closed the door after him. Craigh ground his
teeth; it had been tough keeping his mouth shut. He
would have liked to punch the bastard. He glanced down
at the list of damage done to the manor during the two
raids: deep freezers being turned off, banisters and rails
damaged, the front door, the rear door. Then his jaw
dropped as he read the total figure.

Ten thousand quid? *Ten grand*?

*

as rigid as she waited for Kathleen to be brought
he visiting section. Coming back inside made her
ill, the hair on the nape of her neck standing up as
e kept her eyes down, refusing to look in the direction
of any of the prison officers. All she wanted to do was to
say what she had to say to Kathleen and get out.

Kathleen was led through the door from the prisoners'
section. She was wearing a green overall, her own shoes,
and an Alice band that someone must have given her to
keep her curly red hair off her face. She looked tired,
defeated and bloated.

Dolly reached over and held her big raw hand. 'Hello,
Kathleen, love.'

Kathleen smiled ruefully. 'Well, I'm back. I knew it'd
happen one day but you know I just hoped we'd make
some cash so I could get me and the kids to Ireland. It
was just a dream, really. I should have known I'd be
picked up. I'm just sorry it was at your place.'

'So am I, but I've got you books and there's money
between the pages. Give a few quid out to some of the girls,
ones that knew me. Rest you use for whatever. I got George
Fuller taking on your case, I'll find the money to pay him.'

'I never said nothing, you know, Dolly.'

'I didn't think you would, Kathleen.'

'I'm no snitch.'

'It was Angela. We found out she'd been knocked up
by that young copper.'

'The bastard.'

'She's no better. We've chucked her out on her ear.'

Kathleen flicked through the pages of the paperback novel, seeing the neatly folded fifty-pound notes. She suddenly looked at Dolly, her eyes dead. 'I could have said something, though. I could have said about the diamonds, even the guns, but I didn't.'

Dolly waited, knowing she was going to be hit for more money. It just surprised her that Kathleen would try it on, after she'd hired her a bloody lawyer.

'I'll get at least five this time,' Kathleen said without any emotion. Dolly made no reply, waiting as Kathleen fingered the paperback. 'I want my kids taken care of, Dolly. Sheena, Kate and Mary. They're in a convent but they'll be split up soon, I know it. Not many places can take three kids, three sisters, they'll split them up, so . . .'

Dolly looked at her, hard. 'So what, Kathleen?'

'You take them, Dolly. I've written to the convent, made you their legal guardian. You just got to sign the papers. I want you to look after them until I get out.'

'I can't do that,' hissed Dolly.

'Yes, you can. You wanted kids in that place – well, now I'm giving you mine. You take them, Dolly, please. Please don't make me talk to the coppers about you, just take my kids.' Kathleen bowed her head, as big tears slid down her pale cheeks. 'I was a lousy mother but I'd turn grass for them. I would, Dolly. They're all I've got that's decent. Please, take them, keep them together for me.'

Dolly gripped Kathleen's hand tight.

Just after Dolly had left the manor, Gloria marched up the stairs and banged on Angela's bedroom door. 'Oi, what you doin' in there? We want you out. Come on. Angela?' She tried the door. It was locked but the key was not on the outside.

'Angela?' She banged on the door, turned the handle and pushed hard, but it was securely locked from the inside.

Gloria darted out to the stables and picked up a hammer. Connie appeared and asked her what she was doing.

'That Angela has locked herself in so I'm gonna break down the door and drag her out by the scruff of her neck.'

She went back upstairs and hit the lock hard, while Connie pushed. It eventually gave way and they stumbled into the little box room. Angela was lying on the floor by the bed, face down. Beside her was a bottle of bleach. When the two panic-stricken women turned her over her face was blue, her mouth burnt – but she was alive.

Julia was walking up the driveway when Gloria screamed at her out of the window to hurry. She raced up the stairs three at a time and burst into the bedroom. They'd lifted Angela onto the bed.

Gloria hovered. 'She's drunk bleach, Julia,' Gloria said quickly. 'I dunno how much but look at her mouth!'

Julia barked orders, to call an ambulance, get jugs of water, then pulled Angela into a sitting position, feeling inside her mouth as Gloria and Connie hurried out, glad to be told what to do.

'Angela, can you hear me? Angela? It's Julia.'

The girl lolled forward. Julia tested her pulse, which was very weak, and began to pour water down her throat from a jug Connie had brought in.

Dolly was shown into the Governor's office. She was freaking out: being in the visitors' section was bad enough, but this was terrifying. All she wanted to do was leave.

Mrs Ellis had tea brought in and Dolly sipped from her cup, unable to meet Mrs Ellis's eyes.

'Do you have a job?'

'Not easy at my age but I've got a few things I'm working on.'

'I know about your application to the social services. Dolly, to run an institution requires training and people with qualifications.'

'It was just a home, Mrs Ellis. This place is an institution. But it doesn't matter now, I was rejected, they didn't think me suitable, and if you don't mind I don't want to discuss it further.'

'If you need any help in the future . . .'

'I won't, thank you.'

'You know, Dolly, it isn't wise to keep up some of the friendships you make inside. It's much better to make a clean break.'

Dolly put the cup and saucer back on the desk. 'Thank you, and thank you for the tea, but I've got to go.'

Mrs Ellis stood and put out her hand, but Dolly was already at the door.

'Will we be seeing you again?' she asked, still trying to be pleasant.

'No, I won't come back. Goodbye.'

Mrs Ellis sat back in her chair. Dolly had looked well, but there was a brittle quality to her every move, and she had not smiled once. An unpleasant woman, Mrs Ellis mused, but then her attention was drawn to other matters and Dolly Rawlins was forgotten.

The ambulance rushed Angela to hospital. Julia accompanied her all the way to the emergency department but, once she'd been wheeled in, there was nothing more she could do. By the time Julia returned to the manor, Gloria had got over her shock at finding Angela half-dead on the floor, and sympathy had been replaced by anger. 'She could have got us all arrested,' she was telling Connie.

'She's only eighteen,' Julia snapped.

'Yeah, so was I when I first went down but I still never grassed anyone. She's got no morals, coming here, playing us for idiots.'

'The way we all tried to play Dolly?'

'No, we fucking didn't,' Gloria spat.

'Yes, we did,' Connie said.

'Well, it's all going to change soon, isn't it?' Julia said quietly.

'What you mean?'

Julia sat down. 'We think she's planning a robbery.'

Gloria gasped. 'I knew it – I fucking knew it. Soon as those shotguns went missing I said to Ester, I said to her, "She's got something going down," and I was right.'

Connie shifted her weight to the other foot. 'I wish to God I'd never come here. I never done anything illegal in my entire life.' Gloria snorted. 'I haven't! I'm not like you, Gloria. We all know what you are.'

'Oh yeah, what am I? You tell me that.'

Ester had come in, unnoticed, and answered, 'A loud, brassy tart. So what's all the aggro?'

'Where've you been?' Gloria asked.

Ester took off her coat and chucked it over a chair. 'Talking to that half-wit Raymond Dewey. Dolly wants to know the times of the mail train.'

Gloria's jaw dropped and she drew a chair close. 'Is she gonna hit the security wagon, then?'

Julia crossed to the back door. 'If she does, it's madness. According to Norma they have the place sewn up. The local police come out in force, cut off the lanes. There's no main access, we'd never get a vehicle near, never mind one that'd carry anything away.' She pushed at the broken door and sighed. 'This is crazy, you know, even discussing it.'

Ester looked at her. 'No harm in it, though, is there? Unless you'd prefer to talk about Norma. Do you want to talk about Norma?' Ester repeated the name with a posh, nasal twang. Julia pursed her lips. 'Oh, have I hit a sore point? Don't want to talk about Noooorma, do we?'

'No, I don't. And stop being childish.'

'I'm not being childish. It's you that's got all uptight. All I'm doing is making conversation about Norma.'

Julia glared, then half smiled. 'Jealous?'

'Who, me? Jealous? Of what? Norma? Oh please, do me a favour. I wouldn't touch anyone with that arse.'

Julia opened the door. 'You don't have to, but it's quite tight, actually.' Ester's face twisted in fury. 'She has a very good seat, as they say in riding circles.'

Julia was out of the door, shutting it behind her, before Ester could reply, and smiling to herself. Ester's jealousy was proof that she cared.

Dolly parked outside Ashley Brent's electrical shop. She squinted at the meter and shook her head with disgust:

twenty pence for ten minutes – it was a disgrace! She walked to the boarded-up door of the shop, rang the bell and waited. Eventually she heard a voice from behind the door.

'Who is it?'

'Dolly Rawlins.'

There was a cackle of laughter and the sound of electronic bolts being drawn back before the door opened. Ashley Brent stood in the centre of his shop floor, arms wide, his glasses stuck on top of his bald head. 'As I live and die. So you're out then, gel. Give us a hug. You're looking good, sweetheart. How long you been out, then?'

'Oh, just a few months. Takes a bit of getting used to, especially those ruddy parking meters.'

'Don't tell me. I mean, in the old days you could find a broken one, use it for the day. Now they tow you away if it's busted, tow you if you're a minute over, tow you for any possible excuse. What they don't do is tow the fuckers that block off the traffic. I'm telling you, everything nowadays is geared to get the punter, Doll. You're screwed in this country if you got a legit business, taxed, VAT . . . It's like we got the Gestapo after us for ten quid rates due but then you hear of blokes coining it on social. Makes you sick.'

Ashley was a man who had verbal diarrhoea and it was always the same: he hated the Conservatives, hated the

Liberals, the Labour Party, the blacks, the Jews. In fact, Ashley was a man who lived on his own venom and it was rumoured that, when he went down for a short spell, his cell-mate had asked to be moved because Ashley even talked in his sleep. He offered tea, then more verbals about the council estate across the road and, lastly, his thankless bastard kids. Dolly looked over the equipment in the little shop, while pretending to listen.

Ashley was an electronics genius and ran a business loosely labelled as security devices and trade equipment. In fact, he sold bugs, receivers, transmitters and microphones. You name it, Ashley had it in his well-stocked shop and workroom. He ran a strictly cash business for those wanting certain items and kept no record of their purchase.

Dolly spent three hours with him and left with a briefcase and a small carrier bag. He had taken time to show her how to handle the equipment. It was mostly quite simple but a few items were more complicated. He was patient and gave good advice, but never asked what the items would be used for. Whatever else Ashley was, he was totally trustworthy. But you paid for that. Dolly gave him ten thousand pounds cash.

Susan Withey opened the door.

Dolly smiled sweetly. 'Hello, I'm Mrs Rawlins.'

Susan hesitated. 'Mike's not here.'

'Ah, pity. Well, could I come in? I want to talk to you.'

'I don't think so, actually.'

'I do. It's about Angela, your husband's little girlfriend.'
Susan stepped back and Dolly pushed past her. 'Oh, this
is very nice. You do the decorating yourself, did you?'

Susan shut the door and followed Dolly into the
sitting room.

It was after seven and they were all still waiting for Dolly,
not sure whether to start supper without her, and wondering what she'd been doing all afternoon.

'There's a car coming up the drive now,' Gloria
said, 'but it's not Dolly. Looks like a flash Mercedes or
somethin'.'

Ester ran into the hall and looked through the broken
stained glass in the front door. She raced back.

'Get rid of them. They'll want me. You tell them I
don't live here any more. Get rid of them, Gloria.'

'Why me?'

'Because you're so good at it.' Ester shot into the
kitchen, pushing Julia back just as the doorbell rang.

Gloria opened the front door. Standing there was a
swarthy, handsome-ish man, with dark heavy-lidded
eyes, a slightly hooked nose and thick oiled-back hair.

'Yeah?'

'Ester here?'

'Ester who?'

'F*r*ry.'

tried to shut the door but he kicked it open.

hat you doing?' Gloria shrieked.

nt to speak to Ester.'

e don't live here, well, not any more. She sold house.'

Gloria was lifted off her feet and hurled against the wall. She screamed as he gripped her face between his hands and pushed her head hard into the wall three times until she was too stunned to scream any more. She just stared wide-eyed.

'You tell Ester we need to speak to her, understand?'

Gloria nodded as he slowly released her and then, as if to make sure the message was understood, he slapped her with the back of his hand and she fell to the floor. She didn't try to get up until the front door closed behind him. Then she slowly staggered to her feet as Ester peered out of the kitchen.

'Well, thanks a fuckin' bundle for that,' said Gloria, touching her nose. 'He whacked me into the wall, whacked me in the face and you friggin' let him do it.'

'Was it Hector?' Ester asked as she peered out of the broken window.

'I dunno who it was – he was too busy whacking me to give me his fuckin' name. Look what he done to me face.'

Julia held Gloria's face between her hands an
her nose. 'It's not broken.'

'Oh, great, I should be grateful for that, should i

They all jumped as a car tooted and Ester shrank in
a corner. 'Shit, are they back?'

Connie went over to the door.

'*Don't open it,*' Ester hissed.

'It's Dolly,' Connie said. 'She's driven on round to the
back yard.'

'Don't say anythin' about this, Gloria,' Ester pleaded.

'Well, she might just notice me nose is red and bleedin'
and me blouse torn,' Gloria retorted furiously.

'Look, they want money. I haven't got it so just cover
for me – you know how she can get.'

Dolly called out, and they all turned towards the door.
They couldn't believe their eyes.

Kate and Mary were twins aged nine and Sheena was
five. They all had bright curly red hair like their mother,
round white faces with blue eyes, and were dressed in
an odd assortment of charity-shop clothes. They were
sullen-faced, as if they had been crying, and clung tightly
to each other.

'These are Kathleen's kids. They're moving in.' Dolly
held up her hands. 'Don't anyone say anything. They're
here, there was nothing I could do about it, so let's make
the best of it. Can someone get a room or two ready? Do
you want to sleep together?'

The three little girls nodded in unison and clung even tighter together. 'Right, let's get your coats off. Connie, bring their cases in from the car and someone put some supper on and get a room aired . . .'

Gloria turned away. 'I'll do it. I just fell down the stairs and hit me nose so I need to go and wash me face.'

Mike charged in. Susan was sitting on the sofa, clutching a handkerchief.

'Has she left?'

'Yes. I went into the hall to call you and when I went back she just said she had to leave.'

Mike paced up and down. 'What did she want?'

Susan stood up and slapped him hard. 'She told me about you and that Angela. She's pregnant, did you know that? That bloody tart you've been screwing is pregnant.'

Mike closed his eyes and sank down onto the sofa.

'Well? Don't you have anything to say to me?'

'What else did she want?'

'*Isn't that bloody enough?*'

Mike leaned back. At first it was just sticky mud he'd felt round his ankles, then it felt like cement. Now it felt like someone had fitted him with a straitjacket. Susan waited but still he didn't say a word. She stormed out, slamming the door behind her, and he stayed there, eyes closed, head back, trying to assimilate everything, sort it out in his head. What did Dolly Rawlins want? He never even gave Angela a thought – he was too concerned with himself.

Beneath the coffee table, which was placed against the wall, was a 13-amp adaptor. A table-light plug was fixed into one but in the other socket was a plug, not connected to any electrical appliance. The switch was turned on. The plug was a transmitter, that Mike was even paying for. Not that he ever imagined anyone would be bugging him. But Dolly was. She had inserted the plug the moment Susan had left the room.

'Neat, isn't it?' Dolly said, as she showed the women the second 13-amp adaptor she'd bought. She then showed them two pens that were also transmitters, pens you could even use to write with. They stared like a group of kids at all the equipment: the tiny receivers, the black box and, lastly, the briefcase that would enable Dolly to open up three electronic channels and record anyone she had bugged.

'What's all this for?' Ester asked.

'What do you think?' Dolly said, as she studied the leaflets.

'You planning on bugging us?'

'Don't be stupid, Connie. I'm going to put these to good use.'

Dolly glanced up at the ceiling as she heard a soft cry. She said to Gloria, 'I thought you told me they were asleep.'

'They were last time I looked in but it's a strange house, Dolly, and, well, they're scared.'

Dolly hurried upstairs and along to the room set aside for the kids. She eased open the door and could see them lying huddled together. The twins were sleeping but little Sheena was mewing like a kitten. 'What is it, darlin'?'

'Dark,' came the whimpered reply.

Dolly fetched her own bedside lamp, and covered it with a headscarf. 'There, how's that, then?' Sheena's eyes were wide with fright. 'Would you like me to read you a story?'

The little girl nodded, so Dolly opened one of the cheap plastic suitcases and took out some dog-eared books.

'Which one is your favourite?'

'*Three Little Piggies*,' Sheena whispered.

'Okay, *Three Little Piggies* it is. Oh, you're all awake now, are you? Well, cuddle up and I'll read you a story.'

Dolly read until one by one they fell asleep. Even so, she went on until she'd finished the book then whispered, 'No one will blow my house down, no big bad wolf. This is my house.'

Downstairs, Gloria picked up a transmitter. 'She's obviously serious about it. This gear must have set her back a few quid.'

They heard Dolly coming down and started to make conversation.

'What time did Angela leave?' Dolly asked as she walked in.

'She went out in style,' Gloria said, then told her what had happened, and Julia added that she had called the hospital and Angela was off the danger list. They were unsure, however, if the baby would be all right.

Dolly sighed. 'You go and see her tomorrow, Julia, take her a few things. Just check on her.'

'You won't get me bringin' her in grapes; she deserves all she gets, the nasty little snitch,' Gloria said.

Dolly yawned.

Ester sat next to her. 'So, you gonna tell us what all this gear is for?'

'It's the train, isn't it?' Connie said.

Dolly slowly got up. 'Yes, it is.'

'The mail train?' Ester asked, springing to her feet.

'That's right.'

Julia was resting one foot on the fireguard. 'You'll never do it, Dolly. I spoke to Norma. She said the security for the drops is really tight and there's no access by road. You'd never get a truck or a car up there without the cops knowing. That's why they chose this station: for its inaccessibility.'

'We wouldn't be doing it by car.' Dolly was on her way to the door.

'On foot? How the hell could we carry big fat mailbags?'

Dolly cocked her head to one side. 'We wouldn't carry them and we wouldn't be going by car, or on foot.'

Ester smirked. 'Helicopter, is it?'

Dolly opened the door. 'We hit the train on horseback.' They fell about laughing. Gloria snorted like a braying donkey. Then they saw that Dolly wasn't smiling. She looked from one to the other, her voice quiet, calm, without any emotion. 'Julia gave me the idea, so from tomorrow we all start learning to ride. Every one of us. If we can't do it, then we look for something else. There's a local stable within half a mile of here. They've got eight horses. We're all booked for the early-morning ride so I don't know about you lot but I need to get some sleep. Goodnight.'

She shut the door behind her.

'I've never been on a horse,' Connie said lamely.

'Me neither – well, nearest I got was a donkey ride on Brighton beach,' Gloria said.

'It's bullshit, isn't it, Julia?' Ester said flatly. 'She's joking.'

Julia prodded the fire with the poker. 'I don't think so. One, she's laid out for all that equipment; two, she was up by the woods, checking out the station. I think she's serious. That's why she's made Connie, me, even you, Ester, start checking it out.'

Overhead, the chandelier creaked as Dolly paced the floor above them. Long shadows cast from the fire loomed large across the big dilapidated room. One after another they opened their mouths as if to say something but nothing came out. They were all thinking the same thing. Was Dolly serious? Was the robbery for real? But it was Julia who broke the silence, laughing softly. 'She's pulling our legs. Let's have a drink.'

Chapter 13

Angela was lying curled on her side, a sodden piece of tissue in her hand. She had cried herself into exhaustion. She didn't look up when the door opened, thinking it would be a nurse. She knew it couldn't be her mother – she hadn't called her. She felt so sick and sad; she had never meant to hurt the baby but now it was too late. She was no longer pregnant; she had miscarried early that morning.

'There's grapes and some clothes to change into.'

Angela recognized Dolly's voice but was afraid to look at her so she just curled up tighter.

'I know you lost the baby, Angela, and I'm sorry, sorry for what you've done to yourself.' Dolly laid out the things she had brought. She stood near to the bed, but not close enough to touch Angela. ' It won't seem like it now, but maybe it's for the best.'

'You'd know, would you?' came the muffled reply.

'No, I don't really know at all. I ached for a baby, Angela, all my married life, so no, I wouldn't know what it feels like to lose one.'

Angela sobbed. Dolly was so cold and hard and she so badly needed someone to put their arms around her. 'Please be nice to me, Dolly, *please*.' Angela turned and held out her hand to Dolly.

'Come to the house and . . .'

'Can I stay? I'll cook and clean for you.'

'. . . pack the rest of your things. That's all I came to tell you. You have to leave but we'll keep your things safe until they release you from here. And you should eat those grapes, almost eighty pence a pound.'

The door closed behind her and Angela fell back onto her pillow. She wished she'd killed herself properly, wished she had never woken up because she had nothing to live for, and no place to go.

Dolly walked into the kitchen through the back door, the smell of burning bacon making her wrinkle her nose.

'Oh, sorry, Dolly, it's me. I can never get the hang of this Aga. I dunno whether to put stuff in the oven or stick it on the top there.' Connie shovelled charred bits of bacon onto a piece of paper towel, dabbing the fat off it.

'I been in to see Angela. She lost the baby.'

'Julia told me. She's just bathing the girls – they've had their breakfast.'

Ester appeared. 'Serves the little cow right. Any breakfast going?'

They came in in dribs and drabs but no one seemed inclined to start up a conversation about the proposed robbery. 'You all got boots, jeans to ride in?' Dolly suddenly asked.

Gloria looked down at her wellingtons. Julia arrived with the three children, who hung back shyly at the door. Seeing her, Gloria asked, 'Will these do?'

Julia shook her head. 'No, but there's no point in wasting good money if you're only going to go once. Might as well wait and see, right, Dolly?'

Dolly was eating scrambled eggs and burnt toast. 'I'll need to borrow a pair of trousers. You girls are going to be left alone just for a while, but I got some things for you to do.' They were sitting at the big kitchen table as Dolly laid out drawing pads, crayons and picture books. 'Now you be good, stay put in here and wait until we get back. Don't leave the house, and I'll know if you do because I'm gonna ask the builders to check on you.'

'They not comin' today,' piped up little Sheena.

Dolly patted her head. 'Ah, you don't know, they come and they go. Just be good girls and watch the clock. When the big hand gets to—'

'I can tell the time,' said Kate, one of the twins.

'Good, then you stay put for two hours in here and I don't want to have to tell you again!' Dolly was trying her best but she wasn't used to handling little kids, as well as a houseful of adult ones.

Julia fitted her out in an old pair of her jeans which were too tight and the flies were gaping, but as Julia said, why waste money? They piled into Gloria's Mini, all five of them, and headed for the local stables.

'I see they bleedin' downed tools again,' Gloria said as they drove out of the manor.

'They'll pick them up again as soon as they get paid,' Dolly replied.

'I thought our Connie was supposed to be keeping him happy,' Gloria sniggered.

'I'm already workin' on him and the bloke in the signal box. I don't intend to get through all the ruddy workmen, too. *You* do it.'

'Don't mind if I fuckin' do!' Gloria hooted.

Dolly closed her eyes. 'I wish you'd watch your mouth, Gloria, now we got the girls living in. And that goes for us all. Cut down on the swearing.'

'Well, excuuuuuse me for livin'. I can't help bein' the way I am, it's called frustration. I see her gettng her leg over at every opportunity and—'

'*Shut up!*' roared Dolly.

'It's the truth! I've not had a good seeing-to in years and it's not for want of trying, lemme tell you.' Dolly knew it was pointless attempting to change Gloria. 'Mind you, this horse ridin', they say it gives you a climax, did you know that, Dolly? I'm lookin' forward to it.'

When they got to the riding school Sandy, a young stable girl with a high-pitched Sloane Ranger voice, began to bring out the horses, all shapes and sizes, as her assistant saddled them up. Julia began sorting through hard hats, which were compulsory, and they switched them round and tried them all on. Sandy kept on taking sly looks at the group of women and couldn't help tittering as they appeared to be first-timers, apart from Julia. Just getting them mounted took considerable time, and when Julia left they all looked petrified, including Dolly. When her horse suddenly bent his head to eat some grass, she almost came off with a high-pitched 'Help!'

They had a two-hour lesson and at the end of it they could all mount and dismount, knew how to use the reins, and had been led up and down the field. Gloria wandered into the stables, beaming from ear to ear as if she had just won the Grand National.

'It's quite easy really, isn't it?'

Sandy smiled. 'Yes, if you're a natural.'

'You think I am, then?'

'We'll see. You haven't really been riding yet.'

'Course I have. We been round the field ten times.'

'There's more to it than that, Gloria.'

By lunchtime none of them could walk. Their thighs

were on fire, and everyone was moaning. But Dolly had booked them in for another lesson in a second stable twenty miles away, so reluctantly they squeezed into the Mini again.

'I don't think this is a good idea, you know, Dolly,' Gloria gasped. 'I mean, I'm knackered after just two hours – and my legs! I think I've done myself some serious damage.'

Julia waved them off and decided to take the little girls out for a walk, but before she could set off, Big John arrived and said he needed to speak to Mrs Rawlins. Julia told him she was not at home but asked if she could help. 'Well, it's just that she's supposed to pay me the second instalment. We're behind now, and she did say today. I've got the lads on another job until she pays, but this scaffolding needs finishing and we got all that cement ordered and the sand.'

'I'll tell her to give you a ring.'

He looked unconvinced. 'This was a cash deal and she's put me in a very difficult position.'

'She'll call you,' Julia insisted.

He hung about a moment, then asked, 'Connie here, is she?'

'She's out.'

He returned to his truck; he was determined that until he saw the colour of Mrs Rawlins's money he was not going to finish anything off or order another bag of cement. The reality was that he had been so desperate to get his firm off the ground that he'd stretched himself to the limit. He had a nasty feeling that his inexperience was going to teach him a hard lesson.

The afternoon riding session brought grave doubts that any one of them would ever be let off a leading-rein. Out of the four Connie was the best and the most confident, Gloria the worst. She yelled and shouted abuse to the embarrassment of the others and the prim stable girls. When they returned to the manor, Dolly was certain she would have to think about another way.

She made the children their tea, then sat with them and read them a story. For half an hour Dolly lost herself in the story and in the warmth of the three little girls. They were gradually becoming less fearful and more open. Dolly constantly repeated that the manor was their home, and no one could take it away from them; their mummy knew where to write to them and when she was back she would know where to find them. That was why she had brought them here.

Early next day Dolly drove into the village, toured the second-hand shops, and returned laden with hacking-jackets, jodhpurs, second-hand riding boots and two men's riding coats. Some of the clothes were in good condition, some not so good, so she laid them all out, choosing the best for herself. That morning the lesson was booked for ten and, creaking in agony, the women argued and fought over each item like ten-year-olds. Gloria stuffed two pairs of thick woollen socks inside a pair of men's riding boots as they were far too large; before Gloria could grab them Connie squeezed into a pair that were too small but highly polished. They didn't look any more professional – on the contrary, they were like something out of a Thelwell cartoon and their riding was no better.

Sandy the stable girl led them all into the field connected to the stables and they proceeded to learn how to trot with gritted teeth and loud moans.

Julia remained at the house with the children, cooking breakfast and taking them on a ramble around the grounds. They shrieked with excitement when she brought out Helen of Troy and they each had a turn at being led round the yard. None of them had been in the country before or ridden a horse, and their excitement touched Julia. As a child she had wanted for nothing, she even had her own pony, and it made her realize just how wonderful a place the manor could be for kids like Kathleen's.

It was early afternoon by the time everyone had cleaned themselves up, and the washing machine creaked under the weight of all their dirty clothes. The boots were lined up and the little girls given the task of cleaning them for fifty pence a pair. Soon Sheena seemed to be getting more boot polish on herself than on the boots, but, seeing they were happy, Dolly said nothing and called all the women into the office.

They stood around, waiting, as Dolly closed the door and crossed to her desk. She picked up a small black notebook and sat down. 'Right, it's obvious we're gonna need two lessons a day.'

Gloria leaned on the desk. 'I got to be honest, Doll, I'm not cut out for this riding business. It's me size, you see. Being small I can't get me legs round the horse.'

Dolly frowned. 'We'll get you a small horse, then.'

Gloria pulled a face. 'You're payin'.'

'Yeah, I am paying for everything, so shut up and listen, all of you.'

Julia stood by the window. 'The builder was here, Dolly. You know he's got a delivery of bathroom equipment arriving and he's a bit sore. He could start causing trouble.'

Dolly moistened her lips. 'Yes, I know. We'll start with him.'

Dolly pointed at Connie and told her to keep Big John happy, to see him as much as possible and give him five grand that evening.

Gloria pouted. 'All right for some. I wouldn't mind keeping him happy – got a nice arse.'

No one paid her any attention; they were listening to Dolly as she described the old cesspit half a mile from the house. 'I need to get it cleared, see how deep it is, so this afternoon, Gloria and Julia, that's your job.'

'Oh, great! I just got meself cleaned up,' moaned Gloria, but no one took any notice.

'Connie, when you see John, I want you to order through his firm, without him knowing, some twenty-kilo-bags of lime.'

'Why? What do we need them for?' Connie asked.

'To fill the pit,' Dolly said patiently.

She jabbed a finger at Ester. 'You have an assignment. I want you to find out just how tough it is to unhitch a train carriage.'

'Oh, sure,' Ester said, smiling as if it was as simple as buying groceries.

'I'm serious. The mail carriage is in the centre of the train, it's an ordinary carriage. I want to know how you can unhitch it.'

'How the fuck do I find that out?'

'You've got a big mouth, Ester. Use it. Off the top of my head you can go to the railway museums, chat up a guard, *not* at the local station – any way you think – but I need to know if it's done manually or—'

'Fine, I'll do it,' Ester said.

Dolly made a tick in the notebook, turning a page. 'Tonight, Connie, you go and see your boyfriend in the signal box. This time you find out the layout, how many alarms there are, how long it takes to get the law to the station.'

'You must be joking,' muttered Connie.

'No, love, I'm not. We have to know exactly what goes down when that mail train arrives, what he does, what—'

Connie broke in, 'How do I do that?'

'Find a way, love.'

'Well, one minute you're telling me to be with the builder, then the signal-box guy. I can't do both of them.'

'Yes, you can,' Dolly snapped, and then looked at them all. 'You have to do just what I tell you or this is finished before it's started. I don't want any arguments.'

'Can we ask what exactly you're planning?' Ester leaned forward.

Dolly closed her book and stood up. 'I'm going to London so I'll need the car. I don't want the kids left alone so one of you bath them, feed them and put them to bed. I might be late.'

She walked out and they watched her go, no one saying a word until the door latched. 'She's nuts, you do know that, don't you?' Ester said angrily.

'But you're still here,' remarked Julia tartly.

'Yeah, but not for long if she carries on like this. We got a right to know what she's doing.'

Gloria heaved herself out of the chair. 'Well, like she's always saying, she's paying, so let's get on with it. I mean, I'll do your job if you wanna do the cesspit.'

There was no way Ester was going to dig shit. She was still in agony from the ride. 'I can't. I'm injured.'

'Well then, we just do what the boss says,' Gloria sighed.

Connie said, 'Okay, but I'll never be able to get that information, you know. I'm not supposed to even be in the signal box.'

'Take him a bottle of wine,' Julia said, and stroked Connie's shoulder. 'One for the builder as well.' Connie shrugged her away.

'Right, let's get on with it,' Julia said, and one by one they went to do their allocated jobs.

Angela left the hospital, caught a bus and then made her way down the lane to the manor. No one was in sight so she pushed open the front door.

'Hello? Anyone home?'

Ester appeared on the stairs and glared at her. 'Just stay put, no need to come in.'

'I've come for my gear.'

Ester disappeared along the landing. The three girls peeped out from the kitchen.

'They're Kathleen O'Reilly's kids,' Ester called down.

Angela smiled. 'Hello.'

'Hello,' said Sheena.

'How ya all doing?'

Before they could reply, Ester returned with a suitcase

which she practically hurled down the stairs. 'There's your gear. Piss off and don't come back.'

Angela was near to tears as she picked up her case. 'I got no money.'

'My heart bleeds. Go on, get out.'

Angela walked back down the drive, dragging the suitcase, sniffing back the tears. She didn't see Gloria and Julia way in the distance, digging and clearing the cesspit. Both wore thick scarves round their faces to combat the awful stench. They heaved bucketload after bucketload, chucking it into a wheelbarrow.

'This is making me sick,' said Gloria, retching.

Julia heaved up the wheelbarrow. 'Keep at it. We've only cleared a quarter of it.'

'It's not on, you know. This could give us a disease, it's disgusting. I mean, this is – this is old shit, you know that, don't you?'

Julia paid no attention as she wheeled the thick, stinking mud over to a pile of old bits of furniture and junk. She tipped out the barrow and stood away from the noxious fumes. She turned back as Gloria peered down into the pit.

'Now what? I can't reach in any further with the bucket,' she yelled.

'We'll have to get down into it, then,' Julia said.

'I'm not gettin' in there,' shrieked Gloria.

'Well, one of us has to. We'll toss for it.' Julia picked up a rake and asked whether Gloria wanted the rake or flat side. Gloria bellowed she wanted the rake side. Julia tossed the rake into the air and it came down flat side.

'You bloody did that on purpose,' Gloria yelled. She looked down into the pit again and back to Julia. 'I got an idea. Why don't we get the kids to do it?'

Connie breezed into Big John's yard. He was sitting on the steps of his little hut.

'Hi, how are you?' She beamed as she walked over.

He didn't return her smile. 'Look, Connie, this has got nothing to do with you but that Mrs Rawlins is making me bankrupt.'

Connie sat next to him and passed over the envelope. 'Here you go, and there's more coming in a day or two.'

John opened the envelope and then stood up. 'I'd better go and divvy this up with the men.'

'Oh, right now?'

He looked into her upturned face. 'I got to. When they finish the job they're on, they'll be on their way. If you want that roof done at the manor, I got to pay them.'

'How long will you be?'

'Ten minutes.'

She slipped her arms around him. 'Then I'll wait, but only ten minutes, and we can have a . . .' She kissed him and he gasped for breath when he broke away from her. 'Don't be long,' she whispered, biting his ear.

He blushed, glancing towards the gates then back to

the small wooden makeshift hut. 'You know, anyone can walk in here, Connie.'

She giggled. 'Exciting, isn't it? Besides, you can lock the main gates, can't you? But I think it'll be more fun if they're open and we screw knowing somebody'll walk in any minute. And look, I brought us a bottle of wine.'

He was all over the place, kissing her, groping her breasts, and then he sprinted to his truck. He shouted back that he would be no more than ten minutes.

She was still standing there on the steps of his hut, blouse open, as he clipped the gatepost in his haste to get out. She didn't even wait for the tail end of the van to disappear before she shot into the hut and began to sift through all his papers until she found some order forms. She called a trade supplier and ordered the bags of lime to be delivered directly to the manor for a cash payment. She gave John's firm's reference and as soon as she replaced the receiver she hurried out, picking up her bag with the bottle of wine. Next stop, the signal box.

Mike had just finished his lunch and was about to go back to the station when the call came. He was eager not to let Susan answer it in case it was Angela again. They almost collided in the hall, they were both so desperate to reach the telephone first.

Mike snatched it up. Susan stood with her hands on her hips.

'Hello? Who is it?' Susan said petulantly.

'It's my guv'nor.' He glared at her so hard that she turned away and stomped into the kitchen.

'What do you want?' he said quietly, afraid Susan would still be listening.

'Need to see you, love, it's urgent. I'll be at the Pen and Whistle pub, the one on the corner by your mother's flat, in the saloon bar, six thirty.'

'I can't – I can't see you.'

'I think you can, Mike. Six thirty, just be there.'

The line went dead. He stood there, holding the receiver, and then quickly dialled his station. He was put through to the incident room and he told them he was not feeling too well so he would be in a bit late. Then he looked towards the kitchen. He was sure that Susan was listening. All his anger and frustration welled up as he dropped the phone back down.

Ester, being lazy, called a number of railway museums first but was not getting the information she needed. She then tried another tactic, saying she was making a documentary film for the BBC and asking if she could speak to anyone working at the museum who could assist her. She was given various numbers to call for permission to interview railway technicians and started working her way through them. Permission was not granted by British Rail, so she was now contacting the private railways, saying the BBC documentary had the full backing of the Transport Ministry, who were co-financing the film.

She looked at the list of essential items listed by Dolly: size and weight of the train compartments, couplings and sidings. Underlined was how long it would take to unhitch one carriage from another. She sighed: this was going to take for ever.

Big John had only been gone twelve and a half minutes, more or less flinging the money at his men and racing back to his yard. He quickly ran a comb through his hair, wishing he'd got a spot of cologne, then locked the big double gates before running over to his hut. He threw open the door, his heart pounding.

Connie had left, no note, nothing. She'd even taken the bottle of wine.

Still carrying her suitcase, Angela walked along the road towards Mike's house. It was growing dark and it had taken her hours to hitch a ride from the manor. She saw Mike's car parked outside his house and was in two minds whether or not to go and ring the doorbell. She wanted to confront him, tell him about the baby, but the nearer she got the more her confidence dwindled. She definitely didn't want to see his wife. She sat down on a wall, wondering if he would come out.

Inside the house, Mike and Susan were having one hell of a row. She was demanding to know all about Angela, the phone calls – everything – and he was refusing to answer. 'You stay out all night, and don't speak to me. How do you expect me to feel?'

Mike clenched his fists. 'Susan, I've told you, there is nothing – *nothing* between me and this girl.'

'Then why does she keep calling you? Why was that Mrs Rawlins round here? Is it true that she's pregnant?'

'Leave it alone, Susan. I mean it. Just shut up about it. You're driving me nuts.'

'And *you're* driving *me* nuts,' she said in a fury, watching as he grabbed his coat. 'Where are you going?'

'Out. I can't stand it here.'

'One of these days you're gonna come back here and the locks will have been changed.'

He sighed. 'Sue, listen, give me a break. I've got a lot on my plate right now and I just can't tell you about it.'

'Try me, go on, try me!' she shouted.

He ran his hands through his hair. He didn't even know where to begin. How could he tell her about his mother, the diamonds, the trouble he was in at work? He knew she wouldn't be able to deal with it. Right now, Angela was the least of his problems. He was afraid of what Dolly Rawlins wanted, scared he was heading into even deeper trouble, but he couldn't tell anyone, especially not his wife. Susan broke down in tears as he walked out. She ran up the stairs and was about to open the window, call out to him that they had to talk, when she saw Angela.

Mike yanked open the car door and then suddenly Angela was there. 'We got to talk, Mike.'

'No, we haven't. I got nothing to say to you, Angela, just go away from me. I don't want to see you. Stay away from me and my house.' He got in and slammed the door shut. She rapped on the window and when she wouldn't stop he wound it down.

'I lost the baby, Mike.'

'I don't care, Angela, you hear me? I *don't care.*'

She was sobbing, looking like an orphan with her suitcase. 'I got no one to help me, Mike,' she wept.

He dug into his pocket and pulled out his wallet. He took all the money he had and held it out. 'Here, take this, *take it*, it's all I got on me.'

'I didn't come for money,' she wailed.

He pushed the money at her 'Take it, Angela. I can't see you, so please stay away from me. *Just go away, Angela!*' He threw the money onto the pavement, and started the car. It was six fifteen, and although he was afraid to meet Dolly Rawlins he was more afraid not to, so he drove off.

Angela picked up the four twenty-pound notes, unaware that Susan was watching from the bedroom window, crying just as hard as she was, and wishing she had enough money to get the locks changed there and then.

Gloria and Julia were both deep in the cesspit, clearing away the filth. Their heads appeared at the lip as Ester carried out two mugs.

'All right for some,' moaned Gloria, accepting the tea.

'Blimey, it's deep, isn't it?' Ester remarked.

'I'd say this is for the mailbags,' Julia replied. 'What do you think?'

'I dunno – who knows what the old bat's doing? But as long as it's not for us, who cares?' Ester set off back towards the house.

Gloria looked at Julia. 'What if she's got us diggin' our own bleedin' grave? She shot her old man, remember. I wouldn't put nothing past her.'

Connie was perched on the counter in the signal box, a chipped glass of red wine in her hand, which she clinked against Jim's mug. 'Cheers.'

He moved closer. 'You could get me the sack, you know, Connie.'

'Who's gonna know I'm here?'

'Well, anyone passing can see us.'

She slithered off the counter to sit on the floor. 'Now they can't.' She began to run her hand up his trouser leg.

'Hang on a second – lemme just sort this out. It's the six o'clock, then we got fifteen minutes.'

Connie watched as he pulled levers and answered the phone. She began to ease down her panties. She held them up, waving them. 'Can I have another drink down here?'

Jim began heaving the rail levers faster than he ever had before while Connie crawled across the floor and started undoing his flies. By now she had a good sense of where the phone connection wires ran but she didn't have any knowledge of the alarms. All she knew was that it was going to be a very long night.

Dolly sipped the lemonade, flicking through her little black notebook. Mike stood over her as she looked up, smiling.

'Nothing for me, but do get yourself a drink, love, if you need one.'

'I don't.' He sat down, having a good look around the bar. 'What do you want?'

Dolly shut the book, had another sip. 'Some information – sort of like a trade.'

'What information?' he asked, his heart pounding. He knew something bad was coming but when it came it left him shattered. 'I can't find that out! That's classified!'

She leaned forward and tapped his arm. 'Yes, you

can and you will, otherwise I will have to inform your superiors about those diamonds, about your mother, everything. It's up to you, Mike. Tell me now if you don't want to do it. You must have some old friends from your Army days – they might be helpful, but if you don't want to do it . . .'

'I've just said I don't.'

'Oh, I know you did, but you see, Mike, that's because I don't think you really believe that I'd be prepared to go back to prison. But I would, and I wouldn't be on my own. You'd be sent down as well, and they might even haul your mother back from Spain. So let me ask you again – can you get the information I need?'

He shuffled his feet, took another look around. 'How long have I got?'

'Two days, no more.' She drained her glass, placing it carefully back on the beer mat. 'I'll call you, don't you call me. Two days.'

He sat, head in his hands, as she walked out. The cement was drying, up to his chest now. He didn't know whether to throw the table through the pub window or do as she had asked: find out how much money the mail train was carrying, and if they were going to continue using the same route. He looked at the slip of paper she had passed him with the name of the security firm on the side of the vans she'd seen outside her local station. It was a reputable firm and he didn't know if he'd be able to get any information from them. He needed a drink, a large one. No way would he be able to go in to work. He really did feel ill.

Dolly drove back to the manor and as she turned into the drive the headlamps picked out the large rubbish tip still burning. She got out, leaving the lights on, and walked past it to the cesspit. She nodded to herself, satisfied it was big enough and, most certainly, deep enough.

When she got in she found the kitchen in a mess: dirty soup plates, mince in a pan, dried-out baked beans in another, stacks of used cups and mugs. Every surface was food-stained and filthy. She pursed her lips and dumped her handbag, throwing aside her coat. She found Ester lying stretched out on the sofa with a glass of wine, reading the *TV Times*. Julia was asleep in an easy chair, the television on in the background. Neither heard Dolly. She walked up the big staircase and looked into Connie's room, but it was empty. Then she went up to the second landing to the children's room.

The last person Dolly expected to see was Gloria, wrapped in an old dressing gown, sitting with Sheena on her knee. The other two were fast asleep in the big old-fashioned double bed. 'Oh, said the little pig. What will the big bad wolf do?' Gloria rocked the child, stroking her hair. 'Well, he'll huff and he'll puff and he'll blow the house down.'

Sheena lifted her tiny hand to Gloria's cheek. 'You're not our mummy, are you?'

Gloria shook her head. The little girl's question touched her heart – so many different homes, so many different foster carers, the little girl was completely confused.

Gloria kissed her. 'No, I'm not your mummy.'

'Doesn't she love us any more?'

'Yes, of course she does. But you know, Sheena, a long, long time ago I had a little girl, just like you, and I had to go away, just like your mummy has had to go away. My little girl never had a nice house to live in and I couldn't ever see her again but you will. Your mummy being away doesn't mean she doesn't love you. She does. And she's arranged for us all to look after you until she comes back. Do you understand?'

'No.' Sheena yawned.

'My little girl never understood but then it was too late, you see, I couldn't see her. But you'll be able to see your mummy. One of us will always take you to see her so you won't forget who she is, and in the meantime we'll all be like extra mothers. How's that?'

Sheena was asleep, and Dolly stayed where she was, looking at a Gloria she hadn't known existed, a sad, lonely Gloria who was being so gentle and caring, so unlike the hard, uncouth harridan she showed to them all. They all had secrets, all had hidden pain. Somehow she had not expected Gloria to have so much.

Chapter 14

C onnie was doing up her blouse and Jim had just
finished zipping his trousers as he hurriedly closed
the gates for the nine thirty express to pass through.
John stood at the level crossing, annoyed that he'd just
missed the orange light. As it turned to red, he looked
at the signal box, as if to blame it for his being held up,
and saw her, laughing, her arms wrapped around the
attendant. He was stunned. That wasn't his Connie up
there, was it?

Connie skipped down the steps, looked back and blew
a kiss, then hurried towards the taxi rank. She was in the
cab heading for the manor when the gates opened and
she didn't see John charge up the steps to the signal box.

'Connie here, is she?' John blurted out, when Jim
opened the door.

Jim acted dumb. He didn't know who the big

broad-shouldered bloke was, but he was pretty sure that if Connie had been caught in there with him he'd have been in serious trouble.

'No, nobody here but me, why?'

John looked past him into the signal box. 'No reason. Sorry, mate. Sorry to bother you.'

Jim knew he'd have to ask Connie about the angry bloke but only when the time was right. They'd not even been out on a proper date yet. Half of him still couldn't believe what had taken place – he'd never experienced anything like it. Blown in his own signal box! As if to assure himself that it had really happened, he pulled Connie's lacy panties from his pocket.

'Shit, I forgot me knickers,' Connie said as she walked into the house, slamming the front door. She hurried into the kitchen and began to draw on the back of an envelope everything she could remember. She was just finishing when she heard the doorbell ring.

Ester came in, looking perplexed. 'I didn't hear a car, did you, Connie?'

'No. Who do you think it is?'

Dolly appeared on the landing. 'Just answer it, Ester.'

Ester pushed Connie forward. 'You answer, just in case.'

Dolly thumped down the stairs as the bell rang again. She went for the door and swung it open. Angela stood on the doorstep. 'I'm sorry, I got no other place to go – I thumbed a lift back.'

'Well, love, you can thumb one right out again,' Dolly replied.

Connie felt sorry for Angela. 'Ah, let her stay for just one night.'

Ester scowled. 'You joking? No way! Chuck her out, Dolly.'

'Oh, please don't! I'll cook and clean, I promise,' Angela begged.

Dolly opened the door wider. 'Right, one night. Go up onto the top floor. Your old room's gone so use another, then come down and clean up the kitchen and make us some dinner.'

Angela almost kissed her hand but Dolly stepped away, letting the door bang shut.

'You must be mad.' Ester said, going back into the drawing room.

Connie smiled at Angela but got pushed into the room by Dolly. 'Give us a call when it's ready, will you, love?' Dolly said as she went into the drawing room.

Gloria clattered in a few minutes later. 'I don't fucking believe that girl's cheek. I just seen her making up her bed.'

'Just for tonight,' Dolly said.

'What? Are you crazy?'

Julia yawned. 'Well, the kitchen's a mess, the kids'

room's a mess, we need somebody to cook, do all the ironing and washing, plus she's going to cook dinner so that should keep her occupied for one night, anyway.'

Dolly sat down, took out her notebook, and flicked through it.

'Bit bleedin' risky, isn't it?' Gloria said, warming herself by the fire. 'That boyfriend of hers – what if he's sent her?'

Dolly shook her head. 'He's not made any calls to his station about us. I think we got the bloke by the balls.'

Dolly took out a tape and slipped it into the small cassette player.

'You got him taped?' Ester said.

'Didn't I tell you? Have a listen.'

'What about at the station?' Ester asked, and Dolly frowned, knowing she really needed to do that, too.

They sat round listening to Susan and Mike arguing, with his kids yelling in the background. They all laughed, apart from Ester, as if it was all a big joke. Dolly left them to it, and went to the kitchen to have a private confab with Angela.

Angela was working herself into a sweat, washing dishes, scrubbing the floor, cleaning all the surfaces, as if to prove she was worth her keep.

'You want to stay on, do you?' Dolly asked, as she drew out a chair to sit at the kitchen table.

'I'll do anything to make up for what I done, anything.

I know you won't ever forgive me but ...' Angela sat down opposite Dolly and started trying to explain about the baby and Mike, but Dolly took her hand.

'Shut up. Now, are you still seeing him?'

Angela shook her head.

'I see. Well, you might have to prove yourself, Angela – not just to me but to the others. Does he know you were driving the car that killed Jimmy Donaldson?'

'No! I hate him, Dolly, really, I wouldn't help him. I swear on my life I wouldn't.'

Dolly propped an elbow on the table. 'Well, you remember this, Angela, because if you betray me again, if I find out that you're grassin' back to him, then you'll go down for murder and I'll make sure of it. You understand, don't you?'

Angela nodded. In truth, she didn't have anywhere else to go – even her mum had refused to let her stay. 'I'll make it up to you,' she said, clinging to Dolly's hand. 'I swear I will. I'll do whatever you want.'

'Good girl. Now I want you to keep house, feed us and take care of Kathleen's girls. And I will need you to do a few other things for me.'

The women had obviously been talking about Dolly because when she returned they fell silent. She picked up her notebook.

'Dinner's not ready yet so let's get this sorted before

we eat.' She asked each of them about their day making copious notes, frowning at Ester who, she felt, had not done enough. She was told to go out the next day and get more information on the carriage links.

'Good work on the cesspit, Gloria and Julia.'

They felt a little like schoolgirls and didn't enjoy it.

Dolly then turned her attention to Connie. She was happy that the lime was on its way, but Connie's hastily drawn diagrams were not yet good enough, and they still needed details of the alarms and codes used to contact the local police. Connie said she would have another evening with Jim – even spend the afternoon with him, because he wasn't on duty until four-thirty.

'That's not written down here, Connie,' Dolly said sternly.

'Well, I just told you.'

'That's not good enough. I need to know everything. Is that understood?'

Dolly turned to Julia. 'Do you think you could get hold of Norma's police cape and, if possible, her hat?'

'We could hire some,' offered Julia.

'Yes, we could, and be seen doing it. I've seen them in the back of her car. Go and keep her friendly, just like Connie's doing with the signal-box guy. Plus, Connie, keep your eye on those shotguns at the gym.'

Dolly continued down the list.

'Who's looking after the kids?' Julia asked.

'Angela – and don't argue. Until I say different, she stays. Somebody's got to look after them.'

'I think that's a mistake,' said Ester.

Dolly's voice was icy quiet. 'You want to question me, Ester, then you can pack your gear and leave right now. Either we do this my way or we don't do it at all.'

Angela tapped on the door and peeped round. 'Dinner's on the table,' she said meekly, and scuttled out.

They all started to head for the door, but Dolly caught Ester by the arm. 'Just a second, love, I want a word.' The others left the room.

Ester stood, hands on her hips. 'Don't get me wrong, Dolly, I'm not questioning who's the boss. I just have a few more brains than some of the others.'

'Do you?' Dolly sighed. 'I don't call wheelin' around in a hot car very clever, and I don't call having blokes arrive and knock the hell out of Gloria very clever either.'

'So what do you want me to do?' Ester said angrily

'I want you to sort out this blackmail business. can't afford to have loose ends. Take it back, Ester whole thing is off. I mean it. Something like bring us all down.'

'Oh yeah? And what about you and th must have something going on with you got his home bugged.'

---

he
and

that friend of
er – be a good

n't know if she's

. 'Don't forget we need

of laug

door with a smile and J
pened. 'You're in luck, I'
problem.'

this,' Julia said, taking a
allway while Norma pic
. 'Just one thing, Norma,
know I was in prison,

Dolly rubbed her eyes. 'Just sort out the tape, E̶ Tomorrow.'

Dolly and Julia walked in darkness up th̶ woods and down to the railway line. 'Brin̶ the line, Julia. See if she really is as bomb̶ proof ̶ Norma said.'

'Okay,' Julia replied, not sure why D̶ her along.

They looked down the railwa̶ bridge, the lake, and back to th̶ said nothing but both their mi̶ was trying to visualize step ̶ holding up the train. Julia ̶ reckoned that with or wit̶out ̶ be impossible.

'I think we'll need ̶ lly said, almost to h̶ lia looked back at the la̶ ̶ely she wasn't going to ̶ ̶ But if she was, why wer̶ they ̶ mo̶ of ca̶ uldn't stop sniggering. ̶pated – even with ̶ey were incapable ̶ry ill at ease. They

---

Julia picked up the receiver, but it wasn't her mother at the other end of the phone. It was the housekeeper. Julia's mother had had a stroke, and was very ill. 'My mother's ill,' Julia said unemotionally. T̶ women all looked at her. 'A stroke. I'll have to go̶ sort it out. Can I use your car, Gloria?' 'No, you can't,' Dolly said, clearing the bow̶ 'Well, I'll take the truck.' Dolly turned and smiled. 'Why not ask ̶ yours, Norma? Maybe she'll drive you o̶ chance to talk to her.' Julia shrugged. 'Okay, but I do̶ around. She may be on duty.' Dolly ran the water in the sink̶ the riding cape and her hat.' Norma opened the front̶ explained what had hap̶ for two days so it's no̶ ̶ really appreciat̶ ̶ cottage ̶

Julia gave her a sidelong look. 'Yeah, that's right. First they thought we were hiding some diamonds, then guns. It was ridiculous.'

Norma nodded. 'Mrs Rawlins has quite a reputation.'

'Oh, have you been checking up on us?'

Norma swore as they drew up by the level crossing. 'Oh, bugger it. Let's hope it's not the mail train.'

They sat in silence, watching the gates clang shut, and then Julia leaned back in her seat, slipping her arm behind Norma. 'They have a lot of security on for the mail train?'

Norma pointed along the road. 'Yes, but as you can see, it's quite simple. That's why they pick on this station, no easy access for any car coming up either side of it and they'd never get as far as the motorway, the place is alarmed all along the track, with a special link to the police station. They can be here in under four minutes.'

'Really?' Julia said, trying not to sound too interested.

'You know why they use the security vans?' Norma continued.

'No?'

'Because of the vulnerability of the big stations. Last big robbery was at King's Cross, so now they have armoured trucks and a police escort to an out-of-the-way station like ours, then they put the bags on board and it's a clear run through all the stations. Train goes at around eighty miles an hour.'

Julia began to massage Norma's neck. 'Well, thankfully it's not the mail train today, and no coppers but you!' She leaned over and kissed Norma, only stopping when the gates opened again and they continued on, passing Raymond Dewey on his little stool. He waved to Julia and she waved back.

'Poor sod, what a life,' she said.

'Oh, he's happy enough,' Norma said, and then touched Julia's hand lightly. 'I'm glad you called.'

'So am I,' Julia replied, then stared out of the window. She really did find Norma irritating. It was going to be a long drive.

Dolly asked Connie to come in for a chat. She closed the bedroom door. 'You're seeing that signal-box bloke tonight, aren't you?'

'Yes, I told you.'

'Where's he taking you?'

'Dinner at his place.'

'Good. Slip him a couple of these sleeping tablets. You can have a good search around his place. Maybe he's got papers or something that'll give us the alarm codes.'

Connie took the two tablets wrapped in a bit of tissue and slipped them into her pocket. 'I'll be down the gym first, check on the shotguns.'

'Good girl.'

'Thank you, Dolly,' she said without a smile.

As she was walking out, Dolly caught her hand. 'Something bothering you?'

'What do you think? But, like you said, I owe you for Lennie so I'll do whatever you say.'

'You make sure you do.'

Connie wouldn't meet her gaze as she closed the door behind her. Dolly rubbed her eyes, and pinched the bridge of her nose. God, they infuriated her. She was always having to check up on one or the other of them – it was like having a house full of kids. She would have to start thinking about what she would do with them after the robbery.

Angela was in the kitchen when Dolly came in. 'Want to go into London, love? Only I got to drop Gloria off for her usual visit with her husband so you might as well keep us company.'

It was not until they had left Gloria at a tube station that Dolly told Angela what she wanted her to do. She said it so quietly that Angela didn't get nervous or even ask too many questions; she simply said yes. Not that she wanted to go into the police station, but she didn't really have any choice.

Angela asked at the desk to speak to Mike Withey. The duty sergeant asked her name and then called the incident room. 'What did you say your name was, love?'

'Angela Dunn.'

When Mike was told she was waiting in reception he marched straight out to her, grabbed her by the arm and pulled her out onto the street.

'I told you I didn't want to see you again.'

'Please, Mike, I just want to talk to you, just for a minute. Look, I bought you a present. Please don't be angry.'

'I don't want anything from you, Angela.'

Angela held out the slim little box but he turned away so she took it out and showed it to him. 'It's a pen.'

'Great, Angela, just what I needed.' She slid it into his top pocket, and he turned away from her. 'I don't want it.'

'Please, just give me a few minutes, please, Mike. I got to tell you something – it's important.' He rubbed his jaw. 'Mrs Rawlins said she'll call you tomorrow morning, she wants to know what would be a good time.'

Mike faced the wall, feeling as if someone was about to ram his head into it. 'What else did she tell you?'

'Nothing, just that she would be in touch but for you to tell her what time.'

He bit his lip. 'Tell her I've nothing for her, not yet, but I'll be at home – say in the morning about ten.'

Dolly sat in the car, the briefcase open on her lap. She adjusted the channel and could soon hear Mike as clearly as if he was sitting next to her. She had to know if she could trust him – and Angela, for that matter. So far she had said exactly what she had been told to say, and the added plus was that they were even in sight. She hadn't reckoned on them coming outside to talk.

Angela watched him hurry back into the station before she headed towards Dolly. She could see the aerial stuck on the side of the car. 'Was that okay?'

Dolly beamed. 'Yes, love. Get in, I've a few things I want you to do for me. Can you stay at your mother's?'

'Why? Can't I stay on at the manor?'

'Yes, but I want you to do a few things for me first thing in the morning. Have you got a passport?'

'No.'

'Well, first thing tomorrow I want you to get one and I want you to take mine, with this letter. I'm the girls' legal guardian and I want them put on my passport, just for a holiday. Then you come straight home. And, Angela, you don't say a word about this to any of the others or they'll go ape-shit – you know the way they feel about you.'

'What are you going to do?'

'Oh, drive around a bit. Go on, off you go.'

'My mum won't let me stay, Dolly.'

Dolly counted off some twenty-pound notes. 'Well, here's money for a hotel – just the one night, love, then you get yourself home.'

Dolly watched her walk off down the street, then noticed the channel light blinking in the briefcase and put in her earplug. Mike was making a phone call. She smiled to herself as she listened to Mike arranging to meet someone, and the more Dolly listened the more she smiled. She was sure she was right. She'd got the smart little bastard right by the balls. But better to be safe than sorry.

Gloria saw that Eddie was in a bad mood the moment he was let through the gate to the visiting room. She'd brought a few odds and sods for him, not much, and fifteen quid. He took them without so much as a thank you.

'So, how you keeping?'

'Oh, I'm havin' a really good time in here, Gloria.'

She had known it would start then.

'You look different,' he muttered.

'Yeah, well, it's all the fresh air.'

'So you're still at the farmhouse then?'

'It's a *manor* house, Eddie, and yeah, I'm still there.'

He began to roll a cigarette.

'Anythin' gone down there?' he asked nonchalantly, keeping his eyes on his roll-up. She sat back, watching him, and then he looked up, all innocence, and in that moment she knew she was stronger than him. Maybe she always had been.

Mike had no notion that he was wired up and Dolly Rawlins was taping every word he said. It was as if

she was on his shoulder when he went to visit an old
mate from his days in the Army, leading her directly
to the security firm that handled the money for the
mail train.

He had brought a bottle of Scotch and was shown into
the security firm's office. His friend Colin had been a bit
surprised to hear from Mike as it had been quite a few
years and he wondered what he was after. But Mike soon
got over that, saying he was putting out feelers for work
if he was to leave the police force and a friend of a friend
had told him that Colin had a cushy number going.

Dolly had to hand it to Mike. He was quite a smooth
operator. She listened as he chatted on about his Army
days, about how badly he was paid and how, with a wife
and two kids to keep plus a mortgage to pay, he was getting sick and tired of the Met. She was parked fifty yards
from the security firm's main depot and would have
remained there if she hadn't seen a police patrol car cruise
by. She did one slow tour round the block and then she
was out of range of the transmitter. She decided to call
it quits for the evening. Most important was that she felt
confident that if anything was to go down from Mike's
place she'd be ready for it She headed home, everything
she was planning playing over and over in her mind. It
was all coming together, and yet as the miles clocked
up she became more uneasy. Was she in over her head?
Did she really believe she could go through with it? Just

thinking about it exhausted her. Had it been like this with the widows?

Then he began to talk to her. It didn't take her by surprise – Harry's voice often came to her, not like some whispered menace, nothing like that. In fact, it was the normality of the sound of his voice in her head that had often soothed her. She used to talk to him, silent conversations as if he was in the room with her, his deep, warm tones as clear as if he was sitting in their old drawing room in their house in Totteridge. He used to sit up late many nights. Sometimes she'd take him in a warm glass of malt whisky with just a sprinkling of sugar.

'You all right, darlin'?' she'd ask him.

'I am, sweetheart, but I just need to make sure I'm covered back, front and sideways, because there'll be nobody else looking out for me.'

Harry never told her exactly what he was working on so diligently. But she would sit close and ask him if he wanted to talk about it ... how she loved those times. Harry would sip his drink and rest a hand on her shoulder.

'Well, darlin', I got this tricky little situation. Not sure who to trust with an important delivery and it's only tricky because it could have repercussions.'

She never asked names but in a roundabout way he would tell her who he mistrusted and why, and what he considered the best way to ensure they became trustworthy.

Still driving, one part of her mind concentrating on the road, the other listening to Harry, it wasn't until Dolly stopped at a garage to fill up with petrol that his voice started to fade away. The last thing she heard him say was, 'Cover your backside, Dolly, your sides and your front, before you make the next move.'

Mike remained with his pal Colin as they drank their way halfway down the bottle. He had not asked about the type of work Colin did, taking his time so as not to create any suspicion. Colin was a little ill at ease in case he was caught drinking: as he was the foreman he could get into trouble. But Mike laughed – he was, after all, a copper. Just in case, Colin slipped out to check no one was around to disturb them.

As soon as he left, Mike looked over the time sheets on the desk, and the lists of officers' names, but found nothing pertaining to any mail train pick-up or delivery. It was a big firm and Mike was about to try one of the drawers when Colin returned.

'You're gonna have to go, the night staff'll be on duty any minute and we're not allowed to have anyone in here.'

'Okay. When can we do this again? Only – if I leave the cop shop, I don't want to walk out to nothing. Is the pay decent?'

They talked about the money and Mike brought the conversation gradually round to what kind of work he would be looking at, asking if it was boring and involved just driving around the country. Colin grinned. 'No way, this is one of the top companies, we don't deal in small stuff – this is big. That's why they like us Army boys, you know, men that can handle themselves. We're shifting big loads of money.'

'Oh yeah? What you call big, then?'

Colin gave a shifty look around and leaned in close. 'Come and have a look out in the yard, see the new vans. They're all armour-plated, blow your mind, all work on timers, high-tech stuff. We do the Royal Mail deliveries.'

Mike looked suitably impressed and followed Colin into the yard where he was told in an awestruck whisper just how much money the security firm carried, before Colin hustled him out. They arranged to meet for a drink the following night. By then Colin would have made enquiries to see if there were any openings for someone with Mike's experience.

Dolly switched off the lights and got out of the car. It had been a long night and she was exhausted. She couldn't wait to get to bed but as usual she toured the house first, checking who was in and who wasn't. Julia was still out, so was Connie, and Ester was watching a late-night movie.

'Julia called, said her mother was really bad and that Norma's staying over with her.'

Dolly smiled. 'Well, that's good, give them time to talk.'

Ester made no reply, eyes on the film.

'You've still got to sort out those carriage links, you know, Ester.'

'I'll do it tomorrow, after the morning ride.'

'Okay – and at the same time sort that business out with the tape.'

Dolly was about to go up to bed when Ester asked, 'Where've you been, then?'

She swung the door back and forth. 'Checking out that copper. I think we can trust him.'

Ester turned from the TV set. 'Well, I hope you're right.'

'So do I.' The door closed silently behind her.

Ester went back to watching the film, but she was angry that Julia was with Norma, and couldn't really concentrate on what was going on.

'She's back, then,' Gloria said as she walked in.

Ester switched off the TV. 'She's driving me nuts, wants to find out how to unhitch a train carriage.'

'Well, that's easy.' Gloria yawned 'Get some Semtex and blast them apart, that's what I'd do. She's got a screw loose if she thinks you or me or all five of us could lift one of them heavy links. All you need to do to get a carriage loose is blow it apart, never mind farting around trying to unhitch it. '

*

Dolly listened to them, hearing every word. She wondered if Gloria was right, if they should use Semtex and where they could get hold of some. Then she sat on the bed looking at her notes and plans for the robbery, laid out just like Harry used to do it. She took out the small earpiece and tossed it onto the briefcase, no longer interested in the conversation below. Maybe they were right: maybe she did have a screw loose, because she had now decided that the best place to hold up the train was dead centre of the bridge.

Dolly heard Gloria's bedroom door bang shut. After a few moments she got up off the bed and, pulling her own door slightly ajar, listened. She could hear muffled weeping. She went out into the corridor.

Gloria had her face buried in the pillow, trying to make as little noise as possible. She hadn't expected it to hurt so much. She suddenly jerked back when Dolly touched her. 'You go creepin' around like that you'll gimme a bleedin' heart attack,' she said, shrugging Dolly's hand away.

'What you crying about?'

Gloria shook her head. 'Sad movie on the telly.'

'What happened with Eddie, Gloria?' Dolly sat down on the side of the bed.

Gloria sniffed, wiping her face with the back of her hand, and then decided there was no point in lying. 'He knew the guns was here and he said the filth paid him a

visit, said they was gonna book me on murder, like they
knew I was drivin' that fuckin' car. They told him about
Jimmy Donaldson.'

Gloria pushed her head into the pillow. 'Well, it wasn't
me, an' if they come after me for that then I'll tell them
it was that cow Angela. I'm not taking the rap for that.'

Dolly straightened the candlewick bedspread. 'They
got nothin'. If they had, love, they'd have sorted us out —
and fast. They got nothin' on that car.'

'And you'd know, would you?' snapped Gloria.

'Yes, I'd know. So, go on about Eddie.'

Gloria suddenly deflated and the tears started to fall.
'He grassed us, Dolly, he told them about the guns. He
admitted it.'

'I see,' Dolly said softly.

'No, you don't see, Dolly, you don't see at all. He's my
husband and he stitched me up. All the years I stood by
him, probably would have waited, you know — I mean,
he's not much but he is my husband.' Gloria sniffed again,
and then shrugged her shoulders. 'Well, now you know,
do you want me to pack me bags? I'll understand, I don't
wanna walk but I reckon you got a right to kick me out.'

Gloria didn't expect the gentle embrace, and it made
her want to sob even harder. Dolly held her a moment,
stroking her bleached-blonde hair, and Gloria could
hardly make out what she said, she spoke so softly. "S'all
right, love, I understand. You stay on here because

I understand.' Dolly took out a crumpled tissue and handed it to her. 'You're hurting now, probably always will, but it gets easier, believe me, it gets easier.'

'You're all right, gel, you know that?' Gloria whispered as Dolly left the room.

Dolly washed her hands and face, wiping the tissue across her cheeks. There were no tears, she didn't think she had any left, but she'd felt that hurt, that pain inside, like a knife. She saw his face again, saw him standing waiting for her in the darkness, the lake behind him as dark as the night. And yet his face was so clear, as if lit by a pale flickering light.

'Hello, Doll.' He had lifted his arms to embrace her and she had moved that much closer. She hadn't wanted to miss. She'd wanted to shoot him in the heart.

Chapter 15

Jim hugged Connie tightly. He was feeling very drunk but not as drunk as Connie had hoped. He'd had three pints in the pub and one and a half bottles of wine at home, plus two of Dolly's sleeping tablets, and he was still going strong, his face flushed his eyes unfocused, but no way was he about to pass out.

'I love you,' he said, hanging his head.

'I love you too,' she lied.

'You do? Is that the truth?'

'Yeah, I love you, Jim'

He stepped back, arms wide. 'I don't believe it. You love me?' She was getting really pissed off with him. Then he got down on his knees in front of her. 'Listen, I know we haven't known each other very long but I own this house, I mean, on a mortgage right? But I own it and my car and ... you really love me?' He kissed her hand, getting a bit tearful. She passed him another drink and he gulped it down. 'I need a drink to do this, I never thought I would, okay, give me another . . .' She poured the remains of the bottle into his glass and he swallowed that too, still on his knees. 'Will you marry me?' He looked up into her face as he slowly fell forward, his arms clasped around her legs, unable to keep himself upright.

'Jim. Jim?' She squatted down beside him and gave him a shake but he was out for the count. She slipped his duvet around him and put a pillow under his head before searching his pockets and looking through his wallet. Connie then searched every drawer and closet as he snored away, now curled up on his side. She was about to give up when she saw a small diary at his bedside. She flicked through it: just the odd memo about dental appointments and mortgage payments but listed at the back was a neat row of numbers. She jotted them down, not knowing if they meant anything or not, then turned off the lights and let herself out.

Connie waited for the late-night bus and still had a long walk home at the other end. It was raining and she got soaked, so by the time she got to her bedroom she was in a foul mood. She couldn't sleep straight away because she still felt angry; she was being used, she told herself, almost as much as when she was with Lennie. Well, she wasn't going to take much more of it. Let one of the others get pawed all over, she was well and truly sick of it. She even felt a bit sorry for Jim, who'd obviously fallen hard. She wondered if he'd remember asking her to marry him in the morning.

Connie tossed and turned, and then felt terribly sad. She realized Jim was the only man in her entire life who had asked her to marry him. She gave up on trying to sleep and decided to make herself a nightcap.

Connie was surprised to see Ester sitting in the kitchen in her dressing gown, her hands cupped round a mug of hot chocolate.

'Can't sleep either, huh?'

Ester shook her head. She hated to admit it, but she couldn't sleep for thinking of Julia being with Norma. 'You have a good night?' she asked.

'Depends what you mean by good,' Connie answered, leaning against the Aga. 'I found some numbers in his diary. They may be the codes, they may not be, I dunno. He asked me to marry him.'

Ester looked up. 'What?'

'Yeah, funny, isn't it? He's a nice guy, and so's the builder bloke, but all their niceness does is make me miss Lennie.'

'What?'

'I can't stop thinking about him.' She fetched a mug and spooned in some Horlicks.

'Well, you'd better stop bloody thinking of him. Especially after what we all did to get rid of his body.'

Connie poured hot milk into the mug and stirred it, then joined Ester at the kitchen table. 'Why is it I go for the bastards of this world and not the nice blokes?'

'Because, sweetheart, you're a sucker.'

'I am not.'

'Course you are. Lennie beat the living daylights out of you.'

'He loved me in his way.'

'What way? Who you kidding? He had you on the game and you call it love? He's not worth even thinking about – no pimp is.'

'He wasn't my pimp.'

'Pull the other one and grow up. He wanted you back on the game. That's why you ran off and left him, so don't start fantasizing that it was all lovey-dovey and he'd have you in a cottage with kids and roses round the garden gate. He was a piece of shit.'

'You didn't even know him,' Connie retorted.

'I didn't have to. Know one, know them all. And you got so used to being his punchbag you—'

'I wasn't!'

'*Yes, you were!*' Ester pushed back her chair and took her dirty mug to the sink, slamming it down on the draining board. 'You got loving all confused with being smacked, sweetheart. Wallop, I love you. Beat me up and it means you love me even more – but then, when he's got you on all fours, crawling like a dog, he'll give you one last kick and you're out, used, abused and your head fucked up.'

'You'd know, would you?'

'Yes,' Ester hissed.

'That why you go with women?'

Ester whirled and slapped Connie's face hard. 'You don't know anything about me. But lemme tell you, I know men, know them better than you or anyone else in this house ever will. You make me sick, moaning about that two-bit punk. Instead of bleatin' on about how much he loved you, you should thank Christ he's out of your life.'

Connie put her hand to her cheek. 'Oh yeah, my life's so much better now, is it?'

Ester shrugged. 'It might be. I guess it depends what happens.' Then she walked out.

Norma took her time washing up the supper dishes, feeling awkward in the strange, old-fashioned house. Julia's mother was very ill; the stroke had robbed her of speech and movement, and she lay in her bed, her eyes open wide, as if she was staring at the ceiling.

Julia had been shocked to see her so immobilized and, as a doctor, she had quickly assessed her condition and known instantly she would need round-the-clock nursing. It would be impossible for her to remain alone at the house, even with a housekeeper. She had sat beside her

mother for most of the evening. She had a lot to say to
her, but they had never really talked and now they never
would. Her mother would never speak again. Julia even
had to change her as she was incontinent, had washed
her as if she were a baby, cleaned the bed and tidied
her thinning white hair. She had not said a word but
Norma thought her gentleness was touching. Now Julia
sat staring at the silent figure, knowing a home was the
only option left to her as a nurse was out of the question
financially.

Julia held the frail, bony hand. 'Oh, Mama, we should
have talked. I'd have liked you to know who I was but,
well, it's too late now.'

Norma peeked in. 'I've cleared the dishes and cleaned
the kitchen a bit. It was a bit grimy.'

'Thank you.'

Norma could tell Julia didn't want to talk to her, that
she somehow resented her presence. She crept to the bed
and looked at the old woman. She made not a sound,
didn't move a muscle. There was just the vacant stare.

'You can share the bedroom with me,' Julia said quietly.

Norma whispered that she would go downstairs and
watch television, and crept out again. Norma was trying
her best, but all this creeping around made Julia want
to scream.

She began to pack her mother's nightwear, hairbrush
and toiletries into a small bag, ready for the move. She

would check all the homes that would take her and arrange a private ambulance in the morning. She opened and shut drawer after drawer as quietly as possible so as not to disturb her mother, carrying the garments back and forth to the open case on a low bedside chair. She thought she should perhaps put in some bed jackets or cardigans and started to search through the dressing-table drawers. She saw the newspaper-clippings, hidden beneath a fine wool shawl. At first she didn't think anything of them but then, as she removed the shawl, she couldn't help but notice the headline: 'Local Doctor in Drug Scandal'.

Julia's heart pounded. She sat down on the dressing-table stool and got out the neat stack of clippings. They detailed her arrest for possession of heroin, the charges for selling prescriptions and her trial and sentence. The secret she had so painstakingly kept from her mother, all the years of lying and frantic subterfuge had been a waste of time because all along she had known.

She screwed up the clippings into a tight ball and hurled them into the waste bin but it was a while before the anger rose to the surface, and she turned to the silent figure in the bed.

'You knew! You knew, all those years, and you never told me, you never *talked to me!*'

In the drawing room below, Norma heard the banging and scraping and quickly ran up the narrow staircase.

When she got to the bedroom, she stood at the doorway, frightened, as Julia shook her mother's bed until it rattled, until the old woman seemed about to roll out of it.

'No, Julia! No, stop it! For God's sake, *stop this!*'

Julia then turned her fury on Norma. She was ready to lash out at her, at anyone who came near her, but Norma was quite able to take care of herself and gripped Julia tightly. 'Julia, it's me, it's Norma, stop this . . .'

'She knew, Norma. All the years I've broken my fucking back keeping it away from her, and she knew.'

Julia stormed out of the room. Norma didn't understand what she was talking about but she quickly settled Mrs Lawson back on her pillows and tucked in the bedclothes. She leaned over the bed, touching the frail, wrinkled hand. 'It's all right, she'll be fine.'

Norma felt such sadness as the mute figure's helpless fingers tried to hold on to her and tears rolled down her cheeks. 'Don't worry, you'll be taken care of, Mrs Lawson, and I will look after Julia.'

Only the tears indicated that the old lady understood.

When Norma went into Julia's room, she found her lying on her bed, the bed she had used as a girl, with fists clenched, cursing her own stupidity.

'You shouldn't have done that, upset her like that,' Norma said quietly.

'What do you know?' Julia spat angrily.

'Well, maybe she can't talk but she can hear, Julia.'

'I don't give a shit.'

Norma began to massage Julia's back. 'I understand.'

'No, you don't,' Julia said, her face buried in the pillow.

'Try me,' Norma said softly.

Julia rolled over and looked up into her face. 'This was my bedroom, and you know something? I knew I was gay when I was about twelve or thirteen. She was a stable girl at the local riding school and we came back and we did it in here, then Mother served us tea. We laughed about that.' Julia sat up and leaned against Norma. 'I wanted to make her understand ... I wanted her to know who I was, Norma, but all she wanted was for me to be married and have kids. She still asks ...' Julia mimicked her mother asking if she had a boyfriend and then she bowed her head. 'You know, maybe she's always known I was a lesbian but could never bring herself to talk about it.'

'So what are you going to do?

'Get her into a home tomorrow, sell this place and that's it. There's nothing for me here. Maybe there never was.' She sounded resigned.

Later that night Norma washed Mrs Lawson. She kissed her and switched off the light before going up to bed with Julia. They made love and then Norma fell asleep.

Julia crept out from under the covers and slipped from the room. She removed Norma's police riding cape and hat from the Land Rover, closing the back as quietly as she could. She packed them into a case and left it in the hallway before returning upstairs. But she did not go back to bed immediately. Instead she inched open the door to her mother's room: she had not moved from the centre of the bed, seeming somehow trapped inside the tight sheet across her chest. She appeared to be asleep.

Julia stood staring at her for about five minutes, and then silently left the room. She no longer felt anger, just utterly drained, and it was then she remembered. Her pace quickened as she went into the bathroom. She had to lie flat on the tiled bathroom floor as she unscrewed the cheap Formica surrounds of the bath, pulling them away and reaching around until she found the tin medical box. Only after she had re-screwed the panel into place did she open the old battered white box with the scratched red cross in the centre. She sighed: there was the rubber tube, there were the hypodermic needles, the tiny packets of white cocaine and one small, screwed-up, tin-foil square of heroin.

The following morning Julia made a list of items she wanted from the house. She had arranged for a local estate agent to come in and had also found a home that would take her mother. It was expensive and Norma suggested they ring round a few others. 'Nope. With the money from the house I can pay for it.'

'Are you okay?'

'Yes, I'm fine. Just got a lot to get sorted.'

Norma couldn't quite understand Julia's attitude. She was unemotional, all business. She simply put it down to her way of dealing with the situation and never thought for a moment Julia was high.

Julia didn't see her mother again. Norma got her ready for the ambulance. Julia refused to help when the ambulance arrived, remaining in the drawing room when they took her away. She was still making phone calls, cancelling milk, papers, and the housekeeper.

'She's gone,' Norma said sadly.

'Okay, we can leave in about half an hour.' Julia continued writing, calculating how much the house would be worth. As it had been re-mortgaged three times, there would be little or nothing left from the sale. She was going to need money more than ever, and if it wasn't from the robbery, she would have to find some other means to finance her mother's stay at the home.

Norma did not notice her hat and cape were missing until they left. She didn't seem unduly worried, blaming herself for forgetting to lock the car. 'Probably be some kids. It's a wretched nuisance because I'll have to fork out for the replacements but at least they didn't nick the car.'

'Yeah, that's good,' Julia said, picking up the small case she was carrying out to the car. 'Just a couple of things I thought I'd take back with me.'

Norma started the engine. 'Well, if you need storage

space, I've got a huge barn, and your mother has some nice pieces of furniture, antiques even.'

As they drove off, Julia didn't look back. The house and her mother were in the past now. Her mother was as good as dead and at least there would be no more lies. She stared out of the window. 'Stupid woman. Why did she never tell me she knew?'

Norma said nothing, knowing that Julia wasn't expecting an answer. They headed back to the manor and Norma wondered if Julia would thank her for being with her, for caring, for loving her. 'I love you, Julia,' she said softly.

Julia continued to gaze out of the window, not hearing, wondering if Ester was missing her. Then she began to think about the train hijack and started to smile: maybe it was the drugs, maybe it was just the thought of doing something so audacious, so crazy, that lifted her spirits.

'Feeling a bit better?' Norma asked.

'Yeah, I'm feeling good, really good!'

Dolly was in a ratty mood. She was running low on cash and John was standing in her office, refusing to budge.

'I just want to know what's going on. If I lay the men off, I won't get them back. You got half a roof, scaffolding up, I got cement and sand out there. I've laid out for the equipment, Mrs Rawlins. I've kept my end of the bargain.'

'Look, I'm sorry about this but there have been a few problems. If you give me another day or so—'

'But you say that every time I come here.'

'I know, but I can't help it if people don't pay me. It's not that I like doing this to you'

'The place is unsafe, Mrs Rawlins, and you got kids running around.'

Dolly opened a drawer and took out the last of the cash from the sale of the guns. Five thousand pounds. Now she was almost cleaned out. 'Look, do what you can. If you have to lay a few of the men off then you have to do it but this is all I've got right now.'

John counted out the money, then stashed it in his pocket. 'Okay. At least I'll finish the roof,' he said as he walked out. She scratched her chin. The idea of the robbery was fading fast. They couldn't manage the horses, never mind hold up the train.

Gloria yelled from the yard for someone to get Dolly as the truck arrived with the bags of lime. More money had to be paid over to the driver before he would even lift one of the twenty-kilo bags down from the back of the truck. Dolly then had to pay out for the skip that she had ordered. Money was always going out and nothing was coming in.

'What we gonna do with all this lime, then?' Gloria asked, prodding the bag.

'Tip it into the old cesspit.'

'Oh yeah? Well, who's gonna do that?'

'All of you. Get them out there.'

'Bloody hell,' moaned Gloria.

Dolly clenched her hands. 'Just get on with it!'

Connie, Ester and Gloria changed into old clothes, put on big thick gloves and scarves to cover their faces, and began to slit open the bags and tip them into the pit. The lime clouded and burnt their eyes, making their skin itch, so there were further moans and groans. Julia returned, bright and breezy as she stood looking at the three figures resembling snowmen.

'It's not funny! You get changed and give us a hand,' Ester snapped.

As Julia walked off, Connie called after her, 'How's your mother?' and Julia shouted back that it was all taken care of. Ester then hurled a sack aside and followed Julia. 'Did Norma stay with you?'

'Yep, and I got her hat and cape.' Julia held up the case cheerfully.

'Well, you keep her away from here,' Ester said, and Julia smiled, happy that she was still jealous.

In the kitchen, she found Angela giving the three girls some lunch, and Dolly sitting moodily at the end of the table with her notebook open. She looked up as Julia walked in. 'How was your mother?'

'Mute,' Julia said, and then leaned close to Dolly. 'Got the hat and cape.'

Dolly nodded, then looked to the three girls. 'I don't want any of you going near the big pit out at the back. If you do, you'll get a very hard smack and you won't be allowed to ride Helen of Troy, do you all understand? I see one of you even close to the pit and I will make you very, very sorry.'

Their expressions were glum, and Angela poured another cup of tea for Dolly.

'What's in the pit?'

'Mind your own business, Angela. Take the girls for a nice long walk up to the woods.'

Dolly didn't touch the tea and instead went out to see how the others were doing. She stopped off at the stables to fetch an old canvas bag and walked over to the 'snowmen'. 'When it's finished put this in, see how long it takes to disintegrate. Then fetch some corrugated iron. Take it off the stables roof at the back and put it over the pit.'

Gloria saluted stiffly but Dolly was not amused and walked off round to the front of the house.

'She certainly doesn't get her hands dirty, does she?' Connie said.

Julia poked at the canvas bag with a rake. The bag was disintegrating fast. 'Look, Ester, it works. How was the riding this morning?'

Ester threw her gloves into the pit. 'We're bloody useless. Gloria almost fell off.'

'I didn't,' Connie said proudly.

Julia slipped her arm round Connie's shoulder. 'That's because you, my darling, have a good seat!'

Ester stared hard at Julia. It wasn't like her to be so jolly. 'You been drinking with Norma?'

'Nope.' Julia then single-handedly lifted one sheet of the corrugated iron and dropped it down over the pit. 'Just feeling good, Ester.'

Mike knew something was going down when he saw Craigh and Palmer having a confab in the corridor. As soon as they saw him, they turned away.

'What's going on?' Mike asked casually.

DCI Craigh sighed. 'A lot, mate. Seems the ruddy estimates that bitch Rawlins sent in are now with the Super and he's gone apeshit.'

'Shit,' Mike said ruefully.

'You said it, and it's all over us. We got to get it sorted and, Mike, don't expect to get off with a slapped wrist because I'm not covering for you and nor is he.' He jerked his thumb at Palmer. Palmer gave an apologetic shrug.

Mike hesitated. 'What if I'd got a tip-off about—'

'We don't want any more of your fuckin' tip-offs, we got enough problems.' Craigh prodded Mike with his index finger. 'You sit at your desk. This Rawlins business has left us with a lot of aggro and there are old cases that now take precedence. But if there's to be an internal investigation, I'm warning you, I'm not taking the rap.'

Craigh stormed off down the corridor and Palmer looked after him, then back at Mike. 'Super's in with the Chief now so we just have to wait. Maybe it'll all blow over.'

Mike could feel the pit of his stomach churning. He felt trapped and he couldn't see any way out of it. When he got to his desk there was a message to call Colin. Mike held the slip in his hands, half of him wanting to come clean, to tell Craigh everything. He wanted to tell him about Angela and about his mother, but the more he thought about just how much there was to confess, the more he panicked. He was trapped, all right.

Mike took the pen Angela had given him out of his pocket and sucked at the end of it. Then he looked at the clock. He had another couple of hours' work before he could skive off. Maybe the best plan of action was to see how things played out, go and see his mate again, go and talk to Rawlins, and then make the decision as to whether or not he should spill the beans.

While Angela was putting the children to bed, the women came in to see Dolly as she sat behind her desk. 'Shut the door,' Dolly said quietly.

They lined up, sensing something was going down. Dolly tapped the desk with her pencil, flicking through the little black book. She pointed at Connie. 'You. We have to find out if the numbers you got from the bloke at the signal box are the coded alarms.'

Connie chewed her lip and sighed. 'How do I do that?'

'Get in the signal box and, I dunno, switch on the alarm, see what happens.'

Gloria sat down. 'Well, we really are professionals, aren't we?'

Dolly glared at her. 'I want you to scout around under the signal box, see where their main electrical and phone cables are, see if we can cut them.

'Then there's this.' Dolly took out the pen and opened it, slipping in the small batteries. 'Connie, give this to the bloke in the signal box. This transmitter you place somewhere inside the box. The tail wire, make sure it hangs loose so we get a clear reception. Shove it on a shelf or somethin'. Shouldn't be too hard, it's only just bigger than a matchbox. I've got one under the signal box already but the batteries need changing.'

'We got anything from the signal box?'

Julia snorted. 'Yeah, we know when they eat, fart and go home.'

Dolly was surprised at Julia – she wasn't usually so crude. 'What's the matter with you?'

Julia wiped her nose on her sleeve. 'Got a bit of a cold coming on. Apart from that I'm fine. How are you?'

Dolly raised an eyebrow. 'I'm fine, Julia, but we don't want you in bed sick if we got to ride with you.'

Ester propped herself on the desk. 'Dolly, when are we gonna be told just how we go about the whole thing? I mean, you're a great one for giving orders but we don't really know what we're doing all this for.'

'I'll tell you when I'm ready or when I think you're ready. Now get on with your jobs, all of you.'

Julia sniffed and looked at Ester. 'What do you want us to do?'

Dolly jerked a thumb towards the receiver and the headphones. 'You take it in shifts to listen in at the signal box.'

'Who's listening in to the copper?' Gloria asked.

'I am,' Dolly said as she picked up her briefcase and walked out.

Ester nudged Julia. 'You think she's listening in on us?'

'Put money on it,' Gloria said.

It was a long night, Julia and Ester taking it in shifts, boring hours of listening in at the signal box. It only became interesting when Connie turned up. She hitched up her skirt as she perched on the table and crooked her finger at Jim. 'I got a present for you.'

Jim was hungover and feeling a bit sheepish. 'Look, Connie, about the other night.'

'Forget it, you said a lot of things that maybe you didn't mean.'

'No, I meant every word, I just didn't mean to pass out.'

She wound her legs round his waist. 'Here, this is for you.' She unwrapped the pen and slipped it into his top pocket. 'Keep it close to your heart.'

Ester looked over at Dolly as she walked in. 'He's got the pen. It was a bit distorted to begin with but now we can hear them snogging clear as a bell.'

Dolly glanced at Julia, who had the earpiece in. 'I'm off, be back late. I'm taking Gloria's car.'

Julia beckoned to her and she moved closer. 'I think they're having it away, lot of heavy breathing, you want to hear?'

'All I want to hear is the code for those alarms.'

Connie pulled down her skirt and stepped out of her panties as Jim closed the gates for a passenger train. He didn't mess around when it came to his work, even when Connie nuzzled up behind him and wrapped her arms round his chest.

'Just stay off me a second, I got work to do, darlin'.'

Connie sighed, moving close to the alarm box and special telephone. 'If something went wrong on the rail, Jim, what would you do?'

'Get the sack if they found you here.' He looked towards the station as the train chugged up the tracks.

'I mean if there was an accident,' she asked, sliding down so she couldn't be seen from the station.

'Well, with the alarms I got a direct line to the local cop shop, fire brigade and ambulance. They can all be here within four minutes.'

She watched him as he went about his business, pulling the levers down, moving backwards and forwards across the hut.

'What about the live-wire cable?'

Julia switched on the main speaker and she, Ester and Dolly could hear the train thundering past the signal box. Then they heard something else, a third voice.

John had been playing detective, and now he knew his suspicions were right. He was standing at the gates, his car engine ticking over, when he looked up at the signal box. He knew it was her right away. As the gates opened and the train passed, he saw her more clearly. She was laughing and chatting away. He drove into the yard beneath the box and ran up the wooden steps, then banged on the door.

'Connie, I know you're in there. *Connie!*'

He burst into the signal box, and Jim whipped round.

'What you think you're doing?' John yelled at Connie.

'Seeing an old friend,' she shouted back.

John turned towards Jim. 'She's my girlfriend.'

Jim looked at Connie in confusion. 'What's going on?'

'Nothing!' she shrieked, pushing John back.

'You liar! This is the second time I've seen you up here! I'll get him the sack, that's for starters. You shouldn't be up here.'

'I can go wherever I like, it's no business of yours.'

'Yes, it fucking is!'

John threw a punch at Jim who ducked, looking down at the station, terrified someone would be watching. He backed away.

'Look, mate, I dunno who you are but you'd better get out of here.'

John grabbed Connie. 'She's coming with me.'

'I am not! You don't own me,' Connie yelled, kicking out at him. She was close to the alarm switch, just inches away.

Dolly put her hand over her face. 'One of you had better get up there, get her out.'

The alarm went off. Julia winced, the sound so loud it screamed through the room. 'Jesus Christ, it's the fuck-ing alarm!' Ester yelled.

Jim's face drained of colour. He shouted for Connie and John to get out as he dialled the station to report a false alarm. Connie saw him punch in each number and then

closed her eyes, trying to fix the order in her memory as
John tried to haul her out. They could hear somebody
shouting from the platform below. 'Get out of here!' Jim
roared. He knew if they were discovered in his signal
box he'd lose his job for sure.

By now a passing patrol car had heard the alarm and
was already heading towards the station, siren blaring.

John dragged Connie down the steps and had only
just shoved her into his van when the patrol car hurtled
into the yard. The two uniformed officers got out as Jim
appeared at the top of the steps. 'It's okay, no problem.
It was just a routine test.'

The officers hesitated, one continuing up the steps
while the other crossed over to John.

'What you doing here?'

John grinned. 'Sorry, mate, just having a quickie
with the girlfriend when it went off – talk about being
caught short.'

The officer nodded, looking into the van. Connie
tittered nervously.

'Well, you shouldn't be in this area, so go on, on
your way.'

John drove out, Connie sitting as far away from him
as possible. 'You had no right to do that, you know,' she
said. 'I don't belong to you. I can have as many boyfriends as I like. You even live with a girl and I don't get
uptight about that.'

'I don't live with anyone any more.'

'Well, don't blame it on me.'

John slammed on the brakes. 'I thought you were serious about us.'

'Oh, do me a favour.'

'I just did. You could have been arrested for being up there with him, you know, and he'll probably lose his job.'

'Only if you rat on him.'

John clenched the steering wheel till his knuckles turned white. 'I don't understand you, I thought—'

'You thought what?' she said, her face red with anger.

That maybe you . . . well, I made a mistake.'

'Yes, you did, John. I don't like being told who I can go out with by you or anybody else. If I want to screw—'

'Stop talking like that.'

'Talking like what?'

He turned on her. 'A cheap tart.'

She slapped his face, almost wanting him to slap her back, but he shook his head and turned away.

'I'll take you home.'

He started the engine, feeling sick. 'Why did you lead me on?' he asked softly.

She gently touched his shoulder. 'I'm just not ready to get serious about anyone, not yet.'

He shrugged her hand away. 'It's not as if you're any

spring chicken. How old are you, anyway? You carry on like this and no decent man'll want you.'

Connie felt as if he had punched her, harder than Lennie ever had. 'I'm twenty-five.'

'Well, you got a good figure but I don't think you can count, sweetheart. You're not twenty-five.'

She didn't know what to say. She just felt the tears welling up, trickling down her cheeks. She was only thirty-five but he made her feel as if she was old and worn out. She snuffled as the van turned into the lane by the manor.

'Just drop me here,' she said quietly.

He stopped the van sharply, then leaned across her to open the door for her.

'Jim asked me to marry him,' she said as she climbed out.

'Well, he's a sucker. He can have you and don't worry, I won't rat on him. He's gonna need every penny he can get keeping you – unless you do more of those films you told me about.'

She slammed the door hard and teetered off along the uneven road in her stilettos. John watched her perfect arse as she sashayed along. Then he drove off, wondering whether or not he could make it up with his girlfriend. Maybe he should even ask her to marry him. She was a decent girl. Sometimes it takes a piece of trash like Connie to make you come to your senses, he thought.

Julia passed him on her way back to the manor. She pulled up alongside Connie and wound down the window. 'I was sent out to see if you needed any assistance.'

'I obviously didn't,' snapped Connie, continuing towards the front door. She watched Julia drive round to the stables before she let herself in, and ran up the stairs, trying to avoid seeing anyone else, but Dolly caught her halfway. 'You get the alarm codes? You set it off, didn't you?'

Connie sniffed, refusing to look at her. 'Yes, I got them, but right now I want to be alone.'

'Come on now, Connie, love. Come back down here and tell me all about it.'

'Just stop telling me what to do, I done what you wanted, now leave me alone.' She went on up the stairs.

Dolly looked at her watch and then back to the drawing room. She was tired herself but she had to make sure Mike wasn't setting them up. It was in danger of all falling apart and it seemed, at times, that she was the only adult among them. Maybe she should call it all off, and just get rid of the lot of them. She smiled, imagining pushing each one of them into the lime pit.

Connie sat at her dressing table, studying her face in the mirror. 'Maybe you are old,' she whispered, and then quickly did a movie-star pout. 'Gonna be rich, though, and then you'll always be young and beautiful, and . . .' For the first time she knew for sure she would go through with any robbery Dolly Rawlins had in mind. She stopped making her Marilyn Monroe face, and the real Connie appeared, the other side that she always hid away, the angry, bitter, tough little Liverpool tart that'd give any lad a backhander, just like her dad gave her, like every man seemed to think he could. She'd taken the punches, taken the shit, all her life, but she wasn't going to take any more. She closed her full, sexy lips in a tight line. 'Fuck you, Marilyn.'

Connie breathed on the mirror and, with the tip of her finger, traced the numbers. Now, thanks to her, Dolly had the code for the alarm. Connie beamed: she wasn't as dumb as they all made out, but, as the numbers faded in the mirror, she began to panic, searching for something she could use to write them down. She found her black eyebrow pencil and a piece of tissue, then closed her eyes, replaying in her mind the moment Jim, in his panic, punched in the numbers. She might be no good with words, for reading and the like, but she'd always been able to count. No punter ever short-changed tough little Connie Stevens by a penny.

When Dolly appeared, she asked her twice if she was sure she had the right code, staring at the tissue with the childish figures.

'Yeah. If the alarm goes off, we call that number.'

Dolly gave that odd smile. 'You did good, darlin', very

good.' Connie felt good, but there was no further praise as Dolly left the room, folding the tissue and putting it into her pocket.

Dolly went out alone later that night. If Jim had just used the telephone, then the wires had to be beneath the hut, and all she had to do was cut them because the alarm would also be connected to the central box. She used a map-reading torch, inching her way beneath the signal box, to check for herself. And, sure enough, in the area marked 'No Admittance', was a large, secure, BT fixture, similar to those in residential areas, the ones an engineer sits by with hundreds of tiny wires, and you pass him by wondering what the hell he is doing. Dolly could just make out that she would need some kind of sledgehammer to prise it open. It didn't matter which wire belonged to which telephone; she'd simply slash her way through the lot of them.

Dolly enjoyed the walk back to the house in the darkness. The air smelt good and clean, a light rain had fallen, the ground sparkled in the moonlight, and she smiled to herself as Harry talked to her in that low soft voice.

'Check everything out for yourself. Never leave anything to chance or to anyone else. Remember, Doll, look out for yourself.' Dolly stopped and his voice died. It was strange, because a new thought dawned on her. What if it had been *her* voice that Harry had listened to? Maybe it had been Dolly who had quietly pushed him in the right direction. She had just never been given the credit. At least, not until it was too late.

Chapter 16

Mike was having a few beers with Colin, and pushing him for more details about the 'big stuff' the company handled.

Colin leaned in and lowered his voice. 'We deliver the sacks to the mail trains. After they had the big robberies at the main stations, we were brought in. You know about them?'

Mike took a sip of his pint. 'Nah, they'd be handled by the Robbery Squad, special division, if it's a big one.'

Colin stood up, buttoning his jacket. 'Well, if anyone hit what we're carrying it'd be the biggest in history.'

'Oh yeah?' Mike tried to conceal the tension he was feeling.

Colin leaned even closer and whispered something as Mike looked at him in stunned amazement. 'You kidding me? That much?'

Colin winked, tapped his nose. 'That's classified information but that's how much.'

'Shit. That's mind-blowing.'

'Yeah, and so's the security. Routes change every few months, just to safeguard it ever being leaked.' Colin grinned. 'Think about it and we'll have that curry next week. We'll take the wives, shall we? Make a night of it.'

Ester slipped her arm around Julia, drawing her close. 'What are you taking, Julia?' Julia tried to move away but Ester held on tightly. 'I know, Julia, I can tell by your eyes. And you get very chatty. So what is it?'

Julia shoved her away. 'For Chrissakes, nothing. What's got into you?'

Ester refused to budge. 'Lemme see your arm.'

'No, I won't. Don't you trust me?'

Ester examined her face. 'No, I don't. You've been acting strangely since you got back from your mother's.'

Julia shook her off but Ester grabbed her again. 'Tell me, Julia, or I'll tell Dolly.'

Julia rolled her eyes. 'Okay, look, I took one hit, some gear I'd left at Mother's, just the one, I swear to God. I was feeling so bad, and Norma was getting on my nerves.'

Ester got out of bed and looked around the room. 'I'll find it, if you got a stash here. I'll find it, Julia.'

Julia reached out for her. 'Darling, there's nothing,

on my mother's life. There was just a teeny-weeny bit. I wouldn't get back on it, you know that.'

Ester reluctantly allowed Julia to draw her back to bed. 'I hope not, Julia, because if you *have* started, you're fucked. And if Dolly found out she'd kick you out of here so fast.'

Julia wrapped her arms around Ester, kissing her neck. 'You don't have to worry, Ester.'

They kissed and then curled up together as Julia tried to think of a good hiding place for her stash and Ester wondered if she should warn Dolly. To use Julia in the robbery if she was back on junk would be madness. Maybe she should just piss off and leave them to it, before the whole thing went tits up.

Gloria felt restless. Her back ached constantly from all the horse riding and she kept thinking about Eddie, wondering how he was. Not that she missed him; if she calculated the years they had been married, the time actually spent together was minimal because he had been in and out of prison so much – and she had been inside herself on and off. It hadn't really been a marriage at all. The truth was, he was just somebody who was connected to her, for good or ill, and there was nobody else. Her kids wouldn't even know who she was by now. She wouldn't know them, either, if she came face to face with them. Maybe it was having the little girls around her that brought back the memories. She'd had her kids taken away when she first got arrested. Like Kathleen's girls, they had been shuttled from one foster home to another before she signed the adoption papers. She did it to give them a better life. She wondered if they had one, and then started to cry. She cried for the long, wasted years and eventually fell asleep.

It felt as if she'd only just dropped off when there was a loud bang on her door.

'Come on, get up! Time to ride.'

That morning they had a breakthrough. It happened almost all at once: the fear left them and they went from a canter into a gallop and, at the end of the two-hour lesson, they were all beaming and patting each other on the back. The positive feeling continued as they ate the eggs and bacon Angela had prepared while Julia gave each of them separate hints on improving their performance even further.

Dolly was encouraged enough to ask Julia to find out where they kept the keys to the stable yard and how they could cover the horses' hoofs.

'What do you want to do that for?' Julia asked.

Dolly kept her voice low. 'We'll make a hell of a lot of noise coming out of that stable. We got to ride down the lane, right past two cottages. We got to be silent.' She went back to her coffee and was left at the table with her precious notebook as Angela washed up, while Ester and Gloria checked the tapes to see if there had been any developments at the signal box.

Like Dolly, Gloria had also been under the signal box. She had called out for Buster, a make-believe dog, and nobody had paid her any attention as she clocked the electric cables, the main electricity-power sector and the telephone wires. Gloria had also seen the large danger signs with the red zigzag. Shivers went up her spine because the voltage was so high: Connie had told them at supper one night that a dog got onto the line and was thrown up into a tree!

When Gloria got back to the manor, she didn't mince her words. 'How do we get on the line? We'd get blown into a friggin' tree if any of us hit that cable.' She was drawing a map of the signal box and the railway junction. 'If the gates open and that train moves, it's gonna go over the bridge, right? Well, after that it'll pick up speed and no way is it gonna stop.' Gloria prodded her diagram with a chipped fingernail.

Ester frowned, turning the map round. 'Maybe she's gonna stop it at the crossings, then we ride up to it.'

'No way. She stops it there and we're screwed. There are lanes either side of it – we couldn't stop a cop car with a bleedin' horse!' Gloria sniffed.

Julia leaned over them, arms around each of their shoulders. 'Maybe she's gonna blow it up.'

'Oh shut up,' Ester rapped.

'We still got three shotguns,' Gloria shrugged.

Ester looked at Julia. 'You know, I think it's time we had a serious chat. We're all here being ordered around to do this and that and she's keeping her mouth shut, scribbling in that ruddy black book of hers. I reckon we've got to face her out, ask her just what she intends doing and, more important, how she's gonna do it.'

Gloria crossed to the window and drew back the curtain. 'We got a visitor. Shit! It's that ruddy cop, Angela's bloke. I told you we couldn't trust that two-faced bitch.'

They huddled at the window, watching, as Dolly walked towards Mike, who was getting out of the car. 'Stay put, love, let's just go for a drive, shall we?'

Mike waited for Dolly to get in beside him and then turned the car round and drove out.

'What do you make of that, then?'

Ester sucked in her breath. 'Well, I dunno about you two but I think it stinks. What's she doing driving around with him?'

Dolly and Mike parked in a small turning into a field. He said what he'd come to say and then waited.

'Ex-Army bloke, is he?' Mike nodded. 'You sure it's the truth?'

'All I'm saying is what he told me. Now, I done what I said I would and that's it.'

Dolly pursed her lips. 'How do I know I can trust you?'

Mike leaned back in his seat. 'I have to trust you, that you're not going to stitch me up, Mrs Rawlins.'

'Oh, I know, love, but I've got more to lose than you.'

'I got my job, my kids, my wife. Like I said, I've done what you asked me and that's it.'

Dolly examined her fingernails. 'Sorry, love, it isn't. I need some Semtex.'

'*What?*'

'You heard.'

'I can't get that kind of thing!'

'What about your friend?'

'You must be joking! He works for the ruddy security firm, I can't go asking him for bloody Semtex.'

Dolly shifted her weight in the seat. 'What about some of your other old Army friends? Could they get it?'

'Look, I got to go, I can't do any more.' He gripped the steering wheel tightly. 'Let me off the hook, Mrs Rawlins, and if you want some advice, whatever you're planning, and I've got a bloody good idea what it is, you'll never hit that security wagon. It's armour-plated, they got a convoy, cops at the front, cops at the back, they keep right on its tail. You do yourself a favour and scrap whatever you're thinking of doing.'

'Why? Because you know about it?'

'Because it's a no-hoper right from the start and—'

'And?' Dolly waited, watching him sweating.

'Look, I grass on you and I'm in the frame so hard I'd get time just for what I done to date. All I'm doing is telling you to pull out, forget it. I don't care how many blokes you're using, you'll never do it.'

Dolly opened the car door and looked down at him. 'Thanks for the advice. Maybe you're right.'

She straightened up and could see Angela coming towards her with the three little girls. 'Mike, she doesn't know anything.'

'Well, at least that's something.'

'Hello, my darlin's.' Dolly held out her arms for the girls and they ran to her. One had been collecting some pussy-willow twigs and presented them to her.

'Thank you.' She turned to Angela. 'Have a word with Mike, just a few minutes, I'll wait here.'

Dolly took the girls towards a hedge and began looking for a bird's nest, but she could hear what they said and she'd noticed that Mike still had the pen stuck in his jacket pocket.

Angela sat on the edge of the passenger seat, the door open. 'Hello, Mike.'

'Hello, sweetheart.' He reached out and took her hand. 'Look, I know what I said to you the other day was harsh, but I wasn't thinking. I'm sorry about the baby, I really am.'

She clung to his hand. 'You know I love you.'

He sighed. 'I know, but, Angela, you and me, it can't

work. I got a wife and two kids and I've no intention of leaving them. I never had. If I led you to believe I would, then it was a shitty thing to do, but you have to know it's over, sweetheart. It should never have started.'

'But it did, Mike.'

'Yes, I know, and it's all my fault. But the truth is you're better off without me.'

She started to cry, and he cupped her face between his hands. 'I'm sorry, really sorry.'

Dolly coughed. 'We should go, Angela, love. Say goodbye to the nice man, girls.'

The three little girls waved at Mike, even though they had no idea who he was. Angela got out of the car, her eyes bright with tears. He pulled the door shut, feeling like a heel. He wound down his window. 'Mrs Rawlins, can I have a quick word?' Dolly went to the window. 'You hurt her, get her involved, and I'll see you get busted.'

'Will you now?'

He knew the threat sounded empty. 'Why are you even thinking about it? You got those kids.'

'And you got their mother banged up,' she retorted. 'I'll look after Angela, don't you worry about her. You just worry about me, Mike, love, because remember, I know everything.'

Mike felt worn out. He just wanted it to be over. But it wasn't. He had to get hold of some Semtex and it made him sick just thinking about it.

They walked down the lane, Dolly with a small child's hand in each of hers. 'Don't cry over him, Angela, he's not worth it. You're gonna make your own life now.'

Angela picked up little Sheena

'You ever been to Switzerland?' Dolly asked suddenly.

'No, I never been nowhere abroad,' Angela said.

'Well, as soon as you get that passport, you're gonna get us plane tickets, all five of us, with not a word to the others, because that's where we're going – Switzerland.'

Dolly breezed into the drawing room and was confronted by Gloria, Ester, Julia and Connie, all stone-faced.

'We want to know what the hell is going on,' Ester said angrily.

Dolly put her hands on her hips. 'You sorted out that business with the video, have you?'

'You know I haven't,' Ester snapped.

'Then when it's done, when I'm ready, we'll talk. That goes for all of you, all right?' She pointed a finger at Connie. 'You go and get the shotguns today. You, Gloria, give them all a lesson in how to use them. Go up into the woods and don't come down again until you can all handle them.'

'You know how to use them, though, don't you, Dolly?' Gloria asked sarcastically

'My husband made sure I could always take care of myself,' Dolly replied. 'And you, Ester, sort that video

431

business. You, Julia, get the muffling for the horses, and, Connie, you go to that builder, and tell him to order a leaf–suction machine. I dunno what you call them but they suck up garden leaves.'

'I can't see him,' Connie said petulantly.

'Why not?'

'Because I hate his guts.'

Dolly turned on her, pushing her backwards. 'Then unhate him. Just do it. That goes for all of you. We get through today, and tonight we'll talk.'

She turned, calling for Angela and the girls to get ready.

'We're going on a boat. See you later.' The door closed behind her.

'I think she's bats,' Gloria said.

Ester shrugged. 'Well, she's got until tonight and then we force her to come out with whatever she's got inside that twisted head of hers.'

Dolly began to row. She had one oar, Angela the other, and they began to propel the boat slowly to the centre of the small lake, the three girls perched happily on the seat at the bow.

'Look, look, it's a bridge,' Sheena said, pointing.

Dolly nodded. 'Yes, love, it's a bridge. Maybe we'll see a train crossing it today.'

Neither Angela nor Dolly were adept at rowing, and it

took them a while to get to the centre of the lake where they rested as Dolly caught her breath. She leaned on the oar and looked at the bridge: there was a good twenty-foot drop down to the lake at the lowest point. She then glanced at the boathouse on the other side.

'Is this your boat, Dolly?' Kate asked.

'No, love, it belongs to an old man who lives not far from the manor, in one of those cottages. He lent it to me.'

'Can we come out again?' Sheena piped up.

'Yes, we can borrow his boat any time we want.'

They shouted with excitement and Dolly spotted the floating dock. 'Let's go over to that boathouse, Angela, maybe we can go ashore for a little walk.'

The innocent-looking boating party headed towards a small wooden jetty. Two speedboats were tied up, covered with green tarpaulins. Dolly made each girl remain in their seat until she herself had stepped ashore to guide each one out with Angela's help.

'Can we go in a speedboat?' Sheena asked.

'Not today, darlin', another time maybe.'

Dolly told Angela to take the girls for a ramble, while she remained sitting by the jetty. She began to make notes in her little black book, her eyes flicking from the jetty to the bridge, from the lake to the undergrowth, and then, for a long time, she focused on the bridge.

*

The women lined up with their shotguns. Gloria had showed them over and over how to load and unload before she would allow them to fire. She explained the consequences of not paying attention. She held up her left hand. 'See that? Did it when I was twelve. My dad was showing me at a fairground and I wasn't listening. It wasn't a shotgun, it was an automatic but it snapped back and bang, me thumb was hanging ... off. They all looked suitably chastened. 'Right, put the weight into your shoulder, left hand to steady the barrel, right index finger on the trigger, but gently, they're oiled and you need just a light squeeze, don't jerk it. They got a big kick, these shotguns, so be prepared for it. If you don't hold it right, like what I'm showing you, you'll get a bruise on yer collarbone an' it could whack into yer cheekbone, bring tears to your eyes, I'm tellin' you.'

Dolly stopped rowing when they heard the shotgun blasts. She turned towards the woods and then waved to Angela to stop rowing as she took out her notebook and quickly jotted something down. *Bang!* the shotgun went again.

'Somebody's firing a gun,' Angela said.

'Yeah, be up in the woods. Duck-shooting.'

'What are ducks doing in the woods?' Angela asked.

'Never you mind,' said Dolly, frowning.' *Bang. Bang.* Damn, thought Dolly, that's loud. Some nosy parker's bound to start wondering what's going on. She started rowing. 'Come on, Angela, put your back into it. We need to get back to shore sharpish.'

Julia lowered the shotgun. The tree they'd been aiming at looked as if a tornado had hit it. 'Maybe we've done enough for today.'

Under Gloria's beady eye they unloaded and collected all the spent cartridges before they started back to the manor. The shotguns were now wrapped in their waterproof covers, and they stopped midway to stash them in the trunk of a hollow tree.

Ester had already left for London and Connie had gone to the builder's yard. Julia was sitting at the kitchen table, cutting old sacks with a knife. 'I can use these with a drawstring, pad it out with some sawdust, that should be enough.'

'Fine. Do it in the stables, not in the kitchen. And when Gloria comes back get her to help you.'

Julia snatched up the sacks. 'Right, and we got a ride booked for five o'clock. I found out their key is always left under a plant pot and ...' But Dolly was ushering the girls ahead for an afternoon kids' programme on TV, so Julia went out to the stables, closing the gate behind her. Opening one of the packets of cocaine, she took out a pocket mirror, and laid out a small amount of the powder, deftly chopping it into lines. Then she took an already tightly rolled five-pound note and snorted up each line in turn, sniffing hard, then licking the residue off the mirror. Instantly feeling better, she carefully replaced the mirror and the fiver in her pocket, then started hacking at the sacks. Stacking the squares in a neat pile at her feet, she had cut up about eight when Gloria burst in.

'Bleedin' walked to the local shop. What a load of halfwits! They looked at me like I got two fuckin' heads.'

Julia studied Gloria. She was wearing a pair of jeans that were too tight, a bright purple silk shirt knotted at the waist, with her tits half hanging out from some wire contraption brassiere that went out in the Fifties. Her blonde hair was in need of more bleach, the black roots over an inch long. She was also wearing a baggy man's riding jacket. Julia laughed. 'It's the wellington boots, Gloria, they're very sexy.'

Gloria frowned. 'Piss off. I need them, having to wade through that bloody mud lane. Them potholes get you every time.' She squatted down, picking up one of the cut squares. 'What're these for, then?'

'The horses' hoofs.'

'Oh, of course! Any fool would have known that. What you talkin' about?'

'Dolly's orders, Gloria, so don't ask, just start sewing.'

*

Connie leaned against the hut door and peeked in. 'Hi, John, how you doing?'

John looked over, then went back to opening his bills. She strolled in and leaned closer. 'You were very rude to me last night – you know that, don't you?'

He sighed. 'Don't sit on the desk, it's got a wonky leg. What do you want?'

'Well, you're supposed to be fixing our roof and, like, nobody is there so Mrs Rawlins sent me to ask when you're going to do it.'

He scratched his head. 'Tomorrow. I got a few things lined up for today and the men are all out on other jobs.'

Connie slipped onto his knee. 'Well, that's convenient, then, isn't it?'

'What do you want?' he asked again, leaning away from her.

'What you didn't give me the other day.'

She took his face in her hands and kissed him, teasing his mouth open with her tongue. He couldn't resist for long and his arms were soon wrapped around her. She could feel his erection and started wriggling on his knee. 'Oh, you're very easy to please, aren't you?' she whispered, licking his ear. He started to unbutton her shirt while she kept on licking and kissing, she was half-hoping someone would come in and he'd have to go. When they remained uninterrupted she knew he would screw her. Well, she'd been screwed in some worse places – but never for a machine that sucked up bloody leaves.

Ester leaned forward to the taxi driver. 'Okay, I'm going in this house here. I want you to wait. If I'm not out within five minutes, will you ring the doorbell? And keep this for me.' She passed over the envelope with the tape. He looked at it, then at Ester. 'Five minutes.'

'Okay, but that's all, no more.'

They were parked outside a large, elegant house in The Boltons. Ester stepped out, adjusted her dark glasses and walked slowly up the canopied entrance. She stood for a moment on the steps, noticing the two security cameras before ringing the bell. Part of her was saying what a stupid bitch she was to come here and do what Dolly had told her, but if it kept the old cow quiet, why not?

Hector opened the door and instantly beamed. 'Surprise, surprise! Ester Freeman herself!'

She stepped in and he shut the door behind her. She raised her arms as he frisked her for a weapon, spending more time than necessary patting her down. 'Poor way to get your rocks off, isn't it, Hector? Here, look in my handbag. I've not got the cash for a gun, darlin'.'

Hector searched it. 'What do you want?'

'To get off the hook.'

He smirked at her. 'You got a lot of bottle, Ester. Either that or you're fucking stupid.'

'Look, you prick, right now I'd go down on *you* for fifty quid, I'm that broke, so let's stop the crap and talk.'

Hector ushered her along the thick-piled cream carpet into a double-doored drawing room filled with china cabinets and more Capo di Monte than they have at Asprey's. 'Sit down.'

'Look, I got five minutes. If I don't walk out that cab driver out there will be knocking on the door.'

'That really scares me. Sit down.'

She sat on a peach-silk-covered chair and crossed her legs. 'I've got the video the only copy. You can have it but I just want to know that you'll leave me alone.'

Hector perched on an identical chair, twirling a set of gold worry beads round his finger. 'What you done with the Saab? You nicked it, didn't you? Rooney was screaming about it.'

'You must be joking I wouldn't touch any motor of his, more than likely hot as shit. He's just a liar — but he got his heavies to give me a proper going-over anyway. He gave me the money for a taxi. That was the last I saw of Rooney.'

'So what you after? If it's money, you're even more stupid than I thought.'

'To give you the video of your boss's kids screwing two of my girls. You can have it back and for nothing. I just want to know that it's over.'

Hector chortled. 'Don't be so fucking stupid. You've

been a naughty girl, and you know he won't let you off the hook. You shouldn't have been so greedy – you got paid a lot of dough.'

'I also did three years and I'm telling you, you beat me up, knock me around, and I'll go straight to the cops. This time I'll give them names, all right, and he won't get off with his diplomatic immunity this time.'

Hector was about to hit her when the door opened. Even though Ester couldn't see who was behind it, she knew, from Hector's face, it was the boss.

She saw the cameras at the corners of the embossed ceiling – the whole place was monitored so every word they said must have been overheard. She waited as the two men whispered outside the half-closed door, and began to get a little uneasy, afraid Hector might come back and beat the hell out of her. She was putting a lot of trust in the cab driver.

Hector gestured for her to join him. 'Your lucky day. The tape.'

'I'll go and get it but then it's over, Hector.'

'Yeah. Like I said, it's your lucky day. Come on.'

They came out just as the driver was getting out of the taxi. Ester got into the back. 'Give him that envelope, love.' The cabbie looked at Ester, then at Hector, and reached in for the envelope.

Hector snatched it out of his hand and pulled down the passenger window. 'Ester, this had better be the only copy. If it isn't, you won't just get a rap round the head, you'll get taken out, understand?'

Ester rapped on the glass between her and the driver. 'Marylebone Station.' They drove off, Hector watching from the pavement, as the cabbie eased back the partition.

'I won't ask what that was about, darlin'.'

'Good,' she said, slamming it shut. She sat back in the seat. Maybe it was for the best. It just pissed her off that if she'd had the right back-up, if she'd been able to afford a few heavies, she could have made a lot of dough out of that video. As it was, she didn't have more than a few quid to her name. She was still in debt to the bank up to her eyeballs, but that didn't concern her – that kind of debt never did. She'd just move on. What did concern her was where she would move to. She gazed unseeingly from the cab window. If Dolly really was serious about the robbery, she would live abroad, maybe Miami. All she needed was a break and a lot of cash – she'd always needed both, but she'd never got them. When she'd had the cash she never got a break because she'd been busted so many times. Ester had spent much of her life in prison, all over the country, busted if not for prostitution, then for kiting and dealing in stolen goods. At one time her only ambition was to be top dog in prison and she had achieved it, taking more punishment or solitary than any other con.

Sitting in the cab, remembering, she decided she wasn't going to take any more of Dolly's shit. Either she came clean about the robbery, or she'd let her have it.

Chapter 17

Mike was late getting back on duty after the meeting with Dolly and Angela. When he passed the main desk, the duty sergeant looked up at him, wagging his finger. 'You're in it, mate. DCI Craigh's been in and out looking for you.'

Mike pulled a face and went into the incident room. 'Hear DCI Craigh's looking for me, anyone know where he is?'

Palmer looked in at the door. 'Where the fuck have you been?'

'I was at home, then I got sick and—'

'Never mind that. The Super and the Chief are in with the guv, and they want to see me and you. I think it's coming down.'

Mike slumped into his seat. 'What they want?'

Palmer looked over to the door and back to Mike.

'Well, that bloody ten-grand claim from Mrs Rawlins started it all. Now, well, they're digging into everything.'

'Shit.'

'Yeah, all over us, so get your act together.'

Mike began to get out his files as Palmer was tannoyed to go to the main conference room immediately.

'Is it gonna stay internal?' Mike called after him.

'I bloody hope so,' he said as he disappeared.

Craigh stood, hands clasped nervously in front of him. He had been explaining why they had begun the investigation into the diamond robbery while the Chief listened, tight-lipped.

'I'm not interested in a robbery that went down eight, nine years ago. One minute you got her with a stash of diamonds, the next with weapons ...'

'We had a reliable tip-off,' Craigh insisted.

The Chief shook his head. 'You call Eddie Radford reliable?'

Craigh sat back in his chair. He didn't look up, listening to the flick, flick, flick of the pages as the Chief went through one file after another, and then slapped the top one.

'You want to tell me about DS Mike Withey?'

Craigh loosened his tie. He had tried to cover for Mike, but it was pointless now.

'I am referring to the fact that his sister, a Shirley Ann

Miller, was shot in the armed raid that you and your team have been trying to—'

'Sir, I have to say that at the outset of my investigation I was unaware that Withey had any personal grievances against Mrs Rawlins. But that said—'

'That said, Detective Chief Inspector, Rawlins was never accused in relation to that robbery. She was never accused because there was never any evidence to connect her with it.'

'Yes, I know, sir, but—'

'But I am suggesting that your DS, because of his personal motivation—'

'He believed that Rawlins did, in fact, have something to do with it, sir.'

'Her husband might have, before she shot him, but dead men can't talk.'

'Nor can dead girls,' interjected Craigh.

The flick, flick, flick of the stack of files and reports continued for at least three minutes before the Chief spoke again. 'There is still not one shred of evidence to link Dorothy Rawlins to that robbery, and it's verified by not one but six members of the social services that she was actually being interviewed by them at the time of this man Donaldson's unfortunate accident.'

Craigh looked at his Super, who remained stony-faced with his head bent low, refusing to look at him.

'When questioned about Donaldson, Mrs Rawlins

admitted that she had made contact with him. She also admitted that he was holding certain items for her to collect on her release from Holloway Prison, and I quote, "Mr Donaldson was keeping two Victorian garden gnomes for me. They had been in the garden at my house in Totteridge."'

'That really is bullshit, sir.'

The Chief looked hard at Craigh. 'So is most of this, but we take very seriously Mrs Rawlins's allegations of police harassment, and we also have to take seriously her claim for ten thousand pounds' worth of damages done to her property.'

Craigh knew that had been at the bottom of it all, the bloody claim for damages.

'I would now like to interview DI John Palmer. Thank you for your time, Detective Chief Inspector. That, along with a lot of money, has been wasted. I have also been discussing a backlog of work in your division that should by rights have taken priority over this entire Rawlins situation.'

Craigh stood up and tightened the knot of his tie until it was almost throttling him. 'Yes, sir.'

Palmer took one look at Craigh's face as he walked out and hissed, 'Bad, huh?'

Craigh nodded. 'Look, it's no good trying to cover for that prat Withey. I'm not carrying the can for this, so don't you. They know all about his sister so just tell the truth.'

Palmer would have liked more advice but he was asked to enter the boardroom by the WPC who had been taking notes throughout.

Craigh looked around. 'Where is he?'

Palmer paused at the door. 'He walked in about ten minutes ago, said he'd been sick.'

Mike would be sick all right when they finished with him, Craigh thought, and he knew what the outcome of the internal enquiry would be: that one or other of them would be just that: finished. He just hoped to Christ it wasn't going to be him.

Half an hour later, Palmer left the boardroom. He looked even worse than Craigh had when he walked out, and he just hoped he'd not screwed himself. Mike was sitting with a plastic beaker of coffee in his hand. 'How did it go?'

Palmer gave him a wry look. He went closer before saying quietly, 'They don't know about the diamonds. Seems the big gripe is about Donaldson and that ruddy ten grand.'

Mike exhaled and then swallowed. 'What did they ask you?'

'A lot. But, Mike, they know about your sister – I mean, I never said anything, they knew already. I know the guv wouldn't have told them so you—'

Palmer was interrupted as the same female officer stepped into the room and asked for Mike. Palmer watched him follow her like a condemned man walking to the scaffold. He took off to find Craigh and compare notes.

Mike knew it was going to be heavy but he had not anticipated the icy anger of the Chief.

'You have abused your position as a police officer. You have used personal grievances to instigate a full-scale investigation of Mrs Dorothy Rawlins without disclosing to your superior officer your personal connection.'

Mike remained with his head bowed as the cold voice continued that he had not disclosed on his original papers that his sister had been married to a known criminal and had taken part in and been shot during an armed robbery. He interrupted, 'She was dead, sir. I didn't think there was any reason to put that—'

He was silenced by a wave of the Chief's hand. 'There was every reason and you know it, so don't try and deny it. If we had been privy to this information, it would obviously have been taken into consideration by DCI Craigh and it would have been his decision to go ahead with the investigation without you or not.'

Mike licked his lips. 'I'm sorry, sir, but I feel I should mention that both DCI Craigh and DI Palmer acted with the utmost professionalism throughout, and I apologize for misinforming them as well as for not filling in the required data on my application to join the force.'

The Chief nodded. 'You were accepted by the force because of your exemplary Army record, and the recommendation of your commanding officers. You have proved yourself a highly intelligent and dedicated officer. I do not wish to lose you but at the same time action must be taken ...'

Mike knew he could be up for suspension but he hadn't bargained for the fine and return to uniform for a year. That took the wind right out of him. No way would he be back with the hard hats – not after all he'd been through. Even the job at the security company would be better than that, and probably better paid, too.

Mike resigned there and then, and felt as though a great weight had been lifted from his shoulders. What his wife would think about it what he would do, he didn't give much thought to. He just wanted to get out, have a drink and go home. Both Palmer and Craigh were waiting for him, looking really twitchy. It was Mike who smiled, lifting his arms wide in a big open-handed shrug. 'Well, one of us had to go and it was my decision. I've resigned, so how about a drink?'

Craigh patted him on the shoulder, unable to hide his relief. 'They didn't ask you to leave, then? It wasn't the big heave-ho?'

'No, but the "back in uniform" did it. I'm out. Just get me to the pub.'

Palmer gave Craigh a wink. Mike had let them both off the hook.

Ester took off her best suit and hung it in the wardrobe. She only had a little time before they were due out for the riding class so she pulled on her old jeans and a thick sweater and was just stamping into her right boot when Dolly came in. It irritated Ester that she was expected to knock if she entered Dolly's bedroom, even her tinpot office, but Dolly just barged in.

'Is it sorted?'

Ester stamped into the left boot and stood straight. 'Yep, it's sorted. The tape's back in their hot sweaty hands.'

'You're sure you haven't got any more tapes up your sleeve, are you?'

Dolly walked out before Ester could reply.

Gloria and Connie were in the kitchen getting into their riding boots. Gloria was complaining she'd cut her fingers sewing the sacks and was pissed off that no one else seemed to be doing any work but her. Connie turned on her. 'What you think I've been doing half the afternoon – having a laugh? Well, if you want to take over and screw for—'

'That's enough,' warned Dolly, pointing to the kids, and Connie glared back.

'The leaf machine will be delivered tomorrow morning. It costs fifty-four pounds, cash on delivery, all right?' She flounced out of the kitchen as Dolly drew on a pair of leather gloves and followed her into the hall.

'Right, we all set?' she said calmly, and walked past Ester and out of the front door.

'I swear before God I'll punch her straight in that smarmy arrogant face,' Ester said quietly.

'I'll get one in before you,' Gloria said as they left.

Dolly was worried the stable girl was becoming suspicious, and Julia had arranged for them to take an extra lesson at a different stable. Riding unfamiliar horses, they were unsteady to begin with but soon got their confidence back. Their instructor was an older woman who spoke in a deep, theatrical, aristocratic voice, which they all kept mimicking.

Gloria was still imitating her when they returned to the manor two hours later. They heaved themselves out of the car to Gloria's 'Walk on, come along now, walk on . . .'

Julia galloped down from the wood and called out. They couldn't help being impressed by the way she neatly skirted the plants, wheelbarrows and other obstacles.

'How did it go?'

'Oh, frightfully well,' shouted Gloria.

Connie smiled. 'We're all joining the local hunt, don't you know, we're all so frightfully good.'

Julia laughed and turned Helen of Troy towards the stables. The women followed, grouping outside the loosebox as Julia took off her saddle and carried it inside.

'You've each got to learn how to clad the horses' hoofs this evening so we might as well do it now. Practise on Helen,' Dolly said, scraping the mud off her boots.

'Oh, absolutely, Mrs Rawlins, that would be delightful,' Gloria said, and Dolly actually managed a small tight smile.

Gloria had her hand under the cold-water tap; it was already swelling up. 'The fuckin' thing trod on me hand.' She showed it to Angela.

'I wish you wouldn't swear so much, not in front of the kids,' Angela said, peeling potatoes.

'Oh, fuck off,' Gloria said cheerfully.

They were all famished after their successful riding session, and for the moment even Ester seemed more concerned with eating than with badgering Dolly about the robbery.

'Well, this makes a nice change from pasta,' Gloria said, shovelling more potatoes onto her plate. Dolly noticed for the first time that each one of them had changed considerably. Their skins were fresher, with hardly any trace of make-up; even Gloria's usual thick eye shadow and mascara were no longer evident and Connie hadn't a false nail in sight. Ester retained a glimmer of her old sophistication, but still looked fitter and healthier. But were they up to the job, Dolly wondered?

Mike could have done with some food inside him. He hadn't eaten all day and he was soon drunker than Craigh and Palmer put together. By the time they had driven him home, he was feeling well pissed and stumbled out of the car as they parked outside his house. He leaned against the bonnet, banging it with the flat of his hand. 'Thanks, see you.'

'We'll talk tomorrow,' Craigh said, opening the window.

Mike stepped back. 'Yeah, but I'll be having a lie-in for a change. Goodnight.'

They watched him stagger up his path, knocking over an empty milk bottle before fumbling his key into the lock. He lurched into the house, banging the front door closed, getting as far as the stairs before slumping down with his head in his hands, feeling sick as a dog. 'Are you all right?'

'Yeah, I'm fine.'

Susan stared down at him from the top of the stairs. She had just had a bath and washed her hair. 'Your dinner is in the oven, probably dried to a bone, but if I'd known what time you were coming home––'

'Shut up, Sue, leave it out – just for one night.'

Mike walked unsteadily into the kitchen and she

returned to the bedroom. Well, he could just stay down there, she wasn't going to speak to him. She locked the bedroom door, picked up the hairdryer, turned it on full blast, and opened last week's issue *of Hello!* magazine. She hadn't planned on having an early night but she would now.

In the kitchen, Mike burnt his fingers on the plate, almost dropping it, and then sat at the table, staring at the atrophied stew. He got a bottle of HP sauce and shook it, his chair scraping the floor as he got up and sat down again. He picked up his fork but suddenly couldn't face eating. Instead he sat in a stupor, wondering what the hell he was going to do with his life, how he would pay for the mortgage, the kids' schooling.

'My bloody mother, she got me into this, the stupid cow,' he muttered, shoving the plate to one side.

Ester looked at the dregs of the bottle. 'Well, this is the last of the wine.'

Dolly put her glass down, got up and opened a drawer in the desk. She took out one of the girls' big blank-paged drawing books and a thick black felt-tipped pen. 'Right, this is what I intend to do.'

They sat in front of her, squashed onto the sofa with an air of nervous anticipation.

'I don't want any interruptions, not until I've finished, then you can ask whatever you want.'

They all nodded, eyes fixed on the blank sheet of paper as Dolly started drawing, beginning with the manor which she marked with a big cross, and the stables, explaining how they would pick up their rides and move silently down the lane.

She drew the railway tracks, the bridge and the lake. She then marked in red the danger cables, the areas of vulnerability. No one said a word as, slowly, her plan began to take shape. It was ridiculous, it was insane. She was not even thinking about hitting the security wagon itself. She was aiming to remove the money from the train. And not, as they had supposed, at the level crossing, but *on* the bridge. 'Bloody hell,' Gloria muttered.

Dolly pointed at the lines depicting the rail tracks. 'These are live wires, very high voltage. There's a narrow parapet right along the entire edge of the bridge, two good positions to cover us, and a big notice here.' She smiled. 'One that says "High Voltage, Danger", but it's big enough for one of us to hide behind. There's another boarding here and one on the opposite side of the lake. The railings are lower so we position two of us there.' She made neat crosses and then turned the sketch round. 'We've got to stop the train halfway across the bridge. We'll mark out the position with fluorescent paint. I've paced it and I reckon we can stop it almost dead centre of the bridge.' She continued in a quiet, steady voice, taking them through each stage of the raid. She drew the signal box, the electric cables, the telephone wires and, as her drawings began to take up one page after another, she became more animated, explaining how they would drop the money from the bridge, where the horses would be tethered. 'Well, I think that's nearly all of it. I need to find out if we can get one of the speedboats, and if not, we have to find one. We also need a powerful spotlight positioned here on this jetty. It'll blind the guards but, most important, we'll be able to see the live cables, especially Julia as she is in the most dangerous position of all, right here, up ahead of the train.' Dolly snapped the book closed and looked at the row of stunned faces. 'So that's it.'

Ester let out a long breath. 'It's even more crazy than I thought. Actually, it's not crazy, it's bloody insane – no way can Julia ride her horse up onto the tracks.'

Julia got up. 'I can speak for myself, Ester.'

Ester sprang to her feet. 'But you can't take this seriously, it's impossible!'

Julia looked at Dolly. 'You know how much cash is on the train?'

Dolly ripped up the drawings and threw them on the fire. 'Yes. That copper found out for me.'

'How much?' Connie asked softly.

'Usually between thirty and forty million.'

You could have heard a pin drop. Dolly looked at their gaping mouths and that little smile appeared again as she said, 'Penny for them? Well, if none of you have anything you want to say, I'm going to make a cup of tea.' Still smiling, she went to put the kettle on.

Julia was the first into the kitchen after Dolly. She drew out a chair and began to roll up a cigarette. 'Ester's right, you know.'

Dolly rested her hands on the edge of the table. Her eyes were shining. 'It may be crazy but it's also brilliant. I know it could work, I know it, Julia.'

Julia licked the cigarette paper, her eyes on Dolly. 'We could all get ourselves killed, just like little Shirley Miller.'

Dolly froze. Julia watched her eyes narrow, her hands form into tight fists.

'So what I want to ask you, Dolly, is why? Why take such a risk?'

'Money,' Dolly said simply.

'No other reason?'

'What other reason do you want? With money you can do what you like. Without it in this world you're nothing, you don't count.'

Julia patted her pockets for her matches, the cigarette dangling from her lips.

Dolly turned to the teapot. Behind her Julia struck the match, still keeping her eyes on Dolly's back.

'You're sure this isn't about Harry? You're sure it isn't about emulating him? I don't want to get killed just so you can prove something to yourself, Dolly.'

Dolly took out the milk from the fridge and put the bottle on the tray before picking it up. She stood poised, looking at Julia. 'I killed him, Julia, I looked straight into his face, into his eyes, and I saw the expression on his face the second before I pulled the trigger. After doing that, nothing scares me. I'm not like my husband – I'm better, I always was. I was just very clever at always making sure he never knew it. Now, will you open the door and I'll take the tea in. I'm sure they've all got a lot of questions.'

Julia stayed in the kitchen, smoking until the thin reed of a cigarette was down to nothing but a tiny scrap of sodden paper. She then chucked it into the sink and walked out. She needed a line; she was feeling high but she wanted to get even higher. In the dark old stable, with Helen's heavy snorting breath, Julia laid out her lines and snorted each one, and then she licked the tiny mirror and started to laugh.

'Oh man, if my mother could see me now!'

Chapter 18

J ulia urged Helen of Troy forward. She scouted the
area but there was no one in sight. They had arranged
to have a ride before the stables opened for business, on
the condition that Julia led them. It was not the first time
that Sandy had allowed the women to ride solo with
Julia, and none of them wanted her to see how accomplished they were becoming. They had their ride at six
in the morning and after every lesson they returned the
horses to the stable yard.

Julia and Helen of Troy continued checking the area.
Their breath hung in the cold air, and not until Julia was
truly satisfied that it was all clear did she lift her hand
with the stopwatch as a signal to the waiting Ester, who
then relayed it to the others.

The women nudged their horses forward until they
formed a line over the brow of a hill, waiting for Julia

to join them. Then, stopwatch at the ready, she gave the 'go' signal, and they all set off at a gallop as if they were competing in the Grand National. But they weren't racing against each other; they were trying to beat the stopwatch, each rider trying to accomplish her own specific task in the allotted time. They jumped the hedges, split up, paced their positions, re-formed and started again. Eight times they timed the ride, with Julia carefully monitoring each one, shouting instructions; any more times and they'd have risked being seen.

The horses were stabled and the women drove back to the manor. Julia was waiting with the stopwatch. They were still out of breath, faces flushed, shirts dripping with sweat. Julia ticked off Connie for not being in her position on time and angrily told Gloria and Ester she had seen both of them almost come off and if they fell and injured themselves it would finish the whole caper. She didn't leave Dolly out, admonishing her for holding back too long and delaying by reining in her horse.

'Sorry, I knew I was behind.' She had to bend over as she had a stitch in her side.

Not until they had discussed in detail the entire morning's exercise did they sit down for breakfast, laid out by Angela. Later, Dolly took a boat out with Angela and the little girls. They rowed across the lake and ate crisps and drank lemonade on the jetty. The girls had a wonderful time and when they went off to play hide and seek with Angela, Dolly stashed a can of petrol behind the small boathouse. She shaded her eyes to look towards the bridge and saw Julia and Ester sitting on the wall at the end. She then called the girls to get back into the boat as it was time to leave.

Gloria was out of sight at the opposite end of the bridge. She had an artist's drawing book and was sitting up on the wall seemingly intent on sketching, when the train passed in front of her. However, she wasn't looking at the blank page but counting slowly, pressing the earpiece into her ear, so she could be heard by Julia and Ester at the other end of the bridge. Connie was the only one left at the house. She was on 'listening' duty, recording everything from inside the signal box.

As the days went by, the rehearsals and timekeeping totally preoccupied them. There was no time for worries about whether it could work; they were all too busy making sure they could play their parts.

But there was still one thing worrying Dolly: the stopping of the train itself. It would be done by Julia, on the tracks, with a flashlight, wearing Norma's police cape and hat. She would have to hold her position for some time, giving the driver fair warning that something was amiss. Because the train would be moving slowly, there was no chance of it running into her. The real danger was whether she could hold Helen of Troy steady, standing between the rails side-on, with a massive high-voltage cable beneath her belly.

Julia had rehearsed the sidestepping move many times. On two occasions Helen had bucked and almost thrown her off. She had not rehearsed on the tracks themselves but on mock-ups she had made from logs, and Helen was getting better all the time. What worried Julia was that when she stopped the train and it paused on the bridge, what would make it stay there? If the driver felt any danger, he might start up the engine and move the train forward. 'It's all very well, Dolly, marking out where it's got to stop, but how do we make sure it stays there while we get the bags out?'

'Semtex.'

'Pardon?'

Dolly was listening to the tapes she had collected from Mike's house. She was now sure he hadn't grassed on her. But could he get the explosives? She still didn't know.

'Semtex,' Julia repeated.

'Yeah, we'll blow it on the bridge.'

'Oh, brilliant. And if it's not a rude question, where the hell are you going to get Semtex from?'

Dolly continued checking the tapes. 'I'll tell you when I've got it.'

Julia shook her head, almost wanting to laugh. 'Oh, fine. Which one of us is going to have that job?'

Dolly packed the tapes away. 'I'll let you know that an'

all, but one thing I will tell you is that I'm not prepared
to do anything, not one thing, until I'm sure it'll work.'

Dolly felt at times as if she was a juggler trying to
keep all the plates spinning on the ends of sticks, trying
to keep the women focused, trying to eliminate the
risk factors. Nothing could be left to chance, and if
she needed a few more weeks, months even, she'd take
them. She spent hours with her little black notebook,
jotting down things she had to remember, crossing out
others she had accomplished. Sometimes she sat in the
dilapidated conservatory, wrapped in a coat, staring into
space as she pictured each section of the heist. Could it
work? Would it work? Was she insane? Sometimes the
women seemed more confident about the plan than she
was. Even Ester, of late, had simply got on with the job
in hand and was no longer pushing for supremacy. Dolly
surmised that would probably come. Ester was sharper
than the others, more dangerous, and Dolly suspected
she was just biding her time. She watched each one
closely to see how their nerves were holding up. So far,
so good, but it was still like a game. When it became
a reality, she would see what they were really made of.

In her mind, Dolly kept returning to the bridge,
the train and the damned explosives they still had not
acquired. This was the most dangerous and most daring
section of the entire 'game', and without this piece of the
jigsaw, it could not commence.

The missing piece came from an unexpected person. A call came from Mike: he wanted a meeting but not at the manor. Would this be the moment he grassed? Would he be wired up? She travelled by train to London and met Mike in a small café by King's Cross Station.

Mike was not obviously nervous but a little tense as he put down two cups of tepid tea. It took him a while before he came to the point, looking around then back to Dolly.

'What do you want, Mike?'

'I'm out. I handed in my formal resignation today. It goes without saying they've accepted it and that's thanks to you.'

Dolly sipped the tepid milky tea with distaste. 'So what do you want?'

'Obvious, isn't it?'

'Not really. Why don't you tell me?'

Mike again glanced around and Dolly leaned closer. At no time did he mention the train, the robbery or anything illegal, simply that he would be interested in helping her out with the business she had said she was going into, that he had a contact who might help him get the item she had mentioned.

Dolly nodded, tapping the edge of the saucer with her spoon. 'You ever driven a speedboat?'

Mike breezed into the house where Susan was vacuuming the hall.

She looked at him in surprise. 'What you doing home?'

He switched off the hoover. 'I got something to tell you.'

Susan followed him into the living room. 'I just got fired.'

'What?'

'I just got fired. Well, not quite, I handed in my resignation. So that's it, I'm out of a job.'

'What do you mean, "that's it"?'

'I'm out of the Met. They found out about my sister and—'

Susan sank into a chair. 'Your sister? What are you talking about?'

Mike sighed. 'You've seen her face often enough, the blonde girl in the photo frame at Mum's. She was my sister.'

'Oh, come on, Mike! What's this all about?'

'I'm trying to bloody tell you, if you'd just shut up.'

Susan leapt up. 'You tell me one second you're out of the Met, next you're talking about some sister you've never talked about. How the hell do you expect me to react? What's she got to do with your job?'

'She's dead.'

'I know— I know she is, Mike.'

Susan sank back in the chair and closed her eyes. She was just about to say something when he continued.

'Shirley was younger than me. I'd already signed up

when she was still a teenager. I had a brother in borstal so I wasn't going to lay it on the line about the antics of my family when I joined the Met. A lot of blokes have some member of their family that's a bit dodgy and Gregg's just an idiot. I never had much to do with him, even less than Shirley because he was younger than her.'

Susan leaned forward. 'Will you get to the point, Mike? I'm trying to follow all this, honestly I am, but I don't understand what she's got to do with your job. She's dead.'

Mike put his head in his hands. 'She was married to a right villain, a bloke called Terry Miller. He'd done time for armed robbery, then he was on some job, a big raid on a security van, and he . . . he got burnt to death.'

'What? I don't believe I'm hearing this. If this is some kind of a joke . . . You said he was killed in a car accident.'

Mike snapped, *Just fucking listen!* I don't know all the ins and outs but after Terry died, Shirley got in with some bad people and . . .' The more he tried to explain, the more insane it all sounded. He was almost in tears. 'Shirley was shot during an armed robbery nine years ago.'

Susan was stunned into silence. Mike's face was white as a sheet as he stumbled through the rest of the story: how he hadn't even returned for her funeral, how he had cut her out of his life and tried for years to cut out his mother too.

Susan's mouth went dry. She couldn't go to him to

put her arms around him because she was still so confused. 'Is this . . . this little tart you've been seeing all part of it, then? Is that why you're suddenly telling me all this?'

'No, it isn't. She's got nothing to do with it. If you must know it's Audrey, it's all down to that stupid bitch my mother. She screwed me up but I'm going to get out of it.'

'Does that mean you're leaving me and the kids? Is that what this is all about?'

Mike moved to her side and gripped her arm. 'Sue, listen to me. I have no intention of leaving you or the kids. I've told you that it's all over between me and Angela. It should never have even started. That was me being fucking stupid and I'm sorry I put you through it. But, Sue, you got to trust me now, really trust me, because I need you. I need you to back me up, not fight against me. It's very important I have just a few weeks on my own to sort my head out, okay?'

She pushed him away. 'You *are* leaving me, aren't you?'

'No, I'm not, but I want you and the kids to go and stay with Mum in Spain.'

'What?'

'Don't start with the "what" again, you heard me. Get the kids out of school. I've arranged for you and them to go and stay with Mum.'

Mike put his arms round her and although she

struggled he wouldn't let her go. She broke down and started to cry.

'Don't, please don't. You got to trust me, Sue, you have to. It's for all of us. I'm going to get a job, I mean it, but I'll just need a bit of time before I can join you in Spain. I swear on my life, I'm not lying. I love you and I love my kids.'

Dolly stood ten yards down the road from Mike's house. She could hear every word they said and when she heard Susan agree to go to Spain, sobbing her heart out, she removed the small earpiece and slipped it into her pocket. Now she had him exactly where she wanted him.

Dolly was in a good mood at dinner that evening and after the meal went up to read the girls a story. They had become much more open and smiled freely now. In fact their presence made the entire house more relaxed. No one ever spoke about their plans in front of them and, apart from Ester, the women had become genuinely fond of them, especially Angela, whom little Sheena doted on. They had new frocks and shoes and socks, a big room full of toys and they had even begun to use the word 'home' for the manor. Having so many rooms to run free and play in, and so many adults caring for them, had had the desired effect: the little girls were happy and loved.

Angela peeped in to see Dolly tucking them in. Sheena had so many teddy bears lined up there was hardly room in the bed for her. 'I got everything you told me to get so I'll be in my room if you want me.' Angela whispered.

Dolly turned off the nightlight – the girls were no longer afraid to sleep in the dark – and went into Angela's room. She sat on the neatly made bed and checked all the passports. It touched her to know she really was the girls' legal guardian now.

Angela pointed to hers. 'Me photo's terrible. I look like I'm scared stiff.'

Dolly put them back into the envelope. 'I'll keep these safe, love, and not a word to anyone or they'll all want to come on holiday with us. And if anything happens to me, Angela, I want you to promise me you'll take care of the girls. There'll be money provided for you, I'll see to that.'

Angela slipped her arms around Dolly. 'Have you forgiven me?'

Dolly stiffened and Angela quickly released her. 'Just go about your business here, love. Don't ask me to say things I don't mean. You'll know when I've forgiven you. I need you to make up for a lot of trust you destroyed. That's hard to forgive.' She opened the bedroom door. 'Put your TV on, there's a good film. Don't come downstairs. I'll see to the dishes. Goodnight, love.'

Angela had never known anyone like Dolly before: she seemed so lonely and yet there was something about her that made you frightened of trying to get through that barrier, of breaking the dam holding back her feelings. But Angela had begun to understand how she had hurt Dolly, hurt her more than she could have imagined, because she had shown Angela, and Angela alone, a genuine affection. She was glad they would be going away together. At least she would have a chance to get back to where they had been.

Ester was waiting at the bottom of the stairs. 'You'd better come in and listen to this. It's got us all anxious.'

Dolly switched on the speaker so that they could all hear the tapes from the signal box. There was a series of phone calls from the station master to Jim. The mail train was never mentioned but something referred to as the 'special', due the following Thursday, was being rescheduled due to a fault with the engine. The 'special' would not be arriving as prearranged but at a later time and, as Jim's colleague was unavailable, the station master wanted to know if Jim could do the late shift. Jim was heard to moan about his long hours, and then came the big worrying line:

'Well, we won't have this bloody problem for much longer. After Thursday it'll be rerouted to another station, thank Christ.'

'So what time is it due?'

'Be late, Jim. Around midnight.'

Dolly replayed the last line a few times and then

switched off the machine. 'Shit. I hope that's not what I think it is.'

Ester's hands were on her hips. 'You hope? Jesus Christ, if next Thursday is the last mail train through here we're fucked.'

The women were tired of discussing the taped phone call from the signal box. They sat wondering why Dolly had suddenly upped and left them at eleven o'clock without a word to a single one of them.

'I'm getting sick of this,' Ester said.

Julia yawned and stretched her arms above her head. 'Well, she's a secretive cow, and we all know it, but maybe it's a good thing. We'll never be ready by Thursday, so my guess is it's all off and the question is what do we do next?'

'Oh, shut up.' Ester turned on Julia. 'We've been working our butts off and for what?'

Gloria looked at her chipped nails, felt the rough skin on her hands from the horse's reins. 'I can't believe it, after all we done.'

Connie pursed her lips. 'I never believed it anyway. I mean, I've gone along with it, like everyone, but in my heart I never really believed we'd do it. Did you? Honestly?'

Ester glared at her. 'For forty million quid, sweetheart, I'd believe in anything.'

*

Dolly was waiting for Mike at the end of the lane, sitting in the Mini, smoking. She saw his headlights flash once, twice, as he drew up and parked a few yards ahead of her. She walked over to his car and got in.

'I'm just repeating what Colin said, Mrs Rawlins. Next Thursday he's got to be on duty so he couldn't make dinner with me, something about having problems with the engine, so instead of being back in London he was having to do a late-night drop. He never said the time.'

'Midnight,' Dolly said softly, and Mike stared. Dolly rolled down the window. 'Did he say it would be the last train coming this way? Anything about rerouting it?'

Mike bit his lip, shaking his head. He then leaned over to the back seat. 'You won't be needing this, then, will you?' He unzipped the bag. 'Mate from Aldershot, owed me a favour.'

Dolly turned and looked into the bag and then into his face. 'You fancy a walk, do you? Maybe a nice quiet row across the lake? I'll show you where I plan to blow up the train.'

Mike thought she must be joking, but she wasn't. Feeling sick, he just nodded.

'Drive to the end of the lane, we'll walk through the woods.'

Mike explained how dangerous Semtex was, handing her a diagram showing how it should be used. Dolly listened attentively, making Mike repeat himself a few times, then quietly talked herself through the procedures. He stressed over and over again that only a small amount was needed.

They walked on in silence until they came to the lakeside and gazed into the black water.

'You'll need money now you got no job. I might be able to get a few grand to you.'

Dolly stood still as he slowly turned to face her. 'Can I ask you, and I want the truth, Mrs Rawlins, did you have anything to do with that diamond robbery? Did you set it up?'

She looked into his eyes and lied. 'No, love, it was nothing to do with me. I admit I was after the diamonds but, then, who wouldn't be? Even your mother was after them.' Mike kept staring into her face and she held his gaze. 'I never would have put Shirley at risk. I know I've said things to you in the past, said things about her I shouldn't have but, believe me, I never knew she was on that raid. It was all down to my husband. It was Harry's doing. You think I'd have let her put herself in danger?'

Mike shrugged. 'Just from what you said before, it sounded like you set it up.'

'No, love, it was Harry. All I ever done was kill him. But that was a personal matter.' She could feel him hesitating, and she gestured to the bridge. 'You know how much is on that train, don't you? Now do you want just a few grand in your pocket or a couple of million? Take those kids and that pretty wife of yours to live in Spain for ever. Sunshine, sea and sand, good for kids.'

He was half in shadow, his face caught in the moonlight. 'What would I have to do?'

It was after two o'clock in the morning when Dolly eventually got home. She opened the front door quietly and didn't switch on the lights, but they were not asleep and, slowly, in their dressing gowns, they all appeared on the stairs and landing.

Dolly took off her coat and hung it up, picked up the kit bag Mike had given her and walked over to the bottom stair. She leaned on the banister.

'We do it Thursday. At midnight.' She spoke softly but they could hear every word. 'We've got two days.' She looked at the mute faces. 'Now, let's see who's got the bottle. Are you up for it?'

Ester was the first to say yes. The others hesitated but one by one they agreed.

'Good.' Dolly said it like a schoolteacher satisfied with her pupils. 'Goodnight, then.'

No one could sleep that night. The job was for real and they had only two days to go. Toilets could be heard flushing throughout the night as their nerves hit their bladders. Only Dolly's room remained still and dark as she slept a deep, dreamless sleep, knowing the last piece of the jigsaw was in place. Her only worry was that it might have come too late.

Angela dished up breakfast, aware of the uneasy silence round the table. She put it down to them having had an argument about something, but none of them felt like talking now. She was cutting up toast soldiers for the little girls to dip in their eggs and told Sheena off for using her sleeve instead of the napkin to wipe her mouth. The others could hardly wait for Angela and the children to go on their morning ramble, eager to be left alone to discuss the robbery, but Dolly seemed more intent on making sure they had their wellington boots on, along with thick scarves and hats, before she waved them out of the back door.

As it closed, they all started talking at once, but Dolly ignored them and walked out into the hall. 'I need Gloria and Connie this morning.'

Ester threw down a half-eaten piece of toast. 'That's it? Don't you think we should fucking talk about this?'

Dolly returned and stood, granite-faced, in the doorway.

'No, love. You've got your jobs. The last part is to do with Connie and Gloria, nothing to do with you. When that's done, we'll have a meet later this afternoon after the ride.' Dolly left the room.

Ester glowered at Julia. 'Christ, I'd like to throttle her.'

'Feeling's mutual,' came the reply from Dolly in the hall.

Gloria looked at the kit bag as Dolly unzipped it. 'Now, you don't need much and the most important thing is to know exactly where it's got to go. I've got the instructions . . .'

Connie felt her knees go and she slumped on the sofa. Her mouth was dry. 'I feel a bit faint. I think it's just the time of the month.'

Gloria paid her no attention. She was studying the diagrams and then the kit bag. 'I never handled nothin' like this, you know, Dolly.'

'Well, you'll have to practise, then.'

Gloria goggled. 'Where do I do that, for Chrissakes?'

Dolly waved her hands. 'We got acres of space, Gloria.'

'Who gave you this?' Gloria asked.

'Mind your own business.'

'Well, it is my fucking business because we're dependent on him or her knowing what they're doing for starters. I'm not playing with Lego here, you know. This is high explosives.'

Connie had tried to stand up but then fell back again. She looked as if she was about to pass out.

Dolly felt her head. 'You're not runnin' a temperature, are you?'

Gloria picked up the bag and looked at Connie. 'I

know what it is. It's called shittin' yourself with nerves. You watch her, Doll, she's a liability.'

Connie struggled up. 'No I'm not, you leave me alone. It's my period, I always feel like this.'

Dolly gestured for Connie to come closer. She had a small, high-voltage generator on the floor. 'Right, love. You get this over to the little landing-stage on the lake. I'll get one of the others to carry it with you and then we got to get the light fixed up and hidden.'

Connie's face was ashen. 'But do you think it's a good i–i–idea for us to be lit up? Anyone will be able to see it for miles around and—'

Dolly smiled. 'Don't worry, we're not gonna be doing a cabaret act, Connie.'

Ester moved closer to Julia as they stacked the bags for the horses' hoofs. She pulled away bales of straw to reveal big leather saddlebags they were going to string across the animals' flanks. She tested one. 'I hope these'll hold the weight.'

There was a loud *boom!* followed by the sound of breaking glass. Both women froze and Ester peered nervously out of the stable door. 'What the fuck was that?'

A second boom shook the stables and Ester rushed out. Julia strode after her in a fury, almost knocking her aside. 'I told her not to do it close to the bloody stables.'

Ester looked back at Helen of Troy. She hadn't flinched — unlike the pair of them.

Gloria picked herself up. The old greenhouse had been completely destroyed, leaving nothing but a gaping hole in the ground. She was covered in soil and other debris, shakily holding the dustbin lid she had used as a shield.

'Are you out of your mind?' Julia screamed.

'I got to fucking practise, haven't I?'

'Not inside a greenhouse, you idiot. Look at the glass it's showered everywhere. You stupid bitch! You could have made the horse bolt — and you could have killed yourself.'

Gloria dusted herself down. 'I know what I'm doing.'

'You could have fooled me,' Ester shouted, keeping her distance. 'Just go and blow something up further away from the house.'

Dolly appeared to inspect the damage. 'How much did you use?'

'Not that much,' said Gloria. She looked ruefully at Dolly. 'Sorry.'

Dolly opened her notebook. 'Julia reckons we'll need it at this point of the bridge, here and here.'

Gloria looked at Dolly's tight, neat writing. 'Yeah. We been over it day in, day out. That's the best spot, train moving slowly so it'll get the full impact.'

'Just don't blow the carriage up, Gloria. You do that, the money will be blown to smithereens, too. More important, there are three guards inside that carriage, and I don't want anyone getting hurt unnecessarily.'

Gloria nodded. 'I'll have another go.'

Connie and Julia rowed across the lake, the boat low in the water with the weight of the lamp, the cables and the battery-operated generator. Julia did most of the rowing as Connie still felt faint and couldn't stop shaking. They dragged the boat alongside the jetty and then began to move the equipment, keeping an eye open for anyone who might observe them. Julia wore leather gloves and told Connie off because she hadn't put hers on. They then dusted the lamp down just in case she had left her fingerprints on it, and stashed the gear in the bushes, with the petrol, before heading back to the opposite shore, Julia rowing again as Connie trained the binoculars on the bridge.

Susan and the kids left London the next day. It was Wednesday, and, alone in the house, Mike began to wonder if he really was going to do it tomorrow, if his nerve would hold. But he knew there was no backing out now and took three or four mouthfuls from a bottle of vodka to calm himself down. He had to sell his car and then rent one – there was a lot to get organized and focusing on the details stopped him thinking too hard about just what he had got himself into.

The phone rang, making him jump.

'Hello, love, it's me,' Dolly said softly. 'The wife and kids gone, have they?'

'Yeah, this morning.'

'Good. Angela will be at your place Thursday with the girls.'

'*What*?' He sounded like his wife.

'Two reasons, love. One, you got a nice alibi, just in case you're ever questioned. She'll be there all night and will say you was with her. Might cause a bit of aggro with your wife but if nothing untoward happens she won't know, will she?'

'And the second reason?'

'Because I don't want her and the kids around when it goes down. Like I said, she's not involved in this. Friday she'll get the first train back here. You just go straight to the airport. All right, love?'

His voice was even hoarser. 'Yes.'

There was a long pause. 'Well, you keep out of sight and get on with your business. Goodbye.'

'Norma home, is she?' Dolly asked casually as they drove back from their riding lesson.

'You know she isn't,' Julia said flatly.

'Just checking. You got her keys still?'

Julia sighed. 'You *know* I have. We've been over and over it, Dolly.'

Ester leaned forward from the back seat. She looked at Dolly and then Julia. 'I don't trust that Norma.'

Dolly paused at the level crossing as the gates closed. 'We don't have to trust her, Ester, just use her. What do you think her friends at the nick would say if they found out not only that she was a big dyke but she was slobbering all over a—'

'Shut up,' Julia said.

'Yeah, leave it out, Dolly.' It was Ester now, as she saw Julia's back go rigid.

'No, you leave it out,' Dolly said, her mouth a tight thin line. 'We need Norma. We got to use her place to stash the money, like we used her to get the cop's hat and cape. It's the only place close enough to us the cops are unlikely to search.'

Ester gave Julia's shoulder a squeeze. It was funny, really, Julia being decent enough not to want to involve Norma, and yet prepared to play a major part in the robbery. It really didn't add up. Ester felt more love towards her in that moment than she had for a long time, and she liked it when Julia pressed herself closer, their bodies touching in an unspoken message.

Dolly's beady eyes missed nothing. It was good, she thought, the pair of them backing each other up, because, come Thursday night, she reckoned Julia would need something to stiffen her nerves, maybe even a snort or two.

*

Julia fed Helen of Troy, and checked on the sacking and bags for the umpteenth time that day. When she came back, Dolly was standing at the kitchen door, throwing half-eaten sandwiches out for the birds.

'You're something else, you know that, Dolly Rawlins?'

Dolly brushed the crumbs from her hands and then stared at them, palms upwards. They were steady and she smiled. 'My husband used to say that, only he always called me Doll. Funny, I hated being called that but I used to let him, nobody else.'

'Gloria sometimes calls you Doll, doesn't she?'

Dolly looked up into Julia's face. She was a handsome woman and it was as if only now it struck her just how good-looking she really was. 'Being in prison I got called a lot of things. Got to the point I didn't really care any more, but I used to, in the old days.'

'Prison tough for you?' Julia asked casually.

Dolly hesitated a moment and then folded her arms. 'You know, I reckon there were only a few really criminal-minded women in there. Most of them were inside for petty stuff, kiting, fraud, theft, nothing big, nothing that on the outside a few quid wouldn't have put right. Everything comes down to money in the end. The rest were poor cows put inside by men, men they'd done something for.'

'That doesn't include me,' Julia said softly.

'You were a junkie. That's what put you inside.'

'No, Dolly, I put myself inside.'

Dolly nodded thoughtfully. 'Maybe your guilt put you in there. You tellin' me you really needed to flog prescriptions? I reckon part of you wanted to be caught. I mean, you take how many years to qualify? Doctors when I was a kid were respected, like royalty. My mum was dying on her feet but she got up, made sure the house was clean before the doctor came.'

Julia took out her tobacco stash. She began to roll a cigarette, thinking that she had never, in all the weeks she had been living with Dolly, actually talked this way with her.

'Eight years is a long time inside that place, Julia. Maybe I met only four or five women that deserved to be locked up. The rest weren't really criminals before they went in, but they were when they came out. They were made criminals by the system – humiliated, degraded and, I don't know, *defenalized*.' Is that a word?'

Julia said nothing, carried on rolling her cigarette while Dolly continued in a low unemotional voice.

'The few that were able to take advantage of the education sessions might have gone out with more than what they come in with but most of them were of below average intelligence, lot of girls couldn't read or write, some of them didn't even speak English. Lot of blacks copped with drugs on 'em. They was all herded in together.'

Julia licked the cigarette paper. She found it interesting.

The more Dolly talked, the more fascinated she became by her. The woman they all listened to, at times were even a little afraid of, Julia guessed was poorly educated, maybe even self-taught. This was highlighted by her poor vocabulary and her East End accent, which became thicker as she tried to express herself.

Julia struck a match and lit her cigarette, puffing at it and then spitting out bits of tobacco. 'Out of all of us here, who would you say *was* a proper criminal?'

Dolly reached out and took Julia's cigarette, taking a couple of deep drags. 'You want the truth?'

'Yes.'

'Ester was first sent down at seventeen. She's spent how many years in and out of nick – a lot, right? But as much as I don't like her, I know there's a shell around her. Dig deep and you'll just find a fucked-up kid that stopped crying because there was never anybody there to mop up her tears.'

Julia was surprised. She took back her cigarette and sat on the step. 'What about Gloria?'

'Well, she's been in and out like Ester and, on the surface, you could say she's a criminal or been made one by her sick choice of men. But again there's pain behind that brassy exterior, lot of hurt. She's borne two kids and given them away – you never get over that. You, Julia, have got all this anger inside you, self-hate, and hate for your mother.'

Julia leaned against the doorframe, wanting to change

the subject now, but Dolly continued in the same flat voice. 'Connie's the same. Few years on she'll be another Gloria but she's not as bright. Some man will still screw her up – it's printed on her forehead. But, you know, we all got one thing in common.'

Dolly gave that cold smile and Julia lifted her eyebrows sceptically. 'Come on, Dolly, you tell me what I've got in common with Connie.

'Defemalized, Julia. Not one of you could settle down and lead a normal life. Prison done that, it's wrenched it from our bellies.'

Julia chuckled. 'That's a bit dramatic. Speaking for myself, and being gay, I'm not and never was—'

'You're still a woman, Julia, no matter who you screw. We're outcasts – that's what they done to us, made us outcasts of society.'

'But do we have to be? If every woman in our situation turned—'

'Bad?' Dolly interrupted, and her arms were stiff at her sides. Her voice was angry now. 'They didn't give me a chance to be good, did they?'

Dolly's eyes were so hard and cruel, Julia stepped back, shocked.

'I reckoned there were only five real criminals in the nick with me. Well, I was number six.'

'I don't believe you, Dolly. You had dreams of opening this place, of doing good, fostering kids.'

Dolly smiled, this time with warmth, her eyes soft. 'And with my cut of forty million quid, that's what I'm going to do. I can go down Waterloo Bridge, pick them off the street and bring them back. I won't need any social services, I won't need anyone telling me what I can and can't do because with money you can do anything. That's all it takes, Julia. Money, money, money.'

Julia grinned. 'Well, let's hope we pull it off, then.'

'Oh, we'll do it, Julia. It's afterwards we're going to have to worry about because we're gonna be hit, and hit hard. We foul up one little bit and we will go down. Every cop for miles will be round here, we'll be searched and the house taken apart. We'll be questioned and re-questioned, they'll rip the grounds up ... They'll never leave us alone, for weeks, maybe months.'

'If we pull it off,' Julia said quietly, and Dolly guffawed, a loud single bellow.

'If we don't, we don't. But if we do, every single one of us can go for what we want, do what we want, be what we want.'

Julia's heart began to thud in her chest. Dolly's face was radiant with unabashed excitement. 'I'm not scared, Julia, not for one second. I'm feeling alive for the first time since I killed him.' She lifted both her arms skywards and tilted back her head, like an opera star acknowledging the adulation of a packed house of applauding fans. Julia could see the pulse at the side of her neck beating and felt

suddenly terrified that Dolly Rawlins was insane. As if
Dolly read her mind, she lowered her arms and chuckled.
'When we've got our hands on forty million quid – then
you won't think I'm so mad.'

Chapter 19

Angela arrived at Mike's home with the children at three o'clock, blithely unaware of the drama that was to take place that evening. Mike opened the door, immediately handing her the keys, saying he had to leave but would be back that evening. He didn't touch her, even when she tried to reach for his hand. 'Just settle the kids in, I'll be back later.'

She closed the front door, and went straight to the wall socket receiver as Dolly had instructed her. The girls were already playing with Mike's sons' toys and Angela had a good nose around before she started to cook spaghetti for them. They had been scared of moving to yet another home but felt better when they all called Dolly and said hello to her and were told they would see her the following day.

*

Mike headed for the manor in a hired car. He had plenty of time so he drove carefully, making sure never to exceed the speed limit. The last thing he wanted was anyone to remember him so he didn't even stop at a petrol station.

The women checked and double-checked everything on their lists. Julia went over the cladding and the bags, and the big machine for clearing up leaves. She tested the engine, the suction hose and the long trail of flex ending at the socket in the stables. The machine would be used to hoover up the money and they had already tested it to be certain that the suction was strong enough. Julia then went on to check the lime pit. It was ready for the mailbags to be hurled into; the lime would eat away at the thick canvas, and again it had been tried and tested. The corrugated-iron slats were standing by in position, the builder's skip was in place and already attached to the van so it could be towed across the pit opening.

With a dog's lead, Gloria and Ester headed for the bridge, looking like innocent walkers, calling out for the fictional lost dog. They returned to the house, mission accomplished. Each reported to Dolly and she ticked the jobs as they were done while Gloria collected the shotguns and cleaned and polished them.

Gloves, hats and boots were laid out in the kitchen. Norma's police cape and hat were in readiness for Julia.

The hours ticked by slowly. Eventually dusk came, and Dolly asked if anyone felt hungry. Nobody did.

Mike parked the car and eased the old rowing boat silently into the water. He was wearing a black polo-necked sweater, black ski pants and sneakers, and a black woollen hat. He had a fishing rod and a bag with him, nothing else. He rowed across the lake to the opposite side. The lake was black, the bridge in darkness, lit only by the flash of the signals as a train passed across and on into the distance. He tied up the boat alongside the small wooden jetty and crossed to the anchored speedboat. He pulled back the canopy and climbed inside, checking the ignition and wiring. That accomplished, he went into the woods and searched for the lights. His gloves were sodden but he didn't remove them. He had to pull away the bracken and twigs hiding the gear before carrying each item to the end of the jetty, where he set up the high-powered spotlight. The silence was unnerving, nothing moved and the lake remained still and dark. He could not risk testing the spotlight, just hoped to God it would work. If it didn't, there was nothing he could do about it.

By nine thirty, the women were anxiously waiting for the signal to begin. They didn't speak but the atmosphere was very tense. Connie kept clearing her throat until

Gloria said she should have a drink of water as it was getting on her nerves.

'I'm sorry.'

'That's all right, love. Just a sip, mind — remember what I said about you drinking.' Dolly was reading a magazine.

'I hope we can trust him,' Ester said for the umpteenth time. Dolly ignored her but she wasn't really seeing any of the magazine pages of knit-yourself-a-bolero or the new-fashion beachwear either. She knew Mike had a hell of a lot to lose: two kids, a wife and a future, to put it plainly, but she didn't bother saying anything to Ester. She'd said it before and knew it was just Ester's nerves talking.

Gloria crossed and uncrossed her legs, just as she had been doing for the last half-hour. They were almost at breaking point.

'Time to get dressed,' Julia said, walking out. Connie sprang up and Dolly tossed aside the magazine.

'We've got a while yet, Connie, just relax.'

Julia pulled on her boots, put on a thick sweater over her shirt and began to do up the big rain cape. Like an omen, there was a sudden roll of thunder.

'Oh shit,' Ester said, running to the window. 'That's all we need.'

'Never mind the rain,' Dolly said calmly. 'If it's raining the cops won't hang around.'

'If there's a storm the horses will freak,' Julia said as she picked up Norma's police hat. 'If the thunder makes them edgy, pull the reins in tight,' she said, putting on the hat and turning to the kitchen door.

'Where are you going?' Ester said sharply.

'Just to take a leak,' Julia said, slipping out.

'You've already been,' Ester said, following.

'Let her go,' Dolly said quietly.

Ester drew Dolly aside.

She whispered, 'She'll be snorting coke.'

'I know, but if she needs it to straighten out, then let her do it.' Dolly ignored the other women's gasps, and looked out of the window. 'It's coming down hard. The ground will be slippery.'

'Oh Christ,' Connie said, panting with nerves.

Dolly opened a bottle of Scotch and got down some mugs. 'For those that need a bit of Dutch courage.'

Upstairs Julia knocked back half a tumbler of vodka and then snorted two thick lines of coke, the last of it, but, then, this might be her last night. She stared at her reflection in the dressing-table mirror. She looked huge in the big cape and boots, and she put on the hat, pulling it down low over her face, tucking in her hair. She had a black scarf round her neck, and she practised pulling it over her face. She looked at her reflection for a long time and then held out her hand in front of her. It was steady. She smiled. 'Okay, you can do this.'

Julia returned as the women were pulling on their boots. No one spoke. She walked through the kitchen and a roll of thunder heralded her opening the back door. They could see the rain coming down in sheets outside.

'Well, take care. Hold the reins in tight, let them know who's boss, especially over the jumps.'

They all nodded, and Ester reached up to kiss her. 'Take care, Julia, for Chrissakes. Take care on that live rail.'

Julia smiled. 'It's Helen that's got to take care. I don't want her thrown up into a tree, do I?'

Connie moaned softly. She was chalk-white but at least she'd stopped coughing. One good belt of Scotch had stopped that.

'See you later.' Julia went into the stable to saddle up Helen. She was the only one not to have her hoofs clad as Julia would not be riding on the road. She was to head to the far side of the bridge over the fields. They all had their coats on when they heard Julia moving out. The clock said ten thirty.

Mike blew into his gloves. His hands were freezing and he was already sodden through from the downpour. A bolt of lightning lit up the bridge and lake for a second and he just hoped to God it had not lit him. There was still no sign of a living soul.

*

The convoy was halfway to its destination. The heavy rain did nothing to slow it down and the armoured security wagon was sandwiched between two police cars as it continued towards the station.

Colin was at the wheel, maintaining radio contact between all three vehicles. The empty mail train had left Marylebone Station. The carriage to be used for the collection of the mailbags was at the centre of the four-carriage train. It looked like an ordinary passenger train except for the blacked-out windows. The three guards sat inside playing cards, a good hour to go before they had to pick up the money bags. 'I'll be glad when tonight's over. I hope to God they don't make this a regular thing, I hate getting home this late. Anyone know the next route they're gonna take?' one of the guards asked.

'No one does.'

'Bloody train's clapped out. You'd think carrying this much dough they'd have some kind of high-powered armour-plated job, wouldn't you?'

The rain splattered onto the carriage windows. 'Your deal, mate, and let's hope this doesn't turn into a fuckin' storm, we'll be soaked.'

'I won't. I'm staying here. Let the security blokes carry the gear in. Right, aces wild, this one's dealer's choice.'

His two friends groaned as they heard an ominous distant roll of thunder.

*

Julia moved slowly across the field, concerned to see the thick mud forming in some of the ditches. She opened two gates in readiness, pulling them out of old tractor ruts where they were stuck. She checked the time; the gates had already delayed her by three or four minutes and she'd have to get a move on. Julia urged the horse on through the darkness. She had a long ride ahead to get back to the far end of the bridge, right round the far side of the lake and then up a dangerous high bank to take Helen onto a narrow ledge before moving down onto the line itself. The route didn't worry her – she'd been doing it for weeks – but she felt uneasy about the heavy rain. The steep bank was slippery and Helen could stumble or, worse, she might inadvertently hit the high-voltage cable.

The women parked the Mini in a narrow field-gateway. They kept to the grass verge as they headed towards the stables, passing two small cottages. Lights were on in both and they moved silently in single file: Dolly, Gloria, Ester and, coming up at the rear, Connie.

They saw no one: there was only one street-light to worry them, almost directly outside the cottages. They carried the cladding and saddlebags between them, Gloria, Ester and Dolly with the shotguns. They found the stable key and unlocked the main doors. By torch-light they began to clad the horses' hoofs in the thick sacking bags. It was eleven fifteen; they had three quarters of an hour before the train was due.

When the horses were ready, they rode out one by one, the rain still pelting down. They hoped the sacking would give them some more grip in the mud.

Dolly was first out. She walked her horse down the lane, then made for the woods. It was inky black and not a light could be seen until she broke from the cover of the trees and headed towards the railway line below. She had to cross a small bridge about half a mile from the signal box. She winced as the horse's hoofs thudded on the wooden-planked bridge. She held the reins tightly, keeping to the narrow grass verge, and started to make her way along the side of the tracks. She slipped off the horse and tied him up securely. She began to be glad of the rain as it was really pelting down and would keep potential busybodies indoors. Dolly squeezed under the protective wired fence, already cut in readiness, and moved inch by inch towards the station car park. Above was the signal box, lit up, with Jim inside. Dolly crept beneath it, taking out the wire-clippers and the razor-sharp hatchet. Now she would have to wait and hope to God nobody walked by the slip road and saw her horse tethered there. In the practice runs no one had ever passed even close to it, but maybe tonight would be the night. Half an hour suddenly seemed like a very long time.

Connie and Gloria, using a different route to Julia, also rode to the far side of the bridge. The horses slithered a little in the mud but, on the whole, were steady as they galloped. They had one riderless horse, Ester's, as she had already gone to her designated position, on the other side of the bridge. Once there, with the shotgun ready and loaded, she was to wait for the train. They were going to blow it halfway across the bridge, further down the track, the old railway sign Ester's only protection if too much Semtex was used. She prayed that Gloria now knew the right amount.

Dolly could hear the distant rumble of the train. It was still so far down the tracks she couldn't see it but she tensed up in anticipation, praying that the others were in their positions and ready.

Connie and Gloria tied up the three horses. They were a bit frisky, not liking the heavy rain. Connie followed Gloria as they passed the jetty and Mike appeared. He did no more than look towards them, signal, and start to move to the end of the jetty. He then crouched low, waiting. There was still about twenty minutes to go before the train was due at the station.

Gloria and Connie moved to the end of the bridge, along the railway line, in the opposite direction from Ester. Gloria motioned to Connie to remain behind as she bent low and, keeping pressed to the small parapet at the edge of the rail, checked that the wires and the plastic-covered packages were all intact. She worked quickly and only hesitated once as she double-checked the live and earthed wires. She had gone over it so many times she now closed her eyes tight and swore. 'Please, dear God, have I got it right? Red into the right socket, blue into the left and the earth between them?' She pictured the neat drawings Mike had made that Dolly had told her to burn, wishing she still had them.

'You can do it blindfolded. Come on, gel, don't lose your bottle now.'

Gloria inched her way back towards Connie, who was holding her shotgun. She whispered, 'Can you see him? Is he in position?'

Connie screwed up her eyes to peer over the bridge and looked twenty-five feet down. It was pitch black. 'I can see something at the end of the jetty.'

Gloria nodded. They were under strict instructions not to speak, not to say one word throughout the robbery. She could just make out the outline of the tethered horses by the trees.

Julia had a tough time riding Helen down the steep bank. The horse didn't like it one bit and kicked out with her back hoofs as Julia held on like grim death. She gritted her teeth as they slid further towards the track. Helen tossed and jerked her head but they were on the narrow edge before the line itself so Julia eased Helen forward, one hoof at a time, onto the centre plank. Either side were the live cables but there was an eight-inch-high border and she began to move Helen slowly down the precarious narrow plank. Patted and encouraged, she was as dainty as a ballerina as they got closer and closer to the spot Julia had rehearsed for stopping the train. Now came the really dangerous move: she had to turn Helen to stand sideways on, blocking the entire rail. A roll of thunder made her freeze as Helen tossed her head. Not liking the narrow ledge, the horse lifted one foreleg and almost came down on the cable but Julia shouted sharply. 'Still', a police command, and the wonderful old horse froze her position. Julia waited for her to settle before turning her and moving slowly sideways again.

Mike brought the boat further round. He had the spotlight switch in his hand. He could see none of the women, but knew they must be in position because the horses were tethered.

The lead police patrol car pulled into the station forecourt, and an attendant switched on the exterior lights. The platform was lit up in readiness as the train approached, the level-crossing gates clanging shut. The rear police patrol car remained just behind the security van as the guards waited for the go-ahead to begin moving the money bags onto the train. The rain was bucketing down. Two officers had not got their raincoats with them so they took shelter under the platform awning.

Jim, his hut lit up, watched the train hiss to a halt. He gave the thumbs-up to the driver who waved from the train cabin. He did not get out, simply waited in his cabin for the signal to move on.

The guards opened the central carriage, carrying clipboards and documents. Two guards from the security wagon approached and checked their documents with the other guards and, as the police formed a protective line either side of them, they opened the wagon and began to carry the bags aboard the train. They moved fast, expertly, calling the identity number as each bag went aboard. It took no more than ten minutes for the train to be loaded. As the carriage doors closed, the security guards returned to their empty wagon and the police didn't hang about either. They waited only for the signal from the signal box, and the engine hissed and began to move down the tracks, across the closed level crossing and onto the bridge.

Dolly saw the security wagon move back the way it had come and then the two patrol cars draw away from the station. She was willing them to move off, out of sight, one hand on the electric power switch for the signal box, the other clenched around the hatchet for the alarm wires. She knew exactly which ones they were because this moment, like the entire raid, had been rehearsed over and over again. The mains box opened and closed four times. But when that power went out in the box, the moment of panic for Jim was only going to last a second or two before he hit that separate linked alarm switch. If that went off, the two cop cars could turn back within minutes and they'd have major problems. She had to pull the main switch and slash the wires within seconds of each other.

The train passed, one carriage a second, then the mail carriage, and the last one, and she said to herself, 'Now, now, now.'

The lights switched from red to off – perfect. The signal box went completely dark. Jim didn't panic, went towards the emergency generator but, as he was about to switch it on, he heard something from beneath him. He couldn't tell what it was, his eyes still unaccustomed to the dark.

Dolly slashed down with the hatchet. The wires frayed and two or three remained intact. She slashed again and then pocketed the hatchet before clipping at the cables. One sprang away, then the second. She had four more to go as Jim began to panic. Dolly quickly put the live wires against the generator sides If Jim tried to switch on up in the box he'd get quite a shock – not enough to kill him but enough to stop him trying it again in a hurry.

*

Dolly ran under the fence, and was almost at her horse when she froze. Jim was hurtling down the signal-box steps, having almost been thrown across the signal box when he tried the emergency generator. He leapt down the steps, still semi-shocked, and fell to the ground. He moaned, clutching his ankle, rolling in the grit of the signal-box forecourt. He couldn't hear Dolly, let alone see her, as she mounted her horse and headed towards the bridge, the train moving slowly up ahead. But her horse was nowhere near as well trained as Julia's – he was nervous and skittish and no matter how much she pressed him forward, he refused to go any faster.

The guards aboard the mail carriage had no idea anything was wrong at the station. They could see nothing through the blacked-out windows. The bridge crossing was always slow, but they were moving and would soon pick up speed as usual, so there was no reason to be concerned.

The train driver didn't look back. He was used to the bridge crossing and could do it blindfolded. In fact, he looked over to the lake a moment before the flashlight swung from side to side twenty yards up ahead of him indicating for him to stop. He put his hand up to shield his eyes from the bright light. He began to brake in plenty of time, moving almost at a snail's pace as he leaned out of his cab. All he could see was a police officer standing sideways across the track.

'You fucking crazy?' he screamed. Now he rammed on the brakes but they were travelling so slowly it didn't jolt or jar the rear carriages. The train just slowly eased to a halt. He assumed something had fallen across the tracks. The interphone rang from the centre carriage. He picked it up. 'There's a problem on the line, let me get back to you.'

He was still holding the phone as Julia carefully began to edge closer. He leaned even further out. 'You're taking one hell of a bloody risk – there are live cables under you,' he shouted.

Still she waited. Then she switched on the flashlight again, shining it at the driver's face as she eased the horse onto the narrow verge, moving away from the rail tracks, backing Helen precariously along the stone-flagged parapet towards safety.

'What the hell is going on?' the driver yelled again. The guards were now lifting up the blinds on the covered windows. The train had been stationary for one and a half minutes.

Julia was within six feet of sanctuary when she turned the flashlight on once, twice, three times and Gloria pressed down the detonator. They were only a fraction off-target, but nevertheless the explosion ripped through the second carriage instead of where it was meant to – between the second and the mail carriage. She swore as the carriages rocked and shuddered and the railway line buckled under the impact. Next she crawled to the second detonator and thumped it down. This time it was almost right on its marker as the rear carriage broke loose. The explosion was terrifyingly loud, echoing across the water, glass and metal splintering. There was hardly a window left intact. Inside the guards were stunned, having been thrown across the floor.

Gloria had used too much Semtex and now there was a dangerous hole in the bridge itself. But as they moved frantically on to the next stage of the operation, they didn't realize the imminent danger. Amid the chaos, Julia could hear Dolly's calm voice in her mind: 'Soon as you get away from the track, you chuck this into the main front carriage, as close to the driver as possible. It'll scramble any calls he tries to make from the train to the next station. It won't give us long but it'll be long enough.' Another of Ashley Brent's little toys.

Julia galloped to her next position, then collected Dolly's horse and began to drag it towards the others down below by the lake. Dolly was on foot and running towards the centre of the bridge.

Ester rammed her shotgun through the carriage's broken window. The men inside still lay sprawled on the floor as two more shotguns appeared through the windows on the other side. Dolly was the one to give the order and she screamed it: 'Open the doors! Out!'

Mike switched on the spotlight, turning the powerful beam a fraction to aim directly at the centre carriage. He had seen the train moving off and hoped the driver's phone would be scrambled. Then he jumped into the speedboat and, with the rowing boat trailing behind, headed at top speed for the bridge. He cut the engines as he came directly in line with the spotlight. It covered the doors of the train and the path down to the rowing boat.

The dazed guards came out one by one. Dolly took up her position, screaming orders as she pointed the shotgun at them. 'Lie down, face down!'

Suddenly she saw, to her horror, that the mail carriage was creaking and groaning towards the hole in the bridge. It was going to go over the side.

The guards lay down beside the track, as, unaware of the danger, Connie and Gloria went aboard. Ester walked round to the open doors. The sacks were passed out and dropped into the rowing boat, easily picked out by the beam of the spotlight. Inch by inch, the carriage kept moving closer to the hole as they worked frantically. Below, Mike stacked the bags in the boat, communicating with the women through gestures without saying a word. Dolly stood over the men, who lay face down without moving, listening to the bags crashing down and the awful sound of the carriage as it ground towards the hole.

The guards were helpless to do anything and, if they moved so much as a muscle, they felt a hard dig in the middle of their backs. The women, their faces covered by ski masks, worked on, lifting, passing, dropping the mailbags, the danger now obvious, the carriage continuing to inch closer to disaster.

Jim had limped to the nearest house and called the police. He was almost incoherent, repeating over and over the words 'police' and 'train' and 'bombs'. They would be there in four minutes.

Ester was the first to leave. She ran down to the horses and loosened the reins of her own mount, dragging him towards the water. Julia was already waiting, looking with desperation towards the bridge. Then the spotlight cut out, the batteries overloaded, leaving the bridge in darkness. 'Jesus, God, they're gonna go down with the bloody carriage. It'll hit the rowing boat.'

'Get out, move it,' muttered Ester.

Gloria was next to leave, and the carriage suddenly shot forward by three feet, so that it hung like a seesaw over the bridge. Mike started the speedboat. He didn't care if they lost one or two bags – he wasn't going to risk being under the bridge any longer. He opened the throttle and powered back to the jetty. The next stage was hurling the bags out of the boat and into the saddlebags

on the waiting horses. Mike began helping Ester and
Julia. They turned and saw a mass of bricks and twisted
metal about to crash from the bridge. Connie, still inside
the carriage, whipped round to see Dolly waving frantically for her to get out, but she froze as the creaking
grew louder and louder.

Dolly looked at the men, and back to Connie. She
reached out and grabbed Connie by the arm, dragging
her forward.

'Jump.'

Connie pulled back stiff with fear, and Dolly had to
pull Connie to the edge of the crumbling bridge. Half-
holding, half-dragging her, she jumped the twenty-five
feet to the water below. The shotgun flew from Dolly's
hand as she hit the water.

Connie surfaced first, gasping and flailing. 'I can't
swim!' she spluttered.

Mike had hurled out the last bag, unaware that Dolly
and Connie were in the water and in trouble. Connie
was dragging Dolly down, clawing and scratching at her
in a desperate panic to stay afloat.

Julia lifted the full bags off Helen and climbed back
into the saddle. 'Just keep moving as planned – *Ester, go on!*
We'll catch you up.' She kicked the horse's ribs and set off
into the lake, Helen not batting an eyelid as they waded
deeper and deeper towards the struggling women. Connie
still clung to Dolly, who tried her best to keep them both

afloat, while bricks and concrete slabs began to plummet into the water around them. Then suddenly there was Julia, pushing Helen through the water and reaching out her hand, but Dolly could only grab Helen's tail, with one arm around Connie, as Julia turned in the water and pulled them back to the shore. Gloria and Ester had gone, leaving the tethered horses standing loaded with mailbags.

As they clambered onto the shore, Connie began screaming. Dolly slapped her face hard. 'Get out of here! Get on your horse and get out!'

Connie, sobbing and shaking with cold, stumbled to her horse. She could hardly mount but neither Julia nor Dolly paid her any attention as they heaved Julia's bags onto Helen. They still had a long way to go before they were finished.

Mike left the boat and ran to his car. He tried to stay calm, not allowing himself to put his foot flat to the car floor. If he was caught now, he had two mailbags crammed with money in the boot. He took the route away from the station in the opposite direction from the manor.

Every police force in the county now knew that the mail train had been hit and orders went out to set up roadblocks on all major roads in the area. All vehicles were to be stopped and searched.

So far, though, no police car could get anywhere near the bridge. The guards ran down the sides of the track, their only exit, while the carriage remained precariously balanced. The police who had managed to get to the station tried to question Jim but he broke down, in a state of shock, unable to tell them anything. The three guards were in a similar state as, one by one, they were helped from the bridge. One man was bleeding badly from where the glass in the carriage window had slashed his cheek. An ambulance was on its way.

Mike made it onto the motorway before any road-blocks could be set up, but it was a long drive home and he wasn't safe yet. He wouldn't be truly safe until he'd boarded the plane.

The women were almost crying with exhaustion but not one of them flagged. They pushed themselves on. They had galloped across the fields, up through the woods, keeping to cover as much as possible. Then they galloped down from the woods into the manor grounds, slinging their bags down beside the lime pit, which was open and ready.

Julia leapt from Helen in her haste to start ripping open the mailbags. She hurled the money into the skip and threw the bags into the lime pit. Connie rode up, hurled her bags to the ground and, still sodden from the lake, wheeled her horse round and galloped off, passing Dolly, the last to return, just as she started trotting down from the woods.

Julia grabbed Dolly's bag, ripping it open and throwing the money into the skip, and then, as the pit gurgled and hissed, pressed the empty canvas mailbags down with a rake. Without pausing for breath, she dragged the corrugated iron across the pit, hooked the skip chains to the old truck and began to drag the skip across the pit, over the corrugated iron.

Meanwhile, the rest of the women re-stabled the horses, gathered up the cladding used on their hoofs and took them to the stable yard tip. The horses' tack was replaced in order. No one spoke – they could hardly draw breath from exhaustion and panic – but they were still following their plans, even down to replacing the stable keys in their hiding place. Then they went to the parked Mini, where Gloria was waiting patiently at the wheel. They almost had to haul Dolly inside she was so tired. But it was not over yet.

By the time they returned to the manor, Julia had still not finished. She was hoovering up the money from inside the skip, then emptying it into thick black rubbish bags. Gloria ran from the Mini as the others started lifting the bags and stashing them into the back of the car. They pushed and squashed them inside as bag after bag was tied off and handed over.

Gloria and Connie began a slow, careful walk, eyes to the ground, to look for a single note that might have come loose. They didn't need any torches now as dawn was breaking. The Mini full up to the roof, Julia and Ester drove out. They knew they could be stopped at any second and neither spoke, their mouths bone dry with nerves. They still had not seen a single police car as they drove round the back of Norma's cottage to the barn.

Julia forced open the door of the old coal chute, and they dropped the bags down the hole. The other end of the chute was bricked off in the cellar. They had to shove hard to get the door shut again when they'd finished and Julia applied blackened putty where wrenching the door open had left marks on the wall.

Back at the manor, Dolly now joined Connie on her hands and knees searching the ground. The shotguns had been ditched in the lake, the mailbags were hopefully already rotting, but their work was not finished – not until Dolly was satisfied they were in the clear. One note and they'd be screwed. They found four or five but kept on searching as Gloria raked over the deep tracks left by the skip. She brought stones and branches and stamped them down to cover any movement around the pit.

They didn't stop until Julia and Ester returned. Then they parked the Mini and went into the kitchen. Dolly set light to the black book in front of them and threw the ashes into the waste-disposal unit. All their equipment had already been dumped in the local tip but still they checked that there was no incriminating evidence around the house. It was almost seven o'clock before Dolly ordered them to change and get into their beds. 'They'll be coming and they'll be around for a long time. We just sit tight, stay calm, and carry on here as if nothing has happened. This is the most difficult part. Any one of you can blow it so it's up to you all now, and I dunno about you lot but I'm totally knackered.'

She walked slowly up the stairs and they watched her going to her room. No one congratulated anyone. Connie broke down crying and Gloria gave her a squeeze, telling her to hold it together. They then went their separate ways to bed.

Julia hugged her pillow tightly, the exhaustion still held at bay by adrenalin. She watched as Ester lay back on the pillows. 'Well, so far, so good. We did it.'

Ester drew up the sheets around her chin and turned away. Julia leaned over her. Ester was crying and Julia kissed her shoulder. She didn't say anything because she felt like weeping herself.

Connie cried herself to sleep.

Gloria lay wide awake, waiting for the knock on the door. She was still waiting when she fell into a deep sleep of exhaustion like the rest of them.

Dolly, in her room, couldn't stop smiling. It felt so good – *she* felt so good. She couldn't even think of sleeping, one eye on the clock, waiting to hear if Mike had made it home. In the end she felt her eyes drooping and gave in. She slept with her arms clutching her pillow like a lover.

Mike let himself into the house. He emptied the money bags, putting the cash into two big suitcases and covering them with clothes he'd already prepared. He then sat in the dining room, trying to burn the mailbags. It took a long time and a whole packet of firelighters as the canvas was supposed to be fire-resistant. In the end he poured some white spirit on top of them and they finally caught alight. He took the ashes outside and tipped them into the dustbin, then emptied more rubbish over the top.

Angela was fast asleep in his bed. He stood watching her from the doorway. She looked so young and innocent that he couldn't resist kissing her just one last time. She woke with a start.

'Will you call home and tell Dolly you and the kids are okay? Do it now, so she's not worried about you.'

She yawned and sat up as he walked to the door. 'I'll get the girls dressed and start breakfast.'

Dolly could hardly raise her head. Her whole body felt bruised as if she'd been in a boxing match. She blinked as the phone interrupted her thoughts and she was relieved to hear Angela's voice. They were all fine and she'd get the first train back.

'Good.' Dolly leaned back on her pillow. 'Get a cab from the station, will you? And some fresh bread from that little corner shop.' She hung up and looked at her bedside clock. Mike was home safe. He'd made it. She closed her eyes, wondering if they all would. Any moment she knew the shout would go up and the manor would be the first place they'd start. 'Well, let them come,' she whispered to herself. 'We're ready and waiting.'

Chapter 20

Angela, as instructed by Dolly, had got off the train at the mainline station, not the local one. Dolly didn't want her running into a swarm of cops but didn't tell her that, just that it would be too early to get a cab at the local station.

Angela arrived back at the manor at eight o'clock. The girls were about to run upstairs but she told them to stay quiet and not to wake up the house. She set about preparing breakfast, the girls helping her lay the table.

Angela hadn't known any of the women to sleep in so late and she asked one of the girls to check if Helen of Troy was in the stable, wondering if they had all gone out for an early ride. The girls stayed outside, shouting that Helen was in the stable. Angela had fried eggs and bacon, sausages and some cold potatoes. It was all keeping warm in the oven when the women came down, bleary-eyed and still wearing their dressing gowns.

'Had a late night, did you?' Angela asked as she started getting out the plates.

'Yeah, we did have a bit of a night,' Gloria muttered.

'Aren't you going riding today?' Angela asked. It was unusual for them not to be up and out by now.

'No. Stables have got some kids' party so we can't,' Ester said as she creaked into her chair.

'There was something going on at the station,' Angela said as she served the eggs and bacon.

'Oh yeah, what was that?' Gloria asked, as she poured the tea.

'I dunno, but there were loads of police and all along the lanes more patrol cars. They even stopped us in the taxi.'

Dolly walked in, her hair in pin curls. Unlike the others she was dressed. 'Angela, love, go and get the girls inside. They're getting filthy out there in the yard.'

Angela went out without argument and Dolly sat down. She reached for the teapot, was just about to pour a cup when the sirens wailed. 'Well, here they come,' she said.

The front doorbell echoed through the house, and Angela opened the back door. 'There's police all over the place! They're even up in the woods.'

Dolly jerked her head at Ester. 'Go and see what they want.'

Ester hesitated only for a moment before she pulled her dressing gown round her and they could hear her slippers flip-flopping as she went into the hall.

The Thames Valley police had pulled in every possible man and were searching every house within a five-mile radius of the station, not to mention every outhouse, stable and barn, even every greenhouse. Scotland Yard's Robbery Squad was already at the scene of the raid as hundreds more officers were drafted in to the immediate area to assist in the search. No vehicle had been found, and no witness; the raid appeared to have happened without a single person seeing it.

The police interviewed the women and they all insisted they'd been at home together the entire evening, going to bed some time after eleven. They had heard nothing and kept up a bewildered act that should have won an Oscar as they asked innocently what had happened. A murder? A rape? A kidnapping? But they were told nothing as the uniformed officers began the search. They looked through every cupboard, every chest and wardrobe, the roof, the chimneys, under the floorboards, the sauna area. The police were polite, but diligent, staying there for almost eight hours until they had to move on. They found nothing.

By lunchtime the press were on the scene, and then it was headlines in the evening papers: the biggest train robbery in history had taken place and Thames Valley was using more than four hundred officers to comb the entire area. By now the police knew that a man masquerading as a police officer had daringly held up the train, and the robbery had been committed by possibly five or six others. They had been armed, and the public were warned that, if they were suspicious about anyone, they should act with caution as the men were deemed to be dangerous. The owner of the speedboat had been arrested but released after questioning. The signal-box attendant, Jim, had also been questioned and released. They had, as yet, found no clues, and had no idea of the present whereabouts of the stolen money. The amount in question was not disclosed.

The women did not dare believe they had got away with it as the searches and questioning went on. Even Helen of Troy had been examined, though she had not actually been taken in for questioning, as Julia joked.

Everyone in the area who owned a horse got a visit from the police. Even the staff at the local stables were questioned and their horses examined, but in the darkness the train driver could only describe the horse that had been standing on the line as shiny and black.

Dolly knew she was a prime suspect, but they still didn't take her down to the station for questioning. They didn't take any of them in; they just continued to comb the area. Norma's cottage was the only house that

was not searched. They had a look at her three-year-old
hunter, but she assured them he was in no way capable
of riding across live cables. She suggested they maybe try
the nearest circus.

The officers had laughed. It was the audaciousness of
the crime that couldn't help but hook them all in. It was
called the Wild West Hold-up by the *Sun* and from then
on every paper referred to the raid in cowboy terms.

In some ways Norma was disappointed that when all
the excitement had been happening – a raid at her local
station, no less – she had been on duty outside a cinema
in the West End for some big charity event when the
crowd had got out of hand but nothing much had happened apart from her getting soaked as it had rained all
night long. Luckily, by then she had replaced her lost
cape and hat.

The police now believed that more than one horse
had been involved. They had discovered the scattered
hoofprints in and around the lake but, as the riding
school took pony treks up that way, it became more and
more difficult to ascertain how many horses there had
been, let alone from which direction they had come. The
women had been using the same routes as the stables so
the ground was covered in hoofprints.

There still remained the fact that not one vehicle
had been stopped by the roadblocks put up within ten
minutes of the raid. But as the motorway was only a

short distance from some of the narrow lanes, they could not exclude the possibility that the robbers had slipped through.

The village was agog, the lanes filled with sight-seeing tourists who hampered the police, as did the riders from all the local stables. The ribbons cordoned off certain areas and officers were retained on day-and-night duty, digging up wells, searching every inch of the railway lines, every tunnel and pothole, every drainpipe.

On the fourth day, Dolly almost had a fit when she saw John and his workmen filling the skip over the lime pit. They were stacking it with rubble from the old greenhouse. It remained half-filled and she just hoped that by the time it was moved the lime pit would have done its job.

The women gardened, hoed the vegetable patches, pruned trees, appearing unfazed by the continued search. But the paranoia was starting. They were worried about the dustbin liners filled with money and imagined that the police were just waiting for them to collect them.

Julia was eventually instructed to visit Norma, to ensure the safety of their precious money. She almost had a heart attack when she called on her because, as Norma opened the door, she could see three uniformed coppers sitting in her kitchen. 'Hello, Norma. Long time no see,' Julia said breezily.

'I meant to call you,' Norma said, stepping back. 'Come on in, coffee's on.'

'No, I won't. You've got company.' Julia remained on the doorstep but gave a little wave to the men who clearly recognized her from their stints searching the manor.

'Don't be stupid, come on in.'

'Another time,' Julia said, but the officers began to file out, thanking Norma for the coffee. As Julia hesitated and then went into Norma's hall, Norma hurried past her down the path. The officers stopped, as she called after them, 'It's just a thought, but have you searched my barn?'

They grinned. 'Why? You telling us you got the money, Norma?'

'No, I'm serious.' Norma kept her voice low, stuffing her hands in her pockets. 'That bunch from the manor, they're all ex-cons, you know. She's one of them.' Norma looked back along the path. 'I just remembered she asked if she could store some gear and I said she could. But I just hadn't expected quite so much. Have a look for yourselves.'

Norma unlocked the barn door and opened it. The officers peered inside to see stacks and stacks of black rubbish bags tied tightly at the neck. They went in further as Norma hung back. 'Look, you have a search around. I'll go back and keep her talking, just in case.'

Julia moved fast, her heart pounding. She almost flew down Norma's cellar steps, checking to see if the bricked-up coal chute had been damaged. She peered into the small, dark cellar. 'Stupid, don't be so bloody stupid,' she muttered to herself. The end of the chute was bricked up and even had stacks of boxes pushed up against it. Just as her heart slowed down, it suddenly started hammering again as feet crunched on the gravel outside. They were standing right by the coal-chute door. Would they see that it had been dislodged and then replaced?

Julia tried to keep her breathing under control. She couldn't make out what they were saying. She went back upstairs and looked out of the kitchen window. Norma was smiling as she returned from the barn with the police officers. Julia spun round when Norma breezed in through the back door. 'You want a biscuit?' Norma asked brightly.

'No thanks. I've got to get back, help out, the builders are proving a bit expensive so we're doing a lot ourselves and you know what it's like. Moan, moan, moan, who's doing their fair share becomes the high point of every meal.'

Norma poured more coffee. I'm not good at lying, Julia thought, it's written all over my face. 'What are you doing, Norma? Shopping me to your friends?'

Norma gave a big false laugh. 'No, they just asked if they could look over the barn.'

'Oh dear,' Julia said. 'It's still full of Mother's things.'

The back door opened and one of the officers stood leaning on the doorframe. 'Thanks, Norma, we'll be on our way.'

Norma jumped up and hurried to the door. 'Any problems?' The officer shook his head and went down the path to where his mates were waiting.

Julia pushed back her chair noisily. 'Thanks for the coffee. Maybe we can have dinner one night?'

Norma flushed. 'Sure. I'm back in London for the rest of the week but maybe after that?'

'Scared of being seen with me in front of your pals, are you?'

Norma flushed even deeper. 'No, of course not, but right now this place is worse than Scotland Yard. Every copper in the world seems to be down here and they keep on dropping in.'

Julia just stopped herself from muttering, 'Two-faced cow.' Despite her feelings, so long as the money was hidden on her property, they needed to keep Norma sweet. She smiled, cupping her face in her hands. 'Stay cool, darlin', nobody really gives a fuck who you screw. I like you, Norma, don't turn away from me. Don't make me not trust you.'

Norma leaned against her a moment, and whispered that she was sorry. 'Please see me when I come back next week. Please?'

Julia was smiling as she backed down the path. 'Can't

wait until then. You take care now.' She wanted to wipe her mouth with the back of her hand. She hated the touch of Norma now, but at least the money was still safe, for a while.

They were all lulled into a false sense of security as the days passed and the newspapers stopped screaming out headlines about the robbery. It was now slipping back to pages five and six. They all remained at the manor, waiting. Dolly continued to make them work around the grounds and the house so they were always on show.

Gloria took more and more interest in the children. She turned out to be wonderful at making up games and puzzles. She had unending patience with them but, even so, the waiting was getting to her.

Julia rode every day and sometimes encouraged one of the others to take Helen out, but Dolly was wary of letting the police see that they could all ride so even that created arguments. Julia had started drinking heavily in the evenings. She had sold her mother's house and still had a few hundred left over after paying the bills at the nursing home. She was generous with the money and gave them all a few quid but spent most of it on vodka and always had a half-bottle close at hand.

Ester was the moodiest. She stayed in bed until midday, refusing to help out as she felt it was all a waste of time. Connie began to work out for hours in their gym. She kept well away from John and even further away from Jim. She painted her nails, bleached her hair, content to spend the time daydreaming of a successful career in the movies. She was planning to go to Hollywood with her share of the money, and the dressing-table mirror became the camera. Jim had been questioned so many times his nerves were in shreds but he never disclosed to the police that Connie had spent time with him in the signal box. He did this not to protect her but his job. In the end he had to take two weeks' leave as he was in such a state, and was given sleeping tablets by his doctor.

As the days and nights dragged on Dolly never mentioned the robbery. She was like a rock: calm and always pleasant, trying to keep their nerves from fraying.

One evening Ester freaked and started yelling that she wanted her cut now. If the others wanted to stay then they could, but she was leaving.

'You stay here, Ester, we all stay here until the cops give the place the all-clear. Whether it's weeks or months, we stay on, and we divide it up when I say so and not before.' Dolly was icy calm, her eyes flicking from one woman to the other. 'Let it all out now because nothing will change my mind. You knew this was how it was going to be. Just wait.'

Angela loved the house. She didn't mind cooking and cleaning and enjoyed working in the gardens – and she adored the little girls, who were filling out, rosy-cheeked and boisterous, the only people unaware of the growing tension and the reason for it.

DCI Craigh and his men had read the reports on the robbery in the papers and heard more about it from mates connected to the Robbery Squad at Scotland Yard. They had tipped them off about the women straight away, especially their dealings with Dolly Rawlins. DI Palmer had actually roared with laughter as Craigh had read out the details of the robbery and wondered aloud if Rawlins could possibly have any connection with it.

'Oh yeah! she's a real *Annie Get Your Gun*, guv. I mean, can you see that frosty-faced bitch riding a horse? That's how they reckon it was done, you know. Rawlins's got to be over fifty, nearer sixty.'

Craigh pulled a face but he had sent in a report. He received no feedback so presumed Dolly must have been questioned and dismissed as a suspect. Still, he wondered whether, even if she had not played a part in it, she knew who had, but this was not his department and he had other, more pressing things to worry about. One in particular. George Fuller, Dolly Rawlins's lawyer, having received no reply to his original letter regarding the damage to Rawlins's property, now sent in a reminder, requesting an update. Craigh was confronted by his irate chief as he, too, had received a memo from his superior. The ten-thousand-pound claim was ludicrous, and

Craigh insisted that no way had they created anywhere near that amount of damage. He had hoped the claim was just for show, and it would simply be forgotten. He was told to discuss it further with Mrs Rawlins, and if necessary get an estimate of their own. Craigh and Palmer reckoned she would probably back down if offered a deal, perhaps a quarter of the estimated damages.

It was early evening, and the girls were being bathed and changed ready for bed The women were all watching television. They were more tense than usual because the police had returned yet again and the skip covering the lime pit had been removed, leaving only the corrugated-iron sheets in place. Gloria had eased a part of the sheet back and prodded inside. She had felt a thick lump about three feet down but she was satisfied the mailbags had disintegrated. Still, it made them all uneasy.

Out riding and not far from the bridge, Julia had seen the frogmen searching the lake and was worried they would recover the shotguns but Gloria assured her there would be nothing to incriminate anyone, no finger-prints, no serial numbers.

They all were certain they had never handled the guns without gloves and Gloria recalled that she had cleaned them thoroughly before the raid. However, the pressure of the hunt getting so close made the tension, a constant undercurrent, rise to the surface again. Dolly continued to calm them, telling them everything going on was only to be expected. But they were all volatile, tempers flaring easily, and when, two nights later, the lights of the patrol car flared across the window, they immediately tensed.

Dolly peered through the curtain and drew it back tight. 'It's cops and not local. It's that DCI Craigh and his sidekick.'

'What do they want?' Gloria asked. She sounded scared.

'We'll find out. All of you get in the kitchen and stay there. Let me talk to them.'

DCI Craigh examined the front door and looked at Palmer. 'How much did she claim for this? I reckon this stained glass was already broken.'

Palmer looked at the door and stepped back. 'They done the roof. The place is looking good.'

'Yeah, and it'll be looking a lot better if she gets that ten grand.'

Craigh rang the doorbell and the lights flooded on in the hall. He peered through a broken pane. Dolly was coming towards the front door. Just as she opened it, the children came running down the stairs in their slippers and dressing gowns.

'Come in,' Dolly said pleasantly, opening the door wider for Craigh and Palmer to walk past her. They looked at Angela halfway down the stairs with a bath towel in her hands.

'I'll just say goodnight to the girls then I'll be right with you,' Dolly told the policemen, gesturing towards the drawing room. She kissed Sheena and scooped her up in her arms.

'Will you tell us a story?' Sheena piped up, and Dolly said she couldn't right now but Angela would. She stood at the bottom of the stairs as they ran along the landing to their bedroom. 'Night, night, Auntie Dolly.'

Craigh looked around the ramshackle room. A fire was burning low in the grate. 'Great old house this, isn't it?' he remarked.

Palmer looked up at the ceiling. 'Yeah, needs a lot done, though. These old places always cost a bundle to fix up.'

'Bloody cold.' Craigh rubbed his hands. He sniffed, taking in the torn velvet curtains and the threadbare carpet. Clearly there was not a lot of cash floating around. 'Whose kids were they?'

'Dunno,' Palmer said, as he sat down on a lumpy old sofa. He rose to his feet immediately as Dolly walked in and closed the door.

'So, what do you want?'

Craigh looked at Palmer, cleared his throat. 'It's about that claim for the damage we're supposed to have done to your property, Mrs Rawlins.'

Dolly couldn't help smiling with relief.

*

Ester drummed her fingers on the kitchen table, her eyes on the closed door. 'What you reckon they want?'

Julia poured herself a large vodka. 'We'll find out soon enough. Any of you want a drink?'

'No, and you're hitting the bottle a bit too hard.' Ester pushed back her chair angrily.

'Where you going?' Gloria asked her.

'To the toilet, if that's all right with you.' Ester opened the kitchen door silently and peered into the hall.

'Don't go in there, Ester,' Connie said hesitantly, but she was already out, listening at the drawing-room door.

Craigh was still standing with his back to the fire, and Dolly was sitting in a big, old winged armchair. She gave a soft laugh. 'So what you here for? You want to make a deal, is that it?'

Ester froze. The kitchen door opened wider and Gloria peeped out. Ester scurried back, pushing her inside. 'She's making a fucking deal with them,' she hissed.

'What?' Julia said in disbelief.

'I just heard her. Connie, get out the back and see if they're alone – see if they got any back-up. Go on, do it.'

Connie opened the back door and slipped out. Gloria had dodged behind Ester and gone into the hall to listen for herself. Ester followed then pulled at her arm. 'Go and search her room,' she whispered. Gloria glared but Ester pushed her hard, pressing her ear against the door.

Dolly's voice could be heard clearly. 'No way! You must be joking. I'll do a deal but not for a quarter. Let's say half.'

Craigh looked at Palmer and then back to Dolly. 'You'll get it in cash.'

'Oh, it has to be cash.' Dolly said. She got up from the chair and moved closer to Craigh. 'Fifty per cent.'

'I can't do that,' Craigh said louder.

Ester dived back into the kitchen as Gloria scuttled down the stairs after her.

'Look at this lot! Fucking passports — she's got Kathleen's kids on hers and there's one for Angela.'

Julia could feel her legs turning to jelly. 'Oh, shit.'

Ester looked at Julia 'She's doing a deal for fifty per cent of the cash, I just heard her. She's going to shop the lot of us! How much proof do you want?'

Ester shoved the passports under Julia's nose and then looked back at the closed door. 'Right. We got to get that money. You, Julia, get Gloria's car, get over to Norma's, take Gloria with you.'

Connie came back in from the yard shaking. 'There are police in the lane with dogs and some up in the woods but they're not heading towards us, they're just sort of sniffing around as usual.'

'Shit.' Ester walked to the deep freeze and opened it. She delved inside, brought out a huge twenty-pound frozen turkey and carried it to the sink, turning on the hot water. Julia was putting on her coat, heading for the back door, as Ester removed a .45 pistol from inside the bird. She dug further and scooped out the cartridges.

Julia grabbed her wrist. 'Jesus Christ, Ester, what *are* you doing?'

'She's selling us right down the river! What the hell do you think I'm doing? Go and get the money, as much as you can, and we're getting out of here. I said we couldn't trust her! I *warned* you! Now do it.'

Again Julia hesitated but Gloria gave her a shove. 'I'll come with you, let's go.'

Dolly was chuckling at Craigh, and then she patted his arm. 'All right, you win, gimme three grand and we'll call it quits. You should have been a market trader, you know. But it's got to be cash.'

On Dolly's last line, just as she placed her hand on Craigh's arm, Ester walked in, the gun held in her right hand, her arm pressed close to her body.

Dolly turned, smiling, towards Ester, feeling buoyant because she knew now they had nothing to worry about. Craigh and Palmer weren't there because of the robbery and she couldn't wait to have a laugh about it with them all.

Then she saw the gun.

It was all over within seconds. Dolly was faster to register Ester's intention than either police officer and, as Ester raised the gun to fire at Craigh, Dolly moved in front of him, protecting him with her body as she screamed one word, '*No!*'

She felt the impact of the bullet like a stab from a red-hot poker, her blood splattering Ester's face. DCI Craigh took a step backwards, arms up to brace himself against the next shot. Palmer sidestepped at the same time, Dolly's blood speckling his shirt. Ester's body was rigid, her teeth clenched, her arm still outstretched. She pulled the trigger again. The second bullet spun Dolly a half-step backwards and everything began to blur. She could hear a distant, distorted voice and then saw her own face.

'I have never committed a criminal act in my life.' The social services board looked towards the straight-backed Dorothy Rawlins.

Ester fired the third bullet.

'No, I killed someone who betrayed me, there's a difference, Julia.'

Ester pulled the trigger again.

No pain now, she was urging her horse forward, loving the feel of the cold morning air on her face, enjoying the fact that she had succeeded in learning not just to ride but gallop flat out and jump hedges and ditches – at her age.

Ester fired again.

Dolly's shirt was covered in blood. She was still on her feet, but the impact of the fifth bullet almost toppled her. The images and echoes of voices were fainter now and she could only just make out the figure in an old brown coat standing by a garden gate. 'It's me, Dorothy, it's your auntie. Your mum won't talk about it but that young lad, he's no good. You got a good life ahead of you, grammar-school scholarship and everything.'

With the sixth bullet, her body buckled at the knees, her hands hanging limply at her sides. 'I'll always be here for you, Doll, you know that. I'll always love you, take care of you. Come on, open your arms wide and hold me, hold me, sweetheart, that's my girl. Come on, come to me, it's all over now.'

At last she lay still. In death her face looked older: there was no expression – it was already a mask. Her mouth hung open, and her eyes were wide, staring sightlessly. It had only taken Ester a few moments to fire six shots at point-blank range, but in those seconds Dolly Rawlins's life had flashed from the present to the distant past. She had died a violent death like her beloved husband. Like him, she had not been expecting it; she had been confident, proud of herself and looking forward to the future, looking to make her dreams of a children's home come true. Maybe that had all been a fantasy, maybe this was how it was meant to end. Fate had drawn these women together, and it was fate that it was Ester who killed her, Ester, who she had never really trusted. She had taken such care of them all, checking her back and sides just like Harry had done. And like him, she had faced death straight on, face forward.

Now her cheek lay on the old, dirty, stained carpet, blood trickling from her mouth and her body lying half curled in a foetal position. Her death had been as ugly as her husband's, the only difference being that she had never betrayed anyone.

The sound of the shots brought the officers in the woods running towards the house, shouting into their radios as the others in the lane turned back towards the manor. A patrol car had already received the call and they in turn radioed for further assistance.

Within minutes, the manor was surrounded. Gloria and Julia were hauled out of the Mini, Connie was arrested halfway up the stairs, and Ester was hand-cuffed by DCI Craigh. She said not one word but stared vacantly ahead, her face drained of colour.

One by one the women were led to the waiting patrol cars and taken away. They were in a state of shocked confusion. None of them spoke or looked at each other.

Dolly Rawlins lay where she had been shot, a deep, dark pool of blood spreading across the threadbare carpet. She had been covered by a sheet taken from the linen closet and the blood was soaking through it. Angela sat huddled with the little girls. They had heard the gun-fire but did not understand what had taken place. For the time being, Angela was allowed to remain upstairs with them while the rest of the house filled with more police, plainclothes and uniform, and the women were led out.

Dolly Rawlins's body was removed, after a doctor had certified she was dead, and taken directly to the mortuary. Angela saw the stretcher from the little girls' bedroom window. They stared down, not understanding, and then Sheena asked Angela if she would read their favourite story, *The Three Little Piggies*.

'The big bad wolf huffed and he puffed but no matter how hard he tried, he could not blow the house down.' The tears trickled down Angela's face as she closed the book. It was the end of the story.

The old coal chute at Rose Cottage was never opened by the police. Its black-painted door remained a charming, old-fashioned feature of the 'olde worlde' cottage. So no one discovered the sixteen heavy-duty black bin liners tied tightly at the neck, each containing several million pounds in untraceable notes.

Ask Lynda La Plante

Q. It was ten years between *Widows II* and *She's Out* – why did you decide to write a third instalment of the series?

A In *Widows II*, Dolly Rawlins is sent to prison for nine years after she shoots and kills her husband, Harry Rawlins. As she was the lead character, I had to wait until she was released from prison to write another book!

Q. Of the three *Widows* books, which was the most enjoyable to write?

A. Although I had great success with both *Widows I* and *Widows II*, the most enjoyable novel to write was *She's Out*. By this time, I had learnt so much not only about script writing, but also about writing novels.

Q. In the *Widows* series, which character do you think is most like you?

A. I don't really identify with any of the characters in the series. However, I do bring some of my own traits and quirks to a lot of them.

Q. Which came first, the book or the television script?

A. The television series always came first.

Q. What is the main difference between writing books and writing for television?

A. Television is visual, obviously, so you're mainly concentrating on pace, whereas with a novel, you have to spend more time on description. And, of course, when you're writing a novel there are no restraints regarding budget, so you have a bit more freedom.

Q. How did the television series of *She's Out* come about?

A. I was asked by Verity Lambert if there could be a third series, and of course, I agreed. Dolly Rawlins had been released from prison and knew where the diamonds were located: that gave me the premise.

Q. In the three *Widows* television series, what do you think Ann Mitchell brings to the role of Dolly Rawlins?

A. Ann Mitchell is one of the finest actors I have ever worked with. She really managed to express Dolly Rawlins's complex character, showing her vulnerability and at the same time the strength and toughness that made her a fearful opponent. In *She's Out*, Ann has a smile that can warm you and chill you at the same time. I can think of no other actress who could have brought Dolly to life like this.

Q. *She's Out* was a huge success on television when it aired – did you regret killing off the main character?

A. I know that the network did, because after it had aired and they saw the viewing figures, one of the executives asked if it was possible Dolly could still be alive. But I thought the brutal way her life ended was appropriate, not just because of her criminal past, but because she went out at the top of her game.

Q. Have you ever thought of writing another book featuring any of the characters from the series?

A. I am in the process of writing another book which contains a few surprises. In fact, you can read the first chapter in the following pages. I hope you enjoy it.

Buried

Chapter 1

Rose Cottage had lain empty for eight months. It was a neat, two storey white stone building with thick, black wooden lintels above the central front door and each of the five small windows – three up, two down. On the more sheltered, west side of the front wall, the ivy had completely taken over and was lifting the slate from the roof, but on the exposed east side, the stonework was bare and had been flattened by centuries of strong winter winds swirling down from the hills. From some angles the cottage looked as though it was leaning to the left.

As the cottage was rural, with stables and a hay barn, the land surrounding it had been fairly unkept even before it was left empty, but a small area directly outside the front door had been landscaped into narrow, winding footpaths circling rose beds. The wild roses, left to their own devices, were still fighting against the changing seasons, but today they looked particularly beautiful. In fact, they were the only real reminder of how lovely the cottage had once been.

Suddenly, the small downstairs windows to the left and right of the front door exploded under the immense pressure from the heat inside, sending glass and wood showering into the multi-coloured rose heads. Flames quickly took hold of the black wooden lintels, and within seconds, the smoke from the fire had blackened the white stone wall.

Inside, the furniture had been moved into the centre of the room, just in front of the hearth. A heavy wooden chest of drawers and two bookshelves surrounded a two-seater, horse-hair sofa, which had four occasional tables piled high on top of it. Some of the books from the bookshelves had been forced into the gaps of this makeshift bonfire, and the rest had been thrown into the hearth on top of a huge stack of paper.

The fire had taken hold extremely quickly, and the small lounge was soon consumed by flames, which rose to the ceiling beams, travelled to the wooden staircase and up the stairs. They eventually pushed their way out between the slate roof tiles from the engulfed wooden ceiling beams beneath, and it wasn't long before a spark leapt across to the hay barn, which was full of bales of hay, despite the horses being long gone. The barn went up like a roman candle, and from that point onwards, there was no stopping the fire.

A quarter of a mile away, in a small housing estate, the first of the 999 calls was finally made. Neighbours watched as the dark brown smoke billowed into the clear blue sky. When the house had been occupied, the smoke from the chimney had always been the expected light grey, but this was different. It looked heavy and rancid, and just kept coming.

Speculation was rife as to how the fire had started. Was it 'that bloody tramp' trying to keep warm again? Was it kids taking their games too far?

Fourteen 999 calls were made in total, sending two fire engines racing towards Rose Cottage from Aylesbury Fire Station. By the time the engines arrived, the contents of the cottage had almost gone and the hay barn was a pile of rubble and ashes. However, the stables, which were furthest away from the cottage, were still fully ablaze, with the flames heading for the surrounding trees.

When the fire brigade arrived, they split into two teams – one to tackle the fire inside, and a second on the stables to prevent the flames from jumping to the woodland beyond. The stables were easier to gain control of because, once the wooden frames had gone, there was nothing left to fuel the fire. The interior of the cottage, however, kept re-igniting as the fire found new fuel on the upper floors and from the wooden roof beams. It didn't take much to give the flames a new lease of life.

By nightfall, the grounds resembled a muddy swamp and the rose beds had been completely destroyed by four hours of torture from eight pairs of heavy fire boots walking backwards and forwards. Much of the furniture had been thrown into the front garden, to avoid further re-ignition inside the property, so the once beautiful rose garden looked like a fly-tipping site.

'Stop!' the Sub Officer shouted as he emerged through the hole that used to be the front door. 'Nobody goes back inside!'

Sub reached for his phone and dialled Sally Bown. It was late and the phone rang for quite some time before it was finally answered. 'Sal, this one's for you. We've got a body. Bring your CSI.'

Fire Investigation Officer Sally Bown arrived at the scene at 11 p.m. From the neck down, she was kitted out in her well-worn Fire Officers' Uniform, but from the neck up, she was immaculate. Her long brown hair was in a loose, low braided bun, held in place by an antique hairpin of white beads and silver leaves, and her light makeup enhanced her natural beauty. The whole crew fancied her on an average day, so this post-bridesmaid look was definitely making their arduous night better. She didn't mind. They respected her position, so them watching her arse every now and then didn't bother her in the slightest.

'It's way better than men *not* watching my arse,' was her response to any woman who objected to the glib sexism that came from the male fire fighters. And Sally looked at them, too, so she thought it only fair.

At Sally's side was a child of a CSI with puffy eyes and bed hair. He carried a case almost as big as himself, and he stuck to Sally's side like glue. He wasn't quite used to shift work yet, but if he'd been called by Sally Bown, then he was good at his job. He'd learn the rest.

In the lounge of Rose Cottage, the pile of heavy wooden furniture was now destroyed. The brass hinges and handles from the chest of drawers lay on the floor, just in front of the hearth and, on the obliterated sofa, part-melted into the springs, lay a dead body, charred and blackened beyond recognition.

'Jesus,' muttered Sally, as she got out her camera and filmed the scene, starting at the front door and moving methodically towards the centre of the lounge and the dead body. Her young CSI waited outside until instructed to do otherwise.

'Sally, stop!' Sub shouted. Sally stopped dead. Sub was a man of very few words and everyone who worked with him knew that he only really spoke when he had something important to say. 'Retrace your steps, Sal. Now. Please.'

Sally didn't question his instruction. She started walking backwards, toe to heel, following exactly the same path as she'd taken to come in.

There was a deafening crack from directly above Sally's head. A hand grabbed her belt and she flew backwards with the force of a recoiling bungee rope, to be caught by Sub's waiting arms. Once he had a firm hold on her, he fell backwards onto the floor, taking Sally with him, and in the next split second an iron bedframe dropped through the air and landed right where Sally had been standing. A cloud of ash and debris flew into the air and took an age to come back down. When visibility returned, Sub was still seated on the floor, Sally between his legs and his arms gripped tightly round her waist. The two legs of the bed that were closest to them had smashed deep holes through the lounge floorboards, and the other two were straddling the remains of the sofa and the charred body, which was still, luckily, in one piece.

Sub momentarily tightened his grip around Sally's waist, before letting go completely. That tiny squeeze reassured her that she was safe and protected. As Sally gripped Sub's raised knees to use them as leverage to stand, and he eased her forwards with his hands politely in the small of her back, she couldn't help but think to herself what a massive shame it was that he looked so like her dad.

When he arrived on the scene, Detective Inspector Martin Prescott was frustrated to be held back from entering Rose Cottage until the risk assessment had been done. He couldn't imagine three more infuriating words in the English language than 'risk-fucking-assessment'!

Prescott had been Senior Officer to Sally Bown's older sister for more than twenty years, and so the families were naturally close. This was not unusual for rural Aylesbury or for the local emergency services. Sally knew he'd be impatient, so, whilst the fragile ceiling and crumbling walls were shored up and made safe, she kept him occupied by showing him the video footage of the interior.

'We initially thought he could be a vagrant,' Sally told Prescott.

'He?' Prescott smiled as he corrected Sally's assumption. It was very clear from the video that there was no way of knowing the gender of the charred remains at this point.

Prescott always made Sally smile without even trying. She thought his thick Yorkshire accent made him sound happy, even when they were disagreeing with each other.

'Sorry,' Sally corrected herself. 'We initially thought that the body could be that of a vagrant unlucky enough to have set fire to himself after lighting candles to keep warm. There's no electricity in the cottage, and we found several tea lights scattered around the lounge – on the mantle and in the hearth – but when I looked more closely at the debris on the floor directly next to the sofa, it was clear that the furniture had been piled up around him. I mean, around the body.'

'So, the body was there first?'

'That's for you to decide, Martin.'

'Accelerant?'

'Undetermined as yet.'

Prescott was disappointed when the video footage ended. 'That all ya got?'

Sally started to play a second video, which began by showing the iron bedframe sitting squarely astride the sofa. Prescott closed his eyes and sighed heavily at the sight of his crime scene being buried under a double bed. The quiet breath he exhaled formed the words, 'Fuck me!'.

Prescott took a moment to gather his thoughts. When he was thinking, his eyes flicked from side to side as though he were seeing the various scenarios flashing past inside his head. He appeared to be a very laid back man, but had an intensity bubbling away underneath the surface.

Sally knew that Prescott took this action because he was mildly dyslexic, and soon after joining the force, had made the decision to never write anything down in public. Instead, he had to remember everything, and in a brain that full, it could sometimes take a little longer to process what he was seeing. But Prescott was a clever man, and it was always worth waiting for him. He hid his intellect under Northern glibness, but Sally's older sister had shared all of his secrets with Sally over the years.

'Right, well, ya know the rules, Sal. It's a suspicious death, so I 'ave to assume murder 'til the evidence tells me otherwise.' Prescott walked away from Sally before she could counter and headed for Rose Cottage to see if he could at least peek in through where the window had once been. 'And if it's murder, then I'm wastin' valuable time standin' out here doing naff all!'

Sally raced ahead and stood in his way, forcing him to stop. 'This may be your crime scene, DI Prescott, but you are *not* going into Rose Cottage until I say it's safe for you to do so.'

Prescott looked down at Sally. She was at least four inches shorter than him, but she was a feisty woman, just like her sister, and her calling him DI Prescott instead of Martin told him that she wasn't going to back down.

'And anyway ...' Sally added, '... I hadn't finished.' Sally fast forwarded the second video, stopping it at seven minutes and thirty-two seconds. On the wall above the hearth the word PERVERT could be seen scrawled in red paint. It was mostly covered in a thick layer of black soot, but the letters could still just be made out. 'It looks like you could have a dead sex offender. And I doubt he got here on his own.'

Prescott got his vape out of his left-hand jacket pocket and said, 'See, I know that should make me feel better about havin' to wait to gain access to me crime scene. I mean, a dead perv int' supposed to be as bad as a dead anybody else, but it just annoys me more. I don't know if that word relates to this dead body or not, do I? So now I'm more frustrated than before you showed me.' He dragged on the vape, but couldn't for the life of him get it to work. He put it back into his pocket, and from the other jacket pocket, he got a packet of cigarettes and a lighter. 'You follow ya rules and get that place scaffolded up asap and I'll be over 'ere shortenin' me life.'

Six hours had passed and Martin Prescott had been donned in a blue paper suit and shoes for the last fifty minutes. His white paper face mask sat round his neck as he watched Sally pointing at the partially collapsed roof and muttering to Sub. Sub nodded and Prescott immediately put on his mask. The man of few words had spoken.

Inside Rose Cottage, scaffolding held up the charred ceiling beams and the loose stones from the walls had been removed, leaving behind a relatively solid and safe structure. Visually, the scene was as Prescott expected, based on the preview he'd got from Sally's videos, but nothing ever prepared him for the smell of a body. The stench of burnt flesh and bones overpowers every other sense, and even through his face mask, he could smell and taste the distinctive miasma of 'long-pig'.

'Long-pig is what cannibals call human beings,' Sally had explained on their first ever meeting, more than fourteen years ago. 'By all accounts we taste like barbequed pork and, as we cook, we definitely smell like it.'

'Fuck me,' Prescott had mumbled through his face mask. 'No wonder you're single.' And from that day forwards, Prescott and Sally had got on like the proverbial house on fire. Prescott and Sally paused just inside the jagged hole in the wall that used to be the front doorway of Rose Cottage and watched the dog handler lead her spaniel through the rubble. The dog wore tiny red canvas boots, velcroed in place around the ankles and with thick rubber soles that protected her paws from smouldering embers and sharp debris, allowing her to work safely and comfortably. The single repeated command of, 'Show me, Amber,' was all that could be heard inside Rose Cottage.

Amber's handler kept her off the sofa, as the charred body was still there. The dog worked hard, sniffing and moving around the remnants of furniture. Her tail wagged, her tongue lolled, she jumped and rummaged, but she didn't make one single indication that an accelerant was present.

'Maybe the fire burnt intensely enough to destroy any accelerant?' Sally speculated. 'Or maybe a less common one was used. The dog only knows the most common ones, such as petrol or household flammables. Your Forensics people might still find accelerant on the items you collect.'

'I'll make sure I've got a tennis ball in me pocket if they do.' Prescott signalled for his blue suited CSIs to descend on the scene. He pointed at the sofa. 'There's a body in there, fellas, but it's goin' nowhere, so don't rush and don't compromise evidence just to get it out.'

A sea of nodding blue paper heads dispersed around the room and set about collecting anything and everything that might be useful – wood, brass hinges, plaster, bed springs. All items were individually double-wrapped into nylon bags to preserve any traces of accelerant.

Now that Prescott was inside his crime scene, he had the patience of a saint. He could see the wheels of the machinery turning, see his officers working and progress being made. He followed his CSIs deeper into the mess, allowing them to clear and preserve the way in front of him, and Sally followed after. This was *his* scene now, and she totally respected the shift in authority.

Eventually, and in relative silence, Prescott and Sally made it as far as the sofa. The iron bedframe, which was now gone, had missed the body when it fell. Even so, the body was massively damaged. The face was not only burnt down to the skeleton, but the cheekbones and lower jawbone were smashed and many of the teeth were missing.

'Could that damage to the skull be from falling debris?' Prescott asked.

Sally leaned in to get a better look. 'The ceiling was largely gone by the time we arrived, so God knows what might have fallen through and landed on the sofa. The cleaner looking skull fractures around the temple area could be heat stress. The skull can sometimes just pop, depending on the intensity of heat the fire achieves.'

'Damn shame this fella's teeth are so damaged,' Prescott commented, almost to himself. Then louder, 'Look at the bloody mess your lot has made of this place!'

Sally was just about to tear a strip off him when she looked at his partially hidden face. His eyes were crinkled at the edges and she knew he was smiling.

'Bloody fires,' Prescott continued, avoiding her gaze. 'If the flames don't destroy the evidence, the water does.'

Prescott scratched his head through his blue paper hood and his eyes flicked about again as he thought through everything he was seeing. 'If this is murder, we might be lookin' for someone who's savvy 'bout forensics, you know. I mean, you can't print burnt wood and you can't find shoeprints under water.'

He was suddenly distracted by the contents of the hearth. The water from the fire hose on the floor in this area of the room looked like thin black paint – a result you might expect to get after paper is burnt, creating a fine, soluble ash. Further back in the hearth, untouched by the water altogether, were the remnants of what looked like stacks of dry, charred paper. The paper was now nothing more than tiny fragments of its original form, but the volume was confusing.

Prescott picked up the longest of four fire pokers, and gently nudged the top layer of paper away in the hope of getting to some less burnt samples underneath. He tried not to damage any of the delicate paper. Eventually, he spotted a single in-tact piece, no more than one centimetre in length, showing the instantly recognisable pale blue-green pattern from the bottom left hand corner of an old five pound note. Prescott carefully picked up this fragile piece of evidence and placed into the palm of Sally's gloved hand.

'It's cash, Sal. These stacks o' paper ... it's all cash.'

Jack Warr was a strikingly attractive man. Thick, dark hooded brows hid the deepest brown eyes. He had a cleft chin, which showed the permanent shadow of impending stubble, and when he smiled, two long dimples appeared on either side of his mouth, running from his chin to his high pronounced cheekbones. He had an effortlessly athletic physique that looked great in anything.

Maggie, his partner, always said it was a good job that

his body was so amazing as he made no real effort with the clothes he dressed it in, but she fancied the pants off him no matter what he wore. It was those eyes that had got her in the first instance, though. Eyebrows down, Jack's eyes would express such incredible intensity that if he told you he could take on David Haye and win, you'd believe him. Eyebrows up, he looked like a delicate, innocent soul that any woman would love to care for. This balance between man and boy was why Maggie loved Jack so much. He was her protector and her lover, her rock and her friend.

'Where's the jacket that goes with this shirt you've put out?' Jack shouted from the master bedroom. He liked to call it the 'master' bedroom, regardless of the fact that it was exactly the same size as the spare bedroom. The view over Teddington was what made it masterful, according to Jack.

Maggie didn't answer, so Jack was forced to go into the kitchen to find her. On the breakfast bar was a bowl of cereal and a cup of tea that she'd put out for him, on the back of his chair was his jacket and underneath were his shoes. Maggie's crooked smile said, 'Why do we do this every morning?'

Jack kissed and hugged her tightly. He never tired of just holding Maggie in his arms. She felt the same today as she had when they first met. Jack would maintain that Maggie's exceptional body was effortless, but she tried her very best to go to the hospital gym during every lunch break, and when Jack had the car for work, she'd leave herself enough time to walk to the hospital. For Maggie, this daily exercise was not only good for her body, but also hugely therapeutic, as it took her away from the stresses, pressures and horrors of being an F1 Doctor. Both Jack's and Maggie's jobs weren't always easy. Shift patterns and heavy workloads dictated that junk food was sometimes on the menu, and when they did get a rare day off together, they loved nothing more than going out for dinner, accompanied by casual drinking and a movie.

Maggie exercised to stay beautiful for Jack, and Jack did absolutely nothing to stay fit for Maggie. She was a health-conscious thirty-four-year-old and he was a slobbish thirty-six-year-old. Maggie, in stark contrast to Jack's 'Heathcliff' look, had blonde hair and blue eyes. Jack adored the way she looked when she rolled out of bed in the morning, with her hair ruffled and her pale, flawless skin unhidden by makeup. She was the most beautiful woman he'd ever seen, and would ever see. He had eyes for no one but her.

Maggie had just come off a night shift on the Orthopaedic Ward at the New Victoria Hospital. She was three weeks into her new rotation, and regardless of always coming home exhausted, she still got Jack ready for work before she went to bed. By the time he got home that night, she'd be gone again, so this hug had to last him at least twenty-four hours. Jack nuzzled Maggie's neck. He normally hated the way she smelt when she came home from work – the horrific combination of alcohol hand sanitizer, that chemical smell that hangs in the air in hospitals, moth balls and, occasionally, vomit – but this morning he was running late, so she'd already had time to shower and, therefore, smelt of tangerines.

Fourteen months previously, Maggie and Jack had agreed that moving from Devon to London was the right thing to do for her career. His career, in his words, wasn't as big a deal as hers. Maggie knew she wanted to be an Orthopaedic Surgeon, whereas all Jack really knew for sure was that he wanted to be able to go and watch Plymouth Argyle whenever they played at home. Jack wasn't lazy, but rather discontent. Restless. And, as he explained it, at a cross-roads.

At thirty-six, Jack should, by now, have been a Detective Inspector at least, rather than a lowly DC. When Maggie had asked Jack if they could move to London for her career, he'd said, 'Sure. Gang wrangling will be a bit like sheep wrangling, I expect. Only with knives.' Maggie had asked Jack what it was he truly wanted, and all he could come up with was 'you', which, although lovely, wasn't very helpful. Then he'd answered more seriously, 'I want that look I see in your eyes when you put that stethoscope round your neck.

You're proud of what you do, Mags. You're excited. I want to feel excited.'

London was, in fact, a huge risk, both emotionally and financially, but Jack's commitment to Maggie made it the right decision. They knew no one in the South East, and although Maggie could make a lifelong friend in a supermarket line, Jack was more standoffish. He didn't care about friends – he had Maggie – but the money was a worry. They went from having both time and cash to spend at the end of the month, to being skint ships that passed in the night. And they had to plan two months in advance for any extra expenditure – for example the car's MOT. Maggie dealt with all of this, though. She was the organiser, and she was the one who never panicked when the account turned from black to red.

Jack had agreed to make the life-changing move because he'd always known that Maggie was destined for greater things, and his indecisiveness couldn't be responsible for holding her back. As it happened, Jack's current boss, DCI Simon Ridley, had heard of Jack's transfer on the grapevine and had done a little digging. Jack's reputation in Devon was as a solid foot-soldier with an exceptional eye for detail and a natural ability to talk to people, read them and work out the best way to get what he needed from them. His interview technique was greatly admired, just never pushed to its limits in the small town of Totnes. Ridley had decided to give Jack the opportunity to find his path with the Serious Crime Squad, but very quickly worked out that Jack not being stretched in his previous role was less to do with the location and more to do with Jack's own lack of ambition. However, he was diligent and got on with his work, so Ridley had kept him on … for now.

It was Jack's turn to have the car that morning which, as he sat in a tailback on the A3 near Battersea, he was deeply regretting. His work mobile danced on the passenger seat, pinging and vibrating away as message after message came through, some from the App version of HOLMES, as case related information was shared, and some from DCI Ridley. HOLMES was the Bible for the police force and was normally installed and issued on tablets for use in Court or on cases. But the technology was unreliable, so many officers invested in top of the range mobile phones and installed HOLMES on them instead. It was allowed – just about.

As the pinging and vibrating continued, Jack smiled and shook his head as he imagined Ridley's messages. They would be perfectly spelt and punctuated instructions for the day. Jack knew that Ridley was in meetings all morning, which was why being a little bit late was no big deal. Jack would make the time up at the end of the day anyway, seeing as Maggie would be on her next night shift and he'd be going home to a cold bed.

Ridley led a divisional team of twelve Serious Crime officers. The case that Jack was currently working on started out with one young dad, who happened to be an engineer, realising that the baby monitor in his daughter's nursery was sending a signal to three devices, rather than the two he expected. The monitor had been hacked and an unknown person or persons were watching his daughter sleep.

Once the police had the geography of the rogue signals pinned down, the legwork had begun. Hundreds of hours tracing, interviewing, ruling-in and ruling-out every known paedophile and associate in the area. Over several months, they had discovered hundreds of hacked baby monitors, all within the same fifty mile radius. They visited 756 paedophiles, their friends and their families, and they narrowed the field to thirty-two. Then to one, a Donal Sweeney, who shared a cell with a man whose never-convicted paedophile nephew sold baby monitors to highstreet stores.

It was 8.45 by the time Jack walked down the battleship grey corridor towards CID's shared office. There was nothing remotely dynamic about this part of the station. He paused in the canteen doorway, inhaled the coffee-bean air and diverted inside.

Jack slowly worked his way through all of his text messages and emails over an espresso and a croissant dipped in honey. Jack only drank coffee at work because

Maggie hated the smell and taste of it when he kissed her, and seeing as kissing Maggie was more important than caffeine, Jack did without coffee when he was at home. But Jack needed caffeine to get him through this bloody fraud case.

The canteen was bustling with uniformed officers. Some ate heavy meals, some light breakfasts, depending on where they were in their shift. As Jack made himself a to-do list from Ridley's text messages, he giggled through his croissant, sending a fine spray of loose puff pastry across the table. Ridley had written:

Laura's post-8 p.m. report overwrites yours,
rather than adds to yours from yesterday morning.
Please amend in the system. Print in triplicate and
leave on my desk.

Ridley was the only man in the world who texted in full sentences. Jack sat back in his chair and, wiping the stubborn, buttery crumbs from round his mouth with the back of his hand, he looked around the canteen. He could hear snippets of conversations as officers talked about the cases they were on, the arrests they'd just made, the raids they were about to make. The amount of adrenaline and testosterone flying around Jack was dizzying, and hugely disappointing, because none of it was his. Jack knew that his team would be at their desks, focussed and driven to find the dirty bastard who was watching other people's kids sleep. So why was he late and sitting by himself in the canteen? The truth was that, no matter how friendly and welcoming Ridley's team was, Jack still kept them at arm's length.

Jack had gone from being a normal sized fish in a normal sized pond to being a very small fish in the hugest pond in the UK – the Metropolitan Police Force. And he was out of his depth. After fourteen months of working at the MET, Jack still hadn't found his calling, his passion, his heart in London, and as the months ticked by, he honestly feared that he never would.

When Jack finally walked into the Squad Room, he froze in the doorway. *Shit!* Ridley was *not* in meetings all morning and Jack being a little bit late was a *very* big deal.

Ridley didn't acknowledge Jack's presence, and no one in the team dared look away from him whilst he was talking. This was an impromptu briefing, in response to a phone call from DI Martin Prescott over in Aylesbury.

'We've just been handed a house fire, in which the charred remains of an unknown person have been discovered, together with approximately two million pounds in old money – also burnt. This is being treated as murder, arson and robbery. It's come to us because it's looking like it could be connected to one of our old cases from '95 – the biggest train robbery this country has ever seen. No one was ever arrested and thirty million plus vanished without a trace. We're heading to Aylesbury in twenty minutes.'

Then, and only then, did Ridley look at Jack. Ridley's dark eyes were a frightening combination of anger and disappointment. 'You're with me,' he said, then headed into his office and slammed the door shut.

The team shuffled uncomfortably in their seats, wanting to offer sympathy but, equally wondering what the hell Jack thought he was playing at by being so late. As Jack bowed his head in disgrace and wondered how this day could possibly get any worse, he spotted a blob of honey sliding down the front of his trouser leg. *That's fair*, he thought.

WOMEN L

Adventures, Advice and Experience

6.95

Other available Rough Guides

Amsterdam • Andalucia • Australia • Barcelona • Berlin
Brazil • Brittany & Normandy • Bulgaria • California • Canada
Corsica • Crete • Cyprus • Czech & Slovak Republics • Egypt • England
Europe • Florida • France • Germany • Greece • Guatemala & Belize
Holland, Belgium & Luxembourg • Hong Kong Hungary • Ireland • Italy
Kenya • Mediterranean Wildlife • Mexico • Morocco • Nepal • New York
Nothing Ventured • Pacific Northwest • Paris • Peru • Poland • Portugal
Prague • Provence • Pyrenees • St Petersburg • San Francisco
Scandinavia • Scotland • Sicily • Spain • Thailand • Tunisia • Turkey
Tuscany & Umbria • USA • Venice • Wales • West Africa
Zimbabwe & Botswana

Forthcoming
India • Malaysia & Singapore • Classical Music • World Music

Acknowledgements:

This book would not have been possible without the sustained encouragement, help and patience of our contributors, whom, as far as possible, we have tried to acknowledge within the relevant chapters. But there were many other people who helped in ways less easy to classify, spreading word about the project, passing on information, and lending their judgement to the problems of selecting and editing pieces.

We take this chance to thank: Daphne Toupouzis, Christine Georgeff, Ilse Zambonini, Harriet Gaze, Peggy Gregory, Cath Forrest, Pilar Vazquez, Dörte Haarhaus, Marilyn Hayward, Amanda Sebestyen, Beverley Milton-Edwards, Kate Sebag, Deborah Birkett, Alison Woodhead, Ann Light, Jessica Jenkins, Clare Bayley, Carey Denton, Elaine Wilson, Sara Hovington, Marifran Carlson, Anita Peltonen, Jo Siedlecka, Jackum Brown, Marta Rodriguez, Edie Jarolim, Dana Denniston, Salli Ramsden, Valerie Unsworth, Myra Shackley, Sheena Phillips, Mark Thompson, Amy Erickson, Sabrina Rees, Peggy Jansz, and Clifford Jansz.

Also, thanks to all those connected with the *Rough Guide* office who shared their knowledge and enthusiasm for many of the destinations covered, and through the practicalities of putting this book together, especially Richard Trillo, who also wrote the Africa chapters, Susanne Hillen, Greg Ward, Rosie Ayliffe, Dan Richardson, Karen O'Brien, Shirley Eber, Jules Brown, Mark Salter, Jack Holland, Martin Dunford, Kate Berens, Kate Chambers, Andy Hilliard, Melissa Kim, and Andrew Neather.

We acknowledge a special debt to Bridget Davies, Michael Reed, and Litza Jansz for encouragement and practical help at times of crisis . . .

. . . and Mark Ellingham who, by a combination of unfailing support, editorial prowess, and insistence that the project could work, helped bring this idea to fruition.

WOMEN TRAVEL

Adventures, Advice and Experience

Edited by

MIRANDA DAVIES and **NATANIA JANSZ**

with

Alisa Joyce (USA) and Jane Parkin (New Zealand)

Consultant editors
Laura Longrigg and Lucinda Montefiore

THE ROUGH GUIDES

·Contents

Introduction

1 Albania
Jane McCartan *The Noise of People Walking*

5 Algeria
Jan Wright *Overland with Children*
Janey Hagger *Camel Trek to Tassilli*

13 Anguilla
Viki Radden *An Island in Transition*

17 Australia
Jennifer Moore *Working from Coast to Coast*
Valerie Mason-John *A Black Woman's Perspective*
Nerys Lloyd-Pierce *Six Months in the Outback*
Philippa Back *Alternative Living*

32 Bangladesh
Christina Morton *Working in Development*
Katy Gardner *Learning Village Life*

41 Bhutan
Lesley Reader *From Sunderland to Ura*
Lesley Reader *Walking with Margaret*

51 Bolivia
Susanna Rance *An Inside View*

58 Botswana
Adinah Thomas *A Personal Safari*

63 Brazil
Rebecca Cripps *A Different Rhythm*

69 Britain
Ilse Zambonini *"I am not a Tourist; I live here"*
Luisa Handem *Under the Eyes of the Home Office*
Cathy Roberts *A Scottish Journey*

82 Canada
Geraldine Brennan *A Taste of the Great Outdoors*
Kate Pullinger *Hitching Through the Yukon*

89 Chad
Chris Johnson *Days on the Road*

94 Chile

Barbara Gofton *A Nation of Hospitality*

100 China

Alison Munroe *In Tiananmen Square*
Adrienne Su *An Eastern Westerner in China*
Caroline Grimbly *Striking out Alone*
Alison Gostling *Hitching to Lhasa*

119 Colombia

Janey Mitchell *Taking the Rough With the Smooth*
Susan Bassnet *A Lot of Dire Warnings*

128 Cuba

Jane Drinkwater *Just Another Resort*
Geraldine Ellis *Framing Cuba*

137 Ecuador

Zuleika Kingdon *A Village Film Project*

141 Egypt

Kate Baillie *An Instinctive Kind of Care*
Caroline Bullough *A Student in Alexandria*
Laura Fraser *A Camel Ride in Sinai*

151 Finland

Penny Windsor *A Halcyon Summer*

156 France

Louise Hume *Afloat in Paris*

163 West Germany

Jane Basden *Staying on in Hamburg*

172 Ghana

Naomi Roberts *A "Foreign Expert"*
Helen Scadding *"This Lady, She Takes Time"*

181 Greece

Janet Zoro *A Lasting Idyll*
Mary Castelborg-Koulma *A Part of My Life*
Juliet Martin *What the Chambermaid Saw*

250 Haiti

Worth Cooley-Prost *A Fact-Finding Mission*

197 Hong Kong
Alison Saheed *An Uneasy Path*

204 Hungary
Victoria Clark *Teaching in Pest*
Emma Roper-Evans *In Search of Magyar Feminism*

211 Iceland
Cathryn Evans *Cod Row*

217 India
Una Flett *"Lonely you Come?"*
Peggy Gregory *A Bengali Retreat*
Smita Patel *Between Two Cultures*
Liz Maudslay *Trekking from Kashmir*

235 Indonesia
Janet Bell *A Plant Collector's Dream*

239 Iran
Wendy Dison *A Lonely Journey*

246 Ireland
Hilary Robinson *Behind the Picture Postcards*

252 Italy
Celia Woolfrey *Singled Out*
Valerie Waterhouse *Living in the City of Fashion*
Helen Lee *A Chinese Traveller in Sicily*

263 Jamaica
Mara Benetti *Encounter with a Rastawoman*

267 Japan
Riki Therivel *Finding a place in Kyoto*

273 Kenya
Lindsey Hilsum *Knowing Nairobi*

280 South Korea
Jane Richardson *Accepting the Rules*

285 Malawi
Jessie Carline *A Part of the Truth*

290 Mali
Stephanie Newell *"In and Out of People's Lives"*
Jo Hanson *A Walk along the Niger River*

298 Mexico
Esther Berick *Alone on the Northern Circuit*
Valerie Walkerdine *A Place to Return To*

306 Morocco
Margaret Hubbard *Running Through Fes*
Pat Chell *Three Kinds of Woman*
Jo Crowson *With a Toddler in Tow*

319 Nepal
Deborah Ruttler *Home in a Hindu Valley*

326 Netherlands
Suzie Brocker *Behind the Progressive Myth*
Louise Simmons *Basking in Tolerance*

334 New Zealand
Amanda Gaynor *Back to the "Home Country"*
Viki Radden *"Whose side do you think I'm on?"*

342 Nicaragua
Helen Tetlow *"Welcome to the Republic of Sandino"*

348 Nigeria
Jane Bryce *A Very Nigerian Coup*

355 Norway
Belinda Rhodes *Breaking the Ice*

360 Pacific Islands
Linda Hill *Adventures of a "Snail Woman"*
Carol Stetser *A Nice Life . . . for a Tourist*

369 Pakistan
Sarah Wetherall *A Cautious Enjoyment*
Wendy Dison *Alone on the Overland Route*

378 Paraguay
Mary Durran *"Land of Peace and Sunshine"*

384 Peru
Margaret Hubbard *An Uncluttered Trip*

390 Philippines
Jackie Mutter *Adjusting to the Sight of Guns*
Kate Barker *Working as "One of the Boys"*

CONTENTS

399 Poland
Krystyna Gajda *Guests in Krakow*

402 Portugal
Elizabeth Mullett *"What You Do and What You Don't"*
Jan Wright *Family Life in the Alentejo*

410 Saudi Arabia
Alice Arndt *Back Behind the Veil*

415 Senegal
Daphne Topouzis *Life with the Diops*

422 Sierra Leone
Nicky Young *Working in Makeni*

426 Soviet Union
Lynne Attwood *Touring the Republics*
Sheena Phillips *A friendship visit to Moscow and Riga*
Catherine Grace *A Trans-Siberian Ambition*

443 Sudan
Terri Donovan *Cycling across the Nubian Desert*

450 Taiwan
Kate Hanniker *Taipei without Maps*

455 Tanzania
Sara Oliver *"Slowly, Slowly, Kilimanjaro"*

459 Trinidad
Patricia Jacob *A Health worker in Port of Spain*

465 Tunisia
Linda Cooley *A Surface Liberalism*

469 Turkey
Rosie Ayliffe *In at the Deep End*
Jane Schwartz *Keeping a Political Perspective*

480 USA
Deborah Bosley and Melanie Jones *Just Jump In and Get Cracking*
Deborah Bosley and Melanie Jones *South to New Orleans*
Ann Stirk *Biking from Coast to Coast*
Lucy Ackroyd *New Age Travel*

496 Vietnam
Sarah Furse *A War That Can't Be Forgotten*

503 North Yemen
Gill Hoggard *Qat Country*

507 Yugoslavia
Ruth Ayliffe *Home from Home in Zagreb*

512 Zaire
Chris Johnson *A River Boat Adventure*

517 Zambia
Ilse Mwanza *In Search of Yangumwila Falls*

523 Zimbabwe
Jo Wells *To Harare by Truck*
Kate Kellaway *Caught Between Two Worlds*

530 Further Reading

Introduction

When Baedeker launched the first modern guidebooks in the 1830s it was clear whom he was addressing: gentlemen travelling alone or acting as the guardians, protectors and second-hand guides to the less able travellers accompanying them, namely the "ladies of the party". The fact that many women were making the grand tour of European sites on their own – and often seizing the chance to act as companions and chaperones – could not have escaped his notice. It just wasn't the concern of a travel writer to recognise or encourage this particular phenomenon.

Things are very different now. No one doubts that with the explosion of mass tourism, women, just as much as men, are taking up opportunities to set off abroad. More importantly, no one doubts that we have as much right as men to do so. Yet how many of our super-abundant travel books, guides, brochures, magazines, articles, films and journals really prepare us for the experiences we might have; describe how we are likely to be perceived and treated; deal with the concerns we share about sexism and harassment, or even consider these issues when recommending options for getting around, sleeping and socialising? More radically still, how many break with the Baedeker tradition altogether and talk first and foremost to the woman who is planning the journey?

The problem is not simply that the books and articles are written by men – many are not. But, in following the conventions of "objective" and "authoritative" journalism – where any information of specific relevance to women is considered of marginal interest – women can all too easily write themselves out of the picture.

Consequently, most would-be travellers try to get in touch with other women who have recently returned from a country in order to gain the necessary advice and reassurance. *Women Travel* is an attempt to provide some sort of alternative. The book concentrates on personal accounts, describing the problems and pleasures of travelling in countries as different as Iceland and India. To give some context to the travels, we have added country-by-country introductions, and, as practical pointers, each section ends with contacts for women's organisations and resources, and suggestions for further reading. We don't intend the book to replace regular guidebooks, but instead to fill in some of the gaps, and to give first-hand experience that, hopefully, will both prepare and inspire travels.

Setting off

In our selection of accounts we have concentrated on women travelling alone, with other women or with children. This was not the result of any hardline rejection of travelling with men but a recognition that such experiences tend to be one step removed and therefore less useful to those who want to set out alone. As Margaret Hubbard, travelling in Morocco, put it:

> I used to feel cheated that I was no longer at the forefront and that any contact would be made through (the man) . . . I was prepared to go on alone, however uncomfortable it might become, so long as I was treated as a person in my own right.

Except in cases where there's no choice, as in Albania or Vietnam, we kept the focus on independent travel. Many women, especially those travelling with children, choose package trips as the cheapest, most convenient and "safest" option for setting off alone. But these are, by definition, insulated experiences; encounters with local people, where they occur at all, tend to be brief, impersonal and dominated by the business of buying and services. Some notion of ordinary, everyday human contact seemed essential if we were to provide material of any use. For this reason a large space is given to women who have lived or worked in a country for a while.

Attitudes towards travel were an equally important consideration. Travel, we are told, broadens the mind, but it can also reinforce prejudices. Visiting or working in a country previously colonised by a Western power, there is a pressure to re-enact the old colonial relationships – to treat the problems or pitfalls you come up against as confirmation that we in the West know better. This was graphically illustrated by the experience of Adrienne Su, an American of Chinese descent visiting China for the first time:

> (The privileges accorded tourists, feel more like the privation of the human rights of the Chinese than the extension of hospitality to their visitors . . . When I came across other Westerners on the road their attitude towards me was high-flown and condescending until I spoke English. It wasn't entirely their fault, they had been deluded by the environment into seeing the Chinese as less than people.

We wanted to hear from women who questioned the values they brought to bear in judging societies very different to their own, who were sensitive about their status as affluent Westerners, and who had a genuine interest in crossing cultural divides.

Last, but not least, we wanted to get across the excitement of travel. Not just the adventurous spirit but the fact that for so many women the act of setting off alone, adapting to a new way of life, and coping with the logistics of getting around, amounts to a personal test of ability and independence. As Ann Stirk wrote, having given up twenty years of factory work and cashed in all her savings to ride a motorbike across America:

> I learned my strengths and my weaknesses. I experienced the exhilaration of the ups and the despairs of the lows and most of the feelings in between . . . I learned courage and I learned it myself.

Writing home

Having already been through the process of advertising and sifting accounts for our previous travellers' anthology, *Half the Earth*, we should not perhaps have been surprised by the response we received for *Women Travel*. We were. In addition to the thousand-odd accounts submitted for publication, many other women wrote to share information that they thought might be of help – books to read, contact addresses, women-only resources, gay listings, notes on campaigns of interest to women. And much the same response was arriving in regular packages from our editors in the USA and New Zealand.

In the accounts themselves, it was the depth and the range of experiences that surprised and gratified us the most. If proof was needed of women's ability to embrace new cultures, let go of the comforts and conveniences of a familiar and privileged lifestyle, contend with new customs, and battle with the elements – surely this was it. Some of the travels were astonishingly intrepid: Terri Donovan's epic bike ride across the sands of the Nubian desert; Alison Gostling's illegal hitch across the China/Tibet border; Wendy Dison's lone trip across Iran;

Lesley Reader's account of trekking across the Himalayan mountains of Bhutan; Helen Scadding's motorbike journeys across Ghana. And there were many more.

But demonstrating that women can and do plunge themselves into potentially difficult or dangerous situations did not seem enough in itself. A feature of almost all of the "adventurous" journeys in this book is the extraordinary opportunities they provided for contact and a new depth of understanding between people of entirely separate cultures. The arduous task of hauling a bike over sand dunes was, for Terri Donovan, eclipsed by the unobtrusive warmth and kindness she met from the workers manning the remote transNubian railway maintenance stations. Lesley Reader stayed on for two years with the villagers of Buli, in Bhutan, primarily because these were the people whose friendships she most valued:

> My friends here in Buli are women of all ages. Just as I am a woman alone, the major-ity of them are either widows, women with husbands absent in the army, or single women. They arrived in my house the evening after I reached Buli bearing many bottles of local brew and we all got drunk. We have been together ever since. They teach me to plant, harvest and thresh rice and cook me dinner of rice and chillis when they see that I'm struggling . . . I take their photographs, cook them egg and chips, help out with the cash and tell them about my life and country.

And there were many other, equally inspiring, accounts of finding a new place amongst new people. Naomi Roberts lived for a year and a half in a Ghanaian compound; Rosie Ayliffe (one of many English language teachers) spent a year living in one of the shack dwellings of Istanbul; Valerie Mason-John, a black woman from London, set out to support the Aboriginal cause in Australia; Jan Wright settled with her family in a remote peasant village in the Portuguese Alentejo; Susanna Rance struggled to adapt to the harshness of life in the Bolivian Andes.

Choosing destinations

All in all, a large proportion of the accounts that we chose cover travel to so-called Third World countries. This was not deliberate, but contributors generally felt that they had less to say of relevance or use to women about places closer to home. For every piece we received on Greece, for example, there were perhaps ten or twelve each on India or Morocco. The only country that we actively excluded was South Africa, although we were well aware that many other coun-tries pose a similar moral dilemma for travellers – where your presence and foreign cash might be seen as lending credibility and support to a corrupt or authoritarian regime. As one writer put it, "the nastiest regimes often have the nicest hotels". It is an issue that Jane Schwartz contends with in her account of travelling around Turkey.

As editors, we felt in no position to pronounce judgement on one regime's fail-ings versus another's. We have, however, tried to present a political context in the country introductions and to give precedence to accounts that seem to consider the needs and concerns of the host population; Israel/Palestine is absent because we failed to find sufficient articles which did this.

If we had been able to choose our moment for bringing out a book that covered contemporary experiences worldwide, we probably wouldn't have chosen this one. The world has changed in extraordinary ways since we started work on the project. Pieces on East Germany, Czechoslovakia, Romania and much on the Soviet Union had to be dropped, relegated in the space of a few months to salutary reminders of the old totalitarian days.

It is not that life in these places has altered unrecognisably – social problems and, particularly, attitudes towards women take time to shift – but the premise of travel is different. As borders have opened, so too have the opportunities for contact, and recent cold-war scenarios of reticent conversations and surveillance by the secret police seem strangely out of place. We hope that in those accounts included of places in transition – Christina Gajda's on the dilemmas of being a guest in Poland, for example, or Lynne Attwood's description of the contrasting pressures on women in the different Soviet Republics – the focus on dealings with ordinary people has produced something of enduring relevance.

Harassment and safety

Most women recognise that, much more than bad roads, visa restrictions or poor hotels, it is the fear of sexual attack that most limits the scope of their travels. Yet the issue is still glossed over by the majority of travel accounts. We asked contributors to broach the subject of safety head on, to provide information on the assumptions that were made about them as unattached foreigners, whether harassment was a problem, how they were defined and limited by customs and laws concerning women's roles.

Harassment and safety, of course, are not just an issue for women setting off abroad. It seems easy to forget the limitations we routinely face at home; to forget how habitual it is for us to avoid wandering alone in certain parts of our cities by day and almost everywhere by night; to brace ourselves for comments and jeers if we happen to pass crowds of men; to be far more cautious than men about accepting help from strangers or hitching alone. Belinda Rhodes found Norwegian women "incredulous when they come to Britain and get whistled at by builders", while Susan Bassnett discovered that for Colombians the violence of their own country pales into insignificance against the dangers of New York, "where doors were fitted out with more padlocks than a Colombian would ever dream of and where you cannot be assured safe delivery from a mugger if you simply hand over two dollars or an old watch".

Statistically, we may well be less safe at home. The problem with travel is that we can no longer rely on an instinctive knowledge of what might be considered dangerous, provocative or offensive. In general terms women share an unease about situations where they might feel isolated and exposed. An obvious example is in fundamentalist Muslim cultures where the absence of women on the streets (either actual or because they are hidden behind robes and veils) can in itself be unnerving. Yet sticking to the beaten track is by no means always the safest or easiest option. It is in areas most frequented by tourists, where an easy-going holiday culture has been grafted onto a traditional way of life, that the most damaging stereotypes of Western women have developed – as free-spending, immodest and more available for sex.

Pat Chell, in her piece on Morocco, gives some insights into the sort of attitudes travellers might encounter

As for tourists how do Moroccans see them? If a woman is alone or only with women, what kind of woman can she be? No father would put his daughter at risk by letting her travel unless she was already "worthless". Her nearest equivalent in Moroccan society is the prostitute. She sits in cafés, drinks alcohol, smokes cigarettes or hashish and will even comb her hair in public. She often dresses "indecently" – not even a prostitute would do this. She will also be prepared to have sex if you can charm her into it.

And much the same point was made by Sarah Wetherall in Pakistan;

> The combination of sexually liberated women in the bygone age of the hippy trail, pictures of Sam Fox and widely circulated Western pornography make up a formidable myth of the Western woman as a whore. A myth that cannot easily be dispelled by a single woman traveller wearing a *dupati* (headscarf) for protection.

Attitudes as extreme as this are by no means limited to the Muslim world. Helen Lee in her account of living in Sicily described the commonplace experience of being hemmed in by groups of men "leering and touching". And, as Valerie Mason-John pointed out, a black woman traveller in Europe and Australia is burdened by men's fantasies of her as a more exotic and desirable sex object.

Most women are all too familiar with these forms of sexism. However, in travelling, this picture becomes complicated by the fact that you are also a symbol of the affluent West. You have money, status and can perhaps provide access to a more privileged lifestyle – and you may be resented or desired accordingly. In many Third World tourist resorts (notoriously in Jamaica, Kenya, The Gambia and, according to Jane Schwartz, parts of Eastern Turkey) a gigolo culture has emerged where the exchange of sex and male companionship for money is explicitly made. Travelling in these areas, it may well be assumed that you're looking for a "holiday boyfriend" – someone who you might feel genuinely attracted to and wish to share your holiday funds with, but will nonetheless "dump" when you go back home.

The ambivalence men feel about this reversal of sexual exploitation (and the wider inequalities between North and South that make it possible) can find its expression in propositions and harassment. As Valerie Walkerdine comments:

> The attitudes of Mexican men towards *gringas* are about the hate and envy of an exploited people. White women, especially with fair hair, are about the most hated, envied and desired of all. Any glance at the television screen makes it immediately obvious that white skin equals wealth and class in the Mexican popular imagination. Hence many Mexican men's desire to "have" a white woman is matched by their secret (or sometimes not so secret) contempt.

It is also important to note that local reactions are bound up with differing cultural attitudes towards sex. A woman traveller condemned for being "loose" and "immoral" in Asia or the Middle East might be viewed as "uptight" and "aloof" in Jamaica, Brazil and many parts of Africa, where sex is less ridden by taboo. It can be hard to get used to the idea that sex might be offered in a casual way on the understanding that you have the option of saying no.

Strategies

It's impossible to completely avoid harassment – and a list of do's and don'ts strikes us as colluding with the idea that women create the problem. However, as many women point out, to close yourself off entirely would be to miss a great deal. Once you get accepted as part of a community, once you make friends and learn the language, these problems noticeably fade.

Prior experience of dealing with street hassle certainly helps. Lindsey Hilsum, who had travelled to Kenya after a long stay in Latin America, was amazed by the contrast between her first experiences and those of a woman friend arriving fresh from Norway:

As I showed her around Nairobi that afternoon, men shouted and stared at her. Talking to other women later, I understood the problem. Because I had already learned to walk with confidence and aggression, no one perceived that I was vulnerable. But my friend gave off an aura of uncertainty – she was obviously a newcomer, a tourist, and, as such, fair game.

We found the same observations being made about first-timers in New York.

There were many strategies that women used to try and merge in more easily. Following the lead of more Westernised women in the country (adopting their more conservative style of dress and behaviour) was an obvious one. We point out in each chapter the prevailing attitudes, customs or even laws about clothes. For instance, shorts are illegal in Malawi, and any clothes that indicate (let alone accentuate) the figure or that leave hair, arms and legs uncovered are illegal in Saudi Arabia and Iran. In the Pacific Islands, thighs and ankles are far more taboo than breasts and should be covered. Trousers get a mixed reception in most parts of Africa. The variations are endless.

It should be mentioned, too, that the tendency to dress down, reject ostentatious fashion, or make a personal statement by wearing old or ethnic clothes is very poorly understood outside of the affluent West. People don't flaunt poverty and in many countries bright, colourful, or brand new clothes are a symbolic escape from it. Cleanliness and neatness are similarly valued – it helps to be aware of such factors and to follow suit.

Pregnant women and women with children tend be treated as a category apart and accorded far more respect. As Jo Crowson observed, in her account of setting out as a single parent around Morocco, "having a child labels you as another man's possession". Not only did she suffer less harassment but she found that people welcomed her three-year-old daughter with an openness unthinkable in Britain. She was particularly moved by the hospitality and companionship offered her by Moroccan women. In fact the only undermining encounters she had were with other (male) travellers who took it upon themselves to criticise her for "exposing her child to danger". Despite the dire warnings both mother and daughter had a great time.

Contact with women

In many parts of the world, you're unlikely to have much contact with women. This is not only because men have more interest in making, and following up, the first approaches. But the fact that you are free of family or domestic responsibilities, with time to while away in cafés and bars, places you much more in the male sphere of life; women generally have less opportunities to meet, or leisure to entertain, passing strangers.

In the more developed Western societies this is less of a problem, as there are the possibilities of seeking out women with common interests or politics and tapping into established networks of women-only resources, or lesbian bars and nightclubs. We've either given direct listings or have pointed out ways of getting up-to-date information in the "Travel Notes" section of each country's chapter. Jane Basden in her piece on Germany describes some of the problems and pleasures of linking up with women there.

Elsewhere, divisions are more clearly drawn between the woman traveller as "honorary man" and the women of the country concerned. Many of the travellers who wrote to us expressed an uneasy guilt about identifying more closely with men, whose greater access to education and contact with the outside world provided a more immediate common ground. Language can be more of a barrier with women – who are more often limited to the local dialect – and without the shorthand of shared experience it can be hard to find ways to overcome it.

But beyond this it is the relentless nature of "women's work", and the sheer physical demands of stretching scarce resources to meet the needs of a family (and also any guests that are brought home), that creates obstacles to contact. As Kate Kellaway comments, in her acount of living in a Zimbabwean township, "I wasn't so much lazy as frightened by the routine of housework that shaped the women's day". Her experience, like that of many contributors who lived as guests in village compounds, was that her interest and company were appreciated but her attempts to help were treated as little more than a joke – fortunately one that both sides were able to share.

In such societies, the fact of being childless or husbandless, with no apparent family to protect you, marks you out as an object of pity and concern in many women's eyes – as, too, will ignorance of local custom and lack of any knowledge of importance to women. But it's only on rare occasions that you are blamed for your "unnaturalness". Most of the contributors, such as Naomi Roberts in Ghana, found that concern went hand in hand with a spontaneous urge to offer comfort and help.

In the same way, many women travelling in segregated cultures had positive experiences of being drawn into and protected within the women's community. In Egypt Kate Baillie found:

> There is a communion between women who share and work in and outside the home, in ways that our Western conception of sisterhood could never emulate. In Cairo I experienced this almost instinctive kind of care and protectiveness. On several occasions women who were strangers to me, and who spoke no English, rescued me from situations in which I was unwittingly at risk.

And her sentiment is one that was echoed in most of the accounts of Third World travel.

A final, sensitive issue touched upon by many contributors was the clash between Western feminist values and the very different priorities and concerns of the women they met. It is all too easy for a traveller, disturbed by overt forms of sexism and apparently restrictive customs and laws, to condemn a culture out of hand and view the women who have to contend with it as victims, ignorant of their own oppression. It's a perspective that is rarely well received. As Lindsey Hilsum wrote from Nairobi:

> A Western feminist is often resented. There is good reason for this – many Western women simply do not know about the issues which affect Kenyan women, but nonetheless push their own priorities. On the other hand, the widespread denunciation of feminism (which finds its most outrageous expression in the letters pages of newspapers) is a way of keeping women down, by telling them that any change is "unAfrican" . . . issues such as male violence and access to healthcare and contraception are as important in Kenya as in any Western country, although the starting point for pushing to achieve these things is different.

In Eastern Europe travellers found that feminism got a similarly guarded reaction, but as part of an old and discredited Party ideology. Feminism imposed from above has had little impact on sexual relations and the division of domestic labour. "Maintaining a rightful place in the workforce", often in low-pay, low-

status jobs, has become an untenable burden to many wom[...]
logistics of queueing and searching for scarce foodstuffs. Em[...]
pointed out in her account of life in Hungary:

> The Communist Party has for years issued great tracts on equality an[...]
> certain women who took part in the struggle for communism between the[...]
> nothing was done and nobody believed it was anything but a propagan[...] [...]y.
> Feminism tends to be viewed as something that the West can afford to dabble in but
> which has no place in Hungary.

Obviously you can't and don't suspend your political beliefs and critical abilities
as soon as you set off abroad – it's just that private battles and denunciations are
unlikely to be viewed as expressions of solidarity. Some of the contributors, notably Jane Schwartz in Turkey and Jackie Mutter in the Philippines, used the opportunity of travel to make contact with women's groups, and present an inspiring
picture of the different paths women take towards emancipation. As far as possible we've also tried to point out, in the introductions to each country, the issues
and campaigns that women are organising around, and, in our listings, to provide
contact addresses of local groups who might welcome international support.

Privileges

Our purpose in putting together this book was to bring women's experiences to
the fore – to highlight the invisible travellers who are pounding the beaten track
or finding new paths away from it. Inevitably, this is something of a select group.
Travel is a privilege (a fact reflected in the preponderance of white, middle-class
experiences in this book) and, beyond the Western routes it's a privilege we
seldom share with the people of the countries we visit. In setting out, our hopes
are high that we will be well received, greeted with hospitality and friendship and
accommodated as uninvited guests. But what welcome do we offer in return?
Deborah Rutter ends her account of living in Nepal with a question. We would
like to do the same:

> It is strange now to remember with what trust they took me into their kitchens to
> feed me. They would wave aside any thanks and say, "If we came as strangers to your
> country, you would feed us, wouldn't you?"

Natania Jansz and Miranda Davies, London, 1990.

Albania

• • • • • • • • • • • • • • • • • • •

At the time of writing Albania stands alone – the last closed and determinedly obscure nation in Europe, Stalinist in politics and closely guarded against the prying eyes of independent visitors and journalists. Rumours of revolutionary activity are rife but hard to substantiate in such an inaccessible country. Since the death of Enver Hoxha, president since independence was gained in 1945, small but grudging concessions have been made towards opening up and for the last few years visitors have been allowed in on carefully organised and restricted tours. Visiting is a bit like going into a time warp, so tightly insulated is Albania from the outside world. Private cars are banned, people work the fields with their hands and there is virtually no sign of modern prosperity.

As a foreigner, you will be constantly stared at and women venturing out alone may experience a degree of verbal harassment, though you are unlikely to feel in any physical danger. While all images of Albanian women remain strictly within the framework of mother, worker and soldier, any visitor inevitably tends to be seen to represent the decadence of the capitalist world.

Despite the government's dismantling of any religious buildings, including mosques, Albania's people remain faithful to Muslim traditions, inherited from early centuries of Turkish domination. Women wear trousers under skirts or dresses and usually cover their heads. Except out in the fields, where women do a major share of the work, men are far more visible, monopolising the streets, bars and cafés after dusk.

Officially, there is equality between the sexes: state childcare is freely available and **women** and men receive equal pay for equal work. But old-fashioned attitudes die hard, especially in such a closed society, and women no doubt have their grievances, not least the double burden of paid work and heavy domestic responsibilities. However, there is no recognised forum for dissent and, if Albania's dubious human rights record is anything to go by, any signs of organised protest would soon be quashed.

The Noise of People Walking

· · · · · · · · · · · ·

Jane McCarten went to Albania out of pure curiosity, having gazed at it from the nearby tourist haven of Corfu.

Albania has at least one thing going for it. Or so I thought as I crossed the border from Yugoslavia. The tight security, searches of cases and bags and stern border guards had led to the confiscation of *Penthouse*. Albanian customs are famed for their ferocity, but this was a decision I would have welcomed at home.

It was to be an enlightening few days. When I returned to customs on my way out of the country, I was not surprised to see a soldier poring over that same magazine. Some things are the same the world over.

I'd decided to go to Albania several years before when I was in Corfu. Wouldn't it be great to have Greece without the tourists? This was my bright idea as I looked across the four miles of deceptively calm water which separates Corfu from the Albanian coast. After the death of Enver Hoxha, president since Albania gained independence just after World War II, I had heard that the country was gradually opening up and thought I'd go there before it changed.

It's not possible to travel on your own, and you are always supervised by tourist guides, but at least you can get a taste of the country. A number of companies offer trips ranging from long weekends to a full two week tour. I went for a long weekend. This is probably about right to get the flavour.

So what is it really like? The nearest I can get to describing the experience is that it's like time travel. Albania is a small country, about the size of Wales, extremely mountainous and with one main metalled road running from north

to south. Before I went, I read *High Albania*, an account of travelling in the country in the early years of this century. The author, Edith Durham, found the people warlike and tribal, describing how one night seventeen were shot dead in an argument over which star was the biggest in the sky!

Maybe the book is not so outdated. Enver Hoxha is reputed to have shot one of his cabinet ministers dead in a fit of pique. The men I encountered also seemed to have inherited this tradition of aggression.

"I quickly learned the Albanian for 'whore'. Several men called something out to me and it didn't take long to dawn on me what it was"

Within minutes of arriving at Shkodër, our first stop, we had encountered the Albanian stare. We – two journalists, a lecturer and myself – went for a walk in the main square of the town. Wherever we went, people, mainly men, stopped dead in the street and simply stared at us. It was hard to fathom the expressions on their faces. It could have been curiosity or hostility, or any number of other emotions. Whatever, it was extremely unnerving. The reaction was less ambivalent when I ventured out alone the next morning. I quickly learned the Albanian for 'whore'. Several men called something out to me and it didn't take long to dawn on me what it was! After that, I always went out with a male companion. It is definitely not a country for the faint-hearted.

On the other hand, a young girl we met picked a huge bunch of red flowers for me and thrust them into my hands before retreating to a safe distance.

Albania is a very odd mixture of cultural references. It proclaims itself to be a socialist state, and has been helped at various times by both China and the USSR before breaking off relations with each in turn. It has spent most of its history under the domination of one European country after another – from Italy to Turkey.

What has emerged is a country with an overlay that any traveller in Eastern bloc countries would recognise: prefabricated modern buildings, state rejection of religion, pride in factories and progress, and an obsession with facts and figures, especially those relating to production and output.

But under the surface, what you find is quite different. Despite the painted slogans on the walls, the churches turned into cinemas and the legislated equal rights, people adhere to Muslim traditions brought centuries ago by the Turks. Women sweeping the streets wear crimplene or nylon dresses and, under them, trousers. They cover their heads with scarves.

Rules of dress for visitors follow the same pattern. Despite being told that there are no restrictions, there quite obviously are. My companion brought a whole factory to a halt as he jogged past in shorts, and the men in our party were asked not to show their shoulders in the hotel. You should certainly try to dress unobtrusively if you want to feel at ease.

During our visit we spent a night at the seaside, at Durrës, and there were seemingly fewer restrictions on the beaches. Women and men mixed together, the women wearing bikinis. But when we went to a bar at the end of the pier we found that it was almost exclusively male. The women appeared at the end of the evening to meet their men and go home with them.

Alcohol seems to be accepted, and even quite cheap. Visitors' food is of the minute steak and chips variety and varies from edible to appalling. But this is to judge harshly a country where the standard of living is low and where meat is a luxury. Rejecting food or complaining about it makes life unbearable for your waiters and may subject you to a lecture from your guide, so it's better just to eat. I took snacks with me for variety.

Evening entertainment for visitors was the same as in most Eastern bloc countries – small bands miming to Western records. You can guarantee a rendering of Stevie Wonder songs in any tourist bar from Tirana to the wastes of Siberia, which is a great pity because of the mutual misunderstanding it represents. We would far rather know how they live, and they are only trying to please us by showing us that they understand our culture.

Glimpses of Albanian leisure were a lot more tantalising. One evening we wandered from our hotel and, attracted by the sound of music, crossed the square to a restaurant with a crowd around the door. Inside a wedding feast was in full swing, with two large families and friends drinking, dancing and singing to an accordion accompaniment. The bride and groom sat rather stiffly between their respective parents, he a lot older than her and rather uncomfortable in a suit.

"Sightseeing is a bit surreal in Albania"

Two tourists who had arrived earlier had been invited in and were enthusiastically dancing and drinking. The rest of us stood outside with the local children, craning our necks to see in through the windows. Now and again members of the wedding party waved their glasses at us in an altogether friendly though not very sober way. It looked like a lot of fun.

Another evening we arrived in a hill town to find the municipal brass band playing to a large crowd. We watched them and the crowd watched them and us in equal measure, impassive as usual. When the band stopped, we climbed self-consciously into our coach and drew out. I waved at the old woman who had been standing stony-faced next to me. She grinned broadly. So sometimes the barriers do come down.

Sightseeing is a bit surreal in Albania. In the 1960s the churches and religious buildings were destroyed, so there is very little in the way of monuments to see. The tourist board is now aware of this and is trying to repair what is left of the traditional architecture. The usual trips to museums and workplaces are arranged, but they are very loath to take visitors to farms and rural areas where they perceive themselves to be backward.

One of the most extraordinary things about Albania is the lack of cars. There are buses and ox-carts, as well as ancient Chinese and Russian farm equipment and trucks packed with people, but few cars. When you open the window of your hotel, there is an amazing noise of people walking.

And life for Albanians? It is obviously hard. Women do much physical labour, from hard work in the fields to washing clothes in the river; and there is a government-sponsored population drive to provide much needed labour. On the other hand, the climate is Mediterranean and living conditions have improved out of recognition since the 1940s.

It's easy to deride this small, fiercely nationalistic and independent country which has been the butt of so many jokes for so long. I'd advise going to see and try to understand and enjoy the process as I did. Looking across the water from Corfu, I dreamed of a land which combined the best of the Greek way of life, without the trappings of commercialism and cheap tourism. Looking back across the water towards Corfu, I reflected that reality can indeed sometimes be stranger than dreams.

TRAVEL NOTES

Languages Albanian.

Transport Your movements as a tourist are largely restricted to official buses.

Accommodation Again, there is no choice since all arrangements are made through the state tourist agency, *Albturist.* Hotels are simple and clean.

Tour operators *Voyages Jules Verne*, 21 Dorset Square, London NW1 6QJ, ☎071-730 9841; *Regent Holidays*, 13 Small St., Bristol BS1 1DE, ☎0272-211711.

Special Problems It is best to dress modestly, avoiding bare shoulders or shorts away from beach areas. Journalists, and citizens of America, Israel, the USSR and South Africa are banned from entry.

Guides Philip Ward, *Albania – A Travel Guide* (The Oleander Press, 1983) is knowledgeable, if slavishly official, full of historical as well as practical information. *Albania, A Guide and Illustrated Journal* (Bradt Publications, 1989) is a bit quirky but up-to-date.

Contacts

There are no women's organisations in Albania. **The Albanian Society**, 26 Cambridge Road, Ilford, Essex 193 8LU, is a useful general contact in Britain.

Books

Edith Durham, *High Albania* (Virago, 1985). Account, first published in 1909, of a Victorian traveller's intrepid journeys in the region.

Thanks to Joy Chomley for additional background information.

Algeria

. . . .

Algeria has a reputation as one of the most adventurous parts of North Africa to travel. Having featured for years as the starting point for overland journeys to Mali and the West African routes, the country is now developing its own small tourist industry, centred around the spectacular desert landscapes and ancient sights (such as the Tassilli Plateau rock paintings) within its southernmost borders. As yet, there are few facilities for travellers and getting around requires a great deal of patience and stamina. However, the low-key approach

to tourism has its advantages. Coming from Morocco you will be immediately struck by the relative absence of hustlers and guides; although harassment does occur, it's nowhere like as persistent and oppressive as in, say, Tangiers. Travelling alone you are bound to attract attention (in the more traditional southern areas women have a low profile in public) but the curiosity people may feel about you is often tempered by a traditional and very generous hospitality to strangers. Travelling with a man makes things easier, although you can feel hidden and removed from ordinary contact; as in any Islamic society respect is shown by addressing the man first and foremost.

For many years a combination of Socialist welfare provisions and Islamic charity provided a buffer from the worst effects of poverty but as the oil recession has taken hold this safety net has worn thin. Many Algerians are now struggling to maintain a subsistence living in the face of increased austerity measures and unemployment. The non-aligned socialist government which has been in power throughout the country's 26 years of independence is currently facing an unprecedented wave of protest and dissent, which surfaced in the food riots of October 1988.

There's a noticeable lack of adverts, pornography and Western films in Algeria, in line with the government's rejection of Western cultural influences (though *Dallas*, with its extended family, was shown and proved popular). As yet, this hasn't coincided with any overt antagonism toward themselves; any resentment you experience is likely to be a French colonial war. It took fourteen years up until 1962 for the owners cede independence.

During that struggle, women fought conspicuously and bravely at the front of the resistance movement – and **women's liberation** was a ce nationalist issue. Post-Independence betrayal of revolutionary promises been a key theme, keenly felt, for Algerian feminists. They have had to fight for all advances, and to retain the most circumscribed freedoms. In the 1960s huge numbers of women mobilised against dowry payments, polygamy and disparities in wages, and for better birth control and divorce laws. Twenty years on women organised again, in opposition to a proposed family code, derived from conservative interpretations of Islamic law and directly at odds with the Independence constitution. The proposal was withdrawn after demonstrations led by women veterans of the Revolution, but was passed in secret only three years later. Opposition continues with annual demonstrations on International Women's Day.

With the exception of occasional reunions of veteran revolutionaries, women are unable to hold public meetings or actively engage others in campaigns. Meetings are sabotaged and members physically threatened by Muslim fundamentalists. Algerian women are looking to the international Muslim women's community to co-ordinate legal actions against governments who pass unconstitutional legislation and also to a wide range of international groups to help secure the release of women political prisoners.

Overland with Children

. . . .

Jan Wright travelled through the Sahara by Landrover with her husband and three small sons, aged one, two and four.

It was with relief that I crossed into Algeria from Morocco. I was fed up with being hassled and so hoped that Algeria would be different. It was, and as we steadily made our way along the northern coastal strip our mood lightened and we relaxed.

We had come to see the desert, but before we could do that we had to spend several days in Algiers – fighting our way through traffic jams and looking for goods that weren't in the shops. We were soon feeling frustrated again. Even camping was a problem. There was no campsite and we had great difficulty finding a private spot along the coastal strip, partly because of the heavy military presence and partly because of the spread of the population and cultivation. The seaside resorts offered little consolation. Whilst obviously splendid in French colonial times, they are now decaying and depressed, with rubbish piled high in the streets. Eager to get away from the industrialised and "civilised" north, we drove south.

> "To eat breakfast watching the sunrise, to write by moonlight, and to roll down sand dunes . . . are things I will not easily forget. To the boys it was one big beach"

We were heading down the trans-Saharan highway, which is extremely broken-up tarmac, to Tamanrasset, the centre of the desert. This once sleepy desert oasis is now a tourist centre with visitors being flown in on package tours to luxury hotels. By the time we arrived I was in love with the desert. The freedom and solitude of that great expanse was something I had never before experienced. To eat breakfast watching the sunrise, to write by moonlight, and to roll down sand dunes perhaps previously untrodden are things I will not easily forget. To the boys it was one big beach.

Tamanrasset is also accessible by bus (once or twice weekly from Ghardaia – gateway of the Sahara) and from the town there are organised tours into the desert by Toyota land-cruiser. In many ways to travel with your own vehicle is to do it the hard way. It's tough driving over long distances, but the obvious advantage is the freedom to explore, and we decided to do just that. We drove through the Hoggar mountains and then up north, stopping at the Touareg village of Ideles.

There we were then invited into a *zeriba* – a grass house – by a young Touareg girl to drink tea with her family. The Touareg children were crying with hunger and were given sand to eat to put something in their bellies. Our hostess could speak French and asked us for eye ointment to cure blindness. We learnt later that blindness is very common and could be prevented by the use of antibiotics. Peripatetic teachers reach many of the desert villages but not healthcare. We gave what we could, and left feeling a mixture of anger and sadness for their situation.

Three hundred and fifty kilometres south of Tamanrasset, near the border with Niger, is Gara Ecker, a weird landscape of wind-eroded sandstone rocks. We spent two whole days without seeing another person. It was magic. From here many tourists continue south into Niger. Instead, turning northwards, we set off to recross the Sahara, travelling the lesser used eastern route via Djanet and In Amenas.

This route is much more spectacular than the highway, but it is also much more difficult to drive and there is little traffic. Certain parts have to be driven in convoy for safety. In the hot summer months it can be weeks between one vehicle and the next and a breakdown could mean disaster. We spent the next two weeks in the eastern part of the desert and I enjoyed every minute of it – far more so in fact than the southbound Saharan journey. I think that was partly because I was so much more relaxed with myself and the people, but also because we were so far off the beaten track and there was an unspoilt air about things.

At Fort Gardel, which is 560km north-east of Tamanrasset, we spent several days living in a *zeriba* whilst our excellent Touareg guide showed us famous rock engravings in the Tassilli mountains. He also drove us right out into the desert to where his brother was camping with the camels. Whilst a Touareg boy caught camels for us to ride, we sat in the sand and ate delicious dried meat, which had been wrapped in dung and buried in the sand.

Our guide had two wives, and twelve children – all from his first wife. The wives lived in separate *zeribas* and shared their husband. To marry a second wife is a sign of wealth and status and I believe our guide was the only man of his village to do so. We felt very sad when the first wife asked my husband if, in his eyes, the second wife was pretty.

"Driving into Djanet, you are struck by the absence of women on the streets. The men do all the shopping, socialising and business while the women stay at home"

My memories of the drive between Fort Gardel and Djanet are of baking delicious desert bread in the sand under the embers of a fire, of a hummingbird singing on top of our tent at sunrise, and of a sandstorm which kept us huddled in our tent for twenty-four hours. Temperatures dropped to freezing as the fog of sand completely blocked out the sun.

Driving into Djanet, you are struck by the absence of women on the streets. The men do all the shopping, socialising and business while the women stay at home. Throughout Algeria there are government-run food shops, called national galleries, in an attempt to standardise food prices and it was in one such shop in Djanet that I found myself the only woman amongst a crowd of men pushing and shoving for cheese and eggs after a new consignment had been delivered. These were luxury items.

Further north we visited a really isolated oasis village at the bottom of a canyon. The village chief came out to meet us, or rather my husband Chris, as he totally ignored me. Chris was directed to the chief's house, while I was taken to the women's compound, where numerous women and children were congregated, feeding and washing babies and small children.

I was requested to sit in the centre and breastfeed my youngest son, which I did, much to the delight and amusement of the women. They also insisted on taking off Ed's nappy to discover his sex. Needless to say I was complimented for having three sons and no daughters.

We continued to drive north, over tortuous black rock strewn with corrugations that shook the vehicle nearly to pieces, and past the wrecks of others that had failed to make it. Then, passing Illizi, we picked up a newly scraped gravel road that felt like a motorway in comparison, and a day later we were on tarmac again, and almost out of "our" desert. The last thousand kilometres to the coast were "civilised" as a result of the oil industry, and for us the magic of the desert was already a memory.

Whilst we as a family were not hassled at all in Algeria, we did meet five Dutch girls at Tamanrasset who, travelling together in a van, had been followed into the desert by some Algerian border guards and pestered for sex. It might be worth pointing out that they were dressed in shorts which is usually seen as an invitation in Islamic countries. They did manage to retain control over the situation and nothing dire happened. On the other hand, two French girls we spoke to had hitched across the Saharan highway with truck drivers and had no problems whatsoever. I feel pretty sure that had the Dutch girls been travelling the eastern route they would not have encountered the same problem. One is less likely to be hassled the further one is from the main tourist route. By the same token, however, one can also expect to be treated as invisible the further one gets from the beaten track.

Camel Trek to Tassilli

. . . .

Janey Hagger first went to Algeria to visit her sister, who was working in the north. Looking for a small, remote yet accessible spot they flew to Djanet, an oasis town close to the Libyan border. She has returned there many times on her own, once for a three week camel trek into the desert.

It was early morning when I set out from Djanet with Abdou, my guide and friend, Lakdar, a Tuareg friend and Laura, an Italian woman whom I had met by chance on the day of arrival, for a long trek up to the Tassilli plateau.

We had three camels loaded with supplies consisting of, among other things, four jerry cans of water and a few dozen eggs strapped precariously on the top of the bedding. Throughout our journey we would be alternating between riding and leading the camels on foot, although Abdou and Lakdar would rarely allow themselves a ride.

The first night was spent at the foot of the plateau in a dry *wadi*, where I lay contemplating the great bulk of the cliffs that loomed out of the darkness, against a sky pierced by tiny stars.

My eyes opened as the sun began to rise; it was cold, but the colours gave a hint of what was to come. The fire was already crackling and coffee, bread and jam were produced. There is a Tuareg tradition that says, when travelling in the desert the men do all the work and the women nothing. Cooking being one of my pet hates this suited me fine, although I became an honorary male when it came to learning about camel handling. This latter bit of sexual role reversal was the dubious domain of the Western woman.

The climb began in the pleasant warmth of the early sun when the rocks and boulders were infused with a warm, pink glow. We continued up and up the almost sheer cliff face along a carefully meandering path. The camels seemed hesitant and disgruntled at this with wide feet designed for the soft moving sand they do not welcome steep, rocky climbs.

As the heat became oppressive, I shed some clothes and brought out my *shesh*, a long piece of muslin traditionally used as a headdress by the men and an all purpose sun and wind screen by me. While on their own business the Tuareg move at a near run, but we took a more modest pace, stopping to revive ourselves every so often with mint tea and plenty of sugar. The tea acted as a natural amphetamine helping us to buzz up the slopes.

We reached the top on the second day and rewarded ourselves with a longer than normal midday rest before setting off again across the flat volcanic stone. We paced out the miles on foot, talking to the camels, lizard watching and spotting serpent trails that zigzagged across the ground beneath our feet.

Donkeys are excellent at raising the alarm if there is a snake on or near the route their noses being so close to the ground they can pick up the scent of a fatal reptile, stop dead in their tracks and refuse to go further until the danger has passed. They are also brave rock climbers, leaping across sizeable gaps with grim determination. Camels, with their aristocratic noses in the air, have neither of these advantages but are unsurpassed on the vast tracts of desert dunes.

The rocks began to change formation, some mushrooming out of the earth like small sculptured atomic clouds, others seemed almost fluid, like great waves of rock. We came across fossilised sea-shells, ostrich eggs, arrowheads and the pure white skeletons of camels. Soon the horizon that had seemed like a limitless dome closed in and pillars of rock rose above our heads.

We searched for the most comfortable place to stop for the night. Sometimes we had to make do with a sheltering rock, at other times there would be a small paradise with sand, shade, water and wood offering a respite from the winds. At certain months of the year the winds can blow hot, like air from a hair dryer, for days at a time, but in January we managed to escape the worst of this.

After finding a place we would unload the camels, hobble them and set them free to find their own food. Sometimes the "boss" camel was tethered to prevent him leading the others astray. We collected dead wood, gingerly picking out the thorny branches of acacia trees. The continual need for timber is causing an ecological crisis in the desert, those who live there having to make lengthy excursions from their settlements to find the fuel necessary for survival. A few tourist agencies leave a supply of gas at the more popular places to be used by their tour groups.

Dinner, also made by Abdou, usually consisted of *cous-cous*, a few vegetables and *galet* (bread), baked in the hot embers beneath the fire. During the early part of the journey there was mutton and we also carried some rice and pasta.

As night settled over the desert the silence would be broken by the occasional screech of a jackal searching for breakfast or a mate. We would wait for the fire to burn down, passing round more tea and playing music (the jerry cans doubling up as drums) or telling stories. I would wrack my brains in order to offer a little of my history but the long forgotten art of story-telling can be hard to resurrect.

Sometimes a figure would appear from behind a rock, share tea and pass the time of day with us or rest in silence beside the fire and then rise and disappear in the direction from which he had come. After wrapping up the supplies to protect them from the sand-coloured rodents and sharp-eyed crows, who loved to polish off a bag of sugar, we would bed down for the night. I wore more clothes in bed than at any other time. The nights on the plateau were bitingly cold with frosts that could crack stone. Volcanic rock, however, is tougher than the weather.

"After the fifth day our water supply was getting uncomfortably low. While I had already learnt to bathe in a cupful of water, now even this was forbidden"

After the fifth day our water supply was getting uncomfortably low. While I had already learnt to bathe in a cupful of water, now even this was forbidden. We went to a well-known watering hole and found it dry. A day of hard walking in shadeless countryside stretched out ahead of us. The mountainous rocks had disappeared leaving a plain of black, cracked earth, hard on the feet. Singing kept our spirits up and by early evening we descended into a small valley to find a stairway of three *geltas* (water holes) nestling in its slopes.

The lowest pool was shielded by rocks to offer a perfectly private bathing space. Although we were in the middle of the Sahara, this place, being one of the few water supplies between Djanet and Libya, had become a veritable Piccadilly Circus. Many Malians, fleeing the hardships of the Sahel to find work in Libya, gathered here. We exchanged greetings and gave away some food as is customary for those with the more plentiful supply and being the group closest to its destination. I bathed with the aid of a jerry can and bowl – it is certainly not etiquette to leap bodily into the precious water supply armed with a bar of soap, although, sadly, this is not unknown among tourists.

That evening had a very special quality to it. Having washed the dust temporarily out of my system, cleaned my hair, put on clean clothes and pencilled kohl around my eyes I felt enveloped in a pocket of luxury.

The next stage of the journey was once again among cliffs but this time in the form of alleyways and labyrinths that robbed you of any sense of direction. It is here that some of the oldest rock paintings in the world can be found, providing a clear illustration of a Sahara of water, boats and cattle, a fertile ground where people danced, hunted, fought and made love. Because of these paintings the area is becoming more and more popular with travellers. Our arrival is beginning to threaten the balance of life in the region, although now that border controls and modern transport have almost wiped out the caravan trade routes, the Tuaregs are welcoming the chance of extra work as guides. As yet they are a proudly independent people and hopefully they will be allowed to remain so.

"Everyone, even the Algerian military, has to rely on guides – not least to find the hidden sources of water"

Looking out at the vast horizon, through the large gaps in the rocks, the desert stretched on to Libya in the east and to the edge of the plateau, below which lay Djanet in the west. This, like the land we had just crossed, appeared so different when you turned to look back, that I would have had no chance of finding my way alone. Everyone, even the Algerian military, has to rely on guides – not least to find the hidden sources of water.

The final week of our journey was spent travelling among the main tourist sites. The desert is easily big enough to accommodate all its visitors although a litter problem is gradually developing due to the amount of tinned food consumed by the parties.

In travelling, our hours were set by the sun. We would rise in the pink light of dawn and rest at midday when everything seemed locked in a sizzling heat. My favourite times were the evenings when a golden light saturated the dunes and it would be cool enough to clamber up their slopes and descend in soft, easy cushions of sand.

Eventually we came back down the plateau to re-enter leafy Djanet. The descent the camels disliked even more than the vertical climb. They were tired and hungry. The gravel-like slopes sent us all slipping and sliding, thankfully not all the way to the bottom (not unknown). Once we hit the lower ground, where the air was much warmer, the camels suddenly picked up speed. They were heading for home; I no longer had to guide them towards the easiest path between the boulders as they already had the soft, familiar home ground beneath their feet. It was as much as I could do to keep them in line with the rest of the party.

Soon the palms of Djanet were visible. It seemed like a metropolis after the wide desert landscapes. I dismounted to walk the final mile, turning back as the sun sank low to gaze at the last outcrops of rock.

TRAVEL NOTES

Languages Arabic and (in the south) Berber dialects. French is very widely spoken.

Transport Plenty of buses on main routes, including the Algiers–Ghardaia–Tamanrasset run. Hitching is possible with trucks and other tourist vehicles. Camel treks can be organised through agencies in the south.

Accommodation Most hotels are expensive. Cheaper categories tend to be incredibly basic, like the *zeriba*, a compound of grass huts, which might have a café and camping space for overlanders.

Special problems Sexual harassment – particularly if you're on your own. It helps to dress modestly in long loose-fitting clothes. Coping with a feeling of threat can be difficult. People generally respond intuitively to foreigners and a constantly wary and suspicious approach will lose you many potential friends and guardians. All travellers have to deal with stringent currency exchange regulations, occasional food shortages and a dearth of commodities. You should take any sanitary protection, contraceptives or medicines out with you.

Guides *Morocco, Algeria and Tunisia: A Travel Survival Kit* (Lonely Planet, 1989) is good for general practicalities. *Sahara Handbook* (Roger Lascelles, 1985) is useful for overlanding through the desert.

Contacts

Union Nationale des Femmes Algeriennes (National Union of Algerian Women), 22 Avenue Franklin Roosevelt, Algiers, Algeria. Produces a journal **El Djazairia**.

Books

Fadhma Amrouche, *My Life Story: The Autobiography of a Berber Woman* (The Women's Press, 1988). Born at the end of the last century, Fadhma Amrouche tells of her life in a Berber village, her travels to Paris and eventual acclaim as a singer of the wild and plaintive *Kabylia* songs. Her style of writing draws on the same folk tradition.

"Bound and Gagged by the Family Code" in **Miranda Davies, ed., *Third World – Second Sex*** (Zed Books, 1987). An interview with an Algerian feminist, Marie-Aimée Hélie-Lucas, that details the restrictions imposed on women by an increasingly fundamentalist culture.

Isabelle Eberhardt, *The Passionate Nomad* (Virago, 1987). The recently translated diaries of one of the nineteenth century's most astonishing adventurers. Dressed as a man she mixed freely with the nomadic tribes of the Sahara, even gaining admission to its fiercely protected Muslim Brotherhoods.

Touatti Fettouma, *Desperate Springs: Lives of Algerian Women* (The Women's Press, 1987). Follows the life of one girl growing up in a traditional Berber family.

Ali Ghalem, *A Wife for my Son* (Zed Books, 1985). The painful yet determined struggle of a woman becoming conscious of her own strengths and possibilities.

Juliette Minces, *The House of Disobedience* (Al Saqi, 1984). Introduction to the legal status of women in the Arab world and everyday forms of oppression. Case studies on Algeria and Egypt.

Bouthaina Shaaban, *Both Right and Left Handed* (The Women's Press, 1988). A series of interviews with women from Algeria, Syria, Lebanon and Palestine, highlighting the rapidly changing world that challenges Arab women today.

Pontecorvo, *The Battle of Algiers* (a film – 1965). A classic, clear and powerful on women's involvement in the resistance.

Anguilla

nguilla is a small, serene island at the top of the Lesser Antilles Leeward Islands chain. With a population of roughly 7000, it is dwarfed both in size and in number of tourist trappings by its nearest neighbour, St Martin. Anguilla did not even get electricity until 1977 and the casinos, high-rise hotels and European opulence which are the lifeblood of so many Caribbean islands are thankfully absent.

Anyone planning to visit Anguilla should probably do so in the next ten years. Life is changing so quickly that many of the islanders are reeling from recent events and from developments in the name of progress. The young have become especially disillusioned, and their difficulties in coping with these changes have been exacerbated by the introduction of cable television. These overseas programmes, most of them from America, expose Anguillans to the corruptions of the West: violence, racism, sexism and rampant materialism. Tourism is expanding rapidly as more people discover Anguilla's beauty, the sheer loveliness of mile after endless mile of isolated, quiet beaches, and the kindness of the Anguillan people.

As a lone female tourist you may cause a few raised eyebrows but, provided you respect local custom, people will generally treat you as a welcome curiosity. However, the unsolved murder of two American women on Anguilla in 1988 is a shocking reminder that, even on a remote and seemingly tranquil island, there's no guarantee that you're totally safe.

A dry climate and poor soil long ago forced people to turn to the sea for a living and, at least until tourism catches up, fishing remains the island's prime source of income. People also survive through farming. On top of working on the land and tending the animals, women no doubt carry most of the burden of domestic responsibilities. But the extended family is very strong and, despite the escalating number of teenage pregnancies, there are no signs as yet of organised female discontent.

An Island in Transition

· · · · · · · · · · · ·

A black American, Viki Radden had long wanted to visit the Caribbean, intrigued and inspired by tales of her people's history. When the opportunity finally came, she chose Anguilla for its tranquillity and comparative lack of tourist exploitation.

It has been four months since I heard about the brutal murder of two American women on a deserted Anguillan beach. After having spent some time on this tranquil, idyllic island, I still find the news of these women's deaths shocking and incomprehensible.

As a black American woman, I have had an interest in the West Indies since I was a young girl, when my mother told me that there were black people, descendants of slaves, living throughout the Caribbean. Later I discovered reggae music; the day I first heard Bob Marley, my life was changed forever.

When I was finally able to go to the West Indies, I read extensively so that I could find out just which islands I wanted to visit most. I was looking for an undeveloped island, somewhere without gambling or huge international airports and the maddening sight of black people having no choice but to work in bars, casinos and hotels, helping to keep alive and thriving the very industry which debilitates them and irreversibly alters their way of life. From what I read, Anguilla sounded like the place for me.

I sailed to Anguilla from St Martin on the midnight boat, under a giant full moon. I was escorted there by the island's chief of police, with whom I had shared the flight from Miami. When the boat docked at Blowing Point, the police chief led me through customs and helped me find an inexpensive guesthouse.

When I awoke the next morning I went out on the balcony and saw what was, for me, an especially beautiful sight: black people, some of them as dark as their African ancestors, working, walking barefoot in the summer sun, balancing baskets on their graceful heads. There were goats and chickens everywhere.

"The people are so intact, so sure of their dignity, that there is little evidence of a slave mentality"

Anguillans are unique in the African diaspora in that they, unlike most other blacks brought to the Americas during the slave trade, were never actually enslaved. The British reached the shores of Anguilla with a boatload of West African slaves, but when they saw the flat, arid land, so unsuited to the growing of sugar cane, they packed up and sailed away, leaving behind the Africans, who continued to live according to their tradition as farmers, fishers, and keepers of goats and fowls.

On Anguilla the people are so intact, so sure of their dignity, that there is little evidence of a slave mentality. Anguillans are proud and hard-working, and incredibly friendly. There is also a strong sense of family, not only in individual nuclear or extended families, but in the island as a whole. With such a small population, it is not surprising that almost everyone knows nearly everyone else, and visitors, who can't help standing out, will be regarded with friendly interest.

I am black, but I stood out as well. My light-brown skin seemed absolutely pale compared to the darker-skinned Anguillans. Not only that, but most Anguillans I met told me they had never met a black American woman (or man), but that they were anxious to talk to me and to find out what it was like to live in America, a place towards which they naturally have ambivalent feelings.

The Anguillans I met, young and old, were a little surprised by my travelling alone. Some of the women seemed not to understand my reasons for doing so, and some men immediately assumed that I was looking for a man. But they were more surprised that I was thirty and single and didn't have any children. This is nearly unheard of in Anguilla. Marriage is not seen as necessary, or even particularly desirable, but having children is something Anguillan women are expected to do. A friend I met there told me that when young girls get pregnant, there is a lot of community pressure on them not to have an abortion, but to have the baby and let the extended family help with the childrearing.

I met some wonderful people in Anguilla, although there was an initial language barrier until I became used to hearing Anguillan English. One young woman, a 23-year-old mother of two, worked at one of the larger upscale hotels. She was grateful for her job and didn't seem to worry too much about the influx of tourists and facilities to accommodate them. She lived with her mother and father in a three-bedroomed house on the north end of the island.

But the most meaningful connection I made was with a twenty-year-old rastaman who was the manager of a vegetarian restaurant. One night we hired a rental van and cruised endless back roads that led to once-deserted beaches now filled with skeletons of hotels, houses and restaurants under construction. He told me how Anguillans, mostly the elderly who don't know the long-range ramifications, are selling off their land at an alarming rate. Rich Americans and Europeans, who have no respect for Anguilla and its culture, are buying property, purchasing entire beachfronts and restricting the property from trespassers. These elite newcomers have no interest in maintaining the traditions of Anguillan life,

quite the contrary. It is in their best interests to bring even more tourists and to build more hotels, all of which are priced beyond the reach of most Anguillans.

The rastaman and I drove to the newly-built house of American movie star Chuck Norris, the he-man who is known for fending off attacks from pesky communist invaders with his endless array of big guns. As we sat and looked at his sprawling house, complete with private beach and huge swimming pool, we were silent. My imagination wandered back to a time not so long ago when Anguilla was virtually unheard of, when no one but Anguillans lived there; I began to see the devastation that comes with each passing day.

I must say that I felt completely at ease as a woman travelling alone. During my stay the worst crime that took place was the theft of various potted plants and flowers from porches of the locals' homes. Tourists to Anguilla can expect to be treated with hospitality, particularly if they respect the customs of the island. For example, Anguillans are modest and frown on nude swimming and sunbathing. I had a wonderful time there, exploring the many beaches, the ruins of the island's original inhabitants, the Arawak Indians, and talking with Anguillans, all of whom seemed to have quite a story to tell.

My most moving experience was spending an afternoon with the children of Island Harbour Primary School. The children lit up the minute they saw me, and whisked me off to a stunning white sandy beach lined with coconut palms. We played in the warm aqua-coloured sea, sat in boats that lined the shore, and took each other's pictures. I saw all of the children home that afternoon and I am pleased to still be in regular contact with a beautiful little girl I met that day.

TRAVEL NOTES

Languages English, though it may take a while to get used to the island dialect.

Transport Car rental costs about $25 per day, but Anguilla's size – not much more than sixteen miles long by four miles wide – means that it's possible to explore a fair part of the island on foot. Bicycles and mopeds are also available.

Accommodation During the off-season (May–November) prices are about half the amount you'd pay during the rest of the year. The island has a surprising number of guesthouses, starting at roughly $15 per night. There are no established campsites and camping wild is not worth the risk.

Guides *Insight Guides, Caribbean, The Lesser Antilles* (APA Publications/Harrap) is a bit glossy but contains good detailed information. The section in *Caribbean Islands Handbook* (Trade and Travel Publications) is excellent on practicalities.

Contacts

We haven't traced any specific women's contacts on the island. However, it is worth writing for information to the **Caribbean Association for Feminist Research and Action**, PO Box 442, Tuniapuna PO, Tuniapuna, Trinidad and Tobago. Founded in 1985, CAFRA aims to develop and co-ordinate the feminist movement throughout the Caribbean.

Books

Pat Ellis, ed., *Women of the Caribbean* (Zed Books, 1987). Gives a good general introduction to the history and lives of Caribbean women.

Jamaica Kincaid, *A Small Place* (Virago, 1988). Although the author grew up in Antigua, this often lyrical essay against colonialism and the modern ravages of tourism could apply equally to the changes taking place in Anguilla.

Thanks to Viki Radden for her contribution to the introduction and Travel Notes.

Australia

A ustralia is a vast country, almost the size of North America, yet with
16 million people, concentrated largely on the southern and eastern coasts, it
has the same population as Holland. This enormous scale and emptiness
make it in some ways a difficult place to explore. Temporary jobs, however,
well paid by British standards, are relatively easy to find and travellers often
gain most from working their way around.

Long distances and the high cost of living mean that public transport is
expensive; the cheapest way to travel is to team up with a group and share a
vehicle. Women do hitch, but there are obvious dangers, especially in remote
areas and along the Queensland coast. It is certainly not advisable alone.
Australian men have been slow to accept the notion of women's rights and
the bigotry prevalent in country towns may sometimes make you feel uncomfortable. In general though, people are easygoing and friendly and offer a
warm welcome to strangers.

Australia's population is very mixed. It was not, as popular belief would have it, "discovered" by Captain Cook in the eighteenth century. Aboriginal people had lived there for some 40,000 years when white colonisers arrived to disrupt and destroy their harmony with the land. Thousands were wiped out, either brutally murdered or killed off by imported diseases. Their descendants now form a tiny minority – roughly 1.5 percent of the total population – increasingly prepared to fight for self-determination. The rest of the population are first, second and third generation Australians originating mainly from Europe and, most recently, the subcontinent of Asia.

Aboriginal women hold "Women's Business" involving women only, but their main concerns focus on their people's rights rather than the specific rights of women. Current issues at stake include the high imprisonment rate of their men, Aboriginal and Islander deaths in custody, high infant mortality and a life expectancy rate which is some twenty years lower than that of whites. Aboriginal women also played an active part in protest demonstrations surrounding Australia's 1988 Bicentenary. For years a blank on the political agenda, issues of Aboriginal rights were highlighted during the Bicentennial celebrations which, by their very nature, excluded Aboriginal claims.

Australia has a strong **women's movement**, active on government, local and community levels. The Hawke government has a women's advisory committee and even conservative Queensland has a female senator. Equal opportunity and anti-discrimination laws introduced by the 1970s Labour government have laid the foundations for an impressive network of women's refuges, rape crisis centres and health centres throughout the country. However, recent changes in state and federal governments have meant that women have had to fight hard to maintain these services. Recently feminism has also been very much linked to the environmental and anti-nuclear movements and to issues of racial equality and racism.

Working from Coast to Coast

· · · · · · · · · · · ·

Jennifer Moore runs her own solicitor's practice in Glasgow. Before taking on this commitment she spent a year travelling and working her way around Australia. Her jobs included a gruelling month's fruit-picking and a spell as crew member on a yacht.

Driving through Sydney suburbia from Kingsford-Smith airport, my first impression was one of American-ness: long straight highways, lush green lawns, low, neat, red-roofed bungalows, drive-in movies and McDonalds. Later I was to discover how Australians dislike comparisons with either the US or Britain and that they are very conscious and proud of their national identity. Rightly so, for this huge empty continent is like no other.

Although I enjoyed the bustle and nightlife of the large cities of Sydney and Melbourne, I was drawn by the beautiful rain forests and islands of Queensland and the arid red and ochre plains and escarpments of the outback.

"I found the only real way to meet Australians was to work among them"

Travelling first from Sydney west to Adelaide, then north to Alice Springs, you realise that the "red centre" really is red. Ayers Rock, though crawling with tourists, is well worth a climb despite the commemorative plaques at the bottom to those who have died in the attempt. I did not need to find work until I reached North Queensland. Although it is easy to meet lots of fellow travellers in hostels I found the only real way to meet Australians was to work among them.

Travellers seem to congregate in Cairns, where the emphasis is on partying. Due to the crowds of mainly penniless young people, competition for work is fierce. I moved south to Townsville where I spotted a notice on the hostel board for "female crew on a yacht sailing to Brisbane". Though a bit suspicious of the emphasis on female, I went to the yacht club to meet the skipper and was relieved to find another girl from the hostel. Our tasks were to be cooking, cleaning and generally helping with the sailing. The skipper, who lived aboard his forty-foot yacht, could sail alone, but preferred having company to share the load. We both signed on.

Our journey took us through the Whitsunday islands, calling alternately at deserted bays and resorts. The whole experience was tremendous: warm azure seas, dark leafy mounds of islands, clear skies, the rush of water and roar of wind in the sails. Each day we trawled for fish, catching mackerel and tuna, occasionally supplemented with oysters chipped from the rocks with a chisel. Cooking facilities were cramped, but I soon became adept at

improvising with yet another mackerel and at sieving cockroach maggots from the flour. Our dinghy doubled as a washing machine; when half filled with sea water and washing-up liquid the clothes were sloshed about by the waves.

We often sailed along with other boats and visited them in the evenings to swap stories and have dinner, staying in radio contact during the day. Talking to other female crew members, it seems that on the whole women encountered few problems. Nevertheless I did hear of two or three girls being harassed once out at sea, and in a couple of cases it actually seemed to be expected that they would sleep with the skipper. It is probably better to go aboard with another girl, at least to start with.

I arrived back in Sydney at Christmas to visit friends. It was 25°C, but we had turkey and Christmas pudding and artificial snow on the tree. Having spent all my money in the city I again had to find work. Everyone seemed to be converging on Sydney for the holidays, so once more competition was fierce. I decided to head for the country and, through the Fruit Growers' Association, found a job picking pears in north Victoria.

"By 11am the heat was oppressive and the flies appalling, crawling into your eyes, ears and even mouth as you tried to take a drink from a water bottle"

The main town in the area was Shepparton. Sheppo to its friends. I was stationed six miles away, in the midst of vast orchards at Ardmona. The "barracks" were basic – concrete blocks in a dusty yard, with mattresses on wooden benches and water piped from the irrigation channel. Still, there was all the good money to be earned that I'd heard so much about. My illusions were soon dispelled. It was piecework that was on offer at around $14.50

per large bin, each of which took two or more hours to fill. Expert pickers who follow the seasonal crops each year could fill ten bins a day, but a beginner would be lucky to fill four. My average was three.

We would start in the cold dew-damp early light, but by 11 am the heat was oppressive and the flies appalling, crawling into your eyes, ears and even mouth as you tried to take a drink from a water bottle. Our legs were badly scratched and torn by twigs and my skin came up in a rash from the chemicals in the trees. I stuck it out for four weeks and made about $500.

Despite the hardships, they were some of my happiest days. The warmth and friendship among those staying in the barracks made up for the miseries of the day. We were a mixed bunch: other travellers, whole families with children aged between six and sixteen, all working, lone wolves and students. We were organised into gangs and allotted different areas of the vast orchards.

I shared a trailer, on which were loaded two bins, with my room-mate, an Irish girl. Buried in the branches, we used to sing to keep our spirits up and play guessing games. The voices of fellow pickers would join in from inside the leaves of other trees. We all became quite obsessive and in the evenings could sit for hours discussing pears: how well the trees had been pruned, whether the stalks snapped easily, how best to position your ladder. It was everyone's dream to be moved into the sorting shed and put on wages.

After four weeks, twelve of us hitchhiked to the New South Wales coast where we spent a fortnight camping on the beach, fishing, swimming, eating round the camp fire and generally recovering. It was wonderful to feel clean again.

After visiting friends in Melbourne, my next stop was Perth. I treated myself to a train journey on the Indian

Pacific Railway across the Nullabor Plain. It was a three-day journey and cost $300 for a sleeper and all meals. I think this was when the sheer vastness of Australia finally hit me. Looking out of the window the first morning I could see only a flat, red plain with dull silvery green scrub stretching to the curve of the horizon. The next morning it was exactly the same!

Perth is a very attractive, clean city like a large small town. Work was again quite scarce, but I was lucky enough to find a job waitressing in an Italian restaurant in Northbridge, the arty quarter and rather tame red light district. My employers spoke mostly Italian; the kitchen hands spoke Cantonese and with my own Scottish accent we were often reduced to shouting at each other in an effort to communicate. I rented a room in a flat nearby for eight weeks. Though it was probably quite a bad area, I never felt threatened even when walking home from work late at night.

"Sharing a car is the cheapest way to go and probably the most fun"

My next plan was to travel up the 400km of the west coast to Darwin. Sharing a car is the cheapest way to go and probably the most fun. All the hostel noticeboards have offers and requests for lifts. My notice was only up for a day before I had three offers. I shared a beaten-up Falcon station wagon with one other English girl and two men. We camped most of the time and did our own cooking, stocking up in Perth before we left. The main highway north only has room for two cars, the tarmac simply falling away into gravel and scrub at the sides. You can often drive for half an hour or more without having to turn the steering wheel, the road narrowing to a point at the skyline.

One of my most memorable experiences was at Monkey Mia, a beach on

Shark Bay which wild dolphins have been visiting for over twenty years. They are not fed, but just come to meet the human visitors. The campsite at the beach has resident rangers to protect the dolphins and provide information. We got up to watch the sunrise and the sight of those swooping curved backs cruising in the cold, red stillness was pure magic. Stand knee deep in the sea and the dolphins will approach and eye you up. They will offer strands of seaweed which it is rude not to accept. It was moving to feel that we were perhaps communicating with these gentle intelligent animals.

"The whole town goes to watch the sunset, then wanders round the stalls filling up on Asian food and fruit shakes"

After Monkey Mia, we stopped at a campsite at Carnarvon, a rough little coastal town, where we were woken in the night by wet canvas flapping in our faces. It was Cyclone Herbie. All the campers spent the night in the toilet block, sitting on the edge of urinals, brewing tea. Although it seemed an adventure, the uncertainty of how bad the "blow" would be was frightening. In the end the damage was minor.

Further up the coast, we turned inland to the Pilbara region. Here the only settlements are mining company towns. The area is red and dry, but has some beautiful escarpment and gorge systems around Wittenoom. This was once a thriving town of several thousand people, all servicing the asbestos mine; now it has a population of 26.

Although sad and deserted, it's one of the friendliest places I visited. We were taken walking in the gorges and were roped into the local darts and badminton matches. Life centred around the pub. Heavy rains caused the creeks to flood the roads and we were trapped there for a week. Once on our way again, we were forced by floods to camp on the road, waiting for the water to go down. The four of us felt very small around our fire, pressed by the dark of the desert night.

Our journey continued north through the pearling port of Broome and the largely unexplored Kimberley region, to arrive in Darwin four weeks later.

I spent two months in Darwin doing casual work: cleaning a youth hostel and tourist buses. The city has a tremendous atmosphere: cosmopolitan, lazy, hot and welcoming. It is closer to Bali than Sydney, has temperatures of 32°C every day and a beautiful sunset in the evening, though in the wet season storms and humidity can be trying. My favourite night was a Thursday, when a market is held at Mindil Beach. The whole town goes to watch the sunset, then wanders round the stalls filling up on Asian food and fruit shakes. If you get there early you can find a place for your table and chairs on the grass under the palm trees. It's a great meeting place; I met many travellers who had come to Darwin for a few days and slowed down to the tropical pace so much that they stayed for months.

A Black Woman's Perspective

. . . .

Valerie Mason-John is an investigative journalist and researcher based in London. She travelled to Australia in support of Aboriginal protest against the Bicentenary and to research a book on the Aboriginal struggle.

Seven years old, female and black, sitting in a classroom listening to my teacher tell the class about the world and its colourful people: "Africans and Aborigines are the evolutionary link between man and monkey; they swing from trees and are cannibals", she said. The only difference was that Aborigines were a dying race, almost extinct.

"Miss, what does evolutionary, extinct and cannibals mean?" Each word was explained with vivid images.

Ten years old, female and black, sitting in a classroom listening to my teacher tell the whole class about the world and its discoverers. Columbus and Cook were the heroes, two people we should be very proud of and grateful for. "When Captain Cook discovered Australia it was a vast, empty land with only a few savages who were nomadic", she said.

"Miss, what does savage and nomadic mean?" Both words were explained in vivid detail. I believed my teacher. After all, it was she who awarded the gold stars.

Twenty-five years old, female and black, sitting in the outback, living a traditional life among the Yolngu of Arnhemland in the Northern Territories, I pondered on the facts that I had been brainwashed with eighteen years before. I was visiting Australia, home of the oldest civilisation in the world, and this time my teachers were the indigenous people of that country. I lived on missions, reserves, in urban areas and in the outback. My teachers shared their culture with me, which comes from the Dreamtime when the spirits roamed the universe and created the oceans, rivers, plains, valleys, sun, moon and all living creatures.

During the Dreamtime, these ancestral spirits gave the law to the Aboriginal people. This law is told and retold in *corroborees*, when the people dance and sing their own rituals and ceremonies. Proof of these ancestral spirits lies in the landscape which continues to determine the seasons and cycle of life. Spirits dwell in the caves, mountains, places where the sea thunders against rocks, a pool, a tree or perhaps a spring. These places are the sacred sites today.

"I could hear them asking me: 'Why go to Australia, Valerie? It's so racist out there'"

Historical facts which I had stored for years became historical lies. I soon learned that when Captain Cook first hoisted his flag in 1770 there were over 500 tribal boundaries, clans, languages and dreamings, each clan with its own culture, myths, structures, systems and laws that came from the Dreamtime. Within the first forty years of white settlement, rape, disease, genocide and the partition of land had shattered the fabric of Aboriginal society.

While travelling around Australia, the effects of colonisation became obvious. On the surface Australia appeared so white, only because many of the indigenous population were still tucked away on old government missions and reserves. In Tasmania, Victoria and New South Wales the majority of Aborigines are fair-skinned – those who refused assimilation were wiped out.

Being coastal, these areas were easier for the white man to colonise. Further north, in the Kimberleys, Western Australia and the Northern Territories, the land was rugged and inhospitable for the nineteenth-century settler; and so missionaries were sent in to round up the Aborigines and settle them on reserves. These are the areas where many of the full-blooded Aborigines and traditional elders live today.

"We don't have a colour bar here, we have a dirt bar. The Abos are dirty and drunks; they litter our streets with their filth," I heard the owner of a camel ranch in Central Australia tell a group of tourists. Attitudes like this, typical of many of the pastoralists living in red-neck country, reminded me of my friends back home. I could hear them asking me: "Why go to Australia, Valerie? It's so racist out there."

I was in Australia to support the Aboriginal struggle against the Bicentenary in 1988 – white Australia's celebration of a nation, her two hundredth birthday party. The indigenous people had nothing to celebrate. Inviting them to the party was like asking the Jews to celebrate the Holocaust. The Bicentenary marked 200 years of mourning and colonisation for the Aboriginal people, who continue to struggle for a national form of land rights, self-determination, equal status in society and basic human rights.

Visiting Australia was no easy task. Black women who travel round the globe must be prepared for stress caused by combined racism and sexism. Anyone who says only blond hair, blue eyes and fair skin are a hazard for women travellers is a comedian. Black women travelling in Western attire in Islamic and black countries are considered bizarre, while in Western countries we're regarded as a novelty or exotic.

We black women inevitably encounter different experiences from white women who travel. It is rare to see a black woman travelling on her own. In fact it is only those of us from the African diaspora, Asia and the subcontinent, living in the US and Britain, who have easy access to travel.

Seven years ago I travelled for nine months with another black woman through Palestine and Greece, and then hitched back from Turkey to England. We were picked up so many times because people found it a rare sight to see what they thought were two black men hitching. When they realised we were women, backpacking, most drivers were beside themselves. As black women, we were offered thousands of shekels by Palestinian men to sleep with them, kidnapped by a black cult in Domona, Israel, offered work as prostitutes everywhere we visited in Europe . . . But we survived.

"Because I was a foreign black woman, I was perceived as exotic, beautiful and a whore"

It irks me when I read or hear that Arab or Turkish men are the worst. As far as I'm concerned, men all over the world can be as bad as each other. They just have different ways of harassing you, different chat-up lines and charm. After travelling for thirteen months in Australia I could quite easily complain that white Australian men are the worst. Cars would follow me, beep me, wait for me, the drivers seriously expecting me to hop in beside them. Because I was a foreign black woman, I was perceived as exotic, beautiful and a whore.

In Australia every black looks alike. I was always somebody else, not me. "You're the girl who presents on ABC television, Tricia Goddard," I would be told while out shopping. In most states I was stopped and asked for my autograph, only to be abused because people wouldn't believe that I wasn't Whoopi Goldberg. In Sydney I was often mistaken for Sandra, the black American friend I was staying with.

It can be difficult for black women who travel since there are often no other black women from their part of the world to identify with, or offload on to. And in countries like Australia, with a black indigenous population, foreign blacks can be treated with suspicion because the system uses them to oppress the indigenous blacks. The first black woman to present on ABC, national television, was British. Aboriginal people found this a big insult and felt that in 1988 ABC could at least have found an Aboriginal person to do the job.

"I had to acknowledge that as a foreign black woman I had certain privileges and access, being considered better than an Aboriginal"

I noticed how my status went up while living in Australia. I was no longer at the bottom of the pile. I had to acknowledge that as a foreign black woman I had certain privileges and access, being considered better than an Aboriginal. There were occasions when nightclubs allowed me entry but not my Aboriginal friends. Once I opened my mouth everything was OK. However, I was forced to travel by air because coach stops in Australia refused to serve me. Ten hours to go without refreshments is a long time, and a severe price to pay for the colour of your skin.

The sunshine, the stunning landscape, the ocean and the life of a lotus-eater somehow made life a lot easier to cope with. My skin sparkled, my hair glowed like red embers and I realised that I was not meant to live in a cold climate. Like any other place, Australia is what you make of it, a country where you can choose what you want to see and ignore what you want to miss. Despite the beauty and the fact that it is one of the wealthiest countries in the world, I could not ignore that some of the indigenous population are living in Third World conditions, suffering from Third World diseases; and although they make up 1.4 percent of the population, Aborigines are the most institutionalised race in the world.

Yet with all their hardship I found the communities I visited in Queensland, Tasmania and the Northern Territories immediately friendly and warm – and, living traditionally among the Yolngu of Arhemland, I came across the most gentle men I have ever met.

Six Months in the Outback

. . . .

Nerys Lloyd-Pierce is a freelance journalist, originally from North Wales. After some time in Asia she travelled widely around Australia, starting with six months working on a remote cattle station in the west of the country.

Having spent four months travelling around Asia, a trip to Australia seemed a logical progression. My reasons for visiting that country were ambiguous. On a mercenary note, I knew I would be flat broke by then and had a good chance of earning money. The prospect of warm, sunny weather was also appealing after a succession of chilly English winters.

I arrived with the usual preconceptions about heat, flies and Bondi beach, but was soon to learn that Australia had considerably more to offer. My first preconception was shattered as I flew into Perth. It was green! Greener in fact than the subdued winter face of the England I had left behind.

On the flight from Bangkok I had my first encounter with Australian hospitality. The young guy I started chatting to on the plane was shocked when I remarked that I had nowhere to stay, no connections and very little money, and offered me an indefinite place on his sitting-room floor. This gave me an invaluable base from which to look for the work I now desperately needed.

Finding casual work in Australia shouldn't be a problem and the pay is good. It helps, however, to have a working holiday visa as the government is trying to clamp down on people working illegally. Those I met working without a permit hadn't had any problems, but the penalty if you are caught is instant deportation. Having enough money to tide you over does ease the pressure; I arrived at my first job with only thirty cents left in my purse.

"I saw a newspaper advertisement for a stock camp cook on a remote cattle station . . . Only later did I learn that the job had been advertised for three months and I was the only applicant"

Despite dire financial straits I really didn't want to do a mundane job like waitressing or working behind a bar. Having travelled halfway across the world I wanted to do something which was as much an experience as a job. The chance came when I saw a newspaper advertisement for a stock camp cook on a remote cattle station. I was accepted for the job with an alacrity which surprised me. Only later did I learn that the job had been advertised for three months and I was the only applicant!

To the horror of my Perth friends – urban Australians rarely seem to venture into the bush – I set off, leaving them convinced that I would loathe every minute.

The bus journey from Perth to the cattle station brought home to me the vastness of Australia: close on 2000km

of open space and travel for hours without seeing a solitary sign of human habitation. The station itself was situated 260km from any town with over 600km to the nearest neighbour.

The homestead formed a small cluster of houses in a vast bowl skirted by rugged magenta hills. A deep slow-moving river curled in crescent shape around these homes, creating an effective natural fire break. Families had their own houses while the unmarried stockmen lived in bedsits. I was lucky enough to have a house to myself, which gave me both space and privacy, essential elements in what could very easily become a claustrophobic environment.

Everyone used to meet up for coffee and a chat at morning "smoko" when I, being the "cookie", had to produce vast quantities of cake or biscuit. Food was of great importance to people leading such active outdoor lives. There was no television and evening entertainment revolved around barbecues, fishing, playing cards and scrabble. I was always amazed how the same group of people managed to laugh and joke together in spite of seeing each other every day. On the other hand, living in such close proximity you can't afford to fall out with anyone as there's no way you could manage to avoid them.

Coming from a tiny country like England, the isolation of the outback is hard to imagine. The four-hour drive between station and town naturally made conventional shopping quite impractical; fresh produce was flown in on the mail plane every fortnight. If you ran out of anything in the meantime, too bad.

Every four months a road train brought in supplies of non-perishable goods, absolutely essential in the wet season when it was often impossible for the mail plane to land. During this period the dirt road connecting properties with the outside world would become altogether impassable, sometimes for weeks at a time.

Communications were made by means of a two-way radio with a shrill continuous call sign to clear the airwaves in the event of an emergency. In such a case the flying doctor plane would land on the nearest airstrip, but the patient still had to be transported from the scene of the accident to the waiting plane. Radio also plays an important role in children's education. The school of the air is part of their daily routine, the teacher no more than a disembodied voice. To qualify for a government governess a community must have seven or more children of school age.

"We worked on the basis of three weeks mustering cattle in the bush, when we slept on 'swags' (bedrolls) under the stars, and a week at the homestead"

The cattle station covered one-and-a-half million acres, a distance that I found hard to assimilate. Stand on a high point and literally all that the eye can see is one property. On arrival I naively commented that fifty horses seemed a lot in one paddock, only to be told that the paddock stretched over 12,000 acres.

My job out in the bush was to cook meals for fifteen stockmen, or ringers as they're known, on an open fire. We worked on the basis of three weeks mustering cattle in the bush, when we slept on "swags" (bedrolls) under the stars, and a week at the homestead. Every day we loaded up the gear on to the creaking chuck wagon and moved to a new camp, each of which had a name: Corner Billabong, Eel Creek, Old Man Lagoon.

This itinerant lifestyle led me to discover the hidden corners of a region that might simply appear barren and hostile to the casual observer: an arid outcrop of rocks hiding a tumbling waterfall, a pool framed by the luxuriant growth of pandanus palms, the sudden blooming of hibiscus on a dry plain or the strangely contorted branches of a boab tree clawing the sky.

At first I was afraid of getting hopelessly lost between camps – after all there was no one I could stop to ask for directions – until Phil, the manager, put my mind at rest with the wry observation, "No worries, if you've got the tucker they'll always come and look for you."

Despite the obvious novelty of being in a new place and seeing a different way of life, being a stock camp cook was far from easy. At times I felt very isolated from anything familiar and comforting. Physically the job was often hard work and the hours were long as the cook is always the first up and last to finish. On occasions, struggling to lift billies of boiling water from the fire, sweat dripping down my face and clothes smeared in grime, I wondered why the hell I was doing it.

It's not easy to conquer the vagaries of cooking on an open fire. In order to bake a cake or loaf of bread I had to build up the fire, only to wait for it to die down to a heap of glowing coals. The temperature of these coals was all important; too hot and the cake would burn, too cool and it would simply never cook. I can't remember how many times I found myself frantically piling on more coals in an effort to cook a loaf, while the middle remained stubbornly soggy.

"To his amazement I socked him across the back with an axe handle. Cooks are notoriously bad-tempered and I can see why"

Having put so much effort into cooking you become strangely possessive about the results! On one such occasion I had been labouring over melting moments (biscuits which literally melt in the mouth), a task I wished I had never started, when John, the youngest of the ringers, strolled up remarking, "These look good, cookie" and grabbed a handful. Seeing him munching so indifferently after my labours was too much and to his amazement I socked him across the back with an axe handle. Cooks are notoriously bad-tempered and I can see why.

Eight of the fifteen stockmen were Aboriginals. Relationships between the two communities on the station were amicable but distant. I found the Aboriginal men good humoured, easy-going company. The oldest among them couldn't have been more than fifty, though the deeply etched lines on his face suggested a much older person. He would tell me stories of how he first came into contact with white Australians – how, at the age of fifteen when he saw his first car, he got on his horse and chased it off his land. Despite their superficial friendship, a certain segregation clearly existed between the two communities. The Aboriginals always built a separate campfire in the evenings. This was done by tacit agreement and both groups seemed to accept the arrangement. During the twelve months I lived there I never met a white Australian who mixed socially with an Aboriginal and was shocked to find racial intolerance common, even among the educated elite.

"Male attitudes perhaps resemble those in Britain twenty or thirty years ago"

Generally speaking women in the bush tend to adopt the conventional female roles, and male attitudes perhaps resemble those in Britain twenty or thirty years ago. It is considered unladylike for a woman to swear and, by the same token, it really isn't on to swear in front of a "lady". On one occasion at camp I burnt my foot quite badly on the hot coals; all alone, angry and frustrated, I let loose the tirade of swearing I had so carefully been suppressing!

The three women on the station stayed at the homestead while the men and I went out into the bush. I was worried this might create friction, or that they might simply resent me for being an outsider intruding on their close-knit community, but nothing could have been further from the truth. I was welcomed and accepted from the beginning.

The women's role was different, though no less important than that of the men. They were responsible for the smooth running of the station during the men's absence; they organised the vegetable garden and the orchard and kept chickens. They also provided a balance in a male-dominated environment. The station manager's wife was a nursing sister and fortunate enough to be able to pursue her career as organiser of community health in outlying areas. She told me that without the job she could easily have found the lack of intellectual stimulation hard to handle.

Even though I was alone in the bush with fifteen men, I never at any point encountered sexual harassment. Both women and men went out of their way to make sure I settled in and felt happy and at home. Working on the station was an incredible experience, probably the last vestige of frontier spirit left in Australia. Several things will remain imprinted on my mind forever: the cloud of dust on the horizon heralding the return of stockmen and cattle; riding all day across that immense parched land; the sheer delight of coming across a cool shady water hole.

It was not without regret that I decided after six months that the time was right to move on. I wanted to see more of Australia and now had the finances to do so. As a leaving present the Aboriginal men gave me three boab nuts, carved with the traditional pictures of emu, goanna and kangaroo.

Returning to the city was like emerging into another world, only this time it was urban life that felt alien.

Alternative Living
· · · · · · · · · · · ·

Philippa Back was 21 years old and recovering from the break-up of a five-year relationship when she set off for Australia. She eventually found her peace in Nimbin, a haven of alternative culture.

I started saving with my mind set on India, since I had no reason to stay in London. I ended up going to Australia not by choice but because of the salesmanship of the local travel agent who convinced me it was better value for money and a country where I could work to cover my costs.

Looking back, I would barely have survived Bombay airport. What I needed was confidence boosting and inner strength. I travelled to feel like myself again.

"I was aware that my English accent provided an unjust passport to acceptability"

Now, I really appreciate the advantages of, superficially at least, knowing the language and culture of a country: being able to find out where it is safe to hitch and where to avoid (like Queensland), getting money transferred easily and finding out all those essential travel tips almost straight away. In comparison with my other trips, Australia felt easy. "No worries, mate", as they say.

Arriving in Sydney, however, was a complete letdown: it looked so much like London. Why had I spent three days in an aeroplane travelling to the other side of the world to experience mildly less culture shock than I'd feel landing in Scotland? Three months later I was extending my visa and in love with this continent of astounding variety and quite unimaginable space.

I worked for two-and-a-half months in Sydney, as a waitress, packing boxes and video cassettes, selling soft toys and signing on. (I had a work permit.) Aussie officialdom, like the post, has a rough and ready flavour and tourists are given a welcome blind eye, despite mounting paranoia about the immigrant invasion of the so-called lucky country. At the same time I was aware that my English accent provided an unjust passport to acceptability. Aussies seem predominantly racist and arrogant when it comes to sharing their wealth, and though white Europeans get a good deal, it is not the same for Asian people or for Islanders from the Pacific.

I still had my ticket for India, but through a fateful meeting with an astrologer who showed me the *Nimbin News* I never used it. In good alternative style she convinced me that I needed to visit Nimbin – Aboriginal Sacred Territory, subtropical rainforest and so-called hippy centre of Australia. I arrived two days later and had one of my most memorable experiences ever. Sitting on the bus as we rolled in through the hills, tears poured down my cheeks on first seeing those magnificent Nimbin rocks and I immediately knew that this was where I wanted to be.

Walking into Nimbin I had the remarkable fortune to find a place to rent in the hills almost straight away. I stayed for ten months, working six days a week on the *Nimbin News*, the community newspaper and ecology campaign.

Nimbin is located in northern New South Wales, near Byron Bay, a haven of utopian ideals in a basically conservative land. It is a noble experiment of over thirty communes scattered across acres of hills, jungle, waterfalls and green valleys. Paradise, Bohdi Farm, Dharmananda, Crystal Kookaburra and Heaven are the names of these hamlets of hand-built houses where people grow herbs, keep goats, bake bread and bathe outside; where water wheels in streams provide electricity for televisions and videos; where staircases are built from tree trunks that look like tree trunks; where children go to "free" schools and babies are born at home. Nimbin has community shops, a newspaper, a circus, rebirthing and alternative technology.

"Nimbin is a haven for middle-class drop-outs, for junkies, homeless people, Aborigines, for mystics, astrologers, health freaks and Buddhists"

The community was set up to preserve the rainforest, which it did successfully over years of sit-ins and demonstrations. Living there means spiders and snakes and lots and lots of leeches, and being cut off for two weeks up the mountain in the wet season. My home was on the top of a hill, an hour's walk from the track and a half-hour hitch from the village. I shared it with wallabies, kookaburras, parrots and possums on my doorstep, and sometimes on the kitchen table.

Nimbin is a haven for middle-class drop-outs, for junkies, homeless people, Aborigines, for mystics, astrologers, health freaks and Buddhists. Home too for German and English migrants and the many who fit into no such stereotype, but like myself warmed to the carefree moonlit nights of guitars and festivity, of craft markets, down-to-earth living and wild country. I'll never forget walking into the *Rainbow Café* on the high street, seconds from the cupboard-size police station, to find drugs and carrot cake and an ambiance of gentle rebellion.

Nimbin is laid back yet active. Yet I read more newspapers than ever before. I wrote to more politicians and campaigned more actively for the rights of people in South America, Papua New Guinea and South Africa than during my "right on" days in London. I wrote about incest and women's experiences of violence in the home. I spent five days walking through the bush and waterfalls with a woman friend and her two-year-old child, without seeing a soul, nor fearing if we did. I met women who peed on the beach like men, and for all my feminist training I found myself to be far more romantic, idealistic and naive about men than these Aussie women who, despite driving trucks and working on prawn trawlers, still had a hard time being seen as anything more than a "Sheila". Their lack of willingness to compromise taught me a lot.

Nimbin is an island in Australia, a space that probably only exists because the country is so large, and those who hate its every association live a long way up north. However, survival is not that easy, as people campaign again and again for their community to be recognised by the government so as to ensure its protection. I recommend anyone to visit, for the magnificent countryside if nothing else. Stay a little longer at the Youth Hostel and in the café, and you'll find warm and friendly people and get a chance to visit the communities up in the surrounding hills. It took me a long time to recognise the subtle differences between here and Australia, but they grew on me. I finally left knowing that my experience had changed my life.

TRAVEL NOTES

Languages English is the official language, but you'll also find Italian, Greek, Serbo-Croat, Turkish, Arabic, Chinese and numerous Aboriginal languages.

Transport A good system of trains, buses and planes connects major cities. Public transport is expensive, but prices are competitive and it's a good idea to look around. Petrol is cheap by British standards so it's worth buying your own vehicle if you have the time and money. Hitching alone is not advisable.

Accommodation Suburban motels tend to be much cheaper than those in central locations. Sydney, especially, has lots of hostels geared up to travellers. Australians are very hospitable so don't be afraid to use any contacts you may have. University noticeboards can also be good sources (and for lifts too).

Special Problems Working visas are becoming increasingly hard to get, especially for visitors older than 26. Applications should be made well before you leave home and you will need evidence of sufficient funds to cover your trip.

Guides *Australia: A Travel Survival Kit* (Lonely Planet) is thorough, though written from an Australian perspective and sometimes assuming a bit too much knowledge. *A Traveller's Survival Kit to Australia and New Zealand* (Vacation Work) is the latest in this new series, worth checking out.

Contacts

It would be impossible to include here all Australian **feminist groups**. The following list focuses on some of the major cities – for more details take it from there.

ADELAIDE: **Women's Liberation House**, 1st Floor, 234A Rundle St., Adelaide 5000 ☎223-180.

BRISBANE: **Women's House**, 30 Victoria St., West End 4101 ☎44-4008. For women's radio in the city tune into Megahers on 102FM (5pm Tuesdays).

CANBERRA: **Women's Centre**, 3 Lobelia St., O'Connor 2601 ☎47-8070; **Women's Shopfront Information Service**, Ground Floor, CML Building, Darwin Place, Canberra 2600 ☎46-7266.

DARWIN: **Women's Information Service**, PO Box 2043, Darwin 5794 ☎81-2668.

MELBOURNE: **Women's Centre**, 259 Victoria St., West Melbourne 3000 ☎329-8515. Groups at this address include Women Against Rape, Lesbian Line, Women's Radio Collective and Women's Liberation Newsletter.

PERTH: **Women's Information and Resource Centre**, 103 Fitzgerald Rd., North Perth 6006 ☎328-5717.

SOUTH HOBART: **Women's Information Service**, 4 Milles St., South Hobart 7000 ☎23-6547.

SYDNEY: **Women's Liberation House**, 62 Regent St., Chippendale 2008 ☎699-5281.

Selected women's bookshops

ADELAIDE: **Murphy Sisters Bookshop**, 240 The Parade, Noward 5067 ☎332-7508.

BRISBANE: **Women's Book, Gift and Music Centre**, Cnr Gladstone Rd. and Dorchester St., Highgate Hill 4101 ☎332-7508.

SYDNEY: **The Feminist Bookshop**, 315 Balmain Rd, Lilyfield 2040 ☎810-2666.

VICTORIA: **Shrew**, 37 Gertrude St., Fitzroy 3065 ☎419-5595.

Books

Robyn Davidson, *Tracks* (Paladin Books, 1982). Compelling, very personal story of how the author learned to train wild camels and eventually sets off with four of them and a dog to explore the Australian desert.

Helen Garner, *Postcards from Surfers* (Bloomsbury, 1989). Recommended short stories by one of Australia's finest women writers.
Dorothy Hewett, *Bobbin Up* (Virago, 1985). Entertaining portrait of working-class life in Australia in the 1950s and only novel by one of the country's leading women playwrights, first published in 1959. Also look out for her forthcoming autobiography, *Wild Card* (Virago, 1990).

Pearlie McNeill, *One of the Family* (The Women's Press, 1989). Vivid account of her often unhappy life growing up in Sydney during the 1940s and 1950s.

Glenyse Ward, *Wandering Girl* (Virago, 1988). The author, an Aboriginal from Western Australia, tells her own story of growing up in a white world.

John Pilger, *Secret Country* (Jonathan Cape, 1989). This investigation into Australia's hidden history by one of the country's leading journalists incorporates a strong indictment against the persistent maltreatment of Aboriginal people.

Robert Hughes, *The Fatal Shore* (Pan, 1988). Riveting account of Australian settlement.

Jill Julius Mathews, *Good and Mad Women* (Allen and Unwin, 1984). Traces a history of Australian traditions behind the national ideal of the "good woman".

Susan Mitchell, *Tall Poppies* (Penguin, 1983). These profiles of ten successful Australian women make an inspiring and well-balanced read (the women come from all backgrounds and nationalities). The book has been a phenomenal best seller in Australia.

Sally Morgan, *My Place* (Virago, 1988). A powerful and widely acclaimed account of a young Aboriginal woman's search for her racial identity.

Bruce Pascoe et al., eds., *The Babe is Wise* (Virago, 1988). Excellent collection of contemporary short stories by Australian women writers.

Isobel White et al., eds., *Fighters and Singers: The Lives of Some Australian Women* (Allen and Unwin, 1984). Collection of stories focusing on the lives and strong characters of a number of Aboriginal women.

David Adams, ed., *The Letters of Rachel Henning* (Penguin, 1985). Written between 1853 and 1882, the letters give a vivid account of life in colonial Australia as seen through the eyes of a previously sheltered young Englishwoman.

Also novels by **Miles Franklin, Henry Handel Richardson and Christina Stead** — classics by and about women.

Other publications

Keith D. Suter and Kaye Stearman, *Aboriginal Australians* (Minority Rights Group, Report No. 35, 1977). This excellent report, revised and updated in 1988, includes useful addresses and a select bibliography.

There are many feminist magazines in Australia, among them *Girl's Own, Hecate, Womanspeak, Scarlet Woman* and *Liberation*.

Thanks to Christine Bond, Karen Hooper, Tessa Matyiewicz and Jenny Moore for their individual contributions to these Travel Notes.

Bangladesh

In the minds of most Westerners, Bangladesh remains synonymous with the worst ravages of war, famine and disaster. Whilst a superficial "stability" has been reached under President Ershard, who gained control of the military junta in 1982, the country continues in a state of devastating economic crisis made worse by the ever more frequent out-of-season floods.

In recent years very tentative attempts have been made to entice travellers from the usual subcontinent routes – "Come to Bangladesh before the tourists get here", being the main airline slogan. However this is not a country to visit casually. The degree of poverty experienced in the villages (where most of the country's 100 million people still live) can come as a shock even if you've travelled extensively around

India. Also as a predominantly Muslim country, although not formally an Islamic state, women are expected to conform to Islamic codes of dress and behaviour, a pressure which increases as the fundamentalist movement gains political ground. In the main towns, women are rarely seen in public and those who are, will usually be covered by a *burqua* (a form of veiling).

A number of Western women work in Bangladesh with the development agencies and relief organisations, and reports are that it is easier to travel alone here than in Pakistan. As a stranger (particularly if you are white) you are bound to attract attention – people may be intensely curious about you and astonished by your freedom to travel independently but this is usually expressed in a welcoming, friendly way, often showing great concern for your safety.

Aid and development agencies within the country are increasingly recognising that the long-term survival of impoverished rural communities will depend on how much **women** can be supported in their role as care-givers and providers. Operating at a very local level -- and within the confines of Muslim custom – projects have been set up to educate women in healthcare, nutrition and literacy.

Working in Development

. . . .

Christina Morton went to Bangladesh as a volunteer with a development project. She spent three-and-a-half months there, living mainly with Bengali families in Dacca and the surrounding villages.

During my stay in Bangladesh I experienced complete and profound culture shock – I doubt even now I can write objectively about what it's like to visit the country. I did not go as a tourist – few people do. My purpose was to observe, and as far as possible to participate in, some of the innumerable development projects which have sprung up since the war of independence with Pakistan.

In Bangladesh poverty permeates every facet of human existence, and emotional, cultural, social and political interactions are all to some extent determined by this. I would not, though, discourage anyone from visiting the country provided they were really prepared to open their eyes, their ears, their hearts and their minds to the society around them. This of course takes time and commitment, and it's debatable whether a very short stay would afford great insights.

I was lucky in that for most of the time I wasn't forced to stay in hotels but was able to live with Bangladeshi families, urban and rural, poor and not so poor. Also, though my status of single woman closed a few doors (inevitably of mosques and shrines), it brought me the huge advantage of contact with Bangladeshi women. Having been given initial introductions – most often, from men – I was allowed behind the veil of purdah to see the harshness of women's lives and feel their warmth, their gentleness and generosity.

This process was never easy and I would be emotionally exhausted at the end of a day. Bangladeshi women lack any comprehension of Westerners wanting privacy, and in addition I sometimes felt that I was not appearing as a person with depth, humanity and personality but as a symbol of promiscuity perhaps, of beauty – they have a high regard for white skin – but above all of affluence. Yet it was an unfailingly rewarding process to strip away layers of cultural differentiation, to build a bridge across the gulf that separated us in terms of economic circumstance, and to achieve, on occasion, that truly human contact which is the reward of all travellers.

"One of the names that was called after me was the Bengali word for eunuch"

Language was sometimes a problem. I never picked up as much Bengali as I could have wished, but there are sometimes better ways of communicating – signs, touch, laughter. Indeed there were times when I was positively glad to be unable to understand Bengali. Bangladesh is an Islamic country (not, like Pakistan, an Islamic State but under the influence of aid-giving Middle Eastern countries such as Saudi Arabia it becomes more dogmatically religious every day) and women are simply not seen in public places without the veil, or at least a male escort. Women who do venture out, women who like me walk about alone in the streets, are considered whores and are called after as such.

Sometimes my short hair and my unconventional clothing (I usually wore for modesty's sake – and I would advise any women to do the same – a long-sleeved hip-length shirt over trousers or a longish skirt) invited men to speculate about my sex and one of the names which was called after me was the Bengali word for eunuch. This did not really upset me, because on the whole I had anticipated far worse sexual harassment than I ever actually experienced, and indeed I often felt safer travelling alone in Bangladesh than I do crossing my home town in England.

My hosts, my fellow travellers and the friends I made were often beside themselves with anxiety on my behalf. "Where are your brothers?", they would ask, "Don't you need your father to protect you?", "Don't you miss your mother?" An independent and self-sufficient woman is indeed an enigma to them.

People are what a visit to Bangladesh is all about. There is little point in going if you are more interested in monuments (there are none) or a fun time (forget it). The only places that could be described as being of "tourist interest" are Sundarbans in the south (last remnants of genuine jungle, where people motorlaunch into the forest waterways in search of wildlife) and the 70-mile beach at Cox's Bazaar. But even if the will is there, the near total dearth of tourist facilities makes the usual indulgent "holiday resort" lifestyle impossible.

People, however, are everywhere, over a hundred million of them squashed into a country which is no bigger than England and Wales together. The vast majority live in the villages but even the ten million or so who form the urban population are sufficient to throng the streets and cram the public transport system to bursting. Every bus and railway carriage has almost as many bodies hanging from the outside as are squashed into the interior.

"I would be surrounded by crowds, sometimes scornful, suspicious or even hostile, sometimes merely curious, but mostly, or so it seemed to me, gentle and welcoming"

On a few occasions I visited villages where a white face had never been seen and where England (*Bilat*) was the stuff of legends and faded memories. In any such place I would be surrounded by crowds, sometimes scornful, suspicious or even hostile, sometimes merely curious, but mostly, or so it seemed to me, gentle and welcoming and always ready with hospitality – water, rice, the juice of the date palm, precious eggs.

Women in Bangladesh carry simultaneously the burdens imposed by economic exploitation, from both national and international sources, and a society which in both its religious and secular aspects is stubbornly patriarchal. Uncharacteristically, however, the government has legislated for a quota of ten to fifteen percent of women in employment in all areas of administration and industry, and several of the leading figures in the opposition political parties are women.

Far more significant, I felt, was the relative effectiveness of development schemes which have grasped that the recovery and advancement of the entire country would stand or fall on the improvement of the position of women – their health, their education, their nutrition and their participation in the political and economic organisation of their society.

Bangladesh is, in the villages at least, and particularly where endemic landlessness has rotted the social fabric from within, an embryonic gathering together of the fragments of a ravaged social structure into what is as yet the flimsiest of edifices, so fragile in the face of the odds stacked against it that you tremble for it.

What hope have 100 million souls, half of which hover at or below the poverty line, chronically malnourished, in the face of increasing landlessness among the peasants, a rocketing population (which is predicted to reach 150 million by the end of the century), an escalating national debt, a dearth of commodity resources and a heritage of feudalism and imperialism? All the problems which we now so glibly label "Third World" are concentrated in Bangladesh to a degree which will inevitably shock.

But projects such as *Gonoshastraya Kendra* (the People's Health Centre) just north of the capital, Dacca, and those working under the auspices of the Bangladesh Rural Advancement Committee (both entirely indigenous organisations, incidentally) have recognised the enormous potential for radical change and development which lies in the hands of women.

Women who are healthy, properly fed, basically literate and skilled, who have, in other words, access to the opportunities available in their society now and the chance to create further opportunities for the future – in their hands lies not merely *a* hope, but *the* hope of Bangladesh's future generations I could not avoid reflecting that this is a concept of social development with which the most advanced Western nations have in large measure yet to grapple.

Learning Village Life

. . . .

Katy Gardner, a British research student in anthropology, spent a year-and-a-half living in a village in the north of Bangladesh.

As the plane began its slow descent, a flat expanse of endless paddy fields and long winding rivers spread out beneath us. Closer down, scattered village compounds came into view: men driving bulls through mud, fishing nets spread across waterways, people working in their yards. At last we had arrived in Bangladesh.

It was the beginning for me of a sixteen-month stay. As a student of anthropology my task was relatively simple – to find myself a village and live in it, as much a part of the community as possible, to let the village people teach me about their lives. I had travelled fairly widely in India and Pakistan before, as well as in other parts of the Muslim world, and had always felt strongly drawn to the Indian sub-continent. I had also always found the role of a tourist, unable to speak the local languages, inherently frustrating. This time would be different. I would learn Bengali and actually get close to people where previously I had felt apart.

I made my base in Dacca, a sprawling and chaotic city which by any standards is hard to love, and tried to connect to its modern streets and shopping arcades, its pristine parliament building and ghetto of luxury mansions owned largely by aid donors, to what I felt must surely be the "real" Bangladesh – a country which is mainly rural, with a depressingly large percentage of its population below the poverty line.

Like many of the foreigners I stayed in the district of Gulshan with a friend in a huge house owned by an American donor agency. There was a 24-hour guard service, a full staff, and more rooms than could ever be used. Dacca, like most South Asian cities, is a place of contrasts. Close to this area, although well hidden from sight, were the horrific *bustees* of Dacca – vast areas of huddled huts made from polythene sheeting and jute matting, and down the road, the smog and crowds of the central city.

I was to visit Dacca many times in the months to come, taking breaks from my periods in the village, and although I enjoyed those spells of getting away from it all, I found it disturbingly easy to lead a life there quite separate from Bangladeshi people. Sadly, many of the expatriates have little to do with Bangladeshis socially, and rarely leave Dacca. Perhaps because of this lack of contact, and because the middle classes usually speak good English, many never get round to learning Bengali properly. I was shocked, but perhaps not really surprised by how quickly and easily some of the Westerners took to the master-servant relationships they were involved in. In some ways the Raj, albeit in the form of international aid, still continues.

But although foreigners driving smart jeeps around the city are a common sight, once outside the relative peace of the middle-class suburbs, they attract the usual crowds and stares common in the rest of Bangladesh, especially in the warren-like alleys and roads of the old city.

Foreign women are even more of an oddity; the streets of Dacca are crammed with people, but they are almost exclusively men. In the old city women, if seen at all, are hurrying past, wrapped up in their *burquas*, with faces averted. This does not mean that the atmosphere is hostile to foreign women, but women wandering about alone are conspicuous, an easy target, and I always took the warnings not to walk alone around the city at night seriously.

"A middle-class Bangladeshi said I would never survive the rigours of life without electricity, or eating rice with my hands"

So, after about a month of leading a lifestyle far more luxurious than I had at home, a development worker whom I had met on a trip up north to Sylhet introduced me to a family in his wife's village, and we decided that I should move in. Back in Dacca, a middle-class Bangladeshi said that I would never survive the rigours of life without electricity, or eating rice with my hands. White expatriates talked in terms of rabies injections and medicines, and I bought myself a mosquito net and a hurricane lamp.

I eventually moved into my new home one night in September, travelling by boat from the nearest road with a small group of villagers returning home from a trip to Sylhet. From June to October much of the country is under water, and even under normal, non-flooded conditions (the recent floods which have been so disastrous are not part of this seasonal pattern), many places can only be reached by the painted wooden boats of the villages. In November, the clouds and heat clear, and with the cooler, dry weather, fields and paths miraculously appear from a morass of mud. When the rains start in the spring these are inundated, and the landscape becomes watery once more.

"Although I never enjoyed it, I gradually became used to the excitement my appearance inevitably generated"

That evening we passed straggling villages, waterlogged fields, and groups of children on the paths calling out "Inreji! Inreji!" (English) when they saw me. Very few white people venture outside the urban areas and those that do are always assumed to be English. They are viewed with a mixture of amazement and extreme curiosity.

At the politest end of the continuum this leads to the eternal question: "What is your country?", at the other end huge crowds gather to gape and comment on your every move ("What is she doing? . . . Look, she's alone . . . She doesn't speak our language, she's white . . . Look, she's opening her bag . . . " etc, etc). Although I never enjoyed it, I gradually became used to the excitement my appearance inevitably generated.

Six hours later, and about five miles from the potholed road (the boat being not exactly speedy), long after the sun had set and the Bangladeshi sky turned violet, I arrived. Immediately I was surrounded by clusters of children and the many faces of my new adoptive family. I had of course already met them a month earlier, but I still had no idea who was who, especially as many of the children and younger women had felt unable to come out in front of me and the distantly-related town man who had been my escort.

Now, everyone was present: Amma, my new mother, who took my hand and pronounced immediately that I should be just like a daughter to her; Abba, my dad, who shuffled in to receive my Salaam and then with a chuckle went back to his hookah; and numerous young women – my sisters who were to become my closest friends. I understood hardly anything that was being said to me but it didn't really matter. In a process which was to be repeated many, many times in the following weeks by every family in the village, I was inspected and commented upon. "Look, she's so tall," they said, "Look, she doesn't wear a sari . . . Why don't you wear oil in your hair? . . . Yallah, she's not a proper Londoni, she isn't fat enough . . . Look at her great earrings . . . " and so on.

I didn't really mind these appraisals, since they were a quick way of striking up friendships and of proving that I was no threat and quite prepared to make a fool of myself. More or less everything I did caused outbursts of laughter (whether I'd intended it to or not) and nothing more so than my pathetic attempts to speak the Sylheti dialect. Not surprisingly nobody understood why I should possibly want to live with them and learn. "How can you learn here?", they asked, "Where are your schoolbooks?"

Eventually most people accepted that for some extraordinary reason, I spent hours writing and asking exceedingly stupid questions and wanted to live in their village. "But why come here?", I was often asked, "Your country is a land of peace and richness. Why are you here when we all want to be there?"

Everyone agreed that I had to start at the basics if I wanted to live as they did. "Katy," one of my sisters, Khaola, announced as she eyed me making a mess with my supper of rice that first week, "you're just like a baby, but don't worry, after a year with us we'll make you into a proper Bengali." She was right, I had a long way to go.

Everything I did at first was watched, criticised, laughed at, and corrected. I had to learn how to tie a sari, bathe in the family pond, how to wash out my clothes properly on the stone steps, how to eat my rice, spit, use water in the latrine and much, much more. Compared with the other women, I was a complete oaf and indeed, hardly female. I was clumsy at cutting bamboo or vegetables on the great blades the women squat over, unable to light the fire, and hopelessly inelegant in a sari, which kept riding over my heels. Worse than that, I kept forgetting to cover my head.

As I let the village people mould me, however, I began to learn much about the essence of being a Muslim woman in rural Bangladesh. To be approved of, you must be as feminine and submissive as possible. You must dress in a certain way; your hair must be tied back and smoothed with oil, otherwise you will be seen as "mad" and manly; your sari must be tied properly and your blouse fit in the correct way. There are certain bits of you which must never be shown, especially your legs and ideally your head should always be covered. You must talk quietly, not call out or run; you must be shameful and obedient to your menfolk. An old adage, which village women often quote, is that: "A woman's heaven is at her husband's feet".

"When strange men came into the family compound, I jumped up with the other women and ran inside, feeling genuinely ashamed"

I certainly failed on most counts of modesty, especially as I never succeeded in changing into a new sari after bathing without revealing myself, or in keeping it continually over my head. But slowly, as I stayed longer in the village, I noticed that a transformation had happened in my values as well as my appearance. Not only had I begun to sit, dress and talk like the village women, but to my amazement I began to express the same sorts of ideas. "It is the will of Allah", I heard myself telling people, and when strange men came into the family compound, like the other women I too jumped up and ran inside, feeling genuinely ashamed. If I went out without an umbrella to keep my face hidden, I felt naked.

It was alarming, to say the least. If fourteen months can have effects like that on such a product of Western feminism as I had considered myself to be, what would happen after two years or more? And what did it imply about the security of my beliefs if they could be so easily moulded by a new environment?

Of course this doesn't happen to all Western women who visit Bangladesh. My need to be open to the culture and customs of my hosts left me peculiarly vulnerable. Bangladesh is a very difficult country to get to the heart of, and many visitors leave feeling unsympathetic towards it. This is perhaps because although extremely friendly, Bangladeshis tend to be on their guard with foreigners. The country has had a short, violent and politically unstable history, and foreigners, who originally came to Bengal to rule, now usually come as dispensers of aid or advice. "What project do you work for?", is almost as ubiquitous a question as "What is your country?", and many foreigners inadvertently end up as the patron of a Bangladeshi. I was continually asked for money by people in the village. Poor women would come into my room and ask for saris or *taka* – they felt that since I was rich, which I must have been since I was white, it was my duty to give. I nearly always refused, knowing that I could not manage the stream of requests and people's expectations of me had I taken those initial steps. However frequent this became I never managed to get accustomed to the requests and demands made of me, or my hollow excuses that I wasn't *really* rich. When I left, I gave away all my clothing, bedding, etc and even my bras, which various women had been eyeing all year. One of the last things which one old destitute woman said to me was: "Now you have your own poor, we are your responsibility now."

Just as relationships with foreigners can be coveted, leading as they might to patronage and help, they can also be regarded with horror, due to our dirty ways, loose women and alcohol consumption. This ambivalence is especially strong towards young white Western women. We are respected because we are probably involved in aid, and certainly rich, yet viewed with unease because of our independence. One of the most common reactions I had when meeting people from outside the village was a horrified: "But are you alone? Aren't you married?" So that after sixteen months I too began to see myself as some kind of freak.

Although people may be surprised, even affronted, to see a woman alone, I always felt that Bangladesh was a relatively safe place to travel in. Wherever I went, people were anxious to help me (whether I needed it or not) and get talking. I travelled by trains, local buses, planes and ferries, and always ended these journeys with new friends. Speaking the language helps of course, as does dressing appropriately – I always wore *shalwar kameez* (baggy trousers and long tops), and an *orna* (scarf worn over the chest), or in the village, a sari.

"Why should we be afraid of you, sister?' I was told so many times, 'Aren't we all women?'"

My sex was far more of a blessing than a curse, which I have sometimes felt it to be in other countries. Whilst most rural women would never talk to foreign men, wherever I went I was welcomed into women's quarters. Our Western inhibitions do not exist in these places and friendship is easily and unquestionably offered. "Why should we be afraid of you, sister?" I was told so many times, "Aren't we all women?"

Sixteen months after landing in Dacca, I began to prepare for leaving the village. Many of the villagers asked me to stay, "You can become a Muslim, we'll arrange a husband for you." I wasn't so sure about the conversion or the husband, but leaving was certainly extremely difficult.

The day I went, many people came to our homestead. A tinsel garland was put around my head, and Amma fed me the special sweetmeats she had made. A crowd of people then led me down to the river where a boat was waiting to take me back to the road across the flooded fields, this time for good. As was expected of us, we all cried. The boat punted me away while I looked back at the figures, dwindling against the green fields behind. I knew that my return to Britain would not mean that I would stop being their daughter and that we would write regularly. Now, after a few months in London I am already planning my return.

Bangladesh is a powerful and very beautiful place, with golden winters, lush greenness and kingfishers darting over great rivers of water lilies. My image of the country had been largely of a poverty stricken land, precariously surviving an endless cycle of famine, and bloody coups – swollen-bellied children with begging bowls staring out at me from the TV news or Sunday supplements. That poverty and suffering are very real, yet throughout my time in Bangladesh I was constantly reminded that the ways in which it is portrayed by the Western media conceal in a cloak of sensationalism that the majority of Bangladeshis are extraordinarily resilient. They do as they have always done – they carry on.

TRAVEL NOTES

Languages Bengali. English is widely spoken.

Transport Flights between towns are incredibly cheap. There's a limited rail network and a few buses but these tend to be old, decrepit and massively overcrowded. Boats, paddle launches and steamers are the usual forms of transport in the south. Bangladeshi women tend not to travel without a male escort and can easily be overprotective towards a lone woman. It's often possible to arrange lifts with foreign workers, many of whom have jeeps.

Accommodation Outside Dacca there are very few hotels (or any sort of tourist facilities). You may find rooms in guesthouses but there's nothing like the range in India or Pakistan. Bangladeshis can be very hospitable – the responsibility is yours to pay for as much as you can. As a guest you should always offer some sort of gift.

Special Problems As in any Muslim country, you should dress extremely modestly with loose clothes covering arms and legs. (Non-Muslims are not allowed into mosques or shrines.) Only a few hotels in Dacca sell alcohol and it would certainly be frowned upon for a woman to drink alone.

Guides *Bangladesh – A Travel Survival Kit* (Lonely Planet) is the best-known but can be inaccurate in places. *Bangladesh – a Traveller's Guide* (Roger Lascelles) gives a useful overview.

Contacts

Bangladesh Rural Advancement Committee (BRAC), 66, Mohakhali Commercial Area, Dacca 12. A private, non-profit making organisation of Bangladeshis engaged in development work. BRAC initiated the Jamalpur Women's Programme in 1976, which focuses on skills training, health education and literacy. It has also set up many women's work co-operatives and produces a regular mimeographed newsletter.

National Women's Federation, Rumy-Villa, 88 Santinagar, Dacca. Organises income-generating and health education projects.

Bangladesh Mohila Samity, 104-a New Bailey Road, Dacca. A new group geared towards campaigning for equal status and providing educational and employment opportunities, especially for rural women. It has branches all over the country and runs two educational institutions and a number of cottage industries.

Books

Betsy Hartmann and James Boyce, *A Quiet Violence – View from a Bangladeshi village* (Zed Books, 1983). An account of the role of women in a rural society.

Katy Gardner has written a book of her experiences in a Bangladeshi village, to be published by Virago, 1991.

Bhutan

· ·

After centuries of almost complete isolation from Western influences, the Himalayan kingdom of Bhutan has recently and very guardedly begun to admit Western visitors. It's a privilege, however, well beyond the means of most ordinary travellers. Whilst willing to make some concessions in the interests of foreign exchange, the government of King Jigme Singye Wangchuck is determined to avoid the cultural havoc wreaked by open tourism in nearby Nepal.

His solution has been to limit the number of tourist visas to approximately two thousand a year, and restrict them to visitors arriving on accredited (and incredibly expensive) "luxury tours".

Even after gaining access to the country there are only a few permitted areas of travel. The terrain is difficult and, in order to get away from the capital and into the villages, where the majority of people live, your only option is to trek. There are companies that organise such expeditions but, again, with a hefty charge levied for each day spent in the country. The only way round this is if you arrive on invitation from someone working in the country – foreign workers are allowed a quota of two visitors a year.

Due to its strategic importance, as a borderland between northeast India and Tibetan China, Bhutan was one of the first British protectorates to be established in the Indian subcontinent and English continues to be taught in the state schools. It's a predominantly Buddhist country (with a large Hindu minority in the south) and although formally governed by a constitutional monarchy, the Buddhist clergy still wield considerable power at a local as well as national level. Away from a few urban centres, life continues more or less unchanged from the centuries-old traditions of Himalayan subsistence farming. Communication by roads, wireless, radio and newspaper is still in its early stages and although attempts are being made to introduce formal education to the villages (as part of a general modernisation programme) many still rely on monastic teaching.

Lacking a developed professional class of its own, Bhutan has had to import foreign advisers and teachers, mainly from India and Nepal, although recently work visas have been given to Western volunteers. There are a few women working in the country on two- or three-year contracts. From our correspondence with Lesley Reader (see below) it would seem that Westerners are becoming more familiar in the fairly affluent valley of the capital, Thimpu, but in the more remote Himalayan villages are an incredibly rare sight and a source of both fascination and fear. The conventions and popular beliefs that shape village life vary greatly from area to area. Whilst men on the whole occupy positions of status in the community, **women** are valued as the mainstay of the extended family and in many areas property is inherited through the female line. Attitudes regarding divorce, adultery, illegitimacy, or education for girls can differ even between villages only a day's walk apart.

From Sunderland to Ura

. . . .

Lesley Reader came to Bhutan, from England, in 1986 on a three-year voluntary contract. As part of a project that aimed to improve the quality of state primary schooling she took up a post first in Ura, a small village in the centre of the country, and then in Buli, lower, warmer and more remote. She was the first Westerner to make her home in these villages.

"Well, there are jobs in Zimbabwe, Nepal, Kenya or Bhutan. What do you think?" The voice on the telephone paused. I looked out of the window on to the depressed and depressing Sunderland landscape and tried hard to conjure up the distant and exotic worlds itemised by the woman from the London Headquarters of Voluntary Service Overseas (VSO). It was impossible.

"I'd like to go to Bhutan," I said.

"What do you know about it? Where is it?" she asked. Not unreasonable questions in view of its size, inaccessibility to most people and absence from the world media.

"It's to the right of Nepal and I know enough," I claimed boldly.

I had applied to VSO in a state of boredom with my job, disillusionment with house owning, disgust at the rat race and horror of the increasing materialism of life in England. It seemed to me that I could run away from it all or I could stay and try to improve matters by involving myself in politics at some level. I decided to run.

Four months after the phone call I was actually among the mountains of Bhutan. And two-and-a-half years later, as I write, I am still here. I realise now that I didn't know enough when I arrived, don't know enough now and, indeed, even if I stayed forever, would never know enough about this foreign land and its people where I feel so much at home.

It seems that there are two distinct Bhutans for me. One is the remote Himalayan Kingdom, last remaining Shangri-la, mystical, almost magical place described in guidebooks and glossy travelogues, with scenery beyond words, peace beyond imagining and people of such friendliness, generosity of spirit and contentment that they are special indeed. Remarkable as it seems, this is a true picture.

But it exists alongside the other Bhutan. The Bhutan of sheer slog and drudgery for its people, where ill health, illiteracy, ignorance, and a terrifyingly low life expectancy prevail; where people lead short lives made painful, both physically and emotionally, by hardship. I sat in my friend's house in the village the other evening and her mother looked at me carefully, and said "we go to the fields every day and we become old women very quickly. You teach in school all day and you will become old very slowly". She is right. Yet slowly things are changing.

"I met a group of women on the path a few days ago. They closed their eyes at the sight of me, covered their ears and shook with fear at my approach"

Increased contact with other nations, both by foreigners being allowed into the country and with Bhutanese people being sent abroad to study, has increased the awareness of the potential for improving the situation. But this is only among some. Much of the country is isolated and unvisited either by tourists or aid workers. I met a group of women on the path a few days ago. They closed their eyes at the sight of me, covered their ears with their hands and shook with fear at my approach They had never seen a Westerner before and thought I was a white ghost. It will be a long time before any of the advantages of development touch their lives But it will also be a long time before they have to cope with its disadvantages.

In the more urban centres crime has increased, consumerism raised its ugly head and dissatisfaction at the disparity between rich and poor affected the normal equilibrium of the Buddhist temperament. The balancing act being attempted by the royal government between improving the lives of the people while avoiding the worst pitfalls of "civilisation" makes a tightrope walk across Niagara Falls look like a gentle stroll in the park.

The majority of the Bhutanese are subsistence farmers. In harsh terms that means if you don't farm well you don't fill your stomach. It means working sixteen-hour days of hard physical toil when the work has to be done: dragging yourself weary from your bed well before dawn to get to the fields so as to make use of every second of daylight. The people of Buli did this for more than three weeks at a stretch during rice planting. In my enthusiasm to take an equal part I managed a day- and-a-half with them one weekend and lurched back to the classroom on Monday morning, certain I would never walk upright again. For me it was a new experience, for them the stakes are higher.

In addition to the inexorable demands of the land they must expend considerable ingenuity to find a source of cash as money has become increasingly necessary, perhaps to take a relative to hospital. Sometimes the family or a neighbour helps out, sometimes they can sell butter, cheese or eggs. It isn't easy. They must live with the knowledge that they, their crops and their livestock are at the mercy of unseasonal weather, wild animals or disease. Most cannot read or write although the majority now send at least some children to school in the hope that they will eventually get a job away from the land and so have a steady income. One son, or maybe more if the family is large and the lands sufficient to support them, may be sent to a monastery to become a monk.

"Into this land I arrived from my comfortable terraced house in Newcastle-upon-Tyne"

The main source of information is oral; the weekly government newspaper is incomprehensible to many villagers and any printed matter must be taken to a sympathetic teacher or Lama for understanding. There may or may not be someone in the village with a radio (and the necessary batteries) to listen to the daily broadcasts of news, information or music from the capital which is often many days' journey away. People do not travel much; there is no reason and it is expensive and time consuming.

Knowledge of the outside world is limited, very often, to a few visits to the local "town" and administrative headquarters. In many ways people have little control over their lives, they either have to work to grow food or starve. Fortunately very few Bhutanese go hungry; there is adequate land for a small number of people. But as the government realises, the population is growing and improved farming methods are going to be needed for the picture to remain so rosy.

Into this land I arrived from my comfortable terraced house in Newcastle-upon-Tyne; central heating, automatic washing machine, freezer, a garden that was a wilderness as I knew nothing about growing anything, a car and deep feelings of wanting something different. As I passed my first few days in late winter at over ten and a half thousand feet in Ura, the tiny village in the Himalayas that was to be my home for the next two years, it dawned on me that I had certainly found it.

I was alone and relished what lay ahead, whatever that may turn out to be. I decided to learn the language, find out what life in this beautiful but harsh environment was about and participate in as much as I could. Of course, in some matters there was no choice: I had to adopt local ways; my water was in the stream with everyone else's, I had a pile of wood and an earthen cooking stove to get my food cooked and my pit latrine was out the back. The wind scythed through the myriad tiny cracks in the house walls as it funnelled up the valley every afternoon and the closest electricity was a long way over the horizon. For many weeks I considered it quite a feat just to feed myself, wash my clothes and keep warm. It was to be a long time before I even bothered about washing myself!

In other respects I did have a choice. I could have just spoken English and restricted my social contacts to the staff at school and the few other people in the valley who would understand me. I need not have adopted the national costume. I could have declined to drink the local distillation. I could have stayed in my school quarters and not moved out to live in the temple. I could have refused blessings from the local Lamas. I could have stayed home and not sallied forth with the archery team for a weekend in a neighbouring valley. I could have, but I didn't. And the fact that I had the pleasure of so many remarkable experiences was due to my Bhutanese neighbours.

I was the first Westerner to live in Ura. As such I was the subject of considerable curiosity. For my first two weeks there were twenty faces peering in at my windows each morning watching me eat breakfast. Their disappointment was palpable as they realised I opened my mouth, put food in, chewed and swallowed just like they did. The favourite occupation of some of the smaller children was to stand next to my washing line and watch my multi-coloured knickers, bra, jeans and other exotic clothes flap in the wind.

My entertainment value was considerable and every activity was scrutinised. As their confidence grew I was questioned as to why I took all my clothes off to wash, why I used paper after I'd been to the toilet, why I walked up the mountain at the weekend when I had no work to do there. And to their, and my, delight, after much struggle they could do this in their own language.

> *"'I know who you are,' he said, 'you're the Ura teacher, I'd heard tell there was a teacher there who could speak our language.'"*

At first no one understood why I wanted to learn, then they despaired of me ever managing it, then every person I encountered took it upon themselves to teach me until I thought my brain would explode. Finally after two years they would proudly inform any visitor to the valley, "You know our foreign teacher? She speaks our language."

Once, when visiting a school a day's walk to the north of the village I met an old man walking towards me down the mountain path. We began the usual greetings. He stopped after a short while, "I know who you are," he said, "you're the Ura teacher, I'd heard tell there was a teacher there who could speak our language," he nodded, "it's true, you can." With encouragement like this it was hardly surprising I succeeded. It is the greatest achievement of my life.

In all their curiosity and interest there seemed to be no malice; they enquired, noted the differences and let me carry on, however bizarre they obviously found me. One question that came up again and again related to my family. As an only child (that was considered peculiar and sad enough in itself), they wanted to know how I could leave my elderly parents to travel for so many days across the sea to live amongst strangers. I tried, oh I tried, to convey curiosity, the reality of city life, itchy feet, philanthropy and whatever else my confused motives contained.

But I know that although they might be able to imagine themselves, if they tried very hard, in some of the strange situations I described; living with electricity, driving a car, buying everything from a shop, having a tap in the house, they could never imagine journeying so far from one's family and staying away for so long out of choice. Such a thing was strange indeed.

In Bhutan, the family are your mainstay in times of crisis; they and neighbours will rally round if food runs out, if someone falls sick, if someone dies or if more help is needed in the fields. They are the buffer in misfortune, easing your burdens physically and psychologically. In my case contact with my family was limited to letters. In Buli the postman came every ten days or so, he can rarely have had anyone waiting with such anticipation for him to amble along the path.

The other means by which people achieve control over their fate lies in religion. In the northern part of Bhutan this is Tibetan Buddhism. Seeing its influence on the everyday lives of people, I sought to find out more about this gentle religion. Unfortunately I wasn't fluent enough to grasp the deeper philosophy but I began to attend ceremonies, leave offerings, receive blessings, and later I was given a Bhutanese name. I don't know what much of it means but I do know that it is about living in the present, and that's fine by me.

And where do women fit into all of this? Well, it depends. In the south of the country the majority of the population originate from Nepal and have retained their language, culture and Hindu religion. Of this I know nothing. My life is among the Buddhists in the north. I have been told on many occasions by people far better travelled than I, that compared to the rest of Asia "it's not too bad".

I am not knowledgeable enough to argue. But to my mind there are considerable inequalities. In the village where

I live some work is divided between the sexes; both men and women work in the fields, tend the cows and fetch firewood. Some work seems to be the province of one or the other; men usually do the ploughing, women plant the paddy, women care for the children and do the housework. It isn't rigid and if circumstances dictate then the completion of the work is more important than who does it. However, within the community, the majority of those with status are men; Lamas, village headmen, elected representatives are all men, most teachers and the vast majority of headteachers are men; most health workers, animal husbandry workers and agricultural extension workers are men.

At school the drop-out rate among girls is far higher than for boys. At the local school in Class X, the equivalent to "O" level year, there is one girl and 59 boys. Double standards prevail about sexuality; boys are allowed and indeed expected to be promiscuous, girls are expected to be faithful to one partner. Yet the society is tolerant, the extended family absorbs illegitimate children and the victims of broken marriages just as it absorbs widows and orphans. Many marriages end in divorce, usually when a man tires of his wife and finds a new one. Not many women initiate divorce although there is no legal or social prohibition against them doing so.

My own perceptions have been that more women than men are victims in unsatisfactory relationships, they remain tied to husbands who beat them, are unfaithful to them and generally treat them shabbily. But I admit to a biased view. It needs to be stated that the expectations from marriage are very different from those in the West. In Bhutan it is the cement to bind the social fabric, it brings an additional worker into a household, and through children forms an insurance for old age. Emotional support from a spouse may be an added bonus but in general is found elsewhere.

The women I met were strong, vibrant, outspoken, bawdy and the mainstay of the community. On marriage a man moves to his wife's house and becomes part of her family.

"Coming back late from my friend's house I am warned only about ghosts and bears. I have never met either"

Consequently the birth of a daughter is greatly celebrated as she will later bring much needed manpower to the house. In their everyday lives the women are not constrained as long as the work is attended to. They travel if they need to, they decide on their own work and they drink alcohol if they wish. It's the same for me; I am free to travel where and when I wish. Bhutanese custom dictates that one must offer all possible hospitality to visitors and travellers, and arriving anywhere at any time of the day or night one is immediately looked after. Any man approaching me to ask who I am and where I am going merely wishes to know who I am and where I am going. Coming back late from my friend's house I am warned only about ghosts and bears. I have never met either.

Women speak out at village meetings and, on social occasions, more than hold their own in the verbal sparring that inevitably takes place between the sexes. Yet in their everyday life it would be impossible to have a simple friendship with a member of the opposite sex. These expectations applied to me also; my friends in the village were all women. If any man were seen walking or talking with me it would be instantly assumed we were having an affair. And if he was married the wrath of his wife would traditionally descend upon me, as the "other woman", rather than upon the errant husband.

My friends here in Buli are women of all ages. Just as I am a woman alone, the majority of them are either widows, women with husbands absent in the army or single women. They arrived in my house the evening after I reached Buli bearing many bottles of local booze and we all got drunk. We have been together ever since. They bring me rice, vegetables, local alcohol, they teach me to plant, harvest and thresh rice, and cook me dinners of rice and chillies when they see that I'm struggling.

They try to understand why I don't want a husband and children, they worry about the fact that I will have no one to carry me to my cremation when I die and they answer my innumerable questions about their life, Universe and everything. I take their photographs, cook them egg and chips, read and write letters, cut their hair, help them out with cash and tell them about my life and country.

"As far as people here are concerned, to be on one's own is to be lonely and true friends make sure that I am never in that unfortunate state"

In their attempts to try and understand more about this strange, but entertaining phenomenon in their midst they ply me with questions; why the double-decker buses in the picture of London had no driver on top, where were our rice fields, where did we keep our yaks, how did we cook and keep our saucepans clean? They wanted to know about my parents' house and were astonished to see a picture of a block of flats. They sat mesmerised as I explained how my parents use a lift to get to the thirteenth floor and couldn't understand why I didn't know every single person in my village (London). I fear they have ended up with strange ideas of England. In some ways it doesn't matter, and in other ways it does.

I am rarely completely alone. As far as people here are concerned, to be on one's own is to be lonely and true friends make sure that I am never in that unfortunate state. Sometimes this can feel a burden. I once became sick. As is my habit I took to my bed to sleep. Every five minutes somebody arrived to wake me up and talk to me, they came in relays of two or three for three days. I was demented, I craved sleep, healing sleep. If I had possessed enough strength, the expression "bugger off and leave me alone" might have been verbalised. As it was I lay and suffered.

Inevitably I recovered and questioned my tormentors, although obviously torment was the last thing on their minds. They had come to protect me from the spirits. For spirits are particularly aware of vulnerable souls: those of the sick and anyone who sleeps during the day. They had come to look after me and I in turn have gone to visit sick people for this reason.

So I live all day in a crowd, I live with the constant knowledge that something strange and unexpected may be about to happen; my friends arrive to take me to a wedding, to the temple to get a blessing from an important Lama or from some sticks that have come by magical means from Tibet. I'm aware, however, that I can still only appreciate from the outside what it means to have been born here, to grow up and to expect to die in this tiny valley. To say there is never a dull moment is absolutely true. No it certainly isn't Shangri-la. It's better.

Walking with Margaret

. . . .

Before setting off on a three-day trek from Ura to her new post in Buli, Lesley Reader met Margaret, an English science teacher who had been working in Bhutan for two years. They completed the trek together.

The first hiccup came when I left the monks. Or maybe they lost me, or avoided me, or ran away. I wanted to walk from Ura, ten-and-a-half thousand feet up in the mountains, my home for two years, to Buli, lower, warmer, three-and-a-half days' walk away. The monks were heading in that general direction, perhaps to meet their Lama, escape from work, or do whatever the large numbers of monks who seem forever to be roaming the Bhutanese countryside do. They had been asked by the head-master to take me along; then they had vanished. Perhaps they had heard about my unique walking style.

At that point Margaret came to my rescue. A teacher in the far west of Bhutan, her trekking exploits have entered local mythology. "Ah, the tall foreign woman, no friend", villagers in remote corners of the country reminisce about the solitary visit, her fearlessness, her remarkably fast walking and her consumption of the local booze. Fortuitously she arrived as my plans disintegrated and took me in hand. We'd go to Buli together; I was daunted.

She seemed so much better equipped than I was for striding the hills. Uphill my lungs go on strike, downhill my knees creak and along the flat I look at the scenery and trip over my own feet. Added to this I get vertigo when more than ten inches off the ground, so all in all, wandering about in the middle of the highest mountains on earth I was hardly in my element. Margaret took seven-eighths of the

baggage, leaving me the feeble rest. She said it would even out our walking speeds. It didn't, but she complained not a syllable, looked not a dagger and more importantly, refused to leave me in the wilderness.

We left Ura in the freezing cold with snow swirling in flurries around us. The first day-and-a-half took us 800 feet to bananas in the forest and leeches (indescribably yucky) in the shoes. The path winds down, down and yet more down from blue pines at the top to tropical ferns and lushness at the bottom. It follows a river gorge as the raging, white water plummets down on its southwards journey to India; the roar of its passage a constant counterpoint to my gasping for breath and frequent comments, "Oh, shit" as I slithered once again on my, fortunately well-padded, backside.

> *"I concentrated on putting one foot successfully in front of the other when all I really wanted to do was sit down and cry"*

The scenery is truly remarkable. On either side of the river massive forested hills rise up thousands of feet, enormous spurs of the hillside encroach into the main gorge for as far as the eye can see until they vanish into the mists of the horizon. Perched way up, on what passes as flat land in these parts are small villages; each house surrounded by steeply terraced fields. Pitifully small pools of cultivation are carved painfully out of the oceans of jungle waiting just metres away to take over again.

"We'll sleep the first night in a cave," said Margaret, who'd done this sort of thing before. Her concept of "cave" however was a little different to mine. I couldn't tell you the exact critical point at which a rock turns into a snug, secure and inviting dwelling, but it seemed to me that lying along the bottom of the cliff face with just enough overhang to stop the rain drenching us, we were not even close to it.

I slept the sleep of the dead tired, putting aside all thoughts of bears, snakes, wild pigs and other beasties and woke the next morning with aches I could never have imagined. Every moving part hurt. Stunned by pain (mine) and beauty (Bhutan's), the day passed in a blur as I concentrated on putting one foot successfully in front of the other when all I really wanted to do was sit down and cry.

As pitch darkness surrounded us (why is there never a moon when you want one?) we arrived at the first house we had seen since leaving Ura. The people, obviously poor, and totally bemused at finding two foreign women wandering around in the night, took us in. They gave us floor space to sleep on and the use of their fire to cook our supper. Gradually they became less shy and as I could understand some of their dialect, we began to converse. Suddenly they asked, "In your village foreigner's village, we have heard you have machines to do your housework." I nodded. "Tell us," they demanded.

It would take these people at least two days' hard walk, up the 8000 feet we had already come, to reach a road. They would then need to journey further to find anything even resembling a town. I didn't know if they had ever encountered electricity. How on earth had they heard about machines? My language was simply not good enough to find out. I searched my mind and, hands providing action where words failed, told them about washing machines. I had never seen people stunned into silence before.

When I finished my monologue they looked at each other, shook their heads in amazement and carried on eating as though I had never spoken. Who knows what thoughts of wonder, disbelief and perhaps irritation at the, no doubt, fantasising foreigners were going through their minds.

The next morning we left late. My aches and pains were settling down. Instead of every single part of my body hurting I now had distinct spots of agony; about two thousand of them. Coming over the crest of a hill we saw a beautiful white *chorten*. They dot the Bhutanese countryside containing relics, prayers and sacred objects representing the Buddhist universe.

"Waiting for us and us alone, was a Lama, the Lama from the village near Ura – my Lama who had given me my Bhutanese name"

Sitting resting at the base, as though waiting for us and us alone, was a Lama, the Lama from the village near Ura – my Lama, who had given me my Bhutanese name. Not old, not young, pious, bawdy, serious and startlingly funny, without a word of English, he had the most amazing desire and ability to understand and communicate.

I knew him well and he'd met Margaret the previous winter. He sat and watched us approach as though it was a prearranged appointment. Maybe it was. For him. We chatted, gossiped, exchanged gifts and drank far too much alcohol. He set up a makeshift altar and began his prayers, stopping after a while to pick up a metal statue that had obviously been broken and repaired. Carefully he explained to us that when the statue had been damaged it had been heard to scream. Sitting in the middle of the most dramatic scenery I had ever encountered, beside the Lama, with my brain whirling from the amount I had had to drink, it all seemed perfectly possible. And strangely enough it still does.

Blessings accomplished, regretful farewells completed and promises to meet again sworn, we set off on our separate ways; the Lama back up to Ura, Margaret and I in search of Buli, which I was beginning to imagine was transporting itself by some magical means further and further away from me. By this time it was ridiculously late. Time keeping was not helped when we decided to wash off the worst of the grime and inebriation in a freezing cold stream.

We didn't manage to reach a village that night and slept in a hut on stilts in a rice field. The inadequacies of the roof only became apparent in the middle of the night when the rain began; merely another discomfort to add to the multitude. I was beginning to get the hang of living in agony. I had reached a stage of acceptance of my fate, which seemed to be to slog for the rest of my days up interminable slopes only to slip and slide right down the other side.

As I contemplated the path ahead it seemed to ascend straight up a terrifying looking mountain. Surely my eyes were deceiving me? They weren't. Up we went, then up a bit more, then a bit more, and then further still, round, down a touch, round, down and then steep, steep down some more. Finally, unbelievably, we reached Buli.

In pitch darkness, still no moon, and pouring rain (this was supposed to be the dry season for goodness sake), I staggered to the first house. "I'm the new teacher," I gasped. Traditional hospitality took over. We were fed, watered (with something much stronger and more invigorating than water) and bedded down. The following morning I started school and Margaret left to stroll over some impassable looking mountains and create more amazement wherever she trod.

TRAVEL NOTES

Languages There's a great deal of regional variation in languages and dialects – all of which are hard to pick up. Dzongkha, the national language, is taught in schools but spoken only in the west of Bhutan. English remains the language of instruction, but with formal education being so limited very few people outside of the towns will speak it.

Transport is extremely rudimentary. There are no airports; entry to the country is by bus from Darjeeling in India to the capital, Thimphu. Tour groups usually have coaches laid on but though there are local buses, many villages are a long trek from the roads. Travelling and trekking is sturdy work but helped by the open-handed generosity of the Bhutanese people. From June to September (monsoon season) travel is likely to be severely disrupted.

Accommodation Besides the air conditioned hotel in Phuntsoling built for the luxury tours and a scattering of government rest houses, there are a few spartan hostels for local people.

Special Problems The biggest is gaining entry. Visas are by direct application only to the Director of Tourism, Thimphu, three months in advance; tours available through *Bhutan Travel.* Transit permits can be gained from the Indian High Commission but travelling through can be very expensive ($150 a day at present). Most large overseas voluntary agencies – VSO, VSA (New Zealand), WUSC (Canada), UNV, FAO, WHO, other branches of the UN and Helvitas (Switzerland) – supply workers to Bhutan. Once there, the obvious problems are language, altitude, and the many and various physical demands of rural subsistence in the Himalayas. Take everything you need by way of contraception, sanitary protection and medicine with you.

Guides *The Insight Guide to Asia* (Harrap Columbus) has a small section on Bhutan, with good pictures.

Contacts

As far as we know, no autonomous women's groups have been established.

Books

Katie Hickman, *Dreams of the Peaceful Dragon: Journey into Bhutan* (Coronet, 1989) and **Tom Owen Edmunds, *Bhutan, Land of the Thunder Dragon*** (Elm Tree, 1988). Katie Hickman and Tom Owen Edmunds travelled together through Bhutan. Her version of their epic Himalayan journey is complemented by his book of photos.

Francoise Pommaret-Imaeda and Yoshiro Imaeda, *Bhutan. A Kingdom of the Eastern Himalayas* (Serindia Publications, 1984). A superbly illustrated, informative book by two eminent Tibetologists who have been living in Bhutan for many years.

Thanks to Lesley Reader for help with Travel Notes and introduction.

Bolivia

In Bolivia things are seldom straightforward. Schedules can be disrupted by anything from floods through strikes and road blocks to plain bureaucracy – all hazards you have to take philosophically. The country itself, though, is one of the most exciting for travellers in South America. The scenery, ranging from a height of zero to 16,000 feet, is often spectacularly beautiful and the people (two-thirds Indian) are still steeped in tradition.

From the point of view of sexual harassment, the overwhelming presence of indigenous people make this a relatively peaceful country to travel around. Probably the biggest threat is from black-market money-changers who see a woman as an easy target to short-change. In this case, ignore the sweet talk, be firm and make absolutely sure you check your money. With an inflation rate not far off 450 percent, poverty is rife, even by Latin American standards, so it's hardly surprising if tourists are seen as a tempting source of income.

The **women's movement** in Bolivia continues to develop as more and more women demonstrate for economic and political change. They were a key factor in the defeat of the Banzer dictatorship in 1978 when women from the mines staged a hunger strike in the capital, La Paz, in demand for an amnesty for political exiles. They have also won themselves a strong platform in the COB (Bolivian Workers Federation), where women delegates have long insisted on the need for more representation on its committees and participation in general.

There are women's groups and organisations of all types, from conservative upper-middle-class associations through all shades of the political spectrum to the far left. Two of the most notable are the widespread Women's Peasant Federation and the Amas de Casa de la Ciudad, a group of poor women who run a health clinic and various education programmes in the slums of La Paz. Both are remarkable in being grass-roots women's organisations who believe in the value of excluding men from specific discussions and decisions in order for women to gain the confidence to stand up for their rights.

An Inside View

. . . .

Susanna Rance has been living and working in Bolivia since 1980. Former editor of the bi-monthly news analysis *Bolivia Bulletin*, her special interest is in grass-roots and development journalism, especially relating to popular women's organisations.

When I first arrived in Bolivia nine years ago, I came with the idea of settling here permanently. Not just because La Paz was my husband's birthplace: on previous travels through Mexico and Central America en route for Venezuela, where I lived for two years, I had already got the "bug". I had fallen in love with Latin American culture, music, language, politics, a certain flavour of life which I found – and still find – warming and exhilarating.

On returning to London from Venezuela in 1977, I joined the Latin American Women's Group and became involved in discussion and solidarity work with women from a variety of backgrounds and countries. That experience confirmed my desire to live permanently in South America, and at the same time to change the course of my work, then teaching English as a foreign language, to something linked with the international struggle for social change.

I flew into La Paz airport, reeling from the 13,000ft altitude, in May 1980. Winter, the cold dry season, was beginning, but La Paz was spectacular with its crystal clear air, blue skies and bright Andean sun. The beauty of the descent from the high plateau into the basin of the city has never lost its impact for me. The narrow back road winds down steep hillsides covered with a pastel-coloured hotchpotch of improvised dwellings, a sharp contrast to the avenues and high-rise buildings of the city centre.

"As a gringa, I expected to feel out of place, even rejected. None of my fears were confirmed"

As a *gringa*, arriving in the midst of a fairly traditional Aymara household, I expected to feel out of place, even rejected. None of my fears were confirmed. My husband's extended family welcomed me warmly and did all they could to make me feel at home.

Each of the small rooms around the cobbled courtyard housed several people, yet there were always invitations for us to visit, sit and share a meal or borrow what we needed. Twenty of us used one cold tap in the yard, the only source of water, which frequently dried up. Washing and cooking, both done squatting at ground level, were social activities, a time for the women of the household to chat, complain and catch up on family news. My husband was thought odd for joining in with these tasks, and our attempts to involve our nephews in household chores were firmly rejected.

Although our lifestyle was clearly different from that of the rest of the family, I found an atmosphere of tolerance, generated largely by my mother-in-law, a generous and open woman who was always loving and supportive to me, up until her recent death. "La Mama" was the hub of the household, a true matriarch.

Only three of her nine children had survived. In my terms, the others died of poverty; in hers, from a variety of supernatural causes: the evil eye, a sudden shock which sends the soul fleeing from the body, a strange illness called *larphata* which has all the symptoms of malnutrition.

My parents-in-law lived for most of the year in the subtropical Yungas valley, growing coffee, citrus fruits, bananas and coca on land which they had cleared from virgin forest. Our honeymoon was a month spent with them up in the woods, harvesting coffee, talking in the evenings by candlelight, preparing lunch at dawn on a wood fire before we set off to work. La Mama worked energetically on the land, dressed in trousers and boots, wielding a machete. On her weekly trips to the nearest town, she would run the two-hour stretch down rocky paths, stopping at intervals to take off one of her work garments and replace it with a petticoat, a long vest, a layered skirt, Cinderella-style shoes and finally her bowler hat.

Despite the family's usual openness towards me, there was one period when I felt isolated. In our second year my husband, a folk musician, went abroad for months on tour. I was "sent to Coventry" by his younger brother's family for carrying on my life as usual, going out at night and staying over with friends: unseemly behaviour for a woman, which I could only get away with in their eyes if my husband was around to give his permission.

Nevertheless, I know that even now a lot of allowances are made for me because I am a *gringa*. One of my sisters-in-law, a Quechua from rural Potosi, often feels as much at sea as I do in the midst of Aymara customs and rituals. Yet as a Bolivian, she is expected to merge totally with the dictates of local and family tradition. Only I, as a foreigner, receive praise for any efforts to integrate, and understanding when I opt out!

"After the coup, I felt panicked, ignorant, impotent to do anything about the repression we witnessed daily"

Two months after I arrived in La Paz there was a military coup. I still knew very little about the country, and it wasn't until some time later that I realised this wasn't just another of the frequent changes of government for which Bolivia is notorious.

Being stopped in the street by military patrols after curfew, hearing sinister shots late into the night, seeing tanks blocking the university gates and the media censored – these were just symptoms of the more hidden violence imposed by the cocaine generals. Their two-year rule, ended by the virtual collapse of the Armed Forces, left a trail of exile, massacre and corruption, which remains a brutal reminder of the fragility of the Bolivian democratic system.

After the coup I felt panicked, ignorant, impotent to do anything about the repression we witnessed daily. I looked for ways of finding out more about what was going on. A couple of months later, I was offered the chance to join a small group of people in the clandestine task of collecting and processing information about the abuses committed under the military regime, to send to solidarity and human rights organisations abroad.

Through this work, I started to learn not just about the current situation but also about Bolivia's history and culture. Gradually the information project began to take up most of my time and I was able to leave my English teaching job and change my line of work, just as I had wanted to do before leaving England.

Meanwhile, I had also become politically involved, in the Women's Front of a party active in the resistance to the dictatorship. Our group, made up mainly of middle-class professionals, represented the first attempt to bring women's issues into the forefront of Bolivian left-wing party politics.

We fought against being relegated to tea-making and sticking up posters while the men met to make the "serious" decisions. We were criticised for doing popular education with women's groups in the shanty towns, instead of pushing the party line and rallying female masses to the demos. We were accused of dividing the struggle at a time when the urgency of the situation required unquestioning discipline. Eventually, the Women's Front was dissolved, but a women's education and information centre grew out of that first initiative.

My first three years in Bolivia were a time of almost total immersion in the life, culture and work around me. Most of my friends and workmates were Bolivian and I had little time to miss my own country or people. Then two things happened to change my experience of Bolivia: I got hepatitis and lost a pregnancy; and we moved out of the family house to have our first child.

It wasn't until I was pregnant that I realised I was malnourished. Although my weight had fallen to a little over six stone, I had never given a thought to my diet. When the doctor asked me exactly what I ate each day, I said it was the same as the rest of the family, but I had to admit it wasn't very nutritious: dry bread and herb tea for breakfast, rice or noodle soup with potatoes or boiled bananas for lunch and the same again for tea and supper. No milk, butter or jam. Very little meat, cheese or eggs.

Cooking together at home, we all ate from the same pot, just adding a cup of water to the soup if there was a visitor. The main difference between me and the rest of the family was that they were used to eating large quantities of carbohydrates to compensate for the lack of protein. Often, rice, potatoes and bananas would make up most of the meal, with a tiny sliver of meat and some spicy chilli sauce to give it all flavour. I couldn't take that much bulk, so I just ate less and lost weight.

"I suddenly realised that I couldn't go on subjecting myself to that diet, to that poverty. For the first time since arriving in Bolivia I felt horribly foreign and apart"

Soon after this discovery I got hepatitis and had a miscarriage as a result. The next time a plate of watery rice soup was put in front of me I burst into tears, and I've never been able to eat it since. I suddenly realised that I couldn't go on subjecting myself to that diet, to that poverty. For the first time since arriving in Bolivia I felt horribly foreign and apart. I started to sort out what things I could and couldn't accept in the way of life around me. Some months later, when I had recovered and was pregnant again, we moved out into our own house, on a market street not far down the road.

The birth of my daughter was a wonderful experience. Apart from the joys of motherhood, encountered for the first time at 31, I discovered firsthand how children are welcomed and loved in Bolivian society, how they are accepted as part of everyday life, not segregated into a subculture of mums and toddlers as in my own country. Relatives and neighbours would ask for a turn with the baby. Market sellers would hold out their arms to give her a cuddle. As a mother, I had a new-found bond with the women around me, even if they shrieked with horror to see Nina being carried down the street in a baby sling, unswaddled and hatless.

I went back to my job a couple of months after Nina was born, working partly from home and sitting breast-feeding her in office meetings with the full support of my colleagues. However, I found it impossible to continue my political activity. Carrying my daughter on long, bumpy bus rides to smoky meetings, coming out late and waiting for transport in the cold, arriving home exhausted, with a broken night ahead of me – it was too much. Aside from the incomprehension of the male party mili-tants, the women my age had all started their families ten years before me and weren't into babies any more.

Another isolation point. My life became a shuttle between home and work, and I started to miss the company of other foreign women who were late-starting mothers like myself, or could understand what I was going through. When I did start to find such allies, I was faced with a hard fact of having chosen to live so far from my own culture: the departure of a succes-sion of friends who left Bolivia when their period of work or study ended.

One year, I withdrew and refused to make new contacts, knowing they would just leave again. But gradually I came to terms with the fact that despite the yearly exodus, these friends greatly enrich my life while they are here. Contact with many of them has contin-ued and some, smitten with the Bolivia bug, return periodically to visit.

When Nina was two-and-a-half, our son Amaru was born. I carried on work-ing full-time, thanks to the support of helpers, friends and neighbours. My husband took on the main parenting role during the months he was in La Paz, but continued to tour with his group for several months each year. Like working mothers everywhere, I felt the inevitable strain of combining parenting with a demanding job, and there was little time for relaxation or social activities.

Meanwhile, the work of our small team had grown and developed into a documentation and information centre.

With the demise of the military regime and the return to democracy in 1982, we were able to open an office, print and mail our news bulletins in Spanish and English and offer our services to students, researchers and journalists in Bolivia and abroad.

My own work was taking a clearer line as I alternated writing and editing on general topics with following up my specific interest: popular women's organisations. I started writing for publications in Bolivia and abroad on grass-roots organisations grouping women from the countryside, factories, mines and shanty towns, writing about their experiences and activities on the basis of direct testimonies.

"A stay of several months in England had convinced me that, despite some nostalgia, I far preferred living in Bolivia"

The end of my eighth year in Bolivia marked a watershed in my personal and professional life. A stay of several months in England had convinced me that, despite some nostalgia, I far preferred living in Bolivia, which offered me many more opportunities to develop as a person, worker and mother than Thatcher's Britain. I returned feeling confident in this choice, ready to start a new phase in my life. It was this new confidence which enabled me to make some unset-tling changes: I left my job of eight years and my marriage, also of eight years in the space of three months.

Belonging to the information centre had been a kind of umbilical cord for me almost since my arrival in Bolivia. It was there that I had become accepted as part of a team, made friends, learned about Bolivia and developed a new career. Finally, I was ready to branch out on my own.

As well as writing articles on devel-opment issues, I began to research a report for the National Population Council on the hot debate around (voluntary) family planning versus (imposed) birth control. This work has opened up new channels: the opportunity for training in population and development planning and the prospect of running a programme on legislation and women's rights.

Soon after I changed jobs, my husband and I reached the point of recognising that our lives had become distanced and we had come to relate more as "co-parents" than as a couple. I started to experience the problems of being a single woman in Bolivian society, where stable couples are the accepted norm and *machismo* sets out the rules for most relationships.

But through it all, after nine years in Bolivia, I've finally found my own identity here as a *gringa*, person, mother and worker. I now have close Bolivian women friends with ideas and experiences in common. And I know that this is where I want to stay, where I want my children to grow up, the country I want to keep enjoying, discovering and writing about.

TRAVEL NOTES

Languages Spanish, Quechua, Aymara and other minor Indian languages.

Transport *Flotas*, or long-distance buses, run from the main bus terminal in La Paz to most other towns in the country. Trains are slow, but the journeys often picturesque. Air travel is very cheap.

Accommodation Although prices are rising fast, there are still plenty of cheap, basic hotels by European standards. Only La Paz tends to get booked up, so try to arrive early in the day.

Special Problems Avoid going to a doctor, dentist, clinic or hospital unless absolutely necessary. The Bolivian medical profession has an unhealthy reliance on the prescription of (unnecessary) drugs. Take with you all the sanitary protection you will need as tampons are incredibly expensive. Most varieties of contraceptive pills can be bought at chemists.

Don't bring British currency to Bolivia. If you manage to change sterling it will be at a very low rate. Everything revolves around the dollar.

Guides The excellent *South American Handbook* (Trade and Travel Publications) includes roughly 60 pages on Bolivia.

South America on a Shoestring (Lonely Planet), aimed more at the budget traveller and a lot cheaper to buy, is especially strong on maps and trails.

Contacts

Ms. Guided Tours, 16B Vicars Terrace, Leeds LS8 5AP, UK, organise women-only tours to Bolivia and Peru. Their aim is to combine adventurous travel with introducing and informing Western women about women's lives in the so-called Third World.

Centro de Promoción de la Mujer Gregoria Apaza, Edificio Muritto, 3rd Floor Office no. 2, Calle Murillo, La Paz, ☎327932. Postal address: Casilla 21170, La Paz, Bolivia. Women's centre carrying out research and popular education sessions with poor urban women.

Centro de Información y Desarrollo de la Mujer (CIDEM), Avenida Villazon 1950, Of. 3A. 3rd floor (opposite University). Postal address: Casilla 3961, La Paz, Bolivia. Women's Information and Development Centre – activities include the provision of health and legal advice, participatory research and the build-up of an audiovisual archive on the lives of Bolivian women.

Centro de Estudios y Trabajo de La Mujer (CETM), Calle España 624, Cochabamba, Bolivia. Information and research centre, again concerned with working with women's organisations in poor urban areas. Publishes a weekly bulletin, *Nosotras*.

Books

Domitila Barrios de Chungara, *Let Me Speak* (Stage 1, 1978). First-hand account of the life of one of the founder members of the Housewives Committees of Siglo XX, one of Bolivia's largest mining complexes. A more recent pamphlet by Domitila is included in **Miranda Davies, ed., *Third World — Second Sex*** (Zed Books, 1983). See General Bibliography.

Audrey Bronstein, ed., *The Triple Struggle: Latin American Peasant Women* (War on Want Campaigns, 1982). Includes interviews with Bolivian women.

Alicia Partnoy, ed., *You Can't Drown the Fire: Latin American Women Writing in Exile* (Virago, 1989). Moving anthology bringing together essays, stories, poetry, letters and songs by women in exile.

James Dunkerley, *Bolivia: Coup d'Etat* (Latin America Bureau, 1980); and ***Rebellion in the Veins: Political Struggle in Bolivia, 1952-82*** (Verso, 1984). Excellent, well-informed studies of Bolivia's recent political history.

Susan George, *A Fate Worse than Debt* (Penguin, 1987). Provides a clear account of Latin America's biggest collective problem, debt, including some information on Bolivia.

Thanks to Ruth Ingram of **Ms. Guided Tours** for background information.

Botswana

otswana is relatively affluent by African standards, and it can be an expensive place for independent travellers. The government has a policy of trying to promote luxury tours and squeeze out the ordinary backpackers, and has recently introduced a daily levy for visitors, payable in the game parks and the magical wildlife reserve of Okavango. In these areas there is also little option but to stay in the upmarket accommodation provided. However, if you do manage to escape official tours – possible if you're determined – travel can still be affordable and very rewarding. What's more it is one of the easier African countries for women travelling alone. Harassment, whether on racial or sexual grounds, is uncommon.

Botswana's economic mainstays are diamonds and beef. The country's predominant tribal group, the cattle-herding Batswanas, have benefited considerably from the export of beef to the EC. Few, however, grow rich from the nation's hefty mineral deposits, which are primarily exploited by

South African companies or siphoned off by smugglers. Even before independence from the British in 1966, Botswana's leaders stood firmly against apartheid, but the economy remains heavily dependent on its imperialist neighbour. However, changing expectations in Botswana – largely a nation of young people – combined with upheavals in South Africa, may herald a dramatic shift in relations, as well as other changes in what remains one of the few multi-party democracies in the continent.

Nearly half of all households in Botswana are headed by women, due to male migration to urban centres and to South Africa. The majority work on the land. Though more are beginning to occupy ministerial and embassy positions, women in towns, hampered by lack of education, are mainly employed in the service industries as cooks, cleaners, hotel workers, etc. Widows and single mothers often supplement their incomes by brewing beer.

Botswana has a growing **women's movement** in the sense that, as the backbone of the country's economy, more and more women are demanding respect and recognition for what they do. Women's agricultural co-operatives are on the increase and, largely through the government's Department of Women's Affairs, many are calling for information about their legal rights.

A Personal Safari

. . . .

Adinah Thomas is a writer and dramatist based in London. She went to Botswana at the invitation of two friends, but spent most of her two-month stay exploring alone.

During my visit, I went off alone into the hinterland using a variety of forms of transport. There is basically only one tarmac road in Botswana, running from Gaborone, the capital in the south, to Kasane in the north. Apart from a few good side-shoots, most roads are little more than dirt tracks, some quite reasonable but most impassable in anything other than a four-wheel drive vehicle. A single railway runs from Gaborone to Bulawayo in Zimbabwe. I never travelled by train, but the service is said to be reliable provided you can find someone to explain the timetable.

Despite primitive road conditions, I found travelling through the endless variations of desert fairly easy. I began by catching a bus from Francistown to Nata, a village on the edge of the Makgadigkaki Pans. The bus went on to Kasane where I waited for three hours with six white people and about thirty Batswana, all wanting to go on across the desert to Maun. Eventually I camped in a field belonging to the Sua Pans Lodge, a clean and friendly establishment owned by possibly the most supportive man in Africa, and his efficient wife. That night I had a minor hassle with an extremely drunk and callow youth who wanted to share my tent. I was rescued by "Mr Supportive", who got rid of him with a mixture of firmness and tact. "What sort of opinion do you want this lady to take back to her country about our people?" The youth vanished.

That was the one and only hassle I had while travelling well over a thousand miles alone. The local men were polite, helpful, sometimes amused, sometimes a little reserved and always delighted by my pathetic attempts to string together my few words of Setswana.

I eventually got a lift to Maun with two South African farmers in a massive lorry that averaged 20km per hour. They were kind enough, but every time the engine boiled over, which was often, and we sat in the middle of nowhere, waiting for it to cool down, they would moan about how dreadful it was, not being allowed to shoot everything in sight any more.

The Nata–Maun road is renowned for its bad surface: 300km through desert that varies from scrubby savannah to the vast and lifeless saline pans, empty of water in November, to the palm tree belt, then sandy wastes followed by more scrub and trees, and more sand. It is not soft golden sand like you find in the Sahara, but a much grittier substance, tufted with dry grasses and thorn bushes and the ever-present acacias. When it rains, parts of the road get washed away. I was lucky and actually made the trip four times without either drowning or dying of heat.

In Maun I borrowed floor space from Barbara, an Australian teaching at the secondary school. Maun itself is set on thick, pale sand, with a shopping mall, Riley's Hotel, and a collection of rather upmarket Safari centres. I walked out of town several times, partly to explore and partly to find a swimming pool. On most occasions I got lifts at least part of the way, though I did once walk eighteen kilometres in blazing sun, with a towel draped around my head.

"Travelling on the back of a truck, ostrich-spotting, sharing canned drinks at every bottle store . . . is an exhilarating way of getting about"

Local buses exist, but they are on the erratic side and tend to break down; either all the tyres blow, or the springs give way under the weight of what seems like hundreds of Batswana and their bundles. I frequently found myself with a lapful of parcels, a sleeping baby in one arm and my own luggage in the other. Very local public transport, connecting small villages, can comprise anything from converted lorries to open trucks, and vary accordingly in discomfort. But travelling on the back of a truck, ostrich-spotting, sharing canned drinks at every bottle store on the way and trying to understand what the hell people are talking about is an exhilarating way of getting about..

The Batswana usually charge hitchhikers. The most I ever paid was ten pula from Nata to Maun, and I paid far less for shorter and less bumpy rides. Sometimes I paid nothing at all. Whites don't normally charge, but do get uptight about their insurance policies and tend to make you promise not to sue them if they accidentally almost kill you. Lorry drivers, doing the north–south run will sometimes pick up passengers, but many are forbidden to do so by their contracts. Wherever you are, though, you will eventually get a lift, even if you have to wait a day or two in the more remote areas. Some people will ask for beer (drinking is pretty heavy in Botswana) or food, or even money – if you are white it is assumed you are rich, and by most Botswana standards you are – but it's unlikely that you will ever feel threatened in any way.

Tourism in Botswana concentrates on safaris, aimed pretty exclusively at the very wealthy. It is possible, I was told, to be set down by chartered plane in the middle of the Kalahari amid carpeted tents, with a chance to drink French champagne between taking the occasional blast at leopard from the back of a Landrover. I preferred to spend three unimaginably wonderful days being poled through the watery mazes of the Okavango Delta by a quietly polite and generous-hearted Bushman whose name I never did learn how to pronounce.

It is not only foolish but positively dangerous to roam the ever-changing Delta without the help of an expert, and Kubu Camp, who more or less organised my guide, mentor and transport, came up with a marvel. I was collected from the school gates in a battered jeep, and driven through the bush for three-and-a-half hours to the pick-up point where the *mokoro*, a dug-out canoe, was waiting. My tent, tins of food, lotions, potions and water bottle were carefully loaded and I was arranged equally carefully in the prow, so that I wouldn't upset the balance.

We pushed off into the whispering silence and beauty of the Delta. The poler knew exactly where he was going. Punting soundlessly though great beds of pink, white and lilac water lilies, swishing through reeds and rushes, nosing through rhododendrons, we paused only to gaze at the brilliant birds glittering about their business. At one point, I swam in warm water soft as silk, watching dark red weeds wrap themselves round my legs and getting tangled in lily roots. It was a new, clean, pristine world with its own laws and legends. The Bushman poler knew these laws. Alone, I would have been lost within minutes in those winding secret channels.

I was punted to a small island where I found I was to share a campsite with three Dutch tourists. There was just time to brew a cup of tea and set up my tent before setting off across the bay for a game walk, until the sun did its vanishing act for the day. The Bushman moved softly, perfectly at ease; he belonged to the Delta, his knowledge was awesome and profound. We tracked – he tracked – a herd of buffalo, massive yet gentle until they saw us and vanished. We saw reedbuck, warthogs, assorted boks and beasts, and more species of bird than I could count. We met two giraffe, who loped off with easy elegance, and saw ostrich racing furiously through the grass. There was nothing but the wind, the tart, warm smell of animals and grasses, the clacking of palm leaves, the silky swish of water. The world suddenly made sense.

The next day we set off in the *mokoro* again to do a bit of hippo-spotting. We were lucky to come across a family of hippos, hugely enjoying a late splash, their vast jaws agape, almost grinning at us as they heaved and floundered, snickering to each

other. On land, like elephants, they move almost soundlessly. It seems incredible that all these prehistoric creatures have such grace and gentleness. They won't attack unless they feel threatened, although probably any one of these massive beasts could kill a man. They prefer to back off, to merge into the background, or in the case of hippos, submerge, only their bright eyes alert and visible above the water. A couple of birds dive-bombed the mother hippo, who snapped at one amiably, knowing she would never catch it, and the cabaret continued until slow, warm rain sent the animals underwater and me back to the camp.

"The poler stopped about halfway . . . and led me cautiously through tall grass to stare at what I thought was a tree until it moved forward"

The final day meant another game walk, just after dawn. That night, I heard a lion roaring in the distance, and the poler found its spoor. We tracked it for a while, then lost it in churned-up mud. The poler, while knowing everything, kept his respect and excitement for the wildlife intact. We went back to the beasts and the boks, endlessly graceful, their huge eyes dark and inscrutable.

I left with great reluctance in the *mokoro*. The poler stopped about halfway along the journey, and led me cautiously through tall grass to stare at what I thought was a tree until it moved forward and I found myself so close to a giraffe that I could see its eyelashes. We stared at each other, the Bushman grinning from ear to ear with pride and love and satisfaction before the giraffe became a tree again. We continued pushing through the lilies, pausing to swim and fill our water bottles from the clear river or simply to stop and watch the birds.

There was no sign of the jeep when we arrived at the pick-up point, so the poler and I sat in companionable silence, smoking, dozing, dreaming, until dusk. Out of nowhere a tall, thin man appeared, driving a safari truck with all the trimmings, and offered us a lift. We had gone about 2km when we met our jeep pulling three new *mokoros*. We swapped vehicles and drove at breakneck speed, first to the poler's hut then back to Maun, bouncing over potholes, grinding to a halt in sandpits, narrowly avoiding being pounded to death by startled kudu, and driving into one of the most magnificent electric storms I have ever seen.

TRAVEL NOTES

Languages English and Setswana.

Transport Hitching is widely accepted, as there are few buses away from the main roads, but you're expected to pay. Entering the country from Zimbabwe, it's best to take the train.

Accommodation Hotels are few and expensive, catering to luxury tour groups. There are hostels, mostly run by the different voluntary services, but most places have somewhere you can camp, though clearly at your own risk.

Guide *The Rough Guide: Zimbabwe and Botswana* (Harrap Columbus) has a hundred or so pages on Botswana and is very much geared to independent travel.

Contacts

Women's Affairs Unit, Ministry of Home Affairs, Private Bag 002, Gaborone. Run almost single-handedly by Joyce Anderson, the Department is largely concerned with supporting women's agricultural co-operatives. It also produces publications and helps organise workshops to spread information on women's legal rights.

Books

Bessie Head lived in Botswana as an exile from South Africa until her death in 1988. Of her novels, the best is *A Question of Power* (Heinemann Educational, 1974). Set in the village in Botswana where she lived, this is a beautifully written exploration of a woman's sanity. Heinemann have also published three other of her novels/short story collections: *Maru* (1972), *The Collector of Treasures* (1977) and *Jerowe, Village of the Rain Wind.*

Brazil

· · · · · · · · · · · · · · · ·

Arriving in Brazil from any neighbouring country, let alone from the States or Europe, can be something of a culture shock. Besides the shift from Spanish to Portuguese, the sudden vast distances and extraordinary blend of people and landscapes, the country holds some of the worst pockets of urban poverty in the world. Personal safety has to be taken seriously, as robbery, notably on deserted beaches, in Rio de Janeiro, and in the larger towns of the poverty-stricken northeast, is a very real threat.

Women travellers are also likely to suffer a fair amount of sexual harassment. In general, Brazilians are open, easygoing people with a very relaxed attitude to sex, encapsulated in the often outrageous eroticism of Carnival. At the same time, this is a strongly *machista* society; whether it feels threatening clearly depends on the situation, but a woman alone, especially a foreigner, will inevitably attract a lot of physical attention from men. Hitching is definitely out and it is inadvisable to walk in any city streets on your own at night.

Brazil's diverse landscape, ranging from the threatened tropical rainforest of the Amazon Basin, to partially arid Highlands down to the heavily industrialised coastal strip, is matched by its population. After the centuries of decimation which began with colonisation, only a fraction of Brazil's indigenous Indian population remains. The rest of the population is mainly descended from the Portuguese colonists, the African slaves they brought with them, and the millions of European families who more recently flocked to the country for work. Today whites or near-whites hold most of the nation's wealth, while black and mixed-race people constitute the bulk of the population pouring into the cities in search of work. Along with high inflation, the problem of internal migration is one of the key symptoms of Brazil's ongoing economic crisis.

Despite periods of economic growth and social reform enjoyed earlier this century, Brazilian politics have a tendency to degenerate into turmoil. Instability and corruption finally led, in 1964, to twenty years of military rule, from which the country has only comparatively recently emerged. During the army's most repressive period in the Sixties, hundreds of students, trade unionists and other political activists went into exile. Among them were feminists who later returned with ideas from Europe and the United States. They are just one of the influences behind Brazil's growing **women's movement**. Today groups range from autonomous feminist organisations campaigning on issues such as reproductive health, sexist education, racism, male violence and women's legal rights, to more hierarchical organisations directly linked to political parties. Brazil has a national feminist paper, *Mulherio,* and groups dedicated to working with low-income women, such as the Carlos Chagas Foundation in São Paulo, produce excellent cartoon pamphlets to get their messages across.

A Different Rhythm

. . . .

Rebecca Cripps visited Brazil on the last stage of a year-long trip to South America. She spent much of the time in São Paulo, teaching, writing and helping out at a centre for single-parent families. She works as a free-lance writer in London.

I took the 24-hour "death train" out of Santa Cruz, Bolivia, and arrived in Brazil bone-rattled and worn out. While having my passport stamped at the train station in the border town of Corumbá, sweating in the stifling midday heat, I asked the policeman in the office where I could go for an immediate and everlasting swim. "At my house," he replied, looking at his watch, and he locked up the office for his lunchbreak.

The woman I was with at the time and I refused to go at first; in the previous few months of travelling through South America, we had both already risked our lives more than once, in the cause of spontaneity and the desire to trust. But the man expressed such an earnest wish to have a chance to speak with foreigners – "sin compromiso, you are my guests" – besides which the idea of a cool swim seemed so miraculous, that we finally agreed. Having begged us to stay on, two days later Miguel held a party in our honour and invited forty other federal policemen and their wives for a celebratory barbecue. We became firm friends and two months later he came to stay with me in São Paulo, where I was teaching English.

Such is the generous spirit of hospitality in Brazil that I was constantly invited to stay with people, some of whom I had barely met, and probably I need never have paid for a hotel room. However, I quite often chose to rent somewhere, as basic accommodation is cheap and plentiful throughout the country.

After experiencing Peru and Bolivia, to cross into Brazil involves a certain amount of culture shock. Immediately the atmosphere seems greatly relaxed (police presence is minimal in comparison) and attitudes more liberal, and the Brazilian people move to a different rhythm altogether. They have a languid, graceful motion and a lazy, vibrating way of speaking Portuguese, so unlike the pure clipped tones of *castellano*.

"I was many times touched and stroked against my will by men, and was always unnerved by the strange intimacy inflicted upon me"

Brazilians give the impression of being extremely laid-back – as well as displaying an intense passion for living – while at the same time they are incredibly friendly and open-minded. After the mistrust and hostility I had experienced so often before, particularly in Peru, in Brazil it crossed my mind at first that people were either behaving with extreme cynicism or were overwhelmingly naive. I was wrong on both counts: Brazilians are just unbelievably open.

The whole country seems to breathe in time to some original, sensual drumbeat; sex is everywhere – youth, fire and rhythm. Teenagers make love as soon as their bodies are able and sex is universally proclaimed as the greatest possible pleasure. However, men assume a "liberal" attitude which is often offensively infringing. In São Paulo, where I lived for three months, I was many times touched and stroked unwillingly by men, and always unnerved by the strange intimacy inflicted upon me in often very public places.

I spent a year in South America, my last five months being in Brazil, and by the end of it all I was sick and wary of macho men and their continual harassment. I found it hard not to become cynical, and even harder sometimes not to just give up and go along with it, to save energy. A very few men I met had managed to break away from *machista*, but for most the indoctrination starts too young and is too deeply ingrained.

Once, on a beach, I was offered money for sex by an eleven-year-old boy, whose persistence and expectations of success appalled me. Miguel, the policeman, warned me on my first day in Brazil: "Don't smile at men or they will think you want to go to bed with them", and his assumption proved to be frustratingly correct. He bemoaned to me the virtual impossibility of building a non-sexual relationship with a Brazilian woman and claimed that he was required to "perform" on a first date or risk being considered freakish, and questioned as to his "problem", so expected is the macho way. Although in Brazil there is more acceptance of homosexuality than in other countries on the continent, homophobia is widespread, and the behaviour of men and women is controlled by an uncompromising heterodoxy. If you break the rules you may get into trouble, and if you are rescued it will probably be ironically, by chivalry.

São Paulo, the skyscraping business and finance centre of Brazil, does not attract many tourists, and most sightseeing visitors are warned off by descriptions of its vast and sprawling ugliness and dirt. There is certainly not much to see there in terms of beauty or history or ancient culture, and it is a city motivated by a work ethic which supersedes the traditional siesta-happy image of sleepy Latin America and lazy hammock lie-ins. What makes it such a vibrant, vital place is the inhabitants: over fourteen million people from an astonishingly diverse mix of racial origins and cultural backgrounds.

If you haven't got long in Brazil, a visit to São Paulo will probably not seem worth the trouble of working out its inordinately complex system of buses (it takes about two months!). However, as a place to live in, it has many advantages over other Brazilian cities, the greatest being availability of work. Also, in terms of street crime and violence, it is reputedly much less dangerous than Rio de Janeiro – I certainly found the atmosphere generally much more relaxed.

In certain areas of Rio at night, the tension can reach quite unbearable levels. Romantic as it looks from the lofty peak of Sugarloaf Mountain in the softness of evening, this is a city in decline, and the effects of economic collapse and crippling inflation are apparent everywhere on street level and reflected in its mood of suppressed violence and instability. São Paulo, in contrast, is a place of industrial and economic growth, where opportunities for financial success are there for the grasping. It is one of the few places in Brazil where you can make your fortune, or at least earn enough in order to eat. (To breathe, however, is a different matter – pollution is dense.)

At the same time, against this optimistic background of financial and industrial success, São Paulo has a population of slum-dwellers almost as large as that of Rio. Many are transplanted villagers, attracted from the interior and impoverished northeast by the potent appeal of employment and a vision of existence higher than that of mere survival; many cannot subsist anywhere else. *Favelas*, or slums, which have become a dominant feature in Rio's cityscape – almost a tourist attraction – have sprung up all over São Paulo.

"Children younger than ten have been busted for selling cocaine, often to support their own habit"

There are more than half-a-million homeless children in the city, living on the streets of the *favela* districts in whose dirt and squalor they lack access to even the most basic amenities. Many have been abandoned by their parents, who are simply unable to provide for them, and often at a very early age children are forced on to the streets to live as best they can with no permanent shelter, nor food nor clothes. In order to eat, many have to steal, and the downtown streets of the financial centre of São Bentão and Se are crowded with child pickpockets who are often organised into gangs.

Exposed to the starkness of slum life and surrounded by examples of corruption and crime, children are armed as soon as they can walk and take drugs as soon as they can sell them. Children younger than ten have been busted for selling cocaine, often to support their own habit, but as one policeman sighed to me: "They have to escape like their parents, and I can't blame them. They wake up under no roof, to nothing."

In order to try to curb the increasingly alarming situation and provide at least some support for *favela* children, several schemes have been set up in the city over the past couple of decades, to varying degrees of success. In São Paulo I stayed with an American nurse who works as a volunteer at the Sabia centre, a virtually self-sufficient community of single-parent (mother) families situated about an hour away from the city centre in an area of debilitating poverty. It is run in close association with the Hospital of São Paulo which buses volunteer nurses and helpers to the centre each day, but it remains solely reliant on private investment and donations and has no state funding. Between teaching and writing, I occasionally joined the group to help out.

Sabia was built about fifteen years ago on a site donated by a philanthropic landowner, and constructed out of the rubble and waste found abandoned on the land at the time. The founders were single women with children – from its original four families there are now over forty – and the centre remains as a shelter for mainly women and children, with about four men living and working there at the moment. Apart from the family shacks, Sabia is comprised of a set of common buildings, the most important of which are the creche and the daycare centre. There is also a sewing room, a carpentry workshop and a kitchen and garden, which provide all the children and volunteers with two meals a day. A school has been set up with morning and afternoon sessions, plus provision for learning practical skills during any free periods.

"The Brazilian knack of living with a focus on the present . . . helps put off till tomorrow what could happen today"

There was a wonderful atmosphere at Sabia, a feeling of unity and strength in the face of what seem insurmountable obstacles. But the centre is by no means secure. It could not survive without its private funding, and in a country of such economic and social instability as Brazil its stream of donations could dry up at any moment with a lot of work going to waste. Sometimes it

seems as though the whole country could go down too when inflation rises by thirty percent in one day. But the Brazilian knack of living with a focus on the present, an attitude so often mistakenly identified as hedonistic but simply rising from a necessary short-sightedness, helps put off till tomorrow what could happen today.

After three months in São Paulo, I spent my last four weeks in Brazil on my back on the beaches of the Bahia, eating watermelon. I decided that if I were to choose to live anywhere in South America, it would be in this state, which seems to harbour the essence of Brazil. The people here have an endemic closeness to nature and a habitual knowledge of tides, moon cycles, star formations, trees, plants and animals. They celebrate the full moon without any kind of hippy pretension and constantly express their wonder at the natural beauty of their country.

Poverty here is a way of life and of a different make-up than the consumer-deprivation visible elsewhere; as such it seems far less oppressive than in the cities, where living poor is a struggle with many complications. In the Bahia, which has a mainly black population, life is more immediate. It is yearly attracting more and more visitors seeking palm trees and a good time, and of all the places I have been there is nowhere better for kicking off your shoes, dancing all night and flopping into your hammock without a thought of what is life. Only living.

TRAVEL NOTES

Language Portuguese. Don't assume everyone speaks Spanish. It won't be appreciated.

Transport Cheap, fast and comfortable buses criss-cross the country almost any time of day or night. Hitching is difficult and potentially dangerous. Internal air travel is highly developed.

Accommodation There are plenty of cheap hotels throughout Brazil.

Special problems Avoid going alone to isolated beaches or walking around alone at night in any city. Robberies and assaults on residents and travellers alike are becoming increasingly frequent.

Guide *The Rough Guide: Brazil* (Harrap Columbus) is a new addition to the series – up to date and comprehensive.

Contacts

There are far too many women's organisations to list here; also, groups are forever moving and changing. Probably the best central organisation to contact is **Centro Informação Mulher** (*CIM*). Rua Leoncio Gurgel, 11-Luz 01103, São Paulo/SP, ☎229 4818, or Postal 11.399, 05499 São Paulo/SP, Brazil. *CIM* publishes regular lists of different women's organisations throughout the country.

Books

Elizabeth Jelin, ed., *Citizenship and Identity: Women and Social Change in Latin America* (Zed Books, 1990). Edited by an Argentinian sociologist, this book examines women's increasing involvement in grass-roots social change, from the *favelas* of São Paulo to the Bolivian Highlands.

June Hahner, *Women in Latin American History – Their Lives and Views* (UCLA Latin America Center Publications, Los Angeles, 1976). Includes Brazil.

John Hemming, *Amazon Frontier: The Defeat of the Brazilian Indians* (Macmillan, 1986) and ***Red Gold*** (Macmillan, 1987). Excellent detailed histories tracing the plight of Brazilian Indians from the early days of colonisation.

Jorge Amado, *Dona Flor and Her Two Husbands* (Serpent's Tail, 1986). Exhilarating story set in Bahia by one of the country's leading novelists.

Britain

For many travellers, Britain begins (and quite possibly ends) with London. The capital, with its individuality, cultural mix and entertainment, largely lives up to its myths and reputation. At the same time, along with much of southern England, it can often seem unwelcoming – and for visitors it is outrageously expensive. Without friends to stay with, the cost of accommodation can be crippling, whilst the city's transport charges are the highest in Europe.

Expense, in fact, is a problem throughout Britain and if your funds are limited, you may have to be prepared to rely on youth hostels (or else camp in all weathers), spend a lot of

time hitching and cook for yourself. However, there is plenty of scope for walking and cycling holidays, and there are parts of the north of England, and certainly Scotland and Wales, where you can wander for miles without seeing a soul.

Politically, Britain is at a low ebb, after more than a decade of Conservative Party rule under the increasingly autocratic Margaret Thatcher. Her government has overseen a dramatic widening of the gap between rich and poor, mirrored by the marked differences in prosperity between north and south and the growing number of homeless people and beggars at the heart of commercial London – a shock for many who have not visited for a while. Parts of Wales, Scotland and the north of England have been especially hard hit by government spending cuts, and the poverty and unemployment in cities like Glasgow, Liverpool, Bradford and Newcastle are the worst Britain has seen since the war. But don't be put off exploring these parts of the country. Northerners tend to be more open and friendly, with less of the traditional English reserve; accommodation is cheaper; and much of the countryside is spectacular and wild.

Sexual harassment varies little between England, Wales and Scotland. Apart from the odd wolf-whistle, you're unlikely to be bothered by men in rural areas, except in pubs. Big cities, however, pose a definite problem at night when you're likely to feel uneasy wandering around alone. Racism is an additional problem, rooted in Britain's history as a leading imperialist power. You're undoubtedly more prone to abuse if you're black, but even white Australians report patronising, colonial attitudes, especially at work.

The double issue of racism and sexism has become a strong focus of the **women's movement** in England, which has many more Asian and Afro-Caribbean communities than neighbouring Wales or Scotland; to understand this commitment you need only turn to Britain's long-standing national feminist magazine, *Spare Rib*. The movement as a whole, as in the US and most of Europe, has greatly diversified since its inception in the early 1970s. As well as racism, questions of equal opportunity, reproductive rights, education and violence have been joined by a growing commitment to environmental issues. There is also mounting concern about poverty and homelessness, of which some of the worst sufferers are single mothers. British feminism may have lost its unity as a national movement but all in all, in spite of economic recession and a Prime Minister devoted to traditional Conservative values, its spirit and aims remain very much alive.

"I am not a Tourist; I live here"

. . . .

A German national, Ilse Zambonini lives and works in north London. She has seen many sides of the city over the past twelve years.

The first time I came to Britain, I was eighteen and on my own; I travelled widely, through England, Scotland and Wales, by coach, train and hitchhiking. Protected as much as anything by my naivete, nothing nasty happened to me and I retained a nagging love for this country. In 1976, I decided to return to London for a while, and I have lived here ever since.

I did not know anyone in London, but I had an idea of what kind of people I wanted to meet and where to look for them. I also managed to find a teaching job through the Central Bureau for Educational Visits and Exchanges. Luck – but also my determination to find a way of staying here. Many people who have moved to London from abroad have told me how difficult it is to meet "English people"; they end up in ghettoes of immigrants, give up and go home. I did not find this a problem; it helps if there is a context of shared interest, for instance feminism, politics, education . . . perhaps being a parent.

Within a year, I had moved into a communal house full of English and

Scots. At first I couldn't understand a word the Scots were saying; I thought they were speaking a foreign language. Now, like everyone else in Britain, I can place people by their accents – and people can place me, too.

I have never lost my German accent – it just won't shape into clipped English noises – which puts me outside the class structure. I could be anybody and I enjoy that. The only time I get a little short-tempered is when someone talks to me as if I were a tourist, very slowly and just a little patronisingly. How many English people speak German, let alone accent-free?

However, I never experienced any hostility directed at my being German, except for one English lady in the Portobello Road who called me a "stupid German cow" because I was in the way of her smart car – and she would have found something else to blame me for if I hadn't had a foreign accent. No one has ever complained about my taking jobs away from the British. They are too busy blaming black people for it. And Nazi films on television, where English actors speak with terrible German accents, have thankfully gone out of fashion.

"This was the first time I had come into contact with people who were culturally different from myself and my friends in age, race and class background"

In 1977 I joined a band and found myself in the middle of the Rock Against Racism movement. I was living on Social Security, and upon my return from a tour abroad with the band, I discovered that I had been turned out of the country. I was only admitted back on the condition that I would never again be a burden to the British tax payer. Under the Treaty of Rome, EC nationals are entitled to work and live in any member country. They are entitled to unemployment benefit once they have worked for a certain number of months or years, but not to Social Security benefits. So, I became a resident working alien!

My life changed. I started out as a youth worker and began to get to know intimately the young unemployed of Islington and Hackney: whites, blacks, Cypriots, Asians. This was the first time I had come into contact with people who were culturally different from myself and my friends in age, race and class background. I felt that I was beginning to understand more about London. I had to think about poverty, racism, about being white and working with young black people, and about being a childless woman and working with young single mothers.

When I moved to London, I had been warned about the dangers from muggers, burglars, murderers, rapists, all waiting there for me. At first, I walked about warily. One evening, on my way home, a group of young men walked up to me. "Here it comes, my first encounter with male violence," I thought. They stopped, looked at me, and one of them said: "You look like a hippie." I giggled all the way home.

How exciting, how amusing everything was then: having a key to a boyfriend's flat in Hackney; cycling from Holloway to Mare Street and finding shortcuts through parks; living in a decrepit squat that had open fires in every room but no electricity; having breakfast in my own garden; going on women's day marches dressed in purples, pinks and high lace-up boots, carrying the small children of women friends . . . even the weather was glorious.

Nowadays, I am aware that violent attacks happen all the time, in London as everywhere else. But I move around as though I had a right to, day or night. The area I live in, Archway, in the north of the city, is on the way to "gentrification", though being burgled remains a day-to-day possibility. Sometimes I resent living as if in a fortress, with locks on the windows, locks on every door; lock up after you've let the cat out and unlock when she comes back in (and don't forget to lock up again!). But in a country where the divide between rich and poor is becoming as extreme as in the so-called Third World, this is the price I pay for not being at the bottom of the pile.

In Munich, there are people I know who leave their doors unlocked during the day, some even at night. In London, crime is all around you, and it is just another thing to live with. The dirt, the feeling of neglect, the ugliness of some parts of London, where you find yourself either in a shantytown or in a post-modern theme park, can be extremely depressing. Most of the housing estates are disgusting – full of dogs and dogshit, with dangerous lifts, broken windows and no lighting. But then I go to Hampstead and daydream about living in one of those mansions on the hill, where you breathe London's cleanest air.

"There is a Third World feel to many parts of London"

There is a Third World feel to many parts of London: people queueing outside post offices and benefit offices; beggars; plastic bags full of rubbish everywhere; tatty goods in the shops. In a city with tens of thousands of homeless people, and as many brand new cars, the contrast between private wealth and public poverty has become almost intolerable over the last ten years, and now healthcare is set to go the same way. During the last two elections, I swore to myself that if Thatcher was elected again I'd go back home to Mother, where everything is nice, clean and egalitarian, and ecologically sound. But I never did.

There have also been changes for the better. When I first moved here London was a culinary desert with no decent cup of coffee to be found. The word "café" was synonymous, not with coffee and cake but with greasy food, and wine with overpriced sugarwater.

During my first few years all visitors from Germany had to bring enormous food parcels full of real bread, real coffee, real chocolate, etc. Maybe I felt insecure. Now every supermarket sells ground coffee, and I can buy *Lebkuchen* from my local garage. Everybody knows what *tagliatelle* are (also no one knows how to pronounce them), and cafés with shining espresso machines can be found in Stroud Green Road, Clapham and even Dalston. Thanks to those deplorable yuppies, off-licences now have affordable as well as drinkable wines, and I can swill champagne in wine bars instead of going to a pub – the only British institution I have never learned to love.

London is, of course, different from other big cities in Britain. No other city is so much like a whole country in itself, a whole continent; it is hard to think of leaving, once established. Life in London is anonymous, certainly, and many people are isolated. But isn't this also why they came to live here? If you want to know all your neighbours and all the gossip, you live in the villages. London is a city of privacy, but a place where you can also say hello to the greengrocer or the garage cashier. It is exciting, full of things no one needs, full of useless discoveries, cinemas you will never go to, bands you will never hear, restaurants you might one day go to. The one really negative factor is provided by its size – visiting a friend in another part of town can be a day trip.

I also enjoy the feeling of living in a city I still don't quite know. After twelve years here I still discover new walks by the river or along the canals, parks I have never walked in, or some old bridge or railway station. There are dozens of galleries and museums which I still haven't seen, and I can shop at any time of day or night. In Munich, I hated the deadness that descends on the city at the weekend. Life there stops by noon on Saturday, and if you don't do your shopping by then, you eat out or not at all. No sweat in London.

When I feel like going out to see live music, there is always some band over from Africa, the Caribbean, or some brilliant local musicians no one in Germany will ever hear. There are clubs and events where forty-year-olds can go and dance. There are hundreds of record shops, and dozens of radio stations. In London I'll never run out of music. And the cultural and style climate here is almost anarchic – people wear practically anything. You really appreciate this coming from dull and decent Munich, or from Rome, where you feel like a freak unless you wear something brand new or at least crisply ironed.

What if I get a bit exhausted by all the excitement in London? I have discovered ways of getting out of it. Papers like *Dalton's Weekly* and the Sunday papers advertise cottages all over the country, often incredibly cheap. You don't need to own a second home to have weekends away. I now have two places, one in Cornwall and one in Shropshire, where I go regularly, and I love reading about all the other ones I could go to. The weather, of course, is hardly Mediterranean, but then, if it were, the country would be full of tourists. As one of our cottage landladies said: "We have good weather at the most inconvenient times".

Under the Eyes of the Home Office:

. . . .

Luisa Handem first visited Britain at the age of seventeen from Portugal, where her family had settled after leaving their native Guinea Bissau. She has since made her home in England despite a long history of struggling with the country's forbidding immigration laws.

In Portugal, as a teenager of African descent, I was never quite aware of the fact that, although we all live on one planet, freedom of movement between countries is strictly regulated. Upon my arrival at Gatwick Airport I was kept waiting much longer than everyone else before finally being granted a six-month visitor's visa – and I had only intended staying a couple of months.

"My experience as an au pair was horrendous"

That first hurdle overcome, I went back home to resume my studies, full of wonderful memories of the United Kingdom and its people, and resolved to return the following year to work as an au pair. This time I satisfied all requirements (a letter from my host family inviting me to stay as an au pair for an unspecified period), but the immigration officer decided that only a seven-month visa was appropriate, even though the accepted timespan for an au pair is one year. On being asked what I was coming to do in England, I replied "I intend studying to improve my English." The answer I got was that my English sounded quite good enough and that au pair girls weren't expected to attain a high level of fluency.

My experience as an au pair was horrendous. To begin with the family whose address I had given to the immigration officer had decided not to wait any longer and had taken on another girl. After spending the night at an au pair agency I was allocated a family with one child. A brief interview ensued during which I stated my desire to have some afternoons off to attend a language school. Several weeks later I realised that the agreed two afternoons off a week (plus all of Sunday) were simply not enough.

Unable to negotiate any more free time, I found another family. But my problems weren't over. Not happy with my success in finding an alternative household, the woman I was working for first threatened to have the Home Office deport me and then phoned my next family and told them that I was no good and that I had stolen some envelopes and a half-full can of hairspray (which I had picked out of the rubbish bin in the bathroom). As a result, by the time I moved in they were already looking for a substitute, and, given my bad references, only agreed to keep me for a couple of weeks. The nature and long hours of work aside, I found au pairing a depressing and insulting experience, but it was the only way I could legally stay and work in the UK.

Later on, giving up on the work, I stayed at an all girls Catholic hostel, from where I could at least attend daily classes in English. However, restrictions on closing time (10.30pm weekdays and 11pm on weekends) interfered with my happy discovery of London nightlife and I eventually moved to the newly built YWCA, which doubled as a hotel and youth hostel. From there I attended a full-time "A" level course in order to be able to apply for a university place, applied to a charitable organisation for a grant and worked for up to thirty-five hours a week at a local cinema.

At the age of nineteen I still didn't know enough about immigration laws and the consequences of failing to strictly comply with them. Despite having "employment prohibited" stamped on my passport, I had heard from several people that I could work part-time as long as I was a student receiving more than fifteen hours of tuition a week. Confident of my status, I went on a two-week holiday to visit my parents in Lisbon. Upon my return, I was again faced with a menacing immigration officer and was this time kept waiting for hours while my luggage was taken away and searched in detail. My address book and any letters or notes in my handbag were photocopied and kept for further investigation. One of the letters contained the offer of another cinema job, revealing my intention to work in this country – a point which immigration officers can legitimately use to refuse leave to enter the United Kingdom.

"I was kept for 72 hours in a detention centre at Heathrow, sharing a small cell with three women from Latin America"

I was kept for 72 hours in a detention centre at Heathrow, sharing a small cell with three women from Latin America. When the decision was finally taken to deport me, I was transferred by helicopter to Gatwick Airport where a flight had been booked for my return to Portugal.

All along I was treated as an arrested criminal. One day, while being driven back and forth for questioning, I tried to be human and make a joke about the bitter winter and heavy snow to the woman police officer at the wheel. I was soon shut up by her retort: "If it was so much warmer in Portugal why didn't you stay there?" The only kind words I ever received from officialdom during my detention came from another policewoman. "Why on earth do they keep detaining and sending back polite, decent girls like yourself when we need to be concentrating on dealing with drug traffic?" she said, angrily. I shall always be thankful for those words, which proved to me that not all British people were xenophobic and racist.

After spending nearly a year in Portugal, where post-colonial turmoil was still very much the order of the day, with a huge shortage in housing, work and university places, I was forced once again to contemplate returning to Britain. Despite everything, I stood a better chance of resuming my education. This time I entered successfully as a visitor and, after seeking advice from many friends, decided to apply once again to stay for a year as an au pair.

Months of awaiting a reply from the Home Office followed, during which time I had enrolled at a polytechnic and found myself a family. I finally got in touch to enquire about the fate of my passport. To my astonishment what followed was a visit by an immigration policeman who, using threats and remarks about the poverty of Portugal, wasted no time in suggesting that I was hiding in the country. By the time my hostess's allegiances had switched in favour of the policeman, I was nearing a complete nervous breakdown.

In the end I survived without being deported. My polytechnic supplied good references to back up my assurance that I was only in Britain to pursue my education and I was lucky enough to find a fun-loving Anglo-American family who took such a liking to me that they put in a new application for the extension of my leave to remain in the country. While my case was being considered I managed to secure a university place with a full grant for three years. This in turn helped my case and I was finally granted a visa for the duration of my studies.

Before completing my degree I married a foreign student and, soon after graduating, moved to Sweden where I stayed for two years. I couldn't stand the snow, the country or my marriage, and, refusing to succumb to destiny, I decided one day to return with my young son to Britain. I took the ferry over to Harwich, and as the boat sailed into the port, found myself reassuringly greeted with kindness by strangers.

However, I had come back to join the ranks of single parents struggling in a society which far from meets their needs. I was shocked to find that in London – I still knew nothing of the country outside and the capital was my natural choice – my child was an obstacle. Now that I could neither be sheltered in a hostel, nor housed by a rich family as an au pair, accommodation was very hard to find. Having previously lived in wealthy areas like Hampstead, I now joined the long queues of homeless people waiting to be rehoused.

"I had come back to join the ranks of single parents struggling in a society which far from meets their needs"

Mine was not one of the worst cases; I was kept waiting only six months between bed and breakfast accommodation and incredibly poor temporary housing.

Having grown used to the advanced Swedish welfare state, I was depressed to discover the difficulties of travelling with a child on public transport – something which policy-makers don't seem to take into consideration. This, coupled with the lack of facilities for babies in shops and restaurants, makes it very hard to get around. There are also far too few nurseries to meet the demands of working mothers. My child was on a waiting list for two years.

Despite these setbacks I stayed on. I had been uprooted from my home country as a child and somehow still associated Britain with a sense of liberalism and freedom. Although I'm not so sure about the freedom anymore, to me this is one of the best countries for cultural interchange. I feel I am in the centre of the world. I love the art galleries, the television, the markets; I have been to the Cotswolds, Derbyshire and other parts of northern England and I love these places too. To deal with British people is not always easy, though. The lack of openness, the silence of the London underground, all contribute to a grim picture of the capital itself. And anyone having to face the bottom line here would certainly not view this as a country of hope.

My child is growing up now, with mixed ideas about his identity. I have noticed improvements in race relations over the years but any mention of African origins still triggers racist senti

ments. I have recently noticed that, even in schools, children seem to be confused about the meaning of being African. On being asked by a seven-year-old where I came from, the laughter that followed my reply only served to remind me of my own childhood in what was then Portuguese Guinea, where my dark mother was often an embarrassment in social places and the cause of much humiliation.

A Scottish Journey

Cathy Roberts works for an independent research service in London. Fuelled by childhood lullabies and enthusiastic reports from women friends, she explored Scotland for the first time in autumn with a friend.

I had wanted to see Scotland since the days when my mother would sing me "The Skye Boat Song" as a lullaby, and had a very clear vision of the country – peopled by strong women in shawls and long skirts, either striding across the heather or weaving famous tweeds. The chance to test the reality came when my best friend returned from abroad and we wanted space and time together. What better than the Western Isles, we thought, and set off to gather information from the Scottish Tourist Board. We didn't want to rough it, feeling we were past the backpacking days (always more fun if the sun shone), and coupled with the fact that my friend was pregnant, we decided to find out about train timetables and the availability of guesthouses and small hotels.

Once we had worked out a route on the Scottish mainland which did not

entail a sequence of five-hour stop-overs in Inverness we set off. It was the last week in September. We had wanted to travel from London by sleeper train, then by ferry to Lewis, but the tourist season really ends in mid-September, after which timetables shrink dramatically. In the end we flew to Glasgow, then travelled by train and ferry to Skye.

The train journey, from Glasgow to Mallaig, up the western coast, was superb. There must be something in the atmosphere of the highlands which calms nerves normally shredded by late trains and bad time-keeping. Our train was delayed because it had waited for a steam train to get through on a single track line, making us late for the ferry to Skye, but that was okay, because the ferry waited for us. That first day, the sky was blue, the sun shining and the air cold. We were settling into a marathon talk and boarded the ferry thinking, "Isn't Skye going to be beautiful . . ."

By the time we crossed the narrow stretch of sea and landed at Armadale on Skye, it was raining. It was also the start of a night and a day of upset and anger, as we had been badly misled by the manager of the hotel we were booked into. "Get the bus from the ferry", he had said; we arrived on Skye on the one ferry a bus does not meet, with no transport to travel the 25 miles to our hotel. "I can't help and, no, I can't hold dinner for you if you're going to be late," were the reassuring words of the manager. A fully booked town of Armadale meant we had to get a taxi – an expense we could have done without. Mind you, at least it led us to meet Mrs Morrison, owner of one of the isle's few taxis and lover of Hebridean folk songs and culture. We cheered up a little as she drove us along the night-time roads, explaining the nuances of the songs of the women weavers on the Isle of Harris.

"We felt decidedly isolated and vulnerable, stuck on a cold, wet island, in an ugly hotel"

It was Mrs Morrison we turned to the next day, to take us away from the hotel, which, with its tall tales of original character and sympathetic adaptations of William IV fisherfolks' cottages, had originally attracted us. The reality was 1950s institutional decor. We felt decidedly isolated and vulnerable, stuck on a cold, wet island, in an ugly hotel, with a manager who appeared to have lied about everything when we had phoned from England. I was nervous, and more than a little angry. There was no hire car ("yes, of course, no problem, but you'll find the bus service good"), no buses, no food and certainly no hint of regret. The uncomfortable, noisy rooms were too much for sensitive souls like us, as was the cost of this blot on the harbour.

We called Mrs Morrison, who understood perfectly – in fact, I would swear she was waiting for us to call – and took us to a Victorian hunting lodge in the middle of nowhere, where all the guests but us spent all day standing thigh deep in water, fishing. Here we were handed over to a good old-fashioned house-keeper, began to feel like houseguests and really began to relax.

We did get a car, and discovered how useless they are for sightseeing when there is fog outside and the windows steam up. But it did at least get us around an island where buses are few and far between, leaving little alternative apart from walking. We spent happy hours in and around our wondrous hotel, by Loch Snizort, curled up in comfy old armchairs before a log fire, walking around the loch between rainstorms and seeing the river grow from a pleasant flow to a raging torrent in 24 hours. I phoned my mother, who said, "Well, they do call Skye the 'misty isle'", and giggled. I'm glad I inherited her sense of humour.

We visited Dunvegan Castle to get out of one rainstorm and called in at a few of the many craft workshops during more drizzle. Strange shapes looming in the sky were identified as mountains when the clouds lifted slightly, and we sat coughing in a smoke-filled old "black house", a rebuilt crofter's house made of mud and turf, with a peat fire burning in the middle of the one windowless room. The newer, squat, whitewashed houses dotted over the hills and moors, though bleak, looked beautiful in comparison.

The appalling weather eventually drove us to escape to the mainland. Mrs Morrison, playing us the women weavers' songs as we drove, waved us off at Kyleakin and the sun shone brightly over Skye as we watched the shore recede. We saw more of the isle from the mainland than we did while we were there.

Once on the mainland, we were back on the train. After a few days' pottering on the west coast, we were lucky to stumble upon the tiny seaside village of Plockton, which, together with some of the surrounding hills, is owned by the National Trust for Scotland. And so it should be. There were palm trees and pampas grass in the bay, and pleasant little Bed and Breakfasts where we really did have good value for little money. Our main evening entertainment was to eat out, as pubs and bars didn't hold much attraction. By day, the scenery was all we had hoped for. We spent a wonderful afternoon walking in the new forest nursery owned by the National Trust at Balmacara. We were escorted by a sturdy grey cat who seemed determined to ensure we found the right paths. She stayed with us, fussing and rolling against us, only cross when we stopped too long to enjoy the views. It was beautiful – and dry.

Back on the trains for the journey east and south, we really appreciated rail travel in bad weather. Where the landscape is the main attraction, the problem has to be what to do when the weather stops all but the most intrepid (or waterproof) traveller from getting out into it. The train provided a journey through the mountains, moorlands and lochs, and no steamed-up windows (as long as the carriage was a little draughty!). We felt it was a safe and relaxing way for women to travel together, certainly less stressful than a car. We also appreciated the loos!

We finished up in Edinburgh, in fine weather, and started walking around the city. We didn't appreciate the military presence in the Castle, but we did like the views of the city. I wish we had had the chance to check out some of the women's places in the city, which has quite a flourishing network of groups. I find it hard to make contact in strange places, but I think I would try if I went back. It would help give a female imprint to Scotland as a whole, for I think it sad that a country which has produced some strong women in its history – we were there for the 400th anniversary of the death of Mary Queen of Scots – denies its female past.

Scottish history, like that of most countries, seemed to be all wars and male heroics. We were put off by the blood and guts histories of the castles and museums. The thing that really upset me in Dunvegan Castle, in Skye, was not the sight of the hole in the ground through which prisoners were dropped and left to die, but the hole in the kitchen wall next to it, which had been cut through into the dungeon so that the starving people could smell the food. That's really warped.

"Public transport systems are really important to women . . . and Scotland let us down."

Looking back now, there are general pictures I have, other than rain and puddles. If you are interested in alcohol, then the whisky distilleries can provide a fascinating hour or two in the dry, trying the different types. If you don't like drinking, then the heavy emphasis on pubs, beer and whisky can be off-putting – it certainly doesn't challenge the stereotype of the heavy drinker, usually male, for which Scotland is renowned.

There is some attempt to develop Scottish cuisine, and that is brave in a country famous only for rolled oats and salmon. It is often expensive to eat out, though, and the standard is patchy to say the least. Long will we remember, as food never to be eaten again, "Plaice with Bananas" and weird desserts like strawberry mousse with oats.

Public transport systems are really important to women, whether visitors or residents, and Scotland let us down. Not being able to walk five miles from a station to a hotel, or twenty miles to a ferry, we found ourselves stuck time and time again. Hotels didn't necessarily have transport arrangements either, though the good ones were willing to help out when needed. Perhaps most people take their own cars, which is a shame. The railways have a good network of lines but, out of high season at least, run a slow and infrequent service, much of it stopping in Inverness.

I must admit, I came back wondering a little what my women friends had seen in Scotland. Though I look back fondly now, I'm still left with a very masculine image of drinking, of wars and clans. Then I hear the female voices singing as they stamped the tweed, picture the women cutting peat and living out their lives within its smoke, and think of Mrs Morrison running her taxis and her B & B I also remember the prevailing sense of space, even in towns, and realise how comfortable we two felt travelling around.

TRAVEL NOTES

Languages English and Welsh; plus many dialects and languages spoken by different ethnic groups.

Transport An efficient, if costly, network of buses and trains connects all main centres, coaches being cheapest for long distance travel. Services in remote areas, especially parts of Scotland and Wales, are often slow and irregular. Hitching alone carries the usual risks, although it's fairly easy to get a ride.

Depending on the exact area, big cities can be unsafe at night; if you're going to be out late it's wise to work out in advance how you'll get home. Public transport tends to shut down around midnight and taxis can be extortionate. London at least has a special minicab service, *Ladycabs*, run by women for women, though it doesn't operate around the clock. The service is based at 150 Green Lanes, N16 (☎01-254 3501/3314).

Accommodation In general expensive, especially in London which is renowned for having some of the most highly priced hotels in the world. Rooms advertised as Bed and Breakfast can be reasonable and very comfortable, but fill up quickly in the summer, as do youth hostels. Most tourist information offices carry a list of rooms available in the area. If you don't mind the regulations, youth hostels are widespread and some of the cheapest places to stay. Camping is safer than in many countries and often feasible outside of organised sites.

Special Problems Getting into Britain can be a harrowing experience, especially if you're arriving from a Third World country. Admission is at the discretion of the immigration officer and even marriage to a British citizen won't guarantee you secure entry. Make sure you have all the relevant documents, including

entry clearance from the British Embassy in your home country where applicable, and proof of sufficient funds to cover your stay. Black women have been particularly discriminated against by the UK Nationality Act. If in trouble, contact the *United Kingdom Immigrant Advisory Service* (☎01-240 5176), which has offices at Heathrow and Gatwick airports; and/or the *Women's Immigration and Nationality Group*, c/o 115 Old Street, London EC1V 9JR (☎ -251 8706).

Guides *Let's Go Britain and Ireland* (St Martins Press, US) is good on practicalities, if sometimes a little crass. *Hitchhiker's Manual: Britain* (Vacwork, Oxford) has invaluable route information. *Summer Jobs in Britain* (Vacation Work) is a fairly comprehensive, annual work directory.

Contacts

We only have space for a small selection of **women's organisations** here, but the **Spare Rib Diary** contains a fairly comprehensive list that includes women's centres and local groups, holiday places, bookshops and publications. The diary is obtainable from feminist and radical bookshops (see below) or by writing to *Spare Rib*, 27 Clerkenwell Close, London EC1 0AT.

London (highly selective)

Kings Cross Women's Centre, 71 Tonbridge St., WC1 (☎01-837 7509). Multiracial women's drop in, resource, advice and information centre.

Women's International Resource Centre, 173 Archway Road, London N6 5BL (☎01-341 4409). Mainly geared to linking up and giving solidarity to Third World women.

Lesbian Archive and Information Centre, BM Box 7005, London WC1N 3XX.

Women's Health and Reproductive Rights Information Centre, 52/4 Featherstone Street, London EC1Y 8RT (☎01-251 6332). National information and resource centre.

Feminist Library, 5 Westminster Bridge Road, London SE1 (☎01-928 7789).

London has two feminist **bookshops**: **Silver Moon**, 68 Charing Cross Road, WC2 (☎01-836 7906; and **Sisterwrite**, 190 Upper Street, N1 (☎01-226 9782, closed Monday). There are also a number of radical bookshops, among them **Compendium**, **Housman's** and the **Africa Book Centre**, with extensive women's sections.

England outside London

The following are a few **feminist/radical bookshops outside London**. All of these should be able to provide you with some information on women's activities in the area.

BIRMINGHAM: **Key Books**, 136 Digbeth, Birmingham B5 6DR (☎021-643 8081).

BRISTOL: **Greenleaf Bookshop Co-operative**, 82 Colston Street, Bristol 1 (☎0207-211369). Also a wholefood café.

CAMBRIDGE: **Grapevine**, Unit 6 Dale's Brewery, Gwydir Street, Cambridge (☎0223-61808).

LEEDS: **Corner Bookshop**, 162 Woodhouse Lane (opposite university), Leeds 2 (☎0532-454125).

LIVERPOOL: **Progressive Books**, 12 Berry Street, Liverpool L1 4JF (☎051-709 1905).

MANCHESTER: **Grassroots**, 1 Newton Street, Manchester M1 1HW (☎061-236 3112).

NEWCASTLE: **The Bookhouse**, 13 Ridley Place, Newcastle-upon-Tyne NE1 8JQ (☎ 091-261 6128).

SHEFFIELD: **Independent Bookshop**, 69 Surrey Street, Sheffield S1 2LH (☎0742-737 722).

YORK: **York Community Books**, 73 Walmgate, York (☎0904-37355).

Scotland

EDINBURGH: **West and Wilde Bookshop**, 25A Dundas St., Edinburgh EH3 6QQ (☎031-556 0079).

GLASGOW: **Changes Bookshop**, 340 West Princes St., Glasgow G4 9HF.

Wales

CARDIFF: **108 Bookshop**, 108 Salisbury Road. You should also make contact with the **Women's Centre**, 2 Coburn Street (☎0222-383024), for information about women-only/ lesbian bars and discos.

Women-only hostels/holiday centres

Again, only a selection:

England

Shiplate Farm, Shiplate Road, Avon BS24 ONY (☎0934-14787). Bed and Breakfast in a converted eighteenth-century farmhouse.

The Only Alternative Left, 39 St Aubyns, Hove, Sussex, BN3 2TH (☎0273-24739). Feminist-run Bed and Breakfast, also used for small residential conferences.

The Hen House, Hawerby Hall, Thoresby (☎0472-840278). A large Georgian mansion converted into a women's holiday centre. Slightly more expensive and luxurious than usual.

Women-Only Guest House, 19 Crossroads, Haworth, West Yorkshire, BD22 9BG (☎0535-45711; eves and weekends). Women-run Bed and Breakfast in the heart of Bronte country.

Scotland

Belrose Guest House, 53 Gilmore Place, Edinburgh EH3 9NT (☎229-6219). Women-owned and operated Bed and Breakfast.

Wales

Oaklands Women's Holiday Centre, Glastonbury-on-Wye, nr Hereford, Powys (☎04974-275). Tends to be booked up in advance by groups and can be chaotic and not always very friendly, but worth trying out.

Lan Farm, Graigwen, Pontypridd, Mid Glamorgan, CF37 3NN (☎0443-403606). Traditional Welsh farmhouse run as a hostel by two gay women.

Books

The 1980s saw a rapid development of feminist presses and feminist writing in Britain. Below are just a few personal favourites

Non-fiction

Beatrix Campbell, *Wigan Pier Revisited, Poverty and Politics in the 1980s* (Virago, 1984). A devastating record of the extent of poverty and unemployment in the north of England, and a passionate plea for a feminist socialism that responds to real needs. Also by the same author, ***The Iron Ladies: Why Women Vote Tory*** (Virago, 1987) provides some astute insights into the Margaret Thatcher phenomenon.

Angela Carter, *Nothing Sacred* (Virago, 1982). Collection of essays and writings, many of them autobiographical, by one of Britain's leading contemporary writers.

Jennifer Clarke, *In Our Grandmothers' Footsteps. A Virago Guide to London* (Virago, 1984). The author plus photographer Joanna Parkin have unearthed the memorials to 271 women — famous, infamous and unknown.

Anna Coote and Beatrix Campbell, *Sweet Freedom — The Struggle for Women's Liberation* (Picador, 1982). Two long-term active feminists chronicle the progress of the movement since the late 1960s when it began.

Hannah Kantner, Sarah Lefnu, Shaila Shah and Carole Spedding, eds, *Sweeping Statements: Writings from the Women's Liberation Movement 1981–3* (Women's Press, 1984). Collection of articles and conference papers, demonstrating the range of feminist involvement, analysis and action during this period.

Barbara Rogers, *52%: Getting Women's Power into Politics* (Women's Press, 1983). Compelling argument for the urgent need for more women's involvement in British politics.

Beverley Bryan, Stella Dadzie and Suzanne Scafe, *Heart of the Race* (Virago, 1985). Insights into what it's like growing up as a black woman in Britain.

Sharan-Jeet Shan, *In My Own Name* (The Women's Press, 1985). Autobiographical story of an Indian woman, born in the Punjab and forced into an arranged marriage which brought her to England, where she finally refuses to renounce her right to live her own life. Simply written and very moving.

Amrit Wilson, *Finding A Voice* (Virago, 1978). Experiences of Asian women in Britain recorded in their own words.

Rosalind K. Marshall, *Virgins and Viragos — a History of Women in Scotland from 1080-1980* (Collins, 1983). Over-academic but interesting in its exploration of little known ground.

Fiction

Zoe Fairbairns, *Benefits* (Virago, 1979). Feminist science-fiction set in a not too distant London future where men try to control women's reproduction and the "victims" fight back.

Pat Barker, *Union Street* (Virago, 1982). About the lives and struggles of seven working-class women and their men in the north of England during the 1973 miners' strike. Also recommended is ***The Man who Wasn't There*** (Virago, 1988). An optimistic novel about the bridging of age and class barriers.

Maggie Gee, *Grace* (Heinemann, 1988). Based on the events surrounding the extremely suspicious death of Hilda Murrell, an anti-nuclear campaigner, this novel deals with the threats inherent in British life.

Sara Maitland, *Telling Tales* (Journeyman Press, 1983). Collection of short stories, some set in the present, others featuring women from ancient and biblical history. Very readable. Her latest book, **Three Times Table** (Chatto, 1989), interweaves the lives of three women, combining fantasy with everyday observations.

Jeanette Winterson, *Oranges are not the Only Fruit* (Pandora Press, 1985). A quirky, funny and original book based on the author's own experiences of growing up in a pentecostal community in Lancashire. Barred from expressing her lesbian sexuality she breaks away, establishing her independence via university. Her later novels, ***The Passion*** (Penguin, 1988) and ***Sexing the Cherry*** (Bloomsbury, 1989) are both highly acclaimed works of history, fantasy and magic, inventive if not quite so much fun.

Buchi Emecheta, *Adah's Story* (Allison & Busby, 1983). Having left Nigeria to join her violent husband, Adah finds herself living alone in London with five children to look after. An account of an indomitable woman who fights against the odds to realise her ambition to be a writer. Look out also for Emecheta's other novels and children's books.

Canada

Compared with the US, Canada is a country of less outrageous extremes, more famous for its great outdoors than the hype and excitement of city life. There are far fewer people and, for many, mountains, forests, rivers and vast empty plains really are the principal attraction. You should have little trouble travelling alone or with another woman although, as in the States, most cities have areas it is best to avoid. Getting around to the main centres is straightforward, on buses, trains and internal flights, but public transport services in outlying areas tend to be few and far between. Here hitching, safest through agencies, may be your only option.

Regional differences between people are hardly surprising in a country of this size, but Canada is also very much split along national lines going back to the days of direct French and British colonisation. There has always been a degree of tension between British and French Canadians, particularly in

Quebec Province. The 1970s, when the Quebecois separatist movement was at its height, was an explosive time but since the passing of language laws, making French Quebec's official language relations have been easier. The government is explicitly committed to developing a bilingual national identity, and attempts to do this by emphasising a common cultural heritage, and by regulating foreign, mainly US, influence. Dependence on American investment and technology and the degree to which Canadian culture and lifestyle has been Americanised are a source of continued resentment.

Struggles within national minorities for identity, rights and property have all influenced the **women's movement** and determined its diverse, regional and very active nature. Almost every major town has a women's bookshop, café, feminist theatre, art gallery and local health centre. There are Indian and Inuit (Eskimo) groups, women's causes in national political parties, and active trade union women's groups. The largest national organisation, the *National Action Committee on the Status of Women (NAC)*, is a coalition of just under 6000 groups and represents almost three million women.

Abortion rights, the current rallying call for the American women's movement, is also a key issue in Canada. In January 1989, the Canadian Abortion Law which mandated approval for an abortion by a committee of hospital physicians was ruled unconstitutional. Women's groups hailed this as a major victory for the pro-choice movement. As we enter the 1990s, anti-choice activists are promoting legislation to restrict access to abortions, and, for the women's movement, the struggle now moves to public funding for abortions and equal access for all women, regardless of geography (northern Canada tends to be more conservative on these issues) or financial status.

Canadian feminist groups are facing aggressive opposition from a group called *REAL Women* (Realistic Equal Active for Life), an anti-feminist, anti-choice organisation which borrows the rhetoric of the women's movement to bolster their own traditional family and homophobic agenda. They claim a membership of 20,000 women and have recently been granted funding under a federal programme to promote equality. Feminist groups have yet to find an effective strategy to counterbalance the influence of this sister organisation which in fact opposes most feminist issues.

A Taste of the Great Outdoors

. . . .

Geraldine Brennan spent two months in Canada on the first stage of a year's journey around the world. She stayed with family in Ontario and explored alone in Quebec, British Columbia and Alberta.

When I arrived in Canada I wanted to rest and relish an increase in emotional and physical space. At that early stage in a round-the-world trip, I was not ready for the stimulation and hard slog of immersion into a totally different culture. I have lived all my life on an overcrowded island and for me the chance to watch killer whales playing off Vancouver Island, dodge Pacific rollers as I jogged along a deserted beach, and walk for ten hours with only birds for company was thrilling indeed. I appreciated the Canadians' regard for their environment: relatively clean rivers and streams, no smoking on most transport or in public buildings, bottles and paper collected for recycling with the garbage.

When travelling alone I used buses (with some overnight trips), hitched in emergencies (usually within national parks) and stayed in youth hostels. Attitudes towards me as a woman did not get in the way of many good experiences. Generally, I felt safe – I didn't appreciate how safe until I moved on to the US – with only a few moments of unease in downtown areas at night. The Canadians I met were warm, friendly and accepting. Only one man expressed horror at my travelling alone and asked me what my family thought of it (I'm thirty!). Those with British roots often wanted to talk about the royal family, UK soap operas or their grandparents' home town. It was sometimes hard, but showing interest in these topics paid off and I had many good conversations on long bus journeys.

"The current Canadian ideal is the white nuclear family enjoying the great outdoors"

Early in my visit I spent some weeks in Peterborough, Ontario, a small university town which is also the gateway to the Kawarthas. This network of lakes and canals attracts a stream of weekend and holiday visitors from Toronto and the surrounding area. I passed afternoons watching affluent Canadians at play and it became clear that, while Canada may be multiracial with equal opportunities for women similar to those in the States and Britain, the current Canadian national ideal is the white nuclear family enjoying the great outdoors. This impression was backed up by the Canadian media.

As I watched the lavishly equipped motorised houseboats cruising the canals and scaring away the birdlife, I wondered if the national sport might be collecting expensive leisure equipment in order to relive the pioneer experience. The holiday cabin on a remote lake shore, the camper van with twin mountain bikes or kayaks strapped to the roof and towing a four-wheel drive truck, the roadside picnic tables and barbecue pits are all desirable accessories. My solo attempt to get back to nature without even a car or a tent was often viewed with amusement. Like most Canadian consumer goods, the wilderness is available in neat family-size packages with detailed instructions for use.

I was grateful for the clearly marked trails and helpful information staff found in national and provincial parks. These people offer advice on how to deal with all the natural hazards that equally affect women and men: sudden changes in the weather, potential encounters with bears in some areas or the dangers of a long hike without the right footwear or adequate water. Anyone who chooses to hike alone for more than a day is asked to register, which offers extra protection for women. The park staff can also tell you how to enjoy the landscape and wildlife while making the minimum impact on it.

But it seemed that access to Canada's natural resources is not equally distributed. The country has many well-established ethnic communities: Italians and Asians in Toronto, Ukrainians in the prairie provinces, Chinese and Japanese in Vancouver, Afro-Caribbeans . . . yet I met very few non-white Canadians on my tour of beauty spots and forest-screened campgrounds. This was in obvious contrast to my experience on buses, used by those who can't afford cars, where white faces were in a minority.

Wanting to make contact with North American Indian women, I visited a Kwaitukl reservation in Alert Bay, British Columbia. I was warmly welcomed by a woman running its cultural centre who was only too keen to talk about the past and present life of her people. Museums are a good source of background information on the local Indian bands in whichever part of Canada you find yourself and many have reproduced their own histories in book and video form.

My holiday included a break from any kind of political organising. I noticed active women's organisations within reach of most communities and enormous scope for almost any kind of feminist activity in Toronto, Vancouver and Montreal. Peterborough had a downtown women's centre, two good bookshops and at least one university women's group. Despite all this temptation, my resolve to let the world save itself remained intact.

Canada is a country I could happily live in, preferably in one of the larger cities with greater tolerance for lifestyles outside the nuclear family. I arrived expecting it to be like the United States and found it a much more rational and safe place to be.

Hitching Through the Yukon

. . . .

Kate Pullinger is a Canadian writer living in London. She describes hitch-hiking through the Yukon Territory, a massive area north of British Columbia in western Canada.

The Yukon is basically the "Great Outdoors", and not much else. Exceptionally underpopulated, with less than 25,000 people in an area almost as large as France, it is a mountain-lake-forest-river-lover's dream come true. I think the best way to see it, at least in summer, is to hitchhike. I have always found hitching in the Yukon relatively fast, easy and safe, mainly because towns are far apart and nobody is going to leave anyone standing on the side of the road in the middle of nowhere at -20°C, or, in summer, in all that dust.

Last summer I stood on the side of the road outside the Yukon's capital, Whitehorse. My thumb stuck out, I was heading for Dawson City 333 miles away. The first vehicle to stop was an old Ford truck, bed on back with two extremely large sled dogs hanging out over its sides. They barked at me ferociously. A woman jumped out and asked how far I was going. I told her, and she said she was only going fifty miles, but that was a good start. So I jumped in.

She was young, had long plaited hair, and was wearing men's shorts and a felt hat. Next to her sat a small, dark baby, who looked at me curiously. The woman didn't say anything so neither did I. After a few miles she reached above the windscreen and pulled a cigar from behind the sunshade. She smoked it as she drove, clenching it between her teeth when she changed gear. I looked out of the window over the hills and vast, peopleless landscape.

After fifty miles she pulled off the road on to the dirt track that led to her house and I thanked her and jumped out. I slammed the truck door so it shut properly and she and the baby sped off. The sled dogs barked at me until I was far out of their sight.

I stood again at the side of the road. A small Toyota two-door stopped. I put my pack in the back seat and climbed in front. This driver was also a woman, she wore a skirt and her hair was wet. We began to chat and I learned that she was just driving home from a swimming lesson in Whitehorse – a trip of 200 miles, which she made every Friday. There aren't very many swimming pools in the Yukon. The conversation led to a familiar story: she came up to the Yukon ten years ago to visit a friend and stayed. She said she wouldn't leave for anything, and now her brother lives up here too. I began to think there must be something special about this place.

Where she dropped me it was very quiet. There were trees everywhere I looked. In fact, all I could see was trees. I had to wait here around twenty minutes before I heard what sounded like a truck. I saw the dust before I could see it, great clouds of dirt billowing up into the sky. Then I saw the truck and stood on my tiptoes and tried to make my thumb bigger. The driver saw me and started to slow down. It took him a long time to do so and he went past me. I could no longer see, there was so much dust, and I held my scarf over my mouth. When it settled I walked to the truck – a long way up – and negotiated the lift, another fifty miles.

"I knew about this kind of van: lush interior, shag carpets on the walls, a stereo. They call them sin-bins, glam-vans, or more straightforwardly, fuck-trucks"

After hoisting my pack up I climbed in. The driver started the engine and headed down the road. I smiled to myself, thinking I was in front of the dust now. The truck driver seemed to change gears a hundred times before we were up to the right speed. Steaming along, past the endless lakes and hills, he told me about his children going to school, having babies and

working in Edmonton. I listened and then asked how long he's been here. He said he came for a year thirty years ago. There is something about this place.

Dropped at another turnoff I ran into the bushes for protection from all that dust. When he and his cloud were out of sight, I climbed back to the road. A few more cars went by and then a van stopped. It was a newish van, brown with a sunset painted on the exterior. I knew about this kind of van: lush interior, shag carpets on the walls, a stereo. They call them sin-bins, glam-vans, or more straightforwardly, fuck-trucks. Thinking of my vulnerability, I took a look at the driver. He was male, of course, and looked about forty-five. He was wearing a nylon shirt with bucking broncos on it. He had a skinny black moustache and shiny hair. He asked where I was going and said he was too, he didn't know these parts and would like some company. The voice inside me said he was okay. I got into the van.

The driver was called Dan and came from Fort St John. He talked away about his family and I began to relax. He said he was a professional gambler which made me sit up: gambling is illegal in most of Canada. Dan told me all about the gambling circuit in British Columbia, the late-night games in Trail, Kelowna, Hope, the nights when he'd walked away with $4000 in his pocket. He told me about the cards, the passwords and the bribes to the Mounties. I was astounded; this was a whole new side to "Beautiful But Boring British Columbia". I asked him what he was doing up here. Then I remembered: Dawson City is the only place in Canada where gambling is legal. And Dawson City was where I was headed.

It was evening by the time we arrived and Dan dropped me off at the crossing to the campsite. Satiated with gambling stories, I sat down beside the river and waited for the little ferry to take me across. It was full of other hitchhikers: Germans, Americans, Quebecois. It was 8pm and the sky was as bright as mid-morning. I ate and then took the ferry back across to the town, strolling along the wild west wooden sidewalks, past the false-front saloons, hotels and shops and ending up in front of Diamond Tooth Gerties, the casino. I went in, thinking I wouldn't play, just have a look around. The place was full and everyone was drinking, smoking and gambling. There were dancing girls, and a vaudeville show and card-dealers with waistcoats and bow ties and armbands. I had a drink and wondered if this was what it had looked like in 1905. Standing beside the blackjack table I figured out how to play, and watched as people won and lost. I wasn't going to play, just watch.

"I talked and laughed with all the other gamblers I had met. Feeling rather rich and drunk . . ."

Many bottles of Molson Canadian and five hours later, I came out, $10 up. It was 2am, broad daylight; if the sun ever went down, I missed it. Running to catch the ferry back to the campsite, I talked and laughed with all the other gamblers I had met. Feeling rather rich and drunk, I crawled into my tent. Someone had built a campfire and people were milling about doing campfire sorts of things but it didn't seem right, campfire and campsongs in broad daylight. I closed my eyes and thought that perhaps after a few nights of lucrative gambling I would hitch that brief 150 miles up into the Arctic Circle. There is definitely something about this place.

TRAVEL NOTES

Languages English and French; in Quebec French is the main language.

Transport There are *Greyhound* coaches to most towns, good trains and efficient, fairly inexpensive internal flights. Hitching is possible but not always advisable alone on the open, lonely roads. For long distances, college noticeboards are an excellent source of lifts; they specify people wanting or offering lifts and you get a chance to meet the people beforehand.

Accommodation YWCAs are usually a good bet; full details from the national office in Toronto (571 Jarvis Street, M4Y JJ1 ☎416-921 2117). Universities outside term time are also recommended.

Guides *Canada – A Travel Survival Kit* (Lonely Planet). *Moneywise Guide to North America* (Travelaid) includes a Canada section. Recommended for the Yukon is *The Alaska-Yukon Handbook* (Moon Publications, US).

Contacts

A very good source for addresses and information about the Canadian women's movement is the annual ***Everywoman's Almanac*** (Women's Press, Canada). Distributed in the UK and available in women's bookshops.

The **National Action Committee on the Status of Women** (NAC) is the political arm and largest national women's movement organisation in Canada, comprising a coalition of just under 5000 groups with a combined membership of close to three million women. Main office: 344 Bloor St.W, Suite 505, Toronto, M5S3A7, ☎922-3246.

Also useful, the **Canadian Women's Mailing List** for up-to-date information of events, publications services is published by WEB Women's Information Exchange, 9280 Arvida Avenue Richmond BC, ☎604-274 5335.

Another way of gathering information inside Canada is via the free **networking magazines** available in kiosks in every large city.

These tend to list everything – gay and lesbian groups, ethnic groups, psychodrama, alternative health, ecology groups etc. You could also try phoning the local **New Democratic Party** office, the only political party to seriously consider women's issues on its agenda.

Calgary, Edmonton, Montreal, Quebec, Toronto and Vancouver all have **women's bookshops** and centres. These include:

CALGARY: **Women's Resource Centre-YWCA**, 320-5th Avenue, S.E., Calgary T2G OE5, Alberta, ☎403-263 1550.

EDMONTON: **Commonwoman Books**, 8210-104 St., Edmonton, Alberta.

MONTREAL: **Androgyny** (gay and women's bookshop), 1217 Crescent, Montreal. Should stock the **Montreal Yellow Pages** which lists resources for women.

TORONTO: **Women's Bookstore**, 73 Harboard St., Toronto.

VANCOUVER: **Vancouver Women's Bookstore**, Cambic St, ☎604-684 052.

Books

Margaret Atwood, *Bluebeard's Egg* (Virago, 1988); ***The Handmaid's Tale*** (Virago, 1987) and earlier novels by Canada's leading novelist and poet.

Joan Barfoot, *Gaining Ground* (The Women's Press, 1980). Novel about a woman who leaves her husband, children and suburban security to live as a hermit deep in the Canadian countryside.

Jane Rule, *The Desert of the Heart* (1964; Pandora, 1986) and ***Memory Board*** (Pandora, 1987) are just two of the books we recommend by one of the country's leading lesbian feminist writers.

Ann Cameron, *Daughters of Copper Woman* (The Women's Press, Canada, 1985). Novel of matriarchal secret legends of Nootka women, off Vancouver island.

Willa Cather, *Shadows on the Rock* (1937; Virago 1984). Classic novel about French settlers in Canada.

Alice Munro, *Beggar Maid* (Penguin, 1981). Best-known book of this Canadian author, again set in rural Ontario and in Toronto.

Susan Crean, *Newsworthy: The Lives of Media Women* (Stoddart, Canada, 1985). Examination of how women have overcome the twin barriers of self-doubt and discrimination and established themselves in print and electronic media.

Peney Kome, *Women of Influence: Canadian Women and Politics* (Doubleday, New York, 1985). Somewhat academic but a useful overview of women's place in political life.

Susanna Moodie, *Roughing it in the Bush: or Forest life in Canada* (Virago, 1985). Sharp, enduring account by an early British settler; new introduction by novelist Margaret Atwood.

Thanks to Anne O'Byrne, Catherine Pepinster and Jo Siedlecka for introductory information and Travel Notes.

Chad

. . . .

Not many travellers go to Chad. The country has suffered badly from years of civil war and horrendous drought; there is virtually no public transport and travel is by pick-up truck or lorry, usually on top of a pile of goods.

Despite the ravages of war, evident everywhere in the ruined buildings, untarred roads and general lack of public services, Chad is reportedly going through a period of revival and optimism. What began as a civil war, only five years after independence from the French, has gradually narrowed into war against Libya. The French, only too willing to support their former colony against Colonel Gaddafi, have piled on military assistance and, by 1990, it looks as if Libya may be losing its stronghold. The economy, largely reliant on cotton production, also appears to be improving, though in reality the country is more or less totally dependent on foreign aid.

After a long period of restriction, it is possible to travel almost anywhere in the country; just don't expect to get there quickly. Hotels are few and far between, but in the more populated south most villages seem to have a mission station where, once people have got over the shock of seeing a lone woman traveller, you will probably receive a warm welcome. Also you will nearly always find yourself among travelling Chadienne women, eager to look after you and help find you a bed for the night. Travel in Chad may be unpredictable and hard going at times, but the absence of tourism and subsequent hustle, coupled with vast stretches of wild and beautiful scenery, make it definitely worth a visit.

Oxfam and UNICEF focus a proportion of aid on women's income-generating and health projects but, despite an official Department of Women's Affairs, there appears to be little specific concentration on **women's needs** from within the country. Circumstances vary considerably from north to south, but generally women have only limited property rights and bear the brunt of water and wood carrying on top of childcare and general domestic chores. Though village women's groups exist to try to ease the burden, as long as the country remains hampered by war, it will be some time before Chad sees any kind of concerted movement for women's rights.

Days on the Road

. . . .

A freelance photographer from the northeast of England, Chris Johnson spent a year in Africa, researching into the lives of local women and taking photographs for an exhibition. In Chad she travelled much of the time by lorry, hitching lifts wherever she could.

From the capital, N'Djamena, a narrow strip of pot-holed tarmac runs north; we follow alongside on the broad sandy track through the scrub. There are very few paved roads in Chad, and those that are paved are usually in such bad condition that people prefer making their own tracks. It's hot and I'm thirsty. I look longingly at the bottle of water beside me, but it's the second day of Ramadan and as neither of my companions have had anything to eat or drink since sunrise it seems unfair of me to add to their misery by indulging myself.

At 4pm we stop for them to pray. The road continues through sparse red gold grass and past the occasional dusty tree. Half an hour later we reach a village where we stop to rest. The driver sends off for cans of cold orange juice and hands one to me, brushing aside my protests and insisting I drink. It feels like the height of generosity and is typical of my experiences with Muslim men in Africa.

En route again. We've now lost all semblance of tar, and in places there isn't even much semblance of track, just tyre marks in the sand. At 6.30pm we stop again to pray. The ordeal is over for the day and at last they can drink. They tell me the first three days of Ramadan are the worst; after that one gets used to it. The evening is a pearly grey-pink; above is the thin crescent of the moon. All around is vast emptiness. We drive on again, often through thick sand. A man comes by on his camel, our headlights picking out the rich colours of the woven saddle cloth.

We reach Chaddra, our first port of call, at 10pm. The vehicle is unloaded and we stop for a meal. Inside the courtyard, lit by the flicker of oil lamps, a group of white-robed men sit round the large mat. As a visitor, I am accorded the status of honorary man and sit with them to eat. A woman waits on us silently.

Then it's another two hours' rough driving. Exhausted, I keep falling asleep, only to be jolted awake again. At midnight we stop by a cluster of houses. We roll out our mats and the local inhabitants come across the sands to chat and to bring us more mats. I am aware of the faint sound of someone playing a thumb piano, before falling asleep. Sometime in the early morning the cold wakes me and I crawl into my sleeping bag.

"As a visitor, I am accorded the status of honorary man and sit with them to eat. A woman waits on us silently"

Prayers are at dawn and we are off by six. Apart from the occasional tree, the only vegetation is a pale green plant, about three feet tall and with leathery leaves. Mostly there is just sand. An hour later we pass a small group of rectangular houses with flat roofs; then, coming over a rise, see the village of Mao spread out on the hillside ahead. The single-storey houses are built of the local pale coloured earth which is found in bands by the wadis. They are very Arab looking – rectangular in shape, with flat roofs and little turrets at each corner and halfway along the long walls – and are entered through tiny gateways in the street walls.

One of these houses is my home for the next few days. The thick walls and tiny slit windows keep it wonderfully cool, a welcome contrast to the modern houses of the city. Inside the courtyard someone has planted trees and flowers; an awning keeps off the fierce sun and a gentle wind rustles my papers as I try to write.

Mao is the capital of Karem province and an ancient trading centre. As you enter the village the words "Sultanate of Karem" can be seen written in black over the white archway. The weekly market still brings in people from a wide distance and even the daily market is large, though it has little

fresh food: most things are dried to preserve them. Especially good are the dried dates.

Along one side of the village runs a wadi. Down in its valley piles of bricks lie baking in the sun and there is constant traffic to and from the wall. A line of women, swathed in long black robes, walk back up the hill to the village carrying heavy earthen water pots on their heads.

At 6.30pm the muezzin calls the faithful again to prayer. Looking out across the walls, there are only four colours: the pinky-beige of the sands, which is split by a gash of white – the same white as the houses; the dusty green of trees; and the pale, pale blue of the sky. Veiled women greet me and laugh at my taking photographs.

Northwest of Mao is Nokou. It's definitely remote: if you travel northwest for about 320 miles you might, if your navigation is good, hit Bihua in Niger; travel northeast about 400 miles and, if you are lucky, you come across Zouar in the Tbesti Mountains; otherwise the nearest habitation is about 800 miles away in Libya.

We set off from Mao as soon as the prayers have finished. The empty landscape sweeps up into hills, nothing very high or steep, but on a grand scale. It's windy and the surface sand blows off like spindrift. Occasionally there's a sparse covering of grass which from a distance lends the hills a yellow-green colour; but as soon as you get close it is clear there's far more sand than grass. From time to time we see a few goats or a woman on a donkey, but mainly it's just camels: some roaming free, others ridden by men dressed in long white robes.

The people I am travelling with are involved in a project helping to cultivate the wadis. The water table in the wadis is very close to the surface and *shadufs* are used to lift water to irrigate. Traditionally some people have always cultivated in this area: it's one of the features that distinguish it from the eastern Sahel. But when the drought came and thousands of nomads lost their entire stock and ended up in camps, someone decided that the answer was increased cultivation.

Nomadic people have always had their own way of dealing with drought. A *Fulani* friend explained how, when drought hit and they lost their stock, some of the tribe would go into the villages and work for the settled people, just for long enough to raise money to restock. Then they'd be off again. Maybe many will use the new aid schemes in the same way. Some, though, say desertification has gone too far, that the land can no longer support so many people in that old lifestyle.

It's my last day in Nokou. I get up very early and climb the nearby hill to watch the sun rise behind the small fortress that looks out over the desert. Slowly the village wakes up. Women climb the hill, pots on heads; a man walks off across the desert, the wind tugging at his white robes; a laughing girl comes by on a donkey.

As I walk down and wander along the sandy streets taking photos I am sad to be leaving, but there is little option. If I don't get today's transport there won't be another vehicle until Tuesday; and my visa expires on Wednesday. My original intention had been to go west from here rather than going back to N'Djamena, but being Ramadan there are no vehicles going that way.

We leave at about 9am. Somewhere in the middle of an area of beige and white sand dunes something goes wrong with the vehicle. But, as always, they manage to fix it; meanwhile I go round taking photos.

As enquiries at Mao reveal no transport going either west to the Lake Chad or south to N'Djamena I decide to go out with the project for the day. If there are any vehicles going south we will see them and if not I'll go back to Mao for the night and try again in the morning. For a long time the only vehicles we see are the French Army, and one very broken-down lorry. Then, in the distance, a cloud of dust, out of which emerges a very old blue Toyota. We flag it down, and its occupants, three turbaned Arabs, agree to take me to Mussokori – for a price.

> *"For a long time the only vehicles we see are the French Army, and one very broken-down lorry. Then, in the distance, a cloud of dust, out of which emerges a very old blue Toyota ... three turbaned Arabs agree to take me to Mussokori – for a price"*

Ten minutes along the way we get a flat tyre. They change it and we continue, shuddering our way over the rough ground. My companions speak no French and I little Arabic so our conversation is limited. Almost an hour later the next tyre goes. Luckily we are close by a small settlement. The school-teacher, a slip of a kid who has probably only had a couple of years' secondary schooling himself, comes to greet us and takes me back to one of the huts. I am brought water and Provita – a nutritional supplement in the form of small biscuits, the result of some aid programme.

The hours tick slowly by. Several times I think I hear the sound of a vehicle, but on investigation it is only the wind. It is very hot. Again I think I hear the sound of a vehicle. I go outside and strain my ears; then over the horizon appears a cloud of dust, followed by two very large and very new lorries, each towing a trailer wagon and carrying a handful of passengers. I flag down the first one; the driver is happy to give me a lift and in I climb. It transpires that the lorries are part of a six-truck UNDP convoy returning from delivering food to displaced persons in the war zone.

Such lorries are not fast but they are relatively comfortable and I am well pleased with the lift. The driver has been all over, driving lorries across the Sahara to Tripoli, Algeria, Agadez, Tunis. The only problem with the journey is lack of water – I have stupidly managed to leave my water bottle in the fridge at Mao and by the time we reach Mussokori in the early afternoon I am so thirsty I can hardly speak. In desperation I manage to down 1.5 litres of disgusting Camerounian fizz.

The convoy of UN lorries is staying the night and I should probably stay with them; but I am short of time and anxious to get back to N'Djamena. A pick-up was meant to be leaving "tou:e de suite" so I decide to take it. At 4pm it still hasn't left. I transfer to another pick-up, we leave, get stuck in the sand, push it out, get stuck again . . . "toute de suite" passes us, we push ours out again and pass them, with much glee.

At 6pm we stop in a village where we are all instructed to dismount while the driver simply wanders off. I try to find out what's going on and am told that he has gone to meet his wife and that we'll be leaving again in an hour. I bet. I sit down on a rug, feeling very tired. Not just physically tired, but tired of the endless waits, of the uncertainty, of travelling on my own. At 7.30pm our driver comes back and we pile in, only to find the Surete suddenly want to see my papers – I have only been sitting outside their office for the last hour-and-a-half! Still, at least they are quick and pleasant.

We set off, stop to pick up wood – everyone off, load the cargo of wood, everyone on again – then, on the outskirts of N'Djamena, a motorbike roars up, overtakes us and demands we stop. Apparently we have failed to stop at a checkpoint. Back we go, off we get, and watch them go through all our baggage. Arriving at N'Djamena market at about 9.30pm, I flag down a taxi to take me to the house and collapse.

TRAVEL NOTES

Languages Largely Arabic in the north and French in the south, plus about 70 local languages.

Transport There are few surfaced roads, no buses and no railways. Your only option is to ask around for a lift. Travel this way is slow and erratic, but generally safe.

Accommodation Hotels are in short supply outside the capital. Again, your best bet is to ask around on arrival in a particular place.

Guide *Central Africa: A Travel Survival Kit* (Lonely Planet) – a reasonable section on Chad.

Contacts

We know of no women's groups currently operating. **Oxfam** and **UNICEF** could put you in touch with development projects including women.

Books

We have not traced any books on Chad. However, Chris Johnson recommends the following academic studies for readers interested in the situation of women in Africa:

Niki Nelson ed., *African Women in the Development Process* (Frank Cass and Co., 1981).

Christine Oppong ed., *Female and Male in West Africa* (Allen and Unwin, 1983).

Margaret Jean Kay and Sharon Stitcher eds., *African Women South of the Sahara* (Longman, 1984).

Thanks to Chris Johnson for supplying much of the information for the introduction and Travel Notes.

Chile

. . . .

Since General Pinochet seized power in September 1973, Chile has not seen a great many foreign travellers. In the years immediately after Pinochet's military coup, which toppled the elected socialist government of President Salvador Allende, the country became home to one of the most brutally repressive regimes in Latin America. Thousands of Chileans were imprisoned, murdered, tortured or went into exile.

Sixteen years later Pinochet's rule finally came to an end. Unable to resist any longer the mounting pressure to call a free election he took a gamble on "democracy" and lost. Patricio Alwyn, a centrist politician, now heads a broad but tenuous coalition government in charge of making good the transition to democracy and, most urgently, limiting the role of the army (and with it Pinochet) in the political life of the country. Encouraged by these changes exiles are returning and a spirit of cautious optimism hangs in the air.

Visiting Chile, it is hard to forget the widescale political repression that overshadows the nation's recent past. At the same time, overwhelming hospitality and a general lack of crime against tourists make this one of the more relaxing Latin American countries to explore. Even hitching is reported to be relatively safe for women.

Good roads and an efficient bus and rail network make it easy to get around central Chile, where most of the population is concentrated in and around the capital, Santiago, and in the beautiful lake district, home of the Mapuche Indians. Elsewhere, in the northern desert and south towards Patagonia, transport is more erratic and accommodation can be hard to find. Travel in general can be expensive with prices, including bus fares, at their highest in the south and everywhere during the high season of December to March.

Women have always been very active in the struggle for democracy in Chile. *CODEM* (Defence Committee for Women's Rights) co-ordinates a large network of working-class **women's organisations**. Local groups in different parts of the country develop training schemes for women in areas like health and technical skills; they campaign for women's legal rights, for adequate housing, and for the release of political prisoners; and organise soup kitchens, alternative schools, cultural events and protest activities, especially in the shanty towns. There are also a number of action-oriented research groups, such as the *Centro de Estudios de la Mujer* (CEM), based in Santiago, which has carried out projects with peasant women, including the minority Mapuche Indians of whom only around 150,000 remain.

A Nation of Hospitality

. . . .

At the age of 26, Barbara Gefton gave up her job as a sub-editor to travel around the world. She spent six months altogether in South America, almost half of the time in Chile where she travelled the whole length of the country with a friend, Louise.

To people throughout the world Chile and its president Pinochet are almost bywords for brutality and repression. Only too familiar with the tales of atrocities that have been committed by the present regime, I was surprised to find that on the surface Chile is a land of calm and order where *carabineros* (armed police) maintain a watchful, though usually unobtrusive, presence. Today's methods are clearly more sophisticated and as a visitor you are unlikely to observe them first hand. I was told that these days the regime works partly through an element of fear. Pinochet is frequently to be seen on television carrying out works for the public good. "He speaks in platitudes,"

said a friend. "He says the choice is him or chaos" – the latter being depicted in televised images from the USSR.

Initially I was wary of even mentioning politics, but the days of hushed voices are gone. I heard many points of view, from first-hand accounts of violence in response to public protest to insistence that the foreign press convey a false picture of the country. I learned to keep my mouth shut at times. But overall I felt a spirit of optimism in the air. Since losing majority support in the plebiscite of 1988, Pinochet seems to be fading from the political scene, opening up the way for a new era of democracy.

"In a continent where excessive paranoia can so easily ruin your trip, we felt virtually none of the threat of theft experienced elsewhere"

The peace of mind we enjoyed and the straightforwardness of getting from one place to another were not quite what we had expected from South America, least of all a notorious dictatorship. Things seem so easy here, we'd say, half guiltily (weren't we supposed to be roughing it?) and half relieved. And we'd stay a little longer, in no hurry to confront the hazards we were sure lay ahead. After hearing all the horror stories from visitors newly arrived from Peru and Brazil, Chile was beginning to seem like a travellers' paradise. In a continent where excessive paranoia can so easily ruin your trip, we felt virtually none of the threat of theft experienced elsewhere.

We were also struck by an apparent lack of interest in making money out of foreign tourists who, in Chilean terms, must seem incredibly rich. Perhaps this will change in time, especially if a return to democracy helps to revamp the country's image abroad. For now we should appreciate a nation where people with so little show so much hospitality: like the waiter who brought us free drinks with our beautifully served meal and refused to accept a tip, and the off-duty taxi driver who stopped on his way home to give us a lift.

Yet the trip did not have an auspicious start. Our plans to meet at Santiago airport fell apart when I was over 24 hours late in arriving. Being surrounded by loud emotional family reunions provides little comfort when you find yourself alone in a capital city of four million inhabitants with no sign of the friend you've arranged to meet, nor even a clue to her whereabouts. By this time it was late and the airport information offices where I might have found a message were closed. As people flapped around me and I listened in alarm to the fast and clipped variant of the language I thought I knew so well, I was thankful to be taken under the wing of a bus driver and his conductor. They were about to leave for the city centre and said they would find me a place to stay. Half an hour later on a dark and deserted city street, accompanied by a complete stranger, I wondered if I had lost my head entirely. Needless to say there were no problems and I was simply delivered to a reasonably priced hotel, as promised.

Ironically, this potential disaster may well have been the best thing that could have happened, for it obliged us to put our trust in people who, we soon discovered, take great pleasure in offering all kinds of assistance.

"First impressions of Santiago were of a clean, modern, bustling city full of friendly, helpful people"

I was lucky to meet Rosana who was working in an airline office as part of her studies. When I turned up the next morning she was clearly overjoyed to have a lost English girl to look after. Before I'd been there half an hour I had been invited to stay with her in Santiago and to visit her family in their summer house at the beach (offers we later took up). And when Louise and I were finally reunited via the British Embassy later that day, I discovered that she too had been shown considerable help; a Chilean man she met at the airport had not only gone out of his way to make enquiries as to my whereabouts, but found her somewhere to stay and taken her to see some of the sights of the city.

First impressions of Santiago were of a clean, modern, bustling city full of friendly, helpful people. In fact, smog is so dense in the capital that what would otherwise be a spectacular view of the Andes is blotted out most of the time. I remember my surprise on waking up one morning in the apartment in which we were staying to see snowcapped peaks in the distance: I'd been there a week and had not seen them before. By the afternoon they had disappeared again beneath their grey shroud; that same day on the city streets my eyes smarted and the air was thick and choking.

Santiago afforded the anonymity I take for granted in London and long for in Mediterranean cities once the clicking tongue brigade and the hissers get going. Or it almost did. The only sign of interest you are likely to receive is from the money changers on the street, looking out for gringos, male or female, as potential customers. I don't remember experiencing any sexual harassment, in the capital or anywhere else.

For our first couple of weeks in Chile we stayed in hotels and hostels until we discovered the alternative of staying with families in private homes. Cheaper than hotels, this accommodation provides a good opportunity for meeting people and exchanging information, often leading to contacts in other towns. Another attraction of these *casas de familia* was the chance to use a kitchen and prepare our own food, something of a luxury once the novelty of eating out all the time had worn off. It was interesting, too, to be able to observe something of family life, though these were hardly typical households where the children seemed to take for granted the constantly changing faces, foreign tongues and having to step over bodies on the living room floor.

In a country where women are unable to travel without their husbands' permission, we were treated with courtesy, kindness and a great deal of curiosity everywhere. Certain questions cropped up again and again: Were we German? Were we sisters? (the only likenesses we could see were fairness of complexion, blue eyes and permanently sunburnt noses) and – with great incredulity – Were we on our own? We were also asked, sometimes repeatedly, if we liked Chile.

More than in any other South American country, we met and made good friends with people our own age. Socially, we often found ourselves in male company, spending a few weeks in the far south of the country with a group of students from Santiago we met on a boat trip. The women we got to know, all from wealthy homes in the capital – confident, articulate, and speaking excellent English – were

hardly representative of the nation's female population. All lived at home with their parents, explaining that though they had jobs, they simply couldn't afford to do otherwise.

"Hitching can be a practical as well as economical and interesting way to travel"

Travelling with our Chilean friends was an education. With strict budgets to stick to they hitched lifts everywhere, searched a town for a free place to stay (they once, to our amazement, were given permission to sleep and cook in an empty room in the local fire station) and bargained their way shamelessly through all situations. We meanwhile rather guiltily swanned around on luxury coaches where attendants opened and closed our curtains, reclined our seats for us and helped us disembark, and ate delicious meals in often empty restaurants.

Travelling by bus was a joy, but as Chile has good roads, hitching can be a practical as well as economical and interesting way to travel. Most important, it feels generally safe and we never heard any bad reports.

Louise and I hitched the 1300 miles from Arica, close to the country's northern border, back down to Santiago. Two-and-a-half days and four lifts later we arrived back in the capital having spent over half the time with one lorry driver who was carrying a huge load of salt. There was little transport other than trucks on that road which stretched through an inhospitable desert, dotted with the ghost towns of old nitrate mining settlements. Our driver shared his food with us, treated us to a meal, ignoring our protests, and let us sleep in the bunks in the truck. His seemed a harsh life, spent mostly on the road, hardly sleeping, and rarely seeing his family, but he never complained. When we stopped in a small settlement I watched him unscrew the radio cassette player to reveal boxes containing electrical equipment. He explained that by selling these on the black market he was able to send his elder daughter to university in Santiago, whom, in true Chilean fashion, he insisted we contact on our arrival.

South of Puerto Montt the only transport is by sea or air. The thought of pressing on and reaching what is almost the end of the earth appealed to our imaginations. But to do this we had to first take a three-day boat trip down Chile's coast, through the calm waters of the islands and, for a short stretch, venture into the wilder waters of the Pacific. Chatting to our fellow passengers with dolphins leading the way, I thought there were few places I would rather be. From Punta Arenas, the world's most southerly city, we took a ferry to Tierra del Fuego where we could look out across the Beagle Channel knowing that nothing lay between ourselves and Antarctica.

The Torres del Paine national park in southern Chile is one of the natural wonders of the continent – an unspoilt area of lakes, glaciers, and needle-sharp peaks. To take the week-long trail round the park we needed camping equipment. Luckily we'd made a friend who had all the essentials. With Assi we squashed into a tiny tent, marvelled at the raw beauty around us and bathed in icy streams. He baked us pitta bread in the ashes of the fire for breakfast and we all dreamt of pizzas and chicken and cans of Coke. Once we'd set off we were truly on our own amidst this spendid landscape, meeting just a few people each day coming from the opposite direction.

"As a woman traveller you will inevitably attract attention, but, in this country anyway, it is usually of the most pleasant sort"

Chile is a country of surprises. In Frutillar where we arrived in the week of the annual classical music festival we were amazed to find a mini 'Proms' in the Chilean lake district. In Valdivia, having missed the boat home from a tiny peninsular settlement we were visiting, we were rescued by four yachtsmen who not only returned us to our hostel, but cooked us a meal on the way back. And one day we climbed the smoking volcano Villarrica, rising above the clouds, to peer into the crater to see the occasionally spurting lava before sliding back down in the snow.

Though I did very little travelling on my own in Chile, I would not hesitate to recommend it to anyone who merely lacks reassurance. As a woman traveller you will inevitably attract attention, but, in this country anyway, it is usually of the most pleasant sort. We often wondered if we were just lucky in our experiences here. I don't think so. Other travellers we met, whether alone or in couples, male or female, shared similar tales of hospitality and welcome. When we finally crossed into Argentina, unsure if we would be returning, I felt sadness, wondering if we would be made to feel as welcome in this new country. Later, when we did go back, it felt almost like coming home.

TRAVEL NOTES

Languages Spanish and some remaining indigenous languages.

Transport Buses are many and frequent. Travelling directly from north to south, or vice versa, internal flights are quick and comfortable, but you obviously miss out on much.

Accommodation A wide range of hotels and pensions at all prices can be found throughout the country. There are also quite a few Youth Hostels. Most towns have a tourist information office or it's easy just to ask in the street.

Special Problems Remember to buy Chilean-made products whenever possible. You are usually offered brand-name imported goods at highly inflated prices. Beware of taking part in any overt anti-government activity. A foreign passport doesn't necessarily make you immune to police brutality.

Guides *The South American Handbook* (Trade and Travel) has an excellent chapter on Chile. Also recommended is *Chile and Easter Island: A Travel Survival Kit* (Lonely Planet).

Contacts

For up-to-date information before you leave Britain, contact **Chile Solidarity Campaign Women's Section**, 129 Seven Sisters Rd., London N7 7QG. ☎071-263 8529/272 4298. Or write to **Isis International Women's Information and Communication Service**, Casilla 2067, Correo Central, Santiago, Chile. ☎490 271. Isis has a huge network of contacts, especially in Latin America and the Caribbean, produces publications and houses an excellent resource centre to which visitors are welcome.

Books

Alicia Partnoy, ed., *You Can't Drown the Fire: Latin American Women writing in Exile* (Virago, 1989). Anthology of essays, stories, poetry, letters and songs by 35 Latin American women, including Veronica de Negri, Cecilia Vicuna, Marjorie Agosin and Isabel Morel Letelier from Chile.

Joan Jara, *Victor, An Unfinished Song* (Jonathan Cape, 1983). Moving account of her life with Victor Jara, the legendary Chilean folk-singer who was murdered by the military in 1973.

Marjorie Agosin, *Scraps of Life: The Chilean Arpilleras – Chilean Women and the Pinochet Dictatorship* (Red Sea, US 1987). Arpilleras are artisan women who make lacquered cloth wall hangings; this book is an examination, through their accounts and representations in their art, of their sufferings under the dictatorship. Many lost husbands to the military: they tell stories of jail, torture and bureaucracy. Moving, if a little short on analysis.

Isabel Allende, *House of the Spirits* (Black Swan, 1986) and ***Of Love and Shadows*** (Black Swan, 1988). Two compulsive novels, the first interweaving family saga with political events in an unnamed Latin American country; the second dealing with a passionate love affair against a similar background of violent political turmoil.

Elizabeth Jelin, ed., *Citizenship and Identity: Women and Social Change in Latin America* (Zed Books, 1990). Examines women's roles in Latin American movements for social change from the Mothers of the Disappeared in Argentina to trade union organisations in Chile.

Latin American and Caribbean Women's Collective: *Slaves of Slaves: the Challenge of Latin American Women* (Zed Books, 1980). Portrays women's struggles in eleven different countries, including Chile.

China

N obody can travel to China any longer without being painfully aware of
the politics which grip and strangle this vast and extraordinary country. For a
decade, since the much-vaunted "opening" of China by paramount leader
Deng Xiaoping, millions of Western tourists have romped throughout China's
cities and countryside, marvelling at her ancient wonders and at her more
modern accommodation between communism and capitalism. China was the
world's communist sweetheart – a safe and unthreatening Marxist/Maoist
giant where totalitarian rule could be justified by Confucian tradition and a
historically communal culture.

No more. Justifications for China's current leadership no longer ring true
after the crushing of the students' pro-democracy movement in the spring of
1989. Out of numerous alternative solutions to their crisis, Chinese leaders
chose the most brutal and bloody. To say China's international image has

been tarnished would be a gross understatement. The world was rightly shocked and appalled by the Chinese military's use of brutal force to clean out Tiananmen Square on the night of June 3, and China's international "image" was destroyed. It was revealed to be, in truth, an illusion.

The consequences of the crackdown on students and on a huge segment of the population deemed infected by "bourgeois liberalism" – a euphemism for Western ideology, including market liberalisation, arts and literary freedoms, freedom of the press, civil and human rights – are only now becoming apparent. According to the best estimates, arrests of activists and sympathisers now number in the tens of thousands, and the seemingly unstoppable momentum of China's "opening" to the West has been stalled, if not completely derailed.

This opening had brought prosperity to many segments of society, and had made China more accessible to visitors from the West than ever before. Travelling to China in the Eighties, Westerners could understand and applaud the ever-growing numbers of entrepreneurs who populated street markets and the ever-growing enthusiasm apparent in the general population for change, movement and growth. Yet the opening, the attendant economic reforms, and relaxation of central control, brought with them a host of extraordinary problems. Inflation, running at an estimated thirty percent nationwide, rampant corruption among officials at all levels of the government, an over-taxed and inefficient transportation system that couldn't come close to meeting demand, and a widespread disillusionment with the ideals of communism were just a few of the most obvious problems which accompanied Chinese *perestroika*.

Something had to happen, and it is still a running debate among China watchers whether the democracy movement and its suppression were the victims or the cause of a power struggle between hardliners and reformists within the Chinese government. In any case, the so-called hardliners, orthodox Marxist-Maoists, most definitively won, and China's political and economic future are now careening down a far different path than the one assumed in the early months of 1989.

For tourists and travellers to China, this means a different experience in the Middle Kingdom. For many, and up to this point millions, a vacation or tour through China seems to be in bad taste under current circumstances. Politically, spending one's tourist dollars on a country moving forward, rather than lurching adamantly backwards, is far easier to justify. Yet the people of China remain the same. They are the biggest victims of the crackdown and its economic consequences, of inflation, corruption, and of the disappearance of opportunity and hope. If you travel to China now, the Chinese people may not be able to speak with you honestly, but your presence there will not go unappreciated.

Many people have cancelled their China trips because of the reported violence and out of fear for their own safety. These fears are no longer valid. The pacification of the demonstrators and the wholesale repression across the nation have effectively silenced dissent, for a time. Moments and periods of great tension still occur, especially in occupied Beijing around important anniversary dates, when soldiers jog through the streets in an intimidating show of force. With one frightening exception, the violence that struck the capital in early June was never directed against "foreign friends", but only by Chinese against Chinese. Even the current government, with its seemingly callous disregard for international opinion, realises the importance of safety for Western visitors.

The greatest difference between the China now and the China prior to June is one of mood and climate. The population is, understandably, sullen and far more silent than in the past. On the surface, there are few obvious reminders of the ongoing crackdown and of the campaign against liberalisation. The Chinese people are, as always, polite, welcoming, and even open in expressing their support of the government. In their inner lives, however, nearly impossible to see now, they have different thoughts and different passions, a greater sense of hopelessness than ever before, and a greater fear of speaking honestly with foreigners and of the consequences this can bring right now.

China is as vast and as varied as it ever was, and the further away you travel from Beijing and other large cities the more open and easy your conversations are likely to be. Travelling conditions are greatly eased due to the fact that there are very few Westerners touring China these days. Train and plane tickets are relatively easy to procure, and hotel prices have plummeted as much as fifty percent in the major cities.

If you travel to China these days your presence there will be viewed by the government as an acknowledgement that the situation has returned to "normal". Despite this very uncomfortable impression, there remains much to be learned and explored in this post-Tiananmen China. The repression cannot and should not be ignored, whether you journey to the far edges of the empire in Tibet or Urumqi, or to the centre, Beijing. The traveller under present circumstances must keep in mind that surface impressions of normality are not the true picture, and in fact they never were.

Many of the prominent student leaders during the democracy movement, and some of the most outspoken and brave sympathisers among journalists and intellectuals, were women. Like their male counterparts, most have been arrested and their circumstances are currently unknown. In heralding a new, and as yet unborn China, however, the movement gave voice to a group of women political activists on an equal status with men for the first time. For these women, concern for the future of their nation took precedence over **feminist issues**.

China has always been a patriarchy. The Communist era heralded enormous changes for women, but it institutionalised the problem of dual labour. According to Mao's two zeals, women were expected both to help build the socialist future and fulfil their traditional family role. Many women now have full access to education and employment; contraception is free, abortion legal, and divorce instigated by wives is common. But the traditional view that women are specially suited to certain jobs (childcare and housework) and incapable of others (anything too mentally and physically taxing), as well as the Confucian ideal of the three obediences to father, husband and son, are as strong as ever. The clearest and most frightening demonstration of women's subordinate status has been the increase in female infanticide, associated with the introduction of the one-child-per-family policy.

In Tiananmen Square

. . . .

Alison Munroe, a freelance journalist, writer and television producer, has been a constant visitor to China over the last seven years after living and working in Beijing. In Spring 1989 she returned to report on the progress of the pro-democracy movement for American television. She remained as a witness to its tragic suppression.

I went to China in late April because something was happening. The student demonstrations (of mid and late April following the death of Hu Yaobang) would probably blow over, I reasoned at the time, but their strength and passion were unusual. Gorbachev was coming to China within a few weeks and, given the powerful forces underway in his own country, I believed his visit would make an impact at least in Beijing. His visit and my visit would coincide; we would both see China at a time of change.

What I experienced in China from the end of April through the beginning of July was unlike anything anybody had ever seen in that country before. For a long time China visitor and watcher, it was the most thrilling and the most crushing of experiences, all wrapped up together into one huge convulsion.

Imagine an epidemic of manic depression. Imagine an entire city of twelve million people experiencing mood swings from euphoria and exhilaration to terror, bitter resignation and furious anger, all within the space of a few days, and sometimes in the course of one day.

It seems that, in the West, everybody remembers the "massacre of Tiananmen", but few recall the even more extraordinary events of the weeks before. During that time, most incredi-bly Beijing was a city ruled by the emotions and dreams of her people. It had become a People's Republic, arguably for the first time, and everybody was overwhelmed with a sense of mass power, with the narcotic of an uprising. The stereotypically passive Chinese stunned the world – as they have in the past – with their hidden passions, and all participants and observers were blown away by the storm.

I felt like a revolution in Beijing for a time; less like an "awakening" of political consciousness than a sudden explosion of reality. The Chinese people have always had a great deal to gripe about; poverty, corruption, inflation, repression, deception. But few expected such a passionate, peaceful, and determined effort to redress those wrongs.

For me, watching, reporting, interviewing, it was difficult to maintain a semblance of objectivity. In the early days of the hunger strike and massive demonstrations, I was frightened. "Remember," I said to Western friends who were enthusiastically supporting the students, "remember how powerful this government is." By the end, after the tanks rolled into Tiananmen Square, I was reminded by someone that had warned them early on, and I realised how completely caught up in the movement I had become, how I had forgotten my own warning.

Bits and pieces from my diary and memories of the early days of the movement are more telling, I believe, than a recounting of the terror of the latter days.

May 15: When student broadcasters on Tiananmen Square announced that the welcoming ceremony for visiting Soviet President Mikhail Gorbachev had been moved from the Square to the airport, there was a sense of disappointment, but also of rising jubilation. Students had anticipated a colourful confrontation between protestors and the motorcade but at the same time many began to realise the power of their occupation of the Square.

Some feared that the government had "lost face" and would retaliate against the students with greater ferocity. Yet the hunger strikers were proud. "The government may lose face, " said one student, "but the Chinese people have gained face."

The Square was festooned with incredible banners and slogans. A festival in the making. A hot, sunny, and very happy democratic festival.

May 16: The numbers of supporters who marched to the Square to support the core group of hunger strikers swelled into the hundreds of thousands. Intellectuals from institutes and universities from all over the city marched; journalists from the *People's Daily*, the Communist Party newspaper, marched. An old woman marched, holding up a plate on which was written: "My children are hungry. What are Deng Xiaoping's children eating?"

"All you could hear in the centre of Beijing was the scream of ambulance sirens as they took fainting fasters to the hospital, and the roar and honks of trucks, buses, cars and motorcycles signalling their support"

The students were holding out, and were greatly encouraged by the throngs of supporters. But tension was growing, as was the fear that the government was just going to ignore the millions in the Square. There was talk of suicides. People were frightened that the tinderbox of defiance would explode into massive work strikes and violent rebellion. A rumour spread through the city that two hunger strikers had died. All you could hear in the centre of Beijing was the scream of ambulance sirens as they took fainting fasters to the hospital, and the roar and honks of trucks, buses, cars, and motorcycles signalling their support to the movement. It began to feel eerie.

May 17: At least one million people flooded into Tiananmen. Workers' unions, flight attendants, social scientists, factory labourers, the China Travel Service, the staffs of most newspapers and the central television station. The main street leading to the Square was mobbed for miles. The pedicab purveyors were making a mint. All over Beijing, crowds were singing the Internationale and chanting, "Long Live Democracy". The Square and its immediate environs looked like the scene of a rock concert that had gone on for too long.

Few people in Beijing went to work that day, and after a few hours it became commonplace even miles from the centre of town to see honking brigades of commandeered trucks and buses covered with banners and filled with shouting, laughing, chanting demonstrators. Everywhere they went, people on the street applauded, cheered, and flashed "V" signs of solidarity. The city stopped functioning and the citizens of Beijing just gave in to a new atmosphere of unrestraint.

"This government is corrupt," shouted one hard-hatted construction worker to me, "we need a new one." A factory worker, surrounded by a crowd of gawkers as he talked to me, said, "a man should not act like a slave. It is time Chinese people dared to speak out."

May 18: Another million people marched. Beijing almost resembled those old Cultural Revolution newsreels, every blank place in the city covered with pro-student, pro-freedom, pro-democracy banners. A public bus drove by with the Chinese characters for "support" etched in the dust on the back.

China Central Television, the government-financed and controlled broadcasting network, looked like a revolutionary headquarters. A huge banner swung from its lofty spire, more banners and flags were strewn through the halls inside. Over 1000 employees had marched to the Square that afternoon, and then returned to broadcast footage of the Beijing rebellion to the whole nation. Late that night, they broadcast a dialogue which had taken place earlier in the day between hardline Premier Li Peng and the student hunger strikers. Li was reviled by student leader Wu'er Kaixi, told that he wasn't doing his job. Confucius spun in his grave. The whole nation watched. At the end of the dialogue – at least so went the rumour the next day – Li Peng dismissed the students and thanked them for coming. Wu'er Kaixi turned to the Premier and said, "You didn't invite us, we invited you. And you're late."

May 19: The government had taken no action either for or against the hunger strikers. The workers had joined the movement, Beijing citizens were going into the Square in droves, even Party officials and government functionaries were carrying banners and shouting slogans. In dozens of other Chinese cities, students and citizens were demonstrating. Gorbachev had left China and the centre – China's governmental authority – seemed unable to hold on.

The Square was awake all that night, and so was I. Standing on the monument steps overlooking the tens of thousands of students and their supporters, it seemed impossible that the government could not listen to their demands. We were kept sleepless by continuous broadcasts over the government loudspeakers of a harsh speech by Li Peng warning that the army was coming in to restore order. "It is hopeless," said a female medical student attending the hunger strikers at the square. She was crying as she listened to the speech. "We are really very angry," she said, "We want to kill Li Peng."

May 20: At 10am, as I ran back into the dirty Square, five military helicopters buzzed Tiananmen in formation. It was terrifying, intimidating, and the students awoke shaking their fists at

the power and authority of their government. The imposition of martial law was announced over the loudspeakers, and we all looked at each other in fear, knowing the showdown was inevitable.

> *"Blood was anticipated to flow that night, and the entire city began its 24-hour vigil. Students drove around the city chanting 'Arise, Unite, and Protect the Students'"*

The terror had begun, yet the streets and the Square that morning were once again filled with marchers, trucks crammed with flag-waving protesters, honking, screaming in defiance, "V" waving motorcycle brigades, and one huge bulldozer packed to the brim – even its enormous shovel – with banners and people.

Blood was anticipated to flow that night, and the entire city began its 24-hour-a-day vigil. Students drove around the city chanting: "Arise, Unite, and Protect the Students." All through town people were shouting "Down with Li Peng": words that sent chills down my spine. You could be shot for saying that in China. The peoples' barriers went up on every intersection leading into Beijing, and, incredibly, the people stopped the military from advancing on the Square.

After May 20, and the imposition of the "paper tiger" martial law – a martial law that was unenforceable, even laughable – the exhilaration ebbed and flowed, alternating with boredom, fear, and confusion. Slowly, the students grew tired of their dirty, unhealthy vigil in the centre of the city, and the leaders and vanguard, students from Beijing universities, began to filter back to their homes and campuses. There was one major re-swelling of enthusiasm when art students hauled an enormous statue called the "Goddess of Democracy", modelled after the Statue of Liberty in New York, to the Square. Lined up with cosmically appropriate symmetry between Mao's mausoleum and the Gate of Heavenly Peace, it was the last and most extraordinary gesture of brazen independence. Like a statue of Mao Zedong on the White House lawn. It must have driven the Chinese leadership mad.

The "Goddess" stood out like a very sore thumb and people on the street still dared to stand in front of foreign television cameras, denouncing their government's lies. "Tell the truth," they told us, "tell the world. They say they are enforcing martial law to protect us. We don't need their protection."

Of all the things experienced, this bravery was the most unforgettable. On the night of the assault on Beijing, two weeks after martial law was imposed, the shooting began to the west of the Square in a place called Muxudi. As the hundreds of troop trucks, tanks, and armoured personnel carriers moved east, public buses blockaded the road on a bridge just one mile from the Square. The shooting grew closer; machine guns, rifles, tanks crashing, people running, screaming. They raced to the side streets and watched as the buses were set alight; they roared and cheered as the bus blockades burst into great, dramatic balls of flame.

"People ask me if I was afraid. No, I should have been, but like everybody around me that night . . . I was more shocked, numbed, horrified, and – it must be admitted – exhilarated by the struggle"

The troops were shooting into the crowd, killing some, but at every lull thousands more surged forward again to watch in disbelief as the People's Liberation Army launched its assault on the people. The flames roared, the tanks crashed through, and the two-mile-long convoy of assault troops passed across the bridge while all around them people chanted, "Criminals, criminals!" and "Traitors, traitors".

People ask me if I was afraid. No, I should have been, but like everybody around me that night, including many who died, I was more shocked, numb, horrified, and – it must be admitted – exhilarated by the struggle. Exhilaration rotted with horror soon after, however, as we began to comprehend what had happened and what was happening. My own personal horror came one week later.

A few days after the assault, we interviewed a man on the streets of Beijing for American television. Like thousands of others, he was standing on a street corner, shouting out in despair at what he had seen. We asked him to talk to us, and our cameras, and he told us, and the crowd, of the killing he had witnessed, of his hatred for the government. He said, "After what I have seen, I'm not afraid of death anymore." As he spoke, the small crowd cheered and applauded, and his interview with us ended with a fists-in-the-air crowd chant of "down with Li Peng".

We used a few seconds of this interview in a news piece for American television that night, as part of a larger story about the ongoing defiance and horror in the city. A few days later, exactly one week after the assault, the Chinese nightly news – already a nightly barrage of brazen falsehood about the quelling of the "counter-revolutionary rebellion" – ran a tape of the entire raw footage of my interview with this man.

Apparently, they had "pirated" it off a satellite feed from Tokyo to New York. There was no other explanation for how they obtained the raw footage. They ran the tape, identified the man as a "counter-revolutionary rumour mongeror," and asked anybody recognising him to inform the local Public Security Bureau.

The next evening's news included footage of the man, a 42-year-old accountant named Xiao Bin, beaten and contrite, confessing his crimes to security officials after two enthusiastic patriots had turned him in.

"I could no longer do my job in China, could no longer even attempt to interview people or to find out what was going on. I was quelled, silenced, pacified"

This was the final blow for me. I could no longer do my job in China, could no longer even attempt to interview people or to find out what was going on. I was quelled, silenced, pacified. It was easy in those days to give in to the general melodrama surrounding our circumstances, but still I felt that the government's actions in using me to identify its own malcontents was aimed directly at my personal conscience. They made an example out of Xiao Bin, and taught me the worst lesson of my life. I had forgotten, and had never quite believed, how powerful this government was.

Within a week I left China, determined to go back soon and somehow repay my debt to those people – like Xiao Bin – but I left knowing that my own bitterness and sense of personal defeat would only impair my efforts to continue reporting on China, to tell the truth about what was happening and what had happened.

As a foreigner in China, I have never seen the people full of so much hope, so much true patriotism and passion. The movement was a profoundly idealistic quest, with few concrete goals and little realistic appreciation of how this government was likely to react. It was a feeling, an emotion, a yearning, and eventually almost a hysteria. It was a movement that became a mass narcotic – for those watching as well as those participating – and it swelled up in Beijing and across the country into a euphoric and temporary wave of power. We all forgot about the government, and their personal priorities of power preservation. But the events of May and June revealed, for the first time, the true face of the Chinese government, and of its people.

Earlier Travels . . .

Most of the accounts we received about travelling in China have been rendered more or less irrelevant by the events of Tiananmen Square and subsequent political clampdown. We've selected a few, however, which seem to offer more than a poignant reminder of the days of open tourism. These include a piece on Tibet, which is still open to tour groups flying into Lhasa, though it is currently very difficult to enter as an independent traveller on any of the overland routes from China or Nepal.

An Eastern Westerner in China

· · · · · · · · · · · · ·

Adrienne Su, an American of Chinese descent, completed a year's study at Fudan University in Shanghai in June 1988. Her experiences of being mistaken for a citizen of the PRC forced her to reconsider the privileges foreign travellers routinely depend on.

Not until a customs official at my port of entry into China berated me for speaking halting Chinese did I realise that my Chinese ancestry would exert a powerful influence on all my experiences in this country. My dealings with the Chinese differed from everything I had read in guidebooks. I had never questioned my being an American, but no one in China could tell I was one.

By government policy, a foreigner's dissatisfaction carries more weight than that of a Chinese citizen. If a road accident involves a foreigner, rescue forces arrive efficiently; if only PRC citizens are involved, the ambulance takes its time, if it comes at all. There are not enough ambulances around to accommodate everyone's needs and as a result the Chinese pay for the comfort of foreign guests.

In ticket offices, citizens may have to stand in line for a full day or more, therefore having to take turns with friends and relatives. Foreigners, on the other hand, are free to walk straight to the front. Soft sleepers on trains are available only to an elite few but any foreigner is free to buy a ticket. Large tourist hotels admit Chinese visitors only when accompanied by foreigners and once inside the staff treat the guests of their own nation with contempt while all but kneeling to their foreign companions. Unfortunately this policy is conducted on such a wide scale (the whole country) that it feels more like the privation of the human rights of the Chinese than the extension of hospitality to their visitors.

"I was ashamed of American travellers for riding on their privileges after all their talk about human rights and racial equality"

I detested this policy on arrival, but after a few months became accustomed to it and even grew to expect it. It's not only the expectation of special treatment that changes one's character; the daily observation of the Chinese in a lower position leaves a deep mental image. I was on the verge of thinking myself worth more than the Chinese when I reconsidered my experiences of being mistaken for a local resident. It had been mortifying to be ignored, shouted at, put last in line, and even pushed in favour of white tourists, while fellow Americans enjoyed an attentive service and paid no heed to my abuse. Just as I was appalled by the Chinese acceptance of a secondary status, I was ashamed of American travellers for riding on their privileges after all their talk about human rights and racial equality.

Repeated inhospitable receptions transformed my feelings of sympathy and kinship with the people of my ancestry. Until I made local friends, I found it hard to stay courteous and detached. Acquaintances from Japan, Taiwan, Hong Kong and Korea reported similar difficulties of feeling guilty for using privileges and angry at being denied them. (The black visitors I met faced even more extreme reactions; even in Shanghai, they had to contend with people staring, pointing and drawing away, all of which massively increased the pressures of travelling.) When I came across other white Westerners on the road, their attitude towards me was high-flown and condescending until I spoke English. It wasn't entirely their fault; the environment had deluded them into seeing the Chinese as less than people.

I also, however, found that there was an advantage to blending in, in that I could observe the street scenes without becoming one. Subtle differences in manner made me stand out, even when I dressed inconspicuously, but I could conceal myself in heavy traffic and large crowds, both of which China has in plentiful supply. Most people took me for a citizen of another region in China, or a tourist from another Asian country, and dismissed me as less strange than a Westerner, leaving me at peace to watch and not be watched.

In spite of the inconveniences I faced, I always felt reasonably safe in China. A solo woman is unlikely to encounter violence. Crowded buses make all women (and men) easy prey to wandering hands, and theft is on the increase in touristic cities like Canton

and Guilin. But physical harm to a foreigner invites grave punishment and rarely occurs. It is easy, however, to drop precautions considered routine in the West simply because state media controls keep domestic crime inconspicuous.

Seldom does a Chinese man open a door for a woman, and on trains I have struggled alone to push my bag into a high luggage rack while Chinese men smoked and stared. Their attitude I attribute to the Cultural Revolution (1966–76) and not to Chinese culture itself. In comparison to most Asian cultures, the PRC has made great strides in restoring equal treatment of the sexes. Men and women all receive jobs upon finishing school, with comparable (although scant) salaries. The blue proletarian garb of Mao's China does away with feminine beauty and transforms the visual man and woman into nearly identical units. While many people still wear the old uniform, the streets of Canton and Shanghai boast short skirts, high heels and casual Western-style sportswear for both sexes.

"The sight of a woman on the road by herself evokes concern among the Chinese, who see convenience in numbers, if only to fight the bureaucracy"

Too often, visitors dismiss the Chinese as an homogenous mass of people without considering the many different groups and classes that make up their society. To someone unfamiliar with Chinese ways, general similarities such as black hair, black eyes, plain clothing, and a slighter build than the average Westerner will make people of totally different characteristics seem identical. Until you have developed a sensitivity to cultural differences within China you will blame all Chinese for the offences of a few unhappy encounters. One obstacle is that many who consider themselves well-bred and educated feel it is improper to approach strangers unintroduced, which immediately limits the type of spontaneous contacts you'll make.

An advantage of travelling alone in China is that you do have more opportunities to meet people. The sight of a woman on the road by herself evokes concern among the Chinese, who see convenience in numbers, if only to fight the bureaucracy. Outside large cities, I was invited into homes, given food and escorted around town. One rule to keep in mind is that the Chinese almost always try to pick up the bill even if they haven't the money. Be sure to emphatically resist this and make a genuine effort to pay your share or both; not only is it rude to accept, but most PRC citizens live on minimal salaries that would make one foreign dinner guest a burdensome expense. By tradition a Chinese family gives the best of everything to a guest, even at great personal cost.

"Every Shanghaiese who was there on the eve of the revolution remembers the British sign on the gate of a Shanghai park: 'No Chinese and dogs allowed'"

The extended absence of foreigners has very much increased their mystique, giving rise to rumours about our strange cuisine, etiquette, religions, courtship and rituals. Because no one trusts the government-printed newspapers, reports of the world outside are in high demand. People will treat you as an object in some places, but although you look unusual to them their fascination is more for the world you represent than for your personal peculiarity.

The Chinese conception of the *waiguoren* (foreigner) has been shaped by a dramatic history. Every Shanghaiese who was there on the eve of the revolution remembers the British sign on the gate of a Shanghai park: "No Chinese and dogs allowed." The European "spheres of influence" and the establishment of the Shanghai International Settlement humbled the Chinese, while foreigners enjoyed immunity from local law. Japanese atrocities in the 1930s left indelible memories.

Today, shortages and an enormous population require the pooling of the best resources in order to house, transport and feed foreign guests comfortably, and, considering past injuries, the Chinese are noble hosts. Most live in overcrowded quarters, whole families to a room, without indoor plumbing, and for everyone south of the Yangzi River, without indoor heating. Winter brings a harsh chill to Shanghai, Hangzhou and other southern cities. The discomforts of visitors, such as inefficient service, limited hot water, and difficulties in transport, are minimal compared to the limitations on the local quality of life. The tendency among foreigners, however, is to blame the Chinese for these inconveniences.

And it's easy to feel angry at China; every bus is early or late, many clerks are hostile, crowds push and clamour, and boarding trains, planes and coaches demands a physical struggle. People stare openly at foreigners, sometimes gathering in small crowds to observe while rash youths follow you around, trying to practise English and get a foreign address. You can quickly become overwhelmed by a language you do not properly comprehend and by customs, hemispheres removed from your own.

But beyond all this, there's no denying the grandeur of China's natural scenery, its position on the world scale and the influence it exerts over the rest of Asia. China requires patience, flexibility and humour. The unpredictability of wandering the Middle Kingdom has its rewards, and for women going it alone, it's bound to feel safer than home.

Striking out Alone

· · · · · · · · · · ·

Caroline Gimbly spent five months (January to June 1988) travelling alone around China, covering the major tourist routes and striking out into the lesser-known territories.

This was the first time I had travelled alone and, not being particularly confident, had to grapple with all sorts of anxieties about how, and whether, I would cope. I couldn't speak a word of Chinese at the outset, but got a huge amount of pleasure from trying. Gaining the basics over the weeks helped enormously with the ordinary logistics of travel, buying train tickets etc, as well as giving me opportunities to make contact with people on the way.

Very few spoke English but a phrasebook and dictionary, alongside my own struggling attempts, enabled surprisingly complex conversation. It also created situations ripe for laughter – I found the Chinese invariably displayed a brilliant sense of humour – a perfect tool for making links with people.

"The words for 'I am a woman' came pretty high on my essential phrases list"

Many of the people I met expressed real surprise at meeting someone who had chosen to travel alone. On top of the open, unaggressive curiosity I encountered almost everywhere and the incessant questions about my income and the cost of my camera, people were constantly trying to puzzle out why I would want to be on my own.

Chinese life, in the most stereotypical way, appears to be so very group-based and their concept of a holiday is no exception – if a holiday photo hasn't got people in it, it isn't worth taking. The only snag I did encounter, being on my own, was that because eating is also a social, group occasion, I lost out when it came to ordering in restaurants – a steamed fish eighteen inches long is something of a struggle for one person.

Being a woman on my own seemed barely comprehensible. Being a tall woman with short hair, usually bundled up in a jacket and jeans, created genuine doubt and confusion. I had a number of female communal shower doors slammed in my face by shocked Chinese women and the words for "I am a woman", came pretty high on my essential phrases list. It's an extremely bizarre statement to find yourself yelling out in echoing corridors or dingy backyards. I spent three days sitting on a bus talking to a young Chinese man, who was only convinced I was a woman when, at the end of the second day, I produced my passport.

I wondered whether this was because of my appearance, or whether it was more socially acceptable to talk to me as "man to man". In Kashgar, I was ambling through the main square when a woman walked up to me and, quite matter-of-factly, placed both hands where she thought she may or may not find my breasts. Somehow, it was impossible to be feel angry because it seemed such an honest gesture and she accepted my mock slap across the face in good humour. I also had problems with very tentative barbers, who evidently thought my hair was quite short enough already and were highly reluctant to remove any more.

I cannot remember a time in China when I felt afraid of being on my own, from the point of view of safety. I walked around freely at night, left bags lying around on trains and never felt worried about being amongst groups of men. In Hohhot, I walked into a restaurant after a long day's cycling and was invited to join a table of four young men. They proceeded to engage me in a drinking contest, brushing aside my moans that I would never be able to cycle home by offering to accompany me.

Several glasses of something disgusting later (they manage to eat, drink and smoke at the same time!) they kept their promise, leaving me at the hotel gate after helping me to return my bike to an incredulous attendant. Obviously I was taking a risk (as were they), but it was one I felt prepared to take after four months in the country. I was wolf-whistled once and touched by a man who offered me a lift on his bike, both in Kashgar. This is possibly because it's a Muslim area; I was certainly not welcome at the mosques and was asked to leave one during prayers.

There were many more occasions when I was not only treated extremely hospitably, but was also shown great kindness and a willingness to help, often in quite a protective way. The more surprising of these involved a bureaucrat. A government official drove me all over Hohhot on his motorbike, looking for the relevant person to extend my visa. It's difficult to say who was the more excited; him, having a foreigner in his sidecar, or me, bounc-ing over the pavements in his machine. On top of this, once we had tracked the right person to her home and I had handed over my "foreigner's money", she asked me whether I'd prefer to pay in "people's money", which is only obtainable on the black market. Chinese bureaucracy is unpredictable to say the least.

My most unpleasant brush with "the system" occurred on a train journey and involved a Chinese man I had got to know on the bus coming from Kashgar. Teasing and teaching each other, we shared our very limited knowledge of each other's langauge. A young man of 21, he was born in Suzhou, on the east coast and had left two years previously with his brothers to look for work. He had settled in Kashgar, about as far from his home as possible, and was now travelling hundreds of miles to buy tractor parts.

Though committed to the ideals of communism, he believed China would be capitalist in twenty-five years. Continuing our journey on this train together, our friendship was treated warmly by fellow travellers but any display of affection was treated very harshly by the train staff.

> *"He showed great courage by hugging me at the station when I got off the train, observed closely by what looked like just about every attendant on the train"*

My friend was hauled off to the guard's cabin for a lecture, had his (false) name and address taken and, so he told me later, had to make out he was an ignorant peasant and therefore not responsible for his actions. I, in my turn, was asked into the office where I was treated with great courtesy, which made me feel uncomfortable and angry. My friend became so nervous about what might happen to him that he barely dared talk to me whilst staff were around. He showed great courage by hugging me at the station when I got off the train, observed closely by what looked like just about every atten-dant on the train.

Physical contact in China appears to have laws attached – which, as a foreigner, I was never quite able to grasp. In cramped and seething trains, nobody seemed to mind if you used their shoulder or back for a pillow at night. Touching seems fairly accepta-ble between same-sex friends; I was sad to see one young man rapidly brush his friend's arm from around him when he saw me approaching, as though Western stigmas were affecting his perception of his own cultural rights and wrongs.

However, very few couples display physical affection, even holding hands, married or not. Conversely, in many hotels I came across assumptions that Western men and women would happily share dorms; if I objected, I was always found another room. Generally, personal space felt like a luxury I couldn't always guarantee, leaving me on occasions feeling irritable and claus-trophobic. And, back in England, I still have to check myself, barging my way down crowded main streets.

Hitching to Lhasa

· · · · · · · · · · · ·

Alison Gostling hitched independently and illegally into Tibet with another Western woman whom she had met in central China.

August 1988 found me wandering the bleak corridors of a government hotel in Xining, Central China, trying to find someone willing to attempt a three-thousand-kilometre hitch with me to Lhasa, the capital of Tibet.

Having waited all spring in Kathmandhu without success for the Nepalese/Tibetan border to reopen I had flown to Hong Kong and spent four days crossing China by train. When I arrived in Xining, which despite that distance of three thousand kilometres is considered the "threshold" of Tibet, I was told that individual travel to Lhasa had been banned. Determined not to be cheated, I decided to try and sneak in from the East on long-distance trucks.

Xining was full of disappointed but resigned backpackers. Most thought I was crazy. Then I met a tall French-Canadian woman, Margo, who liked the idea. We checked each other out quite carefully. She still had her childhood love of dirt and discomfort, had mountain-biked around New Zealand, had a great sense of humour and offered me a pair of Chinese silk boxer shorts (secondhand) as an initiation present. By choice I always travel alone, so it seemed extraordinary luck to meet such a good companion.

We decided we would look less conspicuous in Tibetan clothes and, because we are both nearly 6ft, and local men wear broad-brimmed hats and large baggy coats suited to clandestine journeying, we chose to dress as men. Tibetan women, as happens often in mountain areas, tend to be forceful, independent characters who often hitch long distances. But we would have needed long, straight black hair to pass as one of them, even at a distance.

We did feel fairly stupid to be masquerading as men. In hindsight I doubt if this was necessary; it made local people doubly curious about us. From the harassment point of view it probably made no difference; we were treated with great kindness and respect throughout, even when sleeping in a truck packed like a sardine can with Chinese roadworkers.

"Neither of us had done anything like this before, and couldn't believe we were about to set out"

We prepared ourselves by buying whatever "survival rations" we could find – peanuts, biscuits, boiled sweets and dried apricots – and changed lots of money into the local currency on the black market. Neither of us had done anything like this before, and couldn't quite believe we were about to set out. Our biggest concern was that we might be putting local people at risk by helping us – a justifiable fear since security is tight with as many as eight soldiers to every Tibetan, and many informers.

On the other hand, Eastern Tibet (not only the "Tibetan Autonomous Region" but also a huge area now attached to the Chinese provinces of Qinghai and Sichuan) has always been off-limits to foreigners, and we argued that we might be of some service as outside observers of life under Chinese rule.

Woken up by trumpets calling pilgrims to prayer, we set off precipitously one morning before we lost our nerve completely. The suburbs of the town seemed endless as we struggled along in our strange new clothes, our backpacks concealed in unwieldy sacks. A small boy said "hello" (in English!) which was hardly encouraging.

Almost immediately we found ourselves off the beaten track. Sitting in a ditch eating a breakfast of dried apricots, we watched hundreds of identically-clad men being marched out of a compound to work in the fields: a tiny proportion of the vast Chinese gulag said to exist in the region. A few hours later, having skirted some checkpoints, we were heading south on our first truck.

Travelling by truck across the high plateau and passes of Tibet is a world apart. Physically the distances are immense; psychologically they are immeasurable. The grasslands stretch away endlessly from the solitary road.

Once a travelling companion jumped down from the truck and set off into a completely featureless horizon, sure of his lone path. Elsewhere horses grazing around a distant cluster of nomadic tents, strung with prayer flags, were the only hint of human habitation.

"Often we slept in the trucks and ate a supper of boiled rice heated with a borrowed blowtorch"

Switchbacks climb for half a day out of the dead-end valleys. From the crest a magical expanse of peaks extend like waves, with snowy froth on their summits. The clear light dazzles, and the thin air makes everything doubly breathtaking.

On and on for hours, then days, with sometimes no sign of movement for a hundred miles at a time. Mind and matter begin to play strange tricks on each other.

We sprawled on grainsacks in the back of an open truck or huddled together with the rest of the passengers from the wind and rain and dust under a tattered tarpaulin. This is how most Tibetans travel, and a special camaraderie developed, with great whoops of triumph at the top of a high pass and rueful laughter at the bumps when freewheeling for hours down the other side.

Once a half-naked man with matted beard climbed in, carrying only an axe and a kettle. A local chieftain in fur-trimmed coat and knee-high boots, he

was armed with both a silver dagger studded with turquoise and a revolver wrapped in red silk. On a windy plateau we paused to pick up two nomads transporting an assortment of sacks to market: each one contained a section of dismembered yak. A very smelly leg of goat swung beside me, splashing blood.

At night the vehicles rolled into truckstops with high walls and gates like medieval fortresses. Often we slept in the trucks and ate a supper of boiled rice heated with a borrowed blowtorch. I played "Grandmother's Footsteps" with children terrified of the two strangers. One evening a cassette player was produced and Margo's Grace Jones tape echoed in the wilderness.

Set in this raw landscape were sinister new towns with huge walled compounds and a heavy military presence, which we guessed to be prison camps. One road passes through them all, disappearing from and into the emptiness, but guarded by frequent roadblocks.

Sometimes the heart of an old Tibetan town had been ripped out, or else there was just a ribbon development of concrete accommodation for the many Chinese immigrants, with loudspeakers blaring state news and music as if to help them ignore their surroundings. The mud houses of the Tibetans have been squeezed out and huddle low on the edge of the villages, beyond any water or electricity supplies.

We were amazed by the sheer numbers of Chinese we saw – as different from Tibetans in appearance, language, diet and customs as the Japanese are from us. We learnt the facts later. Reeling from the devastation wrought by the Red Guards in the 1960s, and the famines of the 1970s in which more than 300,000 died, Tibet now faces the greatest threat of all – a massive population transfer from the overcrowded mainland.

As far back as 1952, even before the Chinese invasion of Tibet, Mao envisaged that these empty plateaux could house a ten-million overspill from China. As Chinese shops and restaurants proliferate, as good jobs are earmarked for Chinese applicants, as higher education is limited to Chinese speakers, as decent healthcare is reserved for Chinese immigrants, the voice of Tibet is silenced. We grew sadder and sadder over the journey.

For two nights we stopped in a village, which, being a prosperous community, was a cheerful exception. The villagers had made money from the rising value of their yak herds (the Chinese are being re-educated to eat yak meat) and from the endless convoys of trucks that pass through, carrying logs out of the newly-deforested environment.

"No ingratiating friendliness or politeness around here. Locals would look strangers slowly up and down, and only then smile if they liked what they saw"

Central China needs Tibetan wood, but the devastation seemed dramatic to the point of lunacy. We saw whole mountainsides shaved bare, the animals and birds gone and erosion taking over. The Tibetans "steal" the logs that get left behind, and the local bar and store were faced with rough-hewn wood like a Wild West film set.

The place had great style. Fresh yak, a lighter and leaner version of beef, was the only food available for breakfast, lunch or dinner, along with iced gem biscuits which we found in the village store among the socks, stirrups and silks.

The local equivalent of cowboys would ride up and rein in ponies with beautifully plaited tails, tethering them to the telegraph poles. They were Khampa people, famous for their beauty and ferocity. The men wore jade rings and a mass of red silk tassels in their long black hair, the women, chunky ornaments of turquoise, coral and silver.

No ingratiating friendliness or politeness around here. Locals would look strangers slowly up and down, and only then smile if they liked what they saw. Once we were asked back for black salt tea or ly to find the heavy barred door shut in our faces. The kettle was brought out to us.

We arrived in a small town on the eve of a two-day religious festival. It is a famous monastery town (the main temples razed to the ground during the Cultural Revolution were now being rebuilt by local volunteers), but is also in a strategic position across a river gorge and the streets were heavily patrolled by Chinese soldiers. As it now seemed impossible to avoid being spotted we resigned ourselves to the possibility of being sent back and registered with the police. Incredibly, we were given three days' leave to stay with no questions asked – perhaps because we were now in Sichuan, a province traditionally hostile to Beijing. We'll never know, but it was strange suddenly to be ordinary travellers again, wearing our own clothes and wandering about openly.

We followed the Tibetan crowd, gathered from all over the region, down to a shady field by the river with appliqué tents all around a rectangular arena. It had the atmosphere of an English country fair. Everyone milled about meeting friends. Families camped around picnics, horses grazed under the trees and in one corner old peddlars crouched over huge hide bags of jewellery, teacups and devotional objects.

But it was so much more colourful than England: rainbow-striped aprons, men wearing silk brocade shirts under their homespun coats, teenage girls with myriad tiny plaits strung with turquoise hair ornaments. Ninety-nine percent of the women wore traditional dress. A few sported cropped hair and Mao suits; I couldn't decide whether they looked sadder than the rest, or whether it was my imagination.

The previous evening a young Tibetan girl had introduced herself to us in English and for the two days of the festival acted as our interpreter. Her family had fled as refugees in the Sixties (along with thousands of others) and she had received a Western education in a Tibetan children's village in India. Recently the family had returned, bringing her back with them, and she now finds herself an over-educated outsider, lonely for like-minded teenage friends, unable to leave China again. We wished we could have offered her some help. Keeping a promise, Margo sent her a Michael Jackson tape from Bangkok.

"Finally we crept out of the town at dusk . . . and set off for the river on foot, sleeping the night under a bridge"

We were now only thirty kilometres from the Yangzi River which forms the border of the Tibetan Autonomous Region, but our prospects of getting to Lhasa had never seemed bleaker. The one bridge was guarded by machine-gun turrets. Soldiers armed with rifles and bayonets searched every vehicle, and it was rumoured that any driver taking us across could be fined 2000Y (over five years' savings) and lose his licence. Two dubious characters offered to ferry us across at night but we declined. Finally we crept out of the town at dusk (the Public Security Police seemed to go home at 6pm) and set off for the river on foot, sleeping the night under a bridge.

The next day a truck full of Chinese roadworkers just drew up and took us on board. Yet another inexplicable piece of luck. We steamed across the dreaded bridge concealed in life-size

sacks a local tailor had stitched for us. One man helpfully sat on me as I crouched in a yoga dog-pose, wedged up against two oil-cans, every muscle and bone aching.

We didn't believe we had succeeded until we climbed another high pass and emerging from our sacks were confronted with a staggering panorama of peaks, stretching endlessly into the horizon. It really did feel like the "Roof of the World".

Our jubilation was short-lived. At the next stop a plain clothes policeman hauled us out of the truck and arrested us – along with our driver.

At the police station we were left in a room while an interpreter was fetched – a Chinese Christian priest who had just been released after twenty years in jail. He pleaded our case, and managed to gain permission for us to continue, along with warnings of bandits on the road ahead. The driver was fined (we paid) and we were handed certificates of arrest.

Later we heard the priest's story. His wife had accompanied him to jail during the Cultural Revolution, and his children were left destitute. His Bible had been confiscated. I gave him the one that I had smuggled in; it was the least I could do.

As we continued west towards Lhasa, the way became more and more treacherous. The dirt road had turned to knee-deep mud in the summer rain bringing us to a standstill every few miles. Adding our muscle to that of our companions, the roadworkers, we repeatedly heaved the truck out of the mud with ropes.

The real crisis of the trip came when the road reached a dead stop on a high pass and we were forced to walk on alone. We were now at over 16,000ft and experiencing the headaches and breathlessness which are the first signs of altitude sickness. Night found us stranded on the barren mountainside freezing cold and soaked through from the constant downpour, with no food or shelter of any sort. Our chances of survival seemed slender.

"Our jubilation was short-lived. At the next stop a plain clothes policeman hauled us out of the truck and arrested us – along with our driver"

Out of the darkness loomed a tent put up by the Chinese labourers. We appeared at the doorway to their utter astonishment. With some protestation that their home was too humble for two Westerners and that it wasn't suitable for women, they invited us in, shared their meagre rations of rice and boiled water and lent us their own bedding for the night. Living for months on end without electricity, a water supply, fresh food, music, books or female company, their life lacked every human comfort. We spent the evening singing.

The strange sound of "Frère Jacques" wafted over the Himalayas.

Twenty-one days later we turned into the Lhasa valley. The sacred pilgrim route to the magnificent Potala Palace, once the home of the Dalai Lama and the very heart of old Tibet, had been desecrated. The famous golden roofs now preside over miles of soulless military compounds punctuated by wastelands of rubble and barbed wire.

As we got closer we saw nothing but Chinese people on bicycles. Not surprising since in Lhasa itself the Chinese now outnumber Tibetans three to one. Before our feet could touch the pavement we were besieged by a crowd of Tibetan porters begging our custom. A Western girl walked past in a spotless white sweatshirt. She had just flown in with a tour group and didn't even bother to smile a welcome.

TRAVEL NOTES

Languages Standard Chinese (*putong hua* – "common speech" or Mandarin) is based on Beijing Chinese and understood everywhere to a degree. In addition there are major dialects such as Cantonese and Fujianese, plus distinct minority languages. English and Japanese are the main second languages taught in schools, but English is still spoken mainly in the bigger cities and by younger people. It is essential to learn some basic Chinese words and phrases and recognise the basic place names in characters.

Transport Visas are easily obtained from travel agents in Hong Kong and should cover most of the areas you might want to visit. Otherwise Alien travel permits can be picked up, at nominal cost, from the Public Security Bureau. The situation is however constantly changing, especially as regards travel to Lhasa; contact CITS or the Embassy for the most up-to-date information. Trains and buses are fairly efficient but incredibly cramped (unless you opt for first class travel). Hitching is officially frowned upon although it is possible to get lifts from long-distance lorry drivers. The main risk

you'll face is arrest and a fine from the Chinese patrols – your driver, however, could lose his licence, face crippling fines and continuing suspicion by the authorities. It's important to pay as much as you can for your lift.

Accommodation Tourists are designated specific hotels, generally the more expensive; in practice most hotels put you up in their dormitories or cheaper rooms if you are persistent. Men and women are often clumped together but you can insist on a women only room.

Special Problems None which affect women specifically. In general terms you should be sensitive to the political climate and discreet in your dealings with people you meet. The black market for FECs (Foreign Exchange Certificates), especially in the south, is still a going concern. You can exchange your money for "people's money" (*renminbi*) at lucrative rates – but be aware that the authorities are clamping down on this – Chinese can get jailed or shot if caught, tourists deported first class at their own expense. The use of false student cards is also now being cracked down upon by the Chinese.

Health problems include colds, nose and throat infections, caused by the dry atmosphere and industrial pollution. Chemist shops, however, are well stocked and local pills potent.

Special Problems for Tibet Altitude sickness can afflict people quite badly – Lhasa is at 12,000 feet. Don't do anything too energetic for several days after flying in. Outside Lhasa medical facilities are rare and unsophisticated.

Guides *China, A Travel Survival Kit* (Lonely Planet) is a thorough, almost encyclopaedic, 800-page guide, carried by just about every Australian in China. *The Rough Guide: China* (Harrap Columbus) is currently being updated.

Contacts

All China Women's Federation, 50 Deng Shi Hou, Beijing or Box 399, Beijing. Also has branches in most cities, but you will probably need a special introduction by someone at the university or other body of authority in order to meet any representatives. Set up in 1949 under the umbrella of the Communist Party, the federation is often criticised as a Party vehicle, especially as regards the one-child-per-family policies. On the positive side they do provide crucial legal advice and help for women as well as acting as a pressure group to monitor and increase political representation.

Society for Anglo-Chinese Understanding (SACU), 152 Camden High St., London NW1 ☎071-267 9840. A good source of information and also short language courses.

Books

Dympna Cuzak, *Chinese Women Speak* (Century, 1985). Classic, in-depth study of Chinese Women, researched from the 1950s on.

Elizabeth Croll, *Chinese Women since Mao* (Zed Books, 1984). Informed analysis of the effect of Revolutionary policies on the lives of women. Important for understanding the pressures women face in choosing to have children is **Elizabeth Croll, Delia Davin and**

Penny Kane, *China's One Child per Family Policy* (Macmillan, 1985).

Agnus Smedley, *China Correspondent* (1943; Pandora Press, 1985). Compelling account of women's role in the Revolutionary period by one of the US's most unjustly unsung, great, early feminists. Her autobiography, *Daughter of the Earth* (Feminist Press, US, 1987) is an inspiring and engaging read.

Jan MacKinnon and Steve MacKinnon, eds., *Agnes Smedley, Portraits of Chinese Women in Revolution* (The Feminist Press, US, 1988). Eighteen of Smedley's pieces on Chinese women written between 1928 and 1941, based on interviews and observations.

Emily Honig, *Sisters and Strangers: Women in the Shanghai Cotton Mills 1919–1949* (Stanford U. Press, US, 1986). A model of good, readable labour history – though academic. Interesting and with masses of evidence, examining family life, workplace tensions, strikes, and the revolutionary period.

Andrew Higgins and Michael Fathers, *Tiananmen: The Rape of Peking* (Doubleday, 1989). As yet, the best researched piece of analysis and reportage covering the events of June 1989.

Fiction

Zhang Jie, *Leaden Wings* (Virago, 1987). One of China's most popular and controversial writers; her absorbing account of life in an industrial town was both praised and condemned as a powerful contemporary satire. Also translated are her short stories, *As Long as Nothing Happens, Nothing Will* (Virago, 1988).

Yu Luojin, *A Chinese Winter's Tale* (Renditions, US, 1986). Intensely personal chronicle of life during the Cultural Revolution.

Wang Anyi, *Baotown* (Norton Press, US, 1989). A moving account of village life written in the style of a folktale.

Thanks to Alison Monroe who provided the Introduction to this chapter.

Colombia

C olombia is a violent country. Robberies and muggings are
common and, as centre of Latin
America's illicit drug traffic, whole
areas of the country have been
taken over by the cocaine trade.
Smugglers see tourists as an easy
target to use as innocent carriers,
making them a prime suspect for
the police who themselves may not
think twice about planting drugs on
the unwary traveller. Not surprisingly, despite attractions that
include quite overwhelmingly beautiful landscapes and a seductive
popular dance culture, European
travellers are a comparatively rare
sight. Being a woman in a strong
machista culture makes problems
worse, and without a male companion be prepared for continual
sexual harassment. Probably more
than anywhere in Latin America
you will need strong wits and a
good knowledge of Spanish to get
by!

Political conflict adds to Colombia's dangerous reputation. As recently as
1950, thousands of people were being killed in a long and bloody battle
between Liberals and Conservatives. Today there is threat of another civil
war, fuelled by the ruling Liberal Party's failure to meet the basic needs of the
population, let alone confront well-known complicity between sections of the
military and the nation's notoriously powerful drug cartels.

Feminism in Colombia has made a lot of progress since the first groups
started up in 1975. Besides being the venue of the successful First Feminist
Meeting of Latin America and the Caribbean, the country has witnessed
several women's demonstrations, the publication of feminist literature, development of research and the increasing participation of women in cultural
events. Even in such a tense political climate several autonomous groups

survive – some of the most effective dealing with women's health – as well as others, such as *Mujer en la Lucha*, which are directly linked to political opposition parties.

Reaching women of all backgrounds is a major problem for the Women's Movement in a country where social and economic divisions are so rigid. One of the most progressive groups in Colombia is *Cine Mujer*, a women's film-making collective which has made some headway in gaining access to the all-important mass media of cinema and television. Even the poorest families in Colombia tend to have TV, and cinema is a popular form of entertainment. *Cine Mujer* have made several short films about the position of women in Colombian society, which have been shown up until recently in cinemas throughout the country. As long as they don't openly attack the church or the hallowed concept of the family, the group can use this access to a mass audience to challenge many popular myths. As they take advantage of the increasing use of video, there are hopes of achieving an even wider distribution.

Taking the Rough With the Smooth

. . . .

Janey Mitchell spent a year teaching English at a state university in the Andean market town of Tunja, three hours from the capital, Bogotá. She used her holidays to travel around the country, mostly on buses and occasionally hitching.

I was nervous about going to Colombia, a feeling confirmed by the discovery, on arrival at Bogotá airport, that half the contents of my rucksack had evidently flown in a different direction. However, any doubts I had disappeared in the first weeks and today I look back with amusement at my own and others' exaggerated preconceptions of the country.

I cannot deny that Colombia has multiple and currently insoluble problems and it certainly isn't the safest country for a woman to travel alone. I am writing from the point of view of someone who spoke reasonably fluent Spanish on arrival and picked up a great deal more as the year progressed. This is a huge advantage, but you still cannot help drawing attention to yourself. Clad in poncho, local hat concealing any trace of blondness, and dark glasses, I was no less conspicuous than otherwise. It's in your walk, your height, your demeanour. You can't escape it.

"Besides two Moonie missionaries, I was the only so-called alien in the place where I was teaching"

Conspicuousness brings *piropos*, catcalls, comments – even when you have just crawled out of the house with a hangover at seven in the morning. Whistles and psssts from men, as if calling a dog to heel, are blood-boiling, but they are human and once you show yourself to be human too, the situation becomes far less strained.

Your acute visibility as a foreign woman can even be an advantage.

Besides two Moonie missionaries, I was the only so-called alien in the place where I was teaching and naturally provoked considerable curiosity. Blue eyes, white skin and unjustly magic words like Cambridge open all the doors; I was spoilt with constant companionship, invitations into people's homes, VIP treatment, and paid not one peso of rent. I can't help feeling guilty at the undeserved esteem that British nationality seems to inspire and would like to think that the high regard and interest are mutual. However, I fear that Latins in Britain are, in general, poorly received.

During my first month in Tunja the words "es la gringa" followed me everywhere. "Gringa" is the female version of the term for all Western foreigners, although it essentially refers to North Americans, and, as local people regard the States as a rich, powerful, and envied Big Brother, the word is often used derogatorily.

The one conversation when I attempted to clarify the difference between the British and North Americans provoked genuine interest, besides revealing people's far from infallible knowledge of world geography. Many believed England to be a little island off the US coast. By the time a month was up, the words "es la inglesa" echoed in my wake.

Colombian women generally have a raw deal unless they come from affluent families, have perhaps been educated abroad or, for whatever reason, have come to challenge traditional expectations. *Machismo* rules and men with means may have any number of girlfriends. In this respect women simply cannot achieve an equal footing with men, even in the most open of relationships.

In indigenous areas a woman who two-times or is merely seen in public with different men is invariably classified as a whore. Women are a domestic necessity or pastime, yet a pregnant woman, even unmarried, is conceded a level of courtesy. Travelling alone, when I felt most at risk, I sometimes used a small padded rucksack over my stomach and inside a coat as a talisman.

The university environment brought me into contact with a huge range of people. Women were inquisitive and warm, but simultaneously suspicious and envious of my liberty, ability to travel (concomitant with money) and my novelty. I rarely went out with unaccompanied women as most had families and husbands and, for Colombian women, socialising is inseparable from contact with the opposite sex.

Dance is a vital element of social life. *Salsa*, *merengue* and *cumbia* are barely conceivable in a single sex environment. *Merengue* in particular is a fast dance requiring man and woman to swing from side to side with their bodies as close as possible. It wasn't easy to accept that such sudden physical proximity could be less significant than buying someone a drink.

"Though I hardly escaped criticism for mixing with as many men as I did, I probably would have been branded a complete slut had I been local"

I found myself in a unique position in Tunja. Being foreign, I was far less obliged to conform to the unwritten local code of conduct. The vast majority of Colombians are Catholics and in a community rife with gossip and assumed unblemished personal virtue, hypocrisy has the upper hand. Though I hardly escaped criticism for mixing with as many men as I did, I probably would have been branded a complete slut had I been local.

I actually lived with two men for most of the teaching year and was constantly cornered by women demanding to know whether I was sleeping with them both or if just one, which. It was unthinkable that I could be cohabiting with two men without having a relationship with either one. I was incredibly lucky to meet this pair who were like brother-bodyguards to me and unusually lacking in *machismo*. They even cooked and washed up!

Through these two I was initiated not only into the art of dance, but that of drinking *aguardiente*, a sugar-cane based quasi-toxic liquor flavoured with aniseed. It is customarily drunk in liqueur-sized glasses, but don't be misled by the size of the glass. "Fondo blanco", meaning "down in one", becomes a dreaded phrase, but to refuse is impolite and can cause offence.

Women are excused for lacking pride in their stamina for alcohol consumption, but it may take a lot of determination and some strategically placed flowerpots to avoid inebriation. Beware of men using intoxication tactics to try and weaken your will.

As far as travelling in Colombia is concerned, no advice is complete and I can only offer guidelines to bear in mind. A woman alone will inevitably be harassed, but common sense and care go a long way. Thieves and pickpockets riddle bus stations in particular so stick to the obvious precaution of not displaying watch, jewellery or camera in public. Local women have a huge advantage in the Andes in that they wear countless layers of clothing in which to conceal a purse. Most carry notes in their bras.

I wore a money belt and had dollars sewn into the hem of a T-shirt until washing it became a problem and I transferred them to the waistband of a pair of trousers. I once stupidly left the $240 T-shirt in a hotel room (in San Agustin) in a pile of clothes. It disappeared and I still seethe with fury to think of somebody going through every inch of clothing to find my money. Hotel safes are wise but if there was any doubt about the security of money in deposits, I split my cash, wearing half in my clothes.

I would advise women against hitching. I did so rarely, only in daylight and in areas where tourists were few and far between. This may seem to contradict a warning not to wander too far off the beaten track – lone travellers have been known simply to disappear without trace, especially around guerrilla strongholds and the remote foothills used to cultivate *coca* and marijuana.

"A Colombian woman would rarely travel alone and it is difficult for men to envisage a culture that allows women such independence"

But, where foreigners are rare, local people tend to be less wise to means of ripping you off and more likely to take a genuine interest in the whys and wherefores of a woman travelling alone. Here I found that white lies about my Colombian husband did not go amiss. It's wise to explain the reasons for your solitude, whether it means inventing a partner or honestly trying to outline your position. Just remember that a Colombian woman would rarely travel alone and it is difficult for men to envisage a culture that allows women such independence. Hitching also may require a degree of physical and mental stamina as you crouch, squashed between pumpkins and yams, ears deafened by the sound of squealing piglets.

On one occasion, I leapt over the back of a high-sided lorry to find myself landing on a heap of oranges from the valley, in which a bunch of distinctly pickled pickers lay sprawling or half buried. My instinctive recoil was met with a helping hand which then hesitantly offered a petrol can. It turned out to contain their local *trago*, a distilled sugar-cane hooch. They probably thought they were hallucinating as I appeared. However, a spattering of English was successfully dragged out from somewhere in my honour and I even managed to add to it. I soon discovered that making moves to pay the driver is appreciated, but money seldom changes hands.

There were times in Colombia when I knew I was at risk, but after my first few trouble-free months I had become ridiculously blasé about the whole thing. My sense of invulnerability subsequently took a beating.

"Attempted rape radically altered my attitude to travelling alone"

I advise women not to arm themselves with any kind of weapon as men are likely to act more aggressively under threat. I had taken general self-defence classes at the university before setting off alone during the holidays and when I did find myself under attack my automatic reaction was to aim for the organs most likely to debilitate. I was lucky in that in both cases the attacker was unarmed and my aggression won. The scrotal sac is woman's one concession against male physical strength. I remember little of the actual struggle: yelling, uncontrollable shaking afterwards, curiosity on seeing human hair between my knuckles and a recollection of the jelly-like texture of the eyeball as my fingers lunged.

Attempted rape radically altered my attitude to travelling alone. I was astounded by my own physical strength and mental determination to fight off attack. Full accounts of what happened would entail lengthy explanation; it is sufficient to say that, in each case, I had wrongly trusted my intuition and demonstrated a degree of friendliness.

Travelling unaccompanied and without contacts in an unfamiliar city, it isn't easy to reject all approaches from men and I cannot stress enough that these violent incidents came about through a slackening of caution.

Mine was a conscious choice to travel alone and fluent Spanish made it easy to make friends with Latin Americans. Had I been travelling in company and with a person of less fluency, I would not have become as integrated into the communities I visited or have felt as close to their culture. I was often with people so trustworthy that I became blind to the proportion of the population who regard a Western woman travelling alone as a piece of flesh to be bought or taken by force.

Following these incidents, however, I took a great deal more care, making an effort to team up with fellow travellers and, where possible, share rooms with women. Had my attackers been successful, my attitude towards the whole trip would be drastically altered.

As it is, those experiences have given me a deep spiritual resilience. I know that I'd travel alone again under similar circumstances. The good times – visiting Colombia's lesser-known Caribbean islands, dozing in steaming volcanic pools, exploring prehistoric sites on horseback – far outweigh the bad.

A Lot of Dire Warnings

. . . .

As a feminist academic, writer and translator, Susan Bassnett has travelled and lived in a number of countries. With her eight-year-old daughter, she visited Colombia at the invitation of the Universidad de los Andes.

Although I had worked on Latin American Literature for some years and taught courses in Britain on Latin American culture, I hadn't visited a Latin American country until I was invited to go and do some teaching at the Universidad de los Andes, Bogotá, Colombia.

I was given a lot of dire warnings before setting out, many by people who had already visited the country. I was told about the high level of street violence, of areas which are effectively civil-war zones and the dangers of walking anywhere alone. When they learned that I was also proposing to take along my eight-year-old daughter, the warnings increased and I was told horror stories about kidnappings, child prostitution rings and ransom demands. I left Britain in a state of some anxiety. My experiences of the country revealed a lot about the way in which Europeans and North Americans perceive Latin America.

Viewed from afar, the South American continent seems like the final bastion of civilisation: the place to which embezzlers and train robbers flee, the place that harbours undiscovered war criminals and to which people go to lose themselves and change their identities. Seen from the North American fastness, it is source of a steadily creeping communist menace, it is "down below" with all its associations of hellishness and incivility added to the European's image of distance and solitude. And however much we may dismiss these images of another continent, they do exist and consequently colour our own perceptions too. Despite all that I had read, despite the many friends from Latin America that I had made over the years, traces of these negative images remained.

Once I landed in Colombia, after a brief stopover in Caracas, everything changed. The visit remains one of the high points of an extensive travelling life and I can't wait to go back. It is an extraordinarily beautiful country, with a huge range of completely different landscapes, from the high Andes to the glorious Caribbean coast around Cartagena, the great fertile plateau and the Amazonian jungle. It is the only country in Latin America to have a Pacific and a Caribbean coastline, and stands in a unique geographical position, which no doubt is why the conquistadors, the English pirates and later North American profiteers, drug smugglers and the Mafia have always seen it as a prime target for exploitation.

The history of Colombia is a history of violence and there is no denying that it is a country where you have to take certain precautions. When I arrived, the regular traffic police had been replaced by military units, and on every street corner in Bogotá there seemed to be a nervous teenage soldier clutching a sten gun.

"I was careful not to wear jewellery, not even earrings, or anything that might seem in any way ostentatious"

But it is also a country that makes you face up to what it means to be, in the terms of those millions living in appalling shanty towns, a wealthy foreigner. We may not perceive ourselves as rich; but the boy who held up a British Embassy official at knifepoint the week I arrived and stole his coat, his watch, his wallet and his glasses clearly saw the possession of those things as a sign of wealth. Most people carry small sums of money; if you are held up at knifepoint or gunpoint, it is best to hand over a small sum straight away and the thief will then simply take it and vanish.

Colombia, of course, has abject poverty, and stealing from the rich is a way of surviving. I lost count of the number of times Colombian friends told me about their fears in North American cities such as New York, where their doors were fitted out with more padlocks than a Colombian would ever dream of and where you cannot be assured of safe delivery from a mugger if you simply hand over two dollars or an old watch. This difference illustrates two concepts of social crime that cannot fairly be compared.

I lived in Candelaría, the old part of Bogotá, an area reputedly unsafe. I did not walk on the streets at night, but I did walk the fifteen minutes or so to the place where I was working, and never felt remotely uneasy. My daughter and I used to go shopping, visit some of the magnificent churches in Bogotá and walk around quite happily. I used public transport and the ramshackle Bogotá taxis quite normally. However, I was careful not to wear any jewellery, not even earrings, or anything that might seem in any way ostentatious.

Occasionally a shop assistant would remind me not to let my daughter carry a package, in case anyone snatched it from her as we were walking, but otherwise we behaved as though we were in any European city. Bogotá is an extraordinary city, with some beautiful colonial architecture and one of the finest museums in Latin America, the Museum of Gold. Best to walk quickly past the men who hang around outside the museum, with handkerchiefs full of emeralds for quick sale to tourists: a refusal to buy might easily turn into something unpleasant.

Travelling across the country, it is easiest to fly or, if that proves too expensive, to go by bus. The buses may not look it, but they tend to be very efficient and quite safe Nevertheless, I never mastered the rationale behind catching an inter-city bus outside a bus station: you go to the outskirts of the city and then leap out into the road at a passing bus – and it stops! When uncertain, it is always best to go to the central bus station and start the journey from there.

"Responses to children were magnificent everywhere"

I did not have enough time to travel down to the Amazonian jungle, which I would dearly love to do in the future. Crucial to any visitor's itinerary is a trip to Cartagena, the magnificent coastal town that was considered the jewel of the Caribbean in the sixteenth century. Northern Colombia, with its hot coastal flatlands, has been made famous by Gabriel García Márquez who was born

and raised there and who contrasts the fertile plains with their brilliant sunlight with the colder, wetter climate of the high Andes. Bogotá is one of the highest capital cities in the world and although close to the equator is rarely hot. In fact the climate of Bogotá is not unlike that of an English summer, and it can be very wet indeed.

A highlight of our visit was a trip to one of the oldest colonial towns in Colombia, Villa de Leyva, about four hours' bus ride from Bogotá. This amazing old town, constructed around the biggest stone-paved plaza I have ever seen or could ever imagine, stands at the edge of the desert, and the hot, dry winds blowing across the barren landscape have produced a geological miracle.

Close to the town are the skeletons of thousands of prehistoric animals, and all the stonework is full of fossils. Eighteenth-century colonial architects with baroque sensibilities played with the raw materials available, and so there are fountains built out of giant ammonites, courtyards paved with the vertebrae of dinosaurs, ornamental stonework in which the patterns are made out of fossilised bones of all sizes. You can wander around and pick up fossils everywhere, or buy rarer examples for very little from local children who roam around the plaza in groups, looking for likely sales.

The combination of whitewashed houses built around little courtyards that are full of red and purple blossom (apparently all the year round) with the grotesque richness of bones and fossils everywhere was truly memorable. My other, strictly personal, memory to cherish from Villa de Leyva is the sight of my daughter running wildly down a hill in her pyjamas in pursuit of a contemptuous llama who had obviously seen too many enthusiastic small girls before.

I learned a great deal, too, from having a child with me. Responses to children were magnificent everywhere, and something of the wonder of a completely new continent can be lost when adults (and intellectual adults at that) exchange experiences. My daughter kept a home-made diary of the trip, collecting postcards and bus tickets and anything else of interest; and she wrote about the things that most impressed her. I felt that only with a child as a companion would I have sat in a colonial building now converted into a restaurant and stared in amazement at the mummified alligators and boa constrictors hanging from the oak beams above our heads. And having a child with me made me acutely aware of the cruelty of social inequality, where boys younger than mine are out at work or begging in gangs in the streets. One disconcerting fact that my daughter drew to my attention was the absence of girl children either as beggars or as child labour. Though no accurate figures exist, the implication of this absence suggests that the route through life for destitute girls, even at a very young age, is the brothel.

As in many Latin American countries, the position of women is profoundly ambiguous. On the one hand, the cult of *machismo* relegates women to low status as sex objects in the eyes of most men; and yet there are also many powerful women in political and business life who exercise a great deal of authority.

As a centre for Latin American publishing, Colombia is also very much a focal point for the region's culture and there are a growing number of women writers whose work is well-known and widely read. Working in a university context, there was not much evidence as yet that the field of women's studies have begun to gain much ground, but there are women keen to promote them.

Montserrat Ordonez, the feminist writer and critic who has spent some time teaching in the United States, was enormously helpful in introducing me to some of the problems of a Latin American feminist movement – the absence of models except those offered by European or North American women, the need to work specifically with the history and culture of women from Colombia, the problems of class and education that are so extreme in such a hierarchical society.

The first feminist conference in Latin America took place in Colombia in the early 1980s, and women are well represented at the Colombian international theatre festivals that have also become a regular feature over the past decade. Plans are under way for a meeting in 1992 of the Magdalena Project, the international women's theatre association based in Cardiff that has held conferences, workshops and performances throughout Europe since 1986, and it is significant that of all the Latin American countries, particularly those such as Argentina and Chile with a tradition of great women playwrights, it should be Colombia that is preparing to host the meeting.

I would like to go back, ideally in time for the proposed Magdalena Project. That will also be the year when the extent of the changes brought about by Latin American women and Colombian women in particular will be apparent, because it will be the 500th anniversary of Columbus' discovery of the Americas that heralded the centuries of colonialism and reaction against colonialism that is still going on today. Latin American nations will be celebrating their own struggles for independence, and Latin American women will feature prominently – not only celebrating the struggles they have shared with their menfolk, but marking the progress made in their fight for equal rights and status in a *machista* culture.

TRAVEL NOTES

Language Spanish.

Transport Buses are cheap and frequent. All long-distance routes are covered by coaches – comfortable but a bit more expensive. There are few passenger trains. Never travel in a taxi without a meter as you'll be overcharged.

Accommodation The poor exchange rate on the peso makes Colombia one of the most expensive South American countries. However, hotels outside the main cities can be very cheap. Camping isn't advised.

Special Problems Thieves and pickpockets are rife – hang on to your luggage at all times, watch your pockets and don't wear a watch or jewellery. Expect harassment from all kinds of men, including the police and the military. Colombia is perhaps the worst country in South America for *machismo*. Bus stations can be particularly frightening places for harassment of all kinds. The drug scene is very heavy. Buses are periodically searched by the police and it's common for drug pushers to set people up. Never carry packages for other people without checking the contents. Sentences for possession can be very long.

Guides *The South American Handbook* (Trade and Travel Publications) includes 100 pages on Colombia. *Colombia – A Travel Survival Kit* (Lonely Planet) is more in-depth.

Contacts

Casa de la Mujer, Carrera 18, No. 59–60, Bogotá, ☎2496317. Women's centre run by a long-standing collective.

Centro de Informacíon y Recursos para la Mujer, C1 36 17-44, Bogotá; ☎2454266. Rape crisis counselling, family planning etc.

Cine Mujer, Av. 25c 49-24, Apartado 202, Bogotá, ☎2426184. Women's film collective.

Books

Alicia Partnoy, ed., *You Can't Drown the Fire: Latin American Women Writing in Exile* (Virago, 1989). Moving collection of essays, stories, poetry, letters and song, including several contributions from Colombia.

Starting with arguably his best novel, *One Hundred Years of Solitude* (Picador, 1978) it's worth reading any books by **Gabriel García Márquez**. Colombia's most famous contemporary writer brilliantly captures the magic, beauty and madness of his country.

Lyll Becerra de Jenkins, *The Honourable Prison* (Virago, 1989). Part of Virago's teenage list, this extraordinary tale of political intrigue is based on the author's own life in Colombia.

Charlotte Méndez, *Condor and Hummingbird* (The Women's Press, 1987). Passionate novel around North American woman's visiti to Bogotá with her Colombian husband.

Cuba

• • • • • • • • • • • • • • • • • •

In the face of a continuing US trade embargo, Cuba is turning to mass tourism as the most obvious means of importing dollars. Luxury resorts, such as Cayo Largo, have sprung up along its coastline, offering exclusive sun-sea-and-sand holidays for a new, privileged class of hard-currency tourists from Europe and Canada – North Americans still have problems getting visas. Politically motivated tours are also

organised (with visits to factories, schools, hospitals and prisons or to pursue special cultural interests) but the impetus to demonstrate the achievements of the Revolution is gradually giving way to the demands of a more mainstream holiday industry.

For the average Cuban, denied the facilities freely available to dollar-wielding foreigners, resentments are beginning to surface. Cuba has long had a reputation as a safe haven for travellers and for many years street violence was almost unheard of. Tourist muggings are now on the increase, and although the numbers are neglible compared with other South American or Caribbean countries, it's a continuing trend. Travelling independently, you're bound to experience some degree of street hassle from illegal money-changers. Sexual violence, however, is incredibly rare. Cuban men can seem as steeped in *machismo* as their Latin American counterparts, but the propositions and comments you face seldom seem aggressive. If you feel at all uncertain, take stock of the cursory way that Cuban women deal with unsolicited approaches. Despite the tensions caused by tourist privilege, the large majority of Cubans tend to be friendly, helpful and interested in making contact with foreign visitors.

With so much of the Eastern bloc embracing wide-sweeping reforms, the Cuban regime no longer seems the showpiece of progressive socialism that it used to be. Thirty years after the Revolution dissatisfaction is setting in at the apparent unwillingness of Fidel Castro to open up and further democratise the country. A new generation has emerged who can now take for granted the massive advances in health, education and housing. Living with the continual and widespread problems of shortages and bureaucratic restrictions, change, for them, can seem frustratingly slow.

There's no doubt that the **status of women** has improved markedly in the post-revolutionary period. Successful efforts have been made to ensure equal access to education and job opportunities and women have played a leading role in health and literacy campaigns. Most of this work is carried out through the Federation of Cuban Women which was set up by the government in 1960. With well over two million members, the Federation has the ability to organise and change women's lives on an unprecedented scale. Its achievements are impressive, but the fact remains that few, if any, Cuban women hold any high position of power in the government. And "The Family Code", for all its radical stipulations that men should share housework and childcare, has brought about little change in the balance of labour at home.

Just Another Resort?

. . . .

Jane Drinkwater is a professional researcher, formerly in the Trade Union Movement and now in television. She has visited Cuba twice, travelling with a mixed group of friends and occasionally striking out alone.

I first went to Cuba on an unexpected windfall, for what I thought would be the holiday of a lifetime. It wasn't. I liked it so much that I borrowed the money and went back again the following year . . . and as soon as I can afford it, I'll be off again.

British holidaymakers, about two thousand every year, still tend to visit Cuba on group tours organised to meet trade unionists, healthworkers, women's organisations, or attend the cinema or jazz festivals. There's a growing trade from Italian and Canadian tour operators too – though the good time they offer is more usually geared to the traditional, if up-market, holidaymaker. Most of their time seems to be spent at the classier beach resorts, with occasional air-conditioned and fully guided coach trips into Havana for shopping, sightseeing and entertainments. The British tours offer a more rounded view. Visits to factories, schools and hospitals are combined with a trip to the popular Varadero beach resort, with a chance to travel alone from time to time as well.

I went with a small group of friends, both men and women. None of us wanted to be part of a formal tour, so we thought we'd try it the other way around: "buying-in" to the official sightseeing visits, but organising our own timetable and itinerary. This is relatively new in Cuba, but it proved unexpectedly easy – and rewarding. We had to book five nights' accommodation in Havana through the travel agent and after that could set off on our own.

Although Cuba is a big island, travelling its length and breadth isn't as daunting as it sounds. To get to Santiago de Cuba (the hot, very Caribbean "second capital" at the eastern end of the island), we travelled cheaply overnight from Havana on a Russian plane. Pinar Del Rio, to the west of Havana at the heart of the island's tobacco-growing region, we saw from a more expensive hired car. Travelling south, we flew again, this time on a "mini-package", booked from Havana, to Cayo Largo.

"The Bay of Pigs is now a flashy tourist resort with bamboo beach bars that happily accept dollars or travellers' cheques"

Cayo Largo is a tiny island which has been reclaimed from the mosquitoes and cleared of the debris which dropped and drifted on to its beaches in the American-backed invasion of 1961. It is now Cuba's most exclusive tourist resort and offers horse riding, snorkelling, and some of the most spectacular and safest scuba diving in the Caribbean. Exclusive, because it is strictly reserved for travellers in possession of the all-important hard currency, catering for neither Cuban nor Eastern-bloc holidaymakers.

Most of the Cubans working there were on secondment from their regular jobs (we met computer programmers, university professors and Havana hotel porters) and regretted that their only access to the island's attractions was on a working holiday. English visitors were something of a rarity there too. Most of the other guests came from Italy and some from Canada, stopping at Havana only in transit or for an evening's excursion by plane to the famous Tropicana nightclub. They were keen to find out from us what the "real Cuba" was like.

It was much more interesting to explore the mainland by cheaper and more Cuban means – on the network of coaches linking main towns and cities, and by the unofficial collective taxis. You can catch a ride in these *carrios* at most coach stations, where their drivers advertise their preferred destination with a handpainted cardboard sign.

Usually you'll find yourself travelling in a souped-up pre-revolutionary American classic car (a Zodiac, Chevy or Buick). These days they come handpainted, patched, welded and wired together and running on sickly-smelling Russian fuel, with engines that sound more like they belong in an aeroplane. These rides seem to involve any number of ever-changing passengers and can take the most unexpected routes (which on more than one occasion included the driver's home for a cup of coffee laced with rum). The charge is individually negotiated before you set off – but it can alter along the way.

Aiming south and east from Havana we eventually arrived – via any number of small-town suburbs, delivering and collecting passengers on the way – at the Bay of Pigs, America's tried and failed stop-off point in 1961. The area is now a flashy tourist resort with bamboo beach bars that happily accept dollars or travellers' cheques. Many Cubans died fighting off the counter-revolution and the local museum is dedicated to commemorating (movingly) those who fell; beach hoardings proudly proclaim this the site of "the first great blow to imperialism in Latin America".

Much of the land around the Bay of Pigs has also been developed for tourism. Just along the coast is a Butlins-type beach camp, Playa Larga, where Fidel himself holidayed in the early years after the Revolution. It is now used mainly by tourists from the Soviet Union and we joined them there – again the only English tourists – for a few days. The Russians travel in packs, and seemed to be regarded with wry amusement by many of the Cubans I met.

The Soviet Union's relationship and attitude to Cuba is peculiar (although "special" is the usual description given in political circles). That's to be expected: Cuba is the smaller, black and more recently socialist country, with a growing economic dependence on the huge, powerful, and largely white "mother" of socialism. The *Sovietikas* seemed more concerned with their own travelling companions and getting some sun whilst they could, than with exploring Cuban life (they know about it from school, they explained). But they were not disdainful: they protested a real sense of solidarity with Cuba's youthful revolution and respect for its achievements.

Cubans, for their part, seemed open and interested in talking to all tourists – especially to those like ourselves from England, who are still something of a rarity. I enjoyed scores of acquaintances struck up easily over my two trips with many very different people: from the mother who wanted to explain to me what Cubans thought of Margaret Thatcher; to the "revolutionary policeman" who just wanted to share a beer; to the Havana hotel lift attendant (by no means the only Cuban critic I met), who recounted tales from the good old days before the Revolution when he was a casino croupier and mixed with America's rich and famous.

"Cuban women seemed quite confident walking home late"

As in many other relatively poor countries hosting an influx of richer holidaymakers looking for a bargain, there's a brisk currency trade on what seems to be a highly developed informal and illegal economy. This trade brings many tourists' first (and most persistent) contact with the Cubans. It's typically a trade pursued by inner city youths, and because in the main they're young men (sometimes with drugs and prostitution connections, too), their approaches can feel like harassment with a sexist edge.

There were times in Cuba when, on beaches or walking though Havana on my own, I felt uncomfortable, but never more than in any other capital; and I never felt actually threatened. Cuban society generally, even in downtown Havana, is striking for its non-violent atmosphere. Streets in cities may be busy but never, I felt, dangerous. Cuban women seemed quite confident walking home late, and some worked in jobs (like car park attendants or guarding buildings) which left them alone at night in dark, secluded parts of the city – something you would never see in London, for example.

I shared the observations, too, of a black travelling companion, that many of the everyday tensions of racism found in so many other countries seemed curiously absent. It is still nevertheless the case that the higher status the jobs, the whiter the workforce. Life for Cuba's black population, as for its women, seems to be improving – with effort.

We started and finished our holidays both times in Havana, and returned there as a base in between our exploratory journeys. I always left the city needing to slow down and relax, but looking forward to another chance to get to know it better. It is big and busy, but easy to get around, since it's covered by a criss-cross of frequent, if overcrowded, buses.

Shopping – and contrary to popular expectations there is plenty of it – is an experience. Many of the shops in Old Havana are abandoned American Fifties department stores, still sporting original neon signs and laid out to the archetypal Woolworth's formula, some complete with functioning lunch counters. I couldn't resist the Cuban records, and ended up buying far too many to carry.

Unfortunately, it's easy to get a bad impression of Cuban music if you stick to the hotel cabaret circuit. Bands come complete with sparkling bikinis, coconuts, lots of dirty jokes and can be unbelievably tacky. (Strangely, there's a resurgence of interest in this sort of entertainment.) But when the cabaret bands knock off for the night from the hotels, some of them re-appear in the odd jazz club dotted around the suburbs, singing and playing the real thing. Concerts which feature a stream of female ballad singers (sporting ever more impressive ballgowns as you get higher up the bill) are popular. So too, on our first visit, were competitions for the best Madonna look-alikes which every girl under twelve in Havana seemed to have entered. They mimed collectively on the Teatro Karl Marx stage to "Material Girl" and a minor celebrity chose the winner.

On each trip I took some time off on my own. Cuba struck me as a very safe country to travel around; hotels are generally secure, with plenty of staff to call on and the people can be very helpful. You can also use the state tourist office in every major city to book your travel and accommodation ahead as you go, and, of course, living is cheap if you have the right currency.

Needless to say, there are frustrations; some things seem to take forever to sort out, and queueing is practically an art form. The British, proud of their reputation as queuers, have nothing on the Cubans, who go out of their way to find out who is last and then take their place behind them. On any journey it helps to have someone to share the chores and moans with. In a place where seemingly simple tasks can take on epic proportions, travelling alone in Cuba can sometimes be a real strain. But it's undoubtedly worth it.

Framing Cuba

. . . .

Geraldine Ellis, a film-maker and journalist based in London, first went to Havana as a delegate at the International Film Festival. She returned to make a film about the position of women working in the arts and media.

The first time I went to Cuba was for the Annual Festival of Third World Cinema held in Havana. It was easy to get caught up in the Festival and forget to take any account of the host city, but even the most cursory tourist jaunt confirms it as a place rich in character. The architecture bears the stamp of Spanish and American colonisation but the most obvious reminder of the historical rupture with US interests are the cars. You still see vintage American

cars of the Fifties, miraculously roadworthy and often eyed with envy by drivers of modern Ladas. Another high-profile American legacy is the *Capitolio*, a sort of mini-White House in the centre of Old Havana, surrounded by parks graced with tall palm trees and benches where the old men sit.

At around 4pm clusters of schoolchildren in maroon or gold uniforms swarm around the bus stops along the central square. The churches, the Plaza de Alma, the *Bodeguita del Medio*, rub shoulders with community centres, light industry, shops and housing. The rattle of industrial sewing machines can be heard from early morning in a side street which also serves as a playground and baseball pitch. People sit and chat in doorways and washing is pegged out on balconies.

Turn a corner and you find yourself on a building site. Women and men are mixing concrete, loading timber into the open lift, and grinning for the tourist with a camera. These construction teams, or *microbrigadas*, are at work on a variety of sites all over Havana, many of them taking a day off while their comrades cover for them. Some are working on accommodation they will themselves inhabit, and their labour is counted as future rent.

This lively and attractive part of Havana is being refurbished with help from UNESCO; inevitably with an eye to the tourist trade. But there are fears that foreign currency bars would replace residents who would find themselves moved to estates on the outskirts of the city. Like many "Third World" countries, developing the tourist industry is a way of bringing much needed hard currency into Cuba – for instance to buy the building materials essential for solving Havana's acute housing shortage. But ironically it means once again a privileged class emerging – the tourist.

"You can have problems trying to enter a hotel bar with a Cuban friend – it's immediately assumed that illegal money changing will occur"

For instance, two types of taxi operate in Havana: those licenced to deal in dollars and peso taxis which often collect extra passengers en route.

For Cubans, food produce is rationed, and this can entail several hours queueing for something like yoghurt or bread. But this doesn't affect its availability in the hotels. Fruits produced solely for export are sold to tourists yet never reach Cuban tables. Hotel shops are full of unlikely souvenirs like pressure cookers, electric fans, Walkmans, televisions and running shoes – goods which can only be bought with hard currency. Cubans can be imprisoned for possession of dollars but some still wait by hotels to "ride tourists" and change money. They are known as *jenetes*, or *jockeys*, although unfortunately the term often

sticks to any Cuban who develops a relationship with a foreigner.

Because of this you can have problems trying to enter a hotel bar with a Cuban friend – it's immediately assumed that illegal money changing will occur. I met one dissident who, having been caught trying to leave for Miami, claimed to be permanently barred from finding work. He explained that he wanted to leave because, "why is it that you as a tourist have more rights in my country than I do?"

Not surprisingly the US exploits dissent like this for all it's worth. *Radio José Martí*, cynically named after the great Cuban fighter for national liberation, is broadcast from Washington by "Voice of America", with music and politics from Cuban exiles. However most of the Cubans I met regarded the station as a bit of a joke and countered the propaganda with a high degree of political awareness and an impressively internationalist outlook.

On my second visit to Cuba I went with a 16mm camera, one crew member and a Thames TV student bursary to gather material on the position of women in the arts.

Cuba had aroused my curiosity on several counts. Despite the fact that the mainstream British media ignore it as far as possible, everyone seems to have an attitude about it. Take a holiday in Turkey or Tenerife, and people rarely question the politics or human rights record of the country, but go to Cuba and they do. It's almost as if we've subliminally absorbed trace elements of US foreign policy along with Hollywood, TV soaps and chat shows. I spent seven weeks in Havana researching and shooting but had barely enough time to scratch the surface.

For all the economic hardships imposed by the longstanding US embargo, it is clear that irreversible gains have been made. Illiteracy has been almost eradicated in just thirty years and the opportunities available to women, in education, career, and reproductive rights, certainly compares well with more affluent and "developed" countries. The arts are considered the "second wave" of the literacy programme, and concerts, cinema and theatre are very cheap. There are no Cubans who could not afford them. During the 1980s it has become increasingly possible for the photographer, jeweller, or clothes designer to work independently with their home doubling as a studio.

One of the painters I met, Zaida del Rio, earned a monthly salary for which she was obliged to produce three paintings per month to be sold through a government organisation. Anything else she made, she could sell privately. Her work was very popular and she was one of the few who could make a living from it. She works from a small unlit table in her bedroom. Her ten-year-old son has an adjacent room and they share a living room and tiny kitchen.

Caridad Martinez studied at one of the first schools of art to be opened after the Revolution. A dancer and choreographer, she had been with the Cuban National Ballet for eighteen years but in 1987 left to form her own contemporary dance group in conjunction with actors. This break was without precedent and was initially frowned upon by the Ministry of Culture, but they continued to draw salaries as dancers and gained a fair degree of success and recognition.

Many other women have taken advantage of the educational opportunities provided by the Revolution and universities currently have a higher intake of women in nearly all the subjects, not just the arts but also science, engineering, economics and philosophy (so much so, that there was talk of introducing positive discrimination for men). But, whilst women have equal rights, and a strong presence in the workforce, they still face the problem of the double shift.

A few years ago a comprehensive piece of legislation, "The Family Code", was passed, which underlined the principle that all domestic tasks should be shared if both partners work. In other words, men are legally bound to do fifty percent of the housework. Although difficult to enforce, it's reckoned to at best alleviate the shock of embarrassment experienced by the *machista* when he dons an apron. Every woman can choose, under the terms of the Family Code, whether to continue or terminate pregnancy, and equal support is available for either course of action regardless of whether she is married or single, employed or not.

"I used to take the bus back to the Hotel Caribbean in Old Havana, often in the early hours of the morning, without any sense of threat"

Although I couldn't verify the claim that neither rape nor domestic violence are common in Cuba, I used to take a bus back to the Hotel Caribbean in Old Havana, often in the early hours of the morning, without any sense of threat, and in fact many Cuban women were travelling alone at this hour, their activities unrestricted by fear of sexual harassment. This may be due to the self-defence women learn in military training, or to the discreet policing of the CDRs (Committee for the Defence of the Revolution), a sort of neighbourhood watch scheme which governs local affairs.

Even though the past few years have seen an increase in tourist muggings, they're still counted in tens rather than the hundreds that occur in so many capital cities, and the vast majority of Cubans would step in and help if they saw anything happening.

Most of the Cubans I met were open and friendly and it was the contact with people that formed my most enduring memories. Ana, for instance, seemed to have been nearer than most to the hub of Cuba's turbulent history. She brought out photos of herself as a young woman, in light blouse and slacks, crouched with a rifle on the steps of the university and another in army fatigues addressing a large audience of women recruits. She fought at Playa Giron and the Sierra Maestra but is now disillusioned. "No es socialismo," she said, "es Fidelismo." "What will happen when Fidel dies?" I asked. She grabbed the bottle of rum, "There'll be no more of this in the shops, there'll be dancing in the streets!"

The Revolution has its share of successes and failures, and most people dwell on whichever aspect suits their temperament and ideology. Their answer is likely to tell you more about the person than the place. If you're looking for betrayal, blind dogma and the dead hand of bureaucracy, you can find it. And equally if you want to find a triumphant revolution, there's the free and abundant healthcare and education for all. You can be suitably inspired by rent levels fixed at ten percent of income, with transport and food together at about fifteen percent. While for some the experiment has already ended in failure, for others, it's scarcely begun.

TRAVEL NOTES

Language Spanish. Few Cubans speak any English.

Transport Bus and train services are extensive but tend to be slow and generally inefficient. Theoretically, hitching is illegal, but in practice it works quite well.

Accommodation Travelling independently, you're obliged to book five days' accommodation in advance; from then on it's still advisable to book through the official *Cubatur* office, Calle 23, No 156, Velado, Havana, ☎32-4521, as the cheaper hotels tend to fill up quickly, especially in the provinces.

Special Problems You may well be hassled by money-changers, especially outside the main hotels; it's best to steer clear. Shorts and skirts are very rarely worn by adults except on the beach. Many rich Western tourists break the rule but it's frowned upon and will incite critical comment.

Guides *Hildebrand's Travel Guide: Cuba* (Harrap Columbus) is a good short guide with an excellent map of the island. *The Caribbean Handbook* (Trade and Travel Publications) also has a useful chapter. Paula DiPerna's *The Complete Guide to Cuba* (St Martin's Press, New York), though outdated, is still highly recommended.

Contacts

Federation of Cuban Women, Calle 11 No 2ʹ4, La Habana, Cuba. Central organisation for making contact with women's groups throughout the country.

Britain-Cuba Resource Centre, Latin America House, Kingsgate Road, London NW6. Organise places on work brigades.

Books

Jean Stubbs, *Cuba, the Test of Time* (Latin American Bureau, 1989). An illuminating, well researched look at contemporary Cuban life.

Elizabeth Stone, ed., *Women and the Cuban Revolution* (Pathfinder Press, New York, 1981). Collection of speeches and documents, including the thoughts of Fidel Castro.

Inger Holt-Seeland, *Women of Cuba* (Lawrence Hill, US, 1981). Interviews with six women, from farm worker to university teacher.

Margaret Randall, *Women in Cuba: Twenty Years Later* (Smyrna, US, 1981). Good if slightly dated socialist-feminist analysis of women's gains in Cuba in the first two decades of the Revolution. Offers a positive view of advances in legal, political and workplace rights and positions, and in particular gains made by women against *machismo* in family life.

Ecuador

E cuador, one of the smallest
and richest countries in South
America, is commonly considered
the most beautiful. It also has a
reputation for political stability in
spite of a noticeable military
presence.

The country is divided into two
main areas: coast and *sierra*, the
latter dominated by the Andes
mountains. The majority of
Ecuador's large Indian population
eke out a living from working on
the land of the *sierra*. Despite
certain progressive agricultural
policies, both here and along the
more developed coast, a growing
number of people flock to the
towns for work. More than half of
them are women.

For the last two decades, Ecuador has been able to rely on oil resources to
bolster its economy – as the saying goes: "We may be poor, but down there
(Peru) they're dying of hunger." But the crash in world oil prices, followed by
recent earthquake damage to key installations has very much undermined
this financial security. This, together with widespread disillusionment with
the free-market policies of the conservative government contributed to the
election of the centre-left Izquierda Democratica, currently in power. Despite
signs of improvement in the overall state of the economy, political dissent
continues to be fuelled by unemployment, rising prices and the need for
more radical social reform.

Theft is said to be on the increase in Quito and the steamy port of
Guayaquil; otherwise travel in Ecuador is generally hassle-free with few of
the grounds for paranoia experienced in, say, Colombia or Peru. Ecuador has
a gradually awakening **women's movement**, the core of which is dedicated
to developing and working with grass-roots women's organisations. An important group is *CEPAM* (Centre for the Promotion and Action of Ecuadorean
women), whose work led to the opening of the country's first women's centre
in the capital, Quito, in 1983. *CEPAM* runs various training programmes for

rural and urban women; publishes resources on issues such as health and women's legal rights; and helps to co-ordinate most of the twenty or so other women's groups active in and around Quito. The centre is keen to make contact with feminist groups from other countries in order to exchange ideas and promote understanding about the situation and activities of Ecuadorean women.

A Village Film Project

· · · · · · · · · · · ·

Zuleika Kingdon travelled to Ecuador with an anthropologist friend, Harriet Skinner. They spent six months living in an indigenous highland community in Chimborazo Province, where Zuleika was making a film in support of Harriet's field research.

Arriving in Quito with little knowledge of Ecuador and very poor Spanish, our first task was to get to know the country, to travel and make contacts before deciding where to establish our project. A development worker we met through the British Embassy provided useful information about the communities he had worked in, but wherever we went we also encountered Ecuadoreans who were only too happy to pass on the addresses of helpful friends and relatives all over the country, from teachers, university professors and filmmakers, to priests, nuns and community workers. Barely two weeks had gone by when we heard about Cacha.

Situated in the beautiful mountainous province of Chimborazo, Cacha is a small traditional community which, through the help of a certain radical priest, is undergoing great social changes. True to the spirit of liberation theology, this man has spoken out strongly against the oppression within his own church and supports the need for Cacha's self-sufficiency, brought about through the implementation of self-help development projects. Inspired, we decided to contact the priest who, after a hasty breakfast meeting, consented to give us a lift up the rough, dusty road that leads to Cacha's main village.

Preoccupied with having to take a funeral service, the priest was uncommunicative as we bumped and rattled along in his battered old car. Suddenly without warning he stopped at a crossroads: "I'll leave you here," he said, "Walk up to the village and speak to the community leaders." He drove off and we stood coughing in his dust trail, somewhat daunted by the hill ahead. The spot commanded a fine view of the city of Riobamba far down in the valley but, despite its peaceful stillness, the landscape was far from welcoming: hillsides crumbled into gorges, small cultivated patches bore weak and dying crops, and the hard packed ground was punctured only by eucalyptus trees.

In the village we met a young woman who worked in the local health centre though she lived in Riobamba. She was against that we should want to live in Cacha. "What will you eat?" she asked, revealing an attitude we had come across before, namely that women like us (in her mind the daughters of rich *mestizo*, mixed-race, families) grow up with servants and simply do not learn to cook. Nevertheless she introduced us to the council secretary and so the process of being accepted into village life began.

Following decades of acute exploitation and oppression, Cacha's population is now among the poorest in Ecuador. Denied self-sufficiency through the exploitative *hacienda* system, which appropriated the most fertile valley land, these indigenous people were left to make the best of poor arid terrains. The ground was consequently overcultivated, helping to precipitate the landslides and soil erosion we could see all around. Dependency on the richer Spanish communities inevitably limited their economic growth and social advancement, leaving a people understandably sceptical of foreigners. It was therefore very important to all of us that our project should be of benefit to the people of Cacha themselves.

The secretary asked us to submit a written proposal, to be circulated around various village meetings in order for the matter to be discussed outside our presence. Our main contribution was to offer a copy of the film (viewable on equipment supplied by a local development worker) as a resource for popular education campaigns. Likewise we hoped that Harriet's thesis would prove helpful as a historical record of changes taking place in the community.

"The villagers seemed pleased that two young women should be so keen to learn about their community"

This preliminary discussion with the council secretary unexpectedly led to our first encounter with some of the reality of village existence. We were standing explaining our mission in faltering Spanish when a man appeared calling everyone to follow him. The invitation extended to us and we climbed up a steep bank through a maize and *quinua* plantation to arrive at a tiny

mud-brick house that, had it had any windows, would have overlooked the beautiful valley to communities on the opposite sides.

Inside was pitch black save for a solitary candle, the light of which revealed hundreds of little guinea pigs running around the fireplace. On the bed lay a man who had just died, aged 102. I couldn't help being shocked. Women and children gathered around to have a look and then equally nonchalantly wandered out as we learned how, traditionally, villagers must all pay their respects before the body is moved in order for him to leave in peace. They said he had died from loneliness.

The villagers seemed pleased that two young women from a distant foreign country should be so keen to learn about their community, accustomed as they were to having their culture devalued, and I was impressed by the serious consideration they gave to our project. Our obvious sincerity was demonstrated by the fact that we wanted to live in Cacha as opposed to the comfort of digs in the nearest town of Riobamba.

Children were our first visitors when we were finally allotted a little house. Dark-eyed, curious and cheerful, they would come bringing us presents of sweetcorn or invite us to accompany them while they pastured the sheep. The women, being more shy, were harder to get to know. Initially the girls working in the crafts workshop would sit giggling and joking in Quichua, making these encounters far more intimidating than the formal introductions we had to face in village reunions.

Soon, however, one girl was appointed general spokeswoman and translated their questions for us: "Why did we wear trousers? Were we married? Why not? How far from home were we? Why did we leave our families?" They gradually became more relaxed and conversational, wanting to know most what our country looked like and what crops we grew, comparing prices of potatoes and other fruit with wonderment.

Our friendships were further reinforced the day we presented these girls with the photos we had been taking. They were thrilled and, as if it had been proof of our honesty, we were now able to sit among them without being ridiculed; we found ourselves invited to events, music rehearsals, or simply to their houses; talk was less reserved and we were shown how to crochet the brightly patterned *shigras*, bags made to sell in the markets.

I set about crocheting a bag to carry the tripod for my camera. There was plenty of time for I didn't want to start filming until our relations with people had been well established. We had to learn to pace ourselves to a new tempo – the Ecuadorean hour is invariably slower to arrive – and adapt to a very simple, basic daily routine that included new and unfamiliar foods. The local delicacy is roast guinea pig which though well skinned and gutted, comes complete with head and eyes. Served with potatoes cooked in a delicious peanut sauce, this dish is offered to guests as a great honour, so to refuse it would cause deep offence. Fortunately, we quickly got over our squeamishness.

More important than adapting to local food was the need to pick up basic Quichua, as well as to improve our Spanish. The former is very similar to Peruvian Quechua, with just three vowels: i,u and a. Words are given different meanings by adding different structures to the beginning and/or end. As everyone speaks with lightning speed it is far from easy to learn, but when we enrolled for a week's intensive course run by the Church in a nearby community we found that villagers responded very keenly. People greatly enjoyed testing us with phrases, shaking our hands with enthusiastic laughter when we managed to deliver the correct replies. News of our lessons spread and attracted people to join in

and allow opportunities for us to practise. Spanish, however, remained our main language.

Our accommodation turned out to be needed for a student doctor from Quito, who had come to help immunise the children, so we moved on by invitation to share a traditional three-roomed home with a family. Harriet and I were given the largest wooden bed where we slept in our sleeping bags on reed mats in place of a mattress. Washing facilities were very basic: we heated up water in large saucepans and washed out of a huge bucket in the "shower room" outside. Clothes were scrubbed on the block by the water tank in the yard. As in the other house, drinking water had to be boiled for twenty minutes to ensure its safety.

The family offered us food whenever they cooked and so we adopted the same principle. To begin with the children were too shy to eat what we gave them in our presence and would run off with it to their bedroom, but their hesitancy gradually wore off and we became good friends. Despite being fascinated by our possessions, they never demanded anything. They were extremely capable, much of the time having to fend for themselves and take care of the animals while the parents spent most days in another house in the village across the gorge.

"In Cacha it could never be said that women are the weaker sex"

Our offers to help out with daily duties were always accepted, but our clumsiness would invariably cause great hilarity. On one occasion I walked down the hill with Rosa, the mother, to join Harriet who had gone down to help the children cut alfalfa for the animals. In the distance we caught sight of her little figure struggling to load a large bundle on to her back, bent double to prevent it constantly slipping down to her backside. Rosa giggled all the way down the hill, unable to understand the difficulty of doing something that every local child is expected to learn from an early age. Having got this far, Harriet was keen to hand over the load for me to carry back up the steep hill. It was my turn to gasp for breath as I eventually staggered up to the house.

In Cacha it could never be said that women are the weaker sex. Among others, we were constantly impressed by Luz Maria, a mother of five children and the only female full-time worker on the village building site. She seemed burdened with all the labour of fetching and stacking piles of bricks, carrying them in a sling on her back to cart up to the top of the new federation house. She didn't appear to receive any harassment from the men on the site (nor was harassment ever an issue for us), but she had enough problems with her husband who rarely came home and was then invariably dead drunk.

Filming, when it at last began, brought with it many practical and technical challenges, not least of which was carrying around twenty kilos of camera gear at an altitude of over 3000 metres. Fine wind-blown dust also proved a constant nightmare. Yet these problems dwindled in the face of enthusiastic co-operation from the villagers, eager to document the fact that they were taking the future into their own hands, lobbying government and foreign organisations alike to raise the major funds needed for their projects – to bring water supplies to the community; to combat malnutrition; improve education opportunities and generally better the quality of life for the people in the region.

TRAVEL NOTES

Languages Spanish, Quichua, Jivaroa.

Transport Buses are plentiful and very cheap. Trains are also cheap, but erratic.

Accommodation Hotels too are inexpensive, especially outside the main cities, but always ask to see the room.

Special Problems No particular problems for women, but all travellers must carry a passport at all times.

Guides *Ecuador – A Travel Survival Kit* (Lonely Planet) is solid on practicalities. *Climbing and Hiking in Ecuador* (Bradt Enterprises), by the same author, is a good adventure supplement.

Contacts

CEPAM, Los Rios y Gandara, Quito (see introduction); and **Centro Accion de las Mujeres**, Casilla 10201, Guayaquil. Activities include organising literacy campaigns, healthcare, producing audiovisual resources and running a women's bookshop.

A good general bookshop in Quito is **Libri Mundi**, Juan Leon Mera 851 y Veintemilia. The proprietor is European (married to an Ecuadorean Indian) and has information in almost any language. He also keeps a noticeboard for "what's On in Quito".

Books

Audrey Bronstein, ed., ***The Triple Struggle: Latin American Peasant Women*** (War on Want Campaigns, London, 1982). A collection of interviews including discussion about the lives of Ecuadorean peasant women.

Egypt

E gypt is well used to tourism, with a long-established and well-organised holiday industry, geared for the most part towards shunting visitors along the Nile to Cairo, round the Pyramids and on to Luxor and Aswan. If you want to travel independently, it's best to go around February or October when the crowds thin out.

The country, and in particular the capital, Cairo, can seem initially confusing and intimidating. In all the main tourist areas you'll be approached frequently by hustlers and guides, many of them incredibly skilled and persistent in their dealings with foreigners. It can take a while to come to terms with being a symbol of affluence (to some people, the only viable source of income) in a country where unemployment is high and poverty intense. Egyptians routinely give money to beggars and won't easily understand why a wealthy and privileged tourist should refuse. Added to this there are all the prevailing myths and stereotypes of Western women to contend with.

As with any predominantly Muslim country your independence and freedom to travel can be misinterpreted as a sign of immodesty. Much of the attention you'll inevitably attract will have sexual overtones and coupled with more general hustling, this can become quite oppressive. It helps to dress inconspicuously, taking your lead from more Westernised Egyptian women. As ever, these problems become much less intense as you grow more used to travel, or live for a while in one place.

Politically, Egypt's "open door" economic policy has attracted an enormous proliferation of multinational enterprises and their effect has been to widen the already extreme poverty gap. Unemployment and homelessness are approaching ever more critical proportions. Over the last one-and-a-half decades, partly in reaction to these rising encroachments of Western capitalism, and partly due to the influence of Iran, there has been a powerful swing towards Islamic fundamentalism. The government, whilst attempting to subdue fundamentalism as a political movement, has, socially, made concessions.

Women are returning, sometimes voluntarily, but also under considerable social pressure, to traditional roles. The familiar scapegoating of women who attempt to retain their positions in the workplace during a climate of economic recession and high unemployment is particularly strong in Egypt. In rural areas women continue to labour for long hours under arduous conditions to maintain a subsistence living. The **women's movement**, as such, exists only underground. A small number of women have distinguished themselves through feminist writing – Nawaal El Saadawi (see booklist) has perhaps been the most influential, but the development of an autonomous feminist movement appears a distant prospect.

An Instinctive Kind of Care
. . . .

Kate Baillie, a freelance writer, lived in Cairo for two-and-a-half months, teaching English and learning Arabic.

Egypt is the West's pet Arabic country, "moderate" being the favourite adjective. It's important to know that this reflects little of the internal situation, but is simply Egypt's pro-Western economic and diplomatic policy. In reality, Egyptians are imprisoned for criticising the government; censorship of the arts and media is commonplace; political parties are suppressed, and Cairo and the provincial capitals are infested with armed police and soldiers. In the Cairo press and television centre, levelled rifles greet employees from a sandbag emplacement inside the foyer. The oppression is not quite as bad now as it was under President Sadat, but while a few political prisoners are released and the odd paper is allowed to publish again, American enterprise continues to prise apart Egyptian culture, values and economy.

A new polarisation has appeared above the basic division of peasant and bourgeois, villager and Cairean. Those in the pay of the multinationals form their own super class. Speaking only English, adopting Sindy-Doll and grey-suited dress, their living standards leap while their lives become subservient to work patterns evolved for a very alien climate and culture. Speed, greed, glamour and competitiveness are the requisite values. Meanwhile, the majority, who don't or can't choose that rat race, remain in their desert robes and poverty, upholding values and a vision of society derived from a history much older than the West now knows.

The re-emerging strength of Islamic fundamentalism has to be appreciated in this context. An apparently fanatical religious social movement is hard for us to comprehend. What has to be grasped is that Islamic fundamentalism is both political and religious and there is no distinction because of the nature of Islam. The Muslim faith is a set of rules for a state, not just for individuals and it is in this that it differs so much from Christianity. Inevitably, the religious text, the Koran, is open to all manner of conflicting interpretations.

It can be argued – contrary to actual practice in Egypt – that the Koran stipulates the right of women to choose their husbands and to leave them. The financial rights it lays down for women were not achieved by European women until the nineteenth and twentieth centuries. Its banking policy would make you open an account tomorrow. Its precepts on virginity and menstruation would make you run a mile. During the Prophet's lifetime, some women complained that only men were being addressed. From then on, the two words for male believers and female believers appear. There is nothing in the Koran about female circumcision.

"There is a communion between women that our Western conception of sisterhood could never emulate"

Leaving behind the fifth and sixth centuries, the struggle for emancipation was started by Egyptian women at the end of the last century. In 1962, under Nasser, they obtained the vote, access to free education at all levels, and a woman minister for social affairs was appointed. In the last twenty years, women have entered the professions, factories, the civil service and business, though they are not allowed to be judges. In the public sector, equal pay is legally enforceable. Women now comprise almost fifty percent of the workforce though nearly half of those are peasant women working in the fields with their men as they have done for centuries. Abortion remains illegal and clitoridectomy, proving virginity on the wedding night and the punishment of adultery are still practised.

Sadat created an official Women's Movement with his Madison Avenue-bedecked wife Jihan as president.

Although they managed to push through certain reforms, such as allowing women the right to instigate divorce, the movement had little popular support. It was seen as little more than a tea party circle of her friends enjoying the freedoms of power and riches. The real Women's Movement, though inevitably made up of educated urban women, is pan-Arab and takes its position from Arab history and experience not American or European feminist texts.

In the villages and amongst the urban poor, where feminism is unheard of, there is a communion between women who share work in and outside the home, in ways that our Western conception of sisterhood could never emulate. In Cairo, I experienced from women this almost instinctive kind of care and protectiveness. On several occasions women who were strangers to me and spoke no English rescued me from situations in which I was unwittingly at risk. Wandering, heat-dazed and lost, in a slum behind the Citadel, a woman took my arm, smiled at me and led me out of the maze, shooing away the men and little boys who approached us. A few days later I tried sleeping in Al Azhar mosque, unaware that it is is forbidden to women, let alone infidels. A soldier appeared with the intention of arresting me, but I was saved by a woman who sat me behind her and talked at length to what were by now five soldiers and seven other men grouped around. Presumably she explained my ignorance: the only words I could catch from the men were "Police" and "Koran". But she succeeded, the men left and the woman smiled at me and patted the ground to show I could stay.

Aside from the pyramids, the mosques are the sights to see in Cairo, both from the "gaping at beautiful buildings" point of view and to experience the use Muslims make of their places of worship. A note on dress – you always have to take your shoes off and in the more tourist-frequented mosques you may have to pay to get them back. Though not usually enforced, I'd advise wearing a scarf, out of courtesy if nothing else. As for shorts, short skirts, punk hair styles and bra-lessness with clinging clothes, forget it, whether in mosques or in the street.

"I learned to avoid any words the dictionary gave for 'atheist' which carry the same connotations as saying you eat babies"

Mosques can also be the best places to meet Egyptian women – especially where a women's area is curtained off. Not long after the incident in Al Azhar, I was very comforted to be separated from the men. But I still wasn't sure about the sleeping rules, so I gestured an enquiry to a woman, in her fifties I supposed, veiled and gowned to the floor in black. She immediately bounced up to me, talking nineteen to the dozen and then went off to fetch two friends who spoke some English. With their fifty odd words and my fifteen of Arabic, gestures, pictures and a dictionary, and joined by two more women, we passed several hours together in enthusiastic discussion. They asked me the two standard questions that had opened every conversation I had had in Cairo with men or women: "What's your religion?" and "Are you married?" the latter, once answered negatively, would be replaced by "Where's your friend?".

The first question had involved me in metaphysical arguments I had long forgotten, and I learned to avoid any words the dictionary gave for "atheist" which carry the same moral connotations as saying you eat babies. I don't know what these women understood about my religion or lack of it, but they burst into delighted laughter at the fact of my having not one "friend" but lots.

They removed my scarf, combed my hair, called me *halwe* (sweet, pretty) and invited me to eat with them later.

Egyptians are renowned for their kindness, humour and generosity. It was these qualities that I appreciated in the Egyptian men I became friends with. I was treated with great respect and my views were listened to without having to force a space to speak. But when it came to anything to do with sex, they were pathological. One group of colleagues assumed, on zero evidence, that I was having an affair with one of them. They persuaded his wife that I was, expected their turn to be next, and were baffled by my astounded refusals. Their image of Western women and their idea of American companies are similar illusions: free sex and fast money. What I found again and again after similar and worse experiences, was a childlike shame, profuse apologies and misconception of my attitude when I taxed them with their behaviour. These men were all liberals or socialists and well-educated.

However, don't let this put you off getting into conversation with Egyptian men. Though I don't know the statistics for rape and assault, I'd stake a lot on Cairo being a safer place than London for a woman on her own. But even if you encounter no unmanageable difficulties, Cairo is an exhausting experience. Oxford Street during the sales has nothing on every street in the centre of the city all day and most of the night. Crossing roads is like trying to fly a kite at Heathrow. The fumes, heat and dust, the noise of car horns and shouting, and the spilling, squashing buses are a nightmare. And manoeuvering through this you have to contend with constant pestering, mostly verbal, from the passing male masses. There are times when you feel very exposed and wish you were robed and veiled.

A Student in Alexandria

. . . .

Caroline Bullough has travelled extensively around the Middle East. After completing a degree in Arabic and Persian, she moved to the University of Alexandria to spend a year studying Arabic.

The arrival of thirty British students of Arabic (half of them female) caused quite a stir on Alexandria University's dusty concrete campus. I was lodged, along with three other women, in a newly built hut (already falling down) in a far corner of the campus and it was soon surrounded by a gaggle of curious onlookers. For the first few weeks we were showered with invitations and accosted by students eager to practise their English.

Most of these were men. The female students were initially shy and perhaps a little wary of us. Those who did approach us were obviously considered "forward" and therefore disapproved of. It was also clear that many parents disliked the idea of us associating with their daughters – friendships were suddenly broken off or invitations withdrawn without warning. The very fact that we were four girls living in a flat of our own without parents or guardians was enough to guarantee their disapproval. As foreign women it was frustratingly difficult to maintain platonic friendships with Egyptian men as at some stage it was always made clear that more was expected.

Foreign women are well-known as "easy game". Every Egyptian man claims to have at least one friend who can testify to the willingness of a foreign woman he once met. In a society in which pre-marital sex is officially taboo and a complex set of rules govern even informal relations between the sexes, the freedom

enjoyed by most Western women is easily misinterpreted. I was asked constantly what my relationship was with the male students on the course. That they should be my close friends and no more seemed beyond comprehension. Those Egyptians who had begged for invitations to our parties, with the expectation of witnessing orgiastic mass coupling, were disappointed.

"To live each day facing a barrage of comments, whispered or shouted, humorous or insulting, can be a strain"

We could do little to dispel the myths which abound about foreign women (probably fuelled by imported American films and television programmes). However hard I tried to adopt an appropriately decorous way of life, I could not escape the fact that I was foreign and all that it implied. I was evicted from my first flat for having my fellow students (some male) to tea!

To live each day facing a barrage of comments, whispered or shouted, humorous or insulting, can be a strain. I became increasingly adept at avoiding particularly difficult situations, such as passing groups of young boys, who learnt at an early stage to imitate their elders' attitude to foreign women, or crowded pavement cafés. I learnt to ignore, and sometimes not even hear, the comments and asides. I learnt to stride purposefully through the milling crowds, defying passers-by to challenge me. The hassle was often at its worst when we were in groups of girls or pairs, but seldom did I actually feel under any physical danger. I was followed on several occasions both in Cairo and Alexandria but this never happened when I was alone and because we were familiar with the area, it was less frightening than it might have been.

I often went out alone and found a café where I was able to sit undisturbed, my back to the road. I longed to be able to wander at will but it was only when I was with someone else that I felt confident enough to look around me. Alone, it was easier to walk head bowed, ears closed rather than risk attracting anyone's attention. This was the stance adopted by many Egyptian women who are themselves the object of unwanted attention.

Nowhere are wandering hands or, for that matter, wandering bodies, quite such a problem as on crowded buses and trams. Morning tram rides to the university were a constant nightmare of sweaty bodies, grinding hips and whispered comments. However, if you find yourself seriously cornered you should make a fuss, and other passengers will invariably help you out.

"A woman covered from head to foot in a black, Iranian style chador is an unnerving sight"

Egyptian students seemed to pay far more attention to appearance than their British counterparts. Most were dressed in smart Western clothes. Growing support for Muslim fundamentalism with its restrictions on dress was, however, clear. During my last months at the university, there was a student election in which a large number of known members of the Muslim Brotherhood were elected. During the week of the election the walls of the university were plastered with banners exhorting all female students to dress in the prescribed Muslim manners. Bizarre fashion shows were organised on the university campus to demonstrate suitable garb.

Few women in Egypt have returned to full Islamic dress but a woman covered from head to foot in a black, Iranian style *chador* is an unnerving sight. The voluminous garments and thick veils rob her of human shape or form. Her feet are carefully concealed under the floor length folds of her skirt and her hands are covered by thick

black gloves. Once, leaving a crowded bus (all public transport in Egypt is crowded), I was prodded from behind and shouted at by a woman concealed by a thin black veil and cape. Her strident tone of voice and colourful language astonished me and seemed at odds with her devoutly religious appearance. The force of her impatient curses was undoubtedly increased by her anonymity.

Alexandria is more Mediterranean than Arab with its elegant colonial buildings and pavement cafés. The Alexandrians are proud of their city and "Welcome In Alexandria" or "Welcome In Egypt" is on everyone's lips. At night the city is bright and vibrant, the streets teeming. Because of terrible overcrowding at home and particularly in hot weather, most Egyptians spend a large part of their lives on the streets. Coffee houses are exclusively male preserves but respectable restaurants and cake shops are full of women and families tucking into large platters of *ful medames* (a stewed bean dish) and small cakes oozing with honey.

The city is famous for its beaches which attract visitors from throughout the Middle East. In fact they are overcrowded during the summer and rather windswept in winter. Most Egyptian women remain fully clothed on the beach and even in the sea. Hassle is inevitable – Alexandria has its share of rather overweight "beach bums" – but not unbearable. Swimsuits are even now sufficiently rare to arouse interest in all who pass. There's a private beach in the grounds of the Montazeh Palace on the outskirts of Alexandria where we were able to swim and sunbathe almost undisturbed but bikinis are rarely seen even there.

Standards of medical care in urban Egypt are generally high, at least if you are rich or a foreigner. However, although many Egyptian doctors have been trained abroad, there seems to be considerable ignorance of specifically female ailments. Suffering badly from thrush, I visited a doctor associated with the university with whom I had been registered on arrival. Most drugs are available over the counter in any pharmacy so, had I known, I could probably have treated myself. Instead I was subjected to a rather ham-fisted internal examination and a long series of questions. It was clear that the doctor assumed that I must be suffering from a sexually transmitted disease and seemed only partially convinced by my protestations. To be fair, though, the medication I was prescribed, made in Egypt under licence, was extremely effective.

A Camel Ride in Sinai

. . . .

Laura Fraser, an American freelance writer, crossed into Sinai from Israel with two female friends. They took up the offer of joining two Bedouin men on a camel trek into the desert.

My trek into the vast, magical mountains of the Sinai peninsula began when I asked a Bedouin man, Iash, if I could ride his camel.

By that time I felt as if I knew him well enough to ask. I had arrived at his village, Nueva, the previous day with two friends (we had been working together as fisherwomen on a kibbutz). The village, on the coast of Sinai, looked almost medieval, with broken stone structures and makeshift shacks. It appeared to be a common way station however, and we went to a hut near the beach where other travellers were camping. Before long, a couple of Bedouin men, in their cotton djellabas, came over, built a fire, and offered us tea.

Drinking tea with the Bedouins made me realise that as impoverished and primitive as their huts made of cardboard and spiky ferns seemed to me, theirs was a culture with a highly refined sense of etiquette. When Iash poured the tea and gave me a cup, I drank some and passed it along to my friend. Iash told us no, it is the Bedouin custom that each has his own cup of tea, then the other has his, "slowly, slowly". Slowness, relaxation, and calm are highly valued virtues here, which is surely another sign of real "civilisation". We sat by the campfire, quietly, and watched the moon rise orange over the red sea.

After nightfall, one of the men brought out a Bedouin guitar, playing a vibrating, metallic melody, while the others laughed and sang. I noticed how the men all play with their head scarves the way American women play with their hair, arranging them in soft folds accentuating their faces. I felt a flash of resentment; it seemed the men have all the privileges, even of being beautiful and vain. "Why aren't the women sitting here, too?" a German man asked one of the Bedouins. The Bedouin put his scarf over his moustache, covering his face like a veil, and tittered like a Bedouin woman. "The women, they are shy. She doesn't want anyone to see her," he explained. Our only glimpse of Bedouin women so far had been from a distance; one was wading in the sea in her long black garb, catching an octopus with her hands and twisting its head off. We asked whether Bedouin women are ever allowed to sit with the men. "Men here, women there," he replied.

We all went inside an abandoned blue bus, and the Bedouins passed around cans of grapefruit juice, big spliffs, and a booklet of pictures of the Egyptian president. One played music, and the rest clapped. Another got up to dance, imitating a Bedouin woman. The men laughed, not so much at his performance, as at woman in general. He was very funny, but the laughter still rankled.

The next morning, after tea, I asked Iash if I could ride the camel. He seemed quite happy to let me ride, but then he disappeared for a long time. Slowly, slowly, I thought, and then forgot about it. After about three hours, he came back with three camels, loaded with blankets and bags. "What's this?" I asked him, and he told me the camels were ready for the ride. I asked him where. He pointed to the mountains rising out of the desert. I glanced at my two companions. I asked him how long. "Four, five days, maybe a week," he said, smiling. "Ten dollars a day, meals included". We settled on four days.

"Even with our sleeping bags covering the Bedouins' wooden saddles, we were sore from the start"

Camels are as nasty as their reputation. The camel I rode, behind a Bedouin named Psalem, had a tricky habit of calmly letting someone get up three-quarters of the way, and then lurching up violently so the rider had to hang on tight and scramble up the last bit. They are bony beasts; even with our sleeping bags covering the Bedouins' wooden saddles, we were sore from the start.

Before setting off into the mountains, we stopped at a checkpoint run by the multinational peace keeping force, where swarms of military men came to photograph the camels. One man in a helicopter asked Iash for a photo on the camel; Iash insisted he would only let the man sit on the camel if he could sit on the helicopter. After several bits of form-filling and arrangements, we set

off into the mountains. We started up a *wadi*, and a man in military garb chased after us with a sabre-tipped gun. He argued with Iash, who finally gave him cigarettes, and let us go. I was happy to get away from the settlements and into the mountains.

The *wadi* ran through creviced rock, a stream of dust, empty except for an occasional scrub tree, or a group of black-clothed women huddled around the goats. The sun and the camels and the slowly swirling rock were hypnotising as we swayed up into the canyon. The camels showed their spite every so often, frothing and gurgling up a red sac that lolled out of their mouths like a bladder. Soon we didn't care if we never rode a camel again, and were glad to reach a camping place by a small water hole and sheltering rock.

We gathered twigs across a rocky bed, hardly enough in the canyon for a fire. Then we climbed some smooth pink rocks to gaze around us in the evening light. The stillness was complete, except for the noisy crunching of our shoes echoing off the canyon walls. It was so silent and barren we could almost hear the rocks growing.

For dinner, we sat on our saddle blankets (the ones we would sleep under later) and drank tea, then baked bread in the cinders and ate it with sardines. The Bedouins asked us to tell them stories of the world they would never travel. Linda described man-eating grizzly bears, and we compared the southwestern United States with their land. As it grew colder we crowded together and waited for the moon. "She comes", Psalam said, as the sky gradually dimmed. The moon tipped up from the rocks and Iash taught us some Arab words we didn't remember later.

The next day, we rode up the *wadi* to an oasis – a bunch of palm trees and shacks where Iash and Psalam's relatives lived. It seemed more relaxed than on the coast. We sat in a house made of burlap and thin wood, with a dirt floor and fire, drinking tea with the Bedouin women. Their kohl-rimmed eyes smiled at us above their black veils. They admired our jewellery, which we parted with for strings of beads. They smoked our Israeli cigarettes, puffing through the black gauze. A green-bonneted daughter laughed and brought us match covers and bits of plastic as gifts. The women didn't speak much English, but one ventured to ask us how old we were, and whether we were married or had any babies. When they learned we were in our twenties and had no husbands or family, they clucked in sympathy. Then one woman put kohl on our eyes, circling them with dark rims, to improve our luck.

"When they learned we were in our twenties and had no husbands or family, they clucked in sympathy. Then one woman put kohl on our eyes ... to improve our luck"

We rode to another *wadi* where we encountered other travellers from the camp. We listened to an international radio station around the fire, passing spliffs around and talking in the firelight, which now and then flared into a blaze as the dried palm fronds burned. The Bedouin men went from fire to fire; the women never really met the visitors. The men spoke in easy Western slang, "sure, sure", while the women remained hidden and silent, although occasionally we would hear one of them screeching at the goats. It seemed like the men and women were from two different ages. We drank teacup after teacup. Always we must drink first if they will drink. Always they rinse the leaves with water and swish the rim with their thumb before another drink.

By the end of the trip, I was quite ready to get back. I had never been so saddlesore. On the last stretch, all I could think about was swimming, shitting, and cleaning the camel piss off my jacket. And then my camel started to run, and I lost all thought as I marvelled at the swiftness, the smoothness of this beast I had wanted to sit on to have my picture taken.

The camels slowed as we reached some fences and settlements. Iash sputtered with indignation at the fences. "Why do they say this land is theirs?" he said. "Are they crazy that they think they can put fences on the land and make it theirs?" The Bedouin men have adapted to the world as they have had to, whilst resisting anything that has kept them from living on and with the land. The Bedouin women, however, are allowed no such compromise; their lifestyle remains much the same as in ancient times.

TRAVEL NOTES

Languages Arabic. English is spoken in the tourist areas but it's useful at least to be able to read Arabic numerals.

Transport Buses and trains are cheap, but very crowded. Egyptian women would avoid sitting next to a strange man, which is how prostitutes solicit customers. All women, Egyptian and foreign, are subjected to being groped and pinched in the crush. You should make a fuss and enlist the help of women nearby. Efforts have been made to assign sleeper compartments on trains by sex (and complaints are honoured in case of mistakes). Second class cars are not segregated and women have been hassled on overnight journeys. Most Egyptian women travel second class during daylight. Taxis are readily available in the cities and main towns.

Accommodation There are hotels at all prices. In the high season (Oct–March) the expensive places tend to be fully booked, but finding a cheap room is rarely a problem. If you end up late at night booking into a hotel that makes you feel uneasy or unsafe, move on the next day – there are always plenty of alternatives.

Special Problems Harassment – particularly if you're on your own. Though many tourists do wander about in shorts and sleeveless T-shirts, this is considered both offensive and provocative. It's best to keep arms, legs and shoulders covered. It's a good idea to carry coins with you for *Baksheesh*.

Other Information Along the Mediterranean coastline there are both private and public beaches. On public beaches there are few foreign tourists and almost all Egyptian women swim in their clothes. Private beaches do not cost much and you'll feel far less self-conscious as you'll be amongst other women (both tourists and Egyptians) who will be wearing swimming gear.

Guides *Guide to Egypt* (Michael Haag) is well-informed and practical (if not always too helpful for the cheaper hotels). A *Rough Guide: Egypt* (Harrap Columbus) is forthcoming.

Contacts

Arab Women's Solidarity Association, 25 Murad St., Giza, Egypt, ☎Cairo 723976. Strongly supported by Nawal El Saadawi, **AWSA** is an international, non-governmental organisation aimed at "promoting and developing the social, cultural and educational status of Arab women".

Books

Nawal El Saadawi, *The Hidden Face of Eve* (Zed Books, 1980). Covering a wide range of topics – sexual aggression, female circumcision, prostitution, marriage, divorce and sexual relationships – Saadawi provides a personal and often disturbing account of what it's like to grow up as a woman in the Islamic world of the Middle East. Also recommended are Saadawi's novels, ***Woman at Point Zero*** (Zed Books, 1983), a powerful and moving story of a young Egyptian woman condemned to death for killing a pimp, and ***God Dies by the Nile*** (Zed Books, 1985), the story of the tyranny and corruption of a small town mayor in Egypt and the illiterate peasant woman who kills him.

Alifa Rifaat, *Distant View of a Minaret* (Heinemann, 1985). Well-known Egyptian writer in her fifties. She expresses her revolt against male domination and suggests solutions within the orthodox Koranic framework.

Nayra Atiya, *Khul-Khaal Five Egyptian Women Tell Their Stories* (Virago Press, 1988). A fascinating collection of oral histories, recorded over three years, which reveal the lives and aspirations of working-class women in contemporary Egypt.

Huda Sha'rawi, *Harem Years: The Memoirs of an Egyptian Feminist* (Virago, 1986). A unique document from the last generation of upper-class Egyptian women who spent their childhood and married life in the segregated world of the harem.

An excellent article on Egypt by Angela Davis can be found in ***Women: a World Report*** (see General Bibliography).

Thanks to Dana Denniston and Beverley Milton-Edwards for help with the introduction and Travel Notes.

Finland

D espite the obvious attractions
of a wilderness of lakes and forests, a
stunningly modern capital city, and
easy access to neighbouring USSR,
Finland tends to be overlooked as just a
little too remote, obscure and expensive
for most ordinary travellers. For those
who can afford it, however, the tranquility and architectural fascination of the
towns and cities, and the sheer natural
beauty of the countryside, hold an
enduring appeal.

Finland is an easy country to visit
alone or with other women. Besides the
expense, your biggest problem will be
coping with the isolation of travel;
people will offer help if needed but for
the most part leave you to yourself and,
in the more remote countryside, you
might well get a frosty and suspicious
reception from older Finns. It is much
easier to break down barriers of reserve
in Helsinki, a cosmopolitan and
progressive city with a lively alternative
culture.

Since gaining independence from Russia at the beginning of this century,
Finland has struggled to assert its neutrality (and revive its unique culture and
traditions) against the competing claims of the USSR and Western Europe.
Threats of annexation and foreign interference loomed over much of the post-
war period and although these now, in the light of Gorbachev's reforms, seem
far-fetched, the memory of a recent beleaguered period still rankles.

The younger generation tend to be open and confident about their country's security and future. Relations with the USSR are good and travel across
the Soviet border for short trips to Leningrad is fairly routine. With alcohol
heavily restricted, many Finns use the boat and rail crossings to go on drinking sprees; and for this reason it's a good idea to avoid late-night crossings
(and also night ferries to Sweden). Daytime trips are considerably more
sober and sedate.

Finland was the second country in the world (after New Zealand) in which women gained political rights and the current parliament has over 25 percent women representatives. Progressive equal opportunities legislation (backed up by good childcare facilities and maternity leave) has ensured that women retain a high profile in all aspects of public life. Younger women, especially, seem aware of, and confident of, their rights to equality. Sexual harassment and violence towards women are relatively rare (interestingly, in the case of prostitution it is the punters not the women who face prosecution under the law).

The contemporary **women's movement** is now fairly small and centred in Helsinki. Women who were active in the early Seventies tend to have moved into more mainstream politics or joined the various peace, environmental and anti-nuclear organisations and campaigns that have flourished in the post-Chernobyl age. There are a few autonomous lesbian organisations which also operate in the capital (attitudes tend to become more conservative as you move further away from Helsinki), the largest being a group called *Akanat*.

A Halcyon Summer

. . . .

Penny Windsor has worked as a teacher, youth worker, freelance writer and performance poet. She spent a month travelling with her partner around the south of Finland.

All journeys are, of course, personal journeys, but my journey to Finland last summer was a peculiarly emotional one. I was three months pregnant and, at the age of 41, with an eighteen year-old daughter, felt deeply uncertain about my future. My travelling companion had studied Finnish literature and history for many years and had shared his dreams with me of visiting the country. At the end of June, when we had earned enough money to pay the price of the air fare to Helsinki – measured out in potatoes picked in the fields of Pembrokeshire – we began our trip.

Without doubt it was the right country to visit at the time. We had weathered the many curious questions of friends and acquaintances, "Why Finland?", "Where is Finland", "Won't it be cold?", insisting Finland was indeed a European country of considerable interest and beauty and the summers were often warmer than our own.

In bald terms Finland is one of the Scandinavian countries, bordering Norway to the far north and having a long frontier with the USSR in the east. It has a population of about five million people, many of them living in the major cities of Helsinki, Tampere, Turku, Lahti and Oulu. Although a small proportion of the people speak Swedish as a first language and Swedish is the official second language, the overwhelming majority of people speak Finnish, a strange and unique language with affinities only to Hungarian (and a language making no distinction between "she" and "he" – the pronoun for both sexes being *hän*). English is widely spoken but my companion's efforts to speak Finnish at every opportunity were greeted with surprise and delight.

Other than these facts ... Well, Finland is an independent, democratic republic, the first European country to give women the vote (in 1906), has an excellent record in human rights, and a long history of fighting for national independence from Sweden and from its giant neighbouring Russia. (Finnish history makes fascinating reading, a spellbinding account of a David surviving the onslaught of a Goliath.)

We arrived in Helsinki at midnight and put up our small mountaineering tent in Hesperia Park, in the middle of the city, next door to Finlandia House, the international conference centre. It was our first experience of the Finns' "laissez-faire" attitude to all except those who flagrantly break the laws. At no time during our three weeks in the country were we told *not* to do anything. Rules were kept to a minimum and the country seemed to run on the assumption that people would behave well if left to go quietly about their business.

For the rest of our time in Helsinki we camped between fir trees on the island of Seurasaari, a few miles from the city centre. The island is an open-air museum full of historic buildings from all over Finland – a fact we didn't realise until we saw the place in daylight. The red squirrels and even the hares that live there seemed unafraid of people.

From this secluded camping place we explored the city – the National Museum where grand scenes from the Finnish national folk epic, the *Kalevala*, were displayed; the monument to the famous and much-loved musician Sibelius, a vast organ of silver pipes; the island fortress of Soumerlinna, built originally by the Swedes to fight off the Russians; the markets on the harbour fronts; the Academic Bookshop in the main shopping street, which has the largest selection of titles in Europe.

Sometimes I explored the city with my companion, at other times alone. I was never hassled in any way, whether I was wandering about the city centre after dark, whiling away a sunny afternoon reading in the park, or sitting drinking coffee in the green-draped, elegant waiting room in Helsinki station. There were a few drunks, predominantly men, at Helsinki station and various inland stations, but I never felt under any sort of threat from them. Alcohol is expensive and only light lager is easily available, other drinks being sold at state-run stores, called *Alkos*, with mysterious opening hours. Drinking trips are often made to Sweden and across the border to Leningrad where alcohol is cheaper and more readily available.

"Sometimes it (Helsinki) can be too much like the perfect, suburban dream. Full of rosy, stable nuclear families"

Helsinki is a pleasant, restful uncity-city – an orderly place where things work well, people appear prosperous and healthy. Sometimes, perhaps, it can be too much like the perfect, suburban dream. Full of rosy, stable, nuclear families, it rocks along gently with its well-dressed people, nicely displayed museums, beautiful parks and buildings and lovely harbour views. If it lacks altogether that dynamic, volatile, wicked quality of many other capital cities I can only say it was the perfect place for me last summer, a place where nothing I saw was ugly or violent or dirty, where I could wander freely by myself, thinking and writing.

Leaving Helsinki we travelled north to Hameenlinna, birthplace of Sibelius, then east through the cities of Lahti and Imatra to the province of Karelia, near the Russian border and in a wide loop back to Hameenlinna by way of the industrial cities of Varkhaus and Tampere. We travelled by a mixture of train, bus and hitchhiking.

By our standards all prices were high in Finland, particularly the food, but train travel is marginally cheaper than travelling by bus. As with all public places, trains are comfortable and clean and the waiting rooms provide toys which don't appear to get either vandalised or stolen. The toilets have baby-changing rooms and potties, in some cases in the men's as well as the women's sections. This last seemed to me a litmus test of equality – I was truly impressed.

Hitchhiking is difficult. We had a number of short lifts but had to wait long hours for them, even on the main road between towns. We came to the conclusion that this was in tune with the national Finnish character – they are, after all, a nation renowned for their reserve and insularity, wanting, it seems, little to do with an outside world which knows and cares little about them. They treasure the quality of *sisu* – youthfulness, independence of thought, "guts", embodied in the characters of the life-giving, daring Lemminkëinen and the dour, brave Kullervo, the adventurers in the *Kalevala*.

As far as national characteristics can be true, yes, the Finns did seem to be reserved people but, once approached, they proved almost overwhelmingly courteous and helpful. I hold warm memories of the family who gave us supper and breakfast and asked us to camp in their garden outside Lahti, when we stopped to ask the way; the man on the bicycle in Hameenlinna who went off to photocopy a street map of the town for us; the guard who scrupulously looked after our interests on our strange circular journey across the country when we had taken the wrong train.

"We sometimes breakfasted on mustard and onion sandwiches and windfall apples"

We did not use official campsites, preferring to put up our tent in the forest and by the side of lakes. However, the campsites we saw were, like everything else, well organised and clean.

Our biggest problem was money – basic items of food, even in large supermarkets, often cost double the price charged in Britain. Hence we sometimes breakfasted on mustard and onion sandwiches and windfall apples. On the other hand, nobody bothered us in the remote forests where we camped, unless you count the restless midnight mole in the glade above the Aulanko Lake and the early morning woodpecker. Bathing naked in the great quiet lakes of Aulanko Forest and Karelia we were similarly undisturbed. And the sunsets on the lake marshes as we watched the short summer turn to autumn at the end of August were brief, dramatic and perfect.

In those weeks I spent in Finland, I grew accustomed to the gentleness of the country, the mild intimacy of the wilderness forests and the sudden openness of the lakes. It was restful to be in a country which did not seem to deal in unnecessary rules, but where the streets were free of litter, where factories and houses were hidden by trees, lakes and rivers clear and full of plants and bird life.

For me, it was definitely the right country to visit that particular summer, but also the right country for any woman traveller who just wants to sit or wander, reflect and daydream, without comment or interference.

TRAVEL NOTES

Languages Finnish. Swedish is the official second language although many people also speak English.

Transport There are plenty of highly efficient and speedy options – both trains and planes are comparatively cheap (in Finnish terms). It's wise not to join the overnight ferries or train trips to Sweden or Leningrad which tend to be used as cheap boozers and can develop an obnoxiously sexist atmosphere. Hitching is perfectly acceptable and (as much as it can ever be) quite safe, although you'll have to wait a while for lifts.

Accommodation Again the various options are expensive. Many women camp on their own. (See contact listings for the Women's Summer Camp.)

Special Problems None beyond the already mentioned problems of expense and men using boat and train trips for rowdy drinking sprees.

Other Information It's fairly common to find *Naistentanssit* dances organised specifically for women on their way home from the office, usually from 4pm. Women rather than men take their pick of partners. Some mainstream discos also arrange evenings for women (*Sekahaku*), where men and women choose partners freely.

Guide *The Rough Guide: Scandinavia* (Harrap Columbus) has a useful and concise section on Finland.

Contacts

The Women's Movement Union (or Naisasialitto Unioni), Bulevardi 11a, Helsinki, ☎90.64.3158 The oldest and largest of the women's organisations. It's worth dropping by to get information about the range of groups currently operating. The Unioni owns **Ida Salins Summer Home** which houses the Open Women's University. As well as various consciousness-raising courses a Women's Summer Camp is held in the grounds once a year. There are plans to open a "book café" and reading room.

The Organisation for Sexual Equality (SETA), P.O Box 55, 00531, Helsinki, ☎76.96.42 and 76.96.32. Has information about current lesbian groups and provisions.

Akanat, PL 55, 00551 Helsinki, ☎76.96.41. A lesbian collective that publishes a campaigning and listings magazine, **Torajvva**.

Books

We've been unable to track down any translations of books specifically by or about women. Of the others, **Christer Kilman**, *The Downfall of Gerdt Bladh* (P Owen, 1989) gives you a flavour of Helsinki life. It's about a businessman unable to come to terms with his wife's infidelity.

Thanks to Penny Mote and Helen Prescott for help with the Travel Notes.

France

· · · · · · · · · · · · · · · · · ·

By far the most visited country in Northern Europe, France draws more or less every kind of tourist and traveller. Yet despite the obvious appeal of its food, landscape and city life, it can be a hard place to get to know. An image of exclusive *chic* permeates the centre of Paris, the much glamourised Côte d'Azur and the Alpine ski resorts, and the country as a whole has a reputation for cliquishness. Without educational, business or social connections you may find it hard to slot in, no matter how good your French might be. Regional affiliations are very strong and local communities tend to be tightly knit. If you do manage to break down the barriers, however, the rich culture of France, the appreciation of the qualities of life and zest for politics may well have you hooked.

Travelling around is generally straightforward, although in Paris you can come up against a fairly low-key, but persistent harassment – usually running commentaries from men who overtly size you up as you walk past. It's irritating but probably no more prevalent or threatening than street harassment in London or New York. The main difficulties are where sexism merges with racism. French people, and particularly Parisians, will warn you against "les Arabes". If you come from an Arab or North African state, or look as if you do, you may have to contend with some pretty blatant discrimination. (Hotels are suddenly fully booked, etc.) The same applies if you're black (whatever your nationality), and you might find obstacles in gaining entry.

Besides the occasional, often poorly attended, demonstration there's little sign of a resurgence of the **women's movement** in France. The *MLF* (*Mouvement de Libération des Femmes*) which flourished throughout the Sixties and Seventies was declared by the national media to be dead and buried in 1982. Since then, feminist bookshops and cafés have been closing, feminist publications have reached their last issue, and International Women's Day has come and gone without noticeable commemoration. Women have, however, remained active, but in localised areas – running battered wives' hostels, rape crisis centres and organising within the Communist and Socialist Parties, the Trade Unions, or within the wider anti-racism movement.

Yvette Roudy and Hugeuette Bouchardeau, France's two most prominent feminist politicians, have continued to highlight women's issues but with the fluctuating popularity of the Socialists and little outside support, this has proved a determinedly uphill struggle. Although they were able to initiate legislation on equal pay, a motion to change the law against degrading, discriminatory or violent images of women in the media was thrown out of the Assembly. The constant barrage of exploitative images in advertising remains one of the more disturbing aspects of a first-time visit to the country.

Afloat in Paris

. . . .

Louise Hume spent a year studying in Paris. She returned shortly after and, unable to get a job, stretched out her savings by living for nine months on an abandoned barge on the Seine. She is currently back in Paris working as a guide for a British tour company.

My ambition to find out what lay behind the more obvious clichés of Paris began on day one of my first ever school trip. It was a dire holiday with the city lying flat and lifeless outside a steamy school coach window, squashed by endless lists of historical dates and the exploits of Lou s-whoever-he-was. But on the final night the school coach accidently tootled into the middle of a spectacular car chase on the Champs-Elysées where a band of criminals were trying to make off with the contents of a jeweller's shop. I decided the place could be worth getting to know after all.

I next returned under the safe and secure umbrella of studentdom, with a grant cheque, accommodation and a relatively respected identity. Equipped in this way it was all too easy to slip into the role of a spectator, "ooohing and aaaning" at the city in full intoxicating action but hardly experiencing it from within. It was only after I'd lived there for a while as an unemployed foreigner, with next to no money, that I started to break through the glitzy veneer of the place.

I had been lured back to Paris by an old friend with promises of a place to stay and a never-ending succession of occasional work should I need it. I arrived to find that he had left his flat to live on a very bare and very cold barge that he had found abandoned on the Seine – a great and exciting idea if occasionally marred by the pungent reek of boat oil and the wild pitching and tossing whenever a tourist *bateau mouche* swarmed past.

The first few days were taken up with furnishing the boat, using discarded bits and pieces Parisians seem to routinely fling on to their streets. After that I set about finding a job. The most obvious place to look is at the *Centre d'Information et de Documentation de Jeunesse* next to the

Eiffel Tower on the Quai Branly where scores of jobs for mainly young people are displayed on huge noticeboards. It took a while for me to realise just how many of the crowd that gathered around the notices were chasing the same jobs as myself and, after a week of scrambling in and out of a grimy trapdoor that seemed designed to rip off buttons and tear skirts, I was becoming less and less able to compete. I eventually gave up, deciding that for the time being at least I would accept the label "unemployable".

Parisians are considered a cold, unfriendly lot by the rest of France as well as foreign visitors. This I found nowhere so obvious as by their blatant discrimination by appearance. The conventions of neatness, tidiness and feminine prettiness are rigidly upheld. It seems if you can't or don't wish to conform to the high-heeled, well groomed, perfumed and decorated image, then you must expect to meet the sharp end of snubbery and snobbery.

"'Why do you want to go there?', he asked, 'It stinks, it's dirty, It's full of Arabs.'"

In the mornings when I loped along to the local *boulangerie* for bread, the hoards of workpeople dashing to their offices, crisp, white raincoats swishing behind, would often eye me with distaste. If one of them accidentally bumped into me the usual reaction would be to look me up and down, decide I wasn't worth the effort of an "excusez-moi" and stride forcefully on. I was after all living in the richest square kilometre in Paris, where the glut of elegance and glamour could intimidate women and men many times smarter than myself and where the wonderful-smelling restaurants made my bread-and-nothing lunch seem pitifully unappetising.

Of course Paris isn't so restrictively wealthy everywhere. I used to buy vegetables from the comparatively cheap greengrocer shops around the Belleville and Barbès Rochechouart metro stations in the northeast. Both areas are inhabited mainly by new immigrants and, wandering down the narrow sloping streets into the alleyways, you find tiny cafés selling Tunisian sweets – all the more tempting when lit by neon strips – and Arabic music chanting from wide open windows strung with washing. These parts of the city tend to be neglected and cold-shouldered by other Parisians, and trenchant suspicion is shown towards people of Maghrebian origin and expressed in racist graffiti. Once, on one of my vegetable trips, an oldish man, assuming I was a stray tourist, advised me against going further. "Why do you want to go there?" he asked, "It stinks, it's dirty, it's full of Arabs, you'll be pickpocketed." Belleville can seem an intimidating place to wander alone at night, but this is mainly because it is so quiet.

Food is expensive in Paris and prices vary drastically from one shop to another. At the beginning I could still afford to eat in the many student cafeterias (*Restau-U's*) where they don't insist on student identity, although looking the part is an advantage. The countless plates of lentils, ice cream and as much bread as I could sneak kept hunger out of my head even if it didn't supply much in the way of vitamins.

Being vegan and vegetarian is a problem – reasonably priced food co-operatives seemed to exist only as rumours or unfindable addresses on scraps of paper and requests for something without meat were treated with wide-eyed misunderstanding by ordinary shopkeepers or café attendants. Worst of all was when they would look at me and say "Oh, you young girls, always concerned about your figures!". Compassionate eating hasn't made much headway in the tightly guarded bastion of French gastronomy.

In general terms I found that having an entertainment budget of nil helped to emancipate me from the celebrated equation of money equals entertainment equals fun. Some of the sights and monuments are free to the public on certain days, such as Sunday at the Louvre and Sunday morning at the Beaubourg Modern Art Gallery and there were always those spontaneous moments of silence and stillness that form such a memorable part of Parisian life – like sitting on the steps of the white dome of the Sacré Coeur watching the invariably pink evening sky settle the dirt and dust on the rooftops below, or the intensity of the incense-filled darkness inside Notre Dame.

I gradually stopped wistfully eyeing the entrances to cinemas, jazz clubs and lively bars and settled down to more thoughtful activities, sitting on the roof of the barge, wrapped in blankets talking and laughing with the odd passer-by.

"There's a special kind of creep which seems to thrive in Paris which the French call a drageur"

The adventure of our floating home ended when reality produced an owner demanding rent. Even though I had failed to get a job I felt I had at least absorbed Paris. It seemed to me now like a succession of country villages spiralling out from the centre all living on top of each other. I was once told, by a woman I happened to share a bench with, that it was a "woman's city". She was an architect and a staunch believer that the small, curvy streets and light-coloured, soft-edged buildings which lined them, plus the general lack of intimidating high-rise skyscrapers were conducive to female well-being. "It's just the whole irrationality of it all," she enthused, pointing into a direction where the few narrow streets were promising to lurk into obscurity. I knew what she meant and yet it made it all the more disheartening that almost every woman I met swopped tales with me of being threatened and insulted when wandering about this city.

There's a special kind of creep which seems to thrive in Paris which the French call a *drageur*; he smiles, greets, and follows you, pays you the most banal and condescending compliments and then launches into a speech about "love at first sight". Usually *drageurs* concentrate on the most obvious tourist, cashing in on the "nothing-can-happen-to-me-I'm-on-holiday" mood. It could be on any street, regardless of the business, the area, the time of day. If you sit, so much the better, you're no longer a moving target. I have found myself instinctively on the defensive, which I consider an unhealthy state of mind, but unless you are obviously unavailable, say, hanging off a man's arm, it's necessary.

For a long time I would wander around alone at all hours of the day or night, even in the far northern districts which other women had warned me against (it gets more risky the further you are away from the centre). I foolishly believed that my confident stride and air of being able to look after myself would psychologically deter any potential hassler. I was made to think again after an incident in the metro station when an old man, obviously very drunk, began to insult me, push me around and then tried to throw me against a wall. It happened quickly and the train came just in time. I did learn, however, that you can't rely on passers-by to help you – there were five people all watching open-mouthed.

"As in London you're assailed on the streets by advertising images portraying women as glamorous, usable, disposable and weak"

I also learnt that the metro is at its most dangerous, not around midnight when the theatres and restaurants are emptying, but between nine and eleven at night. At these times most people have already got to where they are going and the stations are left to people on the look-out for trouble. Once on the platform you should hang around the exit rather than straying to the deserted ends as one does in vacant moments of waiting.

As in London you're assailed on the streets by advertising images portraying women as glamorous, usable, disposable and weak. Somehow these seemed more offensive and degrading – I think mainly because they seem to come and go without anyone trying to deface or subvert them. I was surprised by how few of the women I met considered these images a problem. When I expressed my own indignation I was accused of showing an unwelcome intolerance amidst another country's culture.

All of which served to bolster a general feeling that there is less feminist sensitivity in Paris. I learnt to attribute this to the intellectualisation and inaccessibility of the feminist movement. It's the same story for the low-profile ecology and peace movements; in fact anything "alternative" seems to live in books and journals rather than as a grass-roots organisation. It was disappointing to find only one haven of female solidarity, although a good one, at *La Maison des Femmes*, Cité Prost. There was always a friendly atmosphere, someone to talk to in English, and feminist publications from all over Europe. On Friday night there is a café run by *MIEL*, the lesbian group and the

Maison puts out a fortnightly magazine "*Paris Féministe*" which contains information on feminist actions all over France as well as the other groups that currently meet there, such as a women against racism and a Maghrebian women's group. There are also noticeboards advertising self-defence courses, holidays and accommodation. Women from all over the world seem to drop by while staying in Paris.

Although I finally had to shrug my shoulders and admit that as I could no longer support myself I would have to leave Paris; within a year I was back.

This time I came with suitcases, strategies, and a series of carefully worded job requests to install in shop windows. Domestic work, cleaning homes in the affluent western suburbs, more than paid my way until, by a combination of timing and great good luck, I landed a job as a guide with a British tour company. At last I can communicate my enthusiasm for this city to over 250 willing ears per week. Paris seems almost a different place from the occupied-and-earning perspective. I'm still here, well-nourished, smartly clothed and securely housed between four wonderfully solid walls.

But even now, as I take a coachload of tourists over the Concorde Bridge, and point them towards the river where my old barge still bobs up and down, I can't resist my private bit of irony; ". . . and here are the houseboats where many people still, in fact, live!"

TRAVEL NOTES

Languages French. Basque and Breton, as well as regional dialects, are still spoken but losing way. Perhaps more important today are immigrant/migrant languages – Maghrebi Arabic, Portuguese, etc. English is spoken reasonably widely but you'll find it frustrating to depend on.

Transport The French rail network is the best in Europe – efficient and extensive; bus services play a relatively minor role. Cycling is big and you can rent bikes from most train stations and in all towns of any size. Few French women would consider hitching, although reports are that it's no more/less safe than Britain. If you have to hitch it's best to make use of *Allostop*, an organisation for drivers and hitchers to register for shared journeys.

Accommodation Plentiful, though if your money is tight you'll need to depend on the numerous Youth Hostels and campsites. There are also a few women's holiday camps (see listings below).

Guides *The Rough Guide: France* (Harrap Columbus) gives a refreshing alternative perspective while also covering all the traditional tourist interests. *Gaia's Guide* (Gaia's Guide, UK) has a good, up-to-date, listings section for lesbian and feminist venues throughout France.

Contacts

French **women's centres**, particularly in Paris, continue in a state of flux. The following are reasonably established and should be able to provide full and up-to-date contacts for other French cities.

Paris

Maison des Femmes, 8 cité Prost, 11e, ☎93.48.24.91. The capital's best-known feminist centre. They publish a fortnightly bulletin, *Paris Féministe*, run a cinema club and radio station, *Les Nanas Radioteuses* (101.6Mhz; Wed 6pm-midnight), and provide a meeting place for most Paris groups including *MIEL*, a lesbian organisation group which runs the centre's café – *L'Hydromel*.

Feminist Bookshops, all of which stock the French **feminist calendar/guide** and *Lesbia*, a monthly lesbian listings and events magazine

can be found at: **Librairie des Femmes,** 74 rue de Seine, 6, ☎43.29.50.75; **Librairie Plurial** 58 rue de la Roquette, ☎47.00.13.06; **Marguerite Durand Library**, 21 Place du Panthéon, 75005, ☎43.78.88.30.

Lesbian/feminist bars: **La Champmesle** 4 rue Chabanais, ☎42.96.85.20; 6pm–2am; a popular bar, the front is mixed, the back is women-only. **Katmandou** 21 rue de Vieux Colombier, ☎45.48.12.96; 11pm–dawn; best-known and most up-market of the lesbian nightclubs, with Afro-Latino and international atmosphere.

Restaurant and Coffee Shops: **Le Mansouria**, 11 rue Faidherbe and **Central**, 3 rue Ste. Croix de la Bretonnerie, ☎274.71.52, are both owned and run by women.

Elsewhere

MARSEILLE: **Maison des Femmes**, 95 rue Benoit Malon, 5. Again a meeting place for all groups with people around on Tuesday and Thursday 6–10.30 pm. **La Douce Amère**, a lesbian campaigning group, can be contacted at the bar *La Boulangerie Gay*, 48 rue de Bruys; There's also a feminist bookshop, **La Librairie des Femmes**, on rue Pavillion.

NICE: **Le Papier Maché**, 3 rue Benoit Bunico. Co-op bookshop, restaurant and arts centre – a friendly, leftist haven and meeting place for feminist, ecology and radical groups.

Holidays

Women's/lesbian holiday houses and campsites. Write first for a prospectus to: **Barriane, Les Essades** (holiday camp), 16210 Chalais ☎045.98.62.37;

R.V.D. Plasse (holiday camp), Les Grezes, St. Aubin des Nabirat, 24250 Domme, ☎053.28.50.28.

Chez Jacqueline Boudillet (guesthouse), Langerau à cere la Ronde, 37460 Montresor, ☎16.47.34.34.63.

Saouis (guesthouse with camping), Cravenceres, 32110 Nogaro, ☎0033.62.08.56.06.

Women's Holiday Centre (Pyrenees holidays), c/o Jean Ginoux Déu Bas, 09 Artigat, Arigée.

Books

Simone de Beauvoir, *The Second Sex* (1949), ***The Woman Destroyed*** (1967). Both published by Flamingo in translation. One of the founders of French feminism – and existentialism, **Judith Okeley's *Simone de Beauvoir*** (Virago, 1986) provides an illuminating revaluation of her life and work.

Claire Duchen, *Feminism in France* (RKP, 1986). Chronicles the evolution of the women's movement in France from its emergence in 1968 to the present. Highly recommended.

Marguerite Duras, *The Lover* (Flamingo, 1985). Autobiographical novel by influential avant-garde writer.

Marguerite Yourcenar, *Coup de Grace* (1957, Corgi, 1983). The first woman to be elected to the Académie Française, Marguerite Yourcenar's novels show an incredible breadth of scholarship and experience.

Eveline Mahyère, *I Will Not Serve* (1958; Virago, 1988). Powerful lesbian fiction set in Paris in the 1950s.

Shari Benstock, *Women of the Left Bank: Paris 1900–1940* (Virago, 1987). Somewhat dry and academic but full of information about women's contribution to the expatriate literary scene and the founding of literary modernism.

Elaine Marks, *New French Feminism* (Harvester, 1981). A part of the continuing debate that divides French feminists – Beauvoir describes Elaine Marks' book as "totally distorted".

Look out for **cartoons by Claire Brétècher and Catherine Rihoit.**

Thanks to Kate Baillie who provided information used in the introduction.

West Germany

At the time of publication, elections are due in both Germanies. Their result, it seems almost inevitably, will be reunification of the states that have existed, since the last war, split between Eastern and Western orbits. Clearly, very great changes lie ahead for the East (the GDR), as its economy and orientation becomes integrated into the European Community and Western free market system. Many Germans in the West (the Federal Republic, or FDR), however, are equally apprehensive as their nation, Europe's wealthiest, absorbs the crisis-ridden and formerly Communist-run territories.

Such an agenda reduces all previous West German politics to a bizarrely minor role. Yet the Federal Republic's post-war years, in which rapid industrialisation and rampant consumerism have characterised its "miracle" economic recovery, have not been without challenge or dissent. Indeed, in terms of political attitudes, the Republic was – in itself – the most divided European nation. Feminist, environmental, civil liberty, and various other left and radical groups, forged over the last two decades, form a full and organised political stratum, continually at odds with the state. They draw support from an extensive city network of housing and workers co-operatives, alternative schools, cafés and bookshops and a flourishing free press – and also from an increasing section of conventional German society, concerned about ecological problems like the acid rain that is destroying the Black Forest. It was from this social fabric that the Green Party was forged and became in 1983 the first ecology party to gain seats in a European national parliament.

More recently, there have been worrying political trends on the right, with the emergence and subsequent election successes of the neo-Nazi Republikaner party. They have capitalised on the already entrenched racism shown towards the country's large migrant worker population, particularly towards Turks. The problems likely to be created by a future absorption of the East German economy are likely only to inflame the situation.

As far as the realities of travel go, if you're Turkish, or look as if you might be, you may well experience some degree of hassle. For any other visitors, sexual harassment is uncommon and money is usually the biggest problem. To take advantage of conventional attractions – and Germany has superb galleries, music festivals and scenery – you'll need to be prepared to spend. On the plus side, there is a well developed network of women's cafés, holiday houses and lift agencies that you can tap into, and some cities run free bus or taxi services for women travelling at night.

The current wave of **feminism** derives from the recent history of alternative politics. Feminist publications (*Courage* and *Emma* are the most widely distributed) proliferated during the 1970s and remain. So too do women's centres, bookshops, and groups, including a large number of lesbian collectives. Many of these, however, are part of an established local scene and are not necessarily open to casual travellers. Activist campaigns – such as organising against pornography and violence against women, "Reclaim the night" demonstrations, etc – continue, but tend to be incorporated in "wider issue" demonstrations led by *Bügerinitiativen* (Citizens' initiatives) or ecology groups. Women have retained a high profile in the Green Party, and not only through Petra Kelly, their best known international spokeswoman. Both the Green Party and Social Democrats operate a quota system to ensure that women are represented on both a local and national level.

Staying on in Hamburg

• • • • • • • • • • •

Jane Basden left Australia after finishing university to travel to southeast Asia, China, Russia and Europe. She ended her five-month journey in West Germany where she lived and worked for eighteen months. She has since returned a number of times in her work as a freelance radio journalist.

My decision to go to Germany was partly due to geography – that's where the Trans-Siberian took me; partly due to economics. I'd run out of money, desperately needed work and it happened to be my first EC port of call. But most importantly it was due to an inexplicable feeling that I ought to understand this country and the people who lived there.

Having said that, I had no real expectation of what Germany would actually be like. There were images of *lederhosen* and Bavarian landscapes, gleaned from uninspired high school language classes. And there were images of Baader-Meinhof news reports, and the ubiquitous American war films. But none of them prepared me for the reality which was at once very normal, very familiar, and yet totally unlike what I'd grown up with in urban Australia.

I arrived in Hamburg on a warm, drizzly summer evening, with very little money, less German, and totally without guidebooks or acquaintances of any kind. It's not the way I'd suggest arriving, although there is something to be said for having to talk to, and depend on, local people for information and directions.

Unlike many other countries I'd travelled in, where contact with local women was limited if not almost impossible, West Germany was an utter relief. When I needed directions on the street I could always find a woman who, hearing my appalling attempts at German, would switch the conversation to English and tell me what I needed to know. (Later experience showed me that many, though undoubtedly fewer, would just as quickly swap to French or Spanish.) A few times these footpath contacts resulted in phone numbers being given, café invitations and, in one case, tips about where to find work. All these offers were genuine, and over the following months I began to realise there was something very German about that.

Hamburg was the first place I'd had time to stop and really observe people since leaving Asia. I felt starved of contact with women, and especially with feminist and lesbian women. One of my first joys was walking through the city squares taking in the sheer numbers of women, walking arm in arm, having animated if incomprehensible conversations, sitting around tables in outdoor cafés . . . women who simply looked like the kind of strong independent women I knew at home.

I began to sense a feeling of tolerance or at least awareness amongst younger Germans (by that I mean people born after the War). It was a difficult thing to put my finger on, and I wasn't sure whether the few people I'd met were representative, but I kept the thought at the back of my mind for future reference.

"German women, if I can generalise, have a certain outward independence about them"

The other thing I very soon noticed was that, as a single white woman walking alone around Hamburg, I didn't feel openly harassed by men. In eighteen months there, I can recall only a few minor incidents. Sexism certainly exists, but it seemed to me that the men I met were more subtle and more anxious to please than their brethren in Australia or England. Nevertheless, for women travelling alone, the absence of overt harassment can often make the difference between a lousy time and an interesting, enjoyable one.

Also, German women, if I can generalise, have a certain outward independence about them. They tend to stand up for themselves and their rights, at least in public. West Germany has a very active women's movement, and if nothing else, "liberated women" are now accepted there. I suppose the point is, if you're a woman travelling alone in West Germany, you won't stick out like a sore thumb from the bulk of women who live there.

And on the question of tolerance: most young people in Hamburg – and I met a wide cross-section eventually, through teaching English – seem to be very tolerant on the question of sexuality; are in favour of the rights of refugees and migrants to live and work in their country as equals; do not seem racist or anti-semitic in any way; and are not prudish or titillated by topless or nude sunbathing. I added this last slightly odd measure of tolerance because, on my "tolerance gauge" of "would this happen in the same situation in Australia?", the ability to sunbathe naked and unharassed with a girlfriend on the banks of Hamburg's many small lakes broke the record.

I wouldn't, however, suggest doing this in Bavaria, nor in fact anywhere outside the more liberal big cities, Hamburg and Berlin being the most notable. My rather limited experience of the south of Germany gave me the distinct impression that, whilst people there were friendly and in some ways less "ordered" than in the north, they were definitely less tolerant of non-white foreigners, people of "dubious" sexual, political or moral persuasions, and so on.

Making the decision to actually live in Germany as opposed to travelling through wasn't easy. On top of all the personal feelings of doubt, insecurity and isolation that typifies culture shock, my decision to stay meant that I had to deal with the immense German bureaucracy. Applying for a residency permit; registering with the area housing office; the foreign police and the tax office . . . there seemed an office for everything, with a language, and a formality, unto itself. As with any government department, the way I was treated depended largely on the personal whim of the official who dealt with me.

In the end, dealing with this red tape wasn't really as bad as I'd anticipated, and in fact, because I had an EC passport, I quite easily became eligible for social security assistance, housing benefit and so on. The hardest part was finding out about these possibilities in the first place. It's definitely worth a trip to an *"Auslanderberatungstelle"* (foreigners advice centre) if you're unsure of your rights.

Having said all of that, living in Hamburg was a mixture of a huge range of experiences, some pleasant, some inspiring, difficult, or even disturbing. In retrospect, it all seemed extremely worthwhile.

As a feminist there were constant opportunities to become involved in active political projects and take part in cultural, craft, academic or manual trade courses, workshops and discussions. There are women's bookshops (*Frauenbuchladen*), holiday houses, cafes, education centres, pubs, advice and support centres all over Germany.

A good place to begin in the search for any or all of these are the bookshops, or backs of the women's, lesbians' and alternative diaries.

"Lesbian households will usually make it clear on the notice"

If you've got the time, inclination and money, the women's education centres and country holiday houses are well worth a visit. Most of the large cities have women's education centres which run courses throughout the year in everything from plumbing and car maintenance, to theoretical analyses of the future of feminism to African music and dance. Many of the country houses like *Osteresch* and *Anraff* run intensive weekend and week-long residential courses along the same lines. The courses aren't all that cheap, though they're usually run on a sliding scale according to means, and the residential ones include all meals and accommodation. When I got sick of the cement and noise of the city, it was good to know that there were places I could escape to.

These courses are a good way of making friends, a difficult thing in any strange city, and also finding out more about what's going on both within and outside the women's movement. Köln, for example, holds a women's film festival every year around October; Hamburg has a *Frauenwoche* (Women's week) each year in February/March; Berlin has a *Lesbenwoche* (Lesbian week) in September/October. There are lots more, so try to find out about them.

The women's bookshops and education centres are also handy for "rooms vacant" notices – for women's, lesbians' or mixed "WGs" (*Wohngemeinschaften* – literally "living communities", or group houses). Other good places to look are university noticeboards, alternative cafés, and the back pages of the left-wing daily *"Die Tageszeitung"* (commonly called *"Die Taz"*). Housing shortages have become quite severe in West Germany in the last couple of years, especially in the big cities like Berlin, Hamburg and Munich, forcing up prices and competition for vacant apartments. Unless you've got lots of money and glowing references about your financial means, you'll probably be better off trying to find a vacant room in an already established household.

If you're looking specifically for a lesbian household, it's worth remembering that *"Frauen WG"* (women's household) usually means that the women are not lesbian, and probably have boyfriends and other male guests staying over. Lesbian households will usually make it clear on the notice. If you're in any doubt, just ask. Even comparatively straight German women don't seem shocked by such questions.

Despite being white, middle-class and speaking English (the language of the tourists opens a lot of doors to work), the pay and conditions in the first two jobs I found were incredibly grim. They were kitchen jobs where migrant workers who, like myself, couldn't speak German were treated as deaf, dumb or stupid and given the dirtiest, heaviest work. Trade unions are fairly inactive in these areas, and workers' rights seem to be explained only in the longest words and the finest print. In one job I was really shocked to find I'd been working an hour per day extra for over three months, and no one had bothered to tell me. The manager and most of the other workers, as it turned out, had known all along . . . and I was one of the privileged workers who could get a legal job with a written contract!

Very little money meant very little choice about which neighbourhood I could live in. But, in my experience, warnings not to live in "the rougher quarters" of the big cities – Kreuzberg in Berlin, Altona or St Pauli in Hamburg – are a bit exaggerated. I lived in and near St Pauli for eighteen months. Despite being Hamburg's

notorious red light district, supposedly teeming with pimps, dealers and racketeers, I never felt directly threatened. I was maddened by the whole industry of prostitution and pornography, and often sorely tempted to lob a few bricks through windows, but it seemed to me like you were either involved in it all or not and the different communities simply moved around each other and rarely met.

Besides, these areas also have the highest concentration of alternative political, social and cultural projects, cafés and so on, with quite a strong feeling of community.

Because cafés, bars and clubs tend to stay open to the smallish hours in West German cities, I found that my waking hours started and finished later than normal. It wasn't unusual to go out for dinner at 10 or 11pm, or to go for a coffee at 1am. So the issue of transport was pretty important.

"For longer journeys elsewhere in Germany, I usually hitched"

German cities are quite compact, and often it's only a matter of a few blocks' walk to a whole night's entertainment. Generally speaking, I felt safer walking around after dark in Hamburg than almost anywhere else I've been, even quite late at night, and especially in the inner city suburbs. That's mainly because the streets were always busy. Walking with a friend, female or male, was usually enough to feel totally comfortable. For slightly longer journeys, or if you feel a bit nervous after dark, bicycles are an excellent means of transport, and one that is completely catered for in all areas of Germany. There are cycle ways on all main roads around Hamburg, and you'll save a packet on the relatively expensive though efficient public transport.

For longer journeys elsewhere in Germany, I usually hitched, though if I wanted to get somewhere by a definite time I often tried the *Mitfahrzentralen*, (lift centres). Most major cities have at least one just for women – drivers and passengers – and the staff can usually cope with English and French. You just ring up and ask if they've got someone going your way and the day/time you want. There's a small fee (roughly half the equivalent train fare), part of which goes to the centre and part pays for your share of the petrol. It's a good compromise between hitching and public transport.

If you do decide to hitch, it's best to start at the Rest Stations on the *Autobahns*, or, in Berlin, at the border crossings on the *Autobahn*.

My rule of thumb was always to trust my gut feeling, err on the side of caution, and never get in with two or more men if alone. Long-distance truck drivers were good because they were usually intent on getting to their destination as fast as they could, to make as much money as they could, which left little time to chat up women passengers. Mostly they were just bored out of their brains and welcomed the company. Some were surprisingly helpful and friendly, even arranging the next stage of a lift with fellow drivers.

I had a couple of minor irritating lifts with private drivers, but never one where I felt in any danger. It was much easier and more pleasant, and a much more accepted mode of transport, than in other countries where I've hitched. Despite that, it's not unknown for hitchers to be attacked, in fact, there's a rather unnerving sign at the hitching point out of Berlin which warns you of the dangers and, to add impact, displays the number of people killed whilst hitching for each of the last few years. So, if you're travelling alone and feel uneasy about hitching, don't do it.

Politically speaking, West Germany is a very intense country, and has been for centuries. There's a very entrenched conservative and wealthy stratum, a great many liberal "free thinkers", and a lot of politically radical groups on the left, far greater in numbers, support and activity than anything similar in, say, Britain or Australia. The effect of this is a serious and long-running struggle for political power – whether parliamentary or not – with huge and sometimes violent demonstrations on the one hand, and stringent, all encompassing police surveillance and muscle flexing on the other (and all manner of things in the middle).

"I found out later that at least a couple of women suspected me of being a police plant"

I had my first taste of this in week one. I met a few women at the women's pub, and after talking to them all evening, one of them suggested I could stay in her flatmate's room for a couple of days while I looked for a room of my own. As I was otherwise doomed to the youth hostel, I eagerly accepted, and said, by way of a "Thank you", that I'd make breakfast in the morning and she could sit down and tell me all about the women's scene in Hamburg. With that, one of the other women at the table stood up, made some obviously scathing comment to my temporary host, and left. "A lovers' tiff?", I thought.

Unfortunately, nothing so easy. I found out later that at least a couple of women now suspected me of being a "police plant" who was going to dig up names and addresses of all the active feminists in Hamburg. At the time I thought this was just a bad case of paranoia, but I soon learnt of instances where exactly that had happened, with an apparent friend, even an apparent lover, suddenly turning out to be a member of the secret service and leaving behind her a string of arrests, questionings, house searches, and the knowledge that files somewhere were being fattened for the kill.

Whether you're politically active or interested or not, even the most inane situations force you to deal with the political realities of West Germany. Proving you're not a police spy is about as easy as convincing the inquisition that you're not a witch, though the result isn't quite as bad. Events in West Germany in the last couple of years, especially raids against over thirty women active in the areas of genetic engineering and population control, have made feminists more wary of police surveillance, and therefore more suspicious of strangers.

Don't go to Germany expecting the warm welcome of sisterhood . . . you may not get it, at least, not straight away.

TRAVEL NOTES

Language German. English is taught in most schools and widely spoken.

Transport Hitching, there are around fifty agencies which arrange lifts – specific agencies for women are *Frauen-Mitfahrzentrale*, in Berlin (Potsdamerstrasse 139), Hamburg (Rappstrasse 4) and Munich (Baidestrasse 8) Ask at the local women's café (*Frauencafé*) for information on free transport at night.

Accommodation Besides hotels, Youth Hostels and campsites there's a fair number of women's holiday houses, some of which offer a range of feminist workshops and courses. (See Contacts listings).

Guides *The Rough Guide: West Germany* (Harrap Columbus) is useful; *Gaia's Guide* (Gaia's Guide, UK) has a wealth of listings.

Contacts

The **Frauen Adressbuch** (Courage, Berlin) lists all women's centres, cafés, bars, bookshops, etc; there are also more detailed *Frauenstadtbuchs* for Berlin, Dusseldorf and Munich. Below is a small selection.

BERLIN: **Infothek für Frauen** (Women's Information Desk), Goldrausch e.V., Potsdamer Strasse. 139, 1000 Berlin 30, ☎215.75.54. Provides tourist information for women.

Die Begine, Potsdamer Strasse 139, 1000 Berlin 30. ☎215.43.25. Women's multicultural centre, with café, theatre, cinema and bar.

BONN: **Nora-Frauenbuchladen** (Feminist bookshop and information centre), Wolfstr. 30, 5300 Bonn 1, ☎65.47.67.

Frauenmuseum (Women's Museum), Im Krausfeld 10, ☎69.13.44.

HAMBURG: **Von Heute An** (Feminist bookshop and café), Bismarckstr. 98, ☎420. 47. 48.

MUNICH: **Lillemor's Frauenbuchladen** (Feminist bookshop and information centre) Arcisstrasse 57, ☎272.12.05.

Frauen Kultürhaus (Women's cultural centre, gallery and café), Richard Strauss-Strasse 21 ☎470 52.12.

Women-only holidays,

Frauenreisen, c/o Gabi Bernhard, Kaiserdamm 6, 1000 Berlin 19, run skiing, hiking, historic trips with the intention of promoting contact between European women.

There's also a network of **holiday houses** with courses and cultural activities. For prospectuses write to: **Frauenbildungsstatte Anraff-Edertal**, Königsbergerstrasse 6, 3593 Anraff-Edertal ☎0.56.21.3218.

Frauenlandhaus Charlottenberg, Holzappelerstrasse 3, 5409 Charlottenberg, ☎0.64.39. 75.31.

Frauenferienhauser Hasenfleet, Hasenfleet 4, 2171 Oberndorf, ☎04.772.206.

Frauenbildungsstatte Osteresch, Zum Osteresch 1, 4447 Hopsten-Schale, ☎0.54.57.1513.

Frauenbildungszentrum Zulpich, Pralat-Franker Strasse 13, 5352 Zulpich-Lovenich, ☎0.22.52.6577.

Frauenferienhaus Tiefenbach, Hammer 22, 8491 Tiefenbach, ☎0.96.73.499.

Books

Petra Kelly, *Fighting for Hope* (Chatto, 1984). Petra Kelly was unhappy about the editing of this, touted as her "personal manifesto". Inspiring ideas nonetheless and good background on the Greens.

Gisela Elsner, *Offside* (Virago, 1985). Revealing portrait of women's life in middle-class Germany.

Paul Frolich, *Rosa Luxembourg* (1939; Pluto, 1983). Original, revolutionary thinker at forefront of working-class struggle and Communist Party of Germany founder. Definitive biography by revolutionary contemporary.

Günther Wallraff, *Lowest of the Low* (Methuen, 1987). An inside view of the cynical (and criminal) exploitation of Turkish migrant workers by one of Germany's most controversial journalists. A political bombshell when released in Germany in the mid-Eighties.

From **East Germany**

Five novels by **Christa Wolf** have been published in England by Virago. A committed socialist, described as East Germany's most formidable woman of letters; her books examine the post-war conditions of Germany as well as evoking life under the Nazis.

Thanks to Dörte Haarhaus for help with the introduction.

Ghana

For many years travellers steered clear of Ghana, deterred by its reputation as one of the most economically distressed countries in the region. Its wealth and resources, amassed during a period of remarkable growth in the Fifties and Sixties, had all but collapsed, leaving an economy floundering in massive foreign debt, political conflict, corruption and famine. Slowly, under the revolutionary council of Flight-Lieutenant Jerry Rawlings things have started to improve. The worst of the poverty has eased, food is again readily available, and although there are few tourists, Ghana is beginning to feature again as part of a West African tour.

Getting around Ghana can be arduous – roads are poor and accommodation limited – but there's a good bus network, and, compared with many nearby countries, it is a relaxed and easy place to travel alone. Ghanaians are renowned for their incredible warmth and openness, and even in the predominantly Muslim area in the north, where travellers are very rare, you're unlikely to face more than a few curious comments. In terms of dress it's worth remembering that, outside of the main towns and the Christian areas along the coast, legs are more taboo than breasts and should be covered. In general, however, the atmosphere is tolerant and very few local customs are imposed on travellers.

Traditionally, **women** have been active in Ghana's economy as subsistence farmers and market traders. The market women's associations continue to wield considerable power over local trade and transport and, under the new regime of the People's National Defence Council (*PNDC*), a small minority of educated women are gaining greater access to the professions and to government posts. It is still, however, a strongly male dominated society with the burdens of child rearing and heavy domestic work falling squarely on women's shoulders. Polygamy is common (usually involving a wife and several "girlfriends"), with women often being left to provide for large families. Even within the semi-matriarchal Ashanti region, where inheritance passes from a man to his sister's son, the secondary status of women holds firm. Mrs Rawlings, who is head of the women's section of the *PNDC*, has toured the country to form local branches. There are also a number of women's development groups geared towards healthcare and helping to set up income-generating projects.

A "Foreign Expert"

. . . .

Naomi Roberts, an English woman in her forties, spent eight months working as a volunteer in a Ghanaian village.

Only a few parts of West Africa have opened up to tourists – little strips of beach backed by new hotels – and even here the slightly adventurous traveller has only to walk past the barbed wire inland for a few hundred yards to discover a very different continent. If you want to you can stick to a life on the fringes – or you can try, with some difficulty, to penetrate the less glamorous and more struggling daily life.

I lived for eight months in a village in the coastal forested region, about 120 miles from Accra. I had been brought out by a British volunteer agency to assist in setting up primary healthcare

programmes. I stayed only eight months because I became uncomfortable in my role as "foreign expert". The undue respect I received seemed to be based on little more than my being English and therefore seemed demeaning to the people who gave it. My job had been worked out between the British agency and a Ghanaian central government department and no one locally had been properly consulted. No effort had been made to see if a Ghanaian could have done my job.

"The job . . . gave me an entry into a shared way of life that will forever make our boxed British existence seem thin"

However, putting these deep objections to the work aside, my time in Ghana was full of interest. I lived with people who were unused to tourists and entirely generous and accepting. They welcomed me into their homes so uncritically that even in such a short time I felt I had gained a new family.

The job, although not working out, gave me an entry into a shared way of life that will forever make our boxed British existence seem thin.

My stay began with a few weeks training, after which I was taken out to the district where I was to work. A truck had been laid on, and loaded up with a bed, a table and two chairs. a few buckets and saucepans, a kerosene stove and lamp and a water filter, as well as my suitcases from England. The journey, although only 25 miles, took about six hours. The truck came at dusk and we drove out into the bush as night fell, over roads which were almost continuous pot holes with vast puddles shining in the moonlight. The towering forest trees and the thick, jungly growth beneath them lined both sides of the road. Occasionally we passed through small villages, crowded and tumbledown, their only signs of life a scattering of roadside stalls, lit by small points of light from oil-lamps. There were dogs tearing along the roadside in the light from our head-lamps and strange birds which crouched on the road waiting to streak off, striped plumage flashing, into the forest darkness.

We arrived in the village at about one in the morning and drove off the road up to a large, low house with its door locked and wooden shutters closed. After pounding on the shutters around the back, the door was pulled back with a great scrape. There was a young woman, a man and a small child, smiling but shy, holding back except to help with carrying my belongings. I didn't know yet just how extraordinary it must have seemed to them, so much stuff arriving with just one person.

I had come to live in a compound house of the chief of the village. It was five miles away from the small district capital where I was to work but no one had been able to find a room for me there. One of my future Ghanaian colleagues, Tony, had found me the room. He lived in the house, too, and

that first night he helped me place my things in my room, hiding them as far from view as he could and warning me to keep my shutters closed at all times. He was a city dweller and convinced that all my belongings would be stolen by these ignorant villagers. When I later stopped following his advice, nothing was ever taken from my room.

Next morning the household was awake well before 6am; banging, chopping, sweeping, talking. As soon as I emerged from my room there were many, many introductions, as half the village had come to see the new arrival. Everyone shook hands and, as I had learned a very few phrases in the local language -- "How are you?", "I am well – how about you?" – there was a great deal of laughter.

"It was clear that I could become an honorary man in this household"

The Chief was referred to as Nana (the name for all chiefs) and was about 65 years old, very tall and erect. He looked benign and wise. I felt that he was pleased and proud that I had come to his house, although very shy and embarrassed too. Through an interpreter he welcomed me and told me that the women would do everything for me that I needed doing – cooking, washing, sweeping. I could go to work and then relax in the evenings with him. It was clear that I could become an honorary man in this household. The other men in the house were Nana's younger brother, called Teacher, because that was what he was, and another lodger – an unattached man whose wife, I later learned, had left him and who was visited by his little daughter who lived elsewhere in the village.

There were many more women. The Chief had four wives, although only two lived in the compound. His senior wife lived in the next village, looking after her ageing mother. The next lived in the compound and so did the youngest wife, who was in her early twenties. Teacher's wife, Beatrice, who was herself also a teacher, became my closest friend. There were three single women relatives and about ten children. Round the back of the compound lived several teenage boys and young men. They did not have much to do with the rest of us.

Over the next few days I began to learn about the first basic, practical problems of everyday life: how to light a kerosene stove and lamp, how to wash myself in a bucket of water, how to get to the wash house at night carrying my bucket, lamp, soap and towel, how to wash my clothes and how to cook. But whatever I did, someone immediately came to help, took over, carried my bucket or washed my clothes for me. I had very mixed feelings about this. I did not want the people I lived with to think that I took them for granted and thought of them as servants, and I really wanted to learn how to do things for myself. Nevertheless I was so slow and clumsy at these tasks, making all sorts of mistakes and having accidents like scalding my hands all over with boiling water when I tried to sterilise my water filter. The young children were much more efficient at so many things: at stripping the skin off plantains and at washing clothes and even sweeping the floor.

I shopped in the local market and bought the same ingredients as the Ghanaians that I lived with: mainly vegetables and dried and smoked fish. But I used to cook them the way I would at home – omelettes when I could get eggs, and stews with large lumps of vegetables and fish, ten times as much fish as any Ghanaian would get to eat. The results were looked on with horror and only a few brave people wanted to try some of my mixtures. Nana was sure that my food would make me ill and urged me again and again to let his wives look after me.

Proper Ghanaian food took hours to prepare. At about 3pm every day the women started to prepare the vegetables for the evening meal: mainly plantains and cassava. After boiling in big pans on wood fires, the vegetables were smashed and mixed together in a large wooden bowl, the children taking turns to pound with a long heavy pole. A steady thud of regular pounding was a late-afternoon sound wherever you went in Ghana. The sticky mixture produced was called *fufu*, and had a texture like uncooked bread dough. This would be eaten in bits torn off by hand and dipped into a very peppery soup made of ground vegetables and fish.

"I attempted nearly everything at least once, including great land snails, though I did baulk at a roasted bat"

The women and children ate together while the largest portions would be taken to the men, who ate alone. I used to prepare my English-style meals over my own kerosene stove and take them over to eat, sitting with the women. We would try bits and pieces from each others' plates. I attempted nearly everything at least once, including great land snails, though I did baulk at a roasted bat. The fruit, however, was wonderful – oranges, avocados, paw-paws, pineapples, mangoes and bananas so good that I haven't been able to enjoy the hard, bright yellow ones in English shops since.

On weekdays I went to work in the "office", sometimes biking there, sometimes catching the passenger lorry or *tro-tro*. Some days of the week all the family went to their farm, which was a good hour's walk out into the forest. They came home at the end of the day laden with plantain, yam, fruit and firewood. On one of my first days off I went with them. At the end of a hot and exhausting walk all I could do was sit on the ground and watch them work: which, at that time of the year (November), involved cutting down the plantain and cassava crops. Women and children worked together and carried the great loads on their heads. Men also went to the farm to work and, on our farm, were involved in tapping palm wine and distilling it in a little dark shed in the forest. But men never carried anything back home. It seems that once a man is old enough to have a wife it is considered improper for him to be seen carrying anything on his head. I had offered to carry a basket of oranges but was defeated by the head carrying; the basket slithered every way on my head and my neck started to ache after a very short while. A little seven-year-old girl took the basket from me, put it on her head and jauntily walked ahead all the way home.

When we were not working, we relaxed together; mainly just sitting and chatting. I loved to be outdoors day and night. My room, despite my attempts to decorate it with a batik tablecloth and postcards and photos of my family stuck to my wall, seemed dark and enclosed. In the evenings we would sit in the courtyard of the compound, an outdoor "drawing room", brilliantly lit on nights with a full moon. Luckily there were few mosquitoes where I lived. Nana would be visited by a stream of people coming up from the village, often consulting him on business or about disputes that he would be asked to settle. They would talk in a little group on one side of the courtyard and drink the palm wine brought home from the farm. The women and the children and I would sit in another group. I could only understand little bits of the language and to learn more I would write down words and phrases in an exercise book. Although my language skills improved, I remained dependent on those people who were able to speak English to me.

"In the evenings Beatrice and I would talk together, sometimes about her life, sometimes about mine"

Beatrice and I soon became friends. At first she must have felt a dutiful concern for me and took responsibility for showing me how to do things and for seeing that I was not lonely, for saying goodnight to me and for enquiring how I felt each morning. If I went for a walk, she would find out and send her nine-year-old son, Kofi, to accompany me.

In the evenings Beatrice and I would talk together, sometimes about her life, sometimes about mine. She asked me questions: what did it feel like to be cold, how did we carry our babies, were there tall mountains in England, which were the biggest towns, what did we export, what did we import? Some of these facts, the sort that must have been in the geography textbooks of her schooldays, really interested her. After a while we talked more intimately. I told her about my frustrations at work and if I was feeling homesick and she gradually and very discreetly began to tell me about Teacher and his other wife, an older woman who lived with her aged mother in the village. I had begun to notice that Teacher was often away at supper time and later on in the evening. On those evenings Beatrice was much more ready to come and talk to me.

Her reaction to the whole affair was mixed in just the same way as an English wife's might be, although she said in a rather defiant sort of way "I don't mind as I don't want to bear any more children". She had five already. As Teacher left the house in the evening, Beatrice would call out "ochina" ("till tomorrow"), embarrassing him by her openness. If I called out "ochina", too, Beatrice and I would laugh together, aware of causing discomfort. When Teacher did spend an evening at home, though, Beatrice was very keen to be with him, leaving me to read my airmail *Guardian Weekly*.

I had other companions, though I could talk less easily to them. Kofi would come into my room to see me in the evenings. He would draw pictures with my coloured crayons and especially liked me to set him rows of sums to do. Nana had a sister who told me that she was adopting me as a daughter. She used to come and sit in my room, smiling at me and holding my hand. She was an old lady whose children had all left the village and who lived with just one grandchild, a little boy of about six. He would be sent up to see me with presents – some mangoes or some beans that she had cooked.

Being in my middle forties, I did not naturally become part of the village courting and coupling activities which took place in the main street after dark. Many of Nana's friends told me that they wanted to marry me and there were lots of jokes with Nana telling them that they would have to apply to him as he was my father now. I did have a more serious suitor, who used to come and talk to me in the evenings and made it very clear that he wanted me to come with him to his room. I did once, but I didn't want to again and he put no pressure on me.

Generally I think women travelling are relatively safe with men in Ghana. I felt no danger from harassment wandering about in the village or in towns day or night. Obviously one should be careful about physical relationships, as aware of the problems of AIDS as you would be in England or America.

Over the months that I lived in the village the family became more and more aware of my frustrations at work and my homesickness. In the spring my plans to return began to shape and

there was genuine sadness – plus, I felt, a bewilderment that I was such a free agent, that I alone decided whether I came or went. Didn't my boss in Accra have to give me permission to go home?

"I questioned the luxury we have as Westerners to pop in and out of other people's lives"

On my last evening we had a party. Earlier in the week I had brought five live chickens and lots of vegetables and that day the women prepared a vast quantity of chicken stew. Even so, Nana had invited so many important men from the village that my friends in the compound stood at the edge of the crush and never got any party food. There was dancing and I tried to get Kofi to dance with me. Like many boys at an age just before growing into manly confidence he hated to show off. He looked on and seemed lost in sadness. That night he just came and slept in my room. After I had left next morning with goodbyes all round the village and was driven off towards Accra, I questioned the luxury we have as Westerners to pop in and out of other people's lives.

If you do manage to stay for a while in a village, there are basic courtesies to observe. Take presents; it is unlikely that anyone will let you pay any rent. Once in a village you must, first and foremost, pay a call on the Chief. He may be able to find you somewhere to stay or will introduce you to the "Queen Mother", the head of women's affairs in every village. If my experience is anything to go by you will be treated with great kindness and generosity as well as being a source of excitement and curiosity. Both sides can give a lot to the other, so much more than when a tourist sticks to a hotel by the beach, getting impatient because of the time it takes to bring the beer.

This Lady, She Takes Time

• • • • • • • • • • • • • •

Helen Scadding has been living in Tamale in the north of Ghana for the last year and a half. Her job, running in-service courses for teachers of the Ghana Education Service, involves a fair amount of travelling, usually by motorbike, around the northern region.

If your first impressions of Ghana are – as mine were – of the airport and the capital, Accra, you're likely to be a little unnerved. Both are frenetic places, with people insistently competing for your custom: taxi-drivers, hawkers and porters, and once in Accra dozens of hawkers for stalls, markets and street food (*chop*). None of this is typical of Ghana, as you quickly realise once you're out in the villages of the countryside.

I came to Ghana in 1987 to work in the northern region, and currently spend much of my time travelling around different districts, running training courses for teachers. During my stay here I have met with a hospitality and warmth that are hard to credit. English is widely spoken and Ghanaians tend to be eager to meet and discuss issues with strangers. The few travellers I've come across, couples and single men and women, were almost all visiting the country as part of a general West Africa trip. They viewed Ghana as a pleasant respite from the tourist traps of Togo, Mali and the Ivory Coast and the more difficult travelling conditions of Sierra Leone and Burkina Faso.

Travelling in Ghana, I have personally felt safer than in any other country (including my own). A single woman, although likely to arouse curiosity and the odd proposal of marriage, will be welcomed, entertained, cared for and protected (especially, I'm afraid to say,

if you are white). It is wise however, as anywhere, to avoid walking aimlessly around in the capital at night, especially near the beach.

Ghanaian women are independent and powerful and many of them are challenging and achieving high status positions in "a man's world". Nevertheless there are very rigidly imposed male and female roles which, even in the strongly matriarchal Ashanti region, are upheld. White women are generally viewed as "different". The men and women that I meet tend to expect and accept that my ideas about relationships and my experiences of life and work will be different to theirs. From my discussions with black female colleagues who visit Ghana, they may feel more pressurised to conform to the image of the ideal Ghanaian woman: a good wife and mother.

> *"A single woman, although likely to arouse curiosity and the odd proposal of marriage, will be welcomed, entertained, cared for and protected"*

However, travelling in Ghana is still quite a challenge. Outside of Accra there are few hotels (although you will find government rest houses), hesitant electricity and water supplies, and some terrible roads. Food, however, is plentiful, healthy and tasty, if a little monotonous. There are also constant improvements and changes in all the infrastructures as Ghana tries to claw her way into the "developed" world. Dehydration and malaria need to be carefully avoided – so come prepared.

My impressions of travelling in Ghana all revolve around one factor – the mode of transport used. At first this was by bus, for the long journey from Accra to Tamale in the north. As with all bus journeys you begin the long, frustrating wait at dawn. It's quite possible that the bus will eventually leave in the early afternoon, after a panic-stricken rush to get aboard (it may even be cancelled altogether). You quickly learn that "take time", "in God we trust", and "no condition is permanent" are well deserved Ghanaian mottoes. Usually you will get where you want to go but there's no way of estimating when. A relatively simple journey of three or four hours can turn into a nightmare of dust, punctures, breakdowns and hours of waiting by the roadside. You learn to save yourself a lot of nervous energy by expecting to be a day late and by always carrying something to read. Still, the dust, sweat and jarring of the bus bumping along the road can take all your concentration. It's nice when you arrive.

One memorable journey from Tamale to Nalerigu started, as usual, after a few hours' wait. As the bus finally swerved into the lorry park men literally leapt for the two open doors, clinging on and fighting other hopeful travellers struggling to reserve one of the few seats. I managed to squeeze on to the edge of a seat, already carrying two others. In front of me, a friend did likewise only to suddenly find his lap, and the others on the seat, occupied by a large woman. Crying out grumpily at everyone in the bus and the bread sellers outside to witness her plight, she continued a jocular tirade against everyone for twenty minutes. Finally my friend moved and she edged her way on to the seat, only to give way seconds later to her friend who had been waiting in the wings.

At last we got going, stopping at every village to let off market women. At each stop the bus became surrounded by small children selling bread, yams, doughnuts, fish and oranges, always amid the clamour of "Ice-water! Ice-water!" At the outskirts of Diare the bus stopped. A large tree trunk lay across the road and on each side there were crowds of men, women and children carrying large sticks, hoes, cutlasses, knives and guns. Men walked up and down the bus, banging on the side and shouting at the driver. Eventually we were allowed through and discovered that the villagers were searching for their chief, who was now banned from the village. All vehicles were being stopped and searched. It took us seven hours to reach our destination, only a hundred miles from Tamale. But not all journeys are so eventful.

Later I bought a motorbike and started using it for most of my travel – both locally and exploring the country. The bike provided a mixture of exhilaration, exhaustion and risk. I once got a puncture on a very isolated road and had to push the bike at noon, with a high sun and no water. I was lucky. It was little more than a mile before I came to a village, where the children rushed to greet me and help haul the bike to the local vulcaniser (puncture-menders). The expertise of mechanics in Ghana is an inspiration in improvisation. Even the most tattered inner tube, sealed over and over again, can be repaired by melting small pieces of rubber over the tube. Bicycles are welded together, plastic bits sewn up, huge tractor tyres held fast with nuts and bolts, anything that will keep the wheels moving. After over 12,000 miles and eleven punctures I have learnt to respect village bike-menders in a way I would never trust my local mechanic at home.

"Returning, I hit a large bush fire, the smoke visible in the sky several miles away, with orange flames burning ominously across the track. There seemed nothing else to do but accelerate . . . and pray"

The most interesting journey I made was to a small village called Kubori in an area known as "Overseas". This was during the wet season when the many tributaries of the Volta flood, making the roads impassable. Arriving at the river I drove down a steep bank and waited for a fisherman to bring his dug-out to the shore. We then lugged the bike onto it and paddled cautiously across the muddy water sitting very still. You try not to think about the "what ifs" when doing this. Once over, I rode along thin ribbons of dust, curtained on either side by six-foot-high bush grass. Not being able to see where you are going, collecting grass in your helmet, shoes, gloves and spokes and knowing you could be lost forever, can be a little unnerving. At every small village I breathed a sigh of relief and greeted the elders who pointed me in the direction of the next thin track. Returning, I hit a large bush fire, the smoke visible in the sky several miles away, with orange flames burning ominously across the track. There seemed nothing else to do but accelerate brazenly through and pray.

Basically, "getting there" is what it all seems to be about. A bucket of water and a plate of T.2 (millet flour and water) can seem like a feast. Arriving with dusk in small towns or villages, stopping at a street stall to drink sweet milo or tea and eat a hunk of bread and egg, while listening to the drumming and high-life music from a tinny tape recorder, is a real pleasure after hours on a dusty road. This is nightlife in Ghana. There is little to do but feel the night breeze, avoid the mosquitoes, wander among the street stalls with their flickering hurricane lamps, read, or, if your luck is in, drink a warm beer in a small bar.

These dry, never changing savannah roads of the north are worlds apart from the cooling sea breeze and easy tarred road of the southern coastal route. Heading out from Accra to Winneba, Cape Coast and Elmina, you meet the beginnings of the confusions and contradictions of Ghana. The coastal towns are very beautiful, with palm-lined beaches and lively fishing ports, but they all carry reminders of the past savagery of the slave trade. Every major town is dominated by a castle or fort built by the British, Dutch, Danish, or Portuguese slavers. "Touring" Elmina Castle with Ghanaians and reading the mixture of tolerance, sadness and bitterness of people's comments in the visitors' book was one of the most poignant experiences I have had in Ghana. Some of this southern route has been developed for tourism with one or two well-known motels and beach villa complexes, but mostly these are used by wealthy Ghanaian business families on a visit to the coast, or development and expatriate workers on holiday.

My memories of Ghana will be mainly of the people who so kindly welcomed me into their homes; of the many hundreds of conversations struck up on buses, in queues and in bars; and of the strength and humour of the women I have met. I will probably even remember those long, red, dusty roads with affection. The biggest compliment I have received in Ghana came from a fellow teacher, "This lady, well, she takes time."

TRAVEL NOTES

Languages English is widely spoken, especially in the towns. Twi, the language of the Ashanti region, is also used in the south, whilst in the north there are many different languages – Dagbani, Mampruli and Wala, to name but three.

Transport State-run buses operate between the major towns. In the towns there are small buses (*moto-way*) and minibuses (*tro-tro*) but these, like the wooden trucks (*mammy-wagons*), are massively overcrowded.

Accommodation There are a few hotels in Accra and in all the state capitals, otherwise you are dependent on fairly basic, but quite safe, guesthouses. It's very likely that you'll be invited to stay at someone's house – be conscientious about the expense this imposes on your hosts, by taking gifts and paying for food and entertainment.

Special Problems Take any health provisions (contraceptives, tampons, etc) you may need – little is available.

Guide *The Rough Guide: West Africa* (Harrap Columbus) has a good section on Ghana.

Contacts

Ghana Assembly of Women, PO Box 459, Accra. Contact Evelyn Amartǝjio or Mildred Kwatchney.

Federation of Ghanaian Women, PO Box 6236, Accra.

African Women's Association for Science & Technological Development, Pecorudos, PO Box 6828, Accra. Promotes self-help projects and is active in education, healthcare and environmental projects.

Books

Ama Ata Aidou, *Our Sister Killjoy* (Longman, 1988). Noted Ghanaian playwright explores the thoughts and experiences of a Ghanaian girl on a voyage of self-discovery in Europe.

Kurei Armah Ayi, *The Beautiful Ones are Not Yet Born* (Heinemann, 1988). Realistic portrayal of a man's struggle against endemic corruption.

Asiedu Yirenkyi, *Kivuli and other Plays* (Heinemann, 1980). One of Ghana's best-known playwrights. *Kivuli* is about the break-up of a family strained by inter-generational conflict.

Greece

· · · · · · · · · · · · · · · ·

Literally millions of independent travellers go to Greece, attracted by the easy-going Mediterranean culture, the islands, legendary ancient sites and relatively low costs. The country seems to get into people's blood, and many return year after year, exploring a different circuit of islands, perhaps, or – increasingly popular – walking in the mountainous countryside of Epirus, in the north. Foreign women also have a strong work presence in Greece, most often as teachers in one of the hundreds of language schools. If you want to spend a year in the country, and to learn Greek, this is by far the most promising possibility.

Travelling about the country is pretty straightforward, with good transport (by bus and ferry) and a pleasingly low-key network of campsites, rooms and hotels. Harassment – from Greek men picking on "easy" tourists – can dampen experiences, though it's more on the persistent, nuisance level than anything more threatening. Even in Athens you rarely feel unsafe. A bigger problem perhaps is the low public presence of women. Off the tourist track, in the villages, you'll find the local *kafenion* (café) is often the only place to get a drink – and that it's completely male territory. As a foreign woman your presence will be politely tolerated, but, travelling alone, you won't always feel comfortable. The major concern for most travellers, though, lies in escaping your fellow tourists. Greece has seen some of the Mediterranean's most rapid development over the last decade and places that one year had character and charm are too often covered in concrete villas the next.

Socially, Greece remains a distinctly conservative country, though one of the few conspicuous achievements of the socialist government (which held power for the best part of the decade until disintegrating in a sea of scandal in

1989) has been a theoretical advance in **women's equality**. The *Women's Union of Greece*, closely identified with the *PASOK* government party, helped to push through legislative reforms on family law – dowry was prohibited, civil marriage recognised, and equal status and shared property rights stipulated. The reforms may have had limited impact in the rural areas, but they at least exist. Another positive, if small-scale, achievement of the socialists was the setting up of Women's Co-operatives in rural communities; these provide loans for women to run guesthouses, and an opportunity for visitors to experience local village life.

In addition to the *Women's Union*, whose influence is uncertain now that the socialists are out of power, several autonomous feminist groups are active in widening public debate around such issues as sexuality, violence and the representation of women by the media.

A Lasting Idyll

· · · · · · · · · · · · ·

Janet Zoro has long held a passion for Greece. Sparked off by an initial visit in the late Sixties, she now makes a habit of returning twice a year, travelling alone to wherever she can get the cheapest last-minute flight.

I fell in love with Greece on my first trip, twenty years ago. I was a student then, surprisingly politically naive at a time when others were sitting down in Grosvenor Square. The Colonels were in power and I should not have gone, but I did and I discovered an almost instant affinity for the place. The affair continued intermittently but it was in 1986, when I made my first solo trip, that the flame rekindled. Now I go in spring and autumn, usually for two weeks, but for longer if I can get a flight.

What is it about Greece? The country is so full of clichés: the perfect blue harbour, the white-cubed houses climbing the harbour slopes, the sunsets and moonrises, smell of oregano and grilling fish, cool, shaded waterside bars, white beaches and brilliant glass-green water; but the clichés work every time. Whenever I arrive and cross the burning tarmac of the island runway, fight through the tin customs shed and head off to yet another idyllic fishing village, my heart beats faster and my spirits lift; I feel as if I am coming home. Familiarity breeds a warm and ever deepening affection.

I am not attracted by the archaeology. I go to Greece to swim and walk and paint and recharge my batteries. I do not want discos or bars or water-skis or umbrella-covered beaches. I want my own vision of Greece: a perfect place to travel alone; no one bothers me if I do not wish to be bothered.

I can sit for hours in solitude over a drink, writing postcards, watching the harbour lights, listening to other tourists talk, or I can strike up conversation with the waiter or a fellow diner. The odd occasions for evasive action inevitably arise: the elderly gentleman from the tailors-cum-shipping agency who presses dinner invitations; the bored boy soldier who ignores my protestations that I am old enough to be his mother; the sailor on the little inter-island steamer who cannot understand that I should choose to be alone, but I would never call it harassment. I find I can accept lifts, drinks or compliments from Greek men and when I smilingly say "no" they shrug and smile and buy me a drink anyway. I never feel worried or lonely.

The Greeks generally welcome foreigners and, though an obvious curiosity as a lone traveller, I feel easily accepted. I have picked up enough words to gather the gist of basic questions and in signs and single words explain that my husband is in England, I am travelling alone, I like to paint and walk, and I have no children. Sitting in the shade of some village square, the old men express amazement while the women offer congratulations. Greek women are slaves to their boy children who, as far as I can see, are allowed to do anything they like as soon as they are mobile enough to elude the maternal embrace.

I wish I knew more Greek. I want to talk to them, the women who run shops from dawn until late, let rooms upstairs, hang out hand-washed sheets each day and still have time to water and weed their miraculous polychrome jam-packed gardens; the women who call to me from balconies as I sit and paint in some un-tourist-frequented hill village, who speak no English at all, but smile and admire my picture and give me apples; the old women who let white cool shuttered rooms with makeshift plumbing and give me coffee and figs for breakfast.

In the Dodecanese, some people speak Italian (compulsory in schools during the Italian occupation), and anywhere in Greece you'll often find men who have picked up a bit of English on their travels as merchant seamen.

Others have Australian connections. In Ithaca a very old woman hailed me as I wandered into a village: "G'day, are you looking for the beach?", and so on. It turned out she had left Australia when she was twelve, but reckoned she'd kept a bit of the accent! In Limnos I was sitting in a tiny bar-cum-shop, slaking my thirst with cold beer, when a woman came in to fetch one of the men for Sunday lunch. Glimpsing me on my perch behind a sack of onions she immediately burst into delighted conversation; home from Austraia, she was going to lunch with her cousin and invited me to join them for tea. The cousin was about to make her first trip out to visit a son she hadn't seen for twenty years and, over sweet Greek coffee and even sweeter honey pastries, my help was enlisted to try and teach her a few words of English. I struggled home hours later, laden down with bags of grapes and peaches.

"There is a new kind of young Greek woman . . . Here, in her tourist empire, the daughter is in charge"

Now that tourism is big money and English taught in all schools, the family pattern is changing. There is a new kind of young Greek woman. Increasingly in small villages I find the local restaurant tends to be run by the daughter of perhaps nineteen or twenty. She speaks good English and/or German, takes the orders, does a lot of the cooking and will talk to the customers about anything: life, politics, tourists, Greece.

She is the pet of her regulars, the English, German and Australian captains of sailing holiday yachts who bring their passengers to eat there throughout the summer. They hug her; she hugs them. They joke and laugh throughout dinner. If she has a husband, he probably builds apartments over the winter, helps in the restaurant during the tourist season or catches fish for her to cook. He may add up the bills. There may be a baby who toddles round the café, harnessed on a long string, tying tables, chairs and tourists into knots. And all the while, in the background, are the parents who, with little grasp of English, cook, carry and watch.

Here, in her tourist empire, the daughter is in charge. At the same time, her education is limited and she has little chance of breaking away. Nor can she escape Greek mores. She can laugh and joke with foreigners, but spend half an hour alone with a village boy whom she has known since birth and there would be hell to pay. No doubt this too will change. Ten years ago these bright, tough girls were with their mothers at the kitchen sink. Learning languages has given them a kind of freedom which in itself has become an economic necessity.

The actual physical business of getting around in Greece is part of the pleasure. Best of all are the boats. They are a sort of game. First, you go to one of the shipping offices which cluster round the harbour. Often these deal with only one line, so you ask for some island and they shake their heads: "Ah no, not there. Try the office next door!" Then there is the timetable; no office will ever admit to its fallibility, though I soon found out that a bit of a gale might well delay a boat for as much as one or two days. However, if you have asked around you will have found a man in the grocery shop who *knows*. He is in actual telephonic communication with the next island and knows that the ferry is running six hours late. Thus the man who sells you the ticket will say 3am, absolutely definitely; the man in the shop will say 9.30am. It makes a difference.

Although it takes a while to get the hang of ferries, the effort is rewarded by the sheer joy of racing through that dark blue sea beneath a cloudless sky, watching for the shadowy shapes of islands in the distance and sometimes, if you are very lucky, seeing a school of dolphins racing and jumping alongside in the creamy wake. Boats are good for sunbathing. They can also be useful for exchanging travellers' information: you'll nearly always meet island-hoppers with news of elsewhere, or someone to team up with in the search for the perfect place to stay.

"I walk miles in totally unsuitable shoes . . . And I take lifts if someone stops, as they generally do."

I love to walk in Greece. There is something about the dry, blue, herb-scented heat that invigorates me. I walk miles in totally unsuitable shoes, armed with my paints and my swimsuit and a beer in case I don't reach a village. And I take lifts if someone stops, as they generally do. Usually, even if I am not thumbing, passing vehicles – anything from German tourists in Mercedes to those rickety three-wheeled trucks full of potatoes – will stop and offer a ride. Again, I've never encountered any problems. Because there are relatively few vehicles in country areas it is the natural thing to do, as it used to be in rural parts of England. I even take lifts at night.

I think what I love about being in Greece is that it is closer to how I feel life should be. I should be able to sit on a balcony overlooking the sea for my early morning coffee and late night brandy; I should be able to go out for a whole day leaving my door unlocked and knowing that nothing unpleasant will happen. The sky should always be blue and the sea transparent.

Greece for its people, though, is not heaven. The Greeks work very hard, particularly the women. Where there are a lot of tourists, the country's character is being sadly eroded by English-style pubs, bars and big hotels. But it is extraordinary how slow this erosion is and I am somehow confident that the Greeks will weather the onslaught of mass tourism: they are intrinsically so much themselves.

I have of course considered living there, but I really think Greece is a hard place for a foreign woman to settle in. I have come across quite a few women who have gone out and simply stayed on; they have a wonderful time, picking up work and drinking with the men in the bars. I met a German girl who stayed just one winter and said she would never do it again, as once the tourists had gone there was really no place for her in society. She could neither drink with the men, nor sit and crochet and talk babies with the women. And the few women I have encountered who have married Greeks don't seem very content, having little choice but to fit into their husbands' life-style, the extended family, the cooking, sewing, gardening, washing and having babies way of life that Greek women lead. As far as I am concerned my spring and autumn visits are perfect.

A Part of My Life

. . . .

Mary Castelborg-Koulma is half-Greek and visited Greece on and off as a child and later as a student. She went for a longer stay in 1974 – and remained for the next thirteen years.

I first went to live in Greece in 1974, the year the dictatorship fell. After a year of teaching in England, I'd had more than enough – and I had always promised myself a long stay in my mother's country.

Although I was brought up in England, I had gained at least a part knowledge of Greek culture, from trips as a child with my family, and later as a student. I was also reasonably at home with the language, which confers an immediate and vast advantage on any visitor. However, I had no idea that I would end up living in the country for the next decade and a bit – nor that it would become so much a part of me, my growth and development.

Like most graduates in Greece, I began life in Athens, working in one of the innumerable language schools, or *frontisteria*, that provide jobs, if not much money, for anyone with a degree and enthusiasm. My school was sited in one of the suburbs, a fact I was thank-ful for in the light of the city's ever-worsening pollution.

Living in this quarter also provided me with an escape route to the sea and the surrounding countryside, and made me feel I had made a wise decision in bringing over my British registration car (an old banger even then), despite endless hassles with the customs. I would never have been able to buy a car in Greece, where prices are about double those in Britain. Driving in Greece was at first a bit nerve-racking, though the necessary survival tactics didn't take too long to acquire.

The mid-Seventies and early Eighties were a good time to be in Greece, as the country basked in the revival of democracy after the oppressive years of the Colonels' dictatorship. When in 1981 the PanHellenic Socialist Party (PASOK) won the elections, the country seemed full of optimism and hope. These years also saw an incredible surge in tourism, which changed from small-scale to mass status in under a decade. Both factors coloured my experience.

On my trips out of Athens, I found myself growing more discriminating about where I chose to visit, listening to the advice of Greek friends in Athens about rural areas as yet unaffected by the tourist boom. Such advice was offered frequently and generously. An incredible proportion of the capital's population are recent emigrants from the countryside. Almost everyone has their "home village", with which they continue to identify, even if they visit just once a year for Easter or the local festival.

Some of my strongest memories are of trips I made in the winter months, when tourism was in virtual hibernation, and naturalness and quietness reigned. I will never forget the swans flying over the near-frozen lake of Ioannina, highlighted against a dark red sky; the gaunt old woman carrying a mountain of wood and sticks on her back, walking unsteadily through the snow on the outskirts of Florina; the night spent sleeping under a huge *flocati* rug near Vergia, when the roads were cut off. The winter was a time for roughing it. Accommodation often had little or no heating, and in these remote parts of the country – the region of Epirus kept drawing me – wolves were known to be on the prowl outside villages.

At Easter I joined up with Athenians returning to their villages for the festivities. The countryside was bursting with spring flowers and the scent of orange blossom filled the air. One of my best experiences was in the beautiful peninsula of Mount Pilion, drinking warm goat's milk for breakfast and helping to roast the Easter lamb on the spit.

"Harassment in Greece takes on a highly predictable and organised form"

In summer I headed for the islands, trying to figure out the least crowded and the least spoilt. One year, with a woman friend, I tried the island of Karpathos in the Dodecanese – then very remote, though changing now with the arrival of an airport. It was a stark insight into the differences between urban and island-rural Greek life. People there asked us why we didn't paint our fingernails or wear make-up – we lived in Athens, after all. I was learning what rural unworldliness meant.

The tourist resorts certainly lost their appeal for me. Travelling through Rhodes in midsummer was unbearable. If I spoke in Greek, the answer came back in English. Nothing was authentic. Harassment, too, was a problem. In Greece, it takes on a highly predictable and organised form: so much so, in fact, that its practitioners have a group name – *kamakia*. A *kamaki* means a harpoon and "to make *kamaki*" means "to fish"; the woman's role in this analogy is, of course, the fish.

Most Greek males have indulged in this practice at one time or another and *kamakia* are to be found more or less anywhere where there are tourists. They can be local, or on holiday from the cities, and their ages run from sixteen to sixty. Motives are varied. Some just want to spend a summer being treated by tourist women. Others might be looking for a prosperous foreign marriage, or even just a way into the woman's country for work or study. They are not often dangerous, though their techniques and persistence – "playing hard to get" is part of the bargaining culture – can be tedious. An indirect result of the phenomenon are the semi-pornographic postcards on sale throughout Greek resorts; depicting "sexually available" women, they probably perpetuate the practice of *kamakia*, too.

Later my experiences of this phenomenon – and my status, generally – changed, as I married a Greek and gave birth to a son. Travelling as a mother, with a child, puts you in a privileged position. Greece is a child-centred society and people go out of their way to give attention and show appreciation to children. It can take the edge off your exhaustion when someone comes up and offers to hold or play with the baby – and you can confidently accept. And a baby lets you off the hook of the *kamakia*, too.

"A positive development, if you actively want to make contact, are the Women's Agro-Tourist Co-operatives"

Greek women often appear peripheral bystanders from the viewpoint of a holiday experience. Yet they play a key role in providing the services that tourism requires in the typical small-scale family enterprise.

Because these jobs are home-bound, however, it can be hard to have any real interaction as a visitor. A positive development, if you actively want to make contact, are the Women's Agro-Tourist Co-operatives that have been set up in various areas of the country. These have been sponsored by the government Sexual Equality Secretariat and are intended to help rural women earn their own livelihood. The co-ops have been geared towards fairly remote communities – and towards local women who are often illiterate or semi-literate and may never have left their village. The women are given a bank loan to fix up a guestroom in their house in traditional style and are asked to provide bed and breakfast for visitors. The co-op arranges stays and keeps a five percent commission on the charges.

Curious to see how the project was faring, I chose to visit the co-op at Ambelakia, a mountain village in Macedonia, five hours' drive from Athens. Most of the co-op rooms had been taken by a large party of Germans, but a widow in her sixties was found, who had space for my family. We checked in and then set off for the huge café-restaurant in the main square, which was also associated with the co-op. I was surprised by the presence of so many local women, the co-op members, who were celebrating with their German guests, whose last evening it was. The women seemed to mingle easily, eating and drinking, and even leading the dancing; the men, by contrast, maintained a low profile. There was a lightness about the whole setting that seemed to confirm what I had been told by one of the co-op organisers in Athens, that the co-ops had "opened the women's spirits". It is a cheering thought, too, to leave the village and know that what you are paying goes directly into the women's pockets.

What the Chambermaid Saw

. . . .

Juliet Martin witnessed another side of tourism, working as a chambermaid on Crete. She explored the island in her spare time, mainly by hitching.

Having spent the first week of a vacation working as a waitress in a pub, I took a one-way plane ticket to Crete to search for similar work in the sun. It is not easy to find. I spent the first week unemployed in Heraklion spending what little money I had. You need a work permit to work there – too many tourist police about.

I ended up getting a job, by word of mouth, in a small resort outside Malia. In return for food and a small room shared with the laundry and cleaning materials I was to work three hours cleaning, occasionally taking the children swimming and doing other odd jobs. The work was tiring in that it took place when the sun was up. Although I was to start at 10am it was often later by the time the rooms were vacated. By midday the humidity made for exhaustion. Weekly, I had to travel up the mountain to clean some villas. For this I was given a moped, which often broke down. Pushing it loaded with linen and cleaning materials was more than tiring, and the mess left was often unpleasant, too. A kitchen table covered with brown sticky glue-like stuff proved a minor challenge. It was hot chocolate. On another occasion my employer's husband shouted at me for failing to remove the shit on the outside of a toilet. Somehow it had escaped my attention.

My boss was English. She'd come to Crete as a courier, "fallen in love with everything" (her words) and stayed to marry. Many of her women friends, also foreign, had fallen for the apparent dream-like existence on the island, married and become disillusioned. They would sit drinking gin and lemonade, discussing their unease. Many husbands were unfaithful, continuing their bachelor existence despite marriage. Nikos took off with a tourist "for dinner" the evening after his Dutch wife gave birth. This was "to celebrate". Such marriages can also cause division in the Greek family who may not accept the foreigner, since she has no dowry. Although it is accepted that men "play around" with tourists, it is still expected that their wives will be virgin locals.

"From the wings I witnessed the Greek beach bums picking out new tourists"

The foreign chambermaid is caught in the middle, neither part of the family/local scene nor a tourist. Many tourists used me to tell their life stories, though, and some included me in their socialising and on their trips around the island. The family frequently entertained relatives and friends for barbecue fish suppers. Although I was welcomed, language was often a barrier to full participation.

From the wings I witnessed the Greek beach bums picking out new tourists fortnightly, declaring unending passion for them, only to find a replacement from the next plane in from Scandinavia. These young men don't work; their mothers do. They are involved in servicing the hotels, usually as cleaners. One woman stood ironing bed linen all day for a hotel, her calves purple-knotted with veins. Such labour supported her son's endeavours to "get to know other cultures" – well, the female side anyway.

Theoretically I worked only mornings so there was plenty of time to see the island, mainly by hitching. Although the buses are cheap and frequent, this is a good option if you're broke. As a woman alone I felt confident hitching by day. Lifts are easy and can be fun if you don't mind the ridiculous conversations in simple English/Greek. Often I'd hitch into Heraklion to walk around the harbour or market or just to sit in the main square with a coffee. It's a big, dusty city relative to the rest of the island, but has its own charm.

Men in the towns or those who give you lifts may ask you for a drink or to meet them later. Refusals are quietly accepted. My trickiest situation was being driven to a deserted beach "to swim". He stripped off; I looked bored. No, I wasn't joining him. He could go ahead. He didn't. We drove on in silence to Ierapetra.

Mopeds and cars are easily hired for those with a bit more cash. Mopeds have a reputation for breaking down, but some places are only accessible in this way. I got to Lassithi Plateau in a tourist's hire car. It's well worth it, to see the thousands of white-sailed windpumps that serve to irrigate the region.

The views are incredible, but take a jumper – it gets blowy.

The most challenging day was spent walking the Samaria Gorge, the longest in Europe. The cheapest way of doing this excursion is to stay in Hania overnight and get the 6am bus to Omalos where the six-hour descent begins. On the way you'll see 1000ft drops, beautiful woodland and springs as well as wild goats. Halfway through is the deserted village of Samaria. At the end in Ayia Roumeli is a restaurant (not too pricey considering its position) and a boat which heads along the coast to Hora Sfakion. There a bus takes you back to Hania; it's a long day but well worth the effort.

Anyone wanting to combine work with travel in this way should take enough cash to get home and to spend during your stay. You may earn a little but not enough to get home. One-way flights from Crete are very expensive. The cheapest way is to get a deckclass ticket on an overnight boat from Heraklion or Hania to Piraeus, the port of Athens. From Athens you may be lucky to get a cheap flight or, failing that, the bus or train.

TRAVEL NOTES

Languages Greek. It's worth at least learning the alphabet to work out bus destinations and timetables. English (if only tourist essentials) is fairly widely understood, as many Greeks have worked abroad and there's a current proliferation of English language schools.

Transport An efficient, reasonably cheap bus service connects main towns and major resorts. Hitching – relatively safe – is accepted, if slow, in the isolated regions where buses do a daily round trip, if at all. Be careful of mopeds, hired out on most islands. Maintenance is a joke and accidents common on the dirt tracks. Island ferries get crowded so arrive early and leave time to get back for your flight – bad weather, strikes and out-of-date timetables make them unreliable.

Accommodation Plenty of cheap hotels, rooms in private houses and reasonably good campsites. Camping wild is illegal but often tolerated (police attitudes vary). On islands you'll be offered rooms as you get off the ferry – usually a good option for a first night.

Special Problems Kafeneia (cafés) are traditionally male territory; kamakia are a pain. See introduction and articles.

Guide The Rough Guide: Greece (Harrap-Columbus). A practical and honest guide, good on background, and which doesn't romanticise islands that are sometimes thoroughly spoilt.

Other Information The Greek Council for Equality in combination with the Greek National Tourist Organisation and Greek Productivity Centre have organised holidays with **Women's Agro-tourist Co-operatives**. Contact addresses are: LESVOS – Petra, Mitilini, ☎0253/41238; HIOS – c/o The Prefecture of Hios, ☎0271/25901; AMBELAKIA (near Larissa, central Greece) – ☎0495/93296; ARAHOVA (near Delphi) – ☎0267/31519; MARONIA (near Komotini, Thrace) – ☎0533/41258.

Contacts

Comprehensive **listings** for all feminist groups and centres in Greece appear in the women's Imerologio (diary) published in Athens by Eyrotyp (Kolonou 12-24), and meetings are often advertised in the English-language magazine, The Athenian (monthly from news stands). Those groups listed below are the more accessible contacts, particularly if you don't have good command of Greek.

Athens

Women's Bookstore, Massalias 20 at Skoufa; **Selana Bookstore**, Sina 38. The capital's two feminist bookshops are useful starting points for all contacts.

Genovefa "Our Ouzeri", 17 Novembriou 71, ☎653-2613. Women's café-bar.

Woman's House, Romanou Melodou 4 (entrance on a side street of Odos Dafnomili), Likavitos, ☎281-4823. The city's main feminist meeting point.

Xen, Amerikis 11. The Greek YWCA offer language courses for women and maintain a library and archive on feminism and women's issues.

Autonomous Women's Movement Contact Marika, ☎363-1224.

European Women's Network, Portaria 22–24, ☎691-3100.

Federation of Greek Women (*Omospondia Gynaekon Elladas*). Focuses on discrimination at work and disparities in pay; active in the peace movement. Main Athens branch at Akademias 52, ☎361-5565.

Union of Greek Women (*Enosis Gynaekon Elladas*). Emphasises the oppression of women in rural areas and Mediterranean women in general. It is responsible for forming the Council of Equality which has branches in all major towns – in Athens at Enianon 8, ☎823-4937.

Outside Athens

Thessaloniki: *Autonomous Women's Group*, Vass Irakliou 19; *Spiti Gynaekon* (women's bookshop), Yermanou 22.

Ioannina: *Steki Gynaekon* (women's bookshop), M. Kakara 25.

Books

Ursule Molinaro, *The New Moon with the Old Moon in her Arms* (The Women's Press, 1990). Witty and passionate novel, set in Ancient Athens, about a young poet who interprets the waning of the Moon Goddess, Circe, as an omen that women's position in society must be strengthened.

Katerina Anghelaki-Rooke, *Beings and Things on Their Own* (BOA editions, US, 1980). Powerful erotic poetry, full of sexual metaphor and sensuality.

Sheelagh Kanelli, *Nets* (The Women's Press, 1983). A short, lucid novel that reconstructs the events leading up to a disaster in a small Greek coastal village. Though British herself, Kanelli is married to a Greek and has lived there for some years.

Dido Sotiriou (author of *Endeli* and others) is perhaps the best known and most respected Greek woman novelist but none of her books have as yet been translated into English.

Journals

Feminist journals include *Dini* (Zoodohou Pigis 95–97, Athens), *Hypatia* (Pilion 1, Athens), and *Katina* (Vass. Irakliou 19, Thessaloniki).

Haiti

• • • • • • • • • • • • • • • • •

Haiti, covering one third of the Caribbean island of Hispaniola, is the poorest country in the Western hemisphere. Despite the achievement of early independence from the French in 1804, when a successful slave rebellion made Haiti the first independent black republic in the world, little has changed in terms of the exploitation of the mass of people by those in power.

From once being the richest colony in the Caribbean, Haiti has become entirely dependent on international foreign aid. Low agricultural productivity, over-population, political instability and the negative effects of deforestation have all contributed to a state of economic chaos which shows few signs of letting up. Any optimism inspired by the comparatively recent forced departure of Jean-Claude "Baby Doc" Duvalier, "President for Life" (a title inherited from his notorious father, "Papa Doc"), in 1986, has since reverted to despair in the face of persistent repression, corruption and a series of military coups. The main issue for Haiti's predominantly rural population is simply survival.

Besides Carnival, which draws hordes of tourists every year, the combination of political turmoil and shocking poverty has prevented Haiti from becoming a large-scale holiday haven for foreign visitors. There's certainly plenty of scope for adventure, though you may well feel better going with a more helpful purpose, for instance to work in some way with a relief agency. Theft is rife in and around the capital Port-au-Prince but elsewhere, provided you treat people with warmth and respect, you will find the atmosphere surprisingly relaxed. Sexual harassment does not appear to be a particular problem.

There are a great many grass-roots organisations in Haiti, working largely on popular education projects with the urban and rural poor. Most of them are affiliated to the church, the only place where people could get together to share their feelings under the Duvalier dictatorship. **Women's groups**, in particular, have multiplied since the departure of "Baby Doc" as women discover themselves gaining far more confidence in separate meetings. Despite some resistance, according to Claudette Werleigh, a leading Haitian educationalist, "the men are very aggressive and sometimes throw stones at them or the places they meet . . . the men think that the women are getting together just to criticise them." These meetings have formed the basis for a growing movement to campaign for women's issues within the framework of fighting for a better society.

A Fact-Finding Mission

. . . .

Worth Cooley-Prost is an American medical writer from Arlington, Virginia. She travelled to Haiti with a group of people from her local parish on a fact-finding visit to their sister parish in the small town of Cavaillon.

The four women in our group included a student in her late fifties, a widely-travelled secretary, a nun with a doctorate in counselling and myself, a medical writer. Our male traveller, a school guidance counsellor, had been to Haiti the previous spring with our parish priest.

Our visit began with a brief but unnerving exchange with the Haitian immigration officer. On seeing from our entry cards that we were going straight to Cavaillon rather than to Port-au-Prince, he became immediately interested and somewhat suspicious, questioning us at length about who we were going to visit and exactly what we were doing in Haiti. He finally proclaimed us "missionaries" and let us go through. It was a good early remin-

der that we were visiting a military dictatorship where anything perceived as unusual was considered potentially threatening.

Once outside the airport, we were immediately overwhelmed by the sea of people, riotous traffic, including small herds of cows, and waves of smells – charcoal, garbage, incense, sewage, cooking. The road was lined with tiny store-fronts and everywhere there were groups of people gathered around small fires and women carrying whole tables of food and other objects on their heads. Added to the visual and olfactory riot was noise: people singing, dogs barking, children screaming, horns blowing and music blaring from *tap taps*, the small brightly painted covered pick-up trucks, always jammed with people, that serve as public transport throughout Haiti. We were grateful that the Cavaillon priest had arrived to act as our translator and guide.

Beyond the city the traffic quickly thinned to nothing. We would drive for miles in absolute darkness, then suddenly come upon a busy late-night throng of people around fires at the side of the road. Twice we encountered *rah-rah* bands, rowdy groups of men and boys dancing in the road with drums and rum late at night. The first simply opened ranks to let us pass, but the second had a hostile air and the priest had to pay them to let us go on. Without his Creole, we'd have been lost in that situation, unable to interpret what was going on and thus unable to gauge the response.

Cavaillon is a town of about 1000 people, some three hours drive west of Port-au-Prince. Electricity is on for four hours each evening, but few houses are wired; virtually none have running water or refrigeration. With the exception of some military jeeps and our own car, about the only motor vehicles we saw were *tap taps* passing through.

We stayed in the rectory, a castle-like concrete hulk towering on a hill at the edge of town, with a distinctly medieval feel. Cold running water, indoor toilets and showers all extremely unusual in this area, had been added only in the past year. The system was very rudimentary: when our toilet flushed, our shower responded in kind. The "kitchen house", a free-standing concrete room in the backyard, held the cooking utensils and three big wood fires. Meals were prepared on a table outdoors and whatever animal was destined to be eaten that day (during our stay, a turkey, several chickens, and a goat) was slaughtered behind the house. A couple of skinny dogs haunted this area. Unconsumed garbage and plain trash got dumped in a pile a little way up the hill behind the yard, left for the elements to dispatch over time.

Visitors were clearly a burden for the three women who lived and worked at the rectory; in addition to having to prepare meals for five extra people, all water used for our coffee and cooking had to be boiled. The women, in their mid-twenties, shared one bedroom and by all appearances functioned as house servants. They were up at six each morning to start the kitchen fires, mop the house and porches, and sweep the yard before breakfast was laid out. The rest of their day consisted of more cooking, cleaning, and doing laundry in the yard. When the electricity came on each night, one of them would immediately spread a sheet on the floor of the meeting room and begin ironing. Later, they would wait for everyone to retire, before locking every bedroom door from the outside – a distinctly eerie feeling.

"Attempts to help with any of the chores seemed to be inappropriate, even mildly alarming"

Only the educated minority in Haiti speak French, while everyone speaks Creole. Language serves as a social barrier within the culture as well as to visitors – all government pronouncements, laws and court proceedings are in French. Our absolute inability to talk to the women in the rectory made us feel very uncomfortable and attempts to help with any of the chores seemed to be inappropriate, even mildly alarming to them.

Every morning I'd wake about six, realise I could sleep another hour or two, then remember where I was and be up for the day. None of the other visitors woke up that early and I used to treasure my time alone on the balcony just watching and listening. Country or city, roosters crowed and dogs barked around the clock. A typical house in Cavaillon consists of a one-room concrete hut without kitchen, water or toilet facilities. Four families, including ten children, lived in the little house below the rectory which can't have been more than ten feet square. Soon after dawn one or two of the children would head down to the river to bring back water in big plastic pails. These stayed in the yard and people gradually came out one at a time to wash, while the younger children sat quietly on a stump in the yard and fixed each other's hair. The process looked so calm and measured in the early light.

Soon trucks began passing on the way to and from the mountains, cows were led down the road toward the riverside marketplace, and hordes of children in various coloured uniforms gathered for school. One morning we visited the priest's school, taking some notebooks and posters we had brought from home. (Paper is very expensive in Haiti; at one mountain school we saw, the children use nothing but slates and chalk.) About 200 children attended, at a cost of around six dollars a month for tuition and supplies. Since the average annual income for a Cavaillon family is only a hundred dollars, many cannot afford to send their children at all.

It was upsetting to see ninety children, crowded three to a rickety desk, shiny little faces reciting in French to one single teacher. These few years of elementary school – no more than three percent of children in rural areas advance any further – are achieved through great family struggle and yet have virtually nothing to do with the everyday reality of people's lives. The illiteracy rate in Haiti is eighty percent – and for women, ninety percent. In 1980 a national adult literacy campaign, Missyon Alfa, was launched by the Catholic Church. Individuals from each community were trained in basic literacy and community organising skills, then sent back to work with their people around local issues.

The programme's popularity quickly led to threats, arrests and even murders. While an educational system that involves a few years of rote drills in French does not threaten any military dictatorship, Missyon Alfa was quite another matter. We were told of a meeting between one of the Missyon Alfa founders and the government Minister of Education. "It's all very well," said the latter, "to teach a peasant to write 'The sun is rising and the day is beautiful', but if you teach that, then he can also write, 'I am poor and I know the reasons'." The violence against Missyon Alfa grew such that the programme was suspended in early 1988.

One Sunday we drove into the mountains. In parts this country is unbelievably beautiful, with primeval forest at every other turn, and, at the beach of Port Salud, the Caribbean a shimmer of unearthly green and blues, the mountains rising right at the edge of the sea. Everywhere, the people showed a friendly interest in us, though language beyond "hello" remained a real barrier. Open markets at crossroads were full of women squatting by baskets of grain, fruits, and an amazing array of plastics from Taiwan.

"The boys either roam around town in small groups or tend cows or goats; only girls under about three years old seemed to be free to play"

We attended a mass with about a hundred Haitians in a tiny mountain chapel. The service lasted almost two hours, with a lot of singing and talking back and forth between the priest and the people. The music was accompanied by drums, wood pipes and rhythm produced by scratching a sort of wand along a metal tube. We could understand none of the words, of course, but were struck by how universal the mass itself is. Without any language, we felt full participants in the service and a bond with people that simply wasn't possible in other settings.

In Port-au-Prince, we stayed in a guesthouse run by a Canadian who moved to Haiti twenty-eight years ago to do quickie divorces. Our rooms were rather seedy by American standards and had neither air conditioning nor hot water, but we were comfortable. The proprietor told us that women were unquestionably the backbone of the country, functioning as the planners, administrators, and marketers. Overtly, the culture is male dominated. When the school day ended in Cavaillon, boys played outside while the girls disappeared to do chores. Among children who don't go to school at all, the boys either roam around town in small groups or tend cows or goats; only girls under about three years old seemed to be free to play. We saw no men cooking, cleaning or washing clothes, although perhaps a tenth of those selling at countryside marketplaces were men.

The degree of poverty everywhere in Haiti is difficult to express. In the huge city slums it is shocking; one of our group commented that even Calcutta was benign in comparison to City Soleil, the largest of the Port-au-Prince slums. Tens of thousands of people live, somehow, in a filthy concrete rabbit warren of tiny rooms and tinier alleys, all connected like a giant maze except for open areas where the sewer trenches serve also as washing and water gathering places. Even so, the people we greeted were usually openly friendly. My most lasting impression of City Soleil was the endurance of the impossible with genuine dignity. Until drawn to the city by promises of factory jobs over the past decade, many of these people lived as subsistence farmers in the countryside, where at least they fed their children: in the city, their apparent powerlessness is overwhelming.

In the countryside, a marketplace appears wherever a river meets a road. In the city, the street itself is the river: everywhere we went, sidewalks and the edges of the street were crowded with people, mostly women and girls, minding a dizzying array of vegetables, clothes, plastics. Much of the food consisted of cans and boxes, mostly American brands, some of it clearly marked as donated by CARE or some other relief agency. Food, especially US food, has a great deal to do with the poverty in Haiti. American policy toward developing nations stresses "food security", the argument being that modern production methods provide more, better and cheaper food. Therefore, instead of growing their own food, these countries should buy food from the US, and in order to have money to buy that food, the people should work in foreign-owned assembly industries.

Haitian friends had counselled us against responding to street children begging, since giving even small change would accomplish little for the child and would result in our being besieged by hundreds of other children. They advised us to say "Later" and keep walking. We also found that persistent vendors generally withdrew when we said "Finis"; otherwise, at times we were unable to walk a block in less than fifteen minutes. Efforts to politely decline an article for sale were invariably interpreted as an invitation to bargain, leaving us feeling confused and hassled and the vendor angry.

"Riding a tap tap would have felt like a tourist lark of some sort"

In terms of getting around, I saw no non-Haitian hitchhiking and wouldn't recommend it. Communicating about such simple things as bottled water is hard enough. You could ride a *tap tap*, but we were uncomfortable, as white foreigners, about being granted a markedly different status than the Haitian women. Riding a *tap tap* would have felt like a tourist lark of some sort and an insult to the local women who are forced to sit on the floor if a man wants a seat. Sexual harassment was not an issue, perhaps in part again because we had no earthly idea what was being said in Creole and because we were rarely out alone. I also thought that, given such complete poverty, if a woman went out stark naked except for a purse, it would be the purse that drew the attention.

Ironies abounded throughout our trip. In the city, with its garbage-filled gutters and people struggling to sell scraps of something to another poor person, we saw beauty shops on every other corner. Advertisements for pain pills were epidemic. Most of all, I was struck with the juxtaposition of beauty and ugliness.

The people themselves have a gracefulness I've never seen anywhere else – the curve of a jaw, the fluid elegance tossed off by a woman swatting a fly, the beautiful open faces. Haitians also impressed me as vibrant, creative and powerful. This grace and power exist within a culture marked from its beginnings by restriction and brutality, both foreign and domestic, whose proverbs observe that laws are made of paper while machetes are made of steel.

TRAVEL NOTES

Languages All Haitians speak Creole, derived from French and African dialects. The fifteen percent or so who have had schooling also speak French and often some English.

Transport Collective taxis, known as *publiques*, and *tap taps* run between all main towns, usually leaving whenever they are full.

Accommodation Low-cost rooms, often including one or two meals, can be arranged through various religious missions. Port-au-Prince has a few major hotels, but lodging in the countryside is best arranged in advance.

Guides *The South American Handbook* (Trade and Travel Publications) has a small but useful section on Haiti.

Contacts

There are a number of **missions and human rights groups** in Haiti. Worth Cooley-Prost recommends first getting in touch with the Holy Ghost Fathers in Port-au-Prince or Mission Wallace outside Petionville.

We have been unable to locate any women's groups. However, it may be worth writing to the **Caribbean Association for Feminist Research and Action**, PO Box 442, Tuniapuna PO, Tuniapuna, Trinidad and Tobago, which is dedicated to developing the women's movement throughout the Caribbean.

Books

Mary Evelyn Jegen, *Haiti: The Struggle Continues* (Pax Christi, US). Excellent 58-page booklet providing an overview of the recent situation in Haiti with an emphasis on the status of women. Available (for US$2 plus postage) from Pax Christi USA, 348 E. 10th St., Erie, PA 16503.

Claudette Werleigh, *Working for Change in Haiti* (CIIR, 1989). This short booklet, published by the Catholic Institute for International Relations, describes the work of Haiti's popular education movement.

James Ferguson, *Papa Doc, Baby Doc: Haiti and the Duvaliers* (Basil Blackwell, 1987). Lively and accurate account of the rise and fall of the country's notorious dictatorship.

Alejo Carpentier, *The Kingdom of this World* (Penguin, 1980). Powerful novel, based on the slave revolt that first created the black republic of Haiti. Out of print, but worth tracking down in a library.

Hong Kong

Hong Kong is in the grips of a deepening crisis of confidence about its future. Since the signing of the Sino-British agreement to return the colony to Chinese sovereignty in 1997, a steady stream of citizens have been leaving the country.

It has now become a flood. The June 4th massacre in Tiananmen Square effectively erased hopes that China will keep to its bargain and allow Hong Kong's economic freedoms to continue for the next half century. For the vast majority who have neither money nor connections enough to emigrate, anger is mounting at the British colonial government's continuing concessions to China and refusal to grant citizens the right of abode in Britain. On top of this there are considerable tensions over the daily influx of Vietnamese refugees, housed in crowded island refugee camps. With space already at a premium, pressure is growing to launch a programme of forced repatriation.

Ironically, Hong Kong remains a land of opportunity for Western expatriate workers, who are offered increasing incentives (low taxes and few currency restrictions) to fill the rapidly dwindling professional class. The cost of living is high but then so are the wages, and many women with British qualifications come here on two- to three-year contracts to boost savings. Luxury hotels, apartment blocks, an amazing range of restaurants and clubs, and the much-touted shopping areas of Kowloon and Hong Kong Island reflect the lavish lifestyle of the multinational business community, as well as catering for nearly three million visitors a year.

Whilst you might well feel bewildered and overwhelmed by the rampant consumerism, crowded streets and the hectic pace of Hong Kong life you're unlikely to feel under any personal threat. Harassment and violent crime certainly occur but they tend to be contained within the different communities. You can expect far more trouble from sexist foreign residents than the Hong Kong Chinese. It can, however, take a while to adjust to being an outsider in this country. The well established ex-pat scene has all the distasteful elements of colonialism and commercial opportunism – creating an independent social network can be a slow and isolating process.

Within the Chinese community women are expected to take on the full burden of domestic work and also to help ensure the family's survival in the economic rat race by working long, hard hours in family businesses, sweatshops etc. For middle-class women these pressures are eased by the use of migrant labour – mainly Filipina maids or Chinese *amahs*. The majority, however, have to rely on support from extended family networks, a resource which is gradually being eroded by the continuing waves of emigration and the move towards living in tiny multistorey flats. With few welfare provisions, no unemployment benefits, costly health and education services, and intense overcrowding, life for most women is fundamentally insecure and stressful. There is little by way of a co-ordinated **women's movement** in Hong Kong and, in general, little interest is shown in feminist debate. The largest and most influential women's organisation, the *Hong Kong Council of Women*, is heavily dominated by ex-pats and, as such, is criticised for being elitist and out of step with the priorities of the Hong Kong Chinese. Its attempts to launch overtly feminist campaigns, against sexual discrimination and harassment, have floundered through lack of support. Much more popular are the grassroots groups (*ying ngai*) based in the larger estates, that offer practical support, communal activities and classes (anything from childrearing to international currency exchange).

An Uneasy Path

· · · · · · · · · · · ·

Alison Saheed travelled to Hong Kong in 1974 to work for a while before journeying across Asia. She stayed thirteen years, worked in various jobs, married and had two children. She eventually had to return to Britain with her family in order to escape the restrictions of the new nationality laws.

Arriving in Hong Kong in the post-summer heat of autumn 1974 knowing no one and with no preconceptions about the place, I little realised that it would be my home for the next thirteen years. Those years threw up dramatic changes for Hong Kong both politically and socially; a shift in attitudes, the emergence of a burgeoning Chinese middle class, Mao Tse Tung's death and the doors opening to China. It also finally became clear that its time as a freewheeling, often exploited entrepot was running out as 1997 crept closer. In that time, I too experienced changes; having arrived young, free and single I left wiser, married, a mother twice over, and with three career switches behind me.

"Above all, I suddenly felt very large and ungainly next to people of much slighter build"

Initial impressions were not favourable; Hong Kong struck me as a hard, harsh place without any softness, its neon-lit buildings perched on the waterfronts, impersonal. The population, all distinctly Chinese as far as I could see, seemed brusque, forever busy, and, contrary to tourist pamphlets, emphatically did not speak English. Humidity, something I had never encountered, seeped from every crevice, interrupted only by blasts of icy cold air conditioning from inside the angular buildings. The smells of cooked food stalls in the streets, and the sights of fresh food in open air markets, so intrinsic a part of life in Asia, were new to me and initially sometimes overwhelming. Above all, I suddenly felt very large and ungainly next to people of much slighter build.

Arriving fresh from an easygoing southern European lifestyle, I was unprepared for the division that appeared to exist between the local populace and the foreign elements. I was shocked by the attitudes of the Europeans I was to meet initally; elitist, racist and snobbish, to me like creatures dragged out of a Somerset Maugham story – characteristics I would later learn were more than equalled by many Chinese.

I met no other European women at that time and to this day cannot fathom where they were. Consequently, the only English speakers I came across were men whom I found to be chauvinistic to extremes. To compound it all, everyone, it seemed, had been in Asia for a very long time. Life, apparently, simply did not exist outside and I grew tired of the catch phrase "You don't

understand, this is Hong Kong/Asia", whenever I queried something unfathomable. All in all, I felt I had inadvertently wandered into the wrong party.

Retreating from this chilly reception, I decided to get on with my life and set about looking for a place to stay and work. The first proved to be easy and I ended up sharing a flat with three Asian career women, two Overseas Chinese women who had grown up in other parts of Asia and had come to Hong Kong to link up with their roots, and a locally born Eurasian woman. I didn't realise then that it was extremely rare for a European woman to live with Asians, nor that the assumption, on the Chinese side, was that only women of loose morals would live away from home. As it turned out, my flatmates saved my sanity through those bleak early times with a sensitive blend of loyalty, tolerance and patience and we remain firm friends today. They also unknowingly taught me a great deal about the Chinese way of thinking and introduced me to aspects which could have taken me years to discover.

Not being particularly career oriented at that time, I continued on the path I had been on in Europe and found a job teaching English in a Chinese-run language school. Here I confronted an impenetrable mask of "no response". I did not know that schools taught by rote method, that the teacher was highly regarded and would be listened to unquestioningly, and that a blank "no" to a question could mask any number of conflicting emotions, ranging from an unwillingness to give the wrong answer and thus lose face or an equal unwillingness to admit that the question had not been understood.

My students were extremely polite, and in casual chats showed great charm and interest, but I was initially baffled by their attitudes. Culture shock by now had well set in. I muddled through, not even realising what it was. Today, there are counselling services available for precisely that in Hong Kong.

"Gaining or losing face" is a concept bandied around a great deal with regard to the Chinese, as if, for some reason, it was unimportant to anyone else. Simply put, it is akin to maintaining your pride but it is much more extensive than that, encompassing many aspects of life whether through openly grandiose gestures or small seemingly insignificant ones. It runs through controlling one's emotions to the meaning behind the spoken word. It has something to do with how you are perceived by those around you and verges almost on a power trip rather than internalised values. I never really came to terms with it.

Breaking through language barriers is also difficult. Cantonese is mastered by few foreigners and is fraught with tonal disasters for the novice. Cantonese love to play with words, much like the English, and words can be changed easily by altering the tones. At one time I lived at an address which, if pronounced incorrectly, equalled a proposition and amused many a taxi driver as I grappled with my "tones". Just a few words of Cantonese can generally evoke a very different open response, particularly in the marketplace if only you can follow the flow of Cantonese that you elicit. I did not manage to learn much though I eventually came to understand a lot of what was being said around me.

But one sure way to crash all barriers is to have a child. I had my elder son in a charity-run hospital in a poor part of town because it was recommended to me. Not having had a child before, I didn't know quite what to expect, but when the time came, it seemed to me to be perfectly adequate. The hospital was run by nuns and men were kept well away while they got on with "women's business". I went into labour, was given a ghastly enema and then sent to lie down in the equivalent of a "waiting room" staffed by an old *amah* who wandered around checking on dilation. I felt very alone and scared

as labour progressed. I was then wheeled into the delivery room where two midwives attached my legs to stirrups and told me in schoolteacherly tones to push. An obstruction in my son's throat after his birth was dealt with briskly and efficiently and he was carried off to be bathed. I was not however, prepared for the painful stitches and more than once was told to behave myself.

Afterwards the staff couldn't have been kinder and I was given all sorts of concessions, including open visiting hours, partly, I believe, because I was the first European to have a baby in that hospital. Although they were at that time promoting bottle feeding, when I explained my preference to breast, they complied.

"I was bewildered when I took my newborn baby to the shops with me as everyone stared at us"

Post-natal care was excellent and when I did develop an infection, they kept me in until they were satisfied and then released me only on condition that I be seen three times a week at home by a nurse, which they arranged. I was in an open ward filled with new mothers whom I shocked by taking a shower and washing my hair after giving birth. Chinese tradition dictates that post-natal mothers do neither until one month after delivery. Special foods, too, are prepared for the mothers and brought to them by visiting relatives. Often soups, they contain vegetables and ingredients to cleanse the blood and act as tonics. After being discharged from hospital, my ex-flatmate very kindly brought me those dishes prepared by her mother.

Superstition runs parallel with tradition regarding newborns and great care is taken to follow the rigid procedures. I was bewildered when I took my newborn baby to the shops with me as everyone stared at us. I was to discover that, according to Chinese custom, a baby should never be taken outside so young for he/she will fall prey to evil elements.

Children are all important to the Chinese family; they secure the lineage and ensure, in turn, that their parents will be looked after when they are old. They are welcomed, protected with a vengeance, and are accepted as a part of life. You will find, in any restaurant, large families including babies and toddlers eating together. Waiters often play with them. They are picked up, cuddled, played with, admired in public wherever you happen to be.

Consequently, I never felt trapped by my child. I took him everywhere with me and never once felt we were intruding. Returning to part-time work shortly after his birth I found, through a friend, a large gregarious Portuguese family who simply absorbed him into their den until I picked him up after work. This is one of the most positive aspects of life in Hong Kong for working mothers; help is available. You pay for it but it is worth it if, like me, you need to work.

This childcare freed me to search for a more satisfying form of employment. This to me is another plus about the place. If you are willing to try, you can break into new fields. Hong Kong pivots on the axle of rapid change so it makes sense to go along with it. You don't have to stay stuck in a rut. Entrepreneurial flair helps too. I am not talking about the white collar professions so much as the person who is vaguely dissatisfied with his or her chosen occupation and wants to venture into something completely different.

At one time I was teaching alongside three female colleagues and all of us knew we wanted out. We each struck out on our own paths. One took up Asian studies at the university, then joined a magazine which concentrated on the politics of the region, was then posted to the Bangkok bureau for a couple of years before returning, with

the same magazine, to Hong Kong. Another did management studies and was hired by an international hotel group to teach her subject in Bali. The third is now near the top notch in an educational publishing house. I worked at a radio station as assistant producer, learning the ropes for three years, while tentatively trying to write articles, had a bash at PR, then freelance writing with a bit of broadcasting thrown in, and finally ended up co-ordinating a new weekly lifestyle publication for one of the English-language newspapers.

For all of us, the transitions and stumbling around in new areas took a long time and lots of hard work, but we found it could be done. The momentum of Hong Kong tends to carry you along and you have the added pressure of not being able to give up because of the very real financial burdens.

"Sexism from Western men is still strong and Asia, with its tradition of submissive women, promotes it"

Money is at the root of the zeal. "No money, no life" goes the Cantonese saying and it is based on reality. There is, after all, no welfare state and no subsidised study. You pay for what you get. Consequently, if you have the fortune, you flaunt it and if you don't then you try to dress as if you do. People in Hong Kong are well-dressed, even if it's casual wear. And there is no excuse for being sloppily dressed because ultra cheap bargains abound on the market stalls. Salaries are wildly fluctuating and uncontrolled with massive disparities of income. This imbalance means a lot of sniping by everyone and you are constantly reminded of the inequality wherever you go. Socialising is to a great degree an extension of work and as such tends to take place outside the home. Needless to say, it places a great strain on personal relationships.

While a fair number of Chinese women marry foreign men, the reverse is not so. In general, Chinese men are not particularly attracted to European women, which leaves you free from any harassment at the office or in the street. It also enables you to function freely at work, deemed as you are as sort of sexless. Sexism from Western men is still strong and Asia, with its tradition of "submissive women", promotes it. Most Chinese women have jobs and those who manage to clamber up the corporate ladder have had to fight tooth and nail for it in hailstorms of Chinese male chauvinism.

"To be British in Hong Kong, if you are remotely sensitive, is to tread an uneasy path fraught with conflicting emotions"

Hence the "dragon lady" syndrome – a fiercely neurotic holder of power, whose tactics in maintaining it make her Western counterparts look like puffballs. Not surprisingly, many of the high flyers are unmarried as the balancing act between being very successful in the workplace, while giving your husband face by being submissive at home, must be a nightmare.

To be British in Hong Kong, if you are remotely sensitive, is to tread an uneasy path fraught with conflicting emotions. It has been, after all, a British colony, ruled by a government which receives its instructions from Britain and as such is terminally out of touch with the population it is supposed to be governing. The Sino-British Treaty regarding the handover of Hong Kong in 1997; the ensuing wrangles over the Basic Law drafting; and the resulting loss of nationality for Hong Kong British passport holders has done little to aid race relations. And the British government's current policy on kowtowing to China for future trade while ignoring the fate of some six million people is impossible to justify.

No one knows what will happen in Hong Kong, one can only go on indicators. What to me is tragic is that the people the place needs, mainly the expanding middle class, well educated, bright and responsible are leaving in droves. The very rich have already set up their families in Australia, Canada or the USA and return to Hong Kong for business, their boltholes secured. The rest are either left there or are desperately trying to figure out where else they can go. No one really wants to leave. With regard to Hong Kong's future, money may well win out. Chinese millionaires have for years now been pouring money into the mainland in the form of hotels, factories and leisure centres. They have smoothed their path and their way of doing it may well prove to be a great deal more successful than the fumblings of the British government.

A year or two ago, I would have advised anyone going to Hong Kong that the localisation policies had tightened up the job market for non-Chinese. Today, I understand this has gone into reverse due to the large numbers of people leaving. It was hinted at recently that Hong Kong will soon have to recruit foreigners again to fill the burgeoning middle management vacancies that are growing daily.

TRAVEL NOTES

Languages Cantonese. English is widely spoken in the main tourist areas.

Transport Easy and cheap by bus, ferry, tram and train.

Accommodation There's plenty of it but it tends to be expensive. Cheapest are probably the YMCAs (Salisbury Rd., Kowloon, ☎3-692-211, and overspill, 23 Waterloo Rd. (Yaumatei), Kowloon, ☎3-319-111), which admit both women and men.

Guides *The Rough Guide China* (Harrap Columbus). Look out for the forthcoming *Rough Guide: Hong Kong* (Harrap Columbus). The local tourist board supply reams of information at points of arrival.

Contacts

Association for the Advancement of Feminism in Hong Kong, Room 1202, Yam Tze Commercial Building, 17-23 Thomson Rd., Wanchai, ☎05 282510. Created in 1984 by local Chinese women, the group collects information on women's social and political participation. They produce a news digest on women in Hong Kong and China.

Hong Kong Council of Women, S 32/F Lai Kwai House, Lai Kok Estate, Kowloon, ☎3 866256. Originally set up by Chinese women to fight for the abolition of concubinage. Now a fully-fledged feminist group, with resource library and telephone information service.

Asian Students Association (ASA), 511 Nathan Rd, 1/F, Kowloon, Hong Kong. The ASA takes a strong anti-imperialist, anti-colonialist and anti-racist stand. Its **Women's Commission** set up in 1975, is currently chaired by the League of Filipino Students (LFS) and promotes the emancipation of women and encourages the formation of national women's groups. ASA publishes a bi-monthly *Asian Students News* which includes regular information about women's struggles in Asia.

Books

J W Salaff, *Working Daughters of Hong Kong: Filial Piety or Power in the Family* (Cambridge University Press, 1981). In-depth study of working women in Hong Kong and the effects of industrialisation upon family life.

Xi Xi, *A Girl Like Me* (Renditions, Washington UP, 1986). A collection of short stories drawing on the traditional Chinese and modern Western experience of Hong Kong.

Thanks to Deborah Singerman for help with the introduction and Travel Details.

Hungary

· · · · · · · · · · · · · ·

After years of experimenting with political and economic reforms, Hungary has now launched itself as an entirely new entity in Europe, a multiparty Socialist state. Yet the outcome and implications of such a vast and rapid change (including dismantling the border with Austria, transforming the Communist Party and instituting the first "free" elections in the Eastern bloc) remains deeply uncertain. A critical issue seems to be how far the West will back up its supportive rhetoric with large and timely foreign loans. This sudden opening up is providing a boost to an already very well established tourist industry – in the summer months there are said to be more foreign visitors than Hungarians in the country. Most are from neighbouring Austria and West Germany, lured by cheap holidays in the resorts around Lake Balaton or in Budapest. But in recent years there have been an increasing number, too, from Britain, The Netherlands and the US.

Arriving in Hungary it can take a while to register that you've crossed into an Eastern bloc country; there are no minimum currency change requirements, few restrictions on where you can stay (many people rent out rooms in their homes), few hassles with black marketeers and a surprising degree of Western-style consumerism. Budapest especially is a highly cosmopolitan city with a lively café scene and numerous hotels, shops, restaurants and bars competing for the tourist trade. Yet unlike its Western counterparts, the capital has a reputation for safety. There are few problems in wandering around alone, even at night, although taxis are cheap enough to make this unnecessary. Outside of the main cities people may seem curious about you or concerned for your safety – old notions of "gallantry" towards women have been slow to fade and although this can seem intrusive at times it's rarely threatening.

Amongst the plethora of oppositional parties that have sprung up over the last few years, there are as yet no autonomous **women's groups** or organisations. In fact "feminism" tends to have negative connotations in Hungary, as an old piece of Communist propaganda, and a distraction from the main business of gaining democratic rights. The state-organised *National Alliance of Hungarian Women*, which campaigns around issues such as equal pay for equal work, is too clearly a party vehicle to gain much support. In many ways the political climate carries echoes of Britain in the Sixties. Pornography, which has long been the cornerstone of Hungary's booming advertising industry, is widely used to express sexual liberation, with little debate as to how such images exploit and degrade women.

Teaching in Pest
. . . .

Victoria Clark, a teacher and free-lance writer based in London, spent two years teaching English in Budapest. She lived alone in a rented flat for much of this time and travelled widely around the country. Since her contract finished she has returned to Budapest for holidays.

How can I explain a relentless pull towards Eastern Europe? I arrived in Budapest pretending to myself that I would stay there long enough to learn a Slav language and would then set off across the Eastern bloc. In fact, as soon as I stepped off the train from Vienna, I had a feeling that I had come home and that night made up my mind to stay on for as long as I could. My vague plans would anyway have proved impossible; Hungarian is of Finno-Urgic not Slavonic origin and is famously impenetrable, spiked as it is with accents, prefixes and suffixes. Also, being employed by one of the privately formed teaching co-operatives, I was paid in non-convertible Hungarian currency which I could not, as a Westerner, spend on travel outside the country.

I was, however, delighted by the astonishing beauty of the city in autumn; by the feverish entrepreneurial energy of a people beginning to shake off the effects of forty years of totalitarian rule; by the Chinese toothpaste, Albanian eels and Vietnamese lychees in the shops. It was easy to ignore the fact that I would surely be leaving Hungary poorer than when I arrived.

After two years of luxurious living in Barcelona, it took a while for my system to adjust to Budapest. I was housed in a ten-storey concrete block on the road out to the airport. My first evening, I emerged from the nearest metro (whose name translates as Sporty Street) to find myself lost in a dark forest of identical concrete blocks, any one of which might have been mine. An elderly gentleman with a rusty command of Hapsburg Empire German called me "Dear Lady", directed me to my flat and clicked his heels before bidding me goodnight. For the first three months I lived off bread and imitation brie, expensive cans of Israeli orange juice and quick-souring milk in bursting plastic bags. Not because there was nothing else to eat, but because I couldn't read the labels on the packages.

My students at the language school were an uneasy but interesting mix. Many were the children of the nouveau riche who lived in new villas on the verdant slopes of the Buda Hills, built from the profits of a greengrocery or Barbie Doll importing business; others were from the tired remnants of the intelligentsia. Even if there were not enough pens, textbooks or classroom space, even if thirty and not fifteen non-English-speaking children turned up for my first class in the living room of a sixth-floor flat, my work was extremely enjoyable. Most of my colleagues were Hungarian women who also worked at the university or in grammar schools and were fantastically committed teachers in a society which respects the profession.

When a private student kindly offered me his flat rent-free for the following year, I had nothing more to ask for. Having a flat all to yourself is an almost unthinkable privilege in this overcrowded capital. I knew of large families who had to make do with a few rooms, and divorced couples who led completely separate lives but remained under the same roof for want of anywhere else to stay.

"The old woman had soon gained enough information about me to conclude that I was a foreign prostitute"

Number 3 Garibaldi utca, its roof graced by three crumbling stone muses, was supported by sturdy wooden scaffolding. Like many buildings in downtown Pest it was due for renovation and had a hallway strewn with dust and rubble and broken glass. On the concierge's door by the wrought-iron lift was a sign which read "House Supervisor" – a tatty relic of the terror-stricken Fifties. Flicking at the greasy curtain over the window in her door, the old woman had soon gained enough information about me to conclude that I was a foreign prostitute and before long I had a visit from a forlorn plainclothes policeman in a bomber jacket. I shouldn't have been surprised that she'd interpret my visits from students in this way. It seemed to me that, much like Britain in the Sixties, sex had become a popular obsession.

I was very happy in that dingy second-floor flat with its high ceilings and badly appointed rooms, and would often just sit there watching street scenes from the window. At one end of the narrow street stood a caravan selling the chocolate pastries I bought for my breakfast. At the other end I could catch glorious sunlit glimpses of the steeples and domes of Buda across the River Danube. The fairy-tale Gothic parliament was just around the corner, my school five minutes' walk away, my favourite cheap restaurant closer still. On March 15th I marched around the city all afternoon to commemorate the Revolution of 1948 and challenge the restrictions of the present day. This was the thick of it!

I never moved across the river to live in Buda. Pest, with its long tree-lined avenues and extravagant Art Nouveau, was the real hub of the city. Like a mini-Vienna, Pest has its opera house and parks and austerely grandiose government buildings, where Buda strikes me as altogether less civilised, more medieval, with its castle, Turkish bath-houses and pattern-roofed churches clustered around the hills. Buda is for the tourists and elegant relaxation; Pest is for the serious business of living and working in the city.

I found Hungarians a serious people – overworked, intense, sceptical and often alarmingly intellectual. It was only in the summer months at the resorts around Lake Balaton that I had a glimpse of a more happy-go-lucky and relaxed approach to life. Staying at a friend's lakeside villa one August weekend, it was refreshing to see my hosts rising late and downing a thimbleful of brandy before tucking into a healthy breakfast of spring onions, green peppers, cream cheese and coffee.

Another summer I stayed at Szigliget, in a country mansion confiscated by the Communists after the war and used as a holiday home for the Writers' Union, where I watched eminent writers in shorts discussing "literature" until the small hours of the morning. I would sometimes retreat to the lake with Agota, a teaching colleague whose mother had a cottage on the northern bank. It had been her grandfather's property before the war and she had spent all the summers of her childhood there. The Communists had confiscated most of the land but there was still a little vineyard and some grassy slopes which they kept up with the help of an old friend of the family, who would turn up with his lawnmower, improvised from a pram and a washing machine motor, and share a glass of wine.

Hungary is changing every day. I hear Agota's mother is confused and not sure that things are improving. Taxes on most commodities are hitting hard. An architect friend tells me no politician has a clean enough record to be entrusted with the awesome task of restructuring Hungary. West Germans are cashing in on property around Lake Balaton; Austrians nip across the border for cheap dental treatment. In Budapest's main shopping street there is now an Adidas shop, a Benetton and a McDonalds. In Gyor there is a Marks and Spencer.

I imagine, though, that for most people life will improve. Hungary's provincial towns will be beautified and upgraded with the help of foreign loans. High speed trains will replace the old blue ones which took the best part of a day to reach anywhere in the small country. I expect the trams in Budapest will be gradually phased out and the cobbled streets, scored with tramlines, replaced with tarmac. They are already renaming the Moscow and Marx squares. A Westerner still, I am already allowing myself the luxury of nostalgia for the "old" Hungary.

In Search of Magyar Feminism

. . . .

Emma Roper-Evans spent four years living and working in Hungary. During this time she had her first child and continued as a single mother working as a freelance proof-reader.

When I first arrived in Hungary in September 1984 I was impressed by a number of things; childcare facilities were free and took children from the age of six months; the streets of Budapest were so unthreatening that I could actually enjoy walking across the city at three in the morning; there was very little pornography of any kind; and virtually all women worked and contributed to the family income. Since then I have come to the conclusion that these advantages (which we in the West are still struggling for) are eroded by the fact that women have no arena in which they can speak for and about themselves, and that they have no access to real power.

Today Hungary is in flux. It seems as if a pluralist doctrine may replace monolithic Communist dogma. Yet out of the 200 independent groups and movements that now exist, no powerful women's voices have emerged. Reform is the word on everyone's lips and yet the only reform affecting women appears to be the one that collapses the traditional image of the courageous, fertile socialist mother into that of the allegedly "liberated" sex bomb, who was displayed pouting and topless in the first Hungarian tabloid of that name, *Reform*. Avant-garde artists and performers, keen to push the limits of censorship as far as they can, also rely heavily on pornography, with women performers using fetishistic gear in their shows.

The family has always been held sacred by the state, especially in a country where the birth rate is lower than the death rate and women are actively encouraged to have as many children as possible. For example, it is much easier to get a prized state flat if you have three or more children. The other side of this is that abortion involves going before a board of doctors, sociologists and psychologists and answering questions about sexual history, financial security and so on, before your case is even considered.

Women might work but when they return home they have the full responsibility of all the household chores. The division of labour in the home is rarely questioned, even though women have been working alongside their male counterparts a good deal longer than we have and Hungary's workforce would not survive without them.

I must explain at this point that my position was considerably better than most men and women in Hungary. I arrived on a tourist visa hoping that I would somehow be able to work. After the initial difficulties of persuading the authorities to give me a work permit, a process which took three months of dealing with bureaucrats and filling in forms, getting a job was relatively easy. English speakers are in great demand, and as soon as I put up notices around the city advertising myself as an English conversation teacher, students flooded in, willing to pay high prices for the dubious pleasure of talking to me in English for an hour or two each week.

Later I taught at International House in Budapest, despite the fact that I have no teaching qualification and my degree was not in English. Budapest is also a great centre for publishing and so I was able to get an official position (written in my identity card which everyone must carry) as a proof-reader of English texts in one of the big state publishing houses. My work was of a freelance nature, with much shorter hours than the usual nine-to-five and earning about twice the average wage. I also found I had access to all sorts of high-powered circles, meeting academics, writers and intellectuals, simply because I was English. They were all intrigued by the fact that I had come to Hungary to work and to learn their language and therefore took me seriously even though I was a graduate still wet behind the ears from university.

"They could not understand the idea of women meeting and speaking about themselves and saw it as very anti-democratic"

My interest in women's issues was, however, met with scepticism and amusement. When I proposed starting a women's group to some of my female friends, work colleagues and acquaintances, many of them said, "but why no men?" They could not understand the idea of women meeting and speaking about themselves, and saw it as very anti-democratic. I think this is partly because the Communist Party has for years issued great tracts on equality and heroised certain women who took part in the struggle for communism between the wars, but nothing was done and nobody believed it was anything but a propaganda ploy. Feminism tends to be viewed as something the West can afford to dabble in but which has no place in Hungary.

Women are of course involved in political activity, either as part of the ruling Communist Party or in dissident circles. The Party has a Women's Section which is run along the lines of a Stalinist Women's Institute, all thick tweed skirts and pamphlets on breast-feeding in which the young mothers are addressed as "comrade", a very disconcerting experience.

Among independent groups I have mentioned a few have women on their executives. One of the best-known women activists is Ottilia Solt, a prominent dissident during the Kadar years. When I went to talk to her she stressed very emphatically that she was not a feminist, saying that there were far more important issues on her agenda to start worrying about whether women have equal rights or not. In a country where everybody is a second-class citizen, why should women receive special treatment? The idea that a struggle for a democratic constitutional state is of paramount importance and that other freedoms will necessarily follow is an old one. Women are co-opted into the radical movements where they must be content to share platforms with angry young men, old revolutionaries and power seekers.

The notion that the personal is political, which has been so central to feminists in the West, does not exist in Hungary. The private sphere is subordinated to the public domain which is concerned with more concrete reforms such as the economy, the political system and environmental policy. This not only affects women but the homosexual community too. There is no concept of being gay, of creating a forum where people can speak openly about sexuality and oppression. Your sexual proclivity is considered a private matter that should not be discussed in public.

The one place you can be sure of women-only company is at the Turkish baths. There you can luxuriate in the warm pools after being pummelled and massaged by middle-aged amazons, wearing amazing, medieval-looking bras. The baths are a traditional meeting place, the last remnant of the Turkish occupation which lasted about 150 years, into the late seventeenth century. Women of all ages sit about in a series of hot pools and saunas, chatting, playing chess and reading the papers. I found them the best cure for a hangover after too much *alinka* (fruit brandy), and the best way of reviving after having to go to work at an unearthly hour in the morning.

One of my jobs was teaching women textile workers in a factory on the edge of the city. This involved getting up at about 5.30am in order to be there at 7am when work started. The hours were arranged so that the women could get home in time to collect their children from school. There were about ten women, mainly in their late thirties, who had arranged special English lessons during work hours. I had to have permission to enter the factory, which is a restricted area for foreigners, although I suspect industrial espionage is hardly rife in a country where manufacture is in crisis.

We had many discussions about the role of women in Hungary; they all agreed that they did too much housework and childcare, but that change would only come about in the next generation and that women are anyway more caring than men. I liked them all and even went on holiday with them to the factory guest house on Lake Balaton. The very funny, but also indulgent, anecdotes they told me about their husbands and boyfriends reminded me of the stories I used to hear from women of my mother's generation.

"All the women on the ward were amazed that not only was I unmarried but I did not even claim a father for her"

I encountered a good deal of conservatism when dealing with such issues as marriage, child-rearing and sexual behaviour. This is perhaps partly due to economic pressures – to support children and have a reasonable chance of getting your own flat you virtually have to be married. There is state child benefit but it is minimal and impossible to live on without an additional income. It would be incredibly difficult to bring up children as a single parent, and I met no women who were doing so.

When my daughter was born in Budapest in July 1986 all the women on my ward were amazed that not only was I unmarried but I did not even claim a father for her. They were all married and were looking forward to a welcome break at home bringing up their children (the state allows up to two years off, with a job guaranteed at the end of this period). All of them had been married in church, as well as the obligatory registry office ceremony.

The only other patient who caused more of a sensation than I did was a middle-aged gypsy woman having her fifth child. The other women were completely unabashed about expressing their racist views. Out came the old platitudes: gypsies are dirty, they steal, are dishonest, abuse their children and so on. Gypsies have lived in Hungary for centuries (and currently make up three percent of the population) but because they look different, speak a different language and refuse assimilation into the state socialist system they have become the nation's scapegoats.

Many of them live in abject poverty in rural areas, especially in the east of the country where I saw gypsy encampments of unbelievable deprivation and squalor. The men tend to gravitate towards the towns to find work. Once there, they live in overcrowded workers hostels, while the women stay behind in the villages working on the collective farms and bringing up their families. I often heard the complaint that the state had allocated a flat to an urban gypsy family, who would only "sell" it (transfer it for a great deal of money – a standard practice) a few months later, rather than to a worker's family who had been on the council list for years.

Hungary is not a classless society at all; gypsies, peasants, workers, professional and Party functionaries are all ruthlessly divided. The urban middle class may have lost everything during the country's wars and revolutions but their manners, attitudes and aspirations have barely changed and they still tell jokes about the peasant politicians and their coarse ways. Interestingly, the few immigrants, some Cuban guest workers and African and Arab students, were usually treated with great courtesy.

TRAVEL NOTES

Languages Hungarian – an incredibly difficult language to pick up. German is widely understood, but English is only spoken in the more heavily touristed parts of Budapest.

Transport Visas are necessary but are issued routinely on entering the country. Travel within the country is fairly straightforward by bus and train and you can go wherever you want. Few Hungarian women hitch – it seems the risks are much the same as in most Western countries.

Accommodation The few cheap hotels in Budapest are usually full but the tourist organisation, *Ibusz*, arranges private rooms. Around the country, *Turistahaza* dormitory hostels are useful and campsites plentiful, as well as the conventional hotel network.

Guides *The Rough Guide: Hungary* (Harrap Columbus). An excellent book – informative, insightful and a gripping read.

Contacts

Hungary Women's Council, Nepkoztarsasag Utca 124, Budapest 5, was set up by the Communist Party. We know of no autonomous women's groups.

Books

Volgyes, Ivan and Nancy, *The Liberated Female: Life, Work and Sex in Socialist Hungary* (Westview Press, US, 1977). Looks at the position of women in Hungarian society from feudal times up to the Seventies.

Iceland

$\cdot \quad \cdot \quad \cdot \quad \cdot \quad \cdot \quad \cdot \quad \cdot \quad \cdot \quad \cdot \quad \cdot \quad \cdot \quad \cdot \quad \cdot \quad \cdot \quad \cdot$

Long popular with geologists and birdwatchers for its weirdly beautiful volcanic landscapes, glaciers and migration grounds, Iceland is now beginning to attract more mainstream travellers. Since the 1986 superpower summit in Reykjavik effectively relaunched the country as a tourist destination there's been a growing trade in package/hiking tours with new hotels opening in and around the capital.

Outside of Reykjavik, however, facilities are very thinly spread. The country's tiny population is centred on the capital and a few small fishing settlements around the coast which makes travelling further afield a lonely and arduous business. Transport is infrequent, with many roads impassable much of the year, costs can be exorbitantly high, and the weather unpredictable – a sudden downfall cutting off your chances of getting your next supplies. Added to this, Icelandic communities have a reputation for being insular and self-reliant, and though ready to give help when needed, people generally seem uninterested in making contact with visitors. It is however, a very safe place to travel (there are few problems with camping or hitching) and, provided you like the hardy outdoor life, you'll find ample rewards in strange and wild scenery, unlike anything else in this part of the world.

The Icelandic **women's movement** has long had a powerful impact at the centre of mainstream politics. *Kvennalistur*, the "Women's Alliance" was the world's first feminist party to win seats in a national parliament. They currently hold six out of 63 seats and are predicted to take the balance of power after the next election. Ten years ago the Movement demonstrated its full collective strength by calling a one-day women's strike for equality in the workplace and parity of wages. In 1985 the action was repeated – again, in protest against discrimination at work. With the unequivocal support of Iceland's first woman president, Vigdis Finnbogadottir, thousands of women walked off their jobs, closing down schools, shops and government offices. More recently the Alliance has become linked to anti-NATO campaigns, and leads the mounting opposition to the US airbase at Keflavik.

Cod Row

. . . .

Cathryn Evans spent ten months working in a fish factory in the northwest fjords before setting off alone on a tour of the country.

I'd spent a few weeks' holiday in and around Reykjavik in the summer and really wanted an extended stay. After searching unsuccessfully for a job and a work visa I decided to try and join the quota of overseas women employed in the fish factories on the coast. Unfortunately the jobs are set up by agents in England who insisted that I return to London for an interview.

They offered me an eight-month contract, with a free return flight thrown in if I lasted the course, and within a fortnight I was flying back to Iceland, heading for the village of Flateyri in the northwest fjords with ten other women. Some were travellers, from Australia, New Zealand and Europe, lured by the chance to fund their fare home in a short time while others from the Southern hemisphere came out of curiosity, knowing only that they were guaranteed a white Christmas.

"Salla, the quality controller, showed us how to sheer the backbone away from the meat, pluck out live worms . . . and cut out some nauseating blemishes"

Before leaving, most of the people I met seemed to think of Iceland as a snow-covered wasteland populated by Eskimos fishing through holes in the ice and living in igloos. They certainly couldn't imagine a socially and technologically advanced nation with a very high standard of living.

The northwest coast is one of the best fishing grounds and, consequently, Flateyri one of the country's wealthiest and best equipped villages. As with most of the settlements outside Reykjavik, the village only existed because of the fishing industry. The factory was run on a co-operative basis, its profits servicing the community of 425 with a swimming pool, sauna, shop, snack bar, library, surgery, school and guesthouse – outstanding amenities for a place of its size. We were given a large house next door to the factory – an instant introduction to the all pervasive smell of fish.

The day after our arrival we were plunged into work. Donning aprons, gumboots, baseball hats and layers of warm clothes we watched apprehensively as Salla, the quality controller, showed us how to sheer the backbone away from the meat, pluck out live worms with a deft flick of the wrist and cut out some nauseating blemishes. It was best not to think too hard about what we were doing and switch to automatic. The hours were long and hard in cold, wet conditions and by the end of the first week we ached all over. Some of the women were already plotting escape plans during the coffee breaks.

I was a little surprised by how clearly the labour was divided, filleting and packing were termed "women's work" while the men unloaded crates, watched over the gutting machines and loaded trays into the freezer. It was a highly mechanised factory but there was no getting round the sheer monotony of packing, alleviated only by the prospect of different fish to work on. Nevertheless it was a comforting routine and very much the focus of life in the village. At the end of the week there was always a rush to finish the week's catch and if there was a particularly big haul at the height of the season the whole village would turn out to help. There was a tremendous community spirit and, as part of the workforce, we gradually felt accepted within it.

At first, of course, we were viewed with what seemed like cold indifference. Foreign workers had been coming to the village for twenty years and we were just another batch. The village mentality, which thrived on gossip and newcomers, focused on us. But they were also shy people and their reticence was taken by some of the foreign women as very inhospitable. There was certainly no great reason for them to be especially welcoming. The younger women, in particular, saw us as coming to their country merely for the money and as potential rivals for the affections of the men. Obviously, there was a precedent to this as it was something of a status symbol to go out with a foreign girl and the trawlermen with money to burn would often shower visitors with gifts, adding to the money-grabber image.

On an individual level the people were very friendly and hospitable and it was a pleasure to share with them their great passion for their country and community. I became closest to a woman called Hjordis, the headmistress of a tiny school. She had represented Iceland at the United Nations and travelled a great deal but had settled on her own in a house at the far side of the fjord from Flateyri. She spent the summer charting the different migratory birds and was dedicated to nurturing a forest in the harsh climate and thin soil. Another good friend was Stina, an imposing figure who had the dubious task of counting the number of worms in the crates of fish and calculating how long it would take us to pluck them out. With a family of three to raise on her own, she supplemented her income by running the swimming pool and gathering expensive eider duck feathers from her farm in summer. She would patiently help me to grasp Icelandic, a language that has changed little from the time the great sagas were written.

The villagers always made sure that we joined in the celebrations of major festivals and would explain to us the different feasts and rituals such as the

pancake feast to mark the last glimpse of the sun before the dark winter days. Men, women and children had their own festivals dating back to the gods Odin and Thor. The feast of Thorrablot, for the single men of the village, was a memorable trial for the tastebuds. Traditional fare such as braised sheep head, rotten shark, rotten eggs and sour ram's testicles was served. The only thing I really acquired a taste for was *skyr*, a sour yoghurt-like liquid mixed with sugar. Most food is bought in from Denmark and is very basic. The tiny store often looked like it was operating food rationing, especially in winter when supplies often couldn't get through by road, air or sea.

"The women I worked with who were not great nature lovers and were used to big city life found it hard going"

Boredom seemed to be a big problem in Flateyri, especially among the younger people; they spent hours cruising round and round the village or burning rubber up and down the road. The women I worked with who were not great nature lovers and were used to big city life found it hard going as well. Dances with live bands were held every fortnight in summer but less frequently in winter.

Being the largest house in the village, our quarters became the party house at weekends and we would often get impromptu visits from people in neighbouring villages. Icelanders are by nature self-contained and undemonstrative and many relied too heavily on alcohol to let their hair down. Sadly, drink problems were common – even in such a small place, there was a regular "Alcoholics Anonymous" meeting. The sale of beer had, until very recently, been illegal, but as fourteen-year-olds would down a bottle of spirits at a time, this, like the high prices, seemed a futile measure. Icelanders put this heavy drinking down to boredom and depression in the winter months.

The whole country had an air of being untouched by commercialism, although it was clear that this was changing. Even Reykjavik, which since the Superpower summit of 1986 became increasingly aggressively marketed to attract foreign investment, had none of the big city atmosphere, not even the usual neon lights. It was striking at Christmas that most adverts were for books. As a legacy of the long, dark winters, writing, poetry, music and chess are still very popular pursuits, with a high number of experts for such a tiny country. However, videos are set to supplant this and mail order mania has taken grip in the villages. Keeping up-to-date with fashions has become increasingly important for both sexes and it's a matter of pride among the free-spending trawlermen to have the latest hi-fi and cars.

Although winter, with only three or four hours of daylight and snowfall cutting off the village for many weeks, seemed a bleak prospect to most of the villagers and foreign workers, its novelty made it the most magical time for me. Every clear winter night there was a fantastic display of the Northern Lights, with whirling, flickering bursts of colour covering the sky. I enjoyed trekking on the mountain slopes on skis and whizzing across acres of snow on a snowmobile, stopping on a ledge and looking out on to the village below.

Flateyri had many houses hugging the sides of the mountains so there was real danger of damage from an avalanche. Sometimes even a walk up the road was too risky. This was brought home dramatically one day, when with a great roar a cloud of snow and dirt subsided leaving a vast mound of snow just short of a row of houses. The risks of making a living by the sea were also made clear as three fishing boats in the region were lost within the space of one stormy week.

"One of the best moments was climbing up the steep mountainsides and crossing the still snow-covered plateau to watch the Midnight Sun"

"Gyllir" was the name of our trawler. A crew of fifteen would go out on voyages of seven to ten days. It was fitted with the latest computerised instruments as well as the comforts of a sauna and videos. For all this the conditions at sea were arduous. When taken on a trip we had to stay below deck while the men struggled above with the nets in fierce winds. The catch was gutted on board, a very tiring process, and the six-hour shifts seemed an eternity. It was a great feeling, however, to sail back into harbour with a large haul which would be turned into neat packets of fillets during the next week. It's strange to think what a high level of job satisfaction there was working in the factory, singing along to the Icelandic pop songs on the radio and picking up pidgin Icelandic, even though this largely consisted of the different names of fish.

After my contract finished I found it hard to break away from the cosy routine of the community, and especially from the beautiful, peaceful environment. It was a total retreat from the hassles of city life and as the summer approached I would spend long evenings walking at the edge of the fjord watching the boats turn into the harbour, seals and eider ducks on the beaches and the snow thawing to create cascading waterfalls. The endless daylight made it hard to stay indoors and, much as I enjoyed the winter, I could see why the villagers were so cheered by the summer sunlight. One of the best moments was climbing up the steep mountainsides and crossing the still snow-covered plateau to watch the Midnight Sun.

However, I had spent ten months hardly leaving the confines of the village, so excitement slowly overtook my regret at leaving Flateyri, as I took off for Reykjavik to begin a tour of the rest of the country. I travelled mainly by bus and hitched to the less accessible spots. Taking advantage of the six weeks in the year when it is possible to travel across the interior, I joined a sturdy bus which was to cross the Spredgisandur route. The whole journey only took a day but it was a battle to keep the bus moving through the glacial desert wasteland of sludge, sand, and ice-cold rivers. Crashing waterfalls, dark volcanic peaks and imposing glaciers contrasted with slabs of multicoloured rocks and steaming hot pools. Only a handful of drivers were qualified to take this route and we had to help out several stranded cars along the way.

"Iceland is not the place to spend time if you don't like the great outdoors"

Hitching can be quite difficult in Iceland. The most interesting places are often off the main road and there may only be a few cars passing. Trudging wearily along in enigmatic weather was quite demoralising, but I never felt at risk and the lack of cars meant that if one did pass me, it would invariably stop. I spent many days exploring Lake Myvatn in the northeast, fortunately picking a time when the midges were taking a breather. This area has always been a magnet for bird watchers as it attracts a huge variety of migrating ducks in the summer. Great geological turbulence has produced many strange features – the barren volcanic cratered areas were used to train the American astronauts.

Close to this is a sulphurous plain with bright yellow crystals and bubbling pools of grey mud. The twisted statues of lava, called *Dimmuborgir* (dark castles), have still not been satisfactorily explained. There is still a suspicion that they might be sleeping trolls. It is usual for any giant boulder to be attributed to these mythical creatures, and often the course of roads has been altered to avoid disturbing them.

The geothermal activity in this area has some unusual spin-offs. In Hveragerdi the hot earth has been used as the basis of a greenhouse centre where exotic flowers and even bananas are grown. It also acts as an oven to bake delicious sourbread. In Svartsengi, the run-off from the heating plant has created a mineral-rich hot pool. It was a real luxury to bathe in the steam rising from bright turquoise water surrounded by craggy black lava. Throughout this time I stayed at Youth Hostels which were always well equipped and sited around the main routes. They ranged from farm outhouses to school halls and were friendly, relatively cheap places to spend the night. Camping was even better as the level of tourism means that there are few restrictions on where you can pitch a tent.

Iceland is not the place to spend time if you don't like the great outdoors and are expecting a bustling nightlife, as outside Reykjavik there are few entertainments laid on. But the spectacular unspoilt landscape and relaxed lifestyle are reasons alone for taking a trip. It will hopefully be some time before the aggressive tourist and business drive now beginning to operate in the capital spreads to the rest of the country.

TRAVEL NOTES

Languages Icelandic and Danish, but most people speak some English.

Transport No particular problems for women; hitching is probably as safe as it can ever be, but be prepared for long waits between lifts.

Accommodation Again, no particular problems for women. Many Icelandic women camp and hike alone. There's a good network of Youth Hostels.

Special Problems Costs can be devastatingly high. Don't underestimate the dangers of hiking or driving into the interior; the terrain can be treacherous and your chances of being found if you have an accident are alarmingly slim.

Guides There's a good section on Iceland in *The Rough Guide: Scandinavia* (Harrap Columbus).

Contacts

Kvennaframbodid, Gamia Hotel Vik, Adalstraeti, 101 Reykjavik. Main office of the Women's Movement, used as a meeting place for various groups and for advice sessions on legal, social and health matters. They also publish a magazine, *Era*, bi-monthly.

Books

We've been unable to find any books in translation by Icelandic women. Any suggestions would be welcome.

India

India provokes intense reactions among travellers. However much you read, or are told, little prepares you for the differences and richness of the various cultures, the unbelievable poverty or the sheer pressure of people. In many ways it is misleading to talk about India as one country. With its six major religious groups, its differing stages of development, its widely varying landscape and proliferation of local cultures and languages, it is a collection of states easily as diverse as Europe. For a traveller on a short trip, one or two areas are more than enough to take in.

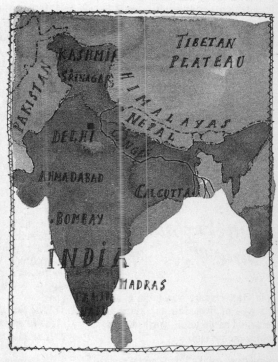

Countless women travel the country alone, and have done so from the days of the Raj through to the hippy era. The lingering hippy stereotype can be burdensome at times, connoting scruffiness, promiscuity and drug abuse, but it also has its positive side in an established trail and a legacy of cheap accommodation. Sexual harassment tends not to be a great problem. This is not to say it doesn't occur; in strongly Muslim areas wandering around on your own is considered a provocation in itself, inviting comments and jeers, and all women in India face the problem of being groped in crowded buses and trains. Actual sexual violence, however, (at least towards foreign visitors) is very rare and dangerous situations can mostly be avoided by making a public outcry – passers-by or fellow travellers are bound to help you.

Much harder to contend with is the constant experience of being in a crowd, the unremitting poverty and the numbers of hustlers and beggars. (Begging carries none of the social stigma that it does in Western societies and Indian people routinely give something.) How you cope with the outrageous disparities of wealth is up to your own personal politics. But whatever you do, or don't do, you'll need to come to terms with your comparative affluence and outsider status – and the attention this inevitably attracts.

The **feminist movement** in India has become established in recent years, though it remains concentrated in the cities and the women involved are predominantly highly educated and middle class. But many women's centres and action groups have been set up and with women's magazines such as *Manushi* and the feminist publishing company *Kali for Women*, the network is widening daily. Local actions like the organisation of lower-caste street workers in Ahmedabad into collectives as a means of protecting themselves from police harassment, and the exploitation of money-lenders (see Una Flett's piece) have been both creative and diverse. One of the chief concerns of the feminist movement is to involve more rural and urban-poor women in various broad-based campaigns – against dowry (the number of dowry deaths remains alarmingly high), discrimination in the workplace and disparities in pay and education.

"Lonely you Come?"

. . . .

Una Flett was born in India but left at the age of five. She has since twice returned as an adult, most recently for a four-month visit.

Somehow, oscillating between resilience and fatalism, India keeps going – keeps going in spite of her 714 million, nearly half of whom are unemployed. This is the enduring image of India, the crowds upon crowds of people everywhere. Most of the population live in rural villages but increasingly they migrate to cities to live in the great sprawls of shanty towns (*bhastis*). The sight of pavement sleepers, beggars and hustlers, tearful young graduates telling you of their destitution, not

enough space on buses, queues like insurrecting armies; these are all part of the day-to-day experience. Everything, from buying a stamp to boarding a train, will be done against the pressure of competing hundreds.

"The first thing to learn is to economise in anger. It gets you nowhere and is exhausting"

As a foreigner, particularly a woman travelling alone, the first thing you encounter is the stare, the open curious gaze, followed usually by the open curious question. Indians are avid "collectors" of foreigners, not by any means always in a predatory spirit. To the crowds of unemployed young men who hang around every public place, the foreigner is entertainment, also – my personal theory – a kind of token substitute for travel. Most of them will never "go foreign" but, because the

West still represents much that is desirable and prestigious, any kind of contact is prized.

There is a difficult ambiguity in these encounters. Are you being chatted up by a hustler or not? I have been enraged by an attempted rip-off – though the first thing to learn is to economise in anger. It gets you nowhere and is exhausting. But there is a long and pushy list of people trying to engage your attention for money; offering to be your guide, find accommodation, rent you a houseboat in Kashmir, or show you the local handicrafts, besides the shoal of aggressive sellers of all kinds of pitiful junk.

In big cities the likelihood of outright harassment is much higher than on trains or in smaller places. "Eve-teasing", the term coined by the Indian press for groping, provokes long, scandalised articles in the "dailies" and is for Indian women as much as foreigners a hazard of city life, particularly on buses (so is pickpocketing and jewellery snatching). Sikh and Muslim men are on the whole much more sexually aggressive than Hindus. A memorably unpleasant experience was being pulled around Lucknow (a predominantly Muslim city) in an open rickshaw, a sight that triggered off shouts, solicitations, jeers and cheers from every man I passed. It was the one place where I chose to go hungry rather than look for somewhere to eat on my own.

I travelled clockwise around India by train, a slow and tiring kind of journeying but a certain way of getting the flavour of the country and above all of the people. For all life takes place in stations. Travelling is endemic among Indians – to visit relatives, to take produce to markets, to make pilgrimages, to look for work. Besides travellers, stations have their quota (sometimes enormous, as in Howrah station in Calcutta) of permanent residents, homeless families who have settled in with their cooking pots and babies and cloth bundles. There is an amazing sense of private family life being lived in the open, among travellers and others. It is, after a little practice, curiously relaxing. You lose the sense of a rigid self-conscious boundary between "public" and "private", as it exists in a Western society. The small space occupied by your bags in the middle of the waiting crowd becomes a sort of privacy. I ended up quite naturally unpacking and repacking my possessions on platforms, settling in to write up notes and generally behaving in a "domestic" manner.

"Both men and women found the fact that I travelled alone quite extraordinary"

I grew to love stations as much as I dreaded them in the early stages. They seem bewildering ant-heaps until you find your way around, but you can always get help from coolies (wearing red waistcoats for identification) who know platforms and departure times rather better than the station staff. Fellow travellers, too, are infinitely helpful. Indians are well aware of the impenetrability of their booking system for foreigners and love to help out. Above all, there is the fun of eating in stations where there are all sorts of oily cooked food snacks, fruit, and hot, sweet tea served in little clay cups which give the tea a slightly earthy taste and which one smashes to shards on the railway lines after drinking.

Both men and women found the fact that I travelled alone quite extraordinary. "Lonely you come?" they would ask, incredulous. Although by their standards bizarre, my choice was entirely tolerated. In some states I found separate compartments on trains for women – good places for conversations. I was asked about our marital system, or lack of it, and asked in turn about theirs. Although love matches do occur across caste and religion (disasters in the eyes of most families), the system of arranged marriages has not been seriously challenged; freedom of contact between the sexes is rigorously proscribed and in many areas college students lead segregated lives and there is no mixing among the young in public.

"To do exactly as it was done before is an axiom of life in India"

Women are still seriously hampered at all levels except at the very top by their subordinate and dependent status. Apart from the small group of highly educated and very able women in academic, professional and commercial jobs – a Westernised elite – the rest of the country's women are restrained either by tradition or poverty or both. The dowry system, though made officially illegal some years ago, persists with all its iniquities. Higher education for girls is more a selling point in the marriage market (read the personal ads column in any English-language newspaper) than a means of entering employment. The large bulk of Indian women do not work after marriage, for that reflects poorly on the husband. Only those at the top and those at the very bottom do so.

However, among women at the desperate bottom of the heap an amazing potential for self-help can be tapped. In Ahmedabad, a union for self-employed women – rag and scrap sellers, quilt-makers, joss-stick rollers and market women of all kinds – was started in the early 1970s. By setting up banking and credit facilities, training schemes and protest groups *SEWA* (Self-Employed Women's Association) has managed to rescue its members from the hold of money-lenders, make an effective case against harassment by police, and to develop – from a baseline of total ignorance – a remarkable degree of financial competence. Women have also asserted themselves in ecological issues, most notably in the Chipko movement to save the deforestation of the Himalayan slopes. However, the power of tradition is vast, a force that locks people into a sense of preordained order. To do exactly as it was done before is an axiom of life in India.

If you visit, don't try to do too much. Your senses will be at full stretch all the time because there is so much to take in. The stimulation is tremendous. So is the exhaustion.

A Bengali Retreat

. . . .

Peggy Gregory spent nearly two years travelling around India. She stayed for three months in an *ashram* and spent six months living alone in a rented house in Bengal.

Before I left for India I talked to people who had already been, attempting to grasp what it would be like, and to gain more confidence about going. Talking helped, but I still had doubts – maybe these other people were simply better travellers, stronger, more open and more resilient than I was.

I had managed through a connection in England to arrange a room with a family in Delhi to cover my first few days. That way the initial shock was softened, as I could make forays out into the hustle for short periods and then retreat into the warmth of a family atmosphere.

It was colder than I'd anticipated (in December) and the city seemed surprisingly pleasant, almost sedate. The old part of the city, however, is less congenial, crowded with people and vehicles, very dusty and chaotic; it was enticing, but I felt too raw, too intimidated by the constant staring, comments and questions that assailed me as I walked around or sat resting for a while. I wanted to merge in with the crowds and observe everything unnoticed.

When I started travelling I compensated for my lack of experience by finding other single women to travel with – either another recent arrival with whom I could share my uncertainties, or people who had been in India for a longer time from whom I could gain confidence. From one woman I learnt to speak some Hindi and to read the alphabet, particularly useful for reading timetables at bus stations. Generally just talking to other travellers was helpful, to find out which places were interesting to visit, how they approached travelling and what they had learnt from their experiences.

There are a lot of foreign travellers all over India, especially in main towns and cities or, in fact, any place mentioned in the guidebooks. I too had set out with a guidebook, which was useful for general hints and finding hotels but soon became redundant. I usually stayed in dormitories in cheap hotels, which are less expensive than rooms, and good places to find companions, although you don't have any privacy. I spent the first month travelling around Rajasthan, an increasingly popular state with tourists.

My confidence grew quickly. With it came the realisation that I wouldn't learn much by confining myself to the tourist route or by hanging around with other Westerners simply for the sake of emotional security. The most important thing I learnt during that time was to judge a situation by its atmosphere and to promote an atmosphere myself of being open to unexpected events or meetings – but not to jump feet first into any situation I was unsure of.

"As a buffer between me and the outside world I developed the persona of a 'nice girl' – strong but odd"

For the next four or five months I stayed in cheap hotels, occasionally with families and once in an *ashram* or sleeping on station platforms or trains when in transit; a passive observer to the life and activity around me. I was gradually changing, relating to things with regard to where I was the month before rather than to England, which began to feel a long way away. The persona I developed was of a "nice girl" – strong but "odd" – as a buffer between me and the world outside: one which both allowed me to communicate and also protected me.

I felt safe, even when walking around at night, travelling in trains or staying in hotels. In cities at night, for instance, many people shop until quite late, and there are women and children on the streets. However, I tried to stay clear of the predominantly Muslim areas at night as the total absence of women made me uneasy. In the countryside it's also not so safe, but when staying in these areas I was often with someone or could use a bicycle. Anyhow, whenever in doubt you can always catch a rickshaw.

I was rarely sexually harassed and never in any sort of aggressive or threatening way, but I did get my share of the street hustlers. Stallholders in the market often pick on foreigners, and leaving a train or bus station with luggage almost invariably brings a rush of rickshaw cyclists and touts insisting on taking you to the "cheapest" hotel in town.

If I felt slightly battered after a journey I'd then hang around for a while and leave the station to look for somewhere to stay, collecting my luggage later. Most situations, however, depend on your reaction and state of mind; if you're feeling bad any hitches or hassles are irritating, but if you're feeling good it is fun. Generally I felt I was hassled less as time went on, partly I think because I had learnt to dress and move around in a less conspicuous manner.

I worked my way southwards over a period of six months. By the time I arrived in Tamil Nadu I began to feel ill. So much so that I had to retreat to a hotel room where I spent a lonely and painful week unable to sleep, eat or do more than shuffle to the toilet twice a day. I had hepatitis. I knew it as soon as I caught sight of my yellow eyes and skin. Gathering the little strength I had, I moved to a local Christian *ashram* at Shantivanam, where I spent a week until they sent me back to Tiruchi to a hospital. *Ashrams* don't usually like people visiting if they are ill but when my symptoms disappeared (after a week) I was welcomed back. I was lucky to have gone to that particular *ashram* as they did genuinely seem to care. They even sent someone to visit me every day while I was in hospital.

Illness of some sort is almost inevitable if you spend any time in India. I was, however, unlucky to catch both hepatitis and later amoebic dysentery, both through contaminated water. I took the usual precautions for the first three months but drinking only sweet tea and soft drinks is expensive and anyway it's extremely difficult if you're staying in rural areas – I lapsed, accepting the possibility that I might get ill.

With a fairly poor diet it took a long time to regain strength so I was at the *ashram* for about three months. Looking back, I realise it was the best place to have convalesced. There was a ready-made structure to the day which I appreciated after so long on the road; and a gentle and open approach to life and "spirituality". I had gone there rather uncertain as to how a casual and unconvinced visitor might be welcomed. The only other *ashram* I'd

been to was a Buddhist one in the north (Igatpur) where I'd gone specifically to do a meditation course. I discovered later that *ashrams* are usually open to anyone as long as they approach with a genuinely sympathetic attitude. Some, however, have become wary as they've been abused in the past for free accommodation – it is often best to write in advance to say you are arriving.

"You can't expect people to become suddenly calm and open the minute they walk through an ashram *gate"*

Most people I met had been disappointed by the lack of harmony they encountered in *ashrams*. It's something I felt myself when I stayed in Igatpur. Everything had been fine during the meditation course, perhaps because we were under a vow of silence and concentrating solely on meditation. Staying on to do some voluntary work (which everyone was asked to do, although this is not so in all *ashrams* – rules vary), I became disheartened by obvious rivalries that emerged between people. Their frustrations and antagonisms weren't particularly new but they seemed out of place. This was true also to a lesser extent in Shantivanam, but by then I was less naïve – you can't expect people to become suddenly calm and open the minute they walk through an *ashram* gate. Often the process of introversion and introspection that people enter into can have paradoxical effects, bringing out hidden aspects of the personality.

Moving on, I began to feel more and more the need for some sort of structure – I wanted to become more involved in learning about Indian culture. In Pondicherry I started to learn *tabla*, the percussion accompaniment to classical Indian music, and for the following nine months was completely involved in learning the technique. I eventually settled down in Bengal in a small town called

Shantiniketan, which has built up around an *ashram*, school and university set up by the renowned poet Rabindranath Tagore. It's an extraordinary, peaceful place. I felt at ease immediately, found a music teacher and rented a room. I also started to learn Bengali and taught English privately. I was extremely happy there, and even when the time came when I wanted to return to England I found it hard to wrench myself away from what had become my home in India.

I could have remained in India, and if I had done so it would probably have been for a long time. Yet I was tired of making the compromises necessary to live in a country as a foreigner; and it was that which eventually made me decide to return.

Returning to England and having to adjust to a more complex lifestyle, having lived so simply for such a long time, was very difficult. I felt disorientated for several months, not sure that I had made the right decision. Looking back, it was a good decision, for what I had learnt there had to be put to the test in another environment; much of it has fallen down and much remained.

Between Two Cultures

. . . .

Smita Patel, a British Asian woman, took five months off from her job at a feminist publishing house to travel with her boyfriend to India and South East Asia.

This was not my first visit to India. Like most second generation Indians I had been taken to India as a child and young teenager. But these journeys had always been considered as a duty or "family visit", not as a means of exploring the country or even mixing with the community at large. I had always been aware that as an Indian girl my role was to accept the guidance and protection of my relatives. Returning as an adult independent woman, I knew that I would face problems and dilemmas, and even more so travelling with a white boyfriend.

Our trip had been planned as part of wider travels to the East spanning over five months. I was fairly confident about travelling independently (having done so alone and with friends to Europe and Africa) but the warnings of other Asian women surprised and disturbed me. India, I was told, would be different and travelling with a white partner I should expect much more harassment and abuse. My mind was becoming full of doubts and pre-judgements but I drew comfort from the fact that India was a country which has witnessed hordes of travellers of almost every race and nationality, exploring every inch of its land.

I remember arriving at Delhi airport at 3am, feeling apprehensive and excited. I was really no more knowledgeable about what to expect than any other Western traveller. After waiting hours for our baggage we ventured out into "independent" travelling. It was now 5am and though the sun had barely risen we were shocked by the sheer volume of people – the first thing you notice about India is how densely populated it is. The whole area outside the airport was packed with families, beggars, police, rickshaw wallahs, fruit vendors, taxi men, and of course the famed hotel sellers, relentlessly directing us to the "best room in town", as well as countless others trying to attract our attention to sell, buy or give advice. Luckily we had met an American woman on the plane who was being met by her brother who had been living in India for three years, and despite being heavily jet-lagged we managed to struggle out of the chaos and find them. As Ben had been living on a low budget for a year we were soon jostled towards India's cheapest mode of transport, the local bus. It looked ancient and decrepit and I was convinced it would never manage the long ride into Delhi city.

"Even though I had witnessed such scenes as a child and heard of India's poverty, I was still bewildered at the extreme deprivation we came across during our stay"

In India there are no such things as queues and you learn quickly how to push and shove to get to the front. We piled on to the bus with what seemed like hundreds of others, all Indian, and I gratefully noticed that as a female traveller and a new arrival people would give up their seats to me. Our first impressions were of the sharp images of life glimpsed through the bus window. It took about an hour to reach the city along a road marked by small dwellings and shanty towns made out of paper, cardboard, rubber, tin, in fact anything that the poor could get their hands on. Even though I had witnessed such scenes as a child and heard of India's poverty, I was still bewildered at the extreme deprivation we were to come across during our stay.

Our first week in Delhi was just as I had visualised it and childhood memories suddenly flooded back. We were staying in the Main Bazaar area of Delhi, near the railway station. This is an old marketplace, full of tiny shops selling everything you could ever need. It's an amazing spectacle of colour and smell, with the persistent noise of fruit and vegetable sellers bargaining over the prices for the day, and rickshaws and bikes swerving through the streets, avoiding the sacred cows that amble in their path. At that stage we were using other travellers' tips and living on a very tight budget. Like most backpackers we tended to be attracted to hotels and eating places where white travellers would meet or end up. To begin with I was unaware that my presence among mostly white men would be seen as strange and immoral behaviour by the Indian men who ran the hotels and eating places.

From the moment of our arrival both Max and I had taken care to dress and act according to Indian customs. At no time did we publicly show affection towards each other such as holding hands, kissing or even being physically close. In England I had been brought up to dress "respectfully" in the presence of family and community so this was not new to me. However, despite our attempts to merge in I soon discovered that being an Asian woman travelling among independent travellers I was perceived very differently by Indian men. People didn't always notice that I was with a white man, especially if Max and I were looking at different things, but as soon as we were together the stares intensified and men would start making comments and even touching me as they walked past. Understanding Hindi made me aware of all the derogatory comments being made about me.

Sometimes this would lead to more direct harassment, with men changing seats so they could touch me in full view of Max. On one occasion, six men got into the compartment and all took turns to insult me, including trying to sit on my lap. I also often heard men describing white women as loose and sexually available. It was clear that to them I was a "white product", a British-born woman doing what mostly white women do, flaunting my independence by travelling around with a white man.

> **"It was clear that to them I was a 'white product', a British-born woman doing what mostly white women do, flaunting my independence"**

We also experienced men approaching Max and talking about me as though I was invisible and had no mind of my own. I was made to feel like an appendage, passive and speaking only through him. Towards the end of our travels I had given up trying to explain my own point of view and simply let Max do all the talking. I felt caught between differing values, having to play an uneasy shifting game of what was expected from an Indian woman. As a child growing up in an Indian family I had experienced a similar "balancing out" of values and had learnt intuitively when to be silent. In India I was silent again, superficially accepting men's behaviour towards me simply to get through a hassle-free day of travelling. But this passivity became much harder as time wore on. Things came to a head in Varanasi, where after only three days I had been subjected to so much abuse and harassment that I retreated to my hotel room and wept. I knew this was not an overreaction or paranoia as white travellers had noticed and commented on how differently I was being treated.

I was left with the feeling that perhaps the two different sides of me just did not fit into Indian life. My attempts to cover up my feminism and, by taking a passive role, to try and gain the approval of Indian men, soon gave way to overwhelming feelings of resentment. It was mortifying when I realised that I was dismissing part of my own culture in a way that can only be described as racist. Unfortunately, being so isolated from other Indian women – I experienced little or no contact with them – my experiences in India were very much male dominated.

These extremely harassing times were also contrasted with some blissfully relaxed moments. After leaving India to spend a while trekking in the Himalayas we returned to spend our last three weeks in Kashmir and Ladakh. Kashmir is known as a tourist attraction and in the month of June many Indians themselves leave the hot plains to cool off in the Kashmir hills. We headed for Dal lake and found a house run by an old Kashmiri man who was obviously respected in the community. We were taken under his family's wing and I experienced no sexual harassment during the stay; due mainly, I am sure, to the fact that his many relatives acknowledged and therefore protected us.

Travelling around India I learnt what it felt like to be an outsider in a culture which I regard as my roots. My experiences, however, were very much my own and I really couldn't say how much they'd apply to other British Asian women travellers. Certainly, the prejudice we encountered as a mixed race couple is not confined to India alone. Returning to England left me in complete culture shock and finding my bearings in British society has again taken time.

Trekking from Kashmir

. . . .

Liz Maudslay made her first trip to India as a student in 1968. Since then she has repeatedly returned, often for several months, and has worked and travelled in many different regions. Her most recent trips have been to the Himalayas for walking and climbing holidays.

"You want houseboat? Five star deluxe. Bathroom attached. Very good houseboat. Very cheap." Arrival in Srinigar can seem the antithesis of the imagined Shangri-la where delicately carved boats rest on tranquil lakes surrounded by snow-peaked mountains. The boats and lakes and mountains are all there. So is the hassling. Tourism has created it; generations of tourists, Indian and Western. And then, unjust but inevitable, it is the tourists who most resent it. However, far from all Kashmiris are the unscrupulous grabbers they are made out to be by the generalising, besieged traveller.

On recent visits I have stayed on a houseboat owned by one of the kindest and most honest families I have ever met. The son, Rashid, also shares my passion for walking and climbing. He regularly takes tourists for short treks and it was while we were talking about these that we developed the plan of sharing a much longer and less frequented trek. We both needed each other for this. I would finance the expedition, paying for the pony men whom he could not otherwise afford, while he would be able to act as guide and translator.

A rich variety of treks can begin in Kashmir, including those which go on into the barer regions of Ladakh and Zanskar. This time we decided to stay in Kashmir and walk from Sonamarg in the north to Bandipur in the west, near the Pakistan border. We estimated this would take us about three weeks.

Unlike Nepal, Kashmir does not have the same small villages where you can find board and lodging; hence you need to take a tent and all your food, and on a longer trek this means pack ponies. Rashid's father, Habib, has been walking in the mountains since he was a boy and knew exactly how much of everything we would need. The whole family joined us in packing up gunny bags full of rice, lentils, tea, oats, sugar and salt and measuring out bottles of kerosene. The next day we caught a bus to Sonamarg where we negotiated with two pony men.

It rained solidly for three days in Sonamarg. Three days of waiting in the tent with only occasional drenched sorties splashing through the mud river of the one main street to buy bread or milk. This can be a problem with Kashmiri treks. The months when the high passes are open are July to September but these are by no means the driest. However, on the fourth day a watery sun emerged and we set off along slippery paths. As we climbed up through the steaming green forest I began to get to know the pony men.

"Why was I wanting to walk in the mountains at all, especially on a route which no one was quite sure of and which no one they knew had ever walked before?"

Manikar was elderly with a grizzled face, very bright eyes, and a thin body which I soon realised would be able to outwalk any of us. He had been on numerous treks and this, along with his age, gave him a licence to tease and play. Aziz was younger and shyer. He had black curly hair and incredibly gentle large brown eyes which would flow through expressions ranging from enjoyment, to bewilderment, embarrassment and shock at Manikar's excesses. Those were my impressions of them but what were theirs of me?

Manikar's previous treks had all been with groups of foreigners. Why was I a woman alone? Where were my husband or brother? Why was I wanting to walk in the mountains at all, especially on a route which no one was quite sure of and which no one they knew had ever walked before? Their way of coping with the situation was for Manikar to become my "father", Aziz my "brother" while Rashid could be the "guide". I accepted my role as daughter and sister. I knew it was the only way which would allow us to become close.

We walked through the forest which smelled of damp pine and up above the treeline to where the grass changed into the dirty snow edge of a glacier. Kashmiri shepherd villages comprise just one or two huts made up of pine trunks and built into the mountainside so that they are six or seven feet high at the front and three or four feet at the back. There are no windows, only a space for a door, and the dank inside smells of the sweet pine needles which make up the floor. The roof is pressed earth where the goats are herded at night. They are inhabited in the summer months by Gujar shepherds who come up from the plains.

This village had only one hut, inhabited by a shepherd, his wife and daughter. As we pitched our tents he came up to talk and asked if I had any medicines for his daughter. This was the first of many such requests and I always felt uneasy and inadequate with the role of the Western omnipotent doctor. But it was also one way in which I could talk easily to the women who otherwise tended to hide shyly as their husbands approached. The daughter was about twelve years old and did look pale and listless. While the summer months give plenty of fresh air and exercise, the diet is a monotonous repetition of *chapati*, made from flour carried up the mountain, washed down with endless cups of *Nun chai* or Kashmiri tea – a reddish liquid made from handfuls of green tea, a little soda and a lot of salt and goat's

milk. Both are delicious after a long day's walk, but not a very balanced diet for months on end. In the end I gave her a supply of vitamin pills which usually seemed the best "medicine" to distribute.

"This was the first time the pass had been crossed for thirteen years"

Each summer shepherds come up with their goats to their own *nai* or meadow. They know every step of the way to their own grazing place (however many days' walk it is) but seldom travel from *nai* to *nai*. Walking for pleasure is a luxury of the rich. When we said we were thinking of going over the pass to Vishnesar the shepherd's first response was "impossible". We had expected this and, several cups of *nun chai* later, the impossible had become merely a strange thing to do. As time went on the adventure began to appeal to him and he volunteered to come with us. We set off the next morning, five of us instead of four.

Although nowhere near "impossible" it proved a very hard walk; a long slog across a permanently frozen glacier followed by a sustained and strenuous rock scramble. It was longer still for the ponies who could not scramble but had to toil up in endless diagonal lines. A few eagles made sudden black shadows; two marmots whistled to each other standing up on their hind legs; a lone bear lurched away in the distance. By the time we reached the top of the pass the sky was midday blue and deep copper-coloured rocks made jagged silhouettes against it. We collapsed on the summit before starting the deep descent. Calculating for a minute, the shepherd announced with indisputable authority that this was the first time the pass had been crossed for thirteen years and the first time ever that it had been crossed by ponies. He said it had no name so we called it Manikar pass. The achievement of a pass which was new to all of us cemented the sense of solidarity between Rashid, the pony men and myself.

The shepherd left us the next morning and we walked the easy few miles to Vishnasar, which is on a route travelled not just by shepherds but also by tourists walking the Vishnesar circle trek. Vishnesar (Vishnu's Lake) is a large lake surrounded by crags. It is incredibly large and deep (considering its altitude) and frozen for most of the year but when we arrived its clear green water reflected the rocks around it. It was tempting, but far too cold for a swim and even a quick splash wash took my breath away.

We set off before sunrise past another lake, Krishnasar, and up the steep Krishnasar pass. From the top you could see Parbat shining in the distance. The route then dropped down to a hidden valley. Entering it was like going into a vision of a biblical Galilee: wild lilies, anemones, little crimson cyclamen, edelweiss, and so many flowers whose names I did not know, speckled the grass. A few tall, silky goats crossed our path and, further away, small lakes shone blue against the grey blue rock. The lakes still had islands of ice although the sun was easily hot enough to walk with bare arms.

"Maybe it was the altitude, but we all seemed touched by the Nil Nai magic. I felt incredibly happy"

We did not run south along the Vishnesar circle route but continued west a few miles when a group of staring and laughing children heralded a village. Zhaudoor was not a Gujar village but inhabited by Telaili people who do not come to the mountains just for the summer months but live here all the year round. Physically they are different from the Kashmiris – broader faced, sturdier and fair. Their houses are two-storeyed, wooden and very solid. They need to be; for seven months the village is covered with snow. Even the river, that wide, leaping torrent where we had pitched our tent, freezes solid. *Zhaudoor* means barley and a few acres of it grew around the houses to be stored for winter. We stayed there for three days and were greeted with much excitement. The children danced and sang for us at night and led us through the one village street where every door was opened to us and every family gave us *nun chai* and *chapati*.

For me, from the outside, it appeared like a self-contained pastoral idyll, but how could I begin to understand what it is like to live there twelve months a year for all of one's life? The men will sometimes walk the two or three days' journey to a road then catch a bus to Srinigar to sell goat meat, eggs, or the socks that were knitted through the winter. Meanwhile the women look after the flocks and do the knitting.

There were two young girls, incredibly beautiful in their bright coloured baggy trousers and long tunics belted with woven shawls. They were poised between childhood and adulthood, not quite old enough to have taken on the shyness of the women. In a year or two they will walk the three or four days to the next Telaili village to be married and continue the same tasks. "Does a teacher ever come?" I asked. "Sometimes. But they find it too lonely here and soon they leave." "And a doctor?" "He should, but doesn't." Sick people can only get treatment if they can manage to walk to the road and, from there, be taken to hospital. One man told me that his wife had died last winter leaving him with four children. I asked him what had been wrong with her. He shrugged. It was a typically Western question; diagnosis is not an option for these villagers.

The route from Zhaudoor went higher still and even further from a road. The highest village, Nil Nai, was not a village at all, just one family living in their hut surrounded by a blue vista of mountains stretching far into Pakistan. The two young shepherd boys were amazed at our offerings of chocolate and balloons, staring at them with as much entranced delight as I kept staring at their mountain view. Maybe it was the altitude but we all seemed touched by the Nil Nai magic. I felt incredibly happy and Manikar teased even more than usual. None of us could sleep that night and from his tent we heard Manikar singing loudly, beginning with traditional prayers to Allah but, as time went on, making up his own words, singing our trek back to us and incorporating all of us into the refrain.

From Nil Nai there was a long descent when we had to jump endlessly over miles of boulders until at last we reached the river we had hoped to find. It was late to find it. The melting snows had made it much fuller than it would have been in early morning. But we locked arms and staggered across. A few miles along the bank on the other side we had been told there was a village called Tressingham.

Tressingham. To me the name seemed more fitting to the southeast of England than to the northwest of Kashmir. A narrow bridge separated us from the six or seven Gujar huts and, as we unpacked the ponies and pitched our tents, people crossed over. The men first, mostly tall, all thin and wiry, wearing long *kurta* and baggy Kashmiri trousers. Then the children, tangle-haired and huge-eyed, and finally, hovering on the outer circle, the women, with their straight hair plaited back from high cheekbones and held under small delicately woven hats.

One woman came through the circle of men. She was older, her body like a rope, her hair grey twine. She cradled a lump of salt brought up from below. She stood erect, too old to have to put on the protection of shyness and withdrawal. Her voice was like a single string of wire. "I want to say as the first foreigner to enter our village you are welcome." British immigration laws came into my mind: Bangladeshis

denied a house because they already had a home in Bangladesh; Sri Lankans moored on a boat; virginity tests. What welcome would she receive as the first foreigner from Tressingham to come to my country? Boundaries may be common to all countries but barriers are not reciprocal.

"'I want to say as the first foreigner to enter our village you are welcome'"

We collected wood and lit a fire. People brought milk, yoghurt and hot *chapati*. We brewed *nun chai*. As it grew dark the men started to sing. Rich praising of Allah simultaneously joyful and soulful. "And this song," said the young man, whose serious air and glasses made him look more like an undergraduate than a shepherd, "is in praise of Benazir Bhutto." Pakistan was only a walk and a border away and far more home for these Gujars than the India which had been thrust upon them. After the singing the dancing began – men squatting, Cossack-style, on their haunches flashing long sticks. Another country linked; another border eroded.

Tressingham was the last of the real magic. Now we were nearing roads on the other side. Already what was almost a path appeared as we dropped down to the next night's village, Hindapani (Rock-Water). This was a much larger affair. Two groups of ten or twelve huts each and what, after the last few weeks, seemed like a mass of people. It was the Muslim festival *Borold* and we stayed two days to celebrate it, giving away what was left of our sweets and balloons and being pressed with goat's meat in return.

Two days later the path became a track and, as if an invisible but definitive line had been drawn, the mountains ended. Paddy fields emerged and proper large houses with farmyards. One by one, signs of civilisation closed in on us: a bicycle, a truck, a small shop. The trek was over. It was in Erin that Manikar and Aziz left us and we said sad goodbyes with promises of photos, letters and more treks. We had shared little actual language but had communicated more than I have with people I have talked with for hours.

Rashid was ill when we stayed at Erin. Kashmiri men, I found out, were no different from English ones when it came to illness. He refused the tea I made him and then insisted on making his own; he grumbled incessantly at the heat and the flies of the apple orchard where we were camping; and he was sure he was dying. "It is always like this," he said "always when I leave the mountains I am sick." I could empathise with that. I too felt an ache at leaving behind the mountains.

When he had recovered we went down to the town of Bandipur and caught a rickety bus to Srinigar. By now the trek had become something different – an adventure to talk and laugh about together, to boast about, and, in my case, to write about. But something of the specialness had to be left behind.

TRAVEL NOTES

Languages Hindi is the official national language but it is by no means universally spoken and there are hundreds of other regional languages and dialects. English is widely spoken.

Transport Trains are the main form of transport. Most tourists use second class reserved seats (second class unreserved gets ludicrously crowded and is best avoided). Some trains also have compartments reserved exclusively for women. Buying and reserving your tickets can take hours; sometimes there are separate queues for women – worth taking advantage of since they massively cut down time. If you've got money you can fly between major cities but there are frequent delays and booking difficulties.

Accommodation A whole range of hotels from expensive luxury palace-style accommodation to bug-ridden cells. There is no shortage of cheap, clean and perfectly safe places to stay. A government tourist bungalow (middling price range) is usually a safe bet. With so much choice there's never any need to stay in a hotel if you feel uneasy there.

Special Problems You're quite likely to get ill in India. Various kinds of dysentery and infective hepatitis are real hazards, though you might get away with just a dose of "Delhi belly". It makes sense not to drink unboiled water or to eat unpeeled fruit.

Theft is common and you should always keep your money and valuables securely on your person, preferably in a money belt. It's a good idea to carry small change to give to beggars, or a little food to share with children. You will also find hundreds of hustlers fighting for your attention. You need to learn quickly how to stay calm and clearheaded.

Guides *India – A Travel Survival Kit* (Lonely Planet) is invaluable, at least to begin with; later you may feel you need to break out of "the circuit". Lonely Planet also publish a regional guide to *Kashmir, Ladakh and Zanskar* and a *Trekking Guide to the Indian Himalayas*. For cultural detail the *Murray's Handbook to India* (John Murray), though originally published half a century ago, remains in a class of its own.

Contacts

AHMEDABAD: **SEWA (Self-Employed Women's Association)**, Textile Worker's Union Building, Ahmedabad (see introduction for more details).

BANGALORE: **Streelekha** (International Feminist Bookshop and Information Centre), 67, 2nd floor, Blumoan Complex, Mahatma Ghandi Road, Bangalore 560 011, Katnataka. Stocks all manner of feminist literature, journals, posters etc and provides space for women to meet.

BOMBAY: **Feminist Resource Centre (FRD)**, 13 Carol Mansion, 35 Sitladevi Temple Rd., Mahim, Bombay 400016. Carries out action-oriented research from a feminist perspective on a range of issues: health, sexuality, violence against women, discrimination at work.

Women's Centre, 307 Yasmeen Apartments, Yashwant Nagar, Vakola, Santa Cruz East, Bombay.

Research Unit on Women's Studies SNDT Women's University; 1 Nathibai Thackersey Rd., Bombay 400 020. Publishes a quarterly newsletter of the Research Unit on Women's Studies – useful resource about organisations and institutions in India involved in research and projects on women and development.

BORIVILI: **Forum Against the Oppression of Women**, c/o Vibhuti Patel, K 8 Nensey Colony, Express Highway, Borivili East 400066.

NEW DELHI: **Institute of Social Studies (ISS)**, 5 Deen Dayal Upadhyaya Marg, New Delhi 2. Voluntary, non-profit research organisation – concentrates on women's access to employment and role in development, also on strengthening women's organisations. The group publishes a newsletter.

Centre for Women's Development Studies, B-43, Panchsheel Enclave, New Delhi 110017. Undertakes research on women and development, and is currently developing a clearing house of information and ideas.

Indian Social Institute (ISI) Programme for Women's Development, Lodi Rd., New Delhi 110003. Aims to increase the participation of women at different levels in the development process through training courses for community organisers.

Indian Council of Social Science Research (ICSSR), 11PA Hostel, Indraprastha Estate, Ring Rd., New Delhi, 110002. Runs a women's studies programme and carries out wide-ranging research. They also organise numerous workshops and symposia on feminist themes.

Manushi, c/202 Lajpat Nagar, New Delhi 110024. Publishes the monthly journal *Manushi* – an excellent source of information on news and analysis of women's situation and struggle in India. Written in English and Hindi.

Kali for Women (feminist publishers), N 84 Panchshila Park, New Delhi, 110017.

The journal, *Manushi*, can be obtained in the UK from *Manushi* c/o Colworth Rd., London E11; in the US from *Manushi*, c/o 5008 Erringer Place, Philadelphia, PA 19144.

Books

Madhu Kishwar and Ruth Vanita, eds., *In Search of Answers: Indian Women's Voices* (Zed Books, 1984). Collection of articles from *Manushi* which provides a comprehensive, powerful and lucid account of women in Indian society.

Jeniffer Sebstad, *Women and Self-Reliance in India: the SEWA story* (Zed Books, 1985). Account of the formation and achievements of SEWA (see introduction).

Joanna Liddle and Rama Joshi, *Daughters of Independence – Gender, Caste and Class in India* (Zed Books, 1985). Reveals the extent to which class and caste define and limit Indian women's lives.

Gail Omvedt, *We Will Smash This Prison! Indian Women in Struggle* (Zed Books, 1980). A compelling account of women's struggles in western India in the 1970s.

Gita Mehta, *Karma Cola* (Fontana, 1979). Still in print, though now slightly dated. This is a sharp and cynical look at the way Indian spirituality is marketed for Western devotees.

Dervla Murphy, *On a Shoestring to Coorg: An experience of Southern India* (1976; Century 1985). More classic adventures by the well-known contemporary traveller, this time with her five-year-old daughter.

There are interesting contributions on India by **Marilyn French** in *Women: A World Report* (Methuen, 1985), by **Devaki Jain** in *Sisterhood is Global* (Penguin, 1985), and by the *Manushi* collective and an Indian Women's Anti-Rape Group in *Third World: Second Sex 1 and 2* (Zed Books, 1983 and 1987). See the general bibliography for details.

Minority Rights Group, *India the Nagas and the North-East* (MRG No. 17), *The Untouchables of India* (MRG No. 26) and *The Sikhs* (MRG No. 65). An exceptionally high standard of research and analysis, the MRG pamphlets will give you a quick and clear overview of the very deep divisions in Indian society.

Fiction

Anita Desai, *Clear Light of Day* (Penguin, 1980), *Baumgartner's Bombay* (Penguin, 1981). The best known titles from a widely acclaimed and prolific writer. Her books chart the changing position of women in a rapidly developing society.

Truth-tales: Contemporary Writing by Indian Women (The Women's Press, 1986). A collection of stories, many of them translated into English for the first time, by contemporary Indian women writers.

Attia Housain, *Sunlight on a Broken Column* (Virago, 1989). Set against the backdrop of Indian Independence this centres on the life of an orphaned girl growing up in a fundamentalist Muslim community.

Padma Perera, *Birthday, Deathday* (The Women's Press, 1985). Short stories, mainly exploring the contradictions for an Indian woman educated in the West on returning to her homeland.

Leena Dhingra, *Amritvela* (The Women's Press, 1988). Stylish account of a middle-aged woman's return to her native India after a life in England.

Sharan-Jat Shar, *In My Own Name* (The Women's Press, 1985). Autobiographical account of growing up in the Punjab, a life that includes forced marriage and emigration.

Shashi Deshpande, *That Long Silence* (Virago, 1988). A middle-class woman retreats to the country around Bombay and reconsiders her past.

Ruth Prawer Jhabvala, *Heat and Dust* (Futura, 1976), *A Backward Place* (Penguin, 1979), and others. Famous as a Booker prize-winner and long-time collaborator on Merchant/Ivory films, her writing charts the more irrational responses to Indian life.

Indonesia

I ndonesia extends over a vast chain of more than ten thousand islands. Though remote and exotic by European or American standards, for millions of Australians and New Zealanders this island nation constitutes the nearest form of abroad. Consequently, at least on better known islands, Indonesians are well used to independent travellers and, alongside the thriving package-tour industry (with developments particularly along the beaches of Bali), there is plenty of cheap, basic accommodation.

Despite being rich in resources, the general standard of living in Indonesia is very low, exacerbated by a rapid growth in population. This is most evident on the island of Java which now holds over 160 million people – most of whom are crammed into its polluted, chaotic, and heavily policed capital, Jakarta. As the nation's administrative centre, Java's influence, known as "System Jakarta", is widely resented and often disparaged as the successor to Dutch colonial rule.

In a nation of so many cultures, religions and languages, it is perhaps surprising that different groups manage to coexist and that the country as a whole has an image of stability. But the underside of this is the harsh, swift, and often brutal suppression of any opposition to General Suharto's regime, that has included the forced resettlement of islanders and the brutal military occupation of East Timor and West Irian. The people of Indonesia are predominantly Muslim but tend to be tolerant towards the different habits of Westerners, and provided you are careful to respect local customs you are unlikely to encounter the sort of aggressive sexual harassment reported by

women travellers in, say, Malaysia. You will however attract a fair amount of attention (often just friendly curiosity) which can feel oppressive at times. Indonesians neither share, nor sympathise with, the Western preoccupation with personal space, and privacy is something you have to learn quickly to do without.

Indonesian women certainly seem more independent and visible than in most Islamic countries. The islands' interpretation of Islam does not demand that women are veiled, government schools are co-educational, and there is relatively little discrimination between the sexes with respect to subjects studied and the number of years spent studying. Whether this will endure is uncertain. Despite government curbs, Islamic fundamentalism has recently gained ground, attempting to reaffirm Malay culture in opposition to Western influence.

There is a long tradition of organisation among Indonesian women. Voluntary women's groups have played an increasingly important role in the provision and delivery of social welfare services throughout the country. The Indonesian Women's Congress (*KOWANI*), a federation of the main **women's organisations** set up in 1928, runs a "legal literacy" programme and helps rural women to understand legal rights. It is campaigning for a more uniform marriage law to prohibit polygyny, child marriage and arbitrary male-initiated divorce, is lobbying for equal inheritance laws, and has autonomous groups focusing on a range of issues including reform of the abortion laws. In some areas these groups have to operate amidst considerable (and escalating) harassment from the emerging Islamic fundamentalist movement.

A Plant Collector's Dream

. . . .

After spending four weeks in the well-travelled islands of Java, Lombok and Bali, Janet Bell spent six months collecting medicinal plants on Seram, a small island in the Moluccas in the far east of Indonesia.

Joseph and Meli were transfixed by the tea bag I had produced from my pack. It wasn't until we lit a fire and made a brew that they were fully satisfied that its contents were what I'd promised.

What delight! Joseph's face lit up at the taste and he chuckled quietly.

The light was fading and the almost saturated mist had become quite chill. I still couldn't believe that we were only two degrees south of the equator and I was craving a woolly sweater. The drop in temperature associated with altitude seemed more pronounced than I was used to, but by now the only too familiar mountainous terrain had also modified my attitude to height, when I considered that we were already about the same height as Ben Nevis.

Indonesia's dramatic and varied scenery continued to amaze me. Seram was completely different from the fertile, highly-populated, volcanic islands of Java, Bali and Lombok, which had served as my introduction to this huge and diverse country.

While I cooked some food for our demanding stomachs, Joseph and Meli collected ferns and made a mattress under the overhang, our shelter for the night. Little did I realise at the time that it was for my benefit, not theirs. We ate our rice with some dried spiced fish from the coastal village we'd left that morning. Rice was something of a treat for all of us since, unlike most of Indonesia, sago was the staple diet in the Moluccas. However, its wallpaper-paste-like consistency scarcely lent it the characteristics of good hiking fodder, and neither did the flavour.

Joseph and Meli experimented with a tea bag themselves while I dealt with my pack. Everything I produced was questioned – "apa ini?" (what is it?), "untuk apa?" (what's it for?); my torch, my knife, my first-aid kit, even my loo roll, for which I could provide no explanation. The things I considered essential seemed trivial, when all my companions' needs fitted into a small pouch. Still, they seemed grateful for the odd garment I offered for the night.

I snuggled down on my temporary bed and contemplated the sky above me. It was rare to have the opportunity to sleep under the stars without fear of a night-time downpour. The overhang would protect me sufficiently without blocking my view. I looked up the steep gorge, which was strongly illuminated by the moon, despite the night being somewhat overcast. I thought that if I were to awake during the night once the clouds had cleared, I would probably think it was morning. Already a long way beneath us, I heard the Wai Lala rushing down from the ridge we were heading over, its swirling blue waters ricocheting relentlessly against the sides of the gorge as it plummeted to the south coast.

The morning was chilly. Meli prepared himself for the climb by viciously rubbing *daun sila* leaves all over his legs and producing huge red welts similar to nettle stings, but far more painful. The locals used the leaves whenever they undertook a long trip to ease weariness in their limbs and to ward off cold at higher altitudes. It seemed more like shock treatment to me. Still, I made a note in my book to add to my ever-increasing list of plants used by the local people.

"The women were surprisingly unin-hibited in their approach; touching me, playing with my hair, and patting my bottom and thighs in sheer disbelief"

That was, after all, my reason for being on this rugged, paradisical island, 1500 miles from Jakarta. This particular trip was taking me inland over an 1800m pass, one of the lowest points in the dramatic ridge that separated the interior villages from the coast, a formidable barrier that still isolates them from the fingers of commercialism which have encroached upon the coastal villages. The ridge, I learnt, is much more than a physical barrier, but has a significant role in the history and mythology related to the Seramese culture. It also represents the division between the northern and southern tribes on Seram, the Manusela and the Nualu.

Further to our west the ridge climaxed in the stark limestone outcrop of Gunung Binaia, the "mother mountain", the greatest spirit force in the eyes of the people and the foundation for the matriarchal lineage that characterises the whole island. This association, coupled with the fact that Islam has no great hold on the island, has meant that the women have rather more of a respected position in society than might be expected. Even in the parts of Indonesia where Islam dominates women have a better position than in the more fundamentalist areas of the Islamic world. This is the reflection of a culture that has evolved by picking up, adapting and modifying the various religious and cultural waves that have swept through its land over the centuries. As a fulcrum of the Indo-China trading axis, Indonesia has distilled diverse influences to create an identity of its own.

Our hike took us up steeply into the mysterious serenity of the moss forest. There was an uncharacteristic calm and quiet at this height, in sharp contrast to the riotous noises of the lowland rainforest. Misty epiphytes hung from moss-covered trees, beards of soft pastel-coloured lichen draped themselves between the branches, the scenery black and white in soft focus; all my senses were muffled by the mist. My feet sank silently into the spongy moss beneath us, giving life and a new spring to my stride. But this was a false paradise; from time to time my legs would crash straight through the luxurious covering, taking me thigh-deep into a limestone gully.

"Taller and broader than most of the men in the village, let alone the women, white-skinned and Western, I obviously didn't go unnoticed"

A rapid descent led us to Manusela, where we received an extraordinary welcome. Taller and broader than most of the men in the village, let alone the women, white-skinned and Western, I obviously didn't go unnoticed. Joseph and Meli had evidently found our little trip together as amusing and curious as I had, and I was frustrated that my Indonesian didn't stretch to interpreting their breakneck account of the hike.

We had attracted quite a gathering of tiny, smiling people. The women were surprisingly uninhibited in their approach; touching me, playing with my hair, and patting my bottom and thighs in sheer disbelief. "Kaki besar!" (big legs), the Bapak Raja's wife had exclaimed. But, for once it wasn't an insult, simply an observation.

The villagers in the interior were even tinier than their coastal counterparts, which is partly accounted for by their more impoverished diet. The creation of a National Park whose boundaries had encroached into their hunting grounds had resulted in dependence on their gardens, a few domestic chickens (which never seemed to be eaten), and a few tiny fish and prawns from the rivers. Where hunting was still permitted, it was generally the man's job, but out of the hunting season they would tend the gardens with the women; these were often situated at least an hour's walk away from the village. It was also a common sight to see a man cradling an infant and looking after the small children.

We were invited to stay in the house of the Bapak Raja, the village leader, literally the "father king". In Manusela the Bapak Raja not only acted as the father figure and the law, but appeared in church on Sunday morning as the pastor, preaching from the pulpit, his head emerging from underneath the festoons of glittering streamers that I usually associated with Christmas. It was a rare sight in that simple wooden building with magnificent views up towards the heavy rounded form of Merkele Besar and its smaller and more elegant partner, the pyramidal Merkele Kecil. No organ here, just a choir of simple pipes and the rich sounds of what are reputedly the best voices in Indonesia.

Despite Seram's geographical isolation and inaccessibility, it didn't survive the invasion of the missionaries. Most of the villages were at least nominally Muslim or Christian. In the interior they were predominantly Christian, although it soon became obvious that the traditional animist beliefs remained very strong. I was told a story about the history of the island by a man who lived in a neighbouring village. Noah's Ark apparently came to rest on the top of Binaia's neighbour, Merkele Besar, the paternal mountain. The villagers in the interior believe that the whole of the human race diversified from Manusela; their Bible stories all seemed to incorporate this strange blend of Christianity and local mythology.

"Plants were such an integral part of their lives that they couldn't look on them objectively or in isolation, as I did"

I had the good fortune to spend a few days in one of a very few villages to fully maintain its animist traditions. The villagers were proud of their culture and looked down on the rest of the island for having succumbed to other religions. They did not travel out of their territorial areas to any great extent and spoke a dialect which was difficult for even my Indonesian companions to understand. On our way to Houalu we stopped a night at another village on the coast where we came across a huge timbered monstrosity amongst the bamboo huts.

This, it transpired, was a missionary house, and its residents were focusing on the last bastion of traditional Seramese culture: Houalu. I couldn't help but smile inwardly when we learnt that although the missionaries had been there for over three years and were constantly trying to gain approval from the animists to build their house in Houalu, so far no permission had been or seemed likely to be granted. So far there were no converts either.

The day began in the same ways every day while I was staying in these villages. I would wake up to the sound of cocks crowing, babies crying and people coughing. At dawn the river was a hive of activity as the children filled the bamboo poles which served as elegant water carriers. The adults would make off for the gardens as soon as it was light to avoid the heat of the day. Sometimes I went with them, picking up endless plants along the way and inquiring about their uses. I soon learnt that direct questions about the way they used plants for food, medicines or construction materials yielded precious little information, simply because they didn't understand the question. Plants were such an integral part of their lives that they couldn't look on them objectively or in isolation, as I did. Most of my records were derived from direct observation or pointing out a plant and questioning its use.

During my stay I collected over 300 plants which served some useful purpose, but I had the feeling even then that I was only scraping the surface. Many of these had medicinal value, but others served quite curious purposes. For example, mashed young pineapple served as a DIY perming kit and the serrated and corrugated leaves of one creeping plant were used as toothbrushes.

The use of medicinal plants is not limited to isolated parts of Indonesia though, for in Java there are small factories which have been set up to produce "Jamu", as traditional medicine is known there. This small but profitable industry is run almost entirely by women and is regaining popularity as the preferred form of treatment, even where Western drugs are readily available.

It was very hard to leave Seram and its peaceful way of life, and I wondered what the next few years would bring; how far the logging road will penetrate into the interior, whether the missionaries will achieve their goals in Houalu, how long it will be before Manusela sees its first shop and the dawn of consumerism, how long before Coke cans clutter the pristeen pathways between the bamboo houses in Manusela. Jakarta brought me down to earth with a bump, the city of the great hypocrisy, attempting to unify and represent a country as diverse in culture and ideology as they come. "Do they hunt with bows and arrows in England?", one Bapak Raja had asked me on Seram. His country's capital would have presented him with as many surprises as a trip to London.

TRAVEL NOTES

Languages The national language is Bahasa Indonesian, relatively easy to learn at a basic level. There are over 200 languages and dialects among ethnic groups. Younger people and those working in the tourist industry generally speak some English.

Transport Boats and *bemos* (buses) are plentiful and cheap; hitching is uncommon but possible and relatively safe.

Accommodation Wide range – from luxury hotels to beach huts.

Guides *Indonesia Handbook* (Moon Publications, US) is a classic guide, so fascinating that it has been banned for sale in Indonesia – though you can carry it in.

Contacts

Organisan Wanita Jakarta Raya *(KOWANI)*, Jalan Diponegoro 26, Jakarta, Pusat. See introduction.

Books

Raden Adjeng Kartini, *Letters of a Javanese Princess* (Heinemann, Asia, 1983). Letters of a nineteenth-century Indonesian feminist and national heroine.

Nina Epton, *Magic and Mystics of Java* (Octagon Press, 1975). Interesting travelogue with anthropological slant.

Hamish McDonald, *Suharto's Indonesia* (Fontana, 1980). Thorough political account of events since 1965.

Minority Rights Group, *Women in Asia* (MRG, 1982). Contains an interesting section on Indonesian women.

A chapter on the rise of the Indonesian women's rights movement is included in **Kumari Jayawardena, *Feminism and Nationalism in the Third World*** (Zed Books, 1986).

Iran

· · · · · · · · · · · · ·

Whilst it is still possible to get into Iran on a two-week transit visa, it is difficult to contemplate travelling through this country with any degree of sanguinity or ease. In ten years of rule, the Ayatollah Khomeini created a climate of oppression unrivalled by even the excesses of the Shah. His successor, President Rafsanjani, has a reputation for pragmatism and a less rigidly anti-Western line, but seems unlikely to significantly challenge the more radically fundamentalist factions. Arbitrary arrests, torture and harassment by the Revolutionary Guards may have slightly abated but still

continue as a day-to-day reality while women, who bear the brunt of the nation's poverty, remain restricted and relatively powerless under Khomeini's interpretations of Shi'ite Islamic Law.

The most obvious laws that affect you as a traveller are those concerning dress – your whole body must be covered and hair hidden beneath a veil. Iranian women who refuse the veil, often as a spontaneous form of protest, run risks of flogging and imprisonment (as a foreigner you're more likely to be severely cautioned and forced to cover up). But however modestly you dress, you are bound to feel conspicuous and vulnerable; asserting your freedom to wander about independently places you in much the same category as a prostitute and you may well be harassed as such.

Against this, however, you can encounter incredible warmth and hospitality. In public, people tend to be constrained from approaching you by the omnipresent Revolutionary Guards, but in the privacy of their homes, Iranians often show traditional generosity and consideration for strangers, welcoming the chance to air their hopes and concerns about the future of their country. You have to be very careful not to compromise your hosts – it's actually illegal for an Iranian man to spend time alone with a woman who is not a relative. Despite these very real deterrents women do still make the journey across Iran. The undeniable beauty of the country and the nostalgic romance of the overland route to India provide the main incentives. Also, in purely practical terms travel is fairly easy. There are good roads and bus networks and plentiful budget hotels.

Whilst the rise of fundamentalism and the re-introduction of Islamic Law has affected the **status of women** throughout the Muslim world, Iran provides perhaps the most extreme example of women's repression under, and resistance to, this trend.

Women had been at the forefront of the revolution that toppled the Shah in 1979. Within the first few days of Khomeini's regime 25,000 women took to the streets of Teheran to protest their rights against pronouncements that women should veil in public. They were beaten and imprisoned. Since then wave after wave of legislation in accordance with Shi'ite interpretations of the Koran has been passed, effectively denying women any economic role, and relegating their status to that of "absolute property" of the man at the head of the family.

With a woman's testimony legally defined as worth half that of a man's, the dangers of being denounced to a popular court (usually for crimes of sexual immorality) are extreme; lengthy imprisonment, flogging and stoning are standard punishments, particularly for working-class women who have no recourse to bribes. Women have continued to oppose these laws, which are seen as threatening their security at the heart of the family and society. Besides mass demonstrations and spontaneous acts of defiance (anything from going unveiled to assassination attempts on Ayatollahs), large numbers of women have supported oppositional parties such as the People's Mujahideen and staged public protests against the Iran/Iraq war.

By the mid-Eighties over 20,000 women had been executed for "counter-revolutionary" or "anti-Islamic" activity. (Holland has been one of the few countries to accept Iranian women as political refugees overtly because of the sexual discrimination they face.) Whilst feminist groups in Iran have been forced underground, many still operate in exile.

A Lonely Journey
. . . .

Wendy Dison has been travelling for the last eight years. Deciding that a career in administration was not for her, she set off first around Europe and Africa and then on to Asia, crossing Iran alone on her way to the Himalayas.

"Salaam, Salaam." The face of the Iranian immigration officer at the border creased with pleasure when I greeted him in Farsi. Over his desk hung a sign which read "No East. No West. Islamic Republic.", and next to it a portrait of Khomeini glared at me.

As the official inspected my passport, looking from my face to the photo and back again, the smile was replaced by a frown. "Monsieur? Madame?" he asked. My short hair confused him and when he realised that I wasn't a man he made urgent gestures that I must cover my head.

I put on a woollen bobble hat which satisfied him, though the young men I talked to on the bus to Tabriz advised me kindly that to comply with Islamic law I must wear a scarf covering my hair and neck. They were students returning from Izmir university and had brought Turkish scarves, prettier than Iranian, for their mothers and sisters and they generously gave one to me. I must wear a knee-length coat too, they said, to hide the shape of my body.

The February sun was warm and the discomfort of wearing a scarf and long jacket increased my resentment. As we travelled through the pale, stony landscape the students talked to me of the repression and cruelty suffered in Iran since the Shah was overthrown in 1979 and Khomeini created his Islamic Republic. Never before had I felt such foreboding on entering a country.

"At one spot we were ordered off the bus and herded behind a wall under spotlights"

Between the border and Tabriz, a distance of 300 kilometres, we were stopped six times. Sometimes the police wanted to check our passports, other times Revolutionary Guards, wearing military-style uniforms, stopped us. Their job was to enforce the strict Islamic code and they searched our bus for drugs, arms and alcohol, forbidden foreign music and indecent pictures. They emptied handbags, confiscated cassettes, and ripped pictures of women with bare arms – or worse – from magazines.

We were treated with contempt and I was taut with resentment while photos of my family were inspected and my journal read. Probably few of them could read English but after this I kept separate notes, buried deep in my rucksack, of anything likely to cause trou-

ble. At one stop we were ordered off the bus and herded behind a wall under spotlights. The guards bullied us and an old woman was crying. I was taken with the women into a hut where we were body-searched by a female guard, all but invisible under a black enveloping *chador*.

It was dark when we arrived in Tabriz; night is a bad time to arrive in a city and the darkness made me more than unusually aware of the security I was leaving. A man I'd talked to on the bus also got off here. He told me he was visiting his sister and when he learnt that I had no plans he invited me to her house. "She will be happy if you stay with her," he said.

In a modern suburb of the city his sister, Eshrat, lived with her two young children and sister-in-law, Parvin. The women were delighted to see their brother and they fussed happily round both of us. They displayed a talent not rare in the East; that of making me feel at once a special guest yet very much at home. We sat drinking tea around a tall wood stove on Persian rugs, their half-forgotten English slowly returning as we talked.

Parvin and Eshrat were married to brothers who had been imprisoned for "being intelligent and lacking sympathy with the government". With bitterness they talked of life before the Revolution, when the Shah's policies of Westernisation and the new wealth from oil had brought a flood of nightclubs, dance halls, cinemas and bars to the cities.

Religion and politics have always been closely interwoven in Iran and with the overthrow of the Shah the religious leaders, angered by the growing materialism, banned these trappings of decadent Western culture. Only religious or classical Persian music was permitted, fashionable imported goods disappeared from the shops, and the menus in restaurants were restricted so much that people no longer ate out for pleasure. For those who weren't religious there was little joy in life.

Far more invidious was the position of women, who had been forced to return to their traditional role in society, denied freedom, further education and the opportunity to work. Parvin's medical training had been curtailed. Because female staff are needed in girls' schools, Eshrat was able to keep her job as a teacher, one of the few occupations still open to women.

Her uniform was a loose, dark tunic and a cowl that left only a circle of her face exposed. Most women wore the *chador*, a black sheet draped over the head and hanging shapelessly to the feet, worn over indoor clothes when outside the house. Those against the regime could keep within the law – though earn disapproval – by wearing a loose knee-length coat and headscarf pulled well forward to cover the hair. I hoped my jacket, which reached mid-thigh, was sufficiently modest, for I was warned that the Revolutionary Guards who patrolled the streets would stop any woman not considered decently dressed.

"All I could see of the women around me were the triangles of eyes and nose visible under the chadors"

The Iranians I met hated the regime they were forced to live under and all talked of leaving Iran. They dreamed of living in Britain or the USA but passports were not being issued and the few people who left the country did so illegally. Demand for hard currency by those planning to leave has resulted in a thriving black market. Of course, because Khomeini's supporters would disapprove of a veil-less woman, I met only pro-Western Iranians and my impressions were necessarily one-sided.

Next day Parvin and I dressed in our street clothes and caught a bus to the bazaar in the city. I was shocked to find separate entrances on the bus for men and women and that inside we sat segregated by metal bars. All I could see of the women around me were the triangles of eyes and nose visible under the *chadors*. When they struggled on and off the bus with a baby and a shopping bag they had difficulty remaining covered and most of them habitually used their teeth to trap the *chador* tightly round their faces. I felt revulsion against a society that treated women like this.

Women took advantage of one area where they could show their individuality. Though they were always black, the fabric of *chadors* varied from plain nylon to finely embroidered silk – reflecting the taste and social standing of their owners. Other clues to identity were given by elegant high-heeled shoes peeping below a hem, the flash of gold rings on well manicured fingers or a hennaed pattern painted on the back of a hand. Except for the odd turban and the popularity of beards, the men, in trousers and cotton jackets, looked like Europeans.

When I left Tabriz, Parvin guided me through the jungle of Persian script at the bus station and wouldn't let me pay for my ticket. We hugged goodbye, both sorry that I couldn't stay longer, but my visa barely gave me enough time to cross the country. We hoped we might meet again in England. As a result of the Iran/Iraq war doctors were in demand and Parvin was to be allowed to complete her training, possibly in London.

The journey to Teheran began with prayers led by the driver, who possibly had his erratic driving in mind. Frilled curtains hung at the windows and an elaborate arrangement of silk flowers obstructed the driver's view. This was a deluxe bus but there was no air conditioning nor did the windows open. As the sun rose so did the temperature inside the bus, and I suffered in my jacket and scarf. On the back of the ticket was printed "Please observe regulations as to the Islamic covering", which seemed unfair under the circumstances.

The restaurant where we stopped for lunch was a large isolated building in the desert – functional and soulless. As in all Iranian restaurants we paid on entry, a procedure simplified by limiting the menu to one item, invariably *chello kebab*, a bland dish of rice and grilled meat. Meal stops were short and people ate rapidly, leaning over their plates. This time I only wanted tea and was directed to the kitchen where, in the dark and confusion, a man beckoned to me. He gave me tea but held my arm to prevent my leaving while another man thrust a hand up under my jacket.

For a long moment I wanted to throw my tea over them, but they laughed at my anger and I fled. I found a seat and sipped my tea, trying to look calm. A woman sat at my table and we exchanged smiles, allies in a man's world. Back on the bus I wanted to share a bag of pistachio nuts with my neighbour but her *chador* enveloped her so completely that I couldn't talk to her. My feeling of isolation was acute.

Apart from the incident in the kitchen I wasn't bothered by men. The stares I often attracted were curious rather than lecherous. Though I received much Muslim hospitality and people were kind and helpful, I didn't relax in Iran. People seemed afraid to show too much friendliness and usually remained distant and guarded. I was nervous too, not knowing the power of the various authorities. In Teheran when I was taken by police to the station for questioning, even though they were courteous I thought anything could happen and I was worried.

With a two-week visa I hadn't time for more than a superficial look at the cities I passed through, and I only saw the countryside through a bus window. Yet I was left with vivid impressions: mud villages that appeared to grow out of the earth, high snow-topped mountains forming a background to arid plains, goats foraging around the black felt tents of tribal nomads, ancient bazaars with lofty brick-vaulted roofs, tombs of medieval poets in rose-filled gardens and, in every village and corner of the city, the graceful turquoise domes of the mosques. I remember in particular the splendid Royal Mosque at Isfahan, decorated inside and out with intricate patterns of rich blue and gold mosaic tiles which completely cover the walls and domes.

"Once we got in his car, his nervousness showed that he knew the risk he was taking"

The beauty of Isfahan was marred, however, by giant paintings of Khomeini which hung in prominent sites. The heavy brows, hard staring eyes and thick lips appeared merciless. Because of the association with this cruel face I no longer enjoyed the singing of the muezzin calling the faithful to prayer. The chant now sounded menacing.

In Shiraaz I became friendly with a man staying at the same hotel as me and accepted his offer to drive me to see Persepolis, the sixth-century capital of Persia. Once we got in his car his nervousness showed that he knew the risk he was taking – Islamic law forbids an unchaperoned woman to be with a man who isn't a relative. "If we are stopped you must say I am your guide and that you are paying me," he said.

Away from the city he relaxed. We explored the ruins, stopped in a village where the best halva in Iran comes from, and had lunch of kebabs and grape juice at a roadside café. It was good to be out in the sunshine even though I couldn't take off my jacket and scarf. My hotel room was the only place I could remove them; even crossing the landing to the bathroom was considered public.

Checking out of the hotel the next day I discovered that my passport, left at reception, was missing. The next 24 hours were a nightmare. The British Consul in Teheran said he couldn't replace the passport but would issue me with papers to enable me to fly back to England. I wept with frustration. The hotel owner suspected my friend. Wasn't he desperate enough to leave Iran? The idea appalled me that the thief could be someone I trusted.

The police were very concerned and treated me kindly. That night they came to the hotel to question the staff and evidently frightened the thief so much that he jettisoned my passport. I found it lying on the stairs next morning and cried with relief. The hotel owner put an arm of comfort round my shoulder but as soon as he realised his indiscretion he pulled away quickly. "What a bloody country" I thought, smiling at him through my tears. I caught the next bus to Zahedan on the Pakistan border.

TRAVEL NOTES

Languages Farsi, Turkish, Kurdish, Arabic. In the main towns and cities quite a number of people speak some English.

Transport Both trains and buses are relatively cheap and efficient. In the former there are women's compartments which provide a welcome feeling of comfort and security. The bus system however is more extensive and generally quite comfortable and efficient. In some cities the buses are segregated, with women seated at the front.

Accommodation Plenty of reasonably priced hotels remain in the medium-sized towns. For your own peace of mind it's best to carry your own padlock.

Special Problems The most obvious one is gaining entry to the country at a time of fluctuating diplomatic relations. The best bet is to apply for transit visas at the Iranian Embassy in Turkey.

There's no option about dress: you need to cover yourself completely, preferably in sombre clothing. This must include a scarf that covers all your hair.

Security is stringent and Revolutionary Guards will stop and search coaches fairly frequently. You might also be body-searched when you cross over the border into Iran.

Guides There are no specific guidebooks to Iran. For limited coverage of the country as part of the overland route to India, there are reasonable sections in *Traveller's Survival Kit to the East* (Vacation Work) and *West Asia on a Shoestring* (Lonely Planet).

Contacts

Committee for Defence of Women's Rights in Iran, c/o London Women's Centre, Wesley House, 70 Great Queen St., London WC2B 5AX. A broad-based solidarity group geared towards publicising women's struggles in Iran and co-ordinating international campaigns to protest the conditions faced by women. They produce an occasional bulletin in English.

Iranian Community Centre (Women's Section), 465a Green Lanes, London N4, ☎081-341 5005. Resource centre producing a women's newsletter in Farsi.

Women & Struggle in Iran. Quarterly publication produced by the Women's Commission of the Iranian Students Association in the USA. Copies available from ISA, (WC-ISA), PO Box 5642, Chicago, Illinois 60680, USA.

Books

Tabari Azar, et al., eds., *In the Shadow of Islam: The Women's Movement in Iran* (Zed Books, 1982). Written by three Iranian women, this book covers the Women's Movement in Iran since the Revolution, focusing on the relation between Islam and the struggle for women's emancipation.

Guity Nashat, *Women in Revolution in Iran* (Westview, US, 1983). Study focusing on the central paradox of women's participation in a revolution that deprived them of many rights. Analysis of the pre- and post-revolutionary periods as well as the revolution itself.

Farah Azari, ed., *Women of Iran* (Ithaca Press, 1983). A collection of papers by socialist-feminist Iranian women which bring a fresh approach to the political debates surrounding the Revolution.

Manny Sharazi, *Javady Alley* (The Women's Press, 1984). An outstanding novel set in Iran in 1953, and seen through the eyes of a seven-year-old girl whose childhood certainties are coming under threat.

Freya Stark, *The Valleys of the Assassins* (1934; Century, 1984). Another world – and another classic piece of travel.

Sousan Azadi and Angela Ferrante, *Out of Iran: One Woman's Escape from the Ayatollahs* (Futura, 1988). Harrowing account of a refugee's flight from her country.

Shusha Guppy, *The Blindfold Horse* (Penguin, 1988). Memoirs of a childhood life amid the intellectual aristocracy in pre-Khomeini Iran.

Miranda Davies, ed., *Third World – Second Sex 2* (Zed Books, 1987). Includes part of a study on crimes against women in Iran by Simin Ahmady.

Ireland

. . . .

Ireland is divided: twenty-six
predominantly Catholic counties
make up the independent
Republic of Ireland (Eire),
while the six largely Protestant
counties of **Northern Ireland**
(The North) comprise a separate
state, ruled by Britain and, for
the last two decades, occupied
by the British army.

Although attempts have been
made to promote **Northern
Ireland** as a holiday destination
and centre for commerce, few
British travellers without relatives or connections would
consider going there. The
British media's insistence on
portraying an area gripped by
sectarian "troubles" and defining
its population as either the
villains or victims of "terrorist"
attack is a strong deterrent. But there's also the more rational fear that resentment of the British army will extend to visitors.

Since it was drafted into the north in 1969 (ostensibly to protect the
Catholic minority from escalating Protestant sectarian violence), the army
has been responsible for a continuing catalogue of civil rights abuses, including arbitrary searches and arrests, detention without trial, the coercion and
torture of suspects and the lethal use of plastic bullets. And the partisan
nature of the occupation has been powerfully revealed by the obvious target-
ting of Catholic communities.

British travellers may, justifiably, feel uneasy about travel in such a
context, yet, with the exception of the Republican bars of Belfast or Derry,
little antagonism is shown. The Irish, on both sides of the border, have an
unrivalled reputation for hospitality and, unfettered by British propaganda
and censorship, a fair number of American, German and Scandinavian
women visit the region.

By contrast, the Irish Republic has a well established tourist industry,
based mainly on its rural attractions – the miles of green, empty landscape

and beautiful, largely undeveloped coastline. Many women return year after year for this, the clichéd (but true) charm of the place, and the relaxed atmosphere you find even when travelling alone. Sexist attitudes certainly prevail but are much more likely to take the form of an old-fashioned male courtesy and genuine bewilderment as to why you should choose to travel alone, than any overt sexual harassment. The cost of living, which is at least 25 percent higher than in Britain, can be an initial shock, but it is alleviated in part by the fact that this is a perfect country for cycling and camping.

Women have played a significant part in Ireland's struggles for self-determination, though the movement for national liberation has not necessarily gone hand in hand with that for women's liberation. Votes for women were introduced into the Republic six years ahead of Northern Ireland and Britain, but women's rights were, and continue to be, severely restricted by a constitution that enshrines many Catholic values. In Northern Ireland, women are, in strictly legal and economic terms, better off, but their rights have always lagged behind those gained for women in Britain.

Northern Irish women played a prominent role in the civil rights movement of the 1960s, and in the 1970s a small but articulate feminist movement emerged, made up mostly of middle-class women. They attempted to operate across the sectarian divide, dealing with issues such as childcare provisions, wife-battering, contraception and abortion (still an imprisonable offence throughout Ireland). They argued that Northern Ireland should be brought in line with British legislation on these issues. At the same time, the Catholic community was facing the introduction of internment without trial. Women as well as men were being arbitrarily detained, more were becoming drawn into direct Republican activism, and women prisoners in Armagh jail were beginning a series of protests for political status, culminating in the "dirty protest" and hunger strikes.

A division arose between those feminists who looked for emancipation through operating within the British government system, and those who saw it proceeding from British withdrawal. The divide still persists today, although notable campaigns – such as that against the strip-searching of women political prisoners and the setting up of the Belfast Well Women's Centre and Rape Crisis Centre – have received widespread support.

Many similar developments were occurring in the Republic, as women began to meet to discuss and act upon the need for specific women's rights. These included access to contraception (at the time banned even for married couples), equal pay for equal work, state benefits for unmarried mothers and legislation for divorce. Twenty years later there has been a slight slackening in the laws against birth control but divorce remains outlawed by the constitution, as does abortion. Since a 1986 court ruling, it has become illegal for agencies even to offer abortion counselling or advice to women.

Lesbians, on both sides of the border, have long had to struggle against entrenched homophobia. It took a ruling by the European Court of Human Rights in 1982 to bring Northern Ireland's homosexuality laws into line with Britain, and gay sex between consenting adults is still illegal in the South. There is, however, a very small but well established network of lesbian groups, and many active gay rights organisations operate within the country.

Behind the Picture Postcards

· · · · · · · · · · · · ·

Hilary Robinson has often visited the Republic of Ireland. In particular, she tries to go every summer to County Clare where she travels with fiddle to the annual music summer school at Miltown Malbay.

It is all too easy to be utterly romantic about the Republic of Ireland. The beauty of the landscape, the numbers of people who still live on a small scale close to the land, and the generosity of spirit of so many of the people that you meet: all combine to encourage an idyllic view. Add to this an almost universal ignorance of Irish history on the part of the British (can you remember being taught any at school?) and the notion of a "Real Ireland" encouraged by the tourist trade and you have the stuff of all romantic dreams – a place with an immutable essence where you can put aside the aspects of the twentieth century that you want to escape

Now, I've spent some of my happiest times in recent years in Ireland, but I feel very strongly that the romanticised "Real Ireland" does not exist, not generally and especially not for women. There are elements, of course, on the visual level. It's very easy to clamber up some hillside in Kerry or Connemara and to sit, breathing in the clean air, and gaze out at the beautiful landscape with its fields of luscious green, the Atlantic in the distance, perhaps a whitewashed cottage with a couple of children out in the yard, a smallholding, a man driving his eight cows home for milking . . . This is when the fantasies start about giving everything up to come and live here on the land, where the children can grow up healthily.

However, each time I go and get to know the country better, the mismatch between the picturesque image of the Tourist Board and the differing realities for the various people I meet seems to become more pronounced.

The parts of Ireland I know best are Dublin, Galway and County Clare, though I have made occasional trips into Connemara and Westport, to Kerry and Kilkenny. I've travelled there for various reasons, but mainly because of Irish music. I play the fiddle a little and try to get to Miltown Malbay in County Clare each summer for a music summer school. It's great fun and draws people from all over the world, even as far as India and Australia, to play and listen. Although most of the traditional musicians who have made recordings are men, and some of the playing in some of the bars is competitively macho, a large number of women also play and attend the school. I found many of the older Irish people, in particular, to be delighted that a non-Irish person should show such an interest in their culture – quite a humbling experience as an Englishwoman.

> **"It's not uncommon for Irishmen to assume that if you're not Irish you must be on the pill and therefore have no good reason to refuse their advances!"**

One of my trips to Ireland was to research part of a thesis about contemporary women artists, when I went to speak to women (mainly in the Dublin area) about their work; another time I went cycling with a boyfriend around Clare, Galway and Connemara, with a tent strapped to the back of a bike.

I have several times had heated arguments with Irishmen who insist that Ireland is a matriarchal society. Their reasoning was based on the romantic ideal that women should be respected simply for being women, mixed with a dollop of mythology about motherhood and strong female figures; I felt it left out any appreciation of the day-to-day realities for their own mothers and sisters, and of the links between

Catholicism and the State in Ireland. The recent divorce and abortion referendums (both won by the church and conservatives) would be a case in point.

The Irish population is nowhere near as dense as in Britain, but it is much more evenly spread across rural areas. Farms are handed down through families and have been important in the past in the support by families of prospective marriages. One of the arguments in the divorce referendum was that women would not only split families but farms, many of which survive only just above subsistence level. Ireland remains the only European country besides Malta to forbid divorce. Not surprisingly, a Dutch friend marrying an Irishman and going to live in Ireland deliberately chose to marry in Holland.

On a practical level, motherhood is held in more esteem than it is in England, something I noticed in little things like the sympathetic attitude of shop assistants to women with children in tow. With regards to sex, it's not uncommon for Irishmen to assume that if you're not Irish you must be on the pill and therefore have no good reason to refuse their advances! On one occasion I realised that a discussion of sexual politics was almost like "talking dirty" to the man I was in conversation with.

In some ways attitudes are similar to those of the British in the Seventies, but for different reasons. The laws around contraception may not be as extreme as they used to be, but the moral climate of Ireland is still a far cry from the so-called permissive era we experienced in Britain. In theory you can buy condoms across the counter in chemist shops; in practice I found it to be a lot more difficult, since many chemists, even in the centre of Dublin, refuse to sell them "on moral grounds". Another difference is that in Britain in the Seventies, men expected sex in the name of "free love". In contrast, the Irishmen that I have met are far more likely to be romantic,

to talk about falling in love, to want to take me across the country for the weekend to meet their parents, to demonstrate a level of romantic seriousness, despite the fact that I am only visiting – in short, to "court".

"This is the only European country I have visited where I've felt happy to hitch alone"

I have heard non-Irish women say that there's a vulnerability in this attitude that can be refreshing after the horribly repressed emotional life of British men. Personally, I've found the "back on top of a pedestal" position, although intended as flattering, deeply uncomfortable. Furthermore, for me to relax into it in a kind of "holiday romance" mode would only end up abusing the man concerned. I learned this the hard way, causing pain on all sides. Irish women would, of course, say something else again; one spoke to me very persuasively of what she called the deep conservatism of Irishmen's notions about women. On looking around a crowded bar in Doolin, County Clare, which every summer is filled with people chasing Irish music, and today seemed mainly to consist of Irish men and German women, she said she was waiting for the first case of herpes to be heard of in the village: then "all the men would soon go home".

There are two aspects of travelling as a woman in Ireland that I especially appreciate. The first, and most practical is that this is the only European country that I have visited where I've felt happy about hitching alone. Obviously, I got offered lifts on my own more easily than when I was one of a couple, either with another woman or with a man; and I am not denying that things can go wrong. But I've never once had cause to feel threatened and, compared to many countries, hitching in Ireland is much more accepted as a way of getting about. Train fares are high, car insurance astronomical, and buses rare out in the country. Consequently you see all sorts of people at the sides of the road, from old men cadging lifts to teenagers trying to get into town.

A number of people said they'd stopped for me because they saw the fiddle case, and was I sure I wasn't Irish? Sometimes families would stop and once I got a lift all the way across the country from a soldier in the Irish army – we shared a similar dislike of Margaret Thatcher, so that was okay. I once got a lift from a single woman driver who told me she always offered lifts to women because she used to hitch herself, and had once or twice been in awkward situations. She never offered lifts to men.

The funniest time was a few miles outside Miltown, the day the summer school ended. It was tipping down, my friend and I were miles from anywhere, had been walking for an hour and were soaked to the skin. A car finally stopped; the man driving had seen the fiddle cases and took pity on us. He'd stopped for another woman (plus fiddle) earlier, and stopped again for another (plus guitar) a few miles further on.

The second thing I'm grateful for in Ireland took a bit of time to notice and that's the absence of pornography. No doubt it's around somewhere in some form, and no doubt it's missing for all the wrong reasons – repressive attitudes towards sexuality in general, rather than radical attitudes towards the representation of women. But it's just not there when you go to buy a newspaper; which is a holiday in itself.

TRAVEL NOTES

Language English and Gaelic.

Transport Buses and trains are very expensive. A good cheap way of exploring the countryside is to hire a bicycle. Hitching is relatively easy and safe, perhaps the greatest problem being lack of cars. Sunday traffic is usually the worst, either cars are packed with families or you get single men with time on their hands looking for some "fun".

Accommodation You can camp more or less anywhere in the countryside, as long as you ask permission of the landowner. Youth Hostels get booked up in the summer so it's wise to book in advance. Bed and Breakfasts are usually relaxed and comfortable.

Special Problems Travelling in the North you may well be stopped by British Army or RUC patrols, and asked for your name, address, date of birth and immediate destination. Whatever your feelings or politics it's best to be civil and to the point.

It is now legal to sell contraception, although some chemists refuse to stock condoms.

Ireland is notorious for its continuing abuse of gay rights. It's a good idea to get advice from a gay group about the local scene.

Guides *The Rough Guide: Ireland* (Harrap Columbus) is easily the most informative.

Contacts

The yearly **Irish Women's Guidebook and Diary** provides a comprehensive list of addresses for individual women's/lesbian groups throughout Ireland. It is available from feminist bookshops in Britain and Ireland or direct from Attic Press, 44 East Sussex Street, Dublin 2.

Below are a small selection of **groups**:

BELFAST: **Women's Centre**, 18 Donegal Street, Belfast BT1 2GP, ☎0232 243363, and **Just Books**, 7 Winetavern St., Smithfield, ☎225426, are good for contacts. You could also try **Lesbian Line**, ☎0232 222023; Mon–Thurs, 7.30–10pm.

DUBLIN: **Dublin Resource Centre**, 6 Crowe St., ☎771974, and **Women's Centre**, 53 Dame St., Dublin 2, ☎710088, will provide you with information about local groups and campaigns. The **Hirschfeld Centre**, 10 Fownes St., ☎910139, is a recommended gay/lesbian meeting place. **Women's Centre Shop**, 27 Temple Lane, ☎710088; **Books Upstairs**, Market Arcade, off South Great Georges St., ☎710064, and **Spellbound Books**, City Centre 23/25 Moss St., ☎712149, all have a good selection of feminist and lesbian literature and stock.

Holidays

The **Southern Ireland Wimmin's Holiday Centre**, "Amcotts", Clonmore, Piltown, County Kilkenny, Eire, ☎Waterford 43371, offers luxury accommodation in a tranquil rural setting, plus good food, a library, cycles for hire and a convivial, hospitable atmosphere.

Magazines

The entertainments guide, *In Dublin*, and the gay magazine, *Out*, both have listings on women's groups.

Books

Eileen Fairweather, ed., *Only the Rivers Run Free: Northern Ireland, the Women's War* (Pluto Press, 1984). A selection of women describe the everyday realities of life in the North.

Eilean Ni Chuilleanain, ed., *Irish Women: Image and Achievement* (Arlen House, Ireland, 1986). Ten essays by specialist authors trace the position of women in Irish society from ancient to modern times.

Nell McCafferty, *A Woman to Blame* (Attic Press, Ireland, 1986). Brilliant study by one of Ireland's most acclaimed journalists of the "Kerry Babies Case". It examines the grip on Irish women by the Church, patriarchy and culture. Also look out for McCafferty's selec-

tion of articles and essays, **The Best of Nell** (Attic Press, Ireland, 1987).

Liz Curtis, *Ireland: the Propaganda War* (Pluto Press, 1984). An excellently researched, clear and unanswerable indictment of the British media's campaign against Irish Republicanism.

Fiction

Frances Molloy, *No Mate for a Magpie* (Virago 1985). Tragi-comic tale of a Catholic girlhood in Ireland.

Emma Cooke, *Eve's Apple* (Blackstaff, 1985). Set against the 1983 Irish abortion referendum campaign, this novel describes a woman's isolation and desperation with middle-class provincialism and the hypocrisy of religious values.

Edna O'Brien, *Johnnie I Hardly Knew You* (Penguin, 1977), and ***The Country Girls*** (Penguin, 1960). Accomplished novels from a popular and prolific author. Both explore issues of emerging female sensuality within the repressive social climate of rural Ireland.

Mary Lavin, *Mary O'Grady* (Virago, 1987). Best-known work by a prestigious Irish writer about a woman who leaves the country life to set up home in Dublin. Also worth reading is ***The House in Clewe Street*** (Virago, 1987). A family saga which uncovers the problems and pitfalls of an Irish Catholic upbringing.

Deirdre Madden, *Hidden Symptoms* (Faber, 1987). A brilliant, hauntingly evocative novel that centres around a woman's attempt to reconcile herself to the sectarian murder of her twin brother.

Julia O'Faolain, *No Country for Young Men* (Penguin, 1980). Devastating story of human and political relations in contemporary Ireland.

Italy

Many Italians regard Italy as two distinct countries: the north and the south. The first, ending at Rome, enjoys an image of prosperity and innovation; the second, encompassing the notorious Mafia strongholds of Calabria and Sicily, is considered poor, corrupt, backward and, at least in the minds of most southerners, cruelly neglected. Compared to the thriving industrial centres in and around Turin or Milan, the south is indeed desperately poor. It's also more traditional and conservative and, in this respect, less easy for travellers.

As a people, the Italians are hospitable and talkative, and it takes little to be drawn into long conversations, however poor your grasp of the language. Train journeys provide the perfect setting and, perhaps surprisingly in the light of widespread street harassment, several women report these as among their most enjoyable experiences. Fellow passengers like practising their English and everyone tends to pool their efforts to keep a conversation going. Travelling with a child, you'll be made even more welcome. All over Italy children are doted on and fussed over, providing a wonderful passport for meeting people and gaining their respect. It's quite common in a restaurant for your child to be whisked off to the kitchen and showered with kisses and treats for a couple of hours while you enjoy your meal.

Travelling alone, or with a female companion, you'll be treated as a curiosity. But the attention you receive can vary from quite genuine concern about your isolation (and possible loneliness) to incredibly brazen and persistent harassment. The cat-calls, propositions and kerb-crawling tend to get worse as you head further south and in Sicily, especially, it takes a tough skin and plenty of determination to stick out a holiday on your own. As usual the hassles and misconceptions face as you become known in a place and even the most frustrating moments can be tempered by singular acts of great warmth and generosity.

Italian society (with the weight of the Catholic Church behind it) is so strongly family-oriented that it's hard for the older generation, at least, to understand any female desire for independence. Mamma may appear to reign at home, but outside *machismo* is irritatingly prevalent. Italian men are stereotypically proud, vain, and not easily rejected, and in any situation like to at least be *seen* to have the upper hand.

Italian women have a lot to battle against and today every city has at least one **feminist organisation**; several have their own bookshops (also meeting places) and documentation centres. The roots of the movement lie in the generation referred to as the "Sixty-eighters", political activists who, during that period of social turmoil, gradually saw the need for women to organise separately from men. Many did and still co belong to the huge Italian Communist Party (PCI)*; feminism and communism have always been strongly linked in Italy. *Noi Donne*, the country's first feminist magazine, was started as an organ of the PCI in the 1940s – but campaigns for divorce rights and against rape, the successful fight to legalise abortion, and a more recent women's peace movement, all indicate a firm belief in the importance of autonomous organisation.

---

*At the time of writing, the PCI, in the wake of events in Eastern Europe, are considering changing the "Communist" part of their name.

Singled Out
. . . .

Celia Woolfrey has travelled widely in Italy, both north and south, most recently to research and write a *Rough Guide* to the country.

I first went to Italy about ten years ago on holiday and have kept going back ever since. However, researching the *Rough Guide* took me to areas less well known to British tourists and revealed a lot more about Italian life. I travelled mainly on my own, though friends came out to join me for the occasional week and I had contacts to look up while I was there. I spent most of my time finding good places to eat and

stay, checking out the tourist sights, visiting art galleries and museums, and occasionally sampling Italian nightlife.

My mode of travel covered the range, from walking and hitching my way through the Dolomites – my best lifts were got by accosting people at petrol stations – to travelling by Vespa in the hinterland of the Riviera. In practical terms it's no problem travelling on your own. Buses and trains are cheap, and in summer there are other women doing the same thing, so if you want company you can meet up with people in Youth Hostels and campsites on the tourist circuit. It's the reaction you get which is difficult.

Actually choosing to go to places on your own can lead people to make strange assumptions about you; Italians are sociable and often go around in big gaggles of family or friends so that being solitary is seen as something weird, and pitiable. People often couldn't work out what I was doing. They would relax visibly when I told them I was in Italy to do a guidebook, but often they weren't convinced. However, there is a positive side to travelling on your own in that you're too much of an oddball to hassle, as people don't know what they are going to get in return.

"Now that I'm 27 and old enough to be called Signora, I've entered a new phase of life"

I was attracted back to Italy not so much by the landscape and architecture, but more by the style and grace with which things are done. Among friends there is a lightness of touch, even when someone is telling you off. Add to this the café life, the posing, women dressing up in furs to eat ice cream . . . it's a very glamorous place. If you are backpacking on a low budget it is worth bearing in mind that Italy today is a far from cheap country and one where appearances hold great store. You get caught out it you're on the way back from a beach holiday with only shorts and espadrilles to wear. Nobody actually turns you away because you're wearing the wrong clothes, but they do something much worse – they feel sorry for you for not having any pride in yourself.

Age makes a big difference; now that I'm 27 and old enough to be called Signora, I've entered a new phase of life. People talk to me completely differently, as though I deserve automatic respect. Conversely, you know there's going to be trouble if someone says "Mah, Signorina . . .", as they begin to explain why you can't do what you were about to. The reaction I got from women of different ages altered too. Older women I chatted to on buses would say "brava" ("well done") when I

told them what I was doing, though I got the feeling they thought I was completely mad. Women younger than me didn't bat an eyelid and were amazingly helpful and open; they would give me lots of information and talk about anything.

It was people my own age who made the most assumptions about me; the question "So what are you really doing here?" would underlie a conversation, as though researching a guidebook must be a cover. For what? Stealing someone's husband? Finding a lover? Messing around before I went back to where I came from and settled down? I came off badly in what one woman wanted to turn into a gladiatorial conversation when we were talking about "courting". She asked what the English word was for the Italian verb *corteggiare*, to which I replied that there was an English verb "to court" but that it wasn't used a lot nowadays. "And what do English women do these days," she retorted, "jump into bed with a man on the first night?" This was an assumption which I came across on other occasions – frustrating in that it's an argument which you can't hope to win. However, you are just as likely to find newspaper articles referring to "Thatcher's Victorian Britain" – a nation of prudes, paranoid about AIDS.

"At a couple of places women hotel proprietors pursed their lips and looked me up and down before telling me that they didn't have a single room"

Attitudes towards me varied greatly from place to place. Big cities and isolated mountains were no problem; it was at family resorts that I had the strangest time. I didn't always get a good reception at some of the seaside towns on the Riviera and the Adriatic. At a couple of places women hotel proprietors pursed their lips and looked me up and down before telling me that they didn't have a single room and that no, they didn't have any double rooms either, at least until next year. The problems occurred when people placed me out of context: what was I doing on my own in a family resort? (They were very sure they knew.)

And family resorts mean just that: holiday towns full of numbered rows of sunbeds, crammed together so the extended family can observe at close quarters other versions of itself. Here tradition and continuity are all important. One Italian women who ran a seaside pension for years told me that the same families came back to her year after year and that some were in tears last season when she told them she was closing down.

In these and regular Italian towns, I was surprised how often the place virtually closed up at night, with shutters pulled down over shops and few signs of life except the occasional bar. This was the time when I was most harassed by men, who tended to assume I was a prostitute if I was walking along the street on my own. This aggravated me a lot because it meant I had to look as if I was on my way to somewhere, even when I wasn't.

In La Spezia, on the Ligurian coast, I was bothered by endless tooting cars as I waited for a bus. It reached extremes in the resort of Rimini after about 8pm, where cars crawl along the main street from the station to the beach, the front passenger door mysteriously springing open as you pass by. Apart from this I was surprised to get more catcalls and stupid comments travelling with a woman friend than when I was alone. I think this was because people just assumed we were on the pick-up – we were obviously tourists.

Most of the time I've felt safe on my own and confident about initiating conversations with people. Comments or overtures from strangers tend to be less offensive than in London, and politely declining someone's offer to accompany me on my way has never

lead to threats, as it has done in Britain and other countries. I often ate alone in restaurants or sat in a bar I felt comfortable in.

Conforming to family life is still a big deal for most of the people I met. It's harder in a practical sense to leave home, and I met quite a few people in their thirties who still lived with their parents because places to rent with friends hardly exist and mortgage arrangements for buying property are quite different from Britain. It was those who had broken away from the rituals of conforming who were most generous with their time and spare rooms, and a lot of fun.

"Many of the assertive women I met would rather have died than call themselves feminists"

Women my age who I met through friends were generally very career oriented, had married to subdue family pressure and were childless. The all-providing mother seemed to be a bit of a spectre for the men as well as the women who have actively rebelled against big dinners and domesticity. This to the extent that they were horrified when I said I liked cooking and eating. "Reactionary women!" they screamed.

As in the rest of Europe, Italian feminism seems to have gone through a quiet patch since the Seventies and many of the assertive women I met would rather have died than call themselves feminists. At the same time, Italian women have achieved some of the most progressive legislation in Europe surrounding maternity benefits and childcare.

Italians have a very positive attitude towards children; they love them dearly which is why they want the best facilities for them to grow up in. Ninety percent of the under-threes are in fulltime nurseries, lessening the burden for women who are working outside the home. Even small villages in the Emilia

Romagna region (admittedly more progressive than most) have purpose-built nurseries. An enlightened communist administration and a slow political process have brought this about. It is ironic indeed that the woman politician with the highest media profile is Scicciolina (Llona Staller), dubbed the *pornodiva* by the press and a whore by her Radical party boss.

Living in the City of Fashion

After two years teaching at a women's university in Hiroshima, Japan, Valerie Waterhouse travelled extensively around the Far East. She has since moved to Milan, where she teaches English at the British Council.

Milan is thought of as the Italian capital of industry and of fashion. The "industrial" label makes the visitor expect a city of high-rise blocks and of factories belching out evil smoke. Yet the centre of the city, dominated by the elaborate Gothic cathedral, is surprisingly grand and beautiful. Wandering through the Saturday markets or exploring the nightlife along the canals inspires excitement, even passion.

It is a city where north meets south, where *casinisti*, chaotic attitudes, combine with a strong work ethic. The Milanese work like maniacs too. For me, these conflicting elements are epitomised in the frivolous extravagance of the cathedral, the Duomo, which took 500 years of hard work to build. Significantly, it took a Frenchman, Napoleon, to get it completed.

Industrial activity is hidden around the outskirts of the city, but it creeps into your nose and lungs invidiously in the form of Milan's most serious problem – pollution. Milan is the most polluted city in Europe and people here regularly develop irritating coughs or bronchitis. Having to wash your hair twice as often as normal can also become wearisome. In early 1989 there was a drought and the pollution build-up became so serious that an emergency was declared. On certain days it was recommended that babies and young children should not be taken outside, and people could be seen in the streets wearing smog masks. No cars were permitted in the centre and people were asked to turn off their central heating. As a result, pollution was reduced; but whether these changes continue to operate once the "pollution emergency" is forgotten remains to be seen.

The fashion industry in Milan is both more attractive and more visible. Milan is an essential stepping stone on the career path of any model wishing to make it big. Models, mostly Americans, come here to collect "tear sheets", photographs in the glossies. Photo shoots near the Duomo or in the glass-roofed arcades nearby are frequent, and tall, pale models of both sexes drift through the streets of the "Golden Rectangle" of expensively labelled designer shops.

Despite this reputation for sophistication, Milan is not as liberal as you might expect. One of the largest differences for a British person lies in the attitudes towards the family. For both social and financial reasons, young people tend to live with their parents until they marry. Students and the unemployed, without state support, cannot afford to live by themselves, and working people see comfort, convenience, and being able to own a car as more important than independence.

In general, less importance is placed on independence than in Anglo-Saxon countries and this is reflected in attitudes to travel. When I told friends or neighbours that my sister was moving to Tanzania, the most common reaction was: "How terrible!" Among older people, the next question was: "How do your parents feel about both of you living abroad?" Even young people were sometimes horrified.

"The 'Latin lover' in a man usually manifests itself in the first, or possibly second, meeting"

Living with another woman teacher, like me in her twenties, provokes some odd reactions. Our neighbour, a middle-aged housewife, thinks nothing of wandering in if the door is open, and commenting if we haven't done the washing up. This of course is double-edged. It is irritating when neighbourly gossip starts intruding on your privacy, but wonderful when you want someone to water your plants, or discover that you've just run out of eggs.

The friendliness displayed by neighbours or people in the street lends justification to the hospitable Italian stereotype. Ask someone on the bus for directions and you will be overwhelmed by people offering you advice. Local shopkeepers are always willing to chat to you about the lack of rain, "La Thatcher", or how your Italian is coming along.

Not surprisingly, friendly social invitations are not uncommon for women. But acceptance of an invitation to a party or to the theatre, even in a group, is often taken as equalling interest in sexual involvement, and it can be hard to counter this macho assumption. The "Latin lover" in a man usually manifests itself in the first, or possibly second, meeting, and with a directness not usually encountered in colder climates. Platonic relationships, as an Italian male I met sadly commented, are extremely difficult to achieve. Of course, not all men behave in this way, but it's in this area that you experience the biggest cultural gulf. Italian women have told me that it is the image of the sexually liberated northern blonde which attracts this sort of behaviour.

In terms of street harassment, approaches are usually verbal. Men do sometimes press up against you in a crowded tram, but no more so than in Britain. However, standing alone or with a female friend at a bus stop at night is taken as an invitation. Men in cars will stop at five-minute intervals and utter those ubiquitous words "Vuoi un passagio?" ("Do you want a lift?"). Generally speaking, a short sharp "no" soon causes them to drive away. If you take the usual precautions, Milan is not an unsafe city to travel in. Public transport is extensive, efficient and safe, and runs until 1.30am. The only place to avoid is the *Circonvallazione*, the city ring road. Prostitutes – many of them transvestites – operate here, so the number of kerb-crawlers can become more than a nuisance, as can harassment from flashers.

Perhaps because it is unusual for women to socialise alone together, I have rarely received a social invitation from a Milanese woman. Riding on a winter tram, you might well think that all women here have fur coats, long hair shoulder pads and jangling jewellery. Bodily conscious femininity is highly prized and foreign women with short hair, flat masculine shoes and ankle-length coats are a definite oddity, though not unacceptable. My closest Milanese friend is Cinzia, a thirty-year-old bilingual Italian who works for an air freight forwarding company. Unlike most women of her age, Cinzia is single and lives alone, since her immediate family have emigrated to Australia. Her Australian connections and perfect English make her untypical, but her example proves that independent women who do not fit the stereotype do exist in Milan.

Amelia, a silk buyer, is another exception. At 35, she is a junior partner in her company and is sent regularly to China, Thailand or India on business trips. Pregnant for the first time, she is still working and intends to return to work soon after the baby is born; she is fortunate in that her career to date has been a successful one. Other women find the path to promotion blocked and feel that less capable men are valued more highly.

Though advanced compared to Britain, Italy lags behind some countries in its provision of crèches, and professional childminders are not always easy to find. But this is partly because of the strength of the family support system. Maternity benefit, on the other hand, is much better than in Britain. Female employees can take six months paid leave, a further six months at seventy percent of their salary, and have a job guaranteed on their return.

Some Italian feminists now believe, however, that fighting for such concrete rights as provisions for small children or abortion on demand should no longer be the primary concern of the Women's Movement. In Milan there is a women's bookshop, run by a group of voluntary workers, whose main activities are political discussion and the publication of feminist books and magazines. The Milan group feel that in society as it is, women are not motivated to become involved or to realise their full potential. We must look within or at our relationships with other women if society is to change. Co-operation between women, for example teachers and pupils in schools, is more important than fighting for individual rights which, in any case, not all women will think worth fighting for. When I asked whether social liberation

for Italian women matched theoretical advancement, the woman in the bookshop said she couldn't comment. "Every woman is different. It depends on the individual."

"For Italians, racism extends to anyone coloured, including their own compatriots south of Rome"

The women's bookshop has a noticeboard containing personal ads and information about cultural events of interest to women. There is a similar noticeboard at Milan's Women's Club, *Cicip e Ciciap*. The club was established by three women, involved in the Women's Movement of the Seventies, to provide an atmosphere where "feminism could flourish". Daniela, a founder member, told us that it is the only club of its kind in Italy, although similar places are planned to open in Turin and Rome. No importance is placed on the sexual preferences of the clientele and in the club women sit talking, their short hair and jeans in this city of fur coats lending truth to the idea that it is ridiculous to talk about women as a homogeneous group with the same needs and wants.

One issue just emerging into media discussion in Milan, as elsewhere in Italy, is racism. Italians I spoke to often mentioned the British reputation for racism, but to my mind the only difference between the two countries is that Italians have yet to confront the problem. And for Italians, racism extends to anyone coloured, including their own compatriots south of Rome. When seeking accommodation, we found that, as white, foreign females in stable jobs, we were perceived as ideal tenants. (It is illegal for landlords to evict their tenants, and they hope that foreigners will not be as well informed about their rights.) However, attitudes may well have been different had we been a different colour. At one accommodation agency, a landlady had specifically requested foreign girls, but "non di colore". We wondered what would have happened when our black or Asian British friends had come to stay.

The issue of racism is one which many Milanese cannot afford to ignore for much longer. There are a growing number of poor black Moroccans, Algerians and Ethiopians living here now. Often we see them sleeping in the parks, where they store their few belongings under bushes. Public reactions vary from sympathy to downright hostility. As a tourist, of course, you will mostly be met with friendliness.

A Chinese Traveller in Sicily

. . . .

Helen Lee, a British woman of Hong Kong descent, spent six months in Sicily with her English husband. Only through giving English lessons did she begin to feel at all accepted.

When the opportunity arose to travel to Sicily for six months with my husband, Jules, I leapt at the chance. It seemed a perfect opening to dispose of the stifling, mundane day-to-day activities of work and life, and to pack my home into one rucksack. This would also be the first time I had travelled with a man and I saw it as a chance to explore a new country with security and ease. It's annoyingly ironic that to escape likely sexual harassment and nuisances from men, you are forced to travel with one of them. However, my experience wasn't as straightforward as that. Although I initially enjoyed the novel sense of relief and safety, and life undoubtedly became smoother, we remained items of fascinating doorstep gossip owing to our unusual pact. This, coupled with my inexplicable "Englishness", not only caused a riot, but seemed to block any further attempts to understand us.

We chose for the first month to live in Taormina, a medieval hill town overlooking the Ionian sea on a spur of Monte Tauro, Sicily's most exuberant holiday resort (mainly for wealthy Germans). I loved strolling through the main Corso Umberto, lined with beautiful palaces transformed into bars, *pasticcerias*, restaurants and expensive clothes shops, and I found it easier to start off living in a tourist resort where people knew English and were accustomed to foreigners.

> *"Despite this lazy and agreeable life, I still felt an undercurrent of tension on account of my colour"*

We had no trouble finding accommodation. All we had to do was ask at the tourist office and keep our eyes open for notices with the word *affitasi* (to rent) displayed on doors and shop windows. An Italian friend gave me the useful tip that rent can often be reduced by straight away offering the landlord a few months' payment in full. Later, when we decided to move again and I felt more confident about speaking Italian, I found a place through an *Agenzia Immobiliare* (estate agent). This was a beautiful two-bedroomed flat in the nearby town of Giardini-Naxos and commanded gorgeous views of Mount Etna from one window and the beach from another – a far cry from our dark, cold and cramped London flat.

It may be a cliché but Sicilians are renowned for their joyous love of life, for their great enjoyment of the simple sensual pleasures of eating, drinking, sleeping, and idle banter with the neighbours. I spent the next few months completely indulging in all my favourite senses: waking to the early morning sounds of the *carciofini* (artichokes) man, calling out his goods as he wheeled his cart through the streets; the aroma of fresh ground coffee and the fragrance of freshly baked pizza and pasta drifting from homes at mealtimes; the flamboyant fish stalls displaying the catch of the day, whole swordfish, heaps of flesh-coloured prawns and great slabs of tuna; the *pasticcerias* with their wicked cakes, pastries and dazzling array of homemade Sicilian sweets; and, best of all, the brilliant sweet-smelling flowers that Sicily is so famous for. Being vegetarian, I loved the wide range of fruit and vegetables available – ruby tomatoes tasting of sunshine.

I grew to thrive on the afternoon siestas, the perfect antidote to our usual substantial three-course lunch of pasta, fish and fruit. And there were many aspects of Sicilian culture that I could identify with, as a Chinese, such as the importance of the family, especially at mealtimes, with their chaotic loud chatterings and adoration of food. In the evenings I'd put on my finest rags, and look forward to the ritual *passeggiata* – a time to stroll leisurely and to admire the beautiful women and frown at their fur coats. The men were even more dashing in their sharp suits, hair greased back, sauntering along the pavements or else driving beaten-up cars or riding wildly, usually in pairs, on noisy mopeds.

Despite this lazy and agreeable life I still felt an undercurrent of tension on account of my colour. It became unsettling to walk into a bar or *trattoria* and always be greeted by hard stares and be aware of people nudging one another. I grew to rely on Jules being with me and could feel my independence dwindling. It was easier travelling in larger cities like the island's capital, Palermo, where I could disappear among the crowds. With its stupendous churches, cathedrals and fountains. I found this a powerful and impressive place. I loved the markets – the confusion of stalls brimming with food and shopkeepers eagerly competing against each other, singing out their prices – which reminded me of the streets in Hong Kong. The many warnings I'd received from tourists about Palermo seemed quite ill-founded and I never came across even a hint of the Mafia.

"Theirs was a familiar story of being hemmed in by groups of men clustering around them, leering and touching"

I spent many days travelling by train along the coast and deep into the countryside, but despite all the horror stories I had also been told about Italian trains, I never encountered an unpleasant situation. Although trains were nearly always late and inevitably overcrowded, passengers were generally friendly and I found this one of the most relaxing ways to travel. Only going inland, where I was more of a curiosity, proved strenuous at times; not to mention frustrating, as Jules's personal experience was so different, he couldn't always understand what I was suffering.

It was a relief when I met a group of American women students at Taormina bus terminal. Homeless and penniless, they ended up spending the Easter holiday with us and in that short time we formed a strong friendship. I vividly recall one incident when they went into the village to shop, excited at the prospect of eating ice cream and practising their Italian, only to return an hour later, angry, flustered and humiliated. Theirs was a familiar story of being hemmed in by groups of men clustering around them, leering and touching. During their stay I noticed that only one woman, of Mexican origin, was repeatedly left alone; Sicilian men seemed to disregard her in the same way that they look down upon Arab women as racially inferior.

My worries about an increasing cultural gap – the Sicilians' misunderstandings of me and my steady intolerance of their ways – were to be proved wrong. As a way of improving my Italian and at the same time earning money, I began advertising English lessons and to my astonishment soon gained a handful of private students.

These ranged from an initially reluctant six-year-old girl to an enthusiastic bank clerk who was determined to develop her vocabulary beyond the monotonous bank conversations with tourists. I was overwhelmed by the generosity of my students who, at the end of each hourly lesson, would nearly always present me with flowers, chocolates or some other gift.

The girl's parents would insist I eat lunch with them twice a week before lessons. Farida was an adopted Sri Lankan and an only child. Because of her colour she had problems with other children at school, so perhaps the parents thought I might provide some comfort. We spent many happy hours sketching and playing together in a mixture of Italian and English. Being with a child, I had less worries about making a fool of myself and learned many new words and expressions.

With these new responsibilities I regained my sense of independence and began to really enjoy myself. I noticed that people were beginning to take me seriously and whenever I walked into the bank to change money, I found myself greeted with nods and whispers no longer of "Chinese" but of "English teacher". It was far too premature to assume their respect, but at least people seemed less suspicious and more willing to accept me.

TRAVEL NOTES

Languages Italian, with strong regional dialects. If you can't speak Italian, French is useful. People working in tourist services usually speak some English.

Transport Trains and buses are reasonably cheap and efficient. Hitching is easy enough but risky, especially in the south.

Accommodation *Pensioni* (and more expensive hotels) are plentiful throughout the country.

Special Problems *Machismo* rules and harassment can be a problem, especially in the south which some women find quite unbearable. Railway stations everywhere are particularly hazardous. You should spend the least possible time in them, and never sleep in a station; you run the risk of theft and sexual assault. In general the most obvious strategy is to avoid eye contact. Whatever clothes you wear, you're still likely to be followed, pushed and touched and have your route blocked. Italians are quite amazing at identifying foreigers.

Beware of the police, too. According to Diana Pritchard who has lived and travelled extensively in Italy: "Their conduct is an unpleasant combination of abuse of authority (even the Italian public are cautious of them) and an apparent lack of respect for foreign women. Some of my worst experiences have involved the *Carabinieri* – the armed police – ranging from the indiscreet fondle of my breast as I walked by, to a time when a group of *Carabinieri* demanded that I open the door of a tiny bedroom in which a female friend and I were staying. Although I eventually managed to get them out of the room, we were followed the next day until we left town."

Guides *Rough Guides* to Italy, Sicily and Venice (Harrap Columbus), all recommended.

Contacts

The following is a selected list of **women's centres and bookshops**. Often bookshops (*librerie*) and centres (*case*) are combined in the same building. A *biblioteca* is a library and suggests a more academic place.

ALESSANDRIA: **Casa delle Donne**, Via Solero 24, 15100.

L'AQUILA: **Biblioteca delle Donne**, c/o A.I.E.D., Corso Federico 11 58.

ANCONA: **Biblioteca delle Donne**, Via Cialdini 26.

BOLOGNA: **Librellula, Libreria delle Donne**, Strada Maggiore 23/e. **Centro di Documentazione Ricerca e Iniziativa delle Donne**, Via Galliera 4. Open from 8am–2pm, the centre promotes research on women's issues and includes a small but growing feminist library. **Circulo Culturale "28" Giugno**, Piazza di Porta Saragozzae, ☎43 33 92. Gay centre, bookshop and library that often holds lesbian meetings, social events, etc.

CIVITAVECCHIA: **Centro Donna 'Terradilet'**, V.G. Abruzzeze, 00053.

FIRENZE: **Libreria delle Donne**, Via Fiesolana 2B; **Casa delle Donne**, Via Carraia 2.

MILANO: **Libreria delle Donne**, Via Dogana 2; **Casa delle Donne**, Via Lanzone 32; **Centro per la Difesa dei Diritti del Donne**, Via Tadino 23. **La Nuova Idea**, via de Castiglia 3, ☎68 92 73. Gay bar. Thursday is lesbian only.

MODENA: **Casa delle Donne**, Via Cesana 43.

PARMA: **Biblioteca delle Donne**, Via XX Settembre 31.

PISA: **Centro Documentazione Donne**, Via Puccini 15.

REGGIO EMILIA: **Casa della Donna**, Viale Isonzo 76.

ROMA: **Libreria delle Donne**, Piazza Farnese 103; **Centro Studi Elsa Bergamaschi**, c/o UDI, Via Colonna Antonina 41, 3rd Floor. Feminist library and archives.

TORINO: **Casa delle Donne**, Via Fiocchetto 13.

Books

Sibilla Alermo, *A Woman* (Virago, 1979). A classic in Italy, first published in 1906, the semi-autobiographical story of a girl growing up, dominated by her love for her father, but determined to break away and forge her own life.

Dacia Maraini, *Woman at War* (Lighthouse Books, London, 1984). By one of Italy's best known contemporary writers, it records, in diary form, a woman's growing self-awareness, beginning on holiday with her husband. The book encompasses weird characters, political argument and a wealth of sensual detail. Also by the same author, ***The Train*** (Camden Press, 1989). This brilliant satire on student life in the 1960s follows a group of friends on their way to an international socialist gathering in Helsinki.

Natalia Ginzburg, *The Road into the City* and ***The Dry Heart*** (1963; Carcanet, 1989) and others. The constraints of family life are a dominant theme in Ginzburg's writing, and her own upbringing is the source for this rigorous yet lyrical work. A radical politician who sits in the Senate in Rome, she is Italy's best-known woman writer, and most of her books are available in translation from Carcanet.

Elsa Morante, *History* (Penguin, 1980). Capturing the experience of daily Roman life during the last war, this is probably the most vivid fictional picture of the conflict as seen from the city.

Mary Taylor Simeti, *On Persephone's Island* (Penguin, 1988). Sympathetic record of a typical year in Sicily by an American who married a Sicilian professor and has lived on the island since the early 1960s.

Lucia C Birnbaum, *"Liberazione Della Donna": Feminism in Italy* (Weslyan U. Press, US, 1983). Good general survey – focuses on post-war developments.

Judith Hellman, *Journeys amnog Women: Feminism in Five Italian Cities* (OUP, 1987). Good, readable study of the womens' movements since 1968 in Turin, Milan, Reggio Emilia, Verona and Casserta. Slightly limited focus – mostly on the activities of the *Unione Donne Italiane* (*UDI*).

Fiona Pitt-Kethley, *Journeys to the Underworld* (Chatto and Windus, 1988). English poet searches Italy for the sibylline sites, a good third of her time in Sicily – though Pitt-Kethley's salacious appetite for sexual adventure often distracts from the real interest.

Thanks to Diana Pritchard and Jane Harkess for useful insights, and Susan Bassnett, who obtained most of the addresses listed above.

Jamaica

Mountains, beaches and a tropical climate attract tourists all year round to Jamaica. Tourism is integral to the island's economy, and strings of discotheques, expensive restaurants and watersports centres line the coast roads. At the same time beaches are never crowded, and outside major resorts like Montego Bay there's plenty of scope for more adventurous travel, though it won't be cheap.

Safety is mainly a hazard in and around the capital, Kingston. The people of Jamaica are mostly very poor; unemployment is high and violence, much of it politically motivated, has become a regular feature of city life. No traveller is advised to walk there alone, especially at night, but tension fades visibly as you move away from the area. You can expect comments from men wherever you go, but no general threat of sexual attack. Communication, however, can prove an unexpected problem. Although British colonisation has left English as the official language, most people speak a local patois which is very difficult for outsiders to understand. It's much easier and probably safer to travel with someone who knows "Jamaica talk".

The importance of reggae music amongst young people, the practice of Rastafarianism (a cult based on the divinity of the late Emperor Haile Selassie of Ethiopia), and moves to achieve official recognition of Jamaican dialect as a language in its own right, are all signs of a nation struggling to define its cultural identity. **Women** are integral to this process, for they have always been greatly responsible for preserving African tradition in the passing down of customs through the family. Recognition of the hitherto submerged role of women in Caribbean history lies at the core of Jamaica's most radical women's group, *Sistren* (meaning sisters), a theatre collective for working-class women. According to founder-member, Honor Ford-Smith, the groups use drama as a consciousness-raising tool, "a means of breaking silence, of stimulating discussion, of posing problems and experimenting with their solutions." This approach is far removed from other women's organisations which tend to focus on domestic and handicraft schemes which do little to challenge the actual position of women in society.

Encounter with a Rastawoman

. . . .

Mara Benetti travelled to Jamaica with friends. During her ten-week stay she found that, though difficult at times, it was more rewarding to explore the island alone.

My first three weeks were a gentle breaking-in period during which I got used to being shouted at in the street – "Ehi! Whitie! Whitie!" – from passing cars and lorries, and learned how to cope with the constant hassling which tourists can expect to suffer. With time I felt stronger within myself and decided to travel around the island.

With its eruptive vitality and alien ways, Jamaica is an intimidating country for a woman to travel alone. However, in the end I much preferred it to travelling with white friends. Alone it was easier to divorce myself from the wealthy tourist hordes and, although I certainly felt insecure and threatened at times, I always ended up having some interesting encounter. I learned to get used to the men who swarm around almost any white woman with caressing looks and sweet words. They are different from, say, the Italian *pappagallo* or the North African male champion; in Jamaica attitudes to sex are more free and easy, sexual taboos appear to be less strong, and I came to the conclusion that the dominant reason behind these seductive approaches was the "subtle charm of the bourgeoisie"

which white skin exerts on people who are very poor. If you go out with a Jamaican man don't be surprised to find yourself paying for two.

Contacts with women in Jamaica aren't easy. Unlike the men, they aren't particularly inclined to strike up a conversation, partly because they're too busy making ends meet, and partly because they see Western women, with the allure exerted on Jamaican men by their wealth, as dangerous competition. From a distance I was struck by the preponderance of strong "mother" figures, mainly a result of the high number of "baby mothers", that is women who are single parents. Relatively little importance is placed on the institution of marriage, but womanhood in Jamaica seems to revolve around children.

"Rastawomen struck me with their strength of character, confidence and self-possession"

With its total rejection of birth control, this emphasis on children is especially strong within the Rastafarian community. The rasta queen is meant to be entirely subordinate to her king. Yet the rastawomen I met struck me with their strength of character, confidence and self-possession. They stood firm and independent. Many lived with their children without men in their lives. The community was generally supportive and the baby's father gave some erratic contribution to the upbringing of his offspring, but it was the women who provided for most of their needs and ran the household.

This was the life of one of the few rastawomen I had the chance to meet.

My encounter dated back to the very beginning of my stay when I made a trip north with Tekula, an American black dreadlock woman I had met through a friend. Tekula was incredibly beautiful and, with her unusual light blue eyes, aroused great interest in everyone she met. She was also very stylish, always dressed in clothes dyed and designed by herself with great inventiveness and skill.

Something must have attracted the rastawoman who approached us as we sat on the beach at Orange Bay. With a sense of purpose she walked straight up to Tekula and, after exchanging a few words, invited her to her hut in the bush. I was taken along as a sort of special concession for the woman took one look at me and announced: "The Bible says woman shall not wear men's clothing," staring at my baggy trousers which, up to that moment, I'd thought very respectable.

Our guide, who was tall, well-built and in about her mid-thirties, led the way up a hill along a path which soon disappeared to leave us scrambling through tropical vegetation. After the first hill we descended into a valley covered with small coconut trees, then up again, past another valley in which grazed half a dozen goats, then up yet another hill.

I can hardly remember how many hills and valleys we walked, but we finally made our way along the edge of a mound at the end of which a couple of bamboo sheds stood on a flattened open space. The first, largish and built on a raised platform, had a couple of beds in it and most of her belongings – a plastic bag full of rags, clothes and several blankets – as well as a wooden table cluttered with tobacco leaves and small parcels of *ganja* characteristically wrapped in brown paper. The other hut was her kitchen, open on two sides, with an open fire and a few makeshift seats made of old beer barrels.

The woman lived alone, although that day several of her men friends were present, all young rastas looking proud and dignified despite their unkempt appearance. They were poorly dressed and no one wore shoes. We were ushered into the first hut and told to make ourselves comfortable and take a seat on her bed. She rolled up a massive joint for herself and offered me some tobacco when I said that *ganja* was too strong.

"Is the only white woman and a 'bald head' . . . I felt so out of place I could only sit in silence and soak up the scene"

It began to rain and everyone came to take shelter and the hut became really crowded. As the only white woman and a "bald head" (the rasta expression for all non-Rastafarians) I felt so out of place I could only sit in silence and soak up the scene. The conversation was in patois, double-dutch to me, and I could only understand the usual "Praise Jah, Rastafari", repeated by everyone so often and regularly that it gave a musical rhythmic quality to what was being said.

Our hostess seemed to rule like a queen. She pointed to the banana and the coconut trees that grew around the hut; at the yam, the green breadfruit she had just collected from the lower branches of a tree, and launched into a thanksgiving litany to Jah. At some point – I didn't understand why or what in the conversation had prompted it – she started to undo her flowery head-scarf. It was an automatic movement, one gesture after another, as she kept on talking to her attentive public. Finally her dreadlocks tumbled down from the top of her head, heavy, long, twenty years of them perhaps? She looked suddenly younger and gave us all a proud satisfied smile before wrapping her hair up again and folding everything into place.

TRAVEL NOTES

Languages Most people speak patois or "Jamaica talk" amongst themselves, but can easily switch into English. Language problems usually depend on the situation you find yourself in.

Transport Buses are cheap, but slow, and the driving can be pretty wild. Minibuses also operate on all the main routes, always jam-packed since they only set off when full. Some taxis have meters, but it's wise to sort out the fare before you set off. Hitching is not recommended.

Accommodation Hotels tend to be expensive and it's usually better to try to find a room for rent. There are lots of houses on the beach at Negril which offer inexpensive rooms.

Special Problems There are varying reports about the safety of Kingston – the shanty-town areas in the southwest of the capital are definitely to be avoided – but provided you feel confident and carry very little money it's worth a visit. Market prices shoot up one hundred percent at the sight of a white face, so bargaining is a must.

Standard medical care is very dubious and medicines expensive, so make sure you are insured and, as far as possible, take your own supplies. *Ganja* or marijuana is widely grown and smoked, but it's illegal. It's also very, very strong.

Guides *Caribbean Islands Handbook* (Trade and Travel Publications) is from the publishers of the excellent *South American Handbook* and includes a good section on Jamaica.

Contacts

Sistren Theatre Collective, 20 Kensington Crescent, Kingston 5. The group works mainly in the shanty-towns and in rural areas, but it's worth getting in touch to try to see them in action.

Books

Sistren, *Lionheart Gal – Life Stories of Jamaican Women* (The Women's Press, 1986). Edited by Sistren's long-standing artistic director, Honor Ford-Smith, this book is based on testimonies collected in the course of the theatre collective's work with ordinary Jamaican women.

Pat Ellis, ed., *Women of the Caribbean* (Zed Books, 1987). This collection of essays provides a good general introduction to the history and lives of Caribbean women.

Michelle Cliff, *Abeng* (The Crossing Press, New York, 1984). Explores the life of a young girl growing up among the contradictions of class, colour, blood and Jamaica's history of colonisation and slavery.

Erna Brodber, *Jane and Louisa Will Soon Come Home* (New Beacon Books, 1980). The author's first novel, written in the form of a long prose poem about life in Jamaica.

Ziggi Alexander and Audrey Dewjee, eds., *The Wonderful Adventures of Mrs Seacole in Many Lands* (1957; Falling Wall Press, 1984). Mary Seacole, who was born into Jamaican slave society, writes about her life and travels.

Pamela Mordecai and Marvyn Morris, eds., *Jamaica Woman* (Heinemann, 1982). Exciting anthology of poems by fifteen Jamaican women.

Also look out for the work of Jamaica's best-known woman poet, **Miss Louise Bennett**.

Japan

For some years now Japan has been asserting its power as the world's richest nation, the pivotal force of international commerce, technology and fashion. Alongside this, a new nationalistic pride has emerged – one that increasingly relegates visitors from less successful nations to a second-class status. This is less of a problem for white Westerners, who tend to be treated with traditional hospitality and courtesy, but black or Asian visitors (of whatever nationality) face fairly blatant discrimination.

The country is an expensive place to visit and the crowds and

hectic pace of the cities can be hard to adjust to. However, Japan does have a reputation for safety. Sexual harassment and violence are relatively rare (at least on the streets) and, even wandering around at night, you're unlikely to feel personally threatened. It is however, easy to feel isolated. People might be curious about you, and want to question you about Western culture or practise their English, but few follow this up. Westerners have a reputation for being clumsy, confrontational, ignorant of etiquette, and very much out of step with Japan's peaceful and harmonious way of life. Even if you speak Japanese you'll find it difficult to cross the cultural divide.

Living and working in the country you'll also come up against a deeply entrenched sexism and conservatism. Pornography is evident and available everywhere – in newspapers, advertisements, even early evening television – and prostitution is a well established industry. So much so, that even a business deal is incomplete without a visit to the nightclub for "hostess" entertainment.

Women in Japan are expected to take a subservient role. The renowned work ethic, the devotion to a company and a job, is greatly dependent on women's unpaid labour as housewives. Women are heavily discriminated against in the workplace and are often only taken on by companies as tempo-

rary, supplementary labour with less pay and none of the security and benefits available for full-time workers. It is also quite common for female employees to be pressurised to retire "voluntarily" when they reach thirty. Much the
same level of discrimination has existed in education and, until very recently,
in almost all levels of government.

This is now changing. After an almost constant stream of government sex
and corruption scandals the Japanese electorate has been casting about for
new political figures. It was in this context that Takako Doi, leader of the Japan
Socialist Party, appointed 200 new women candidates and launched a serious
challenge against the ruling conservative coalition at the last national election.
As a counter-move the Liberal Democratic Party appointed a woman, Mrs
Moriyama, as chief cabinet secretary, a choice that would have been unthinkable only a year or so ago. Whether this impetus will continue, and women politicians will be able to make a significant impact, is still uncertain. Undoubtedly
this political shift has provided a major boost to the **Japanese feminist movement**, which through an expanding network of grass-roots organisations has
been campaigning against sexual discrimination at work, sexual violence in
the home, and pornography. There are also groups campaigning against
Japanese participation in the sex tourism industry in Asia.

Finding a place in Kyoto

. . . .

**Riki Therivel went to Japan on an
American scholarship to study civil
engineering. She lived for almost one-
and-a-half years with a Japanese
family, did a variety of teaching jobs to
boost her savings and travelled extensively throughout the country and also
into China.**

When I left the US for an eighteen-
month stay in Kyoto, I knew almost
nothing about Japan. But I planned to
rectify that by living as much like a
Japanese person as possible. In my
fantasies this involved spending long
hours cross-legged in a remote Zen
monastery and communicating predominantly in haiku verse.

This vision faded more or less as
soon as I arrived. I was taken, at 10pm,
from the airport to the university,
where my fellow students (all men)
were waiting to greet me. Over the next
few weeks I set about learning how to
read and speak Japanese. The other
students were pleasant and polite, and
we got on in very slow and simple
sentences. I noticed, however, that they
seemed uncomfortable with direct
questions and invariably called to their
friends to confirm their opinions. No
one seemed willing to express a
personal view or even enter into a
discussion on their own, although they
asked me many questions, especially
about my views of Japan. At that point I
started understanding how very group-
oriented the Japanese are, and also how
easily the group casts out members
who do not conform. As a foreigner, I
wasn't expected to understand the
group "rules", but, equally, I couldn't
expect to be completely accepted.

People in Japan work long hours, usually six days a week, and generally take only a few days' holiday a year. In the evenings, the men often go out to dinner and then to the bar with their fellow workers, spending little time at home. This leaves little space for other things, like travelling around the country, which I also wanted to do. So after a month of living Japanese-style I started going to lunch with other friends and taking Saturdays off to travel around. Unfortunately this seemed to alienate the other students, and the tentative friendships that had begun chilled quickly. Luckily the university soon matched me up with a host family who had volunteered to help a foreigner to adapt to Japan; the Sueishis took me to festivals, taught me to cook Japanese meals, lent me their sewing machine, and really did become my "family".

I had been provided with an apartment in a foreign students' housing block, a modern Western-style affair, and very luxurious considering that Japanese students usually live in tiny seven foot by seven foot rooms. But three of us soon tired of what we considered to be a gilded cage, so we moved to a Japanese-style house. The move itself was an exercise in formality and ritual: the house had been rented by friends-of-friends who were willing to recommend us, then my host mother and I visited the landlady with presents, and the negotiations reached a crescendo of innumerable phone calls before we were deemed acceptable tenants.

Living in a Japanese neighbourhood was a wonderful way of learning about everyday life. Each morning the women would wave off first their husbands then their children. On my morning shopping trip I would see them all in the street, sweeping the already-clean tarmac, and by the time I returned they would all be in their houses again. The recycling truck would come by with blaring loudspeakers and we would scuttle out with our newspaper bundles. The garbagemen, in turn, were greeted with beautiful piles of neat blue plastic bags. According to a Japanese proverb, "the wife is happy when her husband is healthy and out of the house"; the women in my neighbourhood were happy most of the time.

What struck me was the uniformity of the women's lives. Girls are expected to finish high school and perhaps study English or cooking or fashion at a two-year college. Then they work for a few years and marry. The usual age for marriage is between 23 and 25 and about half are arranged. This initially shocked me, but my host mother reasoned that people from similar backgrounds who have the support of both families will develop love, or at least what she called "warm currents between them".

"I learnt that women walk through doors after men, only after several collisions, with much subsequent apologetic bowing"

The first child comes a few years after the marriage, and the second a few years after that. There is a lot of social pressure to stick to this format. My host mother said that, despite her agreement with feminist principles, she would still suggest this traditional path to a daughter, simply because not conforming would lead her into so many difficulties.

Women in Japan hold their cups and food bowls differently from men, bow more deeply, and use different verb endings. I learnt that women walk through doors after men, only after several collisions, with much subsequent apologetic bowing. Women rarely wear shorts or sleeveless blouses, or even anything very colourful; black and white were definitely *de rigueur* while I was there. Traditional events like tea ceremonies, visits to temples, or trips to the bathhouse also involve etiquette which is best learned from someone who has been before. Foreigners *can* get away with almost any infringement of etiquette and are not expected to master more than the simplest Japanese words. But this only serves to confirm preconceptions that we're invading barbarians.

During my stay I met a lot of Japanese people, but the cultural differences were so strong that I made few friends. The Japanese express themselves predominantly in allusions, ritual phrases and body positions; very different to more verbal and confrontational style of communication I was used to. Also I was brought up with an entrenched belief in egalitarianism, whereas Japan is very hierarchy-oriented, so we had different preconceptions of what friendship should be.

Foreigners have their place in the hierarchy, usually at one of the extremes. White Americans are treated with a mixture of admiration and contempt; admiration, strangely enough, because of their victory in the war, and contempt because Japan is now beating them economically. The Germans are widely respected because of their own post-war achievements, while blacks and Asians are seen as inferior; if Japan could rise from economic obscurity why couldn't they?

Women in Japan are trained (externally at least) to buttress, build up, and coddle their menfolk, and are simply not expected to have any opinions of their own. My conversations with women of my age (mid-twenties) consisted of their questions and my answers, or my questions and their deflections of them. Of course, there were exceptions: the open-minded and incredibly charming Japanese woman who joined me on a journey through China; the woman I met in a crowded and steamy cafeteria who involved me in a wonderful and unintelligible discussion about nuclear war (I think); and my host mother who is one of the most energetic, self-assured and lovable people I have met. But generally the women I met treated me deferentially, tentatively, and often shied away, as though I were a tall and unpredictable extra-terrestrial.

"Foreign women, with their strong opinions and aggressive mannerisms, are considered threatening"

Foreign residents in Tokyo and Kyoto have founded women's groups, and their meeting times are listed in the English-language papers. Japanese women's organisations exist, but these are more like special interest clubs than support groups. Because foreign women tend to be viewed primarily as foreigners and only secondarily as women, I don't think that they would provide much help for the woman traveller in Japan.

Because Japanese women are expected to be so submissive, foreign women, with their strong opinions and aggressive mannerisms, are considered threatening, especially by men. On the other hand, foreign women are also attractive because they are different, and possibly because they are thought to be more sexually available than Japanese women. A Japanese male friend said to me "You're American which puts you above me, but a woman which puts you below me, so we must be equal." One man used to send me and several Western friends an endless stream of postcards and presents, as though we were movie stars. My supervisor asserted his control over me shortly after I arrived by insisting that I go home with him after a drinking party. He woke up his sixty-year-old wife at midnight so that she could prepare snacks for us and then politely insisted that I stay the night as a guest; from then on I avoided the office drinking parties.

However, as unpleasant and frustrating as the sexual discrimination often was, it was never translated into physical harassment. Japan prides itself on its low crime rate, and one can walk around safely anywhere at any time. Public transport is invariably clean, punctual, and safe. The occasional drunken man may mumble "you are beautiful" or "speak English to me", but I never had to go beyond a polite "no" to stop it. Because crime is so rare in their country, many Japanese see other countries, and especially America, as highly dangerous places where drug abuse is rampant and gun-toting hoodlums lurk on every street corner. They were much more afraid of me than I was of them.

I travelled around a lot, predominantly by bicycle. Japan is dotted with beautiful rural villages tucked between steep mountains, and I spent many pleasant afternoons sweating my way up to them and careering back down. The roads are clogged with cars near the cities, making cycling dangerous, but an hour's ride got me away from the traffic and into as much countryside as Japan still has. There aren't many cyclists in Japan, and even fewer women cyclists, but they were friendly and always yelled out a greeting as they sped past.

Hitchhiking in Japan is easy and safe, even for a lone woman. The difficult part is explaining what is wanted, since few Japanese hitchhike themselves. We made big signs, in Japanese, "please take us with you", and never had problems getting picked up, even

with a bike. In fact, once they picked us up, the drivers seemed to feel responsible for the outcome of our journey, and often drove us directly to our destination. We finally learned to ask the drivers where they were going first, and rearrange our journey to save them the sometimes very lengthy detour.

Finding a job in Japan was easy, especially once I had made a few connections. I taught English to schoolchildren, office workers and doctors, corrected translations of Japanese articles, and worked as an assistant at an international Zen Buddhism symposium. English teachers are in high demand and the pay is quite good.

The Zen symposium took place only a week before I left the country and somehow fulfilled my initial romantic vision of Japan. I had worked for the symposium committee for several months, so that when the foreign scholars arrived I felt like a host rather than a visitor. We all went to a traditional tea ceremony and, kneeling to be served by a kimono-clad woman, with a view of a rock garden and pond, I felt that maybe I had learned a lot in Japan after all. I still didn't feel at home and would probably always be treated as a foreigner, but I had learned how to cope with loneliness and a thoroughly foreign culture.

TRAVEL NOTES

Languages Japanese. Little English is spoken outside the cities.

Transport Extensive, efficient and expensive. Hitching is very unusual but fairly safe.

Special Problems The underground is one of the few places where physical harassment is likely. It's worth standing with other women. Racial harassment is more of an upfront problem and applies to all non-Japanese, who may have problems using bathhouses, etc.

You should bring any contraception you need. The pill is illegal and virtually unobtainable and the diaphragm almost unheard of.

Accommodation Japanese-style hotels (*ryokan*) are difficult to cope with and, unless you have knowledge of the language, it's best to go o the tourist office for advice. Look out for "business hotels" which can be up to fifty percent cheaper than normal ones. "Love Hotels" are best avoided although they are not only used for illicit sex – privacy can be hard to come by in Japan's overcrowded cities and people are willing to rent rooms by the hour.

Guide *Japan – A Travel Survival Kit* (Lonely Planet) is comprehensive and useful.

Contacts

TWIN (Tokyo Women's Information Network), c/o BOC Publishing, Shinjuku 1-9-6, Shinjuku-ku, Tokyo 167, ☎358 3941. The best source of information on feminist groups in Japan (both Japanese and English-speaking). Organises feminist English classes and produces a biannual journal, *Agora Agoramini.*

International Feminists of Japan, Fujin Joho Centre, Shinjuku Ku, nr Akebonobashi Station, Exit 4a (meets the first Sunday of every month). Aims to forge better links between Japanese feminist groups and their counterparts abroad. Publishes monthly newsletter, *Feminist Forum.*

Fusen Kaikan (Women's Suffrage), 21-11 Yoyogi 2 Chrome, Shibuya-ku, Tokyo 151, ☎370 0238. Centre for education, research and publishing, with a library and a good permanent exhibition of the life of journalist and political activist Ishikawa Fusae (1893–1980), who was active in the Women's Suffrage League in the 1920s. The staff speak some English.

Gayon House Bookshop, next to Tokyo Union Church (nearest station Omote Sando), Tokyo. Feminist and anti-nuclear books.

Asian Women's Association, Shibuya Coop Rm 211, 14-10-211 Sakuragaokacho, Shbuya-ku, Tokyo 150, ☎592 4950. Campaigning group opposed to the use of cheap female labour in Japan and South East Asia, and also against Japanese sex tourism in Seoul, Taipei and Bangkok. Publishes *Asian Women's Liberation*, a quarterly journal in English and Japanese.

Kyoto Feminist Group, Kyoto YWCA, Muromachi, Demizu-agaru, Kyoto, ☎722 0686. Mainly foreign residents who meet weekly.

National Women's Education Centre, 728 Sugaya, Ranzan-machi, Hiki-gun, Saitama-Ken, ☎355 02. An information centre for study and research, with space for local women's groups.

Lesbian Groups. There is a fairly well established lesbian network in Japan, but Japanese and foreign women tend to organise separately. The main meeting points are lesbian weekends arranged every public holiday. For information, write to **Lesbian Contact**, CPO Box 1780, Tokyo 100-91 (send an International Reply Coupon). The group publishes a regular newsletter, *DD*, with articles, listings and events. There are a few **lesbian bars**, all in the Shinjuku Sanchome area of Tokyo.

Books

Yukio Tanaka, ed., *To Live and to Write: Selections by Japanese Women Writers 1913–1938* (Seal Press, US, 1988). Essays by the first major women writers in Japan, dealing with subjects traditionally taboo for women.

Susan Pharr, *Political Women in Japan: The Search for a Place in Political Life* (California UP, 1981). Exploration of women's images of self and society and of expectations, from first-hand interviews.

Liza Crihfield Dalby, *Geisha* (California UP, 1983). Contemporary study of a living phenomenon. The author, an anthropologist, became a geisha during her stay in Kyoto.

Leonie Caldecott, At the Foot of the Mountain: The Shibokusa Women of Kita Fuji, in **Lynne Jones, ed., *Keeping the Peace*** (The Women's Press, 1983). Moving and extraordinary account of a rural and local peace group at the foot of Mount Fuji and their defence of their community through disrupting military exercises in the region.

Shizuko Go, *Requiem* (1973, The Women's Press, 1986). Diary narrative of the last months of World War II, as experienced by the "daughters of military Japan".

Sachiko Ariyoshi, *Letters from Sachiko* (Abacus, 1984). Letters to the author's sister in the West highlight the constraints faced by women in contemporary Japanese society.

Fiction

Yuko Tsushima, *Child of Fortune* (The Women's Press, 1986); ***The Shooting Gallery and Other Stories*** (The Women's Press, 1988). Lucid pictures of the lives and aspirations of contemporary Japanese women and the pressures they face to accept a subservient role.

Michiko Yamamoto, *Betty San: Four Stories* (1973; Kodansha, 1985). Again addresses the subservient domestic roles of Japanese women – and also East-West incompatibilities.

Junichiro Tanizaki, *The Makioka Sisters* (Picador, 1983). A very well-known novel in Japan, with a quintessential heroine struggling between passivity and self-will.

Thanks to Sylph and Marilyn Haywood for information.

Kenya

- - - - - - - - - - - - - - - - - - - -

Since gaining independence from the British in 1963, Kenya has developed an image of Westernisation and affluence. Its capital, Nairobi, is a major commercial centre crowded with British and multinational firms. Britons also make up a major slice of the country's lucrative and well established tourist trade, attracted by accessible gameparks, beaches, and the country's reputation for political stability. But the economic advantages, which are rapidly levelling off in the context of world recession, have benefited only a small minority. Stretching north from Nairobi into the Mathare valley there are vast urban slums, with up to 100,000 people living in cardboard, tin and plastic bag shanty huts. In the north, the edge of the Sahel region, there are areas devastated by drought.

The country has been ruled as a one-party state since 1982, under President Daniel arap Moi, leader of *KANU* (Kenya African National Union). His government has consolidated its power by ruthless suppression of oppositional groups – literally hundreds have been detained without trial and reports of torture and death in custody are common. In 1989, against a background of international condemnation of widespread human rights violations, an amnesty was announced for political detainees. There are no other signs, however, of a political change of heart and many dissidents, convicted of political subversion, continue to suffer appalling conditions in prison.

Tourism is heavily promoted and, although geared mainly towards expensive safari packages, there are plenty of facilities for independent travellers. Most women, however, tend to travel in pairs rather than alone. Sexual harassment is a fairly persistent problem, especially along the predominantly

Muslim coastline where the experience of mass tourism has fuelled stereotypes of Western women as "loose" and "available". The continual comments and propositions can at times feel personally threatening and on the beaches it's never a good idea to isolate yourself. Statistics for violent robbery are also high, and carrying any symbol of wealth (in fact anything but the bare necessities) can make you a target.

There are numerous **women's groups** throughout the country. Many of them are associated with *Maedeleo ya Wanawake* (Progress of Women), a popular and autonomous organisation responsible for setting up multipurpose centres for health education, skills training and literacy groups (in the 1970s only ten percent of women were literate). In addition to this the *National Council of Women of Kenya*, which is partially funded by the government, campaigns to abolish the practice of female genital mutilation, reform legislation on abortion, and increase women's knowledge of contraception. A continuing scandal is the extent to which untested contraceptives (or those banned in the West) are being foisted on Kenyan women.

Knowing Nairobi
. . . .

Lindsey Hilsum is a journalist and foreign correspondent for the BBC. When she wrote this she had been working in Nairobi as a freelance writer and Information Officer for the United Nations Children's Fund.

It was my first solo walk through the streets of Nairobi. Having just arrived from Latin America, where I learnt that streetwise means ready to run or ready to fend off catcalls, comments and unwelcome hands, I was on my guard. But in Nairobi no man bothered me. I was proffered the occasional elephant-hair bracelet, the odd batik, but no one tried to touch or waylay me. Some months later, a Norwegian woman friend arrived on her first trip outside Europe. As I showed her around Nairobi that afternoon, men shouted and stared at her. Talking to other women later, I understood the problem; because I had already learned to walk with confidence and aggression, no one perceived that I was vulnerable. But my friend gave off an aura of uncertainty – she was obviously a newcomer, a tourist and, as such, was fair game.

It is possible to travel widely in Kenya using public transport. There are hotels and campsites scattered throughout, and people usually go out of their way to help. A lone woman is something of a curiosity in small towns and rural areas but people are more likely to be sympathetic than hostile. "Isn't it sad to be without a husband and children?" I have been asked. My reply that I prefer it that way has started many good conversations. People like to talk – a smattering of Swahili helps, but there are many Kenyans who speak English.

For most visitors, going to a game-park is a high priority. The most comfortable way to go is on an organised tour. I went on one to Masai Mara, and found myself ensconced in a Volkswagen minibus with two cowboy-hatted Texans who were "in oil" in Saudi Arabia, an American couple plus toddler also from Saudi, and a lone geriatric British bird-watcher. Other people have found themselves crushed between Germans and Japanese, straining for a glimpse of a lion through the forest of telephoto lenses, and my sister ended up in the Abedares with a busload of Americans wearing name-badges who turned out to have won the trip by being "workers of the year" at a Coca-Cola factory.

"Hacking my way through the forest at night, in search of two friends and two small children who had not returned from a walk, I realised how threatening the forest can be"

It's more fun to go independently, but only with a reliable, preferably four-wheel drive vehicle. I spent one hot, frustrating, exhausting week trying to get to Lake Turkana in an ancient Landrover, the remnants of a long-since discarded Ministry of Livestock Development Sheep and Goat project. Accompanied by a friend as mechanically incompetent as myself, I never made it to the lake, but now know all the amateur motor mechanics between Baringo and Barogoi.

Only an hour's drive from Nairobi, you reach the natural rainforest. If you want to explore this region you should go with a guide. It's easy and very dangerous to get lost. Hacking my way through the forest at night, in search of two friends and two small children who had not returned from a walk, I realised how threatening the forest can be. One moment luxuriant and enticing, the next, when every coughing sound could be a leopard and every thud an elephant, it becomes sinister. We found our friends, who had lit a fire and tucked the children snugly into the forked foot of a tree when they realised at dusk that they were lost. We would

never have found them without the local Forest Rest House warden, who searched with us as a guide.

One place which has become popular with low-budget tourists is the largely Muslim island of Lamu. With its white sand beaches and curious melée of backstreets, downmarket restaurants and mosques, it is closer in culture and history to Zanzibar and Ilha de Moçambique than to the rest of Kenya. Sometimes I think I'm just prejudiced against it. The first time I went, my friend Laura and I took the sweltering eight-hour bus ride from Malindi, and then the boat. The sun blazed down as we left the shore, my period started, and passed out. Stumbling to the quay at Lamu, I collapsed in the dirt. Laura, pursued by a young man informing her of a nice cheap hotel he was sure she'd like, went in search of liquid. She found a bottle of bright orange Fanta. I took one glance and then vomited. All around me were male voices, saying things like, "get her to hospital" and "why don't you go back to your own country?" Needless to say, it was two women who helped us find a place to stay.

Personal experience apart, Lamu can be difficult for women. The traditional Muslim culture has been sent reeling by the advent of beer and bikinis and while women tourists bathe topless, Lamu women walk the streets clad in black robes from head to foot. Concerned about the corruption of local youth and the rising numbers of "beach boys" who hang around tourists, the local authorities are reported to have forbidden young local men from talking to visiting women. The clash in culture has found expression in sexual violence, and there have been several incidents of rape on the beach. I would never bathe topless, and never lose sight of other people on the beach, however solitary and tempting it may appear.

Back on the mainland at Malindi the beach is fringed with luxurious hotels, complete with bar service, butler service, air conditioning, chilled wine and four-course meals. Not so far away, the town crumbles into ramshackle mud and wooden dwellings where sewage runs along open drains, and household electricity and water are just promises the municipal council has yet to fulfil.

It's this divide between rich and poor that shocks the first-time visitor to Africa. Personally I avoid staying in tourist hotels, not only because the luxury jars alongside such evident poverty, but because guests are alienated from "Africa", as alive in a tourist town like Malindi as in any upcountry village where *mzungu* (white people) are rarely seen.

Generally, I stay in a *hoteli*, a small guesthouse found in any town. They are cheap, occasionally clean, and almost invariably the people who run them will be friendly. But single women sometimes have problems with men knocking on their bedroom door (this happens in upmarket hotels too), so I always make sure that my room can be firmly locked from inside.

I think the only way I've come to understand anything about "ordinary" Kenyan women is by frequenting local bars. In many countries, bars are a male preserve, but in Kenya there are usually women about – barmaids, prostitutes, and in some places women doing their crochet over a bottle of beer. Not many *mzungu* women go into bars, except in tourist hotels, so those that do attract a fair amount of attention. "People say it is dangerous to come here," said the proprietor of one bar in Kisumu, "but you are safe." I agreed with him, and he bought me a beer simply because I'd dared to be there. As I left, some Asian youths cruised by in their Mercedes. "Wanna fuck?" they called. That was when I felt nervous and wished I could find a taxi back to my hotel.

The women tend to assume a protective role. In one bar in downtown Nairobi, a woman kept me by her side all evening. "No one speaks to my sister without my permission!" she insisted, glaring at anyone, male or female, reckless enough to look at me. As I entered a bar in Kisumu, Jane the barmaid, came to sit with me. A young man slouched towards us from the counter. "My friend is talking to *me*," said Jane, and he shrugged and walked away.

"Opening gambits like 'Tell me about free love in'your country' are irritatingly common"

Women like Jane have interesting stories, and they usually like to talk. Many come from rural backgrounds, left home to look for a job in the big city, got pregnant, and have been trapped in the circle of barmaiding and prostitution ever since. Options for women are few once you leave the village; with no education and no money, and with children to support, prostitution is often the only way.

These women may ask you for an address, hoping for a job as a housemaid, or some money to pay school fees, or some clothes. But they're not talking to you because they want something, but because it feels good to talk, and because they're curious, and there is a sympathetic link between women of different cultures, and it is somehow comforting to find common ground with a stranger. "You can so easily end up in a maternity," lamented one woman I know, who hangs around the same bar in Nairobi every evening. "I could be pregnant again. So could you." Later she took a male friend of mine aside. "Don't you get my sister pregnant," she admonished him, "That would be a very terrible thing to do!" Kenyan men do tend to look upon foreign women as an easy lay, and opening gambits like "Tell me about free love in your country" are irritatingly common.

If you have any problems, women around will usually help. But beware "big" men in small towns. If it's the local police chief or councillor who is making advances, it may not be possible for other local people to help out, because of his power and influence. If in doubt get out; preferably accompanied, preferably in a vehicle. I never walk alone at night in Nairobi, because mugging and rape are quite common, and it's always worth the taxi fare to be safe.

I don't think that Kenyan men are intrinsically any more sexist than men from my own country, England. As a person unfettered by family, educated and employed and travelling unaccompanied, I get treated in some ways as an honorary man. But underneath it all, a woman is a woman is a woman, and most Kenyan men I've met agree with their president, who announced in September 1984 that God had made man the head of the family, and challenging that was tantamount to criticising God. And certainly when I've expressed my doubts, the response is generally that in *my* culture we may have different notions, but *their* women like it that way. I'm not so sure about that.

Throughout Kenya there are large numbers of women's groups which have banded together to earn some money, by making handicrafts, growing crops, keeping bees or goats, or other small-scale businesses. Their success is variable. Some groups have made profits and shared them; in other cases the men have sabotaged the group when they felt threatened by the women's success or have appropriated the money. In others, lack of organisation, inexperience, or simply the lack of time among women already overburdened by the day-to-day tasks of survival have built in failure from the beginning.

Women do want better healthcare, contraception, education for themselves and their children, and a higher income. But their needs and wants come a poor second to the concept of "development" which a male-dominated government and which predominantly male-dominated aid agencies promote. The rhetoric of the UN Decade for Women has resounded throughout Kenya, and we all know that small-scale water projects, reforestation, support to women as farmers and access to credit are important. But agricultural extensionists are still men; although it's women who dig the land, women are rarely consulted, and there is a tendency to start "women's projects" as a side line to the more serious business of "nation building".

Women leaders in Kenya tend to take the attitude that gentle persuasion works better than protest. Many of them are middle-class urban women, whose ideas and problems are often seen as divorced from the reality of ordinary Kenyan women. With their emphasis on education, welfare and income-generating projects they have been criticised for supporting the status quo and denying the possibilities of radical change.

"The widespread denunciation of feminism ... is a way of keeping women down, by telling them that any change is 'un-African'"

A Western feminist is often resented. There is good reason for this – many Western women simply do not know about the issues which affect Kenyan women, but nonetheless push their own priorities. On the other hand, the widespread denunciation of feminism (which finds its most outrageous expression in the letters pages of the newspapers) is a way of keeping women down, by telling them that any change is "un-African". I have come to believe that issues such as accessible clean water and getting more girls into school are more important to most Kenyan women than free abortion on demand or the acceptance of lesbianism – and many Kenyan women oppose the latter two. Other issues, such as male violence and access to healthcare and contraception are as important in Kenya as in any Western country, although the starting point for pushing to achieve these things is different.

Foreign women who have lived in small towns and villages, usually as anthropologists or volunteers, have a deeper understanding of Kenyan women than I do. Many such women leave the country thoroughly depressed, as they see Kenyan women, year after year, accepting violent husbands, one pregnancy after another, children dying, endless work and little reward. Most visitors can't see all that, because it takes time, and nor do they get to see the other side of things, such as the sense of community amongst women and the strength of character that outward acceptance and seeming submissiveness belie.

It's not possible to understand so much on a short visit, but I think that many women coming to Kenya could see and understand a lot more if they dared. It took me a year to dare to travel Kenya alone, on *matatus* (collective taxis) and buses; hitchhiking, going to small towns, being open, talking to people. There's no need for every woman to take a year to pluck up courage – it's fun, it's interesting and it's worth it. I haven't had nearly enough yet.

TRAVEL NOTES

Languages Swahili is the official language; also Kikuyu, Luo and Maa. English is widely spoken.

Transport Public transport (buses and a small train network) is reasonable and safe. On well-worn tourist routes there are also collective taxis, usually big Peugeots. *Matatus*, impromptu communal trucks, need more confidence. Hitching isn't advisable.

Accommodation *Board and Lodgings* (B&Ls) can be found in any town and are good value. In gameparks there are very expensive lodges but also *bandas* (small wooden huts with cooking facilities; you bring your own food and sleeping bag) and "tented camps" (tents provided and set up within lodge compounds).

Guide *The Rough Guide: Kenya* (Harrap Columbus) gives an excellent run-through of just about everything you'll need to know about the country.

Contacts

Maedeleo ya Wanawake (Progress of Women), PO Box 44412, Nairobi. Largest and best-known women's organisation with numerous local groups.

National Council of Women of Kenya, PO Box 43741, Nairobi. Produces the publication *Kenyan Women*.

Kenya Association of University Women, PO Box 47010, Nairobi.

African Women Link (AWL), PO Box 50795, Nairobi. A development newsletter aimed at linking development groups and agencies that involve African women.

Viva, PO Box 46319, Nairobi. Monthly magazine combining feminism and fashion in a glossy but appealing package.

Books

Anonymous, *In Dependant Kenya* (Zed Books, 1982). A strident book which you shouldn't take with you, condemning the status quo and Kenya's involvement in the neo-colonial web.

Patrick Marnham, *Fantastic Invasion: Dispatches from Africa* (Penguin, 1986). Sharp, incisive essays on development and politics, concerned in large part with Kenya.

Fiction

Marjorie Oludhe MacGoye, *Coming to Birth* (Virago, 1987). Acclaimed story of a young woman's arranged marriage, its failure and her new life in post-Uhuru Kenya. Set during and just after the Mau Mau emergency.

Rebeka Njau, *Ripples in the Pool* (Heinemann, 1978). Novel, full of myth and menace, about the building of a village clinic.

Toril Brekke, *The Jacaranda Flower* (Methuen, 1987). A dozen short stories most of which touch on the lives of women.

Muthoni Likimani, *Passbook Number F 47927: Women and Mau Mau in Kenya* (Macmillan, 1986). Describes, in ten fictionalised episodes, the impact of the 1950s Mau Mau revolt in Kenya on women's daily lives.

Beryl Markham, *West with the Night* (Virago, 1984; illustrated version, 1989). In 1936 Beryl Markham became the first person to fly solo across the Atlantic. Her biography tells of her upbringing and adventures in colonial Kenya.

Martha Gellhorn, *The Weather in Africa* (Eland, 1985). Three novellas, each set in Kenya and dealing absorbingly with aspects of the European-African relationship.

Karen Blixen, *Out of Africa* (1936; Penguin, 1986) A bestseller and cult book covering Blixen's experiences on a coffee farm in the Ngong Hills between the wars. Evocative, lyrical, sometimes obnoxiously racist, but a lot better than the film.

South Korea

Under the glare of publicity surrounding the 1988 Olympic Games in Seoul, South Korea emerged as a major economic power and centre of commerce. For many years a protegé of the United States, and currently forging close economic links with Japan, the country's foreign trade continues to flourish in the newly built luxury hotels and conference centres. The tourist industry is overtly geared towards the male business traveller, and like Thailand and the Philippines, relies heavily on the exploitation of women as prostitutes, the price of a *Kisaeng* or hostess often being included as part of a package deal. Promoted as a male paradise, South Korea attracts literally thousands of (mainly Japanese) sex tourists every year, many of them arriving in group tours, paid for as part of company incentive schemes. Despite the massive revenue this generates, the hostesses themselves earn notoriously little.

Whilst Korean women frequently face harassment from male tourists, the picture is very different for Western women. People tend to show a great deal of interest in foreigners, but even amongst the hostess bars of Seoul this is rarely intimidating or threatening. Relatively few tourists venture beyond the capital, and travelling alone around the rural areas you are bound to be seen as something of a curiosity. Again this is relatively easy to cope with – you'll most likely be treated with courtesy as a stranger and guest. Without a few words of Korean, however, communication can be a problem.

Tourists have always been very carefully cushioned from the' effects of political dissent. Yet it is hard to ignore the atmosphere of political transition that has begun to take hold of the country. Since the elections of 1988, Korea's new president Roh Tae Woo – the hand-picked successor of the former rigidly authoritarian regime – has initiated a surprising number of reforms. Besides promising various democratic changes, he has begun to pursue charges of past corruption, torture, and general illegality within his own political party. How far he will be able to control the impetus for change, after thirty years of right-wing rule, remains uncertain. An enduring demand amongst many students in the country has been reunification with the Democratic People's Republic of Korea in the north.

Korean culture owes much to Chinese influences but has its own distinctive features, like its unique female *shamans* (religious leaders). In general, the position of women is still dictated by Confucianism, and the disparity in the way daughters are valued in comparison to sons is so glaring that there has been an educational campaign to try and redress the balance.

Conditions of work for South Korean women have long been exceptionally grim – the major employers being the multinational factories that moved to Korea to take advantage of the very low wages and often cut costs further, with unsafe, poorly lit and unhygienic workplaces. Whilst the new regime has introduced an Equal Opportunity Employment Act, with fines imposed for the more blatant discriminatory practices, this has relatively little effect on sweat-shop work, where women comprise most of the workforce. However, attitudes appear to be changing, if very gradually. **Women's groups** both within South Korea and Japan have been militating against sex tourism.

Accepting the Rules

. . . .

Jane Richardson has been living and working in Seoul since June 1988. After a year teaching at a private language institute she moved to a job with the British Council. Throughout her stay she has travelled extensively around the country.

When I accepted a teaching job in Korea I knew little about the country and had only a vague idea of where it was. I knew it was to be the host of the 1988 Olympics, and that, according to the British media, half the population was involved in riots. After many

months here I feel I'm just beginning to know Korea and the Korean people.

The most difficult thing to adjust to initially was the sheer number of people; everywhere I went, pushing, elbowing, jostling, staring, laughing. There were days when I dreaded leaving my apartment or when I would miss my subway stop because I didn't want to push anyone to get off.

After a while I became much more assertive, and also learnt how to avoid, or at least ignore, the staring. The advantage of people staring is that I can also stare without having to worry about offending anyone. I've also learnt what kind of behaviour I should accept from Koreans. A few weeks after I arrived a woman waiting for a subway with me noticed that I had hairs on my arms. She called her friends over to have a look and I ended up with five women trying to pull the hairs out – perhaps to see if they were real. A Korean friend was horrified by this and told me that the women were being very rude. In a country like Korea, with so many customs and social rules, it's very easy to accept things passively out of fear of offending someone.

I lived in an apartment building in a tiny one-bedroomed flat. For me it was a luxury, but for the families and couples living on the estate it must have been impossibly cramped. There were half a dozen other teachers living in the neighbourhood and it was always possible to tell when one was coming home, as the children shouted "Migguk saraam. (American person) Hello. Goodbye. Thank you." They never seemed to get tired of this and were really delighted if you replied to them, rushing off to tell their friends about it.

"One day they decided to take me on a 'girls' trip out' after class, and sent all the men home"

There were also a few people living in the complex who spoke fairly good English – housewives who'd lived in the States, a man who sold eggs in the market, and a delivery boy from a Chinese restaurant. The delivery boy always shouted "hello my teacher", when he saw me, and was convinced that one of the other teachers was my mother simply because she was about 25 years older than me.

As a foreign woman it was very easy to meet people in Korea, but not so easy to make friends. I found that, among my students, the women I had most in common with were the older housewives or the students. However, friendship in Korea is a time-consuming business. Most of the housewives were too busy with their homes and children to go out and the women students were often not allowed to stay out after school hours.

With the men too it was difficult, simply because of the gossip network in the school – if you went to lunch

with a student everyone would know about it. It was also difficult, as a woman teacher, knowing that some of my ideas and way of life could be not exactly shocking, but certainly surprising to some students, and could cause them to lose respect for me.

I usually relied on intuition to tell me what I could say to one student and what to another, but it also depended on how open and interested the students seemed. I had one class which consisted mainly of housewives. One day they decided to take me on a "girls' trip out" after class, and sent all the men home. We went to Imjinga, near the Demilitarised Zone, and they talked about their memories of the Korean War, and also about their husbands and children. I felt privileged that they wanted to discuss these issues with me but it was also depressing – so many of them had been to university and had nurtured ambitions and dreams they had no way of fulfilling once they became married.

One woman I remained friendly with after she had left school, and through her I came to know more about the position of women in Korea. She was evidently unhappy in her marriage, which had been arranged, yet knowing that her own needs and desires would be considered unimport-ant she had decided to try and forget these and live through her children. It struck me that, much more than in the West, women are expected to hide their feelings and be seen to be happy with their lot in life. Complaining seems to be viewed almost as a moral defect, to be frowned upon even by close friends and family.

But the influence of the Women's Movement is growing. More and more women are entering the workforce and demanding better working conditions. Perhaps the increased openness to the West has also made people more aware and receptive to Western ideas about women's rights. In 1983 the Korean Women's Development Institute was set up to provide education and resources, undertake research, and generally attempt to improve women's status. It also provides a counselling service for Korean women and a regular newsletter in English. The atmosphere at the film forum and at the Institute in general was friendly and supportive.

If you're looking for a relaxing, women-only atmosphere, go to the *mogyoktang*, or sauna. These are found in every town and city in Korea, and are indicated by a flame symbol. You can spend, and Korean women frequently do, many hours here, simply getting clean. However, washing seems to be the secondary purpose, the main object being to talk, exchange gossip, and generally relax. As a foreigner you will inevitably attract attention, but it is only friendly curiosity. The women are more than willing to show you what to do.

First you have to wash sitting at a low hand-shower, then you enter the sauna, followed by a plunge in the cold tub, back to the sauna again, and eventually soak in the hot tub or jacuzzi. Later you will be called by a masseuse (mine was bizarrely dressed in black underwear). You lie on a bench and she scrubs you, with something resembling a Brillo pad, until your skin falls off in big grey lumps. A grated cucumber mask is put on your face and oil poured on your body which the masseuse then hits, slaps, pummels and kneads free of aches and pains. The whole process ends with a rinse in warm milk before you stagger, dazed but amazingly clean, to the shower.

In Confucianism women are considered inferior to men and are expected to be submissive, obedient, and to produce sons. A number of incidents illustrate the pervasive nature of these beliefs. In March 1989 a 13-year-old girl and her three sisters from a poor family attempted suicide in order that their parents might have enough money to educate the youngest son. The family had obviously continued to have children until a son was produced, and the girls had internalised the feeling of inferiority. This created an outcry in the country as people started to acknowledge and protest against the sexism in Korean society.

"My biggest problem in terms of harassment comes from drunk businessmen, usually on the subway"

As another example, at the institute where I work, during a money crisis, the manager paid everyone's wages except the female secretaries. After the secretaries went on strike they were fired, rehired, and eventually paid. The very fact that they and their wages were seen as dispensable says a lot about the way women are treated here.

As a Western women, you are also affected by these attitudes. In a shop an assistant will stop serving you if a man wants to be served; men are given empty seats on subways; and some older male students in my classes are obviously disturbed at having a woman teacher. Western women face an additional problem in that the only contact many Koreans have had with foreign women is through soft-porn films, shown regularly at the cinemas here.

Many Korean men assume that all Western women jump into bed with the first man they see. This can cause some harassment, though usually opportunistic rather than intimidating, along the lines of "Do you live alone? You are beautiful. What's your telephone number?" It is very unusual to live alone in Korea – the only women who do so are considered "bad", ie prostitutes.

My biggest problem in terms of harassment comes from drunk businessmen, usually on the subway. From the expressions on their faces and from the reaction of other passengers I presume they are making suggestions about what we could do if we got together. Korean friends have advised me to stare through the men as if they weren't there which causes them to "lose face". "Face" is a key concept of Korean society, and maintaining it is essential to one's feeling of self-esteem and general well-being.

Apart from prostitution, there are various other forms of sex-oriented entertainment in Seoul. "Adult" discos offer strip shows and dancers – young, bored girls wearing swimsuits and white high-heeled boots, who dance on raised podiums between your tables. Both men and women attend these type of discos. Korean women seem angry but accepting of this aspect of Korean life – "It's her job, she has to do it."

If you go to a disco in one of the large hotels you will see countless hostesses – women who are paid to sit with men, drink with them, and, sometimes, have sex. It is difficult to find anywhere in Seoul where entertainment is not provided by women. Even some coffee shops are actually *room salons*, which, like the hotels, have hostesses. I have heard about similar places where women can be entertained by male "hosts", but these are illegal and often raided by police; men's *room salons* are a social necessity, women's are immoral.

Despite all this, travelling in Korea is relatively safe, if not exactly easy. Outside Seoul few people speak English, and most local bus timetables are written in Hangul, or Korean script. Even if you can read Korean it's not always much help since the writing is sometimes handwritten and hence illegible. What does help is if you can pronounce the name of the place where you want to go. People are always really helpful. Take out a map or stand around looking puzzled and at least five people will appear and offer to help you.

The first time I travelled alone, to Tedun mountain, near Taejon, in the middle of winter, I discovered just how unusual it is to travel alone. Everybody I met offered me food, drink, help getting up the mountain, and insisted on taking my photograph. On another occasion, I travelled with another woman teacher to Cheju island, off the south coast, famous for its women divers. These women dive all year round, for shellfish and seaweed, and stay under water for minutes at a time. Postcards show them wearing bikinis, posed provocatively on rocks. Actually they are strong skilled women, proud of their professional skills and reluctant to be photographed, even wearing wetsuits.

TRAVEL NOTES

Languages Korean which has its own alphabet, *Hangul*. Despite the strong American influence, English is spoken in only the large hotels and commercial districts of Seoul.

Transport In Seoul the subway is cheap, easy and safe, though crowded. There are also plenty of taxis and buses. Express coaches, trains and internal flights are all efficient and quite cheap methods of getting round the country.

Accommodation There are plenty of cheap, basic options, including renting private rooms. Camping is possible in more tourist-oriented areas. Many hotels are "Love Hotels", renting rooms by the hour as well as overnight; they are usually quite safe for visitors.

Guide *Korea – A Travel Survival Kit* (Lonely Planet) is the most useful, but don't rely on the maps!

Contacts

Korean Women's Development Institute, C.P.O.Box 2267, Seoul 100, ☎783 7341/7271.

Books

In Korea, look out for the contemporary and historical studies on the position of women from the **Ewha Women's University Press**.

From the Womb of Han: Stories of Korean Women Workers (CCA-URM, 57 Peking Road, Kowloon, Hong Kong, 1982). Collection of stories, many direct transcriptions.

Laura Kendall and Mark Peterson, eds., *Korean Women: Views from the Inner Room* (East Rock Press, US, 1983). Slightly patchy collection, good on Korean women's history, but a bit limited in its portrayal of women's contemporary position and status.

Malawi

· ·

For many years Malawi has been an outcast amongst the African frontline states, condemned for its close links with South Africa and for the dictatorial and incredibly repressive regime of its president-for-life, Dr Hastings Banda.

Recently, under pressure to ensure safe passage for his country's exports and imports, Banda has made moves to ease relations with the neighbour states of Zambia, Zimbabwe and Mozambique, but his diplomatic ventures have been by no means matched by any improvement on human rights. Opposition of any sort is dealt with swiftly and harshly. Pogroms are waged against any group strong enough to pose a threat, thousands are imprisoned or have fled the country, and an all-pervasive network of informers and spies ensure that all criticism – even the most trivial – is silenced.

At the same time, much of Malawi's wealth – its agricultural and mineral resources – have been placed in the hands of a newly formed elite (government ministers, foreign investors and those in favour with Banda); while large estates, cleared of peasant farmers, have been given over to ex-pat "Rhodesian" managers, who have transplanted intact their privileged and isolated lifestyles. For the majority of Malawians, healthcare and educational provisions are minimal and poverty an enduring way of life.

Malawi is the sort of destination that divides independent travellers. There are plenty who visit the country (many of them South African students) attracted by the beauty of its lakeside beaches and its reputation as a more than usually safe place for women travelling alone. Many boycott it, preferring not to sink their foreign cash into such an authoritarian regime. Obviously the decision is yours. The only rules that seem to apply to travellers is that skirts and trousers must, by law, cover the knees and that no attempt should be made to engage Malawians in political discussion. You'll find that most people are extremely friendly and hospitable in their approach to visitors and that harassment of any kind is exceptionally rare.

In keeping with the blanket repression operating in Malawi no autonomous **women's groups** have been allowed. The one official women's organisation is run by Banda's "official hostess" (he is unmarried) and is geared towards reminding women of their traditional role in society. In general terms, women form the backbone of the economy as traders and food producers, but have less status and much less access to education than men.

A Part of the Truth

. . . .

Jessie Carline first heard about Malawi when she was offered a place there as a volunteer for VSO; two years later she is still working in the country. As she intends to stay, she has had to avoid making any comment about the political situation.

When I was told that my two years voluntary service were to be spent in Malawi I had to look it up in an atlas. Now that Mrs Thatcher and the Pope have visited, it may be more commonly known that it is a small (by African standards), thin, landlocked country, wedged in between Tanzania, Zambia and Mozambique. It does not make the headlines because (again by African standards) there is no large-scale famine or fighting.

My job here involves running a department of twenty and it has taken me many, many months to get accustomed to all that this entails. I was apprehensive from the start about being a boss – never having been in that position before – and from this viewpoint alone I knew the post would be challenging. I remember having the list of everyone's names and trying desperately to pronounce them correctly in case I made a fool of myself, only to discover that my name

was equally impossible for my colleagues to say.

There turned out to be many other parts to this post that I had never considered and found myself totally bewildered by. The first was the enormous amount of requests from people for time off work. The range of requests was also startling: "Madam" (being called this was also something to get used to!), "My uncle/mother/son is ill in Balaka so may I go and visit?"; "Madam, I need to go to Liwonde to buy some maize"; "Madam, it's raining may I go and plant my seeds?"; "Madam, I have malaria"; "Madam, someone in my village has died, may I go to the funeral?". How could I refuse?

And perhaps more difficult to cope with were the requests for money: "Madam, my child is unable to go to school because I cannot afford the fees"; "Madam, I would like to buy a bicycle"; "Madam, my brother/daughter/aunt is ill and needs transport to the hospital"; "Madam, my wife is having her fourth child and we have no clothes for the baby". How could I refuse these, either?

After a few weeks I realised half my staff were either away or owing me money and this didn't seem to be a situation that I was in control of. Plucking up courage to ask my Malawian colleagues for their advice, they explained that I'd have to set my own limits. The problems brought to me were real enough – Malawi is one of the poorest countries in the world – but they suggested that it wasn't a good idea to be seen as an endless source of ready cash.

> *"Being 'rich' means that I have leisure time – there is no need to spend hours hoeing a field or walking miles to the nearest clean water"*

Ironically, VSO attempts to pay volunteers a "local wage" so that we are not seen as wealthy ex-pats with more money than sense. But this just doesn't work. However little I earn, I am rich. All my possessions announce my wealth: clothes, motorbike (loaned to me by VSO), radio/cassette player, camera, etc. And at the weekend my time is spent playing tennis or walking up Mulanje because being "rich" means that I have leisure time – there is no need to spend hours hoeing a field or walking miles to the nearest clean water. At the beginning I used to ask my colleagues "And what did you do at the weekend?" I've stopped doing that now.

How I have actually coped with the situation is difficult to explain, but somehow the requests are fewer. Maybe it was because I began to say no, maybe because people began to understand my situation and, perhaps, realise how little I do earn! I'm not so sure about the latter, though. Most of the non-volunteer ex-pats earn a small fortune, plus they receive hard currency back home, so to most Malawians we are all white and rich.

After eighteen months here, however, I am beginning to feel part of the community at work and less of an outsider. It has taken me a long time to make friends. A woman's role in Malawi is in the kitchen, on the land and with the children, and all, bar one, of my professional colleagues are men. It does not make sense to either women or men that I am thirty, single and childless and so far from home (my mother would agree!), and it would be

unheard of for any of the male professional staff at work to invite me round to their house to meet their wife. But the one woman in my department has become my friend and, through her, people have seen that I won't turn my nose up at local food and that I am more than willing to socialise. Without her I'm not sure that I would have coped when I had to go to my first funeral.

That was after a close member of staff lost his wife. She had been admitted to hospital with high blood pressure and heavily pregnant. She gave birth and the high blood pressure continued. This in itself is not unusual and with rest all should be fine. However the hospital needed the "bed" (there are four patients to every mattress on the floor) and so she was dismissed two days later. Having to walk, with her new baby, to the bus station, she began to feel ill – so instead of continuing home she decided to come to the clinic opposite work, where she died soon after arrival. She was in her early twenties and this was her second child.

Everyone at work attended the funeral, along with all the nearby villagers, so it was big affair. I clung on to my friend's hand as we slowly and silently made our way through endless seated women who alternated between great wailing and soft song. We stopped outside the mud hut where the woman had lived and sat on the ground amongst all the other women from work – secretaries, cleaners and canteen staff. I felt horribly conspicuous as the only white woman amongst so many Malawians, but that was something that came from me; I was treated as one of the many mourners and it was appreciated that I had come.

It surprised me that the atmosphere at the end was not heavy and depressing. Mourners had begun to chat and people were smiling. It was a tragic and preventable death but somehow the will to survive, regardless of the daily catastrophes, was paramount. The grave itself was in a cemetery – in land put aside for graves, which is completely untouched and where it is forbidden to cut down and remove the trees. The body then had been lain in an indigenous forest and would not be visited – the woman had been returned to the land, the cycle had been completed. Life continues.

One of the things that I had been forewarned about were the frustrations that I would experience at work – and this has certainly shown to be the case. The problems and difficulties that give rise to frustration are varied, ranging from the telephones being out of order for days on end to the mile of road to work being transformed by a heavy night's rain into a muddy swamp. The machinery I inherited looked impressive until I discovered that four out of the six UN-donated photocopiers lay idle because we cannot afford the spare parts. Other UN machines costing thousands of pounds have not ever been used as there is no-one experienced enough here to operate them, and the UN refuses to let South African technicians show us how, even though they are here to work on non-UN equipment.

"In Africa, you'll find the Malawian lecturers in Tanzania and Botswana"

Lack of foreign exchange means Malawi is in the hands of donor agencies, who at any moment might decide that the way forward is inappropriate new technology that costs a fortune. If the phones don't work, how can desktop publishing? In practical terms, I do not feel that I have achieved a lot and any hopes and aspirations that accompanied me out here have certainly disappeared. I can see others achieving a great deal, but I am increasingly sceptical of the role of the volunteer and aid agencies.

As I write this, Malawi celebrates 25 years of independence. Why then, you

ask yourself, are more than fifty percent of the university staff ex-pats when there are qualified Malawians who could do as well? It's the same with the medical service, and the answer is the same, too. A fully qualified Malawian doctor prefers to stay in Manchester rather than to return to a pitiful salary back home. So doctors here are recruited from Europe, thus perpetuating the myth that whites are more capable. In Africa, you'll find the Malawian lecturers in Tanzania and Botswana.

The extreme of Malawian education is represented by Kamuzu Academy – the so-called "Eton of Africa". This has only white staff and Latin is a compulsory subject for study. The children, after taking their A-levels, will go on to foreign universities. But will they return? If not, Malawi will continue to be one of the few countries left in the world where it is socially acceptable for the minority white population to live in the biggest houses, surrounded by beautiful gardens (plus pool), and serviced by black nannies, workers, gardeners and night watchmen.

If I am fed up at all about working in this country, this is not the case with living here. Malawi calls herself "the warm heart of Africa" and this is certainly true. Malawians are the friendliest and most hospitable people I have ever met (a fact that was reinforced after visiting neighbouring countries). And, on top of this, the country is astonishingly beautiful, with efficient transport and good tarmac roads. Any tourist brochure will elucidate on the mountains, game parks and the stunning lake, where you would be forgiven if you thought you were swimming in an aquarium. And it's all true!

For a woman, Malawi is an easy country to travel alone, without fear of harassment or intimidation. My only caution is that night time travelling, for both men and women, is not recommended, especially in the bigger towns, as the occasional mugging (often accompanied by violence) does occur.

Once, when I found myself travelling alone on the last bus, which didn't take me as far as my destination, the bus conductor himself made sure that, if the hitching didn't pay off, there was some place where I could be put up for the night safely. There aren't many cars on the road late at night.

"For a woman, Malawi is an easy country to travel alone"

Other times I have found it annoying when men have incessantly questioned me whilst waiting for a bus – but it has only been a friendly and inquisitive approach, nothing to do with being "chatted-up", and privacy is an unusual thing to want. And you will be stared at! Staring is not considered rude, so be prepared, especially away from the larger towns, to be the centre of attraction. This is perhaps most trying when, after a long day's travelling, you find yourself surrounded by silent, staring children when all you want to do is relax.

Living, as I do, in one of the larger towns, there is reasonable access to a wide variety of food. Most of it, the *Lilets* or *Tampax*, the tinned coffee and of course, the wine, comes from South Africa. It was very strange for me coming from London, where I boycotted South African goods, to find myself in a black African store full of South African produce. And it is doubly strange to realise that Malawi's precious foreign exchange is being spent on luxury items for the ex-pat community (me!) instead of paper for the children's school exercise books. In fact I feel more guilty living here than I did back home – especially as my living standards have shot up: no dingy London flat on a busy main road for me, but a three- bedroomed house with all mod cons!

TRAVEL NOTES

Languages English and Chichewa and a number of other African languages.

Transport Roads have been improved and there's a reasonably efficient network of express buses. Steamers ply up and down Lake Malawi – which is also one of the few areas where women hitch alone.

Accommodation There are plenty of government rest houses or council rest houses. This is also an easy country for camping.

Special Problems People do not discuss politics with strangers. Attempts to do so are seen as incriminating and compromising. Also be aware that the laws about dress (you should wear skirts that cover the knees) are strictly enforced. Any literature considered critical to the state might be confiscated at the border.

Guide *Africa on a Shoestring* (Lonely Planet) gives a fairly clear overview and has therefore been banned.

Contacts

There are no autonomous women's groups operating within the country.

Books

We've been unable to track down any books by or about Malawian women. *"Malawi from Both Sides"*, in **Joseph Hanlon**, *Beggar Your Neighbours* (CIIR, London, 1986), is a lucid and concise account of the political situation.

David Rubadiri, *No Bride Price* (E. African Pub. House, 1967). A novel of urban Africa centred around the strange and tenacious relationship between Lombe (the main character) and Nuria, his town mistress.

Legson Kayira, *The Detainees* (Heinemann, 1964). A remarkable and stylish novel by a Malawian political refugee.

Mali

• • • • • • • • • • • • • • • •

Mali stands at the edge of the Sahara desert and for overland travellers is the traditional gateway to West Africa. Even during the critical years of the Sahelian drought, travellers would arrive on the desert route from Algeria, attracted by the country's distinctly West African culture and atmosphere, the spectacular Bandigari Escarpment and the views of the great river Niger flowing between its desert banks.

As a predominantly Muslim country, Mali can be difficult for a woman travelling alone – and it becomes a lot easier if you join up with other travellers or an overland expedition. For many Malians, struggling to maintain a subsistence living, travellers now represent an essential source of income. In the cities, especially, you will be continually approached for money and this, coupled with the fairly common experiences of harassment, can become quite oppressive. The police particularly can give you a hard time and it's almost always worth getting someone to go with you if you have to report at a local station. Outside the tourist areas the atmosphere changes. People greet strangers with open hospitality and friendliness – and it's important to carry gifts with you as a means of reciprocating.

For the last two decades, the country has been governed by a succession of Marxist-inspired military regimes. Whilst many of the bureaucratic constraints on foreigners have been lifted in an effort to encourage tourism, travel is still closely regulated. There are restrictions on camping and staying with local people, and accommodation is expensive. Without your own vehicle, journeys can be incredibly slow and arduous.

A **women's movement** is developing in Mali though at present it is predominantly urban-based, made up of well-educated, middle-class women.

The *UNFM (Union Nationale des Femmes au Mali)* is the central organisation and its members campaign for women's rights and participate in meetings abroad. There are also various development centres set up in and around Bamako, mainly co-ordinated by the *Centre Djoliba*, which provide training skills for girls and women as well as education on nutrition and health, and talks on the health hazards of female circumcision.

"In and Out of People's Lives"

. . . .

Stephanie Newell travelled to Mali as part of a six-month overland expedition in a truck heading from Ramsgate, England, to Nigeria.

A fading wooden placard announced our entrance into Mali, and splintered arrows pointed vague tracks across the desert. With the compass as our only guide we headed towards Gao amid rising excitement at the prospect of letters from home. A thick layer of sand covered my scalp from the previous night's sandstorm; I had slept out – the power of the Sahara night sky is impossible to resist.

I was travelling with 25 other people as part of an overland expedition, the cheapest way of covering an unusual route. It started at 4am on the cold front of Ramsgate harbour and took us through many different African countries and climates, ending six months later in the concrete jungle of Nairobi. There were more women than men in our group and we shared tasks equally on a rota basis. We camped out every night, cooked over an open fire, and tried to buy fresh fruit and vegetables from local markets whenever possible. It was not easy travelling with so many new companions, our only common experience being Africa itself. But

when we stopped in a place for any length of time we could always wander off alone, or even leave the truck and meet up with it in another town.

"Arriving in Timbuctou, the group, especially the women, were constantly harassed"

We entered Mali through Tessalit, a desolate area with arid plains all around and the silence of a vast space. Small thick-walled houses crouched at the mercy of black slag-heaps that dominated the bleak landscape. It was difficult for the Western eye to assimilate – flat, orange sand-and-water buildings, a constant haze of dust in the air and a bright, white sun in a white hot sky. In a country that has been devastated by fifteen years of drought I had mixed feelings when we were offered American soft drinks and Dutch lager as an alternative to the tasteless water we had been drinking over the past four days. Overseas companies are dominating a continent where simple, low-cost improvements of water purification facilities could solve so many problems.

The women changed into long skirts as the sprawling town of Gao grew larger on the horizon. Young boys jumped on to the truck, giggling and stumbling as they kicked each other aside to view the new arrivals, calling out for "cadeau" as they fell off and raced behind. The desert's spell of silence became an equally powerful flurry of noise. Our white skins signalled wealth, and we were bombarded with offers of jewellery, metalwork and cloth.

We camped on the outskirts of the spacious town, alongside a mass of Tuareg huts – home to a traditionally nomadic people who have been forced towards the relative security of towns by the widespread drought.

The energy and spirit of these people was overwhelming. Their welcome and curiosity led to constant companionship in whatever we did, whether washing, eating or writing. The young girls were transfixed as a friend applied Moroccan henna to my hair; they watched as it set hard in the sun, then cried out for some as my hair turned from dull brown to bright orange. Likewise the strange ceremony of cleaning teeth with a toothbrush and paste was hilarious to a race who use the far more efficient method of chewing on bark and creating a paste from the sap.

The women and young girls of Gao stayed within the confines of their market stalls, mimicking our high-pitched European female voices, and collapsing with giggles at our hurt looks. They then extended smiles of friendship as we admired their clothes and made appointments to have our hair plaited.

From Gao we turned back into the desert for the three-day drive up to Timbuctou: we navigated the dried riverbeds, stopping to fill our water containers at tall wind-powered pumps gently turning in the winds that sweep along the flat plains. Camels and donkeys were herded to the supply to drink from goatskin watersacks. Arriving in Timbuctou, the group, especially the women, were constantly harassed, so much so that we left after only four hours. Two of us took refuge in the ancient mosque; taking off our shoes, we entered the vast building, climbed some crumbling steps on to a flat roof and then ducked low to climb to the top of the minaret overlooking

the town. We descended from the cool breeze to bowls of clear water from huge earthenware casks before reluctantly joining the bustle outside.

"The circle of tents went up slowly as the group realised that we could be stuck for quite a while; nobody knew where we were and there were no trucks large enough to haul us out"

Speeding on through the ever more green countryside, beside the river Niger, we became more and more lost. A truckload of village men eventually guided us towards Mopti and then turned off as we approached a ford. Our twenty-ton truck ground to a halt in the soft mudbanks midway between shores. The inhabitants of nomadic settlements on either side of the river clustered into the water at this sudden new source of entertainment, leaving their vast herds of cattle to pick at the dried grass. The engine roared and the truck gently tilted to a 45-degree angle at which it remained for almost a week.

The circle of tents went up slowly as the group realised that we could be stuck for quite a while; nobody knew where we were and there were no trucks large enough to haul us out. By dusk, news had spread and running figures approached through herds of cattle. We had 24-hour companions to our shifts of 24-hour guards. Perhaps, to the local people, we were wealthy nomads, certainly we were considered doctors with cures for every ailment. A woman came forward leading another by the hand, blinded by conjunctivitis, infected by the lack of clean water. One of the women in our group couldn't bear to touch this woman, her eyes were so bad; it took twenty minutes to thoroughly clean them with swabs of boiled water and eye drops.

Crowds of people looked in at our first meal by the river, watching in astonishment as we munched our way through soup, then plates of mince, mashed potato and vegetables. A baby was brought to see me, the fifth, sixth, seventh, umpteenth conjunctivitis case in one evening. As its mother opened its eyes for the drops to go in, they looked so sore, almost blind; I broke down, dashing away from the camp in tears. I could never come to terms with the lack of basic health facilities on the shores of the river Niger: a cow keeled over and died in the water as the herd passed through. Eight hours later it was still there, swollen and bloated as the sun beat down.

"We seemed to be a bubble of Englishness with our plentiful fall-back supplies of tinned foods, dehydrated vegetables and packet mixes"

Meanwhile, work on the truck continued as we tried to dig the axle and wheels clear. The vast, yellow lorry had almost become a part of the landscape. Cattle would pass through the river beside it as they were herded across before nightfall; *pirogues* (like gondolas), loaded with baskets and people, navigated around it shouting greetings; and flocks of pelicans would survey the scene from the air as dusk fell over our camp. We seemed to be a bubble of Englishness with our plentiful fall-back supplies of tinned foods, dehydrated vegetables and packet mixes, travelling through communities that had to rely on being self-sufficient. Water and wood, however, are the dictators of health in Mali, and as both ran out for us, we too experienced the discomfort of diarrhoea and conjunctivitis in a relentlessly hot country.

Children pounced on the things we discarded. It was traumatic to watch our waste become prized and fought over; our tins would be thrust forwards through the tight circle of tents as we served up food in the evenings.

Then, in contrast, a group of travelling artists crossed the river and stopped near us one evening. They were on their way to Mopti for a festival of traditional song and dance, and their tuneful passionate singing and relaxed dancing drew some bolder members of our group towards them. We sat in awe at the swaying patchwork of bright African cloth, the togetherness of the musicians who had only a regular drumbeat to set the tempo. The leader of the group sat on the only foam mat and plucked a battered guitar, its three remaining strings held together by elastic bands and the body of a biro. A young boy was called to the front after the main song was over and, strong and rhythmical, his voice rang out in a new song he had created for the group. A young woman with a bold, deep voice that matched her stature joined in with a chorus and presently the whole group were again swaying and singing. We were motioned to leave by the seated man as a passing truck stopped and took them off to Mopti for the festival.

One day three of us negotiated the loan of two donkeys and set out for the local village in search of bread. A young boy was appointed to escort us, or rather the donkeys, who were constantly trying to head back for their owner's hut. Having got used to the rocking movement of the animals we relaxed into the two-mile journey, progressing slowly past the laughing "hellos" of local people and through the occasional herds of cattle. At the edge of the river we scrambled off the donkeys into a *pirogue*, having first spent a while agreeing on a price with the boat owner. I was not wearing shoes and hid from the sun under a long strip of cloth wrapped around my neck and shoulders as we clambered out into the mud on the opposite bank, to be greeted by an excited crowd of people.

The villagers seemed delighted to have three white women visit them and showed us into many one-roomed houses before asking us to take shelter for a while. Our escort of children hovered uncertainly in the doorways, awaiting our exit. Younger children rubbed our arms to prove to themselves that our colour really was not an elaborate paint. All over Africa the children would do this, very softly rubbing our skins, then holding their arms up to ours with wide-eyed enjoyment at finding such a difference.

We came away clasping tiny hands, but no bread. The ovens are fired by the heat of the sun and as it was not yet hot enough for baking to begin we were asked to return later on the following day. The women on the river banks pointed to my bare feet in concern as we climbed back into the narrow wooden boat to leave. Perhaps this was because as a wealthy person I should have been wearing shoes, or maybe because there are so many diseases that can pass up through the soles of one's feet. However, by that time we were drinking and washing in the same river water, but with the knowledge of antibiotics back home.

The truck was eventually heaved out of the river after an SOS message was conveyed via a foreign aid truck to another overland group we had heard was passing through. By this time we had made special friends by the river and seemed to have been accepted as curious residents. It was sad to wave goodbye to the proud people whose world we had somehow stepped in and out of. Our destination was Mopti, where it was encouraging to see variousnew foreign aid agencies working in conjunction with each other on agricultural and health projects. They seemed optimistic about the future of Mali – "All we need now is rain."

A Walk along the Niger River

. . . .

Over several years, Jo Hanson has travelled to many countries in Africa. In the course of one overland trip across the Sahara, she spent a month walking along the Niger River.

If you look presentable, you might easily fall into the foreign aid circuit in Bamako, which consists of men of many nationalities living in styles to which they are probably unaccustomed at home. Exasperated by the two-hour lunches and afternoons beside the swimming pool, I set off to walk up the Niger River towards its source in Guinea.

As soon as I left Bamako and the tarmac road became laterite, good things began to happen. A young man carried my sleeping bag roll and showed me where to buy a cup of condensed-milk coffee, then a half-blind woman took over the bag and led me into a large compound, where I was the centre of attention for several minutes while I put ointment into her eyes (I always carry a few tubes) and lamented the fact that she was in such a plight only a couple of kilometres from the capital. "I can't afford to send her to the hospital," said her husband, but as he was sitting on a good chair surrounded by various sheep and cattle, I wondered where his priorities lay.

Later, in the heat of the day, I was invited to rest by a farmer whose wife was cooking beside the river a delicious-looking fish and groundnut stew.

I was looking forward to a taste of this when he pedalled to the village shop and brought back two tins of sardines and four loaves of French bread, obviously thinking that this was what white people must have! When the heat had lessened he led me back to the road (another thing I didn't really want) and proudly showed me the new table-football game a local entrepreneur had set up, penny-a-go. It was the kind where you manipulate handles at high speed to move model players from side to side, and looked a bit bizarre under a baobab tree with a field of maize nearby.

That night I slept on a handy pile of straw at the edge of an aid project (you can always tell them by the huge size of the fields and the large machinery that is used). Next morning I noticed a Frenchman trying to mend a diesel water-pump, but being an advocate of intermediate technology, I preferred the *shaduf*, an ancient Egyptian device with pole and weight, which was being operated by a market gardener further along the river.

I was invited to a fish stew lunch by a family who this time, far from buying French bread for me, eagerly shared the remains of mine. The six sons seemed to be thriving, but at the expense of their mother who looked utterly sapped as well as pregnant. I couldn't speak her language; even if I could, what would I say? I gave her as many iron and vitamin tablets as I could spare, using sign language to tell her "One a day – only for you"; I often found that men appropriated the little benefits I gave to their women.

All along the way I was repeatedly asked into huts and given rides on bikes, mobylettes, a donkey cart, and even in the car of a gang of hunters out shooting partridges. I met many strange types: a Jehovah's Witness who tried to convert me in French, a Nigerian seaman who had got stranded and was earning enough to get home by selling face cream made from the boiled root of a tree, and a student of English on a motorbike who stopped me to chat about Dickens. Small-scale trading went on in every village, but there was little enough to buy – maybe a few oranges, bananas or water melons or a bowl of rice and groundnut stew in a "café" (a mud hut containing a bench).

"I walked all one afternoon in the shallows of the river wearing only bra and pants, with wading birds hopping round and hippos sighing"

After five days' walking, I had a rest in a metropolis (well, it had a pharmacy and a man who sold matches) called Kangaba. I was adopted by a young unmarried woman called Fatika who was the local community health worker. She took me to the community centre, a large shed where all kinds of classes presumably went on since the walls were plastered with posters about nutritious food and clean, boiled water. I asked Fatika for a drink, thinking this was the right place to be, and she brought me a black cupful from a fetid pot in the corner. As it took so long for my sterilising tablets to dissolve, I surreptitiously threw it away. This gap between theory and practice is often evident in Africa. I saw it again when Fatika's brother showed me his school books, pages full of neat writing in French about hygiene – yet they both had dysentery and pleaded with me for a remedy (the pharmacy had run out).

I stayed the night with a couple of Dutch volunteers. They were marvellous people, up at dawn and out to remote villages with a cold box full of children's vaccines strapped to the back of their motor scooters. For the next couple of days many people I met asked me if I knew "Nelly-et-Harry"!

I crossed over the river by canoe when I reached the border with Guinea (which was closed to tourists at that time), and started to walk back down the other side. This was a wilder part with less population; in fact I walked all one afternoon in the shallows of the river wearing only bra and pants, with wading birds hopping round and hippos sighing and not a soul in sight. The water was so clear I drank straight from the river.

Reaching another large village opposite Kangaba I stayed with a nurse-midwife. She was obviously more committed and practical than Fatika, but stymied by an almost complete lack of medicines and supplies. In the evening she had to make two trips to the river to fetch water, carrying on her head a tin tub that I couldn't even lift when it was full. Other women did the same, many of them pregnant, one even saying that her labour pains had started! That night there was a total eclipse of the moon, marked by much drumming and dancing amongst the population who had been forewarned by news on the radio.

Next day I found myself climbing up a wooded plateau and after several hours' walking through wild, dry scrub, I came upon a gold-mining village. Gold is Mali's principal mineral export, but the people who did the labour obviously had no status at all: they were dressed in rags with no school, clinic or facility of any kind in the place. While I was watching the miners lower themselves into deep holes in the ground, a young man on a bike came wobbling through the trees and introduced himself in French as a gold-dealer. He took me on to his father's village, wading over a rushing cold tributary of the Niger, then bike riding *à deux* amongst a wide area of termite hills like a forest of pointed witches' hats. It would certainly have been a tourist attraction if SMERT (the state tourist agency) had known about it!

After that I paid an old man to pole me a dreamy fifteen kilometres down the river in the evening to a rice-processing factory. I expected to find it a hub of activity, but instead it was empty, deserted, thousands of francs (or dollars, or pounds, or deutsch-marks) just rusting away. Bats and mosquitoes abounded, and for the first time I had to use my net as I spent the night there.

Although the small town attached to the factory had a road back to Bamako and a once-weekly minibus, it wasn't that day, so I resumed my riverside walk. Gradually it got more and more difficult. I followed lonely cattle tracks over rocks and into small fertile areas, but these petered out and I was faced with a huge area of high elephant grass with no way through. I could walk no further – in any case by now I had given away all my spare clothes and presents. I noticed a man standing on a spit of sand and he told me that a ferry-*pirogue* might come across some time. I knew I could get a lift or a squashed paying ride on the laterite road back on the other side of the river, so decided to wait with him.

He was most solicitous, sharing his food and finding a soft place for me to sit and read, his attitude being typical of all the men I had met. Yet I had never seen one offer a bike ride, carry a heavy load or take the hoe out of the hand of his wife, sister or even mother. It is not difficult to find an explanation for this, but I still regret that the friendly assistance I was lucky enough to receive from men did not touch the visibly arduous lives of the women that I saw on my journey.

TRAVEL NOTES

Languages French and various African languages. The most common is Bambara. Some students speak English.

Transport There is only one railway line, connecting Bamako (the capital) with Dakar (Senegal). Roads are fairly rough – tarmac up to certain points out of Bamako, the rest sandy tracks. Hitching is difficult as there are few private cars but you can get rides with lorries where you're expected to pay. Shared taxis are also available as well as *taxis brousses* (crowded minibuses/vans) which go from town to town. When the river is high enough (usually August–December) riverboats run between Mopti, Timbuktu, Gao and sometimes on to Koulikoro, near Bamako.

Accommodation Small hotels are relatively expensive. Travelling outside the towns and tourist areas you will have to rely on local hospitality – you should offer something (money/gifts) in return for your keep.

Special problems Visas are required by all except nationals of France, and can be quite hard to get hold of. Once in, you have to register with the police in each town that you stay in overnight. Sometimes you might be hassled for bribe money – it's best if you check in with another traveller. It can be hard coming to terms with the degree of poverty in Mali. Begging is seen as a necessary part of the social system and you should set money aside for this.

Guide *The Rough Guide: West Africa* (Harrap Columbus) has a good chapter on Mali.

Contacts

Union Nationale des Femmes du Mali, BP 740, Bamako. Formed in 1974 to fight for women's rights, the Union organises literacy programmes, promotes the participation of women in development work, and campaigns against female circumcision.

Books

We have not managed to trace any books dealing specifically with Mali. See other African countries and the General Bibliography for general works on Africa.

Thanks to Jo Hanson who provided much of the information for the Travel Notes.

Mexico

Mexico is a chaotic and exciting country with a tremendous amount to offer the traveller. Between the highly developed resorts lie miles of untouched beaches, but most of the interest lies inland. Large areas of central and southern Mexico are steeped in Spanish colonial history and are rich in Indian traditions and the relics of ancient civilisations – not to mention magnificent scenery. An extensive bus network makes it easy to get around and, depending on the exchange rate (Mexico is in a permanent state of economic crisis), there's plenty of cheap accommodation.

After a very stormy past, Mexico is nowadays regarded as one of the most stable countries in Latin America. This stability is based more on its strength as an advanced industrial power than on just or democratic government. Despite efforts to present a radical face to the outside world, the Institutional Revolutionary Party, in power for over forty years, is deeply conservative. Little has been done to implement the kind of social changes symbolised by the famous 1911 Revolution.

The bulk of the population are very poor and there is considerable resentment of the affluence of their northern neighbours in the United States. This is sometimes focused on tourists, which can be hard to cope with. *Gringas* (foreign women), representing both wealth and a type of sexuality denied to Mexican men, are easy targets for resentment. Approaches from men tend to be aggressive, so you need to feel strong. If s also worth making a great effort to learn at least some Spanish – a relatively easy language – before you go.

Not only foreigners need to arm themselves against *machismo*. **Mexican feminists** have long recognised it as a deep-rooted obstacle in their struggle for equality and freedom. However, as in the rest of Latin America, more urgent concern is given to the denial of basic economic and social rights. Since it began in 1970, a large section of the Women's Movement has had close links with various political parties of the Left. At the same time there is an autonomous movement, for which abortion is a central issue, and there are several organised lesbian groups. Although certain reforms, such as the elimination of discriminatory laws, have been passed on paper, Mexican women see themselves as having a lot more to fight for.

Alone on the Northern Circuit
. . . .

Esther Berick lives in San Francisco and has made several trips to Mexico, most recently travelling by bus and train in the north and central regions.

After four trips to Mexico with friends, I felt confident enough in my ability to speak and understand Spanish to travel by myself. I wanted to experience the train ride through the Barranca del Cobre, the Copper Canyon, which I'd read was the most spectacular rail trip in all of North America. The canyon, which is in the Sierra Madre of the northern state of Chihuahua, is larger than the famous Grand Canyon of Arizona and home to the Tarahumara, the least assimilated indigenous people in Mexico. The photographs I'd seen of the Tarahumara – the women in their voluminous, brightly coloured skirts and blouses, the men in their traditional baggy white pants and shirts – fascinated me. This, I told myself, was worth setting off alone for.

My trip began with a flight from San Francisco to El Paso, Texas, a city which shares a border with Ciudad Juárez, Mexico. It's about a six-hour bus ride from El Paso to Chihuahua, Mexico, where I purchased my ticket for the train ride through the canyon. On the way down to Chihuahua I sat next to a young Mexican named Teresa – a woman of about 25, with black, wavy hair and a wonderful, wide smile.

Teresa was from Chihuahua but lived in El Paso with a wealthy American family, cleaning their house and caring for their children. Her own three young daughters lived in Chihuahua with her mother and every other weekend she made the six-hour trip to visit them. She carried small gifts for her little girls: a child's comb and brush set, candy, a doll. She proudly showed me photos of her daughters and lamented how she had to live and work so far away from them.

The small salary she made in El Paso, however, was more than she could ever hope to earn in Chihuahua. Despite living and working in an American city, she barely spoke English, but was eager to learn. She cajoled me into giving her an impromptu English lesson by promising that she would teach me some Spanish words that weren't in the dictionary. I was glad we had something to share.

"'You must be a writer,' she said, 'there is no other reason for a woman to be travelling by herself'"

Chihuahua City is the capital of the richest state in all of Mexico and this prosperity attracts a broad ethnic mix of people. In the wide streets you see cowboys in their boots and ten-gallon hats, Mennonite women in long sombre skirts and bonnets and, occasionally, some colourfully dressed Tarahumara. This is cattle country, and I'd never been in a Mexican town with so many steak-houses before. I was starving when I got off the bus from El Paso and, after searching unsuccessfully for a café that served simple rice and beans, I ended up at a healthfood restaurant eating a tofu burger with alfalfa sprouts – a unique eating experience in my many trips to Mexico!

The train ride from Chihuahua through the Copper Canyon to Los Mochis, at the other end of the line, takes twelve hours. I decided to break the trip by spending a few nights in Creel, a very small town that serves as a jumping-off point for excursions into the canyon. Creel has unpaved streets, lots of cowboys driving big Ford pickup trucks, and Mexican country-and-western music blaring from every radio.

It's hot and dusty in the summer and, I was told, cold and snow-bound in the winter. There's a bank, a post office, a pharmacy and a small store, run by the local Catholic mission, where the Tarahumara bring their crafts to be sold to tourists. Here one can purchase woven baskets, wooden dolls dressed in traditional indigenous clothing, blankets and excellent, sensitive photographs of the Tarahumara, taken by a Jesuit priest whom they know and trust. The availability of these pictures compensates for not taking your own; the Tarahumara are extremely shy and any attempt to photograph them would be seen as an intrusion.

I arrived in Creel hoping to meet other women travellers, but was disappointed to find that I was one of only three people staying at my hotel. The other two were a Mexican couple on their honeymoon. "Where are your travelling companions?" they wanted to know. The young bride looked at me curiously when I told them I was on my own, then gave me a quick smile: "Well, you must be a writer," she said, "there is no other reason for a woman to be travelling by herself." Thinking of all the years I'd spent travelling and writing in my journal, I thanked her for the compliment.

Because of the dearth of tourists in Creel, none of the fantastic tours I'd read about in my guidebook were being offered. However, the train on to Los Mochis was everything my travel literature promised. The scenery, as we passed through lovely wooded canyons, twisted around sharp mountain curves and chugged over high bridges, was truly spectacular. The train, though primarily a tourist attraction, also serves the local people who live in the tiny towns scattered in the mountains: the men in their ubiquitous cowboy hats and jeans, the women in simple dresses, and nearly everyone holding packages and young children.

It was on this train that I met two Dutch women travelling together, the only women I would meet during my whole time in Mexico who were not travelling with men. I was often looked at with curiosity by the Mexicans I met, though I was never treated rudely. "Pobrecita," (poor little thing) the older women would say when I told them I was on a solo journey through their country. After too many "pobrecitas", I started telling people that I was a student on holiday from my studies in Mexico City. To them that seemed more legitimate than being simply a traveller and quite frankly it got very depressing always having people feel sorry for me.

The men, in general, were bolder in approaching me than the women, and would often ask me about my job in San Francisco and how much money I made. My reply invariably provoked a whistle and the exclamation "That's a lot of money!" followed immediately by the question of whether I was married. At these times I always said yes, and that I was on my way to meet my husband and two darling children in the next town. I made a vow to wear a fake wedding band the next time I travelled to Mexico. Many of the men I met had worked in San Francisco and we would talk about the neighbourhoods and businesses we both knew. These conversations always left me with a warm feeling that I wasn't really so far from home, alone.

There were times, however, when it was very lonely being in a culture that put so much emphasis on a woman always being with her family, or at the very least with an escort. As a result I found myself accepting invitations from men that could have been dangerous. In one situation, I went out to dinner with a man I met at the Guadalajara bus station. We went to a famous *mariachi* nightclub where I seemed to be the only foreigner, and I was delighted when the whole place joined in singing the high-spirited romantic songs along with the performers. My "date" had the idea that the romance would continue in the taxi on the way back to my hotel.

"Just say the word," he told me, trying to pull me close, "and I'll cancel all my business plans just to spend the night with you."

I dealt with both of these situations by acting the part of an incredibly modest and shy young woman"

On another occasion I hired a guide to take me to see some pyramids in Tzintzuntzan, a small town outside Pazcuaro in the state of Michoacan. We'd met the day before at the Regional Museum of Popular Art in Pazcuaro where he worked explaining the folk-art exhibits to tourists. He told me he often took visitors on excursions to see the pyramids, and thinking it would be safer to go with a guide than alone, I agreed to the plan. The pyramids are in an isolated spot on top of a hill and do not receive many visitors. After climbing the hill we sat and chatted for a few minutes; then he surprised me by putting his arms round me and kissing me.

I dealt with both of these situations by acting the part of an incredibly modest and shy young woman. I clearly had no chance of winning a physical struggle, in fact it would probably have made me a more exciting challenge: the feisty *gringa*. It was much safer to appeal to their protective instincts and adopt the role of little sister. How I would have coped if they'd pushed me further I don't know. I'm glad it never happened.

I strongly recommend any woman planning to visit Mexico to have a good working knowledge of Spanish, as relatively few Mexicans speak English, especially in the smaller towns. The conversations I had with local people on buses and in the market places could make the difference between a very good day and a very bad one. Youth Hostels are few and far between, so it helps to have a companion along to share the cost of a hotel room. Although there are some extremely low-cost hotels in Mexico, I often chose to stay in more moderately priced ones as the very cheapest are usually in parts of town that I wouldn't risk going into alone. I avoided being hassled in restaurants by always picking the type of places where families go to eat. While waiting for my meal, I would either read a book or write in my diary. Besides keeping myself busy, it gave the impression that I was comfortable being alone and did not want to be bothered.

A Place to Return To

. . . .

Valerie Walkerdine is a psychologist, writer and artist living in London. Fascinated by Mexico, she has visited the country five times in recent years to travel, work and extend friendships she has made there.

I first had the idea of going to Mexico when I was working for the summer in Canada, from which (like the US) it is possible to get very cheap flights. Although clear that I wanted to see America's so-called back yard for myself, I found it difficult at first to work out where to go. This being the first real solo trip I had made, I suppose I was also slightly afraid.

Cheap flights from North America to Mexico all tend to focus on very Americanised holiday resorts, which are not the best places to go unless you like observing imperialism at work in a particularly obnoxious way. A Mexican woman in one airline office was helpful and found me some literature, but other travel agents just wanted to shunt me off to the beach resorts.

People also suggested that it would be too hot for me in the summer – I have very fair skin – as Mexico is chiefly known as a winter resort. Basic knowledge of the Mexican seasons, however, would have cleared up this mistake; it rains a lot in July and is certainly no hotter in the summer than in winter or spring, though the climate varies according to region.

In the end I decided to start with the city of Oaxaca, some 500km south of Mexico City. My guidebook made it sound interesting, not too full of *gringos*, off the tourist beach scene, and with a strong, relatively intact Indian heritage. It turned out to be a very attractive town, though not exactly off the tourist trail. The surrounding state of Oaxaca was stunning, offering a combination of pre-Columbian remains, tropical forests, mountains and a beautiful coastline, though visiting some of the more remote coastal areas with a friend, I felt that, while they looked inviting, they might well prove dangerous for a woman on her own.

"Men will ask outrageous questions about your sex life"

Getting around Mexico is cheap if you have a European or North American income. For Mexicans it is very expensive, as is the general cost of living. I travelled by plane and bus – trains are very slow, hire cars extortionate. It helps considerably to speak Spanish. On my first trip I spoke none, but can now hold a reasonable conversation, which really repays the effort of learning. I found people on buses eager to talk. Unlike Europeans, who hide themselves in books on journeys, Mexicans like to sit together and chat.

A woman alone, however, is considered an oddity in this patriarchal country and everyone wants to know if you are married and have children. Men will ask outrageous questions about your sex life. It's easy to pass this off as proof of the blatant sexism only to be expected of a macho culture, but it's not as simple as that. Attitudes to *gringos* and *gringas* are also about the hate and envy of an oppressed and exploited people.

White women, especially with fair hair, are about the most hated, envied and desired of all. Any glance at the television screen makes it immediately obvious that white skin equals wealth and class in the Mexican popular imagination. Hence many Mexican men's desire to "have" a white woman is matched by their secret (or sometimes not so secret) contempt.

Travelling alone, the attentions of Mexican men can be both irritating and flattering.

As the Canadian film, *A Winter Tan*, demonstrates, Mexico can feel like a place to let go of the strictures of European morality, but the relationship of the *gringa* tourist to Mexican patriarchy requires some reflection. The film painfully documents the "adventures" and eventual death of a North American woman looking for sex in Mexico. In quite a racist way, it presents the pain of a white woman in search of sexual freedom and, unable to find what she is looking for at home, she is left to pursue the fantasy through another of escape and Otherness. Of course, tales of the promiscuity of *gringa* women abound in Mexico and it is important to try and reflect upon the complex relationship between not only capitalism and patriarchy, but of power and powerlessness between white women and Mexican men.

I have to say that these are issues which I have thought about as I have got to know Mexico and Mexicans better. I was not actually frightened by the harassment at any time, but I do advise caution, for instance when travelling in the metro in Mexico City. The public transport system is stunningly efficient in carrying millions of people at low cost, consequently the trains are always crowded. Where they are available it's wise to travel in women's compartments. You also need to hold on very carefully to your money. In this respect it obviously helps not to go around saying loudly in English (or Spanish for that matter) how cheap everything is: it is only cheap to us.

"It was perhaps the first time in many years that I had actually felt able to let go of some of the attachments to work and begin to recognise that I could relax, that there were other things in life"

Mexico exists with an overt level of corruption and danger in its political and everyday life which can be frightening and shocking. To gain more insight into this complex country it is well worth trying to make contact with feminist groups and to find out what is going on politically. The strongest current is socialist feminism, but the talks I went to were overwhelmingly run by white, middle-class women. However, in both these discussions and the political meetings I attended, people were friendly and more than willing to talk about what was going on. On my last visit, in the summer of 1988, feelings were running especially high in the aftermath of the latest round of corrupt elections. Zapatistas (supporters of the politics of Emilio Zapata, principal hero of the Revolution) marched in the streets of Mexico City and beyond. Elsewhere ordinary people laughed at the very mention of the word *revolución*. "We call it *robolucion*", was a common remark.

Mexico is beautiful in a way that makes you never want to return to northern winters (or summers). There is something about the quality of light and the big skies that is easy to romanticise – as it is to exoticise the country's rich and varied culture. The mixture of indigenous and Spanish cultures can quite take your breath away and makes the West seem horribly obsessive in its post-modernist hype and materialism. I remember stopping in New York on the way home from my first visit in the summer of 1987, having been relaxing with friends north of Mexico City. It was perhaps the first time in many years that I had actually felt able to let go of some of the attachments to work and begin to recognise that I could relax, that there were other things in life. New York after this seemed gross.

For all these reasons and more, it didn't take long for me to dream up an excuse to return. This was provided a few months later by the chance to do some research for a short film about the Mexican painter, Frida Kahlo. My Spanish had improved and I found it fairly easy to wander alone around Mexico City – even with a Super-8 movie camera complete with tripod! I also travelled to Guanjuato and Patzcuaro to the north. The former is a colonial town of great beauty where, in my memory, the golden yellow walls of houses blend with the winter sunshine. In the glorious December light, Patzcuaro, built on the shores of a huge lake, was spectacular. Many Mexicans were on holiday, eating meals of freshly cooked fish overlooking the water. The boat trip out to the central island is lovely, though everything, from the fishermen lifting their nets for the tourist cameras to the souvenir stalls on the island itself, shows how tourism has become a central means of survival for local inhabitants.

I was fascinated by Mexico and yet, as an academic and visual artist, I was aware of how much writing about and seeing of Mexico there had already been through European eyes. D.H.

Lawrence, Malcolm Lowrie and Graham Greene have all set novels here, and all, in one way or another, use the country to explore the fascination and exoticisation of European "man" for the "other" – the uncivilised and primitive, the hot passion against civilised European coldness.

"The women I met in a street market picking through the thrown away rotten produce; they wanted above all not to be photographed in the humiliation of their poverty"

It is all too easy to see Mexico like this, as well as the other version, the big holiday playground south of the border. Of course, there are also writers and artists who want to see and to document oppression and poverty. But this is equally problematic in its way. The role of voyeuristic observer, looking to report to the affluent West, does nothing for, say, the women I met in a street market picking through the thrown away rotten produce; they wanted above all not to be photographed in the humiliation of their poverty.

In the end I made a tape-slide about the relationship between my geographical journey, the problem of the voyeuristic aspects of observing and reporting on other cultures' oppression and poverty, and my own history and personal journey towards liberation. Mexico is an exciting country which makes you look again at all those things most of us take for granted in Europe. The diversity of its cultures, the stunning remains of pre-Columbian civilisations, the wonderful revolutionary artistic heritage, mixed with the complexities and oppression of its present, make it seem both wonderful and terrible. I will keep on going back.

TRAVEL NOTES

Languages Spanish and various Indian dialects.

Transport Buses are the best means of getting around. Trains are cheaper but limited and very slow. Hitching is more hassle than it's worth, with the additional threat of police harassment.

Accommodation Cheap hotels are usually easy to find and it's worth haggling if you feel you're being overcharged. In cities you'll find most of them concentrated around the central square or *zocalo*.

Special Problems Many women have enjoyed travelling alone through Mexico, in spite of sexual harassment. Self-confidence and some knowledge of Spanish seems to help.

Don't get involved with or ever trust the police. Police bribery is a common racket (especially if you're driving). If approached it's best to act as if you don't know a word of Spanish. Talk a lot in English about the British Embassy and *Sectur* (a government agency in charge of looking after tourists), offer them less than half of what they ask and only pay once a reasonable price has been reached. Don't touch drugs. It's usual for a dealer to sell them to someone, sell the information to the police and then get half the drugs once his victim has been arrested.

Guides *The Rough Guide: Mexico* (Harrap Columbus) is one of the best in the series — practical, informed and often amusing. *The South American Handbook* (Trade and Travel Publications) also has a good Mexican section.

Contacts

Movimiento Nacional Para Mujeres, San Juan de Letran 11-411, Mexico DF, ☎512-58 41. National women's organisation, useful for contacts throughout the country.

Colectivo Cine Mujer, Angelas Negoechea, Penururi 19, Sede Casa Oyoacan, Mexico DF. Women's film collective, established in 1974 and, as far as we know, still going strong.

CIDHAL, Apartado 579, Cuernavaca, Morelos. Women's documentation centre primarily concerned with popular education among working-class women.

For information on the lesbian scene in Mexico, write to *Places of Interest to Women*, PO Box 35575 Phoenix, AZ 85069, USA, ☎602-863 2408.

Books

Sybille Bedford, *A Visit to Don Otavio* (1953 Eland Books, 1984). An extremely enjoyable and surprisingly relevant account of travels in 1950s Mexico.

Hayden Herrera, *Frida: A Biography* (Bloomsbury Press, 1989). Biography of the extraordinary Mexican painter who died in 1953.

Oscar Lewis, *The Children of Sanchez* (Penguin, 1982). Chronicles the lives of a working-class family in Mexico City in the 1940s. Oral history at its best.

Octavio Paz, *The Labyrinth of Solitude* (Grove Press, US, 1983). Collection of essays exploring the social and political state of modern Mexico, by one of the country's leading philosophers.

Gisela Espinosa Damián, "Feminism and Social Struggle in Mexico" in Miranda Davies, ed., *Third World — Second Sex 2* (Zed Books, 1987). This article, by a former *CIDHAL* worker, discusses the experience of coordinating workshops on sexuality in a poor neighbourhood of Mexico City.

Morocco

O nly an hour's ferry ride from southern Spain, Morocco is easily the most accessible and certainly the most popular of the North African states. The fact that it's so close to the well trodden Mediterranean routes, and has the familiar feel of recent French colonialism, can however be a disadvantage – leaving you little time to adjust to an Islamic, essentially Third World culture. In line with the precepts of Islam, women keep a low profile, particularly in urban life, and travelling alone (or with other women) you may well find yourself

labelled as a "loose" and "immodest" Westerner, your freedom to travel and mix with men placing you in a broadly similar category to a Moroccan prostitute.

These attitudes are at their most stiflingly apparent in the main resorts and cities where contact with tourists is greatest and where sexual harassment easily merges with the continual and persistent approaches from hustlers and "guides" (many Moroccans have to depend on tourists for economic survival). Tangier, the main point of entry for most travellers, is perhaps the hardest to contend with, and many women stay just a couple of days and then take the ferry back.

To do this, however, would be to miss a great deal. The tradition of hospitality towards strangers runs much deeper than the mutual exploitations of tourism, and just as you can experience harassment you can also experience great friendship and generosity. It's essential to remain polite and even-mannered in all your dealings. At its best – in the high Atlas mountains, in Marrakesh and throughout the southern desert routes – Morocco can be a great country to visit.

Since Independence from the French in 1956, women have looked to the state to take over the traditional functions of providing welfare and educational services for the family. A small proportion of women have managed to gain access to higher education and, despite intense discrimination, professional employment. For the majority, however, modernisation has brought only the erosion of traditional networks of support, with few alternatives provided. This has very much increased women's vulnerability to isolation and poverty.

There is an official government **women's organisation**, the *Women's Union*, which has centres running skills training classes in most of the large cities. More recently, a feminist group, linked to the Left opposition movement, has also emerged in Rabat, printing a women's paper *The 8th of March*; distribution is increasing and the group has also organised various conferences, seminars and events in other cities.

Running through Fes

. . . .

Margaret Hubbard, who works as an English teacher in Scotland, set off to Morocco for a month's holiday. Although she had long been interested in Islamic culture and had already travelled in the Middle East, this was her first trip alone to a Muslim country.

I knew that there were likely to be difficulties in travelling as a woman alone around Morocco. I'd been warned by numerous sources about hustling and harassment and I was already well aware of the constraints imposed upon women travellers within Islamic cultures. But above and beyond this I knew I'd be fascinated by the country. I had picked up a smattering of Arabic and the impetus to study Islamic religion and culture during trips to Damascus and Amman (both times with a male companion). Also I already had enough experience of travelling alone to know that I could live well with myself should I meet up with no one else. So, a little apprehensive but very much more determined and excited, I arrived at Tangier, took the first train out to Casablanca and found a room for the night. It was not until I emerged the next morning into the bright daylight of Casablanca that I experienced my first reaction to Morocco.

Nothing could have prepared me for it. Almost instantly I was assailed by a barrage of "voulez-vous coucher avec moi . . . Avez-vous jamais fait l'amour au Maroc . . . Venez avec moi madame . . . Viens m'selle". Whatever I had to say was ignored at will and wherever I went I felt constantly scrutinised by men. Fighting down the panic I headed for the bus station where, after a lot of frantic rushing to and fro (I couldn't decipher the Arabic signs), I climbed on to a coach for Marrakesh.

It wasn't that the harassment was less, in fact it was almost as constant as in Tangier. But wandering through the Djemaa el Fna (the main square and centre of all life in Marrakesh) amongst the snake charmers, kebab sellers, blanket weavers, water sellers, monkey trainers, merchants of everything from false teeth to handwoven rugs, I became ensnared to such an extent that my response to the men who approached me was no longer one of fear but rather a feeling of irrelevance.

Marrakesh proved to me that I was right to come to Morocco. There was too much to be learned to shut out contact with people and I heard myself utter, as if it were the most normal reply in the world, "Non, monsieur, je ne veux pas coucher avec vous, mais pouvez-vous me dire pourquoi ils vendent false teeth/combien d'années il faut pour faire des tapis a main/ pourquoi les singes (monkeys)". That first night I returned to my room at 2am more alive than I had felt for months.

I'd also stumbled upon a possible strategy for pre-empting, perhaps even preventing, harassment. Moroccan hustlers know a lot about tourists and have reason to expect one of two reactions from them – fear or a sort of resigned acceptance. What they don't expect is for you to move quickly through the opening gambits and launch into a serious conversation about Moroccan life. Using a mixture of French and Arabic, I developed the persona of a "serious woman" and from Marrakesh to Figuig discussed the politics of the Maghreb, maternity rights, housing costs, or the Koran, with almost anyone who wanted my attention.

It became exhausting but any attempt at more desultory chat was treated as an open invitation and

seemed to make any harassment more determined. That isn't to say that it's impossible to have a more relaxed relationship with Moroccan men. I made good friends on two occasions with Arab men and I'm still corresponding with one of them. But I think this was made easier by my defining the terms of our friendship fairly early on in the conversation. As a general rule whenever I arranged to meet up with someone I didn't know very well, I chose well lit public places. I was also careful about my clothes – I found it really did help to look as inconspicuous as possible and almost always wore loose-fitting blouses, longish skirts and occasionally also a headscarf.

"'Is it true that women are opened up by machine?' is a question that worries me still"

After exploring Marrakesh for five days I took a bus out over the Atlas mountain range to Zagora. The journey took twelve hours and the bus was hot and cramped but, wedged between a group of Moroccan mothers, jostling their babies on my lap and sharing whatever food and drink was going round, I felt reassured, more a participant than an outsider.

This was also one of the few occasions that I'd had any sort of meaningful contact with Moroccan women. For the most part women tend to have a low profile in public, moving in very separate spheres to the tourists. There are some women's cafés but they're well hidden and not for foreigners. For me, the most likely meeting place was the *hammam*, or steambath, which I habitually sought out in each stopping place.

Apart from the undoubted pleasures of plentiful hot water, *hammams* became a place of refuge for me. It was a relief to be surrounded by women and to be an object of curiosity without any element of threat. Any ideas about Western status I might have had were lost in the face of explaining in French, Arabic and sign language to an old Moroccan woman with 24 grandchildren the sexual practices and methods of contraception used in the West. "Is it true that women are opened up by machine?" is a question that worries me still.

I arrived in Zagora on the last night of the festival of the King's birthday. It was pure chance. The town was packed with Moroccans who had travelled in from nearby oases, but I met only one other tourist – a German man. We were both of us swept along, as insignificant as any other single people in the crowd, dancing and singing in time to the echoing North African sounds. At the main event of the night, the crowd was divided by a long rope with women on one side and men on the other, with only the German and I standing side by side. I felt overwhelmed with a feeling of excitement and well being, simply because I was there.

From Zagora I headed for Figuig and the desert, stopping overnight en route at Tinerhir. It's possible that I chose a bad hotel for that stop but it was about the worst night that I spent in the entire trip. The men in and around the hotel jeered, even spat at me when I politely refused to accompany them, and throughout the night I had men banging on the door and shutters of my room. For twelve hours I stood guard, tense, afraid, and stifled by the locked in heat of that dismal hotel room. I escaped on the first bus out.

Further south I met up with a Danish man in a Landrover and travelled on with him to spend four days in the desert. It was a simple, businesslike arrangement: he wanted someone to look after the van while he slept and I wanted someone to look out for me while I slept. I can find no terms that will sufficiently describe the effect that the desert had on me. It was awesome and inspiring and it silenced both of us. On the rare occasions that we spoke we did so in whispers.

I also found that the more recent preoccupations that I had about my life, work and relationships had entirely slipped from my mind, yet strangely I could recall with absolute clarity images from over ten years ago. I remain convinced that the desert, in its simplicity, its expansiveness and its power changed me in some way.

At Figuig I parted company with the Dane and made my way in various stages to Fes. I tended to find myself becoming dissatisfied after travelling for a while with a male companion. Not because I didn't enjoy the company, which was more often than not a luxury for me, but I used to feel cheated that I was no longer at the forefront and that any contact with Moroccans would have to be made through him. This is often the case in Islamic countries where any approaches or offers of hospitality are proffered man-to-man, with the woman treated more or less as an appendage. I was prepared to go on alone however uncomfortable it might become as long as I was being treated as a person in my own right.

"I found that Moroccans have such a high regard for sport that the very men who had hustled me in the morning looked on with respectful interest . . . as I hurtled by in the cool of the evening"

In Fes I discovered yet another, perhaps even more effective, strategy for changing my status with Moroccan men I am a runner and compete regularly in marathons and I'm used to keeping up with my training in almost any conditions. Up until Fes I'd held back, uncertain of how I'd be greeted if I dashed out of the hotel in only a tracksuit bottom and T-shirt. My usual outfit, a long skirt and blouse, was hardly suitable for the exercise I had in mind.

After seriously considering confining myself to laps around the hotel bedroom, I recovered my sanity and sense of adventure, changed my clothes and set off. The harassment and the hustling all melted away. I found that Moroccans have such a high regard for sport that the very men who had hustled me in the morning looked on with a respectful interest, offering encouragement and advice as I hurtled by in the cool of the evening. Furthermore I became known as "the runner" and was left more or less in peace for the rest of my stay. After this I made it a rule to train in all the villages and towns I stayed in on the way back to Tangier. Now when I run I conjure up the image of pacing out of Chaouen towards the shrine on the hillside, keeping time with the chants of the muezzin at dawn.

Returning to Tangier I felt as far removed as it is possible to feel from the apprehensive new arrival of the month before. I felt less intimidated by and more stoical about my status as an outsider and I had long since come to accept the fact that I was a source of income to many people whose options for earning a living are sorely limited.

Walking out of the bus station I was surrounded by a group of hustlers. I listened in silence and then said, in the fairly decent Arabic that I had picked up, that I had been in the Sahara and had not got lost so I didn't think I needed a guide in Tangier; furthermore, that I had talked to some Tuareg in Zagora who told me that it is a lie that Moroccans buy their women with camels; please would they excuse me, I had arrangements. I spent the next few days wandering freely around the town, totally immersed in plotting how soon I could return.

Three Kinds of Women

. . . .

Pat Chell lived for two years in Fes, teaching English at the university.

"In Morocco, there are only three kinds of women," I was often told, "virgins, wives and whores." It is as useful a proverb as any to keep in mind when you visit, and a start to understanding the core of the country's culture – Islam and the family.

A woman in Morocco must be a virgin when she marries, and usually she is expected to prove this on consummation of the marriage by showing evidence of hymenal blood. I have known "Westernised", bourgeois women, no longer virgins but about to marry, who have gone to a doctor in Casablanca to have the hymen restitched. This has not necessarily been done to deceive their prospective husbands, with whom they may have been sleeping in any case, but to "observe form" and keep the two families happy.

"All unmarried Moroccan men whom I spoke to about sex had had their only experiences with prostitutes (apart from those who had been 'lucky' enough to meet tourists who would oblige)"

I have also known of liberal families who have given their consent for a couple to sleep together, after the marriage contract has been made but before the wedding ceremony, yet have "satisfied themselves" that the woman was a virgin upon the first occasion.

The only legitimate reason for a woman not being a virgin is if she is a wife. If she is known to be neither, then she will be considered a prostitute. Indeed, once a girl's virginity is lost and her marriage prospects become virtually nil, without family support, she may well have to resort to prostitution as a means of making enough money to live. Prostitution is very common in Morocco. All unmarried Moroccan men whom I spoke to about sex had had their only experiences with prostitutes (apart from those who had been "lucky" enough to meet tourists who would oblige).

On the first occasion this was almost always as an adolescent with a prostitute known for her experience in dealing with "virgins", though Moroccans would laugh at that expression, as the concept of male virginity does not exist. Indeed, many regard childhood circumcision as equivalent to the taking away of virginity. A bridegroom is tacitly expected to be sexually experienced and one who is not is seen as something of a joke.

Homosexuality, though it does exist as a sexual preference, is more likely to be thought of as a substitute for the "real" thing; tourists sometimes misinterpret Moroccan men's show of physical affection for each other as sexual, but this is simply a cultural norm. As for women, I'm not so sure that the concept of sexual satisfaction (let alone sexual preference) even exists. Amongst my students at the university, presumably an intellectual elite, the idea of choosing lesbianism, either for physical or political reasons, was inconceivable. If anything, it was regarded as another example of Western decadence.

Some of my students did have relationships with men but this was a very risky business indeed. If the relationship was "known about" and then ended, the woman could be branded as a whore and her life made a misery. I have met female students who have

been beaten by fathers or brothers simply for being seen talking to a man. Another, who had been raped, did nothing about the attack even though the assailant was known to her, because she was sure that if her family found out she would be taken from the university. Many families are reluctant to allow their daughters to go to university, not because they don't want them educated – they often do as job prospects for women continue to improve – but because they don't want them to be at risk by being in a situation where they can have contact with men.

"Many students ... equated feminism with danger because they saw it as anti-Islamic"

A number of students, male and female, were obviously dissatisfied with the status quo. A married student I knew attempted to help his working wife with chores until he was forbidden to do so by his mother, and his wife was severely reprimanded for failing in her wifely duties. They, like most young Moroccans, were not in a financial position to have a home of their own, even if the family constraints against doing so had not been there. Others of my students wanted to marry Europeans, not so much to have a more equal relationship, nor the financial benefits, but because there was more likelihood of their being able to free themselves from family restraints.

I was only ever aware of one student who did not want to marry. This was Saloua; she was very intelligent and studious, determined to further her studies, which would have meant leaving Morocco, and then returning as a university teacher. She saw this as the best way in which she could help the women of her country.

Although Saloua had a very supportive family, she knew that she had to have a strategy to allow her to carry out her plans. She dressed in Western clothes but very demurely – rather middle-aged "Marks and Spencers". She was rarely seen alone, thus denying any man an opportunity to talk to her. When with women, she avoided the usual "gossip" and "scheming". In a mixed teaching group she spoke only when invited to do so. If she did become involved in a classroom discussion with males, she would be pleasant but distant, humourless and polite. In other words, she always kept a low profile. She was aware of walking a very tenuous tightrope to freedom. She was the most courageous Moroccan woman that I met and I wish her well.

Many students, however, equated feminism with danger because they saw it as anti-Islamic. Some of the most politically active women that I came across were involved in Islamic fundamentalism and wanted nothing to do with Western decadence and therefore nothing to do with me.

Moroccans form their ideas of Western women from two main sources, the media and tourists. The cinema is very popular and there is an abundance of trashy European soft-porn films. I have heard great cheers in the cinema when the "macho" hero has torn off a woman's clothes or physically abused her prior to her becoming a willing sexual partner.

"No father would put his daughter at risk by letting her travel unless she was already 'worthless'"

One of the biggest culture shocks I had in this respect occurred in a very poor home with no running water, toilet or electricity. There was, however, a television and a wire would be run over the roof to a neighbour's when we wanted an evening's viewing. Every Wednesday, neighbours would gather to watch *Dallas*. It was the first time they had spent time socially with a European and so naturally they were curious. My host had to go to great lengths to explain that I was not a "Pamela" or a "Sue Ellen" and that

neither were the majority of Western women. I don't think they were very convinced.

If a woman is alone or only with women, what kind of woman can she be? No father would put his daughter at risk by letting her travel unless she was already "worthless". Her nearest equivalent in Moroccan society is the prostitute. She sits in cafés, drinks alcohol, smokes cigarettes or hashish and will even comb her hair in public. She often dresses "indecently" – not even a prostitute would do this. Why should a woman want to "flaunt" her body? She will also often be prepared to have sex if you can charm her into it. These are the kinds of attitudes I heard so frequently.

And, as a traveller, these are the attitudes which you can expect to meet. The forms the inevitable sexual harassment take vary from the relatively innocuous to the absolutely obscene. The most persistent and annoying is a clicking noise made with the tongue every time you walk past a café, for example. Not terribly serious, you might think, but the cumulative effect is very degrading.

Then there are more direct, verbal approaches. I would strongly advise against confronting anyone who pesters you, as your remonstrations only provide unexpected entertainment. I've never yet seen a woman come out of one of these confrontations without feeling foolish and humiliated. Your anger will simply not be understood. You are unlikely to receive much sympathy from Moroccan women, either. They will either disapprove of you and think that you must be prepared to accept the consequences of being out in public (ie in the man's world) or they will fail to understand your annoyance as there are many young Moroccan women who seek this kind of attention. It is proof of their attractiveness and may be the only kind of contact they have ever known with men.

I don't think as a tourist you can ever avoid sexual harassment completely, but there are certain compromises that reduce its extent. You can dress "appropriately", in skirts, rather than trousers, and in sleeved, loose-fitting tops. You should avoid making eye contact too, and not start up a "casual" conversation with a man – there is no such thing in Morocco. Above all, be as polite and even tempered as possible. Moroccans have a highly ritualised, elaborate etiquette, which you will not be able to learn in a short time, but they do respect politeness. Loss of temper equals loss of face, no matter what the provocation.

What I have written are generalisations. There are Moroccan men and women who do not share these attitudes. There are many students who genuinely want to practise their English and can only do so with travellers. Unfortunately, on a short stay, the Moroccans you're most likely to encounter are street hustlers only after your money or your body. Sometimes, particularly if you are feeling threatened or insecure, it is difficult to tell whether people are being genuine or "hustling". But if you are cautiously optimistic and rely on your instincts, then you might find, as I did, that Moroccans are incredibly hospitable people, many of whom love to have Westerners to stay.

I hope that I haven't put you off travelling to Morocco. Too often, sadly, I met travellers who judged the society with Western values: they saw the men as villains and the women as martyrs.

With a Toddler in Tow

. . . .

Jo Crowson, a single mother, travelled to Morocco from Britain with her two-year-old daughter, Merry. Whilst most of the Moroccans she met seemed very positive in their attitudes towards her and her child, she found that fellow male travellers could be surprisingly critical and unsupportive.

I had already spent some time in Morocco with a group of friends, both male and female, and had a pretty bad time – entirely our own fault. For a start we went in July (temperatures at 31°C plus) and we went straight to the Rif mountains where one of our party immediately got caught with hashish.

We spent the next two weeks trying to get him out of prison and virtually all our combined funds on his fine. So I had a good idea what not to do in Morocco.

Six years later, I found myself a single parent in great need of a winter adventure and my thoughts turned again to Morocco. It was not too far (in case Merry, my two-year-old daughter got ill), it was accessible overland (I wouldn't have to pay for two flights), it was cheap and it was definitely different. I decided to go for it, but with so many doubts, fears and reservations, that I thought I was probably completely mad.

In the following weeks I read as many guidebooks and travel books on Morocco as I could find in the library. This did little to ease my fears. All included warnings about sexual harassment, and the incredibly persistent street hustlers, and they all, without exception, advised women against travelling alone. I decided that if, after a couple of days, I found that travelling with a child was just as difficult as travelling alone, I would go back to Spain and spend my time there. Having established this "escape clause", I felt a lot better.

I managed to get a lift with friends as far as Northern Portugal, which I thought would make the journey cheaper. I'm not sure that it did in the end, but it is good to see the land you're travelling over and watch the gradual changes as they happen. (As a result of this journey I have many tips to pass on to anyone planning to spend three days in the back of a car with a two-year-old.) I was also lucky enough to get a letter sent poste restante from some women friends who were already travelling in Morocco with their children, suggesting a couple of good places to visit and saying what a wonderful time they were having.

"Feeling very brave and excited we boarded the ferry, had our passport checked, and kept a look out for dolphins"

After we left our friends in Portugal we had a great journey into Spain and down to Algeciras, where there are ferries to Morocco. It gave us a chance to get adjusted to our new lifestyle and to gain confidence. It also gave me a bit longer to feel apprehensive about how we'd cope. Finally the great moment arrived and feeling very brave and excited we boarded the ferry, had our passport checked, and kept a look out for dolphins.

I'd decided we'd go to Tangier as it's better connected than Ceuta and I could get a train straight out to Rabat. The south is supposed to be slightly easier for travellers than the north and Rabat sounded like the least problematic (as well as the least exciting) place to acclimatise in.

Despite all my fears, arriving at Tangier was astonishingly easy. We were waved through customs, while most of the other people were emptying out their luggage, shown where to buy our train ticket and pointed in the right direction for the station. There, two unofficial porters grabbed my bags and charged five dirhams for help I didn't need. Ah well. I'd managed the first obstacle although I was still pretty nervous – what if my carriage fills up with men?

At the next stop three young men got on, followed by two women. I began to relax a bit. One of the three started talking to me in English, eating away at my reserves of confidence (not difficult) by saying that we wouldn't be getting to Rabat until very late, it was a terrible city, all the hotels would be full and so on. He was attempting to persuade me to get off at his home town which he described as a beautiful seaside resort full of tourists. This put me off. I looked it up in my guidebook and was put off even more. It was when he insisted that the Youth Hostel where I planned to stay at Rabat would close at 6pm that I suddenly realised I was having my first encounter with a dedicated "hustler". He left the compartment and the women seated opposite me warned me that he was a "bad Moroccan" – a phrase I heard frequently during my stay.

From then on I communicated with my fellow passengers in abysmal French, with the help of an exchange of bananas for biscuits. They were delighted by Merry but seemed very anxious when she fell asleep that she should keep her legs fully covered. I'm not sure if it was fear of her catching cold or the glimpse of bare flesh that particularly disturbed them, but I covered her anyway. Moroccan girls wear loose trousers under their skirts from babyhood onwards and although I had thought about keeping myself covered up, I hadn't considered Merry. From then on I made sure that she wore trousers and/or longish skirts everywhere except at the beach and no one else ever commented.

"Their attitudes ranged from praise for my bravery to criticism of my mothering instincts. More than one warned me of the danger of Merry being stolen and sold into slavery"

When we arrived in Rabat I stomped off, trying to look more confident than I felt. I was a bit worried that the Youth Hostel might not let us stay as, according to the handbook, children under five were not admitted. Either the manager didn't know that or didn't care and we got a place for only a few dirhams a night. The bunk beds were a great hit with Merry and I wanted an uncomplicated place to stay with contact with other travellers for first-hand, up-to-the-minute information. The other travellers at the hostel seemed shocked that I was travelling alone with a small child. Their attitudes ranged from praise for my bravery to criticism of my mothering instincts. More than one warned me of the danger of Merry being stolen and sold into slavery. I treated this prejudice with the contempt it deserved, but I did wonder how they could bring themselves to travel in a place where they believed such things were common. At this point I was still wondering myself what I was doing there, but then one man went too far in his criticisms and I retreated angry but fortified by it. (There were no women staying at the hostel that night.)

Rabat was indeed a mellow city and we wandered around the Medina without hindrance or offers of a guide. At the Kasbah, however, a man approached us and offered to show us around although he said he wasn't a guide. "Good," I said, "as I'm not going to pay you." It was all very amiable and the Kasbah was lovely, like a village within the city, and everyone seemed to know my "not a guide". I relaxed into

chatting while he showed me where he lived and we drank mint tea. He invited me to an evening meal of *couscous* and after I accepted it he went off.

Left to my own devices I began to regret having accepted as I didn't feel completely happy about going to his house alone after dark. I decided to leave a note for him saying I couldn't make it and hoped he would get it. I felt pretty bad about not trusting him, but, with Merry there I had become more than usually cautious and was simply not prepared to launch into any situation where I felt our safety was in doubt. (I still felt bad though.)

All the time I was in Morocco I masqueraded as a married woman. I felt there was nothing to gain in explaining my real circumstances as they would inevitably be misunderstood. Over the course of my stay my "husband" got ever closer. Whilst in Rabat he had been working in England, but on the advice of my Moroccan friend I moved him to Tangier. Later on I occasionally said I was meeting him in a café. (I met a woman who pretended she was pregnant whenever she felt harassed and said it worked.)

Back at the hostel I was happy to meet a woman who had been travelling around Europe on her own. Before coming to Morocco, however, she had gone to a Youth Hostel in Malaga to find someone to travel with. She found a man who was also travelling alone and seemed to have enjoyed her stay. Also at the hostel was a young Moroccan visiting Rabat in order to get a US visa. He was a devout Muslim and we had a friendly and completely uncomplicated conversation about America, the country he was aiming to visit, before he was suddenly and quite aggressively thrown out by the manager. This was despite his being there at the invitation of one of the guests. It seemed to me he was thrown out because he was a Moroccan.

As I spent more time in Morocco I became more relaxed, told "lies" more readily, became better tempered and began to learn who to avoid. Sexual harassment is a problem for women in Morocco, but I seemed to experience less than a lot of other women I met who were travelling with men. I think perhaps having a child labels you as some man's property. "Hustlers", however, still made approaches – and proved incredibly persistent, innovative and subtle. It is important to remember that it is need that spurs them on to such great lengths to part you and your money. Tourists in Morocco are viewed as rich, and in many ways it's true. We're certainly privileged.

Both Merry and I loved Marrakesh immediately. We found a room in a cheap but fairly clean hotel just off the Place Djemaa el Fna, from where we could wander out amongst the stalls, entertainers, travellers and coachtrippers or climb up to the terraces to look out at the views and sip mint tea. I found it fascinating and enjoyed the anonymity of the crowds, while Merry adored the snake charmers and other entertainers. She also loved stopping to buy fruit here, nuts there, and freshly made egg sandwiches from the woman who ran the hard-boiled egg stall. She soon, however, began to miss the freedom to run about and play, and wanted to go to the coast – whilst I would have preferred to stay longer.

"The best part of travelling with my daughter was the contact she brought with Moroccan women"

We went on to a small village just north of Agadir called Taghazoute and rented a room from a Berber family; a mother, grandmother, two sons and two daughters. Although communication was hard – I couldn't speak Berber and they had very few words of French – we smiled a lot at each other. They seemed especially pleased with Merry and would take her out to show her their animals or bring small children in

to see her, and every now and then Yasmina, the mother, would offer us food. It was an ideal place to stay and the beach itself was wide and fairly empty.

I was worried about how safe it would be to swim alone, but resolved this by asking a couple if we could join them for a bit. Later on I became more confident about swimming alone and was happy just to site myself near family groups. I tried to make sure that I was never completely alone with no one in sight, as a woman friend had earlier been assaulted on an isolated bit of beach not far up the coast.

The best part of travelling with my daughter was the contact she brought with Moroccan women. In Essaouira I met a woman called Barka who offered me a room in her house. Again communication was a little difficult but we seemed to manage well on a mixture of French, Arabic, and empathy. She lived alone with her eight-year-old son – her husband was working somewhere in the north (fishing, I think) and didn't come home very often. Eating meals and watching TV together, we soon became very close. Her son Mohammed loved Merry and wanted us to stay much longer than we could. The only problem I had with Barka was that she would refuse to let me help with any chores and wanted to do all of my own work as well. I ended up having to hide in the toilet to wash my clothes.

When it was time for us to leave, she came with us to say goodbye at the bus station. On the way we dropped her son off at school where she introduced us to some of her friends. It was a scorching day and all the women were covered from head to foot in thick white blankets with just their hennaed hands and feet showing and their eyes peeping through above the black veils they wore. I was hot in my light clothing. We were so different in our dress, customs and language and yet somehow we all managed to communicate about our kids and school just as I suppose women all over the world do. Later Barka kissed me goodbye through her veil at the station and made me promise to come back and visit her. I felt I didn't want to leave.

"We were so different in our dress, customs and language and yet somehow we all managed to communicate about our kids and school just as I suppose women all over the world do"

We spent a couple of days exploring Tangier before catching the ferry. For part of this time, we joined up with a couple of English men and I was surprised to find that, with them, I experienced more harassment than I'd ever encountered alone with Merry. I also had my first and only offer to buy hashish.

In the end leaving Morocco wasn't so much of a wrench as Merry caught some sort of stomach bug which made her sick and incredibly tired. Travelling back through Spain to Portugal was awful for us both, although marginally worse for me (she slept through a lot of it). One of the worst aspects of it was the amount of criticism I got from other travellers just when I could have used a little support. I'm not sure why I encountered so much unhelpfulness, especially from male travellers, but fortunately there were exceptions. And Moroccan, Spanish and Portuguese people have a great attitude towards children.

Travelling with a child, I found I couldn't live on as tight a budget as I'd

planned, due mainly to the need for cold, expensive, treats. I also felt pretty isolated at night when Merry was asleep but I still wanted to be out and about. Before I went I didn't expect night-time to be a problem as at home Merry is capable of staying up till all hours. I don't know if it was the fresh air and excitement but her pattern certainly changed and she was asleep by eight every night. I took a pushchair with me so that I could push her around if she slept but this wasn't practical. The roads and paths anywhere other than in the cities were so bad that I would have to carry the pushchair as well as Merry most of the time. Even in the cities there are usually many steps to negotiate. Her pushchair was only useful for carrying our stuff from the bus to the train station. (The lack of personal space will be familiar to all single parents as will the exhaustion you occasionally feel.)

Overall, I think it's a great idea to travel with a child in Morocco, though I wouldn't recommend it to someone wanting a "holiday". It's an adventure above all else and requires a certain amount of work. Other women I know have travelled in Morocco with their children and all agreed that they had a great time. One friend managed to borrow someone else's daughter as well as take her own and so travelled with two ten-year-olds – that has to be the perfect arrangement. And in a way all my earlier fears have left me feeling that I have really accomplished something. When I wasn't feeling a bit scared about what I was taking on I felt incredibly strong and extraordinary – it's not often women get to feel that in their lives.

TRAVEL NOTES

Languages Moroccan Arabic (a considerable variant of "classical" Egyptian/Gulf Arabic) and three distinct Berber languages. French is widely spoken and is taught in schools.

Transport There's a small but useful rail network. Travel otherwise is by bus (plentiful and cheap) or collective taxi (*grand taxi*), which run between towns according to demand. In the Atlas and sub-Sahara you can negotiate lifts on trucks — some of which operate like buses. Hitching is inadvisable, though fellow tourists are sometimes worth approaching at campsites.

Accommodation Very rarely a problem — there are all categories of hotels graded by the state and other (even cheaper) options below them.

Special Problems Arrival can be daunting at both Tangier and Tetouan, where you'll find the country's most persistent, aggressive and experienced hustlers. If it's your first visit it makes sense to move straight on — it only takes a couple of days to get used to things. Many tourists come to Morocco to smoke hashish (*kif*). Although officially illegal, the police tend to turn a blind eye: the main trouble lies with the dealers, who have developed some nasty tricks (like selling you hash then sending friends round to threaten to turn you in to the police unless you pay them off). It's best to avoid the *kif* growing areas of the Rif mountains and the drug centre, Ketama.

Guide *The Rough Guide: Morocco* (Harrap Columbus) is a well-deserved classic.

Contacts

Centre de Documentation et d'action Féminin, 46 Rue Aboudest-Agdal, Rabat. Recently formed and very small feminist group.

8th of March A feminist journal produced at the Mohammed V University, Rabat.

Books

Fatima Mernissi, *Beyond the Veil: The Sexual Ideology of Women* (1975; Al Saqi, 1985). Enlightening study by Morocco's leading sociologist.

Fatima Mernissi, *Doing Daily Battle: Interviews with Moroccan Women* (The Women's Press, 1988). Eleven Moroccan women, from a range of backgrounds, talk candidly about their lives.

Vanessa Maher, *Women and Property in Morocco* (Cambridge UP, 1974). Respected academic study.

Nancy Phelan, *Morocco is a Lion* (Quartet, 1982). Ordinary, lightweight travelogue — but well observed and includes a variety of interviews/experiences with Moroccan women, both rural and urban.

Works by the Moroccan-resident American writer **Paul Bowles** provide an interesting insight into the country. The best of his novels, *The Spider's House* (1955; Abacus, 1988) is set in Fes during the struggle for independence. Bowles's other Moroccan novels, and especially his translations of Moroccan storytellers (notably Mohammed Mrabet), are also worthwhile.

Nepal

• • • • • • • • • • • • • • •

For the first half of this century Nepal was virtually untouched by the outside world, an isolated mountain kingdom and a highly traditional Hindu and Buddhist society. Since the Sixties it has been caught up in a full-scale tourist boom, with travellers pouring into the capital, Kathmandu, and, accompanied by local guides, out along its spectacular Himalayan trekking routes.

As a primarily rural and Hindu society, Nepal is a relatively safe place to travel; Kathmandu has its share of hustlers, eager to gain custom, but they are rarely aggressive in their approach and violent crime, even theft, is uncommon. You'll find that you are treated first and foremost as a foreigner, rather than a woman and, as such, the atmosphere is tolerant. However, it is important to be sensitive to local customs – shorts and skimpy clothes are considered offensive.

A growing number of women trek alone and on the well-trodden, shorter treks this is considered reasonably safe; it would be advisable to have company if you're planning anything longer or more adventurous. What is disturbing, however, is the pattern that tourism is creating; Kathmandu has been transformed into a commercial and cosmopolitan capital, and the trekking industry, for all its supposed "contact with local people", is as prepared as any other to exploit workers with low wages and poor conditions. If you want to feel good about trekking, you'll need to choose your tour with care.

At present the government of King Birenda is locked in a trade dispute with India. Recently this manifested itself in an Indian fuel blockade which has affected transport within the country, but more seriously has caused an escalation in the already critical problem of deforestation as wood is used for fuel in the capital. It is hard to predict what will happen if the blockade continues – such is the importance of tourism that trekking agencies are given priority rations of kerosene and petrol.

Under the partyless political system, autonomous **women's groups** are considered divisive. (It is illegal for any political group to function without prior government consent.) The few officially sanctioned bodies – notably the *Nepal Women's Organisation* – are orientated mainly towards providing educational and social welfare services. They have initiated campaigns on issues of property rights, polygamy, and child and forced marriages, but these have been criticised by Nepalese feminists as being largely tokenistic. The bulk of Nepalese women live in rural villages where their lives are dominated by the demands of subsistence farming and the traditional roles of domestic work and child-rearing. With the recent trend of modernisation, more urban middle-class women are, however, getting access to higher education and the professions. Women are also gaining employment (albeit low-paid) within the tourist industry.

Home in a Hindu Valley

· · · · · · · · · · ·

Deborah Rutter, a post-graduate student in Social Anthropology, went to Nepal to complete research for her PhD. She took along her male partner and thirteen-year-old daughter. None of them had lived abroad before.

The first thing that struck me on arrival in Kathmandu was the filth in the streets; the city had been transformed into a sea of mud by out-of-season rains. Like all first time visitors we headed straight for Thamel, the tourist district, where we picked our way between the small hotels and souvenir shops selling Buddhist wall hangings, Tibetan carpets, bags and outlandish hippy clothing – anything from tie dyes and brocades to cotton ten-tone drawstring trousers and jackets. Young Nepali men took it in turns to try and grab some custom; "Change money? Buy carpet, madam? Clean hotel? Good trekking guide?" As elsewhere in Asia there's a commission on everything. It was a relief to find that there were few beggars although children, with no other English vocabulary, would immediately strike up a chorus of "one rupee, one rupee!"

Staying in Thamel you begin to feel that you are participating simultaneously in several different timezones. Despite all the recent incursions of tourism, the traditional Newar architecture and way of life still holds sway. Nepalese women wearing traditional dress and ornamentation come outside to wash their clothes and hair at the standpipes, bargain for fruit and vegetables at the stalls around the larger shrines, and make offerings to the street deities. At harvest time city and countryside merge into one another as the streets are used to thresh and dry the grain and you'll find that most urban residents have a home called "my village".

Nepalese custom dictates that women are treated with respect and even a casual acquaintance is referred to as elder or younger sister. This doesn't necessarily apply to Western women. There's a flourishing video trade via Bangkok and many young male aficionados apparently cannot distinguish between female tourists and the soft-porn starlets of the screen. My thirteen-year-old daughter had to put up with a public commentary on her anatomy every time she walked down the street. (On only one occasion was she actually touched, being pushed into a sewage-filled gutter.) She regarded these elaborately coiffeured youths with great scorn, dismissing them as ignorant and racist, but it was hard for me, hearing loud and offensive remarks directed at my daughter, not to react in fury.

These incidents are not common, but they are unpleasant and can feel threatening, especially as the antagonisers are always in groups. I realised that such aspects were just another manifestation of being "different", and that the situation had not been helped by some tourists' insistence on wearing transparent clothing or shorts cut above the buttock. Nepali people have little experience of external mores and I suspect that they assume that if you break one taboo you are likely to have no moral sense at all.

As usual it is women's dress and behaviour that attracts the most scrutiny and criticism. If you are interested in meeting Nepalese people you may need to make concessions, such as covering shoulders and legs: many women wear loose skirts for trekking, instead of shorts, with elasticated waists so that, like the indigenous petticoat, they can be drawn up over the breasts to allow privacy while washing.

Of course, most people come to Nepal to trek. How you choose to go about it is very much up to you, but it's worth remembering that the company with the glossy brochure is likely to supply the same standard of food and accommodation on trek as you would get if you just picked up your pack and walked. We did just that, choosing a route which took only seven days of walking into the Annapurna sanctuary region, renowned for its 360-degree panoramas.

"I found it impossible to overcome my reluctance to employ someone to do my 'dirty work', whether washing or carrying"

But we did not get off the ground without the customary debate as to whether we would need to hire a guide. Everywhere we turned we encountered horror stories of fraudulent foreigners with imperialist ideas but dollar deficiency, expecting their guides to struggle under fifty-kilo loads on a bowl of rice a day; or *raksi* (rice wine) crazed guides abandoning their clients in snowstorms, having first relieved them of their Swiss-down trekking clobber.

We ventured only as far as Ghorepani, the most trodden part of the Jomosom–Muktinath trail, and really didn't need a guide. But, in common with many other trekkers, we had a very expansive idea of "necessities" and did wish that we had hired a porter. I found it impossible, however, to overcome my reluctance to employ someone to do my "dirty work", whether washing or carrying: I hated to be called, or treated as, a *memsahib*.

Treks into the Annapurna region normally start with a bus ride to Pokhara in west-central Nepal. Buses and roads, where they exist at all, are appalling. Our first trip involved nine hours of bouncing around with miscellaneous bits of metal stabbing our calves, bottoms stuck with sweat to the plastic seats; we were stunned by heat; and we were starving – having contracted salmonella in the capital's poshest restaurant, we'd become incredibly wary of eating cooked food.

But hunger got the better of us and we joined the other Nepali travellers for a lunch of boiled rice, daal, and vegetable curry at a roadside stop. It was a good nourishing meal and a welcome relief from the pizzas and buffalo, cut up as steak, that the enterprising caterers of Kathmandu are now serving up for foreigners.

"We began to feel ludicrously under-equipped, in our trainers, with a set of thermal underwear and a sweater; all those paperback novels and first-aid kits were just so much dead weight"

Back on the road to Pokhara, cursing the corrupt engineers who applied such a thin layer of tarmac to this important supply route that most of it had worn or washed away, we gazed out at the scenery. Very little of Nepal's mountainous surface is cultivable but every slope where a seed might possibly survive is terraced – the most amazing achievement in human ingenuity and effort. Depending on the season, there are teams of water buffalo churning the flooded rice terraces in preparation for the new seedlings, or teams of scarlet-clad women planting or weeding.

Pokhara was breathtakingly beautiful, the white-iced Himalayas rising like a mirage above the lush vegetation and green waters of its lake. After a day's browsing among the Tibetan-owned stalls (there are several refugee camps in the area), we set off along what's known as the "apple pie trek". The name is a bit of an exaggeration, though the lodges do attempt to satisfy the Western palate with peculiar variants of well-known vegetarian staples – porridge, chips, vegetable omelettes, vegetable soup – and the ubiquitous Coca-Cola. These became progressively more expensive as we climbed the trail, reminding us of the porters who lug the crates up on their backs.

The mountains were as stunning as expected, although the weather proved unreliable and cloud obscured the views for large parts of the day. Still, the English are used to such occurrences and the sheer effort of keeping going left me with little mental energy to contemplate disappointment. I had thought I was quite fit, but I'd never experienced the hills of Nepal.

When you are climbing up you long for a downhill stretch, only to find that every muscle screams and every joint jars going down, so that struggling up seems by far the easier option. I found it a severe challenge, especially for the first three days and my daughter claimed to be too exhausted to even frame the anticipated complaints. For most of the trek we were battling with the heat but as soon as we came to the Ghorepani pass it became foggy, cold and damp. We began to feel ludicrously under-equipped, in our trainers, with a set of thermal underwear and a sweater; all those paperback novels and first-aid kits were just so much dead weight.

It's strange how preoccupied you become by the physical aspects of life on trek but for many, including us, this was the first experience of day-to-day living without any mod cons. You learn that you don't smell any worse after three days without a shower than you did after one. You learn what is really important for human survival, like finding water for drinking, and you get a very real sense of what environmental depletion is all about. I was incensed by those trekkers who accepted the offer of hot water for bathing, knowing that yet more trees would need to be cut down to feed the wood-burning stoves. Of course I didn't cast off the habits of a lifetime, but I did begin to question them.

Equally, the Nepalese need to learn how to deal with the debris of industrial society. They do not seem to realise that the non-biodegradable materials that have flooded into the country in the wake of tourism cannot simply be dropped on the ground. Who of us does not entertain the surreptitious wish that the Nepalese would remain charmingly different and ethnic, unpolluted by the trappings of industrial capitalism. Well, tough luck, it's their choice, not ours, and the convenience of two-minute noodles and plastic bags is much appreciated.

In autumn and spring, the Himalayas are visible from most parts of the Kathmandu valley and there is nothing like the sight of a snow-covered peak to raise the spirits. I don't know why this proof of humanity's insignificance should be so comforting to the soul. But it was for me, and, being stuck in the capital trying to get a research visa, I was often in need of comfort. For six months I traipsed from Ministry to Ministry, grovelling to officials and getting increasingly anxious and frustrated, until eventually I got my permit and was able to set off for the valley slopes. My plan was to live in a small Hindu village for a year in order to see through a full agricultural cycle.

Initially, life in the village was difficult. I knew very little about the practicalities of subsistence living and depended, like a child, on the village women for instruction and help. They never seemed to resent this, claiming that we were a welcome source of amusement and distraction, and showed us great hospitality – offering a constant flow of gifts of food, milk and curd, as we had no cows.

Although we rented our own house, we suffered greatly from lack of privacy; it isn't the Nepalese way to expect great intimacy and intellectual companionship between husband and wife. As a young female, our daughter often felt excluded from conversations with our nightly visitors, but on the whole, having approached the entire trip with dread, she fitted in amazingly well. She would pop in and out of people's houses and kitchens with a freedom only accorded to non-adults, asking about the animals, comparing prize possessions with the girls next

door, and often returning with an infant on her hip.

While I began to feel more weary and, at times, even paranoid about the endless necessity of being "on show", she became more sociable, took part in the rice-planting and did her washing at the tap. Many tears were shed when she returned to England and school; at the awkward age of thirteen, such a radical shift is no joke. In the village she was everyone's sister or daughter and happily free of many of the contradictions about sexuality and behaviour that afflict our own society.

"Initially, life in the village was difficult. I knew very little about the practicalities of subsistence living and depended, like a child, on the village women for instruction and help"

Nepal is a very poor country. Our village was privileged, since they had nearly enough grain to feed themselves, but if there was no starvation there was plenty of malnutrition. Rice is given precedence over vegetables and as a result many people suffer from stomach and eye infections and sores, exacerbated by local remedies. I tried, as far as possible, not to interfere in medical treatment, except with antiseptic cream, or in translating English dosage instructions on medicines haphazardly dispensed at the child health clinic. The only time that I did intervene, when I gave a neighbour some aspirin to soothe her toothache, I felt responsible for a rash that suddenly (and, as it turned out, coincidentally) appeared all over her body. People had very little understanding of our preoccupation with diagnosis; it is assumed that because we all look so healthy we must have the universal panacea.

This is all part of the general assumptions made about foreigners, the most obvious one being that we are rich. The fact of having paid the airfare is proof enough although, knowing that we did not have a house, nor rice fields, our friends were quite puzzled as to where our wealth, not to mention our priorities, lay. I always found myself trying to play down my wealth, by wearing only cheap, cotton dresses and living as simply as possible. But the pressure to keep up an endless round of small gifts, and the even-handedness needed to do this without creating jealousies, would sometimes become a strain.

"At 5am, I would try to ignore the cockerel ... desperate to delay the barrage of questions from early morning visitors, including every child in the village"

Throughout my stay I had many periods of travelling on my own, especially when I was searching for a site for my fieldwork. Invariably it would be women who would invite me home with them; the Nepalese sense of hospitality and general curiosity towards strangers meant that I always had a roof over my head. We would sleep fully clothed on an uncovered rice mat. At 5am, I would try to ignore the cockerel (once, perched at the end of the bed), desperate to delay the barrage of questions from early morning visitors, including every child in the village. I hated the constant observation, the sense of

being alien, and stared at by all, though usually without hostility. But I valued the bridges of shared experiences which I found with Nepali women.

There is only one feasible path for Nepali rural women – marriage and work within the fields and at home. Work is very rigidly divided and, though women have much more to do than men, they rarely complain. My impression was that they placed a high value on cheerfulness and resilience, but this did not make them naturally submissive; a woman might drop to the ground to kiss her husband's feet for religious reasons but she could also be quick to contradict him. For the most part, socialising is segregated and women depend on each other for support and friendship. It helped that I too was married and had a child (though not the son that is so important in Nepali culture) and could take some part in discussions of motherhood and married life.

Leaving was hard. I realised how much I appreciated the bond I had formed with these women, when it became necessary to break it. It is strange now to remember with what trust they took me into their kitchens to feed me. They would wave aside any thanks and say, "if we came as strangers to your country, you would feed us, wouldn't you?"

TRAVEL NOTES

Languages Nepali and regional dialects: some English is spoken on tourist circuits.

Transport Within the Kathmandu Valley there are buses; further north trekking is the only option, other than a small network of flights (expensive and unreliable, though if time is tight you can fly out into the Himalayas and trek back). The recent introduced rationing of petrol has meant that buses are more irregular and crowded – be prepared for long waits.

Accommodation Plenty of cheap places to stay in Kathmandu and surrounding areas; also

small hotels on regular trekking routes. On more remote routes there are virtually no tourist facilities and you'll have to carry your own tent or join a trekking party with porters. The Nepalese are incredibly hospitable and often invite foreigners to sleep in their homes – you should reciprocate with a small gift or some money.

Special Problems Although many tourists wear short summer gear, this is seen as disrespectful. In the more orthodox Hindu areas you may be asked – as a foreigner (and therefore untouchable) – to sleep outside the main living room. Everywhere you should try to avoid touching cooking utensils or food that s being prepared, and if you're given water to drink from a communal vessel avoid any contact with your lips.

For trekking, proper clothing and equipment are absolutely necessary. Altitude sickness is a common problem and should be taken very seriously. There is no clean drinking water, so infections are incredibly common; the numerous stool test laboratories in Kathmandu are an entrepreneurial innovation and have a poor record for reliability.

Guides A *Rough Guide* to Nepal (Harrap Columbus) is forthcoming and should give the best overall view of the country, with information about the many different ethnic minorities and current environmental issues. Best of the specific trekking guides is *Trekking in Nepal* (Mountaineers, US).

Contacts

Centre for Women and Development, PO Box 3637, Kathmandu. A non-governmental organisation established by a group of professional women which collects and disseminates information on women's issues and development projects.

Books

Lynn Bennett, *Dangerous Wives and Sacred Sisters* (Columbia University Press, New York, 1983). Good insight into the life and position of Hindu women in Nepal.

Karuna Kar Varilya, *Nepalese Short Stories* (Gallery Press, US, 1976). A collection of stories by some of Nepal's best writers, on a wide variety of themes.

Lynn Bennett, ed.; *The Status of Women in Nepal* (CEDA, Tribhuvan University, Nepal). Lengthier, more academic study.

The Netherlands

T he Netherlands can be regarded as virtually two separate countries: Amsterdam and the rest. As the centre of West European counter-culture and a gateway to Europe and North America, Amsterdam attracts thousands of visitors every year. The city has a reputation for tolerance – an easy acceptance of race and sexuality – and, compared with other Western capitals, it does feel noticeably relaxed and safe. You can sit on your own in most cafés and bars without feeling conspicuous and there are plenty of women-only resources (bookshops and bars) to tap into. The obvious exception is the red light district where, even in daylight, you can get hassled to buy drugs and may well have to face a stream of comments, catcalls and propositions.

Amsterdam's image as a permissive, "alternative" capital has waned only slightly since its heyday in the Sixties. The municipal authorities have been actively trying to divert attention and funds to more mainstream attractions, such as conference centres, hotel complexes and prestigious arts projects, but the city's progressive politics and policies remain well defended. Squatters continue to oppose urban development plans, the gay community maintains its high profile with plenty of venues and some of the best nightlife in Europe, and the sale of cannabis is still sanctioned in bars and cafés. One disturbing hangover of the "liberated" Sixties has been the proliferation of pornography, seen on newsstands and billboards throughout the city.

All of this stands in marked contrast to the entrenched conservatism of the provinces, where women are largely expected to follow the traditional path as home-makers and child-rearers, and where life can seem parochial and dull. People remain open and hospitable to visitors but it can be hard to gain acceptance as a foreign resident. However, getting around is very easy and Dutch women routinely travel alone. Your major problem will probably be the high standard of living which makes existing in The Netherlands very expensive.

For its size and population, the Netherlands has an expansive and wide-reaching **women's movement**. Since the Sixties, it has staged some impressive and well-publicised campaigns – notably, in the 1970s, to legalise abortion. There are now many local groups, organised around specific issues like sexual violence, unequal education, healthcare and pornography, and many women are active in the peace movement and various squatting campaigns. The Women's Union, a recognised trade union, was set up to improve the position of housewives and unpaid carers by agitating for improved state childcare and benefits.

Behind the Progressive Myth

. . . .

Suzie Brocker, a New Zealander, has been living in The Hague for the past three years. She works as a freelance writer and boosts her income with nannying and cleaning work for Dutch families.

Arriving in Holland is a bit like entering a warm, cosy room which makes you feel comfortable and at home straight away. There's something intimate about the country which I miss elsewhere; from the gabled houses with their overflowing gardens to the little cafés and old-fashioned black bicycles parked outside. People seem friendly and open-hearted, a far cry from the stereotyped image I had of dour-faced Dutch. But then, after living and travelling here for four years, I've had to question a lot of my preconceptions about Holland.

Before coming to live here, the image I had of the country was of a progressive nation at the forefront of moves for social change and equality. I therefore expected that the position of women would be far more advanced than that of many other Western countries. It came as a shock when, on my first day here, I faced a bank manager who was reluctant to open an account for me in my own name, separate from my husband's. Since then I have experienced numerous other incidents which illustrate the problems that many Dutch women face every day.

Dutch women are up against some fairly entrenched attitudes and, surprisingly, less than half of them work – a percentage well below the European Community average. Although the number has been rising gradually, and more and more women would like to work, many services and regulations in Dutch society remain based on the traditional family model, which hinders any attempt to move away from the home. There's a drastic shortage of both public and private childcare facilities, parental leave arrangements are virtually non-existent, and stores and government services are closed outside of regular office hours. I was amazed to find that the school down the road from my house closed between twelve and one, and that mothers were expected to collect and look after their children during this time.

Upon arriving here I advertised for work as a childminder in order to supplement my income, and the number of calls I got from working mums desperate for help was staggering. Most were married women attempting to juggle a career, child-rearing and domestic responsibilities, with little or no help from their husbands. I was perplexed therefore to read a recent survey which showed that eighty percent of the population favoured men and women sharing responsibility for running the house and raising children. From my experiences here there seems to be a big gap between the ideals expressed and actual practice.

"It's nice to be able to walk into a café alone without feeling as if you've invaded a male sanctuary"

I've often wondered why the position of Dutch women is behind that of their North European contemporaries. I think the long-standing influence of the church has had an impact, but beyond that I believe it has something to do with the importance the Dutch have always placed on family life. They are first and foremost home-loving people. They even have a special word for the cosy, comfortable elements of domestic life they treasure so dearly – "gezellig", a word which really has no equivalent in English. And the responsibility for keeping this home together and functioning has always fallen upon the women.

This notion is carried over into Dutch social life too. The small, intimate cafés of Holland which I love aren't intended to supplant the home but duplicate it. Unlike in Greece or Spain where cafés tend to be filled with men flicking ash on the floor and passing comment about any woman that

walks in, cafés in Holland are open to everyone, young and old, alone or in groups, to eat, drink, and mostly just enjoy each other's company. It's nice to be able to walk into a café alone without feeling as if you've invaded a male sanctuary and without having to deal with unwanted attention.

Living in such a tiny country with a population of over fourteen million, the Dutch appreciate the importance of individual privacy, and it's very rare that you'll be hassled. The only time I've ever felt unsafe was when I inadvertently wandered into the red light district of Amsterdam, and then the cause of my unease was a male tourist. The attitude towards pornography and prostitution does mean that certain areas of major cities in Holland, the worst being in Amsterdam, can be hostile places for women, but in response to this, cafés, restaurants and nightclubs have been set up by women and for women almost everywhere.

While there may be many frustrations for a woman living in The Netherlands, I've found travelling on my own here a great experience. The Dutch are incredibly hospitable to travellers and, as English is very widely spoken, language is hardly ever a barrier. The flat countryside lends itself to active holidays, with miles of specially built cycle tracks and walkways leading to the more picturesque areas of Holland not so accessible by car. It's excellently set up for camping, with over 2000 campsites throughout, including several women-only sites.

I've really enjoyed the few camping-biking holidays I've been on as it's an activity in which all age groups and combinations of people are involved, and therefore a good way of feeling part of the place.

One of the most memorable trips I made was a boating holiday on the canals of Friesland in North Holland. Four of us hired an old-fashioned *tjalk*, a sort of flat-bottomed houseboat and set off for a few weeks. We did, however, meet with a lot of sexist flak, even if it was good-natured. Men worldwide seem to think that water is an exclusively male domain, and Dutchmen are no exception. The charter company nearly balked at hiring the boat out when they discovered I'd be the skipper, and men in the villages we stopped at along the way insisted on mooring us up so that it was done "properly". Apart from that it was still magical – there's something very special about the Dutch countryside from the water.

Basking in Tolerance

. . . .

Louise Simmons drove to Amsterdam in a dilapidated VW van, found a job as a secretary and stayed there for nine months. She is now working her way across South East Asia en route from India to Australia.

I left Britain in a flurry of snow and freezing winds. Having driven my fifteen-year-old VW Camper from Birmingham to Harwich in arctic conditions – and in a hurry – I could feel little more emotion at leaving my beloved homeland than relief that sensation was beginning to return to my numbed limbs. I wanted to spend the next few years (extendable) of my life working my way round the world, and chose The Netherlands as my first venture. I hoped to learn something more about this flat land of windmills and finger-in-dike fame (by the way, I never met a Dutch person who knew that story).

Why The Netherlands? It would perhaps be more appropriate to ask "Why Amsterdam?" and make a clear differentiation from the start. During a previous holiday there I'd fallen in love with the intimate atmosphere and romantic architecture of the city; narrowly missed falling in one of the many canals; and had come away with an impression of a laid-back paradise for (ex-)hippies and all lovers of moral and racial freedom. There are reputed to be more different nationalities living in Amsterdam than in any other European city. I have to admit that my own rose-tinted memories, coupled with assurances from a woman friend living there of limitless employment, and an awareness of pro-people legislation from the Sixties had created an idealistic image of the city which seemed unlikely to survive. My woman friend, of Liverpool origin, talked keenly of the equal status of women and the ease of living happily and safely in a single state.

Anyway, I was in such an optimistic mood that not even the manic lurchings of ferry and stomach could upset me. The drive from Hoek van Holland to Amsterdam was relatively trouble-free. For the majority of the time I managed to stay on the right side of the road and trundled through beautifully clean towns and villages, low houses hugging the flat land and canals everywhere I looked.

Living and working as a foreigner in Holland is, in practice, not quite as straightforward as the EC would have us believe. You need an "Eligible for Employment" stamp in your passport to obtain legal employment, which you get from the Foreign Police office. This is a routine procedure (a lengthy wait being the main inconvenience) but you need to have an official residential address (not a hostel) in order to qualify. This can all too easily throw you into the "no money = no flat = no job = no money" pit.

The flat agencies were my first brush with anyone in "authority" in Holland and it was a refreshing experience. Everything was direct and open with none of the patronising comments and questions I've come to expect in these situations. Couples are rarely questioned about their marital status; all Dutch women are automatically the equivalent of "Mrs" after eighteen; and I was told that there was little overt discrimination against gay couples. I had the same positive experience with the private landlord, from whom I finally rented a small studio flat that had been advertised (in English!) in a newspaper.

It just remained to find work! The majority of legal jobs for non-Dutch-speaking women are in the hotel and catering industry – the same exploitative labour as in any other country, but with the comfort of an official (and rigidly enforced) minimum wage. Plodding round job agencies was a depressing task. Not surprisingly, many are loath to consider non-Dutch speakers in view of their own worsening economic situation. I eventually found a job with an academic publishing company (having luckily walked into the right place at the right time) and prepared myself to face the horrors of an office environment.

Living in Amsterdam was surprisingly easy. Virtually everyone can speak English, but this has its drawbacks. Although I took Dutch lessons and spoke Dutch whenever I could, I encountered a problem that seemed common to many foreigners, even those who'd been living in Amsterdam for many years. If people hear an English accent they will often switch into English – and the chances are that their English is far better than your Dutch. Unfortunately, I also found that in Amsterdam the response from shop-

keepers to broken, slowly-spoken Dutch is not as friendly as when you just speak English and they assume you're a tourist. But travelling in the more rural areas of The Netherlands my limited knowledge of Dutch did help, and it was warmly welcomed at work where, with justification, my Dutch colleagues sometimes felt like foreigners in their own country.

Working in a Dutch office was a sharp contrast to what I had known in England. The Dutch women were all strong-minded, independent people and, although it would be hard to say which was cause and which effect, there were none of the inter-sex power games that have infuriated me in English offices. Never once was I asked to make coffee by some smiling male superior. Never once was I assumed to have less intelligence than my typewriter. Never once was I verbally "patted on the head" for my apparently amazing ability to do the most mundane of tasks. (Never ever was I patted on any other part of my anatomy!)

"I sought out women's cafés and spent some peaceful, friendly evenings in the Saarein, *one of the best known of the women-only bars"*

Instead, women and men dealt with each other as colleagues and hierarchy was kept to a minimum. Dress was casual with people wearing whatever they felt most comfortable in. It seemed to me that the Dutch had grasped the point, still missed by many in English commercial life, that a woman doesn't have to wear a skirt and nylons for her brain to function. As such, the office was both cheerful and colourful.

People I met were friendly and helpful and, whilst it was very easy to fall into English-speaking cliques due to the number of English, Irish and Scottish people living in Amsterdam, I did have Dutch women friends who were enthusiastic to include me in their lives. If you live there long enough to have a reasonable grasp of Dutch, there are numerous political, spiritual or environmental organisations and a strong network of women's groups that you can tap into.

The rights of the individual was one of the things that struck me most during my nine months in The Netherlands. People know their rights and, on the whole, seem to respect others'. If I wanted to sit on the pavement and watch the world go by, I could. The police, whilst cutting a frightening figure with guns strapped to thighs, seemed far more interested in towing away illegally-parked cars than hassling harmless drifters.

Women held hands and kissed. Men held hands and kissed. Couples, regardless of colour and age differences, seemed able to show affection in public. I sought out women's cafés and spent some peaceful, friendly evenings in the *Saarein*, one of the best known of the women-only bars (Elandsgracht 119), but this was some way from where I lived in the eastern part of the city and I soon discovered that I could as easily sit and read a book without harassment (if I felt like solitude rather than sisterhood) in a mixed café as in a single-sex one. This didn't mean I was pointedly ignored, but if people spoke to me it was generally in a chatty, friendly manner without any sexual overtones. I travelled freely on my own late at night, but perhaps it is wrong to draw too many conclusions from this: my own conditioning leads me to avoid places or situations I have come to regard as "dangerous".

It took a while to realise that my mood of well-being was due in part to the atmosphere pervading the capital. As opposed to the rat-race of English cities where most people you see look preoccupied, or, at least, determinedly pursuing some goal, people in Amsterdam seemed more relaxed. The rich/poor divide is not as visually apparent as it is in the UK and, as far as

I could gather from my Dutch friends, the standard of living was generally quite high – taxes might be heavier but then there are more benefits available.

"Whilst frightened of the dark alley-ways and bodies leaning in door-ways, I was only ever hassled as a consumer, urged to buy some drugs"

This must sound as though I was living in some socialist paradise for nine months. Indeed not. The Netherlands is as capitalistic and consumerist as Britain and the two countries have much in common ideologically. Some older (and younger) members of the Dutch community that I met were voicing just the same prejudices about colour and sexuality that you come across in the UK. In the red light district, women's bodies are readily available for men's pleasure and it seemed to me that adjacent windows were offering animal flesh and female flesh for sale with very little discrimination. Whilst perhaps preferable to the street-corner hypocrisy of English prostitution, the extent to which this fundamentally exploitative industry has taken root in the city came as a shock.

From my own point of view, however, whilst frightened of the dark alleyways and bodies leaning in doorways, I was only ever hassled as a consumer, urged to buy some drugs. Thankfully, a "no" was always enough. But I only felt safe when I was back in the better-lit and busier streets of the city, away from the rows of neon flashing lights promising "real fucky fucky".

Of all the happy days I spent there, one deserves a special mention. The 30th April is "Queen's Day". This is the Queen's official birthday, but it is certainly not royal pageantry. The whole city is a "free market" on that day and, from dawn to dusk, the streets are full of makeshift stalls or flung-down blankets offering every conceivable sort of item for sale. The smell of foods from many different parts of the world hangs in the air, buskers are out in force and bands, whether reggae or classical, play well into the night. This is Glastonbury in the city, but what amazed me most of all was that, despite the heaving crowds, I never had a moment's worry about drunken violence or street aggression.

TRAVEL NOTES

Language Dutch. But very many people speak fluent English, German and French.

Transport Easy in such a compact country: bus and train routes complement each other and stations are usually adjacent. Hitching is good. Bikes can be hired at all main train stations.

Accommodation Hotels are expensive: pensions less so. In Amsterdam and other cities you'll find *Sleep-ins*, dormitory accommodation heavily subsidised by local councils, and some Youth-Student hotels. There are also a few women-only hotels, guesthouses and campsites (see listings below).

Special Problems The only area where you are likely to experience street harassment is the Amsterdam red light district. There's a growing number of foreign women who get immersed in the Amsterdam drugs scene and resort to prostitution to support their habit. Outside of Amsterdam attitudes are noticeably more conservative – you could feel uncomfortable expressing lesbian sexuality. Bicycle stealing is big business in Holland, especially in Amsterdam (use the bike-pound at the Central Station); there are pickpockets working the Amsterdam's trams.

Guides *The Rough Guide: Amsterdam* (Harrap Columbus) gives an excellent run-through of everything you might need to know about the capital and environs. *The Rough Guide: Holland, Belgium and Luxembourg* (Harrap Columbus) contains a thorough section.

Contacts

Although there are many feminist and lesbian groups throughout The Netherlands they are not necessarily open to casual visitors. Unless you've lived in the country for some time your contacts will mainly be limited to other foreigners. There are however, plenty of **women's centres, bookshops, cafés and bars** that are open to newcomers, only a selection of which are listed below.

Amsterdam

Vrouwenhuis, Nieuwe Herengracht 95. Women's Centre. The best overall contact for local groups and campaigns. Hosts all kinds of cultural events, including regular rock'n'roll

Xantippe, Prinsengracht 290, ☎235854 (closed Sun and Mon). The capital's main feminist bookshop and a good source of local information.

Internationaal Archief voor de Vrouwenbeweging, Keizersgracht 10, ☎244268. International archives for the Women's Movement. Also acts as a referral service for women's studies.

Amazone, Singel 72, ☎279000 (closed Sundays and Mondays). Women's contemporary art gallery and exhibition centre.

COC, National Gay Centre, Rozenstraat 14, ☎268300. Information centre with some congenial bars and a women-only disco on Saturday nights.

Café Saarein, Elandsstraat 119, 1016 RX, ☎234901; **Bar Vivelavie**, Amstelstraat 7. Two of the best known women-only bars.

Françoise, Kerkstraat 176, ☎240145. A women-only café with art gallery and music. Serves lunches as well as snacks.

Amsterdam has a few **hotels and guesthouses** which welcome gay women. None of them are cheap. You could try **The Quentin Hotel** Leidsekade 89, 1017, ☎262187; **ITC Hotel** Prisengracht 1051, 1017 JE, ☎20 230230; and **Hotel New York**, Herengracht 13, ☎243066.

Elsewhere

THE HAGUE: **Vrouwenhuis** (Women's House), Prins Hendrikstraat 33, ☎653844. A meeting place and information centre. **Trix** (feminist bookshop), Prinsestraat 122, ☎645014.

UTRECHT: **Savannah Bay** (feminist bookshop and women's bar), Teelingstraat 13, ☎314410.

ROTTERDAM: **Vrouwencafé Omnoord** (women's café), Sigrid Unsedweg 100, ☎212722. **Krities Boekwerk** (feminist bookshop), Nieuw Binnenweg 115a, ☎4364412.

Camping Holidays

For **women-only camping** contact *Vrouwenkampeerplaats de Hooimijt*, Pieterzijlsterweg 4, 9844 TA, Pieterzijl, Groningen, ☎05948 357. They have a large house with rooms for rent and a number of tents already set up. You can also rent bicycles and boats.

Books

Anja Meulenbelt et al., *A Creative Tension: Exploration in Socialist Feminism* (Pluto Press, 1985). Writings of Dutch feminists ranging across the socialist feminist debate.

Marga Minco, *The Glass Bridge* (Peter Owen, 1989) and ***An Empty House*** (Peter Owen, 1990). First British publication of a popular saga following the life of a Dutch Jewish woman during and immediately after the second world war.

Anja Meulenbelt, *The Shame is Over* (The Women's Press, 1980). Introspective account of becoming a feminist.

Journals

Katijf, Postbus 16572, Amsterdam 10001 RB, ☎020 240382. A bi-monthly socialist-feminist magazine with articles and events.

Lover (pronounced Lowver), Keizersgracht 10, 1015 CN Amsterdam. Review and resources quarterly for the Women's Movement (Dutch and foreign).

Opzij, Raamgracht 4, 1011 KK Amsterdam, ☎10 262375. Feminist monthly.

Lesbian Information Booklet, COC-Magazijn, Rosenstraat 8, 1016 NJ Amsterdam. Annual directory of lesbian resources throughout The Netherlands.

New Zealand

N ew Zealand (Aotearoa) comprises two main islands – North and South – as well as the much smaller Stewart and Chatham Islands. Despite the huge distances separating it from Europe and America, strong links are retained with both, although increasingly the cultural influence of the Pacific is replacing these traditional ties.

Almost all of the indigenous Maori population live on the North Island. Maori society is tribal, traditionally associated in complete harmony with land and sea, and tied closely to the bonds of family life and the village community. Although far more integrated into white European immigrant (*pakeha*) society than, say, the Australian Aboriginals, Maori society has been badly disrupted by rapid urbanisation. Together with age-old land grievances, high unemployment, discrimination in work and education, and low standards of health and housing have contributed to the rapid acceleration of Maori protest in recent years.

New Zealand is a great place if you like the outdoor life. The countryside is wild and beautiful, far more varied than the common image of acres of grazing sheep would suggest. Many travellers are struck by the variety of terrain – mountain, lake and seashore often lie within close proximity. New Zealanders themselves are widely regarded as hospitable and it's generally safe to travel around alone, though hitching on your own is not recommended. Another area for caution is pubs; any unaccompanied woman entering a pub can expect persistent pestering from men, who will refuse to accept that you are not on the look-out for male company.

There is a remarkably strong **women's movement** in New Zealand, illustrated by a range of organisations from Maori women's groups to broad-based women's resource centres and groups working to support the current Labour government's anti-nuclear stance. Campaigns against French nuclear testing and the dumping of nuclear waste in the Pacific are widely supported – particularly as pressure from Britain and the US mounts for New Zealand to abandon its anti-nuclear policy in the Pacific.

Back to the "Home Country"

· · · · · · · · · · ·

Amanda Gaynor is British, though, having a New Zealand mother she was brought up with tales of the "home country". After an initial visit as a teenager, she returned to spend three years living in Auckland, where she worked as a teacher in a large multicultural school.

A customary vision of New Zealand is sheep, burly farmers, thick-set Maori performing *poi* dances and "tourist" *haka*, all backdropped by magnificent rugged scenery. This is the way the country has been marketed, as a kind of outdoor wonderland accompanied by the quaint anachronisms of a cosy "never, never land Britain" of forty years ago. In fact, this was pretty much my impression on my first trip to New Zealand eight years ago at the age of eighteen.

Returning to teach presented me with much more of a paradox. I had a sense of a country in limbo, moving uncomfortably away from its colonial heritage and struggling to emerge as a Pacific nation – compelled to do so, in fact, by dwindling European markets if

not desire. Nowhere is this tension between the Pacific and the European felt more keenly than in the northern North Island city of Auckland, which is now billed as the largest Polynesian city in the world. The city sprawls in an ungainly fashion across a complex network of harbours and inlets, creating an atmosphere of disunity. Yet a broad division between north and south Auckland persists, the former being mainly European and the latter predominantly Polynesian. In general terms, the difference is that between wealth and poverty and respectively low and high unemployment.

I have a New Zealand mother (although I was born and brought up in Britain) and was raised on her Elysian belief in the myth of racial harmony between black and white in New Zealand. So a part of what interested me in coming to this country was to try to gain an insight into the practice of race relations. Owing to the current teacher shortage, I had no problems picking up work in a large, multicultural and rigidly streamed school.

It was immediately apparent that the Maori and Pacific Island pupils made up the majority in classes at the lower end of the ability range (clearly reflecting a discriminatory system) and were hardly present in the top three bands. I was even more startled by the low expectations that many Islander and Maori girls had of themselves; that marrying and having children would take the place of a career. Indeed, for many, the concept of a career hardly figured and the stereotype of homemaker was strongly endorsed by the boys.

However, as I began to understand the differing structures upon which their family groupings were based, I began to question whether it would be appropriate for me to impose upon these children a Western feminist ideal of what constitutes freedom. Historically, Maori women have always held an important and publicly recognised role as homemakers within the *marae* (meeting house). They are endorsed and commended within Maori art as powerful, fertile lifegivers – as women they are creators.

So, it seems that although the urban Maori may have moved away from the traditional lifestyle, they carry with them a cultural heritage of strong womanhood which is then in danger of negation by Western liberal concepts of equality – a system that condemns large families and urges material success in a competitive society.

"European reserve can often be interpreted as rudeness"

By contrast, it has been interesting to step outside my own niche and to go to the mainly Polynesian preserve of the Otara market in South Auckland. The somewhat inauspicious setting of a supermarket car park soon fades amidst the thronging mass of people out shopping and socialising on a Saturday morning. Here, amongst piles of *puha* (a popular edible green) and long earthy kava roots, Samoan music blares and little English is spoken. For me it is the chance to feel in the minority and to catch a glimpse of another way of living. Few white people use the market and, until I started taking my nine-month-old son, I was treated with caution. It was partly because I stood

out and partly because European reserve can often be misinterpreted as rudeness by more outward-going Polynesian people. But now, accompanied by Daniel in backpack, I find a tacit support, especially from women, and a more open friendliness.

Another area in which to experience differing cultures is at the local beach; here an unwritten apartheid seems to operate, whereby black and white gravitate to opposite ends, perhaps because the former tend to come for family picnics and the latter for water sports like jet-skiing. Amongst the picnicking, garlanded Samoans it is rare to find women bathing with their legs uncovered once they have reached puberty, as thighs are regarded as erogenous. From respect I often wrap a towel around me, dropping it only at the water's edge. I enjoy the sense of festivity of these beach outings and the feeling of large family groups settling in for the day with their rugs, windbreaks, fires and volleyball nets.

Yet it is not only the contrast between European and Pacific to which I have had to adapt but also the unexpected differences between me and *pakeha* (white) New Zealanders. "We share the same language but that's about all", was the way one woman put it to me. Again I found fundamental differences in the way we communicated and I am sure that, at times, what I construed as rudeness was in fact a blunter kind of directness with which I was unfamiliar. There are fewer codes of courtesy here, gushing thanks are seldom forthcoming, and consequently I have at times been left feeling taken for granted when this was not the intention. Likewise in performing public transactions it took me quite some time to get away from the "excuse me . . . I wonder if you could possibly tell/help me . . . ?" to the more colloquial and perfunctory "hey, where's the . . . ?". People often visibly stiffened to the former, whereas I was greeted with warm helpfulness by the latter.

Once accustomed to this, I discovered that I made better progress. In my discussions with women I noted frequent reference to the "Kiwi male", often accompanied by a disparaging shrug of the shoulders. When pressed, women are particularly critical of what they view as (white) men's inability to express themselves on an emotional plane and their reluctance to analyse their actions. Many women argue that, by and large, men still maintain traditional attitudes to women. Certainly, from staff-room conversations, I was surprised by the number of women who were still expected to bear sole responsibility for looking after the home, in addition to full-time jobs. But to me the problems seemed comparable to those in England, and the New Zealand Women's Movement correspondingly active and vocal.

"By and large, men still maintain traditional attitudes to women"

What is evident is the solidarity that exists between women in New Zealand. There is a strong sense of companionship that seems to spring from the old pioneer settler mentality. Indeed, there is a practicality about New Zealand women that is reflected in the most popular of the women's magazines, the *New Zealand Women's Weekly*. I have been impressed by the breadth of articles that it runs and the refreshing absence of romantic pap. Women I have spoken to suggest that it is because they are interested in the real issues affecting their lives rather than in escapist fantasies centred on men.

New Zealand is diverse in its facilities for women. In Auckland and other major cities there are women's centres, women-only discos and women's reading rooms at the university. Yet in the rural areas it is not uncommon to receive an invitation to, say, a dance, with the peculiar addendum "and ladies a plate". I was mystified by this on my first encounter but my host explained

to me that it was the woman's responsibility to provide the food. Such traditions die hard in rural communities and the division of labour within the farming sector remains largely clear-cut, with the woman staying in and around the home, preparing food for the men. On farms I have visited it was unusual to see men do more than make a cup of tea when at home. Change is certainly coming, but slowly.

In my travels around both North and South Island I have been astounded by the warmth of strangers toward me. People are eager to meet foreigners and have been happy to go out of their way to help me. But sadly it is no longer as safe as it once was for women to hitch alone, and this is particularly true of more remote areas of the South Island, where there has been an increase in the occurrence of violent rape.

However, there is only one situation in which I have felt directly threatened by men, and that is on my own in pubs. Pubs tend to be utilitarian drinking houses with plastic seating and glaring overhead lighting. They are generally male dominated and the arrival of a sole woman seldom passes without notice. There's the overwhelming assumption that you have come to meet a man, and polite rebuffs are frequently ignored. Men in this situation can be persistent and will sometimes involve others in the bar into the goading of the "reluctant" woman. If possible, it is better to arrange to meet somewhere more neutral and then go on to a pub in a group. Having said this, there are of course pubs where there are more convivial atmospheres and lively bands.

One good way, I found, of discovering what there is to offer in Auckland is to look at the noticeboards of the numerous small health-food cafés. Here I have found adverts for feminist flatshares, womanlines, notices for various discussion groups and alternative women's medicine. If you're looking for accommodation this is an easy place to start and far less bewildering than the reams of adverts in the Saturday *New Zealand Herald*. For me, living in New Zealand for the past two years has been "a looking-glass" experience, by turns frustrating and rewarding. What has been satisfying is the chance to get away from the image of a little England in the South Pacific and come to a recognition of New Zealand as a poly-glot society, striving to achieve a distinct identity. But it is an identity beleaguered at present by an insecure heritage of racial tensions and restrained by the desire to look back to Europe for national origins – as symbolised in the plethora of mock-Elizabethan motels that greet you on the journey from the airport.

"Whose side do you think I'm on?"

. . . .

Viki Radden is a black American, currently living in Japan, where she is working on her first novel, due for publication in 1990. She has both lived and worked in New Zealand.

I first went to New Zealand for love. While living in San Francisco, I fell in love with a man who lived there, and after he returned to New Zealand, I quit school and followed him back. I had certain preconceptions. As everyone knows, New Zealand is an agricultural country, and you see more sheep there in one day than in an entire lifetime elsewhere. I expected to see green, rolling hills; long, endless beaches on the North Island, and alps and fjords on the South; and I was not disappointed. For physical beauty, few countries can equal New Zealand. Two things I did not expect to see, however, were a thriving Women's Movement and a strong indigenous struggle among the Maori, the native Polynesians of New Zealand.

Although racial tensions and problems exist (and they're getting worse rather than better), New Zealand is still serene and safe when compared with other Western countries. It was refresh-ing to be able to come and go virtually free of the debilitating fear of violence that haunts me as a black American woman. I had a feeling during my last visit, however, in 1989, that New Zealand society is now at a critical point in its history. The country is either going to have to extricate itself from its problems – including the new phenom-enon of unemployment – or go into an acute tailspin. In 1988, more than 38,000 New Zealanders left the country, hoping for better times in Australia, where jobs are more plentiful, and where the rights of the Aborigines are so restricted that it is easy for whites to lull themselves into thinking that there is no "race problem".

For the visitor, New Zealand is an ideal country in which to travel. Getting around is easy; there are good bus and train services, and hitchhiking, though always risky, is generally a breeze. Picking up seasonal jobs is no problem either. Though New Zealand govern-ment policy states that visitors who enter the country on a tourist visa are not allowed to work, jobs like fruit pick-ing (in Hawke's Bay, Northland and Central Otago) and sheep shearing are relatively easy to obtain. Employers, as well as the government, seem to turn a blind eye to the rules when it comes to this type of employment.

There are also few problems in trav-elling alone. A well-established women's community makes it easy to forge contacts. All one needs to do is visit one of the feminist bookstores, located in Auckland, Hamilton, Wellington and Christchurch; *Broadsheet*, a wonderful feminist magazine, is a good place for locating women doing political work. As an American, however, you should be prepared for the occasionally frosty reception. Americans are stereotypically viewed as arrogant, money-ridden, and ignorant about how to behave in this country. A particular cause of tension, during my visit, was the US government's threat to place an embargo on New Zealand exports, after it began refusing entry to nuclear-weaponed and nuclear-powered ships. New Zealanders are justly proud of their nuclear-free policy.

"People reacted first to my being an American and a tourist, and then to the fact that I was black"

My experience was in many ways representative of what might happen to any woman traveller who lives and works in New Zealand. People reacted first to my being an American and a tourist, and then to the fact that I was black. This was a new, but not altogether refreshing experience, as white New Zealanders would often complain to me about the Maori, using the same racist terminology I'd heard about black Americans back at home. They assumed that, since I was American, I would sympathise with their feelings. "Look at me," I told the boss of the blueberry orchard where I worked, when she complained that the Maori workers were likely to spend their pay cheques buying beer and marijuana and that they all were violent and

carried knives. "Look at the colour of my skin. Whose side do you think I'm going to be on?"

There was one experience which both disturbed and frightened me. My lover and I were on the west coast of the South Island, a wild, beautiful and sparsely inhabited part of the country. In an incident which I can't help believing was racially motivated, a car with two surly-looking men pulled alongside our car and, without the men saying a word, they stayed beside us for miles, sneering and brandishing a tyre-iron at us.

I had some experiences which changed my life, most notably through my contact with Maori women. I was able to go to several *hui* meetings on Maori land, where problems affecting the Maori community were discussed. The most inspiring of these was a national black women's rape crisis *hui*, followed by an all-women's music concert. Maori events are commonplace in New Zealand but a visitor will be lucky indeed if she is allowed to participate in them. Through this contact, I was able to gain some firsthand knowledge of the deplorable living and working conditions of the Maori – something every visitor should be made aware of.

Time spent in New Zealand will certainly be worthwhile. The sheer beauty of the scenery, most of it pristine and unpolluted, will lighten the spirit and infuse new energy into one's life. Eating is a joy. Never have I tasted such delicious fruit and fresh vegetables; the milk and cream are the best in the world. There really is nothing quite like the thrill of sitting alone on a beautiful beach in the middle of summer, slowly licking an ice cream cone so delicious that it must have been dropped straight from heaven.

TRAVEL NOTES

Languages English and Maori.

Transport The two islands are connected by ferry between Picton and Wellington. If you can afford the hire, a camper van is much the best way of seeing the country. Trains are limited, but buses operate to most outlying areas and quite a few women hitch, though seldom alone.

Accommodation Hotels, lodges and hostels (with dormitories or private rooms) are reasonably priced by Western, or Australian, standards. Camping is very popular and many motor camps have cabins and caravans for hire as well as providing camping facilities.

Guide *New Zealand – A Travel Survival Kit* (Lonely Planet) is practical and comprehensive.

Contacts

The main feminist magazine is *Broadsheet*, based in Auckland. Individual groups include:

AUCKLAND: **The Women's Bookshop**, 228 Dominion Rd., ☎608 583. **Auckland Women's Health Collective**, 63 Ponsonby Rd., ☎764 506/766 838. **Lesbian Support Group**, PO Box 47-090, Ponsonby Rd., ☎888 325. **West Auckland Women's Centre**, 11 McLeod Rd., Henderson., ☎836 6381. **Womanline** (telephone information and referral service), open Mon–Thurs, 9am–noon, 6–9pm, ☎765-173.

CHRISTCHURCH: **Kate Sheppard Women's Bookshop**, 145 Manchester St., ☎790 784. **Lesbian Line**, ☎794 796. **The Health Alternative for Women** (THAW), ☎796 970.

DUNEDIN: **Lesbian Line**, Mondays, 7.30–10 pm, ☎778 765. **Women's Resource Centre** (books, space, ·coffee), Room 10, Regent Chambers, Octagon.

HAMILTON: **Dimensions Women's Bookshop**, NZI Arcade, Garden Place, ☎80 656.

NEW PLYMOUTH: **Women's Centre**, Liardet St., ☎82 407.

PALMERSTON NORTH: **Women's Shop** (books, music, arts), Square Edge, PO Box 509.

TAURANGA: **Women's Centre**, 92 Devonport Rd., ☎783 530.

WELLINGTON: **Access Radio·** (783 khz), Woman Zone 10am Sundays, Lesbian programme 11am. Contact the collective via Radio NZ, ☎721 777. **Lesbian Line**, Tues–Thurs, 7–10pm, ☎898 082.

Books

Lady Barker, *Station Life in New Zealand* (Virago, 1984). First published in 1870, this is a classic story of early colonial life told with warmth and a real feeling of adventure.

Claudia Orange, *The Treaty of Waitangi* (Allen and Unwin, 1988). An award-winning account of the history and implications of the treaty signed by the British government and the Maori in 1840, which gave British sovereignty to New Zealand – an important book for understanding the roots of current Maori grievances.

The Maori of New Zealand (Minority Rights Group Report, No 70, 1986). Excellent background to Maori history and grievances up to the present. Obtainable from good bookshops or MRG, 36 Craven Street, London WC2N 5NG.

Fiction

Keri Hulme, *The Bone People* (Picador, 1985). Extraordinary semi-autobiographical novel weaving in Maori myth, custom and magic, and a wonderful evocation of place. Originally published by a New Zealand feminist co-operative it went on to win the British Booker Prize and international distribution.

Janet Frame, *Owls Do Cry, Living in the Maniototo* (The Women's Press, 1985, 1990), and others. Often psychological novels by arguably New Zealand's finest writer. Also look out for her autobiography in three volumes, starting with ***To the Is-Land*** (The Women's Press, 1985), a haunting tale of growing up in the New Zealand of the 1920s and 1930s.

Rosie Scott, *Glory Days* (The Women's Press, 1988). A gritty, hard-hitting thriller set in Auckland's underworld, and with a marvellously realised heroine.

MacDonald Jackson and Vincent O'Sullivan, eds., *New Zealand Writing Since 1945* (Oxford University Press, 1983). A collection of prose and poetry which brings together the work of many of New Zealand's finest contemporary writers.

Yvonne du Fresne, *The Bear from the North* (The Women's Press, 1989). Spirited stories of pioneering days in New Zealand through the eyes of a child.

Nicaragua

At the time of going to press, Nicaragua is braced for a change of government. The ruling Sandinistas' ten-year struggle to uphold the momentum of revolution against persistent US-backed destabilisation has ended in a surprise electoral defeat. True to his reputation for political integrity, the Sandinista leader Daniel Ortega has pledged to respect the popular mandate and support a process of peace and reconciliation under the new government – to be formed by the politically obscure Violeta Chamorro, "moderate" leader of the broad and disparate coalition party, UNO. How she will manage to reconcile the conflicting claims of commu-

nist and ultra-right factions within her alliance (or contend with the strong Sandinista support within the army and police) is hard to imagine. The only certainty to conjure with is that the US will lift trade sanctions, withdraw from the *contra* war and provide some degree of aid.

For the last decade travel to Nicaragua has taken the form of a personal political statement of solidarity with the Revolution. The country itself had become a powerful symbol of resistance to US intervention and of self-determination in Central America. Foreigners arrived to contribute much-needed skills and labour, or to learn from the initiatives taken in land reform and the massive improvements taken in health and education provisions. As it was assumed that you had a purpose in being in Nicaragua you were unlikely to be considered an oddity travelling alone. Transport and accommodation were cheap, if not the most comfortable. *Machismo* was still prevalent, despite the impressive participation of women in the Revolution, but there was little threat of sexual harassment.

Now that the impetus to express solidarity has gone it seems unlikely that war-torn Nicaragua will get many foreign visitors. It's certainly too early to tell how travellers will be welcomed under the new administration.

The huge involvement of **women in the Nicaraguan Revolution** – at one stage they made up thirty percent of the army including some in high command – has made it a case study for feminists and women in national liberation movements everywhere. Nicaragua has long had an independent women's organisation. Since 1978 this has been the Luisa Amanda Espinoza Nicaraguan Women's Association (AMNLAE), bearing the name of the first women to be killed in the battle against Somoza. At AMNLAE's third congress in 1987, the ruling FSLN presented a policy document stating that discrimination against women would not be "put off or separated from defence of the Revolution" and that *machismo* and other elements had to be immediately combatted as they "inhibit the development of the whole society". AMNLAE was subsequently reorganised and acquired a new status as a "movement" instead of an organisation. The new brief was to work more closely at a regional level within mass organisations, such as trade unions, the Sandinista Youth movement, agrarian workers' co-operatives and the neighbourhood-based Sandinista Defence Committees, including having representatives in each at an executive level. It was also decided to open women's centres (*Casas de la Mujer*) in all regions to offer training courses and provide a focal point for organising social activities. Again we have no notion how this will change under the new administration. AMNLAE is, however, likely to continue its work in opposition.

The piece below was written before the 1990 election. We felt that in its description of Managua life it would have some enduring relevance.

Welcome to the Republic of Sandino

. . . .

Helen Tetlow spent three months working at the University of America in Nicaragua's capital, Managua.

"Nicaragua will get into your blood," said the voice at the other end of the phone, one of a number of people who asked me to deliver letters in Managua,

the only sure way of knowing that mail would arrive. I was due to leave in four days and in too much of a panic about an overnight stay in Miami, a five-hour wait in Honduras (where lengthy questioning of passengers in transit to Nicaragua is not unknown), and about coping with the heat and humidity of Managua, to feel particularly reassured. But she was right.

Probably the main reason I was going to Nicaragua was that it had "got into the blood" of a good friend who had taken out my CV to the university in Managua. Until then I had only felt passive curiosity about this small Central American country whose

Revolution had survived despite all efforts by the US to destroy it; I also had a rather vague notion that I wanted to use my teaching skills in a country which not only desperately needed them, but which was committed to building a society based on socialist principles.

I had been reasonably well briefed about what to expect before I went but, as most of my previous travelling had been confined to fairly developed countries, no amount of words describing the hardship, the food shortages, the minimal transport system and the poverty could have prepared me for the culture shock of my first night in Managua.

"It's like Los Angeles after the holocaust.' A friend's description of the capital was beginning to make sense"

My very first feeling, however, was of tremendous relief. I had arrived safely without becoming a Miami crime statistic and with nothing more threatening in Honduras than a sticky, five-hour, non air-conditioned wait in Tegucigalpa departure lounge. Then came optimism and excitement as I stepped off the plane to face the enormous placard, "Welcome to the Republic of Sandino".

I joined my first long, slow-moving Nicaraguan queue to change the statutory sixty dollars into córdobas. Like many transactions in Nicaragua, this was done without modern technology and took a frustratingly long time. At last I wandered out into the concourse to see if anyone from the university had got hold of a car and enough petrol to come and meet me. They hadn't. Not, it later transpired, because of petrol rations, but because my letter giving arrival times had not arrived and, like several envelopes of tea bags and cassettes, never did.

As I took my first step out of the air-conditioned airport building into the

hot, soupy Managuan night, and peered through the extremely minimal street lighting at a couple of very derelict-looking taxis standing on a road with more holes than surface, I wondered with despair where on earth I had come to. "It's like Los Angeles after the holocaust." A friend's description of the capital was beginning to make sense.

This lack of someone to meet me could have been very unnerving, but I had got talking with four other *internacionalistas* on the plane (two Canadian students and two North American nuns) and shared a taxi with the students to a *hospedaje* (hostel) where they had stayed on a previous visit. It's worth saying that you are unlikely ever to feel isolated travelling alone in Nicaragua. There are a large number of people from many different countries working in solidarity on short and long term projects, making it relatively easy to find a hitching, room or taxi companion with whom you are likely to have something in common.

After the US$48 a night Miami motel room with king sized beds, knee-deep carpet, colour TV, private bathroom with courtesy shampoo and conditioner, the Managua *hospedaje*, which was to be my home for the next three weeks, was a shock. We entered what looked like an untidy back yard surrounded by ramshackle huts.

I remember thinking that I would soon be able to take my crippling rucksack off and then standing paralysed when I was shown my room: bare brick and plasterboard walls, a dusty concrete floor, a tin roof which didn't quite keep out the tropical rain, two very old bedsteads with thin, old, lumpy mattresses, a rickety table and stool, and a piece of string tied across the room to hang my clothes on. I was hot and sticky from a day's travelling in the tropics, but still too accustomed to tiled bathrooms to venture out into one of the unlit tin shower cubicles, where the water supply was a sawn-off pipe running across the top and you could only guess at what insects might be lurking inside.

My stomach turned over many times during my first few days in Managua as I acclimatised from the relative material comfort of my life in London to the hardship and poverty here. I'm glad that I kept a diary to record my first impressions of things which so quickly became familiar. Things which shocked me, like the poor *barrios* (neighbourhoods) with houses built of scraps of wood and metal; pigs and barefoot children everywhere; cars with doors and windows missing, held together with bits of wire; small pick-up trucks bouncing over enormous potholes with sometimes thirty people standing in the back, drenched to the skin by a tropical downpour.

And there was my leaky room in the *hospedaje* which soon became home. Here I met *internacionalistas* from Iceland, Finland, West Germany, the USA, Switzerland, involved in anything from journalism and printing to health-care. I was sorry to leave when I eventually found a room in a university colleague's house.

"I lived in Managua for three months and I would say, without hesitation, that it is the most unmanageable city I have ever visited"

Besides the shock, there were aspects of Nicaragua which I found mesmerising: the beauty of the land-scape with its volcanos and lagunas; the giant, lush foliage; people's faces with their mixture of Indian, Spanish and African blood; walls covered in political slogans or reminders of vaccination campaigns so that walking round Managua was like walking through a social history book; the enormous bill-boards with posters about breastfeed-ing or slogans about the current political situations: "Reagan is going but the Revolution continues".

I lived in Managua for three months and I would say, without hesitation,

that it is the most unmanageable city I have ever visited. Destroyed by an earthquake in 1972, severely bombed during the last months of the Somoza regime, what was apparently a beautiful capital city is now little more than a series of neighbourhoods separated by vast open spaces of scrub and joined by a network of very wide and danger-ously pot-holed roads. It is unbelievably difficult to find your way around because very few of the roads have names, only about a third of the houses are numbered, and so addresses are calculated in blocks away from local landscapes: "Two blocks north, one block south of the shop selling yoghurt" or, even more difficult, "two blocks south, one block north from where the grey tank stood before the earthquake"!

Add to this the vast area now covered by Managua, the debilitating heat and humidity, the skeletal, desper-ately overcrowded and extremely erratic bus service, the almost non-existent street lighting in a city which is plunged into tropical darkness at 6.30pm, and you will begin to under-stand that coping with Managua is a bit of an endurance test.

I would not like to have arrived alone in Managua without relatively good Spanish and colleagues at the univer-sity to help me find my feet. Having said that, I did meet lone women travel-lers who, though unprepared, seemed fine having made contacts and discov-ered Managua "survival techniques" at the *hospedajes*.

Unless you have a car, travelling in Nicaragua is another endurance test. Because of the desperate economic situation, there are few buses and most of these are in bad condition. Usually packed beyond belief, they are rich hunting grounds for razor blade thieves. By day two in Managua, I had heard so many horror stories about rucksacks, bags and even moneybelts under shirts being slashed, that I made my first bus trip carrying nothing more than the two small coins I needed for the journey and a photocopy of my passport tucked in my knickers.

But I quickly mastered the art of bus travel: how to catapult myself on to a bus already bursting at the seams; how to have everything of value wrapped up in a thick towel inside my small rucksack which I would clasp manically to my chest; how to start preparing to worm my way off at least three stops in advance, and how to develop extrasensory perception about where to get off at night.

"When I hitched alone I didn't have any problems but I did worry, more about being robbed than being sexually harassed"

If you manage to get on a bus, it's a very cheap way of travelling, as is the train which runs between León, Managua and Granada. However, the trains have open carriages which means that passengers travelling in the dry season – from January to May – will arrive coated in a layer of dust and, if wearing contact lenses, with streaming eyes. Because of the dire public transport system hitching is very common, particularly at the weekends when many Nicaraguans hitch home to visit families. This can mean long hot or long wet waits.

My experience was that you get there in the end – even if it is on a horse or on the top of a truck load of logs! When I hitched alone I didn't have any problems but I did worry, more about being robbed than being sexually harassed. Nicaragua's desperate economic problems are leading to an increase in robbery, and *internacionalistas* with dollars are an obvious target.

The prospect of surviving alone in Nicaragua was in fact much more frightening than the reality. I had been worried about living in a country at war. However, working in Managua, with only the weekends for travel, meant

that I only visited the Pacific Coast side of the country, well away from the war zones, though I must admit that the *contra* ambushing of a civilian bus and boat put me off trying to squeeze in a visit to the north.

Of course, the effects of the war and the US economic blockade are all too evident. There is a huge military presence and all males over sixteen do two years compulsory military service. But strangely enough, unlike in other Central American countries and indeed Britain, I never felt at all threatened by the army or police in Nicaragua. The Sandinista soldiers really did seem to be the People's Army.

Once, hot, lost and dehydrated in Managua, a soldier walked me home. It's quite customary for army trucks to pick up groups of hitchers and one of my students, who had returned recently from military service, told me that as well as active defence work, he had been involved in literacy work and building projects in some of the villages.

The economy is a disaster, with the country's already battered human and economic resources having to be poured into the battle to maintain the Revolution. Inflation rockets from week to week. When I arrived in May 1988, the exchange rate was one dollar to eleven córdobas. By the time I left in September, it was one dollar to 400.

One week, petrol went up from seventeen to 175 córdobas a litre overnight and bread from ten to forty. The supermarkets and chemists closed without warning for a day to adjust all prices, and for two weeks before the government could implement and backdate a thirty percent salary increase for state workers, some of my Nicaraguan colleagues at the university (who were earning substantially more than school teachers, nurses, the police) were going without meals in order to feed their children.

"Quien sabe?" (Who knows?) is a typical Nicaraguan answer and I think for me it was the uncertainty that even the most basic aspects of daily life would continue to function, which made life so unnerving. There were daily power cuts, water cuts, tropical storms which would paralyse transport, no milk for two weeks, days when there would be little but cheap loo paper and plastic plates in the supermarket, and days when there would be three types of cheese and jelly – but no loo paper!

"I was astounded by the machismo of many Nicaraguan men"

Politics is never far away from any conversation. I heard many moving accounts of people's memories of the fight against Somoza, of participation in the mammoth literacy campaign in the six months after the Triumph when all the schools and universities were closed to release thousands of students and teachers to work in the villages. But I also found it depressing to hear many people, who clearly had been supporters of the Sandinistas, now criticising the government and looking for ways to leave Nicaragua – not because they don't support the basic principles of the Revolution, but because they've had enough hardship. The US may not be able to defuse the Revolution militarily, but economically they are having a profound effect.

I was astounded by the *machismo* of many Nicaraguan men. While producing children and thus proving virility seemed to be a major preoccupation, according to my women colleagues it is rare for a Nicaraguan man to offer any help in the house or with the children, and male infidelity is a hobby. Though I never exactly felt threatened on the streets of Managua, it was hard to take the constant stream of "my queen", "beauty", "my little love", either whispered or shouted by passing men. The women at work were amazed that I objected to these "compliments" and like everything else I got used to them.

The resilience, generosity and good nature of people (and especially women, who face seemingly endless hardship) was something I found extraordinary and inspiring. It is not uncommon for a mother to be supporting three children, possibly by different fathers. "How do you survive?" I asked one woman doing a full-time teaching job at the university, a part-time postgraduate course, and bringing up four children alone. "I make shorts in my spare time," she laughed. In one household to which I was invited to lunch, even though there wasn't enough cutlery to go round, the mother had lost her son in a *contra* ambush, been deserted by her husband and, despite her meagre income, had still adopted a five-year-old war orphan to bring up alongside her own daughters.

One of my students made a special six-hour journey to his mother's house to retrieve a silver pen, clearly one of his treasures, to give me as a farewell present. The pen was presented to me at a very impromptu party which nevertheless included a series of formal and very moving speeches. I was always struck by the Nicaraguans' ability to move from informality to formality without sounding either pompous or self-conscious. Perhaps this has something to do with the very important role poetry plays in this "land of poets". My students loved having parties, which were usually organised at about five minutes notice and always in the middle of the rum and salsa, someone would request a poem.

TRAVEL NOTES

Languages Spanish, with one of the harder accents to understand in Latin America. Creole-English is spoken by a minority on the Atlantic Coast.

Transport Buses are very cheap but over-crowded and uncomfortable. Beware of pick-pockets on buses in Managua. Taxis are safe and reasonably cheap, though be sure to nego-tiate a price in advance. Hitching is very popu-lar and reportedly safe.

Accommodation There are quite a few clean, cheap hotels or *hospedajes* in Managua, though they tend to fill up quickly. Elsewhere accommodation gets more and more basic the further you are from the capital.

Special Problems Dress modestly and avoid wearing shorts, not worn by Nicaraguans despite the intense heat. They are poor but proud dressers and always like to look clean and neat. Don't change money on the black market. It's illegal and there's little difference from the official rate. Bring dollars and make sure you change them into local currency in Managua as you'll only be charged the exorbi-tant "airport official rate" outside. Take a torch with you. Power cuts are frequent and you'll really appreciate having your own light.

Guide *The South American Handbook* (Trade and Travel Publications) has accurate but limited coverage.

Contacts

For up-to-date information and details of study tours, including a yearly two-week tour for women, contact the **Nicaragua Solidarity Campaign**, 23 Bevenden St., London N1 6BH, ☎071-253 2464. Also, **Progressive Tours**, 12 Porchester Place, London W2 2BS, ☎071-262 1676.

Any contact with women's groups is best made through the central office of **AMNLAE**, Apt Postal A238, Managua.

Books

Adriana Angel and Fiona McIntosh, *The Tiger's Milk: Women of Nicaragua* (Virago, 1987). A photographic record of people's lives since the Revolution, backed up by testimonies from a range of Nicaraguan women.

Cain et al., *Sweet Ramparts* (NSC/War on Want, 1983). Traces the history of the Nicaraguan Revolution and assesses achieve-ments and their limitations for women since 1975. Unfortunately out of print, but worth hunting for.

Margaret Randall, *Sandino's Daughters* (Zed Books, 1981). Tells the story of women's participation in the Revolution through a number of interviews made shortly after 1979.

For a general historical summary of Nicaraguan history up to that period, read **George Black, *Triumph of the People*** (Zed Books, 1981).

For an introduction to Nicaragua, it's also worth looking at the handbook ***Nicaraguans Talking*** by Duncan Green (LAB, 1989).

Special thanks to Marta Rodriguez for her contribution to the introduction and Travel Notes.

Nigeria

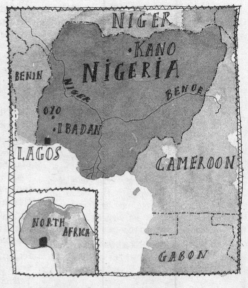

Nigeria has virtually no tourism. The difficulties of obtaining a visa, political instability, and the legendary armed robbers who roam the highways between cities are enough to put off all but the most determined traveller. However, those who do make it often find that the sheer vitality of the country, coupled with the overwhelming hospitality of the people, are enough to make them want to return.

In the thirty years since Independence, Nigeria's progress has been scarred by civil war, assassinations, plummeting oil revenues, economic crises and a succession of repressive military coups. Nigerians are a highly divided people, speaking over 200 languages, and there seems little chance of finding an enduring political solution to their tribal and ethnic conflicts. General Babangida, the current leader of the Armed Forces Ruling Council, has held power since the coup of 1985. While his commitment to widen political freedoms and open the way for national elections in 1990 has been welcomed, he faces considerable dissent over the introduction of widespread and stringent austerity measures – including a fourfold devaluation of the nation's currency.

Women, who have borne the brunt of high prices as consumers and as market traders, are often seen at the forefront of protest. In general, however, Nigerian **women's organisations** seem relatively moderate in their demands. The *Nigerian Council for Women's Societies*, one of the most established bodies, renamed the 1985 International Women's Day "Family Day" to reflect their priorities. These have barely changed. Although many of the women are middle class, professional, and financially independent (the group is often accused of elitism), marriage and bearing children are central to almost all their lives. An infertile woman is likely to be rejected by her husband and fall prey to the many private infertility clinics which advertise every few hundred yards along the roadside.

The country's most radical organisation is *WIN* (*Women in Nigeria*), which was launched in 1983 with the aim of overcoming women's problems within the context of the "exploitative and oppressive character of Nigerian society". Through a nationwide network of state branches and co-ordinators WIN is currently carrying out a plan of action on issues such as domestic violence, sexism in the media and in education, shared housework and childcare with men, and the need for non-sexist alternatives to government and institutional policies. Although men are incorporated into the organisational structure, this programme indicates a radical departure from the traditional, institutionalised and often church-based women's groups.

A Very Nigerian Coup

. . . .

Jane Bryce is white and in her early thirties. She went to Nigeria on a Commonwealth scholarship in order to research African women's writing at the University of Ile-Ife. She stayed five years, married a Nigerian and worked as a freelance journalist. Besides various trips to Lagos, to attend conferences and seminars, she travelled incessantly around the country.

I was so terrified of going to Nigeria that I drank heavily for a month beforehand and arrived in a state of advanced alcohol poisoning. The popular image abroad was of a country riven by extreme violence, lawlessness, and political infighting with a leadership held in place by bribery. I went, however, because I wanted to research a book on African women writers and had decided the best way was to enrol for a PhD at a Nigerian university.

I had lived in Africa before, in Tanzania, I had Nigerian friends, I had read books, but I still felt as if I was severing all ties and jumping off into the unknown, alone. And I was right. Nothing can prepare you for Nigeria; it simply isn't like anywhere else. Or if it is, it's so much bigger, so much more complex, varied, crowded and contradictory, that comparisons seem ludicrous.

Arriving at dawn, I felt utterly elated and totally exhausted. The sun rising red through the seasonal harmattan smog over Lagos, the palm trees, the unmistakable smell of Africa, of my childhood, hit me like a belly punch. I flung myself down by the hotel swimming pool and let the African sun drain the poisons from my body. I lay in a stupor all day, speaking to no one.

In the evening I got dressed and ventured out on to the street. It was New Year's Eve and I wanted to party. I had friends in Festac Village, built for the Festival of Arts and Culture in 1977. All I knew was that it was somewhere in Lagos, so I set out, looking for a taxi.

It was dusk, that sensual, soft, velvety tropical dusk, which caresses your skin and holds you and everything else in its warm embrace . . . the alcohol had left me and instead I was drunk with a feeling of homecoming.

"I spent that New Year's Eve sitting with the other hotel guests . . . listening to radio music interspersed with martial music"

I noticed there were few cars, and they were rushing by at break-neck speed. Nor was there anyone on the street, except a group of armed soldiers guarding a road block, casually wielding menacing-looking machine-guns. "Oh well," I thought happily, "perhaps that's what they do in Nigeria on New Year's Eve." I walked on, flagging taxis. None stopped, though most were empty. Suddenly a car materialised beside me, two anxious male faces peering out.

"Where are you going?"

"To Festac."

"At *this* time? Don't you know there's a curfew?"

"Curfew? Why?"

"Because of the coup."

"Coup? What coup?"

"The government was overthrown today. The soldiers have taken over."

Realisation dawned. The armed soldiers, the empty speeding cars . . . I stood in the road and laughed aloud. I had just arrived and there had been a coup. Nigeria . . . The two men bundled me into the car, turned with a screech of tyres, and drove furiously back to the hotel, where they dropped me off, with just enough time to beat the curfew home. I spent that New Year's Eve sitting with the other hotel guests in the outdoor bar, listening to radio bulletins interspersed with martial music.

Dodan Barracks, the scene of the coup, was a stone's throw from the hotel, the other side of the elite Ikoyi Club and golf course. I was an ignorant outsider with no idea of the significance of the events I had stumbled on: the end of a corrupt civilian regime which had squandered and stolen the country's massive oil revenues, leaving its people no better off than before.

The next morning at breakfast, I was sitting in the dining room when a man entered, dressed in *agbada*, the flowing Yoruba traditional dress. With a dramatic gesture he threw back the folds upon folds of richly coloured cloth, hitching them on to his shoulders and spreading his arms wide to take in the entire room. Enjoying his moment, he shouted to a waiter: "Bring me porridge . . . and champagne!"

Everybody clapped. The universal greeting that morning was, "Happy New Year, happy new government!" I understood, at least, that the civilians had been unpopular. As time went by, I came to understand why. Nigeria's much-vaunted democracy was a sham, the elections had been rigged, huge amounts of money had been spent buying the voters, with unparalleled ostentation and flagrant corruption. Ordinary people, sickened by the display and the waste, and by being forced to look on while their own condition remained unchanged, were all too happy to see the soldiers back. It was not the first time, and it wouldn't be the last.

Unknowingly, my arrival had coincided with an historic moment: the end of the era of oil wealth, the beginning of austerity, foreign debt and IMF-imposed economic stringency. By the time I left, five years later, I had not only seen, I had experienced the effects. Living and working, not as a highly paid "expatriate", but as an honorary member of the Nigerian middle class, I shared the agonising process of impoverishment and the struggle for survival, and I learnt some of the Nigerian strategies for dealing with it – patience, a philosophical outlook, opportunism, and above all, humour.

I've told this story because it illustrates so much about Nigeria, and about the expectations of people who go there: the volatility of the political situation, the love of display and performance, the danger, the humour and warmth, the material disparities. On my side, the ignorance, the shock, the delight and disillusionment, the gradual change of consciousness every sympathetic foreigner undergoes, emerging, in some fundamental way, changed. As a woman and a foreigner, you are exposed in a way both uncomfortable and inescapable. If you're white, you hear everywhere you go:

> *"Oyibo pepe*
> *If you chop pepe*
> *you go yellow more-more!"*
> *(White person, like red pepper,*
> *if you eat pepper,*
> *you'll get more yellow).*

You can never, never be anonymous, you're constantly being reminded of your difference. Even if you're black, if you dress and talk differently, you'll be called "Oyibo" (or outside of the Yoruba areas, "Batoure" or "Amingo"). When I was feeling strong, I could deal with it by laughter, join in the fun. But on bad days, when all I wanted was to be left alone, it could reduce me to tears.

Then as a foreign *woman*, you're a source of curiosity, a challenge to men. There are two roles for women vis à vis men: "wife" and "girlfriend". Polygamy, a fact of life in the Muslim north, was officially ousted by Christianity in the south. Southern men – Yoruba, Igbo and numerous minority groups – instead practice a less institutionalsed form, often having one or more wives and multiple girlfriends.

The effect of this on relationships between the sexes is, to a Western outlook, almost impossible to accept. It means that ordinary, disinterested friendship (though I did eventually achieve this with a handful of men) is almost impossible. For a start, public opinion doesn't allow it. Then, it means that women are perpetually in competition with each other, regarding each other with jealousy and suspicion. As a single foreign woman, your role is automatically that of "girlfriend", since

marriage is a liaison between families, and most families won't countenance a foreign wife.

Having said this, there's a surprisingly large network of foreign wives, with their own organisation, *Nigerwives*. You can go to their meetings as a visitor and they'll be friendly and supportive – often more so than married middle-class Nigerian women, who see you as a threat.

Though, again, I eventually made deep and lasting friendships with several Nigerian women, married and single, it was perhaps my greatest source of loneliness and dismay that women's friendship was so hard to come by. I found myself forced back on the company of men, who were invariably available, eager, and willing to befriend me.

"Like modern Nigerian women, the trick is to learn how to appear to conform, in order to do what you want"

Over and over again, my naive, Western assumptions and open behaviour let me down. At last, I learnt to copy Nigerian women – by not believing anything men told me till it had been proved; by being prepared for sexual advances and not allowing the circumstances to develop where things would get out of control; by standing on my dignity and demanding respect. It was all very alien at first, but it worked, and life became easier.

Like modern Nigerian women, the trick is to learn how to appear to conform, in order to do what you want. And one thing you notice, except in the north where, due to the practice of *purdah*, women are invisible, is how dominant and outspoken women generally are. The markets, epicentre of trade and commodity flows, are ruled by women, who have power over prices and availability.

Trade is second nature to West African women, and many professional women also engage in business, from selling soft drinks to importing luxury goods. There are more women in so-called male professions like law and banking than is common in Europe – indeed the president of United Bank for Africa is a woman. On a more basic level, many women make a living from processing and selling food, whether frying *akara* (bean cakes) on the street, or providing hot spicy pepper soup and beer in the *bukas* and beer parlours.

Overt sexual harassment is rare. In parts of Europe you can't even get on a bus without having your bottom pinched. In Nigeria, this *never* happens. Rape occurs, of course, far more than people will admit, because it's considered a disgrace to the woman and generally hushed up. But as a foreigner you are, to an extent, granted extra licence, and allowed to be eccentric.

I did all sorts of dangerous things before I knew better. Like hitching 400 miles north to Kano, starting so late in the day I had to be rescued and taken home by a man who turned out to have worked on a forestry project in Zaria with my father and introduced me to all his friends as a "very old family friend"; like riding pillion on a motorbike and without a crash helmet from Kano to Benin in the south, sleeping two nights in the bush; like taking *kabu kabu* (unlicensed) taxis to Fela's Shrine at midnight and coming home at three or four in the morning, when fear of armed robbers had driven everyone else off the streets.

I hardly ever felt afraid for my personal safety. Arbitrary accidents, like a blowout on the expressway at 140km per hour, or being caught in the undertow at the beach and breaking my shoulder on the sea bed, could happen to anybody. But the sexual threat was mostly absent.

Deeply entrenched in all Nigerian cultures, though being eroded now by the economic situation, is the automatic protection and assistance of strangers. This manifests itself in all sorts of ways.

In the dreadful discomfort of an over-crowded *danfo* minibus, I would find someone had anonymously paid my 20 kobo fare. Arriving in another city and asking the way, a passer-by would carry my bag half a mile to where I wanted to go. The poorest households would mobilise all their resources to lay on the kind of food they thought appropriate, and exclaim with disbelief and delight if you expressed a preference for "our food".

"Cashing a cheque can take a whole morning – if the bank hasn't run out of money"

The great advantage of the unreal exchange rate of the naira – a contrast to the early 1980s when Nigeria was the most expensive country in Africa – is that anyone with foreign exchange is rich in Nigeria. As a visitor, you can afford to reciprocate such generosity, because to you, everything will be cheap. When my sister came to visit, for two weeks we stayed in the best hotels and flew from place to place, before I reverted to a naira based existence. There's so much to see, such a variety of cultures and traditions, such vitality and creativity, that travel inside Nigeria remained a source of continual excitement.

To some extent, it offset the frustrations of intermittent electricity, phones that didn't work, the unreliability of "Nigerian time" which means that everyone's always late, the sheer *difficulty* of getting simple things done. Cashing a cheque can take a whole morning – if the bank hasn't run out of money. But you can always cool off afterwards in the shade of a palmwine shack, roofed with palm fronds, where you sip from a calabash while eating that great delicacy, bushmeat – wild animals trapped in the bush and smoked over an open fire.

The one certain thing about Nigeria is that you can never predict what's going to happen next, either in politics or everyday life. The president can declare at 6pm that the following day will be a public holiday because the national football team is playing somewhere. Or, you can stand for half an hour in an office while a clerk, being paid to do a job, insolently ignores you while he narrates a story in a language you can't understand to his colleagues,

then tells you indifferently that the boss is "not on seat".

As you splutter with speechless rage, he'll turn to you with a winning smile, holding out a paperful of freshly roasted groundnuts. If his invitation to "Oyibo, come chop!" doesn't melt your fury and make you join in the communal laughter, you shouldn't be in Nigeria.

TRAVEL NOTES

Languages Quite a few people in cities speak English, the official language. Of the 200 indigenous languages, Hausa is commonly used in the north, Yoruba in the southwest, and Ibo in the southeast. Pidgin is the best language to get you around in the south.

Transport Shared taxis run between all major cities. There is also a limited rail service. Internal flights are reasonably cheap. There are long distance buses run by private companies, no cheaper than taxis but considerably safer.

Accommodation Hotels are now inexpensive. Missions also offer accommodation in some large towns for a reasonable price; ECWA (Evangelical Church of West Africa) are the most common. Also, universities often have guest-houses where visitors can stay.

Special problems Nigeria is under military rule and there is the constant presence of army and police checks in the street. You should expect to be stopped and questioned frequently, and occasionally asked for money (bribes are a routine expense). You may get away with innocently misunderstanding this but you should never show anger. Try to avoid travelling between cities or walking around anywhere alone after nightfall. Nigeria's reputation for violent robbery is no myth. In the predominantly Muslim areas, particularly in the north, women are seen much less in public and can be hard to meet. In these areas it's advisable to wear clothes that cover the arms and knees and to avoid wearing trousers. In the Old City at Kano, women have been thrown off public transport or had stones hurled at them for dressing "immodestly".

Nigerians are very dress conscious and you could embarrass yourself and your hosts by

looking scruffy. It's good to try and look as smart as possible.

Guide The Rough Guide: West Africa (Harrap Columbus) gives a full and useful rundown of the country.

Contacts

Women in Nigeria, PO Box 253, Samaru-Zaria. Write for details of WIN groups around the country.

National Council for Women's Societies, Tafawa Balewa Square, Lagos. An NGO umbrella group and a focus for many different women's groups throughout Nigeria, which campaigns around issues of marriage and divorce.

University Groups. There are various women's groups forming at the universities who would welcome contact with western feminists. One such group is **Obafemi Awolowo University** (Ile-Ife) Women's Studies Group (contact Mrs Simi Afonja, Faculty of Social Sciences).

Nigerwives, PO Box 54664, Falomo, Lagos. A network organisation of foreign women married to Nigerian men, which operates as an extended family for attendance at weddings, funerals, etc, and as a pressure group for immigration issues, information and support. They also publish a newsletter.

Books

Women in Nigeria, Women in Nigeria Today (Zed Books, 1985). A selection of theoretical papers on women's subordination in Nigeria from the Women in Nigeria (WIN) conference.

S. Ardener, ed., *Perceiving Women* (John Wiley and Sons, New York, 1975). Revealing essays on Ibo women.

Mary Kingsley, *Travel in West Africa* (1897; Virago, 1982). British woman's journals of her travels in West Africa in the 1890s.

Molara Ogundipe-Leslie, *"Nigeria: Not Spinning on the Axis of Maleness"*, in ***Sisterhood is Global*** (Penguin, 1986; see General Bibliography).

West Africa magazine, published weekly in London, has up-to-date and in-depth news on Nigerian events, as well as many advertisements for cheap flights.

Fiction

Buchi Emecheta, *The Joys of Motherhood* (Heinemann, 1980). Powerful story about the strains of living in a society where women are denied any identity unless they bear children.

Flora Nwapa, *Efuru* (Heinemann, 1966), ***Idu*** (Heinemann, 1970), ***One is Enough*** (Tana Press, Eguru, 1981). Nigeria's first published woman novelist, all of whose work in some way concerns the constraints which marriage has on women. Nwapa now runs her own publishing house as an outlet for African writers.

Ifeoman Okaoye, *Men Without Ears* (Longman, 1984). The frantic chase for money and the obsession with prestige in urban Nigeria today.

Zaynab Alkali, *Stillborn* (Longman, 1984). Story of a young girl in rural Nigeria torn between village life and the lure of the city.

Thanks to Jane Bryce and Deborah Birkett who provided much of the information for the introduction and Travel Notes.

Norway

L ike most of Scand-
inavia, Norway is a relaxed
and easy country to travel
around. Norwegians would
see nothing noteworthy
about a woman travelling
alone or with other women,
and whether you choose to
hike across the justly famous
coastline of the western
fjords or sit in a bar in Oslo
or Bergen you're unlikely to
feel hassled or intruded
upon. The country is,
however, expensive, and
most visitors resort to camping to make ends meet –
though given the spectacular
scenery and general
outdoors culture this is little
hardship. More of a problem
can be the feeling of isolation
that comes from travelling in
a sparsely populated country
with vast, uninhabited
stretches, and where
communities can seem insu-

lar and exclusive. Norwegians tend not to strike up conversations with strangers, foreign or otherwise, so if you want to make contact you have to take the
initiative.

Oslo is often dismissed as a bland, unprepossessing capital. It does,
however, have a surprisingly cosmopolitan atmosphere and a lively street
culture. Bars and cafés are usually well mixed and easy places to enter alone,
although alcoholism, despite high costs and legal restrictions on drink, continues to be a mounting problem for both sexes. There's also a fair scattering of
women-only venues. Again, the lack of people can be a little unnerving; Oslo
has only half a million inhabitants with plenty of room for all, which means you
may well find yourself wandering alone in near-deserted city streets. The

problem is in shifting your perception of city life. Crimes against women are extremely rare and taxis are an expensive and for the most part unnecessary luxury.

After more than three decades of persistent and effective campaigning, the **women's movement** in Norway appears to have entered a quieter, less politicised phase. Women's societies and study centres are well established (the latter internationally renowned) but they no longer have the activist profile that typified earlier years. In part, this reflects the advanced state of equality already achieved within Norwegian society. The last government (which lost office in 1989) was led by a woman, Dr Gro Harlem Brundtland, and parliament has more than 25 percent women representatives. Women are clearly established in most areas of political and public life and, for a new generation of Norwegian women, equal opportunity (enforced via a strict quota system for education and employment) is an accepted legal right. Health and welfare policies are similarly progressive – there are extensive childcare facilities with additional help for single mothers, and abortion is available on demand in the first twelve weeks of pregnancy. Although Norway lags behind Sweden and Denmark in that it has not yet passed equal rights legislation for gay women and men, attitudes towards sexuality are generally permissive, particularly in Oslo and Bergen.

Perhaps one of the more telling examples of women's improved status was a landmark court ruling in 1983, when a pornographer was convicted of slander of a particular feminist activist and of women as a class.

Breaking the Ice
· · · · · · · · · · · ·

Belinda Rhodes followed up an undergraduate degree in Scandinavian studies with a year's postgraduate research at the University of Bergen. When time and money permitted she travelled, mainly on her own, around the southern region and the western fjords.

I had spent time in Norway before and knew more or less what to expect. Nonetheless I arrived exhausted and bewildered after a serious bout of seasickness on the 25-hour ferry crossing from Newcastle to Bergen. The last two hours of the voyage were by far the most pleasant as the boat turned inland, gliding between the superb scenery of the fjord, leaving the high seas behind.

I disembarked with a feeling that I had somehow arrived by accident. The research scholarship I'd applied for, but never really expected to get, had come through suddenly, leaving me very little time to sort out my travel arrangements. It was great, however, to be on firm ground again and to take in the colourful port, harbourside houses and cobbled streets of Bergen, surrounded by a magnificent sweep of Norwegian mountains.

The sight of the student residence where I was to live was far less inspiring. With its eighteen storeys of grey concrete and hundred-metre-long corridors, it reminded me of a prison, and the staff did not seem particularly friendly or helpful either. The latter fact did not really surprise me. The Norwegians are not known for their courtesy to foreigners and, although I had been determined to avoid generalisations when I came here, "cold", "brusque" and "distant" seemed to fit my first impressions of the women and men I met. It is unfair, however, to make such judgements on the basis of what you are used to at home. To a Norwegian there is nothing particularly rude about jostling someone in a queue, not saying "good morning" or "thank you", and there is no word in the Norwegian language for "please". Women are just as likely as men to be elbowed in crowded places, in fact I often found offending elbows belonged to women, but none of this is intended to show hostility or discourtesy, it is simply their way.

Having had previous experience of the unfriendly exterior of the Norwegians (and I must stress that it's only the exterior), I knew it would be up to me to make the effort to meet people and make friends, and I knew it would be worth my while. English is widely spoken so there need never be a language problem. As a foreign student it is always very easy and therefore tempting to get involved with the kind of foreign student subculture which seems to exist at every university.

As I speak Norwegian, I had made a conscious decision to avoid the English-speaking foreigners and to throw myself fully into the Norwegian way of life. Having said that, one of my first friends was an Icelandic woman who was on the same scholarship programme as myself. She was possibly one of the warmest, most liberated and aware women I have ever met, but in a way so natural and non-militant that it suggested to me that feminism must be even more advanced in Iceland than in Norway.

On most occasions I found my knowledge of the language a huge advantage, not only as a means of conversation but also as a talking point. Norwegians were fascinated to find someone who wanted to learn their language. I found the university had a warm, lively atmosphere, though I was surprised to discover that most of my colleagues were men and that there was not a single female teacher in the department of Scandinavian studies where I was to do my research. However, I was always treated as an equal and offered a great deal of help on an academic level. I did spend some very lonely weeks in the library before I began to meet up with any of my co-students socially, but later discovered that, as I hadn't actually approached anyone, it was assumed that I must have already sorted out my own social life.

"I also came across a large number of student single mothers who seemed to feel that they were supported and encouraged to continue their studies"

One of the reasons for the apparent absence of women in the department was that several lecturers had left to set up their own Centre For Women's Studies in the Arts. There the work focused mainly on modern European literature by women, and I attended several of their excellent seminars and talks – often led by notable authors such as Fay Weldon and Angela Carter. It was during a debate in which these authors took part that we discussed why British feminism seemed more politicised than Scandinavian – the conclusion was that it still needs to be in Britain, whereas in Norway many of the goals have already been achieved. I found that many younger women took the great degree of social equality they enjoy for granted, while those in their forties could well remember the period of intense struggle which led to changes in legislation and attitudes in the Fifties and Sixties.

On a social level there were very few women-only events but this was possibly a progressive sign, indicating the ease with which men and women students share whatever's available – most exercise classes, for example, would be mixed. I also came across a large number of student single mothers who seemed to feel that they were supported and encouraged to continue their studies. The local women's group in Bergen was campaigning for less universal causes than we are used to, focusing instead on local issues, like the closure of one particular nightclub in the city, identified as a "meat-market", due to the promotional strategies of the management.

After a couple of months at the stony, silent student residence I decided I would be better off moving into the city. I was lucky enough to find a nice flat in the centre, close to the harbour, which made it a lot easier for me to get involved in the social life of the place. In general I was quite impressed with Bergen after dark. Although it is a busy port and has its large and inevitable quota of drunken sailors and ex-sailors, I never felt threatened when walking home at night. When they are not being hauled off in police vans to sober up in the cells (a regular occurrence), the drunks seem to keep themselves to themselves. The only sexual harassment I remember experiencing was of a very mild nature, and it was only ever from drunks. That Norwegian women are incredulous when they come to Britain and get whistled at by builders would bear out my impression that sexual harassment is relatively rare in Norway.

There were only one or two bars near the harbour where I would generally avoid going alone, and these were extremely easy to spot. Generally, Norwegian bars and cafés have a very relaxed atmosphere and the locals wouldn't find anything strange about a woman going in alone. Tourists are often wary of the strict Norwegian laws on drinking, but in fact these only amount to exorbitant prices and a law in some areas that you have to eat to order a drink. In such places you will often be supplied with a token prawn on a morsel of bread and get a rubber stamp on your hand to show you have consumed something. Beer can be purchased in shops but anything stronger, including wine, is only available at the *Vinmonopol*, the state monopoly store for spirits.

"I enjoyed experiencing life in a society more liberated than my own and where women do appear to have more respect, opportunities and greater freedoms"

Prohibitive prices do not seem, however, to have much effect. Although one might be frowned upon for drinking during the week, people do drink quite heavily at weekends – and always to get very drunk. My impression was that women are just as likely to get very drunk as men, and for this reason, though it may sound odd, I felt much less vulnerable in crowded bars than I would in Britain.

Travelling in Norway should not be a problem for a woman alone. Major hindrances, however, are costs and long distances, although the hours spent on a train are easily compensated for by spectacular scenery. More than once I chose to make the eight-hour journey from Oslo to Bergen by day rather than night for the sake of staring at the landscape and on each occasion found it quite easy to get talking to the other passengers. Norwegians, being very patriotic, are always willing to tell you stories and give you information about any part of their country. Unfortunately there is a limit to where you can actually get to by rail. I occasionally hitched short distances and though it was never easy to get a lift – traffic can be very thin on the more interesting roads – the drivers who did pick me up were very friendly and helpful. I felt that Norway was a relatively safe country to hitchhike in.

One form of travel worth recommending is the *hurtigruta* or coastal steamer which starts at Bergen and calls at all major ports the length of the coast as far as Nordkapp (north of the Arctic Circle). I have yet to experience the midnight sun, but as far as I can gather it is very special. It apparently has something of a magical effect on those living in the far north. Their attitudes and lifestyles change dramatically with the arrival of summer – they sleep less and party more.

Even in Bergen, where it only gets dark for three or four hours in the summer, it was easy to talk the short hours of darkness away or remain at a party until dawn. The whole personality of the city changed dramatically when spring came, the foliage returned to the trees almost overnight, people opened up and the streets became suddenly much more lively. It seemed a more light-hearted place than it had been in the winter.

Overall, Norway was a very agreeable place to live and travel as a woman, and I enjoyed experiencing life in a society more liberated than my own and where women do appear to have more respect, opportunities and greater freedoms. Of course there are areas, particularly in the rural isolated regions, where the traditional way of life still holds firm and where you still come across shepherdesses and "dairymaids", proud of the fact that they represent the "old Norway". One woman I met high in the mountains on a trip from Bergen to Oslo told me with extreme pride that she made the only real goats' cheese to be found in Norway today. It's the peculiar mix of radical social change and valued traditions that makes Norway such a fascinating country to live and travel in and I certainly intend to return to find out more.

TRAVEL NOTES

Languages *Riksmal* or *Bokmal* (book language) are the official Norwegian languages although almost everyone, especially younger Norwegians, speaks some English.

Transport Expensive but very efficient public transport. Some trains have a play space for children. Hitching is apparently safe but slow going, with little traffic even on main routes.

Accommodation Again very expensive – cheap options are university campus rooms and camping (there seems little problem in camping alone even in the more isolated areas).

Guide *The Rough Guide: Scandinavia* (Harrap-Columbus) has a fine, enthusiastic section on Norway.

Contacts

Women's House (Kvindehuset), Råchusgatan 2, Oslo, ☎41.2864 (Mon–Fri 5–10pm, Sat 11am–5pm, closed in the summer). A good place to pick up information regarding the range of women's groups and resources.

Oslo Bookcafe, C.J.Hambros Plass 2, Oslo. Co-operatively run radical bookshop and café.

Women's University (*Kunneuniversitetet*). Contact Berit Aas (Director), Kunneuniversitetet, Joerns adveien 30, NI 360 Nesbru. Courses are exclusively for women.

Books

Bjorg Vik, *Aquarium of Women* (Norvik Press, 986). A collection of short stories by one of Norway's best known feminist authors.

Ebba Haslund, *Nothing Happened* (1948; Seal Press, 1988). First English translation of an early Norwegian novel dealing with lesbian love and friendship.

Gerd Brantenburg, *Egalia's Daughters* (Seal Press, 988). A satire on sex roles by a highly popular feminist writer.

Pacific Islands

The South Pacific is an immense area, dotted with thousands of mostly tiny islands. The main exceptions are the vast island of New Guinea, north of Australia, and the two principal islands of New Zealand in the southeast. The many clusters which lie in between make up the countries of **Fiji**, **Western and American Samoa**, **French Polynesia** (the largest island of which is **Tahiti**), **Tonga**, **Vanuatu** and **New Caledonia**, to name just a few.

New Zealand, with its predominantly white-settler population, is unique in sharing more affinities with Australia than with its Pacific neighbours – whose inaccessibility and limited facilities have kept them relatively unknown, until recently, both to package tourists and independent travellers. Nowadays, a growing number of islands threaten to follow the fate of Tahiti, which commercial interests have succeeded in virtually transforming from a Pacific paradise to a tourist nightmare. In some countries, however, most notably Fiji, New Caledonia and Papua New Guinea, political unrest has reversed the trend, causing travellers to shy away from once lucrative tourist resorts. In the case of Fiji, especially, such caution is not necessarily

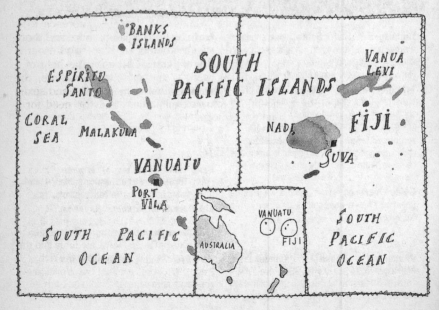

warranted, but sensitivity to the political climate throughout the South Pacific is necessary, and worth learning about in more detail before you set off.

Of the two countries featured in the following accounts, **Fiji** (consisting of 332 islands) is one of the largest and most developed Pacific Island states. It also stands out in having a majority Indian population, whose presence stems from the days of British sovereignty when indentured Indians were brought in to work the sugar plantations. It was the predominance of Indians in the newly elected government of 1987 which provoked a coup by the military who demanded that Fijians be given permanent political control of the country. In contrast, **Vanuatu**, colonised at once by the British and the French, has managed to maintain a degree of political stability – despite mounting Francophone opposition to the chiefly Anglophone government.

Depending on where you go, your choice of accommodation in the South Pacific will vary from luxury hotel to village hut; the cost of food and transport will also fluctuate. In terms of safety, it's again hard to generalise, but provided you're careful and respect local customs there shouldn't be much problem of sexual harassment, at least from the indigenous inhabitants.

A few Pacific nations, among them **American Samoa** and **French Polynesia**, have quite large foreign communities, for they have been maintained as overseas territories by the countries which colonised them. Colonialism is a key political issue, along with escalating concern about French and American nuclear tests and the dumping of foreign nuclear waste into the ocean. In recent decades a vast network of nuclear bases, ports and airfields was set up throughout the region with little, if any, consultation with the indigenous people. Today, heralded by the example of Vanuatu, there is an impressively united and growing movement for a nuclear-free and independent Pacific, a movement in which women play a leading role.

From 1975, when the First Pacific Women's Regional Conference took place in Fiji, the **Pacific women's movement** has spread to more and more countries. Much of its work is co-ordinated by the Pacific Women's Resource Centre which links up groups and spreads information with the help of a satellite communications system. As well as the vital nuclear issue, the concerns of the movement include violence against women, racist and sexist use of experimental contraception, tourist exploitation, and the need for a feminist approach to development projects.

Adventures of a "Snail Woman"

. . . .

Linda Hill, a forty-year-old New Zealander, spent two months in the Pacific islands of Tonga, Samoa and the Cook Islands, before travelling on for another seven weeks to Vanuatu: "Nuclear free, independent, and a different world."

Vanuatu is a scattering of Melanesian islands between New Caledonia and the Solomons. It is too far from the rich tourist markets of the First World to get many visitors. A few package tourists arrive to stay in the overpriced hotels, and regular cruise ships stop for day visits, releasing a flood of very white Australians over Port Vila or Champagne Beach. But backpackers are still virtually unknown – in a six-week stay, I met one Japanese guy waiting out his visa renewal for Tuvalu, and two Australian nurses exploring Vanuatu largely by trading ship, as I was myself. And I would say, from the way news of their later movements reached me through the locals, we five were the only ones in the country at that time.

"It seemed acceptable that, having no family responsibilities, I should be free to do as I pleased"

The crews of the trading ships seemed familiar with the ways of backpackers. Outside Vial and Sano, however, people stopped what they were doing and came over to investigate. "Where are you going? Who are you visiting? Are you a teacher, a nurse or a missionary? And where is your husband?" The Australian women told me that in Hogg Harbour the village women had gone into a huddle at the sight of them and come out giggling. "You are snail women," they were told. "You carry your house on your back and you walk slow!" Though my pack was light and I carried no tent, I was delighted to think of myself as a snail woman too.

My standard answer to the recurrent question, "Where is your husband?" was, "No husband, they're too much work." The women would laugh and agree. It seemed acceptable that, having no family responsibilities, I should be free to do as I pleased. There don't seem to be possible penalties attached to a woman walking or travelling on her own, as in, say Samoa, where a woman who doesn't take her sister along might meet difficulties, especially after sundown.

Certainly, I always felt very safe and welcome – a pleasant novelty for the locals rather than an intruder. The women I met were very friendly and generous and the "house on my back" slowly filled with beautiful hand-made baskets and grass skirts. The best I could do in return was to take addresses and photos, inevitably posed, and send copies when I got home.

As in Polynesia, hospitality is given on the assumption that it will be returned. Where this is unlikely it is important to try and redress the balance of obligation, and not to leave people the poorer. Take enough food with you: tea, sugar, coffee, rice, tinned beef or fresh meat from the town are suitable gifts to offer if you are invited to visit someone's family or village for a few days. If you're uncertain you can always ask another *ni-Vanuatu* (literally, born Vanuatu) to advise you on what is appropriate.

Exploring on your own, accommodation can often be found in one village or the next if you ask around. A church may have a room for guests or there may be a women's committee house, perhaps doubling as their kindergarten, where visitors can be put up. There may be a fixed charge for an overnight stay, but where this is not specified, it is appropriate to make a donation of about the going rate, say, 200–300 vatu, to the women's committee, church or chief.

Interest in you will include concern that you are eating. If you have your own food, it is advisable to make that clear or someone will turn up with a plate of *taro* and "Vanuatu tinned fish" (land crab!). You could share your supplies or contribute some from the village co-op store, or accept whatever arrangement will be made for you and make sure your donation redresses the balance. Someone will show you where women and men go to wash. If camping, it is nearly always proper to check with the nearest village about a campsite. Perhaps safest, too, to be in a way under the villagers' wing, since people will certainly come to see what you are up to.

The 105 languages spoken in Vanuatu present a problem to locals rather than to the traveller, but it is quite usual for totally "uneducated" people to speak two or three languages besides their own. Those with schooling will speak either French or English, as well as the *lingua franca* preferred by independent Vanuatu – Bislama.

Bislama is largely a corrupted English vocabulary, on a Polynesian grammar base, and can be learned easily enough by English speakers with the aid of books available in Vila. People tend to ask standard questions about background and family, and I was soon able to conduct the basic social conversation in Bislama and understand a remarkable amount on more complex subjects. I speak French and met many English- and French-speaking *ni-Vanuatu* with whom I could communicate at a very satisfactory level. I found that I learned a great deal about the country and current opinions and politics.

"I very quickly had to revise any notion that this society was less socially advanced than my own"

Choice of language is a political question in modern Vanuatu. Under the old colonial condominium there were areas of strong French (Catholic, Francophone) and British (Anglican in the north, Presbyterian in the south, Anglophone) influence which still structure politics today. The present Vanua'aku Party government reflects mainly the Anglophone communities, while the gradually consolidating main opposition comes from Francophones.

But large areas are still *kustom*. These villages should not be regarded as "backward" or merely left behind by modernisation. Theirs is often a deliberate political choice, reflecting condemnation of both sides for undermining age-old conventions and traditional forms of leadership by introducing the colonial system of electoral government. There are various expressions of this view, but it has been associated with rejection of churches and education, always the thin edge of the colonial/imperialistic wedge. A recent solution by less remote *kustom* villages has been to send most children to a French-speaking school since the present government is Anglophone, but a few children to an English-speaking school, just in case. This may be supplemented with a *kustom* school to preserve the old ways.

I very quickly had to revise any notion that this society was less socially advanced than my own. Most of the people I met lived in communal, non-cash, village economies, still only peripherally connected to the money economy of capitalism through need for tools, kitchen equipment, clothes, modern building materials, transport, fuel and – less fortunately – tinned goods, tailor-made cigarettes and Fosters lager. A comfortable basis for village life is still provided by food and materials from gardens, sea and bush. "We don't have to pay money for everything, like you," my friend Ernestine told me. "We can take two or three weeks' holiday anytime and there'll still be plenty to feed the kids."

Other criteria of supposed "backwardness" stem from simple lack of access to information and knowledge that our world takes for granted. Access to radio is recent and *battery* (cash) dependent. Books and even writing materials are largely non-existent outside Vila and Santo. Take copies of the government newspaper with you from Vila and pass on any spare magazines, maps, or other material in English or French.

My church affiliation was something I was asked about constantly. Each Sunday I was in Vanuatu I seemed to go to a different denominational church with the different people I met. I had resurrected a brief Anglican background for conversational purposes, but then found myself very embarrassed at being the only person at a service who didn't know the Anglican prayerbook responses by heart, especially as I was the only mother-tongue English speaker.

In the past, bits of information, missionary teaching, and such bizarre experiences as the sudden arrival and equally rapid departure of Uncle Sam with World War II, led to some ingenious philosophical explanations of the world, such as the still popular *Jon Frum* cargo cult in Tanna.

Cargo cults mushroomed throughout Melanesia with the arrival of European-manufactured goods, which being inexplicable according to local technology, were understood in spiritual and millenial terms: "Our ancestors must be sending us things. These Europeans try to make us pay but one day our ship will come." The *Jon Frum* ("frum" means American) variation on this theme seems to have been sparked off by a US pilot's decision to redistribute goods meant for the war front to Tanna locals.

In the more remote islands and villages, people just don't get to hear about things and have no way of checking what they do hear. You will meet with some fascinating opinions and you yourself will be a source of information for people. One thing *ni-Vanuatu* like is a "good story" and I had to repeat again and again the different things that had happened to me on my trip.

I was able to relate first-hand news of the devastation still being caused to villages by the volcano in East Tanna. I told about going to the Friday night *Jon Frum* cargo cult service at Sulphur Bay and dancing with the women in a grass skirt that they gave me to the wonderful funky music. Then there was the walk home in pitch dark across an eerie moonscape of black ash, lit only by thunderous flashes from the volcano, and the deaf man who nearly jumped out of his skin when I tapped him on the arm and pushed my white face into his to ask directions.

My white face often had a similar effect on toddlers, who no doubt associated me with doctors, nurses, injections and nasty tastes. Smiling didn't help – they all do that before they hurt you.

"The sisters were still talking about a young German woman who had turned up in 1978 and stayed a fortnight with them"

Another very popular story I told was about dancing at a Vanuatu wedding in North Ambrym. I had arrived by trading ship at Ranon and walked up to the French-speaking villages around Olal. When I asked about accommodation, I was offered a bed in the New Zealand-donated leper hospital at St Jean's Mission, now just a clinic. But I should just drop my things and hurry, I was told, because the entire village was going to a wedding nearby.

The male teacher from the mission turned me over to some women my age, who talked to me in French, translating for others. With them I joined the line to kiss the beflowered bride and groom sitting under a canopy, leave a small present in a growing pile and have my head sprinkled with talcum powder. With Ernestine, her sister and her four children, I shared a large banana leaf parcel of earth-oven cooked *taro*, *kumara*, pork and beef, flavoured with fern leaves. The sisters were still talking about a young German woman who had turned up in 1978 and stayed a fortnight with them, just "doing what the women do".

That evening there was a wedding disco, with Western pop music, reggae and the local bands in Vila, tea with bread and butter, and *kava* out the back. Everyone was there; men and women danced in separate groups and I got up with the women I had met earlier. When I teased one for dropping out before I did, a man sprang over from the other side of the floor to sweep me off in a foxtrot. My tired partner at once started to beat him about the legs for the impudence of dancing with a woman, and everybody roared with laughter. This was a story that delighted *ni-Vanuatu* elsewhere: that I should have been dancing "Vanuatu-style" with the women. Europeans danced "modern-style" with a man, like people did in Vila. I tried to tell them their way suited me very well.

The "men's house" culture recorded by ethnographers and anthropologists throughout Melanesia seems to be paralleled by an unrecorded but strong women's culture. Women tend to work together in groups (much as they do in the factories, typing pools and other sex-segregated work in the West) and interact socially in groups of girls or women. Women approached me very easily and small groups of girls wanted to accompany me and show me everything. This women's culture is being supported by the liberal Vanua'aku Party government, with a few strong women's rights advocates such as Grace Molisa. Feminism seems at its beginning stages and, like the rest of Vanuatu's development, will, I hope, be a home-grown product.

I came back from Vanuatu with a strong desire to go back in a couple of years, not to be a "snail woman" again but to stay in one of the villages for a month or so, just "doing what the women do". In the meantime I have a plan for subsistence agriculture in my Auckland garden!

A Nice Life . . . for a Tourist

. . . .

Carol Stetser is an American artist and founder of Padma Press. After living for fifteen years in rural Arizona, she and her partner sold their house and decided to spend a year travelling and doing independent art studies in the Pacific. They began their trip in Fiji.

We arrived in Fiji at five in the morning, tired after an eleven-hour flight and not ready for the onslaught of taxi drivers who surrounded us as soon as we emerged from customs.

Our destination was a hotel on Saweni Beach, north of the Nadi airport and south of Lautoka. We drove past barren hillsides covered only with brown grass. Was this the South Pacific? Not a palm tree in sight. The valleys were all cultivated with sugar-cane. We saw long-horned bullocks pulling wooden ploughs followed by Sari-clad Indians. Trucks piled high with cut cane passed us on the road. Narrow-gauge tracks ran parallel to the road, and periodically the long, slow-moving cane train, its flatbed cars piled high with cane, chugged by. We felt like we were in India.

Saweni Beach turned out to be a good place to rest after the long flight, and to unwind into Fijian time. Our room looked out on to a wide green lawn with coconut palms and beyond this were field after field of sugar cane with green leaves standing eight to ten feet high. We could hear the loud horn of the sugar train as it switched back and forth across road junctions on its way to the mill at Lautoka, the sugar capital, the noise rising easily above the crowing of roosters and the bellowing of cows tethered nearby. Early every morning the fishermen would paddle ashore in their fifteen-foot wooden boats to sell their fish from the beach.

There was also a small store where we could buy eggs, bread and beer.

Time is measured in Fiji in terms of the coup of 1987. Before the coup there was a restaurant at Saweni Beach; before the coup the pool was operational; before the coup the taxi driver brought his family to the beach on Sunday. But now the foreign owner doesn't want to put any money into a hotel and the cooking staff has been sent home. Taxis cannot run on Sunday so the taxi driver without a second car must stay at home. All small businesses are closed on Sunday – since the coup.

Only sugar cane mills are supposed to run and this directive has sparked revolt, with workers refusing to harvest their cane on Sunday. Inflation and a devalued dollar has more or less doubled the price of everything. Tourism is down fifty percent since the coup, when the rooms at Saweni Beach were full. Now the lobby and dining areas were empty and maybe half the rooms were rented. Who knows what is going to happen?

It made us uneasy being this close to Lautoka where so much of the trouble had erupted. There were more Indians here than Fijians and an undercurrent of tension was apparent to even the casual tourist. An internal security measure was passed a month before our visit and an amnesty was in effect for the return of weapons shipped illegally into Fiji since the coup. We didn't want to be here when the amnesty ended in July 1988.

We bargained for a taxi to drive us south to the Coral Coast, through the concrete boulevard of duty-free shops and hustle that is Nadi, through the Polynesian Fijian villages, over a mountain pass covered with pine trees, and down into the coconut-fringed coast where the locals and tourists alike come to play.

Our destination, Tumbakula Beach Cottages, was full; so was Sandy Point; the Reef was too expensive; Waratah Lodge was full. The cabby was getting edgy and so were we – tired and hungry after the two-hour drive. The Fijian manager of the Lodge told us of a house for rent. We were sceptical but in desperation decided to give it a look. What luck! It was a luxurious *palangi* house, owned by a New Zealander, right on the beach in Korotogo and set in a compound landscaped in a true Polynesian fantasy: coconut palms and ornamental plants, grass lawn and lovely flowers, even a lily pond with magnificent large pink blooms and a multitude of grotesque bullfrogs that would plop into the pad-covered water whenever anyone approached. "Life doesn't get much better than this," we sighed, as we unpacked our clothes.

A block from the house was the Korotogo store and a bus stop on the Nadi–Suva highway. The buses are an experience. Local buses are air-cooled, and have no glass in the windows; when it rains, a large plastic curtain is rolled down to cover the openings. I have seen the passengers climb out of the windows of a full bus when it stops at the beach with a load of picnickers. The bus crawls along the Queen's Road from Lautoka to Suva so it's a great way to go sightseeing.

"We wondered how all the small shops ever stay in business until we saw the tour buses arrive, full of Australasians"

Once a week we went to town, crossing the Sigatoka River over an old one-lane bridge whose traffic was regulated by a street light that worked periodically. Main Street paralleled the river: hardware stores, sporting goods, banks, tourist tee-shirt shops, handicraft centres, the ubiquitous duty-free shops, milk bars and refreshment stands. A block away from this main thoroughfare was the small bus terminal and the covered market, dark and chaotic, where the smell of curry overpowered the aroma of bananas. We wondered how all the small shops ever stay in business until we saw the four buses arrive, full of Australasians.

Fiji in July (winter in the Pacific) is pretty hot and humid but not unbearable. We couldn't imagine what the summers must be like. Most of the other tourists seemed to restrict themselves to the hotel pools or shopping in Sigatoka, so we had the beach more or less to ourselves. At low tide I could walk for miles from our house, observing all the marine life to be found along the water's edge: coral hiding a blue starfish or the long brown sea snakes, transparent small fish darting away from my shadow, crabs scurrying from my approach to hide in the sand, and big fat slugs.

At full moon, when the tide was exceptionally low, the Fijian women would hike up their skirts and, bending double, root for clams or octopus along the reef. The men, meanwhile, sat in the shade on the beach and drank beer. When their sacks were full the fisherwomen would heave them onto their backs and head back to the village, while the children frolicked in the water and the men shuffled empty-handed behind them.

We rented a car for a week to drive southeast along the highway toward Suva, the capital. Here the lush, verdant jungle was such a contrast to the dry, brown hills of the west. Along the road we visited all the $200-a-day luxury resorts; we browsed in the lobby shops and sat around on their beaches. It was a disorienting experience. There were no Fijians staying in these resorts, only white tourists served by smiling Fijian waiters. "Bula Bula" and "Welcome" to the Fijian or the Sheraton or the Hyatt.

Not a mile down the road from this opulence was a village of thatched *bures*, one-room tin shacks with screenless windows and outhouses; barefoot, often naked children; unpenned animals; and women washing their clothes while squatting in the river. The mind boggles at trying to reconcile these two extremes.

TRAVEL NOTES

Language More than 700 languages are spoken throughout the South Pacific, but you're sure to find someone who speaks English, especially in Fiji. Here the main languages are Fijian and Hindustani, while in Vanuatu it is Bislama.

Accommodation Available in all price ranges on Fiji's main island, though hotels fill up very quickly in winter. Elsewhere you will often have no choice but to accept village hospitality. Such invitations are a privilege and require at least some understanding of local culture and traditions.

Transport A limited selection of trading and cargo ships, and domestic airlines will carry you between the islands. Of the two domestic airlines, Dovair is slightly cheaper. Cargo ship is about half the cost of an airfare and includes

meals. Take a radio to check the shipping news and keep your fingers crossed. They go by cargoes, not schedules. Transport on land varies from place to place, but anywhere of any size has a bus service.

Special Problems Be careful not to offend local customs by your dress. A woman's thighs are considered more erotic than her breasts and are not meant to be exposed in public, so shorts are definitely out.

Guides *South Pacific Handbook* (Moon Publications, US) is very practical and covers even quite remote places. Lonely Planet have individual *Travel Survival Kits* to Tonga, Samoa, New Caledonia, Raratonga & the Cook Islands, Tahiti & French Polynesia, Fiji, Micronesia and The Solomon Islands.

Contacts

The following organisations are all based in Fiji, but should be able to provide information about women's activities in the rest of the South Pacific.

Tok Blong Ol Meri/YWCA, Pacific office, Box 3940, Samabula, Suva. Dedicated to promoting improvements for women in the region, the Fiji office also produces a newsletter, *Ofis Blong Ol Meri.*

The **Pacific Women's Resource Centre**, PO Box 534, Suva. As well as housing resources, the centre publishes a magazine, *Women Speak Out.*

The **National Council for Women**, PO Box 840, Suva. National co-ordinating body for non-governmental women's organisations.

Books

Jan Dibblin, *Day of Two Suns: US Nuclear Testing and the Pacific Islanders* (Virago, 1989). Account of protest amid the atolls and in the international courts against the inhuman appropriation and use of land by the US military. Draws widely on the personal experiences of women and men of the Marshall Islands.

Grace Mara Molisa, *Colonised People*, (Black Stone Publications, Port Vila, 1987). Poetry plus statistics on women in Vanuatu.

Margaret Sinclair, *The Path of the Ocean: Traditional Poetry of Polynesia* (Hawaii U. Press, US, 1982). Fascinating transcription of traditional oral verse.

Thanks to Carol Stetser and Linda Hill for help with the introduction and Travel Notes.

Pakistan

Benazir Bhutto's accession to power in Pakistan in November 1988 was one of the decade's most extraordinary events: a woman elected to the most powerful office of a neo-fundamentalist Islamic state. Yet, almost from the moment of taking her seat at the head of the ruling Pakistan's People's Party, her administration has been under siege, with mounting opposition from the army and growing fundamentalist factions, constitutional wrangles over her prime ministerial powers, and deep divisions and dissent within her own party. Her landmark post-election promise to remove discriminatory laws against women (more particularly to repeal the restrictive Hudood Ordinance that effectively defines a woman as a permanent minor) appears to have sunk without trace, while many other radical policies have floundered in compromise and political concessions. Significantly, she has also changed the image she presents to the public, assuming the more submissive stance of a traditional wife (accepting an arranged marriage) and mother. Calls for another general election are intensifying and it seems unlikely that Benazir Bhutto will be able to retain her mandate.

The atmosphere of political instability (violence has erupted in the province of Sind and along the border with Afghanistan) coupled with widespread and intense sexual harassment makes this a very difficult country to travel around alone. Westerners are viewed stereotypically as morally lax and promiscuous, a notion that's confirmed by the fact that they choose to leave the protection of their homes and mix freely with men in public. Away from the luxury star hotels it takes a fair amount of resilience to cope with the continual propositions, leering and comments. Dressing with extreme modesty helps – for instance wearing the traditional *shalwaar kameez* (loose fitting trousers and tunic) – as does travelling with a man. But unless you're escorted by Pakistani friends, your chances of avoiding unpleasantness are very slim. For some, however, the spectacular scenery of Pakistan's mountains and ravines make it all worthwhile.

The Islamicisation programme introduced during the Zia years ushered in a wave of legislation that very clearly limited women's freedoms and undermined their security at the heart of the family. These rules are still being implemented, most forcefully against working-class women, who cannot protect themselves with bribes or family influence. Under the notorious Hudood Ordinance, women are no longer allowed to testify in a murder case, cannot secure a rape conviction without four *male* witnesses and, unless rape is proved, run the risk of being themselves imprisoned, flogged or stoned for the crime of *zina* (adultery or unlawful sexual intercourse).

Opposition to these laws remains strong. The *Pakistan Women's Action Forum (WAF)*, the main **feminist organisation**, has set up groups in all the major towns and spearheads campaigns for the laws to be repealed. Large demonstrations were staged in Lahore and Karachi even under Zia, though they were dispersed by mass arrests and a brutal show of force. Perhaps the saddest aspect of Bhutto's compromised politics is that having endorsed the WAF charter of demands she has been unable either to prevent or condemn the use of police force in breaking up continuing women's demonstrations.

A Cautious Enjoyment

. . . .

Sarah Wetherall spent six weeks in Pakistan, squeezing in the trip on her way back from India, where she had been working as a volunteer. She is a student of fine art and uses her experiences of travel in her work.

Arriving from India, I had been used to the cultural and social restrictions on women, Indian and Western, and I expected to see few women on the streets and stricter segregation of the sexes in public areas. At first, I was pleasantly surprised to find women walking around Lahore dressed in *shalwaar kameez* (a long sleeved shirt with loose trousers) with a *dupati* (a long scarf) over their head, rather than the full *burqua* that covers the body from head to toe. But my initial impression of freedom proved to be deceptive.

Arriving at the YWCA I found fellow travellers complaining that it was almost impossible to wander out alone; slipping past the matron took hours of intrigue and once on the streets there were continual problems of harassment to contend with. The YWCA had become both a welcome retreat and a prison. It was like some British Victorian boarding house, where middle-class women led chaperoned lives. Piano and typing lessons were held at the beginning of the day and the professional women who lodged at the hostel would go out to teach school-children in the mornings. One woman was allowed to meet her fiancé in a small room in the hostel for an hour each evening and, despite the fact that they were good friends, the door to the room had to be left open. All lights were out at ten.

The mosque and fort in Lahore were the main recreation areas for the Friday holiday. Children played cricket on the grass outside and families picnicked and bought ice creams. The amplified chants from the mosque resounding over the miniature orange trees seemed to conjure up the image that most Westerners hold of Asian Islam. I sat under a tree, nursing a headache, with my *dupati* pulled over my head, and tried to ignore the fact that men were staring at me. A carefully aimed cricket ball landed in my lap, not once but three times, and each time a girl ran across to collect it and gave me a friendly smile. Finally, her mother came up and tried to explain about the attention I was attracting.

"Pakistan men not OK" (*teek na he*), she explained. Her husband and brother had sent her over to save me from the stares. Her son was sent to get me a cup of tea for my headache and I was taken around the old fort with the family. Her husband and sons paid me the customary compliment of not acknowledging or addressing me except to make sure that I wasn't getting lost in the crowd. The family was the first in a long line of people who were to help me out. My vulnerability was double edged. As a woman, I was open to harassment but also equally open to great hospitality and kindness from people amazed to find me travelling alone and unprotected in their country.

The question of religion constantly came up. Before arriving in Pakistan I had been advised not to attempt to explain the casual Western agnostic view. This proved sound advice as your religion defines who you are. I opted for Christianity. One or two women actually approached me to talk about their faith after finding out that I was a Christian too. Their opposition to Islam was whispered as, under the Islamicisation laws, blasphemy is punishable by death. However, I was unsure whether their antipathy to Islam was towards the religion itself or the cruelty that women are beginning to suffer under the fundamentalists.

"The women I met were polite in their bewilderment at my presence in their country"

When I asked for directions in the street, I always approached women first and would act as though affronted if any strange man tried to strike up a conversation with me. But I also made mistakes in this area. At a guesthouse in 'Pindi, I began to wonder at the heavy sighs of the waiters when I sat down for my evening meal. It was only after two days that I understood. I was sitting at the wrong table – a table for four – and, as no man could share it with me, was taking up precious space. I eventually banished myself to the small segregated women's tables, where we ate together below the TV in the corner of the room. My views of the test match were, consequently, coupled with a severely cricked neck.

However, I certainly didn't resent the women's segregation in the buses and minibuses whilst travelling on long journeys. A happy camaraderie exists, at the very back or front of the bus. My huge supply of art materials and drawing pads were soon whittled away as kids energetically pounced on my felt tips and leafed through the pictures in my guidebook.

The actual vehicles were certainly different after India. Auto rickshaws were a uniform blue and decorated with paintings and stickers of animals noted for their prowess, such as tigers and falcons. Shiny Islamic stickers replaced Hindu imagery and there was also a Muslim pin-up of women in lipstick and mascara, pouting through a thin veiled *dupati*. Minibuses were my favourite form of transport, their interiors decorated with pictures of Imrahn Khan, Bhutto and Zia. Outside, Pakistan rolled by – abandoned donkeys next to multistorey car parks, grey-pink sunsets with a train of camels on the horizon, women carrying children and bundles of grass with a herd of goats in tow.

The women I met were polite in their bewilderment at my presence in their country. I had four brothers and sisters, so why was I alone in Pakistan? This incomprehension was also partly the reason for being refused a room at guesthouse counters. What was wrong with me, I despaired. I was polite, I was well-mannered, I was conservatively dressed. The difficulty was in fact twofold. Firstly, if a single room was refused, I would have to stay in a double room at twice the price. The second reason for rejection was wariness of single foreign women for, simply by being there, I would attract men hanging around the hotel. (This seemed to apply only to smaller guesthouses and only in the more rural areas.)

Though I had been advised in advance by a British Pakistani woman to stick to the main cities, I felt more relaxed in the smaller, more remote areas. It was easier to find my way around and the atmosphere was friendlier. I especially enjoyed my time in the Northern Hunza Valley, though this was partly because I spent most of my time with a Western man.

After staggering into a guesthouse in Bhawalpur in the South Cholistan desert, with rucksack and painting materials and being very politely refused a room, I sat down dispiritedly and didn't move.

"You are single?" the manager asked. I affirmed, and a worried discussion ensued with a group of men casting anxious glances at me. I eventually asked the manager what the problem was.

"In Pakistan women never single," he replied.

They eventually gave me the room because I was an artist. "A painter!" they all said in relief.

Bhawalpur was getting used to single women after Zia's assassination nearby. I later cashed in on this and became a self-appointed journalist. My profession gave me a certain amount of respectability. I also learned the key to getting around safely and seeing as much as possible outside of the major cities.

"The tourist office in Bhawalpur provided me with a guide whom they proudly asserted was the only man they would trust in the whole town"

Anywhere vaguely official, such as smarter hotels, newspaper offices or tourist offices, could somehow provide a reliable male escort. The tourist office in Bhawalpur provided me with a guide whom they proudly asserted was the only man they would trust in the whole town. We motorbiked through the desert and I even managed to get some painting done. Resorting to male escorts – in reality, bodyguards – may seem to be copping out, but the alternative, staying in self imposed *purdah* within four walls of a hotel room, seemed a worse defeat. My escort from the tourist office had helped out women travellers before. Two other girls had once come to the office, depressed, upset and terrified of Pakistan. I sympathised with their story. The continual harassment by Pakistani men; low wolf whistles in my ear, oppressive attention, verbal abuse ("fuck me baby"), made my hotel room seem distinctly inviting.

The combination of sexually liberated women in the bygone age of the hippy trail and widely circulated Western pornography make up a formidable myth of the Western woman as a whore. A myth that cannot be exploded by a single woman traveller wearing a *dupati* for protection. Women, on the other hand, did not seem to hold this view of Westerners and were kind, warm, and anxious to gently correct mistakes that I made in public so that I wouldn't put myself in embarrassing or dangerous situations, saying "sit here with us", "queue here for your tickets", etc. I met women everywhere, in the telephone exchange, on buses, in post offices where friendliness and concern bridged all language and cultural barriers. Travelling alone often brings about strong swings of mood and I didn't want my impressions of Pakistan to be coloured by stressful harassment. Women certainly made my time easier in Pakistan. The occasional male escort enabled me to enjoy my time there – albeit a cautious enjoyment.

The codes of hospitality are very strict and it is a delicate task to accept but not take advantage of hospitality, as your hosts adopt your concerns as their own. Soon I learnt not to mention my intention to do anything, or that I was thirsty or hungry, as it resulted in an embarrassing flurry of hospitality that I couldn't accept. Having mistimed my arrival in a desert town, I got off a bus in the middle of the night and was escorted by a couple *and* the bus driver to a "good" hotel. There were no rooms free but instead of turning me away, I was put up in the manager's office with the words: "You are a visitor to our country, it is an honour."

Obviously relying on hospitality is not the best way to travel. I saw few Westerners and only two Western women on their way back to work in Peshawar. There was so much that was regrettably too difficult to see or do, such as eating out at night, walking in the Chitral district, going scuba diving in Karachi, etc. In replying to my letter of thanks after returning to Britain, my escort from the desert wrote that it was a great pleasure to help a "good girl" like myself.

I think back on the restrictions that were formidable, numerous and often trivial. Lighting up a cigarette on a bus on my first day in Pakistan almost caused a traffic pile-up as the driver turned round to gasp! The careful constraint I had to use was quite difficult for a chain smoker and a "good girl" such as myself.

Alone on the Overland Route

. . . .

Wendy Dison has been travelling since 1980 when she realised that a career in administration was not for her. She crossed through Pakistan on her way from Iran to India.

Where the eastern Iranian desert meets the Baluchistan desert of Pakistan a wire fence runs across the sand to mark the border. In the Pakistan frontier town of Taftan a warm wind whipped up the dust in the main street where goats chewed pieces of cardboard and wild-looking men with dark skins squatted in the shade.

Proprietors of shops made of packing cases watched me with friendly interest. One man with a gold-embroidered pill-box hat and a ready smile that revealed large white teeth invited me to rest in his shop until my bus left. During the afternoon he brought bowls of stewed meat and potatoes from the cookshop over the road and showed me how to eat using only a *chapati*. I found it difficult but he encouraged me, ignoring the mess I was making.

A loud two-tone horn announced the departure of the Quetta bus waiting in the bazaar, brilliantly decorated with coloured lights, chrome, plastic cut-out shapes and rows of chains dangling from the bumpers. Men swarmed up and down the ladder at the back to load boxes and bundles on the roof while inside I scrambled for a seat, climbing over enormous quantities of luggage and stools in the aisle. The men stared at me and I was too overwhelmed to do more than stare back.

We travelled east on a dirt road with bone-rattling ridges across the vast stony Baluchistan desert where everything – rocks, bushes, people – had been bleached and burnt to the colour of the earth. The sun set spectacularly and as soon as it touched the horizon we stopped for prayers. The men dispersed, purified themselves with a symbolic "wash" in sand, faced Mecca and started the ritual of praying – bowing and touching their foreheads to the ground, kneeling in the last rays of the sun with their shoes beside them and their loose clothing blowing in the wind.

"After three days in the country I saw my first Pakistani women"

Around midnight we stopped in a small village. In a pool of lamplight outside a restaurant groups of people squatted on rush matting around teapots and bowls. Huge pans simmered on a mudbrick fireplace and unglazed pots of water stood on straw rings with drinking bowls balanced on top. Two men wearing wide Afghan turbans invited me to join them and we ate in a friendly silence, dipping our *chapatis* into a communal dish of meat and drinking bowl after bowl of green tea.

In Quetta, the capital of Baluchistan, the broad avenues lined with plane trees and houses set in walled gardens are unmistakably British but the bazaars, I was relieved to find, are colourful, bustling and very much Asian. On the pavements men are shaved, tailors work at sewing machines and cooks stir smoking pans of *samosas* and sell them in bags made from used school exercise books. Lorries decorated with exotic paintings of tigers and mosques trundle past raising clouds of dust and heavy black bicycles, carrying three people, weave amongst camel-drawn carts and buses groaning under the weight of men clinging on to the outside. I ate in a restaurant with smoke-blackened walls and a choice of either tables and chairs or a raised platform for those who preferred to squat. Men watched me curiously and when I looked up from my spiced spinach they held their gaze. Pakistani men look each other in the eye without embarrassment but I found their steady gaze disconcerting.

After three days in the country I saw my first Pakistani women. Travelling in the ladies' compartment of the Quetta Express the women emerged from their sombre veils and the carriage was filled with glittering colourful fabrics, gold earrings, jewelled nose studs and smiling faces. Delighted to meet a foreigner they spoke to me in Urdu, teasing me when I couldn't understand and enjoying my attempts to pronounce their names. My photos from home fascinated them and one woman, married only two months, showed me her wedding album. They offered me *pan* – a mixture of spices and mild intoxicants wrapped in a betal leaf – and laughed when I screwed up my face at the bitter taste then, in my ignorance, swallowed it with watering eyes. At the stations we reached through the windows and bought hard-boiled eggs, bananas, and tea in disposable clay cups. Later, when it grew dark and sleeping shapes draped with shawls sprawled on the hard wooden seats and carriage floor, the women offered me a turn on the luggage rack and I slept. ·

Multan, a traditional religious city, came as a shock. Women wore the *burka*, a garment that fits tightly round the crown of the head, completely covering all but the woman's feet. She sees the world through a net visor. In traditional society women turn their backs on male strangers. Hurrying along the back streets of the towns they turned away as I passed, mistaking me for a man. My behaviour rather than my appearance was to blame for the misconception; I was doing things that Muslim women didn't do. It saddened me to see them pull their veils over their faces and retreat into the shadows.

"That night, lying awake with men peeping at me through knot holes in the door, my spirits were low"

The men were clearly unused to seeing Western women. Youths trailed me, giggling and jostling, leering rickshaw drivers kerb-crawled, men followed me making kissing sounds and suggestive comments, and boys nearly fell off their bikes in their efforts to turn and watch me. I felt so uncomfortable that I returned to my hotel.

That night, lying awake with men peeping at me through knot holes in the door, my spirits were low. It seemed that the dire warnings I'd been given about Pakistani men were justified. How could I hope to travel in this country? I was heading for the mountains and experience led me to hope that it would be different there. Yet my guidebook gave the disheartening advice that it was dangerous to travel alone in the Himalayas – for women, of course. I left

for Lahore early in the morning, hating myself for giving in but unable to face another day in Multan.

Lahore felt much more European. Unlike their drab veiled country sisters the women of Lahore wear brilliant colours and their *shalwaar kameez* are more tightly fitting – some even have short sleeves, though legs are always covered. However, it was difficult to look around the city. I attracted whistles and leers even though I was modestly dressed. Men stood close to me, staring, oblivious to my feelings, and everybody asked questions, always the same, about my country, my name, my age, my occupation, my qualifications. Few people bothered to listen to the answers.

By the time I left for the mountains I loathed men. The *chai* shop at the bus station smelt of diesel fumes and was crowded with men sheltering from the rains. The wails of a baby came from behind a curtain where women could sit in private. The waiter, confused by my anomalous status, did not seat me with the women but cleared a table for me and protectively kept away any man who tried to sit with me. Outside the rain poured, streaming from the plastic sheeting that vendors rigged up over their stalls and filling potholes in the bus yard through which motor rickshaws lurched. People struggled in the mud in plastic slip-on shoes.

After a twenty-hour bus journey up the Indus gorge we emerged in Gilgit, isolated amongst the high mountains of the Karakorams. In the dusty bazaar swarthy men wearing dun-coloured blankets over their *shalwaar kameez* stared at me curiously. In tiny shops bargaining sessions were conducted over glasses of tea, the customers sitting on sacks of lentils or squatting against piles of rock-salt, smoking cigarettes through clenched fists. If the draped figures of women were seen at all they disappeared quickly.

In the *chai* shop, men lounging on string beds turned to look as I entered.

The sight of a foreigner, let alone a female one, was enough to attract attention and it was impossible for me to break through the barrier of staring eyes and speak to anyone. Maybe the men weren't unfriendly, just ill at ease when a woman invaded their preserve. But the result was the same; I drank alone.

"Maybe the men weren't unfriendly, just ill at ease when a woman invaded their preserve"

Away from the town it was different. Walking on tracks between villages I was stared at by children and tongue-tied youths and young women giggled at me, but everyone greeted me with "Salaam". In the villages so many people invited me in for tea it was difficult to choose one house without offending.

At the end of the day the smell of wood smoke heralded a settlement. Children came whooping down the terraces shouting "angrezi" (foreigner) and led me to an old man sitting outside his house, presumably the headman. Inside, orders were given to his wife and daughters and a meal of *chapatis*, chillied potatoes and rice was prepared on the stove. The women held a water jug for the man and I to wash our hands, then served the meal to us, waiting until we had finished before they ate. I hated the deference they showed me. As a foreigner and an honorary male I felt I was betraying these women.

These women had little variety in their lives and seemed to enjoy my visits as a break in their routine. Away from men they relaxed. Though we had no common language they managed to ask many questions: "Was I alone? Why did I have short hair? How many children had I?" In a land where children are highly valued, I was pitied for being childless. Once I was admonished for my immodesty and advised to roll my sleeves down and button my shirt higher at my neck. Often I was gently teased and it didn't matter that I couldn't understand. It was frustrating however, not to be able to talk to the women other than in sign language. The Urdu I was learning was little use when every village spoke a different dialect, and as girls have only recently started to receive education, few women spoke English.

Being invited into people's homes, forbidden to men outside the family, was one of the privileges I enjoyed in Pakistan. But it didn't outweigh the disadvantages. In many areas I felt threatened. Probably there was no real danger although once I was forced to turn back when a man blocked my way, masturbating. Conflicting emotions confused me as I left. In this country I had felt oppressed even while I was humbled by the hospitality. And three months of being treated as a second-class citizen, albeit often graciously, had left me resentful of being a woman. This was the hardest thing to bear. I can't imagine that Benazir Bhutto's election success will make any difference. It will take more than one woman, powerful but far removed from the lives of ordinary women, to change the attitude of the Muslim male.

TRAVEL NOTES

Languages Urdu, Pushtu and many others. You will find many people speak English in the main towns.

Transport Most buses and trains have special seats or compartments for women and children. There are also different queues for women to buy tickets.

Accommodation A wide range, from top-class international-style hotels to small, very basic inns. Some of the smaller hotels refuse to let out rooms to single women.

Special Problems Harassment can become restrictive and oppressive. It helps to dress conservatively in long, loose clothes or the traditional *shalwaar kameez* (long-sleeved tunic and trousers). It's also possible to hire a guide from a hotel. If you ever feel uneasy you should seek help from Pakistani women.

Guide *Pakistan – A Travel Survival Kit* Lonely Planet) is the best researched, but you' I need to get local information on areas that are closed off by the military.

Contacts

Women's Action Forum (WAF) 103 Basement Raja centre, Main Market, Gulberg 2, Lahore (postal address: PO Box 3287, Gulberg, Lahore). Holds monthly public meetings, and organises workshops, seminars and discussion groups in both Urdu and English.

Asian Women's Institute, c/o Association of Kinnaird College for Women, Lahore-3. Active in the field of education and women's studies, also in rural development projects for women which emphasise consciousness-raising as well as economic growth.

Simorgh (Women's Resource and Publication Centre), 1st floor, Shiraz Plaza, Main Market, Gulberg 2, Lahore (postal address: PO Box 3328). A new women's centre aimed at providing resources, documentation, research etc, for the Women's Movement.

Books

Benazir Bhutto, *Daughter of the East* (Mandarin, 1988). Benazir describes her fabulously privileged upbringing in Pakistan, her Oxford years and the traumatic events surrounding her father's death. There's little that could be considered self-revealing although it's worth reading as a loose chronicle of the more obvious influences on her life.

Khawar Mumtaz and Farida Shaheed, *Women of Pakistan* (Zed Books, 1986). Concise account of women's determined resistance under the Zia regime.

Dervla Murphy, *Where the Indus is Young* (1976 Century, 1985). Lively account of a journey through the more remote parts of northern Pakistan which the author made with her seven-year-old daughter.

Paraguay

araguay is something of a backwater and is rarely visited in comparison to its Latin American neighbours. This fact is entirely to your advantage. There is little of the *gringa* mentality, and, even as a woman alone, you are unlikely to be intimidated by men. The kind of violence and theft against tourists associated with, say, Colombia, Peru or Brazil, is also virtually unknown.

Two bitter wars and several autocratic dictatorships have, however, left their scars on this remote, landlocked country, whose population includes a high proportion of people of Guarani Indian descent. During 34 years of military rule under the notorious General Alfredo Stroessner, when hundreds of political dissenters were killed, imprisoned, or disappeared, indigenous peoples faced extinction as their lands were seized to make way for cattle ranching, intensive agriculture and foreign speculators. At the same time Paraguay became known as a tax-free haven for infamous right-wing pariahs, including the deposed Nicaraguan dictator Anastasio Somoza and several Nazi war criminals. It also became known as an important staging post for drug traffickers.

Recently, however, the country has seen dramatic changes. In February 1989 Stroessner's former right-hand man, General Andreas Rodriguez, mounted a successful coup. Promising democracy and respect for human rights, he had little trouble in winning the presidential elections hastily thrown together some three months later. As he denies widespread accusations of involvement in the lucrative cocaine trade and people wait for signs of concrete reform, there is still hope that the fall of one of the world's most repressive dictatorships has opened up the way for a process of genuine democratisation.

The sleepiness and isolation of Paraguay is reflected in a set of outdated, patriarchal laws that discriminate blatantly against women. A woman found guilty of adultery receives a prison sentence twice as long as a man in the same situation, and, in the eyes of the law, rape of a single woman is a less serious crime than that of a married woman. Women were only accorded the right to vote in 1961 and as recently as 1987 the government passed a law prohibiting women from working outside the home without their husband's permission.

Although **women's groups** have started campaigning for legal changes in the last decade, on the whole they have been nowhere near as vociferous and radical as their sister organisations in the rest of South America. However, the Women's Movement does seem to be gaining momentum and groups have multiplied in the last five years. Since the fall of Stroessner the once censored progressive Radio Nanduti is back on the air and transmits a regular "woman's hour", known as "Palabra de Mujer", which provides women with an invaluable forum to air their views.

"Land of Peace and Sunshine"

. . . .

Mary Durran spent two months in Paraguay at the invitation of a missionary friend, towards the end of the Stroessner dictatorship. She now works for the London-based El Salvador and Guatemala Committees for Human Rights.

In spite of the claims in official tourist leaflets, there wasn't a great deal of sun when I arrived at Asunción airport. But the city was bathed in a wintry haze, dusk was approaching, and there was certainly an air of tranquillity, if not peace, about the place. Bored-looking officials stood around leaning on airport counters, grunting to each other in Guarani, Paraguay's indigenous language. Two of them welcomed the diversion of a thorough search through my rucksack.

I hadn't chosen Paraguay for any specific interest in the country's culture or politics. I had simply followed up the offer of a friend, Paco, who was sent there as a missionary shortly after being ordained as a priest. Caught up with sitting final exams and with my last long summer before me, I had vaguely suggested visiting him to "help with whatever I could", but had made no definite plans as to how I'd spend my time.

As we drove from the airport through the cobbled streets, swerving to avoid potholes, towards the suburb of Lambare, dishevelled-looking barefoot children approached us at traffic lights to sell us newspapers, crying their wares in the curious nasal tones that only a Guarani speaker could utter. I caught a glimpse of a weather-beaten old Indian woman, her wrinkled face blackened by constant exposure to the elements, her headdress a sad mass of flopping, dirty feathers. Cows grazed placidly on grass verges and squalid tumbledown shacks stood beside spacious white houses with gardens and swimming pools. Every street corner displayed the regulation poster of the ailing president of the republic with the slogan "Peace and progress with General Stroessner".

I was later to discover the Asunción depicted by the tourist leaflets: the grandiose white government palace, home to the president and a few dignitaries, which stands only a few yards away from the mosquito-infested shanty town on the edge of the River Paraguay; the impressive Hotel Guaraní and its fashion shows featuring the latest European collections for the Paraguayan jet set; exclusive discotheques where elegant bow-tied waiters address customers in the indigenous language, yet a beer would cost the average Paraguayan at least a day's wages. There was something faintly ridiculous about the sombre grandeur of the dark and cool interior of the Heroes' Pantheon, where the bodies of former dictators are interred.

A few days after my arrival, we drove along a dirt track road, pitted by ditches and potholes. Red sand flew everywhere. I was on my way to Yhu, a small town in the east of the country and home to about 1500 people. As we passed the *ranchitos* (wooden huts with thatched roofs) of the smallholders, old men raised their ruddy hands in greeting, their palms reddened by seasons of contact with the dark soil. The red sand contrasted with the verdant green of the surrounding *estancias* and beautiful brightly coloured butterflies basked in the hot sun.

Having done my homework, I knew that about 80,000 people, mainly smallholders and their families, lived in the district surrounding Yhu. There were only two doctors in this area, about the size of Wales, and I had been invited to stay with a family who were determined to improve the standard of healthcare in their community. Chiquita was a 23-year-old voluntary rural health worker living with her family in San Juan, a small community. Trained by missionary sisters in basic first aid and preventive healthcare, her main task was running the health club which had been set up to encourage villagers to take measures to prevent disease.

"From the advertising and television I saw in Asunción, European women and European lifestyles are presented as the models to aspire to"

As I was introduced to Chiquita's parents, her numerous brothers and sisters and in-laws, I took in what were to be my immediate surroundings for the next few days. The family was housed in four straw-roofed wooden huts in the middle of a plot of land where bananas and manioc (a starchy root crop) were cultivated. A couple of black piglets ran around squealing and several hens pecked at the ground. A crackly old wireless set played the latest American disco sounds alternated with the inimitable strains of Paraguayan polkas – popular folkloric music brought over by German settlers at the beginning of the century. Most of the words were in Guaraní, and sang of the beauty of the Paraguayan countryside and the charms of the indigenous *cunatái* – young women. There's some irony in such eulogies, since from the advertising and television I saw in Asunción, European women and European lifestyles are in reality presented as the models to aspire to.

A log fire in one of the huts served as the kitchen. To prepare a meal (often manioc and cornflour omelettes), water had to be drawn from the well and food was cooked in a pot hanging over the fire. There was no chimney. The fire burned from dawn to dusk providing light, warmth and comfort during the long winter evenings. Its earthy smell permeated everything – clothes, hair and sleeping bag – and remains one of my most vivid impressions of the few days spent with Chiquita and her family.

I was made to feel very welcome. Although not speaking Guarani was a distinct disadvantage (as it is everywhere in Paraguay), Chiquita's parents made sure their Spanish-speaking children translated their greetings and questions. Her teenage sisters and brother were intensely curious about me and never seemed to tire of staring while I wrote letters or read. This made me feel rather uncomfortable, though I tried to bear in mind that, for them, to stare was simply a natural expression of interest and curiosity.

"The family insisted on providing one of the younger brothers as a chaperone every time I went anywhere"

I very quickly became aware that I was an object of absolute fascination for most of the villagers too, many of whom had never been any further than Caaguazu, the main provincial town some sixty miles away. "Did I have a husband?" No, I answered patiently, to at least twenty different people. "Why then, was I not accompanied by at least one of my parents?" (I had to smile at the idea of my ageing parents accompanying me over gruelling dirt tracks to a hamlet where there was neither post, newspapers nor electricity!)

Since I was unaccompanied, the family insisted on providing one of the younger brothers as a chaperone every time I went anywhere, even if it were only a few yards away. I found this quite amusing if sometimes irritating, but realised that the family were genuinely concerned about my welfare and simply couldn't understand the notion that I didn't mind, and sometimes even preferred, going out on my own. Norma, Chiquita's sister, explained to me that women who went out alone were generally badly thought of, considered by men to be trying to attract their attention.

Eighteen-year-old Norma had a boyfriend from a nearby village, who would come to visit her on the traditional courting days: Tuesdays, Thursdays, Saturdays and Sundays. Why such a rigid code? "Normally, the girl's parents would think badly of a novio (boyfriend) who disregarded tradition," she explained. The young couple would often sit in the dusk outside the huts, but always within sight of Norma's mother or one of her older brothers. And for them to go to one of the travelling dances without a chaperone was unthinkable – mother or older brother had to go too. I was surprised to learn that in spite of this strict moral code, there were several single mothers in San Juan and the surrounding area. But it did seem that most families required their daughters to adhere to this convention.

Although Paraguay is unquestionably a male-dominated society, I actually felt very safe as a lone female traveller. I found most Paraguayans gentle and softly-spoken, and if there is a grain of truth in the myth propagated by Stroessner that Paraguay is an "oasis of peace", it lies in the fact that the traveller in Paraguay does not have to be obsessive about devising ingenious methods of hiding money and valuables in their shoes and underwear. The violence and theft that tourists experience in many other Latin American countries are virtually unheard of in Paraguay. Neither are women travellers likely to be intimidated by men on city streets or in the countryside. Paraguayans welcome travellers, who are generally treated with friendliness and curiosity, foreign women receiving probably much more respect than their Paraguayan counterparts.

Almost inevitably, during my stay in San Juan I never once saw a man do any of the traditionally female household tasks. On top of housework, the women seemed to do most of the back-breaking work in the chacra, each smallholder's plot of land, a lifeline for the survival of the family.

Chiquita's family were lucky enough to possess title deeds to their land. I met a family who had no documents proving "ownership" of the tiny plot of land that had housed and fed their ancestors for centuries. Their peace had been shattered one day by the agents of a foreign absentee landowner who had bought the land from the government. Some of the neighbours had refused to move from their plots and were subsequently continually harassed by agents of the landowner. One man had been shot dead in a violent scuffle.

I later found out that Paraguay's land distribution problem is acute. Although there are vast expanses of land available for cultivation, there are approximately 300,000 landless families in the country and eighty percent of the national territory is owned by one percent of the population. Many people in eastern Paraguay had been driven to occupy uncultivated land owned by absentee landlords, and these occupations, although legal under Paraguayan law, have led to several violent conflicts between squatters and army or police-backed landowners.

Malnutrition is also a severe problem. On my first day in San Juan, I woke to the din of cocks crowing and the smell of the fire. I itched all over from mosquito bites. We rose at 6am and walked three miles along the red sand path to the health centre. Already, a queue of patients had formed – old men, mothers with crying children, a man whose arm was in a makeshift sling. I watched Chiquita administer a salt and water solution to a scrawny baby with chronic diarrhoea. She then recommended a simple diet to the mother.

Chiquita explained that many families lived for several months of the year just on manioc, especially if the price of cotton had been low at harvest time. This explained why most of the children were undernourished. Attempts by local farmers to organise to beat the middlemen's price monopolies on cotton had been met with brutal

government repression. Several peasant leaders had been imprisoned and tortured for their efforts.

"Lesson one began: 'William Shakspeer borned in Stratford-upon-Avon'. I reckoned I could at least do better than that"

I left San Juan amazed at Chiquita's dedication and commitment to what was a never-ending task, with few rewards. I returned to Yhu, and spent three weeks living in relative luxury, in a house belonging to missionaries, which had running water, and electricity for a few hours in the evening! During the day, I taught a variety of subjects to some of the 165 pupils at the only secondary school in the district.

Not having come prepared to teach in a school, when this was suggested I felt somewhat daunted by the prospect – until one of the sisters showed me a school 1950s-produced dog-eared English language textbook. Lesson One began: "William Shakspeer borned in Stratford-upon-Avon". I reckoned I could at least do better than that and decided to have a go. I tried to organise my lessons on an exchange basis: I would teach my class an English or a Spanish song, then I'd ask the pupils, aged between 13 and 27, to teach me a Paraguayan song in Guarani. This way, I hoped to place equal value on their culture, and to make the point that things European weren't necessarily better, as many of them believed.

Many were intensely curious about the lifestyle and material goods I had in England; they were very disappointed to discover that my parents lived in an ordinary semi-detached house and not a *Dynasty*-style mansion which they assumed was the norm in Europe. I often asked the young women about their feelings about the status of women in the Paraguayan countryside. What did they think of the fact that the women did all the work in the house, often on the *chacra* and looked after the children as well? Most shrugged and said, "that's the way things are". One girl of about fourteen said, "women are lucky, because if there's a war, it's the men who've got to do the fighting."

There is one image of the national school in Yhu that has stayed with me. Every day, before school began, the pupils would line up outside the building and halfheartedly sing the national anthem. One of the lines referred to

Paraguay as the republic "where union and equality reign". I thought of the Asunción elite and their white houses with swimming pools and contraband Mercedes, and then of the peasant families in their cramped huts who eke out the year with a meagre diet of manioc. That was the reality behind the veneer of the "land of peace and sunshine". There was a very hollow ring to that anthem.

TRAVEL NOTES

Languages Spanish is the official language though most of the population express themselves more fluently in Guarani. Seventeen Indian tribes speak variations of another five different languages.

Transport Buses run between all major destinations, but more remote parts of the country are very hard to get to, even if you hire a jeep. Hitching, though probably safer than in other Latin American countries, carries the obvious risks.

Accommodation Good cheap accommodation is plentiful in Asunción and, apart from some of the *residenciales* around the railway station, hotels are generally clean and safe. The same applies to the roadside hostels which you'll find along all major roads. It's more difficult to find somewhere to stay once you get off the beaten track.

Guide *The South American Handbook* (Trade and Travel Publications) has around 25 pages on Paraguay.

Contacts

For more information write to the **Paraguay Committee for Human Rights**, Latin America House, Kingsgate Place, London NW6.

The only women's organisation we have been able to locate in Paraguay is the women's studies group, **Grupo de Estudios de la Mujer Paraguaya**, El gio Ayala 973, Asunción, who produce a publication, *Enfoquer de Mujer*.

Books

We have found no books on Paraguay, but the **Latin America Bureau**, 1 Amwell St., London EC1R 1UL, has published 2 reports: ***Dominion ... for ever Secured?***, a report of a mission to Paraguay by the British Parliamentary Human Rights Group, May 1987, and ***Paraguay: Power Game*** (1980). A more recent booklet, ***Decline of the Dictator: Paraguay's Crossroads*** is available from the **Washington Office on Latin America**, 110 Maryland Ave., NE, Washington DC 20002, USA. Cost US$8.

Special thanks to Mary Durran for background information.

Peru

P eru is one of the most travelled countries in South America, largely due to its magnificent Inca sites. It also, however, has one of the poorest and most isolated Indian populations in the entire continent. Erratic changes in government, combined with the development of the coast and the Amazon (rich in oil) at the expense of the sierra have restricted any positive moves to improve their position in recent years.

Since the early 1980s, the country has been in the grips of a devastating financial crisis. Inflation has been running at a staggering 5000

percent and, with the denial of any new international loans, the standard of living for those still in employment has plummeted. The embattled young president, Alan García Perez, a social democrat, is leaving office in April 1990. Novelist Mario Vargas Llosa looks set to be his successor on a centre-right coalition ticket, promising to restructure the economy by dismantling state bureaucracy and selling off state-owned companies, increasing prices and devaluing currency.

All this financial chaos and uncertainty is taking place against a background of continuing guerrilla activity, terror and disruption by the *Sendero Luminoso* (Shining Path), a Maoist group allegedly dedicated to achieving self-sufficiency for Peru's largely Indian peasant population. Whatever its motives, *Sendero*'s continuing campaign of bomb attacks, coupled with the government's violent response, have led to a wave of unrest previously unknown in Peru. For the traveller this means that at least one section of the country, the mountainous area around Ayacucho, is completely out of bounds. Most recently, there are reports that Colombian drug barons have begun to transplant their cocaine enterprises across the border into Peru, and in so doing are forging alliances with the guerrillas and the peasant coca producers, beyond the reach of government.

Besides the danger of being caught up in escalating guerrilla activity – the *Sendero Luminoso* have very little sympathy for foreign travellers – Peru is notorious for the skill of its thieves who will try almost any trick to distract you from guarding your belongings. Heed warnings carefully and avoid travelling at night. Women don't report any general sexual threat, but take care: you may well seem a more vulnerable target for robbery.

Peru has a relatively active **women's movement**. As in all Latin American countries, most of its groups are socialist-feminist in outlook, meaning that they are based on the belief that the majority of Peruvian women (seventy percent of the illiterate population) are doubly oppressed, as women and as members of the poorest socio-economic class. At the same time, they are concerned with issues such as the legalisation of free abortion on demand, the right to contraception, and the campaign against male violence, all of which have been consistently neglected by the traditional Left.

An Uncluttered Trip

. . . .

After a disastrous start, Margaret Hubbard spent a rewarding few weeks travelling alone by bus and train to all the better-known destinations in Peru.

My journey from Europe to South America lasted forever. At every refuelling stop the passengers changed – only a handful of worthies who had got on the plane in London seemed destined for Lima. Only then did I feel how very far away South America is.

Perhaps because it does not have for us the strategic importance it does to "Uncle Sam", most Europeans have limited knowledge of South American life and politics. Our media carry little news, so my ideas were shaky and stereotyped. I had one contact in Lima and it was she, along with simple curiosity, who had taken me there.

At Lima airport I faced the nightmare that all travellers dread. My luggage had been lost in transit. Thirty-six hours of travel and only a sparse knowledge of Spanish is not the recipe for dealing calmly with this catastrophe. I stood in Lima airport with nothing but my documents, my money, a camera, one film and a book. The airline assured me the luggage would arrive on Saturday, Monday, Wednesday, mañana; it was in Bogotá, Buenos Aires, wherever. I never saw it again and coping with this disaster turned out to be the key to my holiday and to some lovely moments I would never otherwise have had.

Peru is a difficult place to travel, but being alone did not of itself seem to be a problem. Nor did being a woman; the *machismo* was little different to that in Mediterranean Europe. But being a foreigner, and by definition wealthy in the eyes of the inhabitants of a Third World country, the situation was constantly uneasy and at times positively harrowing. Theft is a big problem. Rucksacks are slit. Thieves jump on to the trains at the switchbacks and the stations to steal luggage not securely tied or chained down. Jewellery is a prime target.

There is a resulting paranoia which sets in and grows worse the longer that you stay. I finished up constantly alert and wary and I met others unwilling or unable to relax their wariness enough even to chat to local people or fellow travellers in case it distracted from the business in hand of protecting their belongings. I was constantly warned to take no notice of any display of local folk culture, children singing or dancing, for example; it was almost certainly a set-up for theft. These warnings were in the guidebooks, but they were also coming from Peruvians that I met.

"In choosing to travel by train I accidentally fell upon a solution to my luggageless state"

The combination of locals warning foreigners against their own people, and an unease about watching some of the attractions of the country became in the end very wearing. I reached the point in Puno of wondering whether the apparently friendly warnings of the apparently friendly locals were themselves part of a set-up. They weren't but that level of unease and distrust is something I have never experienced before in many years of travelling.

Getting around, the roads proved rough and the bus journeys shaky, so trains seemed a better option. In choosing to travel by train I accidentally fell upon the solution to my luggageless state. I had bought the bare minimum of replacement clothing in Lima, the airline constantly assuring me that my

luggage would turn up. On the train to Huancayo, the highest railway station in the world, I told a fellow traveller my tale. She and others in the carriage immediately gave me items I needed. A T-shirt here, three diarrhoea pills there, a pair of socks, a map. All vital items, so carefully planned and packed at home.

That was only the beginning. All along the journeys to Cuyo, Puno, La Paz, people gave or loaned me items. In some ways the loans were most valuable of all. To allow a total stranger use of an item you want to keep is an act of trust seldom met in this world. I spent many happy hours back in Scotland packing up borrowed items and boxes of Edinburgh rock. In some ways I think this could only have happened in a place so fraught with danger.

The journey to Huancayo was exciting. I had read Paul Theroux's *The Old Patagonian Express* and he seemed less than happy on this journey – I loved it. Desemparados Station was a colonial architectural gem, and the train even more fascinating. Up we went on the switchbacks, going forwards, reversing, forward, reverse, and always gaining more height. I began to get breathless and overwhelmed with tiredness. The air was raw and thin.

Huancayo itself is an Indian town, and, despite the fame of the journey, not that heavily geared to tourists. I spent a week up there and used the local buses to get to the villages roundabout. The fertility of the valley astonished me. It also felt safe to walk in the hills alone, although I never went too far off the path. It was cold. Anyone travelling to South America in winter should not underestimate how cold it is at these heights. Proximity to the tropic is irrelevant. During the day it is often in the seventies and at night below freezing.

A friend in Lima afforded me an opportunity to participate in a very different Peru. Very quickly I saw how extensive is the control of the country in the hands of a very few Europeans and their wealthy Peruvian counterparts. The suburban mansions of San Isidro and Miraflores, their shops, cafés, life-styles and values are completely European. The Lima Cricket and Tennis Club is an enclave of a colonial past where you can drink pisco sours and read *The Times*. The ex-pats I met were very friendly and went out of their way to show me around. But I was struck by how small a community it is and how hungry they were for news from home.

"Sadly, this has affected Peruvians' attitude to their own culture, which they regard as second rate"

Peruvian folk culture is a casualty of the country's ambivalent attitude to the USA. Despite a political wariness of its influence and power, North America still symbolises wealth and a better way of life. Sadly, this has affected Peruvians' attitude to their own culture, which, in general, they regard as second rate – a great shame in a country so rich in indigenous music and art.

The centre of folk culture is Ayacucho. However, this city is also a centre of *Sendero Luminoso* activity and thus to be avoided by foreign travellers. I was lucky to see a group of Ayacucho musicians performing in Lima. It was fascinating and I left sad that this music was not more easily available. The lost luggage meant severe tightening of the financial belt, but tapes of Peruvian music were high on the list of necessities to bring home.

For most people, Cuzco, Machu Picchu and Lake Titicaca are the mecca of a trip to Peru. Sooner or later, most, if not all, South American travellers finish up at these sights, and the first two at least were for me no disappointment. I loved Cuzco. It had such charm. The Spanish churches and the halls built on Inca foundations were a mind-bending architectural combination. Through narrow cobbled lanes, up the hill to Sacsayhuamán, the fortress on the hilltop keeping watch over the valley below. Only the columns of Egypt have previously dwarfed me into silence. These massive Inca stones cut

with only the most basic of tools and transported without the wheel left me gazing in awe.

Machu Picchu, too, was everything I hoped for, and more. Stripped of tent, boots, etc. I had to go by train. The Inca trail was no longer possible. I took the local train to Aguas Calientes, a little village one mile before Machu Picchu where there are thermal springs. It was hot and had all the steaminess of high jungle. In the early morning I walked up the railway line to the foot of the mountain and began the climb. It seemed almost indecent to go up any other way. At the top I was seized by a childish unwillingness to look in case it was a let-down. I had nothing to fear. The tiny houses and narrow streets had a sense of identity quite impossible to catch in the photos. The ruins would have been impressive anywhere. But it is the setting which leaves the spectator breathless. Set on a mountain saddle which falls off on each side to the Urubamba river, the ruins are surrounded by a bowl of jungle-covered peaks. It is so remote and so moving that it is difficult to leave behind. Somehow I wanted to parcel it up and take it with me.

I am glad I felt this about Machu Picchu because sadly I felt quite different about the floating islands on Lake Titicaca. There is always an unhealthy contradiction in the juxtaposition of tourism and traditional culture, but at the Lake it verged on the obscene. In one of the most desolate and beautiful places on this planet, I felt a captive source of income, gazing at a human zoo. It disturbed me very deeply indeed.

Peru was for me a strange holiday of dichotomy; stress and beauty, loneliness and moments of rich companionship. I felt a sense of relief when I left to be alive and going home, but back in Britain, months later, Peru haunts me and I search the pages of the newspapers for its news. To me it is no longer on the other side of the world. It is now in me, part of me, and I feel a richer person for having been there.

TRAVEL NOTES

Languages Spanish, Quechua and Aymara.

Transport A fairly comprehensive network of long-distance buses covers all but the most remote Andean towns and the Amazon region. There is no railway in the mountains except between Lima and Huancayo and across the flat *altiplano* between Cuzco and Lake Titicaca. As well as being potentially dangerous, hitching is difficult and you are expected to pay.

Accommodation There are plenty of hotels, most of them cheap but fairly basic. Camping is free since there are only a couple of official campgrounds but you'd be advised not to sleep out alone in remote areas.

Special Problems Peru is the home of very skilled pickpockets and grab-and-run thieves so take care everywhere, especially when arriving in towns at night by public transport. Remember that thieves often work in groups – sometimes families – where *gringas* are caught off-guard by the distracting appealing glances of a small wide-eyed child. It is a livelihood.

Coca leaves, the raw material of cocaine, are freely and legally available for chewing and brewing. However the government, with American help, has mounted a big campaign against smuggling and production of the drug itself. Police have a habit of arresting *gringos*, especially in Lima, and demanding a ransom for their release – otherwise drug-handling charges are threatened. Five years in a Peruvian jail is no joke, so make sure there is absolutely no reason for you to be under suspicion.

The *Sendero Luminoso*, whose activities are spreading, have no love of foreign tourists, so take care to avoid areas where they are active.

Guides *The Rough Guide: Peru* (Harrap Columbus) is probably the best guidebook to any individual South American country, practical and culturally sensitive. Otherwise the *South American Handbook* (Trade and Travel Publications) is always recommended.

Contacts

For up-to-date information on the situation in Peru, contact the **Peru Support Group**, 20 Compton Terrace, London N1 2UN, ☎359 2270.

Among the most longstanding **women's organisations** are:

Flora Tristán, Centro de la Mujer Peruana Av. Arenales 601, Lima. Women's centre dedicated to the growth, development and strengthening of the feminist movement in Peru. Allied to the United Left (*Apron*) party, with the basic tenet "first socialism, then the feminist revolution".

Movimiento Manuela Ramos, Camana 280-Oficina 305, Apartado Postal 11176, Lima 14. Mainly concerned with co-ordinating projects with working-class women. Write first.

There are quite a few **feminist publications** in Peru, published in Spanish. Watch out for *Mujer y Sociedad, La Tortuga* and *La Manzana*. For help, literature, or advice try *Flora Tristán*, the *Libreria de la Mujer* **bookshop** (near the women's centre in Quilca, just half a block from Av. Wilson), which is run by nuns.

Books

Dervla Murphy, Eight Feet in the Andes (John Murray, 1983). Describes the author's journey with her nine-year-old daughter and a mule 1,300 miles through the Andes.

Audrey Bronstein, ed., The Triple Struggle: Latin American Peasant Women (War on Want Campaigns, London, 1982). See General Bibliography.

Carol Andreas, The Rise of Popular Feminism in Peru (Lawrence Hill, US, 1985). Accessible account of the gradual rise of the Peruvian Women's Movement.

Ximena Bunster and Elsa Chaney, Sellers and Servants: Working Women in Lima, Peru (Bergin and Garvey, US, 1989). Using an innovative "talking pictures" technique, presents the lives of women street peddlers and domestic servants from their own words.

Michael Reid, Peru – Paths to Poverty (Latin America Bureau, London, 1985). Good account of the political situation from the 1950s. The author is currently working on a book about the García years, to be published in 1990.

Mario Vargas Llosa, Aunt Julia and the Scriptwriter (Picador, 1984), **Conversations in the Cathedral** (Faber, 1986), and others. Llosa is Peru's best-known novelist – highly readable with incidental, sometimes crazy insights into life in Lima.

The Philippines

Tourists are beginning to steer clear of the Philippines. Its image as a collection of tropical island paradises (replete with luxury hotels and private beaches) has become more than tarnished by the country's obvious political instability. Since being swept into office by the extraordinary "People Power" revolution of 1986, President Corazon Aquino has faced six coup attempts (the latest involving pitched battles with rebel army factions on the streets of Manila), a plummeting economy, and a continuing war in the southern islands with the communist New People's Army.

Although Aquino herself still claims some popularity, the optimism that greeted the end of the twenty-year Marcos dictatorship has become submerged by disillusion that little has really changed. Unemployment has continued to rise and the sprawling poverty-stricken slums that border most cities have been swelled by a new wave of rural poor. Aquino's failure to institute promised land reforms, deal with government corruption, or curb US intervention (from long-established US military bases in the country), are sources of mounting resentment.

Americans tourists particularly, and many luxury holidaymakers, are staying away. But there are still a fair number of European budget travellers stopping off at the Philippines as part of a long haul journey to East Asia. Tourists have in fact never been an ostensible target of hostilities, but travel is limited by army restrictions. However, it's essential to get up-to-date information before choosing to set off.

Uniquely in Asia, the islands of the Philippines are predominantly Catholic and Westernised – the indigenous Malay culture having been subsumed first by Spanish and then American influences – and English is widely spoken as a second language. In general terms Filipino men and women have a reputation for great courtesy and hospitality towards foreign visitors, and women particularly can be incredibly generous with their help and advice. Travelling on your own, anywhere other than the obvious tourist enclaves, you may well attract attention but you'll find that most people who approach you have a genuine (if disconcerting) interest in meeting a Western foreigner.

Sexual harassment from men does occur but it's usually in the form of catcalls and propositions and is rarely personally threatening. If you do have a problem you should turn to the nearest woman for help – it's likely that she'll take you under her wing. It's not unusual to be invited to stay in people's homes, either; in accepting you do need to be sensitive to the costs you impose and look for opportunities to reciprocate.

Women in the Philippines have for many years faced discrimination and exploitation at work. In the Marcos years cheap female labour was used explicitly to attract foreign investment for labour-intensive textiles and electronics industries, with promotional packages advertising the nimble fingers and docile nature of the workforce. Working conditions in these factories were, and continue to be, exceptionally grim. With much of the land taken over by vast agribusiness conglomerates, rural women had little choice but to look for work in the factories or otherwise join the service industries and prostitution rackets that flourished with the tourist trade and around the US military bases. Sex tourism, where the services of a prostitute would be included in the hotel and tour itinerary, became big business in the 1970s and "hostess bars" remain a common sight in Manila and the major tourist enclaves.

As unemployment and poverty have worsened, thousands of women have been leaving the country to find better paid, but often appallingly insecure, work as foreign domestic servants in Asia, the Middle East and Europe. In many countries – Saudi Arabia being a notorious example – Filipina women routinely face harassment and abuse as the bottom-of-the-heap of migrant workers. There are also a growing number of women who work as prostitutes in Japan on short-term entertainment visas – an inverted form of Japanese sex tourism.

In the name of national pride, Corazon Aquino declared a ban on all foreign recruitment of Filipino domestic servants in 1988. This was revoked shortly after as a result of pressure from the women themselves, who felt she was missing the point of their struggle to gain recognition and protection. The main campaigning force for women's rights in the Philippines is the umbrella organisation *Gabriela*. As well as implementing local campaigns against the sexual and economic exploitation of women it has highlighted the problems of women working within the "hospitality industry". The group continues to pressurise the government to bring about the necessary social and economic changes that will provide Filipinas with more equitable options. However, like many other legal organisations associated with the Left, it has to contend with continual suspicion and threat from the army.

Adjusting to the Sight of Guns

. . . .

Jackie Mutter visited the Phil ppines "out of sheer curiosity", almost a year after the overthrow of Ferdinand Marcos. She spent ten weeks in the country, on the first stage of a long solo trip via Asia to Australia.

As I boarded the plane for Manila, it occurred to me that I knew very little about my destination beyond its image as an exotic group of islands, famous for their palm-fringed beaches and, despite political upheaval, still coveted by many as an idyllic holiday location.

Armed with rucksack and carrying a copy of James Fenton's *Snap Revolution*, which offered a restricted though topical insight into the current state of affairs, I arrived in Manila alone, greeted by the onslaught of vivid first impressions that inevitably accompany one's immediate experience of Asia. This was my first "longhaul" trip outside Europe and the Soviet Union and, at 25 years old, I was travelling alone for the first time in my life. I felt apprehensive but my anxieties were lost in the excitement and anticipation of exploring unknown territory and at finally having escaped from the fetters of nine-to-five drudge in London.

My first few days were spent in a constant state of amazement as I survived, one by one, a steady stream of culture shocks. These started with my arrival at the airport and the surge of people who came at me from all angles as I left the arrival hall. Then came a hair-raising taxi ride, where I sat dazed and frozen, watching the suburbs of Manila fly past as if on a some giant 3-D movie screen. As we screeched to a halt at each junction, I caught a glimpse of the barefooted boys dodging in and out of the traffic, selling newspapers, chewing gum and cigarettes to drivers. I gradually became aware of people sitting on the grass verges in the middle of major roadways and the sudden realisation that these people were in fact living on these verges in makeshift homes left me feeling very, very naive. I was riddled with a guilt of decadence as I walked past people lying on pavements, too weak to move, and approached by young children begging and tugging at my clothes. The sight of young armed men guarding the banks, shops and money-changers was totally unfamiliar to me and yet was to become part of the everyday scenery in the Philippines.

"I soon found myself adjusting to the sight of guns and the aggression and underlying tensions that went with them"

Although I never experienced any violence during my two and a half months in the country, I remember being woken one night in Baguio by the sound of gunfire, and seeing a friend return one evening in a state of shock after having witnessed a man being shot dead in the streets of Ermita. One picture that sticks in my mind is that of a child, no more than eight or nine years old, playing with his father's automatic rifle as if it were nothing more harmful than a toy.

However, in the words of a friend, the Philippines is a political time-bomb and I soon found myself adjusting to the sight of guns and the aggression and underlying tensions that went with them. It became apparent after a few days of travelling around and talking to various people in the provinces of Zambales and Pangasinan, northwest of Manila, that life on an individual basis had much less value in a country where people were struggling to survive, where the majority of the population are living under the national poverty line and where "salvaging" (politically motivated murders) were daily occurrences.

Purely by coincidence, I had arrived in the Philippines almost a year after the Revolution which had ousted the repressive dictatorship of Ferdinand Marcos and his notorious wife, Imelda, and replaced them with the extremely tentative government of Corazon Aquino. I was interested in finding out how people felt about their release from the manacles of a dictatorship and was surprised to learn that Marcos still had many supporters, not only amongst the wealthy landowners, but also amongst the rural population. There was a general atmosphere of impatience and disillusionment with the new regime and the distinct lack of political and economic reforms which had been promised before the Revolution.

The long-awaited land reforms were conspicuous by their absence and the majority of peasants remained as tenants or hired agricultural workers. Furthermore, the Philippines has had for many years an export-orientated economy which has made the country a haven for multinational corporations, and consequent bad working conditions and wages which the people are powerless to change. Foreign control of the economy, feudal conflicts, and lack of social welfare seem to be the three major obstacles to redevelopment in the Philippines.

Despite their problems, the Filipinos are among the most friendly and welcoming people I have come across in my travels and I was frequently overwhelmed by kindness. Most of my time was spent in Northern Luzon, although this had not been my original intention. I left Manila after just a couple of days and headed north to Iba and Bolinao, where I was met with endless warmth and hospitality, being invited into homes to meet families, share meals, and spend the night exchanging stories, all of which gradually gave me an insight into Filipino lifestyles.

I discovered that this hospitality was customary and that refusing to share food or a drink would cause deep offence. Of course, there were the very occasional invitations that seemed to have an "ulterior" motive but on the whole – and to my embarrassment – I found that people were "honoured" to be visited by a Westerner.

"It was undoubtedly a trial at times, being a fair-haired, fair-skinned and blue-eyed single woman"

I travelled around the country by bus and *jeepney* (brightly coloured taxi jeeps) and, although crowded and bumpy at times, these journeys were never unbearable and certainly never dull. Sharing my limited space with chickens, pigs, and various other livestock, as well as all manner of produce, was a completely new experience and one that followed me throughout my travels in Asia. Although comfort was not comparable with Western standards, the only major discomforts were usually caused by lack of suspension and dusty roads! Besides, the attitude of the Filipinos was such that they would always create enough space for me and would go out of their way to ensure that I had a pleasant journey.

It was undoubtedly a trial at times, being a fair-haired, fair-skinned and blue-eyed single woman, and my patience and tolerance were frequently put to the test. In Manila there were very few instances when I ventured out into the city and returned without being followed or harassed in some form or other. On one occasion, I was actually kerbcrawled by police officers in a patrol car in the middle of the city! There were many other similar incidences too numerous to mention (one or two of them quite unpleasant) although none impossible to deal with. Being chased around my room early one morning by the 76-year-old hostel owner, who had let himself into my room with the master key, was one incident I found hard to take seriously. Nonetheless it can be a problem and one to be aware of.

My overall impression was that *machismo* seems to rate very highly among the characteristics of the Filipino male. A firm refusal, though, would usually work and I have experienced a far more brutal and arrogant type of sexual harassment in certain other countries. On the whole, I felt quite safe travelling alone and this feeling was reinforced by the attitudes of the Filipinas, who would always come to my aid when necessary and seemed to consider it their responsibility to protect me. I soon built up enormous respect for these women and was keen to learn more about their lives and the conditions in which they lived.

Consequently, I leapt at the opportunity, while in Baguio, Northern Luzon, to attend the first Congress of the Cordillera Women's Movement. The Cordillera is a collective name for the mountain provinces in Northern Luzon and incorporates villages where the cultural minorities of the region continue to practise their own laws and customs. There is an ongoing struggle to maintain their autonomy in the face of various pressures from the government and also from national and international corporations, who have made frequent attempts to take their land over in order to mine its precious metals deposits.

"Around fifty women attended the conference, most of them clothed in traditional dress"

I was introduced to the Congress by Leah, an active feminist who works at Baguio University and who was at the time trying to establish a centre for women in the area. This centre was to act as a much needed refuge, a rape crisis centre, and also as a means to educate women on their rights and the opportunities available to them. Violence against women in the Philippines is a widespread social problem and there is little within the law to protect women and provide them with financial support, should they need it. Entrenched sexual inequality is aggravated by inadequate childcare and maternity benefits, lack of effective family planning, and lack of access to accurate information, as well as the additional hurdle created by corruption and waylaying of funds by local bureaucrats.

The Congress itself was to take place during the three days leading up to International Women's Day and turned out to be the most memorable part of my visit as it gave me the opportunity to listen to and learn about the women in these indigenous groups. I was also given a chance to participate in the conference myself, talking to the women about the Women's Movement in the West, its aims and achievements so far . . . I had to cover a fair amount of ground, needless to say!

Around fifty women attended the conference, most of them clothed in traditional dress, which was usually made up of bright red and black embroidered skirts, with some wearing headbands made from snake vertebrae and others dressed in brightly coloured beads with arms covered in ritual tattoos. The conference was conducted in Ilocano, the local, most commonly used dialect of Tagalog, and was translated for us by one of the conference organisers. We sang songs to start with – a very important aspect of Filipino culture – then various speakers discussed the general situation of women in the country.

However, the most interesting aspect of the conference was the workshops, where we were divided into groups to discuss and exchange our ideas and personal experiences. Women talked about the appalling work conditions within factories and mines, which are generally owned by multinational corporations, and consequent damage to their health (women frequently suffered from urinary infections due to working without breaks, even to visit the toilet), and horrific stories emerged of rape and various forms of sexual abuse. As for maternity benefits, in many cases the sack was almost inevitable for a pregnant woman working in a factory or mine.

Birth control was out of the question for most of the minority women as they have to consult their husbands first and, in some of the villages, lack of children within a marriage is grounds for divorce. On a national scale, even whilst I was there, an Executive Order, endorsed by the Minister of Social Services, had been passed whereby the government would only implement natural methods of family planning – yet another hurdle in women's uphill struggle to achieve some sort of independence.

Undoubtedly, the Philippines will always remain a special place for me: a country of spectacular and varied scenery, exotic rainforests and coastline, and home to a variety of cultures. I left with a profound admiration and respect for the women, in particular, whose courage enables them to maintain their hardworking, generous and kind disposition in spite of the suppression and abuse they endure in their daily lives.

Working as "One of the Boys"
· · · · · · · · · · · ·

Journalist Kate Barker spent five weeks in Manila in 1989 with a film crew, making a documentary about Freddie Aguilar, the Philippines' best-loved popular singer. She has since returned to explore the country on her own.

I never considered my big nose an asset until I arrived in the Philippines. People would come up to me in the street and say, "Hello ma'am. Your nose is so beautiful." Women I met would ask for my photograph to show their friends. The ideal is to be pale-skinned and pointy-nosed, a hankering after Western appearance that is part of the love of things foreign which President Corazon Aquino and her supporters are trying to tackle with a determined promotion of Filipino nationalism. But years of American interference in the country cannot be wiped away so easily. A foreign car, husband or friend remains a status symbol.

I was offered roles in television commercials during my stay, too, despite having absolutely no acting ability or experience. Film-makers are desperate for "white talent" to appear in advertisements, to give the impression that whatever is being pushed is imported, even if it is not.

> **"Every bar door we opened led on to the same scene: skimpily-clad women dancing on bar-tops"**

I don't know if it was this attraction to all things foreign, the natural Filipino amiability, or the fact that I was meeting people through work rather than travelling as a tourist, but I found it very easy to make friends. I have spent a great deal of the last seven years abroad, in Europe, India, the Soviet Union and Turkey, but nowhere have I found myself so quickly accepted, and so few inhibitions or cultural differences acting as a block to friendship.

I was staying with two members of the film crew in a flat in Makati, the business area of Manila, which is also home to the most up-market of the capital's three red light districts. Many of the women working in the *girlie* bars had children to support. While they danced for the tourists, their mothers or sisters looked after the youngsters.

Soon after we arrived, I and another (male) journalist tried to find somewhere to have a beer. Every bar door we opened led on to the same scene: skimpily-clad women dancing on bar-tops, while their colleagues fawned over middle-aged European or American businessmen. Eventually we settled on a bar with an outside terrace and ordered drinks, with me feeling incredibly self-conscious. After a few visits, however, my qualms were eased. "Hello si-ir, hello ma'am," the girls used to shout as we entered. They were always very friendly towards me. They wanted to know how old I was, did I have a boyfriend, what did I think of the Philippines, and could they have my picture?

They often looked incredibly bored as they made flirtatious conversation with the punters. The men could take them away from the bar if they paid a bar fine to the management of between 300 and 500 pesos (roughly £8–14). The women got the money spent on their "ladies' drinks" – about £1.50 for each tiny glass of orange juice – and anything else the client gave them.

Many dreamed of marrying a Western man, or meeting someone who would send them an allowance so they could escape the bars. One such was Benjy who had only been working in the bars for three weeks to pay for her studies in computing. She said her father had died, leaving most of his money to his mistress, and there was nothing left to fund her studies. Benjy struck lucky while we were there and found an Englishman to pay for her education.

Appearances were sometimes deceptive. Not all the women were available for a bar fine. In one place, where the girls arrived for work in red satin knick-ers and vests, high heels and fishnets, the Western owner prided himself on employing only virgins and married women. Joy fell into the first category. She was nineteen and a student. She worked in the bar from 3pm to 3am before travelling the two hours' journey home to the provinces, where she went to school for the morning, then returned straight to Manila. She slept when she could. If there were no punters in the bar, the women got out their books to study. Joy wanted to be a doctor. She told me I looked like the Virgin Mary because I had "tantalising eyes". The remark seemed to sum up the happy-go-lucky attitude to sex and religion. In another bar, Rosa, the Madam, sang the praises of Cory Aquino as a devout family woman. In the next breath, she offered to procure girls for my two companions.

"This is the kind of hardship which drives thousands of Filipinas to Japan each year as 'entertainers'"

Despite their often desperate situation, the bar-girls remained stoically cheerful and optimistic. The same was true wherever we went. Even on Smoky Mountain, an enormous rubbish dump where over 22,000 of Manila's poor eke out a living by scavenging, there appeared to be no resentment towards myself and a friend as we were shown around by a church worker. No one asked us for money. They just wanted to know our names, and asked us to take their picture.

I spent a long time talking to a former cycle rickshaw driver who worked on the heap with his wife and children. They made just over the equivalent of £1 a day, each sorting out baskets of paper, glass, plastic and metal from the garbage. It was easy to see why large families were prevalent when a child could earn as much from scavenging as an adult.

Eva, our guide, said that typically the urban poor married young, did not finish their schooling, and had between six and eight children. Many came to Manila from the provinces hoping to find employment. A mother might work as a maid earning about £12 a month, while her husband could make about £17 a month as a driver. Their combined incomes still put them way below the poverty line. This is the kind of hardship which drives thousands of Filipinas to Japan each year as "entertainers" and to Hong Kong as maids.

"I always felt as if I was going out honorarily as 'one of the boys'"

The capital is bustling, dirty, and not particularly prepossessing, having been extensively bombed during the Second World War. Most tourists seem to head straight out to the fantastic beaches and natural landmarks which abound in the 7107-island archipelago.

Manila's main tourist attraction these days is the Marcos's presidential palace, where Imelda's thousands of shoes and dresses, gallon bottles of perfume, and bedroom modelled on Marie Antoinette's can be seen. But what makes the city fun is just spending time relaxing with Filipino friends. The Philippines is not the place to visit if you want a solitary trip.

Our film crew, all Filipino men, soon adopted the three of us – the director, another reporter and myself – who had come from England, and decided to show us the city, which basically meant the bars and restaurants. Filipinos are incredibly laid back, nothing is rushed and there is time for everything. We soon picked up the expression "Filipino time", which means, as we discovered when filming began four days behind schedule, "late".

I was the only woman involved in the production, and generally the only woman in the group when we went out in the evenings. Young Filipinas do not seem to go out much in mixed parties even after they are married and the crew found it hard to understand that I was staying in a flat with two men who were neither relatives nor boyfriends. They could not believe that in England I lived away from home and did not have a boyfriend. I always felt as if I was going out honorarily as "one of the boys". The crew were surprised when I drank beer and looked shocked if the occasional swear word crept into my conversation.

Nearly all the single men and women we met were still living at home, and so were quite a few of the married ones. Older couples claimed Filipinos mature late as they stay with their parents for so long. Families are particularly strict with the daughters.

Women, however, tend to dominate the family both in looking after the money and having the final say. Of all the couples I met who had any connection with business, it was always the wife who took financial control. One woman running an export company with her husband told me she even preferred to employ women as they worked harder. Of the Filipino man, she said: "Show him a leg and give him a bottle, and nothing gets done."

"There is no need for women's lib here. The Filipina has always been considered equal, even dominant, by the Filipino," Lorena, the Filipino wife of our English lighting director, told me, pointing out that many women worked and occupied high positions. But, without sensing the contradiction, Lorena admitted there was a double standard of morality for men and women. "It is quite acceptable for the husband to play around, but if it is the woman who plays around, she gets into a lot of trouble," she said.

I never found any problems going out on my own despite dire warning from Filipino and Western friends about taking taxis alone and travelling late at night. The nearest thing to sexual harassment came from the rank of tricycle drivers waiting for clients outside our apartment. "I love you ma'am," they called out every time I passed.

TRAVEL NOTES

Languages Filipino (Tagalog) and numerous local dialects. English and Spanish are spoken quite widely in cities and tourist areas.

Transport Boats between islands, and buses around them, are very cheap though far from comfortable. *Jeepneys* (taxis) in towns are also inexpensive.

Accommodation There are few cheap hotels. In Manila and other cities you can usually find dormitories in the university area. Elsewhere negotiate locally for rooms.

Special Problems Due to the continuing NPA guerrilla action, or occupation, many of the southern islands are now impossible (and perhaps unsafe) to visit. On gaining a visa you'll be given an up-to-date list of restricted areas (and activities) and once in the country will have to gain permission from the army for travel to areas outside the main cities and tourist spots.

The evident exploitation of women in the "hospitality" industry is deeply unsettling, so too are the extremes of poverty. Filipina women frequently face problems of harassment, particularly from GIs and foreign tourists in search of cheap sex. You have much less to contend with as a Westerner.

Although people are well used to Western tourists wandering about in shorts and T-shirts, you should remember that this is an inherently conservative society and that you are much more likely to gain respect if you dress modestly.

Guides *The Philippines – A Travel Survival Kit* (Lonely Planet) and, more recently updated, *South-East Asia on a Shoestring* (Lonely Planet).

Contacts

For up-to-date information on what's happening in the country, including women's activities, contact the **Philippine Resource Centre**, 1 Grangeway, London NW6, ☎624 0270.

Gabriela (Women's Movement), PO Box 4386, Manila 2800.

TO-MAE-W (Third World Movement Against the Exploitation of Women), PO Box SM-366, Manila. Very dynamic organisation, established in 1961 to co-ordinate research and action on issues such as tourism/prostitution, sexism in the media, and the plight of women workers throughout the region and the Third World.

Books

Linda Ty-Casper, *Awaiting Trespass (A Pasión)* (Readers International, 1986). the first of Ty-Casper's novels to be published in the West (and a book which could not be published in Marcos's time). Set in the days before the pope is due to visit Manila, it combines a personal awakening with powerful social satire.

Committee for Asian Women, *Tales of Filipino Working Women* and ***Our Rightful Share*** (both 1984). These two excellent short books, available from the Committee for Asian Women, 57 Peking Road, 5.F, Kowloon, Hong Kong, use the personal stories of Filipina factory-workers to describe their working conditions and struggles to stand up for their rights.

James Fenton, *The Snap Revolution* in ***Granta 18*** (Penguin, 1986). Fenton arrived in Manila to cover the phoney election called by Marcos and found himself charting the progress of a Revolution. A sensitive, moving and wild account.

Women Writers in Media Now staff, *Filipina, I: Poetry, Drama, Fiction* (Cellar, US, 1984) and ***II: An Anthology of Contemporary Women Writers in the Philippines*** (Cellar, US, 1985). Two good anthologies of Filipina writers, that draw on the experiences of women from all walks of society.

Rowena Tiempo-Torrerillas, *Upon the Williows and Other Stories* (Cellar, US, 1979). Well-crafted short stories by a female novelist, if from a rather upper-middle-class and Americanised perspective.

Poland

· · · · · · · · · · · · · · · · · · ·

These are deeply uncertain times for Poland. Having ousted the Communist Party from its "leading role" and voted in a Solidarity-led coalition, the Polish electorate are now anxious to feel the benefits of reform. However, faced with a worsening economic crisis, crippling austerity measures, spiralling inflation and widespread food shortages, optimism is wearing thin and support for the new government of Prime Minister Tadeusz Maziwiecki is already

dwindling. Predictably, young Poles are leaving the country – a trend that is steadily mounting. Meanwhile, back at home, people are more than ever having to rely on the black market even for basic commodities.

Western travellers are largely cushioned from these hardships (hotels and "dollar shops" are always well stocked) and, with the new atmosphere of political openness, tourism is on the increase. In general terms Poland is a safe and easy country to travel around alone. Outside the main centres, such as the beautiful city of Krakow, people might seem curious about you as a rare Western visitor, but this is unlikely to feel threatening or intrusive. Harassment, other than the occasional hassle from drunks and illegal money-changers, is rare, and, if you do encounter problems, you'll invariably find other Poles stepping in to help. The Polish people are renowned for their hospitality to strangers and will sacrifice much to make you feel welcome.

As with many Eastern bloc countries it's likely that you'll socialise mainly with men; women tend to have much less time to spend with visitors. It can be hard to come to terms with the entrenched (and largely unchallenged) sexism that you find at all levels of Polish society, even in quite progressive circles. Men still tend to approach women with a degree of old-style gallantry and much is made of hand-kissing and the giving of flowers.

Socially and politically, Poland remains a profoundly Catholic country, and **women's roles** as mothers and homemakers are deeply ingrained. Most women have to combine the tasks of queuing for food and hard domestic labour with full-time jobs – a double burden made increasingly untenable by the worsening shortages. Men for the most part consider themselves exempt from work in the home and, whilst these attitudes persist, the legislative reforms, such as maternity leave (extended to two years by the efforts of Solidarity) and the provision of day nurseries in most workplaces, seem unlikely to bring much relief. There is no feminist movement in the Western sense of the word, and you'll find that feminism has acquired fairly negative connotations, being linked in many people's minds to Soviet propaganda. Under the new Catholic coalition, moves are being made towards repealing the 1956 abortion laws to make abortion illegal. In a political climate that so strongly asserts Catholic values it is proving difficult for women to voice dissent.

Guests in Krakow
· · · · · · · · · · · · ·

Krystyna Gajda is British but of Polish descent. She spent a month in Krakow as a guest of an elderly family friend, with an English companion who had never visited the country before.

I was only eleven years old when I had last visited Poland and the idea of rediscovering the country through adult eyes seemed momentous. In many ways I felt as new to the country as the English friend I was travelling with, though my knowledge of Polish was undoubtedly a buffer when it came to dealing with customs officials on the long rail journey across Europe and with people such as taxi drivers once we reached our destination.

Anyone from the West, however, is at once recognised as such. East Germans and Poles homed in on us on the train journey with a mixture of warmth and curiosity and were bowled over that one of us spoke Polish. As our visit went on, I found myself asserting my Polishness to the point of wearing our hostess's fur hats. I became very conscious of my anglicised Polish language and of being seen as a Westerner who had Polish origins, feeling guilty for what Poles without a doubt viewed as my affluent British lifestyle. I wanted to be accepted as a Pole by the people I met, to dispel any notions of theirs that they had to prove something to me. Unlike my friend, Alison, I was in the curious position of being viewed as a Western outsider *and* a Pole, and I was always aware of this ambivalent identity.

Concerned that my friend might be feeling left out, I worked hard as her interpreter for the duration of our stay. We were based in Krakow, staying with Anna, an old family friend who lived alone. The presence of an "all-English" person put her under something of a strain. She, too, was anxious that my friend did not come away with a bleak, negative image of her country and went to great lengths to provide the best food she could find – bartering, black marketing, stocking up on ration cards and, of course, queueing.

Before long I realised that she was sharing these chores with her closest friend, a woman called Czesia. While Anna whirled us around theatres, art galleries, monasteries and churches, Czesia was organising the food for us all, so it was on the table when we came home. Yet I am sure that we still don't know the *full* extent of the sacrifices made so that we were not forced to take part, or to witness, the difficulties of everyday living.

Travelling around with Anna, I sensed that she became uncomfortable whenever we laughed loudly or behaved flamboyantly. Similarly, when we were shown Krakow's many churches – which are open all day, every day, and are always full of the Faithful – I felt that I was never fervent enough for her liking. It's not unusual for people to attend mass every day of the week. Anna would rise at 6am for church and be back on time to give us her whole day. Even though Alison, like myself, is a Catholic, I know that she found Poland's brand of Catholicism, which is enmeshed in the Polish national identity, overwhelming. I found myself wondering how a non-Catholic, or an unmarried mother, or a homosexual, would cope in a society where one is expected to be Catholic to the letter.

It was quite staggering to walk past Anna's room and see her praying on her knees before a huge portrait of the Virgin Mary. Prayers were always said before meals. Alison was very balanced and detached about all this but it made me feel like an emotional and spiritual cart-horse and not a "proper" Pole.

We travelled to Auschwitz (now called Oswiecim) to visit the camp's museum of martyrdom with a young Polish woman, Basia, a friend of Anna's and a lecturer in English at the university. Basia is married but has no children. As a professional woman she has more chances to travel abroad and more contacts when it comes to finding "luxury" items. She is viewed as a "modern" woman; when Anna found what she thought was a contraceptive device on the floor (I didn't recognise it myself!) she showed it to me and said it was Basia's. When I said I didn't know what it was, she said: "That's good, that's very good. People should have more self-control." It was a view that I realised was quite commonly held.

"Cafés serving alcohol are usually run-down, sleazy looking places filled with men"

There seemed to be a lot of pressure on women to maintain traditional roles although a few professional women have gained some reprieve. But there is no pleasant place – no pubs or clubs – where women from all backgrounds can meet and socialise; when women are not earning money they are queueing for food and running a home; menfolk are "chivalrous" but offer little help in the home. As a result there is little time or opportunity for women to socialise outside of the family circle.

Cafés serving alcohol are usually run-down, sleazy looking places, filled with men – women never darken the doorstep. Spirits are about the only commodity that's cheap and in plentiful supply. Anna told me that alcoholism was an endemic social problem and that it was common for men to drink away their wages.

Foreigners are always welcomed very warmly and are an object of great interest. But they are invariably viewed as well off. Whenever my parents visited their relations, I was always aware of the fact that they never felt they were giving enough. Money always creates tension in our family group. Although anything that is given is gratefully received it must be given with care, as Poles are very proud and want you to have a good impression of what their country has to offer.

I never succumbed to selling dollars on the black market for huge sums of zlotys, as I felt that it would only reinforce the stereotype of the exploitative, wealthy Westerner, only interested in accumulating money to buy furs and crystal. Nor did I shop at the Pewex stores, which accept only Western currency. I will never forget the evening when a chance shipment of oranges made the national TV news bulletin, or the peculiar short propaganda shots shown in between programmes. I soon realised why my cousins loved British TV commercials on their visits!

Most Poles live in tower blocks, which are seen as quite a comfortable and safe form of accommodation. Space, however, is incredibly limited; whole families might live in one partitioned room and there's seldom any choice about which flat you'll be allocated. Czesia, for instance, had to cope with living on the fourth floor despite the fact that her legs were so bad she could barely climb the stairs. Anna told me (she was less concerned about hiding facts from me) that if too many people did their laundry on one day, the water would run out.

Despite the daily limitations they face, Poles do know how to let their hair down. Guests are toasted with plum liqueur (even at breakfast!) and evening gatherings can be pretty wild occasions – with music and conversation rising to fever pitch, and brimming with fervent political discussion. The exuberance and energy of these impromptu gatherings is in complete contrast to the subdued atmosphere and cold, huddled faces of people commuting to work on the trams. My impression was that the Poles are a vital, lively people who make full use of their dry, almost black, sense of humour to cope with the harsh realities of life.

As a visitor, you'll find this contagious and the famous Polish hospitality unforgettable. Beware of saying you like something in someone's home: I mentioned to Anna that I liked her glasses, and before I could blink she was wrapping them in paper for me to take away, saying that I was doing her a favour by solving her dilemma of what to get as a leaving present.

TRAVEL NOTES

Languages Polish. Almost everybody learns Russian at school, although most don't like admitting to it. Some people speak English and older people often speak German.

Transport Mostly by train: make sure you take the *expresobowe* as the alternatives are incredibly slow. Hitching is quite safe but uncommon, and you should expect to contribute towards (rationed) petrol. Public transport in towns is cheap and frequent and so are taxis.

Accommodation You have to stay in state-run hotels, which can be booked through the official travel agency, *Orbis*. Some may only accept payment in foreign currency.

Special Problems Shortages – things you take for granted are unavailable, including: sanitary towels, tampons, paper tissues, toilet paper, shampoo, washing powder, contraceptives, aspirin, coffee, toothpaste, toothbrushes. Western medicines can only be bought from the Pewex shops – most Poles have to rely on herbal remedies. How you deal with the relative privileges you have as a Western visitor is a personal issue. You'll need persistence and ingenuity to reciprocate the hospitality you receive. You might encounter some harassment from illegal money-changers but it is neither persistent nor threatening.

Guides *Eastern Europe – A Travel Survival Kit* (Lonely Planet) has an adequate section on Poland, good on the bureaucracy. A *Rough Guide* is in the making.

Contacts

No information on any women's groups.

Books

Jnina Baumann, *Winter in the Morning, A Young Girl's Life in the Warsaw Ghetto and Beyond* (Virago, 1986). Account of resilience and courage during the Warsaw siege and Nazi occupation.

Wislawa Szymborska, *Sounds, Feelings, Thoughts: 70 Poems by Wislawa Szymborska* (Princeton U. Press, US, 1981). Beautiful poems on simple observations of everyday life.

Portugal

Portugal may be technically an Atlantic country, but its character is – like neighbouring Spain – essentially Mediterranean. The climate is warm, the people a mix of Latin and Celt, and, for visitors, the attractions are a mix of beaches, lush countryside and good, cheap food and wine. It is also distinctively rural, with few sizeable towns beyond the historic capitals of Lisbon and Porto. The culture is relaxed and traditional: the Portuguese talk of themselves as a country of *brandos costumes* – "gentle ways".

The compact size of the country and an efficient network of buses and trains make exploration easy and straightforward, while *machismo* is less rampant here than in other Latin countries; men may hiss and make comments in the streets of Lisbon, but elsewhere traditional courtesy is generally

accompanied by welcome male restraint. It is one of the safest countries in Europe.

Given the persistent strength of tradition, it's sometimes hard to believe that Portugal not so long ago experienced a dramatic and quite extraordinary Revolution. On 25 April 1974 several decades of dictatorship came to an end in an almost bloodless coup, engineered by the army. On top of economic stagnation at home, much of its impetus came from the politicisation of soldiers returning from Africa where their government had sent them, at great expense, to combat the escalating wars of liberation in its colonies. As well as sudden independence for these colonies, the Revolution meant massive changes inside the country; amongst them the redistribution of land, the achievement of workers' rights, better social and living conditions, and alterations in the family law. Portugal also showed an impressive tolerance – in stark contrast to its appalling colonial administration – in coping with the influx of over a million refugees from the former colonies. In the 1980s there has been something of a conservative backlash in politics, with the emphasis placed firmly on handling the economy – the most backward in the EC.

Throughout the period of the Revolution, women campaigned and organised alongside men. Gradually, however, political change seemed to reach a deadlock and with it came the familiar realisation that women's specific needs had been submerged. Despite positive legal reforms, the brief emergence of a woman prime minister, and the high profile of women in higher education, old attitudes die hard and the Portuguese **women's movement** has had difficulties mobilising on any large scale. Compared with, say, Italy or Spain, the movement today is small. However, there are at least a couple of central organisations in Lisbon which can put you in touch with what's happening around the country.

"What You Do and What You Don't"

. . . .

Elizabeth Mullett has lived and studied in Lisbon, as well as travelled throughout the country.

Lisbon is one of the most attractive capitals in the world: a breezy, dazzlingly white city which has somehow escaped the worst of urban expansion. I lived there for a while, with a thesis to research, a long list of archives to visit and an irredeemably student income on which to do it. Not quite a resident, nor quite a tourist, I hired a room and traipsed between libraries and the city sights. I explored the frantic covered market on the river front in the early mornings and, from my landlady, learned to cook the sweet rice desserts and the rich stews, brimming with pigs' ears and calves' shinbones.

I also learned to duck the harassment experienced by most young women in the city, finding in museum gardens and monastery cloisters the perfect places to read or write letters undisturbed. Following the example of other students, I used to take my books and newspapers to one of the big town cafés in the evenings and sit there with a coffee, half-studying, half-watching the world. Local incomes are low but the habit of an evening out universal. I acquired an ability to stay up until four in the morning to listen to the city's *fado* music (a kind of national blues – worth hearing), to eat breakfast standing up in the busy *pastelerias*, to look people back in the eye and to take lunch seriously.

I was so energetically absorbing a new culture that it took me some time to feel a foreigner's isolation. It wasn't that most Portuguese women of my age were locked into family life, married with several children already; more that, despite the relaxing of social attitudes since the 1974 Revolution, women are still essentially seen in the image of their family relationships; somebody's daughter, wife, mother or widow. Acute housing shortages in Lisbon and Porto and a national minimum wage of less than £100 a month mean that most children leave home only after marriage and often not even then.

To be sure, women achieved paper equality within five years of the

Revolution, but male socialism has tended to view women's needs and aims as secondary and feminism has had little institutional and popular support. A liberal family background makes more difference than any legislation and if the corridors of the universities are full of women students, access to higher education (gained by under two percent of the population) is still largely a privilege of the middle classes. Talking to feminists, I found that the most highly valued opportunity had been to travel, either through work or study, and that way gain a sideways look at their culture and sense of themselves as individuals.

My work took me to Evora, a white-washed Moorish town in the Alentejo, a region which seemed to me one of the most fascinating. Since Roman times it has been an area of vast rural estates, most of which were seized from the landowners and transformed into collective farms after the Revolution. Governments responded first by extending, then restricting, agricultural credits needed by these new farms, and now big families are being allowed to return to parts of their estates.

The towns are therefore a focus of both the region's poverty and its provincial bourgeoisie. If the narrow convoluted streets are still lined with sixteenth- and seventeenth-century houses, it's because they have mostly escaped redevelopment; and if the sky on summer nights has more stars than you've ever seen before, it's because electricity has not reached every house in every town.

Every Tuesday, Evora's main square is full of livestock farmers in dark suits and black hats, negotiating business. At lunchtime they swarm into the local restaurants and fall upon the goat stews, dishes of pork cooked with shellfish, and great steaming plates of salt cod boiled with chickpeas. This is a profoundly masculine society – the characteristic music of the region is that of the male voice miners' choirs –

and if you travel from Evora to any of the medieval towns beyond you will find cafés the meeting places of men after dinner. It's rare to see women on the streets after nightfall.

As I moved around the north, to the granite and down-to-earth city of Porto and to Vila Real and the castellated hill towns of the Spanish frontier in Tras-os-Montes, I was confronted with a quite different world. This is the area of the great vineyards, but also of small subsistence farming. On the terraces of the River Douro and in the handkerchief-sized plots, there are jumbles of cows, cabbages and vines, each family holding infinitely subdivided among families by the inheritance divisions of the Minho district. For the visitor, it's an area which repays a good eye for changing styles of domestic architecture – the granite boulders of the Beiras and the drystone walling of Tras-os-Montes; a stomach for the egg-yolk and sugar confections, different in each town; and a taste for the Dão wines and the delicious semi-sparkling *vinhos verdes*.

"The survival of gentle and courteous social attitudes make Portugal one of the easiest Latin countries in which to travel alone"

To the east of the Douro, the journey from Chaves to Bragança takes you through some of the most spectacular scenery in the country, wild and empty. From time to time you pass through villages desiccated by emigration, communities of old people, women and children, whose men work in the cities of Central Europe, returning only for visits in the summer months. It's the most conservative area of Portugal, where adherence to the Church and respect for authority have remained strongest. As "widows of the living", the wives remain rigidly subject to popular criticism of their social behaviour – as one woman put it, "what you do and what you don't".

What you do and what you don't, as a visitor, is very much up to you. There are excellent detailed guidebooks and the tourist offices are friendly and helpful about all sorts of unusual requests – where to go to find the country's remarkable wild flowers, for example, or where to nurse a particular ailment or allergy at a spa. Whatever you can learn of this strangest of the romantic languages in advance will help immeasurably, but many Portuguese speak some English or French and understand Spanish. And the survival of gentle and courteous social attitudes make Portugal, beyond Lisbon or the busy beaches, one of the easiest Latin countries in which to travel alone.

Family Life in the Alentejo

. . . .

After travelling by Landrover around Africa with her husband and three young sons (see Algeria), Jan Wright has settled in a remote part of the Alentejo. Here the family have thrown themselves whole-heartedly into the local peasant life.

A gust of hot air singes my eyebrows and I duck back before swabbing out the clay oven and beginning to shovel in the loaves. One after the other: ten three-pounders, a pizza, a flan, a couple of cakes and a dozen sweet potatoes. Get them in as fast as possible before the oven cools and then relax. Relax? I'll be lucky! Sometimes the weekly bake is a disaster, bread charred on the outside or soggy on the inside. But I'm learning and the disasters are the exception now and not the rule. A small handful of flour on the oven floor – if it goes dark brown the oven's too hot; a knowing tap on the bottom of the first loaf out – if it's too soon pop it back in for another ten minutes. Even the neighbours have to agree it's good.

The neighbours love to help and advise. Even more they love us to be wrong. We are doubly strangers: foreigners and city people. We are ignorant of everything that to them is basic knowledge learned in the early years of life from father or mother. Or more likely grandfather or grandmother, for in this society child-rearing is usually passed back to the older generation to free the parents for the relentless toil which all too often leaves them old beyond their years. "Kill the pig next Saturday?" They look at us in horror. Have we offended some religious festival? We look at each other, at a loss, and eventually they deign to explain: "It's the waning moon." We all look at each other, time travellers, by some fluke caught in the same place at the same time.

Portugal, in the twentieth century. Closer to Africa than to Northern Europe, the Alentejo was, up to fifteen years ago, a semi-feudal society where most people were too poor to afford shoes, where the old starved if they had no family to support them. It's one of the last examples of the peasant society in Europe – a society doomed to extinction among the red tape of EC grants and the glitter of the world on the other side of the TV screen.

Five miles from the west coast and just north of the border with the Algarve, we have a valley to ourselves. Its elements are a continuing wonder to me: native Portuguese trees, Imperial eagles circling overhead in spring, wild flowers, and lots of butterflies. There are no main services and no prospect of ever having them. A track deters all but the most determined visitors. Our building has thick clay walls and a tiled roof; small windows to keep out the sun; an open fireplace and, outside, the great clay bread oven. There's a stream which runs dry in the summer and spills out in furious flood once or twice a year, when we get half the annual rainfall in a few hours. "The worst rain for forty years," they assure us as we all huddle in the local bar. They said that last time, too.

"The prevalent machismo can turn male children into strutting, demanding brats"

We've been here three years now, myself, my husband and our three children. We drive the boys four kilometres up to school in the morning because it's a long steep hill, and who wants to go to school? They make their own way home, stopping to play with friends, getting a freshly baked bun from the old couple who live in the last house of the scattered village, spotting wild flowers and butterflies, birds of prey, the occasional snake. We are a significant minority in the school. There are only ten children, aged from six to ten, including our three. There is just one teacher, an unwilling exile from Porto, who responds to her enforced sojourn in the back of beyond with frequent absences "on business in Odemira".

Predictably it is Sam, our eldest, who has had the most problems settling into our life here. He knew the greater stimulation of primary school in England. He's a great reader and took a long time to develop the skill in Portuguese sufficiently to be able to read the books that interested him. He has had several confrontations with the teacher. "Copy out this passage." "What does it mean?" "I'll tell you later. Copy it out." "I won't copy it out until I know what it means." A sudden reminder of how authoritar-

ian a society Portugal was, and therefore is. After fifty years of fascism many people had forgotten, or had never learned, to think for themselves.

Now, fifteen years after the Revolution, the same attitudes and ideas persist, even though the physical compulsion has disappeared. We can only explain both points of view: that he is right, but that while he is in the school he must go towards the teacher's point of view. The other two boys always have the stimulation of their older brother. Sam suffers from our isolation. Eddie, the youngest, is almost more Portuguese than English. He takes his imaginary cigarettes out of his imaginary breast pocket and taps them on the table: the stance and gestures are completely Portuguese. He was under three when we came here. When we help him with his homework, it's usually in Portuguese. We hope they will all be fully bilingual when they are older and, in their turn, exercise the choice we made of where we would live. Can we also protect them from or show them an alternative to the prevalent *machismo* that can turn male children into strutting, demanding brats?

In choosing the Alentejo, we chose a pre-consumer and almost pre-money society. We all have plastic carrier bags, but the shops charge for them and so we wash and re-use them. There is practically no visible rubbish: anything edible goes to the pig; anything organic disappears in the manure heap; oil cans and paint tins reappear as plant pots. The council provides big square bins at strategic places on the road and we drop off the few bits that are left. Our neighbours usually have one or two money-making lines: peanuts, maize, beans or potatoes, goats, pigs or cheese.

If there is a surplus of something, it is for giving not selling. Giving to family, giving to visitors, giving to those amazing English who are so incompetent that they don't have cabbages coming out of their ears when everybody else does. In return we give the one thing that we have and they don't: transport. Recently I was hailed by one of the ladies of the village and told there was a funeral that afternoon and would I take some of the ladies. Eight elderly ladies in black chose the Landrover in preference to the taxis that were taking the rest of the villagers. I felt rather flattered.

The poorer of our neighbours have very few cash outgoings: they live entirely on their own produce. When they kill a pig, of which every scrap is used, they eat meat; the bulk is salted down to keep them going for months. Potatoes, beans and bread are eaten in quantity and so are a lot of vegetables in season. The cool dark back rooms of the clay houses are ideal for storing vegetables. We were astounded to be given tomatoes in February – they had kept perfectly since the previous October. Cash is spent on alcohol, occasional clothes, and very little else. In the house of our nearest neighbours up-valley there is a bed, a rough wooden table, and a crate for a chair. They cook over an open fire and the only light is a candle.

"My neighbours, Edite and Ze, started with nothing but a couple of goats and a rented house"

The rest of Portugal sees the Alentejans as stupid and lazy. There are Alentejo jokes, just as England has Irish jokes. Lazy perhaps, because they might have seen the Alentejan farmer from their cars, sitting with his back against the cool white walls of his house, looking at the distant sea. They were still in bed when the peasant did half his day's work before breakfast.

My neighbours, Edite and Ze, started with nothing but a couple of goats and a rented house. In a lifetime's work, during which the holidays can be counted on one hand, they increased the herd to 150 goats and 50 cows. The kids and calves are sold once a year; Edite sells goat's cheese of high repute. By local standards they are now wealthy people. Over the years they paid for two daughters at university and now, in their fifties, have bought and paid for the house and acres to which they will retire when a few more calves, a few more goats have added to the security in the bank. The only machine which assists their farming operation is a petrol pump; they do not own a vehicle. A black-and-white TV runs off a car battery; a gas light and the open fire illuminate the kitchen where the life of the family revolves. In an unusually hopeful sign for this way of life, the youngest daughter, after trying several city jobs, has come home to work alongside her parents.

True, the trend is away from the country. The young people want electricity and the tarmac road, and the government encourages this move which pulls people into the money-spending, tax-paying economy. Portugal as a whole is poised between the past and the EC dream of the future. Car ownership increased by eighty percent over the last twelve months, but with a high cost in people defaulting on credit, which was all too easy to arrange.

The older people, though, do not only hold to their way of life through ignorance of any other. Antonio, the local contractor, worked for several years in France to pay for his tractor. Mario, who runs the local garage as a sort of semi-charity for the usually decrepit vehicles around, can afford to do so because of the money he made in Africa and the Middle East. Like many other Mediterranean countries, there are few families who don't have someone working abroad, providing for the present or the future. When the emigrants return they don't want to bring back the ways of more "advanced" countries: they appreciate the way of life here, the importance of the family and friends, the simple pleasures of good company, the beauty of a countryside largely unscarred by man.

It's half-past eight. Still cold at this time of year, and as we mutter greetings to our neighbours, one of the grandmothers, less than five feet tall and dressed in black (she is a widow and widows wear black for life), comes forward with cake and a tiny glass of the local *medronho* spirit, distilled from the fruit of the strawberry tree which grows wild over the hills. Down it in one, and give the ritual exhalation as the spirit burns. We are here to help our neighbours kill a pig: an excuse for a two-day celebration of eating and drinking, music and dance.

The pig is enticed out of the sty, seized firmly by six men and walked to a low table. The fearsome jaw is tied. The pig is lifted bodily on to the table. Two men hold each back leg and one the front against the death throes. The knife goes in deep twists, and within three or four minutes of leaving the sty the pig is dead. We pause for another glass of spirits; nobody enjoys the act of killing and few of the local *matadores* will kill more than once in a day. The women collect and stir the blood for black pudding and the men burn off the hair with a gas burner. (Edite and Ze use burning gorse, but here we are modern.) Then the men scrape the skin white again with the razor sharp penknife that every countryman carries. The pig is opened and the women take the guts and organs for sorting and grading and making into sausages.

My stomach turns as I wash out the intestines, turn them inside out and wash them again. The balance of the work is with us now. Great cauldrons steam over the open fire as the pork fat is rendered down and the skin cut into pork scratchings and the sausages prepared. Meanwhile, since early morning, a separate group of women have been preparing the feast that marks the first major stage of the job; the pig has been halved and the sides separated

from the head and the spine. The men lounge around drinking and smoking. Until the meat sets and they can joint it they have nothing else to do.

"Cassimira . . . found herself insulted by some men at the well. She took down her father's shotgun and fired two rounds over their heads"

As in many rural societies, the division of roles is very marked: women tend to socialise with women, men with men. Some jobs are women's jobs, others men's. The women are strong and often run the families and the farms while the men go away or abroad to work. Cassimira, Edite and Ze's daughter, found herself insulted by some men at the well. She walked back up the hill, took down her father's shotgun and fired two rounds over their heads. She was fifteen. She describes with relish their hasty retreat to their car. Having seen the ease with which she hoists a hundred-weight sack of animal food on to her shoulder, I would prefer to be on her side in any fight!

Interestingly, both men and women are known by their Christian names, with or without the equivalent of Mr or Mrs. So I am Jan or Senhora Jan and my husband is Chris or Senhor Chris, an external sign, perhaps, of the degree to which people keep their own identity.

Our society is poised at a crossroads, firmly divided between the generations. At the moment it's a land of windmills and watermills, of cobblers and cartwrights, blacksmiths and coopers. A way of life very close to nature and based on the village. With a lifetime of immense hard work, the older generation have scraped together a sufficiency and in many cases considerable wealth. The fruits of that thrift are now being lavished on their children.

Our neighbours down the valley have bought their son the car they never allowed themselves. Next they will buy him a plot of land and build him a house. It is almost certain that the son will never return to till the family land.

The alternatives for the future are all too obvious. The paradise that the Algarve once was has been destroyed by piecemeal development, soaking up easy foreign money. The danger is very real that this development will spread up the more austere but totally unspoilt west coast. Inland, as the people move away from the land, the eucalyptus trees move in: mile after mile of mono-culture – the fastest growing tree in the world which, after three crops and thirty years, totally depletes the soil. Many of the plantations are there to guarantee IMF loans, providing secure hard cash in terms of pulp for Northern Europe.

Our own property is an island in this sea. We feel privileged to be experiencing and sharing this life. It seems likely that soon the waves will close over a way of living that has been self-sustaining for the last 2000 years.

TRAVEL NOTES

Languages Portuguese is a difficult language, especially when it comes to pronunciation, but if you know some French and/or Spanish you shouldn't find it too hard to read. English and French are quite widely spoken in cities and most people understand Spanish (albeit reluctantly).

Transport A slow but reasonably cheap and efficient network of buses and trains covers most of the country. Taxis are cheap and reliable; everyone uses them all the time in Lisbon, though outside city boundaries negotiate fares in advance. Bicycle hire is a good, if exhausting, way of exploring the countryside.

Accommodation Reasonably cheap hotels and *pensões* are available, even at the height of summer. In smaller towns it's often best to ask the nearest friendly-looking woman, who will know who lets rooms; it's quite accepted. Youth Hostels are cheaper (there are about a dozen in Portugal, most of them open all year round), but you won't meet Portuguese people that way. There are also about a hundred authorised campsites, mostly small and attractive.

Guide *The Rough Guide: Portugal* (Harrap Columbus) is reliable and up-to-date.

Contacts

There are relatively few **women's organisations** in Portugal. The following addresses, all in Lisbon, are good initial contacts.

Comisão da Condicão Feminina, Avenida de República, 32-1 Lisbon 1093. Researches and maintains a watching brief on all aspects of women's lives in Portugal; organises meetings and conferences, and is very active in areas of social and legal reform. Also a good library and connections with feminists throughout the country.

Informação, Documentação Mulheres (IDM), Rua Filipe da Mata, 115A, Lisbon, ☎720598. Women's centre incorporating a small library and the one women-only café in Lisbon. Run by a collective of lesbian and heterosexual women, very keen to welcome foreign travellers and publicise the activities of the centre. French, German and English spoken.

Editora das Mulheres, Rua da Conceição 17 (4th floor), right in the centre of Lisbon. Feminist bookshop.

Espaço-Mulheres, Rua Pedro Nunes 9a, Lisbon. Art gallery and meeting place for women. Open every day, 3–7pm.

Books

Maria Velho da Costa, Maria Isabel Barreno and Maria Teresa Horta, *The Three Marias: Portuguese Letters* (Paladin, 1975) Collage of letters, stories and poems by three feminist writers. Hard to obtain, but worth the effort.

Few other Portuguese women writers have been translated into English but we'd appreciate any recommendations.

Thanks to Elizabeth Mullet for supplying much of the information for these Travel Notes.

Saudi Arabia

Islam of the stern Wahabite tradition dominates all aspects of life in Saudi Arabia. Although Western technology is welcome, its culture most clearly is not. The country permits no tourism. With the exception of Muslims, who can obtain pilgrimage visas to visit the holy sites of Mecca and Medina, foreigners can only enter the country on work or family visas.

However, due to Saudi Arabia's oil industry – the country is the world's leading exporter – foreign workers make up a significant part of its population. Amongst this large community, the vast majority migrant workers from the Arab world, are several thousand Westerners. Most women among them are on family visas, accompanying their husbands, but a significant number come independently as teachers, doctors, nannies and nurses.

Western women living in Saudi Arabia are faced with numerous restrictions. It is illegal for a woman to drive; it is essential to dress extremely modestly and to keep to the areas marked out for women – the rear of buses, the "family section" of a restaurant, etc. Failure to observe these and many other practices (see Travel Notes) can lead to severe reprimands or arrest by the stick-wielding *mutawa*, the religious police. At the same time, Western women, particularly single workers, are vulnerable to harassment – both from Saudi men for failing to conform to the role expected of women, and from the large numbers of foreign men with bachelor status.

Westerners are usually housed in special compounds, often luxuriously equipped; however, with strict curfews for women, these can become stiflingly insular. Reports are that the various rules and regulations have an infantalising effect and many foreign wives, like their Saudi counterparts, complain of abject boredom. It's not easy to explore the cities, let alone travel around the Kingdom on your own. Most women join up with other expatriates for trips around the country.

Saudi women are expected to lead traditional, secluded lives – their roles strictly confined to that of wife and mother. On the rare occasions when they go out, they are heavily veiled and accompanied by their husbands, fathers or brothers. Their participation in the open labour force is one of the lowest in the world, though, with the widespread introduction of female education in the 1960s, changes have started to take place. Women are now encouraged to work in segregated female sectors (as teachers, doctors, social workers, nurses, etc), and the government has also begun to consider the economic advantages of employing women outside of teaching and social services instead of relying on a large foreign workforce. Moves in this direction provoke much opposition from the conservative Muslims in the country, but at the same time there is a growing movement amongst Saudi women, backed by liberal men, advocating women's greater participation in the economic and social life of the country.

Back Behind the Veil

. . . .

Alice Arndt first went to Saudi Arabia in 1975, on a two-year teaching contract; she returned ten years ater to live, with her husband.

I first arrived in the Kingdom fifteen years ago, washed in on the wave of modern technology, foreign workers and petrodollars. If you had asked me then, I would have told you that, of course, in a few years Saudi women would be driving cars, veils would gradually disappear, the shops which closed their doors at prayer times would constitute an ever smaller minority. I noted the increasing educational opportunities for women, and felt certain that they would soon lead to demands from the women for further work opportunities and ultimately for emancipation in

their society. And the large number of young Saudi men who were being sent to other countries for advanced degrees would surely be infected with more liberal attitudes towards the women at home. I assumed without question that the East-West gap would gradually close up, and took it for granted that exposure to Western customs and values would lead inevitably to their adoption.

Well, it hasn't turned out that way at all. It is still illegal for a woman to drive or own an automobile or to ride a bicycle. Today, virtually every shop closes up tight during the several daily prayers, and any shopkeeper who's slow to lock his door or pull down the shutters is likely to find the *mutawa*, the religious police, brandishing a long stick in his direction. Even television programmes are interrupted by a prayer intermission.

Women in the Kingdom must dress more conservatively than they did during my first stay – and that includes foreigners as well as Saudis. My husband's company issues regular bulletins about the "Dress Code" for employees and their families. The long skirts which I used to wear are now considered to be too form-revealing because they have a waistband; a long, loose dress is preferred. For the same reason, trousers must be covered by a long tunic top. Did I really wear sleeveless blouses in the summer heat one and a half decades ago? Not today.

"When it is necessary for a man to teach a class of women, he lectures to them from behind a one-way glass which functions just like a veil: they can see him but he cannot see them"

Recently, with my family and friends, I ventured into a very old market area of a conservative town in the centre of the peninsula. Although I wore a black silk *abaya*, a long cloak that extends from the top of my head to my feet, covering all but face and hands, the local residents – both men and women – were not satisfied until I was peering out at them in astonishment through three layers of black gauze which hung before my face.

When I first arrived in Saudi Arabia, I got a job teaching English and mathematics to young Saudi men in an industrial training school. Although it was somewhat remarkable for them to have a woman teacher, my skills were needed at that time and most of my students accepted me with friendly good grace. Today, women are not permitted to teach in that school. In some women's colleges, there is a shortage of qualified instructors similar to the situation at my training centre years ago. When it is necessary for a man to teach a class of women, he lectures to them from behind a one-way glass which functions just like a veil: they can see him but he cannot see them.

This is how the Saudis always said it would be. They insisted from the very beginning that they would take

Western technology without taking Western culture. They warned that they would hire foreign workers when they needed them and send them home the minute they had trained Saudis to do their jobs. Today, with oil production at a twenty-year low, thousands of foreigners are leaving the Kingdom every month, returning to homes all over the world.

In addition to preserving their traditions and customs in the face of modernisation, the Saudis are participating in that broad political and religious conservatism which has swept across both East and West. Fundamentalist Muslims, within and without the Kingdom, are urging the Saudi government, as Guardian of the Holy Cities of Mecca and Medina, to be ever stricter in adhering to and enforcing Islamic principles.

Most of the Saudi women I met were disapproving of their sisters in the West. They see Western women as unprotected, living in dangerous cities, and unable to rely on the men of their family to escort them on the streets. A strong sense of sisterhood has always been a part of Arab culture, and constant familial support buoys Saudi women throughout their lives. In contrast, Western women's lifestyles seem full of risk – of loneliness, promiscuity, and abandonment by their children in their old age.

In public, Saudi women and men are separated. Schools are segregated by sex. All museums and public exhibits have men's days and women's days during the week. The few women who venture to worship in a mosque are confined to a special section. Even weddings are celebrated with a men's party and a women's party.

Education for females outside the home is a new phenomenon, which began only 35 years ago. Today there are girls' schools at every level, including women's programmes at several universities. Older women are included in a national literacy campaign.

Opportunities exist for women to study abroad (usually with their husbands). A woman may become a teacher (with female students) or a doctor (with female patients) or a businesswoman (whose brothers provide the interface with the male world). Several banks have established branches just for women. The government has recently begun to consider whether putting their own women to work would be less disruptive to their society than bringing in masses of foreign workers, and is looking for ways to create more "women's jobs".

"There is no political action group in Saudi Arabia, male or female"

I am acquainted with a few Saudi women who refuse to wear the veil – they are fortunate in that their families support them in this move – and a couple who rankle at government censorship and what they see as religious coercion. I know of several who feel depressed by the numerous restrictions placed on them. But they all consider themselves to be good Saudis nonetheless, and are devoted to their

families, culture, religion and country. There is no political action group in Saudi Arabia, male or female. Women are not agitating for "liberation" or "equality". Change in Saudi society will come from the inside, within individual lives, homes and families, and at a pace consistent with the Middle Eastern concept of time – one profoundly different from the Western concept.

Thanks to the oil boom of the 1970s, the Saudis' material needs are basically met. The country is now self-sufficient in food production; electricity has reached a large number of towns and villages; education is free and available to anyone who wants it; hospitals are well-equipped and their number is growing as fast as the staff can be found; even the nomadic Bedouin have access to new water wells drilled here and there in the desert. These material advances can free the people to turn their thoughts and energies to the larger questions of life, to contemplate, perhaps, among other things, the role of women in this modern manifestation of their ancient culture. And that has to be good for Saudi women, for their men, and for both halves of the earth.

TRAVEL NOTES

Languages Arabic. English is widely spoken and understood.

Transport There are frequent and reasonably-priced plane services between all the main cities in the country. There is also a network of good roads and rental cars are available in all areas. However, as a single woman, you will have to obtain a driver (it is illegal for a woman to drive) and obtain written permission for trips further than thirty kilometres! The larger cities have a public bus service. Each bus has a special compartment for women, which is closed off from the rest of the vehicle and entered by a separate door. Employers of Westerners usually operate a private recreational bus service for shopping and beach trips.

Accommodation Special compounds have been built for foreigners. Women are subject to curfews and need a written invitation from a married couple in order to stay out overnight. Cohabitation is absolutely prohibited. Hotels are often reluctant to register single women and, although it is not legally required, you may be asked to produce a letter of permission from your employer, husband or father. During the *Hadj* (pilgrimage) hotels become very full and you'll need to reserve a room well in advance.

Special Problems Visitor's visas are usually only given to workers travelling to a job already obtained in the Kingdom, to women and children on family visas, and to visitors attending a conference or invited by an academic or commercial institution. Tourist visas are not available and it has become more difficult recently for single women to obtain a work permit. Customs officials search luggage thoroughly for alcohol, drugs, medicines and pornography. Penalties for attempting to bring any of these items into the country can be severe.

Western women, in particular single ones, are subjected to a wide array of both verbal and physical abuse – cars hooting, kerb crawling, staring and touching. However, penalties for all crimes are very harsh and actual physical attack (in public at least) is incredibly rare. If you feel uncomfortable you should make a fuss; few men would persist if confronted. It is illegal for a woman to spend time alone with a man who is not a relative. Dress codes are strict and rigidly enforced. Any woman considered immodestly clothed faces severe treatment from the religious police. Many foreigners find it simplest to wear the *abaya*, which covers the body from head to toe.

Guides Madge Pendleton, ed, *The Green Book; Guide for Living in Saudi Arabia* (Middle East Editorial Associates, Washington) is useful to prepare yourself for the regulation. *Saudi Arabia: A MEED Practical Guide* (Middle East Economic Digest, London) gives a good overview and details of sights.

Contacts

Saudi Arabia Women's Association, BP 6, Riyadh. The association provides information about Saudi women's organisations, most of which are organised for social and charitable purposes.

Books

Marianne Alireza, *At the Drop of a Veil* (Houghton Mifflin, US, 1971).

Eleanor Nicholson, *In the Footsteps of the Camel: A Portrait of the Bedouins of Eastern Saudi Arabia in Mid-Century* (Stacy International, 1983).

Soraya Altorki, *Women in Saudi Arabia* (Columbia U. Press, US, 1986). An analysis of life in the rich Jeddah elite. Focuses particularly on Saudi women's efforts to improve their status working within traditionally defined roles.

Useful information on Saudi women can be found in ***Sisterhood is Global*** and in the Minority Rights Group report ***Arab Women*** (see General Bibliography).

Thanks to Jean Grant Fraga for contributing to the introduction.

Senegal

S enegal was the first West African country to be colonised by France and the continuing French influence is immediately apparent in the smooth road networks and transport system, and in the exclusive resorts, restaurants and private beaches along the coast. The country draws around 200,000 French package tourists a year – and it is also one of the most popular West African destinations for independent travellers.

Beneath the French veneer, Senegal has a profoundly African Muslim culture and the precepts of Islam are widely practised and felt. In comparison

with the North African states this imposes relatively few restrictions on women, who maintain a high profile in public life and are easy to make everyday contact with. Politically the country is run as a multiparty democracy and despite the riots of 1988, a continuing economic crisis, and escalating racial conflicts with the Mauritanian minority, it manages to retain its reputation as one of the most stable countries in the region.

Dakar is perhaps the worst introduction to the country. Many people compete to make a living from the tourists and French ex-pats, and the constant pressure and hard-sell tactics of the street vendors and "guides" can give it a coercive atmosphere. The only real danger, however, is in the wealthy commercial centre where muggings are now common. Elsewhere in the country you experience few problems, though you will need to get used to being a symbol of affluence and to having people constantly approach you for money. How you cope with this is a personal issue; most Senegalese routinely give something to beggars and it's vital to remain friendly and polite. Sexual harassment is much less evident. It's advisable, though, and certainly more comfortable in the hot climate, to wear long, loose clothes. Travelling around the country is fairly easy – transport is good, there's a fair amount of accommodation, and the Senegalese people are renowned for their hospitality to strangers. It is quite likely that you will be invited to stay in someone's house, in which case be aware of the burdens you are imposing. There's no offence in paying for as much as you can and it's polite to offer gifts.

The main **women's organisation**, the *Fédération des Associations Feminines du Sénégal* (*FAFS*) was founded by the ruling Parti Socialiste and retains close links with the government. Its chief emphasis is on development and the provision of social welfare and educational services. Although it has a wide membership and has set up a range of local groups, its impact in the rural areas is still small. A more radical group is the *Association of African Women for Research and Development* (*AAWORD*), created by a group of African women dedicated to doing feminist research from an African perspective. Over the last decade they have assisted in numerous schemes, emphasising the need for direct participation of local women in development projects. One of AAWORD's central concerns has been to place the issue of genital mutilation firmly in context as an African problem to be resolved by African people, counteracting Western outrage and sensationalism.

Life with the Diops
. . . .

Daphne Topouzis, a founder editor member of *Africa Report*, an American bi-monthly magazine of African affairs, spent six months in Senegal researching a PhD; she lived with a Senegalese family on the outskirts of Dakar.

My original purpose in going to Senegal was to research into the impact of French colonial rule on the development of Black Politics during the 1930s and 1940s. I also wanted to collect material on the Women's Movement in the cities and on the role of women in rural development. It gradually became apparent to me, though, that living with a Senegalese family was easily the most valuable experience of the trip. It enabled me to meet and get close to a large number of women of all ages, from all walks of life, which would have otherwise been impossible.

A friend who had also researched in West Africa helped me make contact with a Muslim family in Dakar. Though we had never met before, the Diops borrowed a couple of relatives' cars and came to meet me at the airport like an old friend. Hospitality (*teranga*) is central to Senegalese culture and hosts will go to great lengths to provide their guests with everything they possibly can, often exceeding their means.

My first days at the "Keur Diop" (Diop household) in Liberté VI, one of Dakar's suburbs, were overwhelming. Not only was this my first time in Africa but it was also the first time I had lived with a family of twenty. I shared a tiny room with two other women my age and was at once deprived of all privacy and independence, both of which had until then seemed essential to me. Differences in lifestyle and culture initially seemed both fundamental and insurmountable.

Curiosity and shyness on both sides made conversation awkward for the first couple of days, until the youngest children broke the ice. They taught me my first words of Wolof, reminded me of everybody's names, gave me directions to the bus stop and involved me in family activities. Within a week or so I had settled into a daily routine and had learnt a great deal about my host family and its expectations of me.

"We spent long hours discussing polygamy, men, and the lack of choices for women"

Marianne, aged 56, was a secretary in a Dakar hospital, the second of four wives and mother of three daughters and five sons. Just under half of all marriages in Senegal are polygamous (Muslims can have up to four wives), which is a harsh reality and nightmare for many women. It involves economic hardship, neglect of the older wife, favouritism of the younger one, jealousy (wives often share the same bedroom), oversized families and overcrowded households. We spent long hours discussing polygamy, men, and the lack of choices for women. What impressed me most was her good humour, which invariably meant that conversations about grief ended with hearty laughter.

Marianne's daughters (aged 16, 22 and 23) were enormously curious about me and soon became constant companions. One particular incident a few days after my arrival brought us together. After jokingly remarking that my long, straight hair looked dull and ugly, they began plaiting it without awaiting my reply: "Plaits can make anyone look good," they said. But, however graceful they looked on them, plaits made me

look worse than before (not to mention the fact that the children became afraid of me). We laughed about it for hours, and later in the evening, fearful that my feelings had been hurt, my closest friend, Fatou, offered me a *pagne* (square patterned fabric tied around the waist). It felt comfortable and looked good – or so was the general consensus – and I began wearing it regularly.

My relationships with the men in the family were friendly and comfortable except for an isolated misunderstanding with the eldest son. But being always a little uncertain of my status I tried to maintain a safe distance. I rarely saw Mr Diop (a retired postman) as he spent almost all of his time with his third wife. However, I always looked forward to his weekly tea gatherings with his comrades from the Second World War where colonial politics were passionately discussed. They never quite understood how I knew so much about this relatively obscure period of African history, but greatly appreciated my avid interest in their accounts as well as my endless questions and occasional contribution to the discussion.

On the whole, everyone in the family was discreet, never asking personal questions which might have been difficult to answer (on religion, politics or sex). Part of the explanation might be that I was much more curious about them than they were about me. But, like most Senegalese, they were far more tolerant of me than I had expected. For instance, though visibly puzzled by the fact that I did not have children (but less concerned by the fact that I was single), they never pressed the issue.

As a devout Muslim family, the Diops had assumed I also would be religious (the fact that I was Christian did not make us all that different in their eyes) and when I first arrived they gave me directions to the local church. I never went there, and although they realised I did not practice my religion they never held this against me. Similarly, they were perplexed by the fact that despite being white, which meant rich, I dressed relatively casually while they, despite their very tight budget, were always elegant and graceful. In this case, I began to dress visibly better as a result of living with them, but again, they never tried to talk me into it.

In fact, two months after living with the Diops, the differences in culture which had at first seemed so radical began to wane and I was treated like a member of their family: they encouraged me to learn Wolof, dance the *sabar*, wear *pagnes*, and help with the cooking and shopping.

"I was . . . forced to confront why privacy and independence as I understood them were so important to me"

The only two things I found difficult to cope with were the lack of privacy and their unshakeable belief that, being white, I had an inexhaustible supply of money. The lack of privacy meant that I did not have a quiet half-hour to relax, read, or write letters. But there was no way around it as the family was large and the house overcrowded. The real challenge for me, however, was that the women with whom I was closest seemed unable to understand my professed need to be alone once in a while or my occasional spells of gloom and loneliness. I was gently scolded for my self-indulgent attitude and forced to confront why privacy and independence as I understood them were so important to me.

One particular incident has crystallised in my mind: On the last day of Ramadan, all but three young children and a couple of adults had gone to the local mosque to pray. At once, the compound which was full of activity and the noise of many children became unusually quiet. Marianne came to me and said anxiously, "I cannot stand it when the house is empty. It feels so lonely." While in the past I would have relished this rare moment of peace and quiet, I found to my surprise that it did feel lonely and painfully silent without the usual commotion. When the children returned, Marianne was visibly happier and proudly said to me "Now you see why my children (which virtually meant the whole extended family) are my fortune."

This is not to say that I resolved the problem of privacy, but I learnt a lot from doing without it. The problem of money I never fully resolved. Even though I contributed a weekly sum to the family income, regularly bought treats, took the children to the cinema, etc, etc, I was regularly asked for cash. If there was an emergency such as medical expenses or school fees, I gave what I could. But often it was for luxuries like cosmetics, which seemed essential to them but not to me. I learnt to say I did not have money but that always created some tension. In retrospect, I believe it is wiser to give something, even if only a fraction of the amount, rather than refuse altogether and appear insensitive to needs.

Except for those relatively minor problems, my life with the family ran smoothly once I had established a routine of my own. My day began at 7am when after a cup of *kenkilabah* (local herb tea) I would take the bus to the "Building Administratif" where the government archives are held. After work I would return to Liberté VI, often stopping by on the way amid the tiny, dark market stalls, loaded with vegetables and colour.

Marianne's daughters would start to prepare the food in the courtyard while there was still daylight. Evening entertainment consisted of either visiting friends or dancing to the haunting tunes of Dakar's musical superstars Youssou N'Dour (who has now become a celebrity worldwide) and Super Diamono. Social life around the family was so enjoyable that I never went downtown to discos, restaurants or bars. I knew they existed, and they are popular amongst the Senegalese, but it never seemed worth the trip. Liberté VI was relaxing after a hectic day in Dakar. Everybody knew each other, little French was spoken, and no whites lived there. At first I felt uncomfortable being stared at in the streets but gradually people got used to me. As soon as I learnt some Wolof the barrier was broken and I began greeting neighbours regardless of whether I knew them or not.

My first trip outside Dakar was to Fatik, a small town four hours south of the capital. Marianne's son took me to visit his grandmother and her family. The further away we got from Dakar the more we could see the effects of the drought: long stretches of land with dried-up baobabs, cotton trees and abandoned villages. Around Fatik the dry earth had cracked and dead cattle in different stages of disintegration baked in the sun. We visited the local market to get *gris-gris* (protective amulets) and then went to a wrestling match. Wrestling is Senegal's national sport and worth seeing. On a Sunday afternoon you can catch up to thirty matches. They last only a few minutes each and involve mesmerising ritualistic movements.

A second trip to Touba was a little disappointing. Touba is the birthplace of the Mouridyyia – Senegal's fast-growing Muslim brotherhood. A great mosque and Koranic university dominate the town, which itself is very poor. The contrast between the incredible wealth of the mosque and the poverty surrounding it is quite disturbing. Touba has its own militia who can (and do) arrest people for drinking alcohol or smoking cigarettes within the boundaries.

On another trip, with two women friends, I took the Casamance express boat down to Ziguinchor and visited the US Peace Corps house, which is situated right behind the port. (The Peace Corps is an American voluntary development agency.) Even though I initially had reservations about the organisation and its approach to work in Africa, I found the volunteers friendly, hardworking and eager for company. Travellers can stay at the house for a small fee. Also, the volunteers are usually delighted to take travellers to their assigned villages. Their knowledge of the local languages and the fact that they are well integrated in the local community were a positive contrast to the Canadian missionaries nearby who seemed totally estranged from their surroundings.

"I began having all the symptoms of malaria: chills and flushes, headaches, hallucinations and diarrhoea"

After Ziguinchor I went to Diembering, a small village off Cap Skirring. Villagers were drying fish in the sun, mending fishing nets and repairing pirogues on the beach. I had originally planned to stay for a few days at the government *campement*. But the same evening I began having all the symptoms of malaria: chills and flushes, headaches, hallucinations and diarrhoea. Usually, the first 72 hours of malaria attacks are the worst and after that a large dose of Nivaquine begins to work. I was helped on to the boat back to Dakar and went to the Peace Corps doctor. (They usually only treat volunteers but made an exception in my case.) It took ten days for me to recover and when I returned to the Diop family they treated me as though I had been long lost, showing very real relief and concern.

Soon after that episode I was stopped in the centre of Dakar by a *gendarme* who wanted to check my passport. As I didn't have it on me I was taken to the station, where I encountered at least twenty whites picked up for the same reason. (I was later told that every once in a while the police go out on such raids to show foreigners who's boss.) After sitting for hours in the waiting room I began to feel uncomfortable and frightened. The Chief of Police asked me a long series of questions and then calmly assured me that I would be there all day. A few moments later someone offered me a cigarette and I thanked him in Wolof. Suddenly the atmosphere changed, the police became warm and apologetic and I was inundated with invitations and offers of hospitality.

These problems did not cast a shadow over my stay. They were part of the challenge of trying to lead an integrated life in a very different culture and climate to my own. I've kept contact with the family in Liberté VI, whom I consider now part of my extended family, and am returning soon for another six-month stay.

TRAVEL NOTES

Languages French and several African languages – Wolof is the most widely spoken.

Transport The basic transport throughout Senegal is the bush-taxi (*taxi-brousse*). Each passenger pays for a seat, and the taxi leaves only when it is full. Try to travel early in the morning to avoid long waits for other passengers, especially in villages. Prices are government-fixed and fairly low. In Dakar there are taxis and buses.

Accommodation The tourist hotels of Dakar are generally expensive, though you can stay in *campements* (cheap but comfortable accommodation in simple buildings) at Casamance, outside the city. In the rural areas it is likely that you'll be invited to stay in people's homes. You should offer some money or gifts towards your keep.

Special Problems You will often be approached for money by hustlers, beggars and other people who need it and have none. People have their own ways of dealing with this – most give coins or small gifts.

Guides *The Rough Guide: West Africa* (Harrap Columbus) has a major section on Senegal.

Contacts

Association of African Women in Research and Development (AAWORD), Codesria, B3304, Dakar. A pan-African women's federation which carries out research, publishes a journal, and campaigns for women's rights throughout Africa.

Council for the Development of Economic and Social Research in Africa (CODESRA), BP3304, Dakar. Research centre which works, among other themes, on women and development in Africa.

Books

Mariama Ba, *So Long a Letter* (Virago, 1982). Brilliant portrait by a Senegalese feminist of a Muslim woman living in a society of transition. Ba's second book, *The Scarlet Song* (Longman, 1986), focuses on the relationship between an educated French woman and a poor Senegalese man.

Nafissatou Diallo, *A Dakar Childhood* (Longman, 1982). Autobiographical account of growing up in Dakar.

Aminata Sow Fell, *Beggars Strike* (Longman, 1981). Fictional tale of a beggars' uprising in Dakar by Senegal's leading woman novelist.

Sierra Leone

Very few travellers go to Sierra Leone. The problems of an almost defunct transport system and no direct links to neighbouring Guinea and Liberia make it difficult to visit the country as part of a West African tour. And, despite having some of the finest beaches on the continent, tourism has barely developed beyond the odd, isolated resort on Freetown peninsula and a clutch of hotels in the capital.

Escalating foreign debts, high-level corruption and an almost institutionalised diamond smuggling racket have brought Sierra Leone to the verge of economic collapse. The country's British colonial infrastructure, along with many of the state institutions developed since independence from the British in 1963, have either crumbled or fallen into disarray. Education and health provisions are poor and erratic, there's a chronic lack of transport, no internal phone system and a very limited electricity supply. Even the capital, Freetown, is subjected to regular blackouts. General Momoh, who heads the civilian government, has introduced widespread austerity measures in an attempt to prevent national breakdown. But, as poverty and hardship take hold, dissent and opposition are mounting.

Although tourists are very rare, there are plenty of foreign aid workers who travel around the country and there are few obvious restrictions or dangers for women. Men may well approach you with offers of sex – the propositions are usually direct and upfront – but this rarely feels oppressive or threatening. Much the same is true about requests for money. The assumption that you are rich is inescapable and, in a country where you have to rely quite heavily on local hospitality, the onus is on you to be a generous guest. Theft is a fairly common problem, especially if you live in the country for some time, and you'll be warned against wandering alone on deserted stretches of beach.

Attitudes towards women vary as you move from the predominantly Christian and more Westernised south, dominated by the Mende and Krio ethnic groups, to the nominally Muslim and more conservative north, dominated by the Temne. Amongst the Krios, who descend from the freed slaves of the Caribbean, and the Mendes, women have greater access to education and paid work and are expected to take a much more active role in community life. The Mendes still have a fair number of female paramount chiefs, something unheard of in the north. As a foreigner, though, you're unlikely to be affected by the shifts in local customs.

In Freetown there is a fairly well established **women's movement**, set up and run by Krio women to develop and support local education and income-generating projects. But, traditionally, women gain support, solidarity and not a little prestige through membership of the so-called secret societies. Genital mutilation is a central feature of many of these societies' initiation rites and, although campaigns have been set up opposing this practice, it remains a popular and widely accepted aspect of the rites of passage to womanhood.

Working in Makeni

· · · · · · · · · · · ·

Nicky Young has been living for the last eight months in Makeni, the capital of the northern province, where she works as an administrator in a school for deaf children.

When I arrived in Sierra Leone I was prepared for life without some of our normal creature comforts – running water, electricity, railways, efficient public transport, good roads, a national newspaper. What I did find a shock was that only twenty to thirty years ago most of these things were a reliable part of everyday life. The remnants of an economy that once worked is sad to see and incredibly frustrating for the nation who now have to live with it.

If first impressions are important, I can't ignore the arrival at Lungi Airport. The airport, built on a peninsula slightly north of the capital, Freetown, is small, busy and very confusing. You have to push your way through to various desks to produce visas and yellow fever certificates, fill in different coloured forms, and declare and change currency, before going through customs. And then you have to hold tight to your bags in case an over eager taxi driver grabs them and locks them in the trunk of his car. I was lucky in that I had someone to meet me.

Each year sees a small but growing number of wealthy French tourists arriving on package deals to Freetown Peninsula to soak up the hot African sun on the miles of unspoilt, tropical beaches. Besides joining an occasional tour around a "Typical African Village", few of them stray further than the local bars. Travelling up country is a difficult business and has to be treated as part of the adventure, but until you make it out of Freetown you won't really see Sierra Leone.

Hitching is a necessity. The only way of getting around is to wave at a passing car and hope that it will stop. The cars with the yellow number plates and bursting with people are supposed to be taxis, but you may get a lift from someone else, sometimes for free. Outside Freetown, most of the Western people you meet are expatriate workers and volunteers. Those who have transport are usually sympathetic to those who don't and I seem to spend much of my time scrounging lifts. People have mixed opinions of Freetown – most dislike the hassles involved in getting anything achieved, but appreciate the more frequent power and water supplies, Western foods and tropical beaches. It's a welcome break from the heat and commotion of Makeni where I live.

Makeni is about 115 miles inland from Freetown and has the reputation of being the hottest place in the country. I arrived in March, the hottest time of year, having come from frosty English weather. Sierra Leone is divided up into chiefdoms, each dominated by one of several tribes. Makeni is predominantly a Temne area. Temnes are known to be rather vociferous, and since my flat is situated right in the town centre, next to the market, I soon learnt that living in Africa wasn't going to be the peaceful experience I had hoped for.

Every morning at five I am woken by the call to prayer at the town mosque. From then onwards I hear the town stirring into life; market women setting up stalls, cocks crowing, dogs barking, and cassava leaves being pounded down into the staple soft green pulp seasoned with palm oil and fish. The mosque each morning is a constant reminder that Sierra Leone is a predominantly Muslim country. Before I arrived I was warned to dress modestly because of this. But so long as your clothes aren't brief or tight, most local people accept that you'll wear Western clothes, even shorts, and don't seem too bothered.

"'When can we meet to do some loving?' is the usual opening gambit"

Local people greet one another as they pass on the street, whether they know each other or not, and it is considered rude not to return a greeting. However, my trying not to be culturally insensitive was often misinterpreted by men, who took it as an invitation to get better acquainted. Men tend to be very forward in their proposals, "When can we meet to do some loving?" is the usual opening gambit. Life would be much easier if they took no for an answer, but they seldom do and I have often ended up being equally direct. White women tourists are considered both a novelty and a source of funds.

Overall, though, there is a friendliness and openness towards visitors, and people are eager to help you out – sometimes, uncomfortably so. I am rarely allowed to pull water from a well or to weed a garden without someone stepping in to help. And there have been times when I have been given the front seat of a bus, only to find that a frail old woman has been squashed into the back.

My job, as administrator for a school for hearing-impaired children, involves training a local woman the same age as myself. Mankapr had been doing the job for several years already, was used to Westerners coming to "share their skills", and knew how the people in her country expected things to be done. My first few months were spent building up a relationship with her and learning how it all worked.

My arrival coincided with preparations for her tribal wedding. Most of her contemporaries had married long ago and now had large families, but Mankapr had an overprotective brother as a guardian, who had been reluctant to let her go. She had been raised largely by this brother, as her mother had become sick after her birth and had never quite recovered, while her father was busy with his second wife. Mankapr was pregnant on her wedding day, which she explained was a fairly standard occurrence as a man wants to ensure that his wife will be fertile before he agrees to the marriage.

"Sitting in the candlelit room, watching the cockroaches scuttle across the walls, I remember feeling very lost"

I was lucky enough to be invited to attend the wedding, which took place one evening in a dimly lit yard behind the house of the bride's father. I was met by a group of older women, all brightly dressed in batik and tie-dyed *lappas* (fabric tied around their waists and a matching top and head tie), who took me to a neighbour's house. The men, I discovered later, had gathered further down the street.

Sitting in the candlelit room, watching the cockroaches scuttle across the walls, I remember feeling very lost – not understanding any of the Krio being spoken around me. (I learnt Krio fairly quickly afterwards; having so many adapted and assimilated English words it is a fairly easy language to pick up.) Eventually we were led to a yard, lit by a sole kerosene lamp placed in the centre, where the the male representatives of the bride's family were awaiting the entry of the groom's family. The wedding began with the

latter arriving carrying cola nuts – a gift of friendship. The bride's family pretended to be completely ignorant of who they were and why they were there. Then followed introductions of all the important people in the room – including me, because I was white – after which the nuts were accepted and the two groups settled down to negotiate the contract.

Money was discussed for all the groom's specific privileges as a married man, such as being allowed to talk to the bride, take her through the door of his house and, ultimately, to share her bed. This last caused a roar from all the guests, demanding that the price be much higher. The strangest thing throughout was that the bride wasn't even there. She was summoned only when the talks were finished. Then a young girl draped in white, obviously not the bride, was thrust forward and was rejected by the groom to everyone's amusement. Finally Mankapr appeared, was asked if she knew Hassan and if she would marry him and if he would marry her. After each "yes", money was flung in from the guests with much cheering, more cola nuts were exchanged, ground nut stew and *poyo* (palm wine) were distributed and the party began.

Several months later Mankapr and Hassan had a religious wedding, something most people have to forego because of the expense. They are now the proud parents of a healthy baby boy, with a cheeky smile, called Louis. Sierra Leone has one of the highest child mortality rates in the world, if not the highest. A teacher at my school told me that she was the only one of nine children to survive past childhood, and her story was not an uncommon one.

As I walk to school every morning along the dusty streets, children of all ages stop to chant at me, "Porto, Porto, Syrian. Are ya Syrian". The song fades as I pass but rises again with next group. "Porto" means "white". If they stop singing it's usually to greet me and ask for two *leones* (about 2p). School starts at 7.45am and, arriving at the gates, I am usually met by children rushing up for hugs. We have assembly and then Mankapr and I return to our tiny office and attempt to battle through the chaotic task of organising three schools, five bank accounts, and endless problems. It would be easy to spend days just counting out money which arrives in big bundles of old and tatty two *leone* notes – no joke when you're dividing it up for forty people's monthly wages.

"Some women have had things stolen from their rooms at night while they've been asleep, which is unnerving, though personal attacks are extremely rare"

The schoolday ends early at 1.30pm, Mankapr rushes home to cook, wash and clean. I also head home, thankful that I haven't a demanding family waiting for me. On the way I might stop at a bar for a soft drink and a *binche* sandwich (beans, palm oil, fish and onions), using the midday heat as an excuse for relaxing on the veranda with a book and delaying the walk home. Later in the afternoon I'll start to think about the main meal of the day and wander off round the market for inspiration.

Large women with babies tied to their backs, and small children clinging to their ankles, call as I walk past, "Yu no wan jibloks?" (You no want aubergines?). Spread all around in a bright array of colours are bundles of hot red peppers, piles of onions, okra, small squashy tomatoes and sweet potatoes. Green bundles of cassava and potato leaves are heaped into baskets, and rice, beans, groundnuts and spices fill large enamel basins. Dinner is usually an assortment of these vegetables served with rice. Because power is scarce there is no refrigeration and food has to be bought fresh daily. The days and weekends seem to drift past

in a routine of writing home, reading, visiting people, and watching the world pass by from the local bar.

Before I arrived, in March 1988, an economic emergency was declared. The number of checkpoints that appeared on the roads made travelling even slower than usual. These checkpoints have now decreased considerably in number, though foreign currency is strictly regulated and checked for, as well as gold and diamonds, which are frequently smuggled out. Corruption and thieving are a major problem. Makeni is supposed to be particularly vulnerable and during my first few months my flat was broken into twice. Almost all the volunteers living here have been robbed, despite having watchmen, bars on the windows and bolts on the doors. Some women have had things stolen from their rooms at night while they've been asleep, which is unnerving, though personal attacks are extremely rare.

As a volunteer, I currently manage on the weekly equivalent of about ten pounds, but the teachers I work with average only two pounds per week, on which most of them have to support a family. The worst of it is that the salaries don't always arrive. At the time of writing the teachers had been without pay for over four months. They are now on strike. It is no surprise that people resort to stealing.

It is more difficult sometimes to understand how people survive. It seems that family and friends give and share whenever they can. I also give money but it's a problem to know where to draw the line, especially as my own budget is limited. After a few months in the country I felt I was becoming very hard-hearted. I was able to walk away from beggars, people who were hungry and children dressed in rags, without feeling shrouded in guilt.

Sierra Leone is not an easy country to visit, but, once there, you'll find yourself drawn into the local way of life. It certainly makes you rethink old values.

TRAVEL NOTES

Languages Krio (partly derived from archaic English), Mende and Temne. English is widely spoken in Freetown.

Transport There are no trains, government buses are sparse, and *pode podes* (local trucks) are slow, unreliable and packed. Women routinely hitch, which is considered fairly safe.

Accommodation Freetown and the peninsula resorts have a few expensive tourist hotels; the women's hotel, run by the convent on Howe Street, Freetown, is a welcome haven. Upcountry hotels and rest houses are few and far between. If you want to stay in a village you should organise this through the paramount chief and be prepared to reciprocate hospitality with money or gifts. You might also be given sleeping space by VSO or Peace Corps workers; again, you'll be expected to contribute towards your keep.

Special Problems Theft is common. You also face frequent propositions from men, but this is rarely threatening. But there's a real danger of tourist muggings on the deserted beaches. Take everything you'll need by way of sanitary protection, contraception and medical supplies. Supplies are erratic.

Guide *The Rough Guide: West Africa* (Harrap-Columbus) includes a full section on Sierra Leone.

Contacts

Sierra Leone Women's Movement, The Retreat, 40 Main Road, Conge Cross, Freetown. **National Federation of Sierra Leone Women's Organisations**, PO Box 811, Freetown. Both organisations give out information on local development projects involving women, and education and health campaigns.

Books

Olayinka Koso-Thoma, *The Circumcision of Women – a Strategy for Eradication* (Zed Books, 1987). Detailed research and thoughtful analysis focusing on Sierra Leone's powerful women's societies.

Adelaide M. Cromwell, *An African Victorian Feminist – the Life and Times of Adelaide Smith Casely Hayford 1868–1960* (Frank Cass, US, 1986). The compelling biography of an early Krio activist and campaigner.

E. Frances White, *Sierra Leone's Settler Women Traders* (Michigan UP, US, 1987). Charts the historical role of Freetown's "Big Market" women.

Donald Cosentino, *Defiant Maids and Stubborn Farmers: Tradition and Invention in Mende Story Performance* (CUP, US, 1982). Academic study of oral literary traditions amongst the Mende people. Includes analysis of how women are represented.

Soviet Union

At the time of writing surmise is starting to give way to certainty that
the Soviet Union is breaking up. *Perestroika* has clearly taken on a momentum of its own, unleashing a wave of nationalism, urgent demands for self-
determination from many of the federation's fifteen republics – and, with it,
age-old and bloody ethnic conflicts and border disputes (the Azerbaijan-
Armenian war being only one of many potential sites for the outbreak of
hostilities). Many of us in the West have only begun to recognise and appreciate the vastly contrasting races, cultures and religions that exist within
Soviet borders as a result of headlines switching from one area of popular
dissent and unrest to another.

Yet the explosion of nationalism is only one amongst many of the challenges that threatens to destabilise Mikhail Gorbachev's reforms. Within the
Soviet Union, where economic crisis is taking its toll in renewed hardship
and shortages, popular support for the president is waning fast. *Glasnost* has

lifted the lid on the abuses, shortcomings and incompetence of the old monolithic and centralised Communist system (blamed for all current ills – from
Chernobyl to train crashes), while *perestroika* has provided the means to
express dissent through newly legalised oppositional groups.

As far as the West is concerned, much of the excitement generated by the
opening up of the Soviet Union has been reined in by anxiety about its future.
To a frightening degree this seems to depend as much on the abilities and
stamina of Gorbachev himself as on the extent to which the Soviet people can
go on enduring the hardships they face. Gorbachev has stressed that the
changes made (in terms of improved civil and human rights, democratisation,
and moves towards a more market-oriented system) are irreversible – and
that there can be no sudden clampdown and purge of dissenters. To a large
extent he is believed, but the guarantee that there will be no return to a
fortress mentality rests largely on what links can be forged with the outside
world in cultural, economic, political, and simply human terms.

Ironically, at a time when travel is becoming much more open, republics
are being wiped off the tourist map by instability and unrest. Azerbaijan and
Armenia are obvious examples, but many other destinations – the Baltic
states, the Transcaucasian republics, even the Trans-Siberian express – seem
to be hanging in the balance. Obviously it's important to get up-to-date information before deciding to set off. In general terms, though, travel is by no
means the restricted or one-way industry it used to be. More than at any
other time Soviet citizens are being allowed to view the West for themselves
(the US embassy has been so swamped by visa applications that it no longer
treats Soviet immigrants as "political refugees"), while Westerners are being
presented with a range of options for travel.

It is possible to travel without a tour group but it's expensive and you'll be
expected to work out and declare your itinerary well in advance. The most
usual, and still the most popular, way to visit is a package deal arranged
either through *Intourist*, the main Soviet travel organisation, or *Sputnick*, the
youth wing. There are also new co-operatives being formed, however, that
run their own private tours and, more surprisingly, have gained permission to
rent out private rooms. At present these operate exclusively through travel
agencies but they may well soon be on offer to independent travellers.
Already, it is pretty routine to arrange a semi-independent visit through
Finland to the Baltic states.

In the past, state tourist guides were anxious to promote the Party line and
edgy about people wandering off on their own. This is no longer the case.
Itineraries might suddenly change as a result of political unrest but once you
arrive somewhere you are more or less allowed to explore at will, talk to
whoever you wish and even accept invitations to people's homes. If you do,
you will experience first-hand the justly famous hospitality of Russians (or
citizens of the other Soviet republics). It's important, however, to be sensitive
to the burden that hospitality creates and to reciprocate where you can.

Obviously your experience of the Soviet Union depends on where you go –
the European and predominantly Protestant Baltic republics can seem as far
removed from, say, Islamic Uzbekistan, as Holland is from Iraq. Sexism in
the European republics is much more likely to show itself in the form of an

old-fashioned "gallantry" while in the Islamic eastern republics Western visitors, like European Soviets, can come up against fairly persistent street harassment (being propositioned, followed home, etc).

Travelling around, alone or with a group, presents few problems of safety. Crime is on the increase throughout the Soviet Union but these are mainly "economic crimes". You might feel pressurised to change money or barter goods, but sexual assault is incredibly rare. More of a problem can be the feeling of unwarranted privilege that you have as a hard currency tourist. The creation of new and flashy dollar shops and hotels have been amongst the least relevant (but most publicised) of the East-West co-operative ventures and are often pitched well beyond the means of most Soviet citizens. However, there seems to be little resentment shown towards foreigners, and people generally seem interested to meet and talk about their country's pitfalls and promises.

The **position of women** in the Soviet Union is shaped by the different traditions and cultures of its republics. In Russia and the other European republics women have the highest participation in the labour force of any modern industrial society, but they are concentrated in low-pay, low-status jobs. Articles 35 and 53, which instituted sexual equality, have had little impact on sexual relations and the division of domestic, unpaid labour. The double burden of domestic and paid work is an entrenched feature of many women's lives and, in a society where the logistics of looking after a home and family are both complex and time-consuming, can be crippling.

The legislation on maternity leave (one year on full pay and the option of six months unpaid leave) and childcare may seem exemplary, too, but reality again falls far short of the ideal. Daycare centres are understaffed, overcrowded and hotbeds of childhood diseases, and many women prefer to either leave their child with a *Babushka* (granny) or make private arrangements. Abortions are easily available but contraception and sex education are not. Women clearly feel abused by a family planning system centred on the provision of abortions (with poor healthcare and follow-up) at the expense of a safer, more comprehensive, approach to birth control – the average European Soviet woman undergoes six to eight abortions in her lifetime.

In response to concern about the falling birth rate in the European republics, attempts are being made to revive and officially promote the role of the full-time housewife. Women are facing much more social pressure than before to have children, and to take their full quota of maternity leave when they do – articles have suddenly started to appear in state journals alerting society to the problems of maternal deprivation. Whilst there are certainly women who see this as retrogressive, and who have responded with letters and articles defending their right to pursue a career, many are desperate to reduce their appalling workloads and support any move that brings with it flexible work schedules.

A very different picture emerges in the eastern republics. Women tend to follow the traditional pattern of marrying at a very young age, bearing many children (the average being six) and working unpaid on the land or in the home. Poverty is often intense and, for all the claims of the Soviet healthcare system, the infant mortality rate in some areas ranks amongst the worst in the world. The Soviet press has recently started to draw attention to the continuation of outlawed Islamic practices such as arranged marriages and the use of dowry and bride-price. The authorities are similarly running family-planning campaigns in these republics and local activists are trying to persuade women to take up their rightful places in the workforce. Whilst these initiatives might overtly seem pro-women they are understandably viewed as an attempt to lower the birth rate and infringe upon the traditions and strength of Islam. And, as such, they are met largely with hostility.

We realise that in these rapidly shifting times there's little that can be said about the experience of travel in the Soviet Union that would not in some way seem dated – even by the time of publication. The pieces below obviously tell of a particular historical moment but in their descriptions of meetings with Soviet women have, we hope, some enduring relevance.

Touring the Republics

. . . .

Lynne Attwood works as a guide and interpreter for American student trips to the Soviet Union. Her fascination for the country has stood the test of innumerable visits. She has also completed a PhD in Soviet Studies.

I first visited the Soviet Union on a whim, a spur-of-the-moment response to an advert about a New Year student tour to Moscow and Leningrad. Thus began what promises to be a lifetime of fascination with the place. Ten years and more than twenty visits later, I have a PhD in Soviet Studies and a job which takes me to different corners of the country several times a year, as a guide and interpreter to groups of American students.

It has been a love-hate relationship. On the one hand there has been the welter of Soviet bureaucracy to contend with – red tape, delays, rejections, a mass of petty frustrations. On the other there is the warmth of Russian friendships, the coolness of crisp white winters, the delight of coming to understand the rich complexity of the country's cultures.

"I suppose we were some kind of 'exotica' for you!" suggested my friend Larisa, attempting to understand my long-term attachment. (Russians generally seem rather confused by the interest Westerners take in them – or at least they were, until *perestroika* opened the floodgates of media attention and they had to get used to it.) That was probably the case, at least in the beginning. But the Soviet Union – or at least Russia, Georgia, or other of its component parts – just seems to get under some people's skin.

Moscow was blanketed in snow on my first visit, the white pierced by the bright red of New Year decorations. The group I was with was booked into a restaurant for a New Year's Eve dinner, but there were some hours till we were due to meet and I set off to explore the city by myself. Struggling to work out the metro map, I sought the help of a young Russian who spoke some English. His name was Igor. He had a bottle of Soviet champagne tucked under one arm and was on his way to a New Year party.

The champagne did not make it with him. We drank it on a park bench, surrounded by snow-encrusted pine trees, exchanging life histories in painfully fractured English. It was already dark but I was struck by the fact that the curfew which many women in Western cities impose on themselves was not in force here. A number of women strolled past our bench. Some were in twos, arms linked, relaxed and laughing. Others were alone, short-cutting through the park with their shopping bags. I have always felt relatively safe in the streets and parks of Russian cities, a feeling I evidently share with local women. This has to be one of the big advantages of the place.

Two days later I was invited to Igor's home, and was exposed to my first taste of Russian hospitality. Around a table groaning with food and drink (this was some years before Gorbachev would launch his anti-alcohol campaign) I forged friendships which have outlived almost all of those I had at the time at home. Like most people I know, I have lost old friends and gained new ones in the process of growing and changing, so my British friends are a fairly homogeneous bunch with a broad similarity of views. Not so in Russia. Our lives, the ideas we have been exposed to, and our responses to them, have been completely different. We discuss these differences, we argue and marvel over them, but they do not dislodge our mutual affection.

Larisa, Igor's sister, was a seventeen-year-old student when I first met her. Now she is married with a three-year-old child and has become one of a new breed of Soviet women – the rehabilitated housewife. She gently mocks me for my feminism. To her, as to many Russian women, "equality" means that women have ended up with twice as much work. Their full-time professional activities have just been heaped on top of their traditional domestic duties. They get little help from men, nor from the labour-saving devices we take for granted in the West. This has made them a receptive audience for the pro-family propaganda which has been pouring out of the Soviet press since the mid-1970s.

"How long will it be – if glasnost continues – before a Russian version of The Women's Room or The Captive Housewife appears on the shelves?"

It is claimed that women's "equality" in the European part of the Soviet Union has had a number of negative consequences – the divorce rate has risen, the number of births has dropped, and teenage delinquency has increased because children were packed off too young to creches and kindergartens. The catch phrase now is that "being equal does not mean being the same", and unless women are exceptionally career-minded they are being urged to put their paid work in second place and spend more time at home looking after their children.

Larisa admits she sometimes feels bored and isolated in this role, but she insists that her mother – who was the head of a team of architects before she retired – regrets the limited time she spent with her children when they were small. In any case, the women she knows who do leave their children in creches are constantly having to take time off work as their children come home with childhood ailments. She is adamant that she is doing the right thing and I no longer argue with her. But how long will it be – if *glasnost* continues – before a Russian version of *The Women's Room* or *The Captive Housewife* appears on the shelves?

The Soviet Union is the largest country in the world, and a mass of cultural, linguistic and religious variations. Keep moving East, and you'll find that life – particularly for women – undergoes considerable changes. This is certainly the case in the Caucasian republics.

The first time I travelled through the Caucasus was with three British friends, two women and a man, in a hired car. Women drivers are a rarity in that part of the world, and evidently pose a challenge to local manhood. The response was to race past us, horn honking, and then come to a virtual standstill so that we had no choice but to overtake. Then the game would be repeated. We lurched along in this mechanised leap-frog for miles, narrowly avoiding oncoming traffic, on roads which hung precariously over the edge of mountains.

Georgia is the most accessible of the Caucasian republics. Fair-skinned women certainly get a lot of attention there, but in much the same way as they do in Italy. It can be annoying, but it is not threatening. Wandering round Tbilisi alone, I was approached by a succession of men offering to "show me the city". But when I did accept I found the offer was usually genuine, while a refusal was accepted graciously enough. The Georgians are, in any case, a supremely hospitable people. If this characteristic is particularly pronounced when it comes to women, it is not confined to them. I have had some equally friendly encounters in male company.

Our drive through Georgia introduced us into a social whirlwind. When we stopped to sunbathe on a crowded Black Sea beach, we found ourselves the centre of attention. A queue of people formed to practise their English, ask us to find penfriends for their children, and compare notes on problems of everyday life. Turning off the road to have a picnic by a rural stream in the Caucasian foothills we were joined by a group of Georgians on their lunch break from tending the nearby bee hives. Immediately their bottle of vodka was pressed into our hands. In Tbilisi I looked up a complete stranger, a friend of a friend, who at a moment's notice prepared a sumptious banquet.

Sexism certainly flourishes in Georgia, but women do not passively accept it. One of the Soviet Union's finest film makers, Lana Gogoberidze, is from Tbilisi. Her film *Several interviews on Personal Problems*, which has won awards both in the Soviet Union and the West, is a wonderful testament to the strength and resilience of women in the face of the mass of problems and dilemmas they have to deal with.

Armenia is harder to cope with for a woman traveller. I have been there twice, before the uprisings and the tragedy of the earthquake put the republic virtually off limits. I spent one miserable afternoon trying to explore Erevan alone and being pursued relentlessly by one man after another. If I sat down on a bench for just a moment to consult my guidebook, I immediately had company. I was trailed for more than an hour by two men, who followed me on and off a bus and in and out of a shop and took it in turns to make unambiguous advances.

"They thought you were Russian – Russian girls have a reputation here for being loose"

That evening I had dinner with a family who were friends of a friend. As honoured guest, I was placed at one end of the table with the men of the family – two brothers, their father and the older sons. I had little chance to talk to the women, who, after a full day at work, still had to spend all evening cooking and serving and cleaning up. I recounted the story of my day, and, after expressing sympathy, one of the brothers explained "they thought you were Russian – Russian girls have a reputation here for being loose". Not relishing the thought of more battles that night, I accepted an offer to sleep on the sofa – and in the morning, once everyone else had gone to work, was subjected to an unmistakable sexual come-on by this same man.

The republics of Soviet Central Asia present the biggest contrast to life in the Russian republic, though the larger cities bear some heavy imprints of modern Russia. In Tashkent, in particular, the office buildings and apartment blocks which emerged out of the rubble of the 1966 earthquake have stepped straight from a Russian blueprint, and the metro looks identical to the one in Leningrad. But, between the mosques, minarets and bazaars of the Old Town, Asia can still be found. In the labyrinth of dusty alleys, the ramshackle mud houses seem to turn their backs on visitors – they were built around hidden courtyards, and their windows overlook these instead of the streets. Visitors, however, are often invited in.

Walking through Bukhara, I got talking to three teenage girls who told me that there was a wedding in their street. They invited me to come. No questions were asked when I arrived: a plate of food was pressed into my hands and a place made for me on one of the rugs strewn on the ground, on which the guests sat cross-legged. Another time, in the old town in Tashkent, my female companion and I stopped to ask directions from a man leaning against the sun-baked wall of his home. He invited us in to meet his family and "see how we live".

We found ourselves in a courtyard bordered by three low huts and shaded by a cherry tree. There we sat cross-legged with our host, Ahkmet, on the distinctive Uzbeki seat which looks like a huge wooden bedstead. One of the huts had only three walls and served as the kitchen: Ahkmet's wife brought us bowls of soup, *non* (large flat loaves of bread), and green tea. Two small sons sprawled on the ground and played backgammon, while an older daughter sat shyly on the edge of the seat and listened to our conversation.

It was largely about the misguided policies of the Russians. *Perestroika*, Ahkmet felt, was a Russian phenomenon which had nothing to do with Central Asia. He was scathing about most of the Russian innovations in the area, particularly the attempt to moder-

nise housing. Convinced that no-one actually wants to live in these ancient houses, Russian bureaucrats are forcing people into faceless blocks of flats. Yet few people want to move. These houses are cool in the summer and warm in the winter; the courtyards contain vegetable plots and fruit trees, which are a vital counterbalance to the high prices in the markets. They are also the centre of community life.

"While women in the European republics of the Soviet Union seem set to move back into the arms of the family, few Central Asian women have had the chance to leave them"

Ahkmet spoke eloquently and passonately about the benefits of traditional life in Central Asia. It is this kind of attitude which has disturbed the Russians since the time of the Revolution, and now stands in stark contrast to the perceived need to restructure the whole of Soviet society. Yet there is a darker side to the continuation of tradition. The Soviet press has recently drawn attention to the growth of Islamic influence in rural Central Asia, which denies women any control over their own lives, forces them into arranged marriages, and commits them to a life of constant pregnancy and child care. The contrast between the socialist promise of equality for women, and the reality of their own lives, has apparently led to an alarming number of suicides amongst young women.

Certainly the desire to discredit Islam is likely to underlie much of this sudden media interest in the plight of Central Asian women. But published statistics, as well as personal observation, make it clear that outside of the cities, Central Asian women have yet to break out of the traditional mould. While women in the European republics of the Soviet Union seem set to move back into the arms of the family, few Central Asian women have had the chance to leave them.

A Friendship Visit to Moscow and Riga

· · · · · · · · · · · ·

Sheena Phillips, who works for the Campaign for Nuclear Disarmament, visited the Soviet Union on a trip organised by the Quaker Peace Service and the GB-USSR Friendship Society. The official part of her tour included a series of meetings in Moscow and Riga with Soviet officials and researchers on European affairs.

My first view of Moscow was from the air, as the plane started its descent. The city suddenly appeared on the horizon, looking like a white island in a dark green expanse of forest and water. Its isolation and the huge flatness of the surrounding landscape were quite different from anything I had seen before, and this sheer physical strangeness was one of the most exciting things about being there.

Having read books by people like Solzhenitsyn and Kafka (who's Czech, mind you!), I was predisposed to find the Soviet Union dark, dismal and generally downtrodden. As if to confirm my prejudices, it was dark when we arrived, the lighting in the airport was dim, the air was acrid from pollution, and the streets were very bare-looking. Outside the hotel, unsmiling cab drivers stood around sharing cigarettes. Inside, we hung around for ages waiting for our rooms and baggage to be sorted out.

Later, most of these impressions got reinterpreted as aspects of the Soviet Union's economy rather than anything more sinister. Compared to most of Western Europe, the Soviet Union is a strikingly poor country. There is a generally lower standard of amenities like electricity, telephones and plumbing. The supply of most consumer goods, even in the capital city, is erratic. There is also a lot of bad housing. Moscow is surrounded by miles of high-rise apartment blocks and in Riga I visited the most stinking and badly lit block of tenements I had ever been to (though I'm sure parts of Glasgow have rivalled them, at least in the past).

> *"I also experienced the terrifying privilege of being ferried around at high speed in huge black government cars"*

My own accommodation, along with the rest of the group I travelled with, was in a variety of hotels, all booked for us by our hosts. Our first stop was the large and rather ugly Hotel Rossiya in the centre of Moscow, of which my chief memories are faulty telephones, over-heated rooms and large quantities of food (especially bread, meat, yoghurt and fizzy drinks). In Riga we stayed in a much smaller hotel, with better food and some striking local paintings. Then on our return to Moscow we were allocated to a large Trade Union hotel several miles from the centre, crowded with throngs of chattering people from many different parts of the Soviet Union.

In all hotels you are issued with a card that identifies you as a tourist and allows you to eat in other hotels too. You exchange it whenever you come in for your room keys, generally with the *dezhurnaya* – the woman (as it always seems to be) who organises cleaning and other services (sometimes including baby-sitting) on your floor of the hotel. All the hotels I stayed in were clean, comfortable and spacious, and they seemed to have a very unfair share of local food supplies.

Part of my time in the Soviet Union was spent in meetings with researchers and Communist Party officials, discussing disarmament and other issues on the East-West political agenda. I encountered an interesting mixture of frank and restricted conversation – officials are still ideologically bound on some issues, but not nearly as much as they would have been just a few years ago. I also experienced VIP treatment, including delicious (though alcohol-free) lunches and the terrifying privilege of being ferried around at high speed in huge black government cars called *chaiki* (seagulls).

The rest of my time was spent in walking around, sampling sights and wayside snacks and visiting people. Art galleries, museums and swimming pools are all very cheap, and staring at buildings is free! Red Square was stunning, especially at night. There is also some beautiful art in some of the churches open to the public, though in Moscow most are either closed or used as offices. In Riga both the rain and the architecture were more familiar; there was even a true Victorian red-brick church, built by the British in the nineteenth century to serve diplomats and traders.

I also went to a film, which was an interesting experience. The dialogue was in Georgian, but with Turkish subtitles and an occasional voice-over in Russian given by the projectionist, some of which was then relayed to me in a loud English whisper. I wouldn't even have got in without native help. The film had sold out but my Russian companion spotted a ticket-shark and managed to buy tickets (at twice cover price). In general, I was told, it's hard to get tickets without someone who knows the system. Most outings for groups of tourists are arranged days in advance by their Soviet hosts.

Public transport is cheap and on the whole good, though there were long bus queues on some of the main roads in from the residential areas. There are also numerous taxis. The only problem with getting around on your own is likely to be persuading your hosts or official tour guides that you want to; this simply requires firmness. It's a good idea to try and learn the Cyrillic script so that you can make sense of maps and station names more easily –

this is especially useful on the Moscow Underground.

I felt safe everywhere I travelled (and safer than in Britain), including at night, though attitudes vary as to the wisdom of women hitching alone. I have read reports of Moscow street gangs but I didn't see any violence and there was surprisingly little evidence of vandalism. At night, in fact, there was surprisingly little evidence of anything; apart from clusters of artists and musicians in and around the Arbat, Moscow's famous pedestrian precinct, there were few places open and few people on the streets.

"For anyone who wants to, it's easy to make contact with Soviet people"

Walking around, I felt self-conscious as a Westerner looking in on a society out of which many people still cannot easily travel. Westerners are also conspicuous simply by their clothing. On buses and trains I received a few stares and I felt particularly conspicuous in a small café in Riga where my only means of ordering was by pointing at the things I wanted. At least I managed to say "thank you" in Lettish! I didn't ever feel unwelcome, rather as if I had come from a different planet.

For anyone who wants to, it's easy to make contact with Soviet people. English is the first foreign language taught in most schools and people are very interested in speaking to foreign visitors. I was in Russia with people who had personal contacts to follow up in Moscow and we made telephone arrangements to meet. If you have no contacts, one strategy for meeting people (which I am assured works) is simply to sit down somewhere public with a Western brand-name carrier bag, and wait.

I was not travelling alone, so I cannot write in detail about what it would be like to do so as a single woman. But I spent a lot of time talking to women, especially to our translator Tanya and to other women whom we met in their own homes.

From her appearance, I thought Tanya would be a rather formal and conservative person: she was in her mid-thirties, very neatly dressed and made-up, and her speech was very precise and proper. But this was a misjudgement. Soviet codes of dress, hair styles, etc, are very different from those in the West. To us, most styles seem fairly conservative – and faintly Sixties or Seventies – but there is simply not enough choice of clothing for "fashion" to be a sign of social class or personality. Tanya turned out to be very warm, serious and thoughtful. She also treasured the opportunity to meet and work with us: it gave her a break from her normal teaching job, which she described (as always in perfect idiomatic English) as "humdrum".

"Like Tanya, most people seemed very emotional about meeting us: moved that we should have wanted to visit the Soviet Union and eager to tell us about their lives"

The private houses I saw were all tiny but lovingly kept pockets of individuality in the anonymity of the large housing districts. We were always greeted with great warmth and generosity, even in the poorest of conditions. Invariably, tea would be made: first brewed in a small pot until very strong, then diluted. Tea, by the way, is a good thing to take as a gift, as are things like soap, nuts, vitamin pills, batteries, even biros – many of which are hard to get hold of – and almost any Western magazines.

Like Tanya, most people seemed very emotional about meeting us: moved that we should have wanted to visit the Soviet Union and eager to tell us about their lives and to suggest other people we could visit. All our meetings were also tinged, I think, with an awareness of a gulf between our basic experience of everyday life. "You

are richer, in every sense," one woman said. At our partings the separateness of our fates seemed accentuated and I sometimes felt almost guilty about my freedom and, as they saw it, my wealth.

People did not always comment on things in the way I expected. In Riga a young woman studying languages described the distribution of students between the polytechnic (chiefly women taking arts subjects) and the university (chiefly men studying sciences); but she saw this in a very positive light. She was proud of what she was doing and had a cheerful disdain for the university. Another woman, a psychologist, explained that there has been a reaction against the pressures of full-time work while having children. If they can, many women are now choosing to spend more time at home.

Other things also surprised me – like the teams of women painters, decorators and street labourers. I was also disconcerted by the almost sullen manner in which transactions such as money-changing, handing over room keys, and restaurant service, which in the West would be accompanied by professional servility, were carried out.

Except in small pockets of academia there is nothing comparable to the feminist movement in the USSR. According to Tanya, there are various sorts of women's organisations, from the National Committee of Soviet Women to women's councils at nearly all workplaces employing women. They organise things such as daycare facilities and holiday entertainments for children, and clubs for activities – from knitting to aerobics and lectures on family psychology, home economics and fashion. However, these are statutory bodies, not voluntary organisations, and are certainly not feminist in inspiration.

It was hard even to put across the idea of the breadth and diversity of the Women's Movement in the West. A male academic to whom I spoke in

Moscow seemed to think feminism must be an organised political sect with a clear ideology, leaders and virtually a card-carrying membership! In Latvia, which is geographically and culturally fairly close to parts of northern Europe, our guide was a self-confident, casually dressed young woman who had just finished studying English at university. She said she was "probably a feminist" and seemed to know what we meant by it. But, even to her, Latvian nationalism was a much more important issue.

"Patterns of sexuality have changed in the Soviet Union very much as they have done in the West"

With or without an explicit feminist revolution, however, patterns of sexuality have changed in the Soviet Union very much as they have done in the West. Tanya said that people generally live together before getting married. The divorce rate has increased. Tanya herself is divorced but has her own flat, which she said reduced the pressure on her to find a new partner. Contraception is widely used, though the pill is not as popular as condoms or the IUD. There are reportedly a few gay and lesbian orientated bars in Moscow.

One of the best conversations I had with Tanya, sitting on a wall in the popular Latvian seaside resort of Jurmala and eating sickly confections from one of the street stalls, was about Soviet attitudes to the West. To her, first of all, the West meant wealth and choice – though also materialism, which she compared unfavourably with Russian generosity and sentimentality. The word "firma" is used, mainly of clothing, to mean "good quality – made in the West" – and people, especially women, go to great lengths to get and flaunt Western goods. To Tanya this was humiliating, though she envied my freedom of choice and was clearly exasperated by the difficulty of buying the things she wanted.

She, and many other people to whom I spoke, expressed shame about the Soviet Union. Several apologised for the laziness of the Russian people. Latvians, on the other hand, pride themselves on their stronger work ethic and their higher standard of living. Some of the talk about "scroungers" could have been taken straight from Britain, though it was very hard to explain this and many people seemed to have an unrealistically rosy image of material conditions in the West: they saw things like motivation as a peculiarly Soviet problem.

It was also striking, in meetings with Soviet officials and researchers, how closely Western policies on economic management, taxation, etc, are being studied. There is a huge amount of criticism of existing models of state provision: we were told at the new Institute of Europe that Sweden was not a country of much interest to Soviet planners because it was so heavily committed to the idea of the welfare state! Britain's free market approach, on the other hand, was more in vogue.

The watchwords of change under Gorbachev – perestroika (restructuring) and glasnost (openness) – were very much in evidence, particularly in terms of a much freer and more critical media. But the air of excitement and change that permeated the political think-tanks and some of the newly spawned political clubs did not extend to most of the people we met privately, at least in Moscow. The dominant attitudes were: "it's good, but let's wait and see ... in this country, you never know what will happen in five minutes ... maybe in three hundred years you will notice a big difference". For most Moscovites, improvements such as better housing, better consumer goods and (especially for women) less time spent in searching for them, are at least as important as an increase in political freedom. Yet in the short term, at least, the standard of living is likely to sink even lower as the state grapples with an ever more pressing economic crisis.

Most of the people I met who were involved in politics were men (they were also the ones who did most of the talking on television). This left me with a familiar and unwelcome impression! The dominant issues being debated: democracy, law and how to enable the growth of a "civil society", in which certain activities are unregulated by the state, are all important to tackle. But while men took on the task of tussling with the state, I wondered, what happened to the people with no time for late-night meetings and no grounding in political philosophy?

I was more moved and impressed by my meeting with a woman who, at considerable risk to herself, was trying to publish an account she has written of the terrible experiences of many young men, including her son, in national military service – or in trying to avoid it. If published, her book will speak directly to many, many Soviets. However, I don't want to sound too critical of the more formal political developments – the flourishing of discussion and argument in what has been such a closed and tightly controlled society is amazing.

Our last evening was spent in tasting some of the fruits of *perestroika* in a new co-operative restaurant whose profits are shared by its owners and the state. We sat down at a table covered with beautifully prepared cold dishes, drank some wine, listened to a fiddler as he paraded around performing various ingenious feats with his violin, and were presented several hours later with a very handsome bill. The atmosphere was as bourgeois as anything you could find in Hampstead. That left me with mixed feelings. I couldn't help hoping that some of the more useless trappings of consumerism would never reach the Soviet Union – and I shall keep the flimsy wrapping paper from the hard currency export shop as a sentimental reminder of how things were at the end of the Eighties.

A Trans-Siberian Ambition

· · · · · · · · · · · · ·

After years of dreaming, planning and vacillating, Catherine Grace finally set off for the Soviet Union to travel on the Trans-Siberian Express.

From the time I first heard about it, I had wanted to travel on the Trans-Siberian Railway. I even, hopefully, learned Russian at school. When I was planning nine months' travelling, the Soviet Union was the place to start.

I went on my own, catching the train from Liverpool Street. They called out "Mos-Cow" as though it was a huge joke. I felt scornful and brave. My friends thought I was mad, and would I please send a telegram when I got out safely at Japan.

I started to feel lonely in Holland, solitary in a compartment in the only carriage going to Moscow. Then Olga Petrovna arrived – an enormous Russian with an immense amount of luggage. She had been staying with her sister in the West, and the ten vast bundles (including a carpet) were "presents". She was crude, she was kind, she was overwhelming. My limited Russian was not nearly adequate; we shared food and laughed a lot, mostly through incomprehension.

The Polish-Soviet border was my introduction to Russia's other face. The East German and Polish crossings had been no more than a brief disturbance in the night, a quick passport check. Expecting something similar, I was in my nightdress, a full-length ribboned affair which clearly halved my apparent age. A succession of inspectors looked disbelievingly at me. The food inspector (Olga lost all her fresh food), ticket inspector, customs and immigration officers all passed me by and pounced upon Olga, who became more and more flustered. She and all her baggage were taken off for examination.

"I only realised later how generous she had been. Most importantly, I had my first taste of the warmth and generosity of individual Soviet people"

Before we were eventually reunited, I pattered around watching the event of the night – the changing of wheels for the entire train. The Soviet Union retains a different gauge railway system as a defence precaution, even from its closest allies.

This slow introduction to the Soviet Union was useful. I had had no idea how separate and final the Soviet border was compared to other Eastern bloc countries. And the number of officials at the border was just a foretaste of the bureaucracy to come. I was issued with new tickets at every point along my way, retaining the last one (for the boat to Japan) as long as an hour. Similarly, the sheer quantity of consumer goods and food that Olga had brought back gave me an inkling of shortages: I only realised later how generous she had been. Most importantly, I had my first taste of the warmth and generosity of individual Soviet people.

Arriving at the Hotel Metropole in Moscow, I assumed that *Intourist* would be at least a little interested in me and might even tell me what to do. However, once they had my passport, I

was left severely alone. I overheard someone talking (in English) and asked them what to do about theatre tickets. Thus began my rapid disillusionment as the *Intourist* staff demanded "hard" Western currency. They weren't pleased when I produced the exact money – no chance of fiddling the change.

Leningrad lovers don't have a good word to say for Moscow; it's not beautiful people are dwarfed by the gigantism of streets, squares and monuments. I am not in a position to make the comparison: I loved Moscow. I didn't know what I wanted from this new place and I got a little bit of everything. I suspect it is a very Russian city.

A visit to the Kremlin was an initial shock. It is not a great, grey, grim fortress. It contains some stunningly beautiful buildings; from a distance the white towers and golden domes of the cathedral gleam and glint like a fantasy castle. The Kremlin Wall in Red Square looks as though it came from an Italian Renaissance picture (it was in fact designed by an Italian), and Saint Basil's, preposterous onion domes and all is for real.

It's worth branching out, though, from the city's sights and architecture. The centre of Moscow has lots of cinemas and theatres and you can use the workers' restaurants as well as the hotels. You'll have to queue, of course. But queues and waiting are a basic part of everyday life in the Soviet Union. People on buses and in the street were unfailingly kind and helpful when I asked the way; people in food queues were friendly. The only thing there were no queues for was bread.

The longest queue of all, stretching through Red Square and around the Kremlin, was to Lenin's tomb; many of the people were from outside Moscow. As we entered Red Square we were directed to leave anything we were carrying in a cloakroom, made to tidy up our appearance and put in an orderly two-by-two line. The guards

hushed us when we entered the mausoleum, we descended reverently into the
gloom and filed past the body. Early
training will out, and I had to restrain
an impulse to make the sign of the
cross. The evident significance of that
visit for the people around me helped
me to make sense of the huge images
of Lenin found in every Soviet city and
main street.

"It was, I think, one of the most soci-able times of my life"

Rejoining the Trans-Siberian, the
journey took over again. It was, I think,
one of the most sociable times of my
life. The landscape across the Soviet
Union is not striking, and you inevitably spend much of the time talking.
There were many other Western travellers on the train and I discovered for
the first time that to travel alone is to
be vulnerable to the needs of people
travelling in couples who are bored
with each other and not necessarily
interested in you. The same people also
dish out unwanted sympathy for the
(chosen) state of being alone.

I enjoyed myself much more when I
struck up a friendship with a Russian
family in the next compartment. Galia
and Seriozha, a married couple, and
Galia's sister Valia, were travelling the
whole way to Vladivostock to new jobs.
Seriozha had been a chauffeur, Galia a
housebuilder and Valia had been at
school. They did not know what they
would be doing in the east and had had
to leave most of their belongings, but
they were remarkably cheerful about it.
They were also very sweet to me, and
enormously excited at the prospect of
having their photographs taken; there
were kisses and tears when we said
goodbye. I later met Laura, a singing
teacher, who was shy but generous.
We exchanged little gifts every day,
and she attempted the almost hopeless
task of trying to teach me a Russian
song.

Life on the train was complicated by
the fact that it ran on Moscow time,
though we were in fact crossing a time
zone every day. This affected the
restaurant car and you could never
quite predict when it would be open.
Once we were in Siberia I stopped
using it; whenever the train stopped at
a station we would all get out and see
what was for sale. Middle-aged women
would be standing behind stalls selling
cabbage salads, potatoes and onions –
whatever was local. Once it was excellent carrots; once potato pancakes;
another time there were nothing but
pine cones, which aggravated me until I
made the connection with pine nuts
and joined the Soviet passengers who
had rushed out to buy them.

It was important to get out at the
stations as it was the only form of exercise available and it meant fresh air.
Our conductress would never allow us
to open the windows; all carriages were
heated separately by a coal-burning
stove, and it was each conductress's
responsibility to get the coal. There
was, however, hot water available from
urns most of the time, and cups of tea
were brought round at regular intervals. Though there was no hot water for
washing, and the lavatories were grim,
I gathered from more seasoned Soviet
travellers that we should be grateful
they were in working order at all. The
Trans-Siberian is a prestige train.

At Khabarovok all Westerners have
to leave the train, which in fact goes on
to Vladivostock, a military port closed
to foreigners, for a connection to the
ferry across to Japan. We had one more
day and night in the Soviet Union, travelling along the Chinese border.
Autumn was nearly over, the trees on
the horizon were bare and we had seen
our first snow. Crossing the frontier
and leaving the frontier was an anti-
climax. I felt sad, knowing that if I'd
understood more, if I'd been better
prepared, I'd have got much more from
my stay. I knew that I wanted to return.

TRAVEL NOTES

Languages Varies according to republic (Russian, Moldavian, Uzbeki, Georgian, etc), though Russian is the language of higher education, centralised politics and commerce. (Russian linguistic imperialism is fiercely resented and is a major issue behind the nationalist protests.) English is the second language taught in most schools.

Transport Generally by train, with attendant bureaucracy in booking seats through *Intourist*. Internal flights are cheap and are often included in package tours taking in Samarkand, etc. It is possible to rent a car or drive your own, but petrol is expensive and you have to plan and declare routes in advance.

Accommodation Usually arranged through a tour (*Sputnick* being the cheapest). As part of an East-West collaborative venture hotels are being refurbished and new hotels are being built in Moscow and Leningrad; at present, however, standards are pretty basic. A co-operative in Rostov-na-Dony has recently got permission to run tours and arrange accommodation in private homes; more look set to follow. The cheapest option for accommodation (and a good way to meet Soviet rather than Western tourists) are the *Intourist* campsites. They generally have wooden huts if you prefer not to take a tent.

Special Problems Bureaucracy – from getting a visa on. You have to be prepared for sudden changes in your itinerary as a result of unrest.

Sexual harassment can be a problem in the Caucasian and eastern republics, but this is not the case in the Baltic republics and Russia. All foreigners are approached for hard currency and to buy and exchange goods. It's wise to firmly, but politely, steer clear of black-market dealings – both parties can still get arrested.

It's easy to underestimate the conservatism of Soviet society. *Babushkas* (grannies) seem to have the self-appointed role of social police and won't hesitate to put you right if they take issue with your clothes or behaviour. Although there are reports that some gay venues are opening up, any public display of gay sexuality is still extremely risky.

Guides The *Motorists' Guide to the Soviet Union* (Progress Publishers, Moscow) is essential for independent travellers, and the individual city guides produced by Progress Publishers are probably the most detailed you'll find. Most of these are available at *Collets International Bookshop*, 129 Charing Cross Road, London WC2.

Contacts

Soviet Women's Committee, Nemirovitch-Danchenko Street 6, Moscow. Co-ordinates many of the (official) local groups and campaigns. Russian readers should look out for *Rabotnitsa* (Woman Worker) which has begun to include a fair number of radical articles and letters.

Lotus c/o Anastasia Posadskaya, Institute of Socioeconomic studies of Population, USSR Academy of Sciences, Krasikova 27, Moscow 1172 3, ☎129 0653. A small feminist research group who would welcome books, articles or research papers from the West.

The USSR-GB Friendship Society, House of Friendship, 14 Prospect Kalinina, Moscow. (See Sheena Phillips' piece.)

We've been unable to track down any autonomous women's groups or venues. Further information would be welcome.

Books

Tatyana Mamonova ed., *Writings from the Soviet Union* (Blackwell, 1984). A collection of articles and essays that were first printed secretly in Russia by a group known as the *Leningrad Feminists*. Exploding the myth of women's so-called equality, they speak out about the sexism inherent in Soviet society, the unbearable pressures of work women suffer and the abuse of a healthcare system that provides abortions but not contraception. The group was forced to disband under duress from the authorities. Five years later much the same issues are being aired – but this time in the national press.

Barbara Holland, ed., *Soviet Sisterhood* (Fourth Estate, London, 1985). A good, if slightly dated, overview of the position of women in Soviet society. Includes a chapter by Lynne Attwood.

Mikhail Gorbachev, *Perestroika: Our Hopes for Our Country and Our World* (Fontana, 1988). The manifesto for reform. Gorbachev lays out his ideas for the New World, including his thoughts on racial and religious differences, and the emancipation of women.

Martin Walker, *Russia* (Abacus, 1988). A collection of pieces from the Moscow diary of the *Guardian* correspondent. Recommended as an easy but informative glimpse of life in the post-*glasnost* republics.

Fiction

Tatyana Tolstoya, *On Golden Porch* (Virago, 1989). Highly acclaimed collection of short stories that draw on a wealth of Russian characters and settings.

Julia Voznesenskaya, *The Women's Decameron* (Methuen, 1986). This debut novel by a Soviet dissident, now resident in West Germany, became an immediate bestseller. Combining humour with blunt realism it compares the lives of ten women brought together on a Russian labour ward. Voznesenskaya's latest novel, ***The Star***

Chernobyl (Methuen, 1988), deals with the human cost of the 1986 nuclear disaster.

Natalia Baranskya, *A Week Like Any Other* (Virago, 1989). A novella and collection of short stories that passionately and poetically reveal the everyday realities of women's lives in the Soviet Union.

Alexandra Kollontai, *Love of Worker Bees* (1923; Virago, 1977) and ***A Great Love*** (1930; Virago, 1981). One of the most remarkable figures of the Revolution, Alexandra Kollontai was the only woman member of the Bolshevik Central Committee. She fled to Norway, at the height of Stalin's purges, where she wrote these two collections.

Tania Alexander, *An Estonian Childhood* (Heinemann, 1989). A remarkable memoir of the last decades of Tsarist Russia.

Irina Ratushinskaya, *Grey is the Colour of Hope* (Hodder, 1988), ***In the Beginning*** (Hodder, 1990). The first book describes the dissident poet's experiences in a labour camp; the second explores her childhood and faith.

Thanks to Lynne Attwood for her help with the introduction and Travel Notes.

Sudan

For the last six years Sudan has been in the throes of a guerrilla war. The Sudanese People's Liberation Army, predominantly Black African (Christian and Aminist) southerners, have been fighting to end domination by the richer and more populous Arab Muslim groups in the north. It is a conflict which has cost many thousands of lives, draining an already fragile economy and leaving the country open to political instability and corruption. Added to this, thousands of people – many of them refugees from neighbouring Chad and Ethiopia – have been placed at risk by droughts and plagues of locusts. At the time of writing, General Beshir, who recently seized power in the second military coup in five years, has initiated peace negotiations and a ceasefire. Should these fail he appears committed to resuming full-scale military confrontation.

Whilst there seems little place at present for tourism, there are a fair number of independent travellers, foreign workers and volunteers still entering the country. With the south effectively off limits, travel is restricted to the predominantly Muslim areas of the north. The Sudanese are renowned for their courtesy and kindness to strangers, and though a woman travelling alone is clearly seen as a phenomenon, reports are that it's easier to cope with the attention this attracts, and to accept hospitality and friendship, than it is in neighbouring Egypt. Harassment certainly occurs, though, and with relatively few other travellers around it's easy to feel isolated and vulnerable. Dressing inconspicuously in loose, long clothes helps, and you can always insist on the option of joining in with the segregated groups of women and children on trains, buses etc. Travelling with a man you are unlikely to experience many problems.

Women in Sudan bear the brunt of economic hardships, both as providers in the home and as agricultural workers. Whilst cultural constraints vary between the different religious groups, there are widespread problems of illiteracy, poor access to paid employment, and minimal political representation. Sharia Law (introduced as part of a general shift towards Islamicisation in the north) clearly limits the power and status of women to the domestic sphere; although there are still a few middle-class Muslim women in professional roles, their future is uncertain. For many years the most powerful autonomous **women's organisation** has been the *Sudanese Women's Union*. Despite frequent repression it has continued to campaign vociferously against genital mutilation, divorce by verbal denunciation, polygyny, and discrimination in work and pay. Along with various other government-funded groups it has also promoted income-generating projects and launched literacy schemes.

Cycling across the Nubian Desert

. . . .

Terri Donovan, a 36-year-old New Zealander, spent a month travelling by bicycle in Sudan in early 1988, as part of a journey which took her through Europe and Africa. Pushing, riding and hauling her bike across the open stretches of the Nubian desert, she found herself relying more and more on the hospitality of Sudanese workers at the remote railway maintenance stations.

I had already been cycling solo for seven months from London when I arrived at Wadi Halfa, by steamer across Lake Nasser from Egypt. Two months' cycle touring in the Upper Delta, around Sinai and down the Nile Valley to Aswan, had provided an introduction to Muslim customs and Arab culture and also to desert conditions.

I had learnt that it is anathema for women to be seen going about freely and unveiled, and that, although as a non-Muslim I was under less pressure to comply with these strictures, I had to be careful not to cause offence. I found I could escape censorious reactions, as well as the worst effects of sun, by wearing light, loose cotton trousers or skirt and sleeved tops. Entering strange situations, I would try to avoid prolonged eye contact with men (considered an open invitation) and assume an air of quiet purposefulness in what I was doing. Background reading (for example, on the teachings of the Koran) and simple observation helped best in learning to attune myself to cultural and religious nuances.

Everywhere, too, people responded positively to genuine curiosity about their customs and circumstances and, in return, showed an unfailing interest in mine – it was assumed that I had a husband and children and they wanted to know where they were. Most significantly, I had discovered that in places which were popular meccas for tourists, you were much more likely to experience what one guidebook described as "the hustle, the hassle and the hard sell". I anticipated Sudan's culture to be less diluted by Western tourism, but hoped to encounter the same Arab openness and basic good will to travellers.

Overall, I probably experienced less overt propositioning than in Europe, and no more sexual harassment (or hassles generally) travelling alone in Muslim society without the fetters of male patronage than those women I met who did journey with companions. Women travelling with companions sometimes expressed to me the desire to try solo ventures, yet frequently assumed themselves in possession of fewer inner resources to do so than was probably the case. Having travelled both ways, I am aware that responsibility shared can mean initiative halved, and my experiences of solo travel are that confidence soon builds on itself.

"I was amazed to see the shimmering, mirage-like outline of another bicycle approaching from afar along the railway line"

So, with very limited scope for cycle touring in Sudan, owing to restrictions imposed by political circumstances and the sheer lack of roads, I expected that travel would, of necessity, be largely "off the beaten track". I was also prepared to make my way in a much harsher environment amidst more widespread human suffering. I felt an initial trepidation disembarking on to a stark foreshore, bustling with predominantly male, djellaba-clad figures, and seeing only arid desert beyond.

In the township I found a hotel and was directed to the women's quarters – dark, shuttered rooms facing on to an open courtyard in which other women were washing and hanging out laundry. My room-mate, whose husband was in separate men's quarters, was a shy Egyptian woman with a six-month-old baby. She had also arrived on the steamer and, though communication was limited by my rather basic Arabic and her lack of English, we smiled and exchanged food. I welcomed this rare opportunity to meet and talk with other women, and particularly Muslim women, whose traditionally low public profile makes contact very difficult.

The morning after the twice-weekly train had departed to Khartoum, I rose

before the sun to begin my intended cycle trek along the same route across the Nubian Desert. There are no discernible roads and Betty (my bicycle) and I juddered along precariously between the rails, attempting to avoid sinking into the sand by riding over the wooden sleepers.

After several hours I was amazed to see the shimmering, mirage-like outline of another bicycle approaching from afar along the railway line. I had been misguidedly warned by dubious locals in Wadi Halfa about the dangers of lions and hyenas, but had not expected to meet another cyclist in the vast open spaces. I had also received a veiled warning about men I might encounter in the desert: "These are men without women . . ." It was a worker from the first maintenance station returning the thirty kilometres or so to the main station for supplies.

We greeted one another like old friends and I continued on to Station Number One, where the remaining three workers overcame their double astonishment at the sight of the laden bicycle and strange, cloth-swathed figure with cropped red hair who turned out to be a woman. They immediately proffered *chai* (tea) and shade. I began to wonder if I was as crazy as the anxious expressions of the men suggested as I could not cycle self-assuredly away but had to resort to pushing and even dragging Betty through the now loosely packed sand in the direction of Station Number Two.

An hour or more later, as I squatted hunched by the edge of the rail, bike leaning against my back to provide shade while I lunched on a boiled egg, biscuits and fruit, a figure approached.

It was one of the men from Station Number One, carrying a container of water and clearly sent to try gently to dissuade me from continuing. I was touched by the gesture and struck by the fact that I had made as little progress as I would have had I been walking. But I was far from ready to give up. I had more than ample food supplies, and knew that with the maintenance stations located approximately thirty to forty kilometres apart, I could obtain additional water to supplement what I had. I thanked him and sent him back to the station with packets of Egyptian cigarettes for his kindness.

It took all my concentration to keep Betty upright and on course, steering a track, alternately riding over the sleepers or when jarring caused my hands and wrists to ache – parallel to the rails. There was the additional difficulty of a strong, side-buffeting wind, and compensating for that meant little energy for anything else. Occasionally I would stop to absorb my surroundings. Alone in this vast expanse with just the railway line, wind mocking eerily along the telegraph wires, hazy unrelenting sun, and sand stretching *ad infinitum*, Peter Mathiessen's description came to mind: "The Nubian Desert, an hallucinatory void burned by bright winds" (*The Tree Where Man Was Born*). I was glad to be there and felt an inner peace.

"Looks of amazement came from a group of workers passing on a jigger, each one reaching down solemnly to shake my hand"

Progress to the third station proved just as difficult, with the tyres sinking and slithering after short intervals of riding. Hordes of flies clamoured about me whenever I stopped and, attracted by the moisture in the eyes, tried to get behind my goggles. My head and face were shielded by a light muslin shesh, protecting me from the sun and containing condensation from breathing, so reducing dehydration. More looks of amazement came from a group of workers passing on a jigger, each one reaching down solemnly to shake my hand.

One of them introduced himself as the son of the cyclist encountered the previous day and said in English, "Welcome, sister!". The wind at last turned to tail, the sand became firmer and I rattled happily along for several effortless kilometres, singing desert songs as I pulled into the next station.

I was shown the same unstinting welcome and warned that the winds would worsen. I was told I should remain and accept shelter in one of the men's huts rather than risk having my tent flattened. Two of the three men amused themselves by trying on my safety helmet and goggles and directing invisible armies while I took photos.

An extra rope-strung bed was hauled inside one of the conical-shaped outhuts, empty except for a transistor radio and a crucifix on the wall. These were the sleeping quarters of a young man named Belo. I realised he had offered me his own more comfortable bed, and my sudden qualms about sharing the room and lack of privacy were dispelled as he cheerily bid me goodnight and curled up to sleep. The door and window were well shuttered, but sleep was elusive as the wind gathered force during the night.

Next morning, after a shared breakfast of *chai* and a packet of biscuits contributed by me, the men indulged my lifelong whim to ride a jigger. We careered wildly southward, pumping the handle two by two and laughing loudly into the wind. The men laughed even more loudly as I tried to persuade them to join Betty and me in hijacking the jigger to complete the desert journey.

Another man, Khiddr, complained of persistent stomach upsets and diarrhoea, and I dispensed homeopathic and medicinal remedies from my first-aid kit. More difficult to explain than how much to take, and when, was the importance of boiling the brackish water which the men drank. I politely declined to share a communal bowl of okra simmered with spices and eaten with pancake bread – though it looked tasty – for fear of unhealthy repercussions.

Suddenly the air was thick with blinding, choking dust. Less than 300m away, the main station had disappeared. This was the beginning of a weather phenomenon I had heard of: fierce inter-seasonal windstorms which can rage unabated for ten days at a time. The strong winds which had impeded my progress from Wadi Halfa were only a mild precursor. Further movement was impossible and I passed a companionable day under siege with the men, illustrating English and Arabic words and telling stories graphically on the sand floor. The civil conflict between the Arab, mainly Islamic north, and the socialist, mainly Christian/Animist south, did not reflect in the easy compatibility of this mix of Muslim and Christian men.

"The spectre of a single vulture hunched on the overhead wires to spur me on"

With the wind somewhat abated, I experienced the same difficulties in riding with over-thin tyres on wind-loosened sand. Progress towards the next station was confined to pushing, with my usual halo of flies for company and the spectre of a single vulture hunched on the overhead wires to spur me on. There were exhilarating stretches where I could make some speed, and these made it all worthwhile as I sailed along on a sea of sand, alone with lofty thoughts.

Occasionally these were brought to an abrupt halt as I hit a loose patch of sand and was thrown clear off the bike. At the journey's worst, approaching another station, I could manoeuvre Betty through the sand only by balancing both wheels on one of the rails. This required a steady eye (not easy with the loss of one contact lens), and necessitated bending low to push. The picture this must have presented brought out a hasty rescue party of two men carrying water, obviously unprepared for my reaction as I stood tall with a broad grin

and greeted them, clearly far from staggering in on my last legs.

Among the eight or ten men at this station, one young man was aggressively insistent that I should supply him with medication (which I did not have) for a persistent cough. His demeanour was in marked contrast to the excessively polite and unobtrusive manners and easy humour of the Sudanese men I had met so far. The expressions of the others were apologetic, and I later learned that his agitation was a consequence of having suffered from cerebral malaria.

An invitation to join the group for a lunch of freshly chopped tomato and onion salad tossed with oil and seasonings and scooped up with fresh-baked pancake bread was more than I could resist. I squatted eagerly beside the men, scooping heartily from the bowl and remembering in time to keep my left hand away from the food, as this would be considered contaminating. Walking toward the outback toilet (a walled, raised concrete platform with a hole over a bucket), the young man with the pushy manner stepped forward and thoughtfully provided me with a plastic container of water. I was, however, still conditioned to use my dwindling supply of toilet paper from Egypt.

A welcome had been extended to me to stay and wait for the next through train if I wished. Philosophising to myself that had I set out to walk most of the distance, and would have done so unencumbered by my ill-suited companion, Betty, I decided to rail the remaining distance, and passed the interim days in the relaxed company of the isolated railwaymen.

I shared a hut with two mild-mannered men who, like Belo, were from the same area near Djuba in the south. Again, one of them insisted on giving up his own bed for me. Akedj (23) was close on seven feet tall – characteristic of the Dinka tribe – yet the bed was designed for someone my height – five feet six inches. I was aware of how little these men had and the starkness of their existence at these stations. Waal (37) explained his ambition to work at the larger station at Abu Hamed because of its access to the *souk* (market) and the availability of fresh fruit and vegetables to supplement their meagre diet. Akedj expressed a wish to go to London to study, but had neither passport nor financial prospects of doing so.

"In their hospitality these men were unstinting and I was made to feel comfortable and accepted"

In their hospitality these men were unstinting and I was made to feel comfortable and accepted. As at the other stations I found small tokens in my panniers to show my appreciation: mint tea, biscuits, tins of beans and nail clippers.

Before and after meals the three of us would draw water in turns from a clay pitcher outside and pour while the others washed. I was conscious of hiding hands blackened the previous evening from endeavours with my temperamental paraffin camping stove. Despite the largely insanitary conditions in which the men lived, their rituals of washing face and hands were fastidious. We enjoyed the early-morning warmth over games of Ludo in the sand before the sun rose too high and we had to retreat from the gathering forces of wind and flies.

It was curious to be shown a well-thumbed *Oxford English Reader*, adapted for Africa by English speakers, yet with illustrations and references to British Royalty and English lifestyles, outdated and inappropriate to the African context. Akedj and Waal listened attentively to a radio broadcast in both Arabic and English by the Sudanese People's Liberation Movement. It advocated multi-racial harmony, the uniting by law of all national groups in Sudan, and the right of all minorities to an equal say in the National Assembly. The SPLM declared itself committed to the armed struggle against what it called the religious bigotry and racism of Islamic Sharia Law, and to liberating the country from all forms of sectarianism. The men's exuberant reactions after the broadcast provided a suitable opening to explore (within the bounds of the language barrier) the topic.

The late-evening arrival of the train to Khartoum barely left time to say a hurried goodbye as I leaned out the open window to shake hands with Akedj, laughing and easily running apace with the departing train.

There was no time to dwell on sadness; the man behind me in the cramped, unlit compartment put his arm on my shoulder and pressed full body against me. Sinking feeling: it was the first hint of any untoward advances from anyone in this country. When he tried to bustle me backwards to a prone position on the seat behind, under the guise of gauche chivalry offering his place, I sensed differently and reacted swiftly with a firm "No!" and a vice-like grip and twist to his wrists. It effectively repelled him and I had no further trouble.

I soon discovered that the Michelin-marked road from Atbara does not in fact begin until the outskirts of the capital. Reports of bandit activity and a spinal meningitis epidemic weighed the balance in favour of accepting Land-rover rides, first to Shendi and then to Khartoum itself, from British engineers working in the area and concerned to obtain vaccinations. This opportunity provided insight into the shabby splendour and colonial relics of Kitchener's rail-building era in the town of Atbara, and the chance to inspect irrigation projects based on the Nile, designed to overcome the spread of desert into the surrounding parched settlements.

Khartoum at the time was beset with an uneasy tension, exacerbated by the epidemic which was claiming many lives, governmental discord, and, shortly after I left, bombings in which English tourists were killed. It was possible to remain impervious to this whilst wandering the city, tourist fashion, during the daytime, enjoying the delights of fresh mango juice stalls or queuing for fresh-baked bread rolls. However, permits for travel outside the capital were being restrictively issued, as were permits for taking photographs, and travel in the south was prohibited.

Through development workers for aid agencies came the news that starvation and drought were becoming more widespread in the northwest. Families displaced and fleeing from war in the south were being forced to sell their children into contractual slavery in order to raise money to reach Khartoum. But prospects for employment in a city already besieged by the homeless and destitute, many of them refugees from neighbouring Chad, Ethiopia and Somalia, were grim.

Flying north several months later, after touring Kenya and Tanzania, poignant memories of Sudan returned as the plane descended for a brief stopover in Khartoum and we had a bird's-eye view of areas afflicted by recent flooding. The following day even this sight would have been obscured as I read in newspapers of the sky over the capital darkened by a plague of locusts.

TRAVEL NOTES

Languages Arabic and tribal dialects. English, the old colonial language, is taught in schools and quite widely spoken.

Transport Slow and unreliable — expect long delays. Buses are marginally better than trains: *boxes* (collective taxis) are useful. If you're travelling alone it's always best to sit with Sudanese women — they often use separate compartments to men.

Accommodation Outside Khartoum, the capital, hotels tend to be of the dormitory type; many of them have separate women's quarters. Most Sudanese stay with relatives when they travel and hotels are usually a last resort! Catholic resthouses (at Juba, for instance) are good refuges.

Special Problems The southwest of the country is at present in a critical position, devastated by drought and guerrilla war. To visit Sudan at all is probably not realistic or useful other than for work. Visas are granted by the Sudanese Embassy in London but not generally in Egypt or any other transit points. If you do visit the north be very sensitive to the strong Islamic culture, both in dress (cover upper arms and knees) and habit (very harsh penalties for use of alcohol).

Guide *Sudan — No Frills Guide* (Bradt) is good on the basics. *Egypt and the Sudan — A Travel Survival Kit* (Lonely Planet) is also useful.

Contacts

Sudanese Women's National Assembly [SWNA], PO Box 301, Omdurman. The autonomous women's union active in development campaigns with rural women.

Ahfad, University College for Women, PO Box 167, Omdurman. Twice-yearly journal on status of women in developing countries.

Books

Marjorie Hall and Bakhita Amin Ismail, Sisters Under the Sun: the Story of Sudanese Women (Longman, 1981). Regional study with thorough historical background on the position of women in the Sudan today.

Eric Hoagland, African Calliope (Penguin, 1982). Anecdotal stories of Sudanese life.

Thanks for general help in putting together this chapter to Debbie Garlick and Pat Yale.

Taiwan

Not least among the many anachronisms of Taiwan is its pretensions to be the legitimate Republic of China. At the end of the 1949 Revolution the defeated nationalists fled the mainland for the island and took full political and economic control. Their party, the Kuomintang, has remained in power ever since and, under the guise of securing the country from Communist invasion, held it under martial law for close on four decades. This has now been lifted, and a certain element of electoral reform has been introduced, but many Kuomintang deputies remain those who were voted in on the mainland in pre-revolution ballots. Significant change is unlikely.

Political rights, however, have not been a predominant issue in Taiwan. This is first and foremost an entrepreneurial society – money is an abiding obsession and consumerism rampant. Visitors expecting a harmonious and gentle taste of the East will be sorely disappointed. The massive overdevelopment of the main cities, crowded with ugly high-rise blocks and choked with traffic and pollution, can come as a shock, as can the incredibly high cost of living. Taiwan is second only to Tokyo in expense.

Travelling alone, however, is relatively safe. The strong military presence has meant that street crime is uncommon and Western foreigners are generally treated with great courtesy and kindness. Although the country has a fairly large community of expatriates (mainly American businessmen and itinerant English teachers), most tend to lead rarefied and isolated lives. In the less commercial districts of the main cities and throughout the countryside you are likely to attract a great deal of attention. People may well stare and point at you but this rarely leads to more than friendly interest.

As in Hong Kong and South Korea, **women in Taiwan** are caught between the conflicting demands of a modern, Westernised and highly competitive culture and traditional Confucianist values. In constitutional terms women are supposed to have equal rights in work and education but the reality is that they face entrenched discrimination, are ghettoised in poorly paid jobs and are expected to take a subservient role within marriage. Prostitution is illegal but exists on a massive scale (you'll be warned against wandering alone in the red light district of Taipei) and Taiwan has remained a fairly popular destination for Japanese businessmen in search of cheap sex. Under the authoritarian rule of the Kuomintang, autonomous political groups, including feminist initiatives, have been suppressed.

Taipei without Maps

. . . .

Kate Hanniker travelled to Taiwan to stay with a friend who was working there on a temporary contract. She spent a month exploring the capital, Taipei, and made a few trips to the south of the island.

Taiwan is a little island with big ideas. Physically it is half the size of Ireland, with a population of only nineteen million, yet the Nationalist Kuomintang Government still considers itself the only legitimate ruler of the vast mainland and it convenes regularly to pass legislation for the Peoples' Republic. In spite of, or perhaps because of, its exaggerated sense of self importance, it is extremely successful in other ways.

Within the last forty years the country has leapt from rags to riches. Its people are a disconcerting mixture of those men and women who have been caught up in the whirlpool of money-making activity and of those – largely the older generation – whom this frenzied activity has utterly passed by. Life

for this latter category is noticeably more comfortable than it was thirty years ago but essentially their lifestyles remain little altered by the new wave of consumerism.

The bulk of the wealth is concentrated in the five major Taiwanese cities, and especially in Taipei, where the women are streets ahead of their country cousins in their Western dress. For the nouveau riche, life in Taiwan is luxurious and massively consumer-oriented with all shops open daily until 10pm. Unemployment stands at two percent and beggars, touts and pimps are noticeable by their absence. Towards the end of my visit I was thrown by the sight of a beggar and the word suddenly reeled back into my vocabulary (though squalor had not left it).

The cost, inevitably, of this surge of economic growth is overdevelopment, scant accommodation and appalling pollution. In Taipei, apartment blocks stand high and virtually back to back. On the outskirts of the city, homes are little more inviting than chicken shacks and three generations of a family are often crammed into one flat. Traffic is choking and anarchic. The Taiwanese prefer to call it "flamboyant" and the surprisingly low level of road accidents indicate that they employ not a little skill in getting about as quickly and as economically as possible. This same sixth sense is used by the Taiwanese when conducting their business affairs.

What struck me most during my four-week stay was how immediately secure I felt, despite the fact that I had only a limited Chinese vocabulary and a roughly sketched street-plan in English characters which at times impeded, rather than guided, my progress. Being able to roam freely and unaccosted was something I had not expected in Asia.

"Since I was possibly the only redhead in Taipei, I caused something of a stir"

On one of the numerous occasions when I lost not only my way, but also all sense of direction, I felt safe enough to accept a lift from a man I had asked for directions. He spoke no English and was kind enough to leave his work and drive me to my destination on the other side of Taipei.

Whenever I asked the way (most people speak Chinglish to match my Englinese) I would be drawn into a lengthy confab and on occasions an entire family joined me on the street to mull over my map. At times the sense of obligation the Chinese showed towards me as a stranger transcended my (cynical) belief. Finally they would point me in any direction to save the important Chinese "face" and I would embark unknowingly on a vast detour. Yet again I'd have to hail a taxi, defeating my purpose of familiarising myself with the city. With time I came to accept this as simply the most reliable method of getting from A to B without travelling via C and D.

My novelty value as a foreigner was seemingly endless. And since I was possibly the only redhead in Taipei, I caused something of a stir. Children ran up to me grinning as if I was a long lost friend. "Hey, Okay, Number One," they would holler. All foreigners are

American to the Taiwanese. "Ingwor" ("I'm English") was a phrase I soon mastered, but it made no odds, their reaction was still as fervent.

Westerners seem to embody some kind of utopia for the Taiwanese. The fashionable Chinese women have rejected their traditional clothing, opting instead for bolstered shoulder pads. And Western images and models are used to promote even the most oriental of products. It's easy to see how this emulation is interpreted as adulation by the resident ex-pats, who live in isolated splendour in the north of Taipei. Their arrogance translates itself into maudlin attempts to recreate mini-Europes and USAs, epitomised by the disconcerting appearance of a pub or *bierkeller*.

As a European woman I seemed to inspire respect and admiration, especially since I was negotiating the city by myself, unescorted. This is quite contrary to Chinese custom, rooted as it is in Confucianism and chauvinism. Attitudes, I'm assured, are gradually changing, but beyond the more sophisticated work places, sexual discrimination and harassment are still everyday problems. Women may rule over the home, traditionally a power base in Taiwanese society, but they have much less status in public life and double standards are very obvious. For example, it is accepted that men will have "other women" – prostitutes or mistresses – but a wife will be reviled and cast out if she is found to be "unfaithful".

In custodial cases the children will automatically stay with their father. And even where a woman has been subjected to domestic violence, she is ill-advised to seek a divorce, which may result in her social ostracism. Although Taiwanese businesswomen wield considerable power, they are often paid less and work longer hours than their male counterparts and many working-class women suffer harsh conditions in the nation's sweatshops.

The only time that I felt ill at ease in Taiwan was on my final morning when I visited the Lungshan Temple area. There was no obvious threat but the atmosphere unnerved me. A dog twitched to death on the sidewalk and a crowd of old men looked on and shouted useless encouragement. Younger men in string vests stood entranced around a streethawk who measured up a white powder in brass scales. Schoolgirls hovered half-naked in doorways. Later I learnt that I was a street away from the notorious Snake Alley, where women are sold to Japanese businessmen for $1.25 a day and where turtles are tortured for their blood, which is guzzled by the same men to increase their virility.

"Hairdressers and tearooms often operate as hostess-type joints"

The sex industry is big business in Taiwan. All except the most expensive hotels increase their profit margins by letting out rooms by the afternoon and by transmitting soft porn day and night. Hairdressers and tearooms often operate as hostess-type joints, not necessarily brothels, but places where the lonely businessman can fork out large sums of money in exchange for a few hours of female company.

My great joy in Taipei was looking around the temples. The Confucian Temple seemed to be the only public place to have escaped the rest of the city's haphazard development. The Taoist temples on the other hand were home to the same bedlam to be found in the streets. Chickens, children and dogs run amok through the endless passages, up into the small sub-temples. The tiered levels offer panoramic views of the city.

The temples throw up constant surprises to the Western eye accustomed to uniform architecture and solemn devotion. On one floor multicoloured puppets rotate in a perpetual electronic parade, offering gifts to the gods. Somewhere in the grounds an opera may break out. Old men sit around a table playing cards and watching TV rigged up precariously on an altar. A businessman waves joss sticks and throws crescent-shaped pieces of wood to find out if he should change his car.

The state is just beginning to invest money in tourism but as yet there are few concessions to the Western traveller. This has its advantages and its drawbacks. It is pleasant to find areas of natural beauty still unspoilt by the commercialism which has so ravaged the cities. But it can be frustrating when travelling to be faced with the options of a state-run tour or of getting lost trying to decipher Chinese town names. The tours are blatantly commercial, whisking you from site to site with a final compulsory stop at a local factory, where you will be assailed by pretty girls hoping to persuade you to part with your money.

Initially I was irritated by the persistence of the sales people, not only in the tourist shops but also in the village stores, where the shopkeepers wave excitedly and shout at any foreigner passing within ten metres of their shops to come inside and spend. Finally I learnt to laugh at the unashamedness of it all.

Getting around by public transport is cheap and efficient but you're restricted in where you go and what you see. I hired a car which is relatively inexpensive. Cheaper are the mopeds which clog up the streets of Taipei (and often with an entire family aboard one bike), but you have to be brave to contend with the traffic. Driving down the East Coast I found wild and untouched beaches. Central Taiwan was a visual feast – the tranquility of the huge mountains chilling the lakes and paddy fields by night gave way to the intense heat of the March sun and lizards and creepers and luscious foliage.

TRAVEL NOTES

Languages Mandarin is the official language but most people use Taiwanese. English is widely taught although people tend to be shy of trying it out in public.

Transport Taxis are abundant and relatively cheap. There's an efficient bus and train network covering most of the island.

Accommodation The international hotels are very expensive but there are plenty of cheaper and reasonably comfortable youth hostels.

Special Problems Expense. You'll have to fork out for accommodation and food. Harassment is rarely a problem although few women wander alone into the red light districts of Taipei and Kaohsiung, where drug peddling and prostitution breed their own violence.

Although the government is now toeing a softer political line you should be careful not to compromise others in political discussions. The Taiwanese are still exhorted to inform on potential "communist agents".

Guide *Taiwan: A Travel Survival Kit* (Lonely Planet) is the best general guide, though like most books on Taiwan it doesn't really explain why you should want to go there.

Contacts

Women's Research Programme, Population Studies Centre, National Taiwan University, Roosevelt Road, Section 4, No.1, Taipei. A resource for information on women's issues, although most of the literature published is in Chinese.

A useful place to look for contacts, information about jobs, language courses, accommodation etc, is the common-room noticeboard of **The Mandarin Training Centre**, National Taiwan Normal University, 162 Hoping East Road, Section 1, Taipei.

Thanks to Lidi Van-Gool and Luisetta Mudie for help with the Travel Notes.

Tanzania

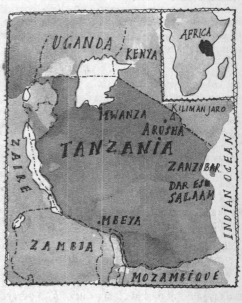

Compared with Kenya, tourism in Tanzania is relatively low-key. Few travellers venture beyond the "northern circuit" of Dar es Salaam, the island of Zanzibar, Arusha (for the ascent of Mount Kilimanjaro), the Ngorongoro crater and the Serengeti. It is in fact a huge country and independent travel, without the money to hire a jeep or a small plane, can be slow and arduous. Most women, however, find the country reasonably relaxed, once outside of the capital, Dar es Salaam, which has definite no-go areas. As a general rule you should dress modestly, particularly in predominantly Muslim areas like the island of Zanzibar.

The population is made up of a diverse range of tribes and cultures – Muslim, Christian, Animist, Hindu. No single group dominates and the official language of Kiswahili affords a very tenuous communal link. Since gaining independence from the British in 1961 the country's politics and policies have been moulded by Julius Nyerere, one of Africa's longest running elder statesmen. He finally stepped down as president in 1985 but continues as chairman of his party, *Chama Cha Mapinduzi* (*CCM*), and still features alongside the current ruler, Ali Hassan Mwinyi, in all government office photos.

Throughout his long rule, Nyerere introduced and determinedly pursued his own brand of Christian Socialism, the most central and ambitious policy of which was *ujamaa*, literally villagisation. This involved the compulsory resettlement of populations on a massive scale with the intention of raising agricultural production through local collective farming. The experiment floundered amidst claims of local and central government corruption, low-level productivity in the villages and increasing scarcity of basic (imported) commodities. Hard hit by the Seventies oil recession, a war with Uganda and a refusal to compromise the country by trade with South Africa, poverty and shortages have become an enduring fact of life. Unsurprisingly theft is a widespread problem and travellers who flaunt their relative wealth are an obvious target.

The **Union of Women of Tanzania** is a government-aligned organisation which was set up to provide and expand education and welfare projects. Its leaders are predominantly urban, middle-class women who work alongside trainers and teachers provided by VSO and other development agencies. Women attached to the church have traditionally had a high social status and are now often seen working at the forefront of education and medicine. Many women community leaders first learnt their organisational skills in the Church. We have been unable to find any additional information regarding autonomous feminist activity.

Slowly, Slowly, Kilimanjaro

. . . .

Sara Oliver describes her ascent of Africa's highest mountain, Kilimanjaro.

Kilimanjaro was given by Queen Victoria to Kaiser Wilhelm as a birthday present, but later reverted to British colonial rule. In the evening sun the magnificent monster looks calm, its white top sparkling out of a shroud of cloud, the foothills dark with forest shadows. An injured young German who had just descended groaned, "Not for a million dollars! Never again", as he limped by.

The National Park entrance at Marangu has a "going up" book and a "coming down" book. Here we begin. With our guide, Anasion Mabando, three porters (who carry warmer clothing and supplies for five days in baskets on their heads), a Dutch volunteer returning from Zambia, and myself, we are a party of six.

The porters soon disappear ahead. The well-trodden path leads past euca-lyptus trees and Japanese cherry blossom. Singing birds are hidden among dense trees and butterflies fly across the stony track. The walk is pleasant, though warm, and we pause where a deep green, shaded stream falls among rocks, refreshing us. After three and a half hours we reach Mandara hut, 9000ft above sea level, where we will stay the night.

We sit watching the lights of Moshi town and the mass of stars. Anasion cooks onion soup, goat, cabbage and potatoes – "food for white people". He urges us to eat a lot as at higher altitudes we may lose our appetites. He has climbed the mountain over 800 times and has progressed from being a junior porter at fourteen to a senior guide. His experience is comforting. We sleep in the wooden huts, well wrapped up against the cold night.

Anasion brings sweet tea at 7am. The morning is clear and quiet but for birds singing, bees humming, and two large white-naped ravens scavenging. We breakfast on paw-paw, porridge and eggs and Anasion suggests we drink a lot of tea. He plans five hours' slow walking. We plod up the path into the forest again while the porters leap ahead with their loads.

The rainforest is dense and dark, with drooping creepers hanging from every branch. Loud screeches come from turacos and red-headed parrots which flash in front of us. Suddenly we are out of the forest and on to high savanna. Blinking in the sun, we see Mawenzi peak and further over, the snow of Kilimanjaro.

Here ferns and long grasses replace the wet green of the forest and the sun burns through the dry thin air. We walk slowly, and stop to watch buck and eland. We meet some porters dashing downward with a radio playing. They are followed by some rotund Norwegians who declare that most of their party reached the top.

Then comes the sound of panting and a group of people appears, running. Two rush by, carrying a grey-faced boy on a stretcher; his companions pause to explain that he has a pulmonary oedema and the only way to save his life is to *run* down to a lower altitude and then take him to hospital. These are fit eighteen-year-old students. Anasion shakes his head and sighs and warns us to move slowly.

Cloud comes rushing towards us and we are engulfed in cold, damp mist. A piercing whistle from Anasion brings back a porter with the down jackets we hired at Marangu. We don gloves and hoods and plod on through the air which shows our breath. We take frequent rests as the track becomes steeper, and I begin to notice the altitude, as any violent movement results in lightheadedness.

We walk silently in single file, saving our breath. Anasion, last in line, walks at the pace of the slowest, which is me. The mist swirls and we seem to be utterly alone on the way to the top of the world. My sinuses ache and my throat thumps strangely, so I realise I must rest.

At last, through the mist, we see the shapes of the huts of Horombo, where we will stay our second night. It is 2pm and we have walked for five hours,

climbing 3000ft. We sleep fully clothed, with hats on inside sleeping bags, tossing and turning fitfully. Breakfast is maize porridge again. Then we start walking. We pass the last water source where we fill our bottles. We cross the saddle between Mawenzi and Kilimanjaro, a vast stretch of empty terrain. We walk for five hours and the last part, just before Kibo hut at 15,520ft, takes a long time; we rest frequently and pant with the effort of moving upwards.

"A German woman vomits continuously and another drifts in and out of consciousness"

We arrive, tired, and eat goulash, which Anasion is delighted we can still manage. We rest, listening to our racing pulses. I sneeze and my nose bleeds. A German woman vomits continuously and another drifts in and out of consciousness, gasping for oxygen.

Anasion rouses us at 1am. We drink sugary tea and put on our warmest clothing. It has been snowing and the bright moonbeams cast shadows as clear as daylight. Anasion leads, instructing us to tell him if we feel unwell. We shuffle off into the night, walking on volcanic scree, using our long sticks to stop sliding backwards on loose gravel. The moonlight is enchanting, the night clear and quiet; our rasping breath sounds insultingly loud.

At about 4.30am a cloud covers the moon and an icy wind begins to batter us between rests we now take eight paces, then six, then four with our lead-like feet. My lungs ache and I feel very tired. Anasion urges us on, chanting "Slowly, Slowly, Kilimanjaro", and we follow. Nothing matters but the next step.

Anasion points to a thin red line in the cloud. "Alleluya!" he shouts, his voice echoing across the mountain. "It is morning! Alleluya! Thank you, God!" I am thankful too. The sun's rays warm us and give us courage to continue as we see the beautiful brilliant dawn of Kilimanjaro. In the growing light Anasion points to something white in the rock. It is not snow. It is a flagpole. It is the top.

Painfully and slowly we ascend the rock, encouraged by Anasion's chanting, scrambling with our hands over the last little bit. Shaking with the strain but enormously exhilarated I look down on huge glaciers, giant steps of brilliant ice dazzling white in the morning sun. The steaming volcano reminds me of my puniness. A wooden box was wedged between the rocks, inside a book full of triumphant signatures. We had no pen.

We had taken eight hours to climb the peak; coming down took only one hour. At Kibo hut the Chaga mountain rescue men congratulated us. "Two white women! Really, that is surprising. It's good, very good." I felt angry, indignant, and pleased.

TRAVEL NOTES

Languages Kiswahili, English, and numerous tribal languages. It helps to speak even a little Swahili, which is far more necessary than in neighbouring Kenya.

Transport Buses, trains and planes are all stricken by shortages of fuel and spare parts. It is often easier to hitch, or, for a small sum, cadge a spare seat on someone else's safari vehicle. Ask around the Asian travel agents who can be helpful. It is possible to go by ferry from Dar to Zanzibar and from other towns like Bagamoyo and Tanga, but can be difficult to arrange as it is thought to threaten national security.

Accommodation The YMCAs are cheap, friendly and admit women too; the YWCA in Dar is a good and secure meeting place. Hotels and guesthouses are similar to Kenya, though fewer and less developed.

Special problems Shortages. Dispensaries and hospitals often lack vital drug supplies, so take your own (Tanzania is in a high risk malarial zone), plus tampons, toiletries, any contraceptives, etc; be prepared, too, for food and drink shortages, even of Tanzanian products.

Official currency rates are abysmal, the black market up to eight times better; but deal at your own risk, penalties are severe on both sides.

If you take any photographs ask first and expect to pay.

Guides *Guide to East Africa* (Travelaid) and *East Africa – A Travel Survival Kit* (Lonely Planet) both have fair sections on Tanzania. *Backpacker's Africa* (Bradt Publications) is useful for hikes.

Contacts

Tanzania Women's Organisation (UWT), Ofisi Kun ndogo SLP 1473, Dar es Salaam, Tanzania. The longest running women's group. Established in 1962, it aims to promote political, economic and social equality.

Women Communicators, PO Box 9033, Dar es Salaam. A Church organisation affiliated to the Msimbazi Centre. Its aim is to promote women's participation in nation-building activities.

Books

Laetitia Mukarasi, Post Abolished: One Woman's Struggle for Employment Rights in Tanzania (The Women's Press, 1990). Brave and fascinating account, not just of the right to work, but of the dynamics of respect within family life.

Goran Hyden, *Beyond Ujamaa in Tanzania: Underdevelopment and an Uncaptured Peasantry* (Heinemann, 1980).

Tepilit Ole Saitoti and Carol Beckwith, *Maasai* (Elm Tree Books, 1980). Photo record with interesting text.

Ophelia Macarenhas and Marjorie Mbilinyi, *Women in Tanzania: An analytical bibliography* (Scandinavian Institute of African Studies, 1983).

Look out too for the work of **Tanzanian writers** like Hanza Sokko, W.E. Mkufya, Agoro Anduru and Prince Kagwema. Also for the writings of Julius Nyerere – essential insights into the present social structure.

Trinidad

The largest island in the Eastern Caribbean, Trinidad has a population of around one million. Outside carnival there is little tourism. Trinidadians themselves take their holidays on the much smaller sister island of Tobago which, as the classic "tropical island paradise", has far more tourist facilities.

Trinidad itself is an oil state, though the collapse of oil prices since the boom period of the 1970s has left the island in bad financial trouble. Even so, the middle classes continue to live a comfortable life, driving around in large gas-guzzling American cars (petrol, despite the odd price increase, is still cheap), eating in overpriced restaurants boasting international cuisine, and building large sprawling houses along the coastal strips beside the capital, Port of Spain, and San Fernando in the south. The poor have been hard hit. Bullock-drawn carts and ploughs co-exist with expensive imported cars and tractors, and many smallholders live in tumbledown shacks in the hills.

Travelling around can be quite a problem since out-of-town bus services are very limited. Without a car, it's almost impossible to get to the beautiful wild beaches and even to established tourist sites such as the mangrove swamps, where stunning flocks of scarlet ibis arrive at dusk to roost. In addition, wherever you go, even staying in small guesthouses or with local families, the cost of living is high. But people are generally friendly and hospitable and, if you love music and dancing (this is the home of the calypso and the steel band), there's lots of cheap entertainment. A drawback is that without a male companion you can expect endless propositions from local men.

Although there are some vociferous feminists within the trade unions, the **women's movement** has been slow to develop. The Secretariat of the *Caribbean Association for Feminist Research and Action* (*CAFRA*), formed in 1985, is based in Trinidad, but it is not easy to gauge how far the organisation has improved the lives of ordinary women. The island is ethnically very mixed – a combination of people of African, Indian and, to a much lesser extent, European, Chinese and Syrian descent. While relations are superficially harmonious, people are always aware of the possibilities of friction between the different groups, especially with rising unemployment. The political parties tend to be split along racial lines, but an attempt is always made to keep some balance of races within the government. People are far more conscious of this issue than they are of sexism.

A Health Worker in Port of Spain
. . . .

Patricia Jacob spent three months working in Trinidad as part of her final year's study at medical school. Wanting medical experience in a tropical country, she chose the island for its comparatively low profile as a tourist resort.

Armed with a Medical Research Council grant, I arrived in Trinidad to help establish a community-based health project. The aim of the project was to teach mothers how to rehydrate their babies at home when they developed gastroenteritis, so avoiding a long, difficult and expensive journey to hospital. Long stretches of deserted palm fringed beaches, copious quantities of rum punch, and the magic of steel pan were also frequently listed on my timetable. But, a little unexpectedly, it was my opportunity to work in the community rather than holiday in the sun that gave me most joy and satisfaction.

My project took me to areas where, as a tourist, I would probably never have gone: the downtown areas of the poor; shanty-towns of cardboard and corrugated iron cluttering the edges of the main city, Port of Spain; old, ramshackle wooden huts perched erratically around the hillsides, clinging desperately to the worn and litter-strewn slopes. In East Dry River, where I was based, there were no roads, no house numbers but always bright-eyed barefoot children to lead you up and down the tumbling paths. Here name and family were your only rank and everyone was related.

"As a doctor . . . I was given a passage into people's houses and treated with a hospitality and intimacy I could never otherwise have expected"

I was surprised how readily the women of these communities accepted and confided in me – for, despite Trinidad's incredibly cosmopolitan people, there is still a powerful racial tension throughout the island. Many whites consider themselves to be superior, while the black population tends to look down on the Indians, who, in turn, condemn the Chinese; finally, everyone seems to hate the Syrians, perhaps because of their remarkable success in business. Even within each race there is racism – or perhaps more accurately "colourism", for the paler black people often mock their darker skinned neighbours and the wealthy Indians in the city use cruel nicknames to taunt their country cousins.

As a white woman venturing into a black ghetto, I was more than a little apprehensive about my reception. But I needn't have worried. In my role as a doctor, going out to help children, I was given a passage into people's houses and treated with a hospitality and intimacy I could never otherwise have expected.

Walking through some of the poorest areas I was often stopped by groups of cold-faced men, especially young Rastas who hang around in clusters on the street, a national habit. As they grilled me about where I was going, and what I was doing, I would explain nervously until their faces relaxed, sometimes smiles broke out, and I was pointed in the right direction for my charge.

In general these areas, like shanty towns in most big cities, aren't safe to wander alone. I was warned, many times too, about going unaccompanied into the countryside, especially into the hills in the middle of the island. Stories of strange goings-on, with hints of black magic and wild half-man, half-beast creatures were wound up into hysteria by the mythical story-telling that Trinidadians love so much. I was sufficiently scared not to go in search of the truth.

I soon learned to master the local taxi service, which runs throughout the city and, in fact, I even looked forward to moving about this way. The taxis (recognisable by their number plates and not to be confused with tourist taxis which carry a proper sign) are shared and thus reasonably cheap. Sitting squashed in the backseat of a vehicle with several strangers soon starts up a conversation and is a great way of hearing local opinion about everything under the sun.

However, getting around the rest of the island is almost impossible; a few buses connect the main towns, but the only railways were ripped up years ago. Hitching is definitely not worth the risk and hiring a car prohibitively expensive; I found myself relying on the excessive Trinidadian hospitality showered on me in order to go further afield.

"Women's stories reflected the ease with which many Trinidadians slip in and out of relationships"

Unlike the men, women I met in the course of my work were always delighted with the opportunity to have someone new to talk to, whatever the colour of their skin. My visits provided just another chance for a chat and a laugh about children, men, rivals, love and sex – the last being a favourite topic everywhere and discussed with surprising frankness.

Women's stories reflected the ease with which many Trinidadians slip in and out of relationships. More children are born out of wedlock than in it, but the problems of the one-parent family are nothing like those in England. In Trinidad there always seems to be someone – grandmother, sisters, cousins, neighbours, friends – to look after the children. At the same time the man's macho role reigns supreme, especially among the poorer communities, and women are often left to cope on their own with the house and children. Even among the wealthier and more educated, women have yet to attain the degree of freedom that many of their Western sisters enjoy.

For much of my stay I lived with a black Trinidadian family, the Bernards, in St Annes, a pleasant district in Port of Spain. Susan, Sandra and Jill-Anne, the three daughters still living at home, were a riot of fun and continual chatter. They adopted me like a long lost member of the family and took me around with them to meet their friends, neighbours and boyfriends, to endless parties and discos; on political rallies, pop concerts, shopping trips, cricket matches, even for a weekend on Trinidad's sister island, Tobago. Life was a constant social whirl and not just for my benefit; the girls lead the same crazy social life as most Trinidadians.

I had my own room in their pretty, if rather chaotic, house and, after initial protest, was allowed to muck in with the rest of the family for chores such as cleaning and shopping. Cooking, however, remained the domain of Mrs Bernard. Meal times were completely relaxed: she would prepare great bowls of traditional food like curry *callalloo* and spicy chicken, to which we just helped ourselves when we felt hungry. Once or twice a week, for a treat, someone would bring home a takeaway; fast foods have caught on in a big way in Trinidad and the influences of both Canada and the USA pervade many aspects of life on the island.

In general the girls had the opportunity to pursue what they wanted to do and seemed to live a modern Western lifestyle. All had good jobs – in banking, as a personal assistant, and with a national airline – but underneath it all they were ultimately expected to fulfil traditional family expectations to settle down (though not necessarily marry), have several children and look after man and home. As in other sides of island life there still hovered an empty promise of something more exciting. The girls' parents, like most of their generation, had been brought up in a rural old-fashioned way.

Modern life only hit Trinidad comparatively recently with the sudden development of the oil industry. Nowadays the shops may sell almost all the material things you could want (provided someone can be bribed to bring it into the country), but it will take much longer for the social structure of Trinidadian life to change. At least the girls I was staying with were able to work in a job of their choice and had money of their own.

Many of the women in my project area had little chance of escape from the drudgery of household chores and childcare. They had to look after every family need on a minuscule income which they only saw if their man hadn't already spent it on gambling and beer. Luckily a close network of family and friends could usually be relied upon to bail them out, but a number had small choice but to struggle from debt to debt.

"Marianne sometimes used to accompany me on my forays into the slums, I think partly because she feared for my safety and partly to pursue her own mission to publicise the health centre"

One woman who had managed to break free from traditional restraints was a beautiful young nurse, called Marianne, half French West Indian, half Scottish. She had trained in England and returned to the island with a determination to improve the lot of Trinidad's women. Together with others in the Catholic community she had helped to establish a community centre in Port of Spain, offering medical help where necessary and tea and coffee to the lonely. The centre provided a welcome bolt-hole, since, while men haunt the streets and bars, there are few places where women can meet and talk outside of their own four walls.

Marianne sometimes used to accompany me on my forays into the slums, I think partly because she feared for my safety and partly to pursue her own mission to publicise the health centre. Commandeering her boyfriend's battered old car, we would drive to the fringes of East Dry River and abandon our escape vehicle to set out on foot along the dusty winding paths.

One visit in particular remains clear in my memory. To enter the house required a careful manoeuvre around a partially collapsed and exceedingly delicate porch platform, the whole hut being raised well above the steep hillside. A slightly insipid smell wafted out to greet us but inside it was pleasantly cool. In the little parlour sat several large and cheery women, dressed in bright but ragged old clothes, slightly faded by the sun and held together in crucial places by safety pins. Gathered pinnis covered their ample laps and gay scarves caught up the bobbly rollers in their hair. Children, probably grandchildren, tumbled and crawled around them as they talked and laughed. Pride of place in the crowded two-roomed hut stood three large, framed certificates, awarded for the best carnival costumes in 1977.

As proof, stunningly colourful intricate masks and headdresses hung from the tatty walls, commanding all attention away from the shabbiness of an old settee, the ragged curtains and mounting rubbish. It was as if all their scarce income had been concentrated on the wild, wonderful, drunken, dancing two days of carnival, a small investment for a momentary release from poverty. During the months leading up to each carnival, people's thoughts overflow with dreams and preparations for the forthcoming spree, while memories of all the fun provide food for months afterwards.

I found Trinidad so full of these contradictions: the wealth amidst the poverty, the gleaming children neatly dressed for school, hair uniformly ribboned, emerging from the smallest hut; the scorching sun followed so rapidly by refreshing torrential rain. The most rickety home would regularly reveal a huge, shiny fridge, trembling gently on the wafer-thin, gaping floorboards and laden with the local brew.

Almost everywhere I was invited to, from shacks to the house of a consultant surgeon, there was always an open invitation to help yourself; in other words march up to the fridge, have a nose around and take whatever you fancied.

Unfortunately the easygoing attitude of the people seems to have a link with their many problems. In a country soused with oil wealth, inefficiency, corruption, and apathetic disorder have contributed to persistent poverty, appalling facilities and massive wastage of precious resources. Nowhere was this more evident than in the government-run General Hospital.

"Patients were sharing beds, head to toe; the place had run out of clean sheets; and the mortuary fridge had broken down"

It's common for expensive equipment, imported into the country with great effort and manipulation of red tape, to lie unused in cupboards, rotting because some simple part can't be found or the official has run off with his bribe to get it through customs. Even if the equipment was intact, the lack of air conditioning would cause it to blow up in the heat, when it would simply return to the cupboard to await supplies for spare parts. While I was out there, patients were sharing beds, head to toe; the place had run out of clean sheets; and the mortuary fridge had broken down, leaving hundreds of corpses to rot, piled up in the courtyard.

A popular saying that I heard several times suggests that Trinidadians are like trees in the forest, growing prolifically in carefree abandon. There is plenty of room for the strong to grow while the weak fall into their shadow. Wherever I went, people offered advice on how to negotiate this forest, telling me about the hundred-and-one things that every Trinidadian needs to know from the day they are born in order to survive in their country: the benefits of goat curry and cow-heel soup, who is planting *ganja*, how to get a brand new car within a week without booking.

Everyone seemed to know how to get items in and money out, legally and illegally; what not to do; where not to go; who not to see. Every Trini, it seems, is a consultant in domestic and foreign affairs, with an ear to the groundbeat and an eye to whatever opportunities a visitor might bring.

Leaving aside the chaos, indulgent hospitality was the most memorable aspect of my trip. No one in the world knows how to look after a visitor like a Trinidadian (it's also said that no people know more how to party, as I surely found out). I came home determined to try my best to emulate their friendliness in Britain's cold climate.

TRAVEL NOTES

Languages English is the main language, though, laced with Creole expressions, it can be hard to understand. In some areas Spanish and a French patois are spoken.

Transport Buses are cheap, but tend to be overcrowded. Out-of-town services are limited, so, if you can decipher the complicated system, it's often best to get a taxi. Make sure you pay after local people in order to determine the fare, or else agree a price in advance. It's not worth hitching. As well as being risky, you'll probably be picked up by a pirate taxi anyway. The *Caribbean Islands Handbook* includes a good run-down on how the taxi system works.

Accommodation Like everything, hotels are expensive and prices more than double at Carnival times. The Trinidad and Tobago Tourist Board (56 Frederick Street, Port of Spain) is very helpful, providing information on a range of places to stay, including guest-houses which are more reasonably priced.

Guide The *Caribbean Islands Handbook* (Trade and Travel Publications) has a good section on Trinidad and Tobago.

Contacts

Caribbean Association for Feminist Research and Action (CAFRA), PO Box 442, Tuniapuna PO, Tuniapuna, Trinidad and Tobago (see introduction).

Books

Pat Ellis, ed., *Women of the Caribbean* (Zed Books, 1987). Collection of essays providing a good general background to the history and lives of Caribbean women.

Merle Hodge, *Crick Crack Monkey* (Heinemann, 1981). Revealing novel about growing up and coping with the caste system in Trinidad.

It's well worth looking out for books by **Michael Anthony**, one of Trinidad's best known novelists, published in the UK by Heinemann. His most recent work, ***All That Glitters*** (Heinemann, 1983), is the story of an adolescent boy infatuated with two different older women.

Tunisia

Tunisia has developed a highly successful package holiday industry over the last fifteen years, centred on its Mediterranean beaches and aided by a comparatively liberal Muslim culture. Most of these visitors, however, stay in or around their resorts – mainly at Cap Bon and the "desert island" of Djerba, and the country sees relatively few independent travellers.

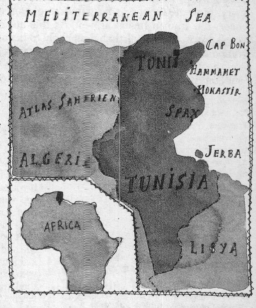

The attention you receive varies greatly between areas with or without tourism. Sexual harassment can be persistent in the more developed resorts and in the Westernised capital, Tunis, though scarcely different to the sort of pestering you find throughout Mediterranean Europe. In the desert south, where you are defined and limited according to Islamic custom, attitudes are harsher. Most women travelling to the sub-Sahara choose to join up with a mixed group. And in these areas, as an independent traveller, you're more likely to be offered hospitality (and you'll find it much easier to accept) if you're travelling with a man.

The official **status of women** in Tunisia has changed radically over the last 35 years. This is due mainly to the liberalising influence of Habib Bourguiba, who led the country to independence from the French in 1956 and remained president until 1987 – when, virtually senile, he was ousted in a palace coup by General Ben Ali, the current president. Bourguiba justified improving women's rights from within original Islamic texts, thus securing the support of Tunisia's religious leaders. Polygamy was outlawed (as Mohammed's stipulation that each wife was to be treated equally was held to be impossible), the marriage age was raised to nineteen, and divorce by *talaq* (verbal repudiation) was outlawed. Legislation was passed on equal pay, and opportunities for work widened considerably following the departure of the French.

Actual social change has, however, been slow to follow these comparatively radical laws – a frequent assertion nowadays being that women have "too much power". It's doubtful, too, whether many of the rural poor are aware of their statutory rights. There remain disparities between the sexes in education and many more women than men are illiterate. In recent years the economic recession, coupled with the rise of Muslim Fundamentalism in the Arab world, have led to an incipient form of reaction. Though many more women work, their wages are often paid directly to husbands or used for dowry. Since 1979 increasing numbers of women have taken to wearing the *chador*, the Iranian headscarf-veil. As this apparent backlash continues, the overall process of social change is likely to become increasingly complicated. Women are finding themselves caught between, on the one hand, the break-up of the extended family – already causing problems of isolation in the cities – and, on the other, new pressures to conform to a traditional way of life.

A Surface Liberalism

Linda Cooley has been working as a teacher in Tunisia for the last six years; she has travelled extensively around the country.

Tunisian women enjoy a measure of freedom and equality under the law unknown in many other Arab countries. Polygamy was abolished in the mid-1950s when Tunisia became independent. Divorce laws have been altered in women's favour. Most girls attend school. A reasonably large percentage of women are in higher education. Many women work outside the home and there are women in the professions and two women ministers in the government.

But the presence of so many women in public can be misleading. It may lull you into a false sense of security when you first arrive and lead to false expectations of what you can and cannot do. If you walk around the capital, you will see women in jeans and the latest fashions, sometimes sitting in cafés, even girls walking along holding hands with their boyfriends. But what you cannot see and should know is that these same fashionably dressed girls have fathers who expect them to be home by 8pm at the latest, who expect them to be virgins when they marry, and who often expect them to marry a relative chosen by the parent.

The clothes may have changed in recent years; the amount of women at work may have changed; but, deep down, social attitudes have not altered. Tunisia remains a traditional Arab society where the idea of a woman travelling abroad alone is still considered as rather strange. It is changing, but very slowly.

It is important, also, to realise how much the Europeanised image, even in Tunis, is superficial. A bar in Tunisia is not like one in France: it's an exclusively male domain and wandering in for a rest and a beer, you are bound to be stared at. Similarly, you can't expect to be able to chat to the man at the next table in the café about the best place to have lunch or the best time to visit the mosque, without your conversation being taken as a sexual invitation. Western movies have done an excellent job in persuading Tunisian men that all Western women are only too keen to have casual sex with any willing male.

"I learnt to cope by evading direct eye contact with men, and above all never smiling at a stranger"

All this must sound somewhat offputting. Yet, in six years of living in Tunisia, I have often travelled alone; I have travelled with my son; I have travelled with another woman. Perhaps I've been lucky, but, apart from the unwanted attentions of a few men nothing has happened to me. There is no part of the country that it is unsafe to visit. (Though, unless you are enamoured of international hotel architecture – miles and miles and miles of it – you may as well avoid Hammamet and Nabeul, the most developed tourist regions.) You can see the ruins of Carthage, the underground dwellings in tranquil Matmata, the fruitful oases of the south, and beautiful Arab architecture all around. You can generally stay in cheap hotels without trouble. The *Mahalas* in particular are very good value and the ones in Djerba and Kairouan are extremely lovely buildings. You can see everything. But, travelling alone, it's incredibly hard to get to know the people.

You will also find it hard to relax, never being sure about how your behaviour will be interpreted if you do. I learnt to cope by evading direct eye contact with men, and above all never smiling at a stranger. I once found myself being followed home after inadvertently smiling at a man as we simultaneously reached for the same tin of tomato sauce in the supermarket.

Really persistent harassment, however, is not common. It may irk you to keep your silence; not to answer like with like; not to show your disdain; but in the long run it will make your day pleasanter. After a while the ignoring game becomes a reality; you really don't notice that anyone has spoken to you!

If you cannot learn to ignore the hassle from men, you will probably find yourself impatient to leave after a very short time, taking with you an awful image of the country and vowing never to return. It is, in fact, an easy country for a woman on her own to dislike.

Travelling with a man makes it all much simpler. The stereotyped images on both sides – yours of macho Arab men and theirs of loose foreign women – can be dispensed with and everyone can act naturally. Men will talk to you both as you're sitting in a café or waiting for a bus. And they're not all hustlers, they often just want someone different to talk to. You may well get invited home to meet their families, where you will be able to talk freely to the women as, unlike in many Arab countries, Tunisian women and men eat together.

You can also go to the *hammam* (public baths) with the women of the house. This is well worth a visit as it is the one place where women meet traditionally as a group, away from all the pressures of what is still a male-dominated society. Unless you speak Arabic it is difficult to talk to the older women there, who rarely speak French, but they are more than willing to show you how to remove the hairs from your body (and I mean your whole body!), to henna your hair, to use *tfal* (a shampoo made from mud), and to give you a thorough scrub with a sort of loofah mitten (and can they scrub thoroughly!). You could, of course, take yourself to the *hammam* travelling alone, but it's much better to go with a Tunisian woman and, as I've said before, introductions are almost exclusively made through men.

Another possibility is that, if you ask around the women, you may well find that you can get yourself invited to a wedding. You don't have to know the bride or groom – hundreds of people attend Arab weddings who hardly know the couple. Total strangers can be very hospitable when it comes to sharing their local customs and food with you. I once had the most beautiful couscous brought out to the field where I was eating my picnic of cheese sandwiches. But then, I was with my son and a man.

Alone or with another woman it is possible to enjoy yourself, but you will miss a great deal of what is, essentially, Tunisian life. Hopefully, through more contact between foreign women and Tunisians, a greater understanding will ensue on both sides, and the lone woman traveller will become more easily accepted.

TRAVEL NOTES

Languages Arabic. French is widely spoken.

Transport Buses cover most of the country, and there's a limited train network. *Louages* (collective taxis) are the fastest form of long-distance transport and operate non-stop. Hitching is a common form of transport, though few women would consider hitching alone.

Accommodation *Hotels Tunisians* are cheap alternatives to the officially graded establishments but some can be on the rough side, occasionally with dormitory accommodation only – unavailable to women. *Pensions familiales* are beginning to appear on the coast, and you are unlikely to leave the country without at least once being offered hospitality for a night.

Special Problems The relative scarcity of foreigners and the more strict Islamic culture of the south can make this an uneasy region to travel around alone.

Guide *The Rough Guide: Tunisia* (Harrap Columbus) is practical, informed and culturally sensitive. It includes an interesting section on women in Tunisia and post-independence reforms.

Contacts

National Union of Women, 56 Boulevard de Bab Benat, Tunis.

All of Tunis Women (Resources and Information on Women), 7 rue Sinam Pacha, Tunis.

Alliance of Tunisian Women for Research and Information on Women, University of Tunis, Tunis.

Books

Norma Salem, *Habib Bourguiba, Islam and the Creation of Tunisia* (Croom Helm, 1985). An uncritical but useful biography of the man at the heart of the modern nation.

Wilfrid Knapp, *Tunisia* (Thames & Hudson, 1971). The best of several history-cum-background books.

Albert Memmi, *The Pillar of Salt* (1956; out of print). Tunisia's most distinguished novelist, and virtually the only one to be translated into English. As a North African Jew, Memmi's work is preoccupied with the problem of identity.

Turkey

· · · · · · · · · · · · · · · · · · ·

Since the military coup of 1980 brought its so-called political "stabilisation", Turkey has been in the grips of a tourist boom. Tour companies, turning their attentions from overexploited Greece, have already transformed vast stretches of the Aegean/Mediterranean coast into a concrete mass of hotels and holiday apartment blocks catering for thousands of Europeans every year. Yet the carefree, Westernised image of the tourist enclaves is misleading. You don't have to venture far to discover a deeply traditional and predominantly rural way of life or witness the strong military presence and atmosphere of political suppression that continues to hang over the country despite its much vaunted transition to democracy

Although Turkey is officially a secular state, women are expected to conform to Islamic customs and values. Westerners who flaunt these by asserting their freedom to travel independently and mix freely with men are stereotypically viewed as "immodest" – a myth encouraged by the portrayal of bikini-clad tourists in the popular press. Travelling alone you may have to contend with fairly persistent sexual harassment. As usual, this is at its most oppressive around the main tourist areas – the coastal resorts, circuit of major sights, and the commercial districts of Istanbul – where men collect in search

of the "easy" tourist. Yet to close yourself off or react suspiciously to all approaches would be to miss a great deal. The Turkish people have a reputation for great hospitality and friendliness and many will go to great lengths to make you feel welcome.

Whilst you can't completely escape unwanted attention, it can help to follow the lead of more Westernised Turkish women, and adopt a fairly conservative style of dress and behaviour. Similarly, if you suffer from any overt harassment you should make your predicament clear to passers-by or fellow passengers. You'll find that Turkish women will be only too happy to take you under their wing.

Under Turkey's secular laws women have been greatly encouraged to take an active role in public life; veiling is officially frowned upon, and in some areas actually prohibited; opportunities in education and work have been expanded and a growing minority of women are entering the professions. But in doing so women are aware of walking a tightrope between meeting the demands of a recently imposed Western capitalist system and upholding the cherished traditions of a suppressed Islamic culture. The contradictions this involves were highlighted in 1988 when veiled students marched with feminists to demand their right to wear headscarves in the classroom.

Despite the repression of all kinds of political organisation in Turkey, an autonomous **women's movement** is gradually becoming established. *Kadin Cevresi* (Women's Circle), a group responsible for setting up the country's first feminist publishing house, has spearheaded many campaigns against sexual discrimination and recently led a demonstration protesting the introduction of compulsory virginity tests for civil servants in the Ministry of Defence. Their activities are currently focused on providing a network of support for battered wives. Women are also taking a leading role in trade union disputes (a woman led the successful *Nigros* grocery store strike) and have been the main force behind *TAYAD* (association of families of prisoners and detainees), a pressure group that highlights the brutal conditions faced by the regime's political prisoners.

The Turkish Left, traditionally hostile to feminism because of its espousal by a "Westernised" bourgeoisie, is now taking a greater interest in mobilising women and the underground Turkish Communist Party recently opened a well-equipped women's centre in Istanbul. The first national women's conference was held in Turkey in 1989 and, despite divisions emerging about priorities for women and the need to organise separately, a manifesto of demands was agreed.

In at the Deep End

. . . .

Rosie Ayliffe spent three years working in Istanbul, as a university teacher, freelance writer and tour leader. She has since returned to Turkey to research and write a *Rough Guide* to the country.

I went to Turkey because I couldn't think how I had finished my formal education without knowing quite where Istanbul was. I was in the university careers library, wondering if I could get one out on loan, when I happened on an advertisement for jobs teaching English in Istanbul. I thought the best way of discovering where the place was and who lived there would be to answer the advertisement.

That same day I was given a job and found myself surveying the prospect of going to Turkey. I "knew" more about Istanbul than I had realised. I knew that it was a Muslim city, and that it was therefore inhabited by people with a sympathy for the Iranian revolution. I knew that the Turks or "infidel" had failed to conquer Vienna in 1683 and that this had been a great relief to the civilised West. I knew from my wide-ranging knowledge of Turkish cinema that Turkish men beat their wives, and from British cinema that you would be arrested and made to walk around a pole indefinitely if you irritated Turkish customs officials.

I arranged accommodation before I went out. A friend who had been living in Istanbul offered to put in a good word with Zahide and Mustafa, who owned the house he was living in. I thought he was joking when he warned me to keep a bottle down the toilet against rats.

September was blistering hot but I sweated cold terror on the flight over. Was I carrying anything that could

possibly cause offence to the customs officials? Would the university give me a job if they knew of my political sympathies? At the time I didn't know that I would have to work for over three months before I saw my first pay packet, not because there was really any serious vetting procedure in operation, but simply because of the sheer inefficiency of a bureaucracy that makes our DSS look like the Starship Enterprise.

"I (always kept) a whisky bottle in the hole in the floor covering an open drain which served as my toilet, but it didn't stop the rats coming in through a hole in the roof"

I arrived on the sixth anniversary of the 1980 military coup. I wasn't surprised to be greeted by machine-gun-toting soldiers, I was only surprised to be allowed to walk freely through passport control. Again, it would be a matter of time before I realised that Western visitors to Turkey are nowadays treated with care and respect by the officials, in a cosmetic attempt to improve a deservedly unprepossessing image.

My new home was situated on the Asian side of the city in the hills overlooking the Bosphorous. One rusty tap sometimes gave me cold clean water. More often it jetted forth a stream of shit-coloured fluid, thick with oxidised iron, or didn't work at all. I did always keep a whisky bottle in the hole in the floor covering an open drain which served as my toilet, but it didn't stop the rats from coming in through a hole in the roof.

The house was what is known as a *gecekondu*, a home "built in the night". An ancient law states that when a roof is put on a house it becomes a legal dwelling place. Contractors have devised methods of building apartments so that the roof is virtually on before the walls are up, and shacks spring up all over the city, literally overnight, before the authorities have time to interfere.

I learnt some Turkish through necessity. None of my neighbours or my landlady spoke any English and nor did the local shopkeepers or restaurateurs. Rather too proud to use sign language, I was hungry by the time I mastered "Could I have a ...?" and "Have you got any ...?".

Mustafa and Zahide were ancient siblings celebrating their approaching dotage in occasional outbursts of screaming, resembling either song or rage as best suited the prevailing circumstance. She was as mean as he was foolish, but they were kind enough to me, and screamed with laughter and "Masallahs!" every time I learnt a new Turkish word.

A rather more interesting companion was the doctor, their older brother, who lived in another wooden house in the same complex. While I watched him go crazy, he had moments of lucidity which seemed to suggest that insanity was a kind of refuge from the glaring injustices of the society in which he had found himself.

He sometimes spoke to me in guarded terms about torture in Turkish prisons and I learnt from him what had happened to the radicals and intellectuals in Turkish universities. Periodically he would rush out while I was doing my washing and implore me not to use detergent in the water since it would do untold destruction to the food chain. I ignored him until three years later, when the press exposed the scandal of phosphates in Turkish detergents.

About eight months after arriving I was told that new neighbours were moving into the compound and was delighted when a young and friendly couple turned up to clean the tiny wooden shack which I had previously taken for an outhouse. The woman, Cybele, was eighteen, and a friend of the doctor's. They had met at English classes in the military academy down in Cengelkoy.

We became friends, helping each other with housework, brewing up pots of tea together and sometimes, when two of her old-crone aunts came to visit from a neighbouring village, we would put on a tape of jangly arabesque music and us two youngsters would be forced to dance while the old women banged on drums, shook tambourines and cackled.

"Many of the women I met had been forced through the pain and humiliation of one or more abortions"

I went to visit her family home one day, in order to take photographs of a new baby for its father who was doing his military service. Three families and countless children appeared to live in a two-bedroom shack and off less than an acre of land. Although it was Ramadan and they were all fasting except Cybele, I was proudly served with a large meal. According to Islamic tradition a guest is given the best food in the house, and I have no doubt that as elsewhere in Turkey this rule was rigidly adhered to in that household, but the food was still virtually inedible.

On the way home I asked Cybele why she wasn't fasting. She was evasive, and it was only when she began to discuss babies that I realised that she was pregnant. Not long after this she came to my house clutching at her stomach. Her aunts arrived and took over, and throughout the evening issued a running commentary on her miscarriage. Cybele and her husband left and I never saw them again. Many of the women I met subsequently stated that they had been forced through the pain and humiliation of one or more abortions before marriage and that this was an accepted form of birth control.

Despite the fact that I was living off the beaten "Stamboul" tourist track, I provoked no more than a passing interest in the village. Perhaps Zahide and Mustafa kept the inhabitants so well informed of my day-to-day activities that there was little left for them to learn from source, but I also suspect that I had developed a well-deserved reputation for haughtiness.

For the first few weeks I seriously expected that unless I behaved with the utmost decorum my house would be surrounded by lusty youths until the early hours of the morning; and I stared rigidly ahead of me at all times rather than risk giving someone an excuse to talk to me. In time I began to realise that my attitudes to Turkish men were shaped by the same degree of unfounded prejudice that served to inform their attitudes toward Western women.

The first incident to bring this home to me happened within a few days of my arrival. Completely lost and miles from home in the street around the covered Bazaar in Cagaoglu, I went into a workshop to ask directions. A boy came out with me, and I imagined he would start to point and gesticulate. Instead he accompanied me down to the ferry port, boarded the ferry with me, then found me the right bus and took me to the bottom of my hill in Cengelkoy. Before I had found any of the words to tell him that I really didn't think it would be terribly wise of me to invite him up to my house, he had grinned, said goodbye, and set off on the two-hour journey back to his work-place. That was the last I saw of him but the first of countless occasions when I was party to acts of altruistic kindness from Turkish men.

While I never felt relaxed enough to make friends with men in the village, this was as much a result of their own personal taboos as of any misconception on my part, and I was quite happy to be assimilated to such an extent that I became *harem*, "forbidden territory".

When I travelled around Turkey I think I was afforded some protection by my appearance. As I learnt more Turkish my manner must have become more confident, and this combined with a dark complexion meant that I was

continually mistaken for a Turk, or at least, cast enough doubt over my nationality to evoke the possibility of a spectral elder brother in the minds of would-be aggressors. My short hair, masculine dress and "boyish" figure further added to the confusion and I was often treated to the familiar epithet of "Agabey" or "big brother".

"Most foreign women I met were rather less fortunate in their experiences with Turkish men"

Only on one occasion did I feel at all threatened by a man, and that was in Trabzon bus station at three in the morning, when I was put into the care of someone who was evidently less than psychologically stable. After escaping from his clutches I took refuge in the company of a group of bus drivers, who realised what was wrong and demanded to know what he had done. They must have taken the matter into their own hands, and a few weeks later some friends travelling through the city returned with the news that my would-be molester had lost his job as a result of the incident.

Most foreign women I met were rather less fortunate in their experiences with Turkish men, and the only advice I could give was to seek the company of women at every opportunity, simply by showing and responding to friendliness. I found I was more comfortable in the company of Turkish women – to whom sisterhood seems a natural concept – and I was especially grateful for the matronly protection I received from older women wherever I travelled in Turkey. While they questioned me about my marital status and wondered at such freedom of movement afforded by independence from any family, I rarely felt that this curiosity had a perjorative edge and by the end of my stay I had been adopted into several Turkish families.

During the first year of my stay I taught English to students of Islamic theology at the university. I had been disappointed in my belief that Turkey would be peopled with religious zealots screaming for their own Islamic revolution, since most people seemed only too happy with the secular state and access to Western commodities and culture. I was warned by teachers in other faculties, however, to expect the worst of my new students.

These people, I was told, wished to annex Turkey to Iran. They were enemies of the Republic and the only English they would ever need would be the vocabulary required to hijack an aeroplane. Islamic fundamentalism is regarded with distrust and distaste among the middle classes in the big cities in Turkey. Most of my students were from villages in the east, from backgrounds of extreme poverty. For many of them, the only form of education they had known to date was religious instruction: rote learning of the Koran, the life and teachings of the Prophet and some Arabic.

I arrived on the first day to find that the students had voluntarily segregated themselves by sex, the women seated in two silent rows on the furthest side of the classroom. Contrary to the rules of *Yok*, the controversial Higher Education Council established after the coup in 1980 in order to depoliticise the universities, their heads were covered in long silk scarves, and most of them wore thick woollen stockings and calf-length coats buttoned at the neck and wrists.

I rapidly discovered that the Western textbook I was using was not suited to the task in hand. There was no way these people were going to mill around a classroom shaking hands with each other. When one of the male students presented me with a picture of Chris Evert Lloyd on which he had biroed a *carsaf* (the black garment worn by fundamentalist women throughout the Islamic world), I conceded that it was time to forego the trendy TEFL teaching text and work on material which

might prove more relevant in the prevailing atmosphere.

Pointing to a picture of Ataturk, founder of the Turkish Republic and official national hero, whose picture must be displayed in all public places, I asked the students what kind of man he had been. My question was greeted by silence and I concluded that this was a taboo subject.

I learnt later that even among devout Muslims there is divided opinion concerning Ataturk and his efforts to Westernise Turkey. Some say that he destroyed Islamic intellectualism and rendered their cultural heritage inaccessible by changing the Turkish alphabet. Others felt that there was no contradiction between Islam and economic and cultural progress. The students were naturally wary of expressing their feelings on such controversial issues since some classrooms retained bullet holes as a result of fights that had broken out before the military coup in 1980.

"I found nothing to argue with in their determination not to be regarded as sex objects"

The majority of the women were serious academics, and some intended to continue their education in other faculties when they had finished their religious studies. They were proud of the emphasis that Islam places on education for men and women, and they didn't feel that Western feminism had much to offer them.

I found nothing to argue with in their determination not to be regarded as sex objects (the reason they gave for covering their bodies in public), nor with a justifiable pride in their academic or artistic achievements. A couple of years after I left the faculty, it was Ilahiyat women who staged the biggest political demonstration since the coup at Istanbul university, when they protested against a ban on covered women in the classroom.

The only aspect of their lives that I couldn't agree with was that the women refused to attend services in the mosque. This was a reaction against feminism in Turkey. By staying away they reaffirmed that the mosque, the traditional forum for political as well as religious debate, was male territory.

I stayed another two years in Turkey after I left my *gecekondu* slum-dwelling and my similarly humble teaching post. I found jobs that required rather less explanation among the leftist and cultural elite, and apartments which required rather less housework.

Most visitors to Turkey opt as I did for a lifestyle which is somewhat more comfortable than that experienced by the majority of Turks. With the possible exception of decent plumbing, all modern conveniences and European commodities are now available in the major resorts and the cities in the west of Turkey. The Turkish people who service and maintain the tourist industry have a better grasp of Western values and behaviour than most of their visitors have of Turkish attitudes.

The people who make money out of tourism may have more time for driving jeeps and drinking Coke than for reading the Koran. The veneer of Western liberalism in Turkey's cities and the process of rapid cosmetic change to which this new generation of Turks is a party, cannot however disguise from them that poverty, year-round physical discomfort, sexual tension and Islamic fundamentalism are the basics of Turkish life for the majority of its population. Most Turks welcome tourism as their most valuable growth industry, but many young people also see tourists as their most valuable allies, as they attempt to improve their country's record on human rights and bring about lasting social change.

Keeping a Political Perspective

. . . .

Jane Schwartz, a feminist journalist, first went to Turkey on a package tour. She has since returned to travel independently round the country, including the east (Kurdistan), south and the Black Sea coast.

I fell in love with Turkey the first night I arrived. It was June 1987 and I'd come on a package, because I was scared of being hassled on my own. I found my carefully chosen destination was a basement room on a concrete construction site in Turkish Benidorm.

After an hour's hysterics I walked out behind the bus station into the town and found a whole street of little shops, all selling delicious food – spices, nuts, dried apricots, roasted corn, watermelons, gold-rimmed glasses of tea. Everything was brightly lit at ten o'clock at night; everyone wanted to talk; Turkish families, from grandmothers to small boys, were touring the streets along with visitors from other countries. Everything was totally safe.

I think I guessed then what I'm almost sure of now: that tourism can only be a kind of ribbon development on a country as huge and old as this. There's a row of Benettons along the seafront in Alanya, but there are goats tethered round the back – one for each household's yoghurt supply – and once a week in front of the blank-faced hotels there'll pass a procession of country people going to market, each one more amazingly and differently costumed than the last.

There are tower blocks in Antalya, but there's also a beautiful Old Town where antique ruins crumble alongside nineteenth-century plaster villas. There are wall to wall discos in Bodrum, but there are also pensions where you can eat your own meals in the centre of a silent orange grove. And next to Kusadasi – that Turkish Benidorm – there's Snake Island, and nothing but a little beach hut where a friendly Kurdish owner will grill you fish caught minutes before.

In Turkey there can be soldiers with machine guns in front of the local bank; there's a growing and nastily complacent class who've got rich quick under President Turgut Ozal – Margaret Thatcher's biggest fan. But there is an enormous culture of resistance, which you will meet in cafés and souvenir shops as much as in radical publishers or on the picket lines, which even springs up at the gates of the Topkapi Palace itself.

At the time of writing, this is a country with 30,000 people on strike. Officially inflation runs at 65 percent and unofficially at over 100 percent. In the big cities the squatted *gecekondu* districts have graduated from shanties to whole boroughs with their own water and power, housing more than a quarter of the town's population. When the new entrepreneurs try to bulldoze this prime building space, women are the ones who link arms in front of the bulldozers.

These were all shocks to my expectations. As, too, were the country's beauty; the Muslim tradition of hospitality to outsiders that extends to women as well as men; and an incredible historical generosity that can leave half the Wonders of the World safely unlocked on their hillsides. Each aspect makes Turkey an extraordinary place for me to visit.

That first year I left my package and went off down the coast: after Kusadasi the market town of Soke, then Ephesus with its wonderful museum tracing the temple of Diana through Cybele to the prehistoric mother goddess. (Her costume, as she squats between her leopards to give birth, is just like the traditional trousers that women wear today.) I went on down the Aegean coast to Bodrum, to a little Turkish resort called Ortakent, and then to the start of the Mediterranean at Fethiye. I didn't want to go home.

"Men cooked me food, carried my heaviest bags, gave me presents, showed me the sights"

The next year I came out for three months, to Istanbul, the south coast, then the east (Kurdistan), Ankara and finally the Black Sea. Although I went to many places and met many different kinds of people, the country is over 400,000 miles square, so I feel very humble trying to describe it. I can only say what I saw.

I had heard about Turkey and its beauty from my sister and her friends, who travelled there in the early Seventies. But they had told me, as well, things that were pretty frightening. They described it as the most hellish stop on the road to India – a place where men pinched you black and blue as you walked the city streets in daylight, and where you had to barricade your hotel door against staff at night.

A lot must have happened to Turkish men since the Sixties (and to me – I'm 42 now). Men cooked me food, carried my heaviest bags, gave me presents, showed me the sights. Very seldom did they even ask – and certainly never seemed to expect – anything in return. Quite a contrast with life in other countries. Undoubtedly, I had rarity value because so many Turkish women are still confined to the home, so my good times were linked to their bad times. Life for emancipated Turkish women is extremely difficult. I was told several times that the expensive Taksim district is the only safe place for a single woman, or even several women, to set up house without a man. Single women buy wedding rings to give themselves a sort of protection in their home neighbourhood.

The feminists I met in Istanbul were all exceptional people. Their march against male violence in 1985 was also the very first event anywhere in the country to break the ban on legal demonstrations imposed by the 1980 military coup. Now the feminists aim to set up Turkey's first refuge, combined with a co-op to give training and a livelihood. They recognise that with no social security and few opportunities for working outside the home, leaving a violent man can be as frightening as staying.

"On the coast there's the beginning of a gigolo syndrome as Northern European women sweep through in search of tourist sex"

I loved these feminists' concern to link *all* women – something which seems to inspire the start of every Women's Movement, but gets lost as the activists become professionals On International Women's Day, the feminists held a fair, with soapboxes for any woman to speak from, and stalls to sell things that they had made. The Turkish feminist publishing house opened their first bookfair stall with no books but a big mirror: they invited every woman who came to "write your life here". Four books later, the publishing house's future is threatened by a new government tax of half a million Turkish lira per month.

Sometimes a rich visitor seems able to reverse the sexual roles in a nasty way. On the coast there's the beginnings of a gigolo syndrome as Northern European women sweep through in search of tourist sex. I met men who'd been picked up and left by German women without another word. The English have a more romantic reputation (and perhaps less money), sometimes marrying Turks or setting up a tourist shop.

"Ordinary" Turkish women were lovely towards me, treating me as an extra daughter or aunt to be invited in for a meal. They were fascinated by the fact that I wasn't married, and by my age – which they'd often underestimate by about twenty years. I think it was helpful to my relations with women that I brought a modest one-piece bathing suit (an old gym leotard) for non-tourist beaches. I also learned to tie a cotton scarf with the ends hanging down in front, to hide the fact that I wasn't wearing a bra. These printed scarves, which cost very little, also make useful headbands. The countrywomen use them for a serious head cover, but it's a measure of Turkey's civilisation that everyone I met was charmed to see them worn by a foreigner, not offended.

The born-again Muslims, whose rise so scares the majority of Turks, would regard the ordinary costume of the country as equally immodest. In the fundamentalist parts of Istanbul and the northeast, women are covered in black from head to ankle – then come nylon tights and stiletto heels, like some S&M fantasy. I noticed that the men got away with Western summer clothes.

I was lucky as a single woman traveller, but you can get pestered in Istanbul and the coastal resorts, especially if you ever take a taxi. I personally never had more than words to worry about, no physical harassment. The east, particularly the fiercely religious northeast, is a weird place for a woman to visit – I was told unsafe by some, quite safe by others. Part of the Turkish racism against Kurds is to give them a sex-mad reputation; but Dervla Murphy has also written that eastern Turkey was the only Muslim country where she got harassed. (She specially resented women trying to get into her bed!)

If you want to look at mosques you'll need trousers or a below-knee skirt, a shirt or jacket with sleeves, a headscarf, and shoes that come off and on easily. I found that sort of costume was convenient and cool most of the time I was travelling, anyway. On the coast, all the visitors wear shorts as so do some Turkish women. For swimming Turkish women wear anything from bikinis to full length whiteshifts, according to the location. The famous tourist beach at Olu Deniz and a few others have topless bathing. Nude bathing – male or female – would cause considerable trouble.

But maybe some of you reading this have bigger problems in mind. For you the unanswered question will be – should we go to Turkey on holiday at all? Kenan Evren, held to be a mass murderer on a level with the Colonels of Greece or Argentina or Chile, is still chief of the military. And during the 1988 "democratic elections", exiled politicians, human rights campaigners and trades union organisers went back home and were arrested as soon as they walked off their planes, in full view of foreign journalists and photographers. From the outside, what does this regime seem to care about world opinion, as long as the pounds, dollars and deutschmarks keep rolling into the seaside resorts?

Well, should we go? The best authority I can think of is the Committee for Defence of Democratic Rights in Turkey, whose English newsletter is crammed with exciting and inspiring as well as horrifying items. This is what they've written:

This year an estimated 400,000 tourists from Britain alone will visit Turkey. Many people, aware of the monstrous violations of human rights in that country, have called for a boycott of holidays.

Our position is based on the views of the victims of the regime – democrats working and struggling in Turkey and those forced into exile. We do not call for a boycott of holidays or visits.

In the darkest days of the junta, from 1980 to 1984, there was some justification for arguing for a boycott of Turkey – just as there is for South Africa today. A boycott was one of the few concrete ways one could protest at a brutal and monolithic fascist state.

However today things are different. There are still torture, political show trials, political prisoners and denial of many rights. But the big difference is the peoples of Turkey are now fighting *increasingly openly* for real democracy. Today the trade unions and human rights bodies need contact with and support from all democratic forces in the world.

A flood of foreign visitors helps to prevent any move to turn Turkey back into a "closed society" where oppression can be conducted on a massive scale unhindered by foreign witnesses and where the population is unaware of new thoughts and outlooks, not to mention world events. The movement of large numbers of people also hinders the regime's attempts to restrict the movement of its own nationals. For Turkey, seeking international respectability and its material benefits, open repression in front of the tourists is not something to make a habit of.

There is one proviso in all this. Foreign visitors to Turkey must be aware of the truth. The tourist enjoying the "sun, sea and smiles" at Bodrum must know that for the millions of Turkish people huddled in shanty towns trying not to starve, holiday is a foreign word.

When tourists go on guided tours or meet people in Turkey they should ask about the human rights situation, and unions. They should express their views on these things so as to leave no doubt in their hosts' minds as to their condemnation of the regime and its crimes . . .

Perhaps this sounds difficult, or joyless, or embarassing. But in Turkey you don't go looking for politics, it comes to you. My own holiday experiences led naturally into "politics". When I visited the Topkapi Palace, I ended up drinking tea with striking printers under the giant plane trees of the courtyard-cum-coachpark. In the south, the owners of a tourist shop took me to visit friends in jail, and I was lucky enough to be able to buy the beautiful bead toys that the prisoners make to support their families. These meetings were as friendly and lively, and as much a part of my trip as bargaining in the bazaar, or taking tea with Turkish families, or chatting with children eager to practise their English.

Not many people are going to tell you their life history in the first five minutes, but at the level of ideas, political conversation in Turkey is amazingly open. My own fears that writing down addresses and contacts might bring trouble on my new friends were waved away.

I'm only a tourist, I didn't share the lives of the people I met. As a visitor I was sheltered, and even fervent supporters of their government (and ours) would listen politely to my opinions. I won't say I had no nasty experiences – from stomach bugs upwards – and living in Turkey might be much less happy than passing through. But the three months I spent there have made me love the place and the people, and believe they're struggling through to a future where the world will look to them for a lot more than sun, sea and sand.

TRAVEL NOTES

Languages Turkish. Some English is spoken but German is more common.

Transport Most people travel by bus; the service is extensive, efficient and cheap. Trains tend to be slower and cover less ground. Shared minibuses (*dolmuses*) are also available – they cost little more than buses and go to even very remote villages. Hitching is not recommended.

Accommodation All main resorts and cities have plenty of cheap accommodation. Some women carry their own padlocks to secure hotel doors. In the east, you'll be able to find places to stay but the choice is far more limited.

Special Problems Sexual harassment – especially in the east, which can be dangerous for women travelling alone. Anywhere in Turkey it helps to dress reasonably modestly, ie cover your shoulders and don't wear shorts. A recent worrying trend has been the rise in tourist muggings – it's wise to avoid any display of wealth. Also avoid drugs; severe penalties are enforced even for possession of a small amount of cannabis.

Guides *Guide to Aegean Turkey* and *Guide to Eastern Turkey* (Michael Haag) are good on historical background and have a fair amount of practical information and listings. Rosie Ayliffe is currently putting together a *Rough Guide: Turkey* (Harrap Columbus, 1991).

Contacts

Kadin Cevresi Yayincilik (Women's Circle), c/o Handan Koc, Klodfarer Caddesi 41/36, Servet Han Cagaloglu, Istanbul. A group of radical feminists and the main point of contact with other autonomous groups. They have a publishing house and produce a magazine called *Feminist*. The group welcomes the donation of international feminist literature.

Demkad (Union of Democratic Women), Tiryaki Hasanpasa Caddesi 60, Toprak Han Kat 4, Aksaray, Istanbul. Part of the Turkish left and hostile to radical feminism. They work with women in the shanty towns and with the prisoners' support group **Tayad**.

Bilsal (cultural centre), Siraselviler Cad, Sogaci Sok 7, Taksim, Istanbul. Regularly hosts feminist events.

Committee for Defence of Democratic Rights in Turkey (CDDRT), 84 Balls Pond Road, London N1. Publishes the *Turkey Newsletter* which includes news of women's campaigns and demonstrations.

Books

Pembenaz Yorgun, "The Women's Question and Difficulties of Feminism in Turkey", in *Modern Turkey – Development and Crisis* (Ithaca Press, US, 1984).

S Tekeli, *Emergence of the New Feminist Movement in Turkey*, in **D Dahlerup** ed., *The New Women's Movement* (Beverley Hills: Sage, 1986).

Freya Stark, *Alexander's Path* (1956; Century, 1984). Classic travels in Asia Minor.

Rose Macaulay, *The Towers of Trebizond* (1956; Futura, 1981). Beautiful, quirky novel of camel-travelling and High Anglican angst.

Thanks to Rosie Ayliffe and Jane Schwartz for help with introduction and Travel Notes.

USA

. . . .

Anyone travelling to the USA from Europe will feel a sense of familiarity about the place: all the exposure to American film, TV and culture does form a preparation. However, it's equally likely that, on a first-time visit, this will be accompanied by considerable culture shock. It takes a while to get to grips with a country that is, genuinely, a continent. A continent where extremes of wealth and poverty can be just a couple of blocks apart – and where whole neighbourhoods, even whole towns, are formed by particular and highly diverse ethnic populations.

The hardest place to arrive, by general consent, is New York City, whose pace and hustle (all part of its appeal) can leave you feeling too vulnerable and too small. The West Coast – Washington State, Oregon and California – is perhaps the gentlest place to adapt, with its more relaxed and laid back ethos an enduring (but true) cliché. But this is only to scratch at the edges. The vastness of Middle America, the distinctiveness of the South, the quieter East Coast cities: all make for a staggering variety of travel or living experience.

As far as issues go, it's important – especially if you're travelling coast-to-coast – to get a grip on the strength of regional chauvinism. Each state has its own legislation as well as political affiliations and, between them, attitudes towards women (and God) vary greatly. On sexual issues, the Moral Majority and associated groups like the Pro-Lifers are continuing to strengthen and

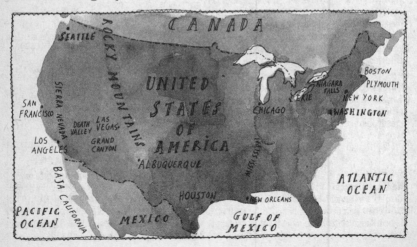

extend their base, proving effective as an anti-abortion lobby and in the simmering climate of hysteria over the spread of AIDS, are receiving growing support for their tough line on "sexual deviance". In terms of race, colour discrimination, notorious in the South, remains an enduring fact of life. Black and Hispanic urban ghettos tend to be the poorest, most deprived in the country, and the recent rehabilitation of Native American culture has done little to halt the erosion of Indian territories and lifestyles. Considering the size and number of America's ethnic minorities, integration remains a reality for comparatively few.

Travel, however, presents few problems in itself. So many American women travel from state to state that you won't generally be given a second glance, and only in situations where you really stand out as a tourist is there likely to be persistent trouble from hustlers. In this case the main thing is to look confident, be firm and at least seem to know where you're going. Big cities can sometimes feel unsafe – all have definite no-go areas – and travelling anywhere in urban America it is always wise to avoid carrying more cash than you need for the day.

It clearly depends on the going exchange rate, but the USA does tend to be expensive for foreign visitors. There are many cheap motels, but these can be pretty sparse, not to mention seedy, catering as they do for migrant people at the bottom of the social heap. On the plus side, the American reputation for hospitality is well deserved and even the briefest encounter can lead to offers of floorspace or a bed for the night. Hitching is considered fairly risky, though quite a few women still do it, especially in Oregon and California, and you may have little other option in some rural areas. Otherwise a choice of *Greyhound, Trailway* bus or the alternative *Green Tortoise* will usually get you to whichever town you want. Flights, too, should be considered – there are always a range of special deals available and, by European standards, they can work out surprisingly cheap

There is a feeling, shared by many women in the US, that the **women's movement** slumbered its way through the dead weight of the Reagan years. While an embattled group of activists tried to tell women that their rights – reproductive freedom, equal pay, the Equal Rights Amendment – were under threat, many American women, feminists and non-feminists alike, experienced the Eighties as an era of private reassessment and reappraisal. It was a defiantly "me-oriented" decade in which activism in any form was unfashionable, and in which personal and independent struggles for success and fulfilment were a priority.

The onset of the 1990s, as Reagan left Washington and his chosen successor, Pro-Life advocate George Bush, came into office, seems to be bringing changes. In April 1989, an estimated 600,000 women, men and children converged on Washington to march for women's rights and reproductive freedom. The immediate inspiration for the march was an impending Supreme Court case which threatened to overturn a woman's constitutional right to have an abortion. The march was an expression of the silent majority finally finding its voice; women who had never before participated in any kind of political activism were marching – mothers, daughters, granddaughters, and men, of all ages – raising their fists and shouting "My body. Not yours".

If the Women's Movement seemed to be in retreat during the Eighties, it may well be that such protest and the participation of thousands of women, young and old, heralds a less introspective, more dynamic new decade.

Just Jump In and Get Cracking

. . . .

Deborah Bosley and Melanie Jones have made several trips to the States, travelling around and occasionally working. Deborah's account concentrates on their experiences of New York and, to a lesser extent, New Orleans.

Perhaps the most maligned and the most adored city in the world, New York is forever on the discussion table. The plethora of information on the city, the media exposure, and stories from friends who have visited, will give you at least a sense of it. Nothing, however, can ever prepare you for arrival.

Reactions vary, so expect every and any: to our minds there are two ways of approaching New York and between us we tried them both. Either, like Melanie, you can remain closeted in your arrival bubble, that haze of defences that is not the result of neurosis but simply the fear of a city whose reputation eclipses the possibility of ever meeting it on neutral ground. Or you can, like me – and I was also scared to death – just jump in and get cracking.

Our experiences, as yours will be, were shaped by circumstances; in a perfect world you would be smack in the middle of Manhattan and able to stay in a roach-free zone in one of the racier neighbourhoods. The outer boroughs may at first seem a more economical option, but commuting back and forth to Manhattan will be a drain on both your time and resources.

Fortunately Americans (even New Yorkers) have a well-earned reputation for extending offers of a place to stay to friends and friends of friends, and we were not about to turn down the promise of a bed in Greenwich Village, even if the offer was third-hand by the time it reached us. An address to head for can make the first few hours in New York infinitely more reassuring. Bearing this in mind, we would definitely recommend that, in the absence of a friend or contact, you book a hotel ahead. Don't just turn up and hope for the best; for women especially this can be a recipe for major headaches and a safe place to stay is vital until you've reached a degree of acclimatisation and are feeling less overwhelmed by the place.

> **"Gay club fiends, though common enough in Manhattan, do nonetheless live in a somewhat self-contained world"**

That said, our own advance arrangements did not make the first few hours in New York any easier. We arrived around midnight to our predestined apartment block only to find a note pinned to the door saying: "Back at 8am – Sorry, Frank". Resigned to a long night, we camped in the lobby, cracked open the duty-free Jack Daniels and decided to ride it out. Bemused apartment dwellers nodded us cautious hellos on their way in and out, and one chap, having walked past us six times or so, heard our story and invited us up to his place to finish the JD in comfort.

We crept back down at the appointed hour and finally met Frank, our host. He was a walking contradiction – at once a man of stifling geniality and, equally, acerbic bitchiness. Only the fortuitous circumstances of immediate shelter; employment (working the stalls in the Soho flea markets of which Frank was a proprietor) and free food (he was also a catering manager at New York University), caused us to pause and reconsider our immediate inclination to get the hell out.

Fifty dollars a day for as long as we liked – we couldn't believe our luck. Not that working, living, eating, sleeping and socialising with Frank wasn't about to test us to our limits. But we believed that his condition, as with many New Yorkers, was symptomatic of where he was and of the survival skills he had acquired in order to exist without being completely discordant from New York's perverse scheme of things.

Our two months with Frank exposed us to a New York we might otherwise have missed and almost certainly steered us away from simpler experiences we might have enjoyed. Gay club fiends, though common enough in Manhattan, do nonetheless live in a somewhat self-contained world. For me this was New York at its best: highly strung, living completely beyond my means and energies and feeling (falsely) secure in the company of strangers who cared little or nothing for my welfare beyond novelty value.

I flourished, using every dexterous social skill at my disposal to charm my way into the circle of New York's terminally trendy and inevitably transient night-time life. One of my more useful acquisitions at the time was a fabulous cliché named Buddy, who was manager of New York's then hot-spot, the Palladium. Like the unfolding of some tacky movie, his character was revealed in all its ungloriousness when he opened the cupboard above his bed and produced a 26 foot python. Too much.

Meanwhile, Melanie was finding the city a little harder to swallow. Ever the realist, she arrived defensive and bristling with indignation at the rudeness and hostility of New Yorkers she had tried and sentenced before arrival. It's hard to take a back seat and feel easy about things in New York unless you're heavily sedated, and for Melanie the experience proved too crushing. Her belief in human sincerity was obscured by too many five-minute friendships: intimacy on contact, and then goodbye. It was all too fast, furious and unfriendly, and she took to adopting a foetal position in the centre of the only air-conditioned room in Frank's smelly apartment for much of the two months.

"Violent crimes against women are high, but your bearing and approach will determine much"

Indeed, New York is weird. Unless you've lived there for years, you can't even really trust your friends. On one particular occasion we were carousing in the Lower East Side's Pyramid Club and could only look on in amazement as Frank removed his shoes and socks and with both hands full, gently manoeuvred his agile feet to the back pocket of a nearby pair of 501's and from an innocent night creature softly prised a $100 bill with his nimble toes. Not that his altruistic nature didn't surface occasionally; but even the sight of Frank thrusting $20 bills into the outstretched palms of passing tramps did little to redeem him in our eyes.

So, seeking some less hurried, more meaningful social contact, we decided to try out New York's women's scene. At the end of our street was a lesbian bar called The Cubbyhole, which strictly prohibited men. It had been recommended to us several times and we arrived with high hopes. But on arrival we found that even getting through the door was a test. Squeezing past the massive, glaring woman who was guarding the entrance shook our confidence, and it wasn't much better inside.

Rather than finding here a good-humoured, supportive and relaxed environment in which to sit and get ploughed with impunity, we found instead a tense gathering of seemingly competitive women pitched against each other, sitting steadfastly in the groups or couples with whom they had arrived. There was little cross-group chit-chat and banter such as you would expect in a place of this kind. Maybe we went on an off-night, but our experience of other women's bars in New York wasn't dissimilar and we were later to find them diametrically opposed in attitude to their far more relaxed (and to our minds superior) counterparts in California.

But New York is known for its extremes, and again we believed that, all things being symptomatic and circumstantial, fear for one's safety surely plays a part. It's a fact: you do have to watch out. Violent crimes against women are high, but your bearing and approach to New York will determine much. The usual rules apply: never walk alone after dark in unfamiliar places; look people straight in the eye, etc – but don't make too much of an issue of it. "There's nothing to fear but fear itself" is pretty applicable here. It really is no more menacing than other large cities and you should be aware of the confidence-destroying vibes of paranoia. Having said that, go on your hunches; everything happens

so fast in New York that you'll have to assimilate many of your experiences in so few moments that your instinctive reactions will be important.

It won't take much to knock your confidence. I'd been riding high for months in New York, felt I had it sussed and knew how to handle myself. Working in the markets in Soho and on Broadway had opened up contacts and engendered a feeling of belonging until, on the day before I left, I took a subway from Broadway alone. Nothing heavy at four in the afternoon, but across the platform from me stood, or rather staggered, a rangy, thin black boy, staring at me. Behind him was a huge poster giving information about AIDS. Suddenly he screamed across at me: "Suck my dick and die." Of course he was completely smashed, or cracked out of his head, and couldn't get to me because of the track between us, so there was no immediate danger. But the experience was chilling and one that has stuck.

To me this typifies some of the completely unbridled aggression that runs beneath everything in New York. Naturalness seems in short supply in the city. Maybe it's not the fault of the people. The madness which surrounds them is absolutely to blame for the rise of neuroses, which feed neuroses, and so it goes on. So don't let it get to you; put yourself in the driving seat and treat New York as an adventure. Lose yourself for a while, and be somebody else.

South to New Orleans
. . . .

After the mania and motion of New York, New Orleans shocked with its stillness. It's the heat. Nothing can move fast; even when it does, it feels

unhurried. But it has its own kind of intensity, like a Tennessee Williams play. This is the Deep South and you'd have to have been living in a cave not to be aware of the implications of racism, oppression and suffering of this unique part of the Americas.

We flew to New Orleans and were sent, through a room-finding service, to a Bed and Breakfast about ten minutes from the French Quarter. At twenty dollars a night per person, we reckoned it was about the best we could do. It was palatial. Jacob, the owner, was renovating the entire house, room by room, to create a period, mid-1800s colonial feel. An antique dealer by trade, he was letting out several of the rooms to help finance the refurbishment. Our room was high-ceilinged with big roof-to-floor windows on one side of the room – quite the place for losing yourself in a few good books, with the overhead fan creaking above.

Not realising that arriving outside of Mardi Gras in February would make much of a difference, we were shocked to find a slightly depressed, mid-sized American city. Instead of all the joviality and celebrations, we found a tacky assortment of bars and shops in the French Quarter, which, without their seasonal crowds, looked bereft and even a little pathetic. Our only real joy was finding the outlawed absinthe (the stuff that sent Verlaine mad and has been responsible for many unwanted hallucinations) on tap.

"Women, black or white, do not walk the streets alone at night"

Otherwise, the French Quarter didn't conform at all to our expectations. Bourbon Street is a row of sad-looking tourist traps, and the once famous Basin Street is now a concrete freeway. But, to be fair, much of New Orleans is startlingly beautiful. In the better parts of town the houses are grandiose structures with pillared entrances, long driveways, and probably a whole squadron of black staff catering to the whims of the white householders. The implications of such wealth were such that they sullied our enjoyment of the more pleasing parts.

Getting over our initial disappointment, we remained largely neighbourhood bound – about ten minutes by trolley-car from the centre, we preferred more local activities. Across

the street was our second home, a bar called the C-Lounge where we often whiled away the afternoons, writing postcards, chatting to the few lizards at the bar and playing over and over our favourite juke box song, "If The Drinking Don't Kill Me, Her Memory Will". Simple pleasures – for us.

In our month there we didn't once find other women out socialising independently. It struck us that white women socialised from the grandeur of their big houses, and black women slaved in the privacy of their little ones. You can't get away from it: black people in New Orleans are massively oppressed. In the street where we were staying, it was literally a case of big houses occupied by whites on one side and shanty-like dwellings for the blacks on the other. The atmosphere at night was heavy. Women, black or white, do not walk the streets alone at night – for very different reasons, but the result is the same.

And so we attracted much attention, most of it unwanted and all of it incredulous that girls really did this kind of thing. Travelling without men? Incredible! We often wondered if maybe the last fifty years had passed this town by and we were amazed that two states in the same country could differ so vastly.

We became friendly with a black girl from New York who was staying in the same house and commanded our rapt attention with her tales of who said what to her that day and the amount of stick she was receiving for being a black girl daring to go it alone in this town. One night she arrived home in tears after being jostled around on the street corner by a gang of young black men, teasing her for her independence. It all seemed a bit too nightmarish.

I'd also stress that there were occasions when we felt easy in mixed company, though this was only in the tourist-hardened French Quarter, and beyond that we found attitudes a little too strained.

Biking from Coast to Coast

· · · · · · · · · · · ·

After twenty years of factory work, Ann Stirk drew out her life savings and fulfilled a lifelong ambition to tour the land of the pioneers. Her account of driving a motorbike alone, from coast to coast, is aimed as a "story of encouragement to all women bored with their everyday existence".

In July 1986, my kids had flown the nest and were fending adequately for themselves. I was 38 years old and free; time was rushing by with reckless speed and my greatest ambition, to visit the land of the Pilgrim Fathers, had yet to be fulfilled. Come August, my mind was made up to tackle this adventure alone. Against the advice of all my friends I drew out my savings, handed in my notice at work, paid three months' rent on my flat and bought a ticket for New York.

I arrived at John F. Kennedy Airport carrying a holdall complete with tent, sleeping bag and an assortment of clothing, and with my crash helmet hanging over my free arm. Altogether I spent three days in the "Big Apple", sightseeing and purchasing a Honda Rebel 450. The motorcycle was more powerful than any I'd previously owned. It had five gears, overdrive and to comply with US law the lights came on with the ignition. Somehow I managed to avoid the entreaties of salesmen on commission, eager to sell me even larger vehicles. This bike was big enough; my feet firmly touched the ground and I could lift it if it should fall over.

The New Yorkers I came into contact with were obliging and friendly, but I didn't tempt fate by walking in Central Park, down 42nd Street or in alleyways. I stayed at Sloane House YMCA, a mixed hostel on 34th Street, and paid reduced rate with my Youth Hostel card. After spending half my travellers' cheques on the Rebel, I worked out a strict budget which I vowed to stick to before setting off.

"He was typical of the people I met all across the States: hospitable, generous and full of useful advice"

Having roughly planned my route, I set out for Plymouth, Massachusetts. Luck was with me in the shape of a guy named Don from Augusta, Georgia, who I met at the first tollbooth. A lot of highways in the East charge tolls and motorcycles pay the same as cars. Don was on his way to Maine and we rode together to Providence, Rhode Island. He was typical of the people I met all across the States: hospitable, generous and full of useful advice. I came into contact with few of the other kind, who tried to take advantage of me, and found common sense by far my best ally.

I spent my first night ever under canvas in a campsite at Plymouth and viewed the plantation the following day. "Plimoth Village" is a reconstruction of the village of 1627, situated inside a high wooden palisade. The interior of the houses is dark and smoky but alive with characters in period costume pursuing the daily tasks of seventeenth-century people. They even take on the speech, attitudes and manner of the time. It was a stifling hot day and my heart went out to the women in their woollen dresses and many petticoats, and the men in their thick hose, jackets and high leather boots, but nonetheless the place lived up to all my expectations. I truly felt as if I had stepped back in time and was hugely impressed by these efforts to retain the aura of seventeenth-century living.

After Plymouth I paid a brief visit to Niagara Falls, the journey marred by a bee which flew up my sleeve and stung me. In my haste to dislodge it my bike toppled over on the hard shoulder and I thanked my lucky stars that I'd used my own judgement and not been persuaded to buy a heavier machine. Arm throbbing, I viewed the Falls and took the boat ride on the river. A year later, if I close my eyes, I can still hear the deafening roar of water, shot through with a multitude of rainbows, and can almost feel the cold spray splashing my face.

My route then took me south along the shores of Lake Erie to Cleveland where the Rebel was due her first service. I had already covered more than 600 miles. Riding through a poor part of town I was struck heavily in the back. I pulled to a halt to discover that some little kids had thrown a soda pop bottle, hitting my bike and dislodging the elastic strap which was holding my camping gear on the pillion. The strap had walloped me. Were they envious of the new bike, I wondered, or was this a national pastime in poor communities? I spent only the time it took to have the bike serviced and ascertain that the YWCA was full before leaving Cleveland to search for a cheap motel. By the time I had found one darkness had fallen. Still the price of a room – $28 – was too high for my $30 a day budget and I moved on. Eventually I noticed a small daytime YWCA, drove round the back of it and camped on the lawn, making sure I was up and away before anyone arrived in the morning.

I camped most nights. State parks are the best places: with showers, toilets and camping shops, they are clean and cheap, as well as being good places to meet people. At a "Kampground of America" in Arkansas, two bikers on Honda Goldwings sprayed my tent with insect repellent after I'd been repeatedly stung. In return I gave them moisturiser for their sunburnt arms. I breakfasted with a couple in Oklahoma who introduced me to hash browns (fried shredded potatoes) and grits (thick white porridge) in their trailer; and I spent the night adjacent to a Cherokee Indian who elaborated on the

Trail of Tears, a true story about the cruel resettlement of several Indian tribes, which had touched me so much at the National Cowboy Hall of Fame in Oklahoma City.

People on the road warned me of possible dangers, such as being surrounded by motorcycle gangs and herded to some lonely spot. They feared for me and commented that my skin wasn't tough enough to withstand extreme weather conditions. I was recommended places to visit and advised to eat in fast-food diners where the food is usually fresh: "Eat where the truckers do. They have the best places sussed out." The Americans I met were generally interested in where I had been and admired my courage.

"After twenty years working in the confines of a noisy factory, the hours spent riding alone across vast spaces gave me a wonderful sense of freedom"

It was some time before I witnessed the violent weather I had been told about. Leaving Albuquerque, New Mexico, to head north, having driven west for many days, I was suddenly frightened by a terrific thunderstorm. My fingers on the clutch tingled from the static as bright streaks of lightning flashed from behind and in front of me. As soon as I could I abandoned the main highway to follow a deserted twisting road that traced the shores of the Rio Grande river. By raising my feet to the petrol tank and putting the bike in first gear I managed to plough shakily through the torrents of red mud and grit that threatened to block my path. It was with a great sigh of relief that I managed to reach that night's destination.

After twenty years working in the confines of a noisy factory, the hours spent riding alone across vast spaces gave me a wonderful sense of freedom and I greatly valued my own company. I took the Rebel high into the Rocky

Mountains, yawning frequently on account of the air's thin quality at 11,000ft. I rode across a grassy saucer-shaped valley which, millions of years ago, had been the crater of a volcano and erupted on a scale ten times that of Mount St Helens. The winding road was quite frightening, with sheer drops into canyons on one side and solid rock walls on the other. Interstate Highway 40 through Arizona is an especially lonely stretch: miles of emptiness and only the distant wind-eroded hills for company. How I loved it. I revelled in the wide open spaces of the Petrified Forest and the Painted Desert, and sat alone on the rim of the Grand Canyon at sunset, at peace with myself.

Bad luck finally struck in Las Vegas, where, suffering from dehydration after crossing miles of arid, stifling desert, I checked into the first motel with a pool. As I lay there, refreshed by a swim and drinking Coke, someone entered my room and stole everything, leaving me stranded 5000 miles from home with nothing but a bikini and a motorbike with no keys.

"Las Vegas must be one of the best places in the world to be destitute"

The cops weren't interested – it takes at least rape or murder to stir them into action. I made a report over the phone, later visiting the police station to pick up a copy of my statement as it is illegal in the States to drive without a licence on you. It wasn't hard to get a replacement set of keys made for the bike, and, three days later, new travellers' cheques arrived and I bought moisturiser for my cracked lips and dried-up face (temperatures reach 120°F in the afternoon). The motel staff were good to me at first, giving me jeans and a shirt, but they wouldn't accept responsibility for my loss and after a week I was thrown out, refusing to pay my bill.

I took refuge in the local Youth Hostel where I was able to work as an assistant until my new passport arrived from the British Consul in Los Angeles. I enjoyed the work, checking in travellers from all over the world, advising them where to eat and suggesting attractions to visit. Las Vegas must be one of the best places in the world to be destitute; if you can prove that you're from out of town, as I could with my English accent and police report, it's not hard to get free or very cheap meals in luxury casino-hotels, as well as the use of facilities. All you need is the nerve to look as if you have a right to be there.

My passport finally arrived and having swapped addresses with my new friends I set off to cross the Sierra Nevada into California. It was far from easy negotiating the high mountain pass. The relentless winds, used to power the army of metal windmills which generate electricity and pump water to the formerly parched terrain, cut through me like a knife, forcing me to ride at a 45-degree angle in order to make any progress at all. By the time I reached Yosemite, to be met by people in ski outfits and dire warnings about impassable mountain roads, I'd caught a bad cold and was forced to lie up for a couple of days. With familiar American kindness the hostel warden dosed me with remedies until I felt well enough to move on.

I only spent a day in San Francisco after crossing the Golden Gate Bridge, for I was impatient to see the ocean and know that I'd achieved my goal. The Youth Hostel I found was in a lighthouse and, that evening, after weeks of observing the sun set behind hills, I was able to watch it silently drop into the magnificent Pacific Ocean. I had made it from coast to coast.

It was now important that I find somewhere under cover to sleep each night. I hadn't replaced the stolen tent and summer was officially over; Youth Hostels were closing down for the winter and I hadn't enough cash to stay in motels.

Chance introduced me to a guy I got chatting to in a coffee shop off the Pacific Coast Highway. He needed temporary help on his secluded ranch in the hills and I accepted his offer of work. I simply kept house, fed the stock and admired the glorious landscape while he conducted business with the various people who called. I never felt threatened, but as my employer spent more and more time away I couldn't shake off the feeling that all was not as it should be.

My instincts were proved right in the early hours of one morning when I was woken by shouts of euphoria coming from downstairs. There I found him with a group of guys celebrating a haul of marijuana which they had just got off a boat from Thailand. Shaking off offers to become involved in future plans, I slipped away, not stopping for gas until I reached Los Angeles.

Here I enjoyed lazy October days on the beach, which was quiet after the exodus of summer visitors, and took in the tourist sights of Hollywood and beyond before selling the Rebel to raise my fare home via New Orleans. By the time I reached cold, damp New York I felt tired but replete. My tour had lasted ten weeks in all, cramming more miles in than many people do in a lifetime. I learned my strengths and my weaknesses. I experienced the exhilaration of the ups and the despair of the lows and most of the feelings in between. Like the lion in *The Wizard of Oz* I learned courage and I learned it by myself.

New Age Travel
· · · · · · · · · · · · · ·

After travelling all over the USA and living in San Francisco, Lucy Ackroyd helped to write and research the Oregon chapter of the *Rough Guide: California and the West Coast*.

America definitively isn't the homogenous mass that the media leads us to believe. Reaganite politics, TV soaps and Hollywood glamour are hardly representative of the American lifestyle and nor does most of the population live in New York or Los Angeles. The West Coast is, however, undoubtedly different. Comprised of the most socially progressive of America's 50 states – with Washington on the Canadian border, California neighbouring Mexico and Oregon sandwiched in between – it is perhaps the most hassle-free destination for female travellers in the big, bad US of A.

The little known northwestern states of Oregon and Washington, so often ignored by California sun seekers, offer a physical and spiritual prize for those who deign to visit. New Age philosophy prevails. Caring communities retrace the footsteps of native American Indian forefathers, moving back to the Mother Earth ideology in an attempt to reverse the self-destruction of Planet Earth. Forerunners in concepts such as environmental groups, organic farming, wholefood co-operatives, arts and crafts revival, Waldorf/Steiner schools, alternative medicine and natural homebirth (which, incidentally, is illegal in most states), and being "green", have long been a way of life.

In some respects this can be seen as a natural progression from the "hippy" communes of the Sixties, an era which played a hugely important role in the establishment of the Women's Movement and other sexual/racial equalities. Also, maybe, as a result of the strong matriarchal role women played back in the pioneer days, when a few brave European immigrants trekked across an unknown continent to settle in the West. Even northwest yokels don't seem to suffer from the small town mentality and bigotry so rife in Midwest and Deep South America.

"I found it comforting to meet many women, like myself, travelling alone"

Whilst travelling around the West Coast I stayed mainly in the Youth Hostels conveniently dotted along Highway 1, the scenic coastal route. I was amazed at the high standard of accommodation for such a humble price ($5 to $10 per night). They are certainly a far cry from the institutionalised Girl Guide specimens located in England's green and pleasant land. My favourite one, in Bandon, Oregon, even had a unique 24-hour open door policy and permitted alcohol on the premises – pretty lax laws for a hostel which, contrary to inviting abuse and wild parties, created a very congenial atmosphere and led to its being the most popular hostel in the state. Of course, its added attractions were spectacular scenery, friendly natives and an interestingly eclectic crowd of visitors. Such hostels are ideal if you want to meet someone to travel with, hitch a ride, or offer someone a lift in exchange for gas money. They are also useful places for gaining first-hand information about areas you're planning to visit from people who have just been there. I found it comforting to meet many women, like myself, travelling alone, with whom to swap travel tips and generally boost each other's confidence from the fact of knowing we weren't the only ones doing it.

Although I usually drove a car or hitched, I did meet quite a few women cycling the West Coast, especially in Oregon, where the famed Highway 1 follows the Pacific Coast through giant redwood forests, atop sheerfaced cliffs and along miles of deserted beaches.

It's ideal for cycling as the route is interspersed with small friendly seaside towns and well used campsites – all of which dispel the threat of isolation usually so unavoidable in America's vast expanses.

In my experience, hitchhiking, alone or with another woman, proved to be a safe and reliable method of travel. Despite the obvious degree of risk involved, it's a good means of getting around the problem of almost non-existent public transport in rural areas. Hitching on quiet back roads guaranteed short rides from locals going about their daily business, but the slowness was more than compensated for by the interesting anecdotes told along the way.

One day, covering a distance of only a hundred kilometres from Bandon-By-the-Sea to Eugene, a college town inland over the Oregon Cascade Mountains, I learnt how to hunt brown bear (apparently quite tasty unless it's been eating skunk cabbage); which of the local lighthouses were haunted; the best place to find magic mushrooms, and what kind of educational exchanges the US Rotary Club organises.

Invariably, lifts will be from single men to whom you're an uncanny reminder of their granddaughter/sister-in-law/second-cousin-twice-removed. But over the past three years and countless rides I have never had a bad time.

Another interesting mode of transport I experienced was the *Green Tortoise*, an alternative bus company based in San Francisco which runs regular trips up and down the West Coast from Los Angeles to Seattle, as well as routes all across the US, including to Alaska and Mexico. *Tortoises* began life in the hippy heydays of the early Seventies and basically go where *Greyhounds* fear to tread. Their converted camper-style coaches are ideal if you can't drive yourself off the beaten track, or just if you fancy some company; unlike most public transport, fellow passengers become instant acquaintances or even close friends as you share the cooking and washing up of communal campfire meals. It really is the answer to laid-back stress free travel for solo females and has enabled a much larger cross section of women to satiate their wanderlust. Grandmas and single mothers are not uncommon riders of the *Tortoise*, as children under the age of twelve get discounts.

"I joined a motley crew of mainly San Franciscan residents ... a British born private eye ... another character who taught Tai Chi on a nudist camp in Southern France every summer; a Jewish/Buddhist witch with her daughter Kaili"

My first experience of *Tortoise* travel was a timid fifteen-hour trip from San Francisco to southern Oregon on their regular West Coast route from Los Angeles to Seattle. Leaving the city at 6pm meant we could have a few beers and a chat to fellow passengers before getting a good night's kip whilst we whizzed up the Highway 15 corridor. The buses are surprisingly comfortable and $5 buys a cook-out meal which everyone helps to prepare. We stopped for breakfast by a creek hidden in the hills, where someone had built a sauna, which my braver companions followed with a dip in the icy creek. I busied myself making blueberry pancakes and fresh fruit salad to provide an excuse for not going skinny dipping (well it was November), but thankfully no one seemed to notice and our only punishment was being left to do the washing up.

This gentle introduction to travel by *Tortoise* inspired me to take a longer trip to Baja California at Christmas. It proved to be a perfect way for a single woman to spend the festive season. I joined a motley crew of mainly San Franciscan residents escaping from the hype associated with this stressful time.

They included a British born private eye investigating a nine-million dollar pistachio swindle; another character

who taught Tai Chi on a nudist camp in Southern France every summer; a Jewish/Buddhist witch with her daughter Kaili (which has nothing to do with Australian soap but means "Ocean Spray" in Hawaiian, as she was born on a beach in Maui); and the infamous Mr Tortoise (aka Gardner Kent), who, needless to say, was quite a character and described himself as a cross between Fred Flintstone and Yogi (smarter than the average) Bear. Christmas came and went in a whirl of windsurfing, snorkelling, clam digging, sunbathing and campfire singing, topped off by an all night Marguerita party. It definitely beat turkey, Xmas pud and a re-run of *The Sound of Music*.

Being homebase for the *Green Tortoise* – and perhaps America's most beautiful major metropolis – are perhaps reasons enough to visit the Golden Gate city of San Francisco. However, its main attraction, for me at any rate, lies not in its physical location, atop seven rolling hills overlooking the Pacific Ocean, but in its cosmopolitan and carefree attitude. I had first visited "Baghdad-by-the-Bay" during a 10,000 mile whirlwind tour of the States, travelling with some friends in a Chevy and Jack Kerouac in my bag, and immediately fell in love with this birthplace of Beat, to which I promised to return as soon as possible. My second visit was a much lengthier affair and as I got to know the city more intimately I discovered many more tangible charms.

The prevailing charm of San Francisco is undoubtedly its laid back, *laissez faire* lifestyle, which allows for racial and sexual harmony to exist in a way no other city has managed to achieve. Undeniably the gay capital of the world, it has matured from the wildly homosexual "sin city" of the early Seventies to a calmly progressive place where all sexuality is accepted.

The current gay scene in San Francisco is such that there are very few strictly men/women only bars and clubs and most welcome anyone of either sex and sexuality. The atmosphere is far more relaxed than the equivalent in, say, London. Perhaps because of this liberal atmosphere, and the high percentage of gay men, San Francisco must be one of the safest cities in the world for women. I really enjoyed the freedom of going out alone at night without male hassle. Previously prohibited pastimes, such as going down to the local bar for a few beers and a game of pool, or to a favourite disco for a good boogie (alone), are just two examples of evening entertainment which men don't have to think twice about and which, in San Francisco, neither did I.

Of course San Francisco isn't a paradise and there are certain areas, as with all big cities, where extra care must be taken, such as the Tenderloin and parts of Mission. But when living in both of these so-called unsavoury districts I never experienced any danger. After finishing work around midnight I often went out dancing with friends to unwind and walked home alone in the early hours without suffering anything worse than a cut foot when I once took my shoes off. Maybe I was lucky but my advice is to heed warnings, but don't take middle-class American opinions as gospel because many tend to overdramatise possible threats to their somewhat cocooned lifestyles. Few will contemplate eating un-prepackaged vegetables, never mind venturing into neighbourhoods like Mission, where Spanish is the leading language and fast-food joints sell *burritos* instead of Big Macs.

Indeed, Mission bears more resemblance to South than North America and is a treat not to be missed, despite the annoying manifestations of Latin *machismo* culture – though these usually amount to nothing worse than verbal abuse about being blond. Although the quarter is as fascinating as Chinatown, the largest Chinese community outside of Asia, or North Beach, the authentically Italian sector, Mission remains well off the tourist track, a fact reflected in the neighbourhood's down-to-earth attitudes and prices. For some reason it's also the sunniest part of town, making the parks full of palm trees as well as people and creating a site for the city's only open-air swimming pool.

Running parallel to Mission is the city's main feminist area of Valencia Street, full of excellent bookshops and cafés. A place I found very useful was the Women's Needs Center, which provides free healthcare and contraceptive advice, charging only the cost price of any medicine prescribed and asking for donations from those who can afford it. This kind of health centre, cheap and friendly, is unusual in the USA, where astronomic medical costs can make going to the doctor a frightening experience. Medical insurance is now compulsory for visitors and residents alike and although expensive it's worth making sure you get comprehensive cover.

Part of San Francisco's magic is that these particular concentrations of ethnic or sexual minorities has not led to a ghetto situation or any noticeable neighbourhood friction as is the case in so many other inner cities.

The city is also a good example of American openness – which can come as quite a surprise to visitors conditioned by the stiff upper lip mentality and insular coldness which pervades parts of Europe. Americans seem to like a great deal of social interaction and it often made my day to be greeted on the street by total strangers. A friendly "Hi, how ya doin?", said in passing, is not a chat-up or come-on line and should be classed in the same category as "Have a nice day" – which, despite its crass reputation, is usually said with sincerity. Unlike the anonymity of large European cities, striking up conversations with strangers on a bus, in a store or at a bar is not uncommon. And although the male chauvinistic slimeball is far from extinct, don't be too quick to assume a defensive stance or refuse the invariably genuine and often very generous American hospitality.

TRAVEL NOTES

Language English – but there's a significant first-generation immigrant population who don't necessarily speak it. This is particularly true of the Spanish-speaking Americans in California, New Mexico and New York.

Accommodation Generally cheaper than Britain though beware of seedy, budget-price hotels in "unsafe" parts of of town. New York and other major cities have a few women-only hotels. Across the country, Youth Hostels, which don't usually require membership, are a good bet. There's also a well-organised network of campsites.

Transport *Greyhound* and *Trailway* buses cover all major destinations; the alternative *Green Tortoise* is more limited, but efficient, fun and a great way of meeting people. Internal flights and car hire are relatively cheap. Hitching, though recommended on the West Coast by Lucy Ackroyd, is reputedly dodgy for both sexes.

Special Problems The cost and bureaucracy of US healthcare is horrific. You must take out medical insurance and if there's any chance you may need gynaecological care, be sure to double-check your policy. Some don't cover it and it's very expensive (as are contraceptive pills).

Guides The *Rough Guides* to New York and California and the West Coast (both Harrap Columbus) are invaluable as ever – both Deborah Bosley and Lucy Ackroyd were involved in research on the latter. For travelling coast-to-coast, *Let's Go USA* (Pan) is dependable.

Contacts

Two important resources:

The Index/Directory of Women's Media (published by the Women's Institute for Freedom of the Press, 3306 Ross Place, NW Washington DC 20008, ☎202 966 7783. Lists women's periodicals, presses and publishers, bookshops, theatre groups, film and music groups, women's news services, writers' groups, media organisations, women's radio, special library collections, and more. Invaluable and updated yearly.

The National Organisation for Women, 15 W. 18th St., 9th Floor, New York 10011 and 425 13th St., NW Washington DC 20004. With groups all over the country, this is a good organisation to get referrals for specific concerns: rape crisis centres and counselling services, feminist bookshops and lesbian bars.

The select listings below comprises mainly **feminist bookshops**, which are nearly always a good source of other local contacts/activities.

ALASKA: **Alaska Women's Bookstore**, 2440 East Tudor Rd., No. 304, Anchorage 99507. Also a resource centre and music store.

ARIZONA: **Women's Place Bookstore**, Dept U, 2401, N 32nd Street, Phoenix, Arizona 85008.

LOS ANGELES: **Sisterhood Bookstore**, 1351 Westwood Blvd. Bookshop and resource centre. **Lesbian Political Action Center**, 1428 Fuller Avenue, Hollywood 90046, ☎874 8312. **A Different Light Bookstore**, 4014 Santa Monica Blvd., Hollywood 90029, ☎668 0629. Lesbian and gay books.

OAKLAND: **Mama Bears**, 6536 Telegraph Avenue. Bookshop, coffeehouse and arts and crafts gallery. **A Woman's Place**, 4015 Broadway. Women's art and bookshop.

SACRAMENTO: **Lioness Books**, 2224 J. St. Feminist and children's books.

SAN DIEGO: **Center for Women's Studies and Services**, 908 E. St. Centre for studies, women's health and therapy services, advice and information; organises educational and cultural activities like free feminist university.

SAN FRANCISCO: **Women's Needs Center**, 1825 Haight St., ☎221 7371. Provides free healthcare and contraception advice, charging only the cost price of any medicine prescribed and asking for donations from those who can afford it. **Old Wives' Tales**, 1009 Valencia St. Feminist, lesbian, Third World books.

SAN JOSE: **Sisterspirit**, 1040 Park Avenue. Non-profit women's bookshop and coffeehouse featuring live entertainment every other week.

FLORIDA: **Pagoda's Women's Space**, Coastal Highway, St Augustine 32084, ☎829 2970. Holiday centre for women; plus **Ellies Nest**, (women's guesthouse) 1414 Newton St., Key West, ☎296 5757.

CHICAGO: **North-Western University Women's Center**, 619 Emerson, Evanston 60201, ☎492 3146. Information about local women's groups. **Jane Addam's Bookstore**, 5 South Wabbash, Room 1508, ☎782 9798.

DETROIT: **Women's Liberation News and Letter** (branches throughout US), 2832 East Grand Blvd., Room 316, MI 43211. **Herself Bookstore** – recently moved, for address call information Detroit.

MINNEAPOLIS: **Amazon Bookstore Inc.**, 2607 Hennepin Avenue South, ☎374 5507. List of rooms, apartments, housing and other interests available. **A Women's Coffee House**, 1 Groveland, nr Franklin.

NEW MEXICO: **Full Circle Books**, 2205 Silver S.E. Albuquerque. New Mexico's only feminist bookshop.

NEW YORK: **Barnard College Women's Center**, 117th Broadway, ☎212 280 2067. Clearinghouse for information on women's organisations, studies, conferences etc. **Womanbooks**, 210 W.92nd St., ☎873 4121. Bookshop, record shop and community centre run by women and stocking a wide range of feminist and lesbian titles; pick up the city's monthly feminist paper, *Womanews*. **Qui Travel**, 165 W.74th St., ☎496 5110. Women's/gay travel agent. **The Saint Mark's Women's Health Collective**, 9 Second Avenue, ☎228 7482. One of the foundations of the New York women's community, offering traditional and alternative medicine at sliding-scale prices.

OREGON: **A Woman's Place**, 1431 NE Broadway, Portland 97232. Resource centre and bookshop carrying over 10,000 titles, plus art, jewellery, music etc.

PENNSYLVANIA: **Women's Center**, 616 North Highland Avenue, Pittsburgh 15206, ☎212-661 6066.

TEXAS: **Book Woman**, 324 E. Sixth St., Austin 78701. Feminist books, records and posters.

WASHINGTON: **Lammas Women's Bookstore**, 321 7th St. SE, ☎546 7299; and 1426 21st St. NW. Bookshop and information centre, with two branches. **Bethune Museum and Archives National Historic Site**, 1318 Vermont Ave. NW. Archive of educational resources on black women and organisations.

WISCONSIN: **A Room of One's Own**, 317 West Johnson St., Madison 53703. Bookshop.

Feminist magazines include:
New York: *Womanews, New Directions, Quest.*
Washington: *Off Our Backs.*
Boston: *Sojourner.*
San Francisco: *Plexus.*
Nationwide (and almost mainstream): *Ms.*

Books

Starting with non-fiction, this is inevitably more an idiosyncratic dip into the pile than any sort of "representative sample".

Maya Angelou, *I Know Why the Caged Bird Sings* (Virago, 1984). First and arguably the best volume of this ongoing (five volumes so far) autobiography by one of America's most extraordinary multi-talented black women writers.

Djuna Barnes, *Djuna Barnes' New York* (Virago, 1990). Collection of essays by a legendary literary figure of the Twenties and Thirties.

Angela Davis, *Women, Culture and Politics* (The Women's Press, 1990). New collection of essays by one of America's leading black activists. Davis's **An Autobiography** (1975; reissued by The Women's Press, 1990, with a new introduction) is also fascinating.

Betty Friedan, *"It Changed My Life"* (Norton, US, 1986). Collection of influential writings, and now historic speeches, that provides a first-hand account of the development and continuing impact of the American Women's Movement.

Zora Neale Hurston, *Dust Tracks on a Road* (Virago, 1989). Reissued autobiography of one of America's most prolific black women writers, folklorists and critics; Hurston is an acknowledged inspiration to most black American women writing today.

Joyce Johnson, *Minor Characters* (Picador, 1983). Gripping memoir of a life as part of the wild 1950s Beat generation growing up in the world of jazz, poetry and black-stockinged New York Bohemia.

June Jordan, *Moving Towards Home* (Virago, 1989). Powerful political essays by yet another multi-talented black American woman activist and writer.

Cherie Moraga and Gloria Anzaldua, eds., *This Bridge Called My Back: Writings by*

Radical Women of Color (Kitchen Table Women of Color Press, 1983). Includes prose, poetry, personal narrative and analysis by Afro American, Asian, American, Latina and Native American Women.

Adrienne Rich, *On Lies, Secrets and Silence – Selected Prose 1966-78* (Virago, 1980). Feminist and lesbian essays, speeches and reviews.

Lillian Schlissel, *Women's Diaries of the Westward Journey* (Schlocken Books, US, 1982). Women's experiences of migrating West in the middle of the last century.

Gloria Steinem, *Outrageous Acts and Everyday Rebellions* (1983, Flamingo 1985). Illuminating journalist/feminist writings of 1960s and 1970s.

Fiction

Toni Cade Bambara, *The Salt Eaters* 1960; The Women's Press, 1982). This brilliant novel by one of America's leading black women writers, is followed by the collection of short stories, *Gorilla, My Love* (The Women's Press, 1984). Bambara writes in a wonderful, racy style, described as "reading like jazz".

Maud Farrell, *Skid* (The Women's Press, 1990). Thriller set among the lesbian dives of New York.

Maxine Hong Kingston, *The Woman Warrior* (Picador, 1981). A beautifully crafted book unravelling the Chinese cultural traditions and myths that helped form Kingston's identity as a first generation Chinese American.

Audre Lorde, *Zami* (Sheba, 1984). Powerful evocation of what it's like to be black and lesbian in a white heterosexual society .

Alison Lurie, *The Nowhere City* (Abacus). Centring on the breakdown of a couple's marriage on moving West for the husband's work, this novel paints an astute, often funny, picture of Los Angeles in the Sixties.

Toni Morrison, *Beloved* (Picador, 1987). Pulitzer prize winning novel centred on the tragedy of slavery. *Song of Solomon* (1970, Triad/Granada, 1982). Complex, beautifully told fable set in the deep south of America. Also recommended is her first novel, *The Bluest Eye* (Triad/Granada, 1981), which chronicles the tragic lives of a poor black family in Ohio through the eyes of a young girl.

Tillie Olsen, *Tell Me a Riddle* (1960; Virago, 1983); *Yonnondio* (1974; Virago, 1980). The first is a collection of four short stories exploring some of the "pain and promise of fundamental American experience"; the second, her only novel, tells the story of a working-class family struggling to better their lives in the Midwest during the Depression.

Marge Piercy, *Braided Lives* (Penguin, 1984). Semi-autobiographical novel covering the youth, adolescence and "college days" of a girl seeking to escape working-class Detroit and the repressions of the McCarthy era. Other Marge Piercy novels include *Vida* (The Women's Press, 1980), the tale of a political activist forced underground in the Sixties, and, most recently, *Gone to Soldiers* (Penguin, 1987), an epic panorama spanning the lives of women and men caught up in a world at war.

Ntozake Shange, *Sassafrass, Cypress and Indigo* Methuen, 1984). Story of three sisters by author of the great play *For Colored girls who Consider ed Suicide when the Rainbow is Enuf.*

Mona Simpson, *Anywhere But Here* (Abacus, 1988). Bizarre and unforgettable saga of a young girl and her ambitious mother as they pursue LA stardom for their daughter.

Betty Smith, *A Tree Grows in Brooklyn* (Pan, 1984). Classic tale set in pre-war Brooklyn of a courageous Irish girl making good .

Amy Tan, *The Joy Luck Club* (Heinemann, 1989). Best-selling novel based on a Chinese American woman's experience of growing up in San Francisco.

Alice Walker, *The Color Purple* (The Women's Press, 1983). Engrossing, deservedly prize-winning novel about two sisters growing up in the Deep South between the wars. Walker's other works include two volumes of short stories and three novels. The latest, *The Temple of My Familiar* (The Women's Press, 1989), is described by the author as "a romance of the last 500,000 years"

Other women writers to look out for include **Joan Didion, Louise Erdrich, Rosa Guy, Tama Janowitz, Paule Marshall, Grace Paley** and **Anne Tyler**. Finally, crime fiction fans must read the novels of **Sarah Paretsky** (published by Penguin), set in Chicago and featuring the indomitable female private detective, V.I. Warshawski.

Vietnam

Fifteen years on from the Communist victory, Vietnam has had little chance to recover from the ravages of war. Immediately after unification, the US imposed an economic blockade which, to their lasting shame, was joined by all other Western nations in 1979. In consequence, this, the country that receives the world's least development aid, is one of the world's poorest. Over the last five years, the well-publicised "Boat People" emigrants have left in a constant, desperate stream, while, at home, the legacies of the war are still everywhere to be seen.

Most Vietnamese refer to the years of fighting, which wrecked so many lives, as the "American War", fuelled as it was by the American government's determination to ward off any southward extension of Communist influence from North Vietnam. In the ten years of fighting up to 1975 over six million tons of bombs and 370,000 tons of napalm were dropped by the Americans (and their Australian allies) on Vietnam; 9000 villages were destroyed and much land is still unusable owing to long-term pollution, craters and unexploded bombs. Close on two million Vietnamese (and 56,000 Americans) lost their lives. Today, women still suffer miscarriages and the tragedy of children born with disabilities as a direct result of chemical warfare.

Despite its bleak economic situation, and painful history, Vietnam is emerging as a destination for tourists. The government, in dire need of international aid and recognition, has liberalised its economic and foreign policies and now welcomes foreign visitors, including Americans. Previously, visitors were pretty much limited to the old Eastern bloc countries. However, independent travellers remain officially frowned upon and, unless you can afford the luxury of hiring your own interpreter and driver, you'll probably have to explore the country from the basis of a group tour. This can still be rewarding, and, as visas become easier to obtain, the opportunities for individual travel are likely to open up. Wherever you go, people will usually be eager to meet you and tell their stories, sometimes in the hope of a passport to the West. Be prepared for an often gruelling experience, but don't be put off. Vietnam is a fascinating country where, as a foreign woman, you'll be more of a curiosity than a target for harassment.

Vietnamese **women**, known as the long-haired army, were active as soldiers in both the Vietnam War and the battle against French occupation which preceded it. In fact their history as warriors goes back to pre-colonial times. But only since 1975 has their status improved and their achievements been fully recognised. Largely through the efforts of the *Women's Union*, the immediate years after reunification saw great progress in work and education opportunities, better healthcare and general women's rights. As the official national women's association, the Union (formed in 1930 and now with ten million members) continues to organise at all levels, from supporting village co-operatives to advising the Prime Minister on new policies for implementing women's rights. But like everything in Vietnam, theirs is a hard struggle. Women undoubtedly bore the brunt of the last war, both in terms of poverty, bereavement, and the hereditary physical effects of dioxin and Agent Orange, described below, and until the whole situation of the country improves there is small hope of even their basic needs being met.

A War That Can't Be Forgotten

. . . .

Sarah Furse went to Vietnam en route from Britain to Australia. It was a brief visit at a time when tourists were only granted short-stay visas for an organised tour. As a result of a meeting with the Women's Union of Ho Chi Minh City, on arrival in Australia she and two travelling companions raised several thousand dollars towards funding a gynaecological research centre for the treatment of women and children still affected by the deadly chemicals used in the Vietnam War.

Day 1: 6.30am. Toula and I are sipping weak coffee and chewing on rubbery omelettes in the coffee shop of our downmarket hotel in Bangkok. We are interrupted: the Diethelm minibus is here to whisk us away to the airport en route for Ho Chi Minh City. We trundle off through the already bustling streets of Bangkok, picking up the four other members of our tour – two German bank clerks, a Scottish farmer and an Australian psychologist – from their decidedly more upmarket hotels, and check each other out for potential camaraderie over the next week.

Two hours later, the ravaged defoliated land west of Ho Chi Minh City is a shocking sight. Alongside the runway the wrecks of military planes sit like rusting cadavers. Customs clearance takes an eternity, with umpteen forms to fill out detailing personal "luxury" effects, the purpose of the visit, etc.

Eventually we are ushered through to the exit area, to be met by our guide, Hinh, a beaming smile lighting up her face. She makes the customary welcome speech in perfect English, which she delivers to every group of Western tourists who arrive here at reasonably regular intervals. We clamber into a minibus and head off into the heart of the city (still known as Saigon), to the Doc Lap Hotel, our home for the next week.

> **"We emerge from the hotel to be immediately surrounded by a mob of children, tugging at our sleeves, calling us 'Mama, Mama'"**

First impressions are of an exhausted, dilapidated city: peeling paintwork on the facades of French colonial buildings; rusty iron gates and railings; rising damp; and thousands of Vietnamese in conical hats, riding all manner of bicycles – two-wheelers, three-wheelers, four-wheelers (with incredibly large loads precariously balanced) and *cyclos* (bicycle taxis). Everyone looks in a hurry to get somewhere.

On the sidewalks French *baguettes* are sold and bicycles are being mended: nearly everything happens on the dusty, cracked pavements of this city. Faded billboards advertise movies and political propaganda. Old women and men, dressed in the customary baggy black trousers, squat down, talking, thinking, chewing betel nuts and absent-mindedly brushing flies from their faces.

We arrive at the Doc Lap, are given room keys and instructions to meet for lunch in the "Rooftop Restaurant". Then we head off upwards in the rickety lift. A brass plaque showing the floor numbers indicates that the Australian Embassy was once lodged on our floor. After a brief glance from

our tiny balcony, over the rooftops of Saigon, Toula and I are eager to step out and wander the streets for an hour or two.

Clutching our map of Ho Chi Minh City, written in Vietnamese, we emerge from the hotel to be immediately surrounded by a mob of children, tugging at our sleeves, calling us "Mama, Mama", and talking ten to the dozen in broken English about fathers in Australia and the United States. Many of these children are Amer-Asian or Austro-Asian street kids. Unwanted and undisciplined, they eke out a living by begging tourists for cigarettes to sell on the black market, and soap, towels, shampoo, disinfectant or pens to trade with. They are eager to show us their city, to tell us their stories and to receive affection and attention from us.

The traces of war are so visible in their faces looking intensely up at us. A little boy, Deng, whose father was a black GI, laughs nervously but does not come as close as the others. Later we learn that he sees himself as "bad, unclean, no good", because he is black. Racism is prevalent, even here. Feeling distraught by this, our first encounter with the children of Vietnam whose lives have been totally shaped by being born out of war, we quickly retreat to the hotel.

Half an hour later we re-emerge. This time there are fewer children and some of them have brought along "souvenirs" for us, carefully wrapped, with little notes of friendship written in shaky English. Nguyen has given me a beautiful black lacquerware vase with a goldfish on it; Thi, a gaudy plaster cat and dog ornament. They slip thin arms through our own rather fleshy ones, and take us for a walk around Saigon, telling us to look after our bags because "bad people will steal". A woman pedals up and asks if we speak French. I say "yes" and she proceeds to tell me that her fifteen-year-old son's father is called Harry Miller and lives in California. She wants to send her son over to him. Can I help? I can't and she pedals resignedly off into the crowded street.

Now the sun is setting and it is time for us to eat and retire, so we say our farewells and go back to exchange experiences with the others over a sumptuous Vietnamese dinner. There is a Russian circus staying in the Doc Lap, and on several occasions in the lift we are spoken to in Russian. I dredge up what little I can remember from my school studies fifteen years ago, to tell them that my mother is Russian but I don't speak or understand the language very well.

"A wave of nausea suddenly takes over, leaving me weeping inwardly at the horrors and perversions of this war"

Day 2: In the morning we visit the enormous, ugly Imperial Palace which once housed the South Vietnamese Government. It is now a museum and the venue for occasional Party conferences. It feels eerie to stand on the rooftop where the helicopters landed to fly the generals, ministers and other top officials off to safety at the fall of Saigon in 1975.

Then on to the Imperial War Museum. Outside it, a large group of "Young Pioneers", proudly wearing red kerchiefs and reminiscent of Boy Scouts, clamber over each other in their eagerness to be photographed next to an old tank. Inside the museum the history of Vietnam's occupation by the Chinese for a thousand years, and more recently by the French, Portuguese and Americans, is vividly displayed in blurred and dog-eared photographs with accompanying texts written in Russian, Vietnamese and English.

A display of guns, bomb shells and the containers used for spraying Agent Orange and other chemicals stands close to the grotesque guillotine which was used by the French right up until

1960. Paintings depict various methods of torture used on suspected revolutionaries. There are photographs of babies horrifically affected by Agent Orange, and a distorted foetus in a jar. An American anti-war pamphlet shows a group of GIs grinning at the camera, surrounded by the dismembered bodies and heads of captured Vietcong guerillas, the caption reading something like: "This is what they don't tell you about the war. You can come and try just to survive and get home in one piece. Or you can come and be turned into a psychopath like the GIs in this photo. They will fuck you over, whatever you do."

A wave of nausea suddenly takes over, leaving me weeping inwardly at the horrors and perversions of this war. We leave the museum emotionally drained and return to the Doc Lap for a subdued two hours at the hotel. Afterwards we are taken across town to a lacquerware factory, an industry which has survived in Vietnam since the fifteenth century. But my mind is still full of what I have just seen – images that will haunt me forever – and I can't take anything in.

In the evening we wander out to buy some books and walk by the river. An Amer-Asian boy of about thirteen, his emaciated spine bent over and twisted so badly that he can only crawl on his hands and feet, follows us, begging for cigarettes. I give him my packets and feel anger and sorrow mounting as I see yet another victim of Agent Orange struggling to survive.

Day 3: Up early, and off in the minibus through the crowded streets where syringes are sold openly to the city's thousands of heroin addicts, and out into the lush green countryside towards My Tho on the banks of the Mekong River delta. Water buffalo, harnessed to antiquated wooden ploughs, plod through the rice paddy fields that flash by the windows of the bus. Lorries pump noxious black diesel smoke from their exhaust pipes; old buses carry a hundred bicycles on top, a hundred passengers inside; neat oblongs of rice line the side of the road, drying in the humid sunshine.

At My Tho we board a tiny boat and are ferried downriver at high speed, to an island bursting with palm trees, grapefruit, coconuts and bananas. Here it is extremely fertile, indicating how the whole of South Vietnam must have looked before wartime defoliation. The islanders make a very good living from fishing, and from farming tropical fruit and vegetables in carefully irrigated jungle.

"The Vietnamese are ingenious at turning abandoned articles of war into useful tools of peace and productivity"

On the way back to My Tho we see a half-sunken US Navy battleship which has been turned into home for scores of Vietnamese people, their huts clinging precariously to the hull of this floating war memorial. The Vietnamese are ingenious at turning abandoned articles of war into useful tools of peace and productivity. GIs' helmets are used as wash basins and watering cans; bomb shells are hammered out and melted down for use in light industry on the communes; brightly coloured plastic electrical wire is woven into beautiful padded teacosies – it seems nothing is wasted.

On the way back to Ho Chi Minh City we stop at a Buddhist monastery to hear about the many monks and nuns who performed public self-immolation in protest at the war. In the evening, Hinh takes us to have dinner at *La Bibliothèque de Madame Dai*, an exclusive restaurant lodged in the former library and law office of Suzanne Dai. A former senator in the South Vietnamese government, she now runs evening classes for illiterate women and children, as well as making visitors to her establishment aware of her love of Vietnam (despite her disa-

greement with Communism) and the needs of her people.

Day 4: Today we are going to Vung Tau, a fishing village and beach resort some two hours' drive from Saigon. On the way we pass an area of scrubland where one of the biggest US Army bases now stands empty and useless on a bleak hillside. Vung Tau itself feels like any seaside town, with its souvenir shops and cafés along the promenade, women mending reams of fishing nets and the ubiquitous Soviet tourists sporting straw hats and sunburn. The Vietnamese are drilling for oil in the South China Sea, with the aid of Russian and Norwegian experts, and a big refining plant – Sovietpetro – sits prominently at the entrance to the village.

After lunch, it's on with the bathers and off to the beach, at one end of which, on top of a high hill, stands an enormous statue of Jesus on the cross, arms outstretched to the heavens. Despite Communism, the Vietnamese are still very religious: sixty percent are Buddhist, twenty percent Catholic, and the rest hold an assortment of beliefs. All seem to be free enough to practise their varying beliefs unhindered.

In the evening, Toula, Di (the psychologist we have befriended on our tour) and I head off for coffee on the promenade and end up having a fascinating, largely mime-based discussion about politics with a group of young Russian sailors.

The next morning, armed with paracetamol to temper our diabolical hangovers from one too many Vietnamese brandies, we are taken up a steep rocky track to the old lighthouse, to look out over a spectacular view and see the remains of what was the largest Australian base in Vietnam.

Day 6: Another trip out of the city, this time westwards to the barren defoliated area around Cu Chi, centre of the extraordinary 300-km network of underground tunnels, built and maintained by the Vietcong despite numerous attempts to destroy them. Many children were born underground. Running beneath villages and even American army bases, these tunnels contained rest areas, kitchens, arms caches, booby traps and latrines.

They measured only 60 x 40cm in the connecting sections; Toula and I crawl through a 50m stretch, slightly enlarged to cope with the size of Western tourists. It is a frightening experience: the guide's torch goes out; it is overwhelmingly hot and claustrophobic, with huge cockroaches, rats and mosquitoes clambering up the walls that we can't see, can only feel. It gives us some idea of what it must have been like to spend weeks, even months underground, and we emerge gasping for air and water. We are then introduced to a woman whose husband had been stabbed to death and disembowelled because he was a Vietcong guerilla and who herself had helped build a section of the tunnel during the war.

In the afternoon we go to Bamboo Shoot 1 Orphanage, where the children learn skills such as weaving, carpentry, embroidery and dressmaking to help them obtain jobs when they leave. They seem to be well cared for and loved, but there is so much more that they need: simple things that we in the West take for granted such as pens, notebooks, milk powder, medicines, shoes, cotton thread, books, etc. How will those needs ever be met in a country that is struggling so hard with a besieged economy and enormous social problems? There is a policy not to send Vietnamese children for adoption outside Vietnam any more. It is very hard to suppress idiotic desires to take half a dozen of them home with me!

Day 7: Today is the big day for Di, Toula and myself. We have written a letter to the Womens' Association of Ho Chi Minh City, asking to meet with them to exchange information about women in Vietnam and women in Australia and England. Our request has been granted, and we leave the men in our group to amuse themselves while we spend a fascinating and very productive afternoon hearing all about life for women in Vietnam since 1975.

"It is estimated that women exposed to dioxin ... have six times more chromosome breaks than survivors of Hiroshima"

The Women's Association comprises women from all walks of life and is dedicated to fighting for women's rights in all areas and at all levels. Though linked to the government Medical Health Department, it remains an independent, self-funded body. Its work includes running rehabilitation programmes for drug addicts and prostitutes; classes for illiterate women and children; medical centres for women and children; creches, orphanages and kindergartens.

One of its greatest needs is the means to try and combat the terrible long-term effects on women and children of Agent Orange. The wartime spraying of this deadly chemical has caused – among other things – a variety of congenital cancers, miscarriages, and babies born with severe mental and physical disabilities resulting in limblessness, severe cleft palate, lack of spine, kidneys, and tear ducts. There have also been cases of women going through a seemingly normal pregnancy only to give birth to their own cancerous reproductive systems and it is estimated that women exposed to dioxin (a highly toxic component of Agent Orange) have six times more chromosome breaks than survivors of Hiroshima.

The Women's Association asked us to try and help them to set up a Gynaecological Research Centre in Ho Chi Minh City to research these affects and attempt to find solutions to a huge problem that does not end simply because the war is over. So we decide to take up their request and set up

"Orange Action", with the aim of raising at least some of the US$100,000 they need.

We left Vietnam on the eighth day, our minds full to bursting with experiences, images, ideas and emotions. More than anything, we left determined to continue the links we made with women in Vietnam and to make "Orange Action" a success.

TRAVEL NOTES

Languages Vietnamese, though quite a few people speak some English picked up during the American occupation. French is also quite widely spoken.

Transport Except on tours, visitors are forbidden to travel by train or long-distance bus. Any breach of these rules can lead to deportation. However, tourists seem free to wander in the cities with little fear of harassment. The main transport here is the *cyclo*, a form of pedal bicycle rickshaw.

Accommodation Hotels are generally cheap and pretty basic, but again you'll have no choice short of organising your own private tour.

Special Problems Vietnam has only minimal health facilities, so be sure to bring your own medicines, tampons, contraception, etc.

Guide *Guide to Vietnam* (Bradt). A bit scanty in places, but written by a photographer who really knows and loves the country and its people.

Contacts

Organised tours are increasingly popular. British operators include **Anita-Regent Holidays**, 13 Small St., Bristol, ☎0272-211 711, and **Bales Tours Ltd.**, Bales House, Barrington Rd., Dorking, Surrey RH4 3EJ, ☎306-885 991.

For more information on the **Women's Union**, write to *War On Want*, 37–39 Great Guildford St., London SE1 0YU, which recently launched a project to raise money for paper, desperately needed for the Union's publication, *Women in Vietnam*, and other educational activities.

Books

Arlene Eisen Bergman, *Women of Vietnam* (People's Press, US, 1975; available in Britain from Zed Books). Interesting material on the history of women's participation in Vietnam's centuries of struggle for liberation.

Michael Herr, *Dispatches* (Picador). Journalist's acclaimed account of the Vietnam War.

Thanks to War on Want for help with background information.

NorthYemen

ountainous and isol-
ated, North Yemen (Yemen Arab
Republic) is a society and economy in considerable flux. It is one
of the world's least-developed
nations, with little industry and no
oil of its own. Yet due to the mass
migration of (male) Yemeni workers to Saudi Arabia, it has acquired
a recent veneer of booming capitalism – at least in the cities. At the
time of writing, there is talk of a
renewed union with neighbouring
South Yemen (the Peoples'
Democratic Republic), which for
the last two decades has pursued a
quite different course, with a
socialist economy and, more interestingly, a break from the region's
rigidly Islamic traditional code.

North Yemen itself is a
completely traditional society.
Foreigners are a rare sight,
though various development agencies are active in the rural areas,
and the startling Arabian architecture of the towns and villages is attracting a
small but growing number of tourists. Visas are obtained without difficulty.
Travel within the country can be arduous but, outside the capital Sana'a,
sexual harassment is relatively rare.

North Yemeni **women** are for the most part bound by traditional social
constraints; the vast majority are veiled and remain secluded from male/
public spheres. The widespread migration of men to work in Saudi has made
this position increasingly problematic for some women. Left behind in the
villages, sometimes with no adult male workers at all, they have had to
expand their work role without the social sanction to do so. Development
agencies have begun to initiate a series of "home economics" projects, involving agricultural training as well as healthcare, literacy and handicrafts education, for rural women. In doing this, they have been lent support by the

Yemeni Women's Association and in some villages have met with considerable success. However the opposition of men to what they perceive as the "politicisation" of women remains a strong barrier.

Qat Country

· · · · · · · · · · ·

Gill Hoggard spent a fortnight travelling around Yemen with a woman friend. They had arrived from Egypt where they had been living and working.

You cannot go to North Yemen without romantic baggage: travelling in the footsteps of Freya Stark, veiled women, austere mountains, clifftop fortresses and swirling cloud. But tempering romanticism with practicality, I stocked up in Cairo with insect repellent, malaria pills and appropriate clothing (baggy trousers and loose kaftans). Bleary eyed from the flight, I watched as our plane circled the mountains and flew low into Sana'a as the rising sun caught a jumble of mud-brick houses, spectacular free-standing minarets, and occasional concrete apartment blocks.

Sana'a airport was in the process of being modernised and on emerging from the concourse into the brilliant morning sun I was met by a cacophony of bulldozers, pneumatic drills and dumper trucks. I was somewhat unsettled by the people – a crowd of fierce-looking men, each of whom displayed a large dagger on his belt, and, unsure how to interpret this, fled back to the safety of a group of American missionaries I had chatted to on the plane.

It was thus, crowded Yemeni-style into a Peugeot taxi, and with the gossip of someone's high school graduation in Milwaukee flowing comfortingly around me, that I caught a first glimpse of Sana'a's extraordinary and beautiful

architecture. Everywhere there was fretwork and tracery, picked out in white against the brown mudbrick. Gutters, drainpipes, latticework balconies and zigzag ramparts rioted over the house-fronts, while on the flat roofs washing flapped in the wind.

"Yemenis regard the modesty and chastity of their women as paramount"

In the course of my stay I saw few women. Like all Arabs, Yemenis regard the modesty and chastity of their women as paramount. They are required to wear not just one veil but two: the inner, covering most of the face except the eyes, and the outer, a kind of thin scarf which may be raised only for close relatives. I found it quite unsettling to attempt a conversation with, literally, an unseen person. Those women seen on the streets, shopping or (rarely) selling food, belong to the poorer classes; it is considered shameful for those of any wealth or position to venture out. Instead you see men doing the shopping and all external business.

Once, manoeuvring my way through the souk, I came upon a whole row of women, side by side, giggling and chattering and selling bread. Unusually they were only half veiled. I surreptitiously took a picture, but was angrily bumped and jostled by the men: they do not want anyone, even another woman, to take pictures of their own women.

I had ventured out into the *qat souk* – the market for the narcotic leaves which Yemenis chew for relaxation.

Serious buying begins around 11am in time for the afternoon, and everywhere earnest groups of men were bargaining over large plastic-wrapped bundles of what looked like privet. Alcohol is strictly forbidden and tobacco rarely smoked, but chewing qat is a national pastime. Everywhere, as the afternoon draws on, you see the unfocused eyes and vacant grin of those under the influence. Qat is easily grown and fetches a respectable sum in the marketplace, and whole mountainsides, which used to grow coffee, have been turned over to its production.

"Although we were often the only women on the buses and always the only Westerners, we were met by unfailing courtesy and friendliness"

Yemeni women as well as men chew qat and throughout one bus journey we made into the mountains, two heavily-wrapped ladies besides us plucked demurely at their bundles of leaves and slowly subsided, like the rest of the passengers, into a quiet and dreamy trance. On that occasion, as on several others, my friend and I had been ushered to the "best" seats at the front, from which we had all too clear a view of the spectacular gorges and canyons which fell away below the road.

Apart from some nerve-racking mountain roads, we didn't find it too difficult travelling around the country. Between all the major centres of population there are good tarmac roads and also a regular and punctual bus service. Although we were often the only women on the buses and always the only Westerners, we were met with unfailing courtesy and friendliness.

The place which left the strongest impression on me was the village of Al-Manakah, high up in the mountains south of Sana'a, and the objective of our qat-powered bus trip. Its "hotel for travellers" proved to be of ancient Yemeni design, a warren of tiny rooms, passageways and mysterious inhabitants, laughing and chattering in the unseen lower quarters.

We had met, briefly, the woman who appeared to be in charge of the hotel in order to settle the business details. From then on our food was served by a heavily veiled and very timid girl of about twelve, probably her daughter, and thereafter, except for the muffled thumps, giggles and bangs emanating from downstairs, we saw no signs of anyone else. The unusual thing about this was that we had seen the woman and the girl at all: normally all strangers would deal only with the men of the house. But Al-Manakah, like so many other villages in the High Yemen, had sent its men to work in the Gulf, leaving the women in charge.

While staying there we followed the track out beyond the village and frequently encountered groups of men, either keeping an eye on their goats or more usually, squatting in the road to brew coffee over a small fire. We called out the Arabic greeting "Peace be on you", both to let it be known that we spoke the language, and to lessen the likelihood of any unpleasantness. Traditionally if one has replied "And on you be peace" it is morally unthinkable to insult or injure whoever you're speaking to. There was, however, not the slightest reason for unease: we were frequently invited to share in the coffee-drinking, or simply encouraged as to what we could find further on.

In Sana'a we met women Peace Corps members who told us differently, citing increasing incidents of sexual harassment on the city's streets after dark. They attributed this to the recent importation of pornographic videos from the West, one amongst a whole number of "luxury" goods that have started to enter the city. American chains such as Hiltons and McDonalds have also been established and the city as a whole is becoming increasingly open to Western influence. Yet it is still expected that these new and gleaming Western establishments will be exclusively staffed and patronised by men.

TRAVEL NOTES

Languages Arabic. It is definitely worth learning the basics before you go (numbers, simple questions) as very few people speak English.

Transport Within Sana'a there are shared taxis which are expensive (as is everything in Yemen) but the only means of getting around. A reasonably good bus service runs between main towns; most buses leaving early in the morning to complete the journey within daylight hours. Once a bus is full the driver will leave, no matter what the clock says, so it's worth arriving in good time. Internal air flights are also available, but besides being vastly expensive mean you miss out on the spectacular mountain scenery.

Accommodation In Sana'a there are several grades of hotels but prices are high even for quite basic accommodation. In the mountain villages you find *funduks*, ancient hostelries which now take in foreign travellers; they are reasonable but very basic — you sleep on floor cushions. Always ask people for a *funduk* and not a hotel if you want the cheaper, more basic accommodation.

Special problems Yemenis are strict Muslims and find bare flesh offensive — they particularly object to women's upper arms being uncovered. Clothing therefore should be loose and voluminous and cover the arms at least to the elbow.

Guide *Yemen — A Travel Surival Kit* (Lonely Planet) covers both North and South Yemen. Its publication is an indication of the country's increasing discovery by travellers.

Contacts

If you are interested in women's development programmes, make contact in Sana'a with either the **Yemeni Women's Association** or the UNESCO-backed **Tihama Development Authority** or **Southern Uplands Rural Development Project (SURDU)**.

Books

Carla Makhlouf, *Changing Veils: Women and Modernisation in North Yemen* (Croom Helm, 1979).

Yugoslavia

Most people think of Yugoslavia as one country: no Yugoslav ever does. The state has existed in its present form – a federation of six republics and two "autonomous regions" – since the end of World War II. Its peoples are a dauntingly complex patchwork of religions – Orthodox Christian, Roman Catholic and Muslim – and ethnic nationalities. And for most of them, the old national affiliations remain far more powerful than any unity forged by Marshall Tito or his successors in the centralised Communist government.

With the frenetic pace of change in Eastern Europe, the Western media frequently run articles on the disintegration of the Yugoslav federation. But, as one local journalist put it, the question is less whether it is going to break up but rather how it is going to be put together. The Yugoslav Communist Party is in crisis, and looks set to fracture into its component republics, but that does not mean the country will follow.

Instead, the republics are likely to pursue ever more individual paths. In the north, Slovenia and Croatia, the wealthiest and most progressive republics, are about to hold free elections, and are making overtures towards the EC for their trade; already, both belong to a trading group agreement with Italy, Austria and West Germany. In the centre, Serbia, and to a lesser extent, Montenegro, seem to be falling back upon national chauvinism, becoming ever more isolated as they attempt to maintain their federal power.

The greatest problems are in the south, where Macedonia has virtually Third World poverty, and where the largely Albanian population of Kosovo, an "autonomous region" officially part of Serbia, are in a state of near-revolution. At the time of writing, the Serbian-dominated federal government has had to bring tanks onto the streets of towns and cities in Kosovo. The state's record on civil rights is not good.

Travelling around the country, it is hard to scratch more than the surface of these complexities. You will be aware, however, of Yugoslavia's deep economic crisis. The calendar year of 1989 saw a staggering 4000 percent inflation and in 1990 the government introduced an extreme austerity budget and tied the dinar to the deutschmark. And if you leave the package resorts of the Adriatic – where the tourist industry is based – you will soon sense the differences between the republics. Like Italy, this has something of a north-south divide: the north, with its European culture and industrial muscle, subsidising the peasant farming regions of the south. But the individual nationalisms and religions play an equally significant role. You come up against a very Catholic Alpine kind of patriarchy in Slovenia and Croatia; a Balkan Orthodox brand in Serbia and Montenegro; a traditional, though far from fundamental, Muslim version in Bosnia-Hercegovina and Montenegro.

The everyday problems in travelling will be familiar to anyone with experience of the southern Mediterranean: *machismo* is a rare, unifying aspect of the various Yugoslav cultures. Attitudes vary from the package holiday mentality of the resorts, where women alone are regarded as available (the locals who swoop down on them are known as *galebovi*, or seagulls), to the Islamic and more backward regions inland where you can be treated with gallantry one minute and as if you don't exist the next. A suitably firm response – or stony silence – should be enough to cope with most situations.

The social system, on paper at least, guarantees Yugoslav **women** equal rights and equal wages in the workplace. They have long had paid maternity leave, state creches and nursery schools, all of which help towards economic independence even if they do little to change chauvinistic attitudes. Women make up a large portion of the student population and all careers are supposedly open to them. However, away from the cities, many remain dominated by fathers, brothers and husbands into a life of domestic servitude. Feminism as a movement scarcely exists, though there are isolated academics in some of the university towns of the north – Ljubljana, for example. Their debate, such as it is, concentrates on the need for open discusssion of issues like rape, health, prostitution and sexism in the media and, above all, the need to acknowledge the existence of a separate "women's question" outside the framework of party ideology.

Home from Home in Zagreb

. . . .

Ruth Ayliffe has been living in Zagreb, the capital of Croatia, since 1988. Free from family or material ties, her decision to make this move was largely inspired by the people she had got to know on a couple of previous visits.

Some four years after my first visit to Yugoslavia, I finally decided to stay. It was now or never, I argued to myself – I had no children, mortgage, or animals, it was time to change my job. So I made the move.

I have been living for two years now in Zagreb. A Yugoslav friend there had wanted to share a place with me, and I arrived to find that she had already rented a wonderfully located flat for us in the centre of town.

I was drawn to this country because I loved what I was getting to know of the people I was meeting – they felt immediately like family. But I was happily surprised by the loveliness of Zagreb itself, which proved a refreshing change from south London. For months after my arrival, every time I set foot outside I was thrilled by the great grey-trunked trees shadowing the streets below in green light; by the mercifully mild winter giving way to a hot spring; by the vaguely Austrian architecture; by the musicians playing in the streets, surrounded by people enjoying the sun.

I spent the first months labouring to learn the language – Croatian or *hrvatskosrpski*. Grammatically it works like a mixture of German and Latin, but to begin with you feel it could take a lifetime to master even the essentials. Eventually, however, I did manage to finish a language course at the university, which qualified me to study for a degree here.

Since my arrival I have moved house a couple of times. My first flatmate had to move back to her home town and I lived for a while with a young family, who answered the advertisement I put in the newspapers. I thought this would help me to learn the language better, while causing them minimal stress. And I was also feeling the need to learn basic etiquette: how to cook, what is considered healthy here, and what isn't.

Ways of thinking and expression are surprisingly different from those in Britain. For example, when speaking with friends, the words "please" and "thank you" and "sorry" are not used very often. It seems more important when handing, for example, a drink to a friend, that you say "here you are" than that your friend answers "thank you". I was considered positively irritating when asking for favours: my friends told me it was as if I thought people don't want to help, as though they were not really friends. I didn't need to labour my requests so much, nor to be so grateful.

Living with a family – eating, working, partying and relaxing together – has made me some very firm friends, and taught me volumes about Yugoslavia. On the health angle, a number of bits of knowledge spring to mind. Walking barefoot is considered quite dangerous; any illness following will prove it. Any kind of draught risks the well-being of your kidneys, even at the height of summer in a train carriage full of smoke. This also means that at home a complicated system develops which ensures that two windows on opposite sides of the room are never open at the same time, while travelling in a car can be interesting, there being a strange law governing which windows can be open, and when, to achieve maximum comfort.

Then there are the perceptions that chilled drinks result in sore throats, and that walking about with wet hair is a health hazard. Tea is considered a medicament: if ever I drink it I'm asked if I'm feeling all right. (While I think of it, I would recommend the tea addict to bring her own. There is a wonderful selection of herb and fruit teas, but nothing resembling the tea to which we add milk – the idea of putting milk in tea is quite strange.)

"There is always someone, somewhere, who will watch you and click his tongue and chatter inanities at you as if you were a budgie"

Currently I am living alone, having found a cheap unfurnished flat with the expectation of sharing with a friend who had furniture; however, she needed to change her plans and I ended up in a flat which I really enjoy but need to furnish. Not that this has proved a problem. I have been amazed at how insistent people have been that I borrow their things: fridge, vacuum cleaner, three stoves, crockery, cooking utensils, bed linen, a table; and now I hear a washing machine is on the way!

As far as being a woman here is concerned, I have usually lived in a very male-dominated environment so am perhaps less than averagely sensitive to hassles from men. Some of the issues are all too familiar, like pornography and erotic films and magazines, which are now rife on street stalls. Socially, though, women face a harder situation than in Britain. It seems that by definition men are the ones who watch women – and that they certainly do, regardless of how many days you have been travelling and how grimy and awful you feel.

There is always someone, somewhere, who will watch you and click his tongue and chatter inanities at you as if you were a budgie. The local girls completely ignore the tongue-clickers, and it seems best to follow their example. Entering into conversation with them is usually taken as an invitation to continue with their pestering.

Other social aspects are, on the whole, refreshing. There are quite a few things that people seem to consider beneath their dignity. These include stealing personal property, taking drugs (alcohol is strongly recommended but taking drugs is generally considered pretty stupid) and, most importantly, rape. Aggressive action towards women is not an acceptable way for Yugoslav men to behave and, on that score, now that I know the language better, I feel much safer here than in London.

Men in fact tend to use ridiculous and sometimes clever tactics to try to win a woman, even for a brief relationship. Tales I've heard range from a heart-rending account of childhood misery, to unbelievable generosity, to infinite tenderness, or a long lecture linking health and psychological well-being to sexual pleasure. If your "No" is insistent, you will be treated to the whole lot. I recently heard someone tell me "I won't do anything you don't want", which, if I add the full meaning to his words, ". . . but I will do everything I can to change your mind", could summarise to date my understanding of the attitude of a man who has taken an interest in a woman.

"Being single at my age (28) is viewed by many of my friends here as a temporary illness"

There are geographical variations to this awful stereotype; the more you travel to the south and east, the more certain you can be that some crisis is going to arise. Travelling in Macedonia, men serving me in shops would give me sweets as I paid for my groceries, doing budgie talk in Macedonian. In cafés, if I was alone, I would be treated to a free drink by the owner. One such decided to fall alarmingly in love with me. He went much further than his Croatian counterparts, buying a round of drinks for my rather large bunch of friends, offering us all a boat ride along the coast, and finally bursting into tears as he told me that he had fallen in love and wanted to marry me.

Being single at my age (28) is viewed by many of my friends here as a temporary illness – and one that requires urgent attention. I was introduced to a lot of men in this way before I realised what was going on. Yugoslavs are confirmed dating agents: if there is a hint of a possible relationship, great discussions ensue and both candidates immediately receive any amount of personal advice.

Living in the family, I came across the concept of "man's work" and "woman's work". In that setting, both seemed very happy with their allotted roles; they worked alongside each other, each left the other to get on with their respective jobs, they worked fast and relaxed at length. Recently I have come across a couple whose roles are almost exactly opposite, though again they work alongside each other, doing their own jobs. I also know couples in which the woman is carrying an unbelievably heavy workload, usually because her husband is ill.

I gather I am considered a bit of a funny kind of woman because I'm interested in discovering how things work, I fix things around the house, and I ride a man's bike. No woman among my friends has ever commented on this but the men are always a bit puzzled, and, yes, they do seem to have the attitude that changing a plug is a rather difficult occupation for a woman.

At university, though, a surprising number of girls are studying what, in Britain, would be male-dominated subjects, for instance physics or engineering, and there aren't many clear distinctions between women and men's work in public office. The role of leadership, however, is usually male, and nursing continues to be monopolised by women and medicine by men.

There seem to be more pressing issues at the forefront of most people's minds than women's issues. Inflation is hitting 2000 percent, with wages lagging behind, while politically the country is in a state of flux. And there's also the matter of the day-to-day enjoyment of life. In summer, for example, all cares suddenly seem to be cast aside, as people work out how they will manage to get to the coast to escape the heat of the city. It's a quality I appreciate – that there is always time to be with friends.

TRAVEL NOTES

Languages Serbo-Croat is the main language; regional languages include Slovene and Macedonian. German is widely spoken in the north and Italian along parts of the Adriatic. An increasing number of Yugoslavs, in the larger cities and in the resorts, can speak English

Transport Buses are plentiful and incredibly cheap, but it's best to book ahead as they get very crowded. Hitching is not recommended for the usual reasons, plus the fact that few Yugoslavs are prepared to give lifts to foreigners.

Accommodation Private rooms are the cheapest option. Hotel prices are strictly controlled but more expensive. Campsites, mainly on the coast, tend to be huge and, again, highly organised

Special Problems Harassment from Yugoslav men can be very persistent. Be firm from the beginning and you should manage to avoid aggressive situations. If travelling alone, avoid bars and walking about late at night; even in large cities "nice" women are expected to stay indoors after 11pm.

Guides *The Rough Guide: Yugoslavia* (Harrap Columbus) has recently been overhauled and is now pretty much definitive.

Books

Rebecca West, *Black Lamb and Grey Falcon* (1938; Papermac, 1982). Erudite and all-embracing, this is the definitive work on Yugoslavia before the last war. Sections are included in *The Essential Rebecca West* (Penguin, 1987)

Edith Durham, *Through the Land of the Serbs* (out of print). Edith Durham was one of the most intrepid of women explorers and her numerous adventures through the Balkans in the early years of this century make captivating reading. Her *High Albania* (Virago, 1985) also contains a fair portion on Kosovo.

Stefan K. Pavlowitch, *The Improbable Survivor: Yugoslavia and Her Problems, 1918–1988* (Hurst, 1989). Forthright collection of essays on modern Yugoslavia and its federal crises by a veteran emigré historian.

Eva S. Westerlind, *Carrying the Farm on Her Back: A Portrait of Women in a Yugoslavian Village* (Rainier Books, US, 1989). An excellent study of the lives of women left to manage the village farms while their husbands work as migrant labourers in Northern Europe. Most of it is told in the villagers' own words.

Barbara Jancar-Webster, *Women and Revolution in Yugoslavia, 1941–1945* (Arden Press, US, 1989). Historical study of women's role in the Yugoslavian resistance and revolutionary movement. A clear, if slightly oversimplified, testimony to the courage and endurance of female partisans.

Zaire

With its wild tropical terrain, volcanoes, vast rivers, and totally erratic public services, Zaire is undoubtedly a place for adventure. Besides the river steamers (described below), there's very little in the way of public transport and, if you're not overlanding, you'll find hitching on trucks the only way to get around. As a traveller, however, most people will welcome you with warmth and hospitality – and, provided you don't brush with authority, you will probably escape any first-hand experience of the unrelenting repression that has dominated the country for the past 25 years.

At the head of Zaire's brutal and corrupt regime stands President Mobutu, who, amid a turmoil of secessionist conflicts, seized power in a military coup in 1965. Having done little, if anything, to exploit the country's rich natural resources for the benefit of his people (only five percent of the mainly rural population even have access to clean water), he has amassed a personal fortune to rival any in the world. His nation, meanwhile, has been plunged more and more into debt. Incredibly, though Mobutu's corruption and political ineptitude has led to a degree of embarrassment among his Western backers, the support appears to keep coming. This is partly through a reluctance to see Zaire radicalise and thus change its position as one of the few African nations to take a "moderate" stand on issues such as sanctions against South Africa.

You'll need patience to travel in Zaire, plus a taste for the unexpected and a willingness to put up with humidity and discomfort – bumping along dirt tracks with thirty other people perched on top of boxes on the back of an open truck can be excruciating. But the sheer vastness and unspoiled beauty of the country and people's friendly acceptance of you makes it an adventurer's dream. The capital, Kinshasa, has its fair share of hustlers and it's clearly unwise to walk around alone at night, but sexual harassment doesn't appear to be a general problem.

Most of Zaire's people live in such poverty that the position of women has yet to become a priority issue. As in the rest of Africa, any **women's organisations** tend to be linked to development schemes and/or the Church. However, even these are very few for in the atmosphere of tight political control most efforts at self-help are deemed subversive and therefore swiftly stamped out.

A River Boat Adventure

. . . .

Chris Johnson, who has also written about Chad, visited Zaire as part of a year-long trip through Africa. She has travelled widely, helping to finance her trips by taking photographs for various development agencies.

By the time I reached Zaire I was more than halfway through my African trip. In all the hours of reading, thinking and planning before I set off from Britain, this was the country that I'd felt most anxious about. Something about its size worried me, and the uncertainty of transport; its reputation for being wild and for having to pay constant bribes.

I flew up to Kinshasa from Zimbabwe – my only long flight in Africa. Though preferable, to arrive overland would have taken too long. Kinshasa is a pleasant city combining tree-lined boulevards, streets of elegant, slightly decaying buildings, and a scattering of the modern constructions which house banks and oil companies. The heart of the capital has good music and warm people; but it's the township of Kimbanseke that I remember best.

Kimbanseke is the outermost of the Kinshasa suburbs and it takes the locals one and a half hours to get into the city to work. The morning I went there I awoke to rain, real equatorial rain that battered on the roofs and ran off their corrugations in steady streams. People walking to work pressed all manner of things into service as umbrellas: one man had a polythene bag large enough to cover his entire body; another, a small piece of soggy brown cardboard over his head. The roads out were full of potholes, and when I visited, were reduced to squelching, churned-up mud. But the women who took me around here, and for a day shared their lives with me, were wonderful. Like most women in Kimbanseke, they are traders, and photographing in the market was enormous fun. Everyone wanted to be in on the act, and there was much extravagant posturing, clapping and laughter.

From Kinshasa I planned to take the legendary river boat north to Lisala. Buying the ticket proved an experience in itself. The road down to the port was lined with women selling things: baskets of huge squirming snails; smoked fish; and gruesome smoked monkeys which looked horribly human, like the blackened bodies of tiny burnt babies. The boat office was inside the port and not at all easy to find but eventually someone rescued me and led me through the docks, past huge logs being unloaded, to the right building. I had intended to treat myself to a first-class ticket, which, at £25 for the eleven-day trip, including three meals a day, hardly seemed extravagant. However, all first-class tickets were booked, so it was to be eight pounds for second-class, including one meal a day. Only advance reservations were being taken and after watching my name written down on a torn off scrap of paper, I was told to return at a later date. Needless to say, I didn't feel too optimistic.

I returned on the appointed day to find a loose crowd already thronging the entrance to the ticket office, where a man and a woman sat doing very little. The woman was tall and looked magnificent. Like many Zairois women, she wore a richly coloured Java print, one length of material forming a wrap-around skirt, another making the blouse and the third being tied around the head turban-style.

I tried to find out what was happening. "Wait a moment." It could be a long wait. I propped myself up against the wall and got out my book. All around me people glistened with sweat, and in the damp heat I felt I was melting away. Suddenly someone took pity on me and waved me inside, pointing to a chair: they must have thought a white female belonged to a delicate species, and for once I was happy to take advantage of the judgement. However, it didn't signify any progress with regard to the ticket. I got out my book again. The man in the corner wrote out the

first-class tickets at the rate of one every ten minutes. The woman laughed and chatted with people.

Eventually someone emerged out of a back room bearing a scrap of paper – the reservation from my previous visit – and I was directed to another office where, after another long wait, someone came along, looked at my bit of paper, disappeared into an office and, to my surprise, produced a ticket. As I emerged back into the hall one man, looking very surprised, said "Fini?" Clearly people don't usually get served so quickly.

"But there was never any shortage of people to talk to and no problems being a woman travelling alone – apart from parrying the endless questions about why I wasn't married and had no children"

I left Kinshasa the next day. There are no roads through this part of Zaire, so unless you can afford to fly the river is the only form of transport. It forms the main link from the south to the north of Zaire and to the Central African Republic and, if you take it through to Kisangani, to the east. Apart from three American women volunteers who joined the boat at Mbandaka (about halfway) I was the only white person on board. But there was never any shortage of people to talk to and no problems being a woman travelling alone – apart from parrying the endless questions about why I wasn't married and had no children. I exchanged English lessons for ones in Lingala, read, wrote and watched the world go by.

The next eleven days were among the best of my entire African trip, chugging gently along in the hot sunshine on top of one of the flat-roofed barges which made up our convoy. There were six barges in all, each lashed to the main boat, the *Colonel Tshatshi*, which took up the rear, pushing four barges in front with a further two lashed along its left-hand side. This huge square main vessel was reserved for first-class passengers; second-class like me got the top deck of the barges, and third-class the bottom deck or any corner they could find.

In fact the roof was by far the best place to be. There must have been well over a thousand passengers below and you couldn't move without stepping over someone. With metal doors and wire mesh on the windows, the cabins were like cages and the toilets were soon foul. But up on the roof it was clean, quiet and peaceful. I looked out towards the hills patterned with trees sloping down to the river, where the occasional village nestled among palm trees at the water's edge. I watched a vast amount of vegetation floating by – great rafts of grass and water-lilies, some with beautiful purple flowers. At one stage a rainbow, formed in a fine gauze of cloud, almost completely encircled the sun. The dominant motion was not that of the boat but of the river, flowing swiftly past while we seemed to remain motionless.

As we progressed upstream the scenery changed, becoming flatter and more jungley until it gave way to real equatorial rainforest, dripping with creepers. A full-scale market had sprung up on board, selling absolutely everything: plastic bowls, mugs, plates, waste paper bins; metal buckets and cooking pots; all kinds of food; clothes, new and second hand; and, as so often in Africa, all kinds of pills – out of date ones, ones that should be on prescription, ones that have been banned. On the roof of an adjacent barge a man was cutting hair; below, another man was busy decanting salt from a sack into small polythene bags – everything gets split up into smaller quantities here and even biscuits are sold individually as well as by the packet. Next to the salt vendor a man sat at a small table selling cigarettes, a single box of matches, orange plastic mugs, biscuits, mosquito coils and chicken stew. A canoe

paddled alongside the boat, its occupants buying bread, salt and beer, and selling fish which was taken straight into a refrigerated room at the bottom of the boat to be eventually taken back to Kinshasa. Someone else paddled up to sell palm wine, a white, cloudy liquid, slightly alcoholic and still fermenting.

For people living along the river, the boat is the only link with the outside world. Each time we passed a village dozens of canoes would paddle out to meet us and buy and sell – I counted as many as sixty tied up alongside us. It was a noisy, colourful scene as everyone struggled to keep the canoes steady in the slipstream of the boat. Both men and women paddled and there were several women-only boats, their occupants strong and full of laughter as they negotiated their canoes alongside, waving fish, or bunches of bananas, high in the air.

"A ferocious storm broke, the wind rose, tossing the trees and sending flecks of white foam scudding across the water . . . we retreated to the shelter of the bank, running aground in the process"

To the local people on board, the most exciting event of the trip was when, just after dark, we passed the other steamer on its way back to Kinshasa. It was bigger and even more crowded than our boat. Everyone was out on the roofs or hanging over the sides, to the extent that one of the barges looked in imminent danger of tipping over. Very slowly we drew alongside, to the accompaniment of great cheers. Then, as we touched, an even louder cheer went up and people leaped from boat to boat, embracing each other. This went on for some time, until finally our departure was heralded by much horn-blowing which sent the gathered multitude into a frenzy of shouting, waving, embracing, and jumping up and down on the roof.

By now we were right on the Equator and it was fearfully hot and humid. Finally, a ferocious storm broke, the wind rose, tossing the trees and sending flecks of white foam scudding across the water. Alongside us men and women in dugout canoes bailed frantically; we retreated to the shelter of the bank, running aground in the process. Driven inside, we went down to the bar on the front of the boat. As we pulled into a small village and the searchlights lit up the colourful crowd the wind tugged at the trees and the storm unleashed its fury once again. Through an open window a solitary palm was lit up in the night, lashed by the wind. The rain ran in through the many holes in the roof, down the rusty cream paintwork and along the wooden floor. The wild vibrant energy of the night ran through the people sitting at tables, drinking beer, talking. Music played loudly, someone shook out the rhythm on a pair of rattles and a lone dancer gyrated. Only later when the gale abated and the fronds of the palm hung limply down its trunk did we turn and go to bed. Some time in the night the boat began to move again.

The final evening on the river was magical. A huge sun hung briefly in the sky, then dropped swiftly over the horizon. It was 11.30pm before we docked at Lisala and midnight before I could finally make my way down to the lower deck, across the barges and through the chaos of people trying to get on or off the boat. José, a Zairois trader I'd met on the boat, had assigned a young lad to escort me to the local hotel. I followed him up the steep narrow path, the stars doing little to relieve the blackness of the night. The hotel proved to be firmly shut for the night but, as always in Africa, he knew someone who would put me up.

TRAVEL NOTES

Languages Lingala and French, the last being the official government language, plus Swahili and a few regional languages.

Transport Public transport is sparse and erratic – there's only one substantial tarred road – so hitching for a fee is widely accepted and – being usually on a lorry with a crowd of other people – generally safe. A journey by river boat is not to be missed.

Accommodation Like everything, most hotels and guesthouses are cheap and basic. In remote areas you can sometimes stay in mission stations; the mission guesthouse in Kinshasa is recommended for being safe and central.

Special Problems Harassment, apart from occasional hustling for money, doesn't appear to be a problem. Bring all your own supplies of tampons, contraceptives, medicaments etc, as such items are expensive and in short supply.

Guides *Central Africa: A Travel Survival Kit* (Lonely Planet) has a reasonable section on Zaire; the chapter in *Africa on a Shoestring* (Lonely Planet), however, is at present more up-to-date and helpful.

Contacts

We have only managed to trace one women's organisation, the **Women's Association of Kibanguist Church**, PO Box 7069, Kinshasa, whose main aim is to encourage women to participate in development projects.

Special thanks to Chris Johnson for her contribution to the introduction.

Zambia

$\bullet \quad \bullet \quad \bullet \quad \bullet \quad \bullet \quad \bullet \quad \bullet \quad \bullet \quad \bullet \quad \bullet \quad \bullet \quad \bullet \quad \bullet \quad \bullet \quad \bullet \quad \bullet$

Erratic transport, the increasing threat of robbery, and a paranoid military, combine to make Zambia one of the more hazardous African countries to explore. As so often there is an organised tourist circuit, in this case focusing on a handful of developed game parks and the famous Victoria Falls. But this has little to do with the "real Zambia", a chaotic nation of escalating poverty, drought, food shortages, rising crime and other problems – many of them stemming from the constant process of internal migration.

Since gaining independence n 1964, Zambia has become the most urbanised of African nations, with nearly half of the population living in towns. Rural production has been consistently neglected in favour of urban/industrial development, leaving the countryside thinly populated by a predominance of women – as chief food producers – and old men and children. This imbalance, coupled with the fallen price of Zambia's main export, copper, lies at the heart of the country's economic crisis.

Added to the problems of ecomonic turmoil are the consequences of the wars of liberation in the region. First Smith in Zimbabwe and then Botha in South Africa carried out the odd bombing raid on towns and bridges in Zambia to try and dissuade President Kaunda from supporting his southern neighbours' struggles for independence. The police and military already have a high profile to curb criminal activities, but it is these acts of sabotage that lie behind the pervasive fear of "spies" or "suspicious characters" which so many travellers comment on. It is to be hoped that a change of events in South Africa will mean transformation here, too.

Women travelling alone in Zambia, however, don't appear to encounter any particular problems – and sexual harassment of foreigners seems virtually unknown. It is the physical limitations that make travel difficult: the erratic bus services, slow trains and dearth of vehicles off the beaten track. From the point of view of people's acceptance of you, being a woman may well even prove an advantage.

In his many speeches on the virtues of humanism, President Kaunda talks continually of a "man-centred" society. Not deliberately making a sexist statement, he nevertheless sums up the position of Zambian women. Traditional attitudes prevail, as does the traditional division of labour. Despite being expected to feed their families and take care of the children, only seven percent of women are in waged employment; they have to try and survive by "informal" activities such as marketeering, beer-brewing, and to some extent prostitution. Discriminatory laws, unchanged since the days of British colonialism, determine that a woman's access to jobs, credit, contraception is controlled by her "guardian" – her husband, brother, father, uncle – and even widows are denied access to their dead husband's estate.

Women who challenge this state of affairs are more often than not branded as "promoters of Western imperialist thinking". However, things are slowly changing. Apart from the apparently ineffectual UNIP Women's League (a division of the national party), there are no political **women's organisations**. But women have an increasingly high profile in the Church, are widely respected as prophets and healers, and there is a growing movement, at least among the educated middle class, to appreciate women's central role in the development process.

In Search of Yangumwila Falls

· · · · · · · · · · · ·

Ilse Mwanza works as a Research Affiliation Officer at the University of Zambia in Lusaka, where she moved in 1968 with her Zambian husband. Her quest in search of the Yangumwila Falls formed part of a two-month trip to the northern provinces, where she was mainly visiting researchers in the field.

Nobody had ever heard of the Yangumwila Falls. I just happened to be travelling south from Nsumbu National Park, where I had spent some days exploring the beautiful countryside around Lake Tanganyika, and, noting these falls on the map, decided to see them on the way. It was still the dry season, so I thought it wouldn't be too difficult.

Rolling into Mporokoso in my old Landrover, I first went to the police station to announce my presence and ask directions. I asked five different police officers, but all claimed to be new to the area and ignorant of such obscure places. They directed me to the nearest mission station on the outskirts of town. Here the Reverend Sikazwe was very kind; he asked his family, his colleagues, even the teacher of the school next door, but nobody knew anything about waterfalls. However, he remembered an old retired teacher from the Njalamimba area who lived nearby and accompanied me to his house.

"Anything out of the ordinary like a mzungu (white) woman travelling alone in the bush is treated with great caution"

Mr Chipopola was also most kind. We sat down on his favourite bench under a big mango tree and discussed my strange request. Why would I want to see these falls, he wondered? I explained that I was from the University of Zambia and keen to know more about the country, and that in over twenty years of living in Zambia I had yet to explore his home area. He agreed that this was a serious shortcoming, but it still didn't explain my interest in waterfalls. Had I any relatives there? I had to disappoint him. Being German by origin and married to a Zambian from the Eastern Province as my name implied (Zambian names are area-specific) – this was highly unlikely. He probed further. So why did I want to go to the falls area? People in Zambia have been exhorted so often to look out for suspicious characters, in the wake of nasty experiences with South African raids, that anyone out of the ordinary, like a *mzungu* (white) woman travelling alone in the bush, is treated with great caution.

I went on to explain how my job at the university was to advise researchers and that I needed to find out about the geological nature of scarp environments; that my description of remote scenic places might even perhaps attract tourists to the region. "Ah, tourists are going to come! Very good." And he finally told me that the Lupupa Falls, marked close to Yangumwila on the map, weren't very far from Njalamimba, from where Headman Chilatu would be able to direct me. He

gave me a note for the Headman and, pointing me in the right direction, wished me well.

After some stopping to ask the way, I eventually found the "clearly-marked track" beyond Njalamimba which led to Chilatu's. The track was so overgrown that I got no further than the end of the village. Screeching to a halt, I looked around helplessly, to be instantly surrounded by a crowd of children. No one understood my poor Nyanja (the language of Eastern Zambia), but someone ran off to return with an adult.

Mr Musonda, it turned out, was the greatest possible gift to travellers. Having once been the house-servant of *mzungu* teachers, he was experienced in their peculiar ways. He knew all about waterfalls, having sometimes accompanied his *bwanas* to visit them. But the Yangumwila Falls? Ah, no. They were a mystery.

By now it was late afternoon. How far at least were the Lupupa Falls? Not far. Mr Musonda willingly agreed to come along and show me the way. He dashed off to tell his wife and came back in a flash – no blanket, no nothing. Ah well, I always carry a spare sleeping bag and enough food, and off we went, through the thicket that proved to be the village exit, along various tracks, across some cassava fields to a huddle of huts that proved to be Chilatu's.

Children scampered in all directions. It later transpired that my Landrover had been mistaken for that of the game-scout who sometimes came in search of poachers, and the children were quickly sent to hide the game-meat that was being smoke-dried. The poor things reappeared with slightly scorched fingers. Headman Chilatu wasn't home; he had gone to visit a relative in town nine months ago! Never mind. After Mr Musonda had shown Mr Chipopola's note and explained my presence, I was warmly welcomed by Chilatu's three wives. The note read: "Please help Mama in her work to see Lupupa Falls. Show her the place. She will be very much pleased to be introduced to that place. She has been sent by the Government. Your brother Chipopola."

It was almost dark by now and there was no question of going on to the Falls, an hour's hike away, so we asked to stay the night. Immediately, one of the Mrs Chilatus hurried to the granary to get fingermillet, another chased the children to fetch more firewood and water, and the third graciously offered us some of their wild pigmeat for dinner. I have seldom eaten so well and, in return, gave them coffee and sugar – for them as rare a treat as wild pig is for me.

"After much talk about which Mrs Chilatu I should stay with, the one with the least children won"

We sat around the fire, talking about our different ways of life, with Mr Musonda, the only man around, acting as interpreter. Most homesteads in this region are female-headed due to male labour migration. Because Chilatu's lies so far off the beaten track, in a heavily wooded and hilly area of Northern province which still has a fair amount of game, the three women can only work small fields. They grow cassava and fingermillet as a staple, some pumpkins and rape as vegetables, and beans as a cash crop. The homestead is surrounded by mango and banana trees. They have to *kraal* (fence with thornbushes) their fields to protect the crops from game, especially wild pigs. The latter are trapped by making an opening in the *kraal* and digging a pit spiked with sharpened stakes. Any surplus game-meat is sold or bartered.

Sometimes the women go into the bush to collect wild arrowroot, a thickener for groundnut paste, much sought after in the 64km-distant Mporokoso *boma*, the nearest market and store. Unfortunately, on leaving nine months ago, Mr Chilatu had locked up his bicycle so the family had no access to market at that moment. The children had to walk 26km to the nearest school, too, where they stayed during the week, fending for themselves from the age of seven. Equipped with cassava roots and dried meat, they set off from home on Sunday afternoons to return the following Saturday morning. On top of doing their own cooking and cleaning at school, they also have to help with chores in the house and fields at weekends or, in the case of boys, go off for a spot of bird or rodent hunting. This week the children hadn't gone. They hadn't felt like making the long trek and the mothers hadn't pressed them. Their school education was elementary in the strictest sense of the word and quite irrelevant to the lives they lived. What good to learn English and maths if they were simply destined to follow in the footsteps of their mothers? No one in living memory had ever heard of anyone from Njalamimba progressing even to secondary school, the only way out of village existence.

Discussion finally came round to where we were going to sleep. Mr Musonda was tucked in with the boys. My suggestion of sleeping, as usual, in the rooftop tent on top of my Landrover was dismissed outright as improper and far too dangerous on account of all the spirits and animals that lurk around at night. After much talk about which Mrs Chilatu I should stay with, the one with the least children won. She had only three to share her bed: a mat on the floor with a *chitenge* cloth as cover.

I was given the part of the room which contained bags of beans and arrowroot awaiting transport to market. With a little rearranging of bags by the light of a paraffin lamp (a vaseline jar filled with paraffin with a twisted cloth for a wick), I was able to spread out my sleeping bag. Not that I could go to sleep yet! My hosting Mrs Chilatu still had to tend the meat, bubbling in two pots on a paraffin stove to prevent spoilage. We drank more coffee and smiled a lot, no longer able to communicate through words, while the three children slept. The youngest, ill I suspected with malaria, kept waking up and crying, and when the light finally went out the rats appeared, busy working their way into the beans. I didn't care any longer and slept.

Next morning, after another meal of millet and pork, while I dished out bread and jam, we set out for the Lupupa Falls. I felt just like the Pied Piper having about twenty children in tow in single file. I was not only shown the way to the Falls, but learned how branches for *chitemene* fields (an age-old slash and burn system) are lopped off trees, what pig traps look like, and how to spot game tracks. We saw zebra and antelope spoor, but no sign of animals.

An hour's hiking took us to the river just above the Falls. Really more of a stream, the Mukubwe drops off a steep cliff in bridal veil fashion for about a hundred metres, deep down into where a circular pool has been formed, surrounded by dense rainforest, before the water disappears, a silver band between the bends of the gorge. I could make out hornbills and swallows, swifts and starlings, gyrating above the pool, and a troop of baboons that had come to drink. We all sat and watched the scenery. There was no way down.

I had asked about the Yangumwila Falls again and again without success so, with Mr Musonda quite happy to accompany me further, we decided to explore the Mumbuluma Falls instead. Back we went to the Njalamimba turn-off to pick up the Landrover.

We parked the car where others had obviously parked before us and followed a footpath along the Luangwa river, which rushes toward the Falls in a series of little rapids and cascades, divided by wooded islands. The Mumbuluma were much wider than I'd expected and about forty metres deep, surrounded by rainforest. The contrast of rushing white water fringed with dark green foliage in an otherwise yellow-brown savanna landscape is quite startling. With only birds for company, the area seemed like a perfect place for camping, but I was still determinedly looking for the elusive Yangumwila Falls and so, after a brief walk round, we resumed our original quest.

"Dense reeds now covered the warthog holes and dismembered trees; the track was totally overgrown"

We bumped along for a time through the forest reserve, narrowly avoiding big potholes and fallen logs, as the road got progressively worse. Dense reeds now covered the warthog holes and dismembered trees; the track was totally overgrown. Just as I was about to give up, Mr Musonda detected another bit of road, so we ploughed on, he running ahead of the car with me bumping after him until we miraculously emerged into open grassland. By now the sun was sinking fast – darkness always falls quickly in Africa – but the assumed proximity of our goal spurred us on. We kept going and with the last light reached a riverine forest, which I took to be that of the Itabu, on which the Falls appeared on the map. I could hear a gurgling brook and even the sound of falling water not too far away. We had made it, we thought, and pitched camp in a clearing.

Next morning we set off on foot to find the Falls. Sound becomes strangely magnified at night and what I had assumed to be the main waterfalls turned out to be only a small rapid. For two hours we walked further upstream, following poachers' tracks along the river. No sign of any falls. The countryside was flat, unlikely to contain cliffs or faults. The river ran quietly between mosses and shrubs. The air was still and the sun getting hot. Thinking the Falls might instead be downstream, we eventually turned back the way we'd come, towards the car.

I should have known better than to try to trace the river on four wheels! Half an hour out of camp I suddenly found myself in wet grassland, up to the axles in black-cotton soil, the kind of muck found in many African wetland areas and which can trap even elephants. It was no use struggling or revving the engine; we would just sink deeper. We were truly stuck, the nearest populated area about a day's walk away. There was nothing else to do but get to work: cut down branches, unload the car, jack it up and push the branches under the wheels. Slowly, very slowly, we inched the Landrover out of the mud. The sun was beating down and I kept pouring water over our heads to prevent dehydration and sunstroke. After five hours of sweating labour, plagued by heat and ants, the vehicle jumped with a last desperate lurch and was free. Was it any wonder that I gave up looking for the Yangumwila Falls?

TRAVEL NOTES

Languages A variety of tribal languages according to region, though English is still the official language and widely spoken.

Transport Slow and erratic; for overlanders, the shortage of spare parts, including tyres, is a permanent problem. Though not necessarily safe, hitching is easy if you don't mind long waits. There is a limited and similarly unpredictable train service.

Accommodation There are few budget hotels in towns though most, according to Ilse Mwanza, are "real dumps". In provincial or district centres, council rest houses sometimes have space, as do missions or secondary schools.

Special Problems Many basic consumer goods, including medicaments, are in short supply so it's important to bring your own. Avoid brushing with officialdom or taking photographs of public buildings. Police and army alike are obsessed with spies and can be very unpleasant.

Guide *Africa on a Shoestring* (Lonely Planet) includes a reliable section on Zambia.

Contacts

Organisation of University Women, PO Box 32379, Lusaka. A resource base for data and research findings on women, also responsible for the **Women's Development Network** which helps to co-ordinate women's organisations around the country.

It may also be worth getting in touch with the **UNIP Women's League**, Freedom House, PO Box 30302, Lusaka.

Books

Barbara Rogers, *The Domestication of Women* (Kogan Page, 1980). By now classic account of missionary and aid-agency influences on women's position in the development process with many examples from Zambia.

Marcia Wright, *Women in Peril: Life Stories of Four Captives* (NECZAM/Institute for African Studies, Zambia, 1984). Four old women tell of their experiences of slavery.

Many thanks to Ilse Mwanza for her contribution to the introduction and Travel Notes.

Zimbabwe

A s Zimbabwe celebrates ten years of independent, democratic rule, the internal conflict which dogged its early years appears to be over – at least for the moment. Caution is still recommended for travellers in the northwest of the country; otherwise all former trouble spots are reportedly safe. And with its "free spirit", beautiful scenery, great music and easy transport, Zimbabwe is a highly enjoyable part of Africa to explore.

Africa's youngest nation, Zimbabwe only gained independence in

1980, after a long, hard war of liberation from white minority rule. Despite overwhelming popular support for Robert Mugabe's ZANU party, shown in his landslide victory in the country's first national elections, the early years of independence saw several isolated but extremely bloody outbreaks of violence, stemming from persistent tension between ZANU and the main opposition party, ZAPU, led by Joshua Nkomo.

Fuelled by inter-tribal rivalry between the Shona (largely supporters of ZANU) and the minority Ndebele (who mainly support ZAPU), political disagreements were further worsened by intense personal animosity between the two leaders. However, tensions have been greatly reduced by a Unity Agreement, signed by both parties in January 1988. Moves like this and the later abolition of the twenty seats guaranteed to the whites in government are all part of Mugabe's long-term plan to transform Zimbabwe into a one-party state. Given the country's political complexity, this seems, at least in the short term, a pragmatic rather than autocratic solution.

British travellers will find an odd familiarity in many aspects of the country's infrastructure – the legacy of a century and a half of colonial history. Perhaps more surprising, for white travellers, is the almost total lack of animosity from the black majority: this is a hugely friendly and hospitable country. The most negative aspect is in the continued racism of white Zimbabweans; though you'll find this population, too, outgoing and generous, the hospitality or lifts that they offer too frequently carry penalties in the form of listening to impassioned racist monologues.

In the wake of a war in which **women** fought equally and as bravely as men, the government has made strident efforts to guarantee the equality of the sexes in society. Several laws have been passed to this end, the most significant being the Legal Age of Majority Act whereby a woman, like her male counterpart, ceases being a minor at eighteen. However, laws have limitations and women have a hard time battling against centuries of tradition and custom. The Ministry of Community Development and Women's Affairs has made inroads through its focus on literacy and self-help projects in rural areas, apparently met with great enthusiasm by the women concerned, and various other organisations encourage income-generating projects with the aim of strengthening women's economic power. But the tendency is still to concentrate on traditional home-based activities, which do little to change fundamental attitudes about women's inferiority. Signs of a growing Women's Movement, and continuing government commitment, indicate the possibility of much deeper, lasting changes in the future.

To Harare by Truck

. . . .

After a spell of casual work in London, Jo Wells and her friend Emma, both in their early twenties, visited Zimbabwe as part of a low-budget trip to Africa. Five months later they returned, "different people"; Jo is now studying African history, while Emma is using her experience in textile design.

I knew Zimbabwe would be good when we arrived at Lilongwe. By this point the oppression of Malawi and its people was getting to us, and the Africans we met from Zimbabwe and Zambia seemed to have a free spirit in comparison. Having originally decided to fly to Harare, we eventually opted for a lift through Zambia with an obliging trucking company. This route was the long way round; most overlanders cut through Mozambique, but Emma and I weren't interested in challenging our bravado by facing that sad, war-torn country amid a barrage of armoured vehicles. Besides, we hoped our passage via Zambia would enlighten us on the sheer massiveness of the continent.

Our driver, aptly named Steady, had the job of transporting a gigantic oil container each week from Harare to northern Malawi. We had caught him on his return run, so he was inclined to travel at a leisurely pace. We spent three days in his truck, sleeping, eating, talking, and all the while watching the vast African landscape spread out before us. I suppose as two white women we were a bit of a novelty, sitting up there in the cab of a young black trucker, and therefore bound to generate attention as Steady stopped at small villages to trade packets of soap powder or bottles of Malawi gin. But everywhere people came out to greet us with the never-ending warm friendliness of the Africans; men and women alike called out "sisters, you're welcome!"

"It was as if we'd left the so-called Third World and crossed back into the West again"

Zambia is a poor country, its people crying out for essentials like bread, meat and vegetables. Throughout the country, we heard endless tales of crime, mainly theft, and every Zambian we met was a "businessman", indulging in various petty dealings simply to earn a crust. Despite all this, we found people to be generous, kind and trustworthy, guidebook rantings about their "dodginess" to be taken with a pinch of salt.

After a three-day diet of Pepsi and popcorn, and the potholed Zambian roads, it was a relief to cross the Zambezi into Zimbabwe. The contrast is remarkable, the first thing we noticed being the abundance of wildlife – baboons careering around the customs buildings and large grey elephants casually strolling in the background. Poor old Zambia is a devastated place. Nothing has been able to restrain the ruthlessness of the poachers who have deprived the countryside of its natural population. There's not even a bird in the sky. The richness of Zimbabwe is luxurious; the roads are straight and smooth and even have cars on them, but wait . . . the people in these cars have white skin.

We stopped at a motel to find ourselves in the grip of yet another culture shock: toasted cheese sandwiches and hamburgers on the menu. It was as if we had left the so-called Third World and crossed back into the West again. Whites were very much in evidence with their big, affluent cars, grand-looking farmhouses, and money. I turned to Steady: "What's happening here? Hasn't the situation changed between black and white since independence?" "Oh," smiles Steady, "we're all friends now; you'll see soon enough." I did see, that night in fact. It takes a while for bad memories to die.

We decided to spend the night outside Harare, so we could arrive fresh and clean in the morning. The clientele of the motel's restaurant was African, an environment in which we had begun to feel at home. As I sat there, wilting over my soup, an old man came over and began to mutter at me in Shona. Being exhausted, I hadn't the energy to try and be enthused by his attention and thought he was drunk. Before I knew it, he was abusing me in English: "White trash, scum," he said. Steady immediately leapt up and led him outside.

It was the first time that I had been insulted on racial grounds. It didn't offend me. On the contrary, I felt fortunate to have avoided it for so long. Steady and the manageress of the restaurant were unbearably apologetic over the whole scene, as I wished desperately that I didn't belong to the race that provoked these people to behave in this way.

The next morning we entered Harare, which, with its colonial mansions and wide tree-lined avenues, again exuded an air of comfort and wealth. This spacious city with its modern planned centre was more what I'd expect of Australia. We began our stay at the Youth Hostel, a fusty old house complete with batty old warden, clinging to her lost youth in Yorkshire with the aid of a few dusty mementoes. Our fellow travellers here were unfortunately fairly obnoxious, all white, and mostly consisting of strapping Afrikaaner women "doing Africa".

To their obvious disapproval, we managed to evade their company that first night by escaping to a township outside the city, accompanied by the hostel cleaner, Geoffrey, and his band of musicians.

"The entry of two whites into the crowded enclosure was an event in itself"

The township of Chitungwiza lies about thirty kilometres from the centre of Harare. Aesthetically, it's a depressing hole, the portaloo-type dwellings bearing no relation to the leafy avenues of Harare. However, despite its inaccessibility by public transport, the place is teeming with atmosphere and undoubtedly the capital's life blood.

It was Sunday afternoon and Geoffrey and his crew were due to perform an eight-hour marathon in the local beerhall. The entry of two whites into the crowded enclosure was an event in itself. We stepped out of the van into silence as people turned in genuine astonishment. Feeling uneasy, I almost climbed back in but a middle-aged woman waddled up and with drunken assertiveness purred "Relax, sisters. You're welcome." From then on we had the time of our lives. Never before had I commanded so much attention; in eight hours there wasn't a minute to collect my thoughts, let alone talk to Emma, though she too seemed to be enjoying herself.

The African crowd at a social gathering is wonderfully uninhibited, no doubt partly due to the endless buckets of *Chibuku* (African beer) that they pour down their throats. People, men and women alike, certainly know how

to "get on down". As the band played a steady rhumba, I could have watched those women swing their hips around for hours, but there were friends to be made, beers to be drunk and spliffs to be smoked.

As night set in it got pretty cold, for this was wintertime below the equator, and we gratefully accepted Geoffrey's offer to take us to warm up at his family's home. Inside the single-storey house it was warm and cosy; people sat in the living room watching *Dynasty* on a large colour television while Geoffrey's mother leapt up to fetch us tea and biscuits. We were introduced to a sister, Gladys, who worked in the city for Air Zimbabwe. Aged around nineteen, her ambition was to save up all her money and emigrate to Dallas the following year. "It's so much better there for black people," she told us, "They can earn a lot and buy nice houses." It was a bizarre dream – she in fact knew no-one who had visited America.

After we returned to the Youth Hostel, I found time to collect my muddled thoughts. This experience of Zimbabwe had touched me in a curious way. Eight years since independence, the persevering divide between races was still very much in evidence and, to a European, appeared both antiquated and crude. I remember my hackles rising when a former South African (intelligent) friend of mine once said: "A revolution could never succeed in South Africa because all the servants who work for the wealthy whites have seen the scope of money. Everyone wants their piece of the cake, even if it means depriving someone else . . ." The occasion in Chitungwiza and Gladys's words rang out in my mind. If there's one thing about Zimbabwe, it makes you think.

Caught Between Two Worlds

. . . .

Kate Kellaway spent three and a half years living as a schoolteacher in Zimbabwe. After a painful period of readjustment, she has finally settled back in London where she works for _The Observer_ newspaper.

Independence in Zimbabwe has meant important legal gains for women. There is a Ministry of Women's Affairs, several women's groups and a steady, growing interest in the Women's Movement. But it is hard to connect these facts to the women I've known and the girls I've taught in Zimbabwe. Only a small educated minority are active in women's affairs – or able to protest – and it is still the exceptional woman who can define her oppression.

The closest I came to Zimbabwean women was when I was living and teaching in St Mary's, a black township outside Harare. The difference between Harare the town and the Harare townships, now euphemistically renamed "high-density suburbs", is so extreme that they shouldn't really share the same name. The luxurious "low-density" suburbs of Zimbabwe's capital are reminiscent of Britain's wealthy stockbroker belt, the style an inheritance of colonialism. The townships, made up of vast complexes of tiny houses, are crowded with people deprived of adequate amenities, a colonial inheritance of another kind.

When I went to live with a family in St Mary's, I was congratulating myself on breaking away from the "British" Zimbabwe to experience the "real thing". But it is terrible to make of someone else's hardship an interesting experience for yourself. Besides it wasn't as simple as that. I was there because it was the home of Moses, my boyfriend. Throughout my stay I felt a conflict between accepting hospitality and looking at what was around me.

St Mary's is the oldest of Chitungwiza townships, 25 miles from Harare yet still without electricity. Imagine row upon row of ramshackle houses, squashed together between miles of dusty streets. You are surrounded by people all day long. There are so many babies that at any given moment one will be crying. Cocks crow dementedly in the middle of the night.

"I wasn't really lazy so much as frightened by the routine of housework that shaped the women's day"

Before I got a job at the local township school my days were spent at home with the women. Moses' sister, Rutendo, had three little girls. She got pregnant at fourteen, her husband treated her badly, and she was glad to be home again. Unlike many women in her position she managed to get custody of the children, whom she brings up with her mother. Moses' father worked far away and, apart from a brother, it was a predominantly female community. Moses' mother was a professional mother. She was my Zimbabwean mother for a while: she accepted me, welcomed and joked with me, and tried in every way to make me feel at home.

I didn't speak much Shona then, just enough to say a few essential things like "Ndipeiwo mutsvairo" (Give me the broom) or "Ndine usimbe" (I'm lazy) or "Ndaguta" (I'm full). I wasn't really lazy so much as frightened by the routine of housework that shaped the women's day. Zimbabwean women keep their houses immaculately clean, but in St Mary's it was an unending fight against dust and dirty feet. Rutendo would rise at dawn and sweep the yard with a broom made of twigs, making beautiful patterns in the dust. Moses' second sister, Musafare, applied strong-smelling wax polish to the kitchen and dining-room floor. The day was punctuated by a trickle of water as children, clothes, floors, pots, shelves, everything, was washed.

Most tasks involved bending. I picture Rutendo and Musafare bending from the hip. Rutendo taught me how to cook *nhopi*, a delicious pumpkin porridge made with peanut butter. She showed me how to scour a pot with sand and how to cook *sadza* – not easy over a wood fire, as it becomes stiff and hard to stir. Zimbabwean women have good strong arms; I felt puny and ridiculous struggling to stir a pot of *sadza* for fifteen, my eyes streaming with tears from the smoke. "Crying for *sadza*", Rutendo used to call it.

"What was I doing here ?.. What sort of image was I trying to create with all this knitting, sewing and cooking of sadza?"

I was the only *murungu* (white) in the township but people soon became openly friendly, shouting greetings when I passed. The men were often easier to talk to, partly because they spoke more English. I also think they felt a freedom to talk to me about subjects they wouldn't discuss with their own women.

One day Rutendo and I went to see her sister, Elizabeth. She was very pregnant – so pregnant it would have been tactless to ask when the baby was coming – and explained that she wanted to be a policewoman after the child was born but her husband was against it. She asked me to check that her application form was correctly filled in. (Later she became a policewoman and her husband beat her up because of it.)

I went to talk to Rutendo in the kitchen:

"Matimati," I stated.

"Matimati," Rutendo confirmed.

"Mafuta ekubikisa?" I asked.

"Yes, cooking oil," said Ruteno, adding it to the pan. In the small black saucepan the *sadza* began to thicken. Using the *mugoti*, a special stick, I stirred. Rutendo was delighted: "I'll tell Moses you are a good housewife now."

Later we sat outside Elizabeth's house, eating *sadza* and sour milk. The sun burnt my calves. I surveyed my pink espadrilles and the pumpkin leaves swaying in the breeze and was suddenly filled with panic. What was I doing here? What was life like for these women? I watched one of them idly stitching a border of little green checks onto a loosely woven yellow tablecloth. "Have a go," she indicated, thrusting the material into my hands. I didn't, afraid of ruining it or showing myself up as an inept needlewoman.

What sort of image was I trying to create with all this knitting, sewing, and cooking of *sadza*? By the time I reached home I felt exhausted from the strain of trying to communicate without enough words. I was so pleased to see Moses' mother, she must have sensed it for she unexpectedly reached for my hand and kissed it.

Women like Rutendo and Moses' mother are authoritative and powerful in the home. One of the most popular subjects my students asked to debate was "Who is the most powerful, the father or the mother?" There was no foregone conclusion. Other popular subjects included bride price, polygamy, and "a woman's place is in the home". Students tended to be reactionary, the girls being the most timidly conservative, although seeds of protest often lay beneath the surface. Most of them, at least, were prepared to express a distaste for polygamy, though few questioned the concept of marriage or women's domestic role in the home. I remember a boy named Launcelot saying: "Women should not go to school. I want a nice fat wife who'll keep me warm in winter and feed me *sadza* all the year round – that's all she will do." The day was saved by a boy, aptly named Blessing, who stood up and spoke passionately and eloquently in favour of women's freedom from the slavery of domesticity and cruel husbands. I'm sure that many girls will eventually gain the confidence they need to express their views themselves.

TRAVEL NOTES

Languages English is the official language. Shona is most widely spoken, followed by Sindebele.

Transport A good railway network connects all major cities. Buses are slow and usually very crowded, but they're cheap and travel almost everywhere. Hitching is easy and seems to be quite safe.

Accommodation All hotels tend to be expensive. Lodges, to be found in all the national parks, are cheaper but nearly always self-catering.

Guide *The Rough Guide: Zimbabwe and Botswana* (Harrap Columbus) has very full, practical coverage.

Contacts

Women's Action Group, Box 135, Harare or 127 Union Avenue, Harare. Initially formed in 1983, in response to a massive and widespread police round-up of women apparently suspected of being prostitutes, the group acts mainly as an advisory body for women on legal rights, health, hygiene and nutrition. It also publishes a quarterly magazine, *Speak Out.*

Zimbabwe Women's Bureau, 43 Hillside Road, Hillside, Harare, ☎734295. The Bureau's aim is to promote the economic self-sufficiency of women outside the formal waged sectors of urban and rural areas. They are helpful if you're interested in visiting various projects; try asking for Mrs Chikwavaire.

Voice, 6 Samora Machel Avenue, Harare. Co-ordinating body of non-governmental or volunteer organisations. Not a women's organisation but very useful for gathering information.

Books

Sekai Nzenza, *The Autobiography of a Zimbabwean Woman* (Karia Press, 1986). Sekai describes her life and shows the issues facing black Zimbabweans amid the contradictions resulting from the long oppression of white minority rule.

Tsitsi Dangaremga, *Nervous Conditions* (The Women's Press, 1988). Set in colonial Rhodesia during the Sixties, this excellent first novel tells of a young black girl's longing for education which she soon learns, comes with a price.

Ellen Kuzwayo, *Call Me a Woman* (The Women's Press, 1985). This remarkable autobiography movingly reveals what it's like to be a black woman in South Africa. Much of the book, notably life in the townships, can be related to Zimbabwe. Look out, too, for Kuzwayo's first collection of stories, *Sit Down and Listen* (The Women's Press, forthcoming).

Zimbabwe Publishing House has a fast-expanding women's list, fiction and non-fiction. Also look out for short stories and/or novels by **Nadine Gordimer** and **Doris Lessing**.

Thanks to Andrea Jarman for additional information.

FURTHER READING

Some of the books detailed below have been included, for their specific concerns, in individual country bibliographies and, in the case of the excellent *Sisterhood is Global* and *Women: A World Report*, more than once. We would like to acknowledge our debt to the whole range of books listed (and often suggested by contributors) in the compilation of *Women Travel*.

Worldwide Concerns/ Anthologies

Robin Morgan, ed., *Sisterhood is Global* (Penguin, 1985). Anthology of articles from feminists all over the world, preceded by statistics and other little-known information on the history and status of women. Especially useful for an overview of the Women's Movement in each country, 70 in all.

New Internationalist, *Women: A World Report* (Methuen, 1985). Published to coincide with the end of the United Nations Decade for Women, this book provides a review of UN information on the status of women, followed by accounts by ten writers, each of whom visited a different country to report on women's experience: for example, Angela Davis on Egypt, Germaine Greer on Cuba and Manny Shirazi on the Soviet Union.

Miranda Davies, ed., *Third World – Second Sex: Women's Struggles and National Liberation 1 and 2* (Zed Books, 1983, 1987). Two collections featuring original material by Third World women activists from over 40 countries in Asia, Latin America, Africa and the Middle East. Topics include women, politics and organisation, the role of women in national liberation movements, the case for autonomy, and campaigns around health, sexuality and work, and against violence.

Cynthia Enloe, *Bananas, Beaches and Bases* (Pandora Press, 1989). Intriguing feminist analysis of international politics, revealing women's crucial role in implementing governments' foreign policies from Soviet *glasnost* to Britain's dealings in the EC.

Women and Development: a Resource Guide for Organisation and Action (Isis, 1983; available from *Isis-WICCE*, PO Box 2471, 1211 Geneva 2, Switzerland). Provides a much-needed feminist perspective to the whole issue of development, focussing on key areas like women's role in food production, health, communication and education, and the effects of migration, tourism and the recruitment of labour by multinational companies. Shows how women are organising and fighting to control their own lives, each chapter being followed by a comprehensive selection of books, groups and other resources.

Kumari Jayawardena, *Feminism and Nationalism in the Third World* (Zed Books, 1986). Authoritative – and pioneering – study of women's participation in the democratic and revolutionary struggles of Asia and the Middle East from the late nineteenth century onwards.

Mineke Schippel, ed., *Unheard Words: Women and Literature in Africa, the Arab World, Asia, the Caribbean and Latin America* (Allison & Busby, 1986). Informative introduction to women's literary achievement in the Third World – including proverbs, essays and interviews.

Joni Seager and Ann Olson, *Women in the World* (Pan, 1986). International atlas packed with satistics on women's position in terms of health, poverty, earnings, media representation, education etc. in different countries.

Gita Sen and Caren Grown, *Development, Crises, and Alternative Visions* (Monthly Review Press, US, 1987). Groundbreaking analysis of the impact of current global economic and political crises – debt, famine, militarisation and fundamentalism – on poor Third World women, including examples of how they are organising to help themselves.

African Women

Margaret Jean Hay and Sharon Stitcher, eds., *African Women South of the Sahara* (Longman, 1984). This coursebook for students is a comprehensive study of the economic, social and political roles of women in Africa, past and present.

Asma El Dareer Woman, Why do You Weep? Circumcision and Its Consequences (Zed Books, 1982). Scholarly survey based on large-scale statistical research of circumcision and infibulation in Dareer's native Sudan. She deals with both women's and men's attitudes to the issues, plus related health problems, the history of circumcision, and suggestions for concrete steps – all relevant to many other areas of Africa as well as the Sudan.

Anne Cloudsley, Women of Omdurman Victims of Circumcision (Ethnographica, 1983, reprinted 1984). The author lived and worked with Sudanese women, learned about their rituals, celebrations, marriages, births. Important book about women in traditional societies, on the social context in which female circumcision is performed.

Charlotte H Bruner, ed., Unwinding Threads: A Collection of African Women Writers (Heinemann, 1983). Excellent anthology of modern African women's writing, covering wide geographical range, including the Islamic Maghreb areas. Good introductions, both general and to each region and author.

Raqiya H Dualeh Abdalla, Sisters in Affliction: Circumcision and Infibulation of Women in Africa (Zed Books, 1982). A good account which provides historical background and a political context to customs and practices within a Muslim framework. Also discusses the economics of marriage and provides community field studies.

Muslim Women

Lois Beck and Nikki Keddie, eds., Women in the Muslim World (Harvard University Press, 1978). An excellent collection of essays, predominantly by anthropologists, on women in different Muslim countries.

Ann Dearden, ed., Arab Women (Minority Rights Group Report no. 27, revised 1983). Useful survey on the position of women in different Arab countries.

Elizabeth Warnock Fernea and Basima Qattan Bezirgan, eds., Middle Eastern Muslim Women Speak (1977, University of Texas Press, 1984). Collection of autobiographical and biographical writings by and about Middle Eastern women.

Fatima Mernissi, Beyond the Veil (1975, Al Saqi Books 1985). Exploration of male-female relations in the Muslim world by a Moroccan feminist academic. The focus is on such themes as the pervasive and often destructive role of the mother-in-law and the constricting physical boundaries of women's lives.

Fatna A Sabbah, Women in the Muslim Unconscious (Pergamon Press, 1984). Detailed exposé of the elements in Islamic culture that combine to ingrain attitudes towards women in Muslim societies.

Juliette Minces, The House of Obedience – Women in Arab Society (Zed Books, 1982). A general study of women in the Arab world with one specific chapter on women in Algeria and Egypt.

Nawa El Saadawi, The Hidden Face of Eve (Zed Books, 1980). Personal, often disturbing account of what it is like to grow up as a woman in the Islamic world of the Middle East.

Germaine Tillion, The Republic of Cousins (1966 reprinted Al Saqi Books, 1985). Thesis by a distinguished French anthropologist on the effects of cultural prehistory of the Mediterranean region on the lives of the women.

Asian Women

Women in Asia (Minority Rights Group Report no 45, revised 1982). Survey on status, role, employment, work, political participation and issues and considerations of women of Pakistan, India, Sri Lanka, Bangladesh, Philippines, Indonesia, South Korea, Japan, China.

Sylvia Chipp and Justin Green, eds., Asian Women in Transition (Pennsylvania State Univ. Press, 1988). Academic but readable studies on women in East South-East and South Asia, covering economic, social and political aspects from a comparative perspective.

Caribbean and Latin American Women

Pat Ellis, ed., Women of the Caribbean (Zed Books, 1986). Essays by Caribbean women encompassing a very wide range of themes from trade-union organisation to women in calypso.

Alicia Partnoy, *You Can't Drown the Fire* (Virago, 1989). Collection of writings by 35 exiled Latin American women.

Audrey Bronstein *The Triple Struggle: Latin American Peasant Women* (War on Want Campaigns, 1982). Women in Bolivia, Ecuador, El Salvador, Guatemala and Peru express in their own works the struggle against the oppression of underdevelopment, poverty and the position of women in male-dominated societies.

Latin American and Caribbean Women's Collective, *Slaves of Slaves: the Challenge of Latin American Women* (Zed Books, 1982). Summary of women's struggles in a number of countries, including accounts of their historical roles in the different wars of independence.

Latin American Women (Minority Rights Group Report no. 57, 1983). Excellent survey of women's exploitation at home and in the workplace, including information on how women are organising, both on specific issues such as health and for wider revolutionary change.

Doris Meyer and Margarite Fernandez-Olmos, eds., *Contemporary Women Authors of Latin America* (Brooklyn College Press, 1984; 2 vols.). Useful general selection and commentary.

Women Travellers: History

Deborah Birkett, *Spinsters Abroad* (Blackwells, 1989). A fascinating piece of research that sheds new light on the attitudes and exploits of the "Lady Explorers" of the nineteenth century, and questions their role as feminist models.

Jane Robinson, *Wayward Women: A Guide To Women Travellers* (OUP, 1990). An annotated bibliography of travel writers ranging from the Abbess Etheria's fourth-century pilgrimage to the Holy Land to Isabella Bird's pan-global travels of the 1870s. A lucky dip of names, dates and journeys with very sketchy biographical details.

Many of the accounts discussed in these two books are published in the **"Virago Travellers"** reprint series.

Guides

Gaia's Guide International (Gaia's Guide, London). Useful, if haphazard, listings of gay and women-only venues in Europe, North America, Canada, Australia and New Zealand, with a few token contacts in "far away places".

Working Abroad

Susan Griffith (ed.), *Work Your Way Around the World* (Vacation Work; updated bi-annually). A mass of ideas and information, with brief contributor's experiences; covers the whole world with particular depth on Europe.

Working Holidays (Central Bureau; annual editions). An invaluable source book including numerous contacts for workcamps and community projects.

Hilary Sewell, *Volunteer Work* (Central Bureau, 1986; new edition in preparation). Contacts and some background on international voluntary agencies and their recruitment.

These books (and a range of other, specialised work directories) can be obtained direct from the **publishers**: *Vacation Work* (9 Park End St, Oxford OX1 1HJ) and *Central Bureau* (Seymour Mews, London W1H 9PE).

A Note on Bookshops

In Britain, the best general sources for most books detailed here are *Sisterwrite*, 190 Upper St., London, N1 (☎01-226 9782) and *Silvermoon Women's Bookshop*, 68 Charing Cross Rd. London WC2H OBB (☎01-836 7906). *The Travel Bookshop*, 13 Blenheim Crescent, London W11 (☎01-229 5260) is useful for the more esoteric guidebooks and travel literature.

Borrowed Items 01/05/2015 14:33
Majchutova, Adriana

Item Title

Skills for success : the personal development planning handbook

08/05/2015

Berlitz cruising and cruise ships 2014 [book]

08/05/2015

Start your own travel business and more : cruises, adventure travel, tours, senior travel

08/05/2015

Personal development and management skills

08/05/2015

Brilliant communication skills : what the best communicators know, do and say

26/06/2015

The reflective practitioner how professionals think in action

22/05/2015

Women travel : adventures advice and experience.

22/05/2015

A QUIET
PLACE
TO
KILL

A QUIET PLACE TO KILL

N.R. DAWS

THOMAS & MERCER

Text copyright © 2021 by N. R. Daws
All rights reserved.

Published by Thomas & Mercer, Seattle

www.apub.com

Amazon, the Amazon logo, and Thomas & Mercer are trademarks of Amazon.com, Inc., or its affiliates.

ISBN-13: 9781542028639
ISBN-10: 1542028639

Cover design by Ghost Design

Printed in the United States of America

In loving memory of my mother, Pam, who taught me to read, and my father, George, who taught me to love reading.

PROLOGUE

Most people don't know the exact time their life will come to an end, but she knew.

The figure looming over her, squeezing her throat, ducked at the sudden sound of scraping metal and stared into the blackout, the nation's wartime defence against death from the night sky. As it was just after ten o'clock, some drinkers were wandering home but she knew the alcohol would have taken its toll and they could not help her. The figure peered over the low wall and across the churchyard towards the Castle pub at the centre of the village.

It was a momentary reprieve

Questions fizzed through her mind. Why was this happening to her? What had she done wrong? Had she said something out of place? Were her hair, make-up, clothing not pleasing? As more unanswered questions piled up she felt another jolt of panic that she'd never do all the things she'd dreamed of or see all the places she'd read about in magazines.

The yew tree cast its deepest shadows over the footpath that ran obliquely from the High Street, between two low, flint-built walls, alongside the churchyard and into the fields beyond. Nobody would notice them here. No one would come. She pleaded with her eyes but the figure's left hand held her right wrist as she flailed her free arm, left hand searching and nails clawing. The air raid warden's nearby call of 'Put that light out' startled them and she felt the grip on her neck tighten.

She'd been stronger and struggled more than she'd ever expected she could, fear triggering the survival instinct, releasing hidden strengths lying deep inside her. But it was not enough. With a powerful squeeze from those fingers, she felt something give way and the fear vanished. Her knees buckled but the hold remained as she slumped to the ground, all sensation leaving her body.

There was nothing she could do now as the pressure increased. Making sure.

CHAPTER ONE

The village of Scotney had been awake for several hours before the throaty rumble of Lizzie Hayes' Norton motorbike announced her arrival.

Scotney, surrounded by a patchwork of fields, hedgerows and pasture, bordered by dense woodland to the west and a nearby stream to the east, matched the picture that had formed in her mind when she'd first heard of it. Having seconds before passed the level crossing and railway station on the Hawkhurst branch line, she paused to get her bearings at a crossroads where two narrow lanes of tiny cottages clad in Kent weatherboard led away either side: Acorn Street to her left; Meadowbank Lane to her right.

The wide High Street carried on northwards, from a small car-repair garage on the right with a single roadside petrol pump, up to where a quaint little bakery, grocer, chemist and butcher lay interspersed between the houses. On the left, past a memorial to the fallen of the Great War, stood a red telephone box. A painted cast-iron sign fixed over a door fortified with sandbags identified the police station, a clock tower above the village hall marked the halfway point and at the extreme far end beyond more houses rose the small bell tower of a church.

Washed clean by overnight downpours, the village brought back memories of life growing up on a small country estate; a far cry from her recent years spent in London. To Lizzie, the capital city still felt too busy, with its lines of narrow brick-built houses huddled together for solace and protection, monumental buildings of stone standing imposing and impersonal, and crowds of Londoners scurrying and getting in each other's way. The smoke from thousands of coal fires and industrial chimneys made her nose and throat itch. The impenetrable pea-souper fogs that often descended on its famous landmarks, bringing twilight in the middle of the day, irritated her lungs. Here, though, the air was as crisp and fresh as apples picked from the nearby orchards. She took a deep breath, her eyes drawn to the distant undulations of low hills, above which, despite the rainclouds, all the sky seemed to stretch.

Lizzie's attention turned to the villagers, most of whom were attending to their shopping and chores. She spotted two who had stopped on the pavement outside the Castle pub, directly opposite the village hall. One wore the dark-blue overalls and black helmet with the white 'W' of an Air Raid Precautions warden, his khaki utility bag hanging from his shoulder. Lizzie opened the Norton's throttle, drove the thundering motorbike towards the pub and drew up beside them, noting the expressions of both puzzlement and disapproval on their faces. Only when the engine gave a final cough as Lizzie turned it off did she realise the ARP warden was speaking.

'Now look here. You can't ride through the village at that speed, my lad. I don't care who you are. If it wasn't for the bad weather I'd have said that racket your machine made was an approaching air raid.'

'I thought it was the invasion,' said his companion, a housewife of not insignificant bulk, who moved behind the warden for protection. 'A Nazi tank or some such.' She hugged her wicker shopping basket close.

4

The warden pulled himself up to his full height at the very suggestion.

It wasn't the welcome she'd been expecting but Lizzie laughed, realising she must look a threatening sight clad in a black greatcoat, leggings, boots and helmet. She watched their consternation turn to shock as she tugged down the black scarf covering her mouth and chin, pulled up her goggles and removed her helmet to reveal dark-brown hair, curled in the latest fashion. Most unmanly, she hoped.

'I'm so sorry, but isn't it beautiful?' she said, patting the black petrol tank. 'It's a Norton. Belongs to my brother but he's been posted to North Weald to fly Hurricanes.'

'Careless talk costs lives, young lady,' the warden scolded. 'Who are you anyway? And where are you going on that thing?'

'My name's Elizabeth Hayes.' She removed a black gauntlet and thrust her hand forward. 'But I prefer Lizzie. I'm with the ATA.'

'Brian Greenway,' the man said, accepting her handshake. 'And this is Ethel Garner. What's the ATA when it's at home?'

'The Air Transport Auxiliary,' Lizzie said proudly. 'I'm a pilot.'

Ethel stepped out from behind Greenway, still hugging her basket. 'Don't be ridiculous,' she snapped. 'Women can't fly. There's a war on, you know.'

Lizzie's smile faltered as she felt the familiar stab of frustration at being dismissed. 'That's rather the point. All the men are flying fighters against the Germans. We're doing our bit behind the front line to make sure all those beautiful aeroplanes get to where they should be.'

'You're having us on,' Greenway said with a condescending smile. 'You can't possibly fly Spitfires.'

'Ah, no, we're not allowed to. Not yet.'

Lizzie was no longer able to maintain a smile. Adapting to new surroundings by mimicking the behaviour of others, like a chameleon trying to blend in against a bush, had always been an important skill for her. But she'd thought she'd get a pleasant reception here. It seemed she'd misjudged the mood of a village at war.

'We deliver small aircraft and trainers at the moment,' she said. 'But one day.'

'One day pigs might fly,' Ethel said with a scowl.

'What are you doing here then?' Greenway asked.

'Trying to find RAF Scotney, as a matter of fact. A whole gaggle of us have been posted there. I take it I'm going in the right direction?'

'Don't tell her, Mr Greenway,' Ethel said brusquely. 'She might be a German spy.'

Lizzie grinned and caught Greenway smiling with her. 'I'm not a spy.' She delved inside her coat and the jacket underneath, and pulled out her identity card. Greenway inspected it and handed it back. 'See, bona fide.'

'She even speaks German,' Ethel said with a grimace.

Greenway rolled his eyes.

At the sound of another vehicle entering the village, they all turned to watch a young woman bring a two-seater sports car to a gentle stop next to Lizzie's Norton. Four wide-eyed schoolboys suddenly appeared from nowhere, surrounding the car excitedly. Two small girls hung back, shyly twisting the hems of their cardigans between their fingers.

'I didn't realise you were driving down as well,' Lizzie said above the chatter.

Greenway looked from Lizzie to the newcomer through narrowed eyes. 'You two know each other?'

'We're friends,' Lizzie explained. 'We were at HQ together at White Waltham. Training.'

'Good grief, not another one?' Ethel muttered as the woman opened the driver's door and stepped out.

'Afraid I am,' the woman replied, hastening to put up the car's soft collapsible roof as the morning's intermittent drizzle began

6

to grow heavier. 'I'm Charlotte Rowan-Peake. *Charlie*. Shame the weather's taken a turn for the worse.'

'Aye,' Greenway agreed, squinting up at the sky. 'Looks like we're in for another pasting. Is this your car, then?'

'Of course.' Charlie pushed the last roof fixing into place. 'I should have taken the train because petrol is already scarce but you can't move for all the soldiers and evacuees.'

Charlie sat back behind the driving wheel and reshaped her wind-blown hair. 'You couldn't be a darling and point us in the right direction, could you?'

Lizzie looked at Greenway, blinking as rain spotted her face. She saw his eyes flick across from her face to Charlie's car as it roared into life and settled to a purr. Lizzie was becoming used to unnecessary delay from officials both major and minor and, with an inward groan, thought they were in for more questions, but then she saw his features relax, a decision made.

'Your papers are in order and I take it you can vouch for this one.' He nodded at Charlie.

'Absolutely,' Lizzie confirmed.

'Right then.' He held his arm out, pointing towards the church. 'Carry on the way you were going and go straight on up Manor Lane for a mile. There's only one road and it stops at the manor so you can't miss it.'

'Whatever next?' Ethel muttered, adjusting her headscarf.

'Thank you,' Lizzie said, pulling on her helmet and goggles, tugging her scarf back over her mouth and slipping on her gauntlet before kick-starting the Norton. Charlie pulled away with a wave and two blasts on the car horn, leaving the schoolboys trailing behind. Lizzie gave the villagers a loose salute and opened the throttle, accelerating towards the north end of the village.

As Lizzie approached the church she noticed two men standing beyond a low wall studying something on the path. One of them, wearing a fawn raincoat and black homburg, bent down and disappeared out of sight while the other, in a police helmet and uniform, remained standing, holding up an umbrella under which they were sheltering. Lizzie brought the Norton to a halt in line with the pathway and saw the man crouched over what looked for a split second like a bundle of clothing on the ground. With a shock she suddenly realised what it was, but another man with an umbrella, wearing a dark-grey, short-brimmed fedora and grey raincoat, stepped in front of her, blocking her view deliberately. She saw his face as he held up a police warrant card. Mid to late thirties, she guessed, despite the drab outfit more suited to someone much older.

'This is a crime scene, not some ghoulish Victorian spectacle for idle sightseers!' he shouted.

Lizzie's face clouded. 'I'm neither idle nor a sightseer.'

'Ah, then you must be a trained detective. I do apologise,' he sneered.

The sarcasm rankled. 'Actually, I'm a trained psy—'

'Move along!'

The detective turned his back on her, which irked Lizzie as much as the blunt rebuke. Knowing it was pointless to pursue the matter, she resumed her journey without a word, her good mood on entering the village well and truly soured.

'Bloody nosey parker,' muttered Detective Inspector Jonathan Kember of the Kent County Constabulary at the receding form of the motorcyclist. Last night's cheese and pickle sandwich was still giving him heartburn, his head cold had smothered any remaining humour and bystanders asking questions always got on his wick. If that wasn't enough, a young girl lay mutilated on his patch, his adulterous wife had asked for a divorce that morning as she'd thrown him out for good, and the rain was lancing down at forty-five degrees.

Again.

He walked a few steps along the narrow path that ran alongside the churchyard and exchanged introductions with the policeman standing over the body, raising his voice over the rhythmic patter on his new umbrella.

'Given the blackout and the weather, this was as good a time and place as any to attack a young woman, don't you think?'

'Aye, sir,' said Sergeant Dennis Wright, trying to adjust his cape so the water from his helmet didn't pour inside his collar, while still holding a large umbrella over the body and the doctor who was inspecting it. 'One of the few secluded spots within the confines of the village, is this.'

Kember had to agree. His only other visit to the village had been a few years before and little had changed. At this end of the busy High Street, the squat Norman bell tower of St Matthew's Church guarded a small burial ground. A quiet place to kill.

'What can you give me, Doctor?' Kember said. 'Anything at this stage would be a great help.'

Dr Michael Headley, formerly a surgeon at St Bart's Hospital in London but now a Home Office-approved pathologist at Pembury Hospital, glanced away from his examination and peered at Kember through the rain-dotted lenses of his spectacles. 'Ah, it's you, Kember. I expected Scotland Yard's *finest*, to be honest.'

Kember gave Headley a wry smile. Almost two years had elapsed since his arrival from Scotland Yard CID on a semi-permanent secondment to his home town of Tonbridge, and Headley remained one of the few people who knew the reason why.

'Violent crime has gone through the roof and the Yard are a bit stretched,' Kember said. 'A shortage of good officers, apparently.' Kember almost laughed at the sideways glance Headley gave him.

'Chief Inspector Beveridge of the Yard has taken most of our men for the triple-murder case a few miles away in Brenchley parish so, as a Yard man myself, I've been pressed into service as a stopgap. I hear the famous Home Office pathologist Sir Bernard Spilsbury is on his team.'

Headley sniffed. 'So you're playing second fiddle in much the same way I am.'

'That's the way of the world.'

''Twas ever thus,' Headley agreed. 'In case you were wondering, I can confirm this has nothing to do with Brenchley, medically at least. By coincidence, I spoke to Sir Bernard this morning – courteously, before you ask. He told me a woman and her daughter had been shot in an orchard near the holiday cottage they owned and their housekeeper lay bludgeoned to death.' He indicated the body with a sideways nod. 'This young lady has been strangled and a knife taken to her.'

Kember had never got used to seeing dead bodies despite his years on the force and turned away, glancing around. 'The Brenchley location is more remote while this is right on the edge of a village, so I suppose we're all in agreement. Different locations, different murder weapons, different modus operandi, different killers. Stands to reason.'

'Hmm. Look here.' Headley nodded as he pointed, drawing Kember's attention back to the woman. 'Despite the cuts to her neck you can see some bruising under the jawline. It appears the perpetrator grasped her throat from the front with his right hand and squeezed. There's not nearly as much blood around as one would expect, even given the weather. That indicates the knife wounds were inflicted post-mortem.'

'Are you saying she was already dead when he did this?' Kember's heart sank. He knew wounds after death suggested premeditation.

'Takes a bit of doing one-handed, let me tell you, but the pattern is specific and commensurate with asphyxia by manual strangulation. I'll be able to tell more once I've got her to the mortuary.'

Kember frowned. 'Why would someone do that if she was already dead?'

'You're the detective, Inspector; I'm merely the quack assigned to give you the how, not the who or why.'

Kember shot Headley an irritated look. 'Was she raped?'

'I suspect not.' Headley dropped a swab into a glass tube and sealed it with a cork stopper. 'Her underwear is in place and there are no obvious bruises in the nether regions to indicate a struggle. I may be able to confirm the presence or absence of semen once I've had a chance to inspect the body more closely, out of the rain. However, and Sergeant Wright may wish to look away at this point—' He lifted the woman's dress high on to her chest and Wright immediately leant over the wall and vomited on the churchyard side.

'Not very Christian, Sergeant,' Kember said, his face impassive.

'No, sir,' said Wright, wiping his mouth and short, neatly trimmed beard with the back of his hand. 'Couldn't be helped, sir. I'm all right now.'

'At least you didn't spew all over the crime scene,' said Headley. 'As I was saying, a chap walking his dog actually found her like this. He wanted to reclaim modesty on her behalf, unaware he was possibly disturbing evidence.'

Kember forced himself to look at the mutilated abdomen of the woman. He grimaced. 'The same knife did all this?'

'Can't say at this point but a sharp, long-bladed knife would have been needed.'

'I take it these were post-mortem too?'

A gust of wind released a deluge of sap-laced droplets from the tree, splattering their umbrellas again.

'Indeed,' Headley said with a shiver. 'They all appear to be very deep but little blood loss again. There may be others but I'll have to clean her first.'

'Any chance you can give a time of death?' Kember asked, aware this question usually brought forth snorts of derision from Headley.

'Difficult to say. The amount of rain we've had already this morning has cleansed most of the exposed parts of the body as it lay here. The blood lividity is fixed along the dorsal aspect. For the uninitiated, that means it's pooled and set along her back. With rigor mortis being total and complete, that would indicate a time of death at somewhere between midnight and four o'clock this morning. However,' Headley said before Kember could speak, 'if you look in here' – he indicated the woman's open mouth – 'there are flies' eggs and already two or three miniscule maggots.'

The twitch of one eyebrow betrayed Kember's inner revulsion as he leant forward to see into her mouth. 'Meaning? She's been here a lot longer?'

Headley groaned in effort as he stood from his crouch. 'I know what you're thinking about: Dr Mearns and the famous Ruxton case in Scotland five years back.' He shook his head. 'According to the literature, and in my experience, flies lay eggs on a body left in the open in very short order and maggots can appear after about eight hours. Within a day, certainly. Given the state of the lividity, rigor, maggots and weather, and if pressed to hazard a guess, I'd give a rough, stick-my-neck-out estimate of between nine o'clock and midnight last night, give or take an hour or so. Quote me and I'll deny everything.'

'That's helpful, Doctor.' Kember inclined his head towards the body. 'Any indication of who she was?'

As Headley packed away his things and prepared to leave, he nodded towards a muddied clutch bag. 'Her purse was on the path beside her,' Headley said. 'Won't be any decent fingerprints on the outside, what with the mud and rain.'

'Sergeant Wright will check for prints anyway,' Kember said as he donned a pair of rubber gloves extracted from his pocket. He opened the bag and looked at a travel permit, feeling a constriction in his throat. Knowing the victim's name always made a case more real, more personal somehow. 'Lavinia Scott. Miss. Aged twenty-three. A ferry pilot in the Air Transport Auxiliary, it seems.' He unfolded a sheet of paper, inside which was a smaller folded note. 'Orders to report to RAF Scotney today.' He opened the smaller note and showed Wright a neatly written address.

'It's a lodging house just down the road, sir,' Wright said. 'Owned by the Taplow sisters, Annie and Elsie.'

Kember returned the papers to the bag.

'The next document is a flight authorisation card. No identity card but her money's still in here. Any jewellery?'

'She has a ring, earrings and necklace,' Headley said. 'All have what look like diamonds. Not cheap, anyway.' He stepped past Kember and trudged towards the road, shadowed by Wright with the umbrella.

Wright signalled to Headley's waiting car.

'Not a robbery then?' Kember called after Headley. 'She looks like she's been left like this on purpose, as if someone wanted us to find her.'

'I agree, and the excess is of particular concern.' Headley jumped back as his car swung in a half-circle and braked to a halt, squirting muddy water at his ankles. He glowered at his driver. 'It looks like someone took great pleasure.'

Rain swept across the countryside like a dirty net curtain billowing through an open window, lashing any trees in its path, drenching anything whether moving or not, soaking everything whether alive or not, and leaving puddles dotted on the tarmac road. The scent of wet leaves and hedgerows, sodden earth and pasture found their way through Lizzie's scarf. Lightning backlit the clouds while thunder cracked and rumbled with malevolence. Through her water-streaked goggles, Lizzie saw the blurry red tail lights of Charlie's car slow to a stop and she pulled up behind. A red-and-white barrier barred access through a chain-link perimeter fence topped with coiled barbed wire that extended into the distance either side. She thought she saw another flash of lightning to the east, but when it remained steady she recognised it as the landing light of an approaching aircraft.

A warder of the Air Ministry Wardens guard force stepped from the shelter of the gatehouse and took up position alongside the car, his rifle at the ready. Lizzie stepped off the Norton and pulled up her goggles, feeling sorry for the young man. A moment ago, he was in the warmth of the gatehouse but now he looked miserable, water streaming off his helmet, cape and rifle.

The driver's window of Charlie's car wound down.

'Papers please,' the warder commanded.

Lizzie saw confusion flit across the guard's face as he peered through his military-issue spectacles into the open window, his bent head allowing rain to run down his neck. She wondered how long he had left on duty, how long he'd have to endure a saturated collar.

'We weren't expecting you until tomorrow,' the warder said. 'Because of the weather.'

'Terribly sorry and all that,' Charlie said charmingly. 'What's your name?'

'Warder Grade Two Freddie Stapleton, miss.'

'Well, Warder Freddie, I was just so eager to meet you all.'

Lizzie looked again towards the aircraft, now identifiable to her as an Ox-box, as the twin-engine Airspeed Oxford was affectionately known. It dropped visibly as the undercarriage descended from the engine nacelles, the starboard wing dipping briefly. Lizzie felt herself in the pilot's position, fighting the crosswind, fighting the fear, tightening her grip on the control column, teeth clenched, determined, pushing hard on the rudder pedals to bring the aircraft back level and pointing along the runway.

Stapleton jumped, almost dropping his rifle as he noticed Lizzie standing next to him clad all in black, shielding her identity card from the rain as she stared across the airfield. He took her card.

Lizzie watched the Oxford flaps lowered, level out and descend foot by foot. She sensed the pilot's anticipation, waiting for the large rubber tyres to touch down, and relief as they sought and found traction on the rain-slicked grass runway.

'Can you remove your helmet, please?'

Her mind clearing, Lizzie became aware of Stapleton glancing from her identity photo to her face and realised she'd been holding her breath.

'My hair's flattened to buggery as it is so I'd rather not get it wet too, if you don't mind.' Lizzie smiled.

'Absolutely,' Charlie said. 'A girl's got to keep up appearances.'

Stapleton's embarrassed thank you as he returned Lizzie's card almost got lost in nervous stutters and the rain's dull drumming on the car's soft roof, but as he stepped over to the counterweight to raise the barrier he managed to squeak, 'Someone at the manor house will take care of you. Welcome to RAF Scotney.'

Lizzie replaced her goggles, got back on her motorbike and both the Scout and Norton grumbled into life. Charlie waggled her fingers at Stapleton and wound up the window. As Lizzie eased her motorbike after the receding car, she glanced in her rear-view mirror and thought she saw a second figure return to the shelter of the hut.

CHAPTER TWO

'Come!'

The commanding officer of the newly arrived women's detachment of the Air Transport Auxiliary clenched her teeth, checked her uniform again and entered. Seeing one officer standing by the window near a large desk on which lay a black-and-white cat, and noting another two officers seated to one side, she closed the door and stood to attention. 'Captain Geraldine Ellenden-Pitt reporting for duty, sir.'

Group Captain George Dallington, commanding officer of RAF Scotney, turned away from his rain-streaked office window, the panes criss-crossed with tape to limit blast shatter, and inspected the empty bowl of his pipe. 'Low cloud base, pissing down, thunder and lightning.' His mouth twitched and his eyes narrowed as he stared at Geraldine for a few seconds. 'That was a damn fool stunt you pulled out there. The weather's atrocious and it's my understanding the chaps are going up only when absolutely necessary. Even Jerry's staying on the deck.'

Geraldine's expression remained fixed. 'I'm afraid I'm unable to comment on the inexperience of other pilots, sir. It was clear enough when we set out. A cloud base of a thousand feet with visibility of at least two thousand. Well within the regulation minimum. I've flown here hundreds of times so I know it like the back of my hand, so to speak.'

Dallington glared at her. 'That was before enemy aircraft and barrage balloons and war, I suspect.' He looked at her over his glasses, which had slipped down his nose a little. He pushed them back with his forefinger and said, 'At ease. Please sit.'

'Thank you, sir.' Geraldine perched on the edge of a leather chair.

'My second-in-command, Wing Commander John Matfield, and Flight Lieutenant Alan Pendry of our RAF Police will be sitting in.'

Geraldine nodded to the men in acknowledgement but otherwise remained quiet and still.

Matfield, enveloped in the comfort of a padded leather chair that would have been more at home in a gentleman's club, ignored Geraldine and scowled at the cat, now sitting up and scratching itself, shedding hairs in his direction.

Seated on a plain wooden desk chair next to Matfield, Pendry looked up from fiddling with the fixings on the back of his black leather gloves and acknowledged her with a single nod.

Geraldine watched Dallington deliberately look her up and down, trying to intimidate. She noticed his eyes lingering on the ATA badges sewn on her field service cap and above the breast pocket of her dark-blue tunic, and her epaulettes with two narrow bands of gold flanked by two wide bands denoting her rank.

'All very . . . showy,' Dallington said.

'My apologies if it offends you, sir.' Geraldine kept her face impassive. 'It's based on the RAF uniform and I'm afraid I had no hand in its design.'

Pendry failed to suppress a smirk and Dallington threw him a sharp glance as his fingers probed beneath the cat. 'Get off my tobacco,' he muttered. The cat retaliated with a swipe. Dallington hissed and gave the cat a shove with the back of his hand, making it skitter across the desk. Matfield made an instinctive grab for two books perched on the edge of the table and Pendry raised his hands against the scrabbling ball of fur and claws, forcing it to jump to the floor.

'Bloody animal,' Dallington snapped. 'I don't know how the feral beast keeps getting in here. And why do we need a station mascot anyway?' He made a show of nursing a scratch. 'I see the blighter got you too.'

Matfield ran his fingers along a scratch on the back of his wrist. 'I'll live,' he said.

Dallington opened his now accessible tin of Old Holborn and scooped an aromatic wad into his pipe bowl. He scraped a match into life and lit the tobacco, squinting through the window.

Sucking the pipe stem with satisfaction on his face, Dallington's head was obscured by a low cloud of blue smoke until he left the window and lowered his six-foot frame into his own padded leather wing-backed chair. He pushed his slipped glasses back to the bridge of his nose with his forefinger and studied a letter on his desk, ignoring everyone for several seconds.

'Do you know what they're calling the ATA these days?' Dallington said eventually.

Geraldine knew and clenched her jaw tighter.

Matfield settled back in his chair. 'Ancient and Tattered Airmen, I believe.'

'That's what they called the old boys and invalids before they let Daddies' little girlies into the club. No, it's Always Terrified Airwomen.'

Pendry looked down at his watch.

Matfield cleared his throat. 'I'm not against progress as such, especially in time of war. Every capable person should be given the chance to do their bit, after all.'

Geraldine enjoyed Dallington nearly choking on his own smoke.

'Good God, man,' Dallington growled. 'You're not one of these liberal types, are you? There are enough jobs at home to keep all the women of this island busy without all this.'

'I agree with you, sir,' Matfield said, 'but there is a war on.'

Dallington, holding the bowl of his pipe, jabbed the stem at Matfield for emphasis. 'How can you say that, John? First, they take away our fighter squadrons, leaving us with a skeleton crew of half-wits and has-beens, then just as the balloon's about to go up, they give us a group of bloody women to look after, for Christ's sake.'

Geraldine resisted the urge to roll her eyes. She considered herself pragmatic enough to realise whatever the RAF, Fighter Command and the Air Ministry wanted, they got. She gave a small cough to get Dallington's attention. 'I appreciate how you must feel, sir, but the Air Ministry were adamant that women can do the jobs required while all of the most able-bodied men, especially pilots, are needed at the front.'

'Front?' Dallington glared first at her, then Pendry, then Matfield. 'Front? If the Luftwaffe jumps the Channel from Calais they've got Hawkinge and Manston to contend with. Lympne too, at a push. If they come from the south, Tangmere's in the way. But what if they come from the south-east? Eh? Forget West Malling, we're the best strategically placed fighter station between the coast and Biggin Hill. Christ almighty, even piddly Detling's operational and they've only got a few airworthy Ansons for reconnaissance. Draw a line from Tangmere to Detling and we're further forward.'

'We may soon need every able body we can get,' Matfield jumped in. 'Male or female. If the invasion comes, the more women who take up support roles the more men are freed up to fight.'

Dallington scowled and puffed his faltering pipe back to life. Squinting through a smoky haze, he said, 'I suppose we shouldn't worry too much. If Jerry does attack, I doubt the delicate ladies will stay around here for very long.' As he paused for effect, a lash of windswept rain filled the gap, rattling against the window like a handful of thrown gravel.

'Seems a little harsh to not give them a chance,' Matfield said. 'In the name of progress, I mean. Could rub off on you most favourably.'

Geraldine inwardly seethed at being talked about as if she wasn't in the room.

'Progress?' Dallington's cheeks reddened at the mention. He took the letter with his forefinger and thumb, holding it as if it was contaminated. 'The whole charade is a bloody experiment by Churchill's cronies and it won't work, you mark my words.'

He tossed the letter loosely towards Geraldine and it landed askew on the desk, but she made no move to take or look at it. If he hadn't the courtesy to pass it to her properly, she certainly wasn't going to reach for it. His next words when they came were slow and deliberate.

'That letter is a directive from Fighter Command, endorsed by the Air Ministry. It confirms RAF Scotney as a de facto operational air station. However, the letter also states that, for the foreseeable, it will play no front-line role. Instead, Scotney will suffer the ignominy of hosting Number Thirteen Ferry Pool of the ATA, under my command.'

Surprised and unable to keep the dismay from her voice, Geraldine said, 'But I thought we were to be under civilian command separate from the RAF.'

'You and me both, Captain,' Dallington said.

'With due respect, sir, I can't see how that can work. We have separate rules and regulations. RAF personnel can face a court martial whereas we can just be sacked.'

Dallington fiddled with his pen. 'Believe me, if there was any way of influencing this arrangement I would have taken it. However, a form of compromise has been agreed.'

'Compromise, sir?' Geraldine had her voice back under control but clenched her hands in anticipation of some draconian restriction.

Dallington pointed to the letter with his pen. 'I retain command of this air station and all of its operational needs, which includes its safety, security, discipline and readiness to act as a fighter base should that become necessary again. It also includes general command of your detachment. In this I am aided by Wing Commander Matfield. You will be in charge of the women's section and all the ATA's daily and scheduled activities, specifically the ferrying of RAF aircraft. Where these two functions meet, you will be treated with the same courtesy as RAF pilots and will obey the same regulations.'

'I'm relieved to hear that, sir.' Geraldine relaxed her hands. It wasn't a perfect solution but it would do.

'Quite,' Dallington said. 'You and your ladies will *not* fraternise with the male ground crews, engineers and other personnel while on this air station. You *will* conduct yourself with decorum at all times, both on and off duty.'

Without looking, Dallington indicated Pendry with a flick of his hand.

'Flight Lieutenant Pendry's detachment ensures security and enforces discipline.' Geraldine saw Pendry's jaw clench. 'Their primary jurisdiction is within the confines of this establishment but also relates to RAF *and* ATA personnel on- or off-site.'

'Understood, sir.' Geraldine tried to keep her tone flat.

'Good. Have you any questions before you settle in?'

'No, sir. We don't expect our first ferrying assignments for a day or two. We'll try our best to keep out of your hair.'

Dallington gave her a hard stare, ran a hand back over his balding head and swapped his pen for his pipe. He took a long suck and expelled blue smoke from his nostrils. 'I really thought Fighter Command had more sense,' he growled. 'Get out of my sight, all of you. I'm going to call Group HQ again. And put those books you borrowed back before you go.'

Geraldine stood, saluted, opened the door and stepped outside as quickly as good grace allowed, noticing Matfield placing the books on a shelf while Dallington's attention had already turned to his telephone.

◆　◆　◆

Out of earshot of Dallington's office, watching Matfield stalk away, Pendry turned to Geraldine and said, 'I'm impressed with the way you handled that. They're not the easiest of characters to deal with.'

Geraldine smiled. 'I was warned by Pauline Gower, head of the women's section. She told me the group captain had not only telephoned the overall head of the ATA, but he'd also called Fighter Command, the Air Ministry and even tried to get through to Number Ten.'

Pendry whistled. 'That's quite a list.'

'Exhaustive, I'd say. I've yet to discover whether he thinks all women should stay in the home but he's made it crystal clear to anyone who'll listen, and many who won't, that women have no business being anywhere near an operational air station.'

Pendry nodded. 'I thought it rather rude of him to sling that letter across his desk.'

'Not very officer-like, was it? No skin off my nose. He even wrote a letter to *The Times* stating that, in his opinion, WAAF stood for Weak, Addled And Fragile, rather than Women's Auxiliary Air Force. I've no illusions this will be an easy posting. Good to know he won't have his fingers all over the ATA's daily operations. With any luck, our paths needn't cross that often.'

'I took a few flying lessons before the war, with the Air Defence Cadet Corps,' Pendry said. 'They taught us to not risk flying in this kind of weather. If you don't mind me asking, why did you?'

Geraldine glanced back at Dallington's office. 'Between you and me, I actually disobeyed a red warning flare fired the second I opened the throttle to take off from Chattis Hill. The trees on the hills were visible and Hampshire, the whole of southern England in fact, was my pre-war aerial playground. I was convinced I knew the way blindfolded. Apart from a bit of buffeting and rain over Kent, I was right. I have better credentials as a pilot than most men but no wish to antagonise anyone this early in my posting, especially not the station commander.'

'I wouldn't worry.' Pendry smiled. 'I think you got up his nose just the right amount.'

◆　◆　◆

Kember fidgeted as he sat in the front office of the village police station, feeling damp to his core. His raincoat and fedora hung drying with Sergeant Wright's police cape on a tall, polished oak stand in the corner. Wright's chair occupied its personal spot at a desk under the window. The visitor's chair was uncomfortable but functional, hard and worn with long use. As senior officer, Kember would have been within his rights to take the better seat, but he was not one for petty posturing. Two large cupboards stood either side of a fire grate beneath a chimney breast where a small fire had been lit, full shelves lined another wall of the office and two waist-high filing cabinets huddled together behind the door. Wafts of sweet wood smoke and the musty smell of wet clothing tainted the air.

Out of his raincoat and hat, Kember felt dishevelled. He hated anything greasy like Brylcreem on his neatly trimmed hair, so he was sure his double crown was sprouting like a clump of reeds at the back of his head. His navy-blue trousers and grey sports jacket, having seen better days, retained random creases despite resolute pressing. His reflection in the office window showed his plain blue tie, although tucked into his dark-blue paisley-patterned waistcoat, occupied its usual position slightly askew of the vertical. His brown shoes currently held a veneer of drying mud to around half an inch up from the soles.

Kember studied his notebook, blinking his gritty eyes and trying to ignore the pressure in his sinuses. Aged thirty-seven, he felt fifty years older. What he wanted more than anything in the world was a pint of ale with a single malt chaser, a tender kiss from his wife and to go back to bed for a much-needed rest; but his wife had ejected him and bedtime was a long way off. He'd decided to get through the day and find somewhere to stay later on, although he'd have to return home at some point to sort through the residual clutter of his now defunct nineteen-year marriage. His large trunk stood against the wall in the back room. The trunk into which his wife had secretly packed his clothes, and as many of his possessions as it could hold, the previous day. Waiting for him to come home from his shift to land the bombshell, she hadn't even looked him in the eye or given him a good reason – except for *the other man*, of course. There had been a few of those before, but without serious consequences. Not that he blamed her entirely. The job took its toll on many marriages. Even so, sitting in this office, he felt mild surprise at this final audacity, as well as concern that she may have inadvertently or deliberately taken some of his personal or treasured possessions, and irritation that the detective in him had not noticed the situation had come to a head.

He had a sudden yearning to see his son and daughter but they had joined the RAF and WAAF respectively and taken up posts away from home. He envied them. He took a worn leather wallet from his jacket and retrieved a photograph, creased from frequent use. Kember studied the happy faces of his grown-up children, twins, taken on their eighteenth birthday a few months earlier. He and his wife, smiling, stood behind them, the epitome of a middle-class family. His own attempt to join up had been thwarted by an old injury to his lower back – a herniated disk that flared up every so often. *Permanently and totally unfit for military service* had come the reply.

Wright came back with two steaming mugs, handing one to Kember before sitting. Kember replaced the photograph and sipped his tea, screwing up his eyes against the hot concoction, bitter without any sugar, its colour somewhere between clay and slurry.

Wright took a slurp as Kember made a show of studying his notebook for a moment longer.

'What do you make of it?' Kember looked across at the sergeant.

'Beg your pardon, sir?' Wright said, as though caught unawares by the question.

'With the few facts we have at present, have you any theories?'

Wright caressed his short beard as if stroking a pet cat. 'Not really, sir. The victim's a well-dressed young lady so I'd say it wasn't a street brawl. If it wasn't for the cutting I'd have said a husband or boyfriend might have had a go at her, out of jealousy, like. The doc doesn't think she was raped and nothing appears to have been stolen.' He shook his head. 'But all that knife work isn't normal by any stretch of the imagination, so I'm guessing it's not a robbery or lovers' quarrel that's gone too far by accident.'

'Exactly.' Kember took another sip of tea. 'The killer didn't seem to want anything from the victim but her life. He deliberately took a long-bladed knife with him and chose one of the quietest spots within the village, but not so secluded the body wouldn't be found. No attempt had been made to cover or conceal. He seemed to want to make a show of her death by leaving her displayed afterwards.' Kember glanced at Wright. 'Shouts *malice aforethought*, not a frenzied spur-of-the-moment attack. Most people desire power and position, wealth and sex, and work hard to get them. Some will kill to get them, or out of anger and revenge if they lose them. As you said, a quick fumble and some loose change doesn't appear to have been the motive here, so I did start to consider whether it could have been a woman.'

'Surely not, sir?' Wright looked incredulous. 'Not the fairer sex.'

'You'd be surprised what women are capable of. But no, I discarded that idea. Dr Headley said death was probably by strangulation and the marks were made by one hand, a right hand. It's more likely a man would have the strength to do that. I saw no signs of a prolonged struggle and I would've expected one woman attacked by another from the front to have at least given a good account of herself. There should have been scratches, a greater disarray of clothing, her bag cast aside and so on. She would've lain crumpled on the ground, not arranged like a window display.'

'It had been raining heavily, sir. Perhaps any signs had been washed away? Also, the ground was churned up by Elias Brown and his dog, police photographers from Tonbridge, the good doctor and ourselves.'

Kember wrote in his notebook. 'Which in itself is a timely reminder about the need for the preservation of crime scenes.' He glanced again at Wright, noting a faint pink hue of embarrassment high on his sergeant's cheeks. Kember took that as a sign no further admonishment was necessary. 'I want you to start with the railway station and two back streets before working your way along into the High Street, interviewing occupants and visitors alike. The doctor estimates the time of death at between ten o'clock and midnight. At that time of night, it would have been dark but several people would still have been out and about. Drinkers leaving the pub, for example. Ask if they saw or heard anything from about nine o'clock until midnight last night. I'll need a word with the owners of the lodgings where Miss Scott stayed. What are the names of the ARP warden and vicar?'

'Brian Greenway and the Reverend Giles Wilson,' Wright said. 'Where you find the reverend you'll find his housekeeper, too. Mrs Jessie Oaks. Widowed.'

'Good, I'll talk to them and the dog walker but I'll visit the air station first, seeing as the victim is one of theirs. They might have had other personnel in the village too.' He glanced out of the window. 'Looks like the rain's eased off for now.'

Wright stood and retrieved his helmet. 'I'll speak to Les Brannan too, he's the publican over at the Castle, and his sister Alice.'

'Ah yes, thank you. Don't forget to dust the clutch bag for fingerprints when you get back. And with any luck, Dr Headley might have something more for us sooner rather than later.' Kember eased himself out of his chair. 'At least let's hope so, so we can get the monster that did this, for the sake of Miss Lavinia Scott.'

CHAPTER THREE

A corridor off the main hallway of the manor house led to the air station briefing room. With cream- and green-painted walls, a blackboard and pull-down projector screen at one end and rows of plain chairs before a desk, the room was utilitarian and functional. Stale cigarette smoke hung in the air, barely disguised by the thick aroma of fresh polish from the parquet floor.

Emily Parker slammed against the open door as a woman barged between her and Lizzie into the briefing room.

'Steady on!' Emily said, rubbing her elbow.

The woman turned back and glared at her. 'Did you say something?'

'Where's the fire, Fizz?'

'Don't you be funny with me, you scrawny wee git.'

Lizzie sighed wearily, as Fizz's formerly mild Scottish accent broadened with aggression.

'We've been together over a month now,' Lizzie said gently. 'I thought we were friends who could get by without being rude.'

Fizz sneered. 'Oh, you'll know when I'm being rude.'

Emily smirked. 'I'm not worried about Fizz. She's nothing more than an angry *Jock* strap.'

Fizz pushed her now flushed face close to Emily's. 'You wanna repeat that?'

Emily laughed. 'The moment we met, you thought you were something special but you're a third officer, just like the rest of us. Good to have around in a scrap, though, what with that temper of yours.' She gave Fizz an exaggerated wink.

'Trouble, ladies?'

Lizzie's heart jolted as she looked left and saw their captain striding across the hall towards the briefing room.

'No, ma'am,' she said, manoeuvring herself between Fizz and Emily. 'A little friendly ribbing, that's all.'

Lizzie concentrated on keeping her smile in place as Geraldine passed them, noting the sideways glance of suspicion the captain gave her. She waited for Fizz and Emily to sit down, as far from each other as they could manage, before finding herself a chair.

Geraldine glanced around the room and consulted a sheet of paper on the table beside her. 'We appear to be one short.' She looked up.

'Lavinia Scott hasn't arrived yet, ma'am,' said Lizzie.

Geraldine frowned. 'I find that most disappointing. We've all had to fight bureaucracy and prejudice to get here and to prove our ability far in excess of that required by men to be allowed to fly. I can't imagine why one of you would throw this opportunity away by not reporting on time.'

'I'm sure there must be a good reason, ma'am. The weather was atrocious earlier.'

'And yet everyone else made it.' Geraldine said coolly.

Lizzie began to pick nervously at the skin around her thumbnails.

'Right,' Geraldine continued. 'You know each other from training but you don't know me from Adam and I've only seen your personnel records. So, introductions.'

Lizzie groaned inwardly. Even though she knew everyone but the captain, this was exactly the kind of situation that could cause her trouble.

'Are you all right there?'

Lizzie's heart put in an extra beat when she realised she'd covered her eyes with her fingers. She dropped her hands and folded them in her lap. 'Yes, I'm fine. Sorry, ma'am.'

'Good. As I was saying. I'm Captain Geraldine Ellenden-Pitt. On duty, I'm ma'am or Captain. Off duty, I'm Geraldine. I am *not*, under any circumstances, Gerry.' A ripple of laughter went around the room. 'I'm in charge of the ATA Number Thirteen Ferry Pool here at RAF Scotney but, although that means anything ATA-related is my patch, I am not in command of the air station as a whole, more's the pity. You'll meet our glorious leaders in a moment. I like all the usual: wine, chocolate, dancing. I also love flying and before the war I piloted sightseeing trips and flew in air shows, even being allowed to do the mystical and dreaded aerobatics most people believe we're incapable of.' She smiled and nodded to Fizz. 'Your turn.'

Fizz half-turned in her chair and put her elbow on the back to maintain the position. 'I'm Third Officer Felicity Mitchell, but I prefer Fizz. I was born in Edinburgh so naturally they posted me as far from there as possible. I too have flown aerobatics and could handle anything the RAF has, if they'd let me.' She flapped her right hand in the air as a gesture of disdain.

The woman behind Fizz and to the right of Lizzie stood up to attention. 'Agata Toroniska, Third Officer, from Warsaw. I escaped when the Germans invaded my country and started to murder Jews. My parents were not so lucky. I can fly better than any man I know and am here to help you kill as many Germans as you can. If I get the chance, I will too.' She sat and relaxed.

In her lap, Lizzie's fingers began to tremble. Mentally she found herself rapidly running through the countermeasures she used in moments like these. The first required taking herself away from the situation and the second involved forcing herself to concentrate on something other than the attack itself, both impossible in her current situation. The third required counting the number of something she could see, like drawing pins on a board, then backwards down to one. As her eyes searched for something to count she heard the captain addressing her again.

Lizzie sat up straight, her heart thrumming in her chest. 'Elizabeth Hayes, ma'am. Third Officer. My father taught me to fly and we had a rather good time around Europe taking part in air races before the Boche spoilt it all. By the way, the gorgeous Norton motorbike in the motor shed is my brother's but he's at the front flying Hurricanes so I've collared it for a while.' She gave the best smile she could muster and concentrated on stilling her breathing, counting each breath until she could feel her heart begin to slow down.

To Lizzie's left, a woman with tawny brown hair took a deep breath and the moment she spoke there was no mistaking her country of birth. 'Third Officer McNulty. I have a Gaelic name spelled N-I-A-M-H but pronounced *Neave*. I was born in Galway but brought up in Dublin. My father was an Irishman in the British Civil Service and my mother was his English secretary. We were despised by the British and the Irish, especially the Irish Republican Army. *West Brits* they called us. You could say I've been fighting all my life. All you really need to know for now is I can fly well enough.'

Fizz emitted a snort of derision, quickly snuffed out by a sharp look from Geraldine.

Geraldine nodded to Charlie in the front row, who cleared her throat before speaking. 'Third Officer Charlotte, *Charlie*, Rowan-Peake, at your service. I've been there and done that. Air shows, sightseeing jaunts, continental fly-ins. Marvellous fun. Dancing is a wonderful distraction at worst and bliss at best. Next to Lizzie's

Norton in the shed is my sports car, a BSA Scout. It's only a two-seater so no group outings, I'm afraid.'

'And lastly . . . ?' Geraldine prompted.

'Third Officer Emily Parker,' Emily announced from her seat in the third row. Lizzie happened to know that at age twenty-two she was the youngest of the Scotney ATA women. 'I've been flying in Tiger Moths since I was old enough to sit in one. My brothers used to take me up for jaunts, and when they began letting me do circuits and bumps of my own I was hooked. They restored an old Royal Flying Corps Sopwith Camel and gave it to me for my eighteenth birthday, bless them. I learn jolly quick and I can sling a kite around the sky as if it's part of me. As soon as they let us fly Spits, I'll be there.'

Geraldine gave a nod of satisfaction. The flying talent in the room was undeniable but so were the black marks Lizzie knew lay on each file, their so-called maverick behaviour having exasperated their instructors the moment they had taken to the air at White Waltham. Their shared talent for trouble should have allowed them to bond quickly as a unit, but it came with its own set of consequences.

Geraldine tapped the pile of personnel files with her fingers for emphasis. 'Welcome to you all. For some of you this will be your first posting and, unless Jerry decides to invade, we may very well remain here for the duration of the war. As you well know, you are not the first women to enter the ATA. The initial intake, or First Eight as they have become known, paved the way for you and me. They may now be famous, their photographs splashed across newspapers like film stars, but fame is not the draw. The lure of flying over the countryside, using one's skills, helping the war effort in the best way possible are laudable reasons for wanting to ferry RAF warplanes. Is it exciting and exhilarating? Of course. Is it risky, perhaps even downright dangerous? Absolutely. We may not be allowed to join the men in aerial combat but all of us have more flying experience in terms of hours logged than most of the pilots anywhere in the Royal Air Force. Never forget you carry a burden on your shoulders: to repay those First Eight for this opportunity by proving every day we can do as good a job of piloting as the men.'

Geraldine pointed to a poster of aircraft types pinned to the board.

'Despite our undeniable experience, we're still not cleared to fly anything beyond Class Three at the moment. Advanced single-engine and light twins, you know the drill. That should mean fighters but the Air Ministry's not playing ball. Pauline Gower is having a crack at the top brass and if she's successful you'll get the go-ahead to fly Spits and Hurries, so fingers crossed but don't hold your breath. In case you were wondering, we'll all take a stint as taxi pilot.'

Unable to help herself, Lizzie could no longer contain the burning question that had been preying on her mind since Geraldine began talking. 'Ma'am,' she said. Geraldine nodded for her to speak. 'Why are we Number Thirteen Ferry Pool? I didn't think there were that many in the country.'

'Good question,' Geraldine replied. 'It's what passes for male humour. Thirteen is the number at the Last Supper when Jesus revealed one of his disciples would betray him. Supposedly, it is also the number of witches in a coven. Therefore, thirteen is regarded as bad luck, as are we, and hence the designation. I'm afraid we're seen as a bit of a joke. It's up to you to prove our detractors wrong.'

Kember pulled up to the air station gatehouse and stated his business. After a moment's delay waiting for clearance, he drove across to the Georgian manor house that now formed the base headquarters and parked on a large semi-circle of gravel at the front.

His father had bought the two-door, soft-top Hillman Minx Tourer brand new in 1937. A follower of British motorsport, he'd insisted on having it painted in the fashionable and rather elegant British racing green, but had only enjoyed driving it for a little over a year. He'd died suddenly of a stroke while watching a racing event at Brooklands race course, leaving his pride and joy to Kember in his will. It had taken Kember another year before he'd even sat in it but now he wouldn't be without this tangible reminder of his much-missed father.

Kember had visited the manor house in the course of his duties before the war, but now its white-painted stucco showed signs of needing a good clean. He knew the building had a main range with two short wings extending to the rear enclosing a large south-facing terrace looking out on a formal garden, and extensive grounds occupied in part by the recently built airfield. Beyond a camouflaged fuel dump, Kember could see scattered blister hangars and aircraft blast pens on the far edge of the airfield. To his right stood regimented lines of corrugated-iron Nissen huts, half-sunk brick buildings with defensive earthworks and an array of sundry buildings from the original estate.

Entering the house through a heavily sandbagged, marble-columned portico into a spacious hallway, Kember noticed changes since his previous visit. All the windows were criss-crossed with tape to prevent blast shatter. Painted signs indicated the officers' mess and lounge off to his right, and various offices to his left. The wide staircase to the first and second floors remained, now leading to more offices and quarters for RAF and ATA officers, but the elaborate crystal chandelier had gone. A few paintings and scattered pieces of polished wood furniture emphasised the gaps where more valuable pieces had been removed to safety.

An orderly emerged from the direction of the offices, led Kember upstairs to the first floor and ushered him into an anteroom. Kember moved to the window and peered through. Beyond the formal gardens lay an expanse of lush green lawn marred by sandbags stacked over and around the concrete portal of an air raid shelter. Beyond this stood an anti-aircraft position, its black-barrelled gun being wiped down by a gunner. Kember looked towards the door of Dallington's office, distinguishable from another belonging to a 'Wg. Cdr. J. Matfield' on the opposite side by its painted nameplate, weighing up whether being kept waiting was a tactic designed to demonstrate power and assert authority over his domain. Kember gave Dallington the benefit of the doubt for two more minutes before deciding to knock, when it opened suddenly.

'*Timber?*' an RAF officer queried.

'*Darlington?*' Kember replied.

Dallington's mouth twitched. 'Group Captain *Dallington*. Commanding officer.'

Kember knew he'd won the first point and stated his full title. 'Detective Inspector *Kember*,' he emphasised, 'from the Tonbridge Division of Kent County Constabulary. I'd like to ask a couple of questions. May I come in?'

Dallington left the door half open, sat behind his desk and puffed out his chest. The framed photographs, certificates and other personal memorabilia on the wall behind him acted like a display of peacock feathers.

Kember remained unimpressed, having often sat opposite Chief Inspector Hartson in an office filled with badges, photographs and other police paraphernalia. Hartson being a man of little theatricality, few of the items belonged to him. He regarded the exhibits as a historical record rather than, as he put it, an ostentatious display of personal frippery.

Kember recalled his superior's ill-disguised awkwardness on one recent occasion, Hartson's mouth opening and closing a few times like a clockwork toy and his tongue flicking at his lips before he managed to speak. 'I've heard about . . . you know?' he'd said.

Irritated that his marriage difficulties had become common knowledge, Kember had suppressed the urge to snap *What? My dodgy back?* Instead, he'd rescued his boss. 'My wife?'

Hartson had frowned. 'Bad business. Sorry, and all that.'

Kember knew Hartson did not normally go in for discussing personal matters and the discomfort had shown on his superior's face. A similar discomfort was now mirrored on Dallington's features, another twitch pulling at the corner of his mouth as Kember sat without waiting to be invited.

'What's so urgent you needed to see me right away?' Dallington said brusquely.

Kember kept his voice calm and flat. 'I think you should call in the head of your RAF Police. He'll need to hear what I have to say.' Kember almost laughed aloud at the officer's petulant pout but Dallington made a telephone call nonetheless. 'And would it be possible to have access to service records, should the need arise?'

On this Dallington refused point-blank and Kember thought he couldn't have looked more horrified if he'd asked him to run naked through the village.

A few moments later another two men entered. After introductions and handshakes, Matfield and Pendry sat at an angle to Dallington's desk. Having never before had cause nor opportunity to study uniforms at close quarters, theirs amused him. Although Dallington's and Matfield's seemed the same, they differed on the number of cuff rings and medal ribbons. Dallington had more of both and Kember wondered whether longevity automatically entitled you to yet another cuff ring, and rank to another medal. Pendry wore the RAF Police Service uniform with a white pistol holster and webbing, a black-and-red band on his right arm with the letters RAFP and a pair of kidskin gloves.

Kember addressed his question to the two newcomers. 'Are you missing any of your women from the Air Transport Auxiliary, by any chance?'

'I've no idea,' Dallington said, cutting off any response from the others. 'Officially they're not my women because they're civilians and I'm RAF. They're the responsibility of Captain Ellenden-Pitt.'

'Perhaps he should join us too?'

'*She* is busy briefing the new arrivals. Look, what is all this?'

Matfield remained impassive but Pendry's cheeks had coloured.

Kember found himself irritated by Dallington's attitude but wouldn't allow himself to show it. 'I'm sorry to say the body of Miss Lavinia Scott was found on a path by the church in Scotney village this morning.'

Dallington's eyes narrowed. 'What has that got to do with us, Inspector?'

Kember's eyes fixed on Dallington's. 'Her bag was found nearby. Her papers state she was an officer in the ATA.'

'Good Lord, well . . . that's terrible news.'

Dallington's face and relaxed body language did not match his exclamation. Nor did Matfield's. Kember felt his already thinning patience begin to ebb away. 'Are you able to confirm she was from the ATA?'

'One moment,' Dallington said. Kember watched as he made a show of scrabbling among the papers anchored on his desk by a Bible used as a paperweight, in an overfull filing cabinet drawer and a cardboard box on the floor. Finally, Dallington waved a sheet of paper in mock triumph and ran his finger down the page. 'I have a list here, Inspector, and according to my information she *is* one of ours.'

Kember noted Dallington's stance shift with the use of the word *ours*. A moment earlier he had seemed blasé about taking responsibility. 'Isn't it a little strange you didn't know she was missing?'

Again, Dallington's mouth twitched and his voice hardened. 'I was about to meet the women for the first time when you called and I'm sure the captain would have informed us of any absences. This . . . Lavinia Scott' – he almost spat the name – 'is one of ours, so we'll take it from here, thank you.'

Kember gripped the fedora on his lap. Keeping the annoyance from his voice, he said, 'Thank you for your generous offer, Group Captain, but as you pointed out, I'm afraid Miss Scott was a civilian killed while off the air station. Kent Police have jurisdiction and I am leading the investigation.'

Dallington's mouth worked like a silent film, the words refusing to come despite its efforts.

'The inspector is correct, sir,' Pendry interjected. He looked at Kember. 'Have you any suspects or leads?'

The genuine interest in Pendry's face reassured Kember that at least someone cared. 'Not at present. Apart from it being a violent and particularly vicious attack, we have few verifiable facts and my sergeant is currently speaking to everyone in the village.' Kember turned his gaze to Matfield. 'I take it that apart from Miss Scott all the ATA women arrived today?'

Matfield stiffened at the question. 'I assume so. Most of them flew in this morning, through the storm. Two others we rather expected to report tomorrow because of the weather arrived by road around the same time today.'

Kember glanced at Pendry. 'The fly-ins can be ruled out as suspects straight away because they weren't here, but the other two—'

'Now look here,' Dallington growled. 'You can't think anyone here is responsible?'

Kember knew if he said nothing, Dallington would be unable to leave the silence. He didn't have to wait long.

'That's preposterous!' Dallington almost spluttered in outrage.

Kember felt his fingers begin to cramp around the rim of his hat. 'Have you had any new personnel at the air station in the last six months, apart from the women, of course?'

'As a matter of fact, we've had people leave,' Matfield said. 'We had three squadrons based here but they've been redeployed. The pilots and most of the air station personnel went with them. We've been designated a reserve station, a satellite of Biggin Hill, left with a skeleton crew and a detachment of ATA women.'

Although said as a matter of fact, Kember detected an undertone of disgust.

'Inspector' – Pendry sat forward – 'as the victim was stationed here, it's my duty to insist that I be part of your investigation.'

Dallington jutted his jaw at Kember and nodded in agreement.

'Of course,' said Kember. 'That's why I asked for you to join us. There are some jurisdictional grey areas your presence would alleviate.' He gave his one warm smile of the meeting. 'May I ask who guards the air station?'

'I have a flight sergeant as my deputy and two corporals,' Pendry said. 'Under our command we have a squad of privates and a full detachment of Air Ministry Wardens, and can call on extra RAF Police from Biggin Hill in an emergency. We undertake all guarding duties, including the perimeter, buildings, aircraft and the gatehouse. The Anti-Aircraft Command are on site too, manning the two search-light positions, two Bofors guns and three heavy machine-gun positions. All their staff at Scotney are Territorial Army but come under the station commander.' He indicated Dallington with a slight bow of his head.

Dallington spluttered like a dying engine and Kember could almost touch the resentment emanating from him and Matfield. Pendry, on the other hand, had the more familiar air of the down-trodden policeman. Kember realised he was still gripping his fedora and made a conscious effort to relax his fingers.

'Gentlemen' – he returned their glares – 'I have the usual routine question to ask of you both before I leave.' He looked at Dallington. 'Where were you last night between ten o'clock and midnight?'

Dallington's already red face became puce with renewed outrage. 'I was here in my office from nine until eleven, then I went to bed. The staff here will confirm that.'

Kember turned to Matfield. 'And you, Wing Commander?'

Matfield's face paled though his voice remained steady. 'I went into the village early evening for a meal and a drink at the pub, on my own. I left about nine o'clock and was tucked up in bed by ten at the latest.'

'Any witnesses?'

'In the pub, and the gatehouse will have a record in the log.'

Kember faked a smile. 'Thank you, gentlemen.' He stood. 'If I can have a word with Flight Lieutenant Pendry before I leave, I won't take up any more of your day. My sergeant or I will be dropping by to speak to the air station personnel and those of the ATA. It shouldn't take too long but I'd appreciate a room to use, so we're not in your way.'

'Very well, Inspector,' Dallington said through thin lips. 'Let Pendry know and we'll put names on the gate list. Is there anything else I can help you with?'

'Not at the moment. Thank you for your time.'

Moments later, standing outside Dallington's office with the door having closed behind them, Kember smiled as he heard the thump of a fist on a desk.

Kember and Pendry walked back through the hall of the manor house and out to the gravel where the Minx remained parked. Being a non-smoker, Kember declined the offer of a cigarette but waited while Pendry lit a Woodbine

'Spiky pair, aren't they?' A stiff breeze whipped away the smoke from Pendry's breath.

'You could say that,' Kember agreed.

'Generally, they're all right, although they have their moments, both good and bad. It has to be said, Dallington hates women on his air station. Come to that, he hates any woman venturing outside domestic or nursing duties.'

Kember looked towards the gatehouse. 'And you?'

'Me?' Pendry looked surprised. 'I got here the hard way: by good work and diligence. Don't get me wrong, I went through boarding school too. Harrow. But Dallington and Matfield don't appreciate the advantages they've had. They don't recognise those same privileges in the ATA women. If the ATA are Daddies' girls, they are Mummies' boys.' He took another long pull on his cigarette.

Kember kept his expression impassive, noting that Pendry had answered a different question. 'Where were you at the time of the murder, Flight Lieutenant?' He gave Pendry a sideways glance.

Pendry didn't seem surprised by the question. 'I commenced walking the perimeter at nine o'clock with my flight sergeant, Ben Vickers. We do that often, to keep the men on their toes and inspect the airfield defences. The men on watch were all at their posts and we got back to the barracks at about ten o'clock or just after. The men not on watch were relaxing in the barracks, with the next watch about to go to bed for a few hours.'

'And you can account for all your men?'

'I can vouch for having seen them all within the space of an hour, Inspector.' He took another long drag on his cigarette.

'Have you met any of the ATA women?'

'Only their captain. I'm due to join Dallington at the ATA briefing.' He looked at his watch. 'Right now, in fact.' He dropped the remains of his cigarette and pushed it into the gravel with his heel. 'Miss Scott's details, next of kin and all that, will be on file. As we're working together and she was stationed here, I'll get in touch with her family, break the news as gently as I can and see if they can shed any light on whether she had any enemies or knew anyone in the village.' He grasped Kember's proffered hand. 'Don't worry, I won't let any cats out of the bag . . . about how she died, I mean.'

'If you could also keep your eyes peeled for anything unusual, I'd be grateful.' Kember opened the door of his Minx.

'Of course.' Pendry nodded. 'I'll see you or your sergeant in due course, Inspector.'

Kember got into his car and watched Pendry return through the portico. In many respects, the RAF policeman seemed decent enough with no apparent loyalty, staunch or otherwise, to Dallington or Matfield. In the coming days, Kember mused, that may prove to be rather useful.

Lizzie noticed an orderly stop Dallington and Matfield outside the ATA briefing room. Moments later, a grim-faced Dallington strode through the door with Matfield. Pendry trailed a few seconds behind. The women stood to attention.

'At ease, ladies,' Dallington said, standing facing them with his hands clasped behind his back, Matfield and Pendry to one side and Geraldine on the other.

The women sat and relaxed.

'Firstly, welcome. I say that with reservation because this was an operational fighter station with its own squadrons until recently. So you will forgive me if I see your arrival as something of a come-down. That's not to ignore the fact you have a job to do, which I hope you will do to a very high standard. The RAF is relying on the movement of aircraft to front-line airfields and the removal of unserviceable aircraft to maintenance units at the rear. Do your job and do it well.' Dallington paused to indicate the man to his immediate left. 'This is Wing Commander Matfield, my second-in-command. Next to him is Flight Lieutenant Pendry of the RAF Police. I would prefer you to raise any issues you have with your captain, in the first instance, and she can bring it to the attention of one of us.'

The women exchanged sideways glances.

'Secondly, I have received important news from Eleven Group HQ. You will be aware that for the last few weeks the German Luftwaffe have been conducting limited night attacks along the coast and harassing shipping in the English Channel and North Sea during daylight. Today, a large formation of German bombers and fighters attacked a convoy in the English Channel. This is the first time such numbers have been used against us and it remains to be seen whether this represents an escalation of hostilities. With a number of losses on both sides, the significance of this act will not escape you, I'm sure.

'Lastly, I came from my office to this briefing having spoken to a Detective Inspector Kember. Regretfully, I have to inform you that one of your expected number, Third Officer Lavinia Scott, was found murdered in the village this morning.'

Gasps rose from the seated women, even Fizz, whose face blanched with shock, and they immediately began to fire questions. Lizzie's mind snapped back to her arrival in the village that morning, remembering the police gathered on the church path and her dismissal by the detective there. Had she unwittingly seen Lavinia's dead body? She clasped her arms around her as her skin tightened with horror.

Dallington raised his hands to quell the uproar and continued unperturbed. 'She was found on a path near the church. I understand her attacker struck last night during the blackout. I tell you this because you have a right to know what has happened to your colleague, to allow you to make informed decisions about how you go about your professional and social business while at Scotney. The world is a dangerous place, even more so now there's a war on. Stay safe. That is all.'

Without a second glance at the officers, Dallington left the room.

Lizzie looked around at her colleagues, some with anguish etched on their faces, others fidgeting with suppressed curiosity, her own head aching with questions. Matfield had remained where he was. She saw his stone-faced military stare change to a benevolent, almost fatherly expression that made her wonder what was coming next.

He held up a pacifying hand. 'I know you have many questions but the CO and I are as deeply shocked and as much in the dark as you. We all must wait for the police to conclude their investigation. Despite this unfortunate turn of events, I echo the CO's words. Your contribution to the war effort must continue so we expect professionalism at every turn. That said, do not let this affect your daily lives. There are bigger killers out there.'

Matfield nodded to Geraldine. 'Carry on,' he said, and left the room with Pendry.

Another burst of chatter exploded around the room before it was silenced as Geraldine rapped her knuckles on the desk. Lizzie raised her hand, questions clamouring to be asked, but the captain ignored her, looking at the women with an expression halfway between serious and sad.

'This has come as a shock to us all. I had braced myself to lose pilots in the air but not on the ground like this. I need to find out more about what happened to Miss Scott and do not wish to lose any more of you in this way, so I must repeat the group captain's warning.' Her face softened but the look of concern remained. 'It's entirely up to you whether or not you wish to socialise in the village but my advice would be to remain on the air station until this man is caught. Whatever your decisions, I urge you to remain vigilant and safe.'

As Geraldine left the room, her command of 'Dismissed' was lost in the returning chatter.

Agata bit a loose piece of tobacco from the end of a cigarette and spat it away. 'Before the Nazis came, if a man tried anything in Poland he'd lose his balls.' She cocked her head on one side to light her cigarette.

Lizzie also lit a cigarette, placing the packet on her lap and taking care to align it with her lighter, watching her colleagues through a curl of blue smoke and half-listening to the conversation. Out of the corner of her eye, she saw Pendry still speaking to Matfield in the corridor, and without giving herself time to think, she rose to join them. Seconds later, with Matfield walking away, she put her hand on Pendry's arm before he could follow.

'Excuse me, Flight Lieutenant,' Lizzie said, uncertain whether she was doing the right thing but unable to stop herself.

Pendry turned, surprise on his face as he looked at her hand. 'I beg your pardon?'

'Sorry, sir.' Lizzie withdrew her hand. 'I know the CO said to go through our captain but I wondered if I could have a quick word.'

Pendry threw her an impatient frown. 'I can spare ninety seconds.'

'Thank you. I wondered if you knew any details about the murder?'

'Such as?'

'Where and when it happened? How she died? The murder weapon? What the crime scene looked like?' Lizzie almost winced at how eager she sounded.

Pendry raised his eyebrows. 'Now why would you want to know all that?'

Lizzie wavered. Perhaps now was the wrong time and he the wrong person. Then she recalled the voice of Beatrice Edgell, her old university tutor and mentor, telling her to believe in herself. '*You can let them underestimate you, that's their problem, but don't ever let anyone convince you that you aren't good enough, because you are.'*

She raised her chin in defiance. 'Because I believe I can help.' She felt colour rising in her cheeks at the benevolent smile he gave her, as if to a child.

'I don't think so, Miss . . . ?'

'Third Officer Hayes. Lizzie.' She caught her breath as Pendry reached out and touched her arm, his smile still in place.

'I understand the loss of your friend comes as a big shock, but—'

'We didn't *lose* her, she was murdered,' Lizzie interrupted, pulling her arm away.

'And that makes it a police matter.'

'And I can help. I'm a trained psychologist. In fact, during my studies at London University, understanding criminals, especially the murderous kind, was my speciality.' Lizzie could see disbelief slide across his features and she almost faltered. 'Certain cases compelled me to dig deeper into the minds of the murderers who had committed them, to learn how to recognise what made them who they were. And I believe that kind of expertise could be invaluable to helping find the person who did this.'

As Pendry glanced at his watch, Lizzie could see his disbelief turning to irritation.

'Well, Miss Hayes.' Pendry's voice was crisp in such a way that made Lizzie's shoulders sink. 'The detective inspector in charge of the case is sending a sergeant to speak to everyone tomorrow. He may even come himself. If you have any questions or information, that will be the time to discuss it. In the meantime, I suggest you relax while you can. Let the men do the job they were *trained* to do.'

With that, Pendry turned away and Lizzie took a long, furious drag on her cigarette, blowing the smoke in a stream of rebuke at his receding form.

CHAPTER FOUR

By Thursday afternoon Kember's cold and mood had not improved. Knocking on front doors and questioning villagers had proved fruitless, and nothing had come from Sergeant Wright's visits to the Brannans and Brian Greenway. The latter was particularly galling and Kember determined to have his own little chat with the ARP warden. Straight after dropping in on the Taplow sisters, and with the previous day's encounter with Dalington running through his mind, Kember knocked on the door of the vicarage. When no answer came, he knocked again. No reply. He leant back and glanced towards St Matthew's Church next door. Within a minute, he had left the vicarage and walked through the small graveyard separating the church from the High Street. Standing at the arched entrance, he could hear a tuneless whistle echoing from within.

'Hello?' he called.

The whistling stopped. Kember took off his fedora as he stepped through the entrance and allowed a few seconds for his eyes to become accustomed to the gloom inside. He caught a waft of disinfectant beneath the sweet scent of roses.

'Can I help you?'

Kember watched a shadow detach itself from others near the baptismal font to his left. As it shifted into more light it was revealed to belong to a short, thin woman with a floral print, wrap-around pinafore and a scarf tied around her hair in a turban style. She held a mop and bucket, her face carrying an expression of polite interest.

'Possibly,' Kember said.

'If you're looking for the reverend, he's in the vestry attending to parish paperwork.' She raised her chin, indicating somewhere over his shoulder.

'Thank you. My name is Detective Inspector Kember. And you are . . . ?'

'Oh.' Her expression changed to one more serious. 'I'm Jessica Oaks. Mrs – well, widowed. You'll be here about that poor girl, I suppose?'

Kember met her gaze. 'I'm afraid so.'

'As I said, Reverend Wilson is busy in the vestry but I'm sure he'll speak to you if you go through.'

'Actually, I'll talk to the reverend in a moment, but I wonder if I could have a word with you first?' Kember motioned towards the rear pew for her to sit.

Her mouth opened without sound for a few seconds. 'Of course, if I can be of any help,' she said at last.

Mrs Oaks put her mop and bucket to one side and perched at the end of the pew, her knees pressed together and her hands resting in her lap. Kember sat at the end of the corresponding pew on the other side of the aisle.

'Nothing to worry about. I have one or two questions to ask. All routine.'

'It's no bother,' she said with a shrug as she picked at the hem of her pinafore.

'I understand from Sergeant Wright that you are Reverend Wilson's housekeeper.'

'I am. I also do a bit of work in the church, putting out hymn books and changing the flowers.' She pointed to a nearby vase of roses. 'Tidying up after services like today's morning prayers.' She gazed levelly at Kember. 'We missed you, I think.'

Kember managed a thin smile. 'Where were you Tuesday night between nine o'clock and midnight?'

'Me?' She put her palm to her chest before gripping the crucifix around her neck. 'I was in the vicarage with the reverend. We had our tea at half past six then he went off for his usual evening prayers at about seven.' She leant forward conspiratorially, her hand dropping back to her lap. 'The reverend always has a bit of private time in the evening in the church. He might do some work or speak to a visitor but he always says a few private prayers.'

Kember nodded his understanding, but to his mind private time provided opportunities for more than just religious contemplation. 'What time did he get back?'

Mrs Oaks sat back and glanced sideways at a clock fixed over the door to the bell tower. 'A minute or so after eight. He usually stays an hour. An hour and a half at most.'

'And then what?'

Kember noticed the flicker of a frown. Country folk knew everyone's business but were notoriously reticent about giving anything away to strangers, even to policemen.

Mrs Oaks clenched her hands together. 'I wash up while he's out and when he returns I might do a bit of ironing or make a pie ready for the following day. The reverend might read, finish some sermon work or listen to the radiogram.'

'Does the reverend work late or does he retire early?'

Mrs Oaks smiled knowingly and held her crucifix again. 'In the winter, he goes to bed at around nine o'clock but as it's summer he goes up between ten and eleven o'clock.' She glanced up in thought. 'About half past ten, on Tuesday, as I recall.'

Kember looked away. Did this provide an alibi or had the reverend slipped out undetected? He'd caught her smile and wondered if there was something between her and the reverend, or maybe she wished there to be.

'Are you all right, Inspector?' Mrs Oaks had her head tilted slightly in concern.

Kember looked back at her. 'At what time did you go up?'

'I don't see—' She cut off the protest, her widened eyes suddenly brimming with indignation. 'I've got a room downstairs at the back so I retire when I've finished my bits and pieces.'

Kember paused.

'Did you hear or see anything outside on Tuesday at about that time?'

Mrs Oaks considered this and when she spoke her voice still had an edge of annoyance. 'No, Inspector.' Then her hand went to her crucifix again. 'Oh, wait.' Her tone had lost its edge and she glanced at the clock again. 'It must have been just after ten o'clock when the reverend called from upstairs. He thought I'd gone out. Don't know why. Anyway, he came down to the kitchen a minute or so later – I'd made our usual Ovaltine – and Mr Greenway shouted for us to put our blackout curtain in place. I'd looked out a moment before to see if it had started raining, seeing as the weather forecast on the radio had said we could expect a storm. I hadn't put it back properly.'

'What did you see when you looked out?'

'Nothing. It was dark by then but it wasn't raining.'

Kember scratched his nose thoughtfully. 'Do many people use the path by the church?'

Mrs Oaks shook her head. 'Not that I know of. Elias, Mr Brown, takes his dog to the field and kiddies play over there sometimes, but it doesn't go anywhere else these days so there's no other reason for anyone to use it.'

Kember glanced along the nave towards the vestry. 'Has Reverend Wilson been here long? As the vicar, I mean?'

Mrs Oaks looked over his head, thinking. 'About three years, I'd say. He's from Maidstone so he knows Kent people.'

'Would you say you know him well?' Kember meant nothing more by his words but saw her face harden again.

'Well enough. He's young but he's got a wise head and a kind heart.'

Kember sensed her defences rising and decided to leave it there. 'Thank you for your help, Mrs Oaks. That's all I need for now.'

A mixture of surprise and relief crossed her face as she stood and smoothed her pinafore. 'I'll get back to my cleaning, then.'

Kember smiled and gestured towards the vestry. 'And I'll just pop in to see the reverend.'

Tea in the officers' lounge on Thursday afternoon was a subdued affair. Charlie slumped in an armchair and Lizzie sat with Fizz and Emily at the low table nearby, to keep the peace more than anything else, their stilted conversation having petered out. The murder of one of their own played on everyone's minds and Lizzie still brooded over being disregarded out of hand by not one, but two policemen.

'What are you doing?' Fizz broke the silence, staring accusatorially at Lizzie.

Lizzie looked down and realised with a jolt that she had aligned their three teaspoons in the middle of the table and Emily was looking at her indulgently, like she was a two-year-old stacking wooden blocks.

'It's nothing,' Lizzie said. 'It's a game I've played since I was little.'

'Doesn't explain why you still do this.' Fizz indicated the spoons.

Lizzie put the spoons back in their saucers, annoyed with herself. She sighed, resigned.

'My mother broke several bones in a riding accident when I was very young and spent weeks in hospital but never rode again. The hospital that made her better was clean and ordered so it seemed to my young mind that washing my hands a bit more' – she didn't dare say how frequently – 'and keeping things in good order was the way to stay safe and healthy.'

'What rubbish.' Fizz laughed. 'Who on earth told you that?'

'Actually, my psychology tutor at university,' Lizzie said.

Beatrice Edgell had noticed her behaviour and diagnosed her with a condition that psychologists had started calling 'obsessive compulsive neurosis', or OCN for short. Lizzie still hated the label but had at least been shown how to manage and cope with it after years of being told there was something wrong with her, some fault, like a crack in bone china.

'Sounds like you needed a better tutor,' Fizz said imperiously.

Lizzie clenched her jaw and fingered one of the thick rubber bands she always wore on her wrists. It was Beatrice who had suggested she use them to ping against her flesh as a defensive measure against rising anxiety. One sharp ping was often enough to shock her back to normal thinking.

'Do leave her alone, Fizz,' Charlie said, sitting forward.

'It's odd, though, don't you think?' said Fizz, circling her index finger by her temple. 'A bit cuckoo.'

'Arranging a few bits of cutlery is no skin off your nose, is it?'

'Not to me, but the local madhouse might be interested.' Fizz laughed.

'Well, if it makes Lizzie feel better . . .' Charlie glared at Fizz with raised eyebrows and Lizzie was grateful to her when Fizz changed the subject.

'Anyway, I'd like to know what Lavinia was thinking, meeting someone in the dead of night?' Fizz snapped a digestive biscuit in half and took a bite.

Emily's cup clinked back on its saucer. 'Ten o'clock is hardly the dead of night.'

'It is in the blackout.' Fizz waved her digestive at the air to underline her point. 'You wouldn't catch me going out alone at night in a strange place, dressed up to the nines.'

Emily looked aghast. 'Are you trying to say it was her fault? That's low, even for you.'

Fizz rolled her eyes. 'I know, I know. We should be able to walk around without fear of being jumped on, but monsters look for the weak and stupid, men and women, so why make it easy for them? Would either of you have gone?'

'I might have,' Lizzie said. 'If I'd known him.'

Fizz tossed the remains of her biscuit on to the plate and spread her hands questioningly. 'She'd been in the village less than a day. Who did she know and why meet him in the middle of nowhere?' She pulled a cigarette from its packet. 'Something dodgy was going on there.'

'She wasn't a tart.' Emily bristled. 'She was by the church in the village, not in the middle of nowhere.'

Fizz shrugged. 'And here's another question. What was she doing down this way so early?' She struck a match.

'Probably because of the storm,' Lizzie said. 'None of us were expected to arrive on time. Perhaps Lavinia decided to come down on the train a day early as a precaution.'

Fizz extinguished the match with a flick of her wrist. 'You wouldn't catch me cutting my leave short by a day, even for this job.'

Emily gave a snort of derision. Fizz's expression hardened but Emily ignored her and turned to Lizzie. 'Why do *you* think he did it?'

'Why do men do anything?' Fizz butted in. 'They whisper sweet nothings but we all know what they're like.' She took a drag and spoke through smoke. 'They're not all bad, mind. The ones I choose, anyway.'

'You're talking rubbish again,' Emily said. 'Before now, I didn't know anyone who'd been killed, or would kill.'

'Don't you dare dismiss me.' Fizz jabbed her cigarette in Emily's direction for emphasis. 'You know exactly what I mean. We read it in the papers all the time. Women raped and killed in dark alleys and lonely places. I don't know about you but having it on your doorstep scares me half to death. There can't be that many women killed by women, can there?'

'Actually, you'd be surprised . . .' Lizzie stopped, suddenly embarrassed by all eyes turning on her. Fizz regarded her coolly and even though she knew she should let her continue to spout her illogical diatribe, the unjustness, the sheer untruth of it, was more than she could stand. 'Look, it's true, many women victims are vulnerable and most murders are committed by men, but there's a big difference in the way they kill, and why.'

'What are you now, an expert?' Fizz sneered.

Lizzie felt her cheeks burn and her chest tighten. 'I told you, I studied psychology at university. I–I've read a lot about things like this.'

'Well, I think you need to read something else.'

Charlie sighed. 'Don't start having a go at her again.'

Lizzie's mouth began to dry and her heart raced in that telltale way, and yet she couldn't help but respond. 'I agree it's probably a man but it could be anyone. We should look out for ourselves and each other. That's all.'

'I'm not looking after Fizz.' Emily laughed. 'But someone should. She's a liability.'

Fizz leapt up, her fists clenched, her face flushed. Emily followed suit, her mocking expression taunting Fizz across the table. A group of male officers sitting by the windows turned their heads inquisitively towards the sudden noise. Two of them stood up ready to intervene, but the flare-up dissipated quickly when Agata and Niamh appeared between the two women.

'Why do the British always want to fight each other?' Agata looked bemused.

Niamh tutted. 'Do you lot not have enough enemies in the world? Sit down. The men are staring.'

Lizzie counted her breaths again, patting her chest with her hand at each one until she could feel her heart rate beginning to return to normal. She paused and wiped a sheen of perspiration from her top lip. Only then did she realise the table had gone quiet. Fizz and Emily had turned their gazes towards her and Agata was looking down at her, curious.

'Are you all right?' Charlie asked quietly.

Lizzie nodded, not yet trusting herself to speak. She suddenly felt the warm pressure of Charlie's reassuring hand on hers.

'You were breathing rather funny just then. Did you know that?' Charlie said.

'Indigestion,' Lizzie croaked. She cleared her throat and managed a more normal voice. 'I'm fine. Really.'

Fizz stubbed out the remains of her cigarette and stood up. 'Good. You don't need me any more then '

'Wait,' Agata said quickly. 'While we're together, Niamh has an idea.'

'Tell me later,' Fizz called over her shoulder as she began to walk away.

As Fizz passed her, Lizzie heard her snarl quietly under her breath so that no one but Lizzie would hear, *'Crackpot.'*

◆ ◆ ◆

Kember left Mrs Oaks to her mop and bucket and sauntered along the aisle towards the altar, looking at the stonework, vaulted ceiling and memorial plaques. He believed the housekeeper, sure nothing more could be gleaned from her at present. Standing before the dressed altar, he saw an arched wooden door to his left leading off from the chancel. He knocked.

After a moment full of scuffling noises, the door opened.

'Hello,' said a youthful face that peered around the door frame.

Kember indicated the nave with a flick of the fedora he still carried. 'I've been speaking to Mrs Oaks. I'm Detective Inspector Kember and I'd like to ask a few questions about last night's incident.'

Reverend Wilson ran a hand back through his mop of fair hair and opened the door halfway. 'Yes, bad business, bad business. Do come in,' he said, stepping back. 'Sorry about the mess. It started as a bit of a spring clean but it's taken a lot longer than I anticipated. More of a summer clean now.' He moved a teetering pile of papers from a chair and placed it beside a fishing rod and basket on the floor.

Kember edged into the vestry, brushing past a rack of ecclesiastical clothing, and took the proffered seat. 'Looks a job and a half.'

Wilson flopped into his own chair the other side of a desk cluttered with paperwork. 'I've been meaning to do this since I arrived at St Matthew's but never got around to it. It's all historical stuff from years ago – accounts, sermons, etcetera. I'm working on the assumption that a third is rubbish and can be thrown away, a third is historically interesting and should be archived, and a third is important to me and the parish right now.'

'A bit like police work,' Kember said.

Wilson smiled. 'Indeed.' He leapt to his feet. 'Good Lord, how rude of me. I know you're on duty and it's still a little early but, by way of friendly introduction, would you like a drink, Inspector?'

Kember held up a hand to decline as he put his handkerchief to his nose with the other.

'Rum, I'm afraid,' Wilson said, 'but it might do that cold some good.' He retrieved a bottle of dark liquid from a cabinet behind him.

'Actually, I will, if you don't mind.' Kember relented. 'I thought you were about to offer me communion wine.'

Wilson laughed. 'It's fine for its intended purpose but it's not my drink of choice.' He found two glasses and poured a large measure into each.

They clinked glasses and each took a mouthful of the strong, spiced spirit.

'Warms the cockles, doesn't it?' Wilson said. 'I acquired a taste for it in the merchant navy. I was a cabin boy and deckhand. Did a few runs from London to the Ivory Coast and a couple to the West Indies before it came to me that I wanted to serve God.' Wilson contemplated his glass before looking at Kember. 'Sorry, Inspector, you didn't come to hear my life story.'

Kember gave him a genial nod. 'As much as I'm sure you have many lively tales, it's what you might know about the death on Tuesday night that I'm interested in.'

'Terrible.' Wilson shook his head sadly. 'Who would do such a thing? I don't think I can help you, Inspector. Mrs Oaks and I have no reason to use that path or be over by that wall unless I'm performing a burial service or doing a little tidying of the churchyard.'

'Did you hear or see anything either side of about ten o'clock?'

Wilson considered this while swilling rum around his glass. 'I had the window open in my room upstairs and thought I heard something, like a scrape of metal and the click of a front door. It sounded close so I called out to Mrs Oaks to see if she'd gone out for anything.'

'Had she?' Although interested, Kember kept his face and voice impassive.

'No, but it would have been odd for her to do that anyway, and she answered so I assumed it must have been Mrs Garner over the road. She likes to know what's going on and pops in and out like a figure in a Swiss weather clock. I shut my window before joining Mrs Oaks in the kitchen downstairs. She'd made Ovaltine.'

'You didn't see anything out of the window?'

Wilson pouted and shook his head. 'Sorry, no, but while we were in the kitchen the ARP warden did shout for us to put our blackout curtain in place. Mrs Oaks did the honours.'

'Anything else after that?'

'I'm afraid not.' Wilson shook his head and drained his glass. 'I went back upstairs to bed after my Ovaltine.'

Kember felt the familiar dead end approaching and gave Wilson a thin smile. He finished the last mouthful of his rum and stood. 'I should be getting on. Thank you for your time, and the drink. I'll leave you to your spring clean.'

'Thank you, Inspector.'

They shook hands and Kember saw a scratch on the vicar's right hand. 'Looks sore.'

'Not too bad actually,' Wilson said. 'Elias Brown cut some roses from his garden to brighten up the church and I scratched myself on a thorn before I got them to Mrs Oaks to put in a vase.' He smiled. 'I had far worse in the merchant navy.'

Kember turned to leave when a display case on the wall by the door caught his eye. He'd not noticed it on the way in. Inside, a jewel-encrusted gold cross from which extended a shiny metal blade hung beside a sheath of similar design.

'Impressive work of art, isn't it?' Wilson said.

'It is,' Kember agreed. 'Is it real?'

'Sixteenth century, from nearby Bayham Abbey. When Henry the Eighth decided to suppress the Catholic monasteries, the clergy made artefacts like these to defend themselves. The long part of the cross is the sheath and the top of the cross forms the handle of the dagger. A bit like a gentleman's swordstick.'

Kember looked back at Wilson. 'Why is it not on display in the main part of the church?'

'Theft, Inspector. It was stolen many years ago but although the cross was recovered, the jewels had been prised off and were never found. The cross was discarded in a ditch because it is gilded, not solid gold, but it's worth more to the parish than its monetary value. The jewels aren't jewels I'm afraid, they're just coloured glass replicas now.'

Gilt and glass or not, the lavishly decorated cross looked incongruous to Kember. 'This is a Protestant church, isn't it?' he said. 'Doesn't this smack of plunder?'

'Four hundred years ago, maybe, but it's been here for centuries and that particular cross is a symbol of the religious persecution that churches of all faiths and denominations experience at some time. Protestants and Catholics alike have always suffered, including at each other's hands.'

Wilson took up his glass and bottle and Kember saw a blanket of world-weary sadness settle on his face.

'Look at what happened in Russia,' Wilson said, pouring himself another small measure, 'and at what's happening in Nazi Germany now.' He lifted his glass and drained the rest in one mouthful.

Kember acknowledged the point with a faint nod. He'd almost run out of ideas but one further thought occurred to him. 'Do you keep the church locked at all?'

'Only at night,' said Wilson. 'The main part is always open during the day but I do keep the vestry locked when I'm not here, and the bell tower of course, for safety. A couple of steps need repairing.'

'Could anyone have taken this?' He indicated the cross.

Wilson shook his head. 'We've had no sign of a break-in. And why would they bring it back?'

Why indeed? Kember thought. 'Can I borrow it for a few days?'

Wilson raised his glass in salute. 'Be my guest.'

Kember lifted the whole frame from the wall and tucked it under his arm.

'Thank you for your time, Reverend. I'll let you get on.'

None the wiser and no further forward, he left the church, waving his hat at the shadowy figure of Mrs Oaks, who whistled notes forming no recognisable tune while swinging her mop from side to side.

Kember frowned. He hadn't expected the case to be straight-forward; these types of cases rarely were. Ordinarily he would have expected a little more in the way of evidence, but the blackout and the storm had taken care of that. Everyone in the village knew everyone else and had done so for years. Scotney seemed to be one of those typical little English villages where nobody's business was their own.

Kember's frown deepened. Experience told him two things: firstly, that female victims had usually met their killer in some way; secondly, that truly random murders, particularly of women and especially of the vicious kind where the killer mutilated the victim, were few and far between. The two facts of the case also told him two things: that Lavinia Scott was a complete newcomer to the village and that she had arrived virtually unnoticed except by the stationmaster, her landladies and the killer. That she'd become the victim of an apparently motiveless murder a mere few hours later, on a church path in the blackout, didn't add up.

The weight of frustration already building, Kember stood looking at the distance between Mrs Garner's house and the vicarage, concluding it would have been easy to hear the sound of her closing door through an open bedroom window in the still of the night. A mortuary quiet lay over this end of the village, even during the day.

Thinking he ought to get the cross over to Headley for testing and have a word himself with the owners of Lavinia Scott's lodgings, he looked at his watch and sighed. Afternoons really weren't the best time to conduct enquiries in a rural village and he could already feel the soporific effect of alcohol on an empty stomach. The rum had helped his cold a little but not his mood.

Never drink rum with a navy man, he decided.

CHAPTER FIVE

The next day, the sombre mood, far darker than any she'd experienced with her colleagues so far, hit Lizzie as soon as she entered the briefing room.

Fizz and Emily sat at opposite ends of the second row of chairs, pointedly avoiding looking at each other. Agata and Niamh had taken positions in the third row, both seemingly lost in their own thoughts. Charlie sat in the middle of the front row, looking solemn while reading a newspaper report about increased attacks in the south-east by German bombers.

Lizzie took a chair in the front row, leaving one space empty between her and Charlie. Her own mind had been working overtime since the rebuff by Flight Lieutenant Pendry. Working on the assumption that the obvious can be discarded first, anyone on the air station at the time of the murder could not have done it. Given that all her ATA colleagues had spent the previous few days together in White Waltham and did not arrive until after Lavinia's body was found, she could discount all of them. That left anyone not on the air station on Tuesday night, including every person in Scotney village. Still her thoughts came back to how and where Lavinia's body had been left and she knew this was where her particular skills could help.

Lizzie did not relish talking to the police again. She'd encountered enough ignorance, obstruction and patronising attitudes from both men and women when struggling to complete her university research, and that had been in the so-called enlightened corridors of academia. Lizzie almost talked herself out of trying, but she couldn't abandon Lavinia to the clueless bumbling of a rude provincial detective and a toy soldier. She had to make them listen to her.

'Good morning, ladies.' Geraldine arrived, closing the door behind her. She stood at the front of the briefing room and placed a typed sheet on the desk. 'Our first chits have arrived at last, available in the ops room after this briefing.'

Lizzie sat up straighter at the mention of the forms allocating aircraft for ferrying.

'Six aircraft, all Moths damaged in recent attacks, need to go to maintenance units,' Geraldine announced. 'A Hornet, a Puss and four Tigers.'

'Christ almighty,' Fizz said. 'My one consolation in coming down south was that I'd get to fly something decent. But what do I get? A swarm of bloody Moths.'

Emily laughed. 'I'm sorry we're not exciting enough for you. Perhaps you should have stayed in Edinburgh, where you can't do any harm.'

'Mitchell, Parker, behave,' Geraldine snapped.

'I thought we were all in this together.' Niamh pulled a strand of tawny hair behind one ear. 'The whole country. The British Empire. Don't they realise half the empire is female? The only way to beat the Nazis is to let us do what we do best – fly.'

'They are letting us fly.' Geraldine's gaze swept over the assembled women. 'But we have to be patient. We have to bide our time and let Pauline Gower work her magic. Let us remember the primary reason we are here and remain focused. Right, Sidcot suits on, please, ladies, and collect your chits.' She clapped her hands twice.

'Chop, chop. Until you've all passed your conversion courses, I'm your taxi pilot.'

◆ ◆ ◆

Lizzie's had been the first taxi stop of the day and the Ox-box had departed moments after she alighted. Now, as Lizzie eased the joystick back she felt the Tiger Moth biplane lurch upwards as its wheels unglued themselves from the West Malling airstrip. Despite being taught blind instrument flying in a Link Trainer, Lizzie and her colleagues had to fly under the cloud base on Visual Flight Rules, keeping an eye on the ground. Annoyingly, this meant enduring the drizzly rain already soaking her in the Moth's open cockpit. But she endured the discomfort willingly for the chance to fly.

The airfield and its buildings receded below as Lizzie gained altitude, transforming the countryside into a giant map. Winding lanes threaded through patchwork fields of green and gold, spreading orchards, dense hop bines and rolling pastures, crossing streams and connecting villages. The market town of Maidstone fell away to the east as Lizzie banked the Moth into a turn to port, flying over the village of West Malling and heading north-west, straightening up for a quick hop over the Thames to RAF Duxford.

With potential bandits behind her, Lizzie strained her ears through crackling interference caused by the steadily increasing rain, listening for alerts over the radio. She took a deep refreshing breath of cold air and wiped her goggles with a leather gauntlet. On the ground, Lizzie often felt clumsy and out of place, awkward in company and anxious in new or difficult situations. In the air, whether in an open cockpit like now or behind the comfortable shelter of a Perspex canopy, she was alive and free. Anxiety never troubled her while flying, panic attacks never gripped her and OCN was banished. This was her element, her true place in the world.

She followed the Thames westward towards London for a while, smoke rising from the myriad chimneys of factories and houses, turning north before reaching the fat barrage balloons protecting the capital city and its docks. The rain eased back to an intermittent drizzle and the temperature rose a few degrees. Bliss. A flight of four Hurricanes came across for a look. *Probably from RAF North Weald*, she thought. She waved, hoping one of the pilots was her brother, and saw the flight leader waggle his wings before powering up through the clouds, followed by the others.

North Weald came and went, and all too soon she had joined the airfield pattern for landing at Duxford. The Moth would be taken further north by another pilot so she savoured her final moments airborne, bringing the biplane around in a graceful bank, straightening up for the final approach and touching down on the grass airstrip with barely a bump or wobble. All Lizzie had to do now was wait for Geraldine to collect her in the air taxi.

Kember stood at the front door of the Garners' house, at the extreme north end of the village across the road opposite the vicarage. He tugged his upturned collar tighter to his neck and buttoned it, recognising too late that this was the kind of rain that drenches you so slowly you hardly realise it's there

He'd gathered from Sergeant Wright that Ethel Garner was a law-abiding woman who didn't smoke and, apart from communion wine on Sundays, drank nothing more than a glass or two of sherry at Christmas, the rest of the small bottle going into her legendary trifle every Easter. If her husband Albert's tales were anything to go by, her only vice, her one real pleasure, was gossip, tittle-tattle and nosey-parkering. Kember had been particularly interested by Wright's final assessment: *If anyone saw anything on Tuesday evening, it'll be Ethel.*

Eventually, the generous proportions of Ethel Garner appeared from behind the opening door, frowning as she wiped her hands on a pinafore apron. When she saw Kember her face softened.

'Oh, hello. Who are you?' she asked.

Kember introduced himself and showed his warrant card.

'Ah yes, I remember you now, from over the road. Wondered when you lot would be around.' She folded her arms, barring the way through her front door. 'Do you know my Albert's had to walk to work again today? The prowler I told Dennis Wright about last week was here again, Tuesday night. Siphoned all the petrol out of my Albert's car, he did.'

'I'm sorry to hear that.' Kember took a step back and saw the flat snout of a dark-red Austin Seven parked at the side of the cottage. 'Could you be more specific about the time? It might be important.'

Ethel seemed to grow an inch at the suggestion her information could have significance. 'Past ten o'clock, shortly after it got dark,' she said. 'Albert had just got home from the pub when I heard a ruckus. There's no real men around here so I went out with my broom but it was too late. I saw a rubber hose sticking out of the car's petrol tank so I called my Albert. He checked. Empty.'

'Did you notice anything else?'

She shook her head. 'No. That poor girl. Such a terrible thing.' She hugged herself defensively. 'Are we not safe in our beds now? And with a war on, too.'

'I'm sure you're perfectly safe and there's nothing to worry about.' Kember immediately regretted the automatic platitude as Ethel froze. He took another half step backwards and cleared his throat. 'Murder is an uncommon offence, Mrs Garner. Almost unheard of round here so I don't expect anyone else to be in danger.'

Ethel relaxed. 'Well, as I said, I heard a noise and went out with my broom. I heard Brian – Mr Greenway – tell the vicar to cover his windows properly with the blackout curtains. I looked over towards the vicarage and saw a chink of light downstairs but Jessie closed the curtain as quick as you like.' She shook her head sadly. 'I saw your lot over by the church yesterday, and Dennis, of course. Did he tell you he used to scrump apples and cherries from old man Glassen's orchard? Lord knows how he became a policeman. His mum was proud though, God rest her. Thought you'd be straight over, to be honest. Have you any clues yet?'

'It's early days, Mrs Garner. I'm still trying to establish if anyone saw anything.'

'Early days? I told Mrs Ware, her down the end, that you looked more lively than most round here. He'll get things sorted out, I said. Don't you make me out to be a liar, now. Where was she from? Mrs Tate, her with the ingrowing toenail – she's a martyr to her feet, has been for years – said the girl was off to the aerodrome. Makes you wonder, doesn't it? What was she doing on that path? All dressed up and nowhere to go, not round here. Have you got *any* suspects?'

Kember put his hands up in a calm-down motion. 'Sorry, but I can't say anything about an ongoing investigation.'

'Well, you should.' Ethel pointed a finger at Kember's chest. 'You need eyes and ears like mine when it's the likes of us who's in the firing line. Anything you want to know about what goes on around here, come and see me.'

'We have to talk to everyone.' Kember gave her his best reassuring smile. 'You never know when someone will remember a detail that cracks the case.'

Ethel laughed and indicated the direction of the police station with a thrust of her chin. 'That's as may be, but Dennis couldn't crack a cobnut with a house brick.'

The door had already clicked shut before he turned and sighed. This could turn out to be trickier than he'd hoped, especially if all the villagers were as prickly as Ethel Garner. He looked at his watch. It was a bit late in the day and he needed to get the cross off to Headley first, but he decided it might be worth having another word with Flight Lieutenant Pendry.

◆ ◆ ◆

Late afternoon found Lizzie, Charlie and Emily looking around the interior of a long, brick-built utility hut with a low, flat ceiling of corrugated iron. The hut, one of the original manor buildings, stood between the perimeter fence and the half-cylindrical Nissen huts erected when the RAF moved in. Holding no more than old mowing equipment and a few tools, the structure had been left unsecured, the door having no serviceable lock.

'What do you think?' Niamh stood beaming at them from the open doorway. 'Looks clean enough and if we do it up I think it will work well as a ladies' club.'

So this was Niamh's big idea, thought Lizzie. The cramped interior didn't bother her but something about the hut made her uneasy. 'I'm not keen,' she said, lifting a tarpaulin to see underneath. 'To be honest, it gives me the willies.'

'It's only a hut,' Niamh said. 'And it's not too far from the house.'

'Exactly. So why do we need this when we have our corner of the officers' lounge?'

The smile dropped from Niamh's face. 'When I was a kid I wasn't always . . . popular, shall we say. My father knew I was unhappy at school so he made me a wooden summer house in our garden as a den where I could invite the few friends I had to come and play.'

Emily opened a wooden box and snapped it shut at the sight of a dead spider.

Niamh continued, 'I'm not saying the men here are unwelcoming, I really don't mind mixing with the fellas, but it'd be nice not having some officer type trying his latest chat-up line, wanting to teach me the rules of chess, a game I already know, or constantly interrupting when all I want is a quiet drink or a game of cards with my friends.'

'Niamh's right,' Charlie said, inspecting a rusty bicycle. 'We could do with a place of our own.'

Lizzie sighed. She wasn't the greatest fan of card games but she did understand the need for a haven where they could relax and chat without being overheard, interrupted and criticised. Feeling like an outcast was nothing new to Lizzie, too. Most of her family hadn't seen the value of her going to university. Her mother had particularly detested the idea of her completing her PhD, citing the success of other young ladies of means in snaring wealthier husbands and producing streams of children.

Suddenly Agata appeared next to Niamh in the doorway.

'Ladies.' Agata grinned. 'If we really are going to open a club, Fizz has found somewhere far better, I think.'

◆　◆　◆

Kember waited for the red-and-white barrier to rise before steering his Minx up the drive to the gravel parking area. Despite the unsettled weather, increased enemy activity had put the air station on alert for enemy bombing raids and most leave had been cancelled. Even Tonbridge Police HQ had recalled men in anticipation of rising tensions and the threat of invasion. Except himself. Labelled as a thorn in his side by Hartson, Kember smiled to himself at the memory of his boss insisting he stay in Scotney to finish the case.

Kember half-expected Pendry to be waiting for him but the RAF policeman wasn't on the portico steps. No matter. He looked skywards, suspecting everyone was busy with preparations.

◆　◆　◆

'Well?' Fizz asked. 'It has its own entrance at the side of the manor house and isn't used as a wine cellar or shelter.'

Lizzie stood with Niamh, Agata and Fizz in a long room leading directly away from the vestibule, front door and steps that gave access to the cellar from outside. The room was about seven feet across with a curved wall at the far end and had two doors leading to two other rooms on the right. The nearest was square and the farthest also had a curved end wall. These were themselves connected by another door. Someone six feet tall could reach up and touch the ceilings with their fingertips but the overall size of each room was not claustrophobic.

'It's perfect,' Emily gushed as she emerged from the farthest of the two rooms. 'We can have games in the long room, with a dartboard at the far end. And the floor's smooth enough for skittles.'

'It's a bit grubby but there's no clutter,' Charlie called, joining them from the other room. 'The back room can be the lounge. It will be cooler in summer and warmer in winter. We can make this other one the bar.'

'I'm not sure that's wise.'

The sudden sound of a man's voice startled Lizzie and her heart thumped a little harder as she held her breath. The officer stomped down the stone steps in his RAF boots and glanced around the cellar.

Lizzie pinged one of the rubber bands on her wrist and managed to take a shallow breath.

'You all right?' Pendry said as he watched her. 'You look a bit pale.'

Lizzie nodded and averted her gaze. 'What's wrong with the idea?' she said, breaking the tension. 'A bar, a lounge and a games room. Just for women.'

'The CO will give us permission, won't he?' Charlie asked. 'If we're down here he'll see less of us and that's right up his street.'

Pendry shook his head. 'The top brass aren't known for letting people wander around without the proper authority.'

'We're asking for proper authority.' Niamh stepped forward and fixed Pendry's gaze with her own. 'There are all sorts of places we can't go and nowhere we can be away from the men. All we want is a place of our own.'

Pendry gave a short bark of a laugh. 'This is a military establishment, not the West End of London. You do know Dallington will have a fit?'

Lizzie waited anxiously with the others as Pendry stepped away from Niamh and wandered through the rooms. She found his body language, one moment relaxed and casual and the next stiff and formal, unusually hard to read.

'You know it's a great idea,' said Lizzie as Pendry brushed past her.

'It's hardly a priority at the moment.' Pendry returned to the entrance. 'The Germans could invade any day and tensions are running high.'

Niamh blocked his attempt to leave. 'We'll do it up, invite the group captain and wing commander to the opening and see where that leads us. You could even buy us some time.'

'I could not.' Pendry straightened his tunic and stepped past Niamh.

Agata took Niamh's place. 'But you could put in a good word.'

Pendry gave Agata an exaggerated frown but then Lizzie watched the corners of his eyes wrinkle as his face broke into a smile and he laughed. 'All right, I admit it does sound fun,' he said, and stomped back up the steps. 'I'll think about it.'

◆ ◆ ◆

Kember reached the top of the portico steps, still contemplating the probability of a German invasion, before he spotted Pendry turning the corner of the manor house. He called and Pendry looked up from his own thoughts.

'Ah, Inspector. I thought you'd bring more men.'

Kember gave Pendry a wry smile. 'The war machine has taken all the best officers, Scotland Yard has taken most of what's left in Tonbridge to a triple murder over at Brenchley, and the local sergeant has to police the village and all the farms hereabouts.'

'Not an ideal situation.'

'That's an understatement I may have to live with for quite some time.'

'How are the villagers taking it?'

'As you'd expect. A mixture of anger and fear, rage and bravado. How's Dallington taking it?'

Pendry smiled. 'He's not best pleased that you're insinuating someone on *his* air station could be responsible. He thinks the RAF is beyond reproach.'

Kember shrugged. 'He may be right, but I have to look everywhere. Actually, there's something you can do for me. I was wondering about the number of personnel on the air station who might have been in the village on Tuesday night. Would you have records to that effect?'

Pendry tried to disguise a momentary flicker of his eyes by scratching behind his ear with a gloved finger but Kember had questioned enough people in his time not to notice such a gesture.

'Will that be a problem?' Kember asked.

'No, no. Not at all.' Pendry said. 'The gatehouse log records comings and goings but it's my understanding the girl was killed during the hours of darkness. At that time of night, those not on duty would have been sleeping in their quarters or the barracks. Easy enough to check. I'll make some enquiries to see if anyone knew her.'

'Thank you.' Kember rubbed his nose in thought. 'Any joy with her family?'

'Actually, yes,' Pendry said. 'Her father returned my call today. He was distraught when I told him his daughter had been murdered, as you can imagine, but I was able to ask a few questions. He insisted she was well liked, had no enemies and, as far as he is aware, knew no one in the village and had never been to Scotney before. I pressed him about other family members, gentlemen friends and so on, but he was adamant she was a nice girl who wasn't currently courting.'

'Thank you anyway.' Kember glanced at his watch. 'I'll need to arrange for written statements to be taken and their alibis checked.'

'No need. I've already arranged for someone to do that.'

Kember couldn't disguise a frown at the thought of someone doing his job.

'Oh, I've overstepped. I apologise.' Pendry held up a hand. 'I know it's your jurisdiction but we've got more than enough men to follow it up, and as you're short-staffed—'

'Inspector!'

The two men turned to see Lizzie hurrying over to them.

'I'm glad I caught you. I wanted to offer my help.'

Kember's eyebrows registered surprise. He had no need of a pilot. 'What kind of help are we talking about?'

'Third Officer Hayes approached me yesterday,' Pendry said. 'She seems to think she has special powers that can identify the murderer.'

'Not special powers,' Lizzie snapped. 'Skills. Shall we talk inside?'

◆ ◆ ◆

Pendry moved a small stack of ledgers, RAF manuals and a tatty-looking Bible to one side and rested his elbows on his desk.

'Third Officer Hayes accosted me yesterday in the corridor after Group Captain Dallington announced the death of the girl at the ATA welcome briefing.' He gave Lizzie a searching look. 'You said you could help the investigation. What makes you think you could do that?'

Pendry's blunt question took Lizzie by surprise. She had been distracted by Kember's tie hanging askew, so to give her time to gather her thoughts, she said, 'Please call me Lizzie, it's less of a mouthful.' She clasped her hands together in her lap and squeezed three times, a signal to herself that all was well. She waited for her brain and body to acknowledge the sign, gave a short sigh and looked at the two men.

'Over a number of years and after a lot of research I have developed an insight into how criminals think and work, how they tick, if you like.'

Kember glanced at Pendry and back at Lizzie. 'That's quite a statement. And how exactly did you . . . acquire this insight?'

The tightness in Lizzie's chest faded as she realised her opening gambit hadn't been dismissed out of hand. She gave Kember a hesitant smile. 'I studied psychology at London University's Bedford

College where I became interested in both crime and criminals. A professor encouraged me to take it further and conduct empirical research into the criminal mind. You've heard of Beatrice Edgell, perhaps? The first British woman to earn a psychology doctorate from *any* university?'

Kember and Pendry looked blank. Lizzie clenched her fingers together and her glare could have cut through sheet metal when she continued.

'It's so nice to know I'm in the presence of such enlightened gentlemen.' She buried a rogue twinge of anxiety beneath a layer of irritation. 'I studied criminals, their crimes, their backgrounds and their thinking to try to get to the heart of what led them to do what they did.'

Pendry cleared his throat. 'How do you know it was successful?'

'I know it was successful because I earned my *doctorate*.' Lizzie noted with satisfaction the impressed looks on their faces at her emphasis. 'Scotland Yard thought I was mad but Oxford City Police and Oxford Prison were most helpful with my research. They thought me harmless and gave me more or less free rein to speak to whomever I wished and read whatever I liked. My peculiar work came to the attention of certain officers and they sometimes asked my opinion. Of the four profiles I provided, the first proved inaccurate but as I progressed, so the accuracy of my work increased.'

Lizzie swallowed hard when she realised how intently Pendry was staring at her.

'That was in Oxford,' Pendry said. 'What makes you so confident you can make a difference here and now? And what's a profile when it's at home?'

Fair questions, she thought. 'I tried to speak to the inspector at the scene of Lavinia Scott's murder but he ignored me.' Kember's eyebrow twitched and he glanced away. 'From that one scene I might have been able to make an initial assessment about the type of person involved. From what I could see, Lavinia's body didn't seem to be lying naturally. It seemed posed, somehow. That suggests to me it wasn't a random act. I wouldn't be surprised if you'd found other peculiarities too.' Lizzie saw Kember's gaze flick back to her and his eyes narrowed in such a way that she knew she was right. She shifted in her chair. 'Similarities emerge when more than one murder has been committed. It becomes possible to compare the two and therefore easier to provide a psychological profile, a character sketch, of the criminal. Even if there is only one murder and one peculiarity I might still be able to provide an assessment, but it won't be as robust.'

Pendry leant forward with a concerned look. 'What puzzles me is why are you not a practising psychiatrist if you believe yourself to be an expert? Why didn't you join the police service? There are a number of women, I believe, and there is the Women's Auxiliary Police Corps too.'

'I'm not a psychiatrist, I'm a psychologist.' Lizzie shook her head. 'And I'll be in my grave before women are allowed to do real police work equally alongside men. I have the ability to help catch criminals but I would be limited to driving, typing and tea-making.' Lizzie noticed Kember wince as the jibe hit home. 'Until I took up flying my fate was to be married off to some rich aristocrat. Now I'm considered too wayward to find a husband.' She smiled wryly.

Kember returned the smile. 'I'm not sure I understand what it is you think you can do for us or how writing some kind of report will help us catch a murderer.'

'All I ask is that you let me look at the file, including the photographs. If the crime scene reveals any specific behaviours I might be able to give you a small insight into the kind of person likely to display them. As I said, I'm very good at what I do. Lavinia's body looked posed and a killer doesn't do that on a whim.'

Kember drummed his fingers on the desk for a moment then stood up. 'I'm sorry, Miss Hayes. I appreciate you're trying to help but this type of quackery is, quite frankly, unhelpful and misleading.'

'But—'

'I can't think of any instance where my chief inspector would countenance your involvement. He has built his career on solid police work and the principles of detection. He hates so-called psychics, astrologers, tarot card readers and fortune tellers, believing them to be no more than fairground amusements, and I have to agree with him.'

Lizzie's mouth opened but she found she couldn't speak. Embarrassment and anger were making the blood rush to her cheeks, blushing like the emotional female she knew they thought her to be. She hated him for it.

'I'm afraid I must go,' he said to Pendry before nodding politely to Lizzie. 'Thank you for your time, Miss Hayes. It really has been most interesting, but ultimately unhelpful. Let's help the war effort by sticking to the things we know, shall we? You fly the aeroplanes and I'll catch the killers.' And with that, he picked up his grey fedora by its narrow brim and left the office, closing the door quietly but firmly behind him.

CHAPTER SIX

Another day and another disturbed night.

Dr Headley had been too busy to perform a post-mortem on Lavinia Scott and the woman's poor family were distraught at not yet having her body back to bury. Kember had spent the night turning the case and its evidence over and over in his mind, seeing the bricks but unable to assemble the building. The information from Pendry seemed to rule out any air station personnel and Sergeant Wright's house-to-house enquiries had yielded nothing but tittle-tattle.

At least Chief Inspector Hartson seemed unperturbed by Kember spending time away from Tonbridge Police HQ. Kember knew Hartson considered him an inconvenience, one foisted on to him by Scotland Yard. Nothing Kember did ever pleased Hartson so he'd long since given up trying. A telephone call to update him had not gone well. Despite offering no extra men on the ground or support from Tonbridge HQ, Hartson had said, 'I expect this case to be wrapped up in a couple of days.' Kember understood fools and accepted that intelligence was variable, but he disliked arrogance. Conveying a few home truths, in the nicest way possible, had left Kember with a headache and Hartson in almost incoherent rage as receivers were slammed down.

'Enjoying your nights in the cells?' Wright asked, placing two mugs of tea on the desk.

Kember grimaced, feeling sheepish.

'Not the most comfortable bed, I'll admit. Not good for my back.'

He sighed. One of the holding cells in the basement of the police station had served as his bedroom since his wife had announced he was being replaced. There had been no point arguing about who should go or stay, who owned what and how the bank account cash should be divided. It seemed she had worked it out well in advance. He retained his own cash, she had the house and most of its contents, and most of his possessions were either in the trunk in the back office or placed in storage in Tonbridge. He took a couple of deep breaths as he felt his face burn with emotion and took a mouthful of hot tea as a distraction.

The cell was warm and dry, if not very comfortable, and at least the bath upstairs in Sergeant Wright's police flat had hot water. With no home to go to he had been trying to avoid the expense of a room, but with Wright dropping hints, his free stay looked like it might be drawing to a close.

'The pub's got some nice rooms, for the short term, like,' Wright said. 'Did a good fry-up breakfast too, before rationing. Still does when there's a rasher of bacon or a sausage going spare.'

Kember's stomach growled at the thought. 'Then it looks like I have a room to take over the road. I'll need to return to Tonbridge today to collect my things and deal with the inevitable paperwork that's been piling up, but I should be back on Monday. Firstly, I need to arrange a telephone call to the Rochester Diocesan Office. I think I need a better idea of what sort of character is holding the religious and moral well-being of the village in his hands.'

The wet mist of the previous day having turned to drizzle over-night had forced Kember to break out his new umbrella again. He'd thought another miserable day of damp clothing lay ahead but as he emerged from questioning the greengrocer, he glanced up at the blanket of grey cloud and thanked God the rain had finally stopped. After two interviews with villagers who once again had seen noth-ing, he crossed the street to a trim little cottage near the village hall, catching the sweet scent of roses and damp, fresh-turned earth. As he opened the gate, he shied away from a brown-and-white springer spaniel that bounded playfully towards him with muddy paws.

'He won't hurt you,' a voice called from his left.

Kember turned and saw the bald dome and slight figure of Elias Brown kneeling by a flower border in the small front garden, the corners of the man's mouth turning up in a developing smile.

'Ah, Mr Brown,' he said. 'I'm afraid I'll take some convincing where dogs are concerned.' Having had bad experiences with so-called friendly dogs, he much preferred the calm aloofness of cats.

'Down, Prince,' Brown commanded and the dog trotted away dutifully.

'I can see you're busy but if you could spare a moment,' Kember said, 'I have to ask you about your dog's discovery on Wednesday morning.'

'Of course, of course.' The smile faded to be replaced by a frown as Brown stood from tending his flowers and offered his hand. 'Sorry it's a bit grubby.'

Kember shook it anyway.

'You don't expect anything like that to happen in a place like this, do you? The whole village has been devastated. Fire away.'

Kember flicked a glance at the nearby church. 'I need you to describe again how you came to find the body.'

Brown scratched his temple. 'I took Prince for his evening walk on Tuesday, along the path to the pastures behind the church.

They're thinking of ploughing them up to plant more crops, you know? Anyway, that was about seven o'clock. We were home by eight and the young lady wasn't there then.' He paused momentarily, as if in thought. 'On Wednesday, I was taking Prince out early morning as usual. The clouds were black and threatening rain again and I almost turned back at the vicarage – but I didn't, and that's when I saw her.'

So far, Kember thought Brown's account accorded with Dr Headley's estimation of the time of death. 'Can you describe what happened next?' He watched Brown wipe the back of his hand across his forehead.

'She had her dress pulled right up, poor lass, so I pulled it down to preserve some semblance of her modesty. There was blood and I could see she'd been stabbed. Her eyes were wide open and staring.'

'And then?' Kember tried to look sympathetic, surprised at Brown's bluntness.

Brown pointed to his dog. 'Prince ran up and down, sniffing and licking so I called him away and went to find Dennis – Sergeant Wright. He telephoned Tonbridge Police Station straight away and came back with me. I took Prince home and helped keep the end of the path closed until the doctor arrived.'

'You seem very calm,' Kember observed. 'Considering you found a body.'

Brown looked at him, seemingly measuring his words before he said them. 'I'm a veteran of the Great War, Inspector. I've seen some terrible things.'

Kember glanced away, slightly embarrassed. 'The path isn't much used, is it? Did you see anyone hanging around Tuesday night or Wednesday morning?'

Brown's mouth turned down and he shrugged. 'I use it twice a day with Prince. I don't think anyone else bothers, apart from a few kids now and again, but even they tend to keep away. There's an old legend about the woods being haunted. The village kids scare the evacuees with ghost stories.'

'Are there many? Evacuees?'

'Four that I know of.' Brown indicated a group of young children playing football in the street with a badly inflated football, jumpers strategically placed for goalposts. A boy and a younger girl stood by.

'See those two watching the game? They're billeted down Meadowbank Lane with Gladys Finch. She owns the tea shop. I think the other two are in Acorn Street.'

Kember looked back at the middle-aged man in gardening trousers and boots. He seemed fairly innocuous, but Kember knew well that appearances could be deceptive.

'Apart from the victim's dress, did you move anything around the body or take anything away?'

Brown looked puzzled. 'No. Why would I do that?'

'Who knows? That's why I'm asking. You never know what people might do when confronted with something horrific. Anyway, that's all for now. I might need to speak to you again and, of course, if you think of anything else, please come and find me or the sergeant.'

'Will do.'

Kember left Brown and stepped back into the street, swearing under his breath as the rain returned in earnest. Annoyed that his best chance of making progress had just evaporated, Kember opened his umbrella and sought the dry sanctuary of the police station. It seemed to him the killer had known precisely what to do and when, to give himself the maximum time to complete his ungodly work unseen.

During a temporary lull in the rain, Kember stood outside the pub where the door was opened by a slim woman of medium height in her mid-thirties, tight blonde curls escaping from beneath a scarf tied in a turban. Her red nose, ruddy face and brandished scrubbing brush were all testament to the cleaning she had abandoned. The woman took one look at Kember and stepped back in embarrassment, wiping her hands on her apron.

'Mrs Brannan?' Kember doffed his fedora.

'Miss, actually, but you can call me Alice. Sorry for . . .' She checked her turban and undid her apron.

'Ah. No, sorry. Entirely my fault. I can come back if you're busy.'

'Don't be silly, duck. You're here now. Did you want to see Les?' She gave Kember a curious look.

'Either of you, really. My name is Detective Inspector Kember and my sergeant tells me you have rooms to let.'

'Well, why didn't you say?' Alice's face broke into a smile. 'Come in, come in. How long do you think you'll need?'

Kember cleared his throat self-consciously. 'A couple of weeks at least. I'm returning to Tonbridge today so I'd like to take it from Monday, if I may?'

'Of course you can, love.'

Kember followed Alice Brannan into the bar, which still smelled faintly of the previous night's beer, sweat and cigarettes, despite the pungent aroma of disinfectant and bleach. She took him through to a cosy living room at the back filled with an overstuffed chair and sofa, a wireless set on a low wooden table and a writing bureau. Shelves on every wall, and even the mantelpiece over the fireplace, were crammed with photographs and ornaments.

Alice opened a book and handed Kember a fountain pen to complete his details as required by law.

'It'll be nice to have another man about the house,' Alice said. 'Especially a policeman. We've not had many visitors since war broke out. I hope you like it here.'

'I'm sure I shall,' Kember said as he signed his name. 'As you will be aware, I'm investigating the murder that occurred over by the church.'

'A terrible thing,' Alice said, her smile gone. 'And a bit too close for comfort.'

Kember nodded gravely. 'I wondered why the young woman didn't take a room here in the pub, instead of with the Taplow sisters.'

'That'll be because we don't accept one-nighters.' She dropped her voice to a whisper. 'Nobody decent comes to Scotney for one night and Les doesn't want our place to get a bad reputation.'

'And the Taplows?'

'That's different. Annie and Elsie can keep a close eye on who comes and goes through their front door. No fooling around goes on there.'

Kember thought the Taplows hadn't kept such a close eye on Lavinia Scott but filed that away, another query ticked off his mental list.

Having completed the necessary transaction, Alice showed Kember his room, departing with, 'I'd best get on, duck.'

The room was small, with a tiny fireplace in one corner, a bed-side table, chest of drawers, a wardrobe and a window that over-looked the High Street. Kember sat on the single, iron-framed bed and was pleasantly surprised at how soft and comfortable it was. The pillows were obviously filled with feathers, as one or two quills poked through the cotton pillowcase. He nodded in satisfaction. This would do nicely.

◆ ◆ ◆

Lizzie hopped down from the back of the Bedford lorry, thanked the young RAF driver with a wave and hurried into the manor house out of the rain. He had collected her from the railway station after she arrived there from RAF Detling by way of a delivery van to Maidstone and a train via Paddock Wood.

It was usual for her to return to base in the ATA's air taxi but today her travel permit had needed pressing into service to get her home. Lizzie's one ferry chit should have taken her from RAF Detling to Croydon but the job had been abandoned when Detling had come under attack. Wave after wave of bombers and fighters had flown over, seemingly undeterred by the rainclouds, and the Kent sky had seemed full of Germans. Talk among pilots and ground crews was of being softened up for invasion.

Now back at RAF Scotney, the first pilot of the day to return, she replaced her gear in her room and went down to the cellar. Work had already started on converting it to a private club for the women, even though it could be in German hands within weeks, but Lizzie had faith in the young pilots risking their lives. She just wished she could fly with them.

On the promise of a drink one night, the few aircraftsmen left at RAF Scotney had whitewashed the walls and moved the old furniture rescued from a storage hut into the lounge and bar rooms. The long sofa had seen better days and a couple of the easy chairs really needed new cushions. Someone had left a stack of three-legged stools in the games room, which Lizzie placed strategically around the bar room. They had yet to find or build a bar and they had no dartboard, skittles or drink, but the whole air station had heard about the ATA's club so Lizzie was confident that families and friends would provide the needed equipment in due course. Charlie had already turned up a few framed black-and-white photographs of Hollywood film stars and Emily had filched a landscape painting and a pen-and-ink drawing of a stag from a little-used corridor on the top floor of the west wing. It was an eclectic collection of artefacts and not all to her taste, but Lizzie had to admit it was coming together and the overall effect was not displeasing.

She took a hammer through to the lounge and began to tap a small nail into position for one of the pictures. As the force of her tapping increased, Lizzie thought she heard someone coming down the steps. She stopped banging and called out.

No reply.

She went back to her picture-hanging, placing the landscape in position before taking another nail and tapping. Once again, she thought she heard footsteps and stopped hammering. Looking over her shoulder, she saw a shadow in the games room and went to see who was taking such an interest.

The room was empty.

Ascending the stone steps, she looked left and right, frowning.

Realising she had the hammer gripped tight and menacingly in her right hand, she swapped hands and flexed her fingers. As Lizzie returned to the cellar she suddenly felt a familiar tightening across her chest. She could smell cigarette smoke where none had been before. Someone was still in the cellar. Brandishing the hammer again, she placed each foot carefully on the stone floor as she moved through the rooms, stalking her prey. Silence pulsed in her ears as she completed the circuit back to the games room but, with no other signs of a visitor, she began to doubt her own senses and had just decided to resume her work when she pulled up short, a shudder passing through her. On one of the stools inside the bar room rested a playing card that hadn't been there before.

As Lizzie carefully picked it up by its edges and turned it over, her heart leapt into her throat. Everyone on the air station knew about the ATA's cellar bar but someone disapproved enough to send them a warning.

It was the Queen of Clubs.

With the eyes pierced through.

◆ ◆ ◆

Lizzie waited impatiently for the operator to connect her call, glancing frequently at the door of the ops room, hoping no one would barge in and start asking awkward questions. She'd telephoned Scotney Police Station first but had been informed by Sergeant Wright that Kember had returned to Tonbridge for a few days.

The seconds dragged by until the operator announced the connection and a man's voice said, 'Police Divisional Headquarters, can I help you?'

Lizzie felt doubt start to flood her thoughts as she asked, 'May I speak to Detective Inspector Kember, please?'

'I'm afraid not, miss,' the policeman replied. 'He's very busy. Would you like to leave a message?'

Biting her lip in frustration and wishing she'd thought it through before ringing, Lizzie sought the right words to ensure her enquiry was passed on and not dismissed. 'Yes, please. Would you let him know that Third Officer Lizzie Hayes called? It's in connection with his investigation at RAF Scotney, but can you make sure he understands that I've received what I believe is a threatening message?'

There was a short pause.

'What kind of threatening message, miss?'

'It's personal so I'd rather not say, if you don't mind. But it is an urgent matter and rather sinister.'

The policeman said, 'Aren't they all,' before taking Lizzie's details and ending the call a little too abruptly for her to be confident of the message getting through. She knew Kember would be back in Scotney in a day or two but anything could happen between now and then, so she rang Wright back straight away. She explained what she thought the significance of the card to be but could tell from the short silence that she wasn't getting through.

'I really think that's something for the inspector to deal with,' Wright said, sounding to Lizzie like the cynical desk sergeant at Tonbridge Police Station. 'I'll pass on your message as soon as I see him, but—'

'I know,' Lizzie interrupted before Wright could say it, her face already burning with disappointment. 'He's away for a few days.'

CHAPTER SEVEN

As it happened, flying was curtailed on Sunday as the rain increased, and still no word came from Kember.

Lizzie sat in Pendry's office, the playing card on the desk between them, trying to remain outwardly calm while seething inside. He was not her first choice – she had asked to see him after being shunned by Kember and Wright – but his lukewarm reaction had not been the one she had expected Here was a solid piece of evidence of the threat towards her and the other women but still he refused to see sense.

'Can't you see that pricking the eyes out of the Queen of Clubs and leaving it in our cellar has to be deliberate?' Lizzie said, aware her cheeks had reddened with exasperation.

'I'm sure it's no more deliberate than throwing a paper aeroplane across the room when you're bored.' Pendry pushed the card towards Lizzie and sat back in his chair. 'I don't understand the significance.'

'Nobody does that without meaning to frighten.' She tapped the card. 'Someone doesn't want women opening a club.'

'I think you've been doing too many cryptic crossword puzzles in *The Times*. I doodle on my blotting pad, tear bits of paper into tiny pieces and push piles of ash around my ashtray with a cigarette all the time. It's absent-minded triviality. It doesn't mean I want to kill you.'

That was the final straw. She pocketed the card, excused herself and left before she said something that would land her in hot water.

Lizzie didn't want to scare the women any more than they had been already, but if Kember and Pendry wouldn't listen how could she not warn her colleagues? As she entered the lounge, her train of thought was derailed by the sound of her name being called from the comfy chairs. She looked across and saw Geraldine beckoning for her to join them.

'Are you feeling all right?' Charlie asked as Lizzie approached. 'You look a bit pale.'

'I'm fine,' Lizzie said with a weak smile, fingering the playing card in her pocket.

'No, you're not,' Fizz said. 'You're acting weird again. Sit down, for God's sake, and get it off your chest.'

'Shove over, Tilly.' Charlie shooed the station's mascot from the seat next to her on the sofa. The disgruntled cat jumped down, flicking her tail with annoyance.

Lizzie took the now empty seat next to Charlie. She could feel the burn in her cheeks and knew a flush would be spreading down her neck, but this was too important to let her mind get the better of her. All the women looked at her: Geraldine, Agata and Niamh inquisitively, Emily and Charlie with worried frowns and Fizz with the beginnings of a cruel smirk.

She cleared her throat. 'I wanted to warn you about the man the police are looking for. Lavinia's murderer.'

'We've already been warned,' Fizz said dismissively.

'I know, but I need to tell you something.'

'Tell us what?'

'Before the war I earned a doctorate in psychology at university.' Lizzie saw the women fidget on their chairs. 'Don't worry, I'm not a psychiatrist who carts people off to asylums or anything like that.' She had their full attention now. 'I studied how people think, act, react and interact. In particular, I specialised in the study of criminals and what makes them tick.'

'They're all loonies, that's what makes them tick,' Fizz said contemptuously.

Lizzie clasped her hands together, desperate to stop the impulse to make them flutter like moths beside her. 'I know you'll find it hard to understand, but my many years of training makes me believe the man who murdered Lavinia is a particular kind of killer, one who will carry on and do it again, to another one of us.' This brought forth a shocked intake of breath from her colleagues.

Tasting metal as her mouth became dry, Lizzie pressed on. 'He doesn't like us as women, or what we stand for, which is the sweeping away of old ideas about our place in the world. We're a threat to the order he believes in and to him personally, and he means to get rid of us.'

Emily, eyes widening, put her hand to her mouth.

Lizzie bit down on her lip. 'I don't want us walking around in fear. All I'm saying is, be very careful. None of us should be on our own until he's caught. I don't want another of my friends to die.'

'So we've got to walk around with the jitters because you read some dusty books at big school? I don't think so.'

Geraldine gave Fizz a stern look. 'Actually, I think Lizzie's sentiments are quite sensible. Try to avoid putting yourself in situations where you are alone. At least for the present.'

Agata shook her head. 'We are ferry pilots. We are alone in the air all the time.'

'Agata's right, ma'am,' Niamh said. 'We visit strange airfields, talk to men we've never met. We can arrive back here on our own, late at night and in the dark. Unless we are going to fly around in twos, we've got no choice.'

'I didn't mean that,' Lizzie said. 'He's not out there, he's here, in Scotney. He's got the blackout on his side, and air raids and countryside and—'

'Why are you so het up about it?' Fizz interrupted. 'What's he done to you?'

'He left a message.' Lizzie tried to look calmer than she felt, her fingers running over the comfort of the rubber band, looping themselves under to make it snap against her skin, keep her focus away from the aridness of her mouth. 'A playing card, actually.'

Fizz snorted in derision. 'A playing card? What, the joker?'

'Leave her alone,' Charlie said. 'Can't you see she's upset?'

Lizzie smiled at Charlie and shook her head. 'Thank you, but I'm agitated, not upset.' She looked at Fizz. 'And you can laugh all you want but he knew I'd understand its meaning. It was the Queen of Clubs and the eyes have been pricked out with a pin.' She produced the playing card from her pocket.

'Card tricks now, is it?' Fizz snorted a laugh.

'This has to be a warning to us all,' Lizzie said as she passed the card around, worry etching lines into her friends' faces.

'You're letting your imagination run away with you,' Fizz said. 'Somebody probably got bored and did it without thinking.'

Lizzie clenched her fists, feeling her nails dig into her palms. 'Don't be an idiot. Lavinia might have been killed in the village but that card was left inside our club, while my back was turned, to let us know he can get to any of us, anywhere.'

Fizz wasn't smirking any more.

'Even here.'

◆ ◆ ◆

Monday also proved a complete washout for flying, with low black cloud and heavy rain, but that didn't prevent Kember following up his next line of enquiry. Seated at his desk in the office he shared in Tonbridge Police Station, telephone to his ear, he waited for the operator to connect his call.

'Speak up, caller, you're through.'

'Rochester Diocesan Office, Jennifer Ward speaking.'

The voice oozed, soft and feminine, just as Kember remembered it from his days as a detective sergeant in the CID at New Scotland Yard. She had been the staff nurse at nearby St Thomas's Hospital, in the ward where he'd been treated after injuring his back. That's not to say they'd been strangers before then. His line of duty had caused their paths to cross many times before.

'Hello, Jenny. It's Jonathan Kember.'

'Jonathan! Nice to hear from you after all this time. I was so surprised when I got your cryptic message.'

'Sorry about that. I'm in the middle of an investigation.'

'I gathered as much. Still surprised me when I heard you wanted to know about the Reverend Giles Wilson. What's happened? Is he in trouble?'

Kember hesitated. 'I don't believe so, but we're trying to eliminate as many people as possible.'

'It's not the sort of enquiry we get in this office. The questions are usually more ecclesiastical than criminal.'

Kember almost laughed. 'Organised religion has attracted crime throughout the centuries, and caused wars.' A silent pause. Worried he'd offended her, Kember pushed on. 'Have you any details or background that might tell me who the Reverend Wilson is, where he comes from, what makes him tick?'

Jenny answered in a hushed voice. 'I made some enquiries as you asked and unearthed his records.' Kember heard the rustle of paper down the line. 'He comes from a decent family who own a furniture business. He did well at school but didn't go on to higher education and wasn't keen on following his father into the family business. He has an older brother and younger sister, both of whom are very interested in that regard, so his father was content for him to go off and see the world. He joined the merchant navy for a while, but being young at the time he had no position of authority. He sailed on a couple of ships to Africa and the Caribbean, I believe.'

'Where he acquired his taste for dark rum,' Kember said, remembering the pleasant warmth of the spirit.

'Oh?'

Kember smiled to himself and fiddled with the telephone cord. 'We had a chat over a small glass.'

'Hmm,' Jenny said, with a tone suggesting she suspected more than one glass may have been involved. 'Anyway, after a few years in the merchant navy he left and applied to become an ordained minister. He said travelling the oceans and seeing exotic lands had made him realise how wonderful the world could be and that he wanted to serve God.'

Kember frowned. The church seemed a far cry from a life on the high seas. 'Is it easy to become a vicar?'

Jenny's laugh bubbled up. 'Of course not. All those who want to be ordained have to study theology for around three years or so. All are trained, some are mentored; attachment to a local parish is not unusual. They have to interact with parishioners, prove to themselves and others that this is their true vocation, and explore their deeper faith. It's all designed to ensure the man is equipped physically, educationally, mentally and religiously to be a minister of the Anglican Church.'

The thought of spending all that time in church, willingly or not, made Kember shudder.

'I take it you found nothing to suggest he is anything less than an exemplary minister?'

'I don't know enough about him to say that but there was an incident you'll be interested in.' Jenny's voice lowered to a whisper. 'Although I'm breaking confidentiality.'

Kember's ears pricked up. 'Go on.'

'It appears the real reason he left the merchant navy was a fight he had where a man died.'

'He killed someone?' Kember was taken aback.

'There isn't much on file, I'm afraid,' Jenny said. 'It seems it was investigated but no charges were brought.'

'Our Reverend Wilson's not a convicted murderer then?' Kember said, puzzled.

'It seems he turned to God pretty soon afterwards, and The Church loves nothing more than a sinner redeemed.'

'Operator here. Your three minutes are up.'

Blast, Kember thought. 'Thanks, Jenny. It's been most interesting.'

'I'm glad I could help. You should come to Rochester for lunch next time.'

Kember let the invitation hang. 'I'd be grateful if you could keep this discussion confidential.'

Jennifer laughed. 'Of course. This is the Church of England, we thrive on keeping secrets—'

The line went dead.

Even though he distrusted both Group Captain Dallington and his sidekick, Wing Commander Matfield, Wilson had risen up this inadequate list of suspects by virtue of the fact he'd killed a man during peacetime. Kember rubbed his eyes. Motive, means and opportunity. Despite this latest revelation, none of his suspects seemed to have all three. Either a key piece of information remained elusive or the short list had, for some reason, excluded the real killer. The former was merely frustrating; the latter, terrifying.

Kember returned to Scotney late Monday evening, his head fuzzy from two days at Divisional Headquarters completing a mountain of paperwork, the rear seats of his Minx full to bursting with some of his things rescued from storage in Tonbridge. He'd been pleasantly surprised to find his possessions in good order, packed neatly and carefully. But then his wife had always been materialistic and set great store by how things looked. Marriage aside.

It took him several trips from his car, through the front door, along a narrow passage beside the bar and up the stairs to his room before all his belongings were in. He could hear Alice's brother, Les, clinking bottles in the cellar and smell a supper of cheese on toast being prepared downstairs by Alice Brannan. His mouth watered as he began to unpack.

CHAPTER EIGHT

By Tuesday morning, which finally brought weather more in keeping with summer, Lizzie had brooded for over two days straight,
unable to think about anything but the playing card. The extra
protection and security demanded of Dallington by Geraldine for
the women, though patchy at best, felt oppressive. Lizzie needed to
talk to Kember again and convince him this was far more serious
than he realised. If he was a man reliant on solid police work as he
claimed, the card could not be discounted as *quackery*. But still she
hesitated, bruised by their last meeting and his thinly veiled derision at her offer of help.

'Come on,' Emily called, interrupting Lizzie's thoughts.
'Geraldine's waiting by the lorry.' She waved her white ferry chit.

Lizzie pointed towards the ops room. 'Actually, I've just got to
make a quick call.'

'You've been acting very strange the last couple of days.' Charlie
placed a hand on Lizzie's arm for emphasis. 'You're not having second thoughts about the club, are you?'

'Of course not.' Lizzie tried to give Charlie her most reassuring
smile. 'Now go, before Geraldine tells you off,' she said, shooing
them away.

Lizzie ignored their glances of concern and entered the ATA ops room. She snatched up the telephone handset, waited for the operator and asked for Scotney Police Station. Moments later, the jaunty voice of Sergeant Wright informed her that Kember was not at the station.

Lizzie gave her compulsion to align all the stationery on the desk free rein as a distraction while she spoke. 'As soon as he arrives can you give him a message?'

'By all means,' Wright assured. 'Pencil at the ready.'

'Tell him this. Lavinia's body was found in a particular place at a particular time and posed in a particular way. That is not random. That is the work of someone who wants to send a message of some kind to those who are left behind to see it.'

She listened to the breathing from the other end of the line and imagined Wright scrawling in his notebook.

After a moment, Wright said, 'Is there anything else, Miss Hayes?'

Lizzie's next words caught in her throat as her vision swam with the image of the playing card. She took a deep breath to clear her head. 'The ATA are opening a women-only club in the cellar of the manor house tomorrow evening. While I was alone there on Saturday evening, someone left a playing card with the eyes put out with a pin. That's a serious warning we can't ignore. Tell DI Kember I want to use my skills and experience to help. The killer won't stop, so you've nothing to lose by giving me a chance.'

Lizzie listened to more heavy breathing, unprepared for the blunt answer when it came at last.

'Thank you for your concern, Miss Hayes,' Wright said. 'I've made another note but the inspector is very busy and really hasn't the time for idle theories. Good day.' And with that the line went dead.

Lizzie clenched her jaw and slammed down the handset, jumping at the sight of Niamh standing in the doorway.

'Don't ask,' Lizzie said, pushing past as Niamh gave her a curious look.

◆ ◆ ◆

Aware of the stares and sideways looks, Lizzie said nothing as she and her friends bounced around in the back of the Bedford lorry taking them to Dispersal. Tension, uncertainty and suspicion marked each of the women's faces.

Lizzie was glad once Geraldine had the Oxford airborne and the women started relaxing, their bodies succumbing to the peace they found when they were in the air.

The smell of aero engines, rubber, grease, leather and canvas soon displaced the scent of fresh air, grass and perfume. As the Oxford gained altitude, its engine noise and vibrations drowned out conversations between Geraldine and Emily in the cockpit, but Niamh and Agata turned to speak to Lizzie.

'What are you doing for them?' Niamh shouted over the loud thrum.

'For who?' Lizzie shouted back.

'You know – the police. What do you know that they don't?'

Lizzie's heart sank. But she was too tired to try to think of a convincing lie. 'I told you, I know about murderers,' she said wearily.

Agata narrowed her eyes and shook her head disbelievingly. 'The police must know more than you.'

Lizzie nodded. 'They do but I know other things.'

The Oxford lurched and shuddered before levelling off. Agata still stared at her.

'What things?' Charlie asked from the seat behind.

Lizzie's chest tightened. This wasn't the time or place to have this discussion.

'What things?' Agata shouted.

Lizzie shrugged. 'How they think.' She looked sharply across as Fizz gave an exaggerated laugh.

'What am *I* thinking, then?' Fizz said.

'I can't do it like that. It's not being psychic, it's more . . . academic. I study people, how they look, behave.'

'Are you watching us all the time? Studying us?' Agata frowned.

'No, of course not.' Lizzie shook her head. *My God*, she thought. *What would they accuse her of next?*

The Oxford banked to port and Lizzie caught a brief sight of the ground before the wings levelled and sky returned in the window.

'How do you *know things*?' Charlie asked.

Lizzie bit her lip. 'I talked to some of them. To murderers.'

Niamh blanched in horror. 'You did what?'

'I wanted to find out how they think, why they do the things they do,' Lizzie said, seeing Niamh's shock transforming into curiosity.

'I read about the Brighton trunk murders in the newspapers,' Niamh said. 'Do you know the ones? Where they found those bodies in luggage trunks? I couldn't believe it.'

'I only know what I read about them,' Lizzie said, unsure what direction this would take.

'What about that chap killed with a carpenter's mallet? That was just awful.' Niamh continued. 'What was his name?'

'Francis Rattenbury, in London,' Lizzie said with a shrug. 'I don't know him either. I did most of my research in Oxford Prison.'

Fizz mouthed the word *freak*, and Niamh and Agata turned back to talk to each other, giving her sideways looks that Lizzie knew meant she was the topic of discussion.

At least she could return to the safe haven of her own thoughts for now, so she tuned in to the drone of the engines, regulated her breathing and allowed her mind to go over recent events. She imagined herself as the killer confronting Lavinia on the church path and seeing her body posed on the ground. She imagined herself outside the cellar, watching and listening, feeling amusement when leaving the playing card on the stool.

Only when Charlie placed a hand on her shoulder did she realise they were landing at Rochester and her mind had been playing the scenario on a constant loop. The time had not been wasted. The images had revealed gaps in her knowledge that only Kember could fill. Whoever Lavinia's murderer was had left a message to taunt and goad them. That the killer felt the need to ridicule and frighten said more about him than it did Lizzie and her colleagues.

She had spent years studying his type, figuring out the terrifying intricacies in the psychology of a killer. He might believe he was the strong one, but she knew she was stronger.

Kember spotted Greenway outside the shops opposite the village hall and strode across the road to meet him. One of the two villagers chatting to the ARP warden nodded towards Kember as he approached. Greenway turned in greeting and the villagers quickly disappeared into the grocer's shop.

'Inspector, I thought I'd see you sooner rather than later.'

'Mr Greenway.' Kember shook his outstretched hand. 'Do you mind coming to the station for a quick chat?'

'I was about to have a slice of rabbit pie for my lunch, if you want to join me?' Greenway indicated the pub. 'Most meat's on ration but we've plenty of bunnies round here.'

A hunger pang rumbled in Kember's stomach as he realised he had missed breakfast. 'That's the best idea I've heard all day.'

Moments later, Kember and Greenway sat in the saloon bar of the Castle pub, each awaiting an order of rabbit pie and each with a pint of bitter in front of him.

'The deceased is one Lavinia Scott of the Air Transport Auxiliary,' Kember said in a low voice. 'The air station confirmed she's one of theirs. What can you tell me about the arrival of Miss Scott into the village last Tuesday?'

'Nothing, I'm afraid. I don't recall seeing her. In contrast, two young women roared through on Wednesday, one in a sports car and one on a motorbike. Upset poor Mrs Garner no end, they did.' Greenway gave a playful wink.

'I'm sure,' Kember said wanly. 'What about the evening? Did you see her about while attending to your warden's duties?'

They paused as a barmaid placed a plate of rabbit pie, boiled potatoes and dark green cabbage in front of them.

'I didn't see hide nor hair of her,' Greenway said, before immediately tucking into his food.

A familiar pattern, Kember thought as he too began his lunch. Amazing how even a pretty young woman, a stranger to the village, could go unnoticed by the busybodies and curtain-twitching brigade, yet the slightest click of a door could be heard from across the street.

'Where were you at about ten o'clock Tuesday night?' Kember continued.

Greenway looked up, thinking. 'I was outside the vicarage, that's the limit of my patrol up that end because there's nobody in the church after dark usually. I was about to cross to Mrs Garner's before returning on the downward leg when I saw a chink of light coming from the vicarage. Now that's unusual, I thought. Mrs Oaks is spot-on with her blackout curtains as a rule. That's why I remember it. I gave my usual cry of *'Put that light out'* and within seconds the curtain had been pulled properly.'

'Did you see anyone else after that?' Kember looked at Greenway over his glass as he took a mouthful of beer.

'No,' Greenway said through a mouthful of pie crust. 'I'd seen a few of the pub regulars at chucking-out time on my way up. There were a couple of staggerers but all well behaved. I saw Bert Garner leave with Andy Wingate, who owns the garage, and both headed home. They live at opposite ends of the village.'

Kember raised an eyebrow. 'You saw Albert Garner go home?'

'Go home, yes. Reach home, no. I conducted a bit of a security sweep around the village hall. I like to do that every couple of days but it does take me an extra ten or fifteen minutes to get to the vicarage on those evenings.' Greenway speared a chunk of meat.

'So there could have been someone on the path next to the church whom you didn't see?'

Greenway paused with his fork halfway to his mouth. 'It's possible.' He put his fork down, his face creased in thought. 'Does it help that I saw nothing?'

'Absolutely,' Kember said.

Greenway nodding slowly as if it all made sense, when it obviously didn't, amused Kember and he had to hide a genuine smile behind a gulp of his beer. On a serious note, Greenway didn't appear to be the most alert ARP warden he'd ever met, but the timing of his patrol was crucial for establishing who was abroad in the blackout around the time of the murder. His sightings of Albert Garner and Andy Wingate, and the incident with the vicarage blackout curtain, were crucial markers that defined the length of opportunity afforded the killer.

Kember clinked his knife and fork down on his empty plate as Wright entered the pub and a cheer went up from the pub regulars.

'Stop messing about,' Wright cried as his constabulary helmet was knocked from his head and disappeared into a huddle of drinkers standing at the bar. Wright chased after it but the men were too quick, passing it left, right and across to another group, always just out of Wright's reach.

'Never too quick, were you, Den?' said one. 'Not even for the cricket team.'

A laugh had Wright's cheeks colouring. 'Give it back, you cheeky sods. That's police property.'

Two old women in hair nets and pinafore aprons sat in a corner drinking half-pints of milk stout. One called out, 'Language, Dennis Wright. I might not be your teacher now but you just remember your Ps and Qs.'

'I remember when you couldn't run in a straight line without falling over and grazing your knee,' said the other. 'Shall I get the Germolene?'

'Was that last year?' More hilarity from the men.

Kember decided to rescue Wright and called him across to his table.

'Sorry to disturb you, sir.' Wright nodded to Greenway. 'Brian.'

'I must get on anyway,' Greenway said, standing. 'I'll catch you later, Den. Inspector.'

As Greenway left, Wright took the empty seat and leant forward conspiratorially. 'I'm glad I've seen you, sir,' he said with a grim look. 'I had a call earlier, from Miss Hayes.'

'The ATA pilot?' Kember's heart sank. 'What does she want now?'

'She said to give you a message.' Wright offered Kember his notebook to read. 'I don't see how she can have some special skill that we don't. I hold no truck with amateur detectives who think they're better than us, especially ladies, but it's a strange turn of events all the same, if you ask me.'

Kember's face clouded as he read the neatly scribed message twice before handing the book back to Wright. He held the same opinion of amateur sleuths as his sergeant, and that included Fleet Street hack journalists, but had to admit the playing card was a worrying development. By itself it could mean something or nothing, but if it was a message from the killer, hand-delivering it to a group of women was surely the action of someone with a warped mind or an axe to grind.

Or both.

'Sir?'

Kember glanced at Wright and saw his sergeant's head cocked to one side in concern.

He took a deep breath. 'I want you to ring Flight Lieutenant Pendry and tell him about Miss Hayes' playing card crank. It's probably one of the men on the air station having a joke at the women's expense, or it could be nothing more sinister than someone picking at it absent-mindedly. Either way, it falls under RAF jurisdiction for the present.'

'And her, um, offer?'

Kember gave a sharp shake of his head. 'I think we have it under control for now.' He pointed at Wright's notebook. 'What else have you got for me?'

The two policemen exchanged reports, which were largely disappointing. Most of the villagers had been indoors after nine o'clock, although a couple of the men living in the first few houses claimed to have been in the pub until ten. One of those had been drinking against the express wishes of his wife. Wright had left him being chastised with a few whacks to the side of his head with a wet dishcloth. No one claimed to have seen anything out of the ordinary.

The old woman who had scolded Sergeant Wright now stood at the bar, straining to hear every word. Kember decided a bit more privacy was required and motioned to Wright that they were leaving. The men at the bar surrounded Wright on his way to the door, patting his back, ruffling his hair and pretending to brush fluff from his uniform.

'Only a bit of fun, Den.'

'A laugh does no one any harm.'

'You're a good bloke.'

Leaving the pub a lot more satisfied than when he went in, Kember saw Wright's helmet returned as he emerged through the doorway and sandbags into the street. Wright grimaced and poured a concoction of beer dregs and ashtray contents from his helmet into the gutter, choosing to wear his steel war helmet instead. Kember smiled, remembering his own days on the beat as a constable, with a wife and two newborn twins to support. Hard but happy days.

The two men walked towards the lower end of the High Street and stopped outside the garage.

'Lavinia Scott arrived Tuesday evening on the last train from Tonbridge,' Wright said. 'Alf, the stationmaster, remembers seeing her alighting from the first-class carriage and collecting her ticket. He directed her to her lodgings with the Taplow sisters, who live next door but one to the Garners.'

'I questioned them both,' Kember said, watching Wright peer through one of the small dirty windows set into the garage's large double doors. 'Elsie Taplow spoke to Miss Scott when she took her room. She'd arrived a day early for her posting so she booked with them for one night. Elsie said her sister Annie had been in bed with a migraine headache that came on in the afternoon and she didn't emerge until the morning so she's no help. Elsie did say she heard something at the front door about half past nine in the evening, but when she checked there was nobody there. She called upstairs but no one answered. Because she'd given Miss Scott a key she assumed she'd gone for a walk, although she thought it a bit late to do so.'

'Aye,' Wright said, checking the lock on the garage doors. 'Apart from the fact that everyone's scared stiff, we haven't got a sausage.' He shook his head. 'Everyone's willing to talk and offer their own opinion but no one saw a thing. None of the shop owners saw anything of Miss Scott or noticed any strangers.'

'So she arrived at seven o'clock in the evening on the train from Tonbridge' – Kember pointed towards the railway station and swept his arm until he pointed at the church – 'and walked the entire length of the High Street, but nobody saw her at all.'

Wright stepped into a passage running beside the garage. 'People have plenty to do at home rather than be wandering the streets. In any case, at that time of an evening most people were having their tea while listening to the BBC Home Service on the wireless, like I was.'

Kember looked thoughtful. 'How many more houses to visit?'

'I've a few people to track down but as far as the High Street goes' – Wright tapped the wall of the garage – 'this one is the last.'

◆ ◆ ◆

An overpowering stench of engine oil, petrol and lubricant hit Kember as he stepped through the open door at the rear of the garage. Even the air felt greasy. A farm truck took up much of the centre space but the walls were lined with shelves of tools and sundry automotive parts.

'Hello, Andy.' Wright smiled as a clunk and a curse came from beneath a farm truck.

The head of Andy Wingate slid into view, peering up at the two policemen. 'You bloody sods, you gave me a heart attack,' he said in mock anger.

'Guilty conscience?'

Wingate gave Wright a quizzical look. 'What have I got to be guilty about?'

Kember made a show of looking at shelves laden with motor parts, products and tools, keeping Wingate at the edge of his vision. He knew from long experience that poking around someone's home ground where they ought to feel safe would start to worry the guilty.

'You tell us,' Wright said.

Wingate frowned and his tone became more serious. 'Stop mucking about, I'm busy. What do you want?'

'Why haven't you been called up?' Kember asked.

'Dodgy ticker.' Wingate patted his chest.

'There's nothing wrong with your heart,' Wright sneered.

'I've got a doctor's note says otherwise.'

Wright opened a bottle of clear fluid, sniffed and recoiled at the stink. 'You've heard about the young lass murdered by the church?' He replaced the cap.

Wingate pulled himself from under the truck and stood, wiping his oil-covered hands on a rag. 'Yeah. Terrible business. I was born here and I've known nothing like that ever happen here before.'

Kember noticed Wingate's grip on the rag tighten almost imperceptibly, though he saw genuine sadness in the man's eyes.

'Need to ask you a few questions, all routine,' Wright continued. 'We're asking everybody in the village.'

'Fair enough.'

Wingate looked expectantly at Wright but it was Kember who next spoke.

'Where were you at ten o'clock last Tuesday?'

'Just leaving the pub,' Wingate said 'I always have a pint and a chat.' He looked at Wright. 'You know that, Den.'

Kember, detecting no relaxing of the tension in Wingate's stance, walked to the other side of the truck. 'People in the pub can confirm that, can they?'

'Of course. I was with Bert – Albert Garner.'

'What happened when you left the pub?'

Wingate looked through the open driver's window to Kember who was peering through the open passenger's window. 'Bert and I said our goodnights and he wandered off towards his place. I wandered off to mine. I saw Brian, the ARP warden, going up the other side of the street on what he laughingly calls his patrol.'

Wright joined Kember in his circling, the pair of them like vultures sussing out a promising cadaver. 'Was he drunk? Albert, that is?'

Wingate smiled. 'Course not. His missus would've killed him.'

Wright smiled too. 'Did you see or hear anything unusual?'

'No, can't say I did. Listen, can you two stay together? I'm getting a crick in my neck looking one way then the other.'

Wright ignored him, stepped over a stirrup pump and nudged a couple of large petrol cans standing on the floor with his foot. Empty. 'Had problems with your petrol?'

The quizzical look returned to Wingate's face. 'What do you mean?'

'Has any of it gone missing?'

'Missing? No, why would it?'

'Been a lot of petrol thefts around the farms and villages.'

Wingate moved the petrol cans. 'Ah, yes. I heard something about that but I keep my stock under double lock and key. Anyone would have to make a bit of a racket if they wanted any of my stuff and I'd clout them with a spanner.'

'Bert had his car siphoned last Tuesday night,' Wright said.

'Good grief,' Wingate responded without hesitation. 'I'll make sure to check my locks. I can't afford for any to go missing. It's my livelihood.'

As Kember walked around the front of the truck, he noticed something on Wingate's arm. 'What have you done there?'

Wingate looked at his right forearm where a sheen of axle grease emphasised a long, angry-looking scratch. 'I was bleeding the brakes on this heap and I caught it on a split pin. Bit sore but I'm a big lad.'

'Best make sure you clean it. You don't want it going septic.' Kember turned to leave, knowing Wingate was one to keep an eye on but prepared to let things lie for the moment.

'Is that it?' Wingate said, his face a mixture of relief and confusion.

'Unless there's anything you want to tell us,' Kember said, pausing before leading Wright from the garage. 'I thought not,' he called back.

◆ ◆ ◆

Ferry duties over for the day, Fizz and Agata were playfully bantering as they completed decorating the lounge room of the cellar club. Niamh had acquired a red rug, no one asked how or where from, which fitted the square floor space only slightly imperfectly, a pretty decent dartboard had appeared and Emily was in the final throes of polishing the brand-new bar, constructed by bolting two solid oak book cabinets together and to the floor. Meanwhile, Niamh and Charlie had found a long string of Christmas tree fairy lights and were in the process of fixing them along one side of the games room, hampered by Tilly wanting to play.

A tendril of anxiety had been throbbing with increasing intensity down Lizzie's spine all day at the indifference shown by Kember. It was one thing to shun her professional advances, demonstrating he had yet to take her seriously, but quite unforgivable to ignore her messages about the playing card, which was surely a valuable piece of evidence. Not only that but she remained convinced that behind it lay a threat to them all. No message had awaited her return from delivering an aircraft to Biggin Hill and only the preparations for tomorrow night's club opening had been able to take her mind away from the playing card.

She took the cloth cover off a beer crate. Instead of beer bottles, inside nestled nine handmade wooden skittles, each about eight inches high, and three wooden balls of a size somewhere between a golf ball and a cricket ball. Along with a chess set, snakes and ladders, Ludo, several packs of cards and two sets of darts, the skittles completed the essential gaming paraphernalia.

'Oh gosh,' Charlie said, seeing the skittles. 'Is this from the ground crew? I haven't played this in age—'

Silence. The room was suddenly plunged into darkness as black as pitch.

'What's happened?' came the unsteady voice of Charlie.

'Probably a power cut,' Fizz said calmly. 'Or a fuse.

But Lizzie wasn't so sure. Her throat tightened at the thought there might be someone down there with them. She sniffed, checking for cigarette smoke, but they'd smoked so many of their own.

Suddenly there was a scream.

Lizzie jumped, felt something warm. Her heart raced and her stomach cramped as panic began to take hold.

'Who in shite's name was that,' Fizz growled.

'Sorry,' Emily squeaked. 'I touched Lizzie's hand.'

Lizzie imagined she could see and feel someone else close but knew it to be false. She greedily took in gulps of air before letting them out slowly, frantically pinging the rubber band wrapped around her wrist, trying desperately to regain control of her body's automatic response to terror.

'Where's the sodding box?'

Niamh lit a match and others did the same, throwing crazy shadows off the walls and ceiling. Fizz found the fuse box in the vestibule by the front door and opened it by the light of Charlie's match.

'There you go. One of the fuses has come loose,' she said knowingly. She checked the wire was still secured by its screws and pushed the holder back into place.

They all blinked as the lights flooded back on. All seemed forgotten in an instant but Lizzie's heart continued to race. Fuses didn't come loose by themselves.

'Somebody needs to get some emergency candles down here,' Fizz said, slamming the fuse box shut.

Emily pushed between Lizzie and Charlie, putting her arms around their shoulders. 'We're ready for anything Hitler has to throw at us now.' She grinned.

Agata emerged from the lounge. 'Well, as there's no booze until tomorrow, who's for a quick one upstairs?'

'Of course,' Charlie said, 'but has anyone got a hankie? I think I've caught the sniffles.'

Lizzie offered hers and caught a scrap of paper from her pocket before it fluttered to the floor. Emily made an 'I don't want to catch anything' face at Charlie and moved away. As the women filed up the steps, chattering excitedly, Lizzie made sure she locked the door and hurriedly chased after the others.

CHAPTER NINE

The next morning at breakfast, all the women except Charlie kept their distance from Lizzie, who rattled cutlery and banged china so hard it could have cracked. Her one piece of toast lay uneaten, decimated under an aggravated assault from the butter knife.

How could Kember, a so-called detective inspector, be so stupid as to ignore professional help when it was offered?

Pendry had told her not ten minutes earlier that Kember had refused her latest offer without any apparent thought. All her education, training and experience, making her more qualified to give an opinion than anyone within at least a thirty-mile radius, had been summarily dismissed. Because she was a woman. Lizzie's mood was not soothed by the women eyeing her with suspicion. Despite becoming friends at White Waltham during training and through a common love of flying, she knew they thought her odd, labelling her frequent periods of vacant staring as daydreaming. She'd heard the words *oddball, scatty* and *loony* whispered about her, though that was generally Fizz, and Charlie had contradicted her.

What really fuelled her anger was being palmed off on to Pendry when the playing card clearly had significance. Even if she could accept that a civilian might not be allowed to assist an investigation, and there were many instances to the contrary, having her messages ignored before being told third-hand through Wright and Pendry that Kember had asked him to investigate the *playing card crank* was more than she could stand.

In that moment, Lizzie resolved to write a letter to Kember. It wouldn't be a full psychological profile of the murderer – only more deaths could provide the patterns to follow – but just enough to whet Kember's appetite.

And the implication would be very clear: if he ignored the letter and anything happened to them, it would be entirely his fault.

◆ ◆ ◆

Kember slouched in the visitor's chair, rubbing the residue of the head cold from his eyes. The weather had prolonged his misery but he perked up when Wright returned with tea.

'We know the routines of both Greenway and Brown, and we know the rough time of death,' Kember began as Wright handed him a mug. 'Mrs Garner heard something she described as *a ruckus* soon after her husband came home, and found the petrol siphoned off. You'd be as quiet as a mouse if you were stealing petrol by siphoning, wouldn't you? Not making a ruckus. The accounts by Wingate, Greenway, Mrs Garner, Mrs Oaks and the reverend all agree.'

Wright sat at his desk and caressed his beard as if he were petting a cat. 'Could Miss Scott have disturbed the thief and been killed to silence her?' he suggested.

'Worth considering,' said Kember. 'Although dragging a struggling person or dead body across the street to hide it behind the wall would have been difficult. Usually, I'd be sure someone must have heard something, but Lavinia Scott arrived on the last train and nobody except the stationmaster, the Taplows and the killer appear to have noticed. Elsie Taplow reckons Miss Scott must have gone out at about half nine, so we need to find out whether she planned to meet anyone. Could she have met someone and trusted them in such a short time?'

Wright shrugged non-committally. It takes all sorts. I'll see if Les Brannan, the publican, can shed any light on things. Then I'll track down the few people we haven't managed to interview yet.'

'Good man,' Kember said. 'I'll call Dr Headley at Pembury to see if he has any good news. At the moment it appears we have little evidence, no weapon, no motive and no prime suspect.'

◆ ◆ ◆

All the women had returned from ferry duties over the last hour and Lizzie had written her letter to Kember, a motorcycle courier promising to drop it in on his way to Tonbridge. Now she sat alone on the terrace behind the manor house, enjoying a quiet cigarette, her train of thought meandering towards Lavinia. In her mind's eye, she saw the footpath and a body on the ground, a police inspector and sergeant blocking her way and moving her on. The grim looks on their faces told her much about the state of Lavinia's body. She needed to see the crime scene and talk to DI Kember.

'Why did someone kill you?' Lizzie's voice split the silence. 'What did they want? Did they know you? Who are they?'

'Who's who?' Agata asked as Niamh placed two cups of tea on the table.

Being caught speaking aloud brought colour to Lizzie's cheeks but she dismissed the question with a wave of her hand. 'Doesn't seem right, does it, with Lavinia gone? I suppose none of us knew her very well, though.'

'I liked her,' said Niamh. 'She was one of the first girls to speak to me when I got to White Waltham.'

'Me too.' Agata looked down solemnly at the cup in her hands.

'Have a good cry and a swig of sherry, it's the best way in times like these,' Niamh said, placing a hand on Lizzie's shoulder before something caught her eye. 'Oh dear.' She pointed towards the motor shed near the barrack huts. 'Looks like Fizz and Emily are having another one of their disagreements.'

Lizzie shielded her eyes with her hand and saw Charlie standing between them, trying to keep the two women apart, her hand on Fizz's arm as the two of them screamed at each other. Fizz shrugged her loose and strode into the shed, followed by Emily.

'They're as bad as each other, have been since training.' Niamh shook her head.

'Now there'll be trouble,' Agata said.

Lizzie gasped in disbelief as Charlie's car shot out of the motor shed, Fizz at the wheel. Charlie waved her hands and shouted but Fizz ignored her and drove towards the far end of the grass runway. A moment later, Lizzie jumped up as Emily chased after Fizz on Lizzie's motorbike.

Charlie ran across from the motor shed, through the garden and up the steps of the terrace, anger and fear on her face as she glanced back at the airfield. 'Someone's going to get hurt,' she said between gasps for air.

'What on earth are they doing?' Lizzie asked.

'Racing. They hurled insults at each other and decided the way to settle things once and for all was to see who could beat the other.'

'Bloody hell,' Lizzie hissed.

The women watched helplessly from the terrace as the tiny figures in the distance got bigger and the roar of engines reverberated around the airfield. It soon became clear that winning was not the primary object but to make the other swerve and crash. First Emily then Fizz pulled ahead, weaving to unsettle the other, but neither could gain the upper hand.

As the vehicles sped towards the hangars, Fizz appeared to lose control and braked hard before skidding into bushes. To avoid Fizz's crash, Emily jerked the Norton's handlebars. The motorbike leant into the ground and slid several yards while Emily rolled over and over to avoid serious injury.

'Christ almighty!' Agata exclaimed.

'Never mind the murderer,' Lizzie said. 'We're trying to kill each other now.'

◆ ◆ ◆

'Ah, Dr Headley,' Kember said in answer to a gruff response from the other end of the telephone line. 'I'm sorry to press you but I'd hoped you'd have something a little more substantial for me – regarding the murdered woman, I mean.'

'You seem to think I'm a miracle-worker,' Headley said.

Despite his irritation at having spent most of the morning trying to reach Headley, Kember tried appealing to Headley's ego, sense of duty and humanity. 'You do yourself a disservice, Doctor, but it's in all our best interests for us to catch this murderer as soon as we can, before he kills again.'

'I'm aware of that, Kember, if you'll let me finish. It just so happens I have completed the full post-mortem, including inspecting her clothing, taking forensic samples and so on and so forth. I had a good old mooch around so I could give you a decent stab at a cause of death, if you pardon the pun.'

Kember rolled his eyes. 'Find anything interesting?'

'Wouldn't be doing my job if I didn't. There is a little U-shaped bone called the hyoid which sits underneath the jawline above the thyroid and larynx. It serves as an anchor point for several muscles, including the back of the tongue. It is crucial to tongue movement, swallowing and speech.' Headley paused.

Kember knew he shouldn't because Headley would enjoy it, but he took the bait anyway. 'And that's interesting because . . .?'

He heard a faint *ha* from Headley. 'In this instance, the hyoid has not been damaged, which suggests insufficient pressure has been applied.'

'Are you saying she wasn't strangled?'

'Hold your horses. I'm saying it's unlikely a ligature was used. The hyoid doesn't become one solid bone for about forty years and Lavinia Scott was only twenty-three. At her age, damage occurs more commonly to two little horns that poke up on either side of the thyroid cartilage, and these *had* been fractured, like a wishbone you might say. The deceased also has evidence of petechiae on the skin around her eyes and subconjunctival haemorrhaging.'

'In English, please, Doctor,' Kember said, and heard Headley sigh.

'Blood spots on the skin and excessively bloodshot eyes. Along with the fractured thyroid cartilage this confirms the initial hypothesis of death by manual strangulation I gave at the scene. As suspected, the killer used the knife once her life expired. You saw the marks on her neck and abdomen. She has the beginning of a bruise on her right wrist but none on her left. She also has some superficial stab wounds around her nether regions. Because there's no bruising there or on her thighs, I was almost certain she had not been raped, and the swabs I took confirmed this.'

'That's a blessing,' Kember said.

'Not really.'

'Why not?'

'Because I found semen on her blouse, which suggests—'

'I know what it suggests,' Kember interrupted, rubbing his eyes with his free hand. 'Jesus Christ,' he sighed, battling a wave of fatigue. Some days the madness that some fellow humans seemed eager to display and unable to control made him tired in both mind as well as body. 'Hitler might be a madman but at least we know he wants to rule the world. What in God's name is this monster playing at?'

'That's not a question I or pathology can answer, I'm afraid.' The doctor continued, 'I tested some of the blood deposits from various parts of her body but it's all type O, which matches the girl's blood type.'

'Nothing that can narrow our list of suspects?' Kember asked, sensing a slight hesitation from the doctor.

'I did find some skin and blood under a fingernail on her left hand, which I tested. It is also human type O.'

Kember's heart gave an extra hard thump. 'Are you saying she marked her killer?'

'I can't see any corresponding scratches on her person,' Headley said. 'There are a couple more things, unrelated to the cause of death but, because of their bizarre nature, I assume will be of great significance to you, Kember.'

A flicker of hope among the confusion. 'And they are?'

'I found some kind of oil residue on her forehead.'

'Oil?' Kember frowned, puzzled. 'What do you mean by residue?'

'Just a smear. Could be nothing of consequence. I also found a piece of paper in her mouth, tucked between her upper gum and her cheek. It had printing on both sides and I thought it might be a piece of newspaper.'

Kember's grip on the handset tightened. 'And was it?'

'No. It was a verse torn from the Bible.'

'The Bible? What did it say?'

'I looked it up. It's from Revelation, chapter nineteen, verse two: *For true and righteous are his judgements: for He hath judged the great whore, which did corrupt the earth with her fornication, and hath avenged the blood of his servants at her hand.*'

Kember shook his head even though the doctor could not see. 'What's that supposed to mean?'

Headley gave a derisive snort. 'You're the criminal investigator, I'm purely medical.'

◆ ◆ ◆

Kember found Reverend Wilson in the vestry again, where the piles of books, ledgers, ecclesiastical equipment and fishing gear seemed not to have reduced or even moved. A smack of head on wood came from beneath the laden desk.

'Oh hel—p.'

Kember smiled at the converted curse. 'You okay there, Reverend?'

'I dropped a pile of papers.' Wilson bobbed up, rubbing his head vigorously. 'There seems to be a never-ending supply of them.'

'I know the feeling,' Kember said.

'I'd offer you a seat, but as you can see . . .' Wilson indicated the chaos.

'Not a problem,' Kember said. 'I can see you're still very busy, but do you mind if I ask you a couple of questions?'

'Not at all. Fire away.'

Kember took out his notebook and opened it at the page on which he'd written the quote from the Bible found in Lavinia Scott's mouth.

He showed Wilson. 'Do you recognise this?'

Wilson nodded. 'It's from the Bible. Revelation, chapter nineteen, I think.'

'We found it at the scene of the crime.' Kember watched Wilson's face and saw only interest and concern. 'I'm not a religious man and therefore likely to take it at face value, but I wondered if there is another interpretation.'

Wilson studied the notebook for a few more seconds. 'The Scriptures tell us that Babylon was a wicked city, *the great whore*, that had corrupted the world with its immorality. Christians had been persecuted and martyred and the people followed a false religion. God sat in judgement and destroyed the city, which was seen as appropriate and just.'

'So it's about wrongdoers getting their just deserts?'

'A bit simplistic, but you could put t like that.'

'Talking of which.' Kember knew a straight answer only ever came from a straight question. 'I understand you had an altercation on board a ship and a man lost his life.'

'Been checking up on me, I see.' Wilson seemed sad but not alarmed. 'I don't blame you. Yes, I killed a man, which is why I turned to God. To atone for my sins.'

Kember was surprised by Wilson's calm confirmation of his guilt. 'Can you elaborate?' he asked. Murder was a capital offence but the reverend had clearly escaped the gallows and Jenny had said nothing about a conviction or long prison sentence.

Wilson took a deep breath and sighed. 'Nothing much to tell, really. The first mate on board a ship I was working on was a petty dictator. He bullied and beat anyone smaller than him or anyone he thought weaker than him. I was often his target, but I took it because it kept him away from the ones who couldn't cope. One day he went too far and I confronted him. To cut a long story short, we had a fist fight. It only lasted seconds until I caught him with an uppercut.'

Kember could see Wilson struggling to keep his composure. In his experience, not the reaction of a cold-blooded killer.

'It wasn't a hard punch, but he hit his head on a bulkhead,' Wilson continued. 'When he saw the blood his eyes took on this wild look and he went for me, but the ship hit a trough in the waves and lurched. He stumbled and fell straight over the bulwark. We searched but couldn't find him.'

Kember rubbed the end of his nose with one finger. 'He wasn't dead when he fell overboard?'

'No,' said Wilson, his eyes full of remorse. 'But if I hadn't punched him . . .'

Kember had seen plenty of hard men who liked a good fight, frightened men who'd lashed out in self-defence and men convinced an accident was their fault. He'd put a few men down himself, in the line of duty. 'Was the incident investigated?'

'Yes, by the captain and the police. They said the fight was self-defence and the drowning an accident, but if he hadn't hit his head . . .'

'It sounds like you could have been the one overboard or lying on a slab,' Kember said.

'I still killed a man,' said Wilson.

Kember opened the vestry door to leave. It was clear the reverend felt remorse – but then there was some truth in his statement.

Geraldine glared at the two women standing rigidly to attention in front of her desk, staring directly ahead at the wall behind her. She could feel her jaw muscles moving as she clenched and unclenched her teeth, her lips pressed together so hard they were almost invisible. She banged her fist on the table in frustration, hard enough to make them flinch, and turned on Emily first.

'To say I am disappointed is to wildly misinterpret my mood,' Geraldine's cold voice snapped. 'To say I am annoyed is a savage understatement.' Her piercing stare moved to Fizz. 'I could say that you have let down yourselves and your families badly. I could even say you have let down the organisation and the uniform.' She looked back to Emily. 'More importantly, you have let *me* down and that is the one thing I cannot countenance under any circumstance. I understand there was a verbal altercation between you two before the incident and that this was not the first time you had antagonised each other.'

'It—' began Fizz, but Geraldine flicked her gaze to her in a microsecond, the ice in her stare freezing the response in Fizz's throat.

'I. Care. Not.' Geraldine said each word individually. 'Your petty rivalries are unimportant. We are all from different but not dissimilar backgrounds and therefore cannot fall back on the excuse of poor breeding or lack of education. I cannot help but visualise how this altercation would have played out in a common public house in a shady district of London. No doubt an unseemly street brawl would have ensued.'

Geraldine saw the corner of Emily's eye twitching and stared at her for a moment, noting a sheen of perspiration settle on the bow of the officer's top lip. She turned back to Fizz.

'That in itself would have been disgraceful behaviour, but when the weapons to hand are private cars and motorcycles, the consequences increase exponentially. At least one aircraft was put at risk today' – she jabbed the desk with her finger for emphasis – 'not to mention personnel, and it has not been a simple task to keep this from reaching the ears of the group captain or wing commander.' She snatched up an apple from her desk and brandished it menacingly. 'To do so I have had to compromise my own integrity and that will take a long time to forgive. I have employed as much guile as I possess and put into practice, as far as I dare, those womanly wiles that my mother said I would one day be grateful for. This is not a stratagem I wished to use in such circumstances and certainly not so early in our tenure here at Scotney.'

Geraldine could feel the anger slowly dissipating and she relaxed her fingers around the apple. With so many other obstacles to an easy life, she had no appetite for prolonging petty squabbles.

'It is within my authority to dismiss you both, but neither the ATA nor I can afford to lose good pilots. I have no wish to give the top brass the ammunition to kick us off this air station but nor can I allow such a serious breach of discipline to go entirely unpunished. Before I issue a sanction, I need to be convinced that this behaviour will cease immediately.' She noted the seemingly sincere nods from Emily and Fizz, but shook her own head with profound disappointment. 'Your actions endangered this air station and could have resulted in a death. I should be throwing every book on the shelf at you, but for the good of this ferry pool I shall not log this incident nor this conversation. However, if any further incident comes to my attention I shall immediately dismiss you from the ATA.'

For the first time since beginning to speak, Geraldine lowered her eyes from the red faces of her officers. She took a deep breath and sighed.

'Enemy action is increasing daily and Scotney may become a target itself very soon. So the only punishment I can deliver without jeopardising operations, and this is non-negotiable, is to confine you to the air station for one month when not on ferry duties. This confinement extends to whatever airfield, station or aerodrome you are assigned to deliver to or collect from and necessary travel between.' Geraldine picked up a switchblade knife from her desk and started to peel her apple. 'Do not test me again. Now shake hands.' Emily and Fizz complied. 'Dismissed.'

The women saluted in unison and turned to leave the room. At the door, Fizz pushed in front of Emily.

Geraldine spotted the exchange and stopped peeling. 'Get out of my sight,' she bellowed. 'Both of you, before I change my mind and shoot you myself.'

◆　◆　◆

After a fruitless day reading and sorting through witness statements and the meagre forensic evidence, Kember considered calling it a day and retiring to the pub. The chat with Reverend Wilson had gone some way to moving him back down the list of suspects but the cross and dagger remained worth pursuing with Headley. He decided on one more piece of paperwork and reached for an envelope addressed to him personally. Kember noticed it bore no stamp, so it had been hand-delivered. He slit the envelope with a letter opener and unfolded the sheets inside, realising with a jolt that it came from Lizzie Hayes.

> *Dear DI Kember,*
>
> *It is disappointing to hear you are not convinced enough by my credentials to allow me to participate directly in the investigation. However, I find myself unable to avoid helping at arm's length because Lavinia Scott deserves our best efforts to find her murderer and achieve justice on her behalf . . .*

Kember stuffed the sheets back into their envelope, leaving the rest of the letter unread. He had no desire tonight to read yet another person's opinion of his failings. Resolving to look at it in the morning, he threw it on the desk, feeling a wave of fatigue wash over him. His wife, his home, the murder, Lizzie Hayes, the final residue of this damnably persistent cold. There was nothing he could do, or wanted to do this evening. He needed to make himself a strong hot toddy, get a very early night and sleep on it. Ordinarily it would be in the warmth of his own bed, next to his wife.

But tonight, it would be in the pub.

CHAPTER TEN

Lizzie watched Matfield standing at the head of the room for the morning briefing, fiddling with the cap in his hands, picking imaginary fluff from its peak, with Pendry standing stiffly to one side. As she listened to Matfield spend the next few minutes conveying Dallington's new rules relating to use of the cellar – the reason for their being called together – she marvelled they had been allowed to use it at all.

Judging by his demeanour, and despite his use of some saccharine phrases, Lizzie suspected Matfield endorsed his superior's views. This came as no surprise, but then she noticed Pendry. It was almost imperceptible, and Lizzie doubted anyone else in the room would have noticed, but she detected miniscule nods, almost twitches, as he listened to Matfield speak. She started to wonder whether his behaviour was entirely unconscious.

Lizzie realised Matfield was winding down, ready to leave, when Charlie spoke up.

'Rumour has it there's a dance in the offing,' she said hopefully. 'Is it true?'

Matfield's face assumed an oddly benevolent look. 'I argued for you to be allowed the opportunity to relax in whatever way the captain sees fit. Against his better judgement, the CO agreed.

Before you ask, that *does* include permission to attend the dance in the village on Saturday evening, to which all off-duty personnel have been invited. However, given recent events, you may wish to consider whether dancing the evening away is worth the risk involved because we cannot protect every one of you out there in the wild, so to speak. Unfortunately, as much as I would like the opportunity to join you ladies for a drink and a dance, the recent increase in hostilities will, undoubtedly, keep me on the station. This does not mean carte blanche to have a free-for-all. You wear a uniform. Respect it.'

He nodded with raised eyebrows for emphasis before leaving the briefing room. Pendry gave Geraldine an apologetic smile before following.

The two officers had left the door open and Lizzie noticed Geraldine's frown at the discourtesy as she strode over to close it before turning back, smiling now, and addressing the women.

'It was me, actually, who persuaded the CO to let you go to the dance. The war is getting closer to us and there's no telling when we might get another chance to let our hair down in the village. The wing commander made a good point about safety, but women take their lives in their hands on a daily basis and I refuse to let another man restrict my freedom. The decision is for each individual to make, but as long as we stay together in the village hall there should be no danger. So, take the opportunity to get to know this place, the locals and each other. It's a farming community and not very affluent, so try not to flaunt your privileged backgrounds.'

Lizzie inwardly cringed at the memory of her entrance into the village with Charlie.

'The CO and wing commander are correct,' Geraldine continued. 'The nearest most of the villagers will have been to an aircraft is when it flies overhead, but that doesn't mean they're stupid. Scotney is their village and we are visitors. Be courteous and play nicely, we're on the same side.'

◆ ◆ ◆

Kember stretched his aching back, the result of several uncomfortable nights spent in the police cells. His soft inviting bed at the pub had begun to soothe his stiff muscles, but hard office chairs did not suit his old injury. As he sat at Wright's desk, Kember noticed Lizzie's letter still peeking from the envelope where he'd left it. He grudgingly retrieved it and unfolded the sheets.

> *Dear DI Kember,*
>
> *It is disappointing to hear you are not convinced enough by my credentials to allow me to participate directly in the investigation. However, I find myself unable to avoid helping at arms' length because Lavinia Scott deserves our best efforts to find her murderer and achieve justice on her behalf.*
>
> *My training and experience tells me the positioning of Lavinia's body was deliberate and designed to gain attention. You have not provided details but I ask you to look at the way she was posed. This was premeditated, most likely to deliver a message, part of a ritual we must decipher.*
>
> *The sad nature of what I can do requires at least two if not more deaths to discern a visible pattern. However, as I made you aware, I received a defaced Queen of Clubs playing card, anonymously, while alone in the cellar we chose as the venue for our new women's club. There has also been another incident*

where fuses were tampered with, which must be connected.

The manner of Lavinia's death was a warning to us all. The playing card was another, and I fear we cannot ignore these without dire consequences.

In my <u>professional</u> opinion, the murderer will kill again very soon. The victim will be killed in a similar way, although I suspect an escalation of the violence, and her body will be left in a similar pose. I fear it will be another of the ATA.

Yours sincerely
Lizzie Hayes
Third Officer ATA

Kember threw the letter on to the desk. He had no idea how Miss Hayes had come to her conclusions with such scant information, but he suspected a hefty dose of assumption generously laced with guesswork. The letter was neat and well written, not the scrawl he would expect from someone frightened about being next on the killer's list. Then again, Third Officer Lizzie Hayes didn't strike him as someone easily scared or deflected.

He yawned.

The murder case was stalling, the morning held more tedium in the form of follow-up interviews and a tiring afternoon of paperwork beckoned at police HQ in Torbridge.

It promised to be a long day.

◆　◆　◆

After much discussion and a few arguments, a name had been chosen for the ATA's new cellar bar and inscribed on a piece of polished wood hung above the door. So it was that Niamh and Emily squealed with delight as they welcomed the first guests to the *Hangar Round* club that evening. The lounge bar had agreed to supply drink at upstairs prices on a sale or return basis, an arrangement that suited everyone. Agata was kept busy as the landlady for the night, ensuring no one took advantage of this new venture on its opening night, while Charlie and Fizz occupied the attentions of some of the senior officers, who had been invited more out of courtesy than for any other reason. Fizz and Emily had been told to keep well away from each other, but their admonishment at the hands of Geraldine seemed to have quietened their rivalry.

Sitting on a stool by herself, Lizzie finally felt content as she absorbed the carefree mood of the club. Sadly, it was a situation that was soon disturbed when Wing Commander Matfield drew up a stool next to her.

'You've done really well here, Miss Hayes,' Matfield simpered. 'Against my better judgement, and that of the group captain, I think you've made this into a really wonderful place.'

'Thank you,' Lizzie said, unsettled by such familiarity from the second-in-command. 'It's . . . good of you to come.' Invitations had been sent to both Dallington and Matfield, but no one had expected either to turn up. Lizzie wasn't sure whether Matfield's presence was a good thing or not.

'Why the odd name?' Matfield asked. 'For the club, I mean.'

'After aircraft hangars, obviously, and the rounded far walls of this cellar. Plus we wanted our own place to *hang around*.'

Matfield's lip curled in a half-smile as he understood the pun. 'I do hope this is a success.' He took a swig from a bottle of light ale. 'The CO was dead set against you taking over this cellar, you know. Pendry and I managed to persuade him otherwise.' He offered a cigarette, which Lizzie accepted and then let him light before he returned to his own.

'What plans have you? I can't hear any music.'

Lizzie shrugged. 'We've had the offer of a gramophone player but it's not arrived yet, and we've some board and card games in the lounge room. No bigger plans than somewhere to get away from you chaps from time to time.' She smiled to take the edge off any perceived slight.

Matfield smiled back, showing a row of perfect teeth. 'I understand. Got to have the girlie chats somewhere, I suppose.' His smile faded. 'How are you all coping after the death of your colleague?'

Lizzie watched him take a pull on his cigarette, tightening his eyes against the smoke.

'It came as a shock, obviously,' she said. 'But we're strong women with a job to do. Can't dwell on it too much.'

'Quite right.' Matfield nodded solemnly. 'We've seen that so-called detective a few times but we couldn't help much as it occurred off the air station. Is he any closer to finding the culprit?'

Culprit? Like a cat burglar or common thief. Lizzie frowned as she blew smoke at the ceiling. 'He seems to be getting somewhere, but criminal evidence isn't the type of thing he'd talk to me about.' She wasn't sure why she felt the need to lie, and stared at her cigarette.

'No,' Matfield said. 'I suppose not.' He finished his beer and stood up. 'Before I go, friendly word of warning. Keep your noses clean. When we discussed your invitation the group captain said he wouldn't be seen dead down here. He doesn't like women being on this air station, as I'm sure you're all aware, and quite frankly he'd do anything to get rid of the lot of you. Flight Lieutenant Pendry will bear me out on that one. Good night, Miss Hayes.'

Matfield crushed his cigarette stub into a glass ashtray, took a final glance around and strolled towards the door.

Lizzie almost jumped as his place was taken by Pendry, who seemed to appear from nowhere.

'Are you all right?' Pendry asked, raising a bottle of brown ale to his lips and taking a sip. 'What was he after?'

'Just being cordial for a change, I think,' Lizzie said, stubbing out her own cigarette. 'He was asking if I knew how the investigation was going.'

'Was he now?' Pendry looked over his shoulder towards the entrance. He turned back, lit two cigarettes and held one out to Lizzie.

The gesture, although gallant, seemed automatic, as if he expected her to want another even though he'd seen her put one out seconds before. Pendry was smiling but the presumption of it made her clench her jaw as she reluctantly accepted.

'What did you tell him?' Pendry stole another glance towards the door.

'That there was slow progress but it wasn't the sort of thing Inspector Kember would discuss with us in detail.'

Pendry turned back again. 'I don't trust him or Dallington one little bit. I'd be careful, if I were you. Keep out of their way.' His face softened and he smiled. 'You've done your duty inviting them to the opening but probably best if you don't do it again.' He crushed his half-smoked cigarette in the ashtray and stood, as if remembering something important. 'Sorry, must dash.'

His abrupt departure left her momentarily open-mouthed. As she sat pondering their commands disguised as warnings, she became more annoyed. Was this just part of a political play between them, a jostling for dominance on the air station? With her as some supposedly brainless pawn? Lizzie angrily ground her unwanted cigarette into the wreckage of the men's. If nothing else, her experience of male criminals had taught her that those who crave power or feel their power threatened will lie, cheat, manipulate, blackmail and even kill for it.

CHAPTER ELEVEN

Two days later, as the sun began to slip from the Saturday evening sky, Lizzie pushed through the doors of the village hall, chatting animatedly with Niamh and Agata. The heads of everyone inside turned as one.

A dirge of a tune drifted across from a gramophone player on the low stage. Bottles of beer, wine and sherry from the pub stood on a cloth-covered trestle table along the left-hand side, arranged in triangles like racked snooker balls. On another table, triangular sandwiches stood to attention on plates lined with doilies, alongside a large bowl of non-alcoholic fruit punch. Home-made triangular bunting cut from multicoloured pieces of cloth hung from lines of string tied to the roof beams. Chairs lined the right-hand wall where most of the current attendees sat as stiff as a tableau.

Already aware of the suspicion with which the ATA were regarded by some of the villagers, Lizzie sensed a further drop in temperature as they approached the drinks table. Tended by a boy Lizzie judged to be fifteen, maybe sixteen, she noticed how he stared at Niamh and Agata as they chatted, and some of the village women tutted at the sound of their accents. With chin up and a smile, Niamh asked politely for a glass of white wine.

The face of the young man reddened as he tried to speak, turning with an imploring look towards an older man sitting on a stool nearby.

The man came over.

'Les Brannan,' he announced. 'Owner of the pub over the road and supplier of the drinks tonight.'

Niamh, her smile evaporating, went to speak but stopped in surprise when Agata put her hand on her arm. Facing the table, Agata stood beside her and looked stony-faced at the boy.

Using a thicker accent than Lizzie had heard before, she said, 'Tomorrow we fly British warplanes to help defeat Nazis. We will risk our lives for this country, for Europe and the world. Tonight, Irish, Polish and British have fun in case tomorrow we die. Red wine. Please. And white for my two comrades.'

The boy looked as if he wanted to run away and glanced again at Brannan, who gave a curt nod. Without turning her head, Agata looked sideways at Brannan who gave her a curious stare.

Having paid for their drinks, they moved towards the stage.

'Frankly, I'm used to that reception,' Niamh said. 'The English split Ireland in two but now can't understand why the southern Irish prefer to stay neutral when the rest of Europe is fighting fascism.'

'The English are stuck in the past,' Agata said, her voice normal again.

'Maybe, but my father is Irish and the papers are full of stories about the Irish from the north and south joining the British Army.'

'Most English are good people but stuffed full of tradition and class and sentimentality and routine. They think the war is somewhere else like twenty-five years ago. France, Poland, Austria, they were all the same. But I have seen it close up. The war is already here, in this country, in this village, and these people are not ready for it.'

A laugh from the door announced the arrival of Charlie and Geraldine. Lizzie saw their hesitation at the sight of the barren dance floor and gave them a wave. They joined the others at the stage by way of the drinks table.

'Just one or two, ladies,' Geraldine said. 'You're flying tomorrow.' She indicated the hall with her glass. 'This is a bit grim.'

'Not very lively for a Saturday night, is it?' Niamh agreed. 'We can't dance to this. It's music to die by.'

'It's a bit solemn at the moment,' Lizzie said. 'But we'll liven it up.' She took a sip of her white wine and grimaced at the warm vinegary liquid.

Charlie patted her canvas shoulder bag. 'It's fine. I've brought along a few records a friend of mine picked up for me. It's a shame Emily and Fizz can't join us, though.'

'I had no choice but to confine them to quarters,' Geraldine said icily. 'I can't have gross misconduct among my ladies. We have to be seen to be better than the men just to break even.'

'Even so, no harm came to anyone, or my car and Lizzie's motorbike.'

'Believe me, it's a small price to pay for their disgraceful indiscipline. I've managed to smooth things over with the ground crew, at my own personal expense, and in so doing have ensured the matter will go no further.'

'What are they doing?' Niamh asked.

'They are cleaning the grass, muc and bushes from the vehicles in secret so the group captain and wing commander are none the wiser.'

Lizzie, thinking the mood had turned as sour as the wine, turned to Charlie. 'Now, Charlie, how about showing us what you've got tucked under your arm?'

Charlie smiled as she pulled a handful of records out of her bag and handed them to Lizzie.

'The Andrews Sisters, "Rhumboogie".' Lizzie read the label of the top one, shaking her head. 'Never heard of it.'

'I've also got three of Glenn Miller's, an Ink Spots and a Vera Lynn.'

'Better get them on,' Geraldine said, 'before we all pass out with boredom.'

Lizzie followed Charlie as she moved with slow, seductive steps over to the gramophone where a young man of about eighteen watched enthralled at the accentuated rolling of her hips.

'Hello,' Charlie breathed. 'Have you got anything a little more uptempo?'

'N-no,' the youth stuttered, his gaze flicking between Charlie and Lizzie. 'I d-don't think so. Mrs Oaks brought these over from the vicarage.'

'Let's have a look, shall we?' Charlie smiled, looking through the collection of records, separating them into two smaller piles as the youth watched, transfixed. 'You seem to have a decent selection of jazz records and they will do nicely. Do try to play those' – she put her finger on the jazz pile – 'rather than those.' She put her finger on the other pile. She took her own collection from Lizzie and offered them to the youth, who took them with reddening cheeks. 'These are precious,' she said. 'Play them too, but guard them with your life.' She winked and turned, Lizzie following and tutting at Charlie's flirting, leaving the young man casting anxious looks around the hall to see if anyone had witnessed the exchange and his embarrassment.

As the sounds of a jazz trumpet filled the air, Niamh and Agata moved into the central void to dance with each other, accompanied by disapproving muttering from the village women. Ever watchful, Lizzie caught sight of a rugged-looking man tucking his bottle of brown ale on the floor under a chair before he walked over to where they danced.

'May I?' he said to Niamh. 'Andy Wingate, at your service.'

Agata made a funny face at Niamh and moved aside to let Wingate in, stiffening as someone else's hand went around her own waist.

Lizzie, seeing Les Brannan bowing his head to whisper in Agata's ear, thought that actually, he looked quite presentable. She smiled as Agata gave her a wink and allowed herself to be danced away.

'One of my favourites,' said the vicar as he passed Geraldine. His smile faltered as she reached out and caught his arm. 'Mine too,' she said. The vicar's smile slid back nervously as she took his hand to dance.

Lizzie watched with Charlie from the side, swaying to the music while nursing drinks in their hands. The faces of the women of Scotney looked as though a bad smell had invaded. Ethel Garner looked as if she could kill someone and held tight to her husband's arm to prevent him from joining in. Lizzie noticed a short, thin woman, her hair tied with a floral scarf into a turban, keep glancing at the vicar while two other women, alike enough to be sisters although one wore round spectacles, sat shaking their heads disapprovingly. Arranged along one side of the hall, the village women looked more like funeral mourners than attendees at a dance.

When the record finished, Charlie instructed the youth to put on one by Glenn Miller and took his hand. He pulled it away sharply.

Lizzie caught a wide-eyed look from him and felt momentary anxiety – empathy for the young man.

'What's wrong?' Charlie said. 'I only want to dance as a thank you for playing the records.'

'I've got a bad arm,' he said, hanging his head. 'It's why I can't join up.'

Charlie lifted his chin with her finger. 'I want to dance, not fight. You don't have to hold me to dance.'

With slow reluctance, the young man relinquished his post by the gramophone and moved to the dance floor. After a few seconds he began to copy Charlie's movements and was soon smiling and moving to the rhythm. As the ATA women regrouped after that second dance, a shout from the door announced the arrival of the ground crew, NAAFI women and others from the air station. What had threatened to become an endurance test ten minutes before was suddenly transformed.

Geraldine nudged Lizzie as one of the ground crew approached, sporting the three stripes of a sergeant. 'Here comes the price I've had to pay for the wrongdoings of Emily and Fizz.'

Lizzie smiled, understanding. 'I'm sure it'll be great fun.'

'I'm sure it will.' Geraldine raised her eyebrows and moved to intercept the sergeant.

Superficially, Lizzie spent the evening dancing, drinking, smoking and chatting. Beneath the surface, she watched how the villagers interacted. Most of the women watched the men watching the air station women, but no one made a move. Young girls sat close to their chaperones as if glued. The boy behind the drinks table remained there, so timid it was almost too painful to watch. The young man whom Charlie had coaxed on to the dance floor, also shy at the beginning, had emerged from his shell to enjoy himself even without Charlie as a dance companion.

As the dance progressed, punctuated with Charlie's uptempo records, the reverend's jazz tunes and occasional dirges, the atmosphere became more genial. Alcohol played its part, but there seemed a genuine thaw in relations between the women of the village and the ATA. After much persuading, even Ethel and her husband took a turn around the floor to a slower tune.

Almost everyone in the hall had danced at some point but the woman in the floral turban, clearly having failed to pluck up enough courage to approach the vicar, looked downcast when she realised he had slunk away. Sergeant Wright and a man with a dozing springer spaniel colonised a corner table, nursing bottles of light ale while deep in discussion for most of the evening, appearing not to hear any of the music at all. Lizzie watched Niamh and Agata being monopolised by Andy Wingate and Les Brannan respectively. Losing sight of her two friends for several minutes gave Lizzie a pang of unease, but this turned to relief when she spotted them returning from the direction of the loo. Lizzie glanced around the hall looking for Wingate and Brannan but couldn't see them. She looked back to her friends and saw them doing the same, a mixed look of disappointment and confusion on Niamh's face but resignation on Agata's. Lizzie collected a drink and waited for the men to reappear, suppressing a ripple of anxiety as she tried to relax. Getting inside people's heads through their words, thoughts and actions was not always as voluntary as she wished and could be exhausting and disturbing.

After a few more minutes, she collected another two glasses of wine and walked over to Agata and Niamh, offering the drinks. Niamh took one and sipped. Agata shrugged, took the glass and downed it in two gulps. Handing the empty glass back, she smiled, crossed her eyes in mock drunkenness and danced back on to the floor.

Feeling increasingly hemmed in by the crowd inside, Lizzie slipped through the heavy blackout curtains and pushed open the front doors of the village hall. She stepped into the street, mindful to remain close to the safety of the door, the balmy evening feeling cool after the warmth of the hall. She lit a cigarette, grateful the recent storms had passed, and watched the almost phosphorescent cloud of smoke drift away. As her eyes readjusted to the enforced darkness, pinpricks of starlight began to appear between scudding clouds.

She froze.

Someone moving to her right, down towards the police station, had caught her eye. Hardly daring to breathe as the seconds passed and feeling for the door handle behind her, just in case, she feared the sound of her thumping heart would give her away. She noticed another movement and almost screamed when her elbow touched the door handle.

With her heart trying to burst its way through her chest, Lizzie let out the breath she didn't realise she'd been holding as moonlight broke through and glinted off the white 'W' of Greenway's ARP helmet. Holding in a laugh of relief, she took a final, calming drag on her cigarette and stepped on the stub just as a faint howl from the direction of Scotney air station fell then rose again. She saw Greenway turn back and unlock a box installed on the wall of the police station before another low moan came from the roof, getting louder and beginning to rise and fall in a warning wail.

With Greenway already running towards the village hall, the door behind her half-opened and the head of Wright appeared, looking skywards. Although unperturbed by the beams of distant searchlights swinging in search of aircraft, the sudden unsettling thrum of aero engines made the hairs on Lizzie's arms stand on end.

'Shelters. Now!' Greenway called, pushing past Wright.

Lizzie and Wright followed Greenway through the blackout curtain as he barged the inner door open and yelled above the music to the startled people inside. 'Air raid. Lights off and get to the shelters. Those at the back follow Sergeant Wright. Those at the front follow me.'

Wright froze for a second as the music stopped, then he threaded across the crowded dance floor to a passage that ran around the stage to a back room and kitchen. 'This way,' he shouted, and stood by a doorway leading into a brick cellar, ushering people below.

'Les, we need your cellar,' Greenway called as Brannan appeared from the rear of the hall with the stub of a smouldering cigarette between his lips.

Brannan weaved between people in the hall, through the door held open by Greenway, and ran across to the Castle pub. He held the front door open and shouted an instruction inside. Seconds later, a crowd from the hall hurried in, across the bar floor and down into the pub cellar. All lights in the hall had already been switched off, the people guided by thin beams from the masked torches of Wright and Greenway. Lizzie and Brannan looked up on hearing anti-aircraft fire and machine-gun bursts. Bright lines of tracer bullets criss-crossed the sky.

'In!' shouted Greenway, following the last villager across from the hall, urgency in his voice.

Brannan bolted the door behind Lizzie and the warden and they ran for the cellar as the first dull crumps of bomb explosions rattled the windows and shook the air.

Emily Parker glanced up at the encroaching darkness as the last remnants of day bled into the west, black shadows barely distinguishable from the indigo sky in the east. She raised her arms, closing first the curtains then the blackout curtain.

She took her cigarettes and slipped out of the manor house. A sliver of yellow light momentarily illuminated a patch of ground before the door closed and darkness pressed in again. She had a routine. A walk in the grounds, a last cigarette, then a sip of water before bed.

She strolled away from the house into deeper darkness, peering ahead as far as she could, looking slightly off-centre so her night vision could see any hazards.

No danger.

Lizzie's being paranoid, she thought. All that stuff about knowing how criminals tick and the killer coming for all of them. What made her think she knew more than the police?

Emily paused, a yellow glow illuminating her face before a cloud of shimmering grey smoke drifted away and a shake of the match extinguished its brief flame. She passed through the gardens and diagonally right, out across the lawn to the long, low, brick-built utility hut.

'Who's there?' she said, barely above a whisper, squinting pointlessly in the direction of some indefinable sound. Was it the scrape of a shoe? The scuffle of a foraging animal? She stopped a short distance beyond the hut, the tip of her cigarette glowing bright in her cupped hand each time she took a drag.

The argument with Fizz had been stupid; she knew that. Emily thought of her friends enjoying the dance and felt a pang of envy. Dancing, theatre and watching Humphrey Bogart at the flicks were among her favourite things to do.

She jumped at the call of the air raid siren, the rise and fall of its warning getting louder as its power increased. The sirens had sounded at least once most nights in the previous weeks, usually without any aircraft appearing, so she wasn't moved to rush for cover. She heard the answering call of the village siren and looked skywards as one by one the distant beams of searchlights appeared and probed the sky for the enemy.

She watched for a few seconds, seeing the bright dashed lines of tracer bullets, like glowing stitches in a fabric sky. Suddenly realising how close the bombers were, she dropped the stub of her cigarette on the ground and stepped on it as she turned to walk back.

Engines thrummed louder overhead and a bomb whistled, exploding a hundred yards away. Anti-aircraft guns began booming and chattering from strategic points around the airfield, adding to the cacophony of noise and the firework display.

Emily was scared now, her heart thumping. The earth trembled with each successive blast as a stick of bombs fell in a staggered line two hundred yards away and threw debris her way. As she hurried past the hut someone grabbed hold of her arm and pulled her into the shadows. She shrieked, off balance and tensing in panic as a strong grip guided her through the door

They moved further inside, brushing tools. Emily felt a workbench against her hip.

'Are we safe in here?' she said, trying to recognise the shape of her rescuer.

No answer.

Her heart pounded in her chest like the bombs that were pounding the earth.

'Who is this?' she said, trying to control the tremor in her voice.

She smelled his breath: cigarettes and booze. Aftershave almost masked the faint aroma of stale sweat.

If Emily Parker could have described the last sensation she felt it would not have been fear, but pain.

CHAPTER TWELVE

Geraldine was sitting on the edge of the desk at the front of the briefing room when Lizzie entered.

'Ah, thank God,' she said. 'I was getting worried about you too.'

Lizzie sat, dread pressing down on seeing the pained expression on Geraldine's face. 'What do you mean, me too, ma'am?'

'As you all know, Emily Parker did not attend church parade this morning. In fact, we believe she went missing last night while most other personnel were at the village dance.'

The women exchanged horrified glances.

'Oh, God,' Charlie exclaimed before she put a hand to her mouth.

'I'm afraid,' Geraldine continued grimly, 'Emily's body was found this morning, inside a hut in the grounds.'

There was a short, stunned silence before it broke, quickly erupting into panicked cries of dismay. Lizzie's eyes stung with tears and she could see her colleagues fighting to hold back their own, their shoulders drooping and bodies slumped. She took deep breaths in through her nose and out through her mouth. The weight on her chest and constriction around her throat persisted.

'At first . . .' Geraldine's voice rose above the bowed heads of the grief-stricken group. 'At first, she was judged absent without leave, but I protested to the group captain that it was not in her nature and so a search was carried out.' Geraldine's face suddenly looked much older than her years as she went on. 'She was found in a damaged utility hut where, although the brick walls were intact, the corrugated roof had partially collapsed. The initial conclusion was that she had been caught outside as the air raid began. Taking refuge in the hut would have looked the best prospect at the time.'

The women started talking over each other again but Geraldine raised her voice.

'However . . .' The clamour died down. 'However, it appears Nazi bombs were not the cause of her death.'

'What does that mean?' Agata exclaimed. If a bomb did not kill her, what did?'

'In the opinion of Dr Davies, the medical officer, her injuries are more consistent with having been killed outside by a bomb blast, which makes them inconsistent with the collapsing of the roof while she was inside.'

'I don't understand.' Charlie looked around the room with frightened eyes and back to Geraldine. 'What does *that* mean?'

'Are you saying she was murdered?' Fizz demanded.

Geraldine hesitated. 'That is for the police to investigate. They're already here and will want to speak to all of us in due course.'

'Lizzie was right.' Strain ripped through the hoarseness of Niamh's voice. 'That's two of us and we've not been here long. How many more of us have to die before they catch him?'

Lizzie couldn't bear to meet anyone's gaze as Geraldine continued.

'We have to let the police do their job, but we also have a job to do and there are aircraft waiting to be ferried.'

'We can't, not today, ma'am,' Charlie protested. 'We need to stick together.'

'No,' Geraldine snapped. 'What we need to do is be professional and fly warplanes where they need to go. That is what we all signed up for and that's what we'll do. There is still a war on. We knew this could be dangerous, just not in this way. Lavinia and Emily would want you to carry on or else you're letting them down. I will not let whoever is doing this dictate how we behave and I'm not letting some coward of a man win as he slinks in the shadows. Chits have come through for four aircraft. Nothing terribly exciting, I'm afraid. I had considered grounding our two miscreants but, given the circumstances . . .' She took a deep breath. 'I think a little routine is called for. Charlie, Agata, Fizz and Niamh, the details are on the ops board. Collect your chits from the desk, get your Sidcot suits on and meet me at the Ox-box.'

Disappointment and apprehension fought for supremacy inside Lizzie. She waited for the other women to crowd out through the door and then looked questioningly at Geraldine.

'Ma'am? What about me?'

Lizzie saw a shadow pass across her superior's face as she stood.

'Flight Lieutenant Pendry wants a word with you.'

'What about?'

'He was rather cryptic, I'm afraid. You'll find out soon enough.'

Lizzie's heart seemed to beat extra hard but she kept her face impassive. She saw Geraldine's penetrating look and felt as though she was trying to inspect her soul.

'I have to speak to Detective Inspector Kember when I return from taxi duties,' said Geraldine. 'The other girls too, after their shifts.' She picked up a file of papers from the desk and moved towards the door. In the opening she stopped and half-turned. 'As women, we have a difficult position on this air station and I fear I will have to lock horns with the group captain on a daily basis.

It helps me greatly if I know what is going on, especially among my women. Whatever the flight lieutenant wants with you, Third Officer Hayes, if it is not too personal, I would appreciate being kept informed.'

'Yes, ma'am.' Lizzie saluted.

Geraldine returned an acknowledging salute as she left.

Lizzie ran to the toilet, pushed the cubicle door shut, put the lid down and sat, shaking so hard her teeth began to chatter. She took in quick gasps of air as if on a hundred-yard dash and clasped her hands together, her fingers turning first red and then white with the pressure. As the pain seared up her arm she felt herself focus long enough to begin counting the number of screws she could see from her seat. After reaching fourteen, she counted backwards to one, repeating the task three times. By the end of the last cycle, Lizzie's uneven breathing had finally regained its natural rhythm and the blurred edges of her vision had begun to clear. She waited a few minutes longer, until she could feel her fingers begin to relax and the shaking cease.

She reached up to pull the flush chain and left the cubicle. At the sink, she allowed herself to wash her hands twice and then once more, each time feeling the tension drain away with the water. Lizzie looked at herself in the mirror until she began to recognise the person reflected back. She ran her tongue over her lips, picked a wayward strand of hair from her tunic and went to meet Pendry.

Inside the utility hut, Kember stood to one side of the doorway to let the light in. The roof damaged in the air raid had been propped up to allow access to the rest of the interior. Emily Parker lay on her back on a wide workbench, legs drawn up with knees bent and feet flat on the wood surface. Her skirt had been pushed up as far as it would go, her left arm lay across her chest and her right lay limp at her side. Dr Sam Davies, medical officer at RAF Scotney, leant grim-faced against another narrow workbench, while Dr Headley bent over the dead body.

'This isn't good form, is it?' Headley said. 'Two in two weeks.'

Kember looked around the interior of the hut. As he would expect on an RAF base, the equipment and tools had a regimented feel, being clean, well-oiled and stored in neat array.

'Do you want me to walk you through the bits and bobs?' Headley asked.

Kember turned his attention back to the doctor and the body. 'If you wouldn't mind.'

Headley continued without looking up. 'As you can see, a lot more blood has been shed here than by the victim found on the church footpath, indicating she wasn't dead before our murderer administered the first cut. Her throat was slit twice.' Headley pointed to her neck. 'Either could have been the fatal wound. She may have been unconscious, mercifully, as there are the beginnings of a large bruise on her cheek and around her eye and dried blood around her nose commensurate with her having been punched violently.' Headley squinted at Kember through his spectacles. 'He didn't stop there, I'm afraid.'

While the doctor itemised the visible injuries, Kember gripped a tool rack tightly, fighting to focus as his mind tried to shut down against the horror. Until Headley's final words jerked him alert.

'. . . that her womb is missing.' Headley looked up.

Kember's mouth dropped open and he closed his eyes for a moment, hearing Wright retching outside.

'Jesus Christ, Headley, what kind of monster are we dealing with?' he said in a hoarse whisper.

'Indeed, Kember. And speaking of Jesus Christ, I thought you might be interested in this.' Headley offered a scrap of paper between two outstretched gloved fingers.

Kember held the paper by its edges, unfolded and read. 'It's the same text fragment as found in the first victim's mouth.'

'Correct. I found it inserted in the same position. I also spotted this.' Headley pointed to a black mark in the middle of Emily's forehead. 'It's a cross marked out in black grease, taken from the gearing in one of the petrol mowers, no doubt. I recall seeing a faint mark of some description on the first victim's forehead.'

'The oil on Lavinia Scott?' Kember said.

'Yes. I only found a smear but it could well have been a cross originally.' Headley flicked a glance at the roof. 'Here, the body was protected, but the rain may have begun to wash the mark off Miss Scott. I didn't think much of it at the time because of the weather and the nature of the death.' He looked back to the body. 'There also appears to be a patch of dried semen on this woman's top.'

'Thank you, Doctor,' Kember said, unable to accommodate any more despair at the mounting revelations. 'I'm grateful for your help.'

Kember turned at a call from the doorway in time to see the remaining colour in Wright's cheeks drain away as he leant sideways and made a grab for the door frame. Dr Davies caught him.

'Sergeant, what's wrong?' Kember said.

Davies held Wright's elbow to help steady him. The sergeant looked dazed.

Headley frowned. 'For God's sake, you're a policeman, you've seen dead bodies before.'

Wright swallowed hard as if trying to keep the contents of his stomach from making another reappearance. 'That I have, sir, but this' – he tilted his head toward Emily – 'I've heard about this manner of killing once before.'

That got Kember's full attention. 'When? Recently? Around here?'

'No, sir. The constable I used to have, he retired then passed away a couple of years back, used to talk about goings-on like this. When he first were a young constable he did his coppering in the Metropolitan Police, when Jack the Ripper were on the prowl.'

Headley snorted. 'You can't seriously believe Jack the Ripper did this? Even if he was murdering when he was eighteen he'd have to be – what – seventy by now?' He stood, wiping his gloved hands on a cloth. 'The whole notion is preposterous and will spread unnecessary panic. We aren't in Whitechapel fifty years ago, and to my mind this is nothing other than the work of a straightforward murderer who is playing games with you. That said, I deal in medical facts, the criminal theatricality is all yours.'

'It's beyond anything I've ever seen,' Davies said. 'I may be medical officer here but I'm more used to patching up people after they've broken themselves and their aeroplane.' He stepped out of the hut and called back, 'I'll have to leave you gents to it, I'm afraid.'

Kember looked at Wright and saw the colour returning to his face. 'Are you all right now, Sergeant?' he asked.

'Yes, sir,' Wright said. 'I'm fine now, sir. Took me aback for a while, that's all.'

Wright's reaction convinced Kember that his sergeant wasn't trying to make spurious suggestions but, nonetheless, he shared the same opinion as Headley. Kember patted Wright on the back as they left the hut for the pathologist to finish his work.

'Inspector.'

Kember looked across the lawn and saw an RAF Police armband on the officer approaching.

'Flight Sergeant Ben Vickers,' the officer introduced himself.

'Pendry's man.' Kember shook Vickers' hand.

Vickers smiled. 'In a manner of speaking.' He indicated the manor house with a jerk of his head. 'He's with the ATA woman you wanted to see.'

Kember instructed Wright to stay with Dr Headley and keep an eye on the hut. As he walked across the lawn with Vickers he said, 'Pendry seems a good man.'

Vickers took a moment to reply. 'He's not too bad, as officers go. Does things by the book. Takes a dim view of any rule-breaking. A policeman through and through.'

They took the few steps up to the garden and a path that took them alongside an ornamental pond.

'Were you on duty last night?' Kember asked.

'I wasn't supposed to be,' Vickers said, avoiding a stone urn trailing foliage, 'but once the air raid hit, all hell broke loose. I was in my quarters when the siren went, then in the shelter. Afterwards, I helped direct the clear-up for an hour before going to bed.'

'Did you see anything, or anyone, acting suspiciously?'

'As I said, it was organised chaos for a while. There were reports of a small fire to the west and people even started seeing paratroops that weren't there. Ridiculous.'

'What about the evening of the ninth of July?'

Vickers stopped on the terrace at the top of the steps leading up from the gardens. 'The night the first girl copped it?'

Kember nodded.

'I thought we'd given you the duty roster.' Vickers shrugged. 'I was on duty that night. I did the usual rounds, walking the perimeter, checking posts and so on.'

'With Pendry?'

'Not that night. He had work to catch up on so I did the inspection alone.' Vickers opened the terrace door and stepped inside.

As Kember followed, he recalled Pendry saying he'd been with Vickers that night. Had Pendry misremembered, or lied?

◆　◆　◆

Kember and Pendry sat behind a desk in the ATA ops room, their expressions solemn. Lizzie sat opposite, hearing the door close behind Vickers, not knowing whether this was to be a welcome or a dressing-down. From their body language, stiff and formal, she suspected the latter.

'When I first read your letter,' Kember said, unsmiling, 'I wasn't convinced.'

Lizzie met his gaze, unwilling to be cowed. 'So why are you talking to me now?'

Kember paused for a moment before he spoke. 'You mentioned in your letter about the posing of bodies as a ritual. You also said the murderer would kill another ATA woman, and that you had received a defaced playing card.'

'So you *can* read.'

Lizzie noticed Kember's mouth twitch.

'It all seemed . . .' He hesitated as if selecting the right word. '. . . fanciful.'

With gritted teeth, she reached into her tunic pocket, retrieved the playing card and flicked it across the desk to Kember. 'Does that particular card, with the eyes pricked out, left in a club opened by women, look fanciful to you?'

Kember picked up the card and held it to the light. 'I'll be keeping this for fingerprinting,' he said, putting it in his pocket. 'I made a few phone calls and checked your credentials.'

Lizzie raised an eyebrow. 'Does this conversation mean they passed muster?'

Kember ignored the question.

'Emily's body has been posed, hasn't it?'

She saw Kember steal a glance at Pendry.

'It appears I owe you an apology, Miss Hayes.'

Well, that was unexpected, Lizzie thought.

'A colleague spoke to me recently about a burglar who smoked a cigarette each time and left the dog-end behind, as though he had not a care in the world but somehow wanted to get caught.'

Lizzie nodded. 'The cigarette was a ritual, his calling card.'

'Like the playing card?'

'That was more of a warning,' Lizzie said.

Kember stared at her. 'If we' – Kember gave a faint nod towards Pendry – 'agreed to you having a limited role in the investigation by allowing you to provide this character sketch you spoke of, what would you need from us? And what's in it for you?'

Lizzie's heart jumped. She couldn't believe Kember had asked her this; it meant he no longer dismissed her as a lunatic. She considered her next words carefully, anxious to avoid spoiling her one chance.

'In the first instance, I need to see the crime scene before Emily's body is removed. Secondly, I need to visit the church path and see any photographs the police took there, including of the body. Last but not least, I need to see the case files and any medical or pathology reports.'

Kember gave another sideways glance at Pendry, who looked shocked. 'That's a lot to ask, considering you're not a civilian or military police officer.'

'There's no other way I can see the full picture and work out the type of person you're looking for. Oh, and there's nothing in it for me except preventing more women dying.' Lizzie stared at Kember, issuing a challenge he avoided.

'You say *type* of person,' Kember said.

'Yes, Inspector. I hope any profile, a pen picture if you like, I am able to give will indicate a person's type to enable you to narrow the field of suspects, but I can't tell you who to arrest.'

Kember crossed his arms and legs, looking thoughtful. 'How did you know the second body would be posed?'

Lizzie's heart thudded. She was right; the ritual had been followed. 'Certain murderers need to complete a set of specific acts each time. A ritual that gives the killing a deeper meaning. I'm not talking about a random or spur-of-the-moment act of violence. This is planned, thought about at length, fantasised about.'

Lizzie sensed Kember coming to a decision and felt herself warm under his gaze.

'I wanted to hear what you had to say, but . . .' Kember shook his head. 'It seems too far-fetched. I believe we are capable of handling a murder investigation.'

Pendry exhaled with relief.

The sudden rebuff hit Lizzie like a physical slap. 'Without the interference of a stupid girl, I suppose?' she said angrily.

'That's not what I mean.' Kember looked hurt. 'I am a trained policeman, as is Flight Lieutenant Pendry. You are not.'

'I may have an insight your detective work can't provide. For example—'

'Miss Hayes—'

'—you crossed your arms and legs,' Lizzie pressed on. 'Crossing either arms *or* legs forms a shield against attack, a closing off of your mind against suggestions that may lead to an undermining of your authority. Crossing both arms *and* legs is doubly defensive. You feel accepting my offer may expose you as weak and ineffectual. You want to protect yourself against any such charges and not leave yourself open to ridicule.'

Pendry smiled at the perplexed look on Kember's face. 'She has you there.'

'And as for you, Flight Lieutenant.' Lizzie rounded on Pendry. 'You are leaning towards the inspector and away from me, your arms resting on the desk and angled towards him.'

Pendry's smile disappeared as he sat up straight and withdrew his arms from the desk.

Lizzie continued, 'You side with the inspector and subconsciously regard him as the leader, the parent in a parent–child relationship.'

Pendry stiffened, his lips pressed into a thin line.

'That was quite a demonstration, I must say,' Kember said.

Lizzie looked down at her hands. 'I apologise. It was unseemly.'

'Not at all. We deserved that.'

Lizzie could no longer resist the urge and surprised Kember further by standing, leaning across the desk and straightening his tie. 'Sorry, everything in its place, Inspector,' she said, her face in full flush. Sensing a corner had been turned, she pressed home her small advantage. 'As long as I'm not interfering with the investigation or getting in the way of your officers, what have you got to lose?'

'I beg your pardon,' Pendry interjected. 'You have duties to perform in your role as an ATA officer. I can't have you running about the air station and countryside like a poor man's Sherlock Holmes.'

Lizzie gritted her teeth.

Kember paused for a few seconds, staring quizzically at Lizzie. 'My chief inspector would never agree to this, and I'm not altogether sure why I am, so any arrangement will have to be kept between us. Even so, you'd need to sign a declaration of confidentiality, and the position would be as unpaid adviser. Any whiff of this gets back to Tonbridge and both our careers will be over.'

'Understood,' Lizzie said without hesitation.

Pendry's eyebrows had risen in alarm. 'But what will Dallington say?'

Kember put a placating hand on Pendry's shoulder. 'She's a civilian, Flight Lieutenant. I'm sure her captain will agree to a short-term secondment.'

'I'll need to see Emily's body before she's moved,' Lizzie said, moving towards the far wall. 'So if you dictate the wording, I can type it here to save time.' She indicated a typewriter sitting on a bureau.

'Are you sure typing is not beneath you?' Pendry said.

Lizzie gave him a cold stare.

'Very well,' Pendry said, shaking his head. 'Let's get to it.'

◆　◆　◆

Sergeant Wright stepped to one side, as did the RAF guard, in response to Pendry's nod, allowing Lizzie access to the utility hut's interior. As her eyes adjusted to the gloom she drew a sharp intake of breath and looked away from the body. She clasped her hands together, each squeeze relaxing her more until her desire to continue outweighed the urge to run. She looked back towards the body, swallowed back the bile in her throat and focused her mind, taking in the positioning, blood and injuries.

'This looks like rage, but it isn't, is it?' she said softly.

'Pardon?' Pendry said. 'It looks—'

Lizzie held up the flat of her hand to Pendry without looking around. 'Forgive me,' she said in a tone that brooked no argument. 'I need to get inside the killer's head, to think like him, and that means I often talk aloud.' After a moment of silence, Lizzie's gaze skating up and down as she took in every detail of Emily's body, she held up a clenched fist. 'You had to hit her, of course you did, to silence her, to make her compliant.' She moved around to one side, now speaking in a calm, muted voice. 'You wanted to kill her. Needed to.' She turned to Kember. 'Was she raped?'

Kember winced at the sudden brusqueness of her tone. 'We won't know until the pathologist does a post-mortem,' he said.

'Was Lavinia?'

'No. The doctor found semen on her top but no bruising around her thighs.'

Lizzie turned back to the body, her voice returning to gentle reassurance. 'You didn't rape them because it's the killing that excites you, isn't it? You stand over them afterwards, enjoying the moment, the quiet intimacy. And why not? You're the master now.'

Kember loosened the tie Lizzie had straightened and glanced at Pendry, who fidgeted nervously beside him.

Lizzie indicated the body with a sweep of her hand. 'This isn't savage or opportunistic. This takes time and planning.' She glanced along a hanging row of tools, noting no empty spaces. 'It takes a sharp blade to do this but you didn't grab a weapon on the spur of the moment. So where's the knife?' Lizzie's frown turned to a look of realisation. 'Oh, I see. You want us to know. You want us to see you're in control, that you can do anything.'

'Of course he's in control,' Pendry said flatly, tapping a cigarette from a packet. 'Look at what he's achieved.'

She glanced back at the two policemen silhouetted in the doorway. 'This is ritualistic. See the way her legs and arms are positioned on display? You can see from the blood patterns that everything has been placed. They were alone inside this hut for a while so he had time to take care.'

During a lull in Lizzie's commentary, Kember forced himself to speak. 'The doctor said her womb is missing'

Lizzie's eyebrows rose in momentary surprise, then she gave a slow nod as the significance registered. 'Along with the breasts, the womb is the most feminine part of a woman.' Lizzie turned back to the body. 'He's taking their femininity from them. That's why he took his time, to make sure he left the right message.'

Pendry exhaled smoke and flicked a match away. 'You're certain it's a message and not some standard madman who just likes bumping off women?'

Lizzie shook her head at the interruption and looked at the surroundings, noting the blood, the tools, the equipment and the general layout. 'Was anything taken or anything unusual left, Inspector? Apart from the body, I mean?'

'Dr Headley found a scrap of paper in her mouth that had been torn from a Bible,' Kember said. 'With the same text as that found in the mouth of Lavinia Scott. It talked about women as whores.'

Lizzie gave Kember a sharp look. 'Emily and Lavinia were not whores in the recognised sense of being prostitutes. That makes me wonder whether something else is going on here, maybe something in the past that's tainted all women for him.' She bent to look at Emily's face. 'What's that on her forehead?'

'We believe it's a cross made in oil or grease,' Kember said. 'Lavinia Scott had one too. Is that all part of the message?'

Lizzie gave a small shrug. 'Ritual doesn't have to mean religious. As I said before, it means something that must be done each time for the act to be meaningful to the killer.'

She stepped away from Emily's body and stood by Kember, trying not to let her revulsion and fear at the mutilation of her friend and colleague gain control.

'Don't worry,' she said, sensing Kember's struggle to understand the significance of her explanation. 'We'll talk again once I've seen the other crime scene and case file. I should warn you, I can only guide and help you narrow the field. Police work and pathology have given you what, where, when and how. Once I really understand Lavinia and Emily perhaps I can discover why they became victims and help with the who. The killer. The *type* of person who would do this. The full *why* may not be revealed until you catch him.'

CHAPTER THIRTEEN

As Kember emerged from the hut, he took out a handkerchief, his nose snorting as he blew it, and looked towards the blue sky of the distant east filled with white patterns, like lines of smoke. He had seen a magazine article that talked about this recent phenomenon: condensation vapour trails marking where high-flying aircraft had engaged in dog fights. Symbols of airborne battles to the death, and yet eerily beautiful. Unlike the scene in the hut.

'Looks like our boys are busy,' Pendry said. 'I hope they give them what for. All we need is some sex maniac running around, making things worse.'

Lizzie joined the men at their huddle. 'Oh, he's not a sex maniac. At least, he doesn't appear to be exhibiting that condition.' She looked at Kember. 'I've seen enough here.'

Kember took the hint. 'Sergeant Wright, please escort Miss Hayes to the police station and allow her free rein over the Lavinia Scott file.'

Wright furrowed his brow, but nevertheless motioned for Lizzie to lead the way.

Pendry leant in to Kember and said in a low voice, 'Are you sure this isn't a mistake? What if she causes more harm or misleads us unintentionally? She's never investigated a crime before.'

'She can't do any harm if we keep an eye on her,' Kember said. 'In the meantime, we have to establish the whereabouts of everyone on this air station not on duty at the time of the air raid.'

'I'll get right on to it.' Pendry flicked his cigarette butt onto the grass. 'But there is a war on, and like last night, it can come our way at any time.'

Kember gave him a single nod.

'Any idea why Miss Parker did not attend the dance?'

'None,' said Pendry. 'Third Officer Felicity Mitchell didn't either. And Flight Captain Ellenden-Pitt is on duty today as taxi pilot for the other women.'

Kember pursed his lips, thinking. 'We know the killing took place before or during the air raid at nine thirty, and Emily Parker will have been alive at . . .'

'Seven thirty, when the girls went to the dance,' Pendry said.

'So we need to concentrate on those two hours. Can you get in touch with the next of kin again, as you have the records? I'll need copies of the files though, and transcripts of the interviews.'

Pendry nodded. 'Of course.'

'Thank you.' Kember tried to rub the weariness from his eyes with thumb and forefinger, the tragedy of more lives ruined weighing heavy on him. 'We might as well have another word with Dallington and Matfield while I'm here.'

'Can't say I fancy that very much,' Pendry said with a watery smile as the air raid siren started up. 'But it looks like it'll have to wait.'

◆ ◆ ◆

A while later, with the all-clear still reverberating and bright sunshine bathing the airfield, Kember and Pendry walked over to the manor house. Uniformed men and women scuttled about attending to their duties, while palls of smoke in the distance bore testimony to the pounding other airfields had suffered. Scotney had escaped unscathed this time.

'You again,' Dallington said gruffly as he saw Kember enter the hallway.

'Can't be helped,' Kember replied. 'You seem to have a habit of losing women.'

Dallington's left eye twitched as if Kember had just spat in it. 'What do you want, *Timber?*'

Kember's features hardened. 'A quick word as soon as possible so we can leave you in peace.'

'That would be a blessed miracle.'

Dallington led them up the stairs and into his office where he immediately took up his pipe and was soon engulfed in a haze of smoke.

'Well, out with it,' he snapped.

Kember turned his gaze towards the bookshelves to the side of Dallington, deliberately choosing not to look at the officer. 'We have reason to believe that Emily Parker was murdered between seven thirty and nine thirty last night. Where were you between those times?' He could almost feel Dallington's glare scalding his cheek.

'Here, of course.'

'Where's here?'

'What type of bloody fool question is that?'

Kember looked at him then, square on. 'Here in your office, here on the station, here in the shelter, your quarters, the mess, bar? Where? Exactly?'

Dallington pressed his lips together for a moment in what Kember recognised as an attempt to stifle an unwise outburst. 'At nineteen thirty I was in my office. I left to go in to dinner at twenty hundred hours in the mess. I had just finished my meal when the air raid siren went off.'

'And you went to the shelter?'

'No, back here to my office. I still had work to do and I won't let the Hun disrupt me or else he's won.' Dallington gave a defiant pout.

'Can anyone confirm that?'

Dallington's eyes narrowed at the challenge. 'Matfield and I could see each other through our open doors before we went to the mess. We try to keep regular mealtimes for all personnel on the air station. I saw no one after that and went to bed at twenty-three hundred.'

So no alibi, Kember concluded. 'The wing commander wasn't in his office when you came back here?'

'His door was shut. I assumed he went to the shelter.'

'Ah yes, that would explain it.' Kember nodded, rising to leave. 'Thank you for your time, Group Captain.' He turned back as he opened the door. 'By the way, do you have any idea why Emily Parker and Felicity Mitchell did not attend the village dance?'

'None whatsoever.'

Kember fought back a wave of exasperation and held Dallington's gaze long enough to impart the hint of a challenge before he closed the door.

Kember glanced towards the closed door of Matfield's office, checking the line of sight. 'What do you think?' he asked Pendry, keeping his voice low.

Pendry thought for a moment. 'Rings true. He has no social life here at Scotney and certainly no friends, so he seems to work a lot more than most.'

'Seems? You think he's a shirker?'

Pendry shrugged. 'Certainly as much of a loner as Matfield.'

Kember sensed something more was coming. He remained silent, waiting.

'When he's not in a temper on the telephone complaining about the ATA or berating their captain for some minor misdemeanour or imagined slight I suspect he spends most of his time sleeping, eating and avoiding people. But that's my opinion and I'll not be sharing it with anyone else.'

Kember rubbed his face in thought. 'Alone a lot of the time, no alibi for Emily's murder, in the clear for Lavinia's. Let's see if we can get any joy from Matfield.'

'I'm not a joyous man, generally.'

Kember saw Pendry start at the sound of Matfield's voice and wondered where the wing commander had been hiding and how much he'd overheard.

'May we have a word?' Kember couldn't be bothered to give even a fake smile.

Moments later, Kember and Pendry sat in front of Matfield, who opened the middle drawer of his desk. 'I have a bottle of blended whisky here some—'

'No, thank you,' Kember said, before Matfield could complete the offer. 'I have a few questions about last night's murder.' Atop a fat book on Matfield's desk stood a hand grenade. Kember picked it up and studied it.

'Ah, yes. A bad business.' Matfield frowned, shutting the drawer. 'I'd be careful with that, Inspector. It's a Mills bomb. A fragmentation grenade, actually. Live.'

Kember felt a jolt of alarm and replaced the grenade with greater care than when he'd picked it up.

Matfield moved the grenade out of Kember's reach. '1918 vintage with a seven-second fuse,' he said. 'In case.'

'In case?'

'Invasion.'

'Is it usual for officers to keep grenades in their office?' Kember watched Matfield relax in his chair, leaning one bent elbow on the arm rest.

'These are unusual times. If the Nazis do invade I wouldn't be averse to taking some of the buggers with me. Blow them to kingdom come.'

Kember held Matfield's gaze. 'The village dance,' he said. 'Some of the air station personnel attended, I believe?'

'That's right.' Matfield leant forward for his cigarettes.

'But Dallington didn't go?'

'He's not really a socialiser.'

Kember watched Matfield put a cigarette between his lips and extract a box of matches from his pocket without offering them around.

'And neither did you?'

Matfield paused and studied Kember's face before striking the match and lighting his cigarette. 'As I'm sure you know, the RAF has a very rigid command structure, even when socialising. Dallington and I tend not to fraternise with the lower ranks and we don't have friends on the air station, not since Fighter Command reassigned our squadrons to other airfields.'

'I understand most of the ATA women went to the dance, including their captain.' Kember began fiddling with a letter opener on the desk, suppressing a smile as Matfield frowned and moved it out of his reach. 'But Emily Parker and Felicity Mitchell stayed on the air station, choosing not to go.'

Matfield shrugged.

'Any idea why?'

'No.'

Kember made a show of consulting his notebook. 'Can you tell us where you were between seven thirty and nine thirty yesterday evening?'

Matfield took a pull on his cigarette and blew smoke at the ceiling, glaring at Pendry as if betrayed by one of his own. 'Apart from dinner in the mess at twenty hundred hours, I had work to do in my office all evening until twenty-three thirty.'

Kember looked up sharply. 'Did you see the group captain before dinner?'

'Only in as much as his office door was open, as was mine, so I could see him at his desk.'

'What about after dinner? Did you leave with anyone?'

'Not with Dallington. He's my superior officer, not my friend.'

Kember sensed an underlying animosity towards Dallington in Matfield's tone. Something deeper than the surface dislike of a superior officer. 'But you ate with him?' he pressed.

'Officers dining together is a ritual, Inspector. Everyone left for the shelters, including the mess staff, so I grabbed my cup of tea and took it back to my office.'

'Not the shelter?'

Matfield sucked on his cigarette and spoke through the smoke. 'I had been led to believe the bombing would be elsewhere but the manor house is sturdy, built to last. The air raid lasted forty minutes or so but it was sporadic.'

'Did you see the group captain at all?' Kember asked, feeling a dead end approaching.

'No. His office door was shut when I returned from the mess and I closed mine. I believed he had gone to the shelter but I heard his door later on and I left my office shortly after.'

Kember thought it time to push some buttons. 'Do you get on with Dallington?'

Matfield stared at Kember for a few seconds then glanced at Pendry. 'This is confidential, Pendry.'

Pendry remained silent, his face impassive.

'We have a professional relationship, no more,' Matfield said. 'Although I must admit there have been times when I've thought this air station needed a stronger character in charge. Someone less pompous, more commanding of respect.'

'Someone like you?' Kember looked at Matfield for signs of ambition, but saw none.

'Good God, no.' Matfield almost snorted with derision. 'I'm happy where I am. What I mean is, Dallington has a lot of bluster and can talk a good game, but when it comes to action he gives the outward appearance of lacking moral fibre.'

The sudden and open accusation sent a shockwave through Kember and out of the corner of his eye, he saw Pendry stiffen. 'That's quite an assertion. In what way?'

Matfield leant forward, resting his elbows on the desk. 'Take the ATA women, for example. I'm perfectly happy for them to be stationed here but Dallington has been shouting the odds for weeks, ringing all his so-called friends at the Air Ministry. It didn't do any good. They still came. If he had really felt so strongly about having women on his air station, surely he'd have done something a little more practical and effective.'

'Maybe he has,' Pendry said flatly.

Matfield sat back, took a long pull on his cigarette and inhaled deeply. 'All I'm trying to say is that this is a man's world and a fighting man's RAF, especially now, in wartime. The arrival of the ATA has made life very complicated for everyone, but Group Captain Dallington appears to have taken it personally.'

Holding Matfield's gaze, Kember sensed something awry, a niggling feeling he couldn't quite put his finger on. Matfield looked away to crush the smouldering stub of his cigarette.

Kember clapped his hands on his thighs. 'Unless the flight lieutenant has anything else to ask?'

Pendry shook his head.

Kember pushed himself up, stretching his back as he stood. 'Then we'll be on our way.'

'Are you all right, Inspector?'

Kember caught the insincerity and returned a thin smile. 'Thank you for your time, Wing Commander. You've been most helpful.'

'Glad to be of help. Dreadful business, dreadful.'

Kember nodded once and led Pendry from the office.

Once the door clicked shut and they had moved out of earshot, Kember said, 'Even if Matfield did hear Dallington's door before he left his own office at eleven thirty, either of them could still be the killer because no one will have seen them after the start of the air raid at nine thirty. What did you make of that business about Dallington not wanting the ATA women here?'

'That's an open secret,' said Pendry. 'But is it sufficient motive for murder?'

CHAPTER FOURTEEN

Once the all-clear sounded, Lizzie emerged from the basement shelter at Scotney Police Station and was shown to a back room used by the officers for taking meals and breaks, holding meetings and interviewing suspects. She skim-read the notices fixed to a board on the wall detailing current policy and procedures, and alerting staff to wanted criminals. A newspaper cutting from the *Daily Sketch* advised 'Dig for Victory' alongside a poster stating 'Take Your Gas Mask Everywhere'. Another recommended 'Be Like Dad, Keep Mum', which Lizzie had to stop herself from tearing down in disgust. A blackboard next to the noticeboard showed the partially erased remains of previous jottings. Against the same wall stood a large trunk, the label tied to a handle identifying: *J. N. Kember*.

Lizzie placed all the paperwork and photographs from the files on Lavinia Scott in a neat arrangement on the table and, with cold determination giving her focus, she started with the witness statements, reading them with great care, then the police report and Lavinia's personnel file, making occasional entries in a notebook. After an hour of pushing grief aside, unable to keep her feelings in check any longer, she let the pain have its moment, tears coursing down her cheeks, her nose running and her eyes becoming red and puffy.

Wright appeared at the door, alarmed and flustered by the emotion. Lizzie composed herself, embarrassed he had witnessed her lapse of control, and fluttered her hands at him to leave. Despite her protestations, he resorted to what he knew to be the ultimate act of comfort and made a pot of tea. With the steaming cup soon in front of her, she thought he'd gone but he returned with a saucer on which stood a lump of bread pudding. The dark, stodgy chunk gave off an aroma of fruit and spice that made her mouth water.

'Gladys made me a batch,' said Wright. 'From the tea shop,' he added hurriedly. 'But it's too much for me.' He patted his stomach.

Lizzie suspected the latter to be untrue by the way Wright looked back longingly as he left. Nonetheless, she was grateful for the gesture and quickly polished off the delicacy. She lit a cigarette and sat in silence, mulling over what her mind had absorbed.

At the end of her tea break, Lizzie washed her cup and the saucer, replaced them with the others, ensuring the handle faced the same way as the rest, washed her hands again and realigned the paperwork. Once everything was in its place, she could proceed.

Lizzie turned her attention to Dr Headley's pathology report from the post-mortem, becoming engrossed in the detail of the injuries, the oil mark and the paper in the mouth with a passage from the Bible. Pulling the photographs towards her and comparing them with the report and her own notes, she crossed her arms and relaxed her eyes, seeming to stare right through the table, allowing her mind to slip into an almost meditative state – something often remarked upon by her teachers in her school reports as habitual daydreaming. This time the image of Lavinia swam into focus, being coaxed on to the path by the church, restrained and strangled. She saw her lifeless body drop to the ground and imagined the thrill that gave. She heard a call off to one side, from the ARP warden? Deep shadows surrounded her as her mind became the killer's, feeling herself completing the ritual.

'Are you all right?'

Lizzie jumped up, knocking her chair over and scattering paperwork across the floor.

'Lizzie?'

Kember's voice, strained and forced, jolted Lizzie's mind from its abstraction. As her vision cleared, his face materialised out of her mind mist. The room became bright again and she realised the sound of panting was her own.

'Let me go, Lizzie.'

Lizzie saw she had hold of Kember's throat with her right hand. He had his hands on her arm, pressing down gently in encouragement. She relaxed her fingers and stepped back, leaving Kember coughing and rubbing his neck.

'What the hell was that about?' Kember yelled when he was free.

'Oh God, I'm so sorry.' She held up her hands, contrite, desperate with embarrassment.

'Assaulting a police officer is a serious offence,' Kember panted.

'It wasn't you I was attacking.'

'It bloody well felt like it.' He rubbed his throat again and raised his chin to stretch his neck. 'What's wrong with you?'

'What's wro—?' She bent to retrieve the papers, concealing the pain she felt. These were words spoken by her family after her decision to study psychology, by students and lecturers who thought someone well-bred should be following more ladylike pursuits, and by a warder at Oxford Prison who only saw her as *a nice bit of skirt*.

'I was doing what I do, to help you,' she said.

Kember righted the chair. 'To be honest, I still have no idea what it is you do or whether it's worth getting choked for. I've had enough of that . . .'

'I really am sorry,' she murmured, as she self-consciously tidied the table of evidence and reports, aware of Kember watching her.

She could hear him breathing but he remained where he was, saying nothing. As she slid the papers back in their file, she heard Kember sigh.

Finally, his voice split the silence. 'So what were you doing?'

Lizzie placed the last file on top of the pile. 'It's my way of seeing through the killer's eyes, to feel for myself the kind of person he is. Do you ever daydream?'

'Not any more. I don't have time.'

'What I do is an extreme version of that.' She forced herself to look at Kember's face. 'I can't really explain because I don't know exactly how it works.'

'It's not that long ago you'd have been burnt as a witch,' Kember said with a crooked smile. 'Does your attempted strangulation mean you succeeded?'

'I'm getting there.' An idea leapt into her head. 'Put your hand around my throat.'

'What?' he said, horrified. 'No.'

'Humour me.' She looked into his eyes, and gave him a gentle nod as he stood there, hesitant and wary.

The table behind Lizzie pressed into the tops of her legs as Kember edged closer. She tilted her head back to look at his face, sensing the same uncertainty in him.

He raised his arm and touched his fingers to her throat.

'As if you want to strangle me.'

'I'm not going to hurt you.'

'I know,' Lizzie said. 'But keep going. I'm right-handed and so are you. My strongest hand can hit you.' She showed him her right hand. 'How would you stop it attacking you?' She pretended to give Kember a slap and froze when he flinched. She frowned, then as he recovered his composure, felt him grab her wrist in his left hand and force her arm down. 'How does that feel?' she said.

'Feel?' He looked confused. 'It feels . . . strange.'

'I'm off balance over the table, you have your hand tightening on my neck, stopping me screaming. You have my wrist restrained so all I can do is flap at you with my other hand. I can't kick you or I'll fall. You hold all the cards. You have control. All the power.' She whispered now, her breathing quick and shallow, 'This excites you. Domination, even for a moment. Payback for past slights. But you don't want sex . . . you want to put my lifeless body on display to show what happens to my kind. To women in a man's world.'

Lizzie whispered something, her voice almost inaudible.

'Pardon?'

She knew he would lean in to listen again. 'You're excited by this and what is to come next. That your fantasy will be fulfilled.'

They stayed like that, in silence, their faces an inch apart.

Then Lizzie pinched him on the back of his right hand.

'Ouch,' Kember said as he stepped back, breaking the spell. 'What was that for?' He released her and rubbed his hand. 'You could have asked me to let go.'

'Did you feel it?' Lizzie asked.

'Yes, and it bloody hurt.'

Lizzie shook her head. 'Did you feel the emotion?' She looked at him enquiringly.

Kember hesitated. 'Yes, I believe I did.'

'Multiply that by a hundred and you will know how the killer feels. And what he feels are the irresistible forces of power and excitement from the realisation that he can do anything he wants to this woman. Any woman.'

'Why now?' Kember said. 'Why start killing now?'

Lizzie selected one of the police crime scene photographs of Lavinia and had to take a breath. 'I would be very surprised if he hasn't killed before. Men who do this have to start somewhere but it tends to be small, like birds or animals, trying out what it feels like, exploring techniques. Most never progress to killing people, but for others the urge is always there, awaiting an outlet. He's killed twice within two weeks so there must have been an incident. Something has happened to trigger this extreme response and release all his long pent-up emotion.'

She placed the photograph back on the table.

'If he's that volatile, he could kill again,' Kember said.

Lizzie nodded, tore a page from a notebook and made a quick pencil sketch. 'When I asked you to hold my neck you unconsciously used your dominant hand, your right hand. The bruising to Lavinia's neck shows the killer strangled her with his right hand. The post-mortem report on Lavinia showed human skin and blood under one nail of her left hand. When you had me by the throat, I pinched your hand with my only free hand, my left. If that had been real, I could have scratched you, in the last throes of a desperate attempt to live, to make you let go.'

'Scratches are a common injury, especially in the countryside. You think the killer has a scratched face?' Kember's eyebrows had risen.

Lizzie shrugged. 'Not necessarily, but anyone with a mark on their face, neck, arm or hand, especially on their right side, can't be ruled out.'

She looked again at the photograph of Lavinia's body lying on the footpath in the cold mud, and felt a heavy weight pressing on her, filling her stomach and constricting her chest.

'Are you all right?' Kember asked. 'You look a bit flushed.'

Lizzie turned away and pushed her tongue hard against the roof of her mouth to hold back the tears. *Of course I'm bloody flushed*, she thought, putting on her coat. *Two of my friends are dead.*

'I'll be fine,' she said.

Not true. She felt fine when investigating, when using her unique skill, one the police didn't have. But looking at the photograph as a friend and colleague rather than as a psychologist or investigator brought home what a terrible tragedy and waste it was, and that she'd never see either of them again. She blinked and brushed away another tear, regaining her composure and professionalism. Whatever the men thought, they needed her and she had to do this for Lavinia and Emily.

As she stepped through the door and pocketed the sketch, she called back, 'I need to see where she died.'

◆　◆　◆

'Hello again, Inspector,' Mrs Oaks called from the vicarage garden path.

'Good afternoon,' Kember called back, in no mood for another chat. He pulled out his handkerchief for a nose blow, his head beginning to throb again. So much for fresh air.

'Hello,' Lizzie said. 'Is the reverend in?'

Kember gave Lizzie a bewildered look. She hadn't mentioned wanting to speak to the vicar.

'He's in the church at the moment,' Mrs Oaks said warily as she walked to the gate. 'He's still very busy, can I help?'

Lizzie took the sketch from inside her coat and passed it across. 'Do you know what this means?'

Mrs Oaks studied it for a few seconds, frowning. 'A cross? Everyone knows what that means.' She made to return the sketch.

'Yes, but this cross looks inverted.' Lizzie tapped the image with a finger.

Mrs Oaks looked again. 'Oh yes, that's the Petrine cross, the cross of St Peter. When the Romans crucified him, he said he wasn't worthy to die in the same manner as Jesus so he had them turn him upside down.'

'He wasn't worthy.' Lizzie nodded. 'Interesting. Thank you.'

'You're welcome.' Mrs Oaks looked a little bemused.

Kember touched the rim of his fedora respectfully before following Lizzie back to the path, irritated she had blundered straight in without consulting him.

'What was that all about?' he demanded. 'I'm supposed to ask the questions.'

Lizzie showed him the sketch. 'The cross is inverted.'

'So?'

'Mrs Oaks said St Peter didn't consider himself worthy of the same death as Jesus. Perhaps the killer thinks women aren't worthy. That would explain the Bible text about women as whores.'

Kember frowned at Lizzie. 'That's an interesting theory, but next time let me know what you're up to so I can do my job.'

Lizzie lowered her eyes. 'I'm sorry.'

A few seconds' silence elapsed.

'I mean, I'm the bloody policeman here,' he said, immediately annoyed with himself for allowing her to employ his own technique of leaving silences for others to fill. 'Look, before we go on, there's something I should tell you.

Lizzie gave him a quizzical look.

Kember hesitated, unsure how Lizzie would take the information he was about to impart. 'Sergeant Wright had a funny turn when he saw Emily's body, a sort of flashback to tales of a similar murder.'

'How similar?'

'Almost exactly the same. Wright knew a sergeant, now passed away, who first joined the Metropolitan Police in 1888 on a posting to H Division in Whitechapel.'

Lizzie looked incredulous. 'Jack the Ripper? You have to be joking.'

Kember shook his head. 'Wright said the old sergeant saw what had been done to the women. He's convinced Emily suffered the same fate.'

'But that's ridiculous. Jack would be over seventy. There's no way a man of that age could commit these murders. He wouldn't have the strength, mobility or allure.'

'I agree,' Kember said. 'But could someone be copying him, taking the Ripper's handiwork as a model for his own?'

'It's possible,' Lizzie conceded. 'I'll have to think about it.'

Kember pointed along the path. 'In the meantime, you wanted to see where Lavinia was killed. Mr Brown walking his dog found the body about halfway along in the shadow of the yew tree. At the estimated time of death, at night during the blackout, it would have been almost impossible to see anything at all unless you were looking straight at them from where we're standing.'

Lizzie walked along the path to the spot where the murder had occurred. 'The report says you found no signs of a struggle.'

'That's right,' Kember said. 'It looks like a sudden attack took her by surprise.'

Lizzie leant against the wall. 'The attack may have been a surprise, but no drag marks were found so she must have walked here, and if the attack had taken place anywhere else, even at the end of the path, they would have been seen.'

Kember looked along the path. 'There's nothing but fields beyond, so why would a young woman be here in the first place?'

'To meet him.' Lizzie sounded certain. 'She knew him in some way.'

Kember still couldn't fathom how that was possible. 'She'd arrived in the village only that day,' he said.

'I knew Lavinia. We were at White Waltham and Hamble together. She was a bit flighty, in my opinion, and irresponsible at times. Got hauled over the coals for minor rule breaches. She used to slip away for romantic liaisons with someone from the ground crew. She sneaked off the air station one evening and returned in the early hours.'

Kember's curiosity was piqued. 'How did she get in and out?'

'One of the gate guards was sweet on her so she could get away with almost anything. She'd had a couple of boyfriends but she could use her charms to get what she wanted without ever having to go beyond flirting. She had a way, you know? With men.'

'Did she go with many men?'

Lizzie rounded on him. 'You think her a tart just because she was gregarious?'

'No, not exactly—'

'Men flirt all the time and no one thinks any the less of them for it. Why can't a woman enjoy life without being labelled a whore? Whatever she did, however she dressed, whatever her behaviour, she did not deserve to die.'

'Of course she didn't,' Kember said, furiously back-pedalling. 'I'm not casting aspersions. What I'm trying to do is get an idea of her character. Maybe the killer took her behaviour the wrong way, wanted more than she offered, perhaps. It pains me to say so, but not every man takes no for an answer.'

Lizzie looked away. Kember reached out and touched her arm.

'From what you say,' Kember continued, 'she may have met someone she already knew or got to know in a very short space of time. I don't expect many strangers pass through Scotney because the road northward ends at the air station, so he must be from around here.'

Kember stopped talking, realising Lizzie was no longer listening. Instead she began talking in that strange manner he'd first heard her use in the hut beside Emily Parker's body. He soon realised it wasn't directed at him.

'You're not laughing and joking because you'll be heard. It's late, you've slipped away to meet so you have to be quiet.' She nodded. 'You can't meet in the tea shop or pub because it's too public and you don't want anyone to see you together, don't want her associated with you, don't want people asking you questions.' Lizzie crouched at the spot where Lavinia's body had lain. 'You knew she'd be found so you wanted us to know what you'd done. Are you trying to teach us a lesson, to show us the way?' She frowned. 'You killed Emily but she was nothing like Lavinia. This is about power, domination, control – it's all here. If that manifests itself in this way, you must feel inadequate in your daily life. A simple murder is not sufficient; it has to be a demonstration, a rebalancing of power.'

Kember had stayed silent throughout Lizzie's conversation with herself, not wishing to break her train of thought. Now, as she paused, he crouched beside her.

'Are you all right?'

Lizzie looked through him at first, her eyes taking time to refocus on his face, helplessly pulled from the horrors of the past to the quiet dread of the present.

'I think I know the kind of man you're looking for.'

CHAPTER FIFTEEN

The following day, Kember sat in the stuffy heat of the briefing room at RAF Scotney. It was the hottest day of the year by far, and a sign that the struggling summer had finally broken through. His jacket had long been discarded, although his waistcoat remained in place as he waited for the latest in a long line of interviewees. The day had not been as fruitful as he'd hoped, as each member of the air station personnel marched in, gave an account of their whereabouts at the time of each murder and marched out again. Most had an alibi for both murders and the rest for at least one.

Kember rubbed his eyes, trying to rid them of the weariness that lodged there like grit. A knock on the door echoed across the room and Pendry consulted a typed list of names on the desk in front of him.

'Next is Warder Grade One Thomas Hammond,' Pendry said. 'Come!'

An Air Ministry Warden marched in, stood to attention before them and announced himself with his service number and rank.

Pendry looked up from his list. 'At ease, take a seat.'

Kember waited for Hammond to sit, detected a faint whiff of petrol, and ploughed straight in. 'Where were you between nine thirty and midnight on Tuesday the ninth of July?'

Hammond didn't hesitate. 'I was on gatehouse guard duty with Frederick Stapleton until twenty-three hundred.'

'Did you see anything unusual or suspicious during your watch?'

Hammond looked down at the table. 'No, sir. Nothing at all.'

'Did anyone leave or enter the air station for any reason?'

Hammond raised his eyes again. 'Wing Commander Matfield went out for a bit and returned at about twenty-two hundred hours, sir. It'll be in the gatehouse log.'

Kember felt Hammond's confidence growing but thought he detected an underlying nervousness or uncertainty. He tried unsuccessfully to make eye contact.

'I suppose you can vouch for Stapleton?'

Hammond glanced at Pendry. 'Of course, sir. We were together in the gatehouse, then we went for some scran before getting our heads down.'

Kember raised his eyebrows. 'Scran?'

'Food, sir. Supper.'

Kember nodded his understanding. 'What about between seven thirty and nine thirty last Saturday night?'

'We, that's me and Stapleton, were back on duty at the gatehouse. Same watch. Because of being short-handed for a couple of weeks, we were doing twelve on, twelve off instead of the usual eight-hour watches.'

'Anything to report?'

'Only Jerry dropping a few friendly messages.' He smiled. Kember and Pendry didn't.

'Did you stay at your post during the air raid?' Kember asked.

'Yes, sir.'

'With Stapleton?'

Kember noticed Hammond glance at Pendry again.

'Yeah, of course. Look, he ain't done anything wrong, has he?'

Kember turned to Pendry. 'Any more questions, Flight Lieutenant?'

'Not from me,' Pendry said. 'Okay, Hammond, that's all. You're dismissed.'

Hammond stood, came to attention, saluted, turned and marched from the room.

Kember placed his pen on the table and sat back, instinct and experience warning him that perhaps more had been left unsaid than had been said.

'You get a nose for who's lying and who's telling the truth in my game.' He couldn't put his finger on it but something bothered him about the man's responses. 'He struck me as nervous and a bit shifty.'

'A bit shifty?' Pendry gave a thin smile. 'That's an official description, is it?'

'Did you see the way he avoided eye contact and stared at the table?'

Pendry shrugged. 'We've already checked the gatehouse log. A record is kept of everyone who comes on to the air station or leaves. That's for security and legal reasons, and so we know how many bodies are missing if we're attacked. The same goes for the air raid shelters, actually. A list of names is written on paper by the person in charge who then puts it into a container and throws it away as far as he can. If the shelter takes a direct hit, we find the container with its list of the dead.'

'Nice.' Kember grimaced.

'Practical.' Pendry consulted his list. 'Hammond's pal next. Warder Grade Two Frederick Stapleton.'

Kember groaned. He'd had enough of interviewing more than twenty suspects ago.

As if on cue, a knock at the door announced Stapleton's arrival and he soon sat in front of the two police officers. Kember took the same line of questioning as with all the other interviews before Pendry dismissed Stapleton and heaved a deep sigh of relief.

'As dodgy as his mate,' Kember said wearily. Mentally drained, he wanted to get away for a bit of peace and quiet and something cool to drink.

'In what way?' Pendry asked.

'He was sweating, gulping and looking like a naughty schoolboy who's been caught smoking, and did you see the fear in his eyes when he got the days wrong? Like he'd rehearsed the answer to the wrong question.'

'I didn't see anything in Stapleton's behaviour to be concerned about. He's short, dumpy and a bit short-sighted. Hardly a master criminal.'

Kember turned to Pendry. 'But an ideal accomplice.'

Lizzie had been sitting in the open cockpits of Tiger Moths all day, having delivered three. She was tired, thirsty and hungry but declined a swift visit to the bar, preferring to go to her quarters and get out of her Sidcot flight suit and boots as soon as possible. She could smell high-octane petrol fumes on her but all thoughts of a bath before dinner evaporated as she reached the foot of the stairs and saw Kember across the hall talking with Pendry.

'Very fetching,' Kember called.

Lizzie smiled, feeling heat rise in her cheeks. 'Did you get my profile? I left it for you this morning.'

'I—' Kember stopped in mid-reply at the sound of his name being called by an orderly crossing the hall from the terrace bar.

The corporal saluted Pendry but spoke to Kember. 'Begging your pardon, sir, but Sergeant Wright asks if you could hurry over to the utility hut. One of our chaps has found something you need to see.'

◆ ◆ ◆

Angered by being forced to trot behind as Kember and Pendry strode ahead, Lizzie was still peeved by the time they had reached the utility hut where Sergeant Wright stood guard at the entrance. She gave a cursory glance to two bored-looking workmen in RAF overalls standing smoking off to one side, and could tell from Wright's expression that they had found something serious. Her throat constricted at the thought of another of her friends lying bloodied and lifeless inside and she pinged the rubber band on her wrist for comfort.

'What have you got for us, Sergeant?' Kember asked.

Wright indicated the workmen with his thumb. 'These lads sent to repair the roof were clearing up inside when they found a folded piece of paper. It'd been dropped behind one of the big lawnmowers and looked like a five-pound note to them, so they had a peek. That's when they called me over. I thought they were having a laugh until I saw what it was. I've left it on the workbench inside for you.'

Lizzie caught Wright's worried glance and her mind began to cycle through the horrific possibilities of what the packet might contain.

With the interior of the hut partially cleared, Pendry and Lizzie had plenty of room to stand and watch as Kember flattened out the neat folds of a large piece of white paper. It turned out to be the reverse of a coloured poster showing a snail moving slowly through the blackout. 'Go WARILY after dark' it said at the top. The words 'and Get there' at the bottom had been crossed out.

Inside was an identity card. Kember opened the cover, his eyes narrowing, and turned it to show her.

'What the devil?' Lizzie exclaimed.

It was her card.

She thought it must be a copy but realised that nobody had asked her for identification all day, ferry chits being the main currency of her job. Her fingers scrabbled at the pocket where she normally kept all her papers but only her travel permit and flight authorisation card were inside.

'How on earth did he get hold of it?' she demanded, glaring at Pendry. 'And why leave it here, next to where . . .'

Her stomach clenched as a piece of the jigsaw fell into place. The killer hated successful, independent women, of that she was convinced, and it was no secret she'd been talking to the police, offering help. Being hunted by her, one of his own prey, someone for whom he had no respect but who nevertheless refused to cower, must be eating away at him.

She followed Kember and Pendry back outside.

'Emily's death was a mistake,' she said.

'A mistake?' Kember echoed, stopping in his tracks. 'Some mistake.'

'I meant a mistake in the sequence. I don't believe Emily was the killer's next choice. I think that was supposed to be me.'

'I doubt that,' Pendry said with a dismissive frown. 'You weren't even on the air station at the time.'

Lizzie returned Pendry's scorn with a glare and held up her identity card. 'This is a personal warning,' she said, taking some comfort from the realisation she must be getting close to the truth. 'He's turned his attention to me.'

'We need to get you and the others more police protection right away,' Kember said. 'The flight lieutenant can arrange that.'

'Are you joking?' Lizzie said, flattered by his instinct to protect her but unable to keep a hint of sarcasm from her voice. 'If the police and RAF couldn't stop two murders, how will they prevent a third? An RAF air station should be one of the safest places on earth, but that didn't help Emily.'

'You're right,' Kember agreed. He turned to Pendry. 'Can you arrange for the ATA women to be evacuated back to White Waltham? Cite the expected invasion and bombing, whatever you like.'

'Don't you bloody dare,' Lizzie snapped. 'We're at war and us women are delivering the warplanes that protect you.' She stabbed a finger at Kember. 'If you don't think that's dangerous enough, you should sign up.'

Kember's face was thunderous.

Pendry gave Lizzie a look that said he was doing his best. 'Biggin Hill are preparing for invasion as much as we are but I'll have a word with them, to see if I can't get a couple more warders down here.'

Lizzie took a breath and put on as reassuring a voice as she could. 'As long as I make sure I'm never alone outside my room at night I should be fine.'

Even as she spoke, Lizzie didn't believe her own words. Not only had someone been in her room to steal her identity card but they had left it with the poster as a warning, at a crime scene that should have been her own. Whatever the case had been before, now it was personal.

'I haven't got the men or authority to offer round-the-clock protection to any one person.' Pendry looked at his watch. 'And I've got other matters to attend to. Shall we walk?'

With Kember striding away beside Pendry, Lizzie was forced to follow again, this time with Sergeant Wright.

'Did you even read the profile I left for you?' Lizzie spoke to Kember's back.

'I haven't had the time.' Kember kept walking.

'It's all mumbo jumbo, if you ask me,' Wright cut in, wrinkling his nose.

'Of course it is.' Pendry glanced over his shoulder at Lizzie. 'After what he did to that body in the hut, I don't believe you'll catch him with guesswork. He's far too clever for that.'

'It's not guesswork,' Lizzie said, feeling the familiar frustration at being dismissed. 'I admit I can't tell you *who* you're after but I can suggest the *type* of person you're looking for.'

'What help is that?' Pendry asked scornfully. 'He's already telling you he's the top man.'

'He's *acting* the top man,' Lizzie corrected. 'Trying to show us he's in control.'

Fed up with hurrying behind and them not listening, Lizzie pushed between Kember and Pendry, who pulled up short as she stood on the steps leading into the garden, blocking the way.

'Will you stop bloody rushing everywhere and listen for a moment?' she almost shouted.

'I mean no disrespect, but how qualified are you?' Wright queried. 'I've been coppering since I were eighteen.'

'I have a PhD from London University—'

'You're a *doctor*?' Wright's eyebrows registered surprise.

'Of psychology, specialising in the criminal mind. You rely on facts such as fingerprints and witnesses. I base my profiles on patterns of behaviour and the balance of probabilities, which is why not all of it may apply to the person you catch.'

'Pretty much useless then,' Pendry said, moving Lizzie aside and almost marching through the garden towards the terrace. 'If you've finished flying for the day, don't you have a debrief to go to?'

Seething as she followed them into the manor house, Lizzie left them to their goodbyes and walked out to where Kember's car stood parked on the gravel. She leant against the driver's door to prevent its opening and waited.

As Kember and Wright emerged from the portico, she saw the flicker of a look between them and prepared herself for battle.

'Sorry about Pendry,' Kember said. 'It can't be easy for him, juggling Dallington and Matfield as well as all of us.'

Lizzie ignored the olive branch, in no mood for placations. Realising a sheet of paper probably wasn't the best way to get her ideas across to these men, Lizzie decided her best option was to explain to Kember face to face.

Alone.

'Seeing as you can't find the time, we'll have to do it here,' she said.

'Liz—'

'Listen, the rest of the girls aren't back yet and I don't want anyone asking awkward questions. Let's go to the Hangar Round club. I can show you where the card was left.'

Lizzie knew cats weren't the only creatures driven by curiosity and Kember was soon inspecting the club while Wright stayed with the car.

Although Kember hadn't seen the basement in its previous guise, he was impressed by the work that had undoubtedly gone into making it a welcoming haven. After a brief tour, he listened to Lizzie describe the playing card and fuse box incidents, but suspected another reason for her luring him here. His wait was brief.

'Most murderers and victims are men, but usually strangers,' Lizzie stated, as if continuing a conversation held in her head. 'Most women are murdered by men and have usually met their killer. That suggests Lavinia and Emily had already met their murderer. The playing card was left when I was alone in the club and destined to find it, and now my ID card has been found wrapped in a warning poster. I think we know he's selected me.'

She moved close enough for him to smell her perfume.

'Do you know how that makes me feel?' she said. 'Knowing I've met the man who wants to kill me?'

'I've met men who wanted to kill me,' Kember said, wincing at his casual insensitivity.

'In the heat of the moment, perhaps.'

Kember saw an odd, faraway look in Lizzie's eyes as if she was looking beyond him, through him, not at him.

'But they've not chosen you and made plans to make it happen.'

Kember had to admit that.

'Think about how intimate you have to be,' she whispered. 'How close you must become to reach out and put your hand or a blade against a neck.'

He felt a strange tension as she reached into his jacket pocket, her eyes locking on his, and took his pen, holding it point down like a dagger.

'The attacks weren't random and frenzied,' she said.

Kember flinched as she mimicked repeated stabbing, stopping as suddenly as she'd begun, and felt relieved when she took a step back.

'There would have been blood splattered everywhere,' Lizzie said, waving Kember's pen at the floor, ceiling and walls. 'He took time and care over the choice of dark secluded places, over the weapon, killing and displaying of the bodies. Have you found the knife?'

'Not yet,' Kember admitted.

'You may not until you catch him. If it's not a personal tool he favours, it might be relevant to his work, or he might have attached some other significance to it, like a talisman.'

'A good luck charm?' Kember scoffed. 'Sergeant Wright would call him a nutter.'

Lizzie glared at him. 'Believe me, he isn't a *nutter*.'

He edged away as she moved closer again and held the pen like a carving knife, but the wall prevented a full retreat. He held his breath as Lizzie drew the pen lightly across his throat.

'He didn't slash.' The pen described lines and curves across his chest. 'He carved – deliberately, delicately – and he placed the organs he removed from Emily's body with great care. Why do you think he cut Lavinia where he did? Why did he bother taking Emily's womb?'

'Because he's a sadist?' Kember suggested, catching the look of disappointment as Lizzie shook her head.

'He's attacking and erasing their femininity. In his mind, he's an artist. He wants us to appreciate his work and its meaning. It's as if he's telling the world he's been emasculated so now he's redressing the balance.'

Kember struggled to marshal his thoughts as Lizzie pressed against him, but there seemed nothing sexual in her actions. It was as if his space was hers, that she'd taken it without his consent, and he didn't know what to do.

'What are you thinking?' Lizzie whispered. 'How do you feel? Not in your head but in your gut, your heart? Are you sure I couldn't kill you, here and now?'

Kember knew it was only a pen but he felt suddenly vulnerable and was glad when she backed away again. Close up, Lizzie could be both alluring and intimidating. At arm's length she seemed distracted but professional. He felt unnerved, as if he was speaking to two sides of the same person. Both potentially dangerous.

'That's how I feel,' Lizzie said, flicking a glance back at him. 'Not about you, of course, but still . . .' She handed him his pen. 'Do you remember what I said about ritual not being religious? That the cutting and display fulfil the personal needs and desires he must *always* express because it's the *only* way he can act out his fantasy?'

'Of course. But the Bible scraps . . .' He shrugged for emphasis.

'Ignore the religion: look at the symbols. Yes, the Bible talks of whores and vengeance but was his wife, mother or sister a whore? Did she act like one? Emily had an *inverted* cross on her forehead, and it's likely Lavinia did too, but were they really unworthy? And of what?'

'Are you saying it's name-calling by other means?' he said, feeling immediately chastised by her annoyed frown.

'No. These are serious signposts. What is the worst untruth someone could say about you? Liar? Wife-beater? Deserter? Bent copper?'

He tried to laugh it off with, 'I've been called worse.'

Lizzie's eyes flashed with anger as she prodded a finger at his chest. 'If someone calls you a bent copper does he really mean you, the system or all police? How does it make you feel when the whole police barrel is called rotten because of one bad apple?'

Kember knew grudgingly that she was right. He hated being tarred with the same brush when one copper took a bribe.

'I believe the killer thinks all women are unworthy whores due to something traumatic in his past,' Lizzie continued. 'He's killing now, judging and getting revenge, having reached a tipping point. He won't stop.'

'Are we looking for a sex maniac, then?' Kember asked, immediately knowing he'd said the wrong thing again as Lizzie's cheeks reddened and she lowered her voice.

'The killer was excited by the planning, chase and execution, that's why he became sexually aroused and . . .' She clasped her hands together and took a faltering breath, letting it out between pursed lips. 'But he's not a sex maniac. He left the bodies on display so everyone would be in no doubt it was the work of someone important and powerful.'

'You think that's what he is?' said Kember.

Lizzie's jaw tightened. 'That's what *he* believes he is. Power and domination lie at the heart of this. Somewhere in his past he was traumatised by something that happened beyond his control and this has given him such a hatred of women that he can't just kill them, he has to show all women he's in charge.'

CHAPTER SIXTEEN

Lizzie hesitated outside the briefing room door, clasping her hands in an attempt to clear her mind, an underlying but illogical sense of dread surfacing and threatening to take hold.

This wasn't the time to be incapacitated by something she couldn't control. The psychological profile she had prepared could save the lives of herself and the women around her. Even so, she knew the three policemen waiting inside would judge and criticise her analysis and conclusions. Her credibility and the progress of the investigation relied on her being at her best, but this knowledge served only to exacerbate her conditions.

Lizzie began to hyperventilate, her throat tightening as she tried to swallow. Any worse and it would prevent her from talking, which would add to her ridicule and humiliation. This made her throat seem tighter, almost as if her brain had disengaged from the reality of her body, indulging itself with a thinking cycle from which it could not or did not want to break free.

Walking into this situation was the exact opposite of what she knew she should do. Taking herself away from the suspected cause of an attack always alleviated the symptoms, as did playing games of concentration like solitaire, or solving a crossword. But these were not viable options at this moment. The one countermeasure she could employ, and one she'd discovered by accident when having a panic attack while suffering from a head cold, was to take a large sniff of Vicks VapoRub.

Lizzie plunged a hand into her pocket and pulled out a little jar made from cobalt blue glass. She unscrewed the lid, braced herself and sniffed. The pungent head-clearing cocktail of camphor, eucalyptus oil and menthol jolted her brain and shocked her breathing out of its unnatural rhythm. She gasped.

'Are you all right out there?'

Lizzie heard concern in Kember's voice as she pocketed the jar, cleared her throat and took a step into full view.

'This had better be good,' Pendry said to Lizzie as she swept into the briefing room. 'I thought we'd said all that needed saying.'

To Lizzie's relief, the three policemen sat on the three chairs she had positioned to encourage them to sit rather than stand. This ensured they were lower than her as she stood at the front, putting her in the dominant position.

The constant struggle to get them to really take her seriously had begun to tire her, but Kember had finally agreed to fetch the reluctant RAF man one more time. Bringing them all together in a proper briefing room away from prying eyes and cramped police stations was the professional way for her ideas to be heard.

Kember and Wright looked expectant but she found Pendry hard to read. With hands resting on knees, he looked relaxed in body, but his eyes had narrowed in suspicion. She needed to make her point fast.

'I know you're all busy, so thank you for allowing me ten more minutes of your time,' Lizzie said. 'I promised you a detailed profile of the killer, and I did leave that for the inspector this morning, but I thought a brief summary would be of benefit.'

'As long as it *is* brief,' Pendry said. 'Dallington has another bee in his bonnet and I need to get on.'

Lizzie started to pace, forcing their eyes to follow her, capturing their attention, focusing their minds. 'As policemen, you take inference and supposition and experience and apply them to any facts you have gathered. Although my extensive research experience and understanding is of the psychology of criminals, I do the same and I came to the following conclusions about the killer.'

She looked directly at the men in turn.

'He targets women, but these are not sex crimes; they exhibit loathing. These types of planned murders aren't a young man's forte, nor are they easy to execute if you're a weaker older man, or easy to conceal if you're married. I'd say he's in his late thirties or early forties and unmarried, certainly living alone.' Lizzie turned briefly to the blackboard and wrote:

MAN, 35–45, SINGLE, HATES WOMEN.

'He's probably socially inept so will be a bit of a loner, using alcohol to relax, but that doesn't mean he's unattractive. He may well use good looks and charm on his victims but don't discount him from being in a position of authority or responsibility. Power has its own allure.' She wrote:

LONER, DRINKER, HANDSOME, POWER.

'The crime scenes showed order and precision, not hurried chaos, which suggests he'll be confident at work, with a neat and orderly appearance.' She wrote:

CONFIDENT, WELL GROOMED, ORGANISED.

'Nobody notices him because he isn't out of place. He's not a wide-eyed maniac. He's confident in his surroundings and knows the area very well indeed, enough to come and go as he pleases without anyone batting an eyelid. I'd say he lives and works around here.' She wrote:

WORKS/LIVES LOCAL.

'He uses the blackout and air raids to cover his attacks, when the victim is isolated and alone. Lavinia was killed out in the open, in the village, in the blackout while she was on her own with him. Emily was killed while walking on her own in the air station grounds at night, just at the start of an air raid.' She wrote:

BLACKOUT/AIR RAIDS.

Lizzie paused, feeling their eyes almost scorching her.

'One last thing. It's not uncommon for this type of murderer to take a trophy, a memento to remember and relive each killing. Lavinia's and Emily's identity cards were not found among their papers so it seems he's collecting identity cards at the moment, but that will escalate when they no longer give him the same thrill. That is why I was shaken by the discovery of my identity card. Emily's murder, more extreme than Lavinia's, was supposed to be mine.' She wrote:

TROPHIES.

Although in a better frame of mind now she'd got that ordeal out of the way, the insistent voice of Lizzie's OCN moved in to replace the panic, telling her the bodies she'd been talking about were unclean and she should wash her hands. Lizzie knew this to be a nonsense, but knew also she would have to comply for the feeling to dissipate. She clasped her hands together as an interim measure and waited.

◆ ◆ ◆

Kember, arms folded against the potential horror they still faced, could almost see the tension in the room, the air thicker and heavier than before. He glanced at the men sitting beside him as his subconscious fought against the dregs of his head cold. Pendry's cheeks seemed to have taken on the extra colour that had all but drained from Wright's face, and Lizzie stood there, looking as if the weight of the world had descended on her shoulders.

Pendry broke the deadlock with a laugh. 'A local, handsome, middle-aged bachelor in a suit who likes a drink but not a party,' Pendry said. 'Are you sure you're not describing your ideal husband, or even the inspector?'

Lizzie glowered at Pendry. 'If that's all you got from it, I can talk you through in detail if you'd like?'

Pendry held up his hands halfway as if in surrender. 'That won't be necessary, at least not for me.'

'It's certainly something to think about,' Kember said. 'Gentlemen, I believe Miss Hayes has given us the edge in this investigation. This is not a large town or city and in spite of the flight lieutenant's reservations, that list on the board rules out most of the population around here. The killer may think he knows us, but he cannot realise we now know him.'

'Still a wide field though, I suspect,' Pendry said.

Kember shook his head. 'Village like this, I'd say fifteen might be worth looking at. As for the air station, you'd be better placed to judge who could've had the opportunity.' He saw Pendry's jaw muscles harden. 'Also, Lavinia had skin and blood under one of her fingernails,' he continued. 'I would expect the killer to have a distinguishing scratch somewhere on his hand, wrist, arm, neck or face; but it's been two weeks so it will have faded by now. Even that won't be there forever.'

'I take it from this you have suspects in mind?'

Kember nodded. 'Certain individuals are under the spotlight.' He glanced at the door to ensure it was secure. 'And the first of those is Group Captain Dallington. I'm aware there's no entry in the gatehouse log showing he left the air station on the night of Lavinia Scott's murder, and his staff did say he went to his quarters at around eleven. However, he has an undisguised hatred of women being on his air station and I recall he had a scratch on his right hand.'

'I would add Wing Commander Matfield to the list,' Pendry said. 'It pains me to say it, but I'm not convinced he doesn't share Dallington's views.'

'I agree,' Kember said, relieved that Pendry seemed finally accepting of Lizzie's work. 'The ATA may well have unsettled his routine and sense of security. He does admit dining in the village pub, but the log shows he arrived back before Lavinia Scott was murdered. Neither of them are recorded as leaving the site on the night Emily Parker died. In fact, like Dallington, Matfield also shunned the dance, has no friends around here and also had a scratch on his right wrist. We only have Matfield's word that he was in his office during the air raid and that he heard Dallington leave at his usual time of eleven. Both have access to ceremonial military swords, daggers and the like. Talking of which, an ornate cross displayed in the church vestry is, in fact, a concealed dagger and its sheath.'

'Sir.' Wright frowned. 'I can't see a man of the cloth being involved but I have to say, the reverend doesn't have an alibi for Emily Parker's murder. I recall him being at the dance but I didn't see him when the air raid started.'

'I was coming to the Reverend Giles Wilson,' Kember said. 'Lizzie may be correct about the religious angle, but the Bible texts and anointing with crosses can't be ignored. He has a weak alibi for the time of Lavinia Scott's murder and had a scratch on his right hand he says was made by a thorn from roses in the church. There is some violence in his past too. Apparently, he had a fight when he was in the merchant navy and his opponent died.'

'Good Lord,' said Wright.

'He said it was self-defence and the man fell overboard after hitting his head.'

'Not murder, then,' Lizzie said.

'No,' Kember said. 'I checked his story through an old friend of mine and no charges were brought, but it's something to bear in mind.' He counted off three fingers. 'Any other potential suspects?'

Wright shifted on his chair. 'Andy Wingate, sir. When we went to see him at the garage he acted a bit funny. Now, I know that's not unusual because he's always had his dirty fingers in other people's pies. He's had affairs with some of the farm women, not all of them unmarried, and he's got form for petty pilfering and handling stolen goods. I'd say the affairs are largely to get him close to other people's property. I wouldn't mark him as a shy loner but he tends to drink alone in a corner of the pub, beer mostly, and he works alone in a garage full of oil, knives and cutting tools. He had a scratch on his right arm but said he'd caught it on a split-pin. In my book, he's a crook, not a killer, but we can't rule him out yet.'

Kember counted off Wingate on another finger, then added two more and said, 'Two more for the pot. Flight Lieutenant Pendry and I interviewed the air station personnel and two caught my attention. Thomas Hammond and Frederick Stapleton, both Air Ministry Wardens, were on guard duty both nights and I'm convinced they know more than they told us.' He saw Pendry open his mouth to speak but put up a quietening hand. 'I know the flight lieutenant doesn't share my view entirely but when we questioned Hammond

I noticed him glance down and left, avoiding eye contact on several occasions. In my experience, that indicates a lie.'

'It's actually a classic tell,' Lizzie said. 'Look down for a lie, look up to access a memory. The guard duty gives them an alibi for both murders but what if they weren't as alert as they should have been? With no disrespect intended' – she nodded to Pendry – 'the gatehouse may not be as secure as everyone thinks.' She paused and looked straight at Kember. 'Charlie and I saw Stapleton when we first arrived. He was on his own at the gatehouse, but when I glanced in my mirror as we left I saw somebody else enter the hut.'

'That had to be Hammond,' Pendry said, shifting on his chair. 'I'll keep an eye on him.'

With such an eclectic list of suspects, Kember felt the familiar weight of despair and responsibility that always preceded a breakthrough. He sat upright to stretch his aching muscles, arched his back and rolled his shoulders. He had hoped to go home and have a hot toddy for his persistent cold before getting an early night, but that possibility was rapidly fading.

He thought of his luggage trunks in the police station and his room in the pub.

Where even *was* home?

Fatigue encroached and Kember closed his eyes as his head and the backs of his eyes throbbed. When he opened them a moment later, the throbbing was still there but his mind had cleared and the others were looking at him with concern, waiting for their next instructions.

He took a long breath and stood up next to Lizzie. 'If Flight Lieutenant Pendry can get hold of Dallington's and Matfield's service records, Hammond's and Stapleton's too, if you can, that would be useful. There isn't anything about Andy Wingate's past that Sergeant Wright doesn't already know but we need to keep an eye on him. Sergeant, please pin down the last of the farm workers and have another chat with the stationmaster and postman, see if they've remembered anything. I need to ask Dr Headley about the cross and dagger, and there is one other person Pendry and I need to speak to immediately. After ATA Third Officers Felicity Mitchell and Emily Parker didn't attend the village dance for some reason, Emily turned up dead.'

Lizzie gasped. 'You're not suggesting Fizz had anything to do with Emily's death?'

'I'm not suggesting anything, but she may have been the last person to see Emily alive and I'd like to know what it was that kept them both on the air station on Saturday night.' He saw Lizzie's body stiffen and almost decided to ask her in private, but this was a murder investigation and his years as a policeman got the better of him. 'Lizzie, do you know why they weren't at the dance?'

He saw Lizzie throw a worried glance at Pendry, who became alert in an instant.

'I'm afraid I can't tell you,' Lizzie said.

'Why not?' Pendry snapped.

'It's not for me to say. The ATA has a rank structure. You should speak to Captain Ellenden-Pitt but I don't think it has any bearing on the case, honestly.' Lizzie stared back at them both in quiet defiance.

'Right,' Kember said, cutting the tension in the room. 'That's all we can do today but I think another little chat is called for tomorrow, here at the air station.'

Kember eased his Minx into the lane and turned south towards the village. Glancing in the rear-view mirror, he watched the gatehouse barrier fully descend, physically and symbolically separating him and Sergeant Wright from the air station. It had turned into an extraordinary day and he welcomed the chance to let his thoughts range unhindered, trying to make some sense of it all. Establishing a list of primary suspects always felt like a huge step forward, but in this instance it felt like no more than a starting line-up. Kember had ruled out strangers, believing it to be someone they'd already spoken to, and Lizzie's profile had narrowed the field. But Pendry was right: there must be many middle-aged men within easy reach of Scotney, suited or uniformed, who fitted the bill. In spite of this, Pendry appeared unconcerned that two of his own men and two officers were listed. Having a man of the cloth and a garage mechanic on the list as well served to emphasise the absurdity of it all.

'Penny for your thoughts, sir?' Wright said.

Kember flicked a glance at Wright as an idea coalesced. 'In my experience, police constables and sergeants are known for their network of contacts.'

Wright said nothing.

'If I wanted a little background on someone in the military, would you have an inkling as to how I might tap into that network? On the quiet, of course.'

'I might have an idea, sir,' Wright said.

'I thought you might.' Kember smiled.

'I have one or two contacts in Scotland Yard and they all have a friend of a friend, if you catch my drift.'

'Is there any chance one of them could get hold of the service records for Flight Lieutenant Pendry?' Kember asked. 'And Flight Sergeant Ben Vickers?'

Wright scratched his beard. 'The war's got people a bit jittery, but I could give it a go.'

'Good man. Also, and I know this is a tall order given your day job, but I'd like you to watch the gatehouse at RAF Scotney for a while this evening. I want to know whether anyone of interest leaves or enters the air station or meets at the gatehouse. I'm not saying this is key to the murder investigation, but if someone is slipping through unchallenged there must be a reason.'

'That won't be a problem, sir,' Wright said. 'But can I ask why you didn't mention it in the briefing?'

Kember hesitated. 'I didn't want to say anything further in front of the flight lieutenant just yet because I still consider everyone on the air station a potential suspect.'

Wright nodded sagely. 'I don't think he's too enamoured with Miss Hayes' technique neither. Can't say I blame him.'

Kember smiled wryly. As his acceptance of Lizzie and belief in her skills increased, the opposite seemed true of his colleagues. Another thought that had bothered Kember even before Lizzie had mentioned it in the briefing room was that the killer had used the blackout and threat of bombing to cover his murders and leave threatening messages for Lizzie. That meant every night, every siren, every air raid could spur him on to kill again, and Lizzie could be next.

They reached the village after a few more minutes and Kember parked the Minx outside the police station.

'I'll stick the kettle on,' Wright said as they went inside.

Kember entered the front office but had no chance to take off his coat before the telephone rang. He snatched up the handset.

'What in God's name do you think you're doing?'

Kember's heart sank into his stomach at the sound of Hartson's voice.

'Investigating a double murder, sir.'

'Don't be facetious, Kember,' Hartson snapped. 'I want it to stop.'

'I don't under—'

'You've taken some girl under your wing. A civilian. Letting her play at being a policewoman.'

'Ah, you've heard,' Kember said, fidgeting with the handset.

'Yes, I've bloody heard,' Hartson shouted. 'So has the whole bloody force, and Scotland bloody Yard, I shouldn't wonder.'

I'm not surprised, Kember thought, *shouting like that*.

'Group Captain Dallington's made a verbal complaint about it,' Hartson continued, 'and I want you to stop wasting everyone's time immediately! Before he puts it in writing.'

'She's a criminal psychologist, sir. A qualified professional providing an insight, for free.'

'Professional?' Hartson spat. 'What insight? You're making me a laughing stock, Kember. I can't be having you traipsing all over Kent with your fancy woman in tow—'

'She's not—'

'And she's a bloody witness, to boot.'

'She has credentials, sir,' Kember complained.

'I don't care if she's got a letter from the King,' Hartson said. 'She's a civilian pilot under the protection of the RAF and Air Ministry, a potential victim and a possible witness. A bloody witness, Kember!'

Kember knew he was technically in the wrong and no amount of explanation would win him the argument. Instead, he listened to Hartson's tirade, imagining his moustache quivering and undulating, waiting for the blustering rage to blow itself out. Regardless of Hartson's vociferous objections, Kember had already decided to carry on using Lizzie's skills, unable to ditch her this far into the investigation.

'The second I get a call from the chief constable your career is over, is that clear?'

Hartson's final words and the slamming down of his handset burst painfully against Kember's ear. Wright's face reappeared inquisitively at the open door as Kember replaced the handset firmly back in its cradle.

'Chief Inspector Hartson is very upset about Miss Elizabeth Hayes helping us with the investigation. It seems Group Captain Dallington has made a complaint.'

CHAPTER SEVENTEEN

The following afternoon, Kember glanced at his watch and sat with growing impatience in the manor house hall, waiting for the day's ATA debriefing to be concluded. The good weather had continued so the women had flown out early that morning and he'd been waiting in the village most of the day for them to return from their ferry duties. He complied with grateful relief when ushered from the hall by an orderly into the ATA ops room to take a telephone call.

'Sergeant,' Kember greeted. 'You have news?'

'That I do, sir. I dropped in on Reverend Wilson earlier, as requested. It seems his departure from the village hall before the air raid was due to him not being much of a dancer.'

'Did you not mention that he *did* dance?'

'That's correct, sir. He did have one, reluctantly, with the ATA captain. He sneaked off to the vicarage a bit later to avoid Mrs Oaks trying to get him on the dance floor and he retired to the church crypt when the air raid siren went off.'

Blast, Kember thought. There would be no witnesses, of course, so he filed the plausible explanation at the back of his mind.

He thanked Wright and returned to the hall, waiting as the chattering Charlie, Niamh and Agata vacated the briefing room before entering it himself. Fizz and Geraldine had remained behind and Kember accepted the offer to sit on a nearby chair. He was still furious about the call from Hartson. Pendry must have said something, as only the two of them knew about Lizzie's unofficial secondment. Kember knew he'd put the RAF policeman in a difficult position but he'd considered him an ally in the investigation and would have expected fair warning at the very least.

Kember tried to put it from his mind and concentrate on the matter at hand, but the stuttering investigation, being kept waiting and his ongoing cold had reduced his tolerance level and he was unable to disguise his impatience.

'Thank you for seeing me, Miss Mitchell. My name is Detective Inspector Kember.'

'Aye, I know.' Fizz looked apprehensive.

'I'll come straight to the point. On the night Emily Parker died, why didn't you go to the village dance with the other women?'

Fizz glanced at Geraldine, who nodded back.

'I was confined to the air station as punishment for a misdemeanour,' Fizz said.

'Would you care to elaborate?'

Fizz hesitated as if steeling herself for the explanation. 'Emily and I argued from the moment we met on the first day of training at White Waltham and disliked each other from then on. We clashed often, but it was usually over in a flash. Only this time, all the old animosity flared up and came to a head. The argument escalated and in the heat of the moment we challenged each other. I took Charlie's car and Emily jumped on Lizzie's motorbike.'

'You stole them?' Kember interjected.

'No!' Fizz looked appalled, her eyes darting as she looked back and forth between Kember and Geraldine. 'We borrowed them to race along the airfield to prove who was better. It was a stupid thing to do and we both ended up crashing.'

'And you knew?' Kember asked Geraldine accusingly.

Geraldine nodded tightly. 'I did, but I decided to keep any disciplinary action within the ATA, which is my right. This is the kind of incident that would have the top brass clamouring for us to be reassigned and in doing so damage the reputation of the whole of the ATA. They have made their feelings about women quite clear.'

Kember noticed Fizz's shoulders, previously held square, had slumped.

Geraldine's face set hard. 'And while we're on the subject, people in glass houses shouldn't throw stones.'

'I beg your pardon?' Kember said, taken aback.

'You used one of my officers for your own purpose, putting her career at risk. Dallington and I have an uneasy relationship on a good day, so he took great pleasure in the dressing-down he gave me.'

Kember felt sheepish. 'I apologise if my investigation has caused you upset. My chief inspector has already conveyed Dallington's views to me.'

'But not mine. Third Officer Hayes may be eager to offer help, but she is under my command and in my care. I've had stern words with her. We all want this maniac caught but please avoid undermining our entire position here. Dallington's already had another try at having us removed, citing the murderer apparently targeting us as just cause. Everyone seems to forget we face death in the air and on the ground every day, but it's a role we've gladly chosen because we love flying and want to do our bit for the war effort. We have a duty and none of us want to leave, but we do demand protection from the RAF Police, and for you to do your job.'

Kember held Geraldine's gaze for a moment before he nodded. Annoyingly, all her points were valid and he had no response. He noticed Fizz looking at him curiously and turned his attention back to her.

'When was the last time you saw Miss Parker that night?' Kember asked.

'About half past nine. I said I was going to get an early night and she went out for her usual walk and cigarette, said it cleared her head. I went to my room and a few minutes later the air raid siren went off.'

'What about the group captain or wing commander?'

Fizz looked away, thinking. 'I saw them both at dinner, before the air raid.'

'Were they in the shelter? Was Miss Parker?'

Fizz shook her head and made a face that said *no*. 'I assumed we took cover in different shelters.'

Kember paused and took a long breath in and out, allowing himself a few seconds to think. Quite frankly, he'd hoped for more, but it seemed to him that Felicity Mitchell's animosity towards Emily Parker was enough for a reckless race but not nearly enough for murder. And she'd been in a shelter at the time and seen no more or less than anyone else on the night of the air raid.

Kember bit the inside of his lip in vexation and stood up. 'Thank you, Miss Mitchell, that's all.'

Geraldine looked confused. 'Aren't you going to report this?'

'It's not within my jurisdiction; no crime has been reported and the incident appears to have no direct bearing on my investigation.' Kember took his hat. 'Seeing as you've dealt with the matter, and given the tragic consequences, I don't wish to give anyone the opportunity to upset another apple cart.' He put on his hat, touched the brim in respectful salute, said, 'Thank you for your time. Good day,' and walked from the briefing room.

The mortuary silence inside the Hangar Round club's lounge conveyed how heavily the two murders weighed on the women of the ATA. It pressed on Lizzie's chest an unspoken but almost physical manifestation of grief. Agata had been reading the same page of a newspaper for the last ten minutes as she sat next to Fizz, who kept staring at Lizzie and dropping her gaze whenever she caught her. Meanwhile Niamh and Charlie held mugs of tea they'd brought down from the mess but which they'd barely drunk.

Ever since Lizzie had issued her warning at the ATA briefing, Fizz had taken to firing questions at her about her psychology studies and criminal research as if she were in some kind of oral exam. Fizz had also taken no time at all in coming straight from her interview to share news of Lizzie's dressing-down by Geraldine, and her work with Kember. Lizzie knew this reflected badly on them all and it had clearly further soured their solemn mood. What's more, she knew Fizz was spoiling for a fight.

Fizz sat forward, resting elbows on knees, and forced herself into Lizzie's eyeline. 'What I don't understand is why the police think someone like *you* can help,' she said, as if they were already in mid-conversation.

Lizzie bit back an angry sigh. 'They want my opinion, that's all,' she said tightly.

'About what? What books you read at university? What good is that to them?'

'I didn't just read books. As I've told you before, I conducted research.'

'Oh hark. *I conducted research,*' Fizz mimicked. 'He's a senior detective and you fly aeroplanes. Being sweet on each other won't catch Lavinia and Emily's killer, will it?'

'Don't be ridiculous.' Lizzie spoke quickly to disguise a rush of anxiety. 'I've learnt how to read people, by looking at what they've done and how they've achieved it. It's a skill to be learnt and practised like any other, like flying. It's just my opinion, but it's an educated one.'

Fizz shook her head. 'I've said it once and I'll say it again – you're not quite normal.'

Tell me something new, Lizzie thought.

'Leave her alone.' Charlie's agitated wave made ash and smoke from her cigarette leave floating patterns in the air. 'Surely anything that helps catch this monster is a good thing?'

But Fizz wasn't about to be deflected. 'Not when it comes from a freak. You think you know people? Read me, then.'

Lizzie shook her head sadly. 'Look, I know you're frightened like the rest of us because the police didn't find him in time to stop Emily being killed. And I know you're taking out your anger on me, because you think I'm somehow different. Like you said, doesn't catch the killer, does it?'

Lizzie saw Fizz tense and thought she was about to launch herself at her and she braced for the impact. But something in her words must have struck home because Fizz paused, her posture deflating slightly as she took in the meaning of Lizzie's words.

'It is all right for the men, it is us being killed,' Agata said flatly, throwing her newspaper to the table.

'Exactly.' Niamh clunked her mug down. 'We must look out for each other. Perhaps we should leave.'

'What for?' said Charlie. 'We'll still be shot at and bombed wherever we go.'

'Not cut into pieces though.'

'I'll tell you something,' Fizz said with a smile. 'The captain didn't want to run and hide. She gave that detective a right telling-off. Said we had a duty to perform and we'd bloody well carry on doing it. Told him he should be doing his job better. That RAF Police lieutenant didn't come off lightly either. He wasn't there, but she demanded he do more to protect us and I reckon he'll get it in the neck when she sees him again. I wouldn't be surprised if she went straight to Dallington.'

'But he doesn't want us here,' Niamh said.

'Makes no odds.' Fizz shrugged. 'The Air Ministry gets what the Air Ministry wants.'

'If we leave,' Lizzie said, 'the killings might stop for a while but they'll never catch him. That's no good for anyone. He'll attack the next group of women they send, and the next. I for one want to stop him before he does it again. I'm not leaving.'

Agata lit a cigarette and left it in the corner of her mouth, bobbing up and down, as she spoke. 'It is the five of us in this room we must protect. And the captain.'

'I agree. We should stick together.' Charlie lit a fresh cigarette from the dying embers of the old. 'He's after all of us.'

Silence returned to the lounge as Charlie's words hung in the air like her smoke. Lizzie looked at Fizz, sullen and hunched into her corner of the opposite sofa. Agata sucked on her cigarette, deep in thought, adding to the heavy cloud of smoke that had formed a halo against the ceiling. How much of her defiance was bravado? Niamh had reclaimed her mug but held it a little too tightly, sipping and grimacing at the now tepid contents. Charlie, worrying a thread on the hem of her skirt with her fingers, had become a chain-smoking shadow of the happy-go-lucky young woman who had danced in the village hall a few nights ago.

Lizzie felt tension of her own across her forehead and worried she might be getting a migraine headache. She felt in her tunic pocket for a handkerchief to wipe her stinging eyes, but instead her fingers touched the forgotten scrap of paper she'd found.

As Lizzie unfolded it and read the small scrap of printed text, she gasped and stood up. Ignoring the worried enquiries bursting around her, she snatched up her things and rushed up the stairs to phone Kember.

◆ ◆ ◆

Lizzie heard the muffled voice of Sergeant Wright and a rustling sound as he handed over the telephone handset.

As soon as she heard Kember's voice she blurted down the line. 'It's me.'

'I know it's you,' Kember said. 'Sergeant Wright sa—'

'It *is* me. I was right. The killer wanted *me* but he couldn't get to me so he went for the next best thing, which was Emily, and used the air raid to get it done—'

'Stop,' Kember said firmly. Lizzie stopped. 'You do know we're in serious trouble over your work for me?'

'I don't care if they give me the sack,' said Lizzie, 'but I do care about catching the killer before it's too late.'

'And you think I don't?' he snapped.

'That's not what I meant,' Lizzie said, her head throbbing in time to the rapid beating of her heart. Kember was clearly concerned about jeopardising his own career but she was certain he would never have agreed to let her help if he'd not wanted to do the right thing.

'I know, but let's be careful,' Kember said. 'Now, what's happened? Slowly.'

Lizzie took a breath, feeling a wave of relief. 'All right. Slowly,' she said, more as an instruction to herself than an acknowledgement. 'Last week, the day we opened our new club, we'd finished all the preparations and were leaving the cellar. I gave my hankie to Charlie and a piece of paper fell out. I thought it was rubbish and put it back in my pocket. I've just found it again and looked at it.'

She paused, seeing whether Kember would work it out.

'Go on,' he said.

She took another deep, calming breath and unfolded the paper to read. 'It says: *For true and righteous are his judgements* . . . Need I go on?' Lizzie waited, listening to breathing at the other end of the line.

'You say you found that at the club?' Kember asked.

'No, it was in my pocket. He must have slipped it in after I found the playing card. He was threatening me, warning me I'd be next.'

'But you weren't next, Emily was.'

'I know, but it's a matter of opportunity.' Lizzie wanted to blurt it all out again but kept a rein on her tumbling thoughts and marshalled them so she could convey them and their gravity to Kember. 'He needs certain criteria to be met before he strikes and it just so happens that Lavinia and Emily met those first. He needs to keep making his point but I haven't put myself in a position to become a victim, albeit unwittingly. The playing card is him taunting me, saying I know who you are, I can *see* what you're doing, and the Bible quote says I can get to you any time you slip up.'

There was a moment's silence, and then Kember said, 'All right. Tell Pendry straight away so he can keep an eye on you. We'll get you out first thing in the morning.'

'Certainly not,' Lizzie said, flooded with indignation.

'I don't want any more blood in the blackout.'

'I'll be fine. I discussed it with the others just now. We're going nowhere.'

She heard a gasp of exasperation from Kember. 'Just make sure you're not alone,' he said.

Lizzie thought Kember's demand, well-meaning or not, to be as patronising as the suggestion she needed Pendry to ensure her welfare, and was grateful when Kember broke the awkward silence that followed.

'If you've handled that paper and had it in your pocket for a few days, the killer's fingerprints probably won't have survived, but keep it very safe nonetheless and I'll collect it tomorrow.'

'That's what I thought,' Lizzie said, calming down. 'I wanted to let you know as soon as I read it but I'll be quite all right if I stick close to my friends. Don't worry.'

Lizzie made sure she sounded more confident than she felt as they finished the call. The last thing she wanted was for Kember to play Sir Galahad and embarrass her in front of the others, especially Fizz. That didn't mean she wasn't scared. The killer was getting bolder and therefore more dangerous, and now her involvement with the police had become common knowledge, she was a prime target.

CHAPTER EIGHTEEN

The sound of aircraft woke Kember earlier than he'd intended and for a moment he wondered where he was. Then it all came flooding back.

He rolled on to his back and tried to drift off for another ten minutes until he heard the first signs of stirring in the pub. A few bottles clinked, a hummed tune filtered under his door and water tinkled musically into a metal pail, the note getting deeper as it filled. He slid out of bed and opened the blackout curtains, allowing light to coat his room. He yawned and attended to his morning routine, finally descending the creaky wooden stairs to breakfast.

'Morning, duck,' Alice said breezily as he sat at a table in the saloon bar. 'Perfect timing.'

She placed a bowl of steaming porridge oats in front of him with thick honey for a sweetener, and a cup of tea. No lucky fry-up this morning, but he demolished the porridge in a couple of minutes. The scalding tea took a bit longer but enabled him to mull over what the day promised, which wasn't much.

After seriously considering going back to bed, he left his breakfast things tidy and shouted a thank you to Alice, whom he could hear working in the back rooms.

'All right, duck,' Alice called back.

Kember closed the pub door and manoeuvred around two schoolboys searching along the High Street for shell casings and shrapnel from the air battles. Hearing the crunch of heavy boots, he looked up and smiled in amusement as the local Home Guard marched towards him from the northern end of the village. Two days earlier, the mishmash of Local Defence Volunteers had been renamed and their brand-new uniforms looked at odds with their motley collection of privately owned shotguns, sporting rifles and Great War pistols.

'Company, company halt,' commanded a short, rotund man sporting the three stripes of a sergeant.

The men stomped to a standstill and Kember watched Elias Brown step from the village hall, march to the head of the company and shout, 'Company, by the right, quick march.'

Kember waited for the men to pass before crossing the road to the police station. Wright greeted him with a scowl and a stifled a yawn.

'It's not as if we haven't got ourselves a double murder investigation to contend with,' Wright complained. 'It was bad enough when they all came to the station to sign up for the LDV. Now Brown and his goons have got a fancy new name they've almost taken over the village hall as their blasted headquarters.'

'What's all the activity about?' Kember asked.

'They're taking ownership of three new pillboxes today,' Wright said in a way that left Kember in no doubt he was unimpressed. 'One to guard the road and railway bridges over the river, one at the junction of the southern approach road and one in a field covering the slope up to the railway station.'

Kember sat as Wright stirred a teapot and poured steaming pale liquid into two mugs.

'The Home Guard finished erecting anti-invasion defences yesterday. They put up sharpened poles in the pastures to stop gliders and paratroops,' Wright continued. 'Elias has new orders to man the pillboxes and a checkpoint at the road junction between first light and dusk. The rest of the time they're on fifteen minutes notice to move in case of invasion.'

'Sounds sensible,' Kember said as Wright handed him a mug.

'That's as may be,' Wright said, eyes watering as he stifled another yawn. 'But Brown's head is bigger than a football now. For some mad reason, probably because he was in the Great War, he was made commanding officer. Scotney Company, Twenty-First Tonbridge Battalion of the Queen's Own Royal West Kent Regiment, they're called. Bit of a mouthful, if you ask me. Insisting on being called *Captain* Brown, he is now.'

'Well, he certainly looks the part.'

Wright laughed and shook his head. 'I spoke to Alf the station-master again, but he couldn't add anything more. I also managed to talk to the remaining farmworkers. They've all got rock-solid alibis.'

'As we suspected.'

'And Mr Pendry asked me to let you know he has the service records you asked for.'

'Good,' Kember said. 'That was quick. I need to catch up with him anyway.'

'There is another thing,' Wright said. 'After I watched the gate-house like you asked, I followed Wingate last night.'

'I wondered what all the yawning was about,' Kember said, taking a sip of tea.

Wright walked over to a map of the area pinned to the wall. 'After he closes his garage each day, Wingate parks his truck in a small dilapidated barn near the railway bridge. I've tried to follow him before in the old police Wolsey I keep behind the station, but could never get close enough to see where he was going. When he leaves his truck he cycles away on a pushbike kept in the back, returning no more than an hour later. I believe he looks to burgle farms. Anyway, about ten o'clock last night, he left his house behind the garage, walked to his truck and drove away.' Wright pointed to a location. 'I followed but lost him here.' He tapped his finger on another location. 'That confused me until I remembered that this track used to be a drovers' road donkey's years ago, passes close to Manor Lane at the point where it reaches the old west gate of Scotney Manor. The archway's been pulled down long since, but it's where the air station gatehouse is now. Anyway I drove back and decided to take another look at the gatehouse from Manor Lane.'

Wright cleared his throat as he continued. 'I drove as far up the lane as I dared before approaching on foot along the other side of the hedgerow. Hammond and Stapleton were on duty. I could see them having words with each other before Hammond left the gatehouse and trotted away, keeping low as if trying not to be seen. Unless there's another way in and out, he never left the air station. He came back less than an hour later and went into the gatehouse. They argued a bit more, then it swung the other way and they didn't speak to each other at all. Whatever else he's been up to, Hammond's guilty of deserting his post.'

The excitement of the chase tingled suddenly in Kember's chest. 'Seems more than coincidence that the night Hammond deserts his post is the same night Wingate drives along that track.'

Kember stood up and traced Wingate's probable route on the map with his finger. Could this be the breakthrough they had been waiting for?

'I have three questions,' he said. 'If Hammond and Wingate did meet, what crimes, if any, can they have been engaged in? If Hammond doesn't leave the air station and Wingate never enters, what's their connection to the dead women? Why would Hammond or Wingate want to kill Lavinia and Emily?'

Wright shrugged. 'Lavinia Scott could have seen something and been killed by Wingate to silence her. And if Emily Parker saw something on the air station, Hammond could have killed her for the same reason.'

War brought out the worst in the worst kind of people, but from what Kember knew, he wasn't convinced these two men were cold-blooded killers. When Lizzie had presented her profile of the murderer it had only enhanced this view but, while Kember still believed her assertion that they were looking for one man, any lead was welcome.

'Good work, Sergeant,' Kember said. 'It'll mean another late night, I'm afraid. Whatever Wingate's up to, we need to catch him in the act, so I'll leave you to draw up a plan of action and we can talk over the details later. But first, I think I need to speak to some of the villagers again.'

Kember and Wright strolled across the High Street towards a man wearing the red-trimmed, navy-blue uniform of the General Post Office. He was crouching outside the grocer's shop that housed the sub-post office, emptying letters and postcards from a bright red pillar box into a beige canvas shoulder pouch. His red-painted GPO-issue bicycle stood propped against the wall, a war-issue steel helmet stamped with GPO hanging from the handlebars. Kember nudged Wright for an introduction.

'Hello, Corky,' Sergeant Wright called.

The postman stood up to his full height, which Kember estimated as a few inches over six feet.

'How many more times, Dennis,' the postman sighed. He removed his peaked cap and ran a hand over his remaining short-cropped grey hair. 'It's Jim, not Corky.'

Wright grinned. 'This is James Corcoran, local postie. And this here's Detective Inspector Kember of Scotland Yard.'

Kember nodded politely and gave a wry smile, well aware of how annoying it could be to have your name said wrong. He was also aware of the effect the words *Scotland Yard* could have on some people, although Jim Corcoran seemed unperturbed.

'If you've seen one bobby you've seen 'em all,' Corcoran said with a smile. 'Although you look a bit more clued up than our Dennis. I've known him since he was a nipper in short trousers with socks round his ankles.'

'Now, Jim,' Wright complained.

'He was a tubby kid back then. Partial to a wedge of cake, was our Den.' He winked at Kember. 'He still is, if his visits to Gladys Finch's tea shop are anything to go by. Although it might not be the cake he's interested in.'

Kember couldn't help smiling at Wright's discomfort. Good-natured ribbing was a fact of life for a bobby on the beat. Although mildly disrespectful, it showed a level of familiarity and trust that police officers relied upon. All the villagers knew Sergeant Wright well and many would have grown up with him. Kember knew from experience that such connections were invaluable.

'How's the investigation going, then?' Corcoran asked.

'We're getting there,' Kember said non-committally.

'Is that all you can tell us?'

'It is for now, unless you've spotted anything untoward on your rounds?'

'As I've already told Den, not a sausage,' Corcoran said. 'Unless you count checkpoints and pillboxes. And Spitfires scaring the horses.'

Kember nodded. 'Then we'll leave you to your letters.'

As they walked on, Kember smiled at Corcoran's call, 'Give my love to Gladys.'

◆　◆　◆

Wright sat at his desk as Kember hung his jacket and hat on the stand and took the visitor's chair by the door.

'Whoever took Albert Garner's petrol must have been out and about at the same time as the killer,' Kember said. 'To get the petrol out must have taken, what, a good five or ten minutes?'

'Aye, sir,' Wright said, 'all of that.'

Kember took a stubby pencil from the desk, turned over a police circular and scribbled a few lines to represent the layout of the village.

'I know it was dark and the angle wasn't perfect, but the thief might have seen the killer. Greenway remembered seeing Albert Garner outside the pub with Andy Wingate and them going their separate ways, but didn't see Garner arrive home.'

Wright frowned. 'Didn't he say he patrolled up that way first? He must have seen him.'

'Greenway told me he took a turn around the village hall to check security, something he does now and again but not every night.' Kember marked the movements with his pencil. 'He didn't get to the vicarage for another ten to fifteen minutes or so.'

'Time enough for the killer to have already done the deed.'

'Perhaps. Greenway didn't see Wingate go home either because his garage is in the opposite direction. What's more, he said he saw the blackout curtains pulled straight but didn't see anyone near the vicarage, nor did he notice Mrs Garner. Not very observant, is he, our Mr Greenway?'

Wright shook his head in disappointment. 'Seems like everyone was going about their own business and not taking a blind bit of notice of anything else.'

'That's human nature, keeping yourself to yourself.'

'Maybe in the towns and cities but not in villages like ours. Everyone knows everyone's business here.'

Kember didn't believe that for a moment. Yes, there were the Ethel Garners and post-office gossip clubs where tittle-tattle was the common currency, but each village had its fair share of Brian Greenways and people who wanted nothing but a quiet life. Criminals always sought and found the shadows to work in.

Wright had his eyes narrowed in thought. 'Brian Greenway saw Bert Garner part company with Andy Wingate, who supposedly went straight home, and Ethel Garner says Bert went home. Ethel, who went out to confront a petrol thief, heard Brian call out, as did Reverend Wilson and his housekeeper Jessie Oaks. Dallington and Matfield have witnesses who saw them on the air station, and the gatehouse log confirms they were there while Miss Scott was being murdered near the church. Hammond and Stapleton were on guard duty but we know Hammond sneaks off and Wingate drives up the lane. Maybe they meet. Even if everyone wasn't quite where they say they were at the times they say they were, and even allowing for a few minutes here and there, are we looking at the right people? Maybe it's not someone from round here.'

Kember rubbed his eyelids, his cold a little better but his eyes still gritty from disturbed sleep. 'I share your frustration, Sergeant, but the whole country is on high alert for the Nazi invasion and no strangers have been reported anywhere around here. Someone must be lying.' He glanced at his wristwatch. 'I must be going. I have to collect those service records from Pendry before I make that telephone call about our Reverend Wilson.' He stood and reached for his hat and jacket. 'Which reminds me. While I'm away, chase your contact for those other service records and see if Dr Headley has anything on the cross and dagger. He must have finished with it by now.'

CHAPTER NINETEEN

Kember drove his Minx up to the manor house, tyres crunching on gravel like boots on fresh snow as he swung the wheel and braked beside a staff car. Moments later, he took the visitor's chair in Pendry's office as the RAF man opened a drawer and pulled out a half-full bottle of Booth's Gin.

'No tonic, I'm afraid.'

Kember nodded in grim approval.

Pendry poured two small measures into china mugs and passed one to Kember.

Kember took a sip. 'Not bad.'

'Last of my old pre-war stock. Tonic, ice and lemon would liven it up a bit but nobody else knows I've got it and I want it to stay that way.' Pendry swilled the clear liquid in his mug. 'Is there any alcohol you would have refused?'

'Right at this moment, probably not.' Kember set his jaw and narrowed his eyes, unable to restrain himself any longer. 'Can I ask why you told Dallington about our arrangement with Lizzie?'

Kember noticed an almost imperceptible flicker of agitation in Pendry's eyelids but the rest of his face remained controlled.

'Look, I wasn't going to but I have a duty to my commanding officer and both he and Matfield were getting suspicious, and the women were all talking. I couldn't very well lie.' Pendry took a sip of gin.

'Surely you must have known he'd tell my chief inspector,' Kember snapped.

Pendry looked discomfited. 'I had no choice. I was just doing my job.'

Kember bit his tongue, choking back the rebuke that he had rehearsed in his mind ever since the call with Hartson. 'Let's just say I'd have appreciated a little warning.'

'Of course, you're right.' Pendry nodded ruefully. 'I'm sorry.'

'Are you also sorry for lying about doing the rounds while Lavinia Scott was being murdered?'

Pendry double-blinked in surprise, giving Kember a slight thrill at having cracked that eerie calm he always seemed to exude.

'Maybe I got the day wrong, but I didn't deliberately lie. I seem to remember saying I walk the perimeter fence often, not every evening. If I misled you, it was a genuine mistake, that's all.'

'Of course,' Kember said, forcing himself to appear relaxed. 'Just doing my job.'

Pendry smiled in recognition and drained his mug. 'Touché.' He reached into another desk drawer, produced a large manila envelope and undid its button and string fastening. 'You'll be pleased to know I managed to get what you asked for.' He pulled out four slim files of folded buff card into which papers had been secured. He placed them on the desk facing towards Kember and fanned them so the names could be read.

Kember sat forward. 'May I?'

Pendry indicated the files with an open-hand. 'Be my guest. A lot of it is redacted but you'll get the gist.'

Kember opened Dallington's file and read aloud. 'Privileged upbringing. Usual career stuff. A commission in the Royal Flying

Corps during the Great War. A bit of an air ace, earned himself a Distinguished Flying Cross, etcetera.'

'Keep going,' Pendry said.

The next entry made Kember pause. 'Ah. Blotted his copybook, I see. *Always had an illogical and vociferous hatred of women in the workplace.*'

Pendry gave a facial shrug. 'He's the product of his upbringing.'

Kember tapped the file. 'There's a further note about his card being marked in that regard. Says here he's been making a nuisance of himself trying to keep women off the air station. Quite the sexist.'

'That's the least of it,' Pendry said.

Kember held Pendry's gaze for a few seconds, wondering what misdemeanour Dallington could have committed, and something in the RAF man's eyes made him dread what he'd find next. He flicked through some more pages until another entry made him stop. This was more than a misdemeanour.

'I didn't know about this before,' Pendry said. 'Not my place to know, actually.'

'Now I understand why he's in charge of this backwater,' Kember said with disgust. 'At his last posting he threatened to slap a WAAF then made her run ten times around the parade ground.'

Pendry looked away. 'You can get away with that with the men, in the name of military discipline, but . . .' His voice tailed off and he cleared his throat. 'You have to understand, this is wartime and all soldiers in any branch of the service have to follow orders, immediately and to the letter. Lives could depend on it.'

Kember recoiled. 'Are you making excuses?'

'Not at all,' Pendry said flatly. 'Just telling you how it is.' He continued as Kember digested the news, 'Does he think slapping a woman brings her to her senses? Yes. Does he think a woman's place is in the home? Yes. Does he think there is men's work and there is women's work? Yes. Does that make him any different from most men and, it has to be said, a sizeable minority of women in the country? No. Does that mean he hates women enough to kill them? Who knows?'

'All pretty emphatic, until the end,' Kember said, keeping his gaze on Pendry.

Pendry shrugged. 'Dallington doesn't want women on his air station but he failed in that regard when the fighter squadrons were based here. WAAFs worked in the operations and signals rooms and all his bluster couldn't dislodge them. They remained here until Fighter Command withdrew them. He reacted the same when he knew the ATA were coming.'

Kember sighed, sensing a *but*.

'But,' Pendry obliged, 'despite what it says in his file, he's always treated the women on *this* air station with courtesy and respect. To their faces. Don't get me wrong, he's not all bark and no bite, but having been in the last war he knows the value of rest, recuperation and morale for the troops.'

Kember lightly tossed the file onto the desk. He was getting mixed messages from Pendry and couldn't decide whether the RAF man despised Dallington or secretly admired him. He reached for Matfield's file. 'What about the dashing wing commander?'

'An altogether more complex background, as you'll see.'

Kember skim-read Matfield's file. 'Joined the Royal Flying Corps, learnt to fly and took to it straight away. Got shot down in one of the last engagements of the war in 1918. Sent out to scout over some woodland, he got pranged by a Jerry fighter and crash-landed. Got caught in a close-quarters skirmish between a squad of British infantry and a German patrol. Pretty gory by all accounts. He returned covered in blood, sole survivor, the rest of the British squad and the entire German patrol having been killed.' Kember looked up. 'This was verified?'

'Absolutely,' Pendry said, pulling a cigarette from its packet. 'Matfield got the Distinguished Flying Cross.'

Despite his dislike of Matfield, Kember found himself quite impressed. 'Was he hurt?'

'Minor scrapes. The doctors patched him up and sent him back to his squadron, but the hand-to-hand fighting played on the mind of a young man used to seeing war from the air.' Pendry struck a match. 'He had a few nightmares, which put the willies up his comrades. Luckily for him, his commanding officer had a brother recovering from shellshock and was more sympathetic than most.' He lit his cigarette and took a drag. 'He got Matfield shipped back to England for some rest and recuperation.'

Kember looked hard at Pendry. 'Do we know the name of this commanding officer?'

Pendry blew out the match before it singed the leather of his gloves, and smiled. 'Dallington.'

'You're kidding?' Kember said, astonished.

'After treatment, Matfield returned to his squadron and stayed in the new RAF, as the Royal Flying Corps became shortly after the Great War.'

Kember flicked over a page. 'Says here he got himself another DFC fighting overseas. DFC *and bar*. A brave man.'

Pendry nodded. 'I bought him a drink on one occasion and asked him why he joined the RAF. He said he'd always fancied flying and there wasn't anything else in Civvy Street he was cut out to do. He also said he liked the camaraderie.'

'Fair enough.' Kember had once enjoyed that feeling in the police.

'And killing from a distance.'

Kember held Pendry's gaze. 'Doesn't make him sound like our man, does it?'

Pendry shrugged. 'He's pleasant to the women but doesn't usually socialise with them. Doesn't socialise with anyone these days, in fact. As we've heard from their own mouths, Dallington and Matfield are both loners in their own way.'

'And therefore both fit Lizzie's profile,' Kember said, frowning at Pendry when the RAF man took a theatrical intake of breath. 'You don't think the profile is valid?'

Pendry made a face that said the jury was still out. 'I'm not so sure that you can judge a personality from looking at a dead body and a crime scene. To go further and predict what that person is like and what they'll do next . . .' He shook his head. 'I don't think people can be reduced so easily.'

'I must admit I was cynical,' Kember agreed. 'But the more I hear, the more logical it seems. As Lizzie said, the basis for her profile comes from academic research and scientific studies. It's not mumbo jumbo, as Sergeant Wright calls it.' Kember could see Pendry remained unconvinced as the RAF man took a long pull on his cigarette. 'I've looked at the interview notes, trying to fathom out this case, and the short list of suspects we settled on all had scratches.'

Pendry still looked sceptical. 'For which they all have explanations.'

Kember rubbed his eyes with finger and thumb. 'One or all could be lying. Anyway, Dallington and Matfield are loners and Wingate, although he drinks in the pub and seems to like the ladies, also lives alone. Reverend Wilson has a live-in housekeeper who is fond of him but he said he left the village dance early to avoid having to dance with her.'

Pendry gave a small laugh. 'Can't say I've ever had that happen to me.'

'Lucky you,' Kember said. 'What do we have on Hammond and Stapleton?' He picked up the remaining two files, Hammond's on top.

Pendry blew smoke. 'Hammond's a bit of a character, by all accounts. Kept getting hauled over the coals, peeling potatoes for frequent indiscipline. His punishment became more severe when he got caught selling goods pilfered from the NAAFI stores. He keeps trying to beat the system in small ways, but he never learns.'

Kember's mouth pressed into a thin line and his brow furrowed. 'Sergeant Wright believes Hammond's up to something. He observed him leaving his post at the gatehouse while on night duty and this seems to correspond with a moonlight excursion taken by Wingate.'

Pendry stiffened. 'You didn't tell me you'd set up an observation post.'

'Relax,' Kember soothed. 'It was a couple of hours for only one night. Wright's theory is that Lavinia Scott saw Wingate doing something criminal outside the air station and he had to silence her. Emily Parker was killed by Hammond inside the air station for a similar reason.'

Pendry poured himself another small measure of gin and, without offering any more to Kember, downed it in one gulp. 'If that theory holds water, I'll hang Hammond myself.'

Kember held his hands up, palms out. 'It's just a theory so I wouldn't go getting carried away.'

'Should I arrest him?'

Kember shook his head. 'Hammond and Stapleton are on duty tonight so Wright and I will be watching Wingate. If you can keep the gatehouse under surveillance we might find out what's going on. It could be that both events are unconnected and innocent.'

'Will do. I'll get my flight sergeant right on to it.'

Kember slid Hammond's file to the bottom. 'What about Stapleton?'

'Stapleton's a run-of-the-mill squadcie,' Pendry began. 'Keeps his head down, for the most part, but he and Hammond know each other from school and have been pals for as long as either can remember.'

Kember glanced up. 'As I said before a worthy accomplice?'

Pendry shook his head. 'I wouldn't say so. He's the weaker of the two and easily led. He'll follow Hammond some way down the path so I wouldn't write him off as a crook, but I reckon he'd pull back from anything serious. Scrumping apples and turning a blind eye, that's his level.'

A sudden thought occurred to Kember. 'Where's the fuel dump on this air station?'

Pendry stared at his cigarette, seemingly transfixed by the rising ribbon of smoke. 'We have two, in case one is hit. The bowsers are filled from the underground main tanks on the eastern side towards the dispersal area. We also have a smaller reserve dump to the west by the wooded copse just north of the drive and a safe distance from both the manor house and operations block.' He looked at Kember. 'Why?'

'Are either near the perimeter fence?'

'Not near, but the reserve dump is easily the closest.' Pendry looked thoughtful. 'What are you thinking?'

Kember knew he should come to the point. 'How often are fuel levels checked?'

'You'd have to ask the ground crew but I'd say the main tank gauges are checked daily.' He tapped ash from his cigarette into a glass ashtray. 'Barrels are stored in the reserve dump prior to being transferred to the main tanks if needed, or used direct if the main tanks are hit. Since the fighters left Scotney the fuel has been needed less, for the odd fly-in and the Ox-box.'

'Ox-box?' Kember asked.

'The Airspeed Oxford the ATA use as their taxi. Anyway, because so little fuel has been used from the main tanks, the barrels in the reserve dump probably haven't been looked at for months.'

Kember said nothing, looking at Pendry but keeping his own face impassive, waiting for the RAF policeman to voice the obvious connection.

'I know what you're thinking,' Pendry obliged, stubbing out his cigarette. 'Hammond steals petrol and Wingate sells it on from his garage.'

'That's a theory,' Kember agreed. 'Easy enough to supplement his petrol with yours to keep the pennies coming in.'

'But it's eighty-seven per cent high octane and would burn out most engines.'

'Mixing the two would take the edge off the high-octane stuff. There's been a spate of petrol thefts in the area but the local boys haven't been able to catch anyone.'

Pendry stood, paced to the door and scratched the back of his head. 'Those barrels are bloody heavy when they're full. They're stored inside an earth-bank enclosure half-sunk below ground level and would make a hell of a racket if anyone tried to move even one. I can't see how it's possible.'

'Neither can I,' Kember said. 'And I have to admit, I don't know how the murders fit in.'

Kember started to feel they were going around in circles so he stood and gathered his things. 'I'm afraid I have to be off for now.' He slipped the files back into the manila envelope. 'May I keep these?'

'Be my guest,' Pendry said. 'Shouldn't really, but if you can't trust a policeman, who can you trust?'

CHAPTER TWENTY

Lizzie turned at the call of her name and saw Kember striding towards her. She felt her face flush and attempted a smile, pushing her hair behind her ears.

'Are you all right? Where's the piece of paper you found? Are you safe?'

'I keep telling you, I'm fine.' Lizzie looked up as a floorboard creaked and saw Dallington and Matfield appearing on the first-floor landing. She took Kember's elbow, steered him into a room used as an occasional office and shut the door behind them.

'Like I said last night, I found the Bible quote a week ago,' she said. 'Three days after the playing card. I thought it was a scrap of rubbish at the time and forgot all about it. I didn't look at it until yesterday.'

Kember frowned. 'He's left two warnings but you didn't think it serious enough to check the piece of paper for a third?'

'Of course it's serious,' Lizzie said. 'I know I'm a target – we all are. But ever since it became well known that I'm working with you to help find him, that's bound to have angered him. I don't show I'm frightened and that must confuse him. He needs to be in control but I'm taking that from him.'

Kember reached for the door handle. 'We really need to protect you.'

'No.' Lizzie shushed him and listened at the door before turning back. 'Don't you see? That's what he wants. If I'm chaperoned, everywhere I go I'll be restricted. He won't be able to get to me but I won't be able to get to him. I need to carry on as normal. He'll make a mistake soon enough.' She looked at the manila envelope in Kember's hand. 'Anyway, why are you here?'

'I came to see Pendry about the service records I asked him for, and I hoped you'd take a look.' Kember held out the envelope. 'I could get arrested for sharing this so it's strictly confidential and off the record. Pendry and I have our opinions, but with your expertise . . .'

'You think me an expert now? That's an about-turn.'

Kember shrugged. 'They're a bit sketchy, information redacted for security purposes, etcetera.'

She forced herself to look him in the eyes, taking the chance to make amends. 'Will you wait while I look over them, Inspector?'

'I'd love to but I haven't the time. And you can call me Kember, or Jonathan if you'd like.'

Lizzie took the envelope, unable to fathom whether he treated all colleagues this way or whether this signified a step forward in their professional relationship, towards acceptance.

'Kember's not a common name, is it?' she blurted, and sensed an instant change in his mood.

'My father told me it's an Anglo-Saxon name meaning royal fortress and my mother told me my hair sticks up at the back because I have a double crown. I made the mistake of saying this at school and the school bullies loved it, doubly so when they heard my middle name.'

Curious but hearing the bitterness in his reply, she tapped the envelope. 'Did you rule out – who was it – Wingate?'

232

'Not yet,' Kember said. 'He may be in league with Hammond regarding theft of stores, possibly petrol. We're keeping watch tonight to see if we can establish what they're up to and catch them in the act.'

'Better take care yourself, then.' She ignored his sharp look. 'By the way, did you get anywhere with the knife?'

Kember massaged the bridge of his nose. 'Afraid not. All our main suspects have access to a long blade of some sort. This part of Kent is covered in farms and orchards, and cutting tools are ten a penny. There are farming tools, gardening implements, butchers' cleavers, fish-filleting knives, kitchen knives, thatching tools, and that's before we get to bayonets and other knives used by the RAF and Home Guard. Then there's the cross with a dagger displayed in the vestry of the church.'

'Have you found anything more about that? About the vicar?'

'No more than you, except that Reverend Wilson doesn't have a cast-iron alibi for the times of both murders and he has access to a long blade. I can't see a motive but that's not to say I've ruled him out entirely. I'm waiting on Dr Headley's analysis.'

'For what it's worth, I'm sure it's not the reverend either.' Lizzie glanced at her watch. 'I should go. Geraldine and Dallington are both still keeping an eye on me, and the girls will be back soon.' She opened the door a fraction and peered through the crack before opening it fully. 'Wait, I almost forgot.' Kember paused as Lizzie fished in her pocket. 'You'd better have this.'

She drew out the folded paper and held it out.

'In case I'm next.'

◆　◆　◆

Agata strode into the lounge, threw her flying helmet on a low coffee table and flopped into an armchair. 'Whose bloody side do they think we are on?'

Lizzie lowered herself into the chair opposite, stretching out a hand to tickle the chin of Tilly as she ambled past. 'You've got to see their side of it. If you're a black speck in the distance, how are they supposed to know who you are when we're not allowed to use the radios en route?'

'That is not the bloody point. They have recognition charts. Spitfires are not shot at by British anti-aircraft guns. It is people like you who get people like me killed.' Agata jabbed a finger for emphasis.

Lizzie pulled a face. 'Don't blame me. I get shot at too, you know.'

Agata shook her head sadly as Charlie, Niamh and Fizz joined them. 'Every day I am chased by Hurricanes, shot at from the ground, shot at by the Bosch, blown by the wind and surrounded by fog. If I survive this war it will be a bloody miracle.'

'You're lucky none of them can shoot straight,' Fizz said. She waved to the barman. 'Have you still got a bottle of that shite left?' The barman held up a full bottle of dry sherry. Fizz grimaced but beckoned for him to bring it over. 'We'd better have the whole thing.'

Niamh rubbed a hand over her face. 'I did three deliveries today. I'm so tired.'

'I delivered two but it's a good job they were going for repair.' Agata scowled. 'They can patch the holes made by English guns.'

'I had *great* fun.' Fizz gave a wry smile. 'Two Tiger Moths to deliver.'

'Well, be careful,' Charlie said. 'The Germans attacked in droves this morning. Fighter airfields and coastal towns copped it. Things are hotting up.'

'Probably why the gunners were so jittery,' Niamh said.

They paused as a bottle of sherry and five glasses clinked onto the table.

'With the compliments of the flight lieutenant,' the barman said, retreating back to his domain.

All five women glanced in mild surprise towards the bar, where Pendry sat on a stool.

'Thank you, sir,' Agata called across the room as Pendry raised his glass in salute. She turned back, grabbing for the bottle. 'I will be mother.'

'I delivered one Moth,' Charlie said. 'It was supposed to be two, one to service and one back to training, but I came over dizzy and couldn't see straight. The station MO said I had a temperature and not to fly back.'

'Now you mention it, you do look a bit peaky,' Lizzie said, noticing how pale her friend had become. 'There's this influenza thing doing the rounds.'

'Whatever you've got, don't give it to me.' Fizz leant away from Charlie as laughter rippled around the group. 'It's all that fresh air you get in a Moth.'

'As sympathetic as ever,' Niamh said, holding out a glass of sherry for Charlie.

Charlie waved the drink away. 'No thanks, darling. I'm not in the mood. I might have an early night and go to bed straight after dinner.'

'That doesn't sound like you.' Niamh passed the glass on to Lizzie.

Fizz stood and looked at her watch. 'I don't know about you but I'm going to get some scran. Coming?'

Niamh and Agata took their drinks and followed Fizz to the mess. Charlie held back and took Lizzie's arm.

'Are you okay?' Lizzie asked.

'Truthfully?' Charlie said. 'Not really. I'll be surprised if I make it to the briefing tomorrow. I think I'll skip dinner, actually. I feel a bit rough.'

'Something to eat might make you feel better,' Lizzie encouraged.

'Thanks, but really, I just need to rest. You lot go and have fun, don't let me spoil the mood.'

Lizzie gave Charlie a hug. 'Make sure you see the MO in the morning,' she whispered.

CHAPTER
TWENTY-ONE

Kember yawned and rubbed his eyes with finger and thumb. He had
sat in the Wolsey with Wright for only half an hour but the darkness and silence weighed heavy on his eyelids. The sun had set in the
west with a glorious tapestry of colours as they had waited for the
Home Guard to return from their pillbox and checkpoint duties,
before setting off on their own mission. As the eastern horizon transi-
tioned through every shade of blue, pale fingers of searchlight beams
had begun probing the sky, drawing lines of glowing tracer bullets.
Whenever clouds passed across the moon, distinguishing the line of
the Lamberhurst road became difficult. Wright had parked inside the
opening to a field where a dilapidated five-bar gate, broken off one
hinge, afforded easy access. A large bush and overhanging tree provided as much concealment as they could have hoped.

The tumultuous turn of recent events churned inside his head,
making little sense and threatening to reignite his headache. The
introduction of the blackout had seen teenage gangs rob passers-by
in darkened streets, pickpockets target families in air raid shelters and
burglars ransack houses of the scared who had sought the safety of the
shelters. With crime shooting up all over the country, he wondered

how long it would be before manpower shortages and a rising caseload called him back to Tonbridge.

This brought his thoughts back to Lizzie, a familiar feeling of dread settling in his chest. They both knew the danger she faced but still she refused police protection. The tension between himself and Chief Inspector Hartson had increased since Pendry's interference and only Kember's status as a seconded officer from Scotland Yard prevented Hartson pulling him off the case immediately, or demoting him.

Kember stared through the windscreen at another distant line of tracer floating up into the darkness, and the realisation he was stuck in a country lane, too far from Lizzie to help if anything happened, made his stomach churn. He bit the inside of his bottom lip, surprised by the intensity of his disquiet. It was irrational; she was safe. Nevertheless, he decided to abandon the surveillance and was about to call it a night, anxious to return to the village, but Wright held up one finger. Kember listened and nodded as his mind and hearing focused on the sound of an approaching engine. He felt his coat pocket, reassured by the bulk of the six-shot Webley that Wright had insisted he carry. Wright had the other police-issue revolver.

Two horizontal bars of dim light made by blackout masks covering headlights bounced and bobbed closer from the direction of the Scotney village junction. A truck with a dark mound silhouetted in the back passed their position and Wright indicated recognition with a thumbs-up. He waited for a moment before switching on the Wolsey's engine, no headlights, and letting the car roll forward on to the road.

Hanging back to avoid discovery, the moon shedding enough pale illumination to follow at a distance, Wright kept Wingate's truck in sight as it turned into the lane carved through the woodland. After several minutes, the lane evolved into nothing more than the old drovers' road it had once been. Ruts cut by metal-rimmed wooden cartwheels caused the car to bounce violently, shaking its occupants and copying the dance that Wingate's truck performed ahead. After about a quarter of an hour, Wingate's truck halted and Wright pulled to the side of the track with the deepest shadows.

Wright leant sideways and spoke into Kember's ear. 'We're near the air station perimeter, past the main gate and north-west of the manor house. It's about seventy feet from the trees at this point.'

Kember waited for a shape to detach itself from the truck and walk away before he eased open his door and motioned for Wright to circle forward, deep into the woods. Sweet and sour scents from the trees and the musty smell of old fallen leaves decaying on the damp earth filled his nostrils. Kember crept closer, his heart trying to force its way out through his chest while silence screamed in his ears.

He paused as he caught a sound like a distant engine. Not a car or truck but more like an aero engine, several engines.

Then the siren at RAF Scotney began its familiar rising and falling wail to warn of the approaching Luftwaffe.

The chatter at dinner had flown around Lizzie's head, pecking at her eardrums and threatening to give her a headache. After her conversation with Kember the previous evening about the Bible passage, which had given her a disturbed night's sleep, the morning encounter with him had done little to calm her active mind. By the afternoon, the hours had seemed to crawl past in a fog of fatigue that matched the tired aircraft she'd ferried for repairs, and even spending part of the evening in the Hangar Round after dinner failed to lift her spirits. A few women from the NAAFI joined them, their enthusiasm merging into one wall of noise, and no amount of persuasion from Niamh could convince her a night on the sherry was what she needed. Besides, flying required a clear head and the 'eight hours from bottle to throttle' rule was strictly enforced. As the telltale pressure at her temples and the black-and-white barber's pole effect rippling on the edge of her vision signalled a developing migraine, Lizzie decided her friend's choice of an early night would do the trick, and said her goodnights.

Even before she'd reached the bottom stair, the plaintive call of the siren signalled another air raid. Lizzie hesitated, caught in two minds – not relishing another night in the cramped shelter, especially while enduring the pain and nausea of a migraine, but unsure whether staying in the manor house was safe. So far, it had escaped the bombs, even in daylight raids, and a direct hit on a shelter still meant almost certain death. That made up her mind, and she climbed the stairs to check on Charlie before returning to her quarters as officers and staff hurried in the opposite direction.

Kember fought back rising nausea as the wail of Greenway's siren came from the village in answer to that from the air station. An air raid gave the murderer the perfect opportunity to kill again and he hoped Lizzie would do the sensible thing by hurrying to the shelters with everyone else. Standing by Wingate's truck, waves of alarm and dread threatened to expose him and ruin the operation. Now was not the time to be distracted by events he couldn't control, and he shook his head to dislodge thoughts of Lizzie.

Kember lifted one corner of a tarpaulin, releasing a pungent waft of petrol that caught in his throat and revealing the unmistakable shapes of several metal drums standing beneath. He let the corner drop back into place and stepped away, watching the shape of Andy Wingate crouch down and begin to belly crawl.

Wingate reached the perimeter fence, where he lay flat but with his head raised above the tussocks of grass fringing its base. After a moment, he moved his arm forward and seemed to poke something through the metal links of the fence. He then shuffled backwards on his belly until he reached the cover of trees and bushes again, got to his feet and moved to the truck.

The rubber hose by the fence uncoiled as someone pulled it across the grass to the reserve fuel dump. The hose lay still for a moment before it gave a jerk, and this appeared to be the signal Wingate had been waiting for. He took his end of the hose, climbed into the back of his truck and flipped back the tarpaulin. He attached the hose to a stirrup pump and placed the nozzle into a petrol can. With the first bombs already falling to the east of the airfield, Wingate put his foot on the baseplate, gripped the handle with both hands and pumped.

◆　◆　◆

A shiver ran through Lizzie.

She could see the door to her room was pulled to, but not completely shut. She tried to remember whether she had closed and locked it earlier, as certain as she could be that she had. Then she noticed the smell of tobacco smoke, her mind jolting back to the moment she'd found the playing card in the Hangar Round, and a cold dread settled across her shoulders.

Lizzie stood as close to the wall as she could and tried to see into her room through a crack in the door. It wasn't wide enough for her migraine-distorted vision to make out anything inside. She gave the door a gentle push with the toe of her shoe and it swung wide open with the slightest of creaks.

Empty.

Lizzie stepped lightly into the room, her shoes making almost no sound but blood pulsing in her ears so loud she thought anyone might hear it. Clenching her jaw and holding her breath, she stooped to look under the bed.

Nothing there except her shoes.

Smiling with relief at the foolishness of her suspicions, she shut the door, unbuckled her belt, unbuttoned her jacket and sat on the end of the bed. She took two Aspirin and allowed herself a drawn-out yawn before slipping off her shoes and massaging her feet. Feeling the tension and aches slowly dissipating from her soles and toes, Lizzie tried to relax her mind too, to let it meander and find its own way through the jumble of memories and recollections, of happenings and incidents, of conversations and snapshots.

The path always led back to Kember, the killer and her lost friends.

Despite the persistence of her thoughts, Lizzie yawned again. She unknotted the tie from around her neck and stood, sliding the jacket from her shoulders. As she reached for the wardrobe door, it creaked and moved, startling her.

Lizzie half-turned to run and drew breath to scream, but a hand shot out from the opening door and covered her mouth while another sought her throat and tightened. She elbowed backwards and heard a grunt of pain. The grips remained. She clawed at the hands but could get no purchase so she kicked backwards with her bare feet. Pain lanced through her heel as it thudded into shins but the move had the desired effect as another cry of pain came from behind her. The hand over her mouth, smelling faintly of leather, cigarettes and whisky, slid higher to cover her nose. Waves of panic rippled through her at the thought of being suffocated.

Lizzie groped up and back, searching for eyes to gouge or hair to pull but his head remained just out of reach. She elbowed and kicked back again but this time he didn't flinch. His hold was tight, his strength far superior, his purpose clear. She did not want to die like this but her burning lungs were fighting for breath now, head swimming, bright-red lights dancing before her eyes.

Ironically, the Luftwaffe saved her life.

Scotney's anti-aircraft guns put up their best barrage, the sky filling with the dotted lines of tracer bullets and fiery red and orange explosions from air-burst shells. A searchlight probing the dark, more in hope than by design, found a target and deadly fire converged on a German bomber. Bombs fell across the airfield, the ground shaking with every hit, chests resonating with each blast. Wingate never looked up, continuing the up-down motion of pumping petrol from the RAF fuel drums into his own petrol cans.

After twenty minutes of sporadic pounding, the Luftwaffe turned for home and the danger abated. Another twenty minutes passed before the air station and village sirens wailed the all-clear, but Kember continued to wait until Wingate had finished pumping and disconnected the hose. He heard the metallic scrape of caps being screwed back on and saw Wingate jump from the back of the truck.

That's when Kember blew hard on his police whistle, jumped up and shouted, 'Police! You're under arrest.'

Wingate turned and ran towards the perimeter, even as an answering whistle and shouted challenge signalled the arrest of his accomplice inside the fence.

Wright stepped out of the shadows into Wingate's path and pointed his Webley at the man's chest. 'The inspector said, *You're under arrest*. Didn't you hear?'

Wingate turned back to find Kember's Webley raised too.

◆ ◆ ◆

The first stick of bombs fell close to the manor house, a close succession of blasts threatening to shake the windows from their frames. Her assailant hesitated for a split second and Lizzie twisted, kicked and elbowed with every ounce of strength left in her. A shove in the back propelled her to the floor between her bed and the window. A sharp pain shot through her elbow and the room went dark. She thought she was losing consciousness but at least she could breathe. Then she realised the lights had been switched off because of the air raid. All she could see was the fading flicker of the barber's pole.

The familiar creak came from her room door followed by a click as it closed again. She sensed she was alone.

Lizzie pulled herself onto the bed, trembling with physical and emotional shock, and managed to light her bedside candle. The meagre flame shed pale light, revealing the room door closed but the wardrobe gaping. Her attacker had fled.

She allowed herself a few sobs of relief until a nearby explosion had her on her feet as if catapulted, expecting the man to be there again, but the room was still empty.

Lizzie considered calling Kember or finding Pendry but the air raid was in full swing. The loud shattering bangs of German bombs rattled the windows, punctuating the cacophony of chatters and booms from the anti-aircraft guns and the throb of her powerful headache. She hoped the raid would be over soon but knew there was nothing either policeman could do tonight. No one could. Short of resigning from the ATA or posting a guard on her door every night, she would have to take her chances with all the other women on the air station.

There was one security measure she could take herself, though. After closing the wardrobe and locking her room door, she tucked the top rail of her chair under the door handle and pushed the legs with her foot until it jammed in position. Barely satisfied, she doused the candle, slid beneath her bed with a pillow as refuge from any falling ceiling plaster dislodged by the bombing, and got ready for what she knew would be another unsettled night.

CHAPTER
TWENTY-TWO

Lizzie rose in the early hours, unable to sleep properly even having returned to her bed after the all-clear. Checking the chair was still wedged in place, she went over to the chimney breast and felt inside for the manila envelope she'd hidden out of sight on a narrow masonry projection. She sat on her bed, tipped out the service records and arranged them in front of her. She read the files of Hammond and Stapleton first but found little of real interest. Then she opened Matfield's file and ran her forefinger along particular entries until she'd finished reading.

Closing the file, Lizzie relaxed her eyes and slipped into her familiar daydream state. She visualised Matfield as he fought the Germans on the Western Front in 1918 after being shot down. She heard the artillery bombardment in her head and physically flinched. She felt the fear of mortal combat, the elation at having survived and the desolation of having witnessed death close up.

Lizzie blinked and forced herself to look at the next file.

Reading through Dallington's service record with the occasional nod, the entry detailing his behaviour towards the WAAF went through her with a jolt. She'd thought Dallington the product of a passing age, one of the old school, steeped in the British Empire, gentlemen's clubs and what they considered to be honour. She disliked his kind but the world was full of such men. In spite of her dislike, she'd rationalised his attitude towards the ATA as a misplaced and extreme version of chivalry, wanting to protect the little ladies from harm. More fool her.

Leaving her room earlier than usual, she checked on Charlie. Finding her still sleeping, Lizzie took the decision to let her rest and went downstairs. Dropping in at the ops room hoping for a first look at the day's work, she was surprised by the absence of ferry chits. After breakfast, she went to tell Pendry about the attack and tracked him to Dallington's office. Intending initially to wait for him, she suddenly found herself close enough to overhear him and Flight Sergeant Ben Vickers giving their report of the previous night's operation and the fate of the petrol thieves.

Lizzie could tell Dallington was not in the best of moods from the tone of his response. She knew that indiscipline was a huge bugbear of his and could guess the fury that thieving would evoke. Another voice Lizzie recognised as Matfield's, muted by the closed door, spoke briefly before a telephone rang. She listened to Dallington appearing to have a one-way conversation until the clunk of a telephone receiver being replaced firmly in its cradle and the rasp of a striking match reached her ears. A noise nearby made Lizzie glance around but, confident she was still alone, she tuned in again to the conversation within the office.

'My prayers have been answered, gentlemen,' Dallington said. 'Mostly.'

'How so, sir?' Matfield asked.

'That was Keith Park of Eleven Group over at Uxbridge. He's been on the telephone to Fighter Command at Bentley Priory this morning. Speaking to Stuffy.'

'Sir Hugh Dowding?' Matfield sounded surprised. 'What about?'

'Us, apparently. They've made us fully operational again.'

'That's excellent news. But you said *mostly*, sir?'

'We're not getting squadrons back on a permanent basis,' Dallington explained. 'We're to become a forward airfield. The squadrons will fly in at first light, wait at readiness for a scramble and fly back to Biggin Hill at night.'

Lizzie could almost hear the self-satisfaction dripping from Dallington and sensed there was more to come.

'Any more good news, sir?' The thinly disguised sarcasm in Pendry's voice surprised Lizzie. 'I get the impression that's not all.'

Dallington coughed theatrically. 'The air raids have increased and Stuffy expects Jerry to come back with a vengeance after last night, so the powers that be have decided it's too dangerous for the little women to fly. They can't ferry Spits and Hurries anyway so they're useless as far as I'm concerned.' Lizzie gasped as, with a note of triumph in his voice, Dallington said, 'I've been ordered to ground those bloody women.'

A moment's silence seeped under the door until Pendry asked, 'Are they being transferred?'

Dallington growled. 'Unfortunately not. Their orders are to stand down and await further instructions.'

As Lizzie turned away in disgust, she heard the clink of a bottle and glasses, and Dallington's voice thick with smugness.

'A toast, gentlemen. One step closer to getting rid.'

Wingate sat opposite Kember and Wright in the back room of Scotney Police Station, the table marking a no-man's land between them.

Kember knew Wingate had been in this position before. With a criminal record containing counts of theft, burglary and receiving stolen goods, he had the air of a man confident his punishment would be the usual. He viewed prison as an occupational hazard well worth the risk. The hint of a smile on his lips and the way he sat back in his chair told Kember that Wingate believed he had the situation under control. His first job was to break that belief.

'Can you take these handcuffs off, please,' Wingate said in a quiet voice.

Kember ignored him and continued to look at the papers in a cardboard file on his lap. He had long ago learnt that the rich and powerful do things at their own pace, believing others should pay due deference to them. If you had the money, information, authority and power, you made others wait until you were ready. Another full minute passed. Kember tapped the top sheet in the file.

'I suspect you know all about the Larceny Act, don't you, Mr Wingate?' Keeping his head bowed towards the file, Kember's eyes looked up. 'You and your accomplice were observed by no fewer than two Kent police officers and several from the RAF Police, using a stirrup pump and a length of rubber hose to siphon petrol into a number of petrol cans and drums placed in the back of your truck. Your intention was to sell it on the black market or top up your own garage petrol tank to sell to motorists from the pump on your forecourt. How am I doing?'

Wingate shrugged in a symbol of submission. 'All right, I admit it; you caught me at it anyway, but it was a one-off.' He threw a quick glance towards the door as Wright stifled a snorted laugh.

'What my colleague is trying to convey, not very eloquently, is that we already know this is not a one-off. Sergeant Wright has been over your truck and found three drums and fourteen cans full of petrol. He had a cursory look around your garage and found a further eight full cans but no paperwork to prove they have been acquired legally. Purely out of curiosity, I had a little rummage around in the old barn where you keep your truck before heading out into the night, as you did last night. Want to hazard a guess at what I found?'

Wingate stared back at Kember. 'Horse shit, pig shit and cow shit. The smell of the countryside.'

Kember gave Wingate a cold smile. 'That too, but I did uncover thirty-five more petrol cans. As a guess, I'd say that once it's been tested it'll prove to be eighty-seven per cent high octane. In other words, aviation fuel.'

'Not mine.'

'Fingerprints may prove otherwise. I take it you thought gloves an unnecessary handicap because you'd never be caught?' Kember waited and was rewarded with a slight flicker of nervousness from Wingate. 'Where were you on the night of the ninth of July?'

Wingate looked puzzled at the change of direction. 'I was in the pub,' he said, his voice not so haughty.

'And after?'

'I left with Bert. Bert Garner. He went his way home and I went mine.'

Kember shook his head and forced a thin smile. 'So you're saying you went nowhere else except home after you left the Castle public house?'

'That's what I said. Brian Greenway, the ARP warden, saw me.'

'Ever seen one of those?' Kember placed a fingerprint sheet on the table.

Wingate glanced at the sheet. 'Of course I have.'

'These are the results of a test carried out on fingerprints recovered from a car belonging to Mr Garner. This sheet tells me those fingerprints, found on the petrol cap the morning after he had all his petrol stolen by siphoning, belong to you.'

Wingate swallowed hard but kept his face impassive. 'They're my fingerprints because I took the cap off when Bert came to fill up with petrol.'

Kember made a face of exaggerated disbelief. 'Mr and Mrs Garner assure us they cleaned and polished his car after visiting your garage. No one else had touched the car. We found their fingerprints on the handles of the doors and boot but nowhere else outside. The only other prints we found were yours, on the petrol cap. Oh yes, and on the rubber hose.'

Wingate's presence seemed to have diminished and he looked smaller. The corners of Kember's mouth twitched but he managed not to smile.

'The boys from Tonbridge Police Station will be all over reported petrol thefts to see whether they can match fingerprints found elsewhere to yours.' Kember retrieved the fingerprint sheet. 'If that was all, you'd be in a lot of trouble.' He paused. 'But that's not all.'

Wingate frowned and opened his mouth in confusion. 'What do you mean, not all? Of course it is. What are you trying to frame me for?'

'The aviation fuel belonged to the RAF, which is fighting to protect this country from invasion. Any act that could aid and abet the enemy or undermine the efforts of the forces of the Crown could be interpreted as an act of treason felony. In fact the Treachery Act was passed this year for such occurrences.'

Wingate was aghast. 'You've got to be joking? I was trying to make some extra money, not help the Germans.'

Wright, who had been taking a note of the interview in stony silence, leant forward, contempt on his face, and growled, 'Every crime helps the Germans when we're at war.'

Kember put another sheet on the table as Wright sat back, and hoped they weren't going too far in rattling Wingate's cage. 'These are the details of the post-mortem conducted on Lavinia Scott. She was murdered on the night of the ninth of July, right across the road from where you were siphoning petrol from Mr Garner's car and at almost exactly the same time.'

Wingate shook his head in disbelief at the inference.

'I suggest Lavinia Scott saw what you were doing and came over to confront you. You tried to keep her quiet and, whether by accident or in anger, you killed her.'

Wingate held out his cuffed hands like a plea. 'No.' He shook his head furiously.

'What I don't understand is why you couldn't leave it at that.'

Wingate leant forward for the first time and put his cuffed hands on the table. 'I didn't, I swear. You've seen my record. I'm a thief. I sell stolen stuff. I don't hurt anyone. I've never even been in a fight.' His furrowed forehead carried a sheen of perspiration and his breathing had become fast and shallow.

Kember returned the papers to the file. 'We're going to search your garage and house and remove all the knives and blades we can find. If any has the slightest trace of blood or we find any other evidence to suggest you were with Lavinia Scott the night she was murdered, we will not be relying on the Treachery Act.'

Wingate's mouth moved but no sound emerged as Kember stood and opened the door. Stepping through, he turned to Wright. 'Keep him in the cells until I get back. No visitors. I don't want him speaking to anyone or being transferred to Tonbridge until Pendry and I have concluded our business at the air station.'

'Aye, sir,' Wright acknowledged.

Kember had reached the front door, his mind already on the forthcoming interviews, when a machine-gun jangle of bells jolted him. He glanced back to the room where Wright was coaxing Wingate to hurry up, and stepped into the office to answer the telephone.

◆　◆　◆

'I heard you had a good night last night,' Lizzie said without introduction when Kember answered her telephone call.

Kember laughed. 'News certainly travels fast in the countryside. Yes, we caught the men behind the petrol thefts.'

Lizzie thought he sounded as tired as she felt as she heard the laughter leave his voice.

'That's good news, surely?' she said.

'Maybe, but I haven't caught the murderer yet and that's what I'll be judged on.'

Lizzie knew Kember's failure to make quick progress troubled him but, as much as she wanted to avoid heaping more onto his shoulders, she knew she had to tell him about her ordeal.

'I . . .' Lizzie hesitated.

'Something wrong?' Kember asked. 'Are you all right?'

'Don't worry when I tell you this because I'm absolutely fine, but I was attacked in my room during the air raid last night—'

'Jesus Christ—'

'He ran off when the bombs got a bit close.' She felt breathless saying it and pinged the rubber band for comfort.

'That's the final straw.' Kember's voice had changed and he seemed completely alert now. 'What did Pendry say? You need to get away from Scotney, quickly.'

Lizzie detected genuine concern for her safety rather than any hint of the knight on horseback rescuing the damsel in distress, but she dismissed his suggestion. 'You know I can't do that,' she said in a way that brooked no argument. 'None of us are leaving or else he's won.'

'I'm coming up there—'

'No need,' she snapped.

'It's my job,' Kember said. 'Anyway, I'm meeting Pendry this morning to question Hammond and Stapleton. Don't touch anything. We'll need to dust for fingerprints.'

'When are you seeing him?'

Kember paused and Lizzie imagined him looking at his watch. 'In an hour.'

'Don't say anything to him. Can you meet me on the terrace beforehand?' She swallowed, her mouth suddenly dry. 'I've read the service records.'

'Of course,' he said. 'I can be there in twenty minutes.'

Feeling the tension rising within her, she opened the release valve and began rearranging the stationery on the desk as she spoke. 'That's great. I have to go but there is one more thing. We've got a special briefing today and I can guess what it's about. I overheard Dallington and Matfield talking. Scotney is now a forward airfield for Biggin Hill. That means the ATA have been grounded.'

'I'm sorry to hear that,' Kember said, 'but it has to be for the best under the circumstances. To keep you safe.'

Lizzie knew he had her best interests in mind, but the insinuation that men were always the protectors and women the protected made her angry.

When Lizzie said nothing Kember filled the silence. 'It'll be until we've won the air battle, that's all, then they'll need aircraft ferrying again.'

'We're not allowed to fly fighters,' Lizzie reminded him, her voice carrying a hard edge.

'They'll soon see sense. You women are good pilots and absolutely capable of flying anything.'

She knew they were platitudes but her mood softened at his words. As she put the handset back in its cradle, something niggled at her that she couldn't put her finger on and she found herself picking the skin around her fingernails, unable to ward off the familiar pressure across her chest. As her breathing became shallower and more rapid, Lizzie retreated to her room to combat the signs of an oncoming panic attack.

CHAPTER
TWENTY-THREE

Unwilling to face further ridicule from Fizz and the others, Lizzie led Kember away from prying eyes and waggling ears on the terrace as soon as he arrived and took him to her favourite spot at the end of the gardens.

'Are you sure you're all right?' Kember asked.

Lizzie disregarded the worry etched on his face. 'That's the tenth time you've asked,' she said, irritated by his persistence. 'And, no, I don't want more police protection, or evacuating.'

'But every time there's an air raid—'

She showed her palm to stop him. 'The killer mucked it up and won't try that with me again. He knows I'm wise to him and we're too close for you to send me away now.' She took out a packet of cigarettes and sat on a low stone wall. 'And don't you dare tell Pendry. He was in the meeting discussing our fate with Dallington and Matfield. I don't want to give them any more reasons for withdrawing us, whatever their motives.'

Kember remained standing and brought out his pocket book, his face pinched with concern and frustration. 'I can't give any guarantees, and I had to tell Sergeant Wright, but we'll keep it under our hats for now. You'd better tell me everything you remember about what happened before and during the attack.'

'It's a bit fuzzy, actually,' Lizzie said as she fidgeted with her cigarette packet. 'I'd checked on Charlie before going to my room because I had a migraine: flashing lights, headache, the lot. It really messes with my eyes and thoughts so I can't give you much of a description.' She pocketed her cigarettes. 'The door to my room was slightly ajar, which I thought was very odd. It's not exactly a spacious suite at the Savoy and I checked that no one was inside or under the bed. I took two Aspirin and was about to hang up my jacket when he burst out of the wardrobe.'

'The wardrobe?' Kember echoed, eyebrows raised.

'Yes,' Lizzie said. 'I had turned to run when I heard something just before, but he grabbed me around the neck and I couldn't scream. As far as I knew, Charlie and I were the only ones not in the shelters anyway.'

'Can you describe anything about him? The smallest or broadest detail would help.'

'I know it was a man, taller than me, and strong. From the feel of his jacket, I'd say he was in uniform.' Lizzie shuddered involuntarily. 'He smelt of cigarettes, leather and booze but didn't say anything. He grunted when I kicked him, so he might have a bruise on his shin.'

Kember blew air through puffed cheeks. 'You do realise that could describe most of the men around here? And I can't ask every man to roll his trousers up. I'm not a Freemason.'

Lizzie suppressed a smile and tapped the manila envelope in her lap. 'I read the files and had a good think about what we know. It's obvious Lavinia went to meet the killer but Hammond, Stapleton and Wingate aren't the suave and sophisticated type she liked. The reverend is handsome, but Lavinia wasn't religious and that would've put her off.'

'You don't think Emily went to meet the killer?'

Lizzie heard the scepticism in Kember's voice.

'Of course not,' she said. 'I think her routine of walking and smoking in the evening combined with the air raid provided an opportunity he couldn't pass up.'

'Could still mean she and Lavinia saw something that got them killed,' Kember said. 'People have been known to kill for less than a gallon of petrol.'

Lizzie almost laughed. 'You'd be surprised what people kill for, or maybe you wouldn't, but Lavinia hadn't been in the village long enough to put herself in that kind of danger.'

'Any thoughts on Hammond?' Kember asked. 'We're questioning him first.'

Lizzie tucked her hair behind her ears and passed the envelope to Kember, aware of him watching her every move.

'I'm sure it's not Hammond,' she said, frowning. 'It doesn't feel right; his background doesn't fit with what I know about serial murderers.'

'Serial murderers?' Kember said doubtfully. 'I've never heard that term.'

'I don't like the label mass murderer because these people kill in a sequence, sometimes over days, months or years, not all at once. I know two victims isn't much of a series but the similarities are too striking to be coincidence.'

'Sometimes crooks get themselves in a tight spot and become murderers.'

'But two tight spots in two weeks?' Lizzie shook her head. 'Hammond's crimes are against authority and for petty theft, mainly of food. This is typical of someone who grew up in poverty. He has the looks but not the sophistication to lure Lavinia and overpower both girls. He might see himself as God's gift to women but I'd be surprised if he's the murderer.'

Lizzie reached for the packet in her pocket, thought about her cigarettes then changed her mind. This was her solitary, private smoking place. Lighting up while Kember was here would sully it somehow.

'If Hammond is sneaking off from guard duty,' Kember said, 'Stapleton must know and be covering for him. As you suggested, that would make Stapleton the accomplice. In your opinion, would either of them be capable of murder if discovered in the throes of committing another crime?'

'Everyone is capable of murder,' she said.

Lizzie's gaze met Kember's and remained locked for a few seconds until the sound of a call broke the spell. They turned and saw Pendry standing on the terrace.

'It seems our chat is cut short,' Kember said. 'Shall we meet later for a pot of tea?'

'Of course,' Lizzie agreed, blushing at the thoughts she imagined going through Pendry's mind.

Hammond sat on one side of a writing desk in one of the smaller rooms in the manor house. On the other side, neither Kember nor Pendry seemed in any hurry. An RAF Police officer sat at a bureau against one wall, its flap down to allow the officer to rest his notebook and record the interview. Another stood guard inside the door. Hammond swiped a film of sweat from his top lip and ran his fingers across the regulation short hair on his head. Kember noted this nervousness with satisfaction while pretending to watch Pendry read a set of typed sheets.

'I've already spoken to your accomplice, Andrew Wingate,' Kember said eventually, keeping his tone neutral. Hammond licked his lips and swallowed. A dry mouth: another good sign.

Hammond's eyes seemed to vibrate in their sockets as he looked back and forth between Kember and Pendry, then he gave Kember a knowing smile. 'You caught us red-handed so it's obvious we were nicking pet—'

'You think you're nicked for pilfering?' Kember interrupted, wanting to snuff out any hint of emerging bravado. 'If the RAF can't defend this country because you've sold their petrol, Jerry can invade when he likes. You are undermining the war effort like some fifth columnist. That, sonny Jim, could be construed as treason felony.'

Kember saw Hammond's inner turmoil displayed on his face, his body slumping as he came to terms with the implications.

Hammond's voice squeaked. 'It was a bit of nicking, that's all.'

With a glance at Pendry, Kember continued. 'We can't think of one good reason why *a bit of nicking* might make you want to kill a woman.'

Hammond's body stiffened. 'What?' His eyes pleaded with Pendry, his response catching in his throat, his jaw flapping without sound.

Pendry continued to sit in silence with jaw set and his stony glare fixed on Hammond's face.

Kember looked at another sheet of paper. 'Did you allow Wingate to access the air station by letting him through the gatehouse?'

He shook his head but Kember saw a tell-tale flicker of his eyes.

'Did you leave the air station on those occasions you deserted your post?'

'No.' Hammond's head shook vigorously again and his voice dropped to almost a whisper.

Kember leant forward, elbows on the desk. 'If both those statements are true, we have to believe the first murdered girl, Lavinia

Scott, saw Wingate and he killed her to keep her quiet. It follows that you killed Emily Parker to keep her quiet.'

Hammond was close to tears, his eyes sparkling as they filled. 'I didn't. I couldn't do that. Not to a woman. Not to anyone. Not for a bit of flippin' petrol.' A sob escaped as tears trickled down both cheeks. 'I've never killed anyone.' He pulled out a square of grey cloth that passed for a handkerchief and rubbed his eyes with it.

Pendry leant forward for the first time and said in a low but powerful voice Kember hadn't heard him use before, 'Tell us what you know about the petrol and I can help you.'

Hammond sniffed, avoiding Pendry's glare by staring at the table. 'I met Andy Wingate in the Castle pub, when me and a few others went down to the village. I got a bit drunk and the next thing I know I've agreed to help him siphon petrol from the reserve dump.' Hammond sniffed again. 'He said he had a nice little earner going, siphoning petrol from cars and trucks and topping up his garage tank. He said if I helped him we'd make a packet and split it fifty–fifty.' He paused.

'Go on,' Kember encouraged in a soft voice.

Hammond swallowed hard. 'He said he would poke a rubber hose on a string through the fence and all I had to do was pull the string until the hose reached the dump, unscrew a petrol drum, stick the hose in and give it a tug to show it was ready. When he'd finished he would give a tug and I'd take it out before screwing the cap back on. Then he'd pull the hose back through the fence.'

He raised his chin and Kember caught his eye. 'Did Emily Parker twig or did she see you?'

'I've told you, all I did was nick petrol.'

'Stapleton must have been in on it?'

The man shifted with discomfort and Kember could sense his internal struggle.

'Yeah,' Hammond croaked. 'Stapleton knew what I was up to but didn't like it. I said he could have a bit of my cut if he kept quiet and covered for me.'

'And did he?' Kember said.

'The first time, he said no, but I went anyway. When I came back he looked terrified. Said we'd been inspected and he'd had to lie about me having a touch of the trots, you know, diarrhoea. I had him, didn't I? He'd covered for me so he was part of the scam.' Hammond paused and looked down to his left, avoiding eye contact. Kember recognised the familiar sign.

'I really don't know any more,' he whined. 'It was just a bit of petrol.'

Hammond looked in real pain and Kember knew they'd pushed him as far as they could for now. He looked at Pendry, raised his eyebrows and glanced at the door.

'All right, Hammond,' Pendry snapped. 'Back to your cell.' He nodded to the guard, who took Hammond from the room and closed the door.

Kember stood and stretched. He wandered to the window and looked out at men scurrying back and forth like ants, repairing the airfield, filling in craters, checking sandbags and rearming the defensive guns. He perched on the window sill and looked back at Pendry.

'Wingate is capable of taking the lead and Hammond looks the type of chap to follow. Below him in the pecking order will be Stapleton, the reluctant accomplice.' Kember grimaced as numbness spread throughout his leg. He stood up and rubbed his thigh. 'Is he capable of murder?' He turned the corners of his mouth down and shook his head. 'He looked genuinely alarmed to be accused of that and became more panicky as we went on.'

He bent to rub life back into his knee and spotted a crumpled piece of paper next to the chair in which Hammond had been sitting. 'What have we here?' He picked it from the floor and smoothed it out on the table, revealing a typed note.

'Keep quiet,' Pendry read. 'Is he being threatened?'

Kember felt a stab of annoyance and prodded the tabletop with his finger. 'I have to see Dallington before I leave.' He stood and opened the door, spoke to the guard outside who listened and left. 'I need a leg stretch before we see Stapleton,' he said to Pendry. 'Fifteen minutes do you?'

Pendry stood. 'Good idea.'

Lizzie was about to follow Charlie into the lounge when Kember appeared on the other side of the hall. The first thing she noticed was his crooked tie and it took all her self-restraint not to reach over and fix it.

'A bit early for that tea but I don't mind,' she said, smiling.

Kember smiled back. 'I can't at the moment, I'm afraid. Still questioning. It looks like Wingate and Hammond are involved with no more than the theft of petrol and I believe neither have it in them to kill. We're about to interview Stapleton, an altogether softer lad. I wanted your opinion on how to handle him.'

Kember's request for advice appealed directly to her professional curiosity as usual, and she looked away, thinking. When she turned back, her mind had retrieved and processed the relevant information. 'From what I remember of his service record, he's the weaker of the two. Hammond will be the leader, the one who has the ideas and carries them through. Stapleton will follow out of loyalty and needing a friend, wanting to be liked, but I doubt his courage or loyalties would run to murder. If he's involved in anything at all it will be the likes of thieving. Hammond is tough on the outside but he needs the support of a friend as much as his schoolmate does. I'd have to say Stapleton is the one most likely to break down emotionally and mentally, so you'll have to be careful. If he starts to crack under the strain it'll not be because he won't want to talk; he won't be able to because his mind will be shutting down to protect itself. Whereas Hammond might respond to a few threats about the consequences, Stapleton should respond to cajoling and gentle questioning.'

Kember looked at her in surprise. 'Good grief. Where did all that come from?'

Lizzie's cheeks reddened and she looked at his chest, unable to meet his gaze. 'I remember stuff, especially if I'm interested.'

'Well, I'm glad you're interested,' he said. 'I'll see you later.'

'Before you go.' Lizzie reached up, unable to resist any longer, wrapping her fingers around Kember's tie, straightening it to his surprise while muttering, 'I hate disorder.'

Stapleton was far more jittery than Hammond. His wide eyes darted looks around the room, hands trembling like a frightened child's, cheeks flushed the red of a postage stamp. Kember found himself feeling sorry for him, the one at the bottom of the food chain in terms of his military, personal and criminal relationships. There always seemed to be a Stapleton – someone needy and vulnerable – at the bottom, trying to be liked, trying to do the right thing, trying to get by and failing on all counts.

After his discussion with Lizzie, Kember had spoken to Pendry and agreed a softer line. Stapleton had accepted the offer of a mug of tea but the warm, mud-brown brew sat untouched on the table, a wrinkled skin forming on the surface. Kember reckoned his appearance seemed even more akin to a schoolboy's than when he'd first seen him. The uniform made no contribution to him looking like a man, and gave the impression that he had got it from a playroom's dressing-up box moments before.

Stapleton proceeded to give a faltering account that pretty much matched Hammond's. After a while, he opened and closed his mouth without speaking, licked his lips and looked away as if searching for an escape route. Kember sensed a wall coming up and suspected the interview had almost run its course.

Stapleton began a gentle back and forth rocking motion. 'I didn't do or see anything, sir. That's the truth. I stayed in my gate-house and looked the other way. Hammond gave me some cash now and again, said it was my hush money. I didn't want it but he stuffed it in my jacket pocket. I haven't spent it. You can have it. It's all in a bag under my mattress.'

Kember leant forward and put a reassuring hand on the man's forearm but the young private jerked his arm away, shooting an imploring look at Pendry.

'All right, son, we'll leave it there.' Kember's voice had softened again. 'All right?'

Stapleton's eyes brimmed full of tears.

At a signal from Pendry, the guard took Stapleton by the arm and they left the room. Before the door closed, another of Pendry's RAF Police officers rapped on the door, entered at Pendry's command and handed Kember a brown paper bag.

'We found this in Stapleton's room, sir, under his mattress, but nothing in Hammond's room.'

Kember had a quick look inside the bag and said, 'Thank you.'

He waited for the man to leave before upending the paper bag, its contents spilling onto the table.

Pendry picked up a small wad of one-pound notes. 'There's a few bob here. Not a lot in the grand scheme of things but if it's for looking the other way and keeping your mouth shut, the other two must be making a packet.'

'A tidy sum,' Kember agreed. He picked up a small piece of white paper that had also been in the bag and unfolded it. It appeared to be blank until he turned it over and saw the typed phrase: *Keep quiet*. He handed it to Pendry. 'Look at this.'

Pendry took a breath. 'Same as Hammond's.' He slid the matching piece across to Kember. 'In common parlance, someone's put the frighteners on them. Still think it could be Dallington?'

Kember shrugged. 'I still think it could be a lot of people, but the field is narrowing and some are looking more likely than others. Until we have something solid against any of them, we'll be on thin ice. We'd better go have that word with the group captain.'

CHAPTER TWENTY-FOUR

Kember and Pendry took the two seats offered, but declined a whisky. Dallington looked at his watch, hesitated and replaced the bottle in his cupboard. He turned back, put his hands on his stomach and interlaced his fingers.

Having waited for Dallington to give them his full attention, Kember remained deliberately silent for a few seconds longer until anger flashed in the RAF officer's eyes. Smiling inwardly with childish satisfaction, Kember said, 'I'm sorry it's become necessary to visit you again, Group Captain.'

'So am I, Inspector.' He glanced at Pendry who stared back mutely, fiddling with the back of his gloves.

'As you are aware, two men guarding the gatehouse were arrested on the air station last night and charged with the theft of petrol.'

'I am aware of that, yes.' Dallington's eyes dulled with obvious disinterest.

'We arrested another criminal last night, a civilian, outside the perimeter fence while engaged in the same theft.'

'And your point is?'

With Dallington's attitude already getting to him, Kember fought back his rising temper. In an effort to calm himself, he studied the bookshelf behind Dallington. As his gaze roamed along the assorted works he saw two misaligned books towards the far end. He stood, brushed the top of his trousers and, enjoying the look of outraged confusion on Dallington's face, moved to the far side of the room to study a framed painting.

'My point is,' Kember said at last, leaning forward as if to inspect the brushwork, 'a good deal of petrol has been stolen from this air station on your watch, under your nose, so to speak, which begs the question as to whether someone senior knew about it.'

Dallington almost spluttered in anger. 'I hope you are not implying that person is me, Inspector?'

Kember ignored the question. 'You see, to my mind, someone had to turn a blind eye, otherwise the whole enterprise would have been impossible.'

'Now look here . . .'

Kember left the painting and moved around the wall with slow, careful steps. 'Flight Lieutenant Pendry and I have interviewed the three men and discovered another issue. It appears someone is intimidating them to keep silent and, judging by their reluctance to say anything, I'm guessing it must be a senior officer.'

Dallington's face turned red with barely suppressed rage. Kember saw Pendry touch the holster where his pistol nestled.

'That is the most preposterous thing I have ever heard. We are gentlemen in His Majesty's Royal Air Force, not common criminals.'

'I'm aware most of you have exemplary records.' Kember gave Dallington a polite bow of his head, despite the incident with the WAAF flashing across his mind's eye. 'The fact remains that the flight lieutenant and I have found evidence—'

Dallington stood up as if catapulted from his chair. 'What evidence? Let me see.'

'Please sit, Group Captain. I'm afraid I can't reveal the nature of the evidence at the moment. Suffice to say, it does prove that two Air Ministry Wardens have got themselves into a bit of a fix.'

Dallington slowly backed down, his face volcanic. 'What kind of fix?' He shot a look at Pendry, who appeared unconcerned.

'We believe this officer discovered the theft and decided to blackmail the two warders into looking the other way or covering for him while he went about other business.'

Dallington frowned. 'What other business could there be?'

Kember turned to the two misaligned books. 'May I?'

Dallington waved a hand dismissively.

Kember pulled one volume from the shelf, a weighty book about an old criminal case. Upon replacing it, he took the other book. His heart almost stopped and the back of his neck prickled. He fought to keep his face impassive as he flicked through the pages.

'What other business, Inspector?'

Kember cleared his throat to disguise his emotions. 'We have reason to believe this officer has a free run around this air station and the village and murdered both Lavinia Scott and Emily Parker.'

Dallington's mouth flapped a few times before a sound managed to escape. 'One of *my* officers? But who?'

'We have our suspects, but in the meantime you should keep this to yourself. I hear the air station has become operational again. You have my congratulations, if that's the appropriate sentiment. I'm sure you're all very busy so you need to focus on your jobs. Pendry and I will be doing ours and will keep you informed, of course.'

Dallington's face had paled at the revelation and all his previous bluster seemed to have evaporated. Kember wasn't sure whether this was real or an act, but he suspected the latter.

He waved the book at Dallington. 'May I borrow this?'

'What?' Dallington seemed dazed. 'No, of course not.'

Kember was taken aback at the refusal. 'May I ask why not?'

'Because I'm not in the habit of letting strangers borrow my personal possessions.'

'But I'm a police officer.'

'Precisely. You're not RAF. I don't know you from Adam.'

Kember hadn't expected such recalcitrance and was annoyed at having to spell out his request in officialese. 'Respectfully, I make a request in my official capacity as a Kent Constabulary officer to borrow your property, this book, for a short period in connection with an ongoing investigation.'

'What do you mean, in connection with?'

'Have you read it?' When Dallington continued to stare, Kember reiterated: 'The book, have you read it?'

'What? Yes, yes, of course I have,' Dallington said. 'I find it interesting. Why would I have books on my shelves I haven't read or that serve no purpose?'

Kember saw Pendry staring at him. 'My thoughts exactly, Group Captain. As my mother used to say, a place for everything and everything in its place.'

'I suppose so.' Dallington still looked puzzled, like a toddler told off for something he was sure he didn't do but was trying to work out if he had. 'Look, if you wanted to read the damn thing, you only needed to ask.'

Kember tucked the book under his arm and retrieved his fedora. 'I did.' He donned his hat and gave a polite touch to the brim. Pendry took this as his cue to stand and they both moved to the door. 'Good day, Group Captain. I'm sure we'll have the chance to talk again.'

◆ ◆ ◆

Once back in Pendry's office, Kember could hardly contain himself. He placed the book on the table as soon as Pendry sat.

'What in God's name was that all about?' Pendry said, reaching for his bottle of gin. He waved it at Kember, who shook his head, before pouring a mouthful into a mug.

'I wanted to rattle him,' Kember said, savouring the feeling while it lasted. It had been a long time since he'd felt such professional satisfaction.

Pendry raised his eyebrows. 'You did that all right. I thought he was going to have a heart attack, or shoot you. Don't get me wrong, having Dallington or Matfield squirming with discomfort is fine by me; all I'm saying is you could have taken it a bit steadier.'

Kember looked thoughtful. 'I agree and I apologise.' He pulled out a clean folded handkerchief, shook it open and used it to handle the book he had placed on the desk. 'But I had good reason.' He turned the book around.

Pendry's eyes widened. 'Good God.' he exclaimed, and then read aloud. '*Jack the Ripper or When London Walked in Terror.*' He reached for the thin volume lying on the table but Kember pulled it away.

'Sorry,' Kember said in response to Pendry's pained expression. 'I want to send this for testing.'

Pendry looked up with the hint of a smile. 'So it *is* Dallington.'

'It's looking that way. I've seen a book with this title before, and a few others like it. If you combine all the details of the Whitechapel murders you can assemble a pretty good picture of each. It appears we owe Sergeant Wright an apology. He said all along the murders looked like the work of Jack the Ripper.' Kember held up a hand to stop Pendry interjecting. 'It's not the Ripper himself but we can be pretty certain that someone is copying him.'

'Even if this points to Dallington, how can we prove it? We have nothing more than circumstantial evidence and you've just put a flare up that we're on to him.'

Kember frowned. 'I'll get this off to Tonbridge for fingerprint testing. I want to make sure who's handled it, for the official record. I'd kick myself if Dallington later denied ownership and his prints weren't actually on it.'

Pendry held out his hand. 'Shall I get one of our couriers to take it?'

Kember waved away the offer. 'I'll need to take the fingerprints of everyone who had access to Dallington's office and this book, to have something to compare it with. Sergeant Wright should still have the kit I brought over from Tonbridge. I'll call him here to take the prints and get them to Tonbridge with the book for transfer to Scotland Yard.'

'Good idea. Wright can set out the kit in the briefing room and I'll wheel Dallington and Matfield in together. They'll have fits, but I can remind them of military law and they'll have to fall in line, however much they squirm and shout.'

'You sound like you'll enjoy it.'

Pendry smiled. 'It's good to get one up on them now and again. Almost as good as a night out at the Ritz picture house.'

Kember smiled back and pointed to the book. 'Have you got something I can put this in, to keep the prints fresh?'

Pendry opened a drawer and extracted a buff internal-mail envelope. A few names had been written in the numbered sections and crossed off when delivered. Pendry took a pen, put two lines through the last entry containing his own name, and reached for the book.

Kember took the envelope instead, slipped the book into the pocket and tucked in the top flap. 'Do you mind if I use your telephone?'

Pendry turned the instrument and Kember dialled Scotney Police Station.

'No time like the present.'

◆ ◆ ◆

Lizzie resigned herself to not seeing Kember for afternoon tea, so long had he and Pendry been engaged in what she assumed were questioning and other investigative pursuits. She was caught unawares by her disappointment and felt annoyed at herself because another let-down should not have come as a surprise.

Kember's hurried, almost flustered entry into the lounge changed her mind immediately, but she tried to feign disinterest as he dragged his chair out with a harsh scraping noise and sat.

Kember was about to speak but he and Lizzie sat back while a steward delivered a tray with two cups and saucers, a pot of tea and a small jug of milk to their table. Four plain biscuits sat forlorn on an over-large white plate. As Kember sat forward again, she found herself leaning in as he spoke in a low voice.

'Before you ask, Sergeant Wright is on his way with the finger-print kit. We questioned Hammond, Stapleton and Wingate and I'm still convinced they're nothing more than thieves, but they are frightened of someone.'

Unable to resist being drawn in, even though being kept waiting still rankled, Lizzie fixed her alert eyes on Kember's.

'They wouldn't say who, but it must be an officer,' Kember said, and followed with a brief summary of the questioning while Lizzie poured their tea.

Lizzie manoeuvred a cup across to him.

'I've been doing some more thinking.' When he smiled, she said, 'I can't switch off once I've got something inside my head.'

'Go on,' he encouraged.

'Serial murderers work alone because they can't trust anyone else to get the details right. It makes sense for the officer to be someone older and more senior.'

'It sounds to me like you're pointing the finger,' Kember said, blowing across his cup to cool the tea.

Lizzie thought for a moment, nibbling at the edge of a biscuit. 'The motive will be entangled in the killer's background and it's up to you to find out who had the opportunity.'

Kember threw a furtive glance around the lounge, snapping a biscuit in half and dunking it in his tea. 'Neither Dallington nor Matfield have watertight alibis, nor Pendry or Reverend Wilson for that matter, but everything else we have is circumstantial.'

'You should add Pendry to your list, then,' Lizzie said, 'if you think he fits the profile.'

She suppressed a smile as his softened biscuit broke off into his tea.

Kember grimaced and scooped out the brown sludge with a teaspoon. 'I don't know what to think.' He glanced up at her. 'You've grappled with the killer, felt him, smelt him. Do you think it could have been Pendry?'

'He can be charming and helpful, but I admit my research did bring me into contact with some very likeable villains,' she said, catching Kember's discomfort. 'You don't think it could be him?'

Kember sighed. 'He seems genuine, but he was the one who told Dallington about our agreement. Said it was his duty.'

'Well, he's a soldier first and a policeman second so I understand where his loyalties lie.' Lizzie shook her head to dislodge her doubts. 'I'm sure that's all it is.' She gave what she hoped was a reassuring smile.

'My gut feeling is telling me Dallington, but my gut's been wrong before,' Kember said.

'In my experience, gut reactions stem from preconceptions.' She ignored his withering look. 'That said, Dallington is commanding officer of this air station and that gives him control and a sense of security. He has his views but he does his job.'

'If that's the case,' Kember said, 'what about Matfield? When Pendry and I questioned him he was less than gushing about Dallington who, don't forget, we discovered was Matfield's CO in the Royal Flying Corps in the last war.'

Lizzie shrugged. 'Matfield is a different kettle of fish. He keeps pretty much to himself and also treats us with professional courtesy, but there's a coolness I can't put my finger on. He's not in complete control because he hasn't got the authority or connections that Dallington has. That makes things difficult for him.'

'As it does for all officers in any chain of command.' Kember smiled wryly and sipped his tea.

'Maybe, but Matfield's background means he could be affected by it more than most.' Lizzie avoided Kember's searching look over his teacup and aligned the handles of the teapot and milk jug, keeping tension at bay.

'What do you mean?' he said. 'Shell shock?'

'I doubt it, but Matfield did have a traumatic time on patrol and that can't have been easy. We know he got sent home for rest and recuperation.'

'That was Dallington's doing.'

'An overreaction because of his brother, I suspect.' Lizzie moved biscuit crumbs into a line with her finger.

'There's nothing on Matfield's file about full-blown shell shock, but he let slip to Pendry over a drink in the bar that he joined the RAF to kill at a distance.'

Lizzie looked up sharply. 'Did he, now?'

Kember played with his teaspoon. 'Matfield told him something else; said he wasn't cut out to be a civilian because there was nothing he was good at. He resumed flying for that reason and for the camaraderie.'

Lizzie frowned. 'Strange thing to say for a man who has few friends.'

'Neither has Dallington,' Kember said. 'Or Pendry, come to that.'

Her eyes widened as a thought hit her. 'Of course!'

'What?'

'Men aren't born hating women, something makes them that way and it could be his hatred of women that turned him away from civilian life and toward the RAF, where women are few and far between. Fighter pilots fly solo and, as you've pointed out, the RAF provides a legitimate way of killing at a distance, to satisfy a compulsion without seeing your hands get dirty.'

'Are you saying all pilots are psychopaths?' Kember said with a puzzled frown.

'Of course not, but the RAF provides an organisation, with all its air bases, infrastructure and hierarchy, for the killer to hide in plain sight. The RAF is more of a home and family than he's ever known.'

At that moment, three fighter aircraft powered over the manor house, bringing everyone in the lounge over to the folding French windows. Kember and Lizzie watched as another fighter, with its RAF roundels flashing in the sun, roared past to join the others.

'Hurricanes,' Niamh said, rubbing her hands together with excitement. 'Probably from Biggin.'

'We are in for it now,' Agata said flatly.

'What, more than before?' Charlie said. 'How many more bombs can they drop on us?' Her nervous laugh descended into a fit of coughing.

'Trust me, more is to come.' Agata shook her head. 'Now the squadron is here, we are a bigger target.'

Another two Hurricanes flew over and banked into the circuit that would bring them into the wind to land. As the last aircraft straightened for approach, so the first aircraft touched down without so much as a wobble or a bounce. The women watched until the last aircraft had landed before retaking their seats on the comfy sofas.

'Exciting stuff,' Kember said as he and Lizzie returned to their table.

Lizzie gave him a funny look. 'Exciting for who, you?'

'Not for you?' Kember looked discomfited.

Lizzie shook her head. 'We're good enough to fly those, and the Spitfires too, but they won't let us because they think we'll break them.'

Lizzie saw Kember hesitate and stare at the half-eaten biscuits on the plate. She gave him a look of concern, tilting her head in query. 'Are you all right? You look funny and you've gone quiet.'

'I've not been entirely honest with you,' he said.

What now? Lizzie thought, as the breath caught in her throat and her heart sank.

'Since before we met for tea I've known something that might have changed your opinions.'

She turned her palms upwards to say *Give it to me*.

Kember licked his lips and swallowed. 'Pendry and I spoke to Dallington again and I noticed two books on the shelf in his office that weren't pushed back in line. I wanted to get up his nose a bit so I wandered over to look at them.'

Lizzie managed to breathe, strangely relieved that he was talking about books.

'One was about Jack the Ripper.'

Lizzie's eyes widened. That wasn't just a book. Not here and now.

'Dallington baulked when I asked to borrow it but could hardly say no. I'm having the fingerprint kit brought here right at this moment. We're going to take sample prints from all the officers, including Dallington, Matfield, Hammond, Stapleton, Pendry. And Ben Vickers.'

Lizzie found her voice. 'That's an extraordinary find, but you don't suspect Vickers now, do you?'

Kember waved away the notion. 'My main concern is, I don't want to scare Dallington away by making him think he's being singled out for special treatment.'

'That makes sense.' Lizzie nodded her approval. Then she clasped her hands together, knowing the sign, feeling her chest tighten. 'But something's bothering me. My profiles deal in probabilities based on statistics, likelihoods and approximations and can't be completely accurate, so some of what I've given you won't fit the killer, but the majority should.' Colour drained from Lizzie's knuckles because of her grip. 'The men here describe Dallington as all piss and wind. He's up-front and bullish but could harbour a mistrust of Matfield due to his subordinate's earlier fallibility. Matfield, on the other hand, is secretive, doesn't give much away and is in emotional debt to Dallington.'

Kember nodded. 'From what I've learnt about the pair of them, you could argue for either being the murderer, but now, finding the book . . .'

Lizzie rested back in her chair for a moment, aware of an inexplicable need to do well for Kember, but this was pushing her expertise and ability to the limit.

She stared into Kember's eyes and leant in closer, conspiratorially. 'Instead of trying to second-guess the killer, try thinking like him. Don't say, *What would I do if I was him?* That keeps him at arm's length. Take what you know of him and put yourself in his shoes. Say, *Who shall I kill next? How? Where? When?* He's already tried to kill me so we know I'm his prime target, but you must think like a killer, not a detective.'

'Easier said than done.' Kember sighed. 'And to be quite honest, I'm not sure I want to. This is your area of expertise, I'm happy being the copper.'

'All right,' Lizzie said. 'The killer is asserting the control he craves through his murders and the way the bodies are displayed. He's sending a message to all women to go back to their homes. We're working in factories, the armed forces, civil defence and the police, ARP and fire services, and he hates that. War broke out last year but the first murder didn't take place until the day the ATA arrived. Don't you see? We were the trigger.'

'So, the threat was always specific to the ATA' – Kember nodded slowly – 'which means you were always at risk.'

Lizzie returned a look of surprise. 'I'm a woman, I was born at risk.'

◆ ◆ ◆

Two hours later, Lizzie's words still permeating his thoughts, Kember's impatient, pacing, foot-tapping, extended wait in the briefing room came to an end. Dallington's throat made a guttural sound as he frowned a greeting and Kember saw the sudden uncertainty in his eyes. Pendry and Vickers stood formally at ease, legs slightly apart and hands behind their backs, but their faces displayed discomfort at the awkwardness of the situation. Wright stood stiff and businesslike to one side. Matfield looked plain bored.

'Glad you could make time, Group Captain.' Kember's voice carried an undertone of sarcasm. 'I needed to speak to you all urgently and Flight Lieutenant Pendry was kind enough to arrange for me to use this briefing room.'

'Get on with it, man,' Dallington snapped. 'What is it that it drags me and my officers away from our work?'

Kember returned Dallington's glare. 'I appreciate your desire to get back to your duties but this is *my* work, which I'm sure you can all agree is of the utmost importance under the circumstances, and should take but a few moments.' Kember paused for longer than necessary and saw, with satisfaction, the corner of Dallington's mouth twitch. 'As you know, *my* officers and I have been investigating two murders that we believe are linked. In fact, we believe them to be the work of one man.'

Dallington nodded thoughtfully. 'Any idea who yet?'

Kember wondered whether Dallington had nodded in agreement or because he *knew*. 'We have a pretty good idea, but we are doing things by the book. That is why I needed to see you.'

Dallington raised his chin defiantly. 'Anything you need from me, just ask. It's a terrible business, terrible.'

'We have evidence that needs testing for fingerprints and we hope to have this on the train to London and Scotland Yard tonight.'

'Quite right, good work.'

Kember almost smiled. He sensed he had the group captain rattled. 'We've taken fingerprint impressions from the suspects but need impressions from yourself, Wing Commander Matfield, Flight Lieutenant Pendry and Flight Sergeant Vickers. This serves the dual purpose of ruling some suspects in and eliminating others.'

Dallington glared at Kember. 'Pendry and Matfield are suspects?'

Kember noted he didn't query his own inclusion, nor that of Vickers. 'Everyone is a suspect until it cannot possibly be them. We've taken dozens of fingerprints from the men and women on this air station to rule out the possibility that they handled any of the items we have recovered.'

Dallington glanced at the table in front of them on which had been laid out all the fingerprint paraphernalia. Realisation dawned across his face. 'You actually want to take *my* fingerprints?'

Kember inclined his head in acknowledgement. 'If you wouldn't mind.'

Some of Dallington's arrogant defiance returned. 'And if I do?'

'I could arrest you for obstructing a murder investigation and preventing a sworn constable from going about his lawful duty, but I'd much prefer you to volunteer so you can get back to your duties before the next air raid. I'm sure you and the wing commander will be sorely missed otherwise.' Kember forced a weak smile.

Dallington pouted and raised his chin to stretch his neck muscles. He took his empty pipe from his pocket, clamped the stem between his teeth before changing his mind and replacing it in his pocket with a grumble. 'Let's get on with it.'

Kember stopped in surprise, glanced to his left and saw Pendry's eyebrows knitted in a frown. They'd expected Dallington to refuse point-blank. Either he was playing some kind of game or none of the threatening notes held his fingerprints. Doubt twisted in the pit of Kember's stomach. If Dallington had worn gloves at all times there might be nothing for Scotland Yard to match. Finding prints on the book alone would prove ownership, which Dallington had never denied.

'If you please, Sergeant,' Kember said to Wright.

Wright stepped forward and moved an ink pad and card nearer to Dallington. 'My apologies, sir,' Wright said. 'I have to hold your fingers to ensure we get a good impression.'

Dallington glowered. 'Carry on.'

Wright took each of the fingers of Dallington's right hand, rolling them first on the ink pad then on the card. He repeated the procedure with Dallington's left hand and both thumbs before handing him a damp cloth and pointing to a bowl.

'You can wipe your hands with this, sir. There's soap and hot water and a towel over there if you want a proper clean before you go.'

Dallington wiped most of the ink from his fingers and stood aside as Matfield nodded to Pendry to take his turn. Pendry indicated the table with his open palm in an offer to go after, but Matfield insisted the RAF policeman go next and stepped behind and to one side to wait.

Dallington washed his hands as suggested and turned to Kember, glaring at him like a snake about to strike. 'I hope that will suffice, Inspector.'

Kember extended his hand for a conciliatory handshake. 'Thank you for your cooperation, Group Captain. I'm sure we have all we need from you.'

Dallington sniffed and ignored Kember's gesture. 'I should bloody well hope so.' He strode from the room, throwing the hand towel onto the table.

Pendry hurriedly pulled his gloves back on after his turn, his lips compressed into a thin line as he watched Matfield grimacing while having his prints taken.

Kember smiled. Only children found enjoyment in having their fingerprints taken. He hadn't found one adult, even the innocent, who had ever been happy to comply.

As Wright cleared away the fingerprint kit after Vickers' turn, putting the ink pad and spare cards back into the large wooden box of powders, brushes and instruction pamphlets, Kember said, 'Thank you, gentlemen, that's most cooperative. Sergeant Wright will send everything off to Scotland Yard on the next train. I'll telephone Tonbridge and the bureau to let them know they're coming and see if I can't persuade them to give us a fast turnaround. As I said, it's for elimination purposes only, at this stage.' Kember tried to give a convincing smile.

'Glad to help,' Matfield sneered, throwing his cloth to Vickers as he left.

Kember raised his eyebrows at Pendry. 'That went smoother than I expected.' He smiled. 'We're making progress.'

◆ ◆ ◆

On her way to bed, Lizzie dropped in to see her friend. Charlie, lying on her back but with her head turned to face the door, gave her a weak smile. Lizzie slipped in, closed the door and sat on a hard wooden chair near the bedside table, moving a flickering candle to set down a glass of water.

Despite Charlie's glamour, few touches in the room displayed femininity. A wardrobe with its door ajar revealed a neat ATA uniform on a hanger for the night. Polished shoes arranged under the bed awaited selection in the morning. Three wild daisies, flowers closed until daylight, drooped over the edge of a glass on the window sill. A packet of cigarettes and a box of matches protruded from an expensive-looking handbag and the faint smell of perfume and cigarettes lingered in the air. Despite the small fireplace, expensive wardrobe and hand-crafted chest of drawers, the room looked like what it was: sleeping quarters on an RAF air station.

Lizzie took off her shoes and rubbed her feet. 'Christ, my feet ache. How are *you* feeling?'

'Like I've been hit by a Jerry bomb,' Charlie murmured.

'Do you want me to stay with you?'

'Not really.'

In Charlie's voice, thick with fatigue and pain, Lizzie was surprised to detect an undertone of resentment.

'Did I do something wrong?' Lizzie asked.

'I've been thinking,' said Charlie. 'You said you have some kind of skill that makes you special.'

'I didn't say that.' *Here it comes*, Lizzie thought. *Not quite normal.* 'I said I've learnt about how certain people think.'

'Well, whatever you think you have, whatever you think you've learnt, it didn't stop Emily being murdered.'

'No. It didn't.' Lizzie said, feeling as though she'd been slapped, her cheeks burning and the familiar ache spreading across her chest.

'You should have used it to keep Emily safe.'

Lizzie gasped, shocked. That's what she'd been trying to do but if her closest friend thought this way, what must the others think? 'Do you want me to go?'

Charlie didn't answer, her eyes already closed.

'I'll sit for a while, anyway.'

Watching Charlie drift slowly off to sleep, brushing away a tear of regret, Lizzie knew her friend was right. Despite everything she said she was and could do, two women were dead. She mulled over the rest of the day's events and only realised she'd been sitting there for almost an hour when her own eyelids drooped and she glanced at her watch. She shook her head to wake herself, licked her thumb and forefinger and pinched out the candle flame.

As her eyes adjusted, a sliver of silver light creeping through a crack in the curtains lay like a slash across the bedclothes. Surprised, Lizzie looked at the window and could see the shadow of tape criss-crossing each glass pane. She tutted. Charlie had forgotten to close the blackout curtains. She moved to the window and drew the curtains into position.

With only the paltry illumination from the bar of yellow light seeping under the door, Lizzie's heart almost stopped. A shadow passed across, came back, then stopped as if someone was standing outside Charlie's door. She held her breath, her mind scrabbling for options. She could think of only two: wait to be attacked again or go on the offensive. With nothing to hand with which to defend herself, but ready to scream her throat raw, she snatched at the door handle and yanked the door open.

There was no one there.

She frowned, confused, certain she'd seen something. With blood pulsing in her ears, she edged into the corridor where weak bulbs cast dim light no better than Charlie's candle. She checked one way but it appeared empty. A standard lamp, its light extinguished, stood sentinel by two small easy chairs huddled around a low table in an alcove. In the other direction, another alcove had been surrounded by boxes that she supposed contained stores. Stationery, most likely. Lizzie pinged the band on her wrist twice and took a few deep breaths. Her hands were shaking but it was ridiculous to think the killer would risk attacking her again inside the manor house. She returned to the room, retrieved her shoes and told herself to stop being so stupid. With a final glance at Charlie, Lizzie closed the door behind her with a soft click as she left and padded barefoot along to her own room.

CHAPTER
TWENTY-FIVE

With the sun burning off sparse cloud as morning drew to a close, the clanging of a bell echoed across the airfield. Lizzie heard a shout and looked across to Dispersal where figures running from a hut towards the Hurricanes signalled the first scramble call of the day. As each pilot slid into his cockpit, the first coughs of life from powerful Merlin engines reverberated across the grass and the ground crews pulled restraining chocks away from wheels. Lizzie watched, full of admiration for their bravery but tinged with sadness that not all would return from the battle. The Hurricanes bounced, wings wagging, towards their take-off positions and lurched forward in a roar of opening throttles. Three Hurricanes left the ground in a V formation followed by three more.

As the air raid siren sounded and Lizzie began making her way to the shelter, more figures detached themselves from another hut, running towards the Spitfires. With the Hurricanes still visible as dots in the sky, the Spitfire squadron became airborne and began climbing to intercept the approaching enemy. Lizzie saw Pendry heading for the shelter and waited.

'Looks like we're off again,' Pendry said.

'I should say so,' Lizzie agreed. 'I bet Dallington and Matfield are in their element.' She swept stray hair from her face.

'Dallington's like a dog with two tails. I saw him this morning at breakfast and you'd think he'd won the football pools.'

'He has, in a way. He's got his beloved fighters back and it looks like we could be sent packing.'

'I'm sure it won't come to that.'

Their heads turned towards a shout and Charlie panted over. She leant forward and put her hands on her knees, gasping and coughing. 'Good gracious,' she said, catching her breath.

'Are you all right?' Lizzie said, putting a concerned arm around her friend. 'You still don't look well.'

'I'm a bit groggy, to tell you the truth. Don't think all the ciggies are doing me any good.' She drew herself upright. 'That's better darling. Are the others here?'

'They're inside already.'

'We'd better join them in the old concrete coffin before someone takes a pot-shot at us.'

'Spot on,' Pendry said, looking towards the south-east. 'Jerry might be here in a few minutes.'

Lizzie took her friend's hand and led her down the concrete steps into the cold confines of the narrow personnel shelter. The rows of chairs lining each long wall, the cloth curtain at the far end concealing a single bucket as the toilet, and the roll-call being taken in case of a direct hit, all seemed so unreal yet terrifying. Each time the all-clear sounded she felt so glad to get out into the fresh air, but here she was again, for the umpteenth time, going underground for safety.

◆ ◆ ◆

Kember sat in the police station basement behind a row of chest-high filing cabinets that partitioned off a small area almost entirely filled by a small table and two chairs. Across the room, Wingate lay on a low bed behind the barred door of one of the two cells that had been installed a few years previously after a spate of thefts around the farms. Kember considered his move over to the pub to be fortunate as it meant he had avoided having to share with the man.

The gloom cast by a weak light bulb revealed the case papers from the files he'd studied the night before arranged in front of him. The package for Scotland Yard had made the connection for the last train to London, but to Kember's annoyance, nothing had come of Wright's attempts to get Pendry's and Vickers' service records. Headley's report on his inspection of the dagger had confirmed the absence of blood. In fact, the blade held an undisturbed film of ancient grime, proving it had remained unused for several hundred years and putting the reverend further in the clear.

Wingate stirred at the sound of the air raid siren and swung his legs off the cell bed. Sitting on the edge, elbows rested on knees, head in his hands, he looked to Kember as if he'd fallen asleep again. Then the man rubbed his face and neck, pushed the heels of his hands into his eyes and coughed. A breakfast brought in earlier consisting of a mug of hot tea and a slice of bread thinly smeared with margarine, now lukewarm and curling respectively, sat outside the bars. Kember allowed Wingate to have his breakfast before he made a noise with his fountain pen.

Wingate jolted. 'Christ almighty, you made me jump. What're you doing, hiding behind there?'

'Sorry about that,' said Kember with mock sincerity. 'Sleep well?'

'No. Cold room, lumpy bed, not the best of company.'

Kember watched in silence, trying to decide whether this man, sitting there as if he hadn't a care in the world, could be a mutilator of women. Wingate seemed so normal and relaxed, and the more Kember looked the more he doubted. There was no denying Wingate might be considered handsome by some and, despite Wright's reservations, could easily have charmed his way into the affections of a vulnerable young woman. But a killer?

Wingate yawned, picked at a bit of food in his teeth, glanced at Kember and scowled. 'Did you want something, Inspector?'

'Catching up on paperwork while there are flying Jerries about.'

'Persistent blighters, aren't they?'

'People who want to take something that isn't theirs usually are.'

Wingate's face softened into a weak smile. 'Fair point.'

Kember paused, allowing the silence to do its work, as he knew it would.

'I didn't kill her,' Wingate said after a while.

Kember's head moved, more a twitch than a nod.

Wingate chewed his lip, rubbed his nose and scratched the back of his neck. He crossed his arms, tapping his right foot on the floor, and sighed loudly, glancing over at Kember. 'Maybe . . .'

Kember watched as Wingate appeared to struggle with making a decision. A confession was too much to hope for but a breakthrough of any kind would be most welcome.

Wingate tilted his head back and looked at the ceiling, as if unable to meet Kember's eyes. 'Maybe . . .' He swallowed. 'Maybe I did see someone that night.'

The whole of Kember's body jerked alert as if electricity had shot through him, but he projected outward calm.

'On the church path. While I was nicking petrol from Bert's car.'

Kember kept still, his eyes never leaving Wingate's face, not wishing to destroy the moment, waiting for a bombshell.

Wingate closed his eyes and winced as if in actual pain. 'No, I can't or I'm a dead man.' He shook his head, an air of sadness about him. 'He's stitched me up.'

'Who did you see?'

Wingate shook his head again and lay back on his bed.

Kember persisted. 'You'll be taken to court in Tonbridge on Monday morning so now's your chance to make amends by helping me. The petrol scam is over so the person you're protecting has lost their hold over you, but he *will* kill another woman if we don't stop him. Tell me who he is and we can arrest him. You, Hammond and Stapleton will be safe.'

He pursed his lips in frustration as Wingate, his knees drawn up, rolled over to face the wall. He'd been so close.

Kember rubbed his hand over his face. Hartson had made his reluctance to take him on secondment from Scotland Yard quite clear, but relished the leverage it gave against the Yard being wheeled in at the drop of a hat. Hartson resented the way the Yard rode roughshod through local protocols and customs and all too often left with the glory after the local constabulary had done the lion's share of the work. But he wanted results and wouldn't wait forever.

Kember looked down at his case notes, his optimism and energy dissipating. Blackmail, intimidation, fingerprints, delay, delay, war, delay. He closed his eyes to marshal his thoughts.

Could this man who Wingate was convinced would kill him be the same man who had intimidated Hammond and Stapleton? And the murderer he was getting ever closer to?

The all-clear sounded around half an hour after the air raid warning, prompting Lizzie and those around her in the shelter to look at each other in puzzlement. Until now, the air raids had lasted a lot longer. On this occasion, they had emerged to find no smoke and no damage but the Hurricanes and Spitfires still away, so the battle must have been going on somewhere.

Lizzie caught hold of Charlie's arm as they walked back to the manor house. 'Are you sure you're all right?'

Charlie looked back through glazed and half-closed eyes. 'I'm exhausted and I've got a stomach ache.'

'Is it flu?' Lizzie studied her friend's face with concern. People died from flu, especially if it turned to pleurisy.

'I don't know. I might have eaten something that didn't agree with me, but it's got worse over the last couple of days.'

Lizzie cursed that she wasn't a doctor of medicine. 'Do you fancy some tea and a biscuit? Settle your stomach?'

Charlie shook her head and took a laboured breath. 'I'll have a doze in the lounge though.'

Lizzie escorted Charlie to the sofa and ensured she was comfortable before seeking a spare blanket. When she returned five minutes later, she spread the blanket over her dozing friend, tucking it around her shoulders, and sat reading in a nearby chair.

'I'm sorry for what I said last night,' Charlie murmured.

Lizzie's heart jumped. 'Don't worry about it.'

'I know you're different somehow.'

Not quite normal.

'You see things differently, things we can't, and the police should have taken notice of you. I know it wasn't your fault Emily died.'

'Forget about it.' Lizzie felt a lump forming in her throat. 'Just get some rest.'

'I just wanted you to know I'm sorry,' Charlie slurred. 'You've been so good to me.'

◆ ◆ ◆

The day had slid into mid-afternoon by the time Kember, irritated by still more delay, managed to get a telephone call through to the air station. He had promised to keep the attack on Lizzie to himself but inaction didn't sit well with him. Without breaking his promise, he needed to make it clear to the one other person who might care enough to do something about it that Lizzie's safety was of increasing importance. Unfortunately, that person had gone down in his estimation. Ever since Pendry had gone to Dallington behind his back, Kember hadn't fully trusted him. He understood Pendry's reasons but he believed a bond existed between police officers. It was a belief he'd fallen foul of before.

Right at that moment, Pendry could not be spared for even five minutes, another irritation, but Kember also wanted to speak to Lizzie. The hours had dragged, with air raids being reported on the wireless all day, and he needed to know.

'How are you?' he said as soon as she came to the telephone, the concern in his voice tangible and genuine.

'I'm absolutely fine,' Lizzie replied.

With those three words Kember felt the tension ease across his shoulders.

'I'm worried about Charlie, though,' she said. 'She's been a bit poorly for a few days and I think she might have flu. Thank God we got away without an air raid but they hit Manston, Hawkinge and God knows where else. Bombed Dover too.'

'They say every cloud has a silver lining,' said Kember. 'Unfortunately, that means every silver lining has its own cloud.'

'On that note, how's the investigation going?'

There's that instant switch again, thought Kember, *from personal to professional.*

'Wingate admitted siphoning petrol from Albert Garner's car the night Lavinia Scott died,' Kember said. 'He's also admitted seeing someone on the church path but said if he talked he'd be a dead man.'

'Did he say why?' Lizzie asked.

'No . . .' Kember hesitated, unsure how she would take what he was about to say. 'But I believe the fingerprints on the book, scraps and notes will match Dallington's and, once we've arrested him, Wingate and the others will feel safe enough to talk.'

The ensuing silence, wasting precious seconds of their three minutes' call time, had Kember fearing the line connection had broken. 'You disagree?'

'I'm getting a bad feeling about this,' Lizzie said. 'Yes, Dallington is arrogant but he's an open book. Matfield is calm but secretive. Both of them have no friends here and both would prefer women to stay at home. None of that makes them murderers.'

'They were high on our list but now you don't think it's them?' Her unease began to sow doubt in Kember's mind.

Lizzie sighed. 'I'm not saying that, but are we being too narrow-minded? I mean, there are a lot of personnel on this air station, a lot of officers, and we've gone straight for the top.'

'With good reason.' Kember knew he should leave it there but the detective in him wouldn't let it go. 'Everything's pointing at Dallington, so what's the problem?'

Kember heard the rustling of her moving the handset to her other hand before she spoke again, her voice quieter as if avoiding being overheard. 'Let me ask you this: from what you know of the pair of them, is there anything in my original profile that rules either of them out?'

He thought carefully. 'Not that I recall.'

'And despite me warning you the profile probably wouldn't fit the killer in every respect, has there been anything glaringly at odds with what you know about either man?'

'No,' Kember admitted.

'You deal in hard evidence to pinpoint one person, but I work with personalities that suggest the type of person. Your technique that leads in one direction is as much open to interpretation as mine that leads in another. So, instead of you asking me why I think it could be someone else, perhaps you should ask yourself why you think it could not?'

Kember felt chastened, like an argumentative schoolboy pulled before the headmaster, and was filled with a sense of dismay at the sudden direction the conversation had taken. He'd called out of concern for her welfare and to ask for her help, but had been given a lecture on evidence.

Lizzie sighed again. 'Look, I've got to go, sorry. My advice is to keep Wingate chatting. As you know, the more he talks the more likely it is he'll slip up.'

The operator announced time up and Kember sat for several minutes after putting the handset back in its cradle. It was true, he'd accepted everything she'd said, almost without question, until he'd come to his own conclusion about Dallington. It was also true that her profile had helped get them this far. Without it they might still be wading through the hundreds of potential suspects living and working within a five-mile radius of Scotney.

Sitting at Wright's desk, Kember rubbed his eyes with finger and thumb. He hadn't seen Wright for some time and supposed he had the usual daily police duties to perform as well as 'war work' – the prevention of looting and other crimes committed during air raids. Not that Scotney was a hotbed of such criminality. Kember listened to the sound of birdsong filtering through the open front door and heard the distant shout of a child. This was how an English summer should be: quiet and peaceful and routine, not spent cowering from bombs and hunting what Lizzie had called serial murderers. After a few moments he got up and returned to the back room where he had moved his papers after the all-clear, leaving Wingate still lying on his bed in the cells, awaiting transfer to Tonbridge.

Kember agonised over whether he'd made his decision to accept Lizzie's profile through a fog of remorse. Guilt that he hadn't listened to his wife very much in the past year. The moment she had told him to go still played on his mind and the weight of failure that came with it troubled him. Failure as a husband, a lover and as a father. The job had always come first and his home life a poor second. His son fighting in the skies over Britain and his daughter doing her bit somewhere in the WAAF gave him a sense of pride that they'd grown up the way he'd hoped. How much of that could be attributed to him was debatable. He suspected they and his wife would say *very little*.

He sighed, worried that listening to Lizzie may have become a way of compensating for his years of turning a blind eye and deaf ear to his wife whenever it suited him. Had his judgement been impaired by this fascinating woman? Was fixating on Dallington his way of swinging the pendulum the other way, back to his former by-the-book self, to prove a point?

She had come to him with bizarre theories anyone else would have laughed at. He was the seasoned detective who relied on evidence.

So he must be right?

Mustn't he?

◆　◆　◆

With another night of the blackout ahead and feeling ready for her bed, Lizzie gave a gentle tap on the door of Charlie's room, opened it and stepped inside.

She gave Charlie a sympathetic look. 'How's your head?'

'Splitting,' Charlie murmured. 'I ache all over and can barely move.'

'Have you eaten?'

'I managed a few nibbles earlier and a glass of water but I keep feeling queasy.' Clearly, Charlie was fighting to keep her eyes open. 'Pendry sent for the quack. He said it's flu and gave me a painkiller and sedative. I should be spark out for hours.'

Lizzie stroked Charlie's hair. 'Another good night's sleep will do you good.'

'The MO's given me sick leave and said he'd pop in tomorrow.'

'All right,' Lizzie said, teasing a damp lock away from her friend's flushed face. 'Goodnight.'

Charlie smiled and closed her eyes, her breathing becoming slow, deep and rhythmic as she slipped into a restful sleep under Lizzie's watchful gaze. Lizzie pulled the covers up to her friend's shoulders and turned out the light.

For a moment, the instant darkness equalled the sound of Charlie's medicated slumber: deep and almost tangible. Lizzie remembered the previous night and checked the bar of light under the door.

Nothing of concern tonight.

She slipped quietly from Charlie's room and returned to her own.

CHAPTER
TWENTY-SIX

Lizzie fancied she could feel the throb of Merlin engines vibrating in her chest as a flight of Spitfires landed and swung towards Dispersal where ammunition trucks and fuel bowsers stood ready by the blast pens. She squinted one last time at the lines of white, wispy cloud highlighted by the early morning sun against the bright blue sky and extinguished the stub of her cigarette, replacing it in its position in the packet.

Lizzie was the last to arrive, following Geraldine into the briefing room. As she found her usual place and slid onto the chair, the captain placed a thin file on the table and stood in front of the detachment. Although her uniform and hair were as immaculate as ever, to Lizzie she seemed to have lost some of the brightness and enthusiasm of their first meeting. Lizzie glanced around and saw in the faces of the others that they sensed a change too.

'You will have seen the daily orders on the ops board,' Geraldine began. 'I've checked with White Waltham. No change, I'm afraid.'

A groan went around the room.

Fizz tutted. 'They don't want us to fly in the rain and now they won't let us fly in the sun.'

'It's rubbish,' Agata said. 'They need new aircraft and we could all fly fighters.'

'I agree,' Lizzie said, feeling the disappointment in the pit of her stomach. 'I'd love a crack at a Hurrie or a Spit but letting me back in anything would do for now.'

'We're not grounded because of the fighting though, are we?' Niamh said, a bitter edge to her words. 'It happened as soon as the men arrived. It's bloody unfair.'

'Look here,' Geraldine said, the sharpness in her voice cutting the conversation. 'Pauline Gower's trying to get the top brass to see sense so we can ferry fighters, but it's a slow process, especially with the air battle going on. We have to follow orders and fly what, where and when they tell us. You've all completed the training so you know they even get to tell us how we should fly.'

'Do you think she'll succeed?' Fizz asked.

'I hope so. She's got a good chance.' She looked at Agata. 'But it won't do the cause any good if we go swanning all over the sky when we're forbidden. We have to be twice as good, twice as safe and twice as disciplined as the men. Is that unfair? Of course it is, but that's the way of the world at the moment.' Geraldine smiled. 'On a lighter note, I've been told some pilots at Central Flying School haven't completed fighter conversion courses due to a lack of dual-control trainers. It's yet to be confirmed, but by this time next week, however the battle is going, I do expect you to be flying again, but we may be pulled further back from the front.'

The room erupted in chatter.

Geraldine rapped the table with her knuckles for silence. 'Ladies, ladies. At least you'll be airborne again. By the end of the year I want you all to have taken the Class Three Plus conversion course so you can fly the Ox-box and Anson without supervision.' She hesitated, looking at her pilots. 'By the way, where's Charlie this morning?'

'She has the flu,' Lizzie said. 'The MO gave her a sedative to help her sleep, and a day on the sick.'

'Ah, right. I'll check on her presently.'

A scream from somewhere within the manor house made all heads turn towards the door. As one, everyone rose from their chairs and rushed through the door, looking for the source of distress. As the women flooded into the main hall, a tiny woman, almost a schoolgirl, dressed in the uniform of the NAAFI, leant over the first-floor balustrade.

'She . . .' was all she could say as her whole body convulsed and a wail escaped her lips, tears coursing down her cheeks.

Lizzie and Geraldine took the stairs two at a time, making a grab for the woman in time to stop her collapsing. They led her to an easy chair by a table on the landing.

'What's wrong?' Geraldine asked as the woman continued to cry. 'Are you hurt?'

As the other ATA women and several RAF men crowded in, Lizzie took a gentle hold of the woman's chin and guided her face to look at her.

'Whatever is the matter?' Lizzie soothed. 'Can we help?'

'No one can help,' the woman said through sobs, her face crumpled as if in pain. 'The mess steward asked me to take breakfast to her room because she wasn't well.'

'Who?' Lizzie asked. She looked at Geraldine, shock widening her eyes. 'Charlie.'

Lizzie pushed past Pendry as he arrived from downstairs, trailing Geraldine and the others along the corridor to the ATA quarters. As she reached Charlie's room she saw a dropped tray of scattered food and smashed crockery in the open doorway.

Geraldine's hands flew to her mouth at the sight that met their eyes.

'Oh my God.' Lizzie almost gagged at the bloody scene in the room.

Niamh peered between the two women and turned away, retching.

Pendry elbowed his way through the shocked women and called, 'Flight Sergeant Vickers.' He moved the broken crockery to one side with his boot and pulled the door shut.

'Sir?' A voice from the back.

Pendry craned his neck to see his sergeant. 'Put a guard on this room. Move all the women into the lounge and get them something strong to drink. If anyone asks, it's on my orders – medicinal.'

'Sir.' Vickers eased himself past the group, already speaking to a uniformed corporal as his men guided some of the women towards the stairs.

'Why are you putting a guard on her door now it's too late?' Lizzie said as a ripple of anger coursed through her. 'Why weren't we guarded like you promised Kember?'

Pendry's face was like stone. 'Because there's a bloody war on and I've barely got enough men to keep Jerry out, never mind play nurse-maid to a group of women too stubborn to leave for their own safety.'

Lizzie raised her chin defiantly, but the truth of his words stung.

Pendry turned back to Vickers. 'This is both a military and civil-ian crime scene. I'm going to call DI Kember. No one enters this room until I say so, and that includes Group Captain Dallington and Wing Commander Matfield, is that clear?'

'Sir.'

Lizzie let Pendry guide her down the staircase, following the crowd, but stopped at the bottom step and turned. She noticed a couple of the women being comforted by the men, but by the time they reached the ground floor it was uncertain who was supporting whom.

'I have to go back to that room,' Lizzie said, her wet eyes determined, her face set hard.

'Not yet,' Pendry said, his voice low but firm.

She put her hand on his arm, the need to go back settling as an ache in her chest. 'The sooner I read whatever's in that room up there, the sooner I can see what happened' – she pointed to her temple with her forefinger – 'in here.'

'We still have to wait for Kember. Once his team has finished you can do whatever it is you need to do.'

'Every minute wastes time.' Lizzie's eyes pleaded for him to relent.

Pendry didn't budge. 'Which is why you need to let me telephone Kember straight away.'

Lizzie's stare of defiance faltered as she lowered her chin. 'You're right, of course.' She felt Pendry's cold fingers prise her hot hand gently from his arm.

'Go and get a drink with the others,' Pendry urged. 'I'll let you know as soon as he gets here. If he says you can go in, that's his lookout.'

◆　◆　◆

Small groups huddled in the lounge, many silent, the hum of murmuring rising from others. Orderlies flitted around, offering drinks and condolences. Tilly wandered through in search of attention as the ATA sat in their usual spot, one of the silent groups.

Niamh, legs folded under her on a sofa, her cheeks wet beneath dark, haunted eyes, occasionally shook her head in disbelief. All of Agata's steel and resolve seemed to have been sucked out of her as she slumped next to Niamh like a bundle of discarded clothing, squeezing an unlit cigarette between two stiff fingers of her right hand. Fizz sat round-shouldered in an easy chair, her head bowed to disguise the tears that trickled with heartbreaking frequency. On another sofa sat Geraldine, legs crossed, her face carrying the expressionless look of someone in a trance, eyes staring and complexion as pale as spilt milk.

Lizzie sat next to her, nursing a small glass of whisky that had scoured the skin from her throat on first sip. Far from being soothing and medicinal, the cheap alcohol had shocked her mind into a state of regret. Regret at not being as smart as she thought she was, at not being able to stop the killer, at ever telling Kember she was good enough. If she'd left him to his own devices he might have stopped this monster by now. She'd got in the way, deflected him from his police work.

And now, upstairs, lay Charlie. Her life taken so brutally, and far too soon.

Lizzie tried to swallow, a lump seeming to fill her throat to choking point. She felt both sick and empty at the same time, numb on the outside, raw on the inside.

She pinged the rubber band on her left wrist, expecting the jolt it usually gave. But this wasn't anxiety she felt. This wasn't panic or OCN. This was close, personal, deep, devastating grief of a kind she'd never experienced, pure and simple.

And upstairs lay Charlie.

No more 'darlings' or tinkling laughs. No more hugs or evenings spent in the Hangar Round. No more 'little drinkies' or shared cigarettes. Lizzie wiped away the tears stinging her eyes and searing her burning cheeks. Charlie was the closest she'd ever got to having a sister, and she'd been taken from her.

Looking up through red eyes, it was the sight of her friends looking so cowed and defeated – the one thing she knew the murderer wanted – that galvanised her thinking. Her mind worked its way through the maze of doubt and self-recrimination and she began to see clearer again. She knew she was close to uncovering the killer because something elusive at the back of her mind still niggled, like a tiny piece of grit in a comfortable shoe. From experience, she knew her subconscious needed time to do its work and the more she mulled it over the closer she would get to discovering the insight, the answer, that was evading her.

But first . . . Lizzie gulped the rest of her whisky and felt the kick as it burnt her throat. She knew what she had to do. She had to see in that room.

◆　◆　◆

When Kember did arrive, he reassured Lizzie he would be with her as soon as he could, but there were protocols to follow. She countered that those protocols had been ignored when he let her in to see Emily's body. In turn, Kember reminded her that Dr Headley had seen the bodies of Lavinia and Emily before even he could inspect them and Headley had precedence over Charlie's too, before anyone else entered the room. Lizzie relented and agreed to wait with the others in the lounge, but made it clear she hated being chastened like a child.

After instructing Wright to guard the bottom of the stairs but let Dr Headley through whenever he arrived, Kember followed Pendry up the ornate stairway onto the ATA landing. He noted the guard outside the door and the remains of broken crockery kicked out of the way beside the skirting board. He hadn't liked evidence being moved but Pendry had explained the circumstances over the telephone.

'What have Dallington and Matfield got to say about this?' Kember asked.

'They've been informed and seemed shocked but, how shall I put it, restrained? Both say you can speak to them whenever you like.'

Kember almost laughed. 'That's big of them.'

Pendry smiled without humour in his eyes. 'Davies, the MO, stuck his head in but declared it far beyond his *ken*, as he put it. He's used to scraping strawberry jam off runways but the poor chap took one look in that room and blanched.' Pendry nodded to the guard, who moved aside. 'I should warn you, it's not a pretty sight. It looks like a butcher's abattoir.'

Kember suspected Pendry's description to be an exaggeration, an opinion he changed as soon as the door opened. The mutilated body of Charlotte Rowan-Peake lay at the epicentre of an extraordinary amount of blood, more than he'd seen at any crime scene in his career, ever. A wave of nausea broke over him and he covered his mouth with the back of his hand. He'd witnessed enough violent death to know the murderer had committed this barbaric dissection moments after he had killed her, the bastard. Through the ripened sweet and metallic stench he discerned another smell: of burning. He leant forward until he could see the fireplace and noted the remains of charred clothing in the grate. When he could stand it no longer, Kember withdrew and shut the door.

Pendry, standing just outside, gave a nod towards the room. 'What kind of monster are we dealing with?'

Kember shook his head, queasy with revulsion. 'One we need to catch, should have caught already.' He moved towards the stairs, struggling to compose himself. 'Headley's on his way. Should be here any minute. Has anyone been in that room?'

'No.'

'Lizzie?'

'Not even her.' Pendry led Kember back to the landing. 'I told her she had to wait for you, which is why she made a beeline for you when you arrived. She did get a first glimpse through the door though. It shook her up a bit.'

'It's shaken me too, to be honest,' Kember said. 'She can have a proper look, if she's adamant, but not until after Headley's poked around.'

'Right, where is she?' came a voice from below.

Kember and Pendry looked over the balustrade as Dr Headley strode from the front door across the main hall.

'Talk of the devil,' Kember said.

Headley looked up, scowled and stumped up the stairs. 'This is getting beyond careless, Kember. How many is this now? Three?'

'Good to see you're as gracious and sympathetic as ever, Doctor. The war treating you well?'

'I've got chronic indigestion from having most of my mealtimes disturbed, and on top of that I accuse a treacherous oyster of giving me a dose of stomach flu. So, no, my war is not thus far very pleasant. What have you got for me?'

Pendry led the way to Charlie's room and pointed to a clean pair of wellington boots beside the door on the opposite side to the crockery. 'You'll need those, Doctor.'

Headley raised his eyebrows in question, but on seeing the answer in Kember's grim expression he removed his polished shoes and slipped on the boots. He took off his coat, lifted a small bag from his larger one and moved to the door.

Kember touched Headley on the arm. 'Prepare yourself.'

He saw the emotional detachment of self-preservation in Headley's eyes transform into apprehension. Kember opened the door and Headley gasped at the carnage revealed inside.

'Good God,' Headley said quietly, solemnly.

He pulled a surgical mask and a pair of surgical gloves from his pocket and donned them, moving straight into his professional assessment. 'There appear to be bloody footprints on the floor and rug but they are smudged and indistinct. He must have worn over-shoes or something tied to his feet to protect them.' He set his bag on a clean area of the wide window sill and took out a notebook. 'I'll not be needing most of my instruments today, gentlemen. Would be nice if I could find a decent secretary, though.' He opened the book and took notes as he spoke, detailing every cut and slash.

Towards the end of the examination, Kember said, 'Is it the same signature?'

Headley glanced at him. 'Most definitely.' He took a pair of tweezers from his bag, delicately pushed the twin prongs into Charlie's mouth and extracted a folded piece of paper, which he passed to Kember.

Using his handkerchief, Kember unfolded the scrap. 'The same Bible text.'

'The same cross on the forehead too. Whoever did this killed your other girls.'

'Any bodily emissions, from the killer?'

Headley gave Kember a wry smile and spread his hands. 'No way to tell unless I test every drop of blood here.'

In his head, Kember heard the unspoken *And I'm not going to do that.*

'It's getting worse,' Kember said. 'He's killing inside now. Getting confident.'

'It's worse than you think,' Headley said.

Kember held his breath, wondering how anything could be worse than the tableau in front of his eyes.

'Her heart's been removed, and by that I mean I can't find it anywhere in or around the body,' Headley said.

Kember was almost beyond being shocked but had to force himself to ask the question. 'Why would someone do that? What does he want with her heart?'

'Search me,' Headley said with a sideways tilt of his head.

Kember ran a hand back through his hair, feeling as old and tired as Headley looked at that moment. 'Thank you for your time,

Doctor. Before you leave the room, is there anything in there that looks out of place or could, in your experience and opinion, be construed as useful to the investigation?'

Headley cast a surprised look at Kember. 'You're the detective, Kember; I'm the poor quack who has to delve into these cadavers.' He sniffed. 'There is a lack of precision throughout and I can safely say this is not the work of a professional. In particular, the cut in the pericardium sac that held the heart, and the resulting damage to surrounding tissue, would have many surgeons choking on their dinner party aperitifs in despair. This man has no medical knowledge or training whatsoever. I would also suggest butchers, fishmongers and vets would have made a neater job of this, so I'd say you can rule those professions out.' He flapped a hand towards the fireplace. 'You'll have noticed the burnt smell in the room. There appears to be clothing in the grate over there.' He moved to the fireplace and bent for a closer look. 'I'll let you have a poke around for yourself, but at first glance it looks like someone's tried to get rid of some overalls, with limited success. There's the charcoal remains of what looks like a pair of gloves and some bloodstained rags that might have been what he tied around his feet. Hold on.' He used his forefinger to lift a flap of dark-grey cloth. 'I can see the embroidered words *Scotney Garage*.'

Kember froze, confusion crowding in. 'How can that be? Wingate, Hammond and Stapleton are in custody, which rules all of them out of being involved in this murder.'

'But there it is,' Headley said, removing the wellingtons as he left the room with his notebook and little bag.

'We'd better have another chat with them,' Kember said. 'I know they're all scared of something and we need to know what that is.'

Pendry looked sceptical. 'Their scam was all about petrol.'

'So who got the overalls, and how? Why wear them in there and leave them half-burnt when he's left no other clues?'

The corners of Pendry's mouth turned down in a facial shrug.

Headley finished tying his polished shoes and put a hand on the wall to help himself stand. 'I'll call for an ambulance from Pembury to collect the poor thing but you should have plenty of time to do your detecting.'

'Can you hazard a guess at the time of death?' Kember asked.

Headley peered at him through his spectacles. 'You don't want much, do you?' He sniffed. 'She was in an enclosed room so there's no insect activity, but from the condition of the body, blood lividity, coagulation and stage of rigor mortis, I'd hazard a guess she was killed in situ, sometime between late yesterday evening and the early hours of this morning. The usual caveats and denials apply, of course, and the usual bits and bobs will follow later.' He placed his small bag inside his larger case and handed a face mask to Kember. 'You'll need that. Good day, gentlemen.'

They watched Headley stroll to the landing and descend the staircase, humming to himself.

'Jesus Christ, Pendry,' Kember said, rubbing his eyes with the heels of his hands. 'Where does he go from here?'

'Headley?' Pendry frowned.

Kember gave Pendry a sharp look but saw no humour in his face. 'This monster; how does he top that? What can he do to his next victim that's even worse than what's in that room? And what's all that about taking her heart? I tell you, Pendry, I've never seen anything like this in all my born days.'

Pendry raised his hands. 'Don't look at me. I'm out of my depth.'

'What about the time of death? Does that fit with station routine?'

Pendry pouted. 'Most people on the air station who weren't on duty, certainly in the manor house, would have been in bed. It would've been all quiet by ten o'clock at the latest. That matches Headley's view she might have died late last night.'

Kember turned at a sound behind him to see Lizzie at the top of the stairs.

'Can I see?' Lizzie said.

'Sorry, sir,' Wright said. 'Miss Hayes saw Dr Headley leave and I couldn't stop her.'

'It's all right, Sergeant. She can stay.'

Lizzie walked the short distance to where Kember, Pendry and the guard stood. 'I need to see.'

Kember hesitated. A strong instinct to protect her from that brutal scene made him step in front of the door, but as he searched her face, he saw a resolute defiance that told him his stance was meaningless. With great reluctance, he pointed to the boots. 'Put those on before you go in,' he said gently, 'and don't touch anything.'

The boots were far too big for her but once she'd slipped them on, Pendry opened the door. Kember watched anxiously as she raised a hand to her mouth, clearly suppressing a scream, and held on to the door frame for support.

'You don't have to,' Kember whispered. 'Let us do this, Lizzie. It's too much.'

'No. No. I do. She was my friend,' Lizzie said, her voice hoarse.

Kember handed her the face mask and watched her move into the room with more care than even Headley had taken, knotting the ties behind her head as her eyes scanned the body and the organs displayed around it. He saw her take in the blood on the floor and walls, glance at the fireplace and stop at the foot of the bed.

When she spoke, the words were professional but her voice cracked with emotion. 'This looks horrific and violent but it is still controlled aggression, not a frenzy. This took time to achieve; look at the candle, almost burnt out. When I left her last night I'm sure it had two or three hours' burn time left. He worked by candlelight to avoid detection and even blew it out when he'd finished. The organs he's removed have been deliberately placed by her body. It has all the elements of perfection. Uninterrupted, dark, peaceful, almost spiritual. A sacrifice.

'She's on display for our benefit, just like the others,' Lizzie continued. 'She's a woman – dispensable, irrelevant, a worthless whore. *Look at what I can do*, he's saying. *You can't stop me, so go. Leave here and never return.*' She looked at Kember standing in the doorway. 'She has the cross on her forehead. Did she have the Bible text in her mouth?'

Kember nodded, seeing the lines of sadness deepen on Lizzie's face, wanting to protect her from the horror but knowing he needed her insight. She'd hate him if he stopped her now.

'He thought killing Lavinia, talking to us through her, would be enough,' Lizzie said. 'We didn't listen, so he killed again. Emily's murder was his way of raising his voice, of insisting we take notice. This . . . this is him shouting at us. He keeps hoping we'll listen to his message. He does this when he thinks we need to be told again.' She closed her eyes. 'I think he tried to make her look ugly, to symbolise how he's come to regard someone in his past. His mother, a sister, a girlfriend, it doesn't matter. It's who she was that's ugly and that's why he needs to do this. Reveal their ugliness, remove it, drive them away.'

Kember's tongue stuck to the roof of his mouth and his throat had become painfully dry. 'I'm afraid he took her heart. Dr Headley couldn't find it.'

Lizzie opened her eyes and looked down at the bed. 'As I said, once the ugliness is revealed, he needs to remove it. Part of the ugliness he sees in women is embedded in the heart. People have long believed it is the heart that rules emotion, especially love and hate. In his mind, this hunk of an organ is one that women give to men and take back again on a whim, that can be warm and loving or cold and forbidding, that in his experience can be loyal for as long as it suits but disloyal and treacherous in equal measure. He has been humiliated or betrayed in some way, so removing her traitorous heart removes the ugliness and the source of his pain.'

Kember could almost reach out and touch Lizzie's grief when she looked across the room at him.

'He disfigured Lavinia, took Emily's womb and now Charlie's heart,' she said, speaking almost in monotone. 'He hates women, so he's taking their femininity.'

'Of course!' Kember mentally slapped himself on his forehead, remembering the Jack the Ripper book. 'He's literally taking a leaf out of Jack's book, copying his style. Lavinia's murder follows that of Mary Ann Nichols, Emily's must be Annie Chapman's, and Charlotte's echoes Mary Jane Kelly.' He could see the energy being sapped from Lizzie with every second she stood there, and beckoned to her. 'That's enough, Lizzie. Come out now.'

She looked over with eyes that appeared not to see him but she moved towards him anyway, pulling the mask from her face. Kember felt no resistance as he took her hand and guided her out of the room, steadying her as Pendry removed the boots and placed Lizzie's own shoes back on her feet.

'You need another drink,' Pendry said. 'Let's get you downstairs.' He put his hand on her elbow but this time she didn't move.

'I don't think we have much time,' Lizzie said, looking at Kember. 'The killer is escalating the violence because he knows we're getting close to him. He needs to get the ATA off this air station quickly, before we catch him.' She turned to Pendry. 'You said you haven't enough men to keep us safe. As far as Dallington's concerned, this will be the final straw. He has all the ammunition he needs to get us withdrawn, not because of Jerry bombing us, but because he'll say it's a matter of our personal safety.' She looked back at Kember. 'You haven't seen Geraldine's face. She's thinking the same thing. Despite hating the thought of giving in to what the men want, she'll allow us to be pulled back to a place of safety. She wants us all to do our best and our duty, and we can't do that while we're grounded and hunted.'

'Perhaps it's for the best,' Kember soothed.

'This . . . creature is able to walk around the air station at will while we have to stick together and look over our shoulders. It has to be someone senior, someone nobody dare question.'

Kember lowered his voice. 'I still think Dallington or Matfield are the most likely. They both fit your profile, and don't forget the book on Dallington's shelf and the way Wingate, Hammond and Stapleton have been frightened into keeping quiet.'

Lizzie nodded. 'You need to talk to them again. Someone is lying.' She seemed to come alive with renewed energy. 'Of course, the playing card.' She gripped Kember's arm. 'There are two heads on a picture card. I thought the eyes being poked out had something to do with me looking into the killer's business, and it does in one way, but it's also a comment on us as women. Two faces, two-faced. He's playing us at what he sees as our own game. He's saying men shouldn't be distracted by what's on the surface into looking in the wrong direction. You need to delve deeper to see the true nature. When are you seeing Dallington and Matfield again?'

'As soon as we've got you a drink downstairs,' Kember said.

'Good. I want to see their faces and body language.'

'I didn't mean you. Pendry and I—'

'I need to sit in when you talk to them,' Lizzie's voice cut in, louder, insistent. 'I need to see how they react when you confront them. I'll be able to see beneath the surface, to tell if they're telling the truth.'

Kember ignored Pendry's shake of his head. 'I can't see any harm in you just watching. If I let you sit in, will you be quiet and say nothing?'

'I promise.' Tears welled in Lizzie's eyes again. 'I just need to see their faces.'

CHAPTER
TWENTY-SEVEN

'Is the manor house not guarded or patrolled at night?' Kember looked up from his notebook as Dallington fidgeted in his office chair.

'Of course it bloody well is. This is a first-class military establishment, not some second-rate provincial cop shop.' The stem of Dallington's pipe came under attack from his clenched teeth.

Pendry cleared his throat. 'I've already assured the inspector that our station perimeter security is tight, sir. I think what he is getting at is whether anyone could have gained unauthorised access to the building while we slept.'

Dallington pulled back as if slapped, the anger in his red face fading as the seriousness of the situation hit home. 'You really are suggesting it is one of our own, aren't you?'

'I'm afraid it's beginning to look that way,' Kember said, watching Dallington squirm. 'Do you have any idea who that person might be? Has anyone been acting suspiciously or out of character?'

'Not that I've noticed.'

As Kember's head cold had faded, so the previously unsettled weather and dashing about had aggravated his old back injury. He uncrossed his legs and leant forward to ease the ache. 'Do you get on with Wing Commander Matfield?'

'What?' Dallington puffed up. 'Yes, of course I do.'

Kember noticed him flick a glance towards Lizzie for a split second, clearly still seething at her presence. Lizzie was looking at Pendry, whose face wore a flat expression of almost cold detachment. Despite the commanding officer's vociferous objections and Pendry's strong misgivings, Kember had insisted she sit in as Captain Ellenden-Pitt's representative seconded to the investigation. This was a lie, any repercussions of which Kember would deal with later.

'He's a fine officer,' Dallington added. 'Keeps himself to himself. Not unusual. The weight of command is often a heavy burden.'

Kember nodded in apparent sympathy. 'He's not in command, though, is he?' He paused to achieve maximum effect. 'At present.'

Dallington's eyes narrowed. 'What are you getting at, *Timber*?' His pomposity flared. 'Are you implying that a commissioned officer of the RAF is an ambitious glory-hunting oaf after my job?' Kember ignored the personal petty insult. 'Ridiculous.' Kember stayed silent. 'Utter tosh.' Dallington sounded less certain. 'Come to think of it, Matfield can be a little stand-offish. Does as commanded to the bare minimum, so to speak. Never considered that a problem before, but now you mention it . . .'

Kember looked straight at Dallington, ready to gauge the man's response. 'In your opinion, does the wing commander have what it takes to be a murderer?'

Dallington stared back. 'Of course he does. He's in a branch of the armed forces. It would be a bloody fool thing to employ someone, let alone give them a commission, if they were patently unsuited to the profession of killing in the name of King and country.'

Kember's eyes were unwavering. 'I mean in cold blood?'

Dallington looked away and took time relighting his pipe, speaking again once the cloud of blue-tinged smoke had dissipated. 'If you stop the man, you stop his next bullet. We are all taught to kill dispassionately, Inspector.'

'Not to mutilate women though, I suspect.' Kember shifted his weight. 'It's no secret you dislike the ATA being here. Does Matfield get on with them?' He enjoyed Dallington's discomfort as the implication sank in.

'As I neither requested to be put in charge of them or agreed to have them on my air station, they qualify as a bloody nuisance.' He shot an icy look of disdain at Lizzie. 'I believe Matfield agrees with me and dislikes them being on an RAF air station as much as I do, but he's a professional and an officer. I don't expect you to believe me, civilians never do, but officers have standards of decency, courtesy and morality. We have to raise our voices to the lower ranks to engender an instant and unquestioning response to an order. Such an order may save lives in battle. Unfortunately, I have little authority over these girls. Captain Ellerden-Pitt is their commanding officer.' He sent another noxious cloud towards the ceiling.

'So they are tolerated.' Kember stood, grimacing as the sudden movement jerked his back muscles. Fed up with Dallington's posturing, he could see little point in going around in circles. 'We'll not take up any more of your time at present, Group Captain. Thank you for seeing us.'

◆ ◆ ◆

Sitting opposite Matfield in his office, Kember held his gaze as the RAF man made a show of leaning forward and sliding a fat book, on which sat the Mills bomb, over to his side of the desk.

'Is that a Bible?' Kember asked, nodding towards the book and grenade. 'I didn't mark you as a religious man.'

'It's a dictionary; I don't own a Bible,' Matfield said with a look of disgust. 'The last war taught me that God doesn't exist.'

From what Kember had learnt, he could quite believe it. 'Where were you last night between, say, ten o'clock and three in the morning?'

Matfield scratched his chin. 'In my quarters.' He sat back in his chair, crossed his arms and looked at Kember. 'It had been a long day. Everyone was tired.'

'Can anyone vouch for you?'

Kember saw Matfield's eyes narrow almost imperceptibly.

'I'm not in the habit of having guests in my room at night.'

That wasn't the question he'd asked, and Matfield knew it. 'Did you see anything out of the ordinary before you went to your quarters or hear anything unusual while you were there?'

Matfield shook his head with slow deliberation. 'The male officers' quarters are in a different part of the manor house so I saw and heard nothing of note.'

'Do you know of anyone who dislikes women so much they would want them dead?'

Matfield glanced at Pendry but addressed Kember. 'I couldn't say, Inspector. If you're trying to suggest Group Captain Dallington had something to do with this, I'd agree it's a possibility.'

Again, that wasn't quite the question he'd asked. Kember tried another tack. 'What is *your* view of having women on the air station?'

Matfield shrugged. 'They distract the men from their duties but are a necessary evil, in my opinion. There are many duties best performed by women, even in the military sphere. While the WAAFs were here they were professional and conscientious in the discharging of their duties.'

'From our previous conversation with you and the group captain, I was left in no doubt he wasn't keen on the WAAFs either.' Kember paused, sensing the officer considering his next response.

'I've been thinking about our last chat,' Matfield said. 'Dallington is a man who is used to getting his own way, getting what he wants all the time. I said I thought him a gutless wonder but, to be honest, that's in relation to military action. His days of front-line duty are long gone and now he's content to sit behind a desk or in a bunker spouting off like a third-rate Churchill. Could I see him hurting women?' He met Kember's gaze and nodded. 'Dallington's opinions about them are well known, as Flight Lieutenant Pendry will attest, and he's more than capable of taking out his frustrations on the weaker sex.'

Kember almost flinched when Pendry leant forward unexpectedly and said, 'Have you seen the group captain acting in a suspicious manner? Have you seen any altercations between him and any of the women?'

Matfield turned his head and appeared to study something on the rug. When he looked up he said, 'Dallington was furious when the ATA first arrived. He had that Elenden-Pitt woman in his office for what should have been a welcome chat. Turned into more of a dressing-down. From that point on, he refused to become involved with them unless absolutely necessary. To answer your question, his relationship with the ATA, if you can call it that, has been cold and distant but no, I haven't seen any unwarranted altercation.'

Kember tried to see past Matfield's eyes to his inner thoughts, but they gave nothing away. Even Pendry, after his one unexpected contribution of the last half hour, had returned to icy, stony-faced detachment. Kember made a show of writing something apparently important in his notebook before continuing.

'Are you happy for Dallington to leave the lion's share of running this place to you?'

A brief smiled flickered across Matfield's lips. 'We have an adjutant to take care of the administrative burden. I am second-in-command, Inspector. It's my job.'

'Ah, yes. You said you are not an ambitious man.' Kember's smile held a challenge.

Matfield accepted the challenge. 'I hope my career will last a while longer yet and, should a promotion be offered, I would be a fool not to consider it. Most probably, I would accept, but I'm not looking for it, nor am I trying to usurp my senior officer. I know which side my bread is buttered, Inspector.'

Kember could feel the interview sliding the same way as Dallington's and decided to retire gracefully. He looked at Pendry. 'Any further questions?'

Pendry shook his head. 'None.'

'I think we'll let you get on then, Wing Commander. An ambulance will remove the body to Pembury Hospital for a post-mortem.'

Kember, Pendry and Lizzie stood from their respective chairs, Matfield already studying some paperwork on his desk as the three of them left his office.

'Chair,' he snapped, as Lizzie started to close the door behind her.

Lizzie's jaw set hard but she remained silent as she retrieved the spare chair and left.

◆ ◆ ◆

Back in Pendry's office, Lizzie seethed. 'Those men both infuriate and scare me.'

'I must admit they're not the most pleasant men I've ever met,' Kember said. 'Did you get anything out of those encounters?'

Lizzie waved away his offer of the chair, her eyes narrowing.

Kember sat in the chair opposite Pendry and recoiled as Lizzie bent forward suddenly, leaning her hands on Pendry's desk, the movement threatening to topple a stack of ledgers.

'Did you hear the language he used?' Lizzie scowled.

Pendry moved the ledgers, a dog-eared Bible and a pile of manuals away from her, sat back and folded his arms.

'He called us *girls, the weaker sex, a necessary evil.* He called my senior officer *that woman* and wasn't bothered one bit that the murder of a young woman had taken place right inside our headquarters. Dallington was also blasé about this latest atrocity and called us *a bloody nuisance.*'

'I've heard many men say such things about women,' Kember said.

Lizzie shook her head and straightened up, a look of disgust on her face. 'They think they're in control, fooling and misleading us, manipulating those around them.' She began to pace the small office. 'Dallington was openly hostile, even giving me dirty looks, not to intimidate but out of bloody-mindedness. Matfield touched his face, scratched his cheek, in fact. The moment you mentioned arguments he didn't look up, trying to remember; he looked down, trying to create a quick story.'

Pendry leant forward and put his elbows on his desk. 'That could be him protecting his senior officer, the one who looked out for him when he needed it.'

Lizzie shot Pendry a frown. 'He never once looked at me or acknowledged I was in the room. Even when we left and he snapped one word, *chair*, he couldn't bring himself to specify me by name or rank. He was in his office, his domain, sitting back like someone with all the power and control but with arms crossed defensively, keeping you out and the secrets in.'

Kember pictured each moment as Lizzie spoke and had to accept her observations, even if he didn't agree with all her interpretations. He recognised Matfield's arrogance and self-importance but couldn't shake off his conviction about Dallington's guilt.

Pendry cleared his throat and scratched the back of his neck. 'I must say, Dallington's cold and distant with an intense dislike of the women. I get the impression he sees them as strong characters, a threat to be eliminated like some kind of strategic target.' He crossed his legs and picked invisible fluff from his trousers.

Lizzie stopped pacing and glared at Pendry. 'Exactly. Matfield took every opportunity to place the seeds of doubt in your minds, mentioning Dallington before you'd said his name, suggesting Dallington was taking out his frustrations at a point where you were talking about Matfield hearing or seeing anything. Dallington did something similar. He turned on Matfield in an instant, calling his character into question before laying down another smokescreen by defending all RAF colleagues.' She shook her head. 'Misdirection. They're both despicable, but something's not right.'

'I value your insights, Lizzie, but I need hard evidence.' Kember saw Lizzie's neck muscles stiffen. Worried for her safety after seeing the carnage upstairs, he decided to take a risk. 'Would it be such a bad idea if the ATA asked to be transferred to another hub, or at least took some leave?'

Lizzie rounded on Kember. 'Then how would we catch him? How would we get justice for Charlie, for Emily, for Lavinia? This is just another case for you, but they were my friends. Thank you for your concern and support.' She spat the last word before opening the door enough to slip through and slam it behind her.

Pendry rolled his head, neck muscles crackling with approval. 'Nicely handled, Kember.'

CHAPTER TWENTY-EIGHT

Having watched through tears falling too fast to be blinked away as the Pembury ambulance took Charlie's body the previous afternoon, Lizzie had pointedly avoided Kember as he too left. Since then, like the other women, she had been in no mood for food or company. Fizz had continued to well up at random moments, sitting near the French windows, dabbing at her eyes with a handkerchief. Lizzie had never seen her so upset and suspected guilt over her feud with Emily as well as grief at the loss of a friend. Niamh had taken to curling up on the sofa as if trying to make herself as small and inconspicuous as possible. Agata alone seemed to be coping with the aftermath of Charlie's death. At first, she had been quiet and withdrawn, but it now seemed as if a decision had been made to not dwell on it and let herself be subdued by a man. But Lizzie knew it was just another manifestation of grief; the stiff-backed and marble-faced woman wanted to lash out but had no legitimate target for her fear, anger and exasperation.

After the initial shock, Geraldine had remained stoic, dispensing kind and soothing words to console, encourage and motivate them. Her verbal fencing with Dallington to keep the ATA on the airfield while demanding security and protection for her women had quickly become the talk of the air station. The men, if they knew what was good for them, were giving her a wide and courteous berth.

Something about the case continued to niggle at the back of Lizzie's mind but its detail still eluded her. It wasn't about the facts; that was Kember's area. No, it was something far less tangible and therefore entirely in her domain.

Lizzie had sat in silence on the terrace for over an hour now, almost chain-smoking, sometimes lighting a new cigarette from the stub of the old, placing the dead butts with deliberate care in a line equal distances apart. She had paid only passing attention as reports of the Luftwaffe bombing other airfields and south-east coastal radar stations had filtered through.

Finishing her final cigarette, she placed the butts back in the packet and walked through the garden where the warm sun shone dappled through nearby cherry trees and birds sang in competition with each other. She strolled down the steps, past the sandbagged shelter protruding from the lawn and around the gun emplacement beyond, still brooding over bloody controlling men. Men who were at the heart of suffering for women and the world.

The nearby Bofors gun swung suddenly, its snout pointing east, the shouts of the gun crew alerting Lizzie to the increasing flurry of activity around her. As observers trained their binoculars and scanned the sky, she looked in the same direction and marvelled at the innumerable black dots of distant but fast-approaching German bombers. Scared but impressed at the same time, the sight brought home to her that Britain stood alone on the edge of invasion, just as Churchill had said.

'Get to the shelter,' a gunner shouted at Lizzie as the siren began again.

She ran back across open lawn and reached the shelter entrance as the sound of Merlin engines reverberated across the airfield, a flight of three Spitfires already rolling. The lead Spitfire's engine noise became a powerful roar as it lurched forwards. The others followed suit, wheels folding under each aircraft as soon as they left the grass airfield.

Lizzie looked east again, alarmed at how close the enemy had come in so short a time. The specks and blobs now formed the recognisable shapes of bombers and fighters. A shout dragged her attention from the sky and she ducked inside the entrance, skittered down the slippery concrete steps and turned a sharp left into the bowels of the air raid shelter with its curved ceiling. A candle in a storm lantern burnt at the far end of the chamber, casting a pale-yellow glow on the shiny faces already occupying thirty of the forty places. Lizzie sat on the thinly padded wooden bench next to a rotund man with glasses who had his eyes closed ready for a short doze. She guessed staff in the front line needed to grab forty winks whenever they could. Seconds later, the bodies of half a dozen vehicle engineers, smelling of oil, sweat, Brylcreem and petrol, crammed into the remaining spaces. A corporal scribbled the final names, fed the paper into a metal canister, threw it outside and slammed the blast door shut.

Locking handles turned.

And then, silence.

◆　◆　◆

As the sound of the airfield's air raid siren reached a mile to the south, Kember and Wright stopped discussing the previous morning's tragic events.

'Good God!' Wright said, pointing towards the eastern sky.

Seconds later, Greenway's front door opened and he trotted across the road, still putting on his black ARP helmet. He unlocked the siren box and turned the switch to 'on'. As the village siren joined in the warning howl, he said, 'Here we go again,' rolled his eyes and yelled, 'Shelters!'

The village came alive like an ants' nest with its top kicked open. Mums shepherded children playing in the street away from danger. A doll's pram stood abandoned on the pavement outside the grocer's as a boy retrieved his football, his mother shouting for him to hurry. Front doors banged shut after disappearing people and cries came from back gardens as scared families without cellars beneath their houses descended into their Anderson shelters. The pub and village hall cellars filled with those unable to reach other safety. Kember helped one elderly resident to the pub door before being told by Sergeant Wright to get to the police station. The sound of distant anti-aircraft fire drifted across like the tinny sound effects of a radio play. Soon, all visible life had disappeared from the village to be replaced with a local silence tarnished only by the distant drone of approaching aircraft. Kember felt a gentle pressure on his arm as Wright, now wearing his steel war helmet with 'Police' in white letters, tried to guide him indoors.

As Kember retreated beneath the police station, he thought of all the villagers cowering in their shelters as the terrifying sounds of war neared their homes. No doubt Elias Brown's Home Guard would be positioned in their pillboxes as Mrs Garner, alone in her Anderson shelter, worried about her Bert working on a nearby farm, and the vicar and Mrs Oaks worked and prayed in the church crypt. Lizzie should be out of harm's way in a shelter by now. He jumped as the door burst open and in bundled Wright, tin helmet askew, breathless from his check of the village and flight to the police station.

'There's swarms of the bastards,' he said, slamming the door shut. 'Here it comes.'

◆ ◆ ◆

No one spoke as the seconds ticked away and tension thickened the air around Lizzie, falling over her shoulders like a shroud. She almost jumped as the guns opened up on the Luftwaffe. The *pom-pom-pom* and *rat-tat-tat* sounded far away through the concrete and earth above them, but the deep *booms* and earthquake shakes from enemy bombs scared her most. The expressions of the people she now faced death or survival with displayed every emotion from terrified to cheerful, worried to indifferent, and tired resignation to stoic stiff upper lip. While the poor souls out there fought against overwhelming odds, Lizzie felt powerless. Multiple jolts from a stick of bombs landing nearby detached a cloud of fine dust from the ceiling, coating everyone in a thin grey film, making a few cough. The explosions became incessant as bomb after bomb fell, nearer or farther away from the shelter but with no respite.

Shockwaves from nearby bomb blasts punched against Lizzie's eardrums, making them ache and ring. As the raid wore on, each face in the shelter displayed fear through a coating of dust, all pretence of bravery erased. Someone passed around a large flat metal flask, about twice the size of a hip flask, containing something indefinable but definitely alcoholic. Lizzie coughed after her swig as the liquid scoured her dry throat and she passed the flask on to an engineer. She wished she was flying. At least in the air she knew what to do and had a measure of control over her destiny. Waiting in this dark, musty, concrete tomb, all the bodies crammed inside raising the temperature, felt like medieval torture.

RAF Scotney's air defences could not fail to register hits, so large and numerous were the formations of aircraft. Stick after stick of bombs fell in jagged lines from the twin-engine bombers, pounding the air station from end to end and side to side. The earth vibrated at each explosion and pressure waves shook buildings. Mud and rock erupted into the air, falling in chunks and splatters, leaving craters pockmarking the land. Inaccurate aiming found many bombs falling outside the air station, blasting holes in fields and smashing woodland.

Stuka dive bombers came next, targeting the anti-aircraft batteries and fuel trucks. As each lead Stuka fell into its dive, another lined up behind and followed, wing sirens wailing and squealing louder and louder as the dive increased, pulling up at the last second, machine-guns raking the ground with lethal fire, flinging bombs away from their bodies and onto the targets. A food store took a direct hit, sending packages and tins flying through the air like shrapnel, and a fuel bowser exploded in a spectacular fireball of orange flame.

The raid lasted another ten hellish minutes before a squadron of Spitfires arrived to reinforce the defensive cover and drive off the enemy, fire crews already pouring foam on burning fuel.

When Kember emerged from the basement of the police station as the sound of the all-clear faded away he found luck had held for Scotney village. Greenway stood at the corner of the police station locking the siren box and watching people take tentative steps back into the daylight.

'Looks like the airfield copped it,' Kember said, looking towards a column of smoke to the north, his thoughts with Lizzie.

'Aye,' Greenway said, grim-faced. 'We nearly did an' all. A bomb fell into the woods to the west of the village.'

'Whereabouts?'

'Out back of the village hall. Far enough away for the trees to protect the houses and hall from most of the shrapnel. I had a quick look. You can see chipped brick and masonry where some got through. The tree trunks took the full force of the blast but branches have been stripped of leaves. The nearer the crater the worse it is. Bloody big hole surrounded by splintered wood, jagged tree stumps and mud.'

'We got away with it, though,' Kember said with relief.

'I'm not sure everyone would say that.' Greenway frowned. 'The rear windows of the Robinsons', the hall and Elias Brown's in between have been sucked out, shattered and thrown into the gardens. The Robinsons said that when they left their Anderson they found a carpet of glass shards between them and their back door.'

'At least it wasn't a direct hit on their houses or the shelters.'

'Aye, we can thank God for that, I suppose.'

Kember caught sight of Wright. 'Excuse me. Mr Greenway, duty calls.'

He strode over to where Wright had his head bent, listening to Ethel Garner outside the grocer's shop.

Wright turned to Kember, his face lined with concern. 'The people are getting scared,' he said. 'They live so close to the air station they're afraid the village might be attacked too, deliberately or by mistake.'

'Can't say I blame them,' Kember said.

Ethel touched Kember on his arm. 'It's not just the bombs. He got another one.'

'I beg your pardon?' Kember said, startled to see her still there.

'That monster,' said a woman in a bright-green coat. 'We heard he killed another poor girl.'

325

Wright turned in surprise. 'Gladys.'

'What are you doing to keep us safe from him, Den?' said Gladys Finch. 'We're all frightened. I'm frightened!'

'There's no need to be scared, Gladys—'

'Easy for you to say,' Jim Corcoran interrupted. 'This bloke's bumping off the ladies. You've been a copper a long time, a good copper, and now's the time to show us what you're made of.'

A bell tinkled as the grocer and his wife left their shop. 'Have you asked him?' the wife said. She looked at Kember. 'What're you doing to keep us safe, then?'

'Well . . .' Kember faltered as the three crowded in. He looked around for support.

Greenway came over to see what the fuss was about and the rapidly expanding gathering drew other villagers towards it like cats to an open box. Questions flew at Kember and the hubbub got louder as each person tried to voice their fears over the shouts of others. Kember and Wright found themselves pinned against the plate-glass window of the grocer's by a crowd of fifteen or more villagers. Kember saw Reverend Wilson striding from the direction of the vicarage and waved hopefully.

One of the men glanced over his shoulder. ''E won't 'elp yer, nor will God. All we wanna know is what're you doin' to catch the bastard?'

Wright took out his police whistle and blew as Wilson arrived. The clamour died down and the crowd stepped back to give Wilson room to get through.

'Ladies and gentlemen, please,' Wilson said. The crowd retreated a little more. 'Give the inspector some air and let him speak. Just because we have a demon among us doesn't mean we have to act like devils ourselves.'

The villagers looked contrite, some bowing their heads, others averting their eyes.

'Thank you, Reverend,' Kember said, regaining his composure. He addressed the crowd. 'I have been a policeman for a long time and understand your concerns better than you think. The truth is these things take time to investigate properly, to ensure we catch and stop the right man.'

'You're sure it is one bloke?'

Kember searched for the face of the speaker to address and saw the man who had spoken before. 'I believe so, and it is the air station he is targeting.'

''Ave you any idea who 'e is, then? Is 'e a spy?'

'Not a spy, no. We have our suspects and I believe we're getting very close.' He glanced around the whole gathering. 'I would guess he knows it too, so please be vigilant in the coming days, to keep yourselves safe and to be my eyes and ears should anything seem suspicious to you.'

'You want us to do your job for you?'

The crowd muttered restlessly.

'Not at all. You look out for each other during air raids and your eyes are peeled for signs of invasion. All I ask is that you do what you can, and so will I.'

Kember sensed a change in the mood of the crowd and took the chance to thread through with Wright. As they walked towards the police station, Kember threw a wave of thanks to Wilson, who nodded back.

'They may be the least intimidating lynch mob I've ever seen,' Kember said to Wright, 'but they're frightened and likely to hit out. The only way to stop them turning really nasty is to catch this monster – before he kills again.'

CHAPTER
TWENTY-NINE

As Kember emerged into the sunny Monday morning from his lodgings at the Castle pub, Alice Brannan stepped out through the sandbags with him and slipped a small packet wrapped with waxed paper into his pocket.

'Don't forget your sandwich,' Alice said. 'It's only chopped egg and cress but it'll tide you over till tonight.'

'You're too kind,' said Kember, patting his pocket thankfully.

'Don't be silly, duck.' Annie stepped back in through the pub door, calling, 'We've all got to take things when they come along. While the hens are laying.'

The incessant fluid warble of a skylark drew Kember's gaze upwards but he could see nothing but blue dotted with white. Dew dripped from his car, creating a rectangular watermark on the road in front of the police station where he had parked it overnight.

On such a beautiful day, it seemed hard to believe Britain was at war. Spared another pasting during the night, Scotney had welcomed back its two squadrons at first light – the last time he had heard the throb of aero engines. Although, as the police station's front door clunked open, Kember feared the battle was far from over.

'Sir, if you wouldn't mind,' Wright called, gesturing towards the open door.

With the fingerprint analysis still not received from Scotland Yard, Kember had intended going straight to the air station to see Pendry. Now he paused, admitting there could be little to gain from making the trip without anything new to discuss.

'What is it, Sergeant?' he said as he entered and went through to the back room. 'Did Wingate get off to Tonbridge all right?'

'Yes, sir. The van picked him up at seven.' Wright had already filled the kettle, lit a gas ring and set it on to boil.

Kember stood, waiting for his sergeant to say more.

'I was about to come looking for you, sir.'

Kember stiffened, not expecting good news.

Wright poured boiling water into a teapot and wiped the inside of two mugs. 'I had a call from the duty sergeant at Tonbridge Police HQ. He said the fingerprint bureau at Scotland Yard had telephoned to inform them an envelope addressed to you was being sent on the first train from London to Tonbridge.' He stirred the teapot and poured the tea through a strainer.

Kember relaxed. 'Excellent news.'

'I got agreement from the duty sergeant there that he'd send it on as soon as it arrived but he couldn't say whether that would be by motorbike messenger or train. It depended on availability and timing.' Milk splashed into the mugs.

Kember's chest tingled with excited anticipation. 'At least we'll have something solid at last. Let me know as soon as you hear any more. When it arrives I have a feeling we'll be needing another visit to the air station.'

The two policemen took their mugs of tea into the front office in time to hear the telephone ring.

Wright snatched up the Bakelite instrument and put the handset to his ear. 'Scotney Police Station, Sergeant Wright speaking . . . Very good, let me have it . . . I see . . . How much was set? . . . What were the reasons? . . . Really? Good Lord . . . Thank you for letting me know.' Wright slammed down the phone angrily and looked at Kember. 'That was the custody sergeant from Tonbridge. He was all set to ship Wingate off to Maidstone Prison but the petty sessions magistrates have given him bail on his own recognisance.'

Kember slapped his palm on the desk. 'But the man's a crook, caught red-handed.'

'He said there's a war on and the whole system's running a bit slower than usual.'

'A bit slower?' Kember said with incredulity, the kick in the stomach all too familiar as the courts let another felon back on the streets. 'What did he put up?'

'His house and the garage,' Wright said.

'Not including the stolen petrol, I hope.'

Wright grimaced. 'No, but they are letting him keep trading for now, as it's his livelihood and all. He's on his way back to the village as we speak.'

'I don't know why we bother,' Kember said. 'I don't suppose he said anything about the officer he's afraid of?'

'No, sir,' Wright said.

Kember took a sip of tea and pondered. 'We'll have to try a little frightening of our own then, won't we?'

Mid morning, as Kember finished the last mouthful of egg and cress far earlier than he should have, a shuffling noise by the police station door announced the arrival of two sets of feet.

Kember stood in anticipation. 'Sergeant Wright, do you have our man?'

'I do, sir,' Wright said.

'He does,' the muffled voice of Wingate came from the hallway, 'but I don't know why.'

'Take him through.'

Kember followed Wright and Wingate into the back room where they all sat around the big table.

'Am I under arrest?' Wingate asked. 'All your guard dog here would say was that you wanted to see me. I've only this minute got back.'

Kember looked past Wingate to the case photographs and notes pinned to the wall board. 'You're merely helping the police with their enquiries, as they say.'

'Listen, Inspector,' Wingate said with a resigned sigh, 'I've been bailed so I can get on with my business until the trial. I can't be sitting here taking tea with you the moment I get back. I haven't done anything for you to bring me here.'

Kember switched his gaze to study Wingate's face, knowing he was on shaky ground. He'd asked Fendry to put pressure on Hammond and Stapleton and now it was his turn to rattle a cage.

'By your own admission, you were at the scene at the time Lavinia Scott was killed.' Kember never took his eyes from Wingate's.

Wingate looked confused, the bravado draining away. 'Now wait a minute. You know I'm a thief, not a murderer.'

Kember twitched his lips into a sneer he hoped wasn't too theatrical. 'Your two accomplices are warming cells on the air station, so scared out of their wits about someone they say has threatened them that they cracked under questioning. That leaves you. So what am I to think?'

Wingate's face noticeably paled as he glanced at Wright and back to Kember. 'If you've got what you want from them, what do you want from me?'

'Your accomplices have done the decent thing. Perhaps if you'd come forward and told us who and what you'd seen, there wouldn't be *three* women lying in the morgue.' Kember looked at the wall display again, ignoring Wingate's stare, confident Hammond would talk when, rather than if, Stapleton broke. Wingate was a more seasoned criminal and Kember wasn't so sure the threat from an RAF officer would frighten him as much as the others. No, he was far more likely to baulk at the prospect of being hanged for murder.

'You're an intelligent man,' Kember continued. 'You know what's right and wrong, and you know the law. From what Sergeant Wright says, and from reading your criminal record, you've never even so much as frightened anyone during your burglaries.' He saw Wingate's head drop a fraction. 'You don't like hurting people, so what went wrong this time? What did you do that got you into this mess?'

Kember saw Wingate's mask slip for a second, the mechanic swallowing several times as if a dry cracker had stuck in his throat.

'You're bluffing.' Wingate narrowed his eyes. 'If you knew anything you'd have arrested him by now.'

Kember noted the use of *arrested him* instead of *arrested me*.

'What I think is that you saw who did kill Lavinia Scott, and your accomplices are mere thieves. I also think the person who frightened Hammond and Stapleton is the same one who warned you off. But my superiors are pushing me to close this case so even though I may think you're a petrol thief, what *I* think is fast becoming less important than getting a result. If that means you hang for murder and your accomplices hang for treason, so be it.'

Alarm returned to Wingate's face. 'You can't nick me for murder.'

'You had plenty of time to go over to the church path after you'd taken the petrol,' Kember said, worried he was overegging the pudding, as his mum always said. 'When your case goes back to court, I won't mention you being threatened. I'll say you were an accomplice to murder. We can get a result with you even if we can't get the actual murderer. My superiors will give me a medal.' Even as the words left his mouth, Kember didn't believe anyone would fall for such an outrageous assertion, but the look on Wingate's face told him he was getting through.

'I *can't* tell you who he is. He was . . . he made me . . .'

'He made you what?'

Wingate bent down, took off his left boot, pushed two fingers inside and extracted a piece of folded, flattened, sweat-stained paper, then flicked it across the table.

Kember took the paper by its edge, unfolded it and froze. Typed on one side were the words *Keep quiet.*

'Who gave you this?' Kember snapped.

Wingate pointed to the paper. 'Can't you read?'

Kember decided to go a step further. He'd been waiting for Wingate to volunteer information about the murderer, or at least hint at his identity, but perhaps it was time for him to do so, to judge the reaction.

He tapped the table with his finger, next to the piece of paper. 'We have two more of these, one each from Hammond and Stapleton, but I still need you to say the name of the murderer or else we can't protect you. I can't understand why you're protecting Dallington.' He paused. 'And Matfield.'

Wingate shook his head, scared but not rising to the bait. 'You've no idea.'

Frustration swirled inside Kember. On one hand, Wingate was a witness withholding vital information that could stop a vicious murderer. On the other, even though Wingate was a thoroughly dishonest man, the killer had created another victim by gaining some kind of hold over him. He could go on like this all day, but without further evidence, he knew it was time to let Wingate go, for now.

'Sergeant,' Kember said. 'Please could you escort Mr Wingate to the door of the police station, but no further. He's on his own.'

Wingate slipped his boot back on, tied the lace and stood. He went to say something to Kember but closed his mouth, shook his head and followed Wright from the room.

When Wright returned, he scratched the beard hairs under his chin. 'He's right scared of someone, that's for certain. It's got to be one of the top brass at the air station, I'd say. Blowed if I know which one.'

Blowed if I know either, Kember thought irritably. 'My fear is, we'll get the killer's fingerprints from the book and notes but that won't be enough. We've Lizzie who didn't see his face and Wingate who knows more than he's saying, no murder weapon, no blood-stained clothing except the burnt stuff from the grate, and no idea what he's done with the identity cards he took.' He caught sight of Wingate in the street through the office window. 'What I said to Wingate was partially true. If we don't get a result soon, we'll all be taken off the case. Far from getting a medal, I'll never be assigned to anything more than sheep theft ever again and you'll have the real Scotland Yard crawling all over the village.'

◆　◆　◆

Excluded from an air battle growing more intense, still grounded and with no word from Kember in a while, Lizzie could not settle, the whole of life around her becoming more jumbled each day. She had been particularly restless since breakfast, although something about the interviews with Dallington and Matfield had played on her mind since she awoke at 4 a.m. with a start. The meetings with the two officers and with Kember, Wright and Pendry had replayed on a constant loop and she could sense her mind getting closer to the truth with each pass.

The killer hadn't struck again, thank God, but Fizz and the others had remained shrouded in grief and fear, a stronger bond of camaraderie slowly emerging from the remains of their shattered group. The initial shock of Charlie's death had dissipated quickly but Lizzie's stomach still ached as though she'd been kicked, so heavy did the blame she took for her friend's murder weigh on her.

Lizzie's mind worked overtime, wanting to know what Kember was doing and how far the investigation had progressed. Staring out of the window, taking sips from a cup of tea she had let go cold long ago, pacing the lounge, chain-smoking: these were her ways of trying to compensate for inactivity elsewhere. They weren't working, and the other ATA women were becoming agitated by her restlessness.

'Can you stop that?' Fizz said from the enveloping depths of an easy chair, her eyes still red with grief. 'You're making me dizzy, pacing like some kind of caged tiger. Sit down, why don't you?'

'Pardon me for breathing,' Lizzie snapped back.

Fizz laughed, but it was mirthless.

Niamh closed her book and said with a trembling voice, 'We really need to stick together to get through this. I'm more worried about your blood pressure. Do you need to see the doctor?'

'I'm fine,' Lizzie said, not fine but offering a thin smile she hoped would suffice. 'Being cooped up in here when all hell's breaking loose out there is making me a bit jittery, that's all.'

'We all are jittery, as you say, but we don't wear out the carpet.' Agata frowned over the top of her newspaper. 'You smoke too many cigarettes, you will be sick.'

Geraldine uncrossed her legs and stood up from the sofa in one fluid motion. 'I know catching this monster has been on your mind a lot since Lavinia died. It's been on all our minds but there's nothing we can do. There's nothing more you can do.'

Lizzie felt a comforting arm ease around her shoulders.

'I know you carried on helping the inspector.'

Lizzie threw Geraldine a look of alarm.

'Don't worry, nothing else has been said about it, but it's time for you to step back and let the professionals do their bit. You need to rest. Sit there and I'll get you a fresh drink.'

'No, thank you. I'm fine, really,' Lizzie said.

Lizzie's mind had been going up through the gears, compelling her to act, to do something to break the deadlock. No new evidence had come to light that she knew of so, bit by bit, the notion had grown that no one could make the breakthrough happen but her. She'd racked her brains trying to work out a strategy, but nothing came to mind and she knew she needed to relax to let her subconscious function.

'I think I'll sit outside for a while.'

'You know it's better not to be alone,' Geraldine said.

Lizzie thought her voice sounded calm but firm, not unlike a schoolteacher, and forced a smile. 'I know, but I'll only be in the garden. He hunts at night anyway. I'll be safe enough for now.'

'Which reminds me.' Geraldine addressed the group. 'I think it's high time I had another firm word with our so-called commanding officer. If Dallington wants to avoid the disgrace of us being withdrawn or being picked off because he is unable to protect a few *lowly women*, he needs to assign more men to our protection, immediately.'

As Lizzie left the lounge, Fizz closed her eyes to doze, Agata and Niamh went back to their reading and Geraldine gave her a supportive smile before heading to the door and Dallington's office.

Keeping her steps slow, Lizzie strolled to her favourite smoking spot on a wall at the far end of the garden as casually as she could. Reports had come in about raids further north over the Thames and Essex and she had seen officers and staff hurrying to the operations block some time ago. Then she had watched Matfield and Dallington walk over too, shortly before the squadrons had scrambled. Lizzie believed they would be ensconced in there for at least an hour, so interruptions were unlikely. She looked around as if taking in the fresh air while, in truth, ensuring the anti-aircraft gunners many yards distant weren't watching, the terrace was clear and she was alone in the garden.

Satisfied with her solitude, Lizzie sat on the wall and lit another cigarette. She believed she knew enough about the killer for her skills to do their work, but the dangerous game she was contemplating could threaten her own sanity. To help her friends, she had no choice. Taking another deep lungful, she let her mind clear itself of the usual daily clutter and relaxed her shoulders as her thoughts turned back to the killer and she prepared to let him in.

It took another two cigarettes before the shrubs and hedges slowly began to lose focus as Lizzie's mind slipped into that contemplative state she could never quite explain to others. She often said that she stepped into the minds of murderers, but that was only partially true. She had realised long ago that sometimes she needed to let them into her own mind first, to imagine that, for a brief moment, their realities were entwined.

She gave an involuntary shudder as she imagined a shadowy figure drifting in the periphery of her mind's eye. She knew she would be forever tainted with this memory. Knew he would leave part of himself behind. Knew she would lose part of herself.

◆　◆　◆

After Kember returned from buying a half-pound mixture of broken biscuits, a week's supply he intended to eke out with his nightly hot drink, Wright donned his helmet and set off on his beat around the village. As agreed, Kember settled down in the back room to take a turn waiting for the letter from Scotland Yard, studying articles of interest in his newspaper before going back through the whole edition a second time to read those he'd skipped during the first pass. The normal routine and tedium of a country village police station intruded throughout the morning as villagers made appearances at irregular intervals: some enquiring tentatively about how the big investigation was going; one or two reporting village gossip as *suspicious activity*; a few popping in to pass the time of day and trying unsuccessfully to engage Kember in conversation; and Corcoran the postman delivering what turned out to be nothing more exciting than routine police correspondence. Underlying all of this surface chit-chat was a deeper layer of fear for their lives at the hands of someone the police – *he* – couldn't catch.

Thankfully, Wright returned from his rounds before boredom and self-doubt got the better of Kember. The sergeant carved two thick slices of bread from a bloomer loaf, gave each one a liberal coating of pale greasy meat fat and rich dark jelly from a metal dish retrieved from the larder. He held out a plate to Kember. 'Bread and dripping, sir? A present from the Taplow sisters.'

Kember accepted the delicacy without hesitation, his mouth already watering at the beefy aroma as his grumbling stomach reminded him that he had finished his sandwich a few hours ago.

'Oh, I'm a daft ha'p'orth,' Wright said, realising he hadn't removed his bicycle clips. Bending low, he slipped off the metal rings clasping his trousers tightly around his ankles and smoothed out the creased material. 'I cycled out to a couple of nearby farms. Been meaning to get around to it but with so much on around here lately . . .' He put the remaining loaf into a bread bin. 'Nice to get back to a bit of routine police work, if I'm honest. You know, show my face and have a chat, reassure them we're still here doing our job, and find out if they've seen anything suspicious.'

Kember took two large bites from his slice, but before Wright was able to take his food to the table he detoured to the front office to answer the telephone. Kember chewed, savouring the strong flavour as he tried to interpret the telephone conversation.

The call finished and Wright returned to the back room. 'That was the duty sergeant at Tonbridge, all apologetic, like. The letter did arrive on the first train from London as promised but someone put it in your pigeonhole while his back was turned, unaware you were based here. It's on its way and should be with us shortly.'

Kember was not amused. He stuffed the last piece of bread and dripping into his mouth, washed it down with a swig of tea and stood. 'I've wasted enough time waiting for letters that don't arrive. I know what "shortly" means in police language. I'm going to the air station.'

A few minutes later, Sergeant Wright stood in the doorway, his head thrown back, searching the sky for the source of a low rumble. The distant white vapour trails of fighting aircraft weaving patterns across the sky showed the overworked RAF giving yet another good account of themselves. He heard Kember's car start and saw him talking to a villager just as a police motorcycle messenger chugged into view and steered towards the police station. Braking right outside the front door, the messenger dipped his hand into a leather pannier.

'DI Kember?'

'He's over—'

Wright had no choice but to grab the package thrust at him by the messenger, who performed a half-circle and roared back the way he'd come. Wright saw Kember's Minx passing the church so, with no time to open the package, he grabbed his helmet and ran to his Wolsey.

CHAPTER THIRTY

Kember parked his British racing-green Minx on the gravel between two air force-blue Bedford lorries and strode across to the manor house. Walking in through the portico, he met one of the stewards from the officers' mess crossing the hall.

'Excuse me. Where can I find Group Captain Dallington or Wing Commander Matfield?'

'They're in the operations block, sir. The squadrons are up.'

'Flight Lieutenant Pendry?'

'I've no idea, sir, but I can get someone to find him.'

'That won't be necessary.'

'Can I get you anything?'

'No, thank you.'

The steward gave a respectful nod before walking on and Kember heard a female laugh as the man passed through into the lounge and closed the door. He knew the ATA had their quarters on the first floor of the main building and the officers' quarters lay a bit further on in the east wing. He took the stairs two at a time and hurried along the landing, stopping in the main corridor to listen.

Nobody around except him. He hesitated.

Searching without a warrant, especially the quarters of a serving RAF officer, was a career-threatening offence. He should've waited for the fingerprint report but had a growing dread that he'd got things wrong and couldn't allow his incompetence to put Lizzie in any further danger.

He moved in silence along the carpeted corridor, not even a floorboard creaking, and found the rooms he wanted. For many police officers, before beginning their careers and even sometimes afterwards, there can be a fine line between poacher and game-keeper and so it was that Kember had the requisite skills to be inside the first locked room within seconds.

The spacious quarters looked pretty much how he'd expected. A small lamp, empty glass and an ashtray stood on a bedside table. Its single drawer held a shaving kit, some loose change and a half-finished crossword torn from the previous day's newspaper. He flicked through the pages of a book from the shelf below the drawer, finding nothing. Two framed photographs stood on a chest of drawers. He picked up one, of a group taken at an RAF flying school, in the process knocking over the other of a young man. He replaced them both. The chest of drawers revealed laundered, pressed and folded items of clothing, both RAF uniform and casual. Two pairs of black shoes and two pairs of black boots had been arranged in a neat line under the well-made bed.

Disillusionment rising again, he yanked open the wardrobe door.

'Christ!'

He jumped back in surprise as a clothes brush clattered to the floor.

Kember took a deep breath and retrieved the brush before looking through every pocket of the trousers and jackets hanging in the wardrobe. Then he turned his attention to a top shelf and two small drawers at the bottom.

Nothing.

Kember frowned. It was unusual for there to be absolutely nothing of interest to a police officer. Could this man's existence be so wrapped up in his service to the country that it left his life devoid of anything else? He went back through everything again, making sure, finishing at the bedside table.

Still nothing. Needing to be thorough to convince himself, he glanced around the room, racking his brains to find other places where evidence might be found. He looked underneath pillows, pushed his fingers down the back by the wall and got on hands and knees to look under the bed. There was nothing on the floor, nor did anything appear to be secreted under the mattress. He tutted and stood, hands on hips. Hearing aero engines, he guessed the squadrons had returned from battle and wondered whether it was worth risking a quick search of another room.

'You cut Lavinia and destroyed her beauty,' Lizzie said quietly, forcing herself to remember each detail, her breath shallow, a dull ache in her chest.

Ash dripped from her cigarette, the shadowy figure unmoved.

'You took Emily's womb, the cradle of life.' Tears flooded her eyes and ran freely down her cheeks, her heart beating faster as the shadow at the corner of her mind stepped closer.

'You took Charlie's heart, because the heart is a symbol of love and your mother gave her heart to someone else.'

Lizzie cocked her head, realisation dawning. *He hath judged the great whore, which did corrupt the earth with her fornication.* A quote from the Bible. The niggle at the back of her mind had not been about the presence of hatred. It was the absence of love.

'She gave her heart to someone else!' She paused. 'And withheld her love from you. Love doesn't exist in your world, it never has.

It's a game women play to get what they want from men. That's a cynical view but you've seen it happen. Ah yes, the two-faced playing card. Say one thing, do another, manipulate, get what you want, move on.'

The shadow had become an overbearing presence. Lizzie stood up unsteadily, her heart racing.

'Your mother's the important one, isn't she? The one who neglected you, rejected you, drove out your father, took a lover, ignored you, blamed you.'

The figure in Lizzie's mind stepped in front of her and she caught her breath. 'That's why you joined the RAF, to surround yourself with men you could trust, an unbreakable camaraderie, to find a strong-willed man to guide you and keep you safe. Not like your weak father submitting to a woman, but someone to look up to. A real father figure.' Lizzie gasped. 'But of course. You still haven't found one so you've had to take matters into your own hands.'

At that moment the shadows of her mind slipped away and it was only then, finally, that Lizzie saw his face.

◆ ◆ ◆

Kember looked around a room similar in decor and furnishing to the one in which he had recently stood, but a little smaller. Embroidered ceiling-to-floor curtains hung beneath an ornate pelmet, and Regency colours adorned the walls. A quilted counterpane of matching design covered the bed. *Very cosy*, Kember thought, remembering his own modest home, now abandoned for a single room above a pub. Regimental tidiness and a couple of framed photographs, one of an RAF Tiger Moth trainer aircraft and another of a group of men in RAF uniform marked this as a military man's quarters.

Kember checked a dog-eared book on the bedside table, finding it to be a trashy detective novel. He flicked through the pages but nothing caught his eye. He opened the small drawer and saw, alongside a small volume of the New Testament, the usual jumble of a man's possessions: a box of matches, nail scissors, loose coins and other bits and pieces. He thought he had the measure of this man, felt certain he wouldn't find anything incriminating here or in his office, but his search needed to be thorough.

After checking inside the wardrobe and all the drawers he could find, Kember moved towards the door, ready to leave. Glancing back at the book on the bedside table's shelf, something occurred to him. He walked around the bed and opened the drawer again, flicked through the well-thumbed copy of the New Testament and froze. Revelation, chapter nineteen, verse two had been underlined in pencil: the Bible passage found in the mouths of the three murdered women.

He replaced the book in the drawer and commenced a deeper search, running his fingers along the bottom of the curtains and feeling for anything taped underneath or behind drawers. He got on his hands and knees and looked under the bed, ran a cursory hand along the top of the wardrobe and along its back.

His fingers brushed something.

He reached further and managed to retrieve two small notebooks from a pouch pinned on the wardrobe's back panel. Kember's heart thumped. Could this be it? Could this be the crucial piece of evidence that would put this man away and bring justice for his victims?

Kember's breathing almost stopped in anticipation as he opened the cover of the top book, and his jaw set the moment he saw the first image: a drawing of a mutilated dog. As he turned more pages, his eyes misted at the sight of sketch after sketch of the same dead animal filling every space. But the worst came next and he fought to keep bile from rising in his throat. Numerous drawings of women covered the later pages, cataloguing horrific ways to kill them. The first drawings were in the grey of ordinary pencil but, as they progressed, more of each drawing had gory additions in red pencil.

Kember closed the first book with a heavy heart and opened the second.

The inked inscription inside the front cover sealed it.

The quotation from Revelation.

Lizzie made straight for the telephone in the ATA ops room as the unmistakable sound of Merlin engines thrummed in the air. She asked the operator to connect her to Scotney Police Station and clunked the handset down with impatience when no one answered.

Finding an orderly in the communications room, Lizzie asked him if he knew the whereabouts of Dallington and Matfield. She was told they'd last been seen in the operations block but had probably left with the return of the squadrons. The same query about Pendry revealed he'd not long entered the manor house. Feeling her chest tightening again right at the time she needed her wits about her, Lizzie hurried out through the portico for some air.

Kember found a pouch at the back of the second book and drew out three identity cards belonging to Lavinia Scott, Emily Parker and Charlotte Rowan-Peake. He heard the scrape of a key and sensed hesitation on the other side of the door at finding it unlocked. As the handle turned and the door swung open without a sound, the thought crossed Kember's mind that the hinges had been oiled to conceal the comings and goings of this monster. As the barrel of a pistol poked into view, Kember patted his pocket and cursed. He'd returned the police-issue Webley to the police station. As an officer's uniform drifted into full view behind the pistol, Kember's mind cycled through the possibilities. Just two: kill or be killed.

◆　◆　◆

Feeling her breaths come even quicker, Lizzie watched as the old battered Wolsey used as a patrol car by Sergeant Wright crunched over the gravel far too fast and skidded the last two feet before coming to a halt next to a Bedford lorry. When it disgorged Sergeant Wright, she ran down the steps and across the gravel to intercept him.

'It's not them,' she panted.

'Pardon?' Wright said, hesitating.

She bent to look through the window. Puzzled. 'Where's Kember?'

'Is he not here yet? He left before me.'

Trepidation gripped Lizzie's heart. 'I need to tell him it's not Dallington. Or Matfield.'

Wright frowned at her. 'It's not?'

'They're not religious.'

'I don't understand.'

'Think about it.' Lizzie straightened up, pushing hair behind her ear. 'Dallington's all about King and country, the British Empire and tradition, but the Bible on his desk is pristine. Absolutely no wear and tear, not even one sign of it ever being looked at. He uses it as a paperweight, nothing more.' She gave a shake of her head. 'And Matfield doesn't even own a Bible.'

'What does that prove?'

Lizzie caught Wright's tone of impatience and moved closer, conspiratorially. 'Pendry has a Bible on his office desk but it's tatty and dog-eared. It's the well-thumbed book of a man who consults it every day, a man who's either deeply religious or . . .' She raised her eyebrows and paused for Wright to take her meaning. She continued when he didn't respond, 'Or obsessed by something specific written within its pages.'

Realisation dawned. 'The quote?'

Lizzie nodded. 'On the surface it talks about whores but underneath it's about a world that has been corrupted. God judges and the judged get what they truly deserve. Dallington and Matfield are not religious men. They saw too much carnage in the Great War and lost any faith they might have had.' She tapped her temple with her forefinger. 'But I knew something was bothering me. Dig deeper and that passage from the Bible is all about the absence of love, and the consequences.

'I sat in when Kember and Pendry questioned Dallington and Matfield. Pendry looked completely unmoved. And he deliberately moved his Bible out of the way when we were in his office after speaking to the officers. Why? On a conscious level he didn't want anyone touching his things. On a subconscious level he didn't want to take the risk of me or Kember picking it up and flicking through. Pendry had probably underlined that passage and knew it would give him away.'

Wright gave her a grim look. 'I can't go arresting senior officers because one uses a Bible and the other doesn't. They'll think I'm mad and lock me up.'

Lizzie's head was thumping in tune with her racing heart and she pinged her bands repeatedly as her breath came in short pants. 'When I sat in front of Pendry and Kember to offer my help I caught both of them out by analysing their body language. Since then something's been bothering me and now I realise Pendry's body language has been all wrong. He's tried to disguise his true feelings by being careful about what he says and altering his physical gestures, but it doesn't matter how hard you try, you can't disguise your body language for long.'

Lizzie could feel anxiety simmering at the blank look Wright was giving her.

'Look. Pendry was always so guarded but often looked annoyed by what I was saying about the killer. That's because I was talking about him. Do you remember in the hut when Pendry said *Look at what he's achieved* about the murder of Emily, someone he called *that body in the hut*? You'd say *Look at what he's done*, wouldn't you? He didn't want to be caught but he did want himself and his crimes to be recognised for the achievements he thought they were.'

'It's still not proof,' Wright said with a pained look.

Lizzie threw her arms wide in exasperation. 'Pendry knew Charlie was sick and asked the MO to give her something. Charlie told me so. Pendry knew she'd had a sedative and would be in her room, drugged and helpless. He had Hammond, Stapleton and Wingate frightened out of their wits because of the petrol scam, and that allowed him to get on and off the air station whenever he wanted. And he has access to bayonets.'

'But Miss Scott scratched her killer and the flight lieutenant wasn't marked.' Wright shook his head dismissively.

'Yes, he probably was, but we never saw it.' Lizzie started to feel desperate at Wight's inaction and tried to keep her voice from rising in pitch like some madwoman. 'I should have realised when he attacked me and I smelled leather. He kept his hands hidden or his gloves on all the time, except after Charlie was killed. Remember the charred remains of gloves in the fireplace? He must have got Charlie's blood on them, but by then the scratch had healed so he didn't need them.'

Lizzie noticed the envelope in Wright's hands for the first time. 'What does that say?'

'Good Lord, I was in such a hurry to catch the inspector . . .' Wright ripped open the flap, took out a thin wad of stapled sheets and looked at the first page.

'Pendry's dabs are all over the evidence.' Wright nodded. 'Bible scraps, warning notes, Ripper book, poster, playing card, the lot.'

Wright and Lizzie moved aside as a group of RAF men left the manor house and headed for the Bedford lorries.

A mixture of emotions swirled inside Lizzie: anger and frustration at not being allowed early access when she'd needed it; relief that her profile had been borne out; fear at what might happen next, despite all her warnings; and concern about Kember's whereabouts. 'What are you going to do?'

'We'll have to wait for – good Lord!' Wright interrupted himself, pointing as the departing lorries revealed Kember's parked Minx. 'That's the inspector's car.'

◆ ◆ ◆

'You,' Pendry said, as if Kember's mere presence confirmed a suspicion. He looked towards his sketchbooks on the bed, one lying open. 'Like what you see, Inspector?'

'Not much,' Kember replied, rising from the bed. 'I prefer the Pre-Raphaelites.'

'Remain seated.' Kember sank back. 'Did you see it all?'

'Enough.'

Pendry nodded. 'My stepfather's precious pet. His broken heart was my reward. The rest . . .' He moved into the room, closer to Kember, eyes narrowed. 'Wingate talk, did he?'

'Actually, no,' Kember said. 'But it was only a matter of time before we whittled it down to you. Lizzie marked your type as suspect right from the outset. I should have guessed the moment you lied about walking the perimeter with Vickers, and then when you betrayed us to Dallington and Hartson.'

Pendry sneered. 'You wouldn't have stood a chance without that ATA bitch. She can't keep her nose out, following you and Wright around like a puppy.'

'Got the measure of you, though, didn't she?'

'I should have killed her as soon as she started poking her nose in. I tried to frighten her but she carried on interfering. She needed to feel the fear of knowing I was coming for her. I wanted to kill her' – he nodded towards the sketchbook – 'like that.'

As Kember instinctively turned his head to look at the open book he realised his mistake, and a flash of pain preceded darkness.

CHAPTER
THIRTY-ONE

A slap across the face brought Kember back to consciousness with a gasp.

'Sit up,' Pendry commanded.

Kember found it awkward to comply, his movements as spongy as the mattress, realising his hands had been tied behind him. His left cheek stung and he could see where a patch of scarlet from a gash on his head had stained the bedspread. He moved and felt something bulky against the right side of his neck, tied in place by string or cord that cut into his flesh.

Kember shook his head to clear it and regretted the action immediately as a flash of pain seared into his skull. When the accompanying nausea receded, he glanced up at Pendry, no more than an out-of-focus shape standing by the window.

'I'd be careful if I were you,' said Pendry. 'That object you can feel on your neck is the Mills bomb I've just liberated from Matfield's desk.'

'What's all this for, Pendry? What's the point?' said Kember, his mouth thick with the metallic taste of blood.

Pendry turned towards him. 'What's the point?' he asked, incredulous. 'Come on, you don't have to pretend with me. You didn't like that ATA freak from the start either, did you? I know you hated her interference, the assumption she knew something us policemen didn't. You had no intention of letting her anywhere near our investigation and you should have stuck to your guns.

'Women are born deceitful. Conniving, dishonest, cheating tricksters. Can't help themselves. Even in the home, you can't escape them – always telling you what to do, how and when to do it. Wives are probably the worst of the lot, don't you think? They make us look like fools behind our backs: having affairs, running off with other men, crawling back when they've had their fun. Nagging, slapping, hitting even, but can you strike back? No, because you're a man and men don't hit women, do they?' He gave a cold, high laugh.

'I could show you a thousand cases of men hitting women.' Kember blinked hard, his vision clearing in increments.

Pendry gave him a blank look. 'Difference is, women get away with it. That's an imbalance.'

'Is that what you wanted, to balance the books?' Kember said, trying to play for time.

Pendry shook his head. 'They're like a virus.'

'That's ridiculous.' Kember blinked again as his vision drifted back to normal.

'It's what they are. If you want to go somewhere, it'll cost you dinner. If you want a kiss, it'll cost you a few drinks, if you want sex, it'll cost you your freedom or a barrowload of pound notes. They are selling themselves all day every day and we are the idiots who buy.'

'You can't think that of all women, surely?' Kember grimaced. 'What about your own mother?'

'Mother,' Pendry scoffed. 'When my father couldn't take it any more, she turned to others. A different man every few nights, with their tokens of appreciation all over our home like a stain. But what did she care as long as her life remained filled with regattas and fox hunts, with shooting parties and lavish balls?' Pendry shook his head, his voice almost wistful. 'Children are innocent, you know, until the adults, the so-called grown-ups responsible for them, hurt them, neglect them, corrupt them.'

Kember wanted to keep him talking, to buy time to think, but the pounding in his head made it difficult. 'Is that what she did, corrupt you?'

Pendry stared at him as if he were mad. 'Corrupt *me*? No, no, she showed me who I was, who she was. She made me understand. It wasn't a kind lesson but I learnt it well. Not all lessons are kind, Inspector,' he said, looking down at him as if he were speaking to a child in a classroom.

'Is that why you killed Lavinia Scott? To teach her a lesson?'

Kember saw Pendry's pitying look.

'Everything was thrown off balance when the ATA arrived. They were a threat to our order, to our honesty.' Pendry lit a cigarette. 'I always knew I'd have to do *something*, but I didn't realise it would be so . . .' He paused as if searching for the right word. '. . . *therapeutic*.' He took a long drag on his cigarette as if for emphasis. 'It was hard work, too. Do you know how much mental and physical effort it takes to kill a woman with your bare hands? Much greater than I'd expected, let me tell you.'

'You planned this from the start?'

Pendry shook his head, disappointed. 'No, no, I took an opportunity. Like my mother always did. I saw that girl standing on her own outside the railway station: so young, pretty. I did have a plan of sorts, I suppose. I always have. By failing to prepare, you are preparing to fail. Benjamin Franklin said that and he was bloody spot on, but sometimes you just have to be . . . flexible. Like when that grubby thief Wingate came scuttling across from that old woman's house and saw me after I'd strangled the girl. He almost wet himself when he saw my pistol. But a man with a gun pointed at him will do almost anything you ask.' He smiled at the memory. 'He handed me his overalls without a word and knelt there in the mud, snivelling and shivering. By the time I'd finished, he knew the score. I had his clothing with the girl's blood on it and could easily get him hanged for murder. Came in handy for the other two as well. All he had to do was keep his mouth shut and make sure he kept Hammond and Stapleton in line.'

'Were Emily Parker and Charlotte Rowan-Peake more *opportunities?*' Kember growled, unable to conceal his revulsion.

Pendry smiled as if amused by a fond memory. 'Oh, don't take it to heart, Inspector. What could I do? No one was listening to me. The ATA women are arrogant, unnatural, expecting the world to bow and scrape at their privileged feet. If only they'd stayed away from here and let me get on with my life in the niche I'd carved out for myself, uninterrupted, uncomplicated and unencumbered, I'd have remained content. I would have stayed apart. They couldn't even let us have that. They're like a creeping mould. Tainting everything.'

'But did you have to be so . . . ?' Kember sought the right words, desperately. 'How could you bear to do *that?*'

Pendry gave a strange cackle that made Kember's scalp tighten. 'When I saw Matfield borrow Dallington's book I knew I had a scapegoat to take the blame should things go awry.'

'You copied Jack the Ripper,' Kember said. 'I thought as much.'

'Copied? God, no!' Pendry looked disgusted. 'I've shown what can be done, how it *should* be done. He was just an amateur. He had the right idea, I'll give him that, but he could have done so much more.'

'*More?*' Kember almost snarled, the bile of anger rising in his throat. 'You've destroyed three lives and the lives of those who loved them, including their men.'

Kember watched Pendry savouring his cigarette. He didn't know why he was being kept alive; all he could hope for was that if Pendry had wanted to kill him, he'd be dead already. Keeping him engaged was his best chance of staying alive, and Kember's mind scrabbled for a question.

'I should have realised all the hindrance was down to you when you reported me to Dallington. Telling me the families had been contacted and statements taken, which I never saw sight of. The personnel files of Dallington and Matfield that were heavily redacted. Trying to convince me that Lizzie was a hopeless interfering amateur. Protection for the women that was never in place for more than an hour or so, with no back-up from Biggin Hill. And no wonder we couldn't get anything out of Hammond and Stapleton, with you sitting next to me.'

Pendry shrugged and laughed.

'Surely threatening Lizzie with the playing card and Bible quote was a bit theatrical for someone as orderly as yourself?'

Pendry's face clouded and he ground the remains of his cigarette into an ashtray. 'She is an aberration. A spreader of this disease of so-called equality. First at university, and then here. The way she pushed herself into this investigation. She is utterly shameless.' He shook his head as if in disbelief.

Kember felt a chill as Pendry looked at him with eyes devoid of emotion.

'None of this is my fault. It's her: Lizzie, and the others like her . . . like my mother. Whores, all of them. They've brought me to this. *Them*.'

Pendry bent down and levelled his gaze at Kember, his eyes unblinking and focused in such a way that made Kember wince.

'Don't you see, Inspector? I've been forced to do this, against my will. They left with me with no choice. So tell me, now you can see the truth, who's the real victim in all this? Them, or me?'

◆ ◆ ◆

Lizzie and Wright found Ben Vickers and, as they told him everything, he listened with a darkening expression before signalling for two of his men to follow, leading the way into the manor house. They had crossed the hall and climbed halfway up the main stairs when Dallington appeared on the landing, pointed his service revolver at the approaching group and shouted, 'Stop right there!'

Confusion crashed in on Lizzie. Dallington? How could she have been so wrong?

'Sir?' Matfield said as he emerged from the corridor behind and to Dallington's left, his hand on his pistol holster.

Dallington turned his head to look at Matfield with wide eyes, but his gun remained trained on Lizzie.

'Ah, Matfield, good man.' He beckoned him over.

Dallington *and* Matfield? A wave of nausea hit Lizzie and her chest tightened, her breathing becoming rapid and shallow. *Not now*, she pleaded in her head.

As Dallington turned back to glare at them, face contorted in rage, his revolver pointed straight at Lizzie and she forced herself to take deep breaths.

Dallington bellowed, 'Which one of you buggers has been in my quarters? Who rummaged through my belongings?'

'That will be this one.' Pendry appeared from the corridor. 'Drop your guns.'

'What the—?' Dallington's question cut off as his eyes took in the scene.

A knot in Lizzie's stomach twisted painfully at the sight of Kember, hands tied and with a grenade secured to his neck. One end of a length of string tied to the pin led to the other wound around Pendry's hand. In his other hand Pendry held a gleaming, honed, long-bladed bayonet. Any relief in realising she had been right after all evaporated when she saw Kember sway as if drunk. She heard a commotion behind her and risked a glance, seeing Geraldine, the other women and a group of RAF men emerging from the officers' lounge to see what the shouting was about.

'Drop the guns and go downstairs.' Pendry said with a flick of his bayonet. As Dallington and Matfield complied, glowering with anger, Pendry made sure everyone saw the bayonet. 'Everyone pull back or Miss Hayes' sweetheart won't survive the day.' The string tightened as he raised his hand for emphasis.

'Don't be stupid, Pendry.' Matfield spoke for the first time.

Pendry laughed high and cold. 'You shoot me and I'll yank the pin out. Try to grab him, and I ll take both our heads off.' He jabbed the bayonet in Lizzie's direction. 'When the ATA arrived here I knew it was high time this saw some action.'

'All right, Pendry,' Lizzie said. 'What do you want?'

'Flight Lieutenant to you, Third Officer,' he spat. 'I want everyone to stay here. You can drive me to Dispersal in Kember's car. Vickers can ring across to get the Oxford ready for take-off. As soon as I'm in and ready, I'll drop the string and you can be the hero.'

Lizzie breathed out slowly. 'How do I know I can trust you and you'll let the string go?'

Pendry gave her a condescending smile. 'You don't.'

Lizzie turned to Vickers who was staring stony-faced at Pendry. 'Get your men to stand down and let me drive him over, alone.'

'Good girl,' Pendry encouraged. 'You're learning.'

Pendry nudged Kember and they both descended the staircase one step at a time. At the moment Pendry flicked his gaze away from her, Lizzie felt something weighty drop into her pocket and she caught sight of Geraldine stepping away from her, lips pursed in a shush.

Pendry and Kember paused at the foot of the staircase before walking out of the front entrance, descending the portico steps and hurrying across to Kember's car. With the last of the Hurricanes becoming airborne again behind the receding Spitfires, the air raid siren broadcast its familiar refrain.

'Is this a trick?' Pendry snapped.

'No, it's an air raid, you bloody fool,' Vickers yelled in alarm. 'Get in.'

Pendry and Kember got in the back as Lizzie took the driver's seat. Elsewhere, the usual evacuation of non-essential personnel to the shelters swung into action. Lizzie started the car and pulled away with a crunch of rubber on gravel.

'Make it fast,' Pendry spat. 'My hand's getting tired.'

Lizzie glanced in the rear-view mirror and saw Pendry showing his teeth in a broad grin. She couldn't remember ever seeing him do that before and the effect was chilling. She had no threat to offer because she suspected Pendry had no real fear of dying. Wanting to get it over with but mindful of the grenade, Lizzie glided the car around the perimeter track and eased to a stop near a Spitfire that, cowling removed but propeller spinning, was having its engine tested.

Vickers' message had got through and the ground crew had wheeled the Oxford from its blast pen. The engineer who had got it running as requested frowned as he watched Pendry lead Kember to the aircraft. Lizzie got out of the car and waved him a warning.

She glanced back and saw an RAF Austin and the police Wolsey racing around the perimeter track towards them, but there was nothing anyone could do.

Lizzie's chest tightened again and she gasped, a panic attack taking hold. *No!* she screamed inside her head, her breath becoming fast and shallow. *For God's sake, not now.* She felt herself hyperventilating, the telltale signs of constriction in her throat preventing her swallowing. She hated that Pendry would mistake the symptoms of her condition as being those of a *typical woman*, weak in mind and body. But her brain was not her own; it wanted to do things its way and this prevented any chance she might have had of fighting back.

Her thoughts cycled in an ever-decreasing circle as her mind sought to disassociate itself from the situation. It would prefer to shut down before facing reality but she couldn't let that happen. Not now. She couldn't let her retreating consciousness get Kember killed.

In desperation, Lizzie scrabbled in her pocket and pulled out the switchblade knife that Geraldine had dropped there, pressing the button and stepping forward as Pendry's head appeared at the pilot's position.

But as she did, Pendry opened the throttle, the string tensing and jerking Kember to his knees, pulling the pin free of the Mills bomb. She lurched forward as the tailplane passed close to Kember's head, dropped to the ground and yanked the knotted string, sliding the knife underneath. She heard someone shout *Grenade!* as she sliced at his neck.

The grenade came free and she threw it, feeling Kember pressing her down, shielding her as it bounced into the blast pen and exploded.

Lizzie held her hands over her ears, trying to stop the ringing in her head as the cars reached Dispersal. Vickers, Geraldine, Wright and her friends flung open the doors and rushed across, crowding around with the startled ground crew helping Lizzie and Kember to their feet. Lizzie's anxiety having been pushed from her head and chest by almost blind fury, she elbowed between Niamh and Fizz and staggered towards the idling Spitfire.

'Are the guns loaded?' Lizzie cried.

With a surprised glance at his mate, the armourer said, 'Yes, but it can't fly. The engine's up the spout.'

Lizzie scrambled onto the wing. 'Chocks away,' she called.

'But—'

'Do it!' She leapt into the cockpit, seeing uncertainty in their eyes.

Lizzie thought for a split second they wouldn't comply, but a shout from Vickers jolted the engineer into action and he ducked under the wing. As soon as he reappeared with a wave, Lizzie opened the throttle and the Spitfire lurched forward, entry flap and canopy still open. Any shouts of protest from behind were drowned by the powerful Merlin engine and spinning propeller.

As the Oxford swung to point along the runway at the start of its take-off run, Lizzie already had the Spitfire taxiing fast, its tail wheel almost off the ground. She swore as the engine suddenly changed pitch and reduced power, a wisp of smoke curling past the canopy. Lizzie cursed that it couldn't fly, but she had a plan. She looked over her right shoulder and saw the Oxford rolling, its twin engines pulling it forward for take-off.

With black smoke beginning to pour from the Spitfire's engine and orange flames licking around the exhausts, Lizzie pushed her foot on the right rudder pedal, pivoting the aircraft to starboard. As the Oxford gained speed and its large rubber tyres left the grass airfield, the range closed rapidly.

Lizzie waited for the Oxford to rise a few more feet and pass in front of the gun sight before thumbing the firing button. The Spitfire juddered as its eight Browning machine guns fired a long chattering burst of .303 bullets, hitting the Oxford just behind its nose and raking the whole length to its tail. Holes appeared and bits flew off, but to Lizzie's disgust it continued its climb.

'Bastard!' Lizzie shouted, stopping firing and letting go of the joystick.

Amid much shouting, Lizzie realised hands were pulling at her tunic so she allowed herself to be dragged from the cockpit. The fire crew were already spraying foam over the engine casing as she scrambled clear of the blazing Spitfire.

Seconds later, the Wolsey arrived, disgorging Kember and Wright.

'Look.' Wright pointed to the far end of the airfield.

All heads turned towards the Oxford as it performed a steep climb. Even from a distance the aircraft seemed to shudder before dipping its port wing, white smoke streaming from the port engine. Pendry levelled and seemed to have gained control before flames devoured the engine, pouring out black smoke. Fire soon engulfed the whole of the wing and lapped at the fuselage as the Oxford lurched into a dive.

'Anyone see a parachute?' Wright asked, shielding his eyes with his hand.

'Too low,' Kember said. 'It would never open in time.'

Lizzie continued to watch as the Oxford's dive flattened, its blazing engine leaving behind a curved stream of smoke. With no sight of a white parachute canopy, Lizzie felt nothing as Pendry's aircraft slid across the treetops and disappeared. A few seconds later, billowing smoke darkened the sky.

'No one's getting out of there alive,' Wright said.

Lizzie continued to watch the oily black cloud until an orange fireball flashed as the aircraft fuel tanks erupted, the explosive *crump* audible a second later. Only then did the ghost of a smile flicker across her lips. Relief brought with it a wave of fatigue as the tension of the past few days left her and she blinked away tears. She felt as though something momentous had happened, that the world she'd known had changed. Pendry, the Scotney Ripper, was dead. It was the first time she'd thought of him by any name other than a flight lieutenant. Scotney Ripper. It took away the familiarity of a man she'd had a professional relationship with and placed him in another category, one labelled *murderer*.

Throughout her years at university and research into criminal psychology, Lizzie had been able to see inside the minds of offenders, walking through scenes as if she was that person. After each case, she had to depersonalise the subject, to distance herself from whatever they had done. It was the one way she'd found to keep herself sane. Lizzie had read about Dr Edmond Locard's exchange principle whereby every contact leaves a forensic trace, both on the person and the scene. Similarly, she'd known many people acquire traces of the accent of a community into which they'd settled; certain traits, mannerisms and customs being absorbed over time.

So it was with Lizzie and killers. The more time she spent inside their minds the more likely something of them would taint her, and the more of her she would leave behind. She was no fool. She knew a certain level of psychological contamination was inevitable, essential even, for her to be able to do what she did. It reminded her of the old saying: you have to set a thief to catch a thief. And she'd killed a killer.

Agata had the doors of the Austin open as Vickers braked next to the Wolsey and she saw Kember and Wright step back as she, Fizz, Niamh and Geraldine emerged in a flurry of chatter.

'That was a stupid thing to do,' Niamh snapped.

'Brave, but stupid,' Agata agreed with a shrug.

Fizz gave Lizzie a small smile. 'I never thought you had it in you,' she said with a hint of admiration.

Encircled by her friends, Lizzie looked across to where Kember stood unsteadily, supported by Wright. She saw him touch his neck, blood oozing from a shallow cut of her doing. Then he looked down and his legs slowly crumpled. Lizzie cried out at the sight of his left trouser leg, dark and wet with blood. Her head pounding with pain and panic, she pushed through her friends and bent to help, fighting her mind's attempts to focus stupidly on the crookedness of his tie, instead taking it from his neck and using it as a tourniquet, shouting for help to get him in the car.

CHAPTER
THIRTY-TWO

Lizzie felt strangely awkward at the sight of Kember perched on the edge of the visitor's chair in Pendry's old office, his trouser leg cut away but his thigh concealed beneath a field dressing and thick bandage. Vickers sat in Pendry's chair while Wright stood nearby with a telephone held to his ear.

'He will be all right?' she asked.

Davies closed his medical bag. 'Two pieces of shrapnel from the grenade hit his leg. He's lost some blood but he insisted on being patched up so he could telephone his boss before he left.' A smile twitched. 'I've given him morphine so he's a bit sleepy and loose-lipped.'

'I may be light-headed but I'm still awake, you know,' Kember complained.

Lizzie saw pain and fatigue in his eyes, convinced she had been the cause. 'I'm sorry,' she said, pinging the rubber band on her wrist, for comfort more than anything else.

'For what?' Kember said. Her heart thumped as he moved his leg and grimaced. 'I got myself into this mess. You were trying to help so I should be thanking you.'

'There's no need,' she said, avoiding his gaze.

'Of course there is. When you offered some mumbo jumbo called a psychological profile of a killer we hadn't even identified, I thought you might be mad, or at least deluded.'

Lizzie felt her cheeks redden. She'd thought he'd had a better opinion of her than that.

'I should have listened to you from the start,' Kember continued. 'You had the right credentials but . . .'

'You're from Scotland Yard and I'm just a woman.' She saw him flinch and regretted it instantly.

'I was going to say, no one had heard of your technique, never mind understood it. But I admit I was wrong.'

'Sir,' Wright said. 'I have the chief inspector for you.'

'We'll wait outside,' said Vickers, shooing everyone from the office.

◆ ◆ ◆

Kember had the telephone pressed to his ear, listening to a tirade from Hartson.

'. . . so don't be flippant, Kember. Losing the perpetrator in any way is less than satisfactory.'

'I appreciate that, sir, but we did get the right result in the end.'

'Right result?' Kember could almost see the bright-red flush of anger on Hartson's face. 'Pendry may be dead but what was required by the chief constable, and by the people of Kent, was a trial and conviction. Justice not only done but seen to be done.'

'I'd say shot down and burnt alive achieved natural justice.'

'If I wasn't so short of men I'd have you on a charge for insolence,' Hartson shouted.

'Thank you, sir.' Kember could sense Hartson's confusion at being thanked so he carried on. 'Wingate, Hammond and

Stapleton have all agreed to give full statements so we're certain of getting convictions for the petrol thefts as well as a full account of their involvement with Pendry.'

'Could've been worse. You might not have caught them either.'

Kember almost sneered. 'I promise you, sir, next time we need an extra man for an all-night surveillance operation to catch a vicious serial murderer or deal with a grenade strapped to a neck, I'll let you know.' He winced as Hartson bellowed at him in reply, and a jab of pain shot through his leg. 'Sorry, sir. I've got to go to hospital now. I'll keep you informed. I wouldn't worry too much. I'm sure you can charm the chief constable at the next senior officers' dinner.'

Kember put the handset in its cradle, cutting off the outraged cries from Hartson that came through the phone right up until the final click.

Lizzie, Wright and Vickers waited at the foot of the steps outside the portico as Davies helped Kember down to meet them. An RAF ambulance, its polished air force-blue paint glinting, waited on the gravel with its rear doors open.

Kember smiled at Vickers. 'I'm afraid the chief inspector's language may have melted your telephone.'

Vickers laughed. 'Upsetting your superiors again? Funny, I never marked you as a rebel at our first meeting.'

'The morphine's kicked in and I've had a bad summer. It seems my lucky streak continues. I've been suspended pending an investigation.'

Wright swore under his breath and immediately apologised. 'They can't do that, sir. Not after what you've done.'

Kember smiled wryly. 'I'll be needing a rest anyway.' He gently rubbed his bandage and regretted it when a stab of pain jolted through his leg.

Vickers thrust his hand forward and shook Kember's. 'Thanks for all your help. To tell you the truth, I've enjoyed myself. Shame it took a serial murderer to break the monotony, that's all. Whatever the outcome, you're welcome here anytime.'

'A pleasure working with you, Flight Sergeant.'

'Call me Ben.' He let go of Kember's hand. 'Don't worry. I'll get word to your son and daughter.'

'Thank you. We must have a beer when I've recovered.'

'That would be good.' Vickers stepped back. 'I'll let you say your goodbyes in peace.' He turned to Wright. 'Come on, Sergeant, duty calls. Let's take a few statements.'

They turned away, climbed the portico steps and disappeared into the manor house. Davies took his medical bag and walked over to speak to the ambulance crew.

Lizzie had watched the exchange in silence with a slight smile on her face at the formality, but now she felt gawky at her turn. Their eyes met and both looked away as if stung. Her heart thumped, her tongue twice its size, rendering speech difficult right at the moment she needed to speak.

Kember raised a hand in acknowledgement of a call from the ambulance crew. 'I extend the offer I made Ben to you too. A drink, lunch, dinner, I don't mind. I'll be recalled to Tonbridge, but it's not far and I know a couple of nice tea rooms and pubs. That's if I still have a job . . . and if I do, Lizzie, I may be needing you.'

'We'll see.'

Lizzie meant to say *That would be lovely*, wanted to give Kember a kiss and a hug, but she recognised the telltale signs of panic rising. As heart palpitations thumped in her chest and sweat prickled on her back, she despaired at her own mind and body's persistence in doing this to her. How long would it be before she could get close to someone without becoming a nervous, incoherent, twitching wreck? Why could she confront a monster and fly aeroplanes into danger zones but not speak to a man she liked?

As she fought to tear her gaze away from the ground, Kember's lips brushed her cheek in a sudden, passing kiss. Lizzie looked at his face as he took an unsteady step back, feeling as giddy and confused as he looked. His wife may have kicked him out but he was still married. He might never be able to get past that, and she would never be able to fully control her afflictions. But it did not stop her heart hammering.

'I . . . er . . . I'd better go,' Kember stuttered, indicating the waiting ambulance crew with his thumb.

Bugger it, she thought, fighting the knot of anxiety in her stomach. She started to lean forward for a full kiss but he was already stepping away, so she disguised her intention with an awkward nod and smile.

Kember allowed himself to be manoeuvred into the ambulance, grimacing in pain as he lay back on the stretcher, declining an offer of more morphine. Lizzie returned his parting wave as the doors closed, shutting her out of the ordeal ahead. Something she'd learnt about him was that he wasn't one who gave up easily.

With bell ringing and tyres crunching on gravel, Lizzie watched the RAF ambulance curve away from the manor house, its red cross on white like spilt blood on a bed sheet.

AUTHOR'S NOTE

When I walked into the Shoreham Aircraft Museum near Sevenoaks in Kent in November 2016, little did I know it would change my life. A wonderfully engaging lady of ninety-three years old was making a personal appearance, chatting and signing prints of a painting of herself. After the small crowd had dissipated, I had the privilege of talking to her on my own for half an hour. And what wonderful stories she had. Joy Lofthouse (1923–2017) was only twenty years old when she took to the skies in 1943 to ferry warplanes for the Air Transport Auxiliary and I could tell by the twinkle in her eyes and the way she reminisced that she'd loved every minute, and still missed it. From this brief encounter came the seed of a story, and a trip to the Air Transport Auxiliary Museum in Maidenhead followed. This provided a haul of books by and about the ATA heroines who had proved they were every bit as good as the men at flying Spitfire fighters and Lancaster bombers. Lizzie Hayes began to form as a character who could assist my detective and make a significant contribution to the investigation.

Then I chanced upon Beatrice Edgell, another real and remarkable woman. She was the first British woman to earn a psychology PhD (1901), became the first British woman to be appointed a professor of psychology (1927) and taught in London University's

Bedford College for twenty-five years (1898–1933). It seemed too good an opportunity for the real Beatrice not to have become a mentor to the fictional Lizzie, turning her into the criminal profiler of my story and an equal partner to Kember.

Despite popular myth, the British at war did not all pull together. In her book *Crime in the Second World War* (Sabrestorm, 2017), Penny Legg says that between 1939 and 1945 the crime rate went up an astonishing 57 per cent. The rate for murder alone went up 22 per cent between 1941–45. Individuals, organised gangs, groups of teenage thugs and personnel from the British and Allied armed forces (including up to 100,000 deserters) took full advantage of the total blackout and chaos of war.

While writing about a serial killer stalking ATA women on an air station in Kent at the start of the Battle of Britain, I discovered a triple murder in Brenchley parish that had occurred on the exact same day I had started my story. Chief Inspector Peter Beveridge of Scotland Yard and famous Home Office pathologist Sir Bernard Spilsbury had been sent to investigate, draining local police manpower from Tonbridge in the process. The post-mortems were carried out in Pembury Hospital near Royal Tunbridge Wells.

Up until the 1970s, those who murdered several people, in whatever time frame, were called mass murderers by criminal justice systems and the media. FBI profiler/agent Robert Ressler is said to have coined the phrase 'serial killer', meaning someone who murders in a time-spaced sequence as opposed to a 'spree killer' who kills in a rush, in 1974. Because Lizzie is ahead of her time, she coins her own phrase of 'serial murderer' to explain the phenomenon.

South-east of Tonbridge and Royal Tunbridge Wells, near the village of Lamberhurst, Scotney Castle sits in a beautiful area of Kent that I have hiked in for many years. I'm afraid I've distorted the actual geography of the area for literary purposes but my fictional village (based on many real ones) and air station (again an amalgam of several) exist somewhere in the area to the east of Scotney Castle, near to where the real but now dismantled Paddock Wood to Hawkhurst railway branch line once ran.

During the course of my research, I discovered many interesting facts. For example, the Francis Rattenbury case and Brighton Trunk Murders mentioned are real, as is the book *Jack the Ripper or When London Walked in Terror* by Edwin T. Woodhall (Mellifont Press Ltd, 1937). After Dunkirk, with Britain under the threat of invasion, the size and shape of conscripted men were less important than skills with a rifle. My character of Freddie Stapleton is a soldier who would have worn British military-issue spectacles similar to the post-war NHS style worn by John Lennon. These were designed to wrap around the ears to prevent them falling off and could be worn under a gas mask.

And finally, the weather – a very British preoccupation. In August and September 1940, at the height of the Battle of Britain, it was famously warm and sunny. However, my story is set at the start of the battle and Meteorological Office records show that the month of July was extremely unsettled, cool and wet with frequent thunderstorms.

ACKNOWLEDGMENTS

Authors and their novels never stagger into the daylight fully formed. Both ricochet about as if on a pinball table until something lights up. Inevitably, there are so many people who have helped me, knowingly or unknowingly, from my first aspiration to eventual publication that it is impossible to list them all. Whether named here or not, please know I shall be eternally grateful.

Firstly, thank you to Emma Haynes and Sara Sarre of the Blue Pencil Agency (BPA), and Nelle Andrew and Beth Underdown, judges of the 2019 BPA First Novel Award. Without this competition I would not have met my fantastic agent, Nelle, who saw something worthy in my entry and took a chance on me. To these I add Rachel Mills, Alexandra Cliff, Charlotte Bowerman and all at Rachel Mills Literary. A big salute too for Jack Butler, Victoria Haslam, Gillian Holmes, Gill Harvey, Jane Snelgrove, Dolly Emmerson and everyone at Thomas & Mercer and Amazon Publishing. You are a big part of making my dream come true.

Thank you to everyone at the Curtis Brown Creative writing school who were part of my step up from wannabe to could be: Anna Davis, Jack Hadley, Katie Smart, Norah Perkins, our brilliant tutor Charlotte Mendelson, and my course-mates, Malika Browne, Lizzie Mary Cullen, Matt Cunningham, Bonnie Garmus, Michelle Garrett,

Simon Hardman Lee, Yasmina Hatem, Ness Lyons, Rosie Oram, Mark Sapwell, Ian Shaw, Melanie Stacey, Elliot Sweeney and Kausar Turabi. Your encouragement and insights (and meeting for 2-for-1 cocktails) were, and continue to be, invaluable. (Mine's a martini!)

To my old schoolmates and hiking buddies: Peter Atkinson, Colin Barwick and the late James Corcoran, I am grateful for the constant discussions about writing while you were trying to enjoy the countryside, and for critiquing early drafts. You pulled no punches, which was exactly what I needed.

A huge thank you to my old Home Office colleague and fellow scribbler, Robert Boscott, without whose encouragement I may have given up on the dream. Keep going, Robert. Your stories are funny and unique and deserve to be seen. Your turn next, my friend.

My thanks go to Roy Ingleton, police historian and retired Kent Police superintendent, to whom I must apologise for asking for lots of advice, only to disregard it when it suited my story! If anything police-related is incorrect, it's entirely my fault.

The biggest thanks must go to my lovely family: my wife Jane, our daughters Laura and Holly and G'ma Mavis, all of whom have seen me chained to my writing desk for many hours and suffered endless conversations about plot points, characterisation, etc.; and my brother Steven, who I spirited away from his wife Kirstie and daughter Belicia to go on many road trips to World War Two sites, events and museums at home and abroad.

Finally, a special mention for two important people at either end of my journey. Firstly, the late Joy Lofthouse, ATA pilot and inspiration for Lizzie Hayes. You were indeed a joy to meet and I loved listening to you talk about your life. Secondly, Mr Sawyer, my English teacher at Lanfranc High School. It was your constant encouragement and interest in my stories that first sowed the seed that I might one day become an author. It took me a while, but I thank you, sir.

ABOUT THE AUTHOR

Born in Croydon, Surrey, in 1959, Neil Daws has been a decent waiter, an average baker and a pretty good printer, but most notably a diligent civil servant, retiring in 2015 after thirty years, twenty spent in security and counter-terrorism. Enthralled by tales of adventure and exploration, he became a hiker, skier, lover of travel, history and maps, and is a long-standing Fellow of the Royal Geographical Society. Following the death of his father and uncle from heart disease, he became a volunteer fundraiser and was awarded an MBE for charitable services in 2006. An alumnus of the Curtis Brown Creative writing school, he achieved Highly Commended in the Blue Pencil Agency's First Novel Award, 2019, where he met his agent, Nelle Andrew of Rachel Mills Literary. He is finally making use of his Open University psychology degree and interest in history, especially World War Two, to write historical crime fiction. Most importantly, he has a wife and two daughters and lives in his adopted county of Kent.

Did you enjoy this book and would like to get informed when N. R. Daws publishes his next work? Just follow the author on Amazon!

1) Search for the book you were just reading on Amazon or in the Amazon App.

2) Go to the Author Page by clicking on the author's name.

3) Click the 'Follow' button.

If you enjoyed this book on a Kindle eReader or in the Kindle App, you will be automatically offered to follow the author when arriving at the last page.

Made in the USA
Coppell, TX
09 September 2021